THE
COMING
OF THE
KING

THE
COMING
OF THE
KING

THE FIRST BOOK OF MERLIN

NIKOLAI TOLSTOY

BANTAM BOOKS
NEW YORK • TORONTO • LONDON • SYDNEY • AUCKLAND

THE COMING OF THE KING
A Bantam Spectra Book/April 1989

Library of Congress Cataloging-in-Publication Data

Tolstoy, Nikolai.
  The coming of the King.

  1. Merlin (Legendary character)—Fiction.
2. Arthurian romances. I. Title.
PR6070.046C66   1988   823'.914   88-47519
  ISBN 0-553-05269-1

PRINTED IN THE UNITED STATES OF AMERICA

DH   0 9 8 7 6 5 4 3 2 1

PRINCIPAL CHARACTERS

ADANC, the Serpent of the Deep
AETLA, king of the barbarian Hunas
ANEIRIN, bard of Gododdin
ARIANROD daughter of Don, goddess
ARTHUR (Artorius), king of Prydein
BELISARIUS, general of the armies of the emperor of Rufein
BEOWULF son of Ecgtheow, lord of the Geatas and Wederas
BRAN the Blessed, son of Lir, a high god
BREICHIOL, king of Rufoniog
BROCHFAEL of the Tusks, son of Cyngen the renowned, king of
    Powys and chief of the house of Cadelling
BROICHAN mac Temnan, druid to King Bruide of the Fichti
BRUIDE mac Maelchon, king of the Fichti
CASWALLON son of Beli, divine enchanter
CEAWLIN the aethling, son of Cynric
CENEU of the Red Neck, son of Pasgen, king of Reged
CEREDIG (Cerdic), king of the barbarian Saeson
CERIDWEN the witch, mother of Merlin and wife to Tegid Foel
CERNUN, god of the untamed wilderness
CIAN "of the Wheat Song," bard to King Ceneu of the Red Neck
COLL son of Collfrewi, divine wizard
CRIST (Iessu Crist) the Son of God
CUNEDDA, king of Manau Gododdin in the North, and great-grandfather
    of Maelgun
CUSTENNIN Gorneu, "the horned," son of Mynwyedig, king of Cerniu
CYNLAS son of Owen of the White Tooth, king of Ros

CYNURIG (Cynric), king of the barbarian Saeson

DIARMAIT mac Cerbaill, king of Eriu (Ywerdon)

DYFNWAL the old, ancestral law-giver

DYLAN Eil Ton, sea god

EAGOR, sea goddess of the barbarian Saeson

EINION son of Run mab Nuithon, one of the three noble exiles of the Island of Prydein

ELFFIN, heir to King Gwydno Garanhir

ELUD son of Glas, king of Dogfaeling

GAFRAN (Gabhran mac Domhangart), king of the Gwydeliod dwelling in the land of the Fichti

GEREINT son of Erbin, king of Dyfneint

GILDAS the Wise, saint, author of libel against Maelgun Gwynedd

GOFANNON son of Don, divine smith

GURTHEFIR the aged, king of Dyfed

GURTHEYRN the thin, king of Prydein

GWEIR son of Geirioed, prisoner beneath Ynys Gweir

GWENDOLAU son of Ceidiaw, king of Godeu

GWENDYD, sister of Merlin

GWRI Golden-hair, herald of springtime

GWYDION son of Don, divine wizard

GWYDNO Garanhir son of Cawrdaf king of Cantre'r Gwaelod

GWYN son of Nud, lord of the Wild Hunt and the hosts of Annufn

HELLADIA, a dancer from Alexandria

HENGYS, barbarian king of Cent

HEORRENDA, scop of the Heodeningas

HERMOGENES, general of the emperor of Rufein

HROTHGAR, king of the Gar-Dene

HROTHWYNN, daughter of Hengys and wife to Wyrtgeorne

HYGELAC, king of the Geatas

IDA son of Eobba, barbarian king of the Beornice

IDNO HEN, chief druid to Melgun Gwynedd

LEU of the Sure Hand, of the Long Arm, son of Gwydion, craftsman god

LIBERIUS, general of the emperor of Rufein

LOFAN of the Murderous Hand, servant to Maeldaf

MABON son of Modron, divine prisoner

MAELDAF the elder, lord of Penardd, counselor to Maelgun Gwynedd

MAELGUN (Maeglcon) the Tall, son of Cadwallon of the Long Hand, king of Gwynedd and chief of the house of Cunedda

MANAWYDAN son of Lir, god of the sea

MATH son of Mathonwy, divine wizard

MAWGAN, abbot of the monastery of Tin Tagell
MELYS son of Marthin, physician to Maelgun Gwynedd
MERLIN mab Morfryn, son of the witch Ceridwen
MORGAN, the washer at the ford
NUD of the Silver Hand, son of Beli the Great, a god
PEIBIO son of Erb, king of Ergyng
PRYDEIN son of Aed the Great, who first settled the Island of Prydein
RIANNON, horse-goddess and mother of the Fair Folk
RUFINUS, tribune of Septem
RUN, heir to Maelgun Gwynedd
SAMO, a merchant of the Freinc
SEITHENNIN, druid to Gwydno Garanhir
SERFAN son of Cedig, bishop to Gwydno Garanhir
SERWYLL son of Usa, king of Cardigan
TALIESIN, prince of poets
THUNOR, war god of the heathen Saeson
UNFERTH son of Ecglaf, counselor to King Hrothgar
URIEN son of Cynfarch, king of Reged
WELAND, smith-god of the Saeson
WIGLAF son of Weohstan, friend to Beowulf
WODEN, one-eyed war god of the Saeson and the Eingl

PRINCIPAL PEOPLES AND PLACES

ANNUFN, the subterranean Underworld, or Otherworld

ARGOED LWYFEIN, hill country beyond the Sea of Reged

BRYTHON, the people of Prydein

CANTRE'R GWAELOD, kingdom by the Sea of Reged

CAER ARIANROD, starry crown in the night sky

CAER CUSTENNIN, city of the emperor of Rufein

CAER GURYGON, city of Brochfael of Powys

CAER GWYDION, starry highway spanning the night sky; ancient causeway crossing the Island of the Mighty

CAER LOYW, shining city on the River Hafren

CAER LUELID, city of King Urien Reged by the wall Guaul

CELLIWIG, Arthur's court in Cerniu

CENT (land of the Cantware), kingdom of the barbarian Saeson in the southeast of Prydein

CERNIU, sea-girt kingdom in the southwest

CORANIEID, hosts of chaos dwelling on the confines of Middle Earth

CYMRY, "compatriots," name bestowed upon the Brython before their hosting against the Saeson

DEGANNWY in Ros, stronghold of Maelgun Gwynedd

DIN BELI, cliff-tower on the coast of Cerniu

DINEIRTH, deserted stronghold on the Plain of Bran

DINLEU GURYGON, sacred hill of Leu Law Gyfes in the land of Powys

DYFNEINT, country of King Gereint mab Erbin in the southwest of Prydein

EINGL, barbarians from the sea, kin to the Saeson

FICHTI, an ancient race dwelling in the mountains of the North

FREINC, barbarians dwelling south of the Sea of Udd

GODEU, forest region north of the wall Guaul

GUAUL, wall spanning the Island from sea to sea, built by the men of Rufein

GURTHEYRNION, kingdom southwest of Powys

GWALES, island off the coast of Dyfed in the Sea of Ywerdon

GWEIR YNYS, island prison of Gweir in the Sea of Hafren

GWENDYD, the Morning Star

GWERYT, river in the North separating the kingdom of the Fichti from Manau Gododdin

GWYDELIOD, inhabitants of Ywerdon

GWYNEDD, kingdom of Maelgun beneath the mountains of Eryri

HAFREN, one of the three great rivers of the Island of Prydein

HEOROT, glorious hall of King Hrothgar

LOIGER, that part of Prydein occupied by the barbarian Saeson

MANAU, island home of Manawydan mab Lir in the Sea of Ywerdon

MANAU GODODDIN, kingdom in the North

POWYS, kingdom of Brochfael, "paradise of Prydein"

PRYDEIN (Bryttene), the Island of the Mighty, fairest island that is in the world

REGED, greatest of kingdoms in the North

RUFEIN, city and empire of the rulers of the world

SAESON, barbarian invaders in the south of Prydein

TEMYS, one of the three great rivers of the Island of Prydein

UDD, Sea of, bounding the eastern and southern coasts of Prydein

UFFERN, a freezing hell

YWERDON, green island west of Prydein, home of the Gwydeliod

CHAPTER ONE

THE FEASTING

OF

KING CENEU

It was on the eve of the Kalan Mai that King Ceneu of the Red Neck was accustomed to hold a great feasting, attended by the noblest of the Men of the North and others of their blood and fosterage from the farthest limits of the Island of Prydein and its Three Adjacent Islands who had wintered at the royal courthouse. Great was his hospitality—as great, it is said, as that of King Ryderch the Generous in former times. No one, so the poets tell, would leave King Ceneu's court at the great city of Caer Luelid, be he king, cleric, or bard, without bearing away costly gifts, and seldom did his breath fail to stink of good ale. Loud was the laughter, merry the games, and gallant the boasting as King Ceneu and his comrades drew the choicest morsels of pork from the seething cauldron in the center of his hall. All was in due order, and the quarreling over precedence no more than was fitting when so many were assembled of the ancient lineage of the Thirteen Tribes of the North.

It was the year that King Edwin of Bryneich was baptized into the faith of Crist, and no one performed that baptizing but Run, son of Urien, the uncle of King Ceneu. The monks of Luifenyd were proud that the sea-bandits looked to the land of Reged for a prince of Prydein to baptize their heathen king, and held that Run and the faith of Crist had brought the men of Bryneich into submission to King Ceneu, Run's nephew. But King Ceneu of the Red Neck held scant store by the faith of Iessu Crist and vowed that, baptism or no baptism, he would before the summer was out drive King Edwin and the whole tribe of the Eingl back into the ocean whence they came.

King Ceneu held to the ways of his forefathers: All that year he wore an adder coiled about his neck. It was larger than snakes of its kind, beautifully marked with a yellow brighter than gorse-flowers in the month of Aust and etched in black darker than the Waters of Annufn. At times it was seen to raise its clever, narrow head and flicker its tongue into the ear of the king. Then King Ceneu mab Pasgen would tell the men of his following of events yet to come, and other secrets known in the Underworld of Annufn from which the serpent had crept. The priest of the court would look a little askance at this, but said nothing aloud. King Ceneu was a prince of uncertain temper, a stamping bull and rampaging boar in the splendor of his rage.

That Kalan Mai the bard of the household sang as was customary the song of Aneirin, the "Gododdin." Each year men were moved to tears as they heard the tale of King Mynydog of Eidyin and his gallant three hundred, slaughtered at Catraeth when striving to drive the barbarian Eingl, invaders of Bryneich, from the shores of Prydein. But one man escaped, and that was the poet Aneirin himself, whose song shall be sung until the world has its ending.

This year, however, haughty pride and fierce defiance were mingled with the regret, for King Ceneu's noble boastings promised bloody battles, which would sweep Eidyin back into the ocean "like the fish-weirs of Reged before the winter cataracts of Erechwyd."

When the poem was finished and the applause died away, King Ceneu fell to talking of his noble relative Morien, famous among the valiant champions who fell at Catraeth. But though he died, he fell gloriously—"defending the blessed muse of Merlin," cried the verse, and it was this that the king repeated thoughtfully over his mead-horn. Afterward, men said they had seen his serpent—seemingly asleep, coiled around the livid blemish on the king's neck—arch its head to its lord's ear and murmur words that none could catch. However that may be, Ceneu mab Pasgen began to speak with his company concerning the famous magician and prophet.

"Would that Merlin yet lived, and could foretell to us our fate!" cried out old Caradog of the White Thigh, whose father, Breichior, had been among the slain at Catraeth. "He passed away from us, none knows whither, and now the future is hidden from us forever. In former days men learned their fate and met it fittingly in consequence. But now it springs upon us, a thief and murderer like the accursed Lofan of the Murderous Hand, causing our spirits to pass unprepared to the land beyond. It might even be that we could order things otherwise than the fates foretell, were we but forewarned."

A murmur of interest sounded through the smoke-filled hall. The words of Caradog spoke to their hearts. A valiant death, the subject of the songs of bards in the halls of their sons and their sons' sons, was what all desired at their ending. But a death sudden and unexpected left the warrior unskilled to guide his fate, and his spirit ill-prepared for its journey. Men told of the shades of men so slain that they were doomed to flit aimlessly like moths for the space of a year in the darkest groves of the Forest of Celyddon. At Catraeth, so Aneirin had sung and Cian the bard but now related, the son of Suino from the land of Gwynedd had comported himself with memorable valor, dying surrounded by a rampart of corpses; *and all had been foreknown by the soothsayer.*

There was a cry for Cian the bard—he who composed "The Song of the Wheat"—to chant a prophecy of Merlin, from whose allusions auguries might be taken, ensuring that the armies assemble on a propitious date and cross the mountains by fortunate routes. But Cian sat muttering and brooding; his *awen*—his muse—was absent, and what verses he recalled made but allusive remarks to the struggles of beasts and dragons, the movements of the constellations, and the rise and fall of unidentifiable kingdoms. None might detect a clear account of the planned campaign, though for a space some desultorily argued this or that point. Cian the bard drew his robe over his head and became withdrawn from the company.

It was muttered by some that the prophet's vision had been spirited away from men's understanding since the faith of Iessu Crist had come to replace the beliefs of their ancestors. At this the priest of the household became angry, declaring that the holy Bishop Cyndeyrn had been possessed of vaticinatory powers fully as great as those of any "mad Merlin," and hinting darkly at the grim fates met by successive kings who had neglected the teachings of Scripture, violated holy virgins, or absconded with church valuables. As forceful as these gathering fulminations was the withering contempt with which he alluded to that dark figure, false prophet to the Brython of old, whose very name it was thought unchancy to invoke without precaution.

At this, King Ceneu himself darted an angry look at the priest and seemed about to deliver a fierce reproof. The livid band about his neck was beginning to glow a deeper crimson, when a cry from the farther end of the hall attracted the company's attention. Cian the bard had abruptly thrown back the folds of his robe from his face and risen to his feet. His face had lost the rapt expression it held when recounting the "Gododdin," and his hand was raised to demand silence. Immediately a respectful hush descended upon the gathering, broken only by the faint singing of a wet log on the hearth and a distant bark from one of the royal bandogs chained by the gateway without.

"Times are not what they were," cried out the poet in high-pitched, querulous tones. "In former times the *awen* spoke from springs undefiled, and the course of time was a bright track whose beginning, middle, and end lay as clear as the Vale of Luifenyd after the passing of a Mai shower. Then the Men of the North were vouchsafed all that had been and all that would be: the destructions, cattle raids, and courtships; the battles, cave-ventures, and navigations; the death-tales, feastings, and sieges; the adventures, elopements, and slaughters of the Island of Prydein and its Three Adjacent Islands. They knew not only the stories of those battles that have passed before: the slaughters of Camlann, Arderid, and Godeu, at which their forefathers fought. Through the honey-touched tongue of the Mountain Seer, the men of Prydein had learned also of wars as yet unnamed and unfought, in which their grandsons and great-grandsons would earn their mead-portion, winning undying fame.

"But now," railed the bard bitterly, "the world is changed utterly. It is a matter of pity to the men of the Cymry, and of scorn to the Eingl, that men of such stature as these should have the Island of the Mighty in their keeping, after the men who guarded it of old. Of what purpose is it to regale ourselves here, in the court of the most generous king that is of the Thirteen Tribes of the North . . ." Here he paused briefly to permit King Ceneu to signal a slave, who crossed the hall swiftly and placed a lustrous embroidered cloak and richly jeweled brooch at the bard's feet. Cian glanced disdainfully at the royal offering—which nonetheless he assigned to his slaves to place with an accumulating heap lying by his hall-pillar. "Of what purpose can it be," he continued, "to look backwards into the brightly lit hall as we leave, only to venture forth into impenetrable darkness without?"

A murmur of approbation mingled with intense curiosity ran through the court-hall. Even the priest sat drawn and silent, filled with a deep longing, and forgetful of the impiety of recalling the words of one who was surely no Esaias but a false prophet of the heathen. Before the waters of baptism had washed away his iniquities, he had as a lad joined with the men of his tribe in dancing at the festival of Kalan Gaeaf around the Rock of Mabon mab Modron, which stands in solitude by the Strand of Reged. Salvation could come only through the Blood of Crist; but had not the blessed Bishop Cyndeyrn himself visited the Wizard in his forest retreat, and then himself uttered a prophecy of events to come in the Island of Prydein?

King Ceneu stirred on his couch. "These things are true," he pronounced reflectively. "But how are we, puny creatures that we are when set beside the giants who lived in my grandfather King Urien's day, to draw aside the curtain when, as you say, the spring of the *awen* no longer flows as it did, and the path of its stream is parched and stony?"

Cian paused before continuing.

"Tomorrow, O king, is, as well you know, the Kalan Mai. This hall will be hung with branches and leafy boughs. The young people of our tribe will dance on the greensward before its gates, and men of good lineage will bring before you their dues of strong beer and sweet roots, mild whey and fresh curds. It is a day when our hearts grow young again, though they be also heavy with remembrance of our friends who have passed away, in hill, in vale, in islands of the sea. It is a day when all things begin to stir: the birds are noisy, the woods green, the plow is in the furrow, the ox at work, the sea green and fretful, and the land many-colored."

The king suddenly recollected sentiments very similar to these having been uttered at the previous Kalan Mai—and the one before that—and began to betray evident signs of impatience. The bard drew abruptly to his point.

"But the Kalan Mai is not only a time for the plow to enter its furrow and the cuckoo to cry from its bough. It is not only the sons of men who will be astir, but also those who are other than the sons of men. Just as your young men and maidens will dance on the greensward of your fortress here, so in upland pastures and woodland glades will the *Tylwyth Teg,* the Fair Folk, sing their enchanted songs and join in silvery dance.

"The Hordes of Annufn are stirring from their halls beneath the earth. Among them are the ranks of the dead, all those of our forefathers whose feats are recalled in the halls of the Thirteen Kings of the North. It is said that they emerge from their burial-mounds, and at times converse with the living. To those with eyes to see, they may be found at the moments of dawn and of dusk, at fords and frontiers, crossroads and stiles."

"True, true!" arose an excited cry; for several there had indeed encountered the shadowy forms of departed ancestors and other men of note from former days. Cian raised his hand to still the clamor.

"Now, you men of Reged, and you, princes of the Thirteen Kingdoms of the North, what say you to this? Last Kalan Gaeaf, while all lamented the passing of summer, I traveled rashly northward by the road which passes over the mountains in the Wasteland of Godeu. I was in search of my *awen,* which begins to fail with the year's ending. It was there, in the heart of the Forest of Celyddon, that I met with a fearful specter gliding through the glades from the land of Prydyn, darting like the hawk from a cliff or the wind from a gray sea, and with his left side ever toward me. When I asked him what he did there, he told me he came from visiting the burial-mound of the Nun's Son on Newais Mountain. On my inquiring further what he meant, he led me a little way up the road to where the trees are thinner and pointed to where the Black Mountain raises its head far above the forest."

"The Black Mountain which lies at the center of the North, whose top, they say, reaches to the sky itself? But who is that Nun's Son of whom the specter spoke?" inquired King Ceneu curiously. The serpent about his neck was writhing in sinuous curves, the yellow and black of its body reflecting the flickering embers of the dying hearth.

The bard nodded and paused for a while in deep thought before continuing. "The Nun's Son, as men are wise to term him when in the Forest of Celyddon, is but a name for the seer Merlin himself. From afar off I saw a ray of the sun lighting on a green mound at the lower skirts of the mountain, that seemed to float suspended like an island upon a black sea beneath a storm-dark sky. That, the specter told me, is the *gorsedd,* the throne of Merlin. Now, O king, what I have to say is this: Tomorrow is the Kalan Mai, when it may be that Merlin the Wild, like others who dwell below the earth, is astir. Why should not all this goodly company be assembled there that morning—and who can say that we may not learn much of what is to befall during the year to come from the lips of the Prophet of Prydein himself?"

Silence fell for a moment in the gloom of the king's hall. A fluttering in the rafters above was caused only by bats that hung in the eaves, but there was that in the air which made the bravest warrior pensive. A moment later, however, a cry of approbation went up from all present. Fresh logs were heaped on the fire, the flames leaped up, and the princes of the Thirteen Tribes of the North gazed about at familiar faces in eager apprehension.

"There is reason in what Cian tells us!" cried old Caradog of the White Thigh. "I have heard my father Breichior tell how Merlin's grave lies on Newais Mountain, and the specter perhaps had good reason to know in which *gorsedd* he sleeps. It is said of that *gorsedd* that any noble who sits upon it shall not depart from it without one of two things happening: Either he will be wounded or suffer some other injury, or he will see a marvel."

"I have no fear of being wounded in the midst of such a host as this," declared King Ceneu, gazing about with pride upon his retinue, "and I would be pleased if I could glimpse a marvel. I will go to the *gorsedd* and sit upon it, that I may see what there is to be seen."

Now this declaration of the king appeared as an impiety to the priest of the court, who saw in it a summoning of devils and demons and imps of darkness.

"Vade retro, Sathanas!" he cried out boldly before the assemblage. "Be it remembered, O king, that whosoever believes in his heart that the Fair Folk continue to dwell within their mounds shall not enter into the Heavenly Kingdom; for then he believes that in which there can be no truth. It is a belief displeasing to Crist Himself."

At this, King Ceneu rose up from his seat in anger and glared upon the priest. It was no ordinary glare, but the poison glance that may do a man great mischief. It was a good fortune for the man of God that he recalled suddenly that the blessed Cadog himself had summoned from the grave Caw of Prydyn, questioning him about former times the giant had known.

"It is true that this miracle became known throughout all the North," explained the priest hurriedly, "the blessed Cadog receiving twenty-four homesteads in recognition of his holy work. It is plain therefore that I was mistaken, and that the opening of grave-mounds in the name of Crist, after fasting and prayers, is a work excellent in the eyes of the Lord."

At this, King Ceneu of the Red Neck seated himself once more, withdrawing his deadly glance from the priest of the household. But he bestowed no homesteads upon him, nor is it recorded that he fasted or prayed.

So it was that three days later, as the sun began to gild the white summits of the mountains, King Ceneu of the Red Neck, son of Pasgen, son of Urien, and the three hundred men of his war-band found themselves approaching the slopes of the Black Mountain. Even in the gray light of the forest depth, as yet unwarmed by the spring dawn, they made a goodly showing. Trotting on strong, fleet-limbed horses, they were gorgeously attired in gold and purple, striped and checkered robes of richest weaving. Golden brooches upon their shoulders and bright sword-hilts at their sides glinted warmly in the somber air. There were shouts and laughter and bursts of merry song as the column wound along its way.

Their route had taken them northward from the fertile Vale of Luifenyd, where bright flowers studded the spring meadows, in profusion as richly glorious by day as was by night the wizard Gwydion's starry stronghold in the purple canopy of heaven. The ox and plow were at work, young men drove dappled cattle to upland pastures, and from hives and dovecotes arose a humming and murmur that spoke of the joy of all the world at its fresh creation. From dusk till dawn the Kyntefin fires blazed from every hilltop, and wheels of flame rolled merrily down the slopes. Only the cry of the cuckoo, on his branch in the Vale of Cuawg, sounded a note that momentarily turned men's thoughts to the melancholy passing of the old year, to the aging and dying of the world, and to those whose momentary span was passed within it.

At the Ford of Erechwyd, hard by the ruined fortress of Arderid, where Merlin once fled the slaughter of King Gwendolau and his war-band, the company of King Ceneu fell silent for a space of time. For now they were following the track pursued by the seer himself, when in his frenzy he departed to the Wasteland of Godeu. They had moreover entered into the envenomed wasteland of the North lying beyond the precinct enclosed by the great wall known as Guaul, which stretches from sea to sea, even from the Sea of Reged to the Sea of Udd, and which is a chain dividing the left-hand region of the Island from the right. To the south lies the land of the Cymry, dwelling each in his courthouse and steading in the fairest isle that is in the world. To the north are bare windy mountains, fetid swamps, wasted uplands inhabited only by poisonous serpents and blown upon with a misty exhalation dangerous to the breath. Among the boulders of the moor and the brakes of the forest flit pale *gwyllion,* shades of the dead, squeaking faint as bats amidst the growling of storm clouds and the howl of moorland winds.

But the mission of the Men of the North was noble and their hearts were high, and even as they began to leave the broad Plain of Reged and ascend the paved road into the mountains built by men of Rufein in days long gone by, they were filled with a great expectation. The forest trees closed about them and the sun barely touched the floor of the valley with his warmth, but there was an excitement and anticipation that set hearts beating faster and even laughter at times upon their lips.

Then it happened that Cian the bard, who was riding at the king's side in the forefront of the cavalcade, placed his harp in its bag and pointed ahead to where a track diverged to their right. It was marked by a great stone planted upright in the leaf mold of the forest floor, its corners incised with strange runes—as if a giant had gripped it with his hand and thrust it hard into the ground, leaving the imprint of his fingers in the sides. The shadow of the slab lay athwart their path, the power of the stone-dweller and the magic of the runes breathing about the glade: warmly strong in the breeze stirring bare branches, and coldly watching from bark and fungus and tree root in the shadows.

Avoiding the great stone, the war-band of King Ceneu wound along the track indicated by the bard. Not a few even of the bravest made the sign of the cross in surreptitious gesture. A silence fell on the company as they traced the forest pathway across the valley bottom, forded a stream, and ascended the farther slope. Before long the path became a barely detectable trail twisting between boulders, where men might pass only in single file. Where the ground was soft the slots of deer were seen, but never a sign of man or horse. They were riding into the empty and unchancy land, abode not of men but of beasts and sprites. It was not the White Crist whose laws and war-bands maintained harmony and order here, but the horned, fanged, furred, scaled legions of Cernun, antlered lord of the untamed Wilderness, who squats cross-legged among wolves upon the summit of Newais Mountain, surveying at a glance all the mist-blown uplands between the Wall Guaul and the River Gweryt on the frontiers of Prydyn.

It was not long before the *gosgordd* of King Ceneu had ridden beyond the shadow of the oak trees and emerged onto a bare, rock-strewn hillside, broken here and there by wind-bent thorn trees and puckered with brown heather and gorse, as yet unquickened by the onset of spring. Beyond towered a vast mountain, snow upon its summit and broad shoulders, whose massive bulk was dimly outlined against a graying sky. No birds were singing, and the only sound was that of the tumbling stream in its rocky chasm, dropping ever farther below their stony path, back into the dark abyss of the forest.

All at once the bard, riding before King Ceneu at the head of his troop, drew up his horse and gestured to their left. He shouted something, but the words were drowned by the crashing of the rivulet and snatched away by a gust of mountain breeze, to be flung across the hillside over the bending heads of the broom. Gazing where the poet pointed, Ceneu mab Pasgen was aware of a patch of level sward upon which a low green mound rose up, rounded and smooth as the belly of a mother great with child. All around lay the bare and rocky mountain slopes, and no other mound could be seen swelling the hillside. By its appearance it was one of those graves of which the poets sing, which the grass covers and the rain wets.

"The grave of the Nun's Son on Newais Mountain:
Lord of battle, Leu Emrys;
Chief magician, Merlin Emrys,"

murmured Cian the bard thoughtfully. "This must be the spot of which the gray specter told. Now is the time to try my bardic lore!"

It was the time that is neither day nor night. The pale pure morning was drawing near. The lords of Reged and Leudiniaun bathed their faces in the dew, strewed about them branches of the rowan plucked in their emerging from the forest depths, and laid themselves down upon the turf. Bard and king alone ascended the *gorsedd*, just as the first ray of dawn sunlight emerged from behind the mountain's shoulder: that shoulder which is named Cadeir Arthur, deep within which dwells the emperor of the Island of the Mighty in his cavernous hall, surrounded by the departed warriors of the Cymry.

Cian the bard it was who poured honey from a vial upon the ground, and spread out a yellow calfskin for his lord to lie upon. King Ceneu mab Pasgen mab Urien, lord of Luifenyd and Erechwyd, of broadest sword and proud in his hall, country's defender and inspiration of battle, stretched himself out upon the yellow calfskin and closed his eyes. Cian saw how the adder about his neck uncoiled itself and flowed through a crevice into the soil below. A thick mist arose and hung about the *gorsedd*, concealing it from the sight of the encircling company. Sweet music seemed to come from the air about them, sweet as that of the Harp of Teirtu or the Birds of Riannon. The princes on the grass below stretched, yawned, and found their eyes closing whether they wished it or not. The false sense had come upon them, and it was visions and dreams that they were to see.

Cian gazed about him at the dense wall of fog that swirled below, even about his feet to the knees, so that he and the king seemed enclosed in a formless space. The mountain and the air upon the mountain became cold, cold, cold: cold as the Ridge of Eryri. The bard raised his arms in supplication, standing alone at the Center of the World, and cried out these words to the vanished hillside and the empty sky:

> "Black your horse, black your cloak,
> Black your head, black yourself,
> Black skull, is it you, O Frenzied One?"

Even as he uttered the words, he too felt a drowsiness come upon him and in a brief spell was asleep with his companions. And as they slumbered, he and the king dreamed a dream.

Now this was one of the Three Great Mound-Openings of the Island of Prydein, and he who witnessed it was Cian the bard, who sang "The Song of the Wheat."

It seemed to King Ceneu and his companion that there arose from the center of the mound a man greater far in stature than the men of their own time. His clothes were but the undressed skins of beasts, his hair thin and gray and flowing, and his aspect pale, emaciated, wild. He lacked his left eye, which was but a puckered, sightless socket. His gaze seemed to portend both pain and anger, and it was with indignation that he spoke:

"What troubles you, O king? You awaken me, that am departed from the world of men."

King Ceneu was seized with a great fear as he gazed upon the tall stranger, for he was not of one time nor of one epoch with the king, to whom he was indeed an increase of the spirit and a broadening of the mind.

"I have come," it appeared to himself he said, "from unknown lands, from known lands, that I may learn from thee the spot in which knowledge and ignorance have died, and the spot where they were born, and the spot in which they were buried. And that I may learn these things I must ask how you are named, lord, and whence do you come?"

The stranger smiled bitterly.

"It is you who should know, O Ceneu mab Pasgen mab Urien mab Cynfarch mab Meirchiawn mab Gurgust mab Coel the Old, for did you not come here to seek me? Some call me Emrys, Holy; others 'the Fortress of the Sea,' which is the Island of the Mighty where you and the puny men of your day exert their sway. Foolish people name me the Nun's Son, and malicious, adze-headed priests, *Merdinus,* 'Dungheap.' Call me what you will, I am Merlin mab Morfryn. I have lain in snow up to my hips for ten and twenty years; I have been pelted by the rain; I have been drenched with the dew. Long, long have I been dead. Now have I named myself, and will fulfill your wish. It is I who am able to prophesy before the ninth wave. What is it that you require to know?"

But King Ceneu tried in vain to reply. He had wished to know who would gain the victory that summer, the men of Reged or the invading hosts of the Eingl from Bryneich. But now it seemed to him that the battle might already have been, though the outcome was unclear in his mind. He saw the kings of the North, their battles, their fortresses, their mountain graves, tumbling as it were in the mist. Time appeared revolving around him, drawing all things with it like the great millstone below the Western Sea that sucked down Brychan the Gwydelian. He no longer knew whether he was the child of kings who had once ruled in Reged, his father Pasgen and his grandfather Urien, or of those whose reigns were yet to come, whose names had been foretold to him by druids at the time of his coming to the kingship. In his ears rang that terrible cry which resounds each Kalan Mai over every hearth in Prydein, piercing the hearts of men and terrifying them so direly that they lose their color and their strength, causing women to miscarry, sons and daughters to be bereft of their senses, and all animals, forests, earth, and waters to be left waste and barren. The land began to heave and roll like the ocean; trees and towers, cliffs and hills, moors and mountains shook and began to topple, one upon the other.

King Ceneu knew that the pivot of the world was loosened, but found that Merlin took him by the hand and led him to safety on the very pinnacle of the Black Mountain. There they found a flat green space, about the breadth of a pig-yard. From it they could see all the many-colored lands of the earth spread out below them, with the encircling blue sea at the rim of the world beyond. The greatest wind that was in the world gusted about them, but it stirred not a hair of their heads.

"Will you play at *gwyddbwyll,* lord?" asked Merlin of his companion.

"I will," replied King Ceneu.

With that, they sat upon the grass and began to play at *gwyddbwyll.* The board was of silver and the pieces of gold. It seemed to Ceneu of the Red Neck in that moment that the pieces bore the faces of men and gods.

"Move your piece!" ordered Merlin before the king could inquire the meaning of the enchantment. As he leaned forward to obey, the seer began to speak, and this is the tale he told. And he that wrote it down from him was Cian the bard, who sang "The Song of the Wheat," and the matter upon which he wrote it was the hide of a dun cow.

CHAPTER TWO

THE BIRTH-TALE OF MERLIN, THE SON OF MORFRYN

MABINOGI MYRDDIN

There are those who say that my birth is a mystery, and others who are less polite. They say I was born in the town of Carmarthen, which (so they think) bears my name, and that my mother was a holy nun living there who was ravished by a king of Dyfed. You may believe what you will, but I will tell you what I know. It was in the Tower of Beli that I first opened my eyes—that dark stronghold which stands on its rocky pinnacle afar off in the south, overlooking the stormy Sea of Hafren over toward Aber Henfelen, where the sun plunges nightly into the ocean depths.

It was the twenty-fifth day of the month Ragfyr that I emerged from my mother's womb. That is no ordinary day, as well you know, for it is also the birthday of the Sun himself, who is also the Son, Mabon. In the sky, Caer Gwydion is opened from the Twins to the Archer, and the souls of the departed ride that path in the wake of Gwyn mab Nud. Perhaps it was that way I came, too, but it is not of that other life that I wish to tell you now.

As is customary at that season of the year, the time of the dead months, the wildest of rain-driven gales was beating in from the Western Sea. The Tower of Beli soars high upon the promontory of Tin Tagell, its base heaved up from the living rock and its walls of seamless slate fused together. It is the greatest of forts that is in the wide western world, and druids tell that the rock face upon which it stands is the brazen cliff that Manawydan mab Lir erected by means of enchantments. Its roots grow deep into the cliff wall, and nothing shall shake down that Tower until the time of all things has come. Yet that night it trembled on its cliff-top, and I myself saw how the spray of the sea mingled with rain that drove in through the window of the topmost turret chamber.

There are those who say that the stronghold was raised up in the infancy of the world through the craft of Gofannon the son of our ancestress Don, aided by enchantments wrought in a tide-washed cave at its base by the wizards Gwydion and Math, who know the books of wizardry and magic. But those who utter such words speak in a fog of ignorance, darker than that which envelops the Tower itself. For how could it be that the company of bright gods should have erected such a place of night and terror and confusion as the Tower of Beli?

There is sea and land between it and the kings of the Brython. There is a great and dark forest that must be traversed, and ill-made is the way there. For it is a quality of that wood that it is as though spearpoints of battle are under men's feet as they pass, like leaves of the forest under their feet. There is an unchancy gulf of the sea full of dumb-mouthed beasts on this side of that immense wood. And before the mountain upon which the stronghold stands is an immense oak forest, dense and thorny, with a narrow path through it, a forked glen full of toads, and a dark dwelling in the mysterious wood at the head of the same path, housing nine hags and a bath of molten lead between them. And each of the hags will proffer a goblet of wine to him who approaches, and of the nine goblets eight are filled with foulest poison.

And after that there is a sword-bridge, a bridge of ice, to traverse; it is guarded by long-maned lions and venomous steeds. About the Tower itself is a hedge of mist and a palisade of bronze with a man's head upon every stake of it—save upon one stake alone. And the skull of each of those heads is pinched in by the grip of the fingers of the baleful Morgan from under the wave. But one man has passed over the stormy gulf, traversed the wild forest, and crossed the bridge of ice, and that was Arthur when he came to wrestle in the halls of Din Beli with Urnach Gawr, who was the porter of that place. And when Arthur approached the gateway, Urnach ran to embrace him. Arthur took up a log from the woodpile as a protection, and Urnach seized upon the log and squeezed it to a twisted mass. In this way Arthur was saved and returned to Celliwig from his raid upon the stronghold of Beli.

Now the purpose of Din Beli was that it should be a fortress and a rampart and a refuge for the destructive people of the Coranieid who dwell within the ocean and in dark chasms of cliffs upon its margin:

Hoarding of plunder in Beli's cold hold,
Blood-bedewed booty seized in crimes untold;
Den of the men of the fen and the coast:
Fortress filled with frenzied Coranieid host.

And the hosting of the Coranieid was a *gormes*, a wasting and an oppression and a destruction inflicted upon the Island of Prydein. They lashed and frothed upon its cliff walls, and hung in fogs and mists and noxious vapors over the land. And throughout the kingdom there was neither food upon dish, nor milk within cow, nor wheat upon stalk. Two thirds of the wheat, and the milk, and the children of the kingdom did they exact in annual tribute.

The king of that place, that is to say the Tower of Beli, was no other than King Custennin Gorneu mab Mynwyedig, whom men call *heussawr* of the beasts of the plain and the forest and the mountain. And no good ruler was he to the land of Cerniu or the Monarchy of Prydein, but a *gormes* to those who judged the Island of Prydein with its Three Adjacent Islands. Such is the account that wise men, *llyfrion,* provide of the Tower of Beli, King Custennin Gorneu, and the *gormes* of the Coranieid.

It was at daybreak, when the tide had reached its highest peak, sounding its deepest roar and driving far into the chasms of the cliffs, that I was born. As the ninth wave spent its greatest fury far below us, my mother gave a great scream, loud as that which echoes every Nos Kalan Mai through all the land of Prydein, shattering the flagstone that lay beneath her. The scream shrieked shrill across every moor upon the wild land of Cerniu, lingering in harsh echoes about the exhalations of its stagnant fens and mingling with a prolonged peal of thunder that rolled across the moors and hills of that desolate land.

It was upon hearing that scream that Henwen the sow of Daluir Dalben, escaping the enchantments of Coll mab Collfrewi, broke out of her enclosure in Glyn Dalwyr and fled across the Sea of Hafren. Upon the slope of Riw Gyferthuch in rugged Eryri she littered a wolf cub and an eagle chick, which Coll gave to Menwaed of Arlechwed and Brynach Gwydel from the North. It is of them that men speak when they tell of the Wolf of Menwaed and the Eagle of Brynach. And the Eagle of Brynach dwelt at Dinas Faraon in Eryri, where Merlin

Emrys uttered the Prophecy of the Dragons before King Gurtheyrn the Thin.

After this the sow Henwen proceeded to Arfon, and rested beside the Black Stone which lay upon the sea marge. There she littered a third beast, and that was the monstrous Cath Palug, which was huge as a young ox or a three-year-old horse. In that dark night the Cath Palug crossed the stormy straits to the corn-bearing Island of Mon. The Black Stone itself slid into the Whirlpool of Pull Ceris, down to the bottom of the sea; but next morning it was found likewise upon the shore of Mon, where it may yet be seen in the Valley of Citheinn.

So it was that the Wolf of Menwaed, the Eagle of Brynach, and the Cath Palug were born in the hour of my birth. They were of equal life with myself, and my nature is of their nature.

After the escape of his beasts across the Sea of Hafren, the wizard Coll mab Collfrewi donned a bird-cloak in Glyn Dalwyr, uttering verses foretelling their appearance in each of the three equal parts of my life, and of their assistance to my *awen* in shaping the destiny of the Island of the Mighty.

And to my mother appeared at that time in her dreaming a single tall, warlike figure. He was clad in a green cloak, and a brooch of white silver upon the cloak, and a satin shirt next to his white skin. There was a torque of gold about his neck, and two sandals of gold under his feet. His form glittered bright as a serpent's mail-coat, he entwined himself about my mother's fair form, and he placed a worm within her womb which was even I, Merlin mab Morfryn. And if any man ask how I know that dream, I make reply that I was of one flesh with my mother and partook of her dreaming.

Thus it was that I came to be conceived at break of day and born between it and evening. It is for this reason men have called me "ever old, and ever young," for day and night between them comprise all eternity.

My time had come, and out I slipped. I was always a precocious lad, and it was gratifying to see what effect my appearance had upon the three midwives gathered about my mother's bed. For a moment they goggled at me stupidly, and then they dropped the rattling eagle-stones and other paraphernalia of their profession and were off! One started yelping and dropped onto the floor in a faint, while the other two screamed like scalded cats and belted out of the room, slamming the door behind them. I could hear the fatuous creatures flying down the steps, shrieking out, "It's as hairy as a badger! Hairy as a badger!"

Well, I ask you! Of course, she was right; there's no denying that.

I was a fair-sized baby in every respect—rather fine-looking, I should say. But I have to admit I *was* hairy. From my neck to my feet I was covered with a beautiful soft pelt of brown hair, or perhaps you could call it fur. It was still wet and sticky from the place where I had lain snug for so long, but you could hardly call that my fault. After biting through and knotting my navel-string (you learn to do these things for yourself when there's no one around to help you), I rubbed myself dry on a blanket and in no time at all was as soft and warm as a young bear cub. You couldn't ask for anything more adorable, though I could hear those silly women yelling away below as if they had just seen the monster that stole Teyrnon's calves. There were men's voices, too, that sounded as if they were trying to reassure them—though I noticed that they seemed no more anxious than the womenfolk to ascend farther up my winding stair. The old hag on the floor was lying in a swoon with her mouth open, so I had no reason to mind her.

I can't say I objected to all the fuss. After all, you want people to take some notice when you make your first entrance into the world. But I did take exception to the words "little hairy devil," which seemed to provide the burden of their repetitive tirade. It was time I looked about me and sorted things out for the future. As a matter of fact, I was extremely glad of my sleek furry skin, I can tell you. The hasp of the window shutter had been dashed open by the angry wind, which with its friend the rain was pelting in on me in a way I was not yet accustomed to. My poor mother (she was *not* a nun, I can assure you—that's a dirty slander spread by idiots who should know better) had fallen back on the bed and was fast asleep, a rowan branch still clutched tightly in her hand. I tucked her up properly, blankets inside, deerskin on top, and managed to jam the shutter to with a stool that fitted the embrasure.

There was clearly no milk to be had for the moment where one would expect it, but still it was time I had something to eat. There had to be a kitchen somewhere below, but as I moved toward the door it suddenly flew open and a crowd of what at first I took to be lunatics burst in. I have heard that in Ywerdon there is a place called Glyn Bulch, where all the madmen of that island are wont to congregate from time to time. If so, I can imagine how the sane inhabitants of that valley (assuming there are any) feel when the visitations take place.

In front of the intruders was a round, cheery-looking fellow dressed in a brown robe with his head shaved over from ear to ear. He was clutching a cross, so I guessed he must be a priest. I was right as usual, and soon discovered him to be Abbot Mawgan from the monastery at Rosnant, tucked away just over the other side of the headland in the lee of the endless gales which drive in off the ocean. The abbot looked just a little dismayed, though he put a brave face on matters. He had been pushed into the room by a couple of soldiers and my fatuous midwives, who were jostling behind trying to peer over his shoulders. (The crone on the floor had sat up by now and added her yelping to the rest.) I stood at the bed's end, waiting to see what they all had to say for themselves. At the same time I gave them a cheery grin, just to reassure them and put an end to any further exhibition of bad manners.

"Is this the child?" asked the priest, after a pause in which he seemed to be collecting his presence of mind.

"Yes, yes, holy father!" squalled out the three old hags, crossing themselves and caterwauling in the most maddening way. "No one knows who is his father: sure, he must have been the Evil One himself!"

"Look here, madam," I began with some dignity, and addressing my remarks to the most vociferous of the three. "In view of your confessed ignorance, I feel you have no call to make such a slanderous assertion, which reflects little credit on my mother or myself. Pray withdraw that allegation, or I may have to take the matter further."

At these words (my very first, you will note), the priest smiled and ordered the soldiers with him to take the women below to the kitchens. As the door closed behind them and their gabbling died away down the spiral of the stairway, Abbot Mawgan turned back to me. He was clutching his crucifix perhaps a little more firmly than was necessary, but otherwise appeared at his ease.

"Perhaps we should have a talk, you and I," he began gently, seating himself in the high-backed chair that stood at the bed's head. This suited me well enough, and I climbed up and perched myself on the foot of the bed, crossing one dear little hairy leg over the other, and resting an elbow on one knee and my chin on my fist.

"Now," began the abbot, firmly but kindly, "what do you mean by frightening these good women in this way?"

At this I felt not a little indignant. I could not help my appearance, which was in any case surely not that displeasing. The priest gazed at me curiously for a moment, and then rose to pick up a broad silver dish that lay on a table at the bedside. Flinging the water in it over the rush-strewn floor, he wiped the interior with his sleeve and held it up before me. I stared at the image imprisoned within and was, I have to confess, not a little startled by what I saw.

The reflected manikin who was myself was as hairy as I knew myself to be. My features, which I now glimpsed for the first time, were (I flatter myself) not undistinguished: rather sharp and sardonic-looking for a newborn baby, but none the worse for that. But what did surprise me was to see that my head was topped by a sort of pink flat cap. Putting up my hand, I found it to be firmly attached to the crown of my head—so much so that it smarted when I gave it a tug. Yes, it had to be confessed that I was a distinctly unusual-looking child.

Abbot Mawgan appeared to sense my discomfort, for he came over and rested his hand on my shoulder.

"You must not repine, my son," he murmured gently. "We are all as God made us. Indeed, you are fortunate that the cap is red. Had it been black, then great misfortunes would have been your lot in life. If what womenfolk say be true, a red cap signifies that you will be possessed in time to come of golden-tongued eloquence, and may also have some presentiments of future events. But first we have to remove it, I fear."

The last words were no sooner out of the priest's mouth than he raised his hand and with a sudden jerk snatched the cap from my head. I felt a sting of pain, but was delighted to find that there was no lasting ill effect.

"There!" chuckled the abbot. "That should make you a little more presentable. Meanwhile you must take care of your birth-cap: it may save you from drowning one of these days. Preserve it, and be certain to keep it from the reach of any ill-wisher." With which he compressed it into a small leather purse, which he knotted by a cord firmly about my neck. I made no objection; he seemed a good man, and so far as I could see sincerely well-disposed toward me.

"Now what?" I inquired curiously. "Is it not breakfast time yet? *You* certainly don't look as if abstinence from good food were much in your line."

"Certainly you must eat, my young friend," returned the good father equably. "But first I think you have to explain one or two small matters—if only to still the tongues of those chattering jays in the kitchen."

"Ask what you like!" I replied cheerfully. "I've nothing to hide, and I'm infernally hungry."

"I'd be careful about that adverb, if I were you," returned Abbot Mawgan with what was clearly intended as a meaning look. I couldn't think what he was on about at all, until his next words put me a bit more in the picture.

"Do you happen to know who is your father?" inquired the good priest gently.

"Not the faintest idea!" I retorted cheerfully. "Why don't you try asking my mother, when she wakes up? I should think I might be the last person to know, seeing I've only just arrived on the scene."

Needless to say, I knew very well who was the author of my being. How should I not? But O You Bright Shining One with Your Sure Arm, even at that time I knew that there are things it is wise to conceal, even from so kindly-intentioned a person as this chubby priest. *We* know who and what we are, but a secret is a secret! My Raven, your secret was safe with me.

Abbot Mawgan glanced to where my mother lay, very beautiful and peaceful in the innocence of her slumber. He rose and went over to the window. The noise of the storm had abated considerably, and he removed the stool I had pushed onto the sill and flung open the shutters. The clear bright light of dawn filled our rough-hewn chamber. Far, far below I could hear the retreating surge lash impotently at the tumbling pebbles, while sea mews shrieked mournfully over the spray. The abbot turned around and gazed at me intently, his expression concealed by the brightness pouring in over his shoulder.

"I hope you like what you see!" I cried impertinently. It is always best to keep the people around you on their toes, I have found. Never give them time to reflect or raise their guard is my motto.

Abbot Mawgan shook his head and came over and sat beside me.

"My poor boy," he began, disconcertingly enough. "I see you have no conception of the danger you are in. We have very little time, perhaps, and I had best tell you how things stand with you and your mother."

"Fire away!" I replied chirpily, though something in my companion's tone told me that my time for joking was probably distinctly limited. Abbot Mawgan nodded.

"It happened in this wise," he began reflectively. "The king of this wild country, as you may or may not know, is Custennin Gorneu, grandson of that Gwrlois whose stronghold was this Tower. It was in this very room, men say, that the lady Eigyr, wife to Gwrlois, was visited by one she took to be her husband. In fact he was none other than King Uther Pendragon, who by a magician's enchantment had assumed the form of Gwrlois, and who that night caused Eigyr to conceive the renowned King Arthur."

"I know that!" I could not resist crying out. After all, I *should* do, should I not, O my Sure-handed One? But the priest ignored my interruption and continued his tale.

"It is for this reason that this chamber has never since been entered by a king of Cerniu, though it is surely strange that King Custennin thought it a fitting place for the confinement of your mother here when the story of her coming child reached him. For he was told by his druids that this lady would bear a son. On that son, so they said, there would be what the pagans call a *dihenydd,* a fate: that he would live to slay the king with a spear of the king's own choosing. The king swore that this should never happen, and kept your mother closely confined here, as if in a prison. As your mother was a virgin, his fears at first seemed groundless.

"Then came that day when all the people of the coast saw a star tumble from the night sky. It fell, so they avowed, upon this, the Tower of Beli. Then they began to speak of prophecies and other portents, until the news reached King Custennin, who was at that time fighting in the East with Gereint mab Erbin, king of Dyfneint. He returned in haste, to learn what all men now know and speak of, that the maiden Ceridwen had conceived a child.

"Upon that he was greatly angered and not a little frightened, and gave strictest instructions for gates with triple locks and bolts to be constructed on the causeway access, and placed the three hundred men of his war-band, turn and turn about, to guard Beli's Tower so closely that not a harvest mouse might come or go without its being detected. Twelve women watched, turn and turn about, within your mother's chamber to see that no man came nigh her. Among the heathen there is a foolish belief—namely, that it is dangerous for a man to approach a woman during her time of travail.

"All hares on the headland were trapped and slain and slips of young rowan planted at the four corners of the promontory. In our cells at Rosnant," concluded the priest, "we naturally kept ourselves from such dark and foolish acts, though I myself at the king's instance spilled holy water upon the causeway linking the promontory with the land, and at the entrance to the Tower."

You may imagine with what feelings I heard this tale. Here was I, not half an hour in the bright world, only to find myself the object of this crazy tyrant's malevolence, and locked in a prison as fast as that of Gweir mab Geirioed himself. Well!

"And what," I inquired boldly (though not quite so bold within, I can tell you), "does this merry monarch intend to do with me now that I *am* born?"

The good father naturally looked a little uncomfortable as he confessed to a strong suspicion that the idea was to do away with me as swiftly as possible. After what he had just told me, this did not come as a great surprise, and I began at once to consider whether there might not be some means of achieving a pleasanter alternative.

"You cannot escape, if that is what you intend, my poor boy," said the monk dolefully.

In my experience churchmen always seem to talk like that, but my motto is "Never say die." I jumped down off the bed and went over to the window. Clambering onto the stool and standing on tiptoe, I was able to scramble up and pull myself onto the sill. At first I saw nothing but the broad sky and the ocean: gray, white-flecked, but somehow comforting in its depth and strength. On the horizon to the northeast stood out the misty form of Ynys Gweir, the island where that other illustrious prisoner, Gweir mab Geirioed, is (so they say) imprisoned. I was in good company, you might feel, though that was scarcely comforting to me in my predicament. Wriggling my body forward, I peered out over the abyss.

The Tower of Beli grew out of the very cliff-edge. My gaze swam straight down its smooth side and on without a break down the black, broken precipice to where ocean breakers lashed and surged on the rock floor at its foot, a hundred span or more below my window. That wasn't a particularly enticing prospect, so I slithered back with some difficulty (you have to remember my age), and got up at the remaining embrasure in the opposite wall. Abbot Mawgan said nothing, but his mournful gaze told me I might have saved myself the trouble.

Again I had a vantage point more suitable to the sea mews that floated past, screaming in desolate fashion (perhaps you think I cannot understand what they say?), than to the child of tender years and delicate disposition that was I. But this time I had a view of the brown-backed headland and mist-swirled cliffs and hills of the rough land of Cerniu beyond—fitting territory for a monarch as rude and violent as its king promised to be. However, this was no time for views rough, rude, or downright revolting.

For below me was the encampment of King Custennin's warband. At a stone's-throw's distance, spread out in a semicircle enclosing the Tower from cliff-edge to cliff-edge, there was erected an array of leather tents; before the entrance of each there stood a spear, bearing on its pennon the emblem of a gaunt-looking chough. There were more choughs on the shields of the rank of soldiers drawn up between the line of tents and the base of the Tower. I estimated that half of the king's war-band was drawn up there, each in his mail-coat, a hedge of spears whose points glinted pale in the morning sea-light. Between the ranks burned braziers of wet driftwood, warming the watchers and, it was easy to guess, lighting up my Tower by night. Their smoke was snatched away by the fierce wind, broken to shreds, and tossed out over the sea. Would that I could follow it!

At that moment I was disconcerted by a movement among the watchers below. A hundred and fifty faces were raised, and a hundred and fifty pairs of eyes stared menacingly straight at my window. I thought of smiling and waving; after all, some of them must have had babies of their own waiting at home. But I decided they were not the sort of men who appreciate lively children, and indeed that their purpose there was not altogether commensurate with my well-being. I confess, too, that vanity played a small part in my reticence in this respect; I had, after all, no teeth as yet with which to smile. I lowered myself back into my little room and returned to where Abbot Mawgan was holding a towel to my mother's hot forehead. She was still asleep, but stirred and muttered as if troubled by bad dreams.

"They are not intending to *kill* me?" I asked the holy man plaintively. He was my only protection—that seemed clear. Still holding the towel to my mother's brow, Abbot Mawgan drew me to him with his other hand. His eyes were full of tears.

"My dear boy, I fear that the king is quite remorseless. He is motivated by fear, which is much more dangerous than mere malevolence."

"But surely you can protect me?" I cried desperately. "Even the worst of kings, surely, must fear the wrath of Holy Church!"

"Would that it were so," replied Abbot Mawgan. "Then might this land be free from all the ills that assail it at this time. King Custennin Gorneu is a devout Cristion in all, I fear, but his thoughts and deeds. It is but a few years since that he, at the head of a party of those lawless robbers you see without these walls, broke into the very church of our monastery, here at Rosnant. Two royal princes, grandsons of King Gereint mab Erbin, whose only crime lay in their royal blood, had sought sanctuary in the arms of Mother Church. I myself witnessed with these eyes how King Custennin broke down the doors and slaughtered the wretched young men even as they clung to our holy altars. They were hewn limb from limb, their royal blood splashing onto the very altar cloths and crucifix of Christ Himself. Not until he had made sure of the boys, thrusting his sword deep into each of their young bodies, did he, like a second Herod, leave us to gather up the scattered remains and bestow them lovingly in consecrated ground. God in the fullness of time will avenge the crime; for, as the Psalmist says, "I will kill and I will make alive: I shall wound and I shall heal, and there is none that can deliver out of my hand." But until that time comes we have no choice but to bend our necks before the proud tyrant."

"What shall I do then?" I cried despairingly; for the abbot had risen solemnly and, making the sign of the cross on my mother's brow, was preparing to leave the room.

"My son," he replied in sorrowful tones, "there is nothing that I or Holy Church can do in this case. What God wills, will be. Perhaps you are fortunate in passing so swiftly from an earth so full of corruption. All I can do is bestow upon you the precious gift of baptism, so that if the worst befall, you may be at once taken up into Heaven, there to dwell evermore with God and His Saints."

None of this was very encouraging, you have to admit, though I could see the force of what the good man said. Certainly the baptism ought to take place, come what may. But even as the thought entered my mind, a sensation of cold dread stole into my heart. If I was fearful of King Custennin and his soldiers, the prospect of baptism aroused what seemed bewilderingly like panic within me. How could that be? Was I damned forever, or had my terrible predicament confused my mind so that I no longer knew what I wanted? Something stirred at the back of my mind, as if a buried thought were trying to obtrude itself. I tried to grasp whatever it was, but before I could do so, Abbot Mawgan interrupted my thinking. From the smile on his face I believe he had some inkling of what was passing within me.

"Well, well, my son," he murmured gently, "perhaps we should leave that matter for the moment. I shall return to see you tomorrow, when we may talk further."

At this I felt considerable relief, not least because the words implied that I should still be alive to see him on the morrow. Not, of course, that the good man was likely to have any knowledge, still less any say, in the matter. But in circumstances like mine one grasps at any straw.

My friend bestowed upon me a final, searching glance and turned to knock on the door of my chamber. There was a clattering of bolts from without, the door opened just wide enough to emit my visitor, and then it clanged to and was firmly fastened again. I was alone with my mother in no very settled frame of mind. She was tossing feverishly beneath her blankets, and to my eye appeared distinctly unwell. I pitied her but, to be quite truthful, felt oddly detached from her fate. Though it was she and no other who had but lately given birth to me, I had this odd sensation of having merely passed through her, that she was but the medium or vehicle of my appearance on this earth—that, and no more. My conception and birth travails had not taken place in this grim chamber, of that I was sure. At least they had, but not in a manner that carried any meaning for me. Oh dear, I feel I am explaining myself with rather less than my customary lucidity. Sure-handed One, with Your Bright Eye, it is *You* who know everything, and doubtless will explain all when it pleases You!

I was left to myself for the next twelve days. The women came to bear away my mother, who, as they explained in reply to my remonstrance, was to undergo proper medical treatment in the monastery at Rosnant, where one of the monks enjoyed a reputation as a skilled doctor. This was no lie, as I was to learn from Abbot Mawgan. My mother recovered in due course; of her cauldron and its enchantments there may yet be a tale to tell.

Before I go on, I must mention something to which I paid little attention at the time, but which was afterward to play an important part in my not uninteresting life. It was the good abbot who drew back my mother's bed coverings as the women prepared to lift her onto the bier provided for her move. Ever solicitous, he bestowed a blessing upon her, touching the bed at its four corners with his crucifix. All at once he gave a cry: As my mother was taken up, still sleeping peacefully, from the bed, he saw that she had left some small thing of herself upon the sheet. I saw it, though at that time I was not to know what it was. I heard Abbot Mawgan draw in his breath and mutter an exclamation of surprise. Then, taking care that the departing women should not witness his action, he scooped it up into the fold of his robe and followed on the heels of the rest of them—not, however, without bestowing a significant glance upon me.

How slowly the following twelve days passed—but not too slowly for me, I can tell you! It was the next morning that Abbot Mawgan was permitted to call again, and he told me that the talk was general that King Custennin would not set foot on the headland during the Dangerous Days (thrice four bonfires were set flaring at the corners of the headland). On the twelfth day, however, he would accompany the Procession of the Horse's Skull during its circuit, and on that day a striking event was to take place. A striking event not unconnected with my small self? I inquired boldly, though my heart was beating like the wings of a kingfisher. Abbot Mawgan did not answer, but his downcast looks told me quite enough—as if I needed to be told anyway!

Oh, those twelve long days! Twelve months, years, and centuries they seemed to me. During the first four, storms continued to howl angrily about my Tower. It was so dark much of the time that I could scarcely distinguish night from day; only the lightning bolts sent blinding light flooding my little world from time to time. On my

Tower-top I felt myself alone and floating far away beyond the earth, the sea and the storm a whirling chaos without. Nothing but the perimeter fires below told me that there was an ordered space to be found when the darkness should pass.

Many, many hours did I spend—by no means wearisome—gazing out on the face of the sea. In my Tower, growing as it did out of the very cliff-edge, I was poised high in air at the very point where earth and sea and sky encountered. Each time I crossed the turret chamber I indulged a fancy that I was moving from sea to land and back again; as yet I did not belong fully to either. It was the sea, however, that exerted upon me a deep fascination. Even when drawn from my observation post at the narrow casement, I remained deeply aware of its abiding presence. Though nothing could budge the mighty rock and rock-grown fastness that harbored me, the heaving and pounding of the deep seemed to roll and swell within me, and in the aether round.

What with the murk and gloom and virtual destruction of time and space, I might still (I sometimes thought) have been within the womb of my mother Ceridwen. I began to think this nighttime of my spirit might never pass. But pass it did on the morning of the fifth day, when the sun woke me at dawn with a cheerful brightness you would not have thought possible at that time of year. This went on for some days, during which I almost succeeded in putting my impending fate out of my mind. I spent my waking hours leaning from the seaward window, watching the sweeping of the gulls gliding past so near I might have touched them. Light upon the tide they were, light as mountain snow or the moon in her fullness; riding at anchor light upon the ocean breakers, fragments of the sunlight, gauntlets of the sea: swift, proud, fish-devouring fowl of Manawydan mab Lir.

What fascinated me was the effortless ease with which they floated upon the invisible element. Scarcely a muscle's movement did they need to dip, to soar, to hover still in air, and then with the smallest tilt of their wings slide away on an eddying gust to land with perfect precision on a projecting pinnacle barely big enough to receive their spread webbed feet. Of all creatures that live upon earth, they inhabit the fiercest and most hostile of elements. The gale shakes the cliff, tears trees up by their roots, and hurls the ocean itself upon the land. Yet the sea birds float upon it with the comfort and confidence of a king lying on his mattress of down. They turn its strength to their own purposes, understanding the nature of its ways, and employ that understanding of the wind's blind strength to climb closer to the sky than all other created beings.

> "Guess who was made before the flood;
> Great creature lacking veins or blood
> Or head or feet or flesh or bone?
> His age on earth may not be known;
> Death neither hinders him, nor fear,
> Nor does he need a comrade dear,"

I murmured to myself, as I watched for hours the gulls' wheeling and crying.

> "Five ages long of ages five
> And fifties more is he alive!
> Broad as the face of earth is he,
> Though never born and yet to see.
> Both good and bad, and unrevealed;
> Ubiquitous, yet fast concealed:
> Well of deep destructive force
> Uncensured and beyond remorse."

I was free also to indulge my absorption in the mystery of Ocean. Below me, indeed, she revealed herself in all her idle display of strength and beauty, advancing rank upon rank of white-maned cavalry in feigned onslaught against the crouching boulders of the shore, playfully shifting them about in grinding pain communicated to me less by sound than by a shuddering passing through the limbs and frame of the Tower of Beli. It intrigued me to stretch out and peer down upon this tumultuous affray at my feet, and then to gaze out in turn upon the more distant surface of the open main. After the heavy rains of previous days the air was brilliantly clear, and to the northeast I could readily see on the horizon that cloud-capped isle where Gweir mab Geirioed groans out (so they say) his perpetual imprisonment.

The ocean surface appeared strangely immobile, wrinkled with numberless waves and spotted at regular intervals by bright breakers. There was no sense of movement or depth; it appeared like the gnarled, shiny skin of some monstrous snake lying frozen at my feet. Only at the point of junction where I was poised could one tell of shift, of depth, of limitless power, and of a devouring obscurity concealing worlds upon worlds forgotten in our fleeting existence above.

I learned to realize, too, how the deep reflects and contains that other world of boundless vastness under whose lowest edge we creep. Shadows large as the cantrefs of an earthly kingdom hung still or flew with incredible swiftness above the placid oily glitter of the sea, changing its aspect in the twinkling of an eye. Beyond the clouds the sun might shine through with low-slanting rays to light up a golden puddle of ocean with marvelous vividness, causing my glance to pass the intervening space in one delighted leap. At night, too, the glittering book of heaven could be read with almost equal facility in the mirrored depths beneath. Thus the Cauldron of Poesy and Wisdom lies above and below and all about, mediated through the passage of the *awen* to inspired bards and seers, for the guidance of the sharp, noisy, and brief world of men.

For all my interest and excitement at the prospect of the bright world in which I had so recently found myself, there were times when I was possessed by the most acute spasms of fear. Looking down upon the louring profundity of the watery abyss, I was at times gripped with giddiness, feeling less a danger than a desire to be sucked down, down past the cliff and the rocks and the ocean bed into the oblivion of darkness beyond. Like the magical insects that Nud Law Ereint broke up in water for the destruction of the noxious race of Coranieid, I would be dissolved once more into the nine forms of elements, essence of soils, water of the ninth wave, bloom of nettles: distillation of three drops seethed after a year and a day from Ceridwen's midnight Cauldron.

On the end of a projecting rib of rock two cormorants appeared one day. There they stood, stiff and black and angular. I laughed as I watched my idiotic guards shooting at them with their bows from the cliff-top. Their arrows struck the rock and pierced the heaving surface of the sea, but the swart, crooked figures never moved. The frightened soldiers ran back within the enclosure bounded by the bonfires. I stuck out my tongue after them, and it was all I could do not to jeer aloud.

About the end of the first week a tiny bird with an upturned tail hopped onto my windowsill and down to where a shaft of pale sunlight threw a long bar along the flagstones. We at once became friends, and I took this mark of confidence as a sign of better things. That afternoon Abbot Mawgan called, urging me again to allow him to baptize me. This move was not unexpected on my part, and now that I had had time to reflect upon the matter I could not see any strong reason for denying the good man his wish. No one was likely to object to the knocking over the head of an unbaptized bastard, but an innocent child newly brought into the fold might not lack supporters. If what Abbot Mawgan had told me concerning the king's charming character was true, then it was a slim chance indeed. But a slim chance is a chance, and the alternative was in any case too unpalatable to contemplate.

"Very well," I conceded grudgingly. My friend was so delighted at this that I felt a little ashamed at not having affected more enthusiasm. However, he was so anxious to proceed that my attitude did not seem to concern him unduly. In a trice he had whipped a sheet over my shoulders, signed me with the cross, and rattled off the following:

"Lord, Holy Father, Almighty and Eternal God: drive out the Devil and all heathenish ways from this person; from his head, his hair, his crown, his brain, his forehead, his eyes, his ears, his nostrils, his mouth, his tongue, the bit under his tongue, his gullet, his throat, his neck, his chest, his back, his whole body's inside and orifices, his hands, his feet, all his limbs, all the sinews of his limbs; and from his thoughts, words, and deeds and all his conduct now and henceforth through Thee, Iessu Crist, who reignest."

Phew! That certainly didn't leave the Devil much of a place to hide. Mind you, I did think of somewhere he might have been perching, but then there's something about these solemn occasions that brings out the worst in me. Luckily the abbot was off again, exorcising the Evil One in still further ingenious ways, and getting me to agree to renounce him and all his works. It all clearly followed a formula; otherwise I might have thought there was something personal in all this talk of the Devil. The good abbot was nervous and anxious to complete the ritual as soon as possible. Next moment he blew in my face, shoved some salt in my mouth, and anointed my chest and back with oil, rattling off a succession of prayers the while.

It was all over quite quickly, but when he came to the final blessing it seemed to me that two items were missing. Firstly, much had been made of the purifying powers of the holy waters in which I had been immersed—except, of course, that I hadn't. Secondly, in his concluding words, he had requested the nonexistent assembly to pray for "our brother"; after which words he hesitated a moment, and I guessed that this was the point where my baptismal name should have been pronounced. I raised these points, upon which the monk gazed at me quizzically.

"There is little, it seems, that may be hid from you, my son," he conceded. "You are quite right, of course. The king in permitting the ceremony refused to allow a vessel suitable for your immersion to be brought up here. There are strange tales concerning your mother, Ceridwen, and her Cauldron which have doubtless reached his ears, and made him foolishly apprehensive. But never fear," he went on with an odd little smile, "I think you will find the immersion has been but briefly postponed, which under the circumstances must surely be allowable."

I was curious to know what he meant, but still more inquisitive to find out what was my name. Without a name, one can scarcely be a person at all; indeed, one does not exist.

"Why do you not baptize me with my name, like other folks?" I asked plaintively.

"Because," rejoined the monk emphatically, "my swearing a solemn oath not to do so was the condition of my being permitted to perform the sacrament at all."

I was astonished. "I thought there was something odd about the whole arrangement," I could not help exclaiming, "but this really does seem too much. Why on earth may I not have a name?"

Abbot Mawgan smiled sympathetically.

"As I told you at your birth, the king's druids have told him that he is fated to die at the hands of a Fatherless Child. This, they hold, can only be you. Now, in their prophesying they named you with a name which, for a reason which must be apparent, I have been forbidden to confer upon you."

"So I *do* have a name!" I could not help exclaiming.

The abbot held up his hand reprovingly. "Have patience, my son, and hear me out. The king's druids have advised him in this manner. The *dihenydd*, all things being equal, must take place as fated. But there is a circumstance under which it could be frustrated. If it be fated that King Custennin is to die at the hands of a man bearing a certain name—and yet at the same time that man does *not* bear the name designated—then, clearly, the *dihenydd* will be nullified. So at least the king and his druids believe. And so, in order to fulfill the oath I swore this very morning on the altar of Saint Docco himself, I must leave you baptized but nameless: a procedure which I trust is canonical, but which I am in any case powerless to improve upon."

Hmm. This was tantalizing. But before I could press the matter further, Abbot Mawgan had raised his hand in the sign of the Trinity, and was pronouncing the last, solemn benediction, urging that my spirit and body be cleansed and purified by the (nonexistent) water. He paused, and stood smiling at me; benign, but with a curious air of expectancy. I began muttering some expressions of gratitude, though I felt strongly that matters had been conducted more than a little irregularly.

"Do you feel any different now, my son?" inquired the abbot, with what looked an almost mischievous smile. It was hard to know what to say. I knew he meant well, but truth to tell I had felt a trifle offended at the continual insistence on the Devil's presence within me. What exactly was he getting at? Anyway, at that particular moment all

I really felt was extremely cold, and longed for my good friend to depart so I could jump back into bed.

"Have you noticed nothing?" he asked again. "Is nothing altered?"

I glanced down, since he seemed to be staring meaningly at my not very large person. At once I gave a yelp of surprise. My hairy pelt, which had until that moment covered my body with stiff short fur like an otter's, had been shed, and was lying like the detritus of a barber's work around my feet. Throwing off the sheet with which I had been enveloped, I found my body to be as pinkly bare as any child of Adaf! I could hardly tell what to think when confronted with this unexpected development. Temporarily overcome by a mixture of cold and embarrassment, I scrambled into bed and pulled the coverlet up to my chin.

"You see," explained the abbot, turning to depart, "though the baptism is not yet complete, the spirit of the Lord has begun to work upon you. Your father the Devil (that is what I term him, though you may prefer another name) bestowed upon you your hairy pelt, and also the power to see all the past set plain before you. Now, through God's good grace, you have shed the outward sign of your beastliness. In addition, you will find you possess the added power to see all the future unfolded to your gaze. I earnestly hope you will put this gift to the service of God, who gave it to you, and totally abandon the service of your former Master."

With which he left the room. As the rattle of bolts and bars died away I began at once to reflect on these strange developments. On the whole I was not sorry to lose my fur, which, though warm and aesthetically pleasing to me, was clearly a prime cause of the fear and disgust that my appearance seemed to arouse in everyone except the kindly abbot. But what was all this about the past and the future? I closed my eyes to see whether I really was possessed of the formidable powers attributed to me. My mind was in a whirl, however. I saw a procession of torque-bearing kings passing before me, some with horrid wounds gaping, others proud and glorious in the splendor of their armor, and one or two clad in drab monastic habits with looks emaciated and stricken with guilt or care. I recognized none of them, but wondered if my malevolent King Custennin Gorneu was among them.

This image dissolved into another. I saw warring armies in the skies, and beyond them the stars twinkling out bright and fierce. Among them moved an endless column of the dead, and to my surprise there was I, passing onward at their head. The heavens began to rotate, slowly at first and then with ever-increasing momentum. A bright light, burning at the center, glowed with pure white fire, and it was toward this that the vortex seemed to be drawing me upward, me and all my company. Glancing wildly about me, I glimpsed looming forms, shaped in stars and swirling multicolored clouds, of gigantic men and beasts, lions, boars, griffins, eagles. They were set about me in a belt around the heavens. When first I gazed upon this colossal panorama it seemed to me that it had both a pattern and a meaning which I might grasp. But even as I tried to do so, all swam apart in confusion, the images intermingling and dividing into broken, vanishing elements.

Suddenly I was alone in the midst of the void; alone, and tumbling through the darkness of space which no longer supported me. Looking fearfully below, I saw the surface of a limitless ocean, motionless and calm, its expanse reflecting the stars and planets, set once more in their appointed places in the panoply of heaven. Now, strange to say, as I plunged toward that great sea my fear passed, and I felt only longing to sink far down into the solitude of its somber depths, safe from the emptiness of the aery space around and above me. I struck the glassy surface of that cosmic ocean without a splash or a tremor, and sank gratefully into its tenebrous depths.

In fact I had fallen asleep, exhausted by all that had passed, and emotionally ravaged by all the ill and strange news I had received. When I awoke, the dawn of a new morning had arisen. The fine bright sun of the last few days had departed and the sky was gray and overcast, as befitted the chill month of Ionaur. So far as I could recollect, I had one more day to live. Was that, then, the significance of my dream, the memory of which still lingered forcefully? All that day I pondered on Abbot Mawgan's strange words. Had I really the ability to survey both past and future? Images came and went in the corners of my mind. At times they glimmered furtively at me in the form of beasts, imps, divine heroes. I seemed to see the Fair Folk dancing around me in a ring, mocking and inviting.

As the day drew on, the elements without grew restless and then angry. At high tide the waves surged raging up the cliff, lashing at the base of the Tower of Beli. They seemed to me to be trying to reach up to my high place and bear me back with them below the returning wash. Once or twice splashes of foam beat invitingly against my shutters, which I had closed to exclude the driving rain. I did not respond, but lay, turning feverishly this way and that, on my bed. I was delirious, and the visions crowded ever more vividly upon my imagination. I seemed to see all the history of the kingdoms of the earth, but not in order, and whether past, present, or future I had no means of knowing. I saw, as vividly as if I were present among them, the unfolding of destructions, cattle raids, wooings, battles, terrors, voyages, death-tales, feasts, sieges, adventures, elopements, and plunderings.

In this way I passed another night, and woke to find that the day appointed by the tyrant for my death had arrived. It was, as I had learned, the day the Cristonogion term Ystuil, the Day of the Star, when Crist was baptized in the waters of Jorddonen and the Spirit of God was seen descending from the heavens. But it seems that King Custennin, though professedly Cristion, still held to the old ways, and was wont instead to attend the Circuit of the Horse's Skull in honor of the Lady Riannon, who visits men's households on that day.

Shortly after the first hour one of the hideous crones who attended upon me entered the room, bearing a covered tray and singing in her cracked voice this strange doggerel:

> "Beneath the shroud, beneath the sheet
> The king is come, the king to greet;
> About him hanging, pair by pair,
> Sweet apples from the orchard fair."

She set her offering down on the floor beside my bed and made off, mumbling nothing very pleasant by the sound of it.

Sitting on the side of the bed, I bent down and gingerly lifted the cloth. Underneath was a square board inscribed with a circle in the center, from the center of which radiated to the corners four diagonal ribs of wood. An apple was fixed at each of the corners, while in the middle was set up a small branch, made to look like a miniature tree. From its topmost twig was hanging by a thread the lifeless body of that little bird with the upturned tail who had befriended me in my solitude. Its neck had been wrung, and there it dangled; as I guessed, a malicious portent of my coming fate.

For some minutes I gazed sorrowfully down at my poor little friend on his strange surround. Then I passed on to puzzling over the meaning of this curious construction, for such it must surely have—whether known to those who made it or not. I was resolved to proceed with due caution, for as we say, "What is collected on Malen's horse's back will find its way under his belly." The board itself struck me at once as bearing a strong (though reduced) resemblance to that used in the game *gwyddbwyll*. In that case, the tree would represent the High King, and the apples at the corners the sub-kings at their Centers, North and South, East and West. The resemblance was so strong as surely not to be fortuitous. But why then, instead of the regular pieces, had there been substituted the apples, and the bird on the branch?

Here was a mystery, and despite my awful predicament I became momentarily absorbed in an effort to unravel it. Absently, treating the little structure as if it were indeed the game of *gwyddbwyll,* I made as if to move one of the apples inward to the space where it protects the king. But without the customary pattern of squares this I could not do, so I fell instead (being hungry) to eating the fruit. As I did so, a snatch of verse floated up unexpectedly from beneath my mind:

> "Sweet-apple tree with blossoms soft,
> Roots deep in earth, crook'd branch aloft—
> What news, pale shade, from Gofan's croft?"

I had inadvertently uttered the words aloud, but before I could ponder their meaning or how I had come by them, my reflexions were rudely interrupted by a rough voice from outside the door:

"The news, my young friend, is that our lord the king awaits the *honor* of your company below!"

With which the door was unbarred with the customary groaning and shrieking of bars and locks, and a burly black-bearded soldier strode into the room. Seeing me sitting with a blanket around my naked shoulders, he came over, scooped me up inside the blanket, and slung me over his shoulder as if I were a badger in a bag. Jolting about on his broad back in the most uncomfortable manner, I found myself being taken swiftly down the winding stairway. I tried to preserve my dignity (and maybe keep up my courage) by continuing to eat my apple, but it is not easy to do any of these things when you are being shaken about all over the place.

Before long the jolting was softened somewhat, and judging by a muffled sound which I took to be the roaring of the sea, I gathered that we had emerged onto the level ground. My captor did not pause, and I heard his rough voice raised in greeting or reply as we moved on— whither? Several times I heard reference made to "the king," and it was not hard to guess I was being taken somewhere I would rather not contemplate. Before long, to my surprise, my guard seemed to be descending a fresh flight of steps. When this became more of a scramble than a regular descent, I guessed we must be descending the cliff-edge. Perhaps we had reached the causeway linking the promontory to the mainland by its narrow neck.

Further jolting and grunting on the part of my bearer suggested that the descent had become a scramble of some difficulty, and then suddenly I felt the man's back straighten and we were moving smoothly and easily along a level surface. A moment later, and I was dumped onto soft ground. My blanket fell open, and the broad sky dazzled my eyes so that I had to put my little fists into them. Not far off I could hear the roll and swell of sea breakers, interspersed with the voices of men and cries of gulls.

Gradually I uncovered my eyes and looked about me. My blanket was spread out on a narrow beach whose sandy inlet had been exposed by the retreating tide. Long black ridges of rock, jagged as jaws of the monsters of the deep, ran out on either side into the water. Among their crevices, and those of heaps of great boulders which the malice of the Coranieid had dragged from cliff-top and ocean bed, lay scattered bones and sea-torn pelts; whether of beasts or men I might not tell. Truth to tell, it was not a matter which at that time I was anxious to contemplate too closely.

Above me, giant cliffs, dark against the rising sun, towered up to the sky itself. Still lying helplessly on my back, kicking my little fat legs in the air, I turned my head in the direction of the voices I had heard. There I saw a score or so of soldiers, fully armed with spears and shields. Beside them, a small ray of comfort in the prevailing gloom, stood my friend the abbot, his arms folded inside the broad sleeves of his robe. I tried to catch his eye, but he had turned his head to look upward at a point just behind me.

Managing to swivel my body around a bit, I followed his gaze and at once guessed that I was in the presence of my terrible enemy. For there, on a low rocky platform at the cliff's base, stood a man dark-haired and dark-eyed, a golden torque about his neck and— unchancy spectacle—a hardened bull's hide drawn closely about him, horns on head, and hoofs and tail dangling low.

Perhaps you will think me prejudiced when I say that I sensed malevolence emitting from every pore of the king's body. But what was sinister by any account in his appearance was the glimpse of his low brow shadowed by the slain bull's mask that cowled his squat skull. For from beneath the heavy dun-colored pelt, with its dead eyes and dried nostrils, projected a pair of knotty protuberances: living excrescences upon the king's forehead, which echoed the borrowed spread of curving cusps above. Now I understood how King Custennin came by the epithet by which he is distinguished among the kings of the Island of the Mighty: "Gorneu." There was a blemish upon him in the form of two squat, blunt horns. In size and appearance they were not unlike a man's fingers. Though he made no overt attempt to disguise his deformity, it was not difficult to divine that it perturbed his spirit greatly. Or it may be that the ugly blemish reflected a perturbation already present within him; that I cannot tell.

The king was leaning upon a short javelin whose finely chased head shone as he twisted it about this way and that—a little nervously, as it seemed to me. This must be King Custennin, and the sulky-looking lad beside him perhaps his son or nephew who would one day succeed to the kingdom. The king had seen me turn, but seemed reluctant to meet my gaze. He jabbed toward me with his little spear, shouting furiously the while to his men. Though my end was clearly imminent, I derived some irrational consolation from a sudden realization that the king was as frightened as I was, or more so. The weapon he bore was no instrument of war but some ritual emblem with which he hoped to avert any malign powers he feared I might possess. Then I recalled the *dihenydd*, and understood his apprehension.

At the king's command his soldiers came forward upon the sand, their spears advanced and shields held up as if facing the fiercest of enemy war-bands instead of a naked baby helpless on a blanket. In a moment the shield-circle closed about me, the spears uplifted and clearly ready at a moment's notice to be driven deep into my defenseless body. I heard the king scream out a further command, a scream taken up by gulls coasting by the cliff-face, and closed my eyes. O now, You Golden Glorious One, now is the moment for You to ward over me!

I waited for what seemed an eternity of blind fear. But at last, when no sharp blades came piercing through my flesh and my bones, my scarcely formed veins and sinews, I half opened my eyes and peered around, still expecting the worst. There stood the soldiers, each with his spear poised toward me, a thicket of points with but one focus. They, however, remained immobile, like the images Dristan mab Tallwch encountered in King March's enchanted gallery.

Into the circle beside me had stepped the plump abbot, together with two slaves (or so, by the collars around their necks, I judged them to be). Abbot Mawgan was rattling off his exorcisms, with an occasional apologetic glance toward me. Between them the slaves bore a large open-ended leather sack. Gingerly, they lifted me up and popped me inside; the king all this while yelling out impatient commands. The men hoisted me up between them and began running down the beach toward the sea. So they were going to drown me! I remembered my dream, and saw it as ominous.

At the sea's marge, where it rolled desultorily back and forth, tumbling loose shells a foot this way and a foot back, my bearers halted, dumped me on the ground, and withdrew as swiftly as possible. A shadow fell across me and I looked up to see Abbot Mawgan gazing down.

"What are they going to do with me?" I asked him, unable to hold back two genuine baby's tears that rolled down each cheek.

"Do?" replied my friend (for so I still took him to be). "They will do nothing. It is the sea that they rely upon to achieve their impious ends, these foolish people: *caeci educti a caecis, foveam cadetis.*"

"So they will drown me?"

"*They* will not drown you; they are afraid to kill you. You will stay here, tied in your bag, until the tide takes you away and the sea draws you down into its ever-open maw."

The prospect of this prolonged and unchancy end seemed more terrible even than a short shrift at the hands of the king's brutal spearmen.

"Can you do nothing for me, holy father?" I pleaded abjectly. "Why does he fear me, and why will he not kill me outright?"

The abbot smiled. "Listen to me, my son. It may be that matters are not so desperate as they appear. The king did indeed plan to have you speared or strangled; until, that is, I took care to point out an aspect of the matter which had eluded his thoughts."

"And what was that?"

An angry shout from the king brought a look of apprehension to the abbot's face. "I must talk no more," he muttered, "lest the blaspheming tyrant alter his mind. I simply asked him, my dear boy, whether he sincerely believed in your fated power to encompass his death. 'Of course,' he replied angrily. 'Why else should I have to do away with him?' 'In that case,' I replied, 'had you not best beware, O king? For if indeed this babe is to cause your death, then it necessarily follows that your end must precede his. Kill him, and if the *dihenydd* is indeed to be fulfilled, then your death *must* come first—if only by a minute!' "

Brilliant! Why had I not thought of that? But Abbot Mawgan held up his hand impatiently. The king was well-nigh berserk with impatience, banging with the haft of his javelin on the rock on which he stood and yelling at the abbot to complete the business.

"So you see," continued my protector swiftly, "you are to be left here for the sea to complete your end. It will not be the king, but the ocean, that takes away your life. Have no fear, though," he exclaimed, "for you have about you that which unless I am much mistaken will save you from a watery end."

He indicated the small pouch on its leather loop which he had strung about my neck at our first meeting. It contained, you will recall, that cap of flesh which the good abbot had taken from my head after my birth, claiming it to be in some mysterious way a sure preservative from drowning.

A scream came from behind us, followed by a cacophony of yelling. My companion and I glanced back in surprise. We had momentarily forgotten our circumstances, and King Custennin, beside himself with fearful rage, had advanced to the edge of his rocky vantage point, shrieking at the abbot to complete his task without delay.

"Fasten tight the sack, and let the sea fulfill the sentence!" he bellowed against the wind. "Do you not see that the waters are lapping ever higher against the foot of my sea fortress?" And he pointed with his weapon to where the breakers were beginning to dash themselves once more upon the base of the cliff wall, above which stands upreared against a wintry sky the dark Tower of Beli, fog-wraithed stronghold of wizardry and enchantments, and dread *gormes* upon the Island of the Mighty.

Abbot Mawgan laughed unexpectedly, a loud laugh. The same sea that had returned to beat against the rocky coast of Cerniu was sweeping up the beach beside us. I felt the tide wash cold against the end of my leather bag.

"O foolish Faraon!" cried out the churchman with startling boldness. "You have named the child! See, the ocean has lapped his foot, and 'sea fortress' have you called him. Henceforth 'sea fortress,' *Merlin,* shall be his name, and a protector shall he be to the noblest sea fortress there is in the world, the cliff-girt Island of the Mighty. The first part of the *dihenydd* is fulfilled!"

King Custennin's face went white with rage and fear, and he took a step forward in unreflecting fury. As he did so his feet suddenly gave way beneath him as he slithered forward upon a strand of green seaweed; dulse and sea-girdle from which the wizard Gwydion once fashioned the leather vessel in which the divine child Leu floated out across the waves to find a haven in fair Arianrod's starry palace. Reaching out wildly with his spear for support, Custennin awkwardly allowed the haft to descend into a rock cleft. In the same instant he fell heavily forward in such an unchancy manner that the bright lance-point was driven through his breast and heart and out between his shoulder blades.

[It is this that the blessed Gildas the Wise foretold, when he railed against the impious king with the words: *"Quid inimicorum vice propriis te confodis sponte ensibus hastis?"* For the saint had received that gift of true prophecy which was denied by God to the false prophets of the idol Baal, druids and soothsayers. And it is I, Cynfael the scribe of the cloister of Meifod, who have written these words, my spiny-clawed cat White-throat playing beside me in the sunlight.]

I caught only the briefest glimpse of the portentous sight: the king's body caught up like a spiked carrion crow, his empty, malevolent gaze fixed upon the shingle beneath, all evil drained out of him. The hood of his cloak had fallen back upon his shoulders, and the hue of the knotty horns upon his brow changed from bloody red to a maggoty pallor. Next instant Abbot Mawgan had thrust me roughly down and knotted a thong about the sack above my head. I heard a muffled confusion of shouting, and at the same time felt the sudden coolness as an incoming wave scooped me up and drew me out to sea with a rush.

In my ears there was a roaring, as of the deep itself, amidst which I heard a farewell cry from my generous friend: "Now, my son, the three waves of baptism are completed!"

As the sea washed about me and I felt myself floating free, I saw that so indeed it was, though this was not the immersion for which I had looked—nor was I overpleased by the course it was taking. Just twelve days old, and I alone on the wild ocean in my leather bag! About me moaned the waves, weeping the anguished cry of drowned Dylan Eil Ton. Tossed giddily upon them was I in my bag: upon the wave of green Ywerdon, and the wave of Manau, and the wave of the North, and the wave of Prydein himself.

Whither was I being borne upon the backs of the breakers, white-maned steeds of Manawydan mab Lir? O Bright Shining Radiant One, I think that You alone can save me now! Reach down with Your Sure Hand, I implore You, and pluck me to safety! Am I to be abandoned helpless and fatherless, or is it You who are my Father indeed?

CHAPTER THREE

THE SERPENT
OF THE DEEP

That was one of my bad times. One moment I was with my fellows (all but one hostile, that is true, but suddenly they appeared strangely dear to me) on the yellow strand. The next I was enclosed in pitchy darkness, bobbing up and down on the surface of the unformed and unknown. For long a terrible roaring never ceased to sound in my ears. I was turned this way and that until I was giddy, was for a time swept high into the air and down into the abyss with a swelling motion that seemed momentarily to separate my spirit from its body, and at others was rolled slowly over and over as if by a playful hand. Fortunate it was that I was enclosed in no ordinary bag but one which, as I have learned since, was marvelously fashioned by Gofannon mab Don himself, toiling for the space of a year and a day in darkness beside the glare of his forge.

It was impossible to know how much time had passed, whether it was night or day, or whether I was still within the little gulf above which looms the Tower of Beli. It was long before I learned the words that could undo the knot securing the neck of my bag, and the first time I did so a renewed storm was loosed upon the ocean in that very instant. Ah, do You remember how I called out to You then, imploring You to reach out with Your Sure Hand to preserve my fragile existence?

> O Thou monarch of the moon,
> Staunch sovereign of the sun,
> Player of the planets' tune
> On Gwydion's starry river-run;
> King of world-encircling stream,

Chieftain of the firmament;
Radiant brow, whose aery beam
Is its brightest ornament!

Velvet cloak of purple hue
Spread about thy limbs so true,
And their iridescent sheen;
Diamonds scattered from thy hands
Glitter over all the lands:
Nine the elements terrene.

I also made a desperate effort to mutter some of the prayers Abbot Mawgan had intoned over me, though with little apparent effect at the time. Some of it may eventually have done some good, for in due course the storm passed away, all fell still, and I in my bag lay suspended almost motionless among the elements. After a cautious delay I again recited the requisite formula and popped my head apprehensively forth. It was nighttime, but a waxing moon hung bright in the vault above me, its mirror's gleam outshone by sparkling clusters of stars of a brilliance I had never seen before. They gazed down upon me from every side, while the moon herself sent a shimmering track directly across the ocean's still surface toward my tranquil resting place.

The whole of creation was still, save for the quiet beating of my heart. Occasional far-off glimmers of lightning beyond the horizon silhouetted the rim of the world, leaving its dark curve imprinted upon my vision, lingering after the momentary flare had passed. I felt no fear; on the contrary, only a sense of comfort that it was my warm little heart that palpitated at the center of all this jeweled stillness. I knew, too (how should I not), that You with Your Sure Hand sustain it all in perfect harmony, and that my heart is but a pulse of Yours.

Across all the dazzling array above me stretched Caer Gwydion, a broad river of spangled light arching itself across the dome. If the dome itself was a meadow filled with celestial flowers whose eyes winked up at a hidden sun, then Caer Gwydion appeared to me like a waving ribbon of dew-spangled cobwebs hung across grass-tips among the dispelling mists of morning. At its summit the River loops about its focus, that Nail of the Heavens which is the center of the celestial mill wheel. One day I would sail that stream, but already I sensed there was much to be done before my time came.

So I floated at peace in the solitude, aware that I alone of all men was awake to contemplate that book whose text it was my task to decipher. Whether the land lay to north or south, east or west, I had no means of knowing. For I was solitary at the center of the void, the still sea extending unbroken on every side. From its farthest encircling bound arose sheer the skirts of the tent of Heaven, through rents in whose sides shone those lamps that even now spoke to me in silence. I strained my ears to catch a faint echo of their matchless music which even now must be resounding through the uppermost aether. Once or twice I fancied I caught some dropping notes of that distant harmony. Then I recovered myself, to find that what I heard was but the lingering remembered strains of a thrush's melody which had enchanted me from a bush below my window in the Tower of Beli. And as for all the grief that I had witnessed and the sorrow experienced, I had no memory of it nor of any sorrow in the world.

As I and the stars stared at each other and reflected, the stillness of the image was jarred: Rending a gash in the upper canopy, a star tumbled from its place like a fiery serpent and vanished. Despite the peace that imbued my spirit at that moment and seemed to pervade the whole iridescent bowl, I felt the burning streamer to be a portent of troublous times to come.

The moon itself was at this time in the House of the Fishes. There were twelve Houses through which I would have to pass along the length of Caer Gwydion before I came to the Door itself, and who knew what perils might lie along the way? That must remain hidden from me until my time came, but in the meantime I sensed that the star tumbling into the House of the Fishes indicated the beginning of my journey, a journey from which there would be no turning back. It is at *gwyddbwyll* that the gods are playing there with those who would lay their oppression on the land, and it was upon this first day of the year that Your Sure Hand reached down to make the first move.

At this I was filled with a sudden dread, and panic seized me. The somber glassy face of the ocean, which until then had been for me a support and floor to the heavens it reflected, I now saw as a void, empty and limitless as that above me. I was no longer the focus of all things that are, upheld by Your Mighty Arm, but a floating speck tumbling endlessly through eternity. I knew not which way to look, for my mind was without direction. Young and rash as I was, I reacted wildly and without reflexion. Had I the knowledge I now possess, had I read the books of Math and Gwydion, I should have paused. But there was a *dihenydd* upon me, just as there was upon King Custennin Gorneu, and it was written in the books as it is in the bright lettering of the heavens.

Up to the surface of my mind there floated a ghastly image: the gory head of a great king, blood dripping from his severed veins and windpipe. The vertebrae of his pillared neck gleamed white where they were splintered; the Tree had been felled by the axe of a woodman with the Murderous Hand. Whether it was the head of Arthur or of Maelgun or of Urien, I do not know. But I guessed what a fearful task was mine, what dread duty, and what suffering I would undergo that the Island of the Mighty might be sustained in the balance of time and space and destiny.

The moon, constellations, and planets began to revolve (so it seemed to me) about their axis with ever-increasing speed, until they became a glittering spiral ascending to the vortex. Their ocean-images paralleled the motion about me, and I felt a great stirring among the waters below.

I was sucked down into an abyss of horrors. The waters, from which I had but recently emerged within my mother's womb, closed over my head; and as I sank downward I saw the moon's face shaken and shattered above me as its light was broken up and dissipated in the opaque, formless mass in which I was engulphed. All became dark, darkness of a solidity that neither light nor life could penetrate. Or so I thought, and gave myself up for lost—until suddenly I was aware of silvery, darting shapes that sported and glided all around. A school of bright fishes had suddenly swarmed about me and bore me along in their eddying course. As I looked about I saw that they were thousands strong, an armored host with glittering scales; so many that they appeared to me a single shape-shifting sea creature that glided and twisted this way and that.

So it came about that I was taken up and was as one with my friends the herrings. There are those who may consider it eccentric or indecorous that I should once have been a mere fish. If so, they know but little of the life I led during those years! Is there anything ignoble in a being whose glistening flanks of emerald and sapphire reflect the watery surface of Ocean herself, and whose silvery belly matches to perfection the dappled lights and shades of that element in which he has his being? As if this were not sufficient glory, his luminescent form alters its gorgeous hues to harmonize with the ever-changing colors of the sea: a rich golden-brown imperceptibly transformed into an ethereal grayish-green. What was the loricated armor of Arthur to this? Could even Gofannon mab Don forge mail so glorious in its perfection?

I will bore you no further with my herring-life, O king, for I see you growing restless on my *gorsedd*; take care how you irritate me, though! I will say only this. Your days and those of all your fellow princes are passed in bitterness and strife. Even now you are here to learn how your armies will fare this summer against those of the men of Bryneich. It is true, is it not? Nor is this all; this year you war with the sea-robbers who are sworn foes to the Thirteen Princes of the North. They are foreigners, scavengers, foxes of deceit; a black host, wandering up every estuary, who worship the one-eyed demon they call Woden. But last year did you not enter into battle with your relatives in Aeron, and the year before that with the men of Stratclud—princes who speak the same tongue and profess the same faith as you? And whom will you attack and slay next year? Could it be your cousin Morgan of the Gap Tooth, with whom you have sworn a treaty of eternal friendship? I see I startle you; well, be that as it may.

I say nothing of your wars and manslaughters: I saw enough of them during the slaughter of Arderid. What I do say is this. Among the herrings of our shoal were we a thousand million in number? Ten thousand million? I cannot tell: Manawydan mab Lir it is alone who counts and knows. True it is, though, that we are as the grains of sand upon the ocean floor beneath us. Each year we travel a thousand miles or more from the Isles of Orc to our spawning grounds in the southern channel of the stormy Sea of Udd. During all that journey, traveling for two months or more, think you that strife breaks out within our ranks? Do we war over our feeding grounds, limited as they are, or struggle for room to drop the spawn? As we return northward with the current that encircles the Sea of Udd, it may be that we encounter another shoal of equal size. Do we rush upon each other with bows bent and swords drawn, eager for the place of battle?

I tell you that strife has not been nor ever will be among the herring-folk. There are neither sieges, nor cattle raids, nor hostage-taking among the herring-hosts. But why talk of strife? Picture to yourself numberless millions speeding through the depths, packed close together yet never touching, their faint vision in the darkness no greater in span than the score or so of fish about them. Each flickers and turns in never-ceasing feeding without possibility of collision. Then, when our feeding ground is exhausted or our spawning complete, we turn as one body—a body, be it remembered, a hundred miles in length and fifty in breadth—and swim together to our next destination. Not one of us gives a command; we *know* and *feel* and *act*. Among us are neither kings nor counselors, yet that perfect harmony of purpose and execution which is our *gwir deyrnas* prevails.

So I lived for forty years. Forty times we encircled the sea; forty times, a thousand million laid each her ten thousand spawn, and forty times we rose in gladness to the surface to sport beneath the full moon of the Nos Kalan Gaeaf, the Autumn Calends. But now my time was come, and the Hamper of Gwydno beckoned. One day, as I plunged on my endless course through the depths of Manawydan's watery halls, I found myself suddenly alone. Not for long, though, for there approaching me was a great fish more splendid by far than I had encountered during the term of my wanderings.

I knew it to be the Salmon of Lyn Liw, the oldest of all created beings, who acquired wisdom from eating the hazelnuts that float up from the Spring of Leudiniaun. He was of great size and ponderous movement, his flanks scarred and worn, but his bright eye told of unfailing youth. No word passed between us, but I knew well that he had come for me. I was drawn to his side and there I stayed, my course reflecting every turn and dart of his. Whither he was taking me I did not know, but I sensed well enough that what had been fated at my birth was taking place, and I had no choice but to obey my *dihenydd*.

Farther and farther out into ocean the Salmon of Lyn Liw pursued his course with myself drawn by his side. We were gliding above a huge mud-covered featureless plain, a plain whose grayish-black expanse was broken by neither trees nor hills, lakes nor rivers.

Vegetation there was none, unless you except small scattered fernlike growths swaying uneasily in the deep-water current. We were now far below the depths frequented by my former comrades the herrings, or the mackerel, sprats, and other species of the upper waters with whom I had become familiar in the course of our perennial voyaging. Now we encountered myriads of tiny lantern fish whose eyes glowed like red coals as they glanced upward at our passing; or still vaster shoals of hatchetfish, minute silvery discs gleaming like a hoard of coins spilling forth from the treasure chests of kings in Rufein and Caer Custennin.

We were swimming low along the surface of the underwater plain, which stretched level and featureless for mile after mile beneath us. I sensed we were passing ever farther toward the west, where Beli's steeds rest after drawing his golden chariot on its bright diurnal course, but I never dreamed of questioning my companion as to the purpose of our journey. His air of calm deliberation told me that it was for no light motive that he had drawn me from the familiar company of herrings out into this uncharted world, far from the familiar Sea of Udd. With him I felt no danger; indeed, these emptier depths contained no threat that I could see. Close below me I saw from time to time a slow-moving cloud trail across the mud level where crimson and orange amphipods pursued their ungainly path, or a cuttlefish shot out his long projecting tongue to seize a wretched prawn. Among them, too, arose faint dusty swirls as bristle worms or sea urchins buried themselves in haste at the passing overhead of our faint shadows.

To an observant eye there was beauty to be found even in this uncultivated world. It possessed its own exotic vegetation: floating sponges shaped like lilacs or elf-caps; others growing up to all appearance like Venus flytraps such as you, O king, may see in wayside bogs about us here on Newais Mountain; yellow, red, and purple sea fans, plumes, ferns, stalked streaming moss; all interspersed with gentle, wash-colored starfish, languorously arching and stretching their studded limbs on the soft sea floor.

It was only as we began to pass beyond the seemingly endless plain that I became unpleasantly aware that in this tranquil wilderness danger lurked as elsewhere. From time to time I was amused by the antics of small squids, who changed their color several times over in agitated anticipation of our approach. Then, as we came almost upon them, they would disappear angrily behind an inky squirt discharged for our benefit. My indulgent mockery swiftly passed, however, when it was brought forcibly home to me how much all in this life is a question of proportion. For there, suddenly, a little way to our right, was another squid of very different stamp. From his blunt tail to the tip of the two long tentacles that streamed out before him he must have stretched fifty or sixty feet in length. His eight shorter tentacles curled and uncurled a little at our passing, but beyond this he gave no indication of being perturbed by our presence. Still, I intensely disliked the gaze of his bold eye and the curve of his beak where it nestled at the heart of those streaming tentacles.

Almost immediately after this disturbing encounter, the featureless plain of mud over which we had been traveling for what I took to be several weeks came to an abrupt end. I had kept no track of time or distance, but the passing of night and day had been faintly distinguishable even at the great depth at which our journey was being conducted. Now, suddenly, the familiar seascape below us had vanished, to be replaced by an impenetrable pitch-black void. These must be the Waters of Annufn, I reflected with a pang of alarm; I must turn back before it is too late. But a glance from the calm, all-seeing eye of the Salmon of Lyn Liw stilled my panic.

So powerful was the influence of this extraordinarily ancient being over me that I did not hesitate to follow when he deliberately turned over on his side and plunged down into the darkened abyss. For a time I could see nothing as we dived ever deeper and deeper. Then, gradually, as my eyes became accustomed even to this region of eternal night, I became aware of hundreds of pinpricks of light all around. Many were bright as the stars that smiled down upon me as I floated in my bag upon the waters of Hafren, after my liberation from the Tower of Beli. Others glowed with faint luminosity, like dull, staring eyes glimpsed by shepherds from their campfire in the forest night.

It did not take long for me to realize that we were surrounded by myriads of light-emitting fish. Some bore luminous bands or spots upon their sides and bellies, while others were equipped with staring, gleaming eyes. Some of these emitted a lanternlike beam, lighting up an area before them. It was by following these brief rays that I became gradually aware that we were swimming down the face of an immense black cliff. As we plunged downward, so everything grew colder, darker, stiller, and more other than this world above.

How long we continued this descent I have no means of knowing. Were you to tell me it was weeks or months, I could not contradict you. I only know that eventually we came up against a floor of black slime: we had gained the bottom of the gulf!

I will not describe our further travels in detail. It is unlikely you will ever have occasion to visit that infernal region, and should you do so it would in any case be with me as your guide. Suffice it to say that for five ages of the five periods we traveled monotonously onward over a grim rocky landscape of mountain ranges and hills, interspersed with the dead level mud floor to which we had become accustomed during the first part of our journey over the plain.

This region, which is many, many times bigger than the earth on which we live, is the nethermost level of the Waters of Annufn. Nothing there is ordered rightly. There are creatures squatting or creeping upon its floor which comprise nothing but mouth and anus. Continually they devour the ooze before them and discharge it in a thin stream behind. They are the living symbols of this nether Wasteland, one where everything has been broken down, atomized into annihilation. For it is in reality nothing but a huge stagnant midden. From the surface of the great waters, thousands of feet above, the debris of life sinks down unceasingly onto the dead surface of the earth's necessary-house. For millions upon millions of years it has received everything the earth rejects: not merely dust, clay, and rocks slipping from melting ice-islands, but the excrement and corpses of millions and millions of birds, fishes, sea beasts, and—on occasion— men. All is absorbed into the shapeless slime, whose level is rising imperceptibly in the darkness. Let a sailor's foot slip unchancily on the gunwale of his boat, a stricken bird fall from the air, a blazing fire-mountain discharge its clouds of smoking ash: All, all seeps below and sinks forever to the level surface of the primeval quagmire, there to be ingested and excreted to all eternity through the mucus-spit of spiraling slime-worms.

Within the chaos lie the nine elements of creation. There was a time when I traveled straight as an arrow to the warm southland, to the borderlands of the Middle Sea, where dwell the people of the Groeguir. And there I spoke with a wise man, a *llyfrawr;* the wisest there was at that time of their people. He it was who showed me that in the beginning there existed no conjoined forms, but faces without necks, arms without shoulders, eyes detached from foreheads, ox-headed, with rolling gait and thousand hands; all sterile, without progeny. "Many a head," said he, "comes to birth without its neck." Yet there came a night, and a fire in that night, from which the lovely limbs of men and maidens emerged whole, natural, and entwined not in the profusion of deformity and chaos but the blessed ecstasy of love. It was love that brought about the transformation: the love that gleaming Arianrod bore for her son Leu Law Gyfes, Dristan for fair Esylt, and I in my turn (as perchance you shall see, O king) for my sister Gwendyd.

But I knew none of these things during the time of my apprenticeship with the ancient Salmon of Lyn Liw, and it was with disgust and fear growing upon me with every mile that I began to sense we were approaching our goal. Though no word passed between us, I never once doubted that my guide had brought me here for some transcendent purpose. For you must recall, O king, that this bright world, within which you and the men of your kingdom dwell, is to that Otherworld at the summit of Caer Gwydion but as the sluggish murk of the sea bottom is to this.

We had come at last to a mighty range of mountains, up whose steep, valve-enclustered sides we skimmed with ever-increasing speed. Now we had attained its ridge, over which we passed onward. I saw beneath me a tortured landscape: mountains whose hollowed summits told of once-belching sulphurous fire and boulders hurtling upward until they tore through the sea's surface and vented their rage against the skies beyond.

Before long I saw a dramatic change come over the ground below. The suffocating mantle of sediment which hung on the flanks and peak of every oceanic mountain and hill, and which filled plains and valleys with flat layers, immeasurably deep, began to recede and then abruptly ceased. Now we could see the bare, craggy heads of mountains more jagged than any encountered so far, with clean rocks tumbled about and everywhere slipways, puddles, and excrescent accu-

mulations of molten rock which had—not very long before, it appeared—
poured from the soaring crests of these sleeping furnaces. That the
discharges had been relatively recent was evidenced by a perceptible
warmth wafting up from the lava beds, where once-fiery rocks, cooled
instantly by the waters as they emerged, had been molded into rounded
pillows with sides serrated in curvaceous patterns.

Above this clear, clean, but dreadfully disfigured landscape we
floated. We no longer followed the curves of the hills as hitherto, but
passed directly above the volcano tops. At times we were shifted
forcefully from our course by warm lateral currents, which made me
wonder whether mountains farther along the ridge were exploding
through their thin crusts. Once the earth shuddered perceptibly, its
face blurring for an instant before my startled gaze. Despite my confidence in my guide, I was becoming ever more alarmed, and once or
twice (I confess) contemplated flight.

But it was at that moment of impending crisis that we attained
our destination. Skimming the ridge of a sharp-backed range, we
suddenly found ourselves poised above the edge of an enormously
deep rifted valley, whose course stretched away on either side far to
unknown limits. For the first time since our initial encounter the
Salmon was undoubtedly troubled. Instead of pursuing our arrowlike
course across the breadth of ocean, we wheeled to our left and coasted
southward along the frontier ridge, I following my companion's gaze
as he peered from time to time into the great cleft which lay like a deep
wound gouged into the flank of earth. He had become unexpectedly
cautious, pausing and fluttering his fins from time to time before
proceeding.

It was not long before I saw what we had come for. For some
time I had sensed disturbing shocks in the water, and felt warmer and
yet warmer currents strike me. We passed through thin clouds of a
grayish sediment not encountered before, and then . . . there it was
before us! Halting and hovering over the concave summit of a massive
peak, we had a perfect view of the next mountain in the chain, a gaunt
crag towering high above that over which we floated. Its huge hellish
bulk was girded about with clouds and smoke of disturbed sediment.
Its brink was of an appalling height, so that we could scarcely see the
top of it. But about that towering peak, steep as a fortress wall, we
glimpsed firebrands and red sparks leaping about like frenzied imps
and demons of the Underworld.

All of a sudden its top detached itself without any warning and
flew upward in silent explosion, shattering into a myriad pieces of
various sizes. Under the dense pressure of the great waters all appeared

to take place in slow motion. As yellow and orange flames spouted from the neck of the decapitated mountain, the splintered summit was hurled leisurely upward and outward, giant boulders, broken rocks, and streams of molten lava pouring out until they began tumbling lazily over into the depths around.

I watched, fascinated and terrified. I pictured the fiery contents, seething and bubbling like the enchanted brew in Ceridwen's Cauldron. I saw glowing lava spurt and slither over the rim, like that bloody froth which trickles from the lips of a slain warrior. The open tip of this suppurating tumor of the tormented earth vomited forth mounting cataracts of steam, pouring upward in a vertical river of bubbles and ash. Even as the lava began pouring down the mountain's flanks, the icy water cooled it so that on the lower slopes it turned to rolling boulders such as we had seen around the extinct volcanoes lining this huge world-cleft.

The turbulence around us grew ever greater and the water warmer. Eddying shocks pulled us this way and that, and as I struggled to maintain my balance and keep near to my protector, I caught glimpses of other mountains still farther off along the chain beginning to give off sudden spurts of steam and then ponderously breaking up. The row of blazing cones glowed fiercely as the furnaces of Gofannon mab Don—assuming that is not what in reality they were. One by one they burst out into cascading showers of boulders, raging cataracts of steam and boiling slime. Shaken by successive explosions, I saw from time to time a sudden discharge send a group of rocks spinning directly upward with such force that I could picture them bursting through the surface of the waters thousands of feet above us and rising high into the sunlit air of the empty ocean.

I glanced appealingly at the great fish beside me, and noted to my surprise that he was not contemplating the stupendous series of explosions taking place in the silent waters around us but, with an intentness I had never seen before, directed his reflective gaze at the bed of the great valley below its parallel ranges of flaring peaks: a fiery pathway lit by glaring torches (so it seemed to me), leading down to the icy horrors of Uffern. Following his glance, I saw that the floor of the valley was rolling and swelling in enormous waves as the earth's crust began to split into huge jagged-edged chunks. All at once a deep crevice split the center of the valley down its middle, opening up what appeared to me a fathomless seam. And from within the seam there now heaved up twin walls of rock, driven upward and outward by some unimaginably powerful subterranean force.

As these rock layers emerged, falling on their sides and thrust away from the ever-widening fissure, they were driven with irresistible pressure against the existing valley floor. Through the water I felt a juddering lurch, and was stupefied to see the whole floor—the mountain beneath me, the great crust of the world—begin to slide away on its base and draw slowly but perceptibly away to our rear. At the same time it was possible to see a similar cataclysm taking place on the opposite side of the cleft; the twin mountain ranges were being prised apart!

Mountains were exploding and shattering on every side, the waters of the ocean boiled in a swirling flurry of splintered rocks, mud, and ash, and blinding broken flashes of flame flared amid the gathering darkness. Tossed this way and that, I was losing all sense of balance and perception. The primeval chaos was reasserting itself, the breaking up of the nine elements into a meaningless congeries outside time and space and coherence. Good Abbot Mawgan had told me I possessed power to survey both past and future, but what I was witnessing was the destruction of past, present, and future. Just as the ordered objects of upper air disintegrated into primeval ooze as they filtered down to the ocean bottom, so now I saw all elements of the cosmos diverging and settling into the directionless, timeless, disjunct void from which they had emerged at the dawn of the gods.

Fear gripped me such as I had not known even when I thought the spears of King Custennin's guards were poised to grind together within my thumping heart on the strand below the Tower of Beli. For death is assuredly the gateway to life, our own and others'. But now I knew how delicately poised is all that creation which Your Sure Hand sustains in harmonious balance; a tilt in the balance of the scales, an unchancy fall of the dice on the *gwyddbwyll* board, and all that beautiful harmony is unhinged forever. The bottom of Brychan's Whirlpool is opening, the abyss into which all things are drawn and emerge no more.

Then, as I hung suspended in fear and loss, I caught the steady gray eye of the Salmon of Lyn Liw fixed reproachfully upon me. At once my cold herring's heart grew warm within me. The gaze of that wise creature, the oldest of all created beings, recalled me in a flash to understanding. For how could the primordial chaos be, when *I* was there to contemplate it? For *I* was there, and I sensed with a thrill of strength that, were all to dissolve into shapeless, unrelated atoms, I by my observance alone drew all to order. For I am Merlin, son of Morfryn, who was born in the Tower of Beli and played with my friend the wren and watched the cormorants from my turret window, and lived twelve days of sun and wind and storm before my baptism. *I* exist in time and space; I see (not clearly, but sufficiently) the succession of kings who have reigned and will reign over the Island of Prydein with its Three Adjacent Islands—and what I see possesses order, direction, and purpose. I have mapped it, limned it, and made it be: simply by *my* being!

O You Bright Glorious One! How could I have doubted? When You encircled the dark host of Oeth and Anoeth at the Battle of Godeu, moving on one foot and with Your One Eye fixed upon them, that bright eye numbered the kings and over-kings, free and unfree, and more; the things that no man knows but which are: the counting of the stars of heaven, and the sands of the sea, and flakes of snow, and dew on lawns, and hailstones, and grass beneath the feet of horses, and the white horses of the Son of Lir in a sea storm. All these *You* know, and will I think vouchsafe me to know in my time. I am not afraid!

When first I sank beneath the ocean waves in the Gulf of Hafren I had experienced unexpected placidity and content, much as a man feels when falling asleep after a troubled day. I had felt as if the great waters, enclosing me within their dark bosom and gently supporting me by the pressures of their depths, had benignly removed me from the cares and agitation I had known on earth. It had been almost with gratitude then that I had accepted my sinking below the surface. Now, however, I knew a mounting horror. I longed for the daylight, and welcomed the invigorating prospect of lurid life with my fellow men, its hardships, struggle, and brevity, as well as the warmth of its pleasures. I sensed with relief that my companion was preparing to leave the scene of chaos before which we had hovered for what seemed like endless time. I paddled with my fin and turned to flee. As I did so I could not resist glancing for the last time down into the great fire-swollen chasm between its twin mountain chains. What I saw astonished me, and the image will remain with me to the end of my days—should that time ever arrive. Think you it will, O King Ceneu of the Red Neck, son of Pasgen?

As the subterranean river of fiery molten rocks disgorged the thick hide of earth on either marge, I perceived among the heaving debris stretches and patches of something that writhed and shifted painfully beneath them. They appeared like sections of scaly skin on a half-buried undulating body, which ground the rocks with its ribs and dripped eternal fire from its valve-encrusted flanks in its retching labors. Below the trench, I now sensed, there lay that mighty Beast they call the Adanc of the Deep, whether serpent or dragon I know not, whose form encircles the world itself. I was, as are all men, familiar with the tale of the monster Chaos, and how You, O Bright

One, with Your Sure Arm consigned it after a terrible struggle to the darkest recess of Ocean. But to gaze upon its hideous form myself!

Oritur nauis et desuper Draco mortuus, uocatur Terra.

To my alarm I saw that the Salmon of Lyn Liw had already turned away. For one brief, dread moment I glanced back to where the Beast writhed in its tortured bondage, discharging noxious flames and gases from the numberless hidden orifices of its encircling strength. Seized with an overwhelming fear, I made after my guardian as swiftly as I was able, and in no time at all we were speeding back across the tracts covered in our voyage outward. Over my gleaming flank I caught a last glimpse of the great mountain above, belching out all its flame into the juddering waters and swallowing it again, so that it seemed all one ball of fire.

So it is also with the Adanc of the Deep, I reflected, if all that men say be true. For it is his own tail that he constantly devours, where he encounters it at the girdling of the earth. Devouring himself, he is self-slain and then, regurgitative, gives birth unto himself anew. Why is it, think you, that you bear that writhing gold-black torque set about your throat, O King Ceneu of the Red Neck?

Time and necessity encircle all creation, the new being reborn from the old. There is the shadow below the sea and the light that gilds its surface. One requires the other, opposites though they be, and Beli's golden chariot must sleep nightly within the darkened cave if it is to achieve its auroral ascent upon the arc of upper air.

As druids and *llyfyrion* teach us, "Men's souls and the universe are indestructible, although at times fire and water may prevail," which I take to be a revelation of continual cycles of death and reparturition. And what is the encircling Adanc of the Deep, his tail in his slavering jaws, but the pitiless cycle of renewal which contains itself and is preserved in the salt: tormented in his subaqueous travails, continually creating the cosmos anew through breaking of the waters?

And so once again we directed our course straight as an arrow through the watery abyss, leaving the seabed far below. In my present state of fear and horror I would have found the sight even of a clumsy sea slug familiar and a little comforting, but the choice of route did not lie with me. Indeed, I had reason to be thankful, for our journey seemed to pass with unexpected rapidity.

Within what may have been a week or so there came the happy moment when we abandoned our monotonous traversing of the featureless deep, and began ascending swiftly through ever warmer and lighter waters until our heads abruptly emerged above lapping waves. Looking about me, I saw that we had arrived in a broad estuary, from whose banks stretched away meadows of a verdant lushness that I never recall seeing before or since. Clearly I was influenced by my forty years' sojourn in the watery wastes, for though a bright sun shone down cheerily upon the wavelets I could see that it was already late autumn. Southward stood a serried row of mountains, whose peaks had already received their first dusting of snow. Crowning them uprose a lofty peak, thick sweeping snow mantling his ridge. Beautiful full-bellied clouds, bright and fleecy as the sheep of Gwenhiduy tossing upon the tide's edge, hung upon the summits of the great mountain and his sisters. The sun, smiling down through gaps in the moving cloud-rack, appeared to bestow upon them some of his effulgence; so that it glowed within them, darting out bright lantern rays below the gray roof of cloud, which reflected the gray expanse of the wide estuary and ocean beyond. Lovely was the junction of mountain and cloud, and beautiful the play of light upon them.

It was approaching the time to bid farewell to my mentor, the wise old Salmon of Lyn Liw, who now bore me on his back through the shimmering strait. Perched on the back of the oldest of all created beings, I watched the sea pass from sight as we rounded a level grassy headland.

As I took my last glance behind me, I beheld an extraordinary vision. I believe I saw the ocean raised up to the western sky, its surface turned over toward me like a glassy wall. There, as if on land, I saw through the water, which was so pellucid, bright, and clear that all the fish and monsters of the ocean appeared in their teeming myriads like so many herds of cattle on a broad level plain. But how immeasurably vaster and more densely populated! My old companions the herrings passed by in bodies large as floating kingdoms, pausing and moving onward in their grazing as one great single-purposed cloud. There, too, dark against the sky, sailed ponderously mighty whales whose shadows darkening the land below were broad as your ramparted stone and mortar fortress at Caer Luelid, O king.

I heard the hoarse booming of the main thunder in my ears; saw salmon, iridescent, white-bellied, plunged through its waves; in their wake huge bull-seals, thick and dark, and ravening reptiles rough-ribbed and ragged-toothed. Then the blast and rushing roar of wind and water uprose, so that the ocean was transformed into heaving hills and unscalable mountains; squalls, tempests, hurricanes: the maelstrom of the deep, whose vortex is dissolution of time and space in annihilation unimaginable.

Even as this vision faded and the glassy wall leveled once more with the horizon, it was brought home again to me how immeasurably vaster is that broad deep than the active sunlit world above its surface which we, kings, warriors, and poets, inhabit. Well it is for us that we look outward and upward, on the world of men and the bright abodes of the gods. For below lies the unshaped void with its dim floating images from which all has emerged, and to which all will one day return. As the verse foretells,

The sea shall roll across green Ywerdon in one flood.

But it may be that green Ywerdon, and our fair Island of Prydein, too, with their woods and lakes and beautiful women, will rise once more from the depths. Of that I may have more to tell, though not at this time, O king!

I return to my story. The Salmon was bearing me swiftly along with the tide into a river mouth. I became aware of this quite suddenly with the closing in of the banks on either side. The incoming tide had all but covered the mud flats, which merged into broad grassy levels. Here, I reflected, is the point at which the Serpent's Wasteland becomes the bright earth, the marge along which poets like to wander. It was the frontier, too, which lay between my chaotic existence in the unreflecting profundity of the watery void, and the testing time of thought and action I sensed lay before me.

How came it that the void acquired form, and the sleep of death awoke into life? But even as I asked the question, the answer came to me with the sunshine that warmed my blue-green back. O Golden Glorious One! With Your Skilled Hand, Bright One, Light One, You plucked up the earth from its glassy prison, and set it free beneath the heavens!

The tide, which seemed to race with extraordinary swiftness, was lapping at the grass tussocks bounding its limits. Its vigor was gradually ebbing, and it was clear the race must before long resume its outward flow. The time had come for the wisest and oldest of all created beings to abandon me to my destiny. Setting me gently on a sandbank, he circled me three times with his right flank set toward me, all the while observing me with his calm gray eye; and then, with a switch of his tail, he turned and made off down the eddying channel.

Now I was myself again, enclosed in the leather bag just as when Abbot Mawgan consigned me to the deep at the cliff's foot those forty long years ago. In it I lay helplessly, watching the tide scooping around my tiny islet. Now I found to my alarm that the Salmon had miscalculated; a breeze got up, sufficient to stir the waters, and the ninth wave of the receding tide scooped me up and bore me off with incredible swiftness. I was being carried out to sea again! I howled and cried for help, but much good did it do me in that desolate spot, where there were neither men nor flocks but only soaring, mocking seagulls.

No longer a lissome, strong-swimming herring, I was a helpless baby tied up to the neck in a strong sack. I tried desperately to remember the words that would release me, as the muddy shoals passed swiftly by at ever-increasing speed and distance. Just as I was abandoning all hope, however, my bag fetched up against an unseen barrier and came to an abrupt halt. Twisting my head around, I saw to my surprise and intense relief that the dropping tide had exposed a broad fishing-weir of stakes, which traversed the mouth of the river from bank to bank. Constructed of hurdles and brushwood, it held me fast while the sea raced away through the interstices.

For the present I was saved, but I found myself in a dreadfully exposed and uncomfortable position. An upright stake had passed through the thong-loop of my bag, so that there I dangled above the wet sand and retreating tide. All efforts to free myself proved of no avail. My puny limbs were lacking in strength, and my fat little fingers could do no more than pluck feebly at the noose about my neck. The sole result of my wriggling about in this way was that I twisted myself into a position where a projecting wattle came to protrude painfully into my side, causing me no small anguish.

I desisted from the impotent struggle and gazed about me. I was raised up high enough to see above the banks, but twist and turn my head about as I would, my gaze rested upon nothing but an interminable waste of mud flats and tussocks of wiry grass. Apart from the weir itself, there was no sign of human presence in this dreary wasteland. The occasional gull wheeled past, eyeing me curiously, and once a huge flock of greylag geese passed overhead, honking desultorily. Their indifference to my plight brought about within me a sharpening sense of loneliness and abandonment. I was truly alone, a helpless speck in this empty wilderness. The sky had turned gray and chill, and in the absence of the sun there was neither east nor west, south nor north. Save that I was growing increasingly chilled, there was no indication of time of day nor season of the year.

The sea had withdrawn far from sight and sound, but as time drew on it was borne increasingly upon my mind that within a few hours it must return racing along the inlet, to sweep high above the fence where I hung like a piglet in a bondsman's sack. Renewed efforts to release myself, however, only resulted in the thong's becoming still more tightly attached to its stake. Exhausted by the fruitless effort, I eventually succumbed to an uneasy sleep.

My sleep was troubled by a strange dream. Beyond the crying of the gulls I could now hear the deep distant roar of ocean from which I had so lately emerged. The stake on which I hung had grown to an enormous tree reaching high above the clouds. The twig digging into my side had become a sharp spear, driving ever deeper through my flesh, while the knotted thong about my neck was tightening to the point of strangulation. As if this were not enough, I fancied I could hear the tide coming silent and deep up the inlet, like a stealthy murderer unchecked by fear of intervening hand. From somewhere up the river I thought, too, that I could hear an eerie wailing chant, as if the Fair Folk in chorus were inviting me into their mounds.

Why am I being tortured in this way—I, a harmless babe, who wish mankind only good? The intensity of pain and despair grew increasingly insupportable, and I began to pray with desperate intensity to You, that You might reach down to me. It is Your Sure Arm that balances and protects all within its compass. You would not abandon me, I thought. But no word came from You. Ah, is it the throw of the *gwyddbwyll* dice that has gone against me, or are the gods in their sport enjoying the cruel game of Badger in the Bag? The spear is piercing my little beating heart, the cruel noose is throttling me, and now I am certain I can hear the water stealing and swirling through the weir about me!

CHAPTER FOUR

THE
WILD HUNT

The Port of Gwydno Garanhir in the North is one of the Three Chief Ports of the Island of Prydein. It is situated at the gullet of the Sea of Reged, and men say it is the most fortunate and the least fortunate citadel in the Island; a bridge from this world to the Other and from the Other to this, a stronghold which is on sea and on land, in the North and in the South; neither within nor without the golden-green meadowlands of Crist and Mabon, the blighted Wilderness of Cernun, or the deep-flowing waters of Nud Silver-hand. It is at the end of the Wall and at its beginning, on the hither side and the farther.

There are those who say that, standing as it does upon the Wall, it must have been built in a past age by those men of Rufein who made the great roads and Twenty-eight Cities of the Island of Prydein, now laid to ruin by the barbarians from across the sea, savage sea-wolves of the Eingl and the Fichti. Others hold that, since it stands on the sea marge at the Wall's ending, Porth Gwydno wards the land from the sea and the sea from the land, being established by Beli the Great when he raised up this Island from the sea. On the Wall's right-hand side lies the great dyke which was (so they say) torn out of the earth by the white tusks of the boar Turch Truith and his sow-wife Henwen, when they traversed the Island of Prydein from Caer Weir to Caer Luelid. Porth Gwydno stands between dyke and Wall, and who is to say whether it was raised by the hands of man or beast, god or demon?

Be all these things as they may (and nothing is said here concerning the holy orchard without its gates), Porth Gwydno in the North was the four-cornered fortress where King Gwydno Garanhir was accustomed to hold his court. In former years the wealth of his lands in

Cantre'r Gwaelod had been as great as that of King Mynydog of the rock-fortress of Eidyn, whose host perished gloriously on the field of Catraeth, the warriors' breath still smelling of the strong mead bestowed without stint upon them in the hall of the generous king.

Regrettably, though, the largesse King Gwydno dispensed at his mead-drinking had become yet more profuse than that of Mynydog of the Great Treasures, or even that of Ryderch the Generous of Alclud; and of late his coffers had been stripped bare as the bosom of Gwenhuifar the Unchaste. It was long since captives had languished in his hostage pit or been paraded in the northwestern corner of his banqueting hall; and the lords of Cantre'r Gwaelod were not so swift to pay tribute of cattle and swine, mantles and brooches, copper cauldrons and pails, as they had been in former times when the eight royal packhorses called for their annual tribute-gathering.

And when King Gwydno Garanhir traveled on his yearly *cylch* about the kingdom, niggardly was the *gwestfa* of pork and beef, mead and ale, cheese and butter, laid out before him in his nobles' halls. He had been a great king, but was held to be growing old and unfit for cattle raiding. It was at this time, too, that the power of his neighbor, King Urien of Reged, was becoming great in the land, where he was famed as Bull-protector among the Thirteen Kings of the North.

However, Gwydno's resources were not so scanty, nor was he so foolhardy, as not to undertake ceremonies customary among all men at the time of the dread night of Nos Kalan Gaeaf. He knew as well as any of the Thirteen Kings of the North that banquets and royal feasts prove the worthiness of a king's reign, causing the *gwir deyrnas* to prevail throughout his kingdom. Moreover, the guard he placed upon the gates of the North at that unchancy season was a guard for all the Tribes of the North. To Gwydno came costly gifts at this time from the tribe of Cynfarch, the tribe of Cinuit, and the tribe of Coel. In return their emissaries bore back the sacred fire from the king's hearth which kindled the fires of all the Men of the North.

The feasting of the Kalan Gaeaf lasts for three nights before and three nights after that dread day, and King Gwydno's druids saw to it that all was conducted as the safety of the realm demanded. Outside Porth Gwydno's stone-and-mortar walls, Beli's bonfires burn on every hilltop, as they do throughout the Island of Prydein and its Three Adjacent Islands. The land is wild and desolate; the wind as swift as a storm tossing about the leaves, the berries hard, the ponds full. Yellow are the tops of the birches, their branches bending and shaking like angry words from the mouths of the disputatious. Upland steadings are all deserted beneath the wind, their yards now frequented only by lean deer driven by rain and snow from mountain grazing.

Now, too, are the windy, wet, and empty places of the earth filled with mischievous and evil beings from the Underworld, the realms of Annufn. The Adanc of the Deep and his children of the lakes begin to stir and writhe on their sandy resting places, causing the sea to dash against the land in raging turmoil and rivers to burst their banks. Despite the blazing of the bonfires, the Witch of Ystafengun rides overhead among the racing storm clouds at the head of her Nine Daughters, mocking at the flames guttering below her in the downpour, shrieking in the gale and brandishing her flashing trident over the huddled huts of stricken men. The Hall of Afarnach has opened wide its portals and sent abroad its noxious brood.

Thrown open, too, are the mounds of the Fair Folk, who pour forth and swarm about the habitations of mortal men. Now even the bravest of the Thirteen Princes of the North may feel terror without disgrace, for it is the time when the mountain graves of heroes and churchyard tombs yawn open wide, and their dwellers stalk the earth in death as once they did in life. Let a rash householder cross his yard with lantern in hand to make fast a slamming byre door, and he will hear their footsteps treading in the mud behind him. At fords and stiles and crossroads they lie in wait; they cluster beneath the eaves of houses, and when men sleep at night they troop into their halls and gather squeaking about the hearth. Let no man be so foolhardy as to obstruct their way, leaving his door barred or his hearth untended on that night!

Next day in the grayness of dawn, men witness the mischief wrought by the destructive sprites: plows and carts tumbled into ditches and ponds, gates flung from their hinges, cattle and horses driven afar off among the fields, uprooted cabbages flung about every threshold. Still, men must venture forth to tend the hilltop bonfires, heaping them high with branches until the moment comes for the whole company to fly in terror down the hillside, never turning their heads until within doors once more.

> "The cropped Black Sow
> Seize the hindmost!"

goes up the frantic cry, as those at the rear trip and stumble in their fright, sensing the cold shadow fall upon their shoulders. For it is the Black Pig (as they in their fear term the Horned One) whose power reigns on that chaotic night. Horrible it is to see her:

> The cutty Black Sow
> On every stile,
> Spinning and carding
> Each Winter Calends.

Even when they crowd back through the gates of the fortress, men fancy they hear a grunting and a squealing beneath the log pile or beyond the smithy forge, and do not rest until they are once more gathered about the blazing hearth.

Kalan Gaeaf is the name borne by that unchancy day, but in truth it could be called "No-day." For it belongs not to the year or the seasons, or to the ageing of the world. It is the allotted time of Him they call the Black Pig, and so it stands beside time. It is said that when the gods first divided up the mounds of the Fair Folk and the inhabited places of the earth among themselves, that deceitful Horned One came to where Bran the Blessed and the company of the gods were gathered about the dark-blue Cauldron of Inspiration, demanding that he, too, receive his portion from that cauldron from which no one may depart unsatisfied.

"I have nothing for thee," replied the Fisher King, his brow darkening. "The division is completed."

"Then give me," pleaded the Trickster, "a day and a night in your own dwelling."

"That will I do willingly," replied Bran smiling.

Next day the Trickster was ordered to depart to his own people, for his time was up. The nine maidens blew upon the fires that heat the cauldron, and the gods looked mockingly upon the enemy of mankind. But he it was that laughed scornfully as he left their company; for, as he said, "I see now that Night and Day are the whole world, and it is that which you have given me."

Then Bran and his company saw how they were deceived, for there is Time and No-time, and Space and No-space, and in each case it is the latter that the horned maleficent one has appropriated to himself. So it is that from that day forward it is he who rules over the Wasteland, and the gap between the years when there is no time and the frontiers of kingdoms and the rule of kings are annulled. The dead are as one with the living; men are as women and women as men, there are neither husbands nor wives, all being commingled in amorous communion without adultery; all is as it was before the gods took up the scattered elements, set the stars in the tent of heaven and the earth upon its firmament of waters, and kings established order and justice in their realms.

Porth Gwydno is set within the Wall that divides the Wasteland from walled townships and hedged pastures, the heaving ocean from snug woodlands, and it is there that watch and ward must be kept throughout each Kalan Gaeaf. Its high stone-and-mortar walls face east and west and north and south, and it is every day that King Gwydno must mount the ramparts to gaze on to the four corners of the earth to ensure that the People of the Mounds do not steal upon the stronghold unawares. Above its southern entrance is set a stone image of divine Belatgaer, the Bright Shining One, bringer of life, wealth, and fertility. Opposite, shrouded in a shadowy niche above the northern, left-hand doorway, lurks a statue of crooked Cernun, horned and baleful. The fortress is square, as is the board upon which is played the game of *gwyddbwyll*, and it was at *gwyddbwyll* that King Gwydno was playing every Nos Kalan Gaeaf with the hosts of the Fair Folk without.

In the center of the square-walled enclosure was the pillared hall of the king, and within its walls, to north and south, east and west, were erected four hostels. To the north was the hostel of Seithennin the druid, to whom were vouchsafed all runes, enchantments, and spells. To the south was the hostel of Serfan the bishop, who used to bless the food and drink of Gwydno's court for the daughters of the gold-torqued chieftains of this Island. To the west was the hostel of Elffin mab Gwydno, the king's son, to whom men looked forward for the succession. To the east, facing the king as was fitting, was the most illustrious of his guests, Prince Run, son of King Maelgun the Tall of Gwynedd. At the feasting their couches were bestowed about the king's in like manner, and so the king himself faced ever to the east. As for the nobles of Cantre'r Gwaelod, they were disposed along the benches of the hall, each according to precedence of rank, of calling, of legitimacy, and of immemorial custom.

Joyous was the revelry at the banquet of Gwydno Garanhir that Nos Kalan Gaeaf, and numerous were the nobles who sought his hospitality, each receiving the oldest of every liquor and the newest of every meat. The number of the assemblage delighted the heart of King Gwydno; for, as he said, "We are princes so long as chieftains frequent our courts. The greater the favor we bestow, the greater shall be our nobility, our fame, and our honor."

The assembled chiefs marveled at the plentiful wine of Eden, each quaffing his fill of sparkling wine and mead and bragget from brimming vessels of glass and horn. Of contentions and quarreling there was no more than is customary when King Gwydno Garanhir, rejoicing in purple and gold, dispensed the drinking horn in his luxurious palace. And when the yellow ensnaring mead came to capture the minds of warriors, each one a leek in battle and serpent on the track of the enemy, causing hot words and challenges to be exchanged, then did the judge of the court pronounce judgment acceptable to all. And for himself he received from the victor in the contention a buffalo horn and a gold ring and a cushion for his chair. And these gifts were acceptable to the judge of the court.

Merrily blazed the fire beneath a copper cauldron worthy of Diurnach Gwydel, and choice were the gobbets of pork that the company drew forth from it with their flesh-hooks, each in order of precedence. To the glorious preeminent triumphant King Gwydno were apportioned the loins, to the chief princes the limbs, to the noble ladies the curving lean part, to the poets the lard, and to the stewards the lungs. With what laughter and gibing, too, was the rump bestowed upon the jesters, the kidneys upon the buffoons, and the intestines upon the household slaves—the portion fit for boors.

Not forgotten either were the tiny folk who dwell within the ground, floor, walls, and hall pillars of a fortress: elves of the earth, gnomes of the earth. When bread crumbs and meat scraps fall from careless hands, let no reveler be so rash as to retrieve them from the rush-strewn floor. For among the rushes is a scuttling and a rustling and a squeaking, which tells of the merry feasting of little people, small as shrews but strong in spells. All recall the tale how once, amid that silence which follows a long night's revelry, a waking warrior heard amid the sterterous breathing of his companions a little voice that spake from beneath his ale-bench:

> "Hush my bonnie, hush my pet,
> Hush my dearie, do not fret:
> When King Gwydno's board is set
> Flesh and fowl will thine be yet."

Then he knew that the elf-child, no bigger than a beetle as he guessed, was receiving from its mother due meed of the king's comestibles. And this is the *gwestfa* which the men of Cantre'r Gwaelod grant in tribute to the rock-elves; for though small, they may wreak dire mischief if angered.

Now a troop of jugglers from Aeron flew like squirrels up the hall pillars, tumbling, falling, bounding from the floor to the tables without breaking ever a dish, and running along the fence that divides the upper and lower parts of the hall. They crowed like cocks, fought like cats, and flew about the feasters with outstretched necks and arms like geese whilst King Gwydno and his company laughed until the tears coursed down their cheeks. The brew of Hydref was of rare strength, ale and mead tasting as if they flowed from the cup of Luir mab Luirion; the thirst of the king and his courtiers was deep as if each had swallowed a mayfly, and the deeper they drank the merrier appeared the jugglers.

Finally the king rose in jovial mood and emptied his goblet over the head of the leader of the troop, who at once made marvelous semblance as if water were spouting from his mouth, his nostrils, his ears, and his fore- and back-passages. Then the laughing company began to pelt those skilled men with half-gnawed bones, which the jugglers in turn caught deftly and flung up and down in increasing and decreasing arcs, circles, and ellipses, passing each around or through another. The air was filled with flying bones, and men fell rolling to the ground in mirth as wolfhounds and mastiffs sprang up and bounded forward, chasing the somersaulting and cartwheeling jesters out into the night and so to the booth where household slaves had prepared for them a lavish feast worthy of men possessed of such deft accomplishments.

The laughter continued for a space as the princes spoke about what they had seen, and some of the more ribald among them made foolhardy attempts to emulate the skills they had just witnessed. Then the laughter died away among sooty rafters and behind shadowed hall pillars as a troop of musicians entered to take up their stance before the king and assembled princes. They bore neither harps nor bells nor instruments of any sort. Across the sea from green Ywerdon had they come, and enchanting was the beauty of their art. Twenty-seven were they in number, and it was humming that was their skill.

From end to end of the rank of the hummers of Ywerdon uprose a gentle harmony. At first it resembled the low moaning of a spring breeze caressing the strings of the Harp of Teirtu. Then was it louder: a swarm of bees moving about bright flowers spangling lush meadows in the verdant Vale of Luifenyd. Next arose a weaving and spiraling of themes; birds, breeze, and bees hummed in harmony, one tune and one song and one faint echo rising and falling above the other. So it was that the Men of the North forgot the cold, wet blight of winter, each fancying himself riding out on the Kalan Mai under the warm sun, a beautiful slender-waisted wanton maiden by his side.

Slowly the humming died as it had arisen: The bees returned heavy-laden with sweet honey for their royal hive; the birds flew each to his own nest, sporadic twittering dying with the onset of evening; and the breeze dropped back behind the hillside as the Mai moon sailed up into a soft blue-black sky. One note alone sounded on, and one hummer alone sustained his note. He it was who was the leader of the twenty-seven hummers of Ywerdon, and if their humming was worthy of the courts of the Thirteen Princes of the North, his was a humming that might have wafted from the pipes of Hafgan's three organs, playing over the paradisal plain of Caer Sidi.

Raising his beard in the air, the hummer hummed on as King Gwydno lay back upon his seat with his eyes closed and his lips smiling the smile of those that dwell in the Isles of the Blessed. At length there came a time when the hummer's strength began to wane, but no sooner did he appear to be faltering to a stop than the king awakened and signaled to him to continue. On and on went the magical humming, to the delight of all assembled there in the court-house of Porth Gwydno in the North. But finally an exhaustion came upon the chief of the hummers of Ywerdon, and in straining for an effect beyond his failing strength it happened that one of his eyes popped out of its socket and lay upon his cheek.

At this the poor man was angered, and cried out, "Would that I had not come on a visit to this court to be put to shame in this manner! For with this blemish I cannot behold the land I have come to; and, as for the land I have left, I cannot return to it now."

Then the king awoke from his pleasant dreaming, as did the princes and nobles of his household, and King Gwydno was greatly distressed at witnessing the hummer's blemish. It was fortunate that the physician of the household was there, seated as is his right by the chief of the king's bodyguard. It was with herbs and enchantments and skill of his fingers that the physician replaced the hummer's eye secure again within its socket.

Content with their reception, the hummers received their due guerdon and retired to their hostel to partake of food and drink and rest. A murmur of appreciation followed them in their departure—to be replaced of a sudden with a wild shout of welcome. Not finished yet was King Gwydno's royal entertainment, and the seven solemn-faced men in short kirtles who entered were recognized by all as being as skilled in their special art as were the hummers in theirs. Long-snouted and sharp-heeled were they, foxy-faced and bald.

Low before the king bowed the seven newcomers; and bowed low they remained, with buttocks bare gleaming from the ruddy glare of the king's hearth. For they were the far-famed farters of the Island of the Mighty, whose skill in farting surpassed any that might be found in Prydyn, or Ywerdon, or distant Lydau across the Sea of Udd.

Wonderfully loud was the farting of the royal farters at the feasting of King Gwydno Garanhir upon the Kalan Gaeaf; wonderfully loud, skillfully sonorous, and evil-smelling beyond the achieving of all others of their calling. At first they emitted with rare delicacy the seven notes of the scale, moving up and down the line in harmony, high and low. Then they blew forth tunes such as cowherds and milkmaids sing. They whistled high and they whistled low in semblance of the whistling of the keepers of the king's kennels, or of unseen birds that pipe in the brake.

But these wonderful feats were as nothing to what followed, and an ecstasy came upon the Men of the North as each of the performers excelled his fellow with some new and marvelous display of art and skill. Marvelously true to reality was the snorting of war horses, the braying of trumpets, the roaring of stags, the rumble of thunder, the bellowing of bulls, the snarling of wildcats, and the long, low drone of a homing cockchafer on a summer's eve.

Well-fed were the performers upon dulse and lentils and beans, but not beyond the space of half an hour were they able to sustain their skillful performance. There came a moment when their conductor gave vent to a long, low whistling sound like a serpent retiring to its heathery lair; so sibilantly soft, stealthy-sounding, and stalely stinking as to instill an awed silence upon the assembled company. It was a signal for the departure of the troop, and with a final effort of mind and spirit and body they thundered forth a fanfare of such loudness and force and vigor that men swore afterward it set the goblets rattling upon the royal board, and all but extinguished the pine torches flaring in their sockets and even the great hearth burning beneath the royal cauldron.

Like the gale before which no man is able to stand upright, which blows without ceasing from the mouth of that Cave in the land of Gwent which men call Chwith Gwynt, was that mightiest of farts which was in the North at that time. There were those in the king's hall, however, who feared lest the performance might arouse storms and tempests in the winter sky, avowing they could hear afar off in the mountains the rolling of Taran's Wheel.

It was amid smoke and confusion and stench that the king's farters flew from the banquet hall to the hostel set apart for them. It was long before the pleasure passed and laughter died away and tongues were stilled, so delightful was their performance to the Men of the North.

Finally, as the mirth waned and men were ware of the drumming of rain on shingled roof and the creaking of shadowy rafters above their heads, there was a change of mood. King Gwydno called for Taliesin, chief of bards, to sing a song of glorious conflict, reminding those present of heroic feats of gallantry performed against overwhelming odds on the field of battle.

At once a respectful silence descended upon the hall, and all glanced shyly at the great poet. But Taliesin sat silent and moody, wrapped in his purple mantle of bardhood, whether because the *awen* had not entered into him or because he was irritated by the excessive applause bestowed upon the band of ignoble buffoons, it was hard to tell. His expression was pensive, frowning, and his bright far-ranging eyes remained glazed over in inward contemplation.

Gradually, as the bard continued mute with head bowed, an increasing murmur of conversation resumed—until the king raised his hand and gave a sharp cry. All glanced across in surprise, and saw that the chief of bards had raised his head and stared before him in an attitude of ecstatic concentration. Upon his lips the honey-foam was forming. Seeing this, the boy beside him plucked a gentle chord from his harp. Taliesin smiled approvingly, upon which the harpist struck up a soft, rippling scale worthy of the Harp of Teirtu which brought to mind the gentle plashing of a lakeland rill in high summer.

Now began the song, a song in which the princes were glad to recognize a skillful compliment paid to their noble guest. For it was a paean of praise to the undying glory of Run mab Maelgun's greatest forefather, his great-great-grandfather, bulwark of the people of Manau and Gododdin, Cunedda mab Edeyrn mab Padarn—he who was first to receive the scarlet mantle of sovranty from the emperor of Rufein.

At first the verses struck a disturbing note. Between hill and sea and river, sang Taliesin in a low and solemn chant, the strongholds of Cunedda are shaken along all the length of the Wall, from Caer Luelid to Caer Weir. Is it the power of the pirates of Bryneich that threatens the security of the Men of the North? No, continued Taliesin in tones of mournful indignation, the pagans have been harried without mercy by the glorious kings of Baptism, fleeing like foxes into every estuary. It is conflict between the Men of the North themselves of which I sing, cruel and senseless strife among the kindred.

Like the waves of the ocean, rising up one upon another, continued the poet, his voice rising in anger, the brave devour one another. Like a breeze stirring young ash trees, cousin fights against cousin. The house of Edeyrn wars with the house of Coel, while the bards of each household goad their kings to ever more bitter enmity. And who is it who laughs in his lair, as the kings of the North harry each other with sword and with spear? Is it not the Flame-bearer, as he approaches our coasts with his hundred ships? The Men of the North shake the trees, but it is the wolves of Loiger and Bryneich who pluck the fruit that falls.

"Are you bewitched or drunken, O Men of the North, that you

war like beasts with your fellow Cristonogion?" suddenly cried the bard
in a ringing tone that recalled the trysting horn which summons
warriors to battle. "Have you forgotten the fame of Cunedda, how a
hundred times he fought and overbore the men of Bryneich before he in
his turn was borne home on a hurdle by his sorrowing people? Like a
pack of hounds about a hart, the traitors laid him low, but before he
was slain he slew! And even in death his name was uttered in fear and
trembling; a hundred thousand of the men of Bryneich he left upon
the place of battle, their sightless eyes glaring upward as the crows and
kites begin to circle overhead!"

A murmur of approval and excitement ran about the hall, and
men glanced eagerly to where goodly ash-spears and whitened shields
hung about the walls. But even as the battle heat began to throb
through their veins, the song of Taliesin swiftly changed its mood.
Now his strain was melancholy and bitter. In low and suffocating
tones he mourned the untimely end of the noble Cunedda, his court
and his girdle. "The tide of the sea has receded, the salt-water salmon
departed; of herds and abundance there is nought but loss. Only the
bards' songs maintain his glory now, and they will continue forever
without number. Ah, most generous of kings, openhanded without
stint, dispenser of wine and oil, horses and milch kine, would that you
were with us today! Before the son of Edeyrn, the land of the enemy
was laid in ashes; he was a lion and a dragon in the forefront of the
armies, his followers a rampart of shields and forest of spears without
number."

Taliesin ceased his song with unexpected suddenness, the harpist
striking a single sharp high note. The poet sank back on his couch as if
exhausted, a foam upon his lips. There followed a hush within the hall
as each warrior sat pinioned by his thoughts. Then a great shouting
burst from every throat. The swift, fleeting images conjured up in the
poet's magical phrasing brought within the compass of a half-dozen
words a picture more vivid even than the events themselves. One
replaced another, and yet all lingered as if they had never passed. The
princes were no longer seated beneath the smoky rafters and flickering
shadows of King Gwydno's courthouse, but saw before them the Wall
and its fortresses basking beneath a summer sky in sinuous undula-
tions, like an adder on a heath. They saw the distant smoke of burning
townships, the trampling and glitter of Cunedda's array, the noble
figure of the great king himself riding in the vanguard. They saw, too,
his dreadful end, borne down by the spears of the sons of Coel, his
own kinsfolk. Cunedda is slain, and his betrayers flee before the pale-
faced men of the Eingl! Remorse and anger filled every breast, and

solemn vows of retribution were announced before all the glorious
company by torque-wearing heroes who were as greedy for corpses as
for drinking mead or wine.

King Gwydno glanced toward the couch where Taliesin sat, the
hood of his purple cloak drawn forward so as to enshadow his features, and smiled inwardly. The poet's *awen* had transformed men's
purposes, making them of one heart and mind. The renown of Cunedda
was dear to the Men of the North, whose sovereign he had been in
generations gone by. He was also the ancestor of Run mab Maelgun,
Gwydno's favored guest, whose father's aid he sought. The death song
of Cunedda had aroused shame and regret among the descendants of
Coel, many of whom were present among the company.

It happened that King Gwydno had recently cast in his lot with
Urien of Reged, chief of the tribe of Coel and greatest of the Thirteen
Kings of the North. Now Urien's thoughts ran thus: Next summer he
planned to confederate with the kings of the North, and march against
the lands of Bryneich on the eastern seacoast. For he had resolved upon
a reckoning with the pagan sea-wolves and the destruction of their
king, Ida.

King Urien's soothsayers had assured him that the mongrel hosts
of the Eingl (haunters of estuaries and woodland foxes that they
were) would be driven through the forests and slip away with the ebb
of the sea. But these auguries had ended in cloudy images of blood and
treachery, and it had not escaped the far-ranging thoughts of the great
king that Ida might receive aid from the fleet and armies of Cynurig,
king of the Iwys, Saeson of the Southland. For it is known that all the
princes of the Saeson are united by a blood tie, being (as they claim)
descended from their one-eyed god whom they name Woden.

Three years earlier Cynurig had defeated in battle Cynin, doughty
prince of the Brython, and his confederate force from the southland
towns and fortresses of Prydein, driving them into a strong hilltop
fortress built of old by the men of Rufein. After a fierce siege, the
barbarians took the fortress by storm and drove out King Cynin, who
fled like a stricken deer into the wooded combes of Dyfneint, seeking
there refuge with Gereint mab Erbin. In consequence Cynurig was
become more powerful than any king of the Saesons or Eingl before
him, not excepting the wily Hengys and astute Ceredig, and impudently arrogated to himself the title of Guledig of the whole Island of
Prydein! Were Cynurig to march northward and come to the aid of Ida
with his full strength, then even Urien of Reged might find himself
sorely pressed to obtain the victory he sought.

But were Cynurig in his turn to be attacked by Maelgun the Tall of

Gwynedd, lord of the corn-bearing Island of Mon, then would the armies and fleets of the Saeson of the South be hard-pressed at home, and unable to lend aid to their fellow wolf Ida of Bryneich. Then surely would he, Urien of Reged, and Maelgun of Gwynedd, the two most powerful Bull-protectors of the Island of Prydein, be enabled to drive the whole race of pale-faced Saeson from all their vantage points on the eastern and southern coastlands of Prydein, back into the sea forever.

Only the ancient blood feud between the sons of Coel, ancestor of Urien, and the sons of Cunedda, ancestor of Maelgun, had stood hitherto in the way of King Urien's great scheme. Now the song of Taliesin had dispelled four generations of hatred and mistrust, and all about the hall, princes of both houses were clasping the hands of their neighbors and vowing battle-brotherhood. King Gwydno Garanhir wondered for a moment within himself whether this had been the bard's set purpose—the bounty bestowed upon him by Urien of Reged this past summer had not been niggardly—but nothing of Taliesin's inner thoughts was detectable on the poet's radiant, quick-glancing features.

So the heroes filled their horns and glasses with sweet yellow ensnaring mead, growing ever more joyful with songs and shoutings. They laughed loudly as King Gwydno's satirists, garbed in dog masks, appeared before them to recite rhymes of ridicule and blistering and blemishing, slighting the fame and courage of Gwalaug of Elfed and Ida of Bryneich. All had become drunken and glorious, and none more so than their illustrious guest, Run mab Maelgun. A handsome yellow-haired prince he was, renowned throughout all his father's kingdoms for his conquests over brave men and fair women. Indeed it was a saying in those days that neither woman nor maiden with whom he chose to spend a merry moment came away with her reputation what it had been before his visit to her bower.

King Gwydno Garanhir was anxious that the prince Run should return to his father's court in Gwynedd with good reports of his reception at Porth Gwydno in the North. It was now that three beautiful slave girls were brought forward to be bestowed by the king upon Prince Run: the first a fair-haired and blue-eyed sea-king's daughter from Bryneich; the second, the dark, flashing-eyed daughter of a king of the Fichti, whose fastness is in the mountains of the North; and the third, a comely auburn-haired princess from the green Isle of Ywerdon— the last captured but a month before when King Gwydno's ships had raided her father's coastland.

Prince Run studied each slave girl with approval, kissed them tenderly, and ordered the men of his household to make all comfortable for them that night within his hostel without the king's hall. With a smile of approval, he turned back to the king and raised his gold-rimmed horn in salute. However, fair though all this seemed, the king was sore perplexed how to proceed further. He shifted uneasily on his high seat, the lovely maiden who was his foot-holder reaching up to rub his long thigh soothingly.

The slave girls were all very well in their way. But there could be no shortage of beautiful women at the court of King Maelgun Gwynedd in Degannwy, if what men said was true; and it was clear the king must bestow upon the prince some gift of sufficient splendor to arouse the admiration of the men of Gwynedd, so setting them talking of the glory of King Gwydno Garanhir and of the prowess of the Men of the North. But his coffers were well-nigh empty, so lavish had been his hospitality of late. Though none of the men of his tribe in Cantre'r Gwaelod was aware of the fact, the stone-lined cellar beneath his court-yard contained little of its one-time display of golden ornaments, soft furs, and rich cloaks. Even the brooch the king himself wore could not match that which Run had but now carelessly unpinned in order to cast aside his cloak for the mead-feasting.

What was to be done? King Gwydno glanced appealingly toward his cousin, the bishop Serfan; a true pilgrim in heart and soul like Efream, gentle and forgiving as Moessen the seer, a psalmist skilled as Dewi who was king of old in Iudea. So virtuous was the blessed saint's conduct that there would not be weariness upon a midge that bore the burden of his sins; and so pious his praying that of him it is related that corn-blades grew through his hair from the perfection of his prayers.

If ever a miracle were needed, surely it was now. But old Serfan lay back half sleeping, stroking his white beard meditatively. At King Gwydno's summoning he nodded approvingly, rising to pronounce certain words of the prophet Esaias, which he took to be a fitting grace for the laity:

" 'They are swallowed up of wine, they have erred in drunkenness; they have not known Him that seeth, they have been ignorant of judgment. For all tables were filled with the vomit of their filthiness, so that there was no more room.' "

At once all the company rose to cross themselves devoutly. To King Gwydno, however, the words conveyed no message of advice or encouragement. He turned, beckoning in desperation to Seithennin the druid, who occupied the couch on the northern side of the hall. Unmarked by the laughing revelers, a deep conversation ensued between king and druid. The king frowned a little at first, but concluded by nodding reluctantly and, as the druid resumed his couch, held up his hand for silence.

"Hear me, O Men of the North!" cried Gwydno Garanhir with an imperative shout. All who were still awake looked up expectantly.

"The prince Run mab Maelgun, heir to the Pendragon of the Island, honors us by his presence at our feasting, and now will I mark our appreciation by the bestowal of a gift worthy so noble a prince."

Here the bishop and Prince Elffin, Gwydno's heir, were unable to avoid betraying some little surprise. As the king's nearest relatives, they had of late gained some inkling of the dire straits into which his extravagance had led him. Was their king to shame the men of his tribe by some gift unworthy their guest's high rank?

Gwydno marked this, but continued unabashed: "We have pondered long and carefully upon this matter. As all men know, in our stone-walled cellar we possess wealth superior even to that of Ryderch of Alclud: torques, brooches, jewels, and richly embroidered tunics and cloaks beyond counting. But what are these to the heir of Cunedda? Does not his father, King Maelgun, also possess treasures without limit in his fortress at Degannwy? And what he does not possess, will he not seize next summer from the king of the Saeson in the Southland, Cynurig, when he ravages his lands as far as the ninth wave of the stormy Sea of Udd?"

At this a growl of approval ran around the glorious smoke-filled hall, and the warriors were gratified to see Prince Run nod his handsome head in apparent assent.

"There is nothing in the way of wealth that King Maelgun does not hold in his coffers," continued King Gwydno, "or which he cannot take unto himself from his foes when they come to lie at his feet—as to be sure they will. Yet it may be that we in the North hold among us objects more precious and powerful than gold or silver. Surely, O prince, you will have heard tell beyond Dygen of the Thirteen Treasures of the Island of Prydein?"

It was now for the first time that Run's air of easy superiority slipped from him as he gazed in surprise and expectation at his host, who glanced proudly about the pillared hall. Prince Elffin betrayed still greater marks of astonishment, half rising from his seat with what appeared an expression of protest upon his youthful features.

For who there had not heard of those marvels, believed to be in the possession of one or other of the kings of the North, and guarded from the prying eyes of men by locks and knots and spells of druids and smiths? A hubbub of talk broke out as men told of the powers and attributes of the Whetstone of Tudwal, the Knife of Lawfroded, or the Sword of Riderch. Men who had earned their mead-portions in different courts of the North reported what they had heard and seen. Others entered into the age-old discussion as to their origins, some asserting roundly that the Treasures had been discovered at the opening of the prison of Caer Oeth and Anoeth, others as confident that they had been revealed when Gorneu mab Custennin first raised the Stone of Echymeint. A third viewpoint, confirmed by the authoritative voice of Seithennin the druid, was that the Thirteen Treasures had all been fetched away by Arthur, when he and his company traveled in the ship *Prydwen* to the Glass Fortress.

It was a matter of pride to those present who were of the retinue of Gwydno that one of these Treasures of enchantment was in the possession of their lord. This was that celebrated receptacle termed the Hamper of Gwydno, which when food for one man was put in it and it came to be opened was found to contain food sufficient for a hundred. It was at this very time, indeed, the Kalan Gaeaf, that the opening of the Hamper took place. Visiting warriors from other kings' courts could however speak of similar marvels in possession of their kings, so that there was ample justification for fierce words and angry looks.

King Gwydno raised his hand for silence, but it was not until his chamberlain had called out thrice that the outcry subsided. The king bestowed a significant glance around the hall and then, when he judged expectation to have reached a satisfactory degree of impatience, announced that he would that night bestow on his most favored guest a gift such as no king—no, not Arthur the emperor nor Emrys Guledig—had ever proffered since the Island of Prydein first arose dripping from out the ocean.

"As the men of my retinue know full well, and it may be some of you guests too, my stone-walled cellar contains riches without measure. Yet there is one Treasure that is greater than all of these, a Treasure which even the chosen heir of Maelgun the Tall would receive honor in the accepting."

At these words a murmur ran around the hall; among the retinue of Gwydno it included a note of displeasure. Surely the king could not be thinking of bestowing even upon Run mab Maelgun the fabled Hamper of Gwydno, the source of all his wealth? But with a glance of impatience, soothed by the ministering hand of his foot-holder, the king continued his discourse.

"Among the Thirteen Treasures of the Island of Prydein it is the Hamper of Gwydno that is the portion of our tribe. I will now reveal a secret, known hitherto only to myself and Seithennin the druid. There exists a fourteenth Treasure, here in Porth Gwydno, and it is that which I shall bestow upon Prince Run. I will tell you in what manner I came by so great a prize.

"It was upon this night a year ago that Seithennin and I, as is the custom, rode out to kindle the great fire on the height of Talyntir, which gazes over the land of Cantre'r Gwaelod and the white-rimmed Sea of Reged. By nine nines of first-begotten sons was the oak-log bored with the auger, until the Yellow Flame began to play upon the snow. Swiftly (I confess it) did we recite the Blessing of Beli upon all kine and crops from sea to sea and ridge to ridge, from wave to wave to the cataract's falling. And until the cattle come to depart their stalls, the sheep to forsake their folds, and goats to ascend to the mountain of mist, may the tending of the Three and the blessing of Beli be upon them!

"Afterward, as we rode fast for the sanctuary of Porth Gwydno, with the tailless Black Pig laughing in the gloaming woods behind us, we came to the windy upland of Torpen, where lie the twin mounds of the Fair Folk which men call the Paps of the Mother's Blessing. Darkness was coming upon us, and as we drew nearer we saw fires blazing on either side of the road. The mounds were open and the Fair Folk inside them. Our horses reared up, frightened (as were we), and as we strove to urge them on we heard voices on either side of us. They were discussing an exchange of gifts between the peoples of the two mounds, and we saw how a man of small height came from out of one of the mounds and passed to the other, bearing a kneading-trough, upon it a pig, a cooked calf, and a bunch of garlic.

"From the other mound came another small person with a chest of yew wood in his hands. I flung my spear at them, and at the passing of the iron over their heads they screamed and the fires in the mounds went out. Then, when our eyes became once more accustomed to the gloom, we saw that the wooden chest lay upon the ground where its bearer had dropped it. We bore it home and, when we opened it in my bedchamber, found it contained the precious Mantle of Tegau Eurvron. It was Seithennin who revealed its marvelous nature to me."

"The king speaks truth," cried out the druid, rising from his couch at the north side of the assemblage. "It is the Mantle of Tegau Eurvron which has this property: It will not serve any woman who had violated her marriage or her virginity. For whoever has been faithful to her husband it will reach to the ground; but for whoever has violated her marriage it will reach but to her lap, so revealing her shame to all men. But its color no man knows, for it is changeable."

Then the men of Gwydno's following and his guests smiled and looked wisely upon one another. The women, too, waxed merry in their part of the hall, gazing kindly upon the fierce eyes and strong limbs of the heir of Gwynedd. It is said that there were those among them who would not have minded a shortening of Tegau's Mantle upon them, could they but find a trysting-place for an hour's space beneath a yellow gorse bush with Prince Run. For was he not one of the Three Fair Princes of the Island of Prydein, and the lustiest man, and the man most favored by the beautiful women of the Island?

> "Upon his course croaks loud a cloud of crows,
> Where fiercely stabs his spear among the foes:
> From fallen foeman drawing deepest groan—
> Upon mild maiden working wilder moan."

Clearly there would be much diversion and profit from the Mantle of Tegau Eurvron at the court and house of Degannwy. Prince Run rose to express his gratitude for this signal honor, speaking not only of the glory it would bring to the tribes of Gwynedd, its brave men and beautiful women, but also in passing alluded to coming victories of the confederated tribes of Reged and Gwynedd over the treacherous Saeson. Gwydno smiled at this, drinking deeply from the mead-horn before him.

But now Gwydno's son, Prince Elffin, rose up in anger before his father. "How comes it, O king my father," he cried out wrathfully, "that you bestow a gift beyond price upon this stranger, the son of Maelgun the Tall—when of late you have refused me the gold I require to dispense among the men of my following? For do not our laws state that he who is to reign after the king should be honored above all in the court except the king and the queen? I am dishonored in my father's house! I believe, too, that there will be those who hold this action to be a dishonoring of the king, even excrement upon his face."

Prince Elffin was heir to Gwydno Garanhir, *gwrthrych* of the kingdom of Cantre'r Gwaelod, "looker forward" of his tribe and people. Though young and as yet untried in war, to him had been sung the hunter's charm, enjoining him to kill hind on the hoof and bird on the wing, sparing the white-bosomed swan and the duck with her yellow brood and taking only that prey which is lawful in wilderness and forest:

> Eat not, and ever leave alone
> Fish, beast, and fowl that's not thine own!

And that summer he had displayed his fitness for the kingship by conducting a cattle raid in Stratclud, returning from his wolfing with kine in such quantity that it was said of Elffin mab Gwydno: "When he returned to Erechwyd from the land of the Cluduis, not a cow lowed to her calf."

So it was that Prince Elffin's followers looked darkly upon Prince Run, and the judge of the court, who sat in his accustomed place between Elffin and his hall pillar, nodded in concurrence. At this, Prince Run looked grim and King Gwydno dismayed. What could he give his son, whom he loved dearly, when there was nothing to be found behind the locked doors of the royal strongroom? Between the demands of these two young hotheaded princes there seemed no middle way.

It was that peace-loving man of God, renowned for his wisdom throughout all Reged, Leudiniaun, and even among the remote fastnesses of Prydyn, the sainted Bishop Serfan, who rose to propose a solution.

"Hear me, O king, and you, O princes of the North! Let there be no disputations at our feasting. Hearken to what the holy prophet Micheas hath said: 'Hear thou, O tribe! What shall adorn a city? Not fire? Not the house of the unjust treasuring unjust treasures, and injustice with injury?'

"Nay, my children, if the king hath bestowed one Treasure upon his illustrious guest, he still possesses another. Have you forgotten the Hamper of Gwydno, into which the wealth of our kingdom flows, and from which the most generous king in the land of Baptism dispenses his gifts? It is at this time, the feasting of the Kalan Gaeaf, that the Hamper is filled; 'a snare unto watchfulness, and like a net spread upon Tabor, which they who have set the hunt have fixed,' as the holy prophet Osea pronounced."

The saintly old man in his excitement had half risen from his stall, his voice piping and quavering like those of women as they call to each other in their clothes-washing at a river's edge.

" 'Hear now, ye princes of the house of Jacob. Is it not for you to know judgment, though ye hate the good and the evil, plucking their skin from off them, and their flesh from off their bones? How have they eaten the flesh of my people and flayed their skins from off them, have broken their bones and chopped them as flesh in the cauldron?' "

There were those among King Gwydno's guests from distant kingdoms who surreptitiously let fall the gobbets of pork which they were yet absently gnawing, fearing spells and enchantments from the holy man's words. But the men of the king's household remained rapt and unperturbed, for they were aware that the saint spoke often in words of veiled meaning—words uttered by druids of Crist in long ages gone by and distant lands far from the Island of the Mighty.

The old man paused, muttering for a while within his white beard. Then he spoke again, once more uttering words from the book of enchantments of Cristonogion: " 'Do men gather grapes of thorns, or figs of thistles? Even so every good tree beareth good fruit. . . .' Let the king this year bestow the contents of his Hamper (the which is a tree that beareth good fruit, excellent fruit, rare fruit of great price) upon Prince Elffin; as he himself has told us, he has wealth sufficient for his own needs within the coffers of Porth Gwydno!"

As the ancient bishop resumed his couch, a shout of approbation echoed through the hall. Only Seithennin the druid cast a malicious glance in his colleague's direction. The king rose up in relief, the yellow ensnaring mead driving from his mind any thought of how he might fare between now and the next Kalan Gaeaf, when the Hamper came again to dispense its riches.

"Hear me, O Men of the North and Men of the South!" he proclaimed aloud. "Let it be known to all present that to my son Prince Elffin shall be all the takings of the Hamper of Gwydno, when men come to gather up its profusion in the morning. Chamberlain, see to it that the vats be opened! Cupbearer, take about the mead and wine! Let there be an end to discord, and let the merrymaking last until sunrise!"

Then did laughter and song resound again through the pillared hall of Gwydno Garanhir. Taliesin, chief of bards, arose and sang two odes which will be sung each Kalan Gaeaf until the end of time. He extolled the Mantle of Tegau Eurvron and the Hamper of Gwydno Garanhir in such brief, brilliant images of luster, wealth, and musical alliteration that men marveled and brooded a while in silence. But soon the revelry broke out again, and all was shouting and laughter.

There came a time eventually when the uproar ceased. Prince Run departed to his chamber in order to engage in converse with the three beautiful slave girls bestowed upon him by King Gwydno. There were those who lay back upon their couches, grunting and snorting in their slumbers like the swine of Puil, lord of Annufn. The fire on the central hearth burned low, and men feared to go out to the woodsheds to replenish it. The wind moaned around the timbered walls, a wounded beast in the outer darkness. Tapers guttered, sparked, and began to go out one by one, like stars at dawning. The shadowy places of the hall grew, the sooty rafters were hidden from view in smoke and blackness, and to those who still lay waking about the dying embers the hall pillars appeared as tree trunks, and they as travelers lost in thickets of the Forest of Celyddon or the Wasteland of Godeu. At times, dripping resin from pine torches flared briefly, and they seemed as the flickering elf-fires that dance upon the sullen, sodden Moss of Lochar.

Then, as is the custom at the feast of the Kalan Gaeaf, men began to tell tales of ghosts, of deaths of kings by burning and drowning and spear thrusts, and of those hellish beings who emerge when the gates of Annufn and Uffern are opened wide. There were tales, too, of the Black Man of Ysbidinongyl, the Man-eating Birds of Gwendolau, and the Witch of Ystafengun—she whose names are Sigh, Sough, Storm, Rough Wind, Winter-night, Cry, Wail, Groan; and who conjured for King Gwendolau two warring hosts: the one blue and the other headless.

"*Vade retro, Sathanas!*" cried out old Bishop Serfan in tremulous tones. All started and turned, and saw the holy man was crossing himself repeatedly and plucking agitatedly at the long white flow of his beard. Sensing a good tale in the offing, King Gwydno courteously inquired whether the bishop had ever encountered the hag.

"Not the hag," muttered the saint with some scorn, "but he who is master of all hags and evil beings. On my journey home across the mountains from the city of Rufein it happened that I came to a steep, narrow valley, roofed over by a dark, hanging mist."

A murmur of appreciation ran around the hall.

"The earth was quaking beneath my feet," continued the saint without pausing. "Thunder and lightning played all around, there was a stink of sulphur in the air, and all at once . . ."

"All at once what?" cried out a dozen excited voices, waking all but the heaviest sleepers. Bishop Serfan sat silent with head bowed for a minute or so before resuming his tale.

"All at once I was surrounded by fearsome beasts of all kinds, some with two legs and some with four, filling the valley from side to side so they crammed it to the highest mountain peaks. Not only that; the place was swarming with dragons and serpents and . . ."

The old man's memory appeared to be failing him, and he twisted and untwisted a lock of his snowy beard. In the obscurity its tangled tresses gleamed like the foaming Cataract of Derwent. In response to pressing appeals, however, he continued falteringly: ". . . dragons, serpents"—now it seemed to come back to him in a rush—"and regiments of gnats, bony gnats, bony gnats with long beaks; verily, I say, they and all the other hellish sprites that Satan has at his command."

An audible gasp sounded softly in the gloom, echoed mockingly by gusts of the night wind sighing about the eaves of King Gwydno's courthouse. The bony gnats were good, quite as good as the blue and headless hosts paraded before King Gwendolau.

"But what of their Master?" called out Prince Elffin. "You saw him, too, at the head of his host?"

"Not then," answered the venerable man, shaking his head slowly. "Not then, but after my return home. It was here, in the North, I met him—and confounded him. I traveled far beyond the Wall, into the Wasteland below the mountains of Prydyn."

He glanced toward the northern portal of King Gwydno's hall. The company followed his gaze and shuddered. In the darkness they could no longer see, but could still picture too readily, the image that was set above it.

"I traveled ever northward, floating across the Sea of Iodeo on my altar-stone, until I came to the realms of Bruide, son of Dargart, king of the Fichti. There I visited a certain holy monk dwelling in a cave beneath the ground. My friend was sick, and Satan, sensing his soul might shortly be flitting from his unworthy body, came to see what opportunity offered. Then I saw him face to face, in all his majesty and power and cruelty. But I confounded him and drove him from that desert place; not through my own poor strength, but in the name of God and the Holy Trinity."

"It seems you had an easy victory," muttered Seithennin the druid sourly, echoing some general disappointment.

"Not easy," responded the bishop sharply. "We fought long and hard, not with swords and spears but with weapons of the spirit. The Evil One sought to tempt me, but I was too much for him. This is the way it was: He asked me questions he thought I could not answer. His serpent's cunning was great, but assisted by divine inspiration I out-witted him."

"What were his questions and your answers then?" asked Seithennin curiously—he who was learned in spells and enchantments and wizardry.

"It was in this manner," replied the saint. "He began by asking me, very politely, whether I was a wise priest, and if so whether he might ask me some questions. 'Certainly,' I replied. 'Ask away.' 'Very well,' replied the Devil with a smirk. 'Where did God live before He created Heaven and earth?' 'Easy,' I replied. 'He lived nowhere but within Himself, since He is bounded neither by time nor space.' 'Hmm,' said the Devil, pretending to look disconcerted and then sud-denly springing another on me: 'Why did God create living beings?' I laughed; this was too easy. 'Why, if He had not created creatures, He would not have been the Creator, would He?' "

The saint's pert responses hugely delighted the valiant Men of the North, and they moved forward to the edge of their couches to listen intently, storing them up to recount at future feastings. Clearly it would take more than the Devil to outwit this learned man of God, master of riddles, who even now resumed his tale.

"Next the Evil One shot questions at me thick and fast. Where did God form Adam? In Hebron. Where was Adam afterward driven out of Paradise? Same place. How long did he stay there after committing his sin? Just over seven hours. 'Aha! Why did He allow Adam and Eve to sin; try answering that!' 'Oh dear,' I replied, 'is that all? Crist could not have been born in the flesh unless Adam and Eve had sinned, could He?' 'Ah, but,' said the Devil, grinning, 'why did not God make a better man after Adam went wrong?' I just had to laugh at that. 'What good would that have done us men, who are descended from Adam?'

"By this time Satan knew he was beaten, and concluded by asking me spitefully why we men were freed by Crist's Passion, and not the demons also? I dealt with that one as easily as with the rest, and Satan stood downcast and sulky, confessing that it was no good arguing with me at all. 'That's right,' said I, 'and now you can clear off as quick as possible. Get out, and don't ever dare come back to tempt poor men with your wicked wiles!' Off he went without a word, though he left behind a mighty stink of sulphur. And from that day to this he has never been back to that cave. You see how it is, my brethren. Amen."

As he relived the dread encounter in the halls of his memory, Bishop Serfan's speech had become excited, almost youthful. The skill with which the saint had dealt with his opponent was greatly admired by his audience. He might have overcome him with magical enchantments, but instead answered the riddles every one correctly. Men repeated the questions and answers, so far as they could recall them, with appreciative chuckles. Soon the Kalan Gaeaf would be over, and for another year men could live free from the threat of the Horned One and the Adanc of the Deep. Their laughter made them confident and strong, and they disposed themselves at last to slumber.

Unfortunately someone chose this moment to speak of the story of Teyrnon Turf Liant, who held vigil in his hall one Nos Kalan Mai, and saw a great claw come stealing through the window to snatch at a colt tethered within. At once all men were wide awake and spoke together for comfort. All thought of sleep departed from their minds.

So the night passed, that terrible night when time and space cease to exist and the Hosts of Annufn threaten to lay waste this world of men. A gray, pallid light began to filter wanly through the great chamber, and men saw on all sides the white, exhausted faces of their companions, looking strange and alien as the shades of the departed that flit through the groves of the Forest of Celyddon.

Dawn was approaching, and with it arose the hour of mortal danger. In the mountains of the North, in the heart of the forests of Godeu and Celyddon, lies the great rock-cleft men term the Cauldron of Cernun. Its dark-rimmed, smooth-sided, mist-hung abyss may be glimpsed from the paved road that ascends the wilderness of forest and mountain between Caer Luelid and Alclud. On golden days of high summer, when larks sing clear above bright gorse-covered hills, it is the Cauldron alone that lies dark and ill-boding, a place of terror even to the high-spirited warriors of the Thirteen Tribes of the North. Now, at the Kalan Gaeaf, the Cauldron's throat is opened, and in the depths of the abyss below is a boiling and heaving of the earth, a melting and burning in the Halls of Annufn.

In the forest depths around there hangs a strange stillness. No breath of wind stirs the black, leafless branches of the oaks of the Forest of Celyddon. In the gaunt unreality of pallid predawning is heard only the hum of invisible insects, the faint whistling of plovers, and the hoarse screaming of wild geese winging far above a spreading fog. Above the white fog the moon rises bright and solitary, casting its unearthly light upon mountain peaks rising like islands from a level sea of seething cloud. Eddies and currents faintly stir the surface of this silver, empty ocean; level save where a spiraling motion troubles its surface hard by the upthrust peak of Newais Mountain. The sinuous circle of mist uncurls itself like a striking serpent, the coiled spiral of the self-devouring Adanc of the Deep, opening up a dark vortex through the mantle of fog: a vortex whose base is the abyssal pit, the Cauldron of Cernun. The Underworld and the upper sky are linked by this swaying stairway, up which floats a wailing scream—that scream which causes the hearts of men to lose their color and their strength, women to miscarry, sons and daughters to lose their senses, and all animals, forests, earth, and waters to be left barren:

Jet-black the dark, unformed the hills; trees are bare and bleak;
Roars in the racing ocean since first I heard that shriek.

There is also a well-hole in the firmament above, a fissure ruptured by a falling star in the tent of heaven five fifties of ages before the first of the three greatest upheavals that have been in the world. "The Smoke-barrel," men call it, and it lies far to the south beyond the Middle Sea, where rises the spangled path of Caer Gwydion. It is sealed by a mighty altar-stone, guarded by the Archer, Medyr mab Medredyd, and his companion the stinging Scorpion, Esgeir Gulhwch Gonyn Cawn. And it is said that if at the Kalan Gaeaf a man gaze into a swart peat bog upon the wind-racked wastes of Godeu, he will see as in a mirror the raising of the altar-stone in the night sky. And from it will he hear faint and far, echoing about the four corners of creation, that wail which is stealing about him in rising mist from the Cauldron of Cernun; and with horror, from below the lifting stone will he glimpse the hosting of the hordes of Uffern.

Within the dressed stone walls of Porth Gwydno in the North, princes and nobles sit immobile in expectant hush. The hour moves on in silence, save for the dripping of the last drops of resin from dying pine torches. Then comes the distant sound awaited by all: faint and far-off in the gates of the North, then louder and more insistent, louder and yet louder until it gathers like the beating of winter waves on rocky shores. It is all about them now, humming in the air like clouds of insects in a summer-heated wood. Now comes an insistent roaring like the Cataract of Echuid, a gusting mighty wind in the treetops, and the tempest bursts about the shingled roof of the hall of King Gwydno Garanhir.

The Wild Hunt is passing overhead, the host of fiends and goblins that ranges the earth each Kalan Gaeaf, coursing through a storm-laden, livid sky behind their master, Gwyn mab Nud. Fiends and goblins, swart and hairy, extinguishing fires, ripping slats from roofs, and plucking babies from their cradles, they course in reckless exultation over the lonely homesteads of abandoned men. One night of lawless rule was Bran the Blessed deceived into granting the Trickster, and on it he exacts his toll of terror. Before the Wild Hunt flies the baying pack of the Hounds of Hell; glittering bright white is their color, and their ears red; the redness of their ears glitters as brightly as does the whiteness of their bodies. Behind skims a shadowy flock of copper-red birds, wide of wing and crooked of beak, blighting crops and slaughtering cattle with their poisoned breath.

The timbers of King Gwydno's hall are splitting and stone blocks loosening in their mortar shells. Bars and bolts are loosened, and the doors fly open wide with a gust of gale and rain that extinguishes every torch and taper. King and courtiers crouch like frozen images, poised in mid-movement like the sleeping warriors gathered about Arthur in his chamber beneath Newais Mountain. The earthen floor trembles and heaves. All about them in the shadow of hall pillars and roof trees the stricken princes hear the squealing of an impish crew, laughing, capering, spitting, and farting. Some descend like huge

spiders from the rafters, dangling and grinning in men's faces, displaying the malevolent features of tiny pigs, toads, adders, rats.

The full, fiery rush of the first band of the hellish host had broken
into the hall. They burst in with such fury that there was not left a
spear on a rack, nor a shield on a spike, nor a sword in an armory that
did not fall clattering down. One would think it was the sea that had
come over the walls and over the recesses of the world to them. The
forms of countenances were changed, and there was chattering of teeth
in Porth Gwydno.

Only the rowan branches affixed by Seithennin the druid to the
outer hall pillars served to fend off a general onslaught of the demon
band, and even now their leaves and twigs were drying, withering and
dropping under the fetid exhalations and spiteful plucking fingers of
the invading tormentors. Old Bishop Serfan threw himself forward
from his couch, to lie spread-eagled on the rush-strewn floor in the
attitude of the cross-vigil. Amid the mocking laughter of imps, bogles,
and dogheads, the good old man gabbled out in tremulous tones the
Litany of Confession:

"Many and vast are my sins in their number,
Penetrating the breastplate of my flesh.
O King, they cannot be numbered;
Deprive me of them, O God;
Break, smite, and war against them;
Ravage, bend, and wither them;
Take away, repel, destroy them;
Arise, scatter, defeat them;
See, repress, waste them;
Destroy, summon, starve them;
Prostrate, burn, mangle them;
Kill, slay, and ruin them;
Torture, divide, and purify them;
Tear, expel, and raze them;
Remove, scatter, and cleave them;
Subdue, exhaust, and lay them low."

On ordinary occasions a prayer of such piety might cause a flock
of demons to dive like black birds to drown in the sea, or consign the
maleficent Devil himself to the interior of a dunghill. But now, as the
defiant stanzas proceeded, so the devils' anger and scorn increased.
They became bolder, passing over the tables in the guise of great bears,
wolves, lions, and leopards, and creeping about the floor as serpents,

asps, scorpions. They filled the air with clouds of hornets big as
sparrows, and capered like monkeys about the boards, oversetting
goblets and dishes. Of the feast that was set upon the boards they left
neither fat nor lean, hot nor cold, sour nor sweet, fresh nor salted,
boiled nor raw.

To distract the blessed saint from his orison, these venomous
visitants created images of ignorant armies fighting blindly in the
night, of fleets destroyed by raging storms, and great cities burning
with ruddy glow in blighted landscapes scourged by disease and corruption. From the shadows around came sounds as of babies crying for
their absent mothers and women weeping for lost children, cattle
lowing deep from black swamps that sucked them under and lions
roaring in exultation as they ripped their prey to bloody shreds.

Finally, when none of these vain shows seemed to daunt the holy
man's courageous spirit, fortified as it was by the aid of God's warlike
Son, two sable dwarfish beings, with unseeing slabbed faces and asses'
feet turned backward, sprang upon the old man's back and began
scourging him with spiked thongs.

With the words "Subdue, exhaust, and lay them low," Bishop
Serfan swooned away, all strength departed from him. A scream of
exultant laughter went up from every nook and cranny, and warriors
who had faced unflinching the hosts of the pale-faced Saeson crouched,
sweating and trembling, gripped by unconquerable fear.

For now the square of stars glimpsed through the smoke-hole of
the roof was extinguished from view, as through it rushed Gwyn mab
Nud and his Wild Hunt, pouring in, whirling down toward the
king's hearth. King and courtiers glimpsed through a blood-red fog
horrible figures mounted on sable steeds: kings and bishops, nobles
and ladies, witches, adulteresses, and harlots. Some bore their heads
fixed backward on their necks, others sported the heads and antlers of
stags and wolves, or faces that grinned out from their chests. Others
were maimed, headless, lacking an arm, a hand, a leg, or an eye.
Others, lizard-skinned, glowed with a chill luminosity, or swung
helplessly with livid entrails hanging from open wounds in their bellies. There were those who rode astride iron-spiked saddles that gored
thigh and groin and rump, causing them to drip with blood, rolling
and screaming in unending pain.

Out of the heart of this satanic brood a huge black horse appeared,
from whose saddle sprang the colossal figure of the Master of the Wild
Hunt. Over the recumbent form of the stricken saint he limped, a
dreadful figure, naked save for a golden torque about his neck, green
and hirsute, towering far above the height of mortal men. Forth from

his bony forehead branched antlers broad as those of a roebuck in his prime, sprouting amidst upswept, spikey, flamelike hair—hair of the barbarians who yearly violate the coasts and frontiers of ordered kingdoms. His gaze was fierce and smoldering, his saturnine features furred by a reddish-colored beard, and his full-spread scarlet lips twisted into a malevolent grin. His hands were long and clawed, his belly buttoned by parallel rows of naked udders, while a great hairy phallus swung between his sinewy goat's thighs. About his left arm was coiled a broad-backed, writhing, ram-headed serpent, and in his right hand he bore an ebony-handled trident. This, then, was Gwyn mab Nud, in whom God has put the ferocity of the fiends of Annufn.

As he stepped over the recumbent cleric, the apparition's stiff tufted tail rose up erect, and forth from his gaping red-lined hair-fringed anus belched a noxious spume of billowing yellowish vapor, repugnant to sight and smell. The mocking laughter in the air grew ever more strident, dying away to a low twittering as the prince of Annufn settled himself cross-legged before King Gwydno Garanhir. The king sat pale and upright; as befitted a descendant of Dyfnwal Hen, he betrayed no fear beyond a certain pallor about his lips. The Laws of Dyfnwal decree that "whoever shall say a rough or ugly word to a king in his hall, let him pay him twofold *camlwrw* of wrongdoing." But for the laws of men Gwyn mab Nud cared not a rush, nor so much as would cover the eye of an ant.

"How fares it with thee, O king?" inquired the demon.

"Well enough, lord," answered Gwydno slowly. "And what, may I ask, brings you to our royal hall at this time—an uninvited guest, if I may make so bold as to say so?"

"Uninvited and unwelcome, you would say, my king?" the visitor said, laughing, and his unseen tribe gibbered and scoffed about the corners and eaves of the hall.

"I say nought of that," returned Gwydno in a firmer voice. "The dawn is breaking, and I take it your stay cannot be of the longest?"

"Not long, but time enough for a cast of dice at the *gwyddbwyll* board. The game will be played out whether you choose or not; know you that, O Gwydno of the Long Shank?"

Gwydno nodded in assent; the checkered board was placed between them, and the play began. It fell to Gwyn mab Nud to cast the first die; the number being uneven, he moved a man from the northern edge of the board before the row that protected Gwydno's king on its center square. Next, Gwydno threw an even number; his pegged pieces rested solid in their four-square central block. Five times did his gigantic visitor throw with his left hand the crooked, uneven numbers he desired, and five times did Gwydno Garanhir suffer the misfortune of the even throws. Gwydno's northernmost man was trapped and taken from the board.

Now Gwydno grew pale indeed, for he saw the game was to be played in deadly earnest. Three further moves upon each side, and the sweat was gathering upon his brow. His northern men were taken or scattered, one of his dreadful opponent's pieces stood beside the king, and an unchancy fall of the dice or unskillful response on his part could see the king taken within the space of a single move! Gwyn mab Nud scratched his hairy belly, belched long and loud in the king's face, and laughed exultantly. Unnoticed, the host of attendant devils had crowded forward and encircled the two players, chattering, scoffing, and squealing in high delight. One or two, neutered newts and five-legged frogs bolder than the rest, reached up to pluck impudently at King Gwydno's royal robe, and tweak surreptitiously at his beard.

The Lord of the Wild Hunt cupped the die within his taloned hands, shaking it long between hairy palms and grinning wide in his opponent's face. At last, eking out his anticipated triumph to the end, he let fall the die upon the board. King Gwydno trembled violently. Again an uneven throw, in an uneven game! The adversary had but to advance to the vacant right-hand space, and the king, the precious king, was his. Gwyn mab Nud raised his pegged piece and poised it gloatingly for untold moments. From a rafter above, a gross squat spider with bloated torso and long hooked nose spun down on a line of web, dangling in spite and mockery before the wretched King Gwydno's pale face, while emitting a foul-smelling thin stream of smoking urine into the king's goblet.

It was time that Gwydno Garanhir had need of now, which being the night of Kalan Gaeaf is No-time. Pale and shrunken and near to death he seemed, as he gazed down at the gold and silver board and up at the demon's poised peg. Through the smoke-hole in the hall roof one present glimpsed a cluster of stars, which he knew to be the Fishes hanging far out over the Sea of Reged. Between them lay the celestial *gwyddbwyll* board, where You, Bright Guardian of the Spindle of the Earth, first played the game of the gods. With Your Sure Arm You moved the pegs, until the broad firmament was stablished firm and the waters of chaos, hosts of the Coranieid, were driven to the borderlands of chaos which fringe the frail universe. To a watcher's straining gaze the square seemed void and empty, but he prayed that even now You might extend Your Sure Hand to poise the pegs, that King Gwydno might not err in his playing, succumbing to strife, discord, and deception.

The world of men is but the gods' game of *gwyddbwyll*. The moving of the pegs set upon the board at the game's commencing is restricted by those laws which You established at the beginning with Your Sure Hand. Yet though the pegs be few and the laws so simple a child may master them, the multiplicity of moves which may be made is numberless as leaves of the forest.

Does this then mean that the game is without pattern or meaning, since each successive die-throwing must multiply by myriads the moves that may be made? That can scarcely be so, it seems to me, since every game must have its ending. As the ending is of necessity foredoomed from the game's beginning, so every careless dice-throw unwittingly plays its purposed part in encompassing that ending. Just as the Adanc of the Deep girdles the earth, so time bends ever over until it encircles the whole of that which Gofannon mab Don wrought at creation's beginning; with its stars to our wishing, with its sun and its moon.

We say that casting of dice is but a contention of chance, and is not chance blind, favoring neither creation nor destruction, the maintenance of the truth of a kingdom nor its wasting by famine or forays of foemen? So men say, but in many matters it is men themselves who appear blind. For may it not be chance that tests and sorts the disordered elements; chance, the explorer and orderer of the unformed and disordered? A rotten branch drops from a tree, breaking the back of a goat that grazes the greensward beneath. It was chance that the branch broke in that instant and not another; it was chance that brought the goat to graze that spot in that moment and no other. But was it chance that brought them both to do these things together?

Take that die which even now you shake this way and that in your cupped hands, O king. On five sides you see ascending in successive clusters the numbered dots; the fifth alone is a rune, which is the letter B. Cast six throws in succession! There, you have six numbers, each of which must lie between one and six: 1, 3, 5, 2, 2, 6. Next, reckon up the instances where the number obtained is equal to or less than three, and term that the Golden Number. In this case, as you see, there are four such numbers. Now repeat with six more throws, and make a new Golden Number which is the tally of instances where the number obtained is less than or equal to the previous Golden Number. You have thrown 3, 3, 2, 1, 1, and 4. All are equal to or less than four, so your fresh Golden Number is the sum of all: six. Continue the throwing and scoring in this manner, and you will find that the Golden Number continually veers to 0 or 6, oscillating with the regularity of the sun's rising and setting.

Though every throw has its chance result, and the path of Golden

Numbers leading to 0 or 6 varies randomly, the regular achievement of
0 and 6 is as inevitable as the movement of the tides. Chance varies the
path in many ways, but the goal is nevertheless inescapable. Thus
chance determines the anticipated result. Consider hard, O king: How
can this thing be? For chance is chaotic, and what is determined is
ordered. Is it possible that chaos may be order, and what is destined
regulated by disorder? The dice tell you the answer, throw as you will
the length of a summer's day.

Nor is this all the interplay of chance and necessity which is found
in the throwing of dice. We call that which governs the fall of the dice
"chance." Yet is it in truth so? Is not the fall governed by motions or
roughness of hand and finger which, though too secret and subtle for
us to detect, are nonetheless in every detail determined? In truth it may
be said that chance and that which is preordained are as inextricably
entwined as is the convolvulus about the blackthorn bush.

It is not for mortal men to see the beginning and end of time, but
only the immortal gods. How can we then, fallible sons and daughters
of time, see aught but confusion in all that has arisen from the nine
forms of elements which were at the beginning? Rules there may be;
but how may we, who enter the *gwyddbwyll* game each in his generation to depart with the game as yet unplayed, know in truth what rules
prevailed at the beginning, and whether they play any part in the
fluctuations of the struggle?

Hard it is to answer this question, though the books of *llyfyrion* and
the precepts of druids be consulted for five ages of five periods. For are
we not part of the game, and how may that which is a part contemplate the whole? But if we may not contemplate the game at large, yet
is the *awen* of the poet and the prophet attuned to awareness: awareness of the presence of the nine elements of creation, the rules of the
game that govern creation, and the purpose which He whose Sure
Arm embraces all has laid upon the board and the pegs which move
about it.

But here was no time for contemplation, for the game was being
played out within the courthouse of King Gwydno, as well as upon
that greater board which is set between the Fishes. Now it was that
Gwydno Garanhir pleaded in a voice thin and quavering for *naut*, that
protection and immunity which a noble may by right claim of his
king:

> "Bull of battle, fierce, malign
> Prince of plunder and rapine,
> Dost thou grant me *naut* benign?"

The giant figure shadowing the checkered board, horned and hirsute, parting his blood-red lips in a mocking grin, nodded.

"As your country's conquering lord,
Head of hosts, and slashing sword:
Naut I grant as my award."

King Gwydno's brow glistened damp in the ruddy hearth-glow, and his gaze of terror remained fixed upon the *gwyddbwyll* peg poised in the fiend's crooked grasp. It was in the ingratiating tones with which a vassal addresses his chief that he made reply:

"Since you grant your royal due,
Tell me how I speak to you;
Whence your royal retinue?"

Shrill was the laughter of the swart imps and multilimbed deformities that lurked behind each rafter and within each goblet, momentarily dissolved in drink like those insects which Nud Silver-hand ground into liquid for the destruction of the Coranieid. Mischievous, tormenting, and quarrelsome were the thoughts the demon huntsmen placed within the minds of the Men of the North, as each in turn sipped unwarily at the yellow ensnaring mead. Gwyn mab Nud laughed louder and longer than all, the long red tongue within his black gullet flickering livid as flames out of the gates of Annufn, as he made mocking reply:

"From stern slaughter red and grim,
Where by shielded rampart rim
Lie splintered skull and severed limb!"

King Gwydno trembled, but made reply as is the right of a chieftain becoming man and kin of his overlord, at whose coming to kingship is recitation of origins and genealogies, donation of *cyfarwys* in return for gifts and hostings and hostages:

"Headstrong hero, pray define—
Shield of shattered battle-line—
What thy race and royal line?"

The cold eye of Gwyn mab Nud glinted dull as that of a lizard as he made contemptuous reply:

"Stern my steed, barring quarter;
Gwyn my name, grim in slaughter:
Lover of Nud's fair daughter."

Strange it was to hear so grim a specter name himself as a lover. Yet true it is that antlered Gwyn mab Nud fights with Gwithir mab Greidawl every Kalan Mai from this until Doomsday for love of Creidilad, daughter of Nud Law Ereint, the most majestic maiden there ever was in the Island of Prydein and its Three Adjacent Islands.

Now the leader of the Wild Hunt had named himself, it was for Gwydno to do likewise, though he knew that in so doing he was delivering himself into his power and becoming one of his tribe and people.

"Since thou art Gwyn, lost souls' guide,
My name too I shall not hide:
Gwydno, ruling Reged's tide."

But the Sea of Reged was dark as the inside of a stone at this time, by reason of the swarm of maleficent beings that clouded all air and winds that blew above the Island of Prydein and its Three Adjacent Islands. Gwyn mab Nud laughed long and bitterly, his hobgoblin horde twittering and squeaking about him in the night. Behind him loomed up in the darkness a great black dog, high as the rooftree, lame, ragged-fanged, eyes burning like coals and hanging over its jaws. And the stench of the breath from its nostrils, its maw, and its anus hung upon the night air in fumes fetid and foul as those of a foumart; it was the stench of corpses dragged by ravening curs to be devoured from deserted fields of slaughter. It seemed to Gwydno Garanhir that the creature crouched ever closer, and as much as its bladed teeth did he fear the mildewed stench of its matted hide.

Gwyn mab Nud scented the king's fear with a maleficent grin of satisfaction. Toying with the *gwyddbwyll* peg above that slot King Gwydno had cause to dread, he spoke sneering words of taunt and mockery:

"Fair and strong is hound of Gwyn,
Fair without and fair within,
Dormach, dog of Maelgun."

The dog, too, grinned, its slavering jaws opening wide as the fifty broad rafters that were in Gwydno's hall, its pitch-black lips brushing the sooty eaves. Like jagged pinnacles of a mountain ridge were its grinders and fore-fangs; like those rocks, sharp as the dagger of Osla Cylelfawr, which jut out from the seashore below King Custennin's dark Tower in distant Cerniu, with their bloody intersticing of bleached bones and battered bodies. Let Gwyn mab Nud but give the word, one thought to himself, and the monster would devour all men in the hall from hunger: king, princes, and warriors for his tearing and gnawing and swallowing.

A man who was there longed to intervene with a riddling question of his own, but he knew too well that only the king could play at *gwyddbwyll* in his hall with Gwyn mab Nud at the time of the Kalan Gaeaf. And King Gwydno, it has to be said, played his part well enough.

"Red-nosed Dormach, staring hound,"

he asked tremulously,

"Tell me what it was you found,
On that misty hill renowned?"

Then all fear-frozen folk in the beleaguered hall shuddered for the space of a broken moment as Dormach growled foully upon them all from within his great black belly. And worse than that grim growling was the neighing laugh of his great bare-shanked master, Lord of the Wild Hunt and leader of the souls of the departed. Fiercely laughed the specter, as he closed his fingers upon the head of a feaster, pinching in his skull like an eggshell and presenting the brains upon his taloned fingers for the red tongue of Dormach to lick and lap. Fierce and cruel was Gwyn's laughter, and fiercely and cruelly did his venomous crew echo it up from rafter and bench-end and doorjamb.

Whether it was the black dog or his master who made reply, none could recall afterward. But the words that blew about their brains were of such nature that they shall not be forgotten so long as the rain wets the graves of the princes of Prydein on uplands and headlands. All that were assembled at Porth Gwydno in the North heard them screamed derisively in their ears, as did all who dwell in the land of Cantre'r Gwaelod, and throughout all the sixty cantrefs of Prydein.

For my part, it is the demon's opening words that are most terrible to recall. Even now, as I suffer sickness and sorrow in the Forest of Celyddon, torture of ten and forty years, snow up to my hips

among wolves of the forest, I hear wailing down the wind from
Newais Mountain the gloating refrain:

> "Gwendolau's white corpse I saw,
> Poets' patron, mab Ceidaw:
> Ravens croaking on his gore!"

Then followed other verses of similarly sinister import, each as all
knew to be irrevocably true, inscribed in runes upon granite slabs, and
written in illuminated letters in the velvet-bound book of bright lettering that hangs suspended above the aery world. Would that it could
have been *that* book I destroyed, rather than that other of which
Taliesin sang! But in Iweryd is destruction and desolation and death of
all things.

> "I saw Iweryd, where fell
> His son Bran, whose fame men tell:
> Ravens croak on him as well!

> "Lacheu's death I also saw,
> Arthur's son, of magic lore:
> Filled with blood the raven's maw!

> "I have been where Prydein's soldiers died
> From eastwards to the North,
> Entombed: while I ride forth!

> "I have been where Prydein's soldiers died
> From southwards to the east,
> My life endures: but theirs has ceased!"

Loud and long was the Huntsman's exultant laughter. Even as the
great hound Dormach dwindled back into the shadows, Gwyn mab
Nud seemed to swell in strength and stature until his antlered helm all
but reached the rooftree. No more would he taunt the paralyzed king,
who with each adverse throw of the dice had sunk into the ground
beneath his feet, until it was his chin that rested on the level surface of
the earth. The final move must be made, and the king swept from the
board! Gwyn thrust forward his peg, keeping his terrible gaze fixed
hard and taunting down upon King Gwydno's pallid face—then leaned
across to place it on the fatal spot.

It was hard to tell how long the moment passed, at a time when time itself was suspended. Then an apprehensive spasm unexpectedly shadowed the demon's masterful gaze, as he abruptly darted down his piece toward the vacant square upon which every eye was bent.

But in the splitting of a moment before the peg could be inserted in its hole, a ringing cry echoed throughout the hall, causing all to gaze about them in surprise. It came from Prince Elffin, who until now had been immobile as all the rest. He had risen abruptly to his feet and was pointing in high excitement at a square of light in the center of the rooftree.

"The dawn!" he cried. "The dawn has broken, and the game is ended!"

Even as Gwyn mab Nud glanced upward in irritation, a thin shaft of pale sunlight darted through a crack in the timbered wall, setting a faint but perceptible ray upon the carved figure of Gwydno's king in the center of the *gwyddbwyll* board. A terrible scream burst from the throat of the victorious player as he saw how narrowly he had been deprived of his victory. As the screaming died away, echoing ever more faintly about the halls and walls of Porth Gwydno in the North, a red-combed cock was heard raising a spirited clarion cry from his exultant perch in the yard.

Flinging his piece upon the board, Gwyn bounded high in air and flew to where his coal-black steed awaited him by the hearthside. After him streamed his infernal crew, scuffling and clawing at one another in frantic endeavor not to be left within the building as the burgeoning light of dawn brought back suspended time, space, and reality to the Island of Prydein and its Three Adjacent Islands. Upward through the smoke-hole they poured, that chaotic crew of perverted deformity. For a moment the troop hovered in upper air like a gathering swarm of bees, then broke away to stream northward toward the mountains and forests of the Wilderness of Godeu. Behind them, in the hall of King Gwydno Garanhir, they left only the stench and miasma of vomit, excrement, urine, phlegm, froth, saliva, sweating, and spitting, filthy fumes of flatulent foulness, lurking in every corner and crevice.

For a few moments the sky over the whole Island of the Mighty, from Penrin Blathaon in the north to Penrin Penwaed in the south, was darkened by the passing of the fleeing host of Hell. Then, as the sun rose in glory above the coasts of Manau Gododdin and Bryneich, bathing in light and warmth the fairest island that is in the world, the dazzling white, red-eared Hounds of Hell bounded over the Wall, passed across the gilded expanse of the Sea of Reged, and with horrid yelping coursed homeward above the wind-tossed expanse of the Forest of Celyddon. Pressed hard by their antlered master and his frenzied troop, they streamed down through the chasm that yawned open—not a moment too soon—at the base of the cloud-capped cliffs that wall in the abyssal Cauldron of Cernun in the heart of the Wasteland of Godeu. Open, too, was the great altar-stone of the sky, at the foot of Gwydion's glittering arc.

Morning was up, birds trilled from the tops of oak and ash, streams sparkled in their rocky courses, and the world of gods and men resumed its wonted course. Not for a year would the mounds of the Fair Folk again be opened, the gates of the Halls of Annufn and Afarnach loose bolt and bar, and the Wild Hunt of Gwyn mab Nud ride out on the gusts of the storm cloud.

In the hall of Porth Gwydno the princes' limbs and lips were loosened, and in the expansion of relief from oppression, tongues wagged gloriously eloquent once more. Only King Gwydno raised himself from out of the earth to sit silent, gazing fixedly at the *gwyddbwyll* board. Once or twice his fingers strayed toward a piece, only to withdraw themselves in perplexity. Bishop Serfan rose unsteadily from the floor and, leaning upon his crosier, that holy crook with which he gathered in Crist's flock to safety, pronounced holy words of exorcism, destructive to imps and demons, spells of smiths and druids:

"Let the envy, whether of human feeling or spiritual wickedness, cease, that I may be worthy to attain unto Iessu Crist; may fires, crosses, beasts, wrenchings of bones, hacking of limbs, and pains in my whole body, and all tortures devised by the art of the Devil be fulfilled in me alone, provided I be worthy to attain unto Iessu Crist."

Then, assisted by the priest of the household, did the sainted bishop totter away in search of holy water with which to sain the polluted steading. He sensed a lingering evil that hovered about the cobwebbed recesses of the great hall, behind sooty rafters, under benches, and in unscoured pots. What he was not to know was that, following his mischievous wont, Gwyn mab Nud had placed thorn-apples of discord and envy and boasting in the minds of the young princes Elffin mab Gwydno and Run mab Maelgun. Escaping in the direction from which he had come, he left trouble brewing between them such as seemed good to him.

Prince Elffin sat upon the edge of his couch, glancing sleepily about him. He cocked his ear. What was that distant sound? A moment later, and he cried aloud. All men paused, gazing about them expectantly. Far off they could hear a faint, level moaning, a dull distant roar that grew perceptibly in volume even as they listened.

"The Wild Hunt is returning!" cried Prince Run mab Maegun,

snatching a spear from the wall and gazing fiercely about him. Emboldened by the daylight, warriors sprang to arms and prepared to defend the hall, even against the Hosts of Annufn.

It was Taliesin, chief of bards, who broke in with a smile.

"That is no Wild Hunt!" he exclaimed sharply. "Do you not hear the wave-voice of the strong-maned sea, and the storm of the green-sided waves? Do you live so near the shores of the Sea of Reged, and fail to recognize the murmuring of Gwenhudwy's daughters and the pounding of the white-maned steeds of Manawydan mab Lir?"

Enlightenment dawned, and the confused minds of the princes became crystal-clear once more.

"Of course!" shouted Elffin, laughing. "You are right, prince of poets; it is the tide returning between the flats!"

And then, as memory, too, flooded back, he cried out gleefully, "The king's gift! The Hamper of Gwydno! This year its contents shall be mine; who rides with me to retrieve the richest Treasure that is in the North?"

With laughter and with gladness the lords sprang from their couches and ran to the royal stables. Mounting their noble, fleet-limbed, long-maned steeds, they rode rejoicing through the western gateway of Porth Gwydno, mocking as they passed the grumblings of King Gwydno's surly porter while he fumbled with bolt and bar. Past the huddled reed-thatched houses of the bondsmen clustered without the gates trotted the joyous company, marking the wreckage wrought by the Wild Hunt in its passing. Cattle were wandering loose, women chasing their scattered fowl, men repairing roofs despoiled by the malicious sprites, and bees humming angrily around tumbled rope-hives.

Through the gap in the ruined Wall that divides the North, from the Sea of Reged to the Sea of Udd, trotted Prince Elffin and his splendid, finely dressed, yellow-haired companions, accompanied by their white-toothed wolfhounds and mastiffs. Before them the land was bare and open; barren, tussocky, and reedy. But above them the upper air was bright and free of malign beings, the breeze was warm and gusty, and all created things reflected the joys of a world born anew. The nobles galloped along the flats by the Pull Brook, calling to each other with gleeful shouting. From the rivulet a low band of mist was dispelling, so that the horsemen appeared as the plunging coursers of Manawydan mab Lir rolling in from the surging ocean, whom even now they raced to encounter. Ahead lay the gray, white-flecked expanse of the Sea of Reged, where its inmost gulf thrusts in between the rich estuarine grazing meadows of Reged and Leudiniaun, and beyond towered the heaped-up mountains of Godeu, caps of snow upon their heads. A flock of white-fronted geese swooped inland before the rising tide, their harsh laughter mingling with that of the torque-bearing, silken-clothed princes on their broad-thighed, small-stepping, broad-backed steeds.

It was not long before the cavalcade approached the Aber Eden, and as they did so their ears were assailed by a wailing chanting. Now high, now low, its melody meandered like the course of the Eden. Permeating the harmony flowed a deeper mournful measure, moving and moaning, soughing and sighing like the distant main, murmuring in majesty beyond the mudbanks of Erechwyd. Above the ceaseless sighing of the sea and its accompanying plaintive chanting arose from time to time the shrill scream of a seafowl, caught up in its turn by a wild ululation from the hidden chorus.

Leaping a small rivulet trickling through the yellow muddy level, Prince Elffin and his company came upon a bend in the river, not half a mile before it joins the greater flow of Erechwyd. There upon a low flat promontory, their faces uplifted toward the salt breeze blowing off the Sea of Reged, knelt a group of men and women who sang as sweetly as any chorus cadenced in church or monastery. These were the fisherfolk of Porth Gwydno, singing the ancient song of enchantments which draws salmon into the river mouth, and on into their wide nets.

Now the troop had left the broad level, with its stumpy gorse bushes and rough grass tussocks, and cantered across a drear expanse of mud flat, which lay between them and their goal. Before him Elffin glimpsed at last the long dark line of the weir spanning the Eden from bank to bank, a risen tide coursing through the wattled palisade.

> "I hear the wave of heavy roar
> Growling on the shingled shore;
> God preserve the outcast poor,"

murmured the poet Taliesin at the prince's side. Prince Elffin glanced at him with an impatient word upon his lips, then drove his heels into his horse's flanks and rode down the riverbank into the swirling foam.

His following waited respectfully upon the river marge while their prince, boy in years but man in vigor, waded forward through the foaming tide, the waves washing his horse's tail. The waters sucked and swelled about the legs and flanks of the well-fed steed, as if mischievously enticing mount and rider to descend into the glassy halls of Manawydan mab Lir. Elffin thought little enough of that; his heart was bounding as he approached within the arms of the weir. For well he knew how each Kalan Gaeaf his father's Hamper was filled with broad-backed speckled salmon beyond counting. It was said indeed that if the whole world should come, three nines at a time, each would get all the food he wanted. The Hamper of Gwydno Garanhir was famed as the milch cow of the waters of Prydein for the number of fish that it held at this catching; each one as great, so the men of Cantre'r Gwaelod were wont to boast, as the famed Salmon of Drobess in remote Ywerdon.

But what was this? From each stake streamed out the sea wrack, and the wattling between was as sound as when woven after the Kalan Mai. However, gaze as he might, Prince Elffin mab Gwydno saw there neither head nor tail of a single young salmon. Nothing was trapped by the angled fence of King Gwydno's great weir—nothing save a dark shape that hung from the great central post at its apex, the keystone as it were of the fish rampart. Prince Elffin gazed in sorrow and anger at that small thing within the enclosure, swept his glance once more the breadth of the empty Hamper—and lowered his head to return in shame and poverty to his expectant following.

Halfway back through the tugging swell he encountered Taliesin. The bard, reining in his horse alongside him among the wavelets, smiled a quizzical smile that angered the prince.

"At what do you smile, chief of bards?" he growled. "Do you not see the Hamper is empty?"

"Not so, O prince," responded the poet with a short laugh. "Are your eyes bent so low that they do not see what thing it is that your father's Hamper holds this Kalan Gaeaf? Turn back your horse's head, and see what gift Manawydan mab Lir has bestowed upon you!"

With a grunt of impatience Elffin turned his bridle and waded back with the poet toward the center of the strong-flowing Eden. Only the firm-footed stockade saved them from being swept out into the billowing Sea of Reged. There, on the central pile, hung by a thong a black leathern bag, sodden and streaming from its immersion beneath the foaming crest of the turning tide.

"What is it?" asked the prince, with a quick leap of expectation.

"Draw your knife and slit it open!" urged Taliesin, his smile broadening. "Only take care how you cut. Whatever lies within may not take kindly to a throat-slitting!"

CHAPTER FIVE

THE CONSOLATION
OF
ELFFIN
DEHUDDIANT ELFFIN

It was to the Hamper of his father, King Gwydno Garanhir, at the Aber Eden that Prince Elffin had ridden with his company on the morning following the feast of the Kalan Gaeaf. But to his dismay there was neither silver salmon nor speckled trout within that Hamper, but only a small leathern bag. At the bidding of Taliesin, chief of bards, Elffin leaned forward in his saddle and, drawing it to him, gently severed the knotted cord about its neck and gazed curiously within. What he saw peeping out at him—great was his surprise—was the broad fair brow of a sturdy radiant child.

For so I think with due modesty I may describe myself, O king. You surely did not need *my* wisdom, King Ceneu of the Red Neck, to guess that it was I within that leathern bag? Yes, after my forty years' stay with the Salmon of Lyn Liw in the watery realms of Manawydan mab Lir, I had fetched up in this awkward predicament. Now, at the very moment it really seemed my promising career was about to be unfairly nipped in the bud, here I was rescued by this dashing if not overintelligent young princeling. I gave him a beaming smile while I struggled to draw my plump little dimpled arms out of the bag.

"What in the name of Mabon is this?" snorted Elffin to his

companion. "Some wanton's bastard, flung out upon the river for the fishes to devour?"

Grateful as I was to Prince Elffin, I could not but be gravely affronted by these offensive words. True, the circumstances of my birth *were* a trifle irregular—well, "unusual" I think would be a fairer description—but gratuitously rude allusions of this sort have never greatly appealed to me. We are none of us responsible for the precise manner in which we emerge from the portals of the Otherworld, and for some the entry may be more unconventional than for others. However, I felt more than a little vulnerable (I still could not extract my puny arms), and thought it best to placate the hotheaded youth with fair words.

"Fair Elffin, wipe that tear!" I began appealingly.

> "There's no use in despair;
> No catch in Gwydno's weir
> Was ever half so dear.
> Let no man come to rue
> A fate he can't see through:
> Gwydno receives his due;
> God to His word is true."

Doggerel though it was, my precocious speech greatly startled the prince, who nearly dropped me and my bag back into the water. With an expression of comical astonishment upon his handsome face, he turned to Taliesin for an explanation.

"The babe is right," returned the bard in tones of emphatic meaning. "If you are wise you will treat him with respect; and it may be that in time you and the Men of the North will learn from his lips much concerning the lore of the stars, the playing of the greater *gwyddbwyll* game, and marvelous matter concerning the future of the Island of Prydein with its Three Adjacent Islands. There is more than one cause for sending adrift a child in a boat of one hide, and it is not for you to prefer one to another without inquiry."

"Very true, O poet!" I piped up confidently, though none too sure within myself as to what he had in mind. "You see, my prince, that there may be much virtue in me: I am well worth preserving, I assure you."

By now we were at the river's edge, and scrambled up the eroded mudbank to where Prince Elffin's comrades were sitting their horses in a half-circle, agog with curiosity to know what lay within the bag they had seen him hoist from the stake. The prince, by now in more

equable mood, drew me out and set me before him on his saddlebow.
I looked cheerily round at the ring of puzzled faces, resolved to divert
them, too, with my precocity. (How were they to know I was in
reality forty years old?) I took up my verse again:

> "Prince Elffin should be glad
> At gaining such a lad;
> There's not much to be had
> From being vainly sad.
> Small and frail I may be
> And damp from Dylan's sea,
> But time will prove, you'll see,
> That I'll be wealth to thee."

A shout of approbation greeted this sally, which passed from lip
to lip in merry repetition. By now Elffin seemed largely reconciled to
his strange catch, and turned to Taliesin for final reassurance.

"Do you indeed think this young imp will bring me good fortune, O bard?" he inquired earnestly. Taliesin nodded shortly, turning
to stare penetratingly into my eyes. I did not altogether like that look; I
sensed I was dealing with someone almost as clever as myself. I could
see I had best have my wits about me, for I did not relish being tossed
back into the river to sink or swim.

Now Taliesin's eyes began to roll upward until the dilated pupils
were concealed behind the lids. His lips mumbled together, foaming a
little as words began to form upon his tongue. The princes edged their
horses back respectfully; they could see that the *awen* had come unexpectedly upon the divine versifier, and that he was inspired. To me he
addressed words which from their truth and perception I saw came
without falsehood from the Cauldron of Poesy.

> "Black your horse, black your cloak,
> Black your head and black yourself,
> Black skull, are you the Frenzied One?"

Deprecatingly I replied:

> "I am the Frenzied One learned in booklore,
> But a frenzied one lacking in guile.
> For the burning of churches and killing of cattle,
> And most evil of all the drowning a Book,
> Will bring down a penance most grievous to bear.

Creator of all things, Helper of all men,
Forgive me that sin!
For it was I was betrayed by him betrayed you,
And so I suffer the span of an endless year
Hanging over the flood on the stake of a weir,
Gnawed through to the bone by worms from the sea.
Were I to know then what now I know
—Clear as wind whistling wild through branch of tree—
Never that way would I choose to go."

Nobody understood our colloquy; indeed at that time I am not certain that I did myself. If you hear out my tale, O king, perchance you will learn in time what was its meaning. The main thing is that it served its purpose. Prince Elffin was greatly impressed by all this rigmarole, for like most people he believed that the more incomprehensible an explanation, the deeper its import.

So it was I found myself bobbing along in my sack hanging from Elffin's saddlebow, until at last we rode triumphantly into Porth Gwydno. Everybody crowded out to see what their prince had brought back from his father's enchanted Hamper, and were agog to clap eyes on little me when they learned of his unusual find. I was naturally on my best behavior, smirking and nodding away to the huge delight of all—especially the womenfolk. After I had been paraded about the court, dandled by King Gwydno on his Long Shank, and tossed high in air by Prince Run mab Maelgun, I was taken to receive the blessing of Bishop Serfan.

The good old man was propped up in his high-backed chair when I was borne in before him. They wanted him to baptize me, and the priest of the household made all ready for that end. The bishop to my mind appeared rather the worse for wear after all the previous night's excitements, which considering his age was scarcely surprising. During the preparations he lay back with glazed eyes fixed upon the roof. His reaction seemed all the odder in consequence when I was in due course presented to him at close quarters. Wearily he raised the chrism, and was about to apply the oil to my "radiant forehead" (as the ladies were kind enough to term it), when abruptly he sat upright and gave an exclamation of surprise.

"Who is this infant?" he cried out. The account of my appearance in the Hamper of Gwydno was repeated, but this time the saint shook his head angrily.

"No, no!" he shouted indignantly. "This child has undergone the rite already. The canons of Holy Church do not permit a second baptism. Take him away!"

Mighty shrewd, thought I to myself, while everyone gabbled away at sixes and sevens. As you who hear this tale will know, I had indeed been baptized by Abbot Mawgan soon after my birth in the land of Cerniu. But that was forty years ago; could the mark be still upon me, after my long bath in the ocean? However, I certainly was not going to make a fuss. During those forty years I had undergone more in the way of total immersion than most people are likely to encounter, and for the moment was more than content to keep out of water, hot, holy, or whatever.

But as questions broke out on all sides, I quickly appreciated that the old fellow was less of a wizard than I took him for, and had made a simple error. It was a case of mistaken identity! It made a great impression on everyone there, except me, when the old fellow began a rambling account of his baptizing a baby on a previous occasion, a baby he swore was the precise image of me. When he was still at his church on Pen Celyn in the kingdom of the Fichti, he told us, he happened one day to be praying alone after mass within the building. All at once he heard companies of angels singing wonderfully sweetly, so that he joined in the chorus (*not* quite so mellifluously, I fear) with a "We praise Thee, O Lord."

Next, some shepherds (I think I've heard this story somewhere else) found a young girl lying sleeping beside their fire, with a baby dressed in rags clasped in her arms. They fed her and brought her to the saint, whose mouth was "filled with spiritual laughter" (that's how he put it, and gave a toothless cackle just to show us how).

"He is a most lovable babe," went on the saint, nodding confusingly down at me. "I baptized him with the name Cyndeyrn—that is, "chief lord," as I believe he will one day become within our Holy Mother Church. His was a strange story: His mother, Taneu, as she told me, was a virgin who had been cast out to sea in a leathern coracle by a cruel king, a veritable Herod in those parts. But the Lord, who preserved Jonah within the belly of the great fish and thrice saved the apostle Paul from shipwreck, guided the course of that frail vessel until it fetched up on the beach below our church. As she slept by the shepherds' watchfire the unhappy maiden gave birth to this miraculous babe, of whom I have prophesied many great things. The monks of my household offered up the calves of their lips to the Lord, and since then He has marked the lad out by manifold signs. On one occasion, I recall, he cured a pet robin of whom I was inordinately fond. On another he raised from the dead our most excellent cook (who was even then lying in his tomb), just in time for dinner."

It was an odd story, in some respects not a little like my own. The bishop's strength appeared to have returned to him, and he continued a succession of anecdotes about the lad Cyndeyrn, who was clearly a great favorite with him. King Gwydno eventually grew a little impatient and, together with many of his company, stole away, leaving me to suffer the interminable history of this precocious youth upon whom none of us had so much as clapped eye. I felt myself trapped, until I had the wit to vomit into the old gentleman's lap. He was glad enough then to be rid of me, though as we departed I could hear him still intoning his anecdotes to a couple of young monks as they wiped him down.

After this abortive encounter, I was to receive a fuller and final initiation into the workaday world. Elffin bore me to the booth of the druid Seithennin, who to my relief did not confuse me with other babes of similar appearance. The rite which followed was quite simple. His slaves carried me to the central hearth of the hall, where they laid me down on a calfskin in an awkward posture, my knees being drawn up to my chin. Next the druid made obeisance to the carved images of the Bright Shining One (Belatgaer) that stands over the southern doorway, and to that of the Horned One (Cernun) above the northern entrance. He then uttered a lengthy prophecy in verse which I won't give you here, since much of it was to prove correct—and *that,* needless to say, would spoil the effect of my story.

Lastly came the most significant item, without which I could not be held properly to exist. I was named after Porth Gwydno itself, so that my luck might attach itself to the king's fortress. *Mer-lin,* "Sea-fortress," was what I was now called. This was most fortunate in that, as you may recall, it happened to be my name already! So, Merlin I became henceforward, though I was to receive additional names in due course. There would come a time, too, when many feared to call me by any name at all. But that was not a happy time, and I gladly leave the subject for the present. "Black Frenzied One," Taliesin had called me at the weir; I think he knew something of what would come to pass.

So it was that I became accepted at the court of King Gwydno, and found my earliest home among the folk of the Cantre'r Gwaelod. I was given over for upbringing to the women of the court, among whom I became a great pet. At night I slept in the bed of Elffin's princess, where, too, lay her handmaidens. They termed me a mischievous child, and laughed much at the pranks I got up to at night while they lay languorously unguarded in sleep. That was no unpleasant time for me, as you may conceive, O king! Slim white limbs in profusion, and soft breasts like those of the mother I scarcely knew.

Until the festival of Nadolic, I saw little of my protector, Prince Elffin, who was out riding with hawk and hound for much of the time. I feared that he might have forgotten his unlooked-for ward, being a rather lighthearted young man, and resolved to bring myself to his attention when opportunity offered.

My chance came at the time of Nadolic, which is the feast of Iessu Crist, pure son of a woman who knew no mate. As usual I was confined to the women's quarters, and had to hear afar off joyous sounds of revelry denied poor me. Above all I repined bitterly when the brawling suddenly stilled and I heard a lone voice raised in song. Being something of a poet myself I longed to be present when the *awen* unlocked the precious store held in the Cauldron of Poesy. For that man Taliesin was a poet and a half! Ah, if you could but have heard him! His words cast a spell upon us all, even those who like me were not permitted to be present at their singing. For his words became images and the images overlapped reality, until the praise of kings, the lamentation of kings, the trumpet clamor of cattle raiding, the stillness of the abandoned battlefield, and the glorious, drunken march of heroes riding resistless as the foaming Cataract of Derwent, swept the audience up into an ecstasy rapt as that of the bard himself.

Then would he play them a tearful melody, so that the company began to weep and lament and grieve, finally imploring him to cease. Accordingly he played them a laughter-provoking strain, so that all laughed until their lungs were almost visible. Finally he would play them a sleep-inducing air, sweet as that of the Birds of Riannon, so that all fell asleep until the next day.

At that time of Nadolic, the yellow ensnaring mead wrought its customary effect upon the assembled princes. The quarreling over the Champion's Portion at the division of the pork-joints was more ferocious than usual, and the boasts that followed of an extravagance extreme even among the glorious, spear-showering Men of the North. When the revelry finally died down there were many who found themselves unable to regain their couches and so snored the night away comfortably enough upon the rushes.

To those who remained within the darkened hall, Bishop Serfan uttered before his retiring words of reproof and chastisement for their edification, in the form of certain words of the prophet Ioel:

" 'Awake ye that are drunk through your wine, and weep and

lament all who drink wine unto drunkenness, because joy and gladness is taken away from your mouth.' ''

And true it was that for many, joy and gladness were taken from
their mouths, which were parched as withered reeds; and from their
heads also, which were sore and sad as is the life of an exile; and from
their stomachs likewise, which knew sudden lurchings and swellings,
such as tossing billows inflict upon the frail barks of fishermen.

We (the princess and I, that is) were woken abruptly in the early
hours of the morning when our door curtain was roughly drawn to
one side. A taper was still burning dimly within our chamber, and by
its light we saw Elffin standing swaying in the entrance. Presuming he
had come for her, the princess swiftly passed me into the hands of her
maid (a very pretty girl called Heled) and signed to her to remove me.
But Prince Elffin raised his hand in a gesture as if to let me stay.
Lurching over to the bed, he sat down heavily and cupped his head in
his hands with a deep groan.

"What is it that ails you, lord?" asked my princess, moving across
to place her arm across his shoulders. "Can I be of help to you? Say
but the word, and if I can do it, I will, be the cost what it may."

The princess was a very beautiful young lady. Yellower was her
hair than the flowers of the broom; whiter her skin than the foam of a
wave; whiter, too, were her palms and fingers than the bloom of
marsh stitchwort by a sandy sea marge. Neither the eye of a mewed
hawk nor the eye of a thrice-mewed falcon was brighter than her own.
Whiter were her breasts than that of a swan, her cheeks redder than the
foxglove, and all who saw her were filled with love for her.

Prince Elffin, for all his willful ways, loved her dearly, and showed
no signs of wishing to take a second wife. Without looking up, he
groaned once more.

"Ah, wife," he said at last, "least of all folk can you help me. My
honor is lost, and never after this night's work shall I be able to hold
up my head among the Men of the North. The bards of Prydein will
utter satires against me to the value of a hundred stags or, worse,
raising blisters upon me of deserving and repentance and wretchedness.
Oh, that I should live to see this night!"

"Tell me, my prince!" cried out the lady, clasping her arms about
his neck, kissing his cheek and lips, and pushing back his curly hair
from his feverish forehead. But Prince Elffin gave a loud sob of anger
or remorse, and made as if to thrust her from him. I decided it was
time I intervened to help these two charming young people, who had
been very kind to me.

"You must excuse my interfering in what appears to be a matter of domestic concern, my lord," I interposed, standing before them both and bowing respectfully. "But will you not tell *me* what has happened? It may be that I can help sort out your problem."

Without removing her arms from about her husband, the princess turned her head to look at me. Tears were rolling down her soft cheeks, but she raised a half-smile when she saw my confident look.

"Tell our wise child what perplexes you, lord!" she urged. "I have several times found him more learned than his years would appear to allow."

Elffin groaned a third time. "I have been a fool thrice over," he muttered distractedly. "A fool and a vain boaster. Listen, and you shall hear the shame of Prince Elffin, who will never be king in Cantre'r Gwaelod after this night's work!"

I said nothing, but settled myself on a stool to listen. My lady bestowed on me a grateful look and smile, which made my heart give such a jump I feared she must have seen it. Enough of that.

Prince Elffin, his gaze bent fixedly on the floor before him, told us what I concede was indeed a sorry tale. It seems that when the drinking was at its highest, he had risen to boast of the powers of the Hamper of Gwydno: how of all the Thirteen Treasures of the Island of the Mighty it was the most profuse; how when food for one man was put in it, food for a hundred would be found within; and how Seithennin the druid had foretold great things for the babe (myself, I need hardly tell you) found within it that Kalan Gaeaf.

The men of Cantre'r Gwaelod rejoiced at this, but the principal guest at Gwydno's court had then risen to take up what he chose to regard as a challenge. The prince Run mab Maelgun, a young man as fiery and unpredictable as our own prince, sprang up to ask why in that case King Gwydno had bestowed upon him what now seemed to be a gift of inferior degree. For what was the value of the Mantle of Tegau Eurvron to a prince like himself, who was as yet unmarried?

"I told him that doubtless he would marry before long, when the Mantle would prove most efficacious in determining the chastity of his bride," explained Elffin sheepishly.

"Very true!" cried I. "And what then?"

"He then flared up, declaring that it was other men's wives whose virtue lay in danger from his attentions, not his own. Moreover, he went on, 'I need to know now whether the Mantle be a worthy gift to the heir of Gwynedd. Why should we not try its power this night?' Then I knew what he was about, and that he had been planning this move for some time. I have seen the looks he cast upon you, wife; woe is me that I should then have fallen so readily into his trap!"

The princess and I exchanged a glance. By now we had guessed the rest without difficulty. (I should point out that she was a great deal more intelligent than her torque-bearing lord.) Prince Run had demanded that he be allowed to spend a night with his host's young wife. Then would it be seen next morning whether the Mantle of Tegau still reached about her to the ground, or but to her lap. On hearing this the young lady blushed angrily, then turned pale and defiant.

"If your word be given, lord, I must submit myself to the test. But I promise you, let him stay so long as he will, he will receive nothing of me that would shorten the Mantle by the thickness of a blade of grass. It needs no sword to lie between us for me to preserve my honor and thine, lord! Come, be of good cheer"—stroking his cheek. "What night is it that I must suffer this importunate guest?"

My heart went out to this brave lady, but from Elffin's miserable face I sensed that the test might not prove as easy to resist as she fancied. He looked about him wretchedly.

"Would that it were so simple," he muttered. "The night is . . . tonight."

"Tonight?" exclaimed the wife, startled.

"Aye, tonight," replied the prince grimly. "Even now his slaves are combing his hair, and he will be here shortly. Oh, my dear"—he gave a sob and clasped her to him—"he is a great prince, and he is drunken and angry and lustful."

"Surely he will not seek to take me by force?" cried out the princess, suddenly frightened. "Your father the king would never permit it!"

"My father the king is an old man and much beholden to Urien Reged, who in turn sets great store upon an alliance between the Men of the North and Maelgun Gwynedd. I doubt he will wish to interfere in this matter."

I could see the force of all this, and set myself to thinking swiftly. There was certainly no time to be lost, and I would do what I could to see these young people through a very nasty business. You may think I bore a proprietary interest in the young lady, but I can assure you that had nothing to do with my thoughts at that time.

"Now, Prince Elffin," I ordered sharply, "depart at once for your own lodgings in the king's hall, and take care the woodman secures the doors fast. Go at once, and remember it may be as well to restrain your boasting at the banquet in future!"

Elffin began to ask questions and the young lady to wring her hands, so that I was obliged to give them a very sharp look and order them to act on my words without delay. This was the first time I acted as became Merlin mab Morfryn; I was sorry to have to frighten them, but this was no time for the elaborate niceties of courts and kings. Elffin left pretty sharply, pausing to convey a last imploring look to his wife, so that I was obliged to take him by the hand and drag him from the room by main force. Already I could hear a stirring about the booth of Run mab Maelgun, and I knew I had but a moment alone with my sweet young princess.

During the next three days the skies above Porth Gwydno remained gray and louring, with rain beating in from time to time from off the Sea of Reged. Flocks of large black birds never seen before circled above rooftrees and battlements, floating silently down toward the salt marshes about Aber Eden. The atmosphere of King Gwydno's court was correspondingly chill and oppressive. Men could not shake off the fear aroused by the dread visit of Gwyn mab Nud and his hellish troop. It was no unusual thing for the Wild Hunt to career through the night sky above men's dwellings at the time of the Kalan Gaeaf, but never before had the Black One entered a king's court and conversed with him, as had happened on this occasion.

The druid Seithennin remained for long hours with his cloak drawn over his head. Those who ventured near heard him muttering of much ill that would befall the land before the coming year was out. Half-remembered stanzas from the colloquy that had passed between the demon and the king were repeated, but though their tone was unmistakably ominous, none was able to interpret them to general satisfaction. Taliesin, chief of bards, withdrew himself to a darkened room, where he chewed raw pork and lay in the attitude of inspiration, the palms of his hands pressed against his cheeks, and his eyes staring upward into the obscurity. The boy who sat at his door did not know whether knowledge would come to his master within two, three, or even nine days. Once the bard's voice was heard babbling loudly, but none could tell what the words imported. Only afterward was the story told that Taliesin was preparing the death-song of Urien Reged, he who even now ruled as greatest of the Thirteen Princes of the North. But this was disbelieved when messengers arrived soon after from King Urien himself at Caer Luelid, demanding tribute (in vain, of course, on this occasion) from the annual opening of the Hamper of Gwydno.

During those three days neither the prince Run mab Maelgun nor the wife of Prince Elffin was seen about the court. Men of Run's company stood on guard outside the princess's quarters, grinning and jesting in a manner highly offensive to the lords of Cantre'r Gwaelod.

Only the sternest injunctions of King Gwydno Garanhir prevented an
open quarrel from disfiguring the time of festival. As for Prince Elffin,
he skulked about the courtyard and ramparts, a pale shadow of his
former lighthearted self. He neither ate nor slept. He spoke to no one,
and only once during that time did I encounter him. I was playing by
the blacksmith's forge when he passed by on his endless pacing to and
fro. Our eyes met by chance, and I could not forget the look of
anguish and reproach he darted at me in that moment.

King Gwydno, too, was moody and ill at ease. Once he dispatched an envoy to Caer Luelid, hovering about the porter's lodge until
his return. But whatever the reply, it brought our king little satisfaction. He returned to the hall and resumed his chair of state, drinking
deeply with his lords of the yellow ensnaring mead.

This is the way things were on the last night of the feasting of
Kalan Gaeaf. All were assembled as usual, and among the men of
Gwynedd there was much merriment. But among the men of Cantre'r
Gwaelod there was only misery and shame and dishonor, each lord
seated despondently in his place without addressing his neighbor or
lifting his flesh-hook to the cauldron. Suddenly the king's chamberlain
entered the hall and announced the appearance of Prince Run mab
Maelgun.

A ringing cheer went up from the men of Gwynedd as their prince
entered. He was splendidly arrayed, sleek of hair and flushed of feature
as he swaggered thrice about the hall, bowed low before the king and
the bishop, and lounged into his seat opposite the king. Watching
Prince Elffin anxiously, I saw him turn deadly pale, and resolved to do
what I could to right matters as swiftly as possible before terrible
mischief were done in the royal hall.

"What news, lord?" cried out a chieftain of Run's following,
winking and nudging his neighbor. Loud and long laughed the men of
Gwynedd as their prince rose to his feet, a silver-chased buffalo-horn in
his hand, and gazed smiling about the company.

"The news?" shouted Prince Run, throwing his head back in all
his boastful pride. "The news, my friends, is that Elffin's bride is likely
to gain scant warmth this winter from the Mantle of Tegau Eurvron!"

Then, looking about him with a grin of triumph, he drew a small
packet from within his tunic and held it up for all to see. I shared the
eager surprise and curiosity of all about me: Here was a development I
had not expected.

"Prince Elffin, I have tidings for you!" cried out Run in ringing
tones which were echoed by the sooty imps that lurk about the rafters
of a kingly hall at this time of year. Elffin did not look up, but a hush

of expectancy lay upon the rest of us. Even the aged bishop snorted and awoke from his slumbers.

"Prince Elffin," repeated Run, "I think you should know now that it is nothing but foolishness for any man to trust his wife in the matter of chastity any farther than he can see her. You are in no worse plight than others in this regard. No women in Prydein are fairer or chaster than the maidens of Gwynedd, yet none in my father's dominions has yet been found to deny Prince Run the comforts of her flock-mattress. Come, hang not your head in shame! I tell you this: Never in the leaf-hung bowers of Gwynedd have I spent so merry a time as these past three nights have proved to me. Sweet is the bright-billed, snowy-breasted swan that nestles within the bower of Prince Elffin mab Gwydno; sweeter than the songs of the Birds of Riannon are the nights I spent in her company, in the storerooms of my memory."

Loud and long rang the laughter of the men of Run's household at this sally, and paler and more desperate looked the wretched Elffin. Talk arose about the endless infidelity of womenfolk, and men shook their heads in assent that was merry or gloomy, each according to the circumstances in which he fancied he stood with his own lady.

> "Steady and bold is the wind from the north,
> And yielding the heart of a maid;
> Dashing the youth who from Gwynedd rides forth,
> To sit where the banquet is laid;
> Wretched the rising from revelry's rout!"

"Your words are true, prince," called out the druid from his chair to the north of the hearth. "Faithless and false are the hearts of womankind. Why, even Arthur the emperor had his fickle Guenhuifar, who was taken by magic and enchantment to that green wood where Melwas enjoyed pleasures as great as those of which you speak."

Hitherto the blessed saint, Serfan the bishop, had remained silent, considering the topic unsuited to people baptized into the faith of the Cristonogion. Irritated as he customarily was by Seithennin's words, however, he spoke up to confirm before the company that the evil of women was as the sands of the sea or the stars of the firmament, unnumbered and beyond reckoning. "Let a holy man remove himself never so far into the wilderness among the wild beasts, and women round of breast and smooth of limb will seek him out with their devilish temptations. Do not I myself recall how once in my desert refuge within the land of Prydyn, when I was kneeling at my orisons under the shade of a sweet-apple tree . . ."

But the good old man's reminiscence was drowned by the clamor of the exultant companions of Run. The prince of Gwynedd smiled indulgently upon the cringing Elffin, and continued his evil, taunting speech, each word a piercing, barbed arrow.

"So happy a time have I passed that I think men will talk of the hospitality of Porth Gwydno in the North as long as the Island of Prydein and its Three Adjacent Islands remain above the blue-rimmed depths of the realm of Manawydan mab Lir. And for this I shall not bring shame upon your lady by inviting her to try on before this company the Mantle of Tegau Eurvron. For it is not merely her white leg and shapely side it would reveal to all men here, but other delights that should remain known only to you and me, Prince Elffin! Let her remain to blush unseen within her chamber—though whether her blushes are those of shame or pleasure I willingly leave the judge of the court to decide, and the poets of Reged to picture! I have here that which will enable you and all here to harbor no doubts that Elffin's princess broke her marriage vows with me these past three nights."

And breaking open the packet in his hand, Run held up what we could see to be a lady's little finger. About it, lest any doubt remain, was a golden ring known to all as the property of Prince Elffin. For it was a ring of enchantment which Prince Elffin found when once he went to the sea to seek seafood, and behold! he saw a corpse floating in on the flood. Never had he seen a body so fair as that one, and upon its finger he found this ring.

"As a mark of her love for me," continued Prince Run, smiling in pleasurable memory, "the princess permitted me before she slept after drinking much wine to remove this token of her love. With a cobweb was the wound healed, and so long as I possess this fair finger, be I never so far away in my father's court at Degannwy, her, too, do I possess."

I saw that Elffin believed himself destroyed forever. He had known his honor to be stolen, and now his wife was taken too. For Prince Run spoke but the truth: If he owned part of the lady, he owned all. Moreover, since the severance of the maiden's finger was a sacrifice to God and a releasing of her sinful action, it was the wanton part of her nature that was possessed by Run mab Maelgun. Elffin's misery was too great to be borne, and I saw it was high time for me to intervene.

"Just a moment, prince!" I cried, springing up onto a fleece-covered couch in the midst of the company. Run smiled down on me genially enough in the pride of his swaggering triumph.

"Talk away, boy!" he cried. "Though we do not speak of matters fit for babes of your tender years."

Now my blood was up. I might appear a child to those around me, but after forty years I was beginning to feel that men might recognize me for what I am, even though my time was not quite come.

Jumping down from my vantage point and going up to Run, to his great surprise I reached up and snatched the finger from his grasp, to brandish it above my head.

"Before the prince Run completes his instructive address," I piped up in my most bitingly sarcastic manner, "there are three things he might care to note about the little item upon which he lays such emphasis."

"And what are those, pray?" cried out Run, winking around at the joyous men of his company.

"No great matter to you, O prince," I replied smartly, "but of interest enough it may be to the satirists and poets of Gwynedd and Reged. There is here a small matter of law, upon which one so little as I is ill-suited to pronounce."

A silence fell upon the courthouse, followed by muttered murmurs of surprise and curiosity which have ever proved frivolous food for my vanity. I turned to the judge of the court, who sat in his accustomed place between Prince Elffin and the hall pillar.

"Correct me if I be wrong, O judge," I piped out boldly, "but after such an assertion as the prince Run mab Maelgun has made here within the courthouse of King Gwydno, is it not permitted for another to express a contrary view?"

The judge looked awkward, and shifted upon his couch.

"It is, of a certainty," he replied. "But we have seen the ring, and the princess . . ."

"The princess is not here to answer for herself," I interrupted shortly. "Is it permissible for me to speak in the case? Has not any man that right of appeal and counter-swearing which is called *gwrthdwng,* and which is recorded in the Books of Dyfnwal Moelmud?"

The judge and all men there looked startled at this, for they were unaccustomed to hear babes such as I speak of the intricacies of the Laws of the Island of the Mighty, clustered over as they are by judgments and precedents and customs, clinging like convolvulus about the tree of justice which King Dyfnwal established throughout all the land in times immemorial.

The judge pondered a moment while all present gazed at him expectantly.

"The child is right," he conceded. "There is but one tongue

making the charge, and another is entitled to use his one tongue to deny him."

"And is it not also right, O king, that the judge should take relics in his hand, and say to him who makes the charge: 'The protection of God before you and the protection of the bishop of Rome and the protection of your lord, do not attempt a false oath?' "

The judge was impressed by my erudition, as was everyone else. At the same time they were clearly puzzled as to the relevance of my questioning. Still, the judge was obliged to concede my point.

"True, my child," he replied. "You, or anyone else here, may resort to the *gwrthdwng*, for counter-swearing is good law. Now, if there is indeed to be counter-swearing, then he who would avail himself of the right must counter-swear while the asserter is putting his mouth to the holy relics after he has sworn. Is it your wish, O king, that the prince Run mab Maelgun should submit to the counter-swearing?"

King Gwydno nodded cautiously at first, then more vigorously as he sensed expressions of approval among the nobles of his following and the warriors of his bodyguard.

"Have we a relic?" inquired the judge of the household.

"We have a relic indeed," replied Bishop Serfan, rousing himself and signing to a priest, who departed to the church which lies within the walls of Porth Gwydno in the North.

Soon it was that the priest returned, reverently bearing in his hands a reliquary covered by a veil which he proffered, kneeling, to the sainted bishop. Reciting the *Suscipe, sancta Trinitas, hanc oblationem,* the bishop removed the veil, allowing the company to gaze upon the precious vessel.

Cunningly constructed of silver and crystal, it contained the little finger of the blessed Nynio, whom, with his brother Peibio, God turned into oxen for their sins. Before that pious transformation came about, a young monk of his household asked the saint for something of himself, that it might be preserved with other relics of the apostle of God. "That is hard," replied Nynio. "Nevertheless it must be done," replied the monk. The saint agreed, and with that he severed his little finger, declaring, "What thou hast collected will be thine, and also thy relics gathered heretofore."

Afterward it came about that the holy relic was brought upon two clouds from across the Mountain Bannog to Cantre'r Gwaelod, and preserved from that day onward within the hollow of an ancient apple tree in the sacred grove which lies beyond the southern gate of Porth Gwydno in the North. And when woodmen attempted to fell that tree, every chip that they struck from it flew back into the tree, so that it might not be felled. It is that relic which has effected many miraculous cures among the Men of the North; and its especial property is that no matter how much a man may consume at a banquet, he will suffer no hurt, let the surfeit be never so great.

The relic being transferred to the holding of the judge of the court, he summoned Prince Run to approach him nearly.

"Do you swear to the truth of this tale you have told before King Gwydno and all this noble company, O prince?" he inquired.

"I do," replied Run mab Maelgun in a loud and cheerful voice.

"Then place your lips to the holy relic, while this boy delivers his counter-swearing!"

The prince obeyed, not without a swaggering glance at the leading men of his following, who, as I perceived, were concealing their merriment with difficulty.

Next, the judge beckoned me to come forward, lifting me upon a settle so that all might hear my words. At his prompting, I piped up loudly:

"By the relic which is there I am a surety given by you upon what I shall now say, and that you, O Prince Run mab Maelgun, have sworn a perjury; and because of the counter-oath that I have sworn against you, I wish to have the judge give judgment for me."

"And what is it that you have to say, my little man?" inquired Run jovially, as he withdrew his mouth from the reliquary. "Have you not heard the saying 'Boys are nimble and grimy?' "

Waiting for a predictable chorus of obsequious guffaws to die away, I remarked pertly that I knew of another proverb.

"And what is that, pray? There appear to be many big words concealed within that little body!"

"Well, prince, since you have asked me, I will tell you. I have heard it said that 'Usual with the wanton is excessive laughter.' "

Contrary to expectation, I saw that my little sally aroused less amusement among the men of Cantre'r Gwaelod than it did among those of Gwynedd; for it was, after all, the latter who had reason to feel the game had gone their way.

"Very sharp, little squirrel!" Run said, laughing. "And now are we permitted to learn what it is upon which you base your counter-swearing?"

I looked about me with one eyebrow cocked and an irritating little smirk upon my lips. Prince Elffin appeared glum and restless, and his father, King Gwydno, ill at ease. This was not the time, I sensed their thought, for buffoonery and jesting. It was time for me to proceed to the matter of my business.

"It is true that I have some small points which the judge may wish to consider with regard to your claim concerning the princess, O prince. They are small like myself, but no less worthy of notice in my humble view."

Glancing about me, I saw one or two faces raised expectantly. Already there were those about the court who had found reason to respect the sharpness of my wits. Holding up that finger which Rhun claimed he had severed from the princess's fair hand, I cried out in a clear, officious voice:

"Now, you men of the North, and you, men of Gwynedd: I ask you to look hard upon the ring that adorns this white finger. Then pray consider these points, which I doubt not occurred to you as swiftly as they did to me.

"One. It may be that this is the ring of Elffin's princess, and that it matches her finger to a nicety. But, as you see, it encircles *this* finger here as well as a newly forged hoop fits a staved-in barrel.

"Two. The princess is in the habit of paring her nails once a week before going to bed. This I know full well, because mine is the task of stowing away the parings where witches and sprites may not come at them. This nail—please note—has not been cut for at least a month.

"Three. Have a close look, please; yes, gather 'round if you wish! *This* finger belongs to someone who is accustomed to kneading rye dough. There, you see some even now beneath the fingernail. Now, correct me if I am wrong, but it is my impression that the princesses of the Island of the Mighty are little given to the work of the kitchen. Or are matters arranged differently among noble ladies at the court of Degannwy in Gwynedd?"

This sally aroused a sudden roar of laughter from the assembled lords of Cantre'r Gwaelod, on whom it had dawned that things might not be altogether as they had at first appeared. King Gwydno sat up in surprise, Elffin darted an expectant look at me, and even Bishop Serfan was aroused from his reverie over devil's work wrought long years ago under the apple tree at the entrance to his cave in the Desert of Fife. Run mab Maelgun frowned angrily.

"What are you driving at, little fellow? Do you think I do not know with whom I have lain lip to lip and white arms twining 'round me these past three nights?"

"That is precisely the point," I replied. "I see your wits run more swiftly than I had at first assumed. That is, you are grievously mistaken if you imagine your bedfellow was the chaste wife of Prince Elffin. Is it possible that your conversation with the lady was not so close as you would have us think, that you seem to know so little of her?"

I turned and winked at Prince Elffin, whose color was returning to his cheeks. His expression was a comical mixture of incredulity and dawning relief. A yell of laughter went up from the Men of the North, while Run's followers looked glum and puzzled. I was rather tickled by my pert responses myself, though given the circumstances it was not so hard to be witty.

Prince Run glared furiously about him, and then started as he saw the princess enter the hall. Very stately and aloof, dressed in her finest, she moved with measured tread to the center of the hall. She wore a blue cloak of single hue about her, with a gold pin in it over her breast, and her long golden hair flowing about her shoulders. Fair she was indeed: fair in form and in wit, in wisdom and embroidery, in chastity and nobility. A hush fell upon the company, so still you could have heard a needle drop from roof to floor. Run mab Maelgun gazed at her in stupefaction, looking more than a little foolish as she sailed like a swan on a lake past him without ever a glance, and went up to her husband.

"Is it your wish, lord," she asked in a soft voice, though audible enough to all the company, "that I should wear tonight the gold-fringed Mantle of Tegau Eurvron?" With which she threw her arms about his neck and, resting her head upon his shoulder, began to murmur in his ear. He was a remarkably lucky man, I remember thinking, though it was no time for the wanton thoughts of a forty-year-old bachelor. A gasp echoed about Gwydno's hall as everybody, straining forward, saw that the princess's hands lacked never a finger nor even a nail's paring.

"What is the meaning of this? What witchcraft have we here?" cried Prince Run in heated tones. There was fear in the hearts of some at these words, for well is it said that "a lord is like a stone along the ice." But even as the heir of Gwynedd glared about him, seeking for a cause of offense, first his eye and that of every other person present was caught by a movement of the hangings that shrouded the entrance to the princess's chamber. There stood the handmaiden Heled, blushing a little before the concentrated gaze of a hundred and fifty pairs of eyes.

But it was not her face, pretty enough as it certainly was, at which men gazed, but at her bandaged left hand. Not hard was it to see that her little finger was missing, and as she slipped across the rush-strewn floor to take up her accustomed place behind her mistress's chair, a roar of laughter like the approaching surge of the tide swelled up, until all present, from King Gwydno to the very slaves who bore in the mead-vat, were grasping their sides in the extremity of their mirth. Seizing their opportunity, the royal jesters sprang into the hall and bounded about before the couches of the princes. They had blackened their faces and reddened their lips, like men from beyond the Middle Sea, and their trippings and leapings and tumblings and vaultings proved a delight and distraction to the Men of the North and the warriors of Gwynedd.

Prince Run alone continued scowling, and flung himself back upon his couch. But as the men of his household perforce joined in the merriment like the others, it seemed there was little he could do at that time. Nor was it long before he was brought to overlook the deception to which he had been prey, and the foolish predicament in which he found himself.

There were indeed strong reasons why he should not allow the affair to become matter of quarrel between himself and Prince Elffin. First, there was the presence at Porth Gwydno in the North of Taliesin, chief of bards. Not once or twice only did Run fancy he caught the poet's eye fixed upon him in sardonic reflexion, and he feared exceedingly lest he be satirized even to the extent of the three blisters: shame, blemish, and disgrace. Second, he feared the anger of his father, King Maelgun, should he return to the court at Degannwy by Kalan Mai having given offense to King Gwydno Garanhir, with whom at that time Maelgun Gwynedd desired to be upon terms of amity. Lastly (and this was no small reason) he began to recall that his three nights spent in the princess's chamber had been far from unpleasurable, whosoever had been the fair form that lay beside him. And when once or twice he caught the maiden Heled's bright brown eye fixed upon him with no cold look, he began to reflect that there might be more pleasant ways of passing the winter than in quarreling with the formidable Men of the North.

Then Prince Run mab Maelgun declared affably before the company that he believed himself to have been indeed in error.

"I am not uninstructed in matters of law," he announced, with a quizzical eye cocked in my direction, "and, as I see it, matters stand thus. I doubt not that the princess's maiden here will swear as to the truth of her mistress's tale, and the law avows truly that 'a maiden is one of the nine-tongued ones, and it is for this reason she is to be believed.' Am I right, O judge?"

The judge of the court nodded approvingly, opening his mouth to recite more than one precedent; but Prince Run held up his hand and gazed smiling about at all who sat within the mead-hall.

"We in Gwynedd are not unlearned in these matters, as I hope to show you. I have heard (and the judge will confirm whether I am right) that this, too, is the Law of Dyfnwal Moelmud, which is binding upon all who dwell in the Island of the Mighty:

" 'Should it come about that a maiden claims ravishment upon a man, and claims, too, that if he has not ravished her she is a maiden yet, then the law requires that it is proper to test whether she be a maiden or no maiden—for such is her plea.' Is this the law in Cantre'r Gwaelod, O judge?"

"It is," pronounced the judge. "Moreover—"

"If you permit, I will conclude the passage myself," interrupted Run cheerfully. "I believe it runs something like this:

" 'It is proper that the heir to the throne should test her, and if he finds her to be indeed a maiden, the man will be free and she will not lose her status as a maiden.'

"Now it appears that there is some confusion as to which of these ladies has suffered ravishment, for certain it is that one or the other lay with me these past three nights. And since it is claimed that it is this maiden rather than that, the law compels me as heir to the throne of Gwynedd to put the matter to the test. Now shall I prove to you, O judge, that Run mab Maelgun is as mindful of the law as any prince in Prydein!"

With which the prince Run swept the maiden Heled up onto his broad shoulder, and departed with long strides for his chamber. The cheerful smile upon his lips was matched by a merry glint in the maiden's brown eye, and after brief reflexion, all in the smoky hall joined together in loud laughter. I saw Taliesin purse his lips as he gazed intensely into the blazing hearth, but it was in my mind that there would be no satires of blemish pronounced upon Prince Run that winter.

So the season passed in feasting and merriment as men drank King Gwydno's sweet pale mead, for which they would pay in combat with his foes when the time came around once more for cattle raiding and sieges and battles before ramparts and fords. Each day was divided into three parts: In the first the young men trained with their weapons and played at sports beside the kingly fort; in the second they played at talbwrdd, gwyddbwyll, and other board games; and in the third they consumed food and drink in profusion until sleep came upon them all, when minstrels and musicians lulled them to slumber.

That I was a favorite of Prince Elffin and his wife is not hard to guess. Their love for each other seemed to me greater than it had been at the time of my coming from the sea. How often did I come upon the young couple alone and content within their bower. There lay the young prince, his head in her lap, while she, his beautiful princess, sang in a low sweet voice the lays of her own country, patiently searching his hair for vermin.

Then, too, I saw they fussed together over a pretty little lap dog which the prince of Gwynedd had brought as a gift at the time of his coming. It fitted on the palm of my princess's hand, with a silver chain about its neck and, on that, a little gold bell. It did not require the inspiration of my *awen* to guess that before the summer was out, there might be a plump little pledge of their love lying in the royal cradle, a coverlet of marten-skins upon him, and eight slaves by to croon "Dinogad's Lullaby."

Prince Run forgave me my interference, too, when he saw that the affair had ended not badly for him. Indeed, he soon resolved to take back with him to Degannwy not just the little finger but the rest of the bright sparkling maiden Heled, warm as she was as sunlit downs in Aust; white, curved, and soft of breast and smooth of thigh as gracious Esylt or wanton Gwenhuifar. He even declared he would take me, too, in order to impress the men of his father's court with my skills!

With King Gwydno, I played frequently at *gwyddbwyll*. He had greatly taken to me with the rest; indeed, he had cause to do so, since the predicament from which I had saved his heir had been brought about in large part by his own extravagance and folly. He declared that I might have what my head and tongue might claim, as long as the wind dries, the rain wets, the sun moves, as far as land and sea reach, in the land of Cantre'r Gwaelod.

The king and Taliesin and I were much closeted together, and they listened with great interest to my story. My birth in the Tower of Beli particularly intrigued the king, who told me it was from a stronghold of that name that in past times fleets of raiders were said to have come each Kalan Gaeaf to lay waste the Cantre'r Gwaelod, abducting two thirds of the children, of the corn, and of the milk in the country. These depredations were held to be the work of sea demons, swarms of the Coranieid, and as they had ceased some years since it was thought that the coming of the faith of Crist had forestalled them.

Each year at the Kalan Mai the bishop and priests went down to the beach singing hymns. Saint Serfan declared that the invaders would not be able to pass a certain large rock he took care to strike with his bagl, that holy crook which had come to him from the fair starry vault of heaven. This Gwydno believed effective, but was at the same time not displeased when the druid Seithennin secretly inscribed certain runes on the farther side of the rock for the same purpose. For the rock, it was said, had been hewn from a mountain by the axe of Gofannon mab Don, and placed by him upon the strand as a mark above which floods and demons and oppressions might not arise. And who but a druid may unravel the spells of a smith?

Once, when the king and I were playing at *gwyddbwyll*, I asked him to place the pegs as they had been set out that Kalan Gaeaf when he played his dread game with Gwyn mab Nud. He did so, and I gave great satisfaction by demonstrating how his king could have avoided entrapment by the advanced pieces of the Black One. It was impossible to conceal from him, however, that his western flank remained exposed, move the pegs about as he might.

"What of that?" remarked the king confidently. "We have no foes now that sail the Sea of Reged. I have supplied hostages to King Urien, whose fleet is strong, as is that of his ally King Gafran of Dalriada in the islands of the sea. No host can invade us from the west."

My own thoughts floated for a moment upon the element, in contemplation of that other host, whose white-maned horses ride twice daily against the shores of the Cantre'r Gwaelod—the host of Manawydan mab Lir, king in his Glass Fortress of the Ocean. There is a weeping amid the foaming watery ridges, the lamentation of Dylan Eil Ton. Only a poet may understand the words of that lamentation, for it is as he paces the seashore that the *awen* steals upon him. The inspiration of the *awen* was not yet mine, but a day was to come when I, too, would be enabled to place an incantation on the wave, so that it might be revealed to me what was the meaning of that moaning which the westerly wind wafted about the walls of Porth Gwydno in the North.

THE HAWK
OF GWALES

For four years an uneasy peace
had reigned in the Southland of
the Island of the Mighty. Some time after the Battle of Camlann,
when Arthur and Medraud fell, the mongrel hosts of the Iwys
withheld the tribute which was due from them to him who judged the
Island of Prydein with its Three Adjacent Islands. The princes of the
Brython thereupon slew a nobleman of the Iwys named Wigmaer,
together with others of his people whom they held in their hostage
pits. It seemed then that devouring war would rage again in the south
country, but before that could occur, there came an Oppression upon
the Island more terrible by far than the worst of wars.

For the space of a year, warriors, priests, and herdsmen alike were
ravaged by horrible black erupting pustules, large as lentils, which grew
beneath their groins and armpits. The victims of this Oppression were
neither able to sleep nor eat, for buboes of poison grew within their
bodies as well as without; they vomited blood, suffered persecution by
demons unnumbered in their dreams, and ran about screaming until
for the most part they died. And of those who suffered the Oppression
and lived, they were altogether withered in body and deficient of
speech.

He who inflicted this Oppression upon the Island of Prydein with
its Three Adjacent Islands was none other than the evil enchanter
Caswallon mab Beli. As he stalked the land he moved muffled within a
magic mantle, so that none might see him passing among the people.
But there were those who saw his sword flash as it inflicted the

pustules of pain and putrescence upon men, women, and children, Cristonogion and heathen, Brython and Iwys alike. Free alone from this sea of suffering were the men of the green Island of Ywerdon, and the Fichti dwelling among the snow-peaked mountains of Prydyn beyond the River Gweryt. It was the druids of their people who erected about the bounds and frontiers of their lands a hedge of mist which repelled the Oppression of Caswallon mab Beli.

It was long after the lifting of the Oppression of Caswallon mab Beli before the warriors of the Island of the Mighty were in a fit condition to take up their ash-hafted spears and white-limed shields and set forth for the spring hosting. Now, however, more than a dozen years had passed since that cruel time of dread and crying in the night, and men's minds were drawn once more to the struggle between the baptized princes of the Brython and the heathen sea-kings of the Iwys, which had been foretold from the beginning, when the Red and White Dragons were revealed at the Center of the Island to Nud of the Silver Hand. All summer long during four still, heavy years, men held watch on green dykes and stockaded watchtowers, scanning that blue expanse of forest and plain to southward which had long been cleared as a sword-land.

But the king of the Iwys, some said, was at war with his cousin of Cent. Others believed him to have departed over the sea, to fight for the king of Freinc who was warring in Gulad yr Eidal. Merchants from the South who bring wine to the Island of the Mighty each summer told, it is true, of battles in Italia between the Freinc and legions sent from the East by the emperor in Caer Custennin. These men judged the emperor's cause lost, since his general, an able commander, had for some crime been deprived of his testicles before setting out for the campaign.

Be all these things as they may, beyond some cattle raiding in the borderlands, the mongrel hosts of the Iwys made no attempt during this time to violate the great chain of earthworks and fortresses established in our grandparents' time by the emperor Arthur. Peddlers and spies brought word that their settlers were peacefully at work clearing woodland in the valleys and expanding their settlements. As the people of the Brython, lovers of light and truth, for the most part dwell upon sunny upland downs, the settlement of the pale-faced foreigners along swampy valley bottoms far below was held to be matter of small concern.

In any case there was war also among the princes of the Brython; war among the kinship, greater and more terrible far than the distant squabbles of emperor and king by the far-off Middle Sea. It was at this time that King Maelgun of Gwynedd, son of Cadwallon of the Long Hand and heir of Cunedda the Guledig, established himself as greatest among the kings of Prydein. With the men of his following, young men with the aspect of lions in battle, he had in successive years raided far to the south of his kingdom of Gwynedd, mountainous Land of Bran.

After receiving hostages from the kings of Buelt and Gurtheyrnion and felling the holy tree at the center of each cantref, he marched through their passes and appeared unexpectedly by the stream Brittrou in the kingdom of Gwynliog. King Gwinliu led out the men of his following to resist this attack and, but for the intervention of the blessed Cadog, a bloody war must certainly have been waged between the two kings.

The saint it was who made peace between them, King Gwinliu for his part agreeing to pay homage and fealty to Maelgun, and Maelgun in return granting his protection over the monastery of Cadog, with sanctuary rights of seven years, seven months, and seven days, and tribute of four hundred and fifty cows until that day when Crist shall appear in judgment upon false, oath-breaking kings. So at least it is written in the Book of the Blessed Cadog, preserved in his monastery at Lancarfan: the witnesses of this are Cadog and his clergy, Pachan, Detiu, Bodfan; whoever shall preserve this pact, God preserve him; and whoever shall break it, God will break him. Amen.

When news of this and other oppressions spread throughout the land, all kings beyond Dygen hastened to make their peace with King Maelgun the Tall of Gwynedd. They dispatched heralds to his court at Degannwy, agreeing to attend his annual hosting with their warbands. They entered into bonds of fosterage, supplied hostages, and paid to him annually one hundred cows from each cantref with as many calves of whatever kind he might choose, male or female as he wished it. As lord of the corn-bearing Island of Mon, Maelgun had been known as "the island-dragon"; now was he Dragon of the Island— that is, the Island of the Mighty, white-cliffed Prydein of beautiful women. Four years after the shameful victory of the heathen Iwys at the Siege of Caer Caradog, Maelgun felt himself powerful enough to avenge that ill day, and march against Cynurig their king with all the hosts of Prydein save those of the North.

As soon as the winter floods had subsided, messengers came from Maelgun's court at Degannwy to Porth Gwydno in the North, summoning Prince Run to return home and attend the hosting of the kings of Prydein which his father had ordered to be assembled at the Kalan Mai. Great was Run's excitement and pleasure when he heard the news, for he was as greedy (so the poets sang) for corpses as for drinking mead or wine. Swift therefore were his preparations for departure, arising early in the morn and raising the shout of battle.

Now, following the affair of the Mantle of Tegau Eurvron, a deep friendship had been unexpectedly struck up between the two young princes, Run and Elffin. King Gwydno, too, had taken the heir of Gwynedd to his heart. The feast of Pasc in that year fell upon the sixteenth day of the month Ebril, and at the seasonal banquet King Gwydno Garanhir took into fosterage Run mab Maelgun, cutting his hair with silver-handled shears and combing it with a golden comb as the prince knelt before all the company with his head in the king's lap. So Run and Elffin became brothers, and Elffin vowed to travel south to join the men of Gwynedd in their hosting against the pagan Iwys.

Permission for this was granted by Gwydno's overlord, Urien of Reged, who was himself making more leisurely preparations for an onslaught that summer against the mongrel hosts of Bryneich. A prior victory over the Iwys in the South could only make his task easier, so his consent was the more ready. Horns were sounded throughout the Cantre'r Gwaelod, whose nobles eagerly flocked to join the *gosgordd* of Prince Elffin at its mustering before Porth Gwydno in the North.

Four days after Pasc the two princes bade farewell to King Gwydno, and rode forth in gallant array through the eastern gateway of Porth Gwydno in the North. The king stood with the ladies of the household upon the battlements, gazing out with swelling heart as the splendid cavalcade, three hundred horsemen strong, trotted out onto the paved causeway below the shadow of the great Wall built by the emperor of Rufein long years ago. The spring sun shone down on burnished torques of gold, bright lance-heads, white-painted shields, and on yellow and purple and tartan cloaks. At the head of the company rode Elffin and Run, splendid gray, high-stepping steeds neighing beneath them.

On the walls of Porth Gwydno the young wife of Prince Elffin wept in silence, straining her eyes (bright they were as those of a falcon) to retain a last glimpse of him she loved with all her heart. The beautiful base-born Heled traveled in Prince Run's baggage train, bound for the court of King Maelgun at Degannwy, but the princess must needs remain behind in the North in her bower with the women of Gwydno's household.

Thus it was that we set out on our great adventure: three hundred proud men, united, fully armed; three hundred spirited horses hastening beneath us; three great hounds accompanying and three hundred. It would surely fare ill with the mongrel hosts of Loiger when this gallant host came up with them, a bright shining array eager to earn their mead-portion gained in the halls of Gwydno Garanhir.

As has been seen, King Maelgun the Tall, son of Cadwallon of the Long Hand, had sent two noble heralds, Graban and Terillan, to summon his son Prince Run mab Maelgun to attend on the Kalan Mai at a great hosting to be held of all the kings and under-kings who owed fealty to the Dragon of Mon. The trysting place was at Dinleu Gurygon in the fair land of Powys, where the great king would await his son's arrival. Run's heart beat high as he foresaw his father's delight at finding the host of Gwynedd unexpectedly strengthened by the noble *gosgordd* of Prince Elffin mab Gwydno. The two princes laughed and shouted in the clear warm air, clasping each other by arm or shoulder and merrily exchanging torques and brooches as they rode southward to the assemblage of the greatest host that was in the Island of the Mighty since the time of the emperor Arthur.

Behind the young princes, in a place of honor worthy our exalted station, rode myself, Merlin mab Morfryn, and the bard Taliesin. During the winter's feasting I had come to know the chief of bards, and great were my love and admiration for him. Never was there a poet for rhyme and ornament and alliteration and tantalizing obscurity like him; none was there like him to bring a dazzling image forth from his word hoard to float before you more real than the world itself; none ranked higher in bardic contests; none could pluck verses from the threefold listings as did he, each of the value of three poems and three score and three hundred. The *awen* poured from the head of that man as if it were the Cauldron of Poesy itself. His words, variegated like flowers on a spring lawn, flowed from his honeyed lips like the crystal spring in Leudiniaun as it gushes forth in its purity from the Halls of Annufn.

I think I may say without boasting, too, that Taliesin valued likewise my own poor essays in the matter of praise-poems, of songs of reconciliation, and of death-songs of princes. We sang together, composed together, and talked much of bardic lore and of those secrets of the earth and the heavens which may not be known to the uninitiated. So close were our thoughts together that at times it was almost as if we worked with one mind. Indeed, I think that in aftertimes there may be those who find it difficult to distinguish between verses written by the one and the other of us, so like are they in conception, meter, and kenning-allusions. As we rode behind our lords we, too, felt exalted, and longed for the day when ravens would scream above slaughter and our harp-strings sing out new odes of triumph in praise of valiant warriors: leeks of battle, bears upon the trackway, dragons in bloodshed.

It was not long, as you who know the North will guess, before we passed through the great city of Caer Luelid, with its gates and towers and temples and arches and bathhouses and mead-halls and other wondrous mighty works of dressed stone made by the men of Rufein when they ruled all the world. There, Urien of Reged, son of Cynfarch, greatest of the Thirteen Princes of the North, came forth to greet us and watch us pass by. I caught a fleeting glimpse of his stately figure and haughty eye as our throng passed below him and the nobles of his household in the crowded street. There he stood, exalted among the warriors of Reged, great Bull-protector of the Island of the Mighty. Little did I know (or well I knew) how close our destinies were interwoven, the great king's and mine. Of that you may hear in due course, and much more.

As its name bears witness, Caer Luelid is a city under the especial care of the Bright God, Leu mab Gwydion. It was even said in those days that the prince Owen, son to Urien and since so famous, was in reality a son of the god; and all this seemed to provide good augury for our expedition, whose assemblage was to be held before the stronghold of the god in the land of Powys. So the soothsayers of King Gwydno had declared before our departure, sweet honey upon their lips; but Taliesin and I exchanged looks and held our tongues.

How happy were our hearts within us at that memorable spring-time! Today I am cold and racked with pains, snow up to my thigh, and King Ryderch neglects me as he feasts within his brightly lit hall. Sore is my heart with the affliction of melancholy. But it was not so then. It was still the month of Ebril, that lovely time when the upland is misty, oxen trudge before the brown furrow, and gulls settle in the path of the plow. Everywhere woods are green with the fair colors of spring, birds noisy on branches heavy with budding blossom, and the plaintive call of the cuckoo rings out over meadow and brook to call men and maidens to wantonness beneath the shade of flowery branches. So it was at least in the green pastureland of the Vale of Luifenyd through which we were passing.

From time to time the breeze bore upon its wings from the surrounding hills an enticing acrid smell. On hillslopes and fells men were at work firing dead heather, that the young green shoots might emerge into the sunlight. Long plumes of smoke like advancing ranks of warriors accompanied us high on the hills upon either flank, recalling to the young men of our company that they were bound for no bridal feast but for the place where black ravens are glutted, corpses are counted, and men wade in blood up to the knees.

It was not long, however, before we had left the lush land of Luifenyd and found ourselves ascending to the upland country of Argoed Lwyfein: a wild region of mountains, lakes, and forests. On our right the mountain summits were still crowned with snow; it was a land peopled by roebuck, wild boar, and foxes. Instead of deriving their wealth from pasture or tillage, the bold men of Argoed hunted boar and speckled grouse with javelin and bow, speared the speckled salmon at the Cataract of Derwent, and supported themselves richly on game, fish, and honey.

Ahead I could hear Run mab Maelgun telling Prince Elffin of a great wolf hunt held by the men of his father's court in the mountains of Eryri. Elffin listened, as I could see, with eager attention and, when his companion's tale was done, cried out how he, too, would scour the forests of Gwynedd at Run's side that autumn, vowing to perform the feat of seizing a wolf by his mane and slaying him without spear or javelin. But meantime, before them lay the prospect of wilder hunting even than that of wolf or boar: the harrying of the heathen Iwys, splitting of skulls, widowing of women, and seizing of cattle! Run nodded in eager assent, and began to speak of the kings who would appear at his father's hosting.

Elffin, however, was too intoxicated by the sweet freshness of the springtime, the joyous singing of the birds and sprouting of green leaves, the bounding of his war horse, to listen long; and to the delight of those who rode within earshot he broke out into lusty song. It was that ditty, known to all the Men of the North, which every mother chants at her boy baby's cradleside.

> "Stripy, stripy, Dinogad's coat
> Made from skin of a stripy stoat,
> 'Whew! Whew! Whew!' Let's whistle shrill:
> Eight fond slaves to sing and trill.
> Dada's gone a-hunting grand,
> Spear on shoulder, club in hand;
> Calling to his clever hounds:
> 'Giff and Gaff, now make your rounds!'
> From his little tiny boat,
> Spearing all the fish that float;
> Next, climbing up the mountains big,
> Kills buck and stag and tusky pig,
> Fat grouse that from the hillside soars

And fish in foaming Derwent falls.
So, all at which he aims his spear—
Wild boar or fox or swift red deer—
Must learn to fly when Dada's near!"

Run mab Maelgun and the men of Elffin's *gosgordd* laughed uproariously at this, bellowing out the last three lines in a chorus that surged rippling back along the column of gaily clad horsemen:

"So, all at which he aims his spear—
Wild boar or fox or swift red deer—
Must learn to fly when Dada's near!"

My companion and I alone remained silent and brooding. Taliesin glanced sideways, observing how the rough prospect about us at once drew and terrified me. Then he spoke with a still voice of the mind that I alone heard, glancing at the broad highway ahead traversed by the silken-robed horsemen of Reged and Gwynedd which leads from gateway to gateway through the twenty-eight cities of the Island of Prydein:

"If this be destined for me, may it be grain and milk yield that I see! But if it be not destined for me, then let it be wolves and deer and traversing of mountains and young men of an outlaw band that I see!"

I knew his meaning well enough. Upon a stream in the woodland beside us, which tumbled on its way headstrong as the princes who paced the paved pathway, hung a hedge of mist. Now, that hedge is the deception of Gwyn mab Nud, and beyond it lies a land of unbroken woods and waters, moors and mountains, swamps and rivers, which was upon the Island of Prydein before its peopling by the men of the Brython. It is a land beyond bounds, without the enclosure; an outer realm, where mark of man is seen only in slabs of rock, those graves which the rain wets and the thicket covers. Men enter that land when the false sense steals upon them in the nighttime, faring forth as beasts or birds, fishes or snakes.

It is a dreadful realm of murk and loss, kingdom of antlered Cernun, with his wolf-packs, with his bears, with his boars, beavers, and roebuck. Dark One is he by name, and dark, rain-pelted and fogbound is the wilderness over which he holds sway. Yet is it not to be avoided by those whose *awen* seeks truth and understanding of the bright world of men, its design and destiny. It is to the cave beneath the cataract or the slippery ledge upon the mountainside, where the swooping eagle hovers in the spray, that the initiate pursues his painful path. Not for him is there free and easy verse upon an open road, but a dark distant refuge with hardship; a grassy scaur, a mountain prospect, an aery landscape.

For it is outside ourselves that we must be if we are to glimpse the truth that is greater than ourselves. The expositions of the learned are very well, gaining knowledge and learning for bards and *llyfyrion*, whose matter they display and dispute. They provide contentious entertainment and far-flung fame for generous princes who sustain them at their banqueting. But it is not in the books of *llyfyrion* that the greater truth is to be read. *That* lies in remoter realms, existing beyond the ramparts of reasoned thought.

Who should know these things better than I, Merlin mab Morfryn, who have endured pain for ten and forty years in the Forest of Celyddon? Now the hair of my head is thin, my cloak tattered, acorns and mosses my scanty portion. Wind and frost flay and nip my wasted body, while wolves howl close in the darkness. King Ryderch is feasting tonight in purple and gold, and tomorrow his hounds and huntsmen will leave the tilled land of Stratclud to track me through the thicket. Torment and tribulation are mine in full measure.

Yet is it I who speak with the shades of the departed, who understand the language of birds, who witnessed the Battle of the Trees, and lay in the rampart with Dylan Eil Ton! And when I tell of these things, men call me mad, *wyllt*. Once I ascended the Rock of Molendinar which overhangs the monastery of the blessed Bishop Cyndeyrn. I cried out to him and his monks of what I had learned, that they, too, might acquire understanding. But they mocked me from within their ordered enclosure, deriding my prophecy, even when it was of my own ending that I shrieked down to them.

All this lay many years ahead of the time of which I speak, O king, with your Red Neck and your Serpent which breathes wisdom into your ears. But I knew even then that I must be as a serpent, entering the dark fissures of the earth that lead to Annufn, grasping there the secret of eternal life. Drawing on our bridles, Taliesin and I abandoned the busy highway, riding out onto the boundless waste that stretched away on either side of the paved road of the loricated legions which, straight as a spear-shaft, alone gave direction and demarcation to the empty landscape.

Once or twice the chief of bards opened his mouth as if to speak, only to close himself up within his thoughts as before. Then, as we passed by a place of broken rocks and fallen trees, he told me how once he had stood before the opening of a strange cave.

"Inside I saw a flap, and around the flap twelve spikes. Above the opening were two bellows, and above the bellows two lakes, and above the lakes two peaks, and behind the peaks hills and lava, and down from the hills and lava descended four pillars with twenty-four sharp curved things on them. Did you ever stand before that cave entrance, son of Morfryn?"

I laughed at this. "Indeed I did, prince of poets, and that not long ago! I believe you were present, too, when the cat of King Gwydno's household came and mewed to me for milk, were you not?"

Taliesin laughed merrily in his turn as I informed him of a strange sight I had seen: a dun-covered hill with two caves below, two mountain-pools above, and two leafless nine-branched trees growing from its summit.

"Not hard to guess, my Merlin; I fancy we may see stags enough about us here in the forests of Argoed Lwyfein!"

Knowing his mind, I trotted on beside Taliesin through a thicket of birches that lay athwart our path. As yet the birds of spring had not come to that chill region to break the silence with their singing.

"There are matters of which we must speak, you and I," cried my companion after a while, "which may not be spoken within earshot of the foolish. At the center of this solitude there is a place where our conversation may not be heard even by Clust mab Clustfeinad: he who, though he were buried seven fathoms below the earth, might hear an ant fifty miles away stirring within its hill of a morning."

Alone we accordingly rode some way beneath the trees until we came upon a deer's track, marked with the slot of roebuck, leading around the skirts of a hill before us. Our way was clear, with the open bracken-covered hillside swelling up to the sky, and our horses at once broke into a canter which soon became a gallop.

Faster and faster we flew, our steeds floating over stream and ford and hill and dale, until it seemed to me that I rode upon the enchanted Horse of Guedu upon which Mabon mab Modron hunted the boar Turch Truith. Valleys I saw, and hollows, and crags of wondrous height, and rugged precipices. Taliesin kept pace beside me, and we traversed the upland dales of Argoed Lwyfein with the speed and ease of Henwas the Swift, beneath whose step no stalk of reed or grass would ever bend because of his lightness. Not swifter in their coursing were squirrels sporting below us in the treetops of sunken combes, the eagle skimming the aery abyss among rocky pinnacles above, or startled roebuck dashing headlong from a brake.

As we galloped furiously onward, Taliesin flung a question at me: "What is sweeter than mead?"

"Not difficult!" I called back. "The conversation of friends."

Without pause he shouted out a succession of such questions, which I answered with equal facility: What is swifter than the wind? —Thought. What is sharper than the sword?—Understanding. What is whiter than snow?—Truth. What is lighter than a spark?—The mind of a woman between two men.

Taliesin's laugh rang out clear among the boulders and rippled in the bright bed of the mountain rills as he saw (what I fancy he knew already) that he had met his match in word cunning and wisdom. We had come to the head of a great pass among the mountains, whose whitened summits gleamed bright in the sunlit upper air. Beyond, at the end of this rocky, darkened trough, lay the sparkling waters of a lovely wood-fringed lake. We reined in our panting horses on a grassy knoll, ourselves in the warm sunshine, to gaze the length of the shadowed glen at the inviting waters and distant mountain rampart. It was a time and place I loved well. In clefts and gullies, smudges of birch were turned chestnut-brown in the slanting light of the low spring sun. The hills too were ruddy-colored in the failing light of late afternoon. Beside us, not many paces off, stood a great heap of stones upon a raised mound.

"That is the cairn of King Dyfnwal the Old," shouted Taliesin through the wind. "He it was who gave laws and righteousness to the Men of the North, and from him is descended the tribe of Cinuit."

I gazed upon the cairn, a focus for the order and justice that kings confer upon their kingdoms, without which all would be tumbled and strewn in confusion, like these stones before they were gathered up and consecrated to the memory of the wise king whose bones lie within the mound.

> Whose is the grave in the fastness of Argoed?
> The grave of Dyfnwal Hen, leader of hosts,
> Whose justice was strong in the land.

I sensed Taliesin had not brought me all these scores of miles to gaze upon a king's grave, famed though his name might be, and gazed at him expectantly. He smiled and, turning his rein, pointed to the rugged chain of fells upon our right. Beyond them a gigantic mountain rose soaring upward into the clouds. I nodded, and together we swung our horses' heads around. My companion clearly knew the path— which was as well, since for my part we soon seemed quite lost. After ascending a scree-ridden track among bare wind-beaten trees fringing a bright cascading beck, we plunged into a maze of winding narrow glens, traversed seemingly trackless swamps, and wound our way through deep forests whose fresh leaves excluded all but the most suffused light, opaquely green as the watery world I once traversed with the Salmon of Lyn Liw. Then all at once we emerged from the last of these thickets to find ourselves at the base of what from its size and splendor I knew to be the mountain we sought.

The ascent became rough and steep, so that we were obliged to dismount and tie our steeds to a lone thornbush. Suspended by a scarlet baldric from a branch of this bush was a golden horn. Taliesin took it down and examined it closely for a moment. Then he placed it to his lips and sounded a long clear note, whose echoes rolled about the mountainside, crag replying to crag, until they died away tossed and broken in distant unseen corries.

Replacing the horn, my companion led me forward along a rough track that wound ever up the bare mountainside until we found ourselves trudging high above the region we had so recently traversed. Glancing back from time to time, I judged that much of mountainous Argoed Lwyfein lay stretched before my gaze: a blue-hilled haze; faery forests far; and deep below, the leaden sullen waters of a great lost lake. No sign of human habitation was there, nor wisp of smoke, nor ring of woodsman's axe. The sole sound was that of a river coursing far, far below, filling the empty valley with its faintly vibrant voice: that, and the sough of the wind whistling faint in my ears.

The mountaintops were still crowned with snow, upon which the sun was attempting to shine through a wan belt of cloud. After a long, weary, trudging ascent, we came upon pockets of snow lying among the brown winter's heather. Despite the time of year I found myself sweating heavily from the exertion, and it was with relief that I joined Taliesin in pausing to cool our faces in snow gathered up in our cupped hands. Moving on, we found ourselves before long among snow lying heavy upon turf and shale. The river's roaring in the distant vale had become so faint as to be almost inaudible, and approaching the summit of our ridge we could see that the mountain of our ascending was hemmed about at a distance by grim, towering cliff walls.

The wet snow upon which we tramped caused our feet to slither back with each pace, so that our ascent dwindled to a snail's pace. My limbs ached, my heart throbbed fast, and I breathed in great gulping gasps as the air grew thin and my endurance flagged. How long we had been clambering on our way I no longer knew. Ten and twenty, ten and forty: how many years was it since I last lay nestled on the great bearskin beside King Gwydno's hearth?

I began to feel I could go no farther, and summoned up courage to appeal to Taliesin for a pause in his remorseless plodding. Until that moment he had neither spoken nor glanced at me, but as if sensing my frailty, he now plucked me by the arm. Dragging me almost by main force, he compelled me to stagger up, onto the brow of the hill before us. There indeed he permitted me a brief stay, while I panted like a dog in the burning month of Aust when streams by upland *hafodai* run dry.

Before me was a sight worth the seeing which, with the short rest, gave me strength to proceed upon our strange journey. A broad white valley of snow lay stretched out ahead, sparkling and glinting in a manner dazzling to behold. On either side the white basin was walled in by ascending precipices, while overhead it was roofed in by clouds gray, monotonous, indifferent to human plight. The parallel ramparts of rock led ever upward toward a cloud-cumbered mountain, soaring high into the unknown upper air; its ponderous bulk sealed the farther end of this vista of desolation.

It was up one of these stone staircases—that on our left—that we continued our ascent. Trudge, trudge, trudge: ever harder did it become to gain a purchase upon the steep, coarse-crystaled snow. Worse was to come, as the thick slush became half-melted ice upon the narrowing ridgeway. Once I all but lost my foothold as a great black crow flapped out of the depths and past my face.

Now, to my alarm, we found ourselves slipping along the icy, sharp, narrow edge of the ridge itself; so sharp and narrow, indeed, that it resembled a blunted sword-blade extended edge-upward. In my apprehensive fancy I found myself wondering whether we might not be traversing the blade Bronlafn, borne by Osla Cylelfawr? That is a blade short and broad; and when Arthur with his retinue would come to the edge of the dark river, seeking a narrow crossing, the knife would be placed across the filthy water. It was bridge sufficient for all the hosts of the Island of Prydein and its Three Adjacent Islands, together with their baggage.

A track ran out before us along that edge, so strait that two men might not walk abreast. On either side the rock descended sheer, with a face smooth as burnished steel. As we set foot on this dreadful bridge I ventured a rash glance below on either side. Wisps of cloud drifting close to the skirts of the mountain broke at intervals to reveal, far, far below, a river shining motionless like a sleeping snake. The distance itself seemed to suck me down, and I turned with a shudder to peer over the right-hand edge of the sword-bridge. There, too, my gaze was plucked from my head and flung dizzily downward to where a small pitch-black lake lay sullenly in a dark surround of cruel cliffs.

Trembling, I fixed my eyes firmly on my companion's back as he tramped resolutely on before me. A drizzling mountain mist soon enveloped us, so that the rocks beneath our feet became treacherously slippery beyond even what we had so far experienced. The mist hid the ghastly drop from sight, though not from imagination. One false footfall, and I would plunge spinning down to the bottom of the abyss. So lofty was the path, and so remote the valley lost below, that I no longer felt I moved on earth. Ours might have been the ascent of Caer Gwydion in the night sky for all I knew. Time, space, and memory were dissolving. Once again I was floating among the elements, though this time it was the fog and not the ocean through which I passed without support or direction.

Soaked with rain and wrapped in mist, I found myself becoming a prey to fantastic visions. Menacing shapes loomed out of the obscurity: snakes and dogheads, and a terrible raging lion. In the outcome they did me no harm, though I freely confess they filled me with terror. All around at one point I heard the galloping of an unseen host, the sounding of horns and baying of hounds. The track beneath my feet appeared to my deluded senses to be narrowed till it was but the breadth of a hair, slippery as an eel's tail. It even seemed at times to writhe like a serpent, coiling upward to the height of a ship's mast.

My brain swam with reeling visions of danger and desolation. Brambles, nettles, and thornbushes clung to my clothes and skin. As I dragged myself painfully through them, my movements became leaden, plodding, slow. Now I suddenly saw blazing ahead a rolling fire, which plunged furiously toward me. I closed my eyes and bowed my head feebly, but when I looked again the conflagration had disappeared as abruptly as it had arisen. From behind arose a roaring thunder, as if the ocean in all its fury were rolling in one great wave upon me. Whether it was from fear, obduracy, or exhaustion I know not, but I could not bring myself to turn about. A raging and crashing and thundering filled my ears for a long space, but once it had passed by, no effect of the deluge appeared to remain.

It is impossible to say how long this ordeal lasted, but to me at the time it was fifty ages of ages, even from creation to the Doomsday death of divine Leu. Eventually there came a moment when the mist lifted briefly, and I saw before me a rough, almost perpendicular ascent where our sword-bridge buttressed the mountainside. Mist hovered above and below, and what I presumed to be chasing clouds sent swift shadows flying like bats up and down the rugged wall of rock. A dazzling blaze of light momentarily illuminated the whole eerie scene, followed by a deafening crash that resounded shatteringly through my befuddled brain. Taran's Wheel was trundling past the cliff-face; and, even as it passed by, darkness more opaque than any I had experienced before was flung like a cloak about me.

Jagged striations incised upon the rock face, momentarily thrown into relief before my distraught imagination, took on the form of runic writings whose meaning my ignorance and fear obscured. In the state in which I found myself it came as unexpected consolation to hear a raven croaking in the darkness. At least it was a creature of flesh and blood, though the burden of its harsh speech was scarcely reassuring—so far as I could understand it.

Now we had to scramble as best we could up the precipitous rock wall above us. My clothes were torn and drenched, my limbs bruised and cut, and my mind filled with a thousand images of terror. It was long since Taliesin had turned his face to me, and now all I could see of him were the soles of his shoes as he scrambled from toehold to toehold. Hitherto I had presumed his purpose beneficent, but now I began to have my doubts. Where and to what was he taking me?

I was too far gone now to turn back, and all my mind went to marking each crevice by which my guide was making his painful ascent. It was bitterly cold, and there was scarcely a moment when the wind did not gust angrily along the cliff-face, striving to dash us from the precipice. I muttered charms over and over to myself, invoking the protection of Your Sure Arm and not scorning further to conceal my fear. Suspecting now upon what place it was I found myself, I was reminded of the terrible lines of the poem "Cad Godeu":

Wake, watch, and ward each midnight hour,
By Mellun Mountain's gloomy lour:
Thigh-deep in blood you'll cringe and cower!

My shoes of strongest deer's hide were worn to flayed shreds, and my trousers likewise ripped to ribbons. Whether it was saturation of mountain fog or blood that kept the sodden rags stuck to my torn limbs I could not tell; it was long since I had turned my gaze from Taliesin's heels.

It would be weary work to describe an ascent that proceeded in the same painfully laborious manner for what may have been days or weeks, for aught I could tell. We were undoubtedly far, far above the earth's surface, somewhere I judged in the middle sky. There came in the end a moment when Taliesin seemed to plunge forward into the fog that pressed ever around us, and I found myself alone in space.

Then I set my hands upon a ledge, dragging myself up and plunging over, collapsing exhausted upon a small level space. And it was the spring and twist of the Salmon Leap, taught me by the wise old Salmon of Lyn Liw, that saved me in that moment.

We were upon the summit of Mellun, a round space about as broad as King Gwydno's courtyard, walled about and roofed in by fog, despite the greatest wind that was in the world that shrieked and eddied about its wet and slippery rock surface. By a square boulder in its center stood Taliesin, the greatest wind that was in the world buffeting his cloak and setting his dripping hair and beard streaming in the blast. Upon the stone was laid a board of *gwyddbwyll*, with its pegs set as they had been when the game was left off in Porth Gwydno after the visit of Gwyn mab Nud and his Wild Hunt. Taliesin's lips moved, and though the raging of the gale prevented my hearing the words he spoke, I knew within me what they were:

"A babe, a man and graybeard he,
Who limbless swam beneath the sea;
Named and nameless, wolf and stag:
Baptized son of maiden hag;
Know you this man, if man he be?"

I smiled insofar as my chattering teeth would permit, and nodded acknowledgment. Clearly this man knew much more about me than I had thought.

Crouching cross-legged upon the rock floor, I examined the board. We had, I sensed, resumed the *clas* of Leu—the same that had been violated by Gwyn mab Nud upon the Nos Kalan Gaeaf at the court of Gwydno Garanhir. There was the *clas* of the mountain peak upon which we squatted, among filthy fog and rain-rack; and there was the royal *clas* at the center of the *gwyddbwyll* board. And each is a *clas* against wounding, against drowning, against fire, against spells, against wolves, against every evil.

It fell to my opponent to make the first move, which he did with confident alacrity. I looked up expectantly, for now was the moment to declare the stake. To my alarm I saw that a great glossy blue-black raven was perched on Taliesin's shoulder, its beady eyes fixed upon the *gwyddbwyll* board. So He had joined the game, and it was His Sure Arm that would direct the play! The stake was a great one: no less than the coming fate of the Island of the Mighty. For the blackness of the Raven is the darkness of the void that was before the beginning, His flight is that of the creative wind that breathed upon the earth at its forming, and His croak is the voice which gave ordering utterance to life.

Despite the bitter cold and lashing rain I found myself becoming a little lightheaded, and my heart began to pound warmly within me. The outer rim of my consciousness was a little blurred and dizzy, but the core began to swell and glow. The *awen* was coming upon me as I saw by the light froth upon his lips that it was upon Taliesin likewise. His dark bold eyes held mine, and we made our respective moves without ever a glance at the board. The fog closed in so that the ground was covered by clouds rolling up the mountainside and settling about our feet. Taliesin and I and the Raven were alone in the unformed chaos that was and will be, and through our moves at *gwyddbwyll* those who direct the endless reordering of the cosmic fragments were shaping the world anew. Soon we would glimpse that which I have ever dreaded knowing: those things which are yet to be. For in foresight lies the ending of freedom. Destiny is a path from which even the gods and their offspring may not stray.

Our minds were fused as one, I felt. Cautiously we began our play with the recent past, hoping perhaps to stave off contemplation of that which—to mortal men at least—appears as yet fluid and changeable. Our theme was last autumn's war in Dyfed, when Maelgun established his overlordship in the South. There died Cedfiu and Cafan, choicest warriors of their race, leeks of battle who glutted black ravens before the rampart, preferring death on the field of slaughter to the fitting burial that was theirs by right:

"Bright and fierce those swords that hewed
Shattered shields and warriors' blood."

Taliesin's face was set and grim:

"I saw King Maelgun's hosts advance
With angry shout and brandished lance."

But my heart bled still for the vanquished men of Dyfed, whose shades I pictured now as flocking the dark road winding down to Annufn, even before death seized them:

"Each monarch and army in combat bleeds
At Errith and Gwrrith on pale-white steeds;
Treading the road where Elgan led
The serried ranks of the newly dead
Through the grim gates where all life leads."

All I could see was a rain of blood splashing the faces of fighting men and pouring from the wounds of pale stripped corpses, a woeful vision. To Taliesin, though, the triumph of Maelgun over Elgan, champion of the king of Dyfed's *gosgordd*, was a glorious prelude to the restoration of the Monarchy of Prydein—ETBRIT PRITEIN (were those the words I had read inscribed upon the cliff-face?)—and the right ordering of the fairest island that is in the world:

"One-toothed Rhys, with buckler broad,
Sweeping on high his flashing sword—
Bold Cyndur falls, his people's pride,
Their hopes have with their hero died;
Three who fell for Elgan's lord."

The game was a strange one. Taliesin, who controlled the king, was moving his pieces toward the board's perimeter, while I in vain strove to repel them or draw the king into a trap between two of my pegs. Pieces and board dripped with moisture from the heavy fog which obscured them even from the cloaked figures twain poised above. The board alone, with its precincts of gold and silver, gleamed at the heart of the dank obscurity. Sensing that Taliesin was turning to the true purpose of our colloquy, I brought my elegy to its climax:

"Wave upon wave, and throng upon throng,
(My heart will break for Elgan's wrong)
In this their grimmest, last affray
Did Dywel son of Erbin slay."

With his next stanza, Taliesin appeared at first to press the victory of Maelgun and downfall of Dyfed, but suddenly his theme switched and he named that place of dread which was the ruin of my hopes, and will one day, if prophecies speak truth, be the end of all things, men and gods and the bright world itself:

"Like boars of battle ride Maelgun's lords,
Pillars of conflict with piercing swords . . ."

and then:

"For the strife of Arderid provides the cause
From their lives' preparing till the last of wars."

The king was now in mortal danger; but for which king did it

stand? Maelgun the Tall of Gwynedd, or Gurthefir of Dyfed? The hedge
of fog about us became streaked with a ruddy tinge, as if a great fire
were burning around the rim of the mountaintop. I shuddered and bent
my thoughts to our game. I could not drive from my mind the next
occasion on which I would stand within such an encircling bloody mist.

"A rampart of spears in the deep of the fray,
Unbroken their battle-peers' dauntless array—
A rampart now shattered, a rampart now rent,
Hosts frantically fleeing, their valor all spent."

But Taliesin interposed a silver-corseleted *uchelwr* to save his beleaguered king, and I sensed that I could no longer hold him to the matter
of Dyfed. The worst was to come, and with a smile of undisguised
triumph he whispered this distich across the shining gold-and-silver
checkered board:

"Seven sons of Eliffer, seven dragons of war,
Seven spears are repelling, seven hosts to the fore."

The bard's gaze held mine in an eye-grasp that compelled me to
meet challenge with defiant challenge, hopeless though I knew the
contest to be:

"Seven blazing pyres, seven hosts all told;
Seven fierce chiefs with Cynfelyn the Bold."

But Taliesin knew full well the outcome, as did I. He shook back
the hood of his cloak from off his head, allowing the drizzling wet to
drip from his matted black elflocks down his sinewy neck. His face
was glowing with an inner frenzy, his flesh almost translucent, and I
could see he was sickening fast. It occurred to me all of a sudden that
he might be dying, and that I would be left to descend alone from this
island poised among the clouds.

At that moment, however, he rose with a desperate effort to his
feet and stood swaying for a minute or two, the froth rising on his
lips, words forming in soundless bubbles. Then he raised his hand in
triumph and pointed upward to where, through a funnel penetrating
the fast-whirling vapor, I saw in a puddle of empty blackness the
bright face of the Nail of the Heavens glittering in the endless night of
the outer sphere. With a harsh, tortured cry that seemed to arise from
the aether about us rather than his own mouth (which was gulping like

that of a drowning man), Taliesin croaked out the verse I would have given my life to avoid hearing:

"Seven spears of Gofannon, seven streams at their flood,
Swollen foaming and crimson with the chieftains' clear blood."

The eerie flames in the murk about us leapt up higher and yet higher, as violent and horrifying as the eruption of the fire mountains shown me by the Salmon of Lyn Liw. The shifting fog formed itself into a thousand distorted, horrible shapes, grinning, leering, mocking. The Raven on Taliesin's shoulder fluttered its wings continuously to avoid being swept upward into the ascending vortex. I glanced about me, groaning in anguish. No longer could I conceal the extent of my despair. "For the strife of Arderid provides the cause!"—the words buzzed in my seething brain, destructive of stanzas that rose and languished exhausted within the failing stronghold of my skull.

Frantic, I tore what shreds of clothing still remained on my back from off me, and stood up naked in shrieking wind and pelting rain. The fate of the Island of the Mighty rested on my white shoulders (I knew it), and mine alone were the terrors imposed as the test. I had crossed the sword-bridge and ascended the world-mountain; might I not yet surmount this last and grimmest of ordeals? As if in scorn of my puny hopes, a mighty crack of thunder exploded about the small space on which we stood, Taliesin and I, and a lance of lightning flashed between us, enveloping the king on the *gwyddbwyll* board momentarily in iridescent flame as it passed on to splinter the boulder upon which we played into a thousand fragments.

As the fire burned all around us, I saw suspended blazing in the fog at that moment the glorious towering image of the Eagle of Brynach; that wondrous bird which was born in the hour that was also that of my birth. It was upon Riw Gyferthuch, the Ascent of Labor in the North, that the sow Henwen was delivered of her chick, after flight and escape from the enchanted precinct of the magician Coll mab Collfrewi. The Eagle's feathers seemed of beaten gold, his noble eyes glowed like huge rubies, and the sheen and sweep of his mighty pinions were like the sun's path across ripples of ocean. Next instant the image was gone, however, to be replaced by a darkness of an opacity more drear even than that of the gaping galleries of unplumbed Uffern, as my blinded gaze recovered from the spear-stroke of the lightning shaft.

But I knew what was the Eagle's message. Hope was not destroyed, and the ending is but a beginning. Horizons multiply as you ascend a mountain slope, clouds lift, and there are gods of stone who bear two and three faces gazing out toward opposing aspects. In the hall of Gwydno Garanhir, had I not glimpsed in his recess above the sullen northern entrance a dark effigy of dun-pelted Cernun, the Horned One, squatting cross-legged before his treasure hoard; while over the sunny southern portal gleamed noble Belatgaer, the Bright Shining One?

Trembling, though with an unwarranted confidence gained at last, I stumbled sunwise thrice about that stony platform, encircling Taliesin and the fatal *gwyddbwyll* board upon one foot and with one eye closed. And as I spun upon one leg I became as the axletree of a corn mill. And just as oxen, fastened to the cross-post of the mill, trudge around at shorter, middle, or longer distances, so fixed upon the inner and outer rims of time does the circle of stars and planets rotate, supported by the Tree of Leu, propelled by the wind, and ranging in every direction until the culmination of an aeon's cycle.

The bard sat cross-legged in the center with his head bowed, as I chanted, "Fo! Fo! Fe! Fe! Cle!" Faster and faster I spun around, until the jewels of the firmament appeared before my giddy vision extended into long starry streamers. Greater grew my torment with every passing of the pivot, and my shrieks were the shrieking of the ungreased axle as the corn mill grinds about it. It was only when the lines of light were linked, each conjoined with its own tail like the Adanc who lies coiled about the earth beneath the ocean, his tail within his jaws, that my travail came to a close.

Weak and faint of body but resolute within, I returned to my place before the board. Hopping like the Raven of Leu, I was poised to deliver the concluding verse of our strange colloquy:

"Seven score chieftains slipped off with the shades,
To dwell with the dead in Celyddon's glades."

Then, glancing mischievously down at my rival, whose eyes I could see glinting strangely in the gathering darkness, I made my impudent declaration, since so famous in the land:

"Can ys mi myrtin guydi taliessin
Bithaud kyffredin vy darogan."

"Thus is it I, Merlin, following Taliesin,
Whose prophetic verse will prove the blessing."

Taliesin laughed harshly in the murk, which had been stealing up the mountain wall and now suddenly enveloped us in a cloak of total

obscurity. The *clas* on the summit of Mellun Mountain became all at
once a place of utter dread, chillingly cold and chokingly black. We
stood upon a holy, forbidden spot and were in the presence of that
which is not hostile to men, but is nonetheless death to approach. The
space allowed us had passed, and we must be gone lest we be consumed utterly in the fire that devours blindly all that lies in its path.

I turned and stumbled frantically to gain the edge of the precipice.
That its smooth sides descended unending fathoms into the abyssal
gloom I knew full well, but fear had gripped my whole being. Crouching on all fours, I fumbled at the freezing, clammy rock floor, until all
at once I was clutching at the ocean of emptiness that stretched away
on all sides to the farthest limits of eternity. With a strangled cry I
pitched forward and found myself plunging downward through space,
turning over and over until I was overwhelmed with giddiness, confusion, and terror. I felt that hours were passing, that I must have passed
through a hollow in the roots of the mountain and beyond, or that
perhaps I was not moving at all but spinning endlessly a few bare yards
from the cliff-wall.

I was frail as a leaf at winter's end whose tracing is all that
survives; I was old as man may be, and older. I had sung at the courts
of Maelgun and Arthur, and prophesied before Gurtheyrn Gurtheneu. I
had observed the departure and the arrival of the loricated legions of
Rufein, saw the people of the Coranieid with their ears ever to the wind,
and was here when Prydein son of Aed the Great first settled the Island
that bears his name and mine. I was beside Nud of the Silver Hand when
he discovered the dragons at the navel of the Island of the Mighty, and I
saw the Island itself spreading upon the sea from its navel-string. It
was then that the earth groaned and sobbed with my mother in the
sea-girt, seal-haunted Tower of Beli, at the bursting of the waters
when I emerged fresh and glistening into the light of day. The navel-
string was severed, but the link remains, and all will be drawn back to
its beginnings when the time be come.

But time was ebbing fast, slipping away on every side through the
dissolving fog. I had lived out the ages of mortal men, and more
besides. I had survived the spans of horses, of stags, of eagles—of
salmon even; and now, after three life-spans of a yew, I found myself
at the spot on the last plow-ridge, where Gwydion with his wand
first conjured the nine elements from which I am made: fruit of
fruits; fruit of God; pale primroses and scattering of soft-scented
flowers over hillsides; scented blossoms of woods and trees; nettle
bloom; primeval soil; water of Gwenhudwy's ninth wave; and the
mother that bore me.

By the plow-ridge I halted and struggled vainly. I was drawn from before and impelled from behind, and could resist no more than a floating branch when it arrives at the headwater of the Cataract of Echuid. Though I rooted my heels in the ground with all my strength, they slid from under me, driving two dykes through the furrow into the encircling wastes of ocean beyond. I felt the pitch-black Waters of Annufn flow fiercely in past my knees, with a gush and a roar like the eruption of the Lake of Syfaddon.

With leaden, unresisting steps I waded forward through the successive lapping swell of eight foam-crested waves—my sisters—until the ninth swept me from my feet and launched me floating, helpless as at the moment of my birth, out into the void:

Swift as a sea mew glides the sand-colored steed,
For 'twixt seashore and sea not great is my need.

Gently, gently did the horses of Manawydan mab Lir bear me onward and, heaving me higher than the tallest ship mast, deposited me upon the smooth rock-roof of Ynys Gweir.

From a chasm far below I could hear what I knew to be the groaning of Gweir mab Geirioed, one of the Three Famous Prisoners of the Island of Prydein, and the rock trembled under me as he writhed in his anguish. Far above him, a mile's depth of gray rock between, it was I who lay spread-eagled on my back in the coldest night I have ever experienced, with the ice like a blue wall above me.

Then a Hawk out of cold Gwales landed beside me, walking a little to and fro on the sea-washed slab. It was he who peered hard into my salt-stained face, and then plucked out my left eye. I felt great pain but could not stir, and cried out:

"Why have you taken my eye, O Hawk? What *sarhad* will you pay me for the loss?"

Replied the Hawk: "Small is the *sarhad* due to thee, O Merlin son of Morfryn. I would pluck out the eye that remains in thy withered head, for thou art old and thy body shrunken." With which he rose from the rock and flapped heavily off, leaving me alone, pinioned to my crag by invisible bonds. Then I began to suffer pain beyond all endurance, abandoned one-eyed in the gloom. It seemed to me that at times I slept, my tortured frame exhausted beyond support. I dreamed in my agony that the Eagle of Brynach alighted on Ynys Gweir and tore unceasingly at my liver with his crooked beak. Waking, I saw the yellow bill of the Blackbird of Cilguri poised to peck out my remaining eye; and sleeping again I felt myself tossed and gored upon the branching antlers of the Stag of Redynfre, as if a host of spearmen were making cruel play with me. It was in this fashion I passed a night on the western wave, on Ynys Gweir of the seals; a night such as I never felt from the beginning of the world to its end.

At daybreak the Hawk returned and perched upon a pillar-stone, gazing at me with its bright eye. I turned my face, gaunt, gory, and salt-stained as I knew it to be, up to him.

"Why did you take my eye, O Hawk of Ynys Gweir? Or, if take it you must, why do you not pay me my recompense?" I asked faintly—so faintly that the wind whipped the words from me, and all I could hear was the moaning of ocean (or was it Gweir in his prison house?) and the lovely singing of seals upon the rocks below. But I believe that great bird possessed the hearing of the Coranieid, or else his bright eye read my thoughts as clearly as I the runes running up and down the corner of his pillar-stone.

"I have not brought thee thine eye, nor yet art thou due *sarhad*," croaked the Hawk in response. "Thou hast an eye such as is possessed by no man in the Island of the Mighty: no man that was, no man that is, and no man that will be. Last night I dropped your eye into the Fountain of Leudiniaun. The Salmon of Lyn Liw, oldest and wisest of living creatures, bore it downward to where it shall rest until the world's ending."

"And where is that?" I cried hoarsely and angrily. But I knew the answer before he told me.

"Your eye is in the well beneath the roots of the Tree, where lies the Uther Ben; and from *that* you possess all knowledge and fore-knowledge. All this I have bestowed upon you, and I think you will be hard put to it now to claim *sarhad* compensation! Those who sailed to Annufn in the ship *Prydwen* were a goodly company, but they never succeeded in winning the gift I have now given you freely. You are as a god, seeing before and after!"

"Release me from your gift, O Hawk!" I pleaded, raising myself from the pool of blood in which I lay. "You have bestowed upon me power like that possessed by those who last night rent the night sky to peer down upon me. But I am a mortal, and how can a mortal live with such knowledge? O Hawk out of cold Gwales! How long is it since you were hatched from your egg?"

The Hawk fluttered down beside me and stared hard into my sound eye.

"Neither longer nor shorter than your hatching, my Merlin, son of gentle Morfryn of the foaming tresses! Do you remember nothing of the shattering of Ceridwen's Cauldron, and the tufted Black Hen,

and the grain of corn? And how were you named before you became
Merlin?" He laughed harshly, cocking his head on one side and gazing
sardonically into my face, and screamed against the tempest of the
Western Sea that lashed the rock of Ynys Gweir:

"Black your horse, black your cloak,
Black your head, black yourself,
Black skull, is it you . . . *Afagddu?*"

Afagddu! So he knew; he knew everything. "Utter darkness" had
I been in truth; Abbot Mawgan knew it when he saw my hairy pelt that
day of wind and storm in the sea-girt Tower of Beli. It was during certain
days and hours of utter darkness that Ceridwen had gathered herbs of
the earth. In utter darkness had she tossed them into her Cauldron and
set the Cauldron over the fire. For a year and a day of utter darkness
had she patiently kindled the blaze, squatting upon her bony haunches,
so that by its ending she might distill the three drops conferring skills
in hidden arts, and power to penetrate that which is utter darkness for
all men: knowledge of those things which are yet to be. *Afagddu!*
     For all her watching and waking, Ceridwen had been deceived at
the last. It was upon my twin brother, my *llallogan,* that the drops fell
when the Cauldron screamed and shattered, spilling its poison across
the left-handed places of the earth. He became a hare when he saw the
poison in her waking eyes. She pursued him as a greyhound. He fled
along his furrow, while I was left in utter darkness that hung about the
dell where lay the Cauldron's broken shards; and the only sound
beneath a cloak of starless sky was the hissing of the spilled venom as it
seeped across the barren land of Cerniu.
     Henceforward it was I who was to take the left-handed path,
Afagddu, with its unasked-for gifts and torments, winding across the
blighted Wasteland. He, on the other hand, my *llallogan,* with his
radiant brow, brings light and joy to all men, singing before the king
in his hall with its well-fed fire, its pine logs blazing from dawn till
dusk, its lit-up doorway for the purple-robed traveler. Mine is the
rock-strewn gully in the Forest of Celyddon, snow up to my hips and
icicles in my hair. Wolves are howling on the moonlit mountainside, but it is not for them my sweat is running, nor for them King
Ryderch's hounds are baying:

"Chill is the nighttime in Celyddon Wood;
Rain without ceasing on my refuge rude,
Laughter and shrieking of the wild wet gale,
Breaking of branches and lashing of hail."

My Hawk gave me a reproachful look. "And yet if all these things be true," he urged, "is there not light beside the darkness? Can there be darkness without light, or light without darkness? Does not the one create the other? The brighter the light, the blacker the shadow; where you see the shadow, look for the light! That is your gift, *Afagddu,* placed within you for good as well as ill. See this pillar-stone. In winter it casts no shadow. Sky and rock and sea are all as one: gray, gray, gray as a seal's back. Yet return here in the month of Mehevin, when the strands are yellow, the sea smooth, and the sun burning as the eye of Beli the Great, and see the beautiful-beaked puffins hatching their young on the warm ledges of these cliffs! Approach this stone, whose rough markings you see now, when the morning sun directs its bright rays upon its side. What do you see then? With His Sure Arm, He will paint upon it with shadow-tracings the name of one who played no small part in the making of wonders in the Island of the Mighty. For beneath that stone lies she who was wife to Gwrlois, and mother to Arthur: Eigyr from sea-washed Cerniu."

That was no new tale for me, as the Hawk well knew, and we fell to talking of the Island of Prydein, its destructions, cattle raids, wooings, battles, terrors, voyages, death-tales, feasts, sieges, adventures, elopements, and plunderings. Each in his turn recited the historical traditions and takings of Prydein since the Flood, until the whole was set out in verses recounting the reigns of kings who had held the Island from the time of Prydein son of Aed the Great until that of Emrys and Arthur.

Now I felt my heart beating within my hollowed breast like the hammer of Gofannon upon his bent anvil. For the Hawk spoke of the kings of our day, Maelgun Gwynedd and Urien Reged, looking to me to continue. With faltering tongue I told of Morgan mab Sadurnin, of Ryderch the Generous, and of Gwendolau mab Ceidiaw: kings whose reigns were yet to come. I saw them with that inward eye the Hawk had plucked from its socket—and I saw that which I would have given the remaining eye not to see. I felt blood welling out of the sightless socket, and the fog closed about me: the bloody battle-fog of Arderid! There lay my lord Gwendolau, lifeless and gored by the spears of his foes, a black raven upon his white breast, a heap of corpses beneath him. They were bodies headless and red, heads without bodies, limbs lying hacked and gashed, heaped like salmon in a net. Naked as a heap of white maggots were they piled, twisting and writhing, cursing and groaning.

Though severed arms grasped bright swords, and lips muttered upon severed heads, there was neither life nor meaning about the field of Arderid that day. The shades of the slain had fled, squeaking like bats, into the darkened groves of Celyddon, on the left-hand side of the

Wall dividing the living from the dead. Everything was dissolving into its component parts. The Adanc of the Deep shuddered convulsively within its trench, lashing furiously across the abyssal depths. The waters of Ocean were loosened, the sea rushed in great waves upon the land, and the sun turned black and still in the firmament. Great tongues of fire leaped out from the northern ice into the darkened sky. The Adanc opened his rough-toothed jaws, yawning wide from earth to sky; the black disc that was the sun tumbled in, and the whole horrible vision, with myself in it, was blotted out in the blood-red battle-fog of Arderid.

There was neither up nor down, left nor right, shape nor form. I was dead beneath my *gorsedd* on Newais Mountain. The Island of the Mighty and its kings no longer existed, had never existed. The well of knowledge was dried up; without poets and poetry the pedigrees of kings were forgotten, the twelve battles of Arthur no more than a churl's plowing of twelve furrows, the greatness of Urien Reged and Cynan Garwyn and Mynydog of Eidyn blown away with the vanished praise-poems of Taliesin and Aneirin.

Verses that conjured fish in creeks, fruit on trees, cataracts and forests about mountain-skirts, setting Ynys Prydein in its four parts with its Center; they were broken up, disordered, running this way and that like the square called ROTAS-SATOR, or the fragments of tessellated floors from ruined palaces puzzling the wise with here an eye, there a section of flowing robe, and there a fragment of a dolphin's tail.

The wand of Gwydion was broken, and all the objects of the created world, linked no longer by time and space, floated in insignificant disorder. There were no generations to count, no distances to span; and without an eye to survey the past, the past could not have been, for what is the past but that which the poet summons before his inward eye?

I cried aloud and withdrew myself from this unchancy conversation with the Hawk from cold Gwales. He had departed, and all the gulls that floated above the Sea of Hafren screamed in response to my screaming. The sea below me was still and level as a board, gleaming bright as the Silver Hand of Nud, and seals on the rocks at its edge sang in lovely unison, calming my troubled spirit. I understood now the two-edged gift bestowed upon me, with its left-hand side and its right-hand side. I had drunk too deep of the Well of the Wondrous Head, and learned for myself that excessive understanding without the binding of vision is, at the end of all things, the end of all things.

And this is called the Conversation between Merlin and the Hawk of Gwales.

★   ★   ★

Descending the black cliff to the water's edge, I found awaiting
me the one-eyed Salmon of Lyn Liw. Across the waves with the rising
tide he bore me upon his back to Caer Loyw, the Shining Fortress. It
was there that Mabon mab Modron would heal the bleeding of my
empty eye socket, leaving the blemish with me but not the pain.
Wantonly and splendidly did the mighty sea lap the coasts of the Sea of
Hafren. Upon my right hand I saw frail coracles plying merrily along
the coast below the rounded hills of Dyfneint, the fishermen's faint cries
borne to us by the salt breeze as they called to boys gathering seaweed
upon the broad level strand. It is a lovely land, Dyfneint of wooded
combes and sunny ridges and variegated pastures. But deep is its
name—*dyfn*—and deep the dark sea that laps its shores.

Beautiful to me was the sea of gulls, the home of ships; and
beautiful and bold were the white-maned steeds of Manawydan that
coursed about us on our way. It was with *this* eye that I would
contemplate Gwydion's fair creation: the poet's eye of radiant-browed
Taliesin. All this—the laughing ocean, foaming, turbulent, white-
gulled, and gliding with cloud shadows—could be snatched away and
enclosed by the poet's gift—his *awen*. Where does the breeze bear the
poet's breath? Do his words die when he falls silent amid the acclaim
of kings and princes? No, they live forever within winds wafting the
music of the spheres about the canopy of heaven, and in jeweled
writings traced upon that canopy.

Once in the Vale of Luifenyd I passed a green enclosure. To me it
was like any other in that fertile land; but chance, causing me to glance
back, revealed that a skillful host of spiders had woven gossamer
threads over every blade of grass. The meadow was silvered across
with the lightest of veils, of an intricacy and beauty that could scarcely
have been matched by the Fair Folk, spin though they might for a year
and a day beneath their green mounds. Yet would I never have seen
that marvel were it not for a sudden shaft cast by the golden sun,
all-seeing eye of Beli mab Benlli, which picked out what had lain
hidden from view. Golden is Taliesin's glance, and immortal his vision!

But where was Taliesin? Taliesin of course was riding beside me,
nodding and smiling as he joined in Elffin's childish strain:

"So, all at which he aims his spear—
Wild boar or fox or swift red deer—
Must learn to fly when Dada's near!"

I stared about me in bewilderment for a moment or two: at Elffin

and Run trotting before us, and back at the brave cavalcade that
wound along the paved highway leading southward through Reged.
At first horrified glance I fancied I saw them all filing in death down to
the grim Halls of Annufn, their faces pale and eyes staring upward,
their garments spotted with blood, their mouths agape and arms flung
about in rigid contortion. But then I perceived at once that they were
merry, too, with that idiotic ditty of Elffin's, throwing their flushed
faces back in lusty chorus and brandishing their fists as accompaniment.

Turning back to Taliesin, I caught him bestowing upon me a look
of appraisal or curiosity, I was not certain which. Catching my inquiring glance, he grinned and shrugged. For my part, furtively drawing
forward the hood of my cloak, I sought to conceal in shadow that
bloodstained recess from which the Hawk of Gwales had torn my left
eye. Taliesin gave me a searching glance, and I knew forthwith not to be
so foolish as to believe that I could hide my secret from him. But the
burble of the rivulet beside the highway and a plaintive cuckoo's
calling in the warm sun cheered my flagging spirits. A cloud had
passed its shadow over me, but once again I was my old cheery self. I
had missed the words of Baby Dinogad's song (being caught up in a
private reverie), but I hummed jauntily enough a little nonsense ditty
which one of the attendants of Elffin's princess used to croon to me as
I played on the floor of her bower in Gwydno's hall.

It was in this manner that we passed the next week or so. By day
we rode as far and fast as was possible, and at night we slept in leather
tents set up by slaves marching in the rear with our baggage train. It
was surprising to see how swiftly the men of Reged had cleared and
made good the highroad after the ravages of winter. Teams of tonsured slaves had toiled unceasingly, clearing tree trunks toppled by the
gales of winter, refilling puddled potholes with gravel, and laying
logged causeways across sodden fens where swollen torrents had brought
broad tracts of countryside beneath their temporary sway.

Once only, and then in the southern marches of Urien's domains,
did we find a bridge down. That was at a fort called Brewuin, whose
guards informed us that the river (whose name here means "roaring"),
or the goddess who dwells in it, had come raging down three weeks
earlier, breaking all the fishing weirs and bearing the bridge away.
However, warned of our approach, the soldiers had set up a row of
stout stakes by means of which we were enabled to ford the stream,
whose flood had by then much abated. Thus our march continued.

CHAPTER SEVEN

THE HOSTING OF KING MAELGUN GWYNEDD

S o it came about that we arrived upon the last day of the month of Ebril in the kingdom of Powys, where Maelgun Gwynedd had ordained the gathering of the hosts of Prydein. Leaving the land of Reged, we had passed by the gray Sea of Terwin, marching on through the walled city of the legions, Caer Legion, until we assembled with our brave company from the North at the trysting place.

I must now inform you of the appearance of our great hosting, and of the deep plans laid by Maelgun and his fellow kings whereby they intended to spread fire and sword throughout the land of Loiger. In this manner would be fulfilled the Prophecy of the Red and White Dragons uttered in a former age before the treacherous King Gurtheyrn Gurtheneu, as may be read in the Book of the Blessed Garmawn.

Throughout the previous winter, heralds had gone forth from King Maelgun's court at Degannwy to all the kings of southern Prydein. Loud sounded their horns before each royal gateway, summoning the princes to assemble on the Kalan Mai at Dinleu Gurygon in the kingdom of Powys. Those whose kingdoms lay afar off or on the farther side of large lakes or tidal waters were permitted a fortnight's grace, and those who dwelt in adjacent cantrefs, three days. Early in the year Maelgun the Tall assembled the hosts of Gwynedd and Mon at

Degannwy, and awaited there the war-bands of his royal cousins, princes of the house of Cunedda.

Of Maelgun Gwynedd it is said truly that he was greater than all other kings in stature, in wealth, and in generous gifts to those skilled poets whose songs tell of these matters. In his youth he deprived his uncle of the throne of Gwynedd in no ignoble fashion, but in open warfare, with sword and spear and fire. Then did he wisely purge himself of the blood of his kinsman, donning the cowl of a monk. For the space of a year he lived a humble and devout life under the tutelage of the blessed Iltud, most refined teacher of almost the whole of Prydein.

Then to his cell at Laniltud Fawr came one day from Gwynedd, Maeldaf the elder, lord of Penardd. With words of cunning, Maeldaf represented to Maelgun the danger in which he stood. For his kindred of the house of Cunedda (so the wise counselor explained) purposed to divide up his patrimony of Gwynedd, electing one of their number as king of all the tribe. Maelgun listened intently, expressing himself before the blessed Iltud as loath to abandon a crown of righteousness for one of fleeting earthly power.

"Unhappy is he," he exclaimed, letting fall tears of regret, "who leaves the cloister for any worldly life, who leaves the great love of God to be a king in the land of worldly men. Wretched is he who takes up arms in this world, unless he do dire penance. Better occupied is he in studying white books for recitation of the offices of Holy Church. Though the art of war is a worthy art, it is a great labor for a little gain; it is a meager life that comes of it, and Hell is its reward. Unhappy he who abandons holy Heaven where the saints abide for the gloomy Hell of the damned, who abandons the Great Lord, O Crist thou Lord of Battles!"

Upon hearing these pious words, and seeing the tears of the king, the blessed Illtud was likewise moved to weeping. Embracing King Maelgun, he blessed him and magnified him with the prayer *horum atque harum,* praising him as a splendid flame over a sparkling wave, great champion of Crist and of the baptism of Saint Dewi.

Nevertheless King Maelgun the Tall of Gwynedd saw no good reason why a nephew should take what he himself had seized from an uncle, and returned in haste to Gwynedd. There, following ever the advice of Maeldaf, he summoned the chiefs of the tribe of Cunedda to meet him at that place in Meirionyd men still call the Strand of Maelgun, where the River Dyfi flows into the Sea of Ywerdon. This was (so it is said) the beach on which landed Maelgun's great-grandfather Cunedda, who sailed out of the north with his tribe to drive the Gwydelian invaders from Eryri and establish his sons as kings in their place.

There on the yellow sands, beyond the three hundred salmon nets of the loud-voiced rippling Dyfi, Maelgun sat upon his golden chair with its wings of wax, and there was he reinstated with the hazel wand of kingship. His cousins of the tribe of Cunedda, ruling over the wide lands of Cardigan, Meirionyd, Osfaeling, Rufoniog, Dunoding, Aflogion, Dogfaeling, and Edeyrnion, came in some fear to King Maelgun upon the open sea-blown strand, where they duly hastened to suck the king's nipple, pinch hold of his cheek, and exchange gifts of fealty. To each in turn Maeldaf the elder whispered barbed words of promise or warning, that they might know the Dragon of Mon had indeed returned to his lair. And each in return gave all the elements as surety that they would never contest the kingship against him or his descendants.

Since then, as I have told, Maelgun's hosts had spread fire and sword as far from home as Gliwising and Dyfed, and his fleets had even crossed the Sea of Hafren, extracting tribute and hostages from kings in sea-girt Cerniu, which men call the Horn of Prydein. And after that great hosting, were heard throughout all the Island of Prydein and its Three Adjacent Islands the three demon cries of plunder: that is, whistling and shrieking and groaning. Then did King Maelgun the Tall make a great *cylch* of the Island of the Mighty, proceeding sunwise from kingdom to kingdom until he returned to his fortress at Degannwy in Ros. And in every cantref and kingdom that King Maelgun visited, the princes and nobles of those kingdoms and cantrefs assembled to clean the hoofs of his horse, swearing by the elements to do him fealty. Hostages, too, they all delivered to Maelgun Gwynedd, that they might be held in chains in the hostage pit of Degannwy. For wisely has it been said that the king who has not hostages in keeping is as ale in a leaky vessel.

In every kingdom and cantref the kings hastened also to light before every sacred yew tree fires of rowan branches, whose smoke rose upward and, combining, encircled and covered with its darkness the whole Island of Prydein with its Three Adjacent Islands. And but one place remained free of that smoke, and that was the cell of Gildas the Wise. For the blessed Gildas was even then writing that great book which enumerates the sins of King Maelgun the Tall, his apostasies, adulteries, and murders: a book whose contents were displeasing to the king. When Maelgun saw that the smoke of his sovranty did not cover the saint's cell, he came in anger and in wrath with his horsemen riding night and day to the doorway of Saint Gildas.

"Thou hast done ill," cried Maelgun, "to undo my sovranty in this manner. And for that cause I say this unto thee: 'May thy cell be the first that is ruined in the Island of Prydein, and may thy monks desert thee!' "

To this the saint made reply: "May thy kingdom fail speedily!"

Maelgun: "Thy see shall be empty, and swine shall root up thy churchyards."

Gildas: "Degannwy shall be desolate, and dilapidated shall its dwellings be."

Maelgun: "Mayst thou suffer a disgusting and shameful blemish!"

Gildas: "May thy body be mangled by enemies, and thy limbs be dispersed so that none be found together within a single spot!"

Maelgun: "May a wild boar come to grub up the hill in which thou comest to be buried, and thy relics be scattered. Likewise at Nones let there be in thy churchyard howling of wolves every evening, so that neither thee nor thy monks derive the least pleasure from it!"

Gildas: "May thy body suffer putrefaction and pustules, that the poison pour forth from every pore!"

And that was one of the Three Great Cursings of the Island of Prydein.

Thereupon Maelgun Gwynedd returned in anger to his courthouse at Degannwy in Ros. Through fear that the curse of Saint Gildas might consign him to everlasting torment in Hell, King Maelgun caused a certain prisoner within his hostage pit to be piously scourged every day for a year that he might in the king's place provide commutation for his sins.

So it was that, when the king of Gwynedd's horn sounded before every king in each cantref of Prydein, the mustering of hosts was not slow to follow. The greatest of all the hosts was by right that of King Maelgun himself. For he was lord of the Land of Bran: Bran, immortal son of Lir, in whose thigh was lodged the red Spear, and whose Head was borne home by his companions from the green Island of Ywerdon as a protection for the Island of the Mighty. And that was one of the Three Concealments of the Island of Prydein. When Maelgun son of Cadwallon of the Long Hand ascended his ivory throne in Degannwy, the light of his brow and his power extended far over corn-bearing Mon and green-pastured Arfon. His was the wealth of rich cornlands, of sheltered valleys, and of lakes teeming with fish. Among the snowy mountains of Eryri, eagles screamed above glens stocked with fat kine and sheep, and sailed over oak forests roamed by broad-antlered stags and herds of swine.

On the western shores of Maelgun's realm, descendants of the invading Gwydel from across the sea still lived each in his own fort and knowing his friend's dwelling. These were those who had not been expelled by Cunedda at his restitution of the Brython, and who afterward, in token of fealty, sucked the breasts and grasped the cheeks of Maelgun's father, King Cadwallon of the Long Hand. Maelgun's

grandmother had been of the race of the Gwydel, so that he himself
spoke their tongue, which was regarded by them as a mark of particular favor. Set aside from the lords of the Brython by language and
ancestry, and worshipping the gods of their own people, they bore
especial loyalty to the king's person. And it was no small thing to be
able to rely upon the fierce spearmen of Leyn and bowmen of Mon,
should the men of his own tribe become stirred up into the impiety
of rebellion.

The fame of Maelgun the Tall is familiar to all, and I do but remind
you of these things that you may remember his greatness, and why it
was men had reason to believe that this summer's hosting would be
the greatest since the emperor Arthur fought with the mongrel hosts of
Loiger upon Din Badon. At the Kalan Gaeaf, Maelgun consulted
with his druids and soothsayers, who told him that the time was
indeed come for a fulfillment of the Prophecy of the Dragons.

As a pious son of Holy Church, the king spoke, too, with the
blessed Saint Cubi, upon whom he bestowed the fortress of Caer Gybi.
The man of God forgave the proud king the offense that lay between
them in the unfortunate matter of the abducted goat, and spoke likewise of a mighty victory of the soldiers of Crist over the heathen.

"They have burned with fire Thy sanctuary in the land;
They have defiled the tabernacle of Thy name,"

he cried, and the time was now ripe for the destruction of the sons of
Anak. King Maelgun smiled upon the blessed Cubi, bestowing land
worth annually six vats of beer with bread and flesh to the monastery
of Saint Cubi from this till Doomsday. And who shall observe this
donation, God preserve him, and who shall violate it, let him be
cursed by God. Amen. So is it recorded in the Book of the Blessed
Cubi.

All winter long the warriors of Gwynedd, Gwydel, and Brython
alike received their mead-portion in the fair fortress of Degannwy in
Ros. Loud was the revelry of bards over mead-horns, a throng of free
men keeping festival. Outside that fine fortress on the broad ocean the
swift wave surged against the shore, and beautiful all around it was the
flying spray; pure white was the seagull, his wings long and his voice
hoarse as he flew by the cliff-top! But those who made loud revelry
about a generous lord, bold and brave, left the gray-green ocean to the
tribe of the Fichti, while they drank mead and wine out of a crystal
bowl.

Then, a fortnight before the Kalan Mai, Maelgun Gwynedd and

the men of his *gosgordd* rode forth to the trysting place at Dinleu Gurygon, where he was to meet with his son Run and the tributary kings of Prydein. This memorable year was, as they say, the one hundred and thirty-second since Cunedda and his sons came from Manaw Gododdin in the North to expel the Gwydel from Gwynedd. As it is recorded in the Chronicle of Gildas the Wise, that was the ninety-ninth year of the Cycle of Victorious of Aquitaine; or, as others claim, the thirty-first in that of Dionysius Exiguus. That is to say, it was five thousand three hundred and sixty-seven years since the creation of the earth. Such is the reckoning of learned men in monasteries, who record with care the years on tables by which they calculate the coming of the festival of Pasc.

Such men know all that may be known, of that we may be certain, placing small value upon the ravings of those who chew upon pork and lie upon the yellow calfskin. What should Merlin mab Morfryn know of the seven words that brought about the creation of the earth and the spangled tent set above it, or the passage of time, or the generations of kings? Today all wisdom belongs to adze-headed monks, with their crooked-headed staffs and hole-headed cloaks. Is that not true, O king? It was surely not to learn the wisdom of the Island of the Mighty that you came here to raise me from my *gorsedd* mound, was it, O my king Ceneu of the Red Neck? I, after all, am long departed from the land of the living.

But I must return to my tale, since you insist. Or whether you insist or not, still must you listen if you are wise, son of Pasgen! Maelgun and the men of his household journeyed by the coastal road through Tegeing to the walled City of the Legions that stands on the River Dyfrdwy. Thence they traveled southward, pausing for three days to do penance at the monastery of Saint Deiniol at Bangor Iscoed. In this manner they came to the rich land of Powys, which men call the Paradise of Prydein.

Meanwhile, others of Maelgun's following had ridden by the upland causeway which was constructed by Helen of the Hosts in the time of Macsen Guledig, over the mountains to the land of Pryderi by the Western Sea. There they demanded that King Gurthefir of Dyfed deliver up to them one of the sacred stones that lie upon the summit of Presseleu Mountain; a gift from the land of Pryderi to the Land of Bran. The old king gave his assent, and the stone was borne off screaming within a wagon, that it might accompany the Island Dragon in his hosting against the Iwys.

A mighty wagon that was, drawn by a team of dappled oxen of a strength fit to drag the Adanc from his slimy lair at the bottom of Lin

Syfadon. Foolish people still tell a tale of the two leading oxen: that they were the kings Nynio and Peibio, who had become oxen for their sins. And when they came to a great hill in Cardigan which they might not pass, King Nynio burst his heart and died on the southern side. And King Peibio bellowed nine times in his anguish, which noise split the hill and opened up that pass which is known to this day as the Furrow of the Oxen. Believe that tale who will.

So it was upon the eve of Kalan Mai that King Maelgun the Tall began the great hosting at Dinleu Gurygon. That night he entered his tent and prepared to sleep. But sleep avoided him as he pondered upon the likely outcome of the summer's hosting. For a space of time he stood before the entrance of his tent, gazing out on the thousands of red fires that glowed upon the plain, and upon the thousands of stars that blazed in the dark-velvet sky above. His thoughts were of victory, of plunder and cattle raiding, but when he returned to his couch, sleep still eluded his summons. So he rose again in impatience, took a yellow calfskin that lay on the ground beside his couch, and bestowed himself to sleep upon it in the open air by the fire that burned before his tent door. And so it happened that before long he fell into a deep sleep and dreamed a dream, the Birds of Riannon singing softly about him in the shadows.

As soon as sleep had come upon his eyes, Maelgun Gwynedd found that he was crossing a vast, empty plain under a louring sky that shimmered from time to time with distant lightning flashes. Though his journeying seemed in the dream to be brief enough, yet in his mind he knew it to have been one that had lasted all his life until that time. At length, after wearisome plodding, he came upon a ring of huge stones, standing gaunt in the center of that wasteland. About the stones were grassy mounds, like those that cover the graves of long-dead heroes. A strong wind blew across the plain, causing the long coarse grass with which it was covered to ripple in slow-gliding waves which, shifting about the mounds, made it appear as if the buried chieftains beneath were straining to dislodge the heavy turf that held them down.

Gripped with fear, Maelgun moved on between the heaving mounds and passed through a darkened portal of the ring of stones. The foot-holder who watched by the king at his fireside saw his royal master tremble violently, but dared not wake him. Now in his dream Maelgun found himself approaching the very heart of the sanctuary, and there he saw a marvel. For there grew in the center a noble fruitful Tree that ascended far, far into the sky above him. As he craned to look upward, he saw that its branches and top stretched as a protection over the whole Island of Prydein with its Three Adjacent Islands. The fruit of that Tree went forth over the sea that surrounded the Island, and the birds of the world came to feast on that fruit.

At the foot of that marvelous Tree arose a stone pillar greater in height than the mighty columns that formed the circle in which the king stood. At the foot of the pillar were gathered nine fair maidens, who crouched about a cauldron that seethed upon a low fire. Each maiden in turn bent low to blow upon the fire and rouse its glow. From the cauldron arose a greenish vapor, which ascended about the pillar-stone and obscured a pale shadow crouched upon its summit, which before the king's gaze appeared to assume the shape of a being, whether male or female at first he could not tell.

The sweat broke out upon him and he felt gripped by a deadly cold. Upon his left-hand side he sensed that there were those who drew closer from among the shadows of gray boulders. Soon he might feel their touch upon his back. As befitted so great a king, hero of a hundred battles, he resolved to turn and face his adversaries manfully; but try as he might he could not bring himself to turn about.

Then all at once he heard within the chambers of his brain and from the stones and the air about him that horrible piercing cry which resounds every Nos Kalan Mai about every hearth in Prydein; that scream which travels through the hearts of men, terrifying them so much that they lose their color and their strength, women miscarry, sons and daughters lose their senses, and all animals, forests, earth, and waters are left barren. The screaming echoed and resounded among the boulders; and as Maelgun fell trembling upon the cold ground, groaning and turning, so his foot-holder, who remained outside the dream, saw his royal master writhe and mutter in distress upon the yellow calfskin.

When he had recovered he gazed upward again, seeing among the smoke and vapor on the pillar's peak a figure he guessed came from the uttermost confines of Annufn. She was old and wrinkled and haggard, as old almost as the Stag of Redynfre. Her long gray hair straggled down over her blood-red robes, upon whose surface played the reflected flames of the fire beneath. In her hand she bore a trident, from whose prongs dripped gouts of blood that trickled down her withered arm. Her mantle was not so long that it covered her repulsive shriveled shanks, nor the open chasm of her pudenda, dry as a snakeskin and hollow as the parchmented hide of a long-dead rat. Her livid gaze was directed full on Maelgun's upturned eyes, and in no way might he turn or flee, strive as he might.

"Who art thou, O hag?" asked the king in a trembling voice.

"I am the Witch from the Mountains of Ystafengun, O Maelgun

son of Cadwallon Lawhir son of Einion Yrth son of Cunedda," responded the crone in a voice that croaked like that of a raven.

"What do you want with me?" cried the king in anguish. The witch's gaze held his in so strong a grip that it seemed to him her face loomed nearer until the warmth and fetid stench of her breath lay upon his face. But still she squatted high upon her pillar-stone.

"How is this?" cried the witch. "Did I summon thee, or didst thou call upon me? Is it true, or is it false, that you desire to know the outcome of your summer's hosting against the men of Loiger, followers of the White Dragon?"

"It is true or it is false, O witch," cried Maelgun boldly. "But what do you do here?"

The Witch of Ystafengun laughed, and her laugh was like the cry of a vixen in the nighttime of her mating.

"I am here to work for you, great king! I and my nine maidens are gathering and mustering the four quarters of the Island of Prydein to march with you into the land of the Iwys in Loiger."

"Why do you do that for me, whom as I guess you wish no good?" demanded Maelgun.

"Why do you think that, great king?" mocked the witch. "I am a humble bondmaid of your people."

"Who of my people are you, and whence do you come?"

"That is not hard to tell. I am the Witch of Ystafengun, but in your country I and my nine daughters dwell in the forests hard by Caer Loyw. I know all your desire."

"Tell me then, O witch, how do you see our army?"

There was a pause, and only the sound of the wind sighing across the long grasses upon the graves of the plain and moaning about the pillar-stones. The vapor of the cauldron burned green and blue and yellow about the witch, whose form appeared now as a night-black raven with bloody beak, now as a wolf with gaping maw, and now as an upreared serpent with fanged grin and flickering forked tongue. Then she was herself again, and answered with a grin:

"I see red upon them. I see crimson."

Maelgun replied confidently: "Cynurig, king of the Iwys, is departed over the sea with the men of his *gosgordd* to fight for the king of Freinc by the Middle Sea. My spies report that his land is empty of soldiers. There is nothing for us to fear in Loiger. Speak truth, O Witch of Ystafengun: How do you see our army?"

"I see red upon them. I see crimson."

"All the kings of the Island of Prydein with its Three Adjacent Islands have assembled at my hosting. We have nothing to fear from the warriors of Iwys, were they still present in Loiger and joined by all the men of their kindred from the coasts of Deifr and Bryneich, and from across the Sea of Udd. Speak truth, O Witch of Ystafengun: How do you see our army?"

"I see red upon them. I see crimson."

"I care nothing for your prophecy, O Witch," rejoined Maelgun, "for when the tribes of the Brython are gathered in one place, among them will be strife and broils and affrays, in dispute as to who shall lead the vanguard, or bring up the rear guard, or be the first to cross ford or river. So speak truth to me, O Witch of Ystafengun: How do you see our army?"

"I see red upon them. I see crimson."

Then Maelgun in his dream grew impatient, and prepared to leave that unchancy place with its wind and spattering rain and darkness from Annufn. But the prophetess raised her bloody trident and stayed him with her prophecy:

"I see the White Dragon and the Red, lashing and coiling in deadly strife. I see a fair fortress, with brave men slain in the gap. I see a host lying dead upon the field, the light in their eyes and a black raven upon each white breast. I see Maelgun the Tall, greatest that is among the kings of the Island of the Mighty, wearing a scarlet cloak beneath whose protection are gathered all her kingdoms, cantrefs, and cymwds. It is a mantle whose name is Pain, as well as Protection, however. Lastly I see the long sleep of Maelgun in the church of Ros. And this is the prophecy of the Witch of Ystafengun whom thou, Maelgun the Tall, hast summoned from the Halls of Annufn."

Then the column of vapor that swirled about the witch upon her pillar-stone closed in about her until she was hidden from sight. And when Maelgun gazed at the pillar's foot he saw that the nine maidens and the cauldron they tended had vanished likewise. And the darkness and the storm passed, so that Maelgun found himself seated on his wax-winged throne on the strand by the estuary of the Dyfi. The open sky and sea were about him, and his fear passed away. But the memory of the prophecy remained, and he rejoiced. For had he not been promised a glorious victory and the Monarchy of Prydein? And after all was achieved, was he not to die a peaceful and hallowed death, lying by his father in the church of Ros, and received into the blessed arms of Iessu Crist at the last?

But even as King Maelgun exulted in this manner, he found himself transported a third time within his dream. Now he was within the little church of Ros, hard by the walls of his great castle of Degannwy on its hill above the white-tossed sea. He was kneeling before the altar in prayer, when he felt a chill upon his back. Turning about, he could see the door of the church opening a little space, and yet a little more. There was a coldness and a dankness and a sweating that broke out upon him, and he stumbled back to close the door. He set his mighty shoulder against it and strove with all his strength to set it shut once more. His heart was like ice within him, and he knew fear such as he had never known in battle or siege or fights at fords. But push as he might, the door continued to open, and through the widening gap came stealing yellow, cloying, and pitiless torments more chilling to the king's heart than all the Hosts of Annufn. The door was open wide now, and Maelgun gave a smothered shriek of terror, a shriek that was taken up by the white gulls that glide about the sea-girt promontory of Degannwy.

The king's body was the kingdom of Prydein, lying prone in the ocean while waves lapped his limbs and sides. His nose and chin were mountains, his eyes and mouth were great lakes, and from the dirt within his navel grew a sapling which extended to the rooftree of the church of Ros. He struggled to raise himself, but could not. Within his body there was the pain of hidden fires that shake the earth's surface, and his veins coursed with a burning liquid. As his torment increased, Maelgun, peering down, saw that upon the whiteness of his naked body was the clustered growth of a myriad mounds, like downland graves of mighty warriors of former days. Now the mounds heaved and swelled and began to open, as they shall do at Doomsday, and from each was discharged a stream of sticky golden honey.

Then Maelgun the Tall, as he writhed helpless in his agony upon the earthen floor of the church of Ros, recalled the name that the Island bore before it was conquered by Prydein son of Aed the Great: Y Vel Ynys, the Island of Honey. But the honey was fermented and seething as if in preparation for a mead-brewing, and stank as foully as the urine and dung of cats. Maelgun felt his great body to be rotting and loathsome within, and the wells of honey that frothed up from the ducts in his chest and belly burned like glowing rivets set in his flesh. His torture and fear increased beyond bearing, and he strove convulsively but unavailingly to turn his head toward the cross of Crist upon the altar behind him.

Then he awoke, to find that in his troubled slumbers he had rolled about, lying with his back upon the cold, damp, stony ground, and clasping the yellow calfskin about his face. His foot-holder was stroking his legs apprehensively, but it was some time before the king could shake off the wild images which had so disturbed him. For sleep is ever near to death, and it was near to death the king knew himself to have been that night. Returning within his tent, he tossed long upon his couch before sleep drew him away once more from the camp by Dinleu Gurygon, disposing him this time to calm repose until daybreak.

And this dream is called the Dream of Maelgun Gwynedd, and here it ends.

Next morning King Maelgun rose with the dawn to hold his great hosting at the Kalan Mai by Dinleu Gurygon, the sacred hill. It is the day that Gwyn mab Nud and Gwithir mab Greidawl must fight from this till Doomsday for possession of Creidilad, majestic maiden of the Island of Prydein with its Three Adjacent Islands; and it is the day that the combat of the Red and White Dragons causes terror throughout the land.

These are matters of dread and surmise, but glorious and joyous is the arrival at the Kalan Mai of Gwri of the Golden Hair from out of his winter's captivity. As he rides through forests, woods, and meadows, his hand it is which makes the greenwood branches grow. Strong and virile is the young prince, and light the touch with which he brings healing herbs to sprout within woodland shade, crops to pierce the brown, furrowed earth with their fresh lance-heads, and smooth meadows to glow with verdant sheen. Noble hosts of bees go a-plundering among the spring blossoms, birds are conjured in flocks up into the blue singing sky, while great white-bellied clouds sail overhead in cheerful majesty. Blessings on you, Gwri, and would that you might linger on past the three months allotted for your golden reign! Hearken to the cockerels in each homestead, hailing you with their trumpet tongues from each lofty dung-fortress!

All the world is a-hum, like the bold honey-gathering bees Prince Gwri Golden-hair brings in his radiant train. Up betimes are the men of the Brython, warriors, priests, and herdsmen. Early, too, in their rising, braiding and brushing their yellow hair by rivulets and ponds, are the golden-torqued daughters of the Island of Prydein, the fairest isle that is in the world. Many an Esylt dreams that on the Kalan Mai she will meet her handsome Dristan in a woven leafy bower set amid birch and hazel: home not of man's making, but of Him who brought into being this bright world!

Above all this beautiful busy world reborn rings out the cuckoo's clear and clamorous call, remembrancer of lost loves near chilled from memory by the icy winds and sodden rain of winter.

From topmost twig of mighty oak
I heard the choir of feathered folk;
The cuckoo's plaint my longing woke.

Then are the hearts of lusty lads and lovely maidens exalted, too, by the magical touch of gracious Gwri as he rides smiling upon his verdant way, yellow primroses spangling the lawns across which his steed is softly stepping. Lying beneath the broom upon a warm hillside, or lingering in a mist-rising twilight copse, many a youth will find lips and cheeks warm, soft, and waiting, before the Kalan Mai be out.

The Kalan Mai is a day of merriment, love, and renewal of hope. Gwri Golden-hair is son to Riannon of maned steeds, and it is upon this day that the young men of Powys bring their finest high-stepping horses to the racing. About the long ridge of Dinleu Gurygon they ride with the wind before the slanting sun, when the king has given his signal. Each with harsh voice and holly-wand urges on his bounding, wide-coursing mount to feats worthy of Meinlas, gray steed of Caswallon mab Beli, or (best of all) Melyngan Mangre, upon whom rides Sure-handed Leu himself, whose bright-bushed lovely hill it is. From their strength and stamina and vigor, and upon the order of their running, do the horses sustain the hill upon its rocky foundations and provide portents of the summer's doings.

Afterward there takes place the combat of the armies for posses-sion of the summit. Upon the crown of the hill stands the king of Powys, Brochfael of the Tusks, son of renowned Cyngen mab Pasgen mab Cadell. Head is he of the princely house of the Cadelling, whose great-grandfather Cadell of the Gleaming Hilt it was whom the blessed Bishop Garmawn raised to the kingship of Powys, from whose seed is the whole region of the men of Powys governed until this day.

Brochfael of the Tusks stands surrounded for protection by the men of his bodyguard, and he it is who is Leu of the Sure Hand. Then from all sides ascend others, their faces painted black, shrieking, howl-ing, frenzied, yelping like wolves and screaming like lynxes: the hate-ful host of the Coranieid. From the cold mists and baleful fogs that hang about the coils of the River Hafren and dew-ponds of the plain, blighting crops and rotting produce, they rise up in hordes to assail the proud hill. Swarming like bluebottles about a carcass, they crowd in chaotic ranks about its peak. Now clubs are wielded and swords drawn, blood is shed while watching women wail and weep, and fierce is the fight until the impious array be driven in disorder down to the level plain once more.

It is this battle, like that being fought by Gwyn and Gwithir in the upper air, which must be waged each Kalan Mai until there takes place the final conflict at the time of the ending of all things.

After this all men and women leave the hill, save King Brochfael mab Cyngen, who remains alone upon the pinnacle with the druids of his household. Now is come the dangerous hour, when the one they call the Daughter of Ifor emerges from a hole in the hillside. It is said she can be heard whistling low among the heather as she glides long as a stream: smooth, steady, and venomous. She is somewhere upon the knoll, and unseen her leaden eye is watching the king. If she can, she will steal upon him unawares and slay him by stealth. Thrice the king paces sunwise around the summit, and he must be possessed of a lion's courage if he is to make that *cylch* of the world and survive.

Ifor's daughter is watching and waiting. Her back is brown as the heather, her side gray as the rock, and her coiling when still but the rampart of the hillside. And it is still she lies, waiting for her opportunity, year by year. The whistling the king hears ever in his ears may be but the wind that ever plays about the hilltop, it may be the writhing of twisted beech branches within a wooded dell, or it may be the mournful cry of the plover to his mate. It may also be Ivor's cold daughter waiting by a bank, coiled among the bracken, glinting between boulders.

King Brochfael's druids bear rowan sprigs, and beat unceasingly with clubs upon the ground about the king, muttering charms and incantations the while. They know not whether, among thickets of gnarled and twisted oak, dark groves of yew, or below the white-splashed birch, the enemy may not be peering predatory upon them. Nestled within a knotted trunk, rustling stealthily within a leaf-spray, is Ifor's evil daughter. And when she strikes, it is sudden as a spearpoint from within a thorny gorse bush, dropping upon bared neck from drooping bough, or streaking for upturned throat swift as an arrow from below the rotten bracken. Of what avail are the druids' murmured runes? Ifor's daughter, lying close within the cold hillside, knows them all and smiles within her cold heart. She knows full well her hour will come: if not this year, then the next.

This year, it is true, she is caught and bruised by the heel of the king. He catches her in the noose of his Belt of Prowess, which he encircles about the ribs and flanks of Ifor's daughter, as surely as the ocean flows about the earth and Caer Gwydion encompasses the heavens. Bound is the dragon as ivy binds a tree trunk; belabored is she as flax is beaten by a flail; ground is she as a millstone grinds malt; pierced is she as an awl pierces a plank.

Back into the stony heart of the hill she slips, wounded, bleeding, vengeful; dissolving once more into the nine elements of creation, water of the ninth wave, dust about the empty distance of the nine spheres. Dispelled for the space of a year, she lies hid, consumed with a deadly hatred nurtured until the Kalan Mai makes its inexorable return. But that is a year hence, and for the present time fertile Powys, Paradise of Prydein, her crops, cattle, and fishes, are saved!

The druids' cry of triumph echoes down the slope, to be caught up by a joyous crowd waiting in dread anticipation in the fields below. Up into the pure warm Mai air rises a rapturous paean of praise to the Lord of the Hill, who once again has with His Sure Arm preserved his people from their adversary, crushing the crooked head of the dragon, driving her back into the depths, spilling her noxious blood beyond the windy coasts of creation.

As king and druids descend the winding path, pausing only to drink from the Raven's Bowl and pass through the Eye of the Needle, they are met by weeping, laughing crowds; garlands; dancing, happy chorus:

> "Bright Leu, whose love is all,
> Here unto you we call,
> Preserved beneath your caul:
> Remember us!
>
> O You with Your Sure Arm,
> Who saved us all from harm,
> Teach us the holy charm:
> Protect us all!
>
> Send flocks upon the hills;
> Free from wolf and fox's skills,
> Giant's grasp, specter's chills:
> Avoid them all!
>
> Cows and herds safely keep,
> Encircle all our sheep,
> Foiling foumart's cruel creep:
> Likewise the vole!
>
> Drop dew upon our kine,
> Greening grass, corn, and vine,
> Burdock, cress, rushes fine:
> And daisy bright!

Leu, dauntless and daring,
Across the sea faring,
Ninth wave your barque bearing,
By sea and land steering:
Come to our aid!"

Now was the Island of the Mighty become once more the fairest isle that is in the world, with its Thirteen Treasures, its Three Adjacent Islands, its Three Chief Rivers, and its Twenty-eight Cities. Poised in the divine balance that sustains the whole earth, it contains within its coasts plains and hills suited to perfection for winter and summer pasturage of cattle, meadows spangled with flowers like a bride's dress with jewels; all richly irrigated by clear streams flowing upon snow-white gravel beds into broad lakes mirroring meadows and mountains.

It was the season when kings and queens, young men and maidens, ride out a-maying with green branches in their hands. To the greenwood they wound their path, toward Mai's snug bowers of plaited leaves and sweet-scented blossoms. And there among the balmy forest shadows were played delightful games, goodly men and gentle women in couples, each beneath a sheltering bush. There was neither sin nor blame, restraint nor regret, upon them in that hour. Ah, my sweet little apple tree that grows beyond Run, upon your gentle breeze-wafted knoll: would that now as at one time I lay beneath you, seeking my yielding maiden's pleasure!

Heat in the hollows of the hills where deer are drowsing, swallows darting to drink from Hafren's hazy rippling surface, cuckoos calling from the copse, the lark caroling in the clear upland air; a bright arrow has pierced the cold heart of winter, and the gold of the iris reflects its passing. The cool cheerful waterfall tumbles greetings down to smiling reflective pools, while the mistle thrush leads all the woodland birds in merry chorus from the heart of the hazel grove. The lyre of the woods, the Harp of Teirtu, imparts its gentle melody throughout the leafy shades, drawing into order the nine forms of elements, bloom of bluebells, and blossom of primroses. The sun smiles down over all the land, grass shoots are green, sap and blood flow vigorously in limbs of trees and men, seeds sprout, and women's wombs are quickened.

Ah, Mai, poets' jeweled treasure, leafy-mantled maiden, season of swooping hawks and warbling blackbirds, how long have we awaited thee! All creation is linked in love and laughter as Winter's grim specter, tattered mantle about his wasted flanks, flees northward over the snow-topped mountains of Prydyn toward his refuge amidst eternal ice and snow. Farewell, joyless tyrant, and return no more!

It was the following day that was appointed for the gathering of
the hosts, for it is of the Kalan Mai that poets sing:

> There is racing of blood for coursing of horses;
> While each king in his cantref marshals his forces.

At dawn the Dragon of the Island, King Maelgun Hir mab Cadwallon
Lawhir, ascended the base of the hill of Dinleu Gurygon, with his face
toward the sun's rising, that he might view the hosting of the Island of
the Mighty. Together with King Maelgun ascended Brochfael mab
Cyngen of Powys, who was brother-in-law to Maelgun Gwynedd, and
monarch of the fair land of Powys.

Upon the kings' right hand sat the blessed Gwydfarch, the holy
anchorite whose rocky bed lay upon the grim side of the Mountain
Galt yr Ancer overhanging Meifod. His was the task of blessing the
hosts of the Island of the Mighty. And upon the kings' left hand was
Maeldaf the elder, by whose wisdom King Maelgun the Tall was guided.
Not far off upon the green slope were stationed also the bard Taliesin
and myself, most curious to witness all that should pass. The sun had
but freshly arisen, his rays lancing the mists of the Mai morning. The
air was bright and very clear, so that we saw spread before us much of
the fair land of Powys, and beyond in the dazzling distance the hills
and forests of Loiger.

A clear, cold breeze blew briskly across the top of the gorse, and
cool were the hollows where the hoarfrost lingered. But hills and
woods were radiant with every hue, larks singing clear in the upper
air. Our gaze rested upon the rich pasture-plain stretching northward
up the Vale of the Tren, and reached out eastward where the broad
paved highway travels a day's march and more to Caer Luitgoed. Most
glorious of all was the shimmering coiling track of Hafren, where
the broad river winds her way around the southern skirts of Dinleu
Gurygon. At times the silver goddess glides swiftly between grassy
banks, where cattle come down to drink under the willows' shade; at
others she spreads abroad among the meadows in languid flooding, her
sparkling wavelets idly stirring the reed beds around her marges. For
tribes of beavers, skilled carpenters of the water banks, had constructed
log-dams of willow and poplar and made fair lakes for their pleasure.

The sky was pale-blue and dazzlingly clear; clouds lay only upon
the earth, where mists were dispersing above meadow streams, and
thin spirals of smoke arose from homesteads scattered over that fair
plain. The sun smiled over every land; truly is Powys named the
Paradise of Prydein!

On either side of the highroad that leads from Caer Gurygon to Caer Luitgoed, at the foot of the mountain beneath which we stood, lay a broad green meadow upon which we saw set out tents and pavilions, and heard the distant clamor of a mighty host advancing toward the point where King Maelgun sat.

The king scanned the plain. He seemed to see a great gray mist which filled all the space between earth and heaven. He seemed to see islands in lakes above the slopes of the mist. He seemed to see yawning caverns in the forefront of the mist itself. It seemed to him that pure-white linen cloths or sifted snow dropping down appeared to him through a rift in the same mist. He seemed to see a flock of varied, wonderful, numerous birds, or the shimmering of shining stars on a bright, frosty night, or the sparks of a blazing fire. He heard a noise and tumult, a din and thunder, a clamor and uproar.

The king inquired of Maeldaf the significance of these things: "Is the sky descending upon the earth, or is it lakes bursting up and splitting the soil asunder, or is it the ocean overwhelming the earth that I see? For it appears to me that the land of Prydein is in turmoil, as if the end of the world were come upon us."

"Not difficult to answer, O king," replied the elder. "The gray mist you see is the breath of horses and heroes, and a cloud of dust from the road which they traverse. The islands in lakes are the heads of heroes and warriors rising above that breath and dust. The yawning caverns are the mouths and nostrils of horses and heroes breathing in and out the sun and the wind with the swiftness of their riding. The pure-white linen cloths or sifted snow dropping down are the foam and froth that the bits of the reins cast from the mouths of the strong, stout steeds. The flock of varied, wonderful, numerous birds which you see is the clods of turf which the horses fling up with their hoofs. The shimmering of shining stars on a bright night, or the sparks of a blazing fire, are the fierce eyes of the heroes glittering from beneath their helmets full of fury and anger. Against men such as these neither equal combat nor overwhelming numbers can prevail at any time, nor will they until Doomsday."

Then the noise and tumult drew near to where the king sat, and they were the shock of shields, the smiting of spears and the clashing of swords, the clangor of helmets and breastplates, the trampling of horses' hoofs, and the loud vehement cries of heroes and warriors as they approached. Foremost among them was a troop of horsemen in green cloaks, at their head a handsome youth bearing two silver-hafted javelins, and two brindled white-breasted greyhounds coursing beside him. This was the host of Gwynedd, with the men of Arfon of reddened spears in the van as was their privilege, and Run mab Maelgun riding at their head.

Next came a troop of horsemen in yellow tunics, with fair yellow hair flowing down to their shoulders.

"Maeldaf," inquired Maelgun, "to whom does this troop belong?"

"Not difficult to say, lord. That is the host of the men of this country. Cynan Garwyn, son of Brochfael of the Tusks, it is who rides at their head in his white chariot of fine wood and wickerwork, moving on wheels of white bronze and drawn by his horses, Tall, Black-tinted. Of the warriors of Powys it is said that they are dauntless in battle and dauntless in defeat."

"That is as it should be," declared Maelgun. "And whose is the noble band of horsemen following, each with his silver brooch and golden torque?"

"Not difficult to say," replied Maeldaf. "They are the men from Cantre'r Gwaelod in the North, and the prince with the eager gray eye and purple-fringed mantle who leads them is Prince Elffin mab Gwydno, foster-brother to your son Run."

Then Maelgun stepped down and struck the horse of Prince Elffin on its muzzle with the sheathed blade of his sword: such a blow that, had it been with the bare blade, it would surely have gone as hardly with the bone as it did with the flesh.

"Why did you strike my horse?" demanded Elffin hotly. "Was it in insult or in counsel?"

"In counsel, prince: that you ride not too furiously or proudly."

"I take your counsel, king," answered Elffin, and rode modestly on his way at the head of his troop.

After the household of Elffin mab Gwydno came six war-bands wearing mail-coats: six contentious war-bands armored in battle, winged in battle, dragons with great blades who gave no quarter, bounding forward together. And their kings were six men of valor: six equally strong-necked ones, six equally bright flames, six equally bright torches; six who attacked harshly, who collected booty. No need was there for Maelgun the Tall to inquire after these, for they were the six kings of the tribe of Cunedda: even Cadwalader mab Meriawn from rocky Meirionyd; Dinogad from Dunoding of the hardy spearmen; Serwyl mab Usa, lord of the four cantrefs of Cardigan; Cynlas the Red-haired of Ros, son of that Owen of the White Tooth whom Maelgun slew in his youth and whose kingdom of Gwynedd he took unto himself; Elud the Gray-haired of Dogfaeling, guardian of the Red Fort; and Breichiol of upland Rufoniog, proud boar from the banks of the River Aled and destructive ravager of every lowland.

Great was the pride and the eagerness and the ferocity of King Maelgun the Tall of Gwynedd when he gazed upon the array of the kings of the tribe of Cunedda, for truly it is said that never did they flee for fear of sword or spear or arrow, and that Maelgun was never shamed in battle on the day that he saw their faces in the field. So they passed by like a stormy wave that engulphs the land.

And Maelgun saw approaching him where he sat upon the hill of Dinleu Gurygon a company like the overwhelming sea, blazing fiery red, in numbers a mighty host, in strength a rock, in pugnacity like doom, in violence like thunder. Before them rode a wrathful, terrible, fearsome king wearing a striped cloak and bearing a great spear with thirty rivets in the socket about its head.

"Who is that warrior," inquired Maelgun of Maeldaf the elder, "who I think is a bull in battle and terror to the pale-faced men of Loiger?"

"Not difficult to answer," replied Maeldaf. "For that is Louarch mab Rigeneu, heir of Brychan of Brycheiniog in whose kingdom lies that city which was drowned at the bottom of Lake Syfaddon. It was Brychan's son, Rain the Red-eyed, who tried with teams of oxen to draw forth the monstrous Adanc who sleeps among its ruins. But all was in vain; as it is said in the *englyn*:

> " 'Nor ox nor cart will ever take
> Me from my home beneath the lake.' "

Then Maelgun swore a great oath by the bones of Saint Garmawn that one day he would try that adventure; but it was not to be.

After the host of Brycheiniog, there passed by three great armies, like forests in number, like mountains in strength, and like rivers in turbulence. Each war-band was twenty-one hundred in number.

"Who are these warriors, the most mettlesome that ever I saw?" asked Maelgun.

"Not difficult to answer. They are the warriors of Gwent, of Gliwising, and of sea-girt Dyfed," replied Maeldaf the elder. "Their battle chiefs are Meurig mab Caradog of the Mighty Arm, Gwynllyw father of the blessed Cadog, and Pedyr mab Cyngar, grandson of King Gurthefir the Aged. Three Pillars of Battle are they, whose swords when once drawn must needs be sheathed in blood."

It is of this hosting that the poets tell, when they sing of "Long-haired Gwentians about Caer Gurygon." For the warriors of the battle-host of King Meurig of Gwent are permitted to take neither knife nor razor nor shears to the locks of their hair, which grows thick and dangling down their broad backs. Like thick-woven cloth is the texture of their dirt-encrusted, matted tresses, which may no more be washed than cut. For within them lurk the power and strength of their god, immortal Nud of the Silver Hand, who watches from his temple over the fish-teeming Estuary of Hafren.

Last in the hosting of King Maelgun the Tall at Dinleu Gurygon came a mighty legion in dark-blue armor and bearing lime-white shields. At their head rode one who seemed a goring beast in battle, a soaring eagle in counsel.

"Who is that who rides as boldly as if he were Cunedda the Guledig himself?" inquired Maelgun.

"Not difficult to answer," replied Maeldaf. "He is indeed a reaper in combat, a bear in the trackway, a bright arm of battle. That golden horn that hangs about his neck is the horn that was wont to be sounded by Glewlyd Mighty-grasp at Arthur's gate in Celliwig. He is Gereint mab Erbin; and those behind him are brave men from the land of many-combed Dyfneint beyond the seal-frequented Sea of Hafren, fierce in battle like lions with bloodstained paws."

So all that day the kings and warriors of Prydein mustered about the hill of Dinleu Gurygon from early morning until sunset; and ever were their right hands turned toward the king. During that time the ground about was hardly clear of them as they came, with every *gosgordd* about its king, and every king with the full complement of his army, his muster, and his gathering. Thus was gathered the greatest host that was in the Island of the Mighty since Arthur the emperor laid siege to Din Badon in our grandfathers' time. And as for numbering the host of warriors that was assembled before King Maelgun the Tall upon the Plain of Powys: Until the stars of heaven be counted, and the sands of the sea, and flakes of snow, and dewdrops upon a lawn, and hailstones, and grass beneath the stepping hooves of horses, and the horses of the son of Lir in a sea storm; until all these be counted, there will be no counting that host at all.

Then Maelgun the son of Cadwallon of the Long Hand declared: "Let us pitch our tents and pavilions, and let us prepare food and drink, and let music and melody be played within the camp. For never was such an army assembled in the Island of Prydein and its Three Adjacent Islands; and even were the men of Loiger, and the men of Prydyn, and the men of Ywerdon opposed to it in one place and one meeting and one muster, in one camp and on one hill, it would give them all battle, it would win victory, and it would not be routed."

CHAPTER EIGHT

THE COUNCIL
OF THE KINGS

As the warriors made merry over the mead-vats in their camp, the kings with their *mechdeyrns* and other principal men of their tribes to the fourth degree of kindred rode around the mountain to the city of Caer Gurygon that lies on the banks of the River Hafren, just below the point where it is joined by the Tren. The city is set upon an open plain, ending in a wall of mountains to the westward, across which was passing a trailing skirt of rain; a gray and louring rampart smudged the horizon, which to me momentarily appeared a presage of distant menace about the glorious hosting of Maelgun Gwynedd at Caer Gurygon.

Splendid was the spectacle of the city as we approached it, with its high stone walls, parapets and towers, and its tiled roofs glinting ruddy in the western sunlight. Not by earthen banks and wooden stockades was it protected, but by smooth-faced shining ramparts of dressed stone. No fairer fortress is to be found, so those who rode beside me related, throughout the whole Island of Prydein—search as you may from Penrin Blathaon in the north to Penwaed in the south.

As we approached the gates of the stronghold, I glanced back over my shoulder—to see the head of the ridge of Dinleu Gurygon heaved up and watching from the east, the descending sun gilding its dark summit with a coronet of gold. It was not hard to sense the god's presence, nor that of the goddess, for hard by across the meadowland I glimpsed the encircling swell of the silver Hafren.

I rode in the train of Prince Elffin mab Gwydno in the cavalcade, which wound through the eastern gateway of the great city. We of the North were struck by its great size, which straddled an area twice or thrice that of Urien Reged's Caer Luelid, largest of the cities of the

North. Above us towered a bridge trodden by neither men nor horses, but one which once brought an unending flow of water to the baths and fountains of the city. Within the walls we passed a great square stone-built temple, shops, and houses belonging to wealthy citizens on either side of a noisy street which brought us to the marketplace. With the Kalan Mai had come chapmen and hucksters who set up their booths and cried their wares in a discordant variety of languages and dialects: merchants from the highlands of Prydyn, from green Ywerdon over the sea, and even dark-haired foreigners from across the stormy Sea of Udd.

It was easy to see that King Brochfael of Powys was a ruler of greater possessions and riches and wealth than any of the kings of the Island of the Mighty, possessing rings and torques and brooches of gold, cloaks purple and checkered and striped, flocks of sheep upon fields and lawns and open plains, steeds from grazing lands and meadows and paddocks, swine from woods and glens and remote dells, and herds of cattle even now departing for upland slopes and hills and headlands.

None of the Twenty-eight Cities of the Island of Prydein had escaped devastation in the wars that had ravaged the Island from coast to coast before the Restitution of Emrys and Arthur, but Caer Gurygon had clearly suffered less than most—at any rate, that I have seen. It is true that there were buildings wholly or partly ruined, with walled-up windows and breaches closed with heaps of rubble or hurdles of willow. Timber houses had been erected where once stood splendid mansions of dressed stone, the wreckage of splendid palaces heaped about them. Twice we came upon places where a house had collapsed into the street, causing a troublesome diversion and permitting the proliferation of improvised shelters inhabited by the more wretched of the poor. But many fine public buildings remained in evident use, and it was the most magnificent of these that we now entered.

Passing through lofty portals, we found ourselves within the great hall of a building which, as I learned from an officer of King Brochfael's court who hovered near us, had been termed by the men of Rufein who built it long ago the *palestr*. This great chamber, with its stone colonnades, splendid tessellated floor covered with images of sea gods, nymphs, and dolphins sporting among curls of spray so realistic we feared momentarily to get our feet wet, overawed everyone who entered it.

Accustomed to the bleak strongholds of upland Ardudwy or Arlechwed, the kings of the house of Cunedda and its federated tribes gazed mutely about them, the murmur of their excited talk dying away in odd echoes about remote corners of the hall, or sounding confusingly from high above in the vaulted roof over the central aisle. It was upward to this vault that time and again men's gaze involuntarily traveled. It seemed to float in the air like the vault of the noonday heaven, and it might be thought that sunlight grew in it.

The walls were covered with painted frescoes and patterns, waved or curling for the most part to provide an involuntary impression of a space adrift upon a gentle, swelling sea. There were paintings, too, of a beauty unimaginable. One that particularly struck me portrayed a young man, in appearance a god with winged sandals, in the moment of alighting by a rock to which was chained a girl of a beauty that caught at my heart. She was gloriously naked but for the tresses of her dark hair, which the sea breeze fanned about her. In this wonderful painting the maiden's breasts and limbs seemed as warmly soft and sweet-scented as those of Elffin's princess, by whom I slept as a precocious child in her bower at Porth Gwydno in the North. At the feet of this divine couple lay a monstrous, misshapen beast—the Adanc of the Deep. Beauty, symmetry, and love were seen to triumph over the dragon of chaos, as they now did in the warlike hearts of the assembled kings of the Island of Prydein.

On the far side of the hall, tall windows opened out onto a sunny courtyard, beyond which we could see another mighty edifice of stone. Our guide whispered to us that it was in former times a great bathhouse, but now that public bathing had long passed out of fashion its chambers were used as granaries housing the rich harvests of the fair land of Powys.

Gazing in wonder and delight about them, the kings were guided to their couches by the steward of King Brochfael's household and his attendants. The disposal of the kings and their principal followers was arranged in this manner: In the midst of the hall was the couch of Maelgun the great king, Dragon of Mon. It was the Center of Prydein that was about Maelgun in that house. The king of Powys sat on the couch opposite in the east, the king of Dyfneint on his right hand, the kings of the tribe of Cunedda and its dependent kings at his back, the prince Elffin mab Gwdyno on his left hand. To those kings and princes were granted equal *galanas* and honor-price. Behind the kings were seated the lords of their followings in the four quarters of the hall.

Before the kings was a mighty cauldron of bronze suspended above its hearth, and within it broiling the succulent flesh of swine fattened upon mast of beech and oak in the forests of Mechain. Before the kings fell to their feasting, the holy bishop Gwydfarch, abbot of that privileged monastery of Meifod which shines as a beacon among the flooded meadows of Efyrnwy, blessed the good meats with the sign of the cross and the words of the *Hymnum Dicat*. The grace sanctified the food; and the *gwir* of King Brochfael was within that cauldron, so that it created and established the flesh which was in the mouth of the god which is the cauldron, causing it to be choice as meat from the Dish of Rygenyd the Scholar, plentiful as that from the Hamper of Gwydno Garanhir, and as unpalatable to the taste of a coward as any from the Cauldron of Diurnach Gwydel.

Then the feasting began in the customary manner, each king taking his allotted portion of pork from the cauldron with his flesh-hook in due order of precedence. And it is a wonder told of that great council-feasting that there was neither bloodletting, nor setting-up of blood feuds, nor disputations among the fifteen mighty kings there assembled. All was peaceful and orderly as it had been when Arthur ruled as chief prince at his court at Celliwig in Cerniu.

As men feasted in the court of Brochfael of the Tusks, skilled storytellers recounted tales of the battles and triumphs of the Brython over the mongrel hosts of the heathen in Cent and Loiger from the time of Gurthefir the Blessed to that of Arthur. The assembled kings drank deeply of the sweet yellow mead, laughing as they recalled their forefathers' victories and speaking of rich booty to be taken from the halls of the kings of the Iwys. In shining array were the princes of the Island of the Mighty at that feasting, feeding together around the cauldron of Brochfael, setting their hands to wine and mead and malt.

Then the storytellers dispersed, and it was the turn of Taliesin, chief of bards, to sing before the company. It was easy to see from his foaming lips and shining brow that the *awen* was upon him, and all men fell silent, so that you might have heard a needle drop from the roof to the floor. Firstly in subdued but moving tones he sang a praise-song to their generous host, Brochfael of Powys. He began by recalling how beforetimes he had been household bard to Brochfael, who loved his *awen*, had sung to him by green banks in the meadows of winding Hafren. Then had he served the king, mighty descendant of Cadell of the Gleaming Hilt, immovable in battle, boundary-extending, the glory of armies, the light of his flame spreading as a mighty fire. The fame of Brochfael of the Tusks could never die, for his generosity to poets was a byword throughout the Island of the Mighty, from Penrin Blathaon in the north to Penwaed in the south. Had Taliesin himself not received from him a hundred horses with silver-embossed harnessing, a hundred purple mantles, a hundred

bracelets and fifty brooches, and a splendid yellow-hilted sword with
jewel-encrusted scabbard?

Here Taliesin paused to drink of the yellow mead, while King
Brochfael's household slaves dragged before his feet chests filled with
choice gifts from their grateful master. With a disdainful glance at the
rich treasures spilling from their caskets—treasures which in ages to
come will be consumed by mice and moths and dust—he rose to
resume that which can never perish: immortal song, for which the
poet's utterance is but the mouthpiece of the godhead, the outpouring
of the Cauldron of Poesy. Casting aside his embroidered mantle, Taliesin
rolled his eyes upward, his forehead gleaming with radiant light, and
men knew that he was to sing the enchanted song of the Island of the
Mighty, "The Monarchy of Prydein."

I shall never forget the singing of that song—the greatest that is,
chanted by the greatest poet that has been—though I live for century
upon century until that day when the seas roll over the green earth and
the sky collapses above us. We were no longer within Brochfael's
great hall, the *palestr* of Caer Gurygon by the silver Hafren; but flew
with winged thoughts wherever Taliesin's honeyed words bore us.

It was poetry that formed this, the fairest Island that is in the
world. First it was called the Precinct of Merlin, for it was Merlin of
old who uttered the charmed verses which invoked the Island of
Prydein, its fruitful orchards and forests and rivers teeming with game
and fish, its flower-strewn meadows, and its lofty mountains grazed
by the dun deer. As the strings of the harp, of different lengths and
tension, when struck by the skilled harpist acquire a perfection of
attunement not possessed by the unlike elements of the instrument, so
did the invocation of Merlin meld discordant rocky screes and heaths
and swamps into a harmonious whole of sunlit flowers, birdsong, and
gentle breezes.

Next, Merlin secured the Island at its Center, where he imposed
the rites that consecrated Prydein son of Aed the Great as king: lofty
oak that separated earth and sky, incarnation of Leu of the Sure Hand,
and husband of the goddess Don. So the kingship was from the
beginning, and it is that which sustains the Island with its Three
Adjacent Islands, its Three Chief Estuaries, its Twenty-eight Cities,
and its Thirteen Treasures. For the Dragons of Nud of the Silver
Hand lie concealed in the stone chest which is at its Center, the head of
Bran the Blessed is buried in the White Hill in Lunnein, and the bones
of Gurthefir the Blessed are disposed in the chief ports of the Island.
And so long as they lay undisturbed in their concealment, no oppression could come upon the Island of the Mighty.

But then the Dragons were revealed at the command of Gurtheyrn the Thin, false king who brought the pale-faced foreigners into the land: Horsa and Hengys, scavengers from over the sea who destroyed the land of the Brython, crown-wearing churls whose oppression was great! Through lying and deceit they obtained the Isle of Ruohim, and from it they extended their oppressive rule among the noble princes of the Brython. They trampled upon the privileges of the Church and ruined the palaces of the kings. Yet who are they? Where is their home? Of what stock are they come, and to whom are they of kin or fosterage?

Great has been their oppression. But the poet's *awen,* which established the harmony destroyed by the perfidy of Gurtheyrn in his lust and drunkenness, foretells an awakening, a candle in the darkness. Merlin foretells, the druids foretell, that there will be a hosting among the Brython, a gathering of the tribes of Cunedda and Cadell, a rushing like mountain-bears upon the foreigner, a thrusting of spears and hewing of swords, a spilling of brains and widowing of wives, and a fleeing of the Iwys to their ships. Before Maelgun the Tall—Merlin's prophecy does not lie—sea and anchor shall be their counselors, blood and death their companions! On foot will they flee through the forests, perfidious foxes as they are, and with the ebb of the tide will they slip back into the ocean. War will depart with them, and peace will be upon the Island of Prydein.

There was silence in Brochfael's courthouse as Taliesin finished his song, while that last proud note sounded in each princely heart like the pure, clear stroke of a hermit's bell heard in a woodland glade. Then there arose one joyous shout of triumph and vengeance, echoing and crashing among the vaulting of the pillared hall, until the giant form of Maelgun the king arose in the midst with his hand upheld for silence.

"The prophecy cannot lie," he cried, "and certain it is that our armies will crush the mongrel hosts of Loiger! All who partake in the slaughter shall be honored until the end of the world, and receive the blessing of Crist and his angels who watch over our hosting."

Maelgun paused, to allow a fresh shout of acclamation to subside. Then he resumed his speech, his expression serious and masterful.

"And now it is time for us to take counsel among ourselves as to the best way in which we may conduct the march of our hosts southward into Loiger. God is with us, of that we may be sure; but it would be as well to ensure that our plans are laid with skill and foresight. There is a man here among the men of Gwynedd who will give us good counsel, and my advice is that you should heed his words attentively."

With which the king resumed his couch, and a man stepped forward from behind him to address the company. That man was Maeldaf the elder, a man of great wealth in the land of Gwynedd. Though he was of middle age, his beard was gray and he stooped somewhat. But his glance was sharp and shrewd, and his skill in counsel was famed far beyond the mountains of Eryri. He stepped forward, his arms folded within the sleeves of his tunic as if to conceal the secret-hoard locked within his bosom.

"I thank you, great king," began Maeldaf, speaking at first in a voice so quiet and low that men feared to move upon their couches lest he let fall words that failed to reach their ears. "I thank you, too, noble princes of the Brython, for listening to my humble counsel, which must surely be of little moment where so many of the wisest of the Island of the Mighty are gathered together under the rooftree of the munificent ruler of Powys, Brochfael, son of Cyngen the Renowned."

King Brochfael beamed affably, and there was laughter in the hall; for all knew and Maeldaf knew that he was wise as that king Selyf who reigned over Israel of old, and that there was none present so wise as he—unless it be Taliesin, whose inspired knowledge was of a different order. (Of myself I say nothing, for as yet it was but my name that was known among the Brython, and as yet they knew not that I and the name were one.)

Maeldaf permitted himself an inward smile, waiting until the full-bellied laughter of the kings had died away.

"I thank you, noble princes. And now to my tale. Never since the time of Arthur has there been such a hosting as this, where a hundred thousand of the bravest of the Brython have gathered to wreak destruction in Loiger, driving the kings of the Iwys from our land forever. We have good reason to expect the victories foretold by Taliesin, chief of bards. Indeed, we have a right to triumph."

There was a murmur of approval, and a brief pause while those present drank deep draughts of mead and bragget.

"However," Maeldaf continued sharply, "men do not always receive what is their due. The proverb tells us 'The heart is stronger than a hundred counsels.' But though the hearts of the Brython are ever valiant, it has to be said that they have not always brought victory to the cause of the just. Was not Nuithon mab Cathen one of the greatest of our kings, of ancestry more illustrious than most? And yet in our grandfathers' time he and five thousand of his following—men bold in battle, mighty when hard-pressed—were slain at the hands of the heathen Iwys. And they were engaged in just such a hosting as that upon which we are now set. Moreover, they fought in the land which had belonged to their forefathers time out of mind. They knew the hidden tracks through forest and swamp, and yet the cunning men of Iwys laid an ambush for them in the thickets. Not by courage did they win the field, but by skill and treachery!"

Men nodded approvingly over their mead-horns. Their hearts were high and their pride lofty, yet they knew full well that the perfidious Iwys would long ago have been driven from their land, were they not greatly skilled in battle cunning.

"It is for us to match their cunning!" cried out Maeldaf with sudden vigor. "We must be before them with our stratagems, and it must be they who fall into our snares. I gave you one proverb just now, but you will recall another common among us: 'Empty each achievement which lacks its proper talent.' But I will prepare your ears no more for that which I have to say. I see we are in accord, and I will to my point."

Then Maeldaf set out in words of brevity and clarity the way matters stood at that time between the baptized and the heathen in the Island of the Mighty. For four years there had been peace on the frontiers. Beyond cattle-raiding proper to lords who watch over the borderland, no armies had taken the field on either side. Among the Brython their own affairs had been troubled. King Custennin Gorneu had died a mysterious death at his own hand (so it was said), and Maelgun the Tall had been active in subduing the subordinate kings to his overlordship. During this time the land of Loiger had been still—so still that it was rumored that the king of the Iwys, Cynurig son of Ceredig, was no more, and that his cousin the king of Cent had taken his land into overlordship. Then had come further rumors the last summer that Cynurig lived indeed, but that he had departed over the sea with the greater part of his following to take service under the king of the Freinc. Great wars were reported to be raging around the Middle Sea, and the lure of rich plunder was as close to the heart of Cynurig as that of any other dog of an Iwys.

So far so good. But what if the tales were false? What if Cynurig had returned before the winter to store his plunder? Most alarming of all, what if it were Cynurig himself who had spread abroad the rumors of his absence in order to lure the Brython into ambush, as the hunts-man catches the wild bull in his net? Truly is it said, "Let the wily conceal his plan." But do we not also say, "The malicious do not deceive the righteous?"

"For," concluded Maeldaf, with a sudden bitter smile of triumph, " 'man's reason is a bright candle,' and the whole of our foes' scheming has been made known to me, as I will now make it known to you. Stand forth, Samo the Freinc, and tell your tale!"

There was a movement among the men of Gwynedd, and a man stepped forward. He was middle-aged, inclined to stoutness, and plainly dressed. Yet there was that about him which told of the disposal of great wealth, love of comforts, and skill in disputes. To few of those craning their necks for a glimpse of the stranger did it come as a surprise to learn that this Samo was a rich merchant from the land of Freinc, accustomed to plying his trade impartially with heathen and Cristion alike, provided their wealth sufficed for his purpose.

The merchant looked about him with an ingratiating smile, appearing confident of a friendly reception among the great men assembled. To many indeed of the princes present he was a familiar figure, bartering every year before their courts wine, corn, and oil from beyond the seas for the gold and slaves and wolfhounds of the Brython. To Maeldaf the elder in particular was he well known, for Maeldaf was a rich man whose wealth had been greatly increased by dealings with Samo and other foreigners.

"Great king and princes all, my greetings and obeisance!" cried the merchant. He spoke the speech of the Brython well, though with the broken tongue characteristic of all barbarians.

"The lord Maeldaf has requested me to inform you of what I learned concerning the heathen Saxons as I passed through their land on my way hither. For I have bargained with them in their halls, and know much of their doings. I can tell you that what men guess is true: Cynric their king and ten thousand of his boldest thegns have departed their land for more than a year. They sailed from Cerdices-ora to join the army which the late king of my country, Theodebald, dispatched to fight alongside the Goths in Italia."

Samo paused, permitting the company to repeat the good news to one another. Then he continued: "Reports differ as to what has happened to them. Some say that they suffered fearful losses when the Imperial general defeated the Gothic army at Capua. Others on the contrary hold that our people defeated the eunuch Narses utterly, and are at present occupying the island of Sicilia. Be that as it may, the truth is that the Saxons' army has not returned, and all that has been seen of it is a rich consignment of plunder dispatched a year ago or more from Italia. I myself purchased some of the finer wares—fine glass, silken robes, curious brooches of delicate workmanship—which

I shall be happy to display before the generous princes gathered here when this council has completed its work."

As Samo paused for his words to have their effect, there came an interruption from the group of nobles standing behind him. A warrior stepped forward who was not of the race of the Brython. He was a man of some fifty winters and of no very prepossessing appearance, for his nose was red and he suffered from the affliction of baldness. He wore a weather-stained white tunic with broad purple border beneath a handsome coat of loricated armor, decorated upon the chest with nine embossed discs. Despite his plain looks and broken tongue, however, he spoke with an air of authority and appeared a personage of some consequence. He spoke in Ladin, the tongue of churchmen and the Rufeinieid, a tongue which fortunately King Maelgun and some others present understood.

"You should know, O kings, that not all the words of this huckster are true," began the stranger with contemptuous abruptness. "He claims that the barbarians have conquered Sicilia. That I know to be false, since I have good reason to believe that the Imperial fleet evacuating part of our army from Baetica has passed this winter in Sicilia. If this be false, can the rest be true? It may be, but it would be wise to question him closely and check his replies against other knowledge you may possess. Such men as this are accustomed to proffering fair words and dealing even-handedly with Roman and barbarian alike."

The kings glanced at each other in some surprise. They were not accustomed to interruptions of this sort. Their royal councils were held in this manner: In the presence of a great king such as Maelgun, whom all feared, each man should have his say and then listen to his fellow. Should the kings be of an equality, having the same *galanas* and honor-price, then might they wrangle fiercely indeed, without paying heed one to another. But who was this stranger, who by his manner regarded himself as worthy to tell the princes what they should or should not do?

All gazed expectantly at the great king, Dragon of the Island. Maelgun the Tall, however, appeared in no way discomposed, nodding politely toward the interrupter and signing to Samo to continue his account.

"What this lord says may well be true," conceded the merchant with an affable nod toward his critic, who stepped back among the ranks of his companions with a dissatisfied expression. "I did not say that I knew that the Franks were in Sicilia, but merely that such a report had reached the ears of King Theodebald in Paris, while the king was yet alive. I myself heard it from Priscus the Jew, whose dealers buy corn from Africa in the markets of Massilia. Sea captains report that at present they are unable to put in at Panormus or Neapolis, for fear of having their cargoes seized by Franks or Goths. Speaking as a simple man of business, this appeared to me good enough authority; but I am far from vouching for it myself."

The foreigner whose interruption had brought about this digression was seen to shake his head, though whether in criticism of Samo's judgment or the value of the report he cited was unclear. The merchant, whose profession accustomed him to disputations at all times, took no offense and concluded his report:

"All I can say, great kings and counselors all, is that I am certain from what I have seen and heard that Cynric and the greater part of his warriors are absent from the shores of this Island. Whether they were victorious or defeated in Italia, I cannot say. Perhaps this man knows more of the matter than I. But, as you may see if you visit the marketplace tomorrow morning, I found no market for my goods among the Saxons, whose halls are well-nigh bare of men of wealth. I am no man of war, but what I have seen with these eyes enables me to vouch that warriors are few among the Saesons today, and their land lies open to conquest. So at least it seems to me, O king."

Maelgun Gwynedd nodded approvingly, and signed to Samo to pause a moment while the kings considered the matter. Various opinions could be heard urged in the brief hubbub that followed. There were those who expressed dissatisfaction, wishing the whole brood of the Saeson, or Iwys as we generally call them, to be present at the destruction of their vipers' nest; whilst others held there would be sufficient work for sword and spear among those who remained. Prominent among the latter was Run mab Maelgun, a prince as greedy for the blood of foemen as for drinking mead or wine, who urged a swift and immediate march upon the enemy strongholds, regardless of their strength.

"Let us put the whole country to fire and sword," he cried, "restore the bones of Gurthefir the Blessed to every port, and ensure that the pollution of the heathen be purged from the Island of the Mighty for all time!"

At length Maelgun nodded to Maeldaf the elder, who raised his hand to demand silence.

"Certain it is that we must be cautious in our counsels," he pronounced in a level, compelling tone, "though here I see no difficulty. 'Evil does not conceal itself where it occurs,' and certain it is that no false person has complete power of his speech. I see no reason for us to doubt the account this man has brought us; he is cautious and cunning, and there is no contradiction in what he has told us. Now he has more to say, and that unless I am mistaken of greater import by far than that which we have heard already."

Samo bowed his head toward the great king and proceeded with his tale. Though his manner of speaking was that of merchants—polite, practical, and to the point—one could see by an occasional glance he bestowed about him that he was well aware of the mounting excitement his narrative aroused in his audience.

It seemed that, though greatly reduced from the strength they had known before Cynurig's departure overseas, the Iwys still possessed a small but determined host, commanded by the young prince Ceawlin, heir (edlyng in their rough tongue) to Cynurig. And even now they were assembled with what following they could muster at Ceawlin's timbered stronghold: in the crude language of that people, their heal-reced; in ours, flowing and beautiful, the language of Paradise, their llys. This lay, so it appeared, not far from the ruins of the great stone city they call Wintanceaster, but which we of the Brython call Caer Went. Though the city still bore remnants of a strong wall, the Iwys feared to make use of it as a fortress (so they told the merchant Samo) because they believed it to have been constructed by giants and to be peopled by devils, especially at nighttime. Yet the stockaded fortress they had built beside the old city was shrewdly sited, since from Wintanceaster paved roads radiated like the spokes of a chariot wheel west and north and east to all the frontiers of their kingdom. Alerted by beacon fires or messengers, their host could in a short time make its way to any threatened point.

At this arose Gereint mab Erbin, warlike king of Dyfneint, to confirm that the merchant's assessment was worthy of acceptance. "For," he explained to the council, "it happened that this was the principal cause of the slaughter inflicted upon the men of my gosgordd four years ago. As we marched deep into the heart of their territory, opposed by a lesser host, King Cynurig passed by us with his great war-band by another road and seized Caer Caradog to our rear. Thus we were compelled to withdraw lest they strike at us from front and rear, and in addition the great fortress remained in their hands—as it does to this day, a shame and reproach to the men of the Brython. It was by deceit and not courage that we were defeated; but if we are to destroy the kingdom of the Iwys as fully as the prince Run mab Maelgun contends, then must we match their deceit by cunning of our own."

Here the ruddy-nosed stranger who had spoken earlier nodded vigorously, seeming to look upon the merchant with new approval. I think he would have spoken, but all men were attentive to Samo's words.

"Now I come to my point, O king," he concluded. "It happened by a fortunate chance that the whole battle plan of the Saxons came to my ears, and with this knowledge it should not be difficult to forestall the advantage which the spider must always possess at the center of the net he has constructed."

"Tell the council how you came by this knowledge," ordered Maelgun Gwynedd with a gruff laugh, indicating that he had heard the tale already.

"As you wish it, great king. It so happened that one of my slaves, a Saeson whom I bought five years ago from the Syrian dealer Eufronius, is brother to one of the women in the kitchen of Cynric's royal hall. On a certain occasion this slave was assisting in the hall when Ceawlin and his thegns were holding their war council, and so he was able to bring me word of all that passed. Though how so cunning a prince as Ceawlin could have permitted such an indiscretion passes my poor understanding, I confess freely."

Samo looked about him with a half-smile, which became a gale of laughter throughout the council chamber. Information could be as valuable a commodity as figs and dates from Egipt, as all well knew, and it was clear the wily merchant had not neglected his opportunities during his sojourn among the Iwys. Great wealth at the hands of Maelgun the Tall would undoubtedly be his for the purchasing of this word-hoard. Samo delayed no further, preparing to unfasten his baggage thongs for all to inspect his wares.

Firstly, however, there was a hubbub in a corner of the hall, as Maeldaf the elder signed to two officers of the household to come forward. One of them bore what appeared to be a section of leather tenting wrapped about two poles. Unwound and held up before the company, it proved to be a large map painted upon a tanned bull's hide. Roads and towns were set out upon it in red, the latter depicted as small squat towers. I noticed that the names of towns were written in a neat clear Ladin script, VENTA BELGARVM, CALLEVA, ATREBATVM, and the like, and that the distances between them by road were marked down also in those neat numerals which are still to be seen inscribed upon the milestones of the Rufeinieid beside their great paved roads. It was, as I guessed, an old army map from the time when the emperor of Rufein ruled with his legions over the Island of Prydein. Superimposed upon the network of straight roads were markings in another hand, which upon examination I took to be a representation of the system of

fortresses and earthworks constructed by the emperor Arthur in the
time of the grandfathers of the present generation.

"The Saxons' stratagem is simple and effective," declared Samo
briskly. "See here upon the map: Venta is the city you call Caer Went,
and it is beside its walls that the Saxon host is to assemble. Last
Christmastide, when the heathen held the great feast they call
Modranecht, Ceawlin declared to his people that a great hosting and
warring against the people of Christendom would take place this
summer. The hosting, I believe, is intended to take place at the time of
full moon in the month of Thrimilchi; that is to say, about ten nights
from now, as I understand the workings of their calendar."

I glanced at Maelgun, catching as I thought a look of satisfaction
upon his bold, intelligent features. The Brython were gathered well in
advance of their wily foe!

"This, then, is Ceawlin's battle plan," continued Samo, sensing a
rising impatience among his audience. "In the absence abroad of his
father the king and the better part of his nation's warriors, he sees that
he must rely more on guile and stratagem than on the bravery of his
followers. He has, it seems, been well advised—I believe by certain
chiefs of my own people who have taken service with him."

At this there was a murmur of suspicion among some present, but
to most this came as no surprise. The kingdom of the Freinc was so
powerful, and its warriors so numerous, that many had long been
accustomed to seeking service in foreign lands—even so far east as
with the emperor in Caer Custennin. Indeed, there were those of the
kings of Prydein who maintained Freinc warriors among their body-
guards. They were greatly valued as champions of proven valor;
fighting in the first rank after the manner of their people, naked but for
their leather trousers, and wielding battle-axes of enormous size. Their
loyalty and valor had been proved in many a hard-fought combat,
even where men of their kinsfolk were to be found in the ranks of the
enemy host.

All heads were craned toward the merchant as he indicated points
upon the map with a rod of office borrowed from the steward of King
Brochfael's household.

"There is the kingdom of the Saxons about its royal palace beside
Caer Went. To the south it is bounded by the sea, and to the west and
north by the line of dykes and fortresses fortified by the emperor
Arthur after his victory at Mount Badon. Thus the heathens are
hemmed in as if locked within a strong chest. The chest itself is
fastened as it were by two great locks, devised by Arthur in his
wisdom. In the center of the western frontier lies the fortress of Caer

Caradog, and in the center of the northern line is the impregnable stronghold of Caer Vydei.

"To emerge from the chest in which Arthur secured him, the king of the Saxons knows full well he must loose one of those two locks. Four years ago, indeed, King Cynric attempted to do this, succeeding by a ruse in capturing Caer Caradog. Unfortunately for him he was not to know that one side of the chest in which he is confined rests as it were against a wall, and it was this wall that he now faced beyond Caer Caradog. For to the west of the fort are further great dykes, some old and some new, and beyond them lies the impenetrable forest of huge extent which you Brython call Coed Mawr, and the Saxons, 'Mearc-wudu.' "

Maeldaf the elder swept the company with his sharp gaze, judging the effect of the merchant's words. Each king upon his couch at once sat upright, with bright attentive eye fixed upon the map. It had happened before to some that Maeldaf the elder had spoken words of blemish and satire when their attention had wandered, momentarily ensnared by the sweet strong mead.

"During the four years which have passed since the taking of Caer Caradog," continued Samo equably, "Ceawlin has been seeking and seeking a new method of breaking out of the box in which you hold him. He is well aware that, since the taking of Caer Caradog, the kings of the Brython desire only to harry him and his people out of the land altogether. Equally, he wishes to perform some great feat before old King Cynric, his father, returns from his warring abroad.

"What is he to do? The taking of Caer Caradog proved that there was no passage to the west; and yet the north is held by Caer Vydei, which is too strong to be taken, the barbarians having no engines of war with which to storm city walls of dressed stone."

I could sense an atmosphere of unease about me in the hall. That the Iwys were confined within Arthur's strongbox was an article of faith throughout the Island: Had not two full generations passed since Din Badon, and was not the lid as securely fastened as ever? Yet Samo's words clearly implied that Ceawlin believed he had devised a means of breaking free from his captivity. My own thoughts turned to that dread nighttime scene in the hall of Nud of the Silver Hand, when the lid of the stone cistern containing the fated Dragons had slowly begun to rise. For upon the outcome of the combat of the two Dragons, the Red and the White, there rested a prophecy, the interpretation of which (to my mind at least) remained equivocal.

It was not hard to see that Samo was enjoying the atmosphere of expectation his words had aroused. His peculiar talent, I surmised, made him adept at arousing an audience's expectancy to maximum pitch before granting satisfaction at precisely the appropriate moment. At the same time he knew not to provoke too far the impatience of the hot-blooded kings of the Brython. He came swiftly to the point.

"The words spoken by Ceawlin to his counselors, as reported to me, were much as follows: 'The Wealas' (so they term the Brython—the word signifies 'foreigners' in their rough tongue) 'have locked us into their chest. If we find we cannot force the padlocks, then why do we not try the hinge?' "

At this a babel of voices was raised in disputatious talk. There was anger at the reminder that these impudent invaders, the pale-faced mongrel host of Loiger, frequenters of fens, mud flats, and estuaries, should dare to term the Brython *foreigners* in the land in which they had dwelt since it was first settled by Prydein, son of Aedd the Great. Others, more learned, asserted that their ancestors had come to Prydein with Brutus the Trojan, and that it was he from whom the Island derived its name. There was anger and contention between kings of rival descent, but the discord was swiftly brought to an end by an admonition from the steward of King Brochfael's household. The great king of Powys, lord of the tribes of the Cadelling, was curious to learn the meaning of Ceawlin's ominous-sounding suggestion.

"The hinge?" cried out Cynan of the White Chariot, generous son of Brochfael. "To what does this impudent huckster refer? Is it not a saying among our people: 'The carpenter's son to the adze, to fashion planks aright; the smith's son to the coal; it is fitting that each should follow the calling of his family'? Who is this Freinc to talk of battles and sieges? I have heard that the walls of Caer Vydei are impregnable, above all to barbarians who lack siege-engines. The dykes and forts established by Arthur the emperor are like bands of triple steel. Where is the 'hinge' in our trap, which this fox hopes to prise open?"

Samo pointed with his rod to the point on the map where the western and northern defense-works joined at a right angle.

"There, high on open downs, lies the great fort named after Arthur, the Bear of Prydein: Dineirth. The Saxons, too, term it 'Bear's fort': Beran-burh. I believe I am right in saying that it lies at the very fulcrum of your defense system? If so, you may perceive what Ceawlin had in mind when he referred to 'the hinge' in that chest which encloses his people!"

King Maelgun gazed intently at the map. "We see indeed, O Samo. You should lead a war-band, and not deal in wines and oils! But, great fortress that it is, Dineirth is no new work but a stronghold of kings of old who built it long before the men of Rufein came hither. So at least

it is said. It is but one of many works of which our people will make
use in time of war. Of what advantage can it be to the Iwys to attack
this among so many earthworks?"

The foreigner who had spoken earlier in criticism of the merchant
rose as if disposed to intervene once more, but Samo's words which
followed grasped the attention of all and checked him.

"I do not know all that lies in that heathen barbarian's mind, I
confess. But on my journey hither, traveling on the great road between Caer Vydei and Caer Ceri, I passed over the downs hard by
Dineirth; and what I saw and heard enabled me as I believe to conceive
what his stratagem may be. Having learned that the Saxons planned to
assault this fortress (of which I had never heard speak before), I was
curious to learn more of its significance. I made inquiry of a party of
turf-cutters whom I espied from the wayside, who told me freely all I
wished to know.

"Dineirth, they said, is a huge fort, bounded by earthen dykes
topped by a palisade of stakes. But these are now old and rotten in
places, it seems, and the place lies undefended except for twenty
soldiers of the Brython who guard a beacon set upon the rampart. It
struck me that what I learned with such facility could also readily have
been discovered by the spies of Ceawlin. Indeed, I learned that not far
off lie settlements of Saxon folk. They have long been under the
domination of the Brython' lords; but tame the wolf as you will, he
looks ever back to the forest.

"Ceawlin's plan, as I see it, is this. From Caer Went he will dispatch
a small party of picked warriors northeast to Caer Vydei. He knows he
cannot take the city, but with a large body of bondsmen and others of
the folk he will make a great display beyond its gates. Thus your
garrison will be held to the spot, and may even be persuaded to draw
in men from the dyke-defenses westward.

"Meanwhile, Ceawlin, with every warrior he can raise, marches up
the northwestern road with great speed and throws himself into Dineirth,
swiftly fortifying it into the impregnable stronghold it must once have
been, and could so readily be again."

"How will that avail him?" shouted Run mab Maelgun, wolf of
the army and herb-garden of the king's war-band that he was. "With a
host such as ours, we can besiege him there—or march on past him
into the heart of Loiger, laying waste all his father's lands, as we have
planned in any case to do!"

His father, Maelgun, who was doubtless already party to the merchant's revelations, raised his hand and signed to Maeldaf the elder to
take up the argument.

"What you say is true, Prince Run mab Maelgun," returned Maeldaf in polished, measured tones, "but it is necessary to consider other matters. Once master of Dineirth, Ceawlin may at his discretion attack our defenses in flank or rear. Indeed, we shall have either to withdraw our watch-parties from the vicinity or to fortify them to such an extent that our mighty host here is deprived of the greater part of its strength.

"Moreover there is a danger more pressing still, which will not have escaped the attention of so wily a fox as our ancient adversary. To north and east below the downs upon which stands Dineirth are numberless villages inhabited by the heathen Iwys. Since they were conquered after Din Badon they have owed fealty to the lords of the Brython, living in peace with us and delivering up their annual tribute freely. But were Ceawlin's dragon banners to fly from the hills above them, how long think you would their loyalty last? He would have but to raise his finger, and the whole valley of the Temys would be his—as for a time it was his grandfather Ceredig's! The danger is great, it must be confessed. The wolfhound may with justice ever scorn the fox; but to catch the fox, men must employ a fox's cunning. It is with the net and not the spear that you will take him. Ceawlin thinks to prise open the hinge of the chest in which he is imprisoned. But let him beware, lest it prove not a hinge but the spring of a steel-jawed trap!"

At this, men laughed in King Cynan's chamber. For who was so cunning as Maeldaf the elder? From his expression it was not hard to guess that he had already conceived a method of outwitting the wily Ceawlin, whose battle plan was now in the possession of the Brython. Slaves hurried about with the mead-vessels, as the lords of the Brython drank to one another, vaunting the mead-portion they would earn in the coming campaign.

Amid the joyous din, Maelgun Gwynedd and the confederated kings rose and left the great *palestr,* with its gorgeous painted walls, lofty hall pillars of polished stone, and soaring canopied roof. Together with their principal counselors, they made their way to an inner chamber to discuss their plans in secret. With them went also Maeldaf the elder, together with that foreign soldier who had spoken earlier in the discussion, and myself. The princes Elffin and Run had informed Maelgun of my not-unskilled intervention in the matter of the Mantle of Tegau Eurvron, and my advice was not despised.

True, I fancied that Maeldaf the elder looked upon me a little askance, but other men's envy has never disturbed me. Indeed, I regard it as a form of tribute. Just as the greatness of kings is measured by the weight of booty seized from their enemies, the tribute exacted from their vassals, and the number of princes chained within their hostage pits, so brilliant men of letters, *llyfyrion*,may judge of their ascendancy by the virulent hatred their abilities arouse in men of inferior capacity. To the present discussion, however, I contributed but little. I knew no more of the facts than those laid but now before us, and from what I had seen, Maeldaf's responses were precisely what mine would have been. I resolved to bend my mind carefully to every issue as it arose, however; for come what may, the Monarchy of Prydein must be preserved.

Reassembled in the small council chamber, kings and counselors were enabled to speak their minds more freely. The intelligence brought by Samo, it was generally agreed, was likely to be accurate. He was a man of shrewd parts and, though no man of war, was accustomed to conversing with kings and assessing their wealth and the numbers and capacity of their armies. His news, too, was recent and unlikely to have been overtaken by any fresh development or change of plan on the part of the Iwys. Samo's baggage train consisted of the swift-moving four-wheeled wagons termed by the people of his nation *rheda*. A bare month had passed since he was in the court of Ceawlin by Caer Went. At that time the barbarian king was still, so Samo averred, awaiting reinforcements from his nephews whose kingdom lay to the south, upon the Island of Weith. And after their gathering, the lords of the Iwys would be obliged to repair to a sacred grove to make customary sacrifices to their war god, without which they could not proceed on a summer's hosting.

In view of all these considerations, concluded Maeldaf, Ceawlin could scarcely be expected to begin his march until about the time our host would make its departure from Dinleu Gurygon. Thus there should be ample time to adopt stratagems calculated to frustrate the Iwys' impudent endeavor.

"What further measures are needed?" cried out Run mab Maelgun. "Our host is mightier far than that of the pale-faced Iwys, whose king and greatest men of war are far beyond the sea. Let us march in all haste upon Dineirth and there meet with these impudent heathen, making of them food for carrion!"

King Maelgun glanced at his wise counselor, and rose to speak: "You forget, my son, that the Iwys must reach the fortress long before we may do so. Look here upon the map: From Caer Went to Dineirth is a bare forty miles or so. Our own march thither is thrice the distance or more, our host is huge and encumbered with a great baggage train, and on our way we must make tryst with the kings who rule over the borderlands at Caer Loyw, Caer Ceri, and Caer Vadon.

We will be a month upon the road to every week of our enemies' march. During that time they may fortify Dineirth so strongly that it will be a great work for us to besiege it. *That* is what we have to avoid, if we are not to risk an uprising of the tributary Saeson along both banks of Temys in our rear."

"What do you suggest then, O king?" inquired Run. "Or"— here I thought I detected a touch of bitterness—"what does Maeldaf the elder commend to us as a battle plan?"

At a nod from the king, Maeldaf took up the matter with a fluency which confirmed my surmise that the strategy had already been discussed at length between them.

"At all costs," replied the cunning counselor, "must we prevent the Iwys from making use of the strength of Dineirth. We must be there before him, so that he remain confined within the strong chest devised by Arthur the emperor. Then indeed may we march in force into his dominions, destroying his host and laying waste his land. What I therefore propose is this: that we send a single war-band, unimpeded by baggage or foot soldiers, riding night and day to Dineirth. There they will repair the stockade, and defend the stronghold until relief may come."

"Let it be my *gosgordd* that rides on that expedition!" cried Run eagerly, looking from the counselor to the king. Maeldaf lowered his gaze to the rush-strewn floor; this was a matter for the princes to decide between themselves. Maelgun the Tall gazed with pride upon his stalwart son, remarking with approval: "That were a worthy task for the heir of Gwynedd, son Run; it shall be thine."

Run gave a shout of triumph, while beside him sprang up Elffin son of Gwydno Garanhir.

"I will ride by thy side, my foster brother!" he shouted joyfully. "Together will we await the enemy on the rampart, we will smite them with sword strokes by the gate, and with our bright lances give over their corpses to glut the wolf and the raven!"

The young men's faces were flushed with mead and battle ardor.

"What think you, Maeldaf?" inquired the king of his counselor. "Does this accord with your plan?"

Maeldaf raised his head and replied with deference that he could conceive of no better prince to hold the false Iwys in check than Run mab Maelgun: boy in years yet man in vigor, boisterous in courage, fierce and rash. No man who donned armor for battle, with his spear and his shield and his sword and his knife, would be better than Run mab Maelgun. It should not be hard for two such princes with their retinues to hold so great a fortress. "For is it not a saying among the wise, that 'mighty is the shield upon a brave shoulder'?"

"Then is that matter settled," pronounced the king. "And what think you should be the battle path of the hosts of the Brython? Should we not also march upon Dineirth and beyond, meeting the mongrel hosts of Loiger in battle?"

There was a murmur of assent from some at this. The king looked ever to his counselor, and once more it was easy for me to see that a plan had already been concerted between them.

Maeldaf stroked his beard, standing with eyes downcast until the murmuring had ceased, and then spoke again: "That we must seek out the wolf in his lair, all men are agreed. See here upon the map: There is Dineirth, hinge of the strongbox in which the emperor Arthur closed up the princes of the Iwys. That the princes Run mab Maelgun and Elffin mab Gwydno will seize and hold, holding Ceawlin and the pale-faced hosts of the heathen in check."

Here the princes rose, smiling and nodding to the assembled kings.

"Now," pursued Maeldaf the elder, turning to the map and pointing with his wand of office, "cast your eyes to the eastward, along the line of ramparts and fortresses. That tower there is the northern lock of the chest in which the White Dragon lies bound: Caer Vydei. With its dressed-stone walls and towers, defended by the valiant war-band of Prince Einion mab Run, Caer Vydei stands like a rock before the tumbling wave of the sea. Besides, as the merchant tells us, the enemy before its walls is but a rabble, dispatched to deceive us into believing that Ceawlin intends to attack by that path.

"Einion mab Run has no need of further men, yet the enemy must be brought to hold that we have indeed fallen into their trap, believing the host of the Brython to have marched to the relief of Caer Vydei. In reality, though, our host will march by the nearer route to Dineirth, joining with the princes Run and Elffin who await us there, and so our whole host will fall upon that of the heathen, who will have no rampart behind which he may conceal himself. After that will we march on into the heart of Loiger, there to put Ceawlin's royal hall to the flames and root out his brood of whelps from the land."

On a table before the company lay a magnificent board of *gwyddbwyll,* its pieces of gold and silver, whose splendor had attracted the gaze of all present. It was the board "Fair-head," which it is said was taken long ago from an elf-mound at its opening at the time of the Kalan Gaeaf.

"See here," explained Maeldaf the elder, stepping beside the board, "where Ceawlin squats like a spider in the center. To the south is the sea, to the east the Forest of Anderhyd, to the west the Forest of Coed Mawr. He moves a piece northward—thus—seeking to convey to us that he marches against Caer Vydei. Meanwhile he and all his host prepare in reality to march toward the northwest corner, which he believes to be undefended. However, it is there *we* swiftly set a piece: the princes Run and Elffin in Dineirth.

"This will not deter Ceawlin, who will lay siege to the strong place, believing his host great enough to overwhelm a single war-band. At length he receives tidings that the great king, Dragon of the Island, has arrived in the east at Caer Vydei with the whole host of the Brython, coming as they believe to aid Prince Einion against the chief attack. This of course is what the fox hopes will happen; now he believes he can storm Dineirth without delay!

"But Ceawlin is fallen into a trap of his own digging. For the hosts of the Brython are by no means, as he believes, at Caer Vydei, but hard by him upon the downs beside Dineirth. It is the Brython who will fall upon the unwary host of the Iwys where they stand before the rampart of Dineirth, crushed between the wave and the rock!"

The kings studied the board, those whose realms paid tribute in cattle and hostages to Maelgun Gwynedd nodding their agreement with the wily proposal of Maeldaf the elder with especial vigor.

Pedyr of Dyfed it was who voiced the first objection. What would induce Ceawlin to believe that the hosts of Prydein had assembled at Caer Vydei rather than Dineirth? Here Maeldaf permitted himself a smile of deep satisfaction, exchanging a glance with Maelgun.

"The trap will be baited in this fashion," he explained: "King Maelgun himself will indeed be seen upon the walls of Caer Vydei, and beside him the Dragon Standard of the Brython. Those who espy him there will believe him to be accompanied by his host, whereas in reality he will have with him but the three hundred picked men of his *gosgordd*, together with the men of Einion mab Run who guard the city.

"Each player seeks to mask his chief move upon the board," concluded Maeldaf the elder. "Since it is we who know our adversary's thought, and not he ours, it is we who will be enabled to compass him about and cast him from the board."

When Maelgun was seen to nod in approval, the kings were pleased and laughed among themselves. For who could mistake the giant frame of Maelgun the Tall, whose massive frame towered a head above his fellow princes? Cunning as he was, Ceawlin would undoubtedly believe that the army must have accompanied the king, and that

Dineirth would be his for the taking, while King Maelgun and all the hosts of the Brython fruitlessly awaited an attack within Caer Vydei.

All this was well enough, conceded Louarch of Brycheiniog, but what if Ceawlin, finding Run and Elffin within Dineirth, were to seek to break through the dykes at some other point? To this, Maeldaf replied that he did not believe such an event likely. However, were it to happen, precautions might be taken without overmuch difficulty. The host of the Brython was the greatest that had been seen in the Island of the Mighty since the time of the emperor Arthur, while that of Ceawlin was but the runt of the fox's litter. The boldest warriors of the Iwys, as Samo discovered, had crossed the sea with Ceawlin's father, Cynurig. There would be men and to spare who could be detached to hold the length of the rampart from Dineirth in the west to Caer Vydei in the east.

Gereint of Dyfneint, whom all heard with deference, provided strong reasons for adopting this course rather than the other: "It seems to me, O Dragon of the Island, that it were indeed best to halt upon the frontier and repair ramparts, dykes, and forts before proceeding into a fen of which few men know the trackways. I think that there are few here who will term me coward"—darting a fierce look about him— "but it was rashly venturing far into their territory that lost us Caer Caradog, the western padlock. I say this: Let us repair the stockade before venturing within to rope the bull! Not for nothing did the emperor Arthur construct works so mighty that the heathen think them the handiwork of their one-eyed god."

As Gereint's kingdom marched with that of the Iwys, and there were few who matched him for valor and renown, there were those present who murmured that he spoke truth. Sovereigns each in his own country, it was not right they should allow one to speak for all. The fear of Maelgun was great upon all who ruled between the Seas of Hafren and Reged, but when Gereint mab Erbin spoke, then might princes in council voice other views—with decency and caution, be it said.

"There is wisdom in what you say, Prince Gerontius," interposed the rough voice of the stranger among us, whom I had observed taking a very keen interest in Maeldaf's proposal. "But nevertheless I believe the king's counselor here has the right of it. Have I your permission, O king, to address the company?"

While Maeldaf played at *gwyddbwyll,* this man had stood stooping over the map, examining it narrowly. Now he turned to face the company. He spoke as before in Ladin, which Maelgun the Tall (who, it will be remembered, had studied under the blessed Iltud, enlightened instructor of the youth of Prydein) took upon himself to translate.

But before he could utter more than a few words, Serwyl of Cardigan, after Maelgun first of the tribe of Cunedda, interrupted with some indignation:

"Who is this foreigner, with his broken speech, that he dares to sit in council among the kings of the Brython and advise what it is they may or may not do? Let him go below and take his place at the feast among his equals—whoever they may be. Of what tribe is he? Who among us are of his kin or fosterage?"

There was agreement among the assemblage upon this point, and from each king went up the cry of "Gray wolf! Gray wolf!" There were those, too, who spat to void themselves and those with them of the infection of the foreigner, whose entry into their councils violated the hedge of protection which druids have set about the Island of the Mighty.

The contention of the kings was, however, stilled in a moment by Maelgun Gwynedd, who arose towering above the company and spoke thus: "Truth it is that this man is come as a foreigner among us, and does not speak the pure tongue of the Brython. But he is no mere *aillt,* a kin-broken fugitive who must suffer servitude even unto the ninth generation. He is the king of Gwynedd's foreigner, an *alltud* with *galanas* of sixty-three cows. He is also a chieftain of high renown in the hosts of the emperor at Caer Custennin, whose loricated legions have even now, as travelers tell, reconquered all the lands about the Middle Sea that are his by right in descent from his royal ancestors. From this man you will learn much concerning the right disposition of hosts, and of stratagems and deceptions of war. *Who* he is, and *what* he is, you may hear further from the noble Gereint mab Erbin, king of Dyfneint, in whose train he traveled hither."

The anger of the kings was swiftly dispelled by these words. For who among them was not aware that the realm of the emperor of Rufein (now dwelling in Caer Custennin) is the last realm of the world? Impossible it is to reckon up the ranks and the degrees of the men of his following, because of the multitude of their consuls and their founders and their legates and their counts and their dictators and their patricians, their satraps and senators and judges and centurions.

Then up again rose Gereint from the South, whose hilly land of Dyfneint reaches from sea to sea. He was one of the Three Seafarers of the Island of Prydein, and his was the fleet that plied the foam-crested Sea of Udd even as far as the coast of Lydau. Great was the renown of his feats of arms, and with him more usual was a shattered shield

than an ox to the noonday rest. As yet he had not formally acknowledged the supremacy of Maelgun Gwynedd over the Island of Prydein
and its Three Adjacent Islands, and it was requisite to treat him with
due respect.

"This man," explained Gereint, "came from the Middle Sea to
our coast in the last ship to arrive before the storms that follow the
Kalan Gaeaf. He passed the winter in our palace at Din Gereint in
Dyfneint, where I had many an instructive conversation with him. He is
a man of great skill and experience in all matters pertaining to battles
and sieges and expeditions, and it is my view that you would do well
to listen to his words and weigh deeply his advice. I believe he shares
the view of Maeldaf and not those I have urged upon you, but nevertheless he is a man whose words are weighty. Now I leave it to him to
tell you who he is, and what course he recommends in this our great
hosting."

These words of Gereint mab Erbin were sufficient to gain the
stranger a respectful hearing, and all sat still and expectant. He stood
before us, his back straight as a spear-shaft, with a confidence that
suggested the council chambers of the kings were not unfamiliar to
him, and launched abruptly into speech. Of those present, I believe
only Maelgun Gwynedd and three or four others were able to understand
his words, which were however afterward translated by a monk summoned to act as interpreter. The remainder restrained their impatience
at having to remain silent during the temporarily unintelligible flow,
being sufficiently impressed by the attentive expression on King Maelgun's
face to sense that they were words of power and skill and worth.

"My name is Rufinus, of the senatorial family of the Rufii Festi in
Etruria," began the speaker in a flat recitative monotone. I guessed that
what followed comprised a regular prolegomena to speeches delivered
before assemblages of this sort. Later I was to find out what an
amazing panorama of events and experiences underlay the brief, dry
catalogue.

"I became a soldier in the eighth year of the late emperor. I have
served in the Empire's wars against the Persians, the Vandals, and the
Goths. For long I commanded on the frontier in Mauretania Tingitana,
where I held the post of tribune of Septem. Lastly I served in the army
of Liberius at the invasion of Hispania. Twenty-eight times have I been
rewarded for bravery by my generals, I have been decorated seven
times with the *corona aurea*. I have performed thirty years' service and
am nearly fifty years old."

Those who understood nodded in approval. This man must surely
know more of the skills of warfare than any Freinc. For my part,

though, I could not help wondering whether his were skills of great practical use in the sort of warfare which is waged in the Island of Prydein. As you will see, I was to be proved wrong.

"It appears to me," continued Rufinus, with a change of voice and manner that alerted the attention of all, "that your armament is great, your intelligence good, and the advice tendered by this personage"— indicating Maeldaf—"in general sound. This expedition is in good hands and should not fail, provided our plans are expeditiously laid, each commander knowing precisely what is expected of him, and as little as possible left to chance. I have one amendment to make to the plan proposed, and it is for you, O princes, to decide whether you think my advice worthy of adoption."

After the monk had rephrased these words in the tongue of the Brython, the assembled kings nodded approvingly to one another. The speaker's frank approach had engaged their confidence, while his studied courtesy stilled the ire of the more hot-blooded. His tactful manner impressed me greatly, for with skills and experience such as his it might have come readily to him to speak in imperious tones unsuited to the fiercely proud kings of the Brython, ever swift as they are to take offense. Maelgun signed to him to continue without further interruption.

"In war there are two major aspects to bear in mind, and for each of these aspects there is a guiding principle. This is what Count Belisarius used to say, and where he held undivided command I never knew his approach to fail.

"One. In battle, much depends on chance, on the bravery of particular officers or troops, and on a will to win that the best commander may fail to instill into the best of soldiers. As it is said: 'In all battles, it is the eyes which are conquered first.' At the great battle of Ad Decimum, which we fought on landing in Africa, the day started with our army falling into as pretty an ambush as I have seen. It was the brother of their king, though, who spoiled their plan, by advancing too soon and giving us a chance to prepare. Ammatas was his name, and he was killed on the spot. Then our Huns smashed through in the Plain of Salt to the east, and it looked as if the day was ours. But it seems our flanks were overextended, for next moment King Gelimer himself with his main force drove in our center. There was our commander with his staff (I saw it myself) riding about, thrashing Uliaris' cowardly guards back to the line, when we saw the main Vandal strength appear on the hill before us. I felt we were done for, and so, I could see, did the general.

"But what happened? The attack never came. Afterward we heard that Gelimer was so distressed upon learning that his brother was killed he forgot all about making sure our forces really were beaten, and set about supervising a work party to bury his brother Ammatas on the field. Naturally, Belisarius lost no time in rallying our people, who this time fought with such a will that they drove the Vandals out into the desert.

"So you see how first the enemy was beaten, then *we* were, and then the enemy again—and all in the same day! That night, when we celebrated with a great feast in Carthage, Belisarius congratulated the officers, pointing out nevertheless how much luck had played a part in our victory. If our Huns had not come unexpectedly upon Gibamund in the Plain of Salt, if Ammatas had not been slain, if Gelimer had exerted more control over his grief—then it would have been Gelimer feasting here, and not ourselves! For you see, there was great amusement in the army on account of the feast we enjoyed that night being that which the Vandals had prepared for the victory they were certain they would gain that day."

"True," responded Maeldaf. "Not easy is it to escape disaster when one's luck is poor. Death and misfortune come to all, and uncertain is the day when they arrive."

"Precisely. But if it be luck that frequently rules the battlefield, it is *before* the battle that one may grasp that luck for one's own. It is the strategy of the campaign, skillfully determined, which decides when, where, and on what terms the battle is fought. And in strategy it is skill and not luck which is the prevailing factor. So at least my master Belisarius used to say, and many are the times I have been present to witness the proof of that. It is our strategy, the course of our marching and the place of our fighting, that we should now consider with care."

Maelgun Gwynedd, stilling with a glance the mirth of those who continued to dwell with delight on the spectacle of Belisarius devouring the Champion's Portion from the cauldron of Gelimer, signed to Rufinus to continue.

"Just so. Now, gentlemen, I would ask you to look again at this map. Your *primicerius* (if that be his rank) has suggested that your army assembled here should proceed by forced marches until it reach the threatened fortress, which it will prepare to defend against the enemy's postulated attack. Here is where I disagree. It seems to me you risk committing a cardinal mistake, which I am certain my master, the count Belisarius, would never have permitted. 'If you have the power to choose,' he used to say, 'hit the enemy anywhere you like—but *not* where he expects it, and above all not on ground of his choosing.' We know the barbarian force intends to seize this fort in your frontier defenses, and you propose to meet and fight them there. Wrong, if I may say so!"

The kings gazed wisely at the map, nodding their heads in agreement, though unable to divine what considerations led this soldier to draw such a conclusion. Most had been unable to understand a word, speaking as they did only the pure tongue of the Brython, and each preparing an eloquent speech of rejoinder during the time the monk translated. However, it was clear the stranger was all for some hard fighting one way or the other, and the manner of it was for King Maelgun and his counselors to decide between them. It would be a summer when kites and crows would gorge their fill of blood, and men had good reason to wax merry now over their mead-horns. Rufinus resumed his address, which I will summarize briefly here, since you will see in due course how the fighting went. Also, as is customarily the case, not everything went according to plan.

Rufinus insisted, in short, that the plan propounded by Maeldaf was good in its essentials. However, it was vital not to stand upon the frontier, as Gereint had urged, but to seek out the enemy and bring him to decisive battle on terms and ground of our own choosing. As had been noted, there were two roads leading out of Loiger: that passing by the threatened fortress of Dineirth, and that blocked by the impregnable walls of Caer Vydei. Let Run and Elffin reinforce the former without delay, as suggested: It was vital the enemy should be unable to turn our flank, which would assuredly be the case were they to arrive there first.

Meanwhile, the main army, proceeding by forced marches, should direct its march toward Caer Vydei. Masked by the city, beyond which the enemy could not advance, its approach might hope to pass unmarked. The king could there conveniently marshal his forces, and then march with all haste upon the barbarians' capital. Then one of two things might reasonably be expected to happen. Either Ceawlin would return to defend the seat of his power, or (less likely) he would proceed to besiege Dineirth. Whichever he chose, the army would swiftly be enabled to bring him to battle in open field.

"Do not imagine I speak from inexperience," Rufinus concluded. "For long years I held a command on the Roman frontier in Africa, after the reconquest, and so I know much of what passed there even before my time of service. No summer passed without an attack by our enemies, who greatly outnumbered us. Despite this, our generals Belisarius and Solomon mounted expedition after expedition, harrying the tribesmen and gaining victory over them in battle on numerous occasions. Then, in an evil hour, the emperor appointed as our commander his nephew Sergius as master of soldiers in Africa. *His* policy was that of defending the frontiers, never venturing to seek out the enemy beyond. Thus it was they who decided the place and timing of attack, with disastrous results.

"Matters were not remedied until John Troglita took over the command. The soldiers knew and admired him, for he had held command under Belisarius and Solomon. They knew they would soon see action—which they did, as much and more than they desired. You will know what was the outcome: the glorious victory of the Fields of Cato, where King Carcasan and sixteen kings of the Mauri fell."

Rufinus paused, and I noted the quick glance he directed at his audience. The brief murmur of discussion which arose was clearly one of approval. The power of the emperor of the Rufeinieid was equally over the center of the world and over the islands of the east and the west, so that everything which passed in the world became known in due course to his judges and counselors and commanders of his armies. Besides, the kings desired a great battle, one which would live forever in the mouths of bards and storytellers; not a series of inglorious skirmishes along the line of dykes.

Sensing his advantage, Rufinus concluded with these words: "I am told that the fortified *limes* which lie between your kingdoms and those of the barbarians were constructed by that Artorius whose fame spread even to the court of the emperor in Byzantium. He corresponded, as I know, with my master the count Belisarius before the siege of Rufein, undertaking to conduct a campaign in Armorica against the Franks, to prevent their king from coming to the aid of Witigis. As I understand it, the policy of Artorius was never to rest upon the earthworks his engineers erected as a barrier between your people and the barbarians, but to harry them far within their own territory. If Artorius was your Belisarius, then it seems to me that it is you, O king, who will be a John Troglita, whose strategy will recover the fortunes of your people and the Empire. Such at any rate is my advice, which you may heed or not as you wish: Do not rely on ramparts and forts, however strongly constructed, but on the spears and swords of your soldiers. Pursue your enemy, give him no rest, and hunt him down until he is compelled to give you battle!"

The kings murmured among themselves, uncertain whether this advice should be heeded or not, looking ever to Maelgun to decide. For myself, I glanced from beneath my cowl at Maeldaf the elder. It was he, I guessed, who had devised the ingenious plan approved by Maelgun, and I wished to see whether he resented the counterproposal of Rufinus. He, however, remained silent, smiling quietly and looking like the others to Maelgun Gwynedd for judgment.

Maelgun the Tall pondered a little, before addressing himself to the council.

"What think you, princes of the Brython?" he inquired after this pause, looking about him at the expectant faces. "Do we strengthen that mighty barrier, which Arthur bequeathed to us and which has penned in the heathen for more than a generation? Or do we advance our host into the heart of his lands, venturing all on the field of battle?"

Many voices were at once raised in disputatious outcry. Run and Elffin were all for flinging themselves upon the foe without further consideration. Gereint of Dyfneint proposed a strengthening of the frontier, coupled with a raid by his fleet upon the Island of Weith. Rufinus referred to strategic errors committed by the Imperial general Narses, following his victory over the Goths at Mons Lactarius. It was at length Cynlas of Ros, Rider of the Chariot of the Bear, whose wisdom was respected by all and who had as yet said nothing, who rose and spoke his mind before the assembled kings.

"Noble princes of the Brython," he began in measured tones, "allow me to suggest that this foreigner has the right of it. Our dykes and forts are strong, and wise was the emperor Arthur when he marked them out after the memorable victory of Din Badon. But stronger than ramparts in our defense was the renown of Arthur, and it is my belief that it was dread of him which held the wily Ceredig and (in these our days) his son Cynurig in check. Then, after the slaughter of Camlann, when Arthur was slain, it was the plague that came to ravage the heathen.

"Now, however, Arthur and the plague have departed, and it seems to me that sooner or later the heathen Iwys will seek an opportunity to ravage the Island of the Mighty as they did in the time of Gurtheyrn the Thin, when once again the savage fire of their vengeance will lick the Western Sea with its fiery tongue.

"Walls are strong, but never so strong that they cannot be breached when those within have the choosing of where and when to breach them. Only recall the prison constructed by Bran the Blessed, in which he shut up the giant Lassar Laes Gyfnewid together with his monstrous wife, Cymidei Cymeinfoll. He summoned all the blacksmiths that were in Ywerdon in those days, and all the owners of tongs and hammers, and they piled coal high as the chamber of iron which they constructed. Then were food and drink served to the woman, her husband, and the hideous brood to which she had given birth. When it was seen that they were drunk, then was a fire kindled about the house, and men blew upon bellows—one man to each two bellows—and the bellows blew until the chamber was white-hot about those that lay within. And then did Lassar Laes Gyfnewid and his family awake and take counsel in the midst of the chamber. And the result of that counsel was that the giant waited until the walls were white with heat, and he charged the wall with his shoulder and shattered it, escaping with his wife.

"The storytellers say that the monstrous pair came to the Island of the Mighty, giving birth to a new generation of children with yellowish-red hair, who made themselves loathed throughout the Island, insulting, molesting, and defiling noble men and women. It is in my thought that it was from among those children that the heathen tribe of the Iwys arose; for they, as we know, have hair upon them which is yellowish-red. Be that as it may, it is to be seen that not even Bran's iron wall could contain the giant brood. It were better to have entered the chamber and slain the giant and his wife, sleeping or waking."

Uttering these measured words, Cynlas of Ros resumed his couch and was silent once more. All but one of those present approved the tale and advice of Cynlas. Maeldaf the elder alone spoke against them, but briefly and moderately. He reminded the council of the Prophecy of the Dragons before Gurtheyrn the Thin, foretelling that the White Dragon would extend its ravages over the Island of Prydein for a hundred and fifty years. The hundred and fifty years being not yet passed, it were better to contain them in the manner he suggested, rather than risk the Monarchy of Prydein in an unpropitious battle.

But the kings had heard before the prophecy of Gurtheyrn, and it was a matter of argument whether or not a hundred and fifty years had passed since its revelation. They preferred the tale told by Cynlas of sea-girt Ros, wise son of Owen the White-toothed. They would follow the advice of Rufinus, who seemed a warrior of wide experience and favored by Maelgun Gwynedd.

The great king accordingly gave orders that the princes Run and Elffin should muster their war-bands without delay, so that when the time came they should ride night and day without resting to hold Dineirth before the host of Ceawlin might appear before the stronghold. Meantime, the hundred thousand men of the host of the Brython would, with what speed they could command, march to Caer Vydei, upon whose walls floated the banner of Einion mab Run mab Nuithon. There would they hold a mustering, and then go forth to sack the halls of Ceawlin and bring his soldiers to battle.

The matter settled, King Brochfael's steward was summoned to guide the kings back to his *palestr,* where that night's feasting was to take place. The kings departed, exultant and triumphant, leaving me and Maeldaf the elder alone in the council chamber. We sat for long in silence, pondering the *gwyddbwyll* board. At one point Maeldaf's hand strayed forward as if to move a piece, hovered a moment above the board, and then withdrew.

"What think you, Maeldaf?" I inquired. "It has to be said that the king has adopted the counsel of the stranger, rather than that which you proffered."

Maeldaf rose to depart. "There are many counsels a man may give," he replied equably. "I have one; the stranger whom the waves cast up upon the coast of Dyfneint has another. Think you he is to be trusted?"

I made no reply, nor did I raise my eye from the king upon the board "Fair-head."

"All I have to say is this," concluded Maeldaf: "When the hosts of the Brython and those of the Iwys meet in battle, King Maelgun should not be there. We have heard the Prophecy of the Dragons which was delivered at the Center of the Island. Should the Dragon of Mon chance to be slain, then will there be an end of the Monarchy of Prydein."

With which he, too, departed.

I did not join the kings and nobles at their feasting that evening. My mind was deeply troubled. The room darkened, and the *gwyddbwyll* board seemed gradually to gleam silver, floating before me in the obscurity. So must the world have appeared at its beginning, when Gwydion's wand gathered its elements together from the surrounding chaos, Gofannon mab Don fashioned within his white-hot furnace the bright firmament on high, and Leu with his Sure Arm made an enclosure that fenced out the formless Hosts of Annufn. That was before he set the king in his Center with protective pieces disposed about him. The sky had likewise been an empty *gwyddbwyll* board, black as the wing of a crow, until it, too, was given its bright Center and glittering pieces set in a revolving household.

Now that an ordered space had been set in the midst of the turbulence, it became necessary to play out the dread game which would preserve it from being swallowed up once more by the Hosts of Annufn that compass it about: the Witch of Ystafengun, the swarms of the Coranieid, the Adanc of the Deep. Twice every day since the beginning of the world are the white-maned steeds of Manawydan mab Lir hurled in fury against the rocky cliffs of the Island of Prydein and its Three Adjacent Islands. And it is twice a year, at the Kalan Mai and the Kalan Gaeaf, that the king of the Island of the Mighty musters the flower of the warriors of Prydein about him, and the best of the war-bands of Prydein, each encircling the other about the king in the midst, without and within, and the king and the queen in the middle of the house, and the courts locked. It is in this manner that they await the approach of those who gather about the shadowed margins of the world.

Now it appeared to me that the board before me bore an ugly aspect, and that rather than the name "Fair-head" there was that about it which brought to mind the unchancy *gwyddbwyll* board of the Black Man of Ysbidinongyl, which was cast into the lake that lies about the Castle of Wonders. The half-light that was in the chamber came and went with the chasing of clouds before the moon, and silence descended upon the banqueting hall of King Brochfael of the Tusks in the *palestr* beyond the courtyard, as every king and prince assembled, each with his war-band, about the seat of King Maelgun the Tall, son of Cadwallon of the Long Hand.

What with the gloom, and the pain of my eye, and the shifting of shadows, it seemed to me that the pieces of the *gwyddbwyll* board made play of their own accord. The king had moved outward to the north-eastern corner, to the edge of the enclosure. I saw that the piece that should have protected him from his assailants appeared now of their coloring, and that a check had been placed upon the king. It was bitter cold in the empty chamber and I trembled, drawing my cloak closer about me.

How long I sat thus musing in the watches of the night, I know not. The arguments we had heard presented themselves in turn before my inward eye, and it was hard for me to see the safe path. For in truth there was no path that was safe. Talk of Arthur brought to my mind the tale they tell in the North of his expedition to the cave of the Witch Ordd, daughter of the Witch Orwen, of Penn Nant Gofud in the backlands of Uffern.

With his company he arrived at the mouth of that cave, which I have since seen with my own eyes. Halted before its dark and dismal entrance, Arthur's men disputed long as to what should be done. For this much was known: that there were chambers within the cave, one leading to another. Would the hag be in this one, or in that one? Were the monstrous whelps of her brood at home, or abroad scavenging about the land of Prydyn?

At last Cacamuri and his brother Hygwyd entered the cave stealth-

ily and cautiously, not wishing to blunder into a snare. In the fetid air
about them lingered smells dank, reeking, tainted; and their feet
slipped upon rotting remnants of the hell-hag's prey. There in the
pitch darkness they heard her low laugh behind them, where she lay
concealed in a cleft of the rock. Then they turned upon her, but she
had the advantage of them. She seized Hygwyd's hair in her taloned
grasp and threw him upon the ground. And when Cacamuri came to
his brother's aid, she gripped him, too, and between them both they
returned to Arthur bloodied and bruised and torn.

Seeing this, Amren and Eiddil the Tall drew their swords and
dashed forward boldly into the black chasm, hoping to give the witch
no time to recover from her combat with Cacamuri and Hygwyd.
They fared no better, but worse; for they blundered into a snare which
the sorceress had set for them, and she took them and flayed the skin
from their bodies, sucked the blood from their veins, and licked out
the brains from their skulls.

It seemed to me that the land of the Iwys beyond the frontiers of
Prydein was just such a cave, and it was as hard to know what we
might encounter upon entering it. Should we fence its mouth about
and wait for the cave dweller to emerge; should we make our way
within by caution and stealth; or should we advance boldly forward,
spear and sword in hand, to its innermost recesses? Each of these
courses had been suggested at the council of the kings, and each
possessed its dangers and advantages.

Difficult it was to decide between these measures, so long as the
interior of the cave remained in obscurity. The Island of the Mighty did
not lack for fierce, rash, active princes; bears in the trackway, reapers
like leeks in battle, who made of biers a necessity—as my friend
Taliesin put it in his songs. It was not for want of courage that we
would gain the victory, if victory were indeed to be ours. But for my
part, when it came down to it, I laid great store by the presence of a
warrior such as was this foreigner, Rufinus. Were matters by some ill
chance to fare badly with the host of Maelgun Gwynedd, then I felt we
possessed a cool head among us of which we might well have need.
With this consolatory thought I abandoned my reflections with a sigh
of lingering misgiving.

At this there came a dry laugh in the darkness, and from all about
me in the enclosing murk came squealings and mutterings and scrap-
ings beyond reckoning, as if it had been the mice that stripped
Manawydan's fields in Arberth. Then I knew I had to deal with Gwyn
mab Nud and his following, and laughed myself. We were at the
same *gwyddbwyll*-playing that I had watched on Nos Kalan Gaeaf

in the hall of Gwydno Garanhir in the North. I saw, too, that the deceiver was up to his old mischief, and under cover of the failing light would very likely attempt to place a fog of deception before my eyes.

However, I resolved to outwit Gwyn mab Nud, employing no unusual powers, neither spells of druids, smiths, nor women. The Lord of the Wild Hunt guessed my thought, and laughed mockingly again.

"I have your king in check, O Merlin son of Morfryn!"

Not so, I thought fiercely. But a moment earlier the king had been safe enough, and the pieces skulking on the board's fringes held convincingly at bay. My mind raced with the swiftest of all created things: thought. But study the board as I would, I could see no move the king could make to save himself, nor yet a supporting peg to intervene between him and the forces that threatened him.

Gwyn mab Nud divined my thought, his laughter gathering, echoing, resounding in the caverns of my skull. A nauseous stench filled the room, causing my brain to reel and totter. The demon was squatting and defecating somewhere in a corner upon the rushes of the floor, while the swart imps of his following swarmed about my body in the shape of vermin and parasites of every kind. As I writhed upon my seat I began to long desperately for fresh air and purifying water. All about me was a thick-shadowed miasma of decay and corruption. It was almost impossible to breathe, for now my tormentor was, as I could hear, vigorously urinating in successive corners of the room.

While my body and all about began to twist and turn and swim, I continued to stare with all the concentration at my command at the king and his neighboring piece. How could the game have reached so swift and unwarranted an end? A waft of fetid breath gusted hot upon my cheek, and I felt my adversary close beside me.

"I have been where Bran was slain,
Far across the western main,"

sniggered a voice at my ear. I declined to be distracted by this dog-gerel, or by the ludicrous malpractices of his obscene crew, and bent my mind to close out all but the one problem from my mind.

But try as I would, I found the doggerel distich drumming in my head, repeating itself over and over again as I feverishly considered moves the king's attendant pieces might make. What had our game to do with Bran, or Bran's death? Maelgun's kingdom of Gwynedd was also known as the Land of Bran, and the god was believed to have made his home somewhere among the white-topped mountains of rugged Eryri. But were Maelgun to die in battle with the Iwys, it would not be in his rocky homeland, but somewhere in the green south country. Bran in any case had died in far-off Ywerdon, across the blue-green Western Sea. Perhaps the demon huntsman (oh, the lice! their bites would drive me crazy before long) was referring to the manner of the king's death? How had Bran died? I fumbled desperately to recall the story. Worms or small snakes were, I felt certain, creeping about my thigh—doubtless to distract me. Distract me they assuredly did, with their twining and slithering and nipping upon my white thigh. My thigh! It was through his thigh that Bran had received the fatal wound that treachery had inflicted upon him. Yes, treachery.

Why treachery? . . . Ah, but I had it now! *Treachery* had lain Bran low in Ywerdon, and I saw now it was treachery that had manipulated matters upon the *gwyddbwyll* board. Who had played the last move, before Gwyn mab Nud had entered the game? Maelgun the Tall or Maeldaf the elder? No matter now; the game had not been played fair, of that I was now certain. No defending player—Maelgun, Maeldaf, Rufinus, or anyone—could have permitted a hostile piece to come so near the king unopposed.

Now I recalled the game as it had been set during our council: The piece next the king had been his own. It had been changed for another!

"Treachery!" I cried aloud in triumph. "There has been deception and lying and falsehood, and the game is no more!"

A screaming and gibbering and groaning broke out all around me such as I had never heard before or am like to again, but it was nothing to me. With a shout of triumph I seized the false piece, and flung it to the farthest corner of the room. All was at once plunged into utter darkness, *Afagddu*, as the moonlit rectangle of the window was blotted out by a gush of distorted figures, winged, hoofed, and horned in indiscriminate profusion. Squeaking and spitting in anger, breaking wind each in the other's face, beating leathern wings in desperation to be away, they were gone almost before I could collect my thoughts. I ran to the window and gazed out. Above the moonlit rooftops and turrets of Caer Gurygon, I saw them spiral northward like a stream of bees at swarming.

Nauseated by the stench and filth left behind by my persecutors, I flung open the door and tottered down the stairway. From the *palestr* came joyous shouts and bursts of song, but my need was for fresh air and thought. Wandering through the empty streets, I came upon the eastern gateway of the city. The guards were drunk or asleep, or at any rate did not see me as I passed by.

In this way I departed from the city of Caer Gurygon, with its purple-clad kings, its fierce warriors in their blue armor, its judges and priests and cunning gold-merchants, its bakeries, smithies and marketplace. Behind me now were stone-dressed palaces, buttressed towers and gateways, and ordered streets crossing each other straight and true as planks after skilled wrights in noisy yards have divided and smoothed the gnarled, writhing trunks of oak and elm dragged by paired teams of oxen from dark forest groves.

There was a moment when the bright lanterns at the gateway blinded my gaze, so that the landscape without was obscured from my view: a well of darkness, jagged by dizzying images of light that dazzled my single eye and confused my weary brain. But as I struck out off the broad highway across the neighboring meadowland, leaving the light behind me, I swiftly became accustomed to the night, glimpsing about me still shapes of trees and cattle, floating above a rising evening mist; while ahead of me, thrusting its great head somber among the stars, loomed the peak bright-knolled beyond all hills, with its hilltop round and gray and rugged: Dinleu Gurygon.

CHAPTER NINE

THE CONVERSATION
OF MERLIN WITH
THE TRIBUNE

I had fled from Caer Gurygon in a state of agitation amounting almost to frenzy. I felt near to the end of my tether, blundering onward as if as drunken as the kings at their feasting. It was a still, warm evening, with low swathes of mist hanging among the meadows. From them trees emerged gauntly at irregular intervals, while all about stood cattle without motion in the fog, like a flotilla of coracles on a still, moonlit ocean. There was no noise, save afar off it seemed to me I heard the faint plopping of fish breaking the heavy surface of the swollen River Hafren. Up from the wellsprings of my mind floated the memory of a long summer's day I would enjoy as respite from my torments, passed half sleeping in my delightful orchard beyond Run, apples dropping one by one into the long grass about my refuge.

After stumbling across open ground for a considerable time beneath the moon, I found myself at the foot of the steep side of the sacred hill Dinleu. My purpose was to ascend the height upon whose summit lay that broad green enclosure where the mysteries had been enacted by king and druids the previous day. There was no time to be lost, and without looking about me for a path I began to scramble up the steep ascent that rose above me.

At first there was little difficulty, though much effort, in trudging up the bracken-covered slope, dead stalks snapping beneath my feet. But as I began to draw nearer the summit, the walk became a climb, and I was glad of the moonlight which enabled me to espy rocks and branches upon which I could obtain purchase and grasping.

I was compelled to move more slowly by reason of the difficulty, and this with the invigorating night air served a little to recover my scattered wits and depleted strength. Without desisting from my efforts, I was enabled gradually to reflect upon my predicament and purpose. There were frequent moments when I was obliged to pause and contemplate which of several difficult courses I might pursue. As I did so, plunged in a medley of confused reveries, I thought from time to time I could detect the steps of one who followed furtively in my track. Once or twice I halted abruptly and gazed below me, but neither sight nor sound betrayed the presence of another living being upon the sheer hillside.

The upland air increasingly revived me, and eventually I paused a moment to look below at the city. There it lay, a tiny cluster of twinkling light, a glowworm beside the serpentine length of shining Hafren, as she wound her sinuous curves through the fertile plain. There is no river more holy, *glanos,* in all Prydein, to my mind. She rises from the breast of gray Pumlumon, upon whose peak is perched the cairn Guilathir where Cai and Beduir played out their game of *gwyddbwyll* in the greatest wind that was in the world. It was then that they saw the column of smoke that hung without movement in the gale far off in the south.

From her spring upon Pumlumon the goddess tumbles foaming through mountain passes, and dropping headlong in cataracts, until at length she emerges into the kingdom of Powys, the Paradise of Prydein. Full-bellied and wanton, she glides through lush orchards and verdant pastures until at long last she passes under the bridges of the Shining City, Caer Loyw, where Mabon mab Modron has lain imprisoned since being taken from his mother when but three days old. But the loud-voiced, rippling, crested wave, gray flood with a splendid voice, does not pause for all Mabon's dreadful groaning, for before her lies the Battle of the Two Kings of Hafren. The shining river meets tide of the sea, with its great fishes and porpoises and fierce sea otters, and there the two kings rush raging upon each other in masses of spray, colliding like fighting rams, recoiling and falling back to the onslaught more furious still. This have they done from the beginning of the world until this day.

Finally, as the battle subsides, the broad river flows into the broad-bosomed Sea of Hafren, a myriad sea birds singing overhead, the monsters of ocean plunging in delight, while watching over all sits

Nud of the Silver Arm, his trident of guidance in his Silver Hand, within his temple upon the hill in the fair land of Gwent.

And that is the road which all men traverse: at their begetting welling up out of the dark Abyss of Annufn into the clear, cold dawn; now pursuing a course rocky, turbulent, dangerous; now idling through days of ease and comfort, lounging purple-clad in the brightly lit courts of kings; now departing with the green dawn to rampart, ford, or triple-fossed fortress, where spears are splintered and shields shattered, and ravens gather above corpses.

Finally, after the time of strife, we are borne out onto the boundless swell of ocean, guided by the trident of Nud, passing through crystalline gates into the four-cornered fortress of Caer Sidi. And there, as Manawydan and Pryderi learned, are found neither the afflictions of sickness nor age. About its peaks flow the streams of Ocean, and above is a fountain from which cascades water sweeter than white wine. Within the gates is a tree whose branches are burdened almost to the ground with apples of eternal youth, while beyond lie green meadows spangled with flowers more numerous than clustered stars in Caer Gwydion. Cushioned upon soft mosses, young men and maidens are caressed by warm breezes wafting music from Hafgan's three organs. Wandering among golden buttercups by trickling rivulets, they hear among the rushes the singing of the Birds of Riannon, and the music of the spheres played by warm winds upon the seven strings of the Harp of Teirtu.

It is a long and hard journey, beset by many a trial and torment, before we gain that blessed haven. And yet how strange it is, I have often thought, that the wellspring of the river gushes forth within sight of the golden ocean, smell of the salt sea spray, and sound of crying gulls. Like the shimmering course of Caer Gwydion in the heavens, the young river may not join the bourne to which it lies so near, but must traverse a great arc through light and shadow, until it returns to the point from whence it came. I have in my time sat upon the cairn Guilathir gazing out upon the Western Sea, and have spied amid the horizon haze the Island of Gwales. To my thought it was but a salmon's leaping; but to attain it I knew full well that I must set my back to the sea, and follow the tortuous course of Hafren for many a weary year's struggle.

My spirit was troubled by these reflexions, bringing me to a pause upon the last shoulder of the hill before gaining the summit. As I did so, I heard once more what I became certain was the sound of a footfall below me, halting even as mine halted. Immediately ahead lay a rugged outcrop of lichened crags, sheltered by a cluster of yews clinging precariously to the rough flank of the hill. Without glancing back or altering my tread, I made as if to clamber past them, then sank back into a cleft between two rocks.

There I lay, grateful for the thought that the wind which ever gusted against the hill, pinning me to my precarious sanctuary, effectively drowned the sound of my own poor gasps of exhaustion. It was but a moment, I feared, but I derived respite from my brief haven, held as I was against the wall of the world by the greatest wind that was in the world.

Across the shaking treetops I could glimpse a section of silvered level land about the city of Caer Gurygon. Clouds hurrying overhead intermittently extinguished a reflected shimmer of dew-ponds puddling the plain about the languorous length of Hafren. But there was a line of hills lying distant on the western skyline which loomed menacing to my mind as a suspended breaker. It was in all a peaceful, majestic spectacle, yet my heart palpitated with fear. Below me to my right wound up the track upon which I had ascended, and by which another than myself was approaching fast. I shrank back into my crevice; so fast that the sharp rock-face bruised my back. It was impossible not to think of Ifor's daughter, upon whose precinct I now lay pinioned.

I was right: Someone was hastening up the track that wound toward me through the shadowed yew grove; someone cautious not to be detected, but anxious not to lose me. A dim shadow loomed close beside, peering about among the rocks in which I was ensconced, and made as if to press on. It flashed into my mind that my pursuer might be Maeldaf the elder, King Maelgun's druid. For who but he who knew the rites of entry would dare to intrude upon the *clas* of Leu alone and in darkness?

I decided to reveal myself, to discover who was my rash companion upon the bare hilltop. That the stranger was aware of my presence was certain, for had I not paused two or three times, and that against the eastern sky?

"Do you wish to converse with me, friend?" I cried after him, skulking still within my recess. I had laid my hand upon a knife I kept beneath my cloak, for Nos Kalan Mai is an unchancy night to be abroad, and as every man knows, it is cold iron that provides protection from the Fair Folk.

I heard a muttered exclamation, and then the sound of returning footsteps. A moment later a figure stood before me, enshrouded like myself in long cloak and hood. His face was in shadow, but I caught the glint of his eyes as he peered among the heap of rocks.

"Where is he?" muttered the stranger, with a movement of his shoulders which I took to imply the laying of hand upon sword or knife.

"I am here!" replied I, stepping forward with a smile.

The other started back a step, swiftly recovering himself. I could see that he knew me, and I had recognized him the moment I heard him speak. He was the emperor's officer, Rufinus, who had spoken so eloquently at the kings' council.

"You are there, then," he muttered. "Just where I looked. Were you inside the rock, or have you a cloak of invisibility?"

I laughed, and seated myself on the edge of a grassy bank. Rufinus came a step nearer.

"Are you the wise man they call Merlin, who came with Prince Elffin from the North?" he inquired.

"I know not if I be wise," answered I, "but I am Merlin son of Morfryn, a friend to the prince Elffin. How may I help you, on Dinleu at the Nos Kalan Mai?"

Rufinus came and sat beside me, turning back his hood so that I could distinguish his long nose and bald head.

"Time and again have I been obliged to join in the feasting of federate kings," he grumbled, "and never once that I remember have my liver and head been in good order when I rose next morning. I was proceeding to my quarters as soon as I could decently do so, when you passed me in the street. I will tell you directly that I became suspicious, and decided to see what you were up to. Security is extremely lax here, in my view, and it is vital the enemy should not discover the true course of our march. The plan which I put forward, and which the king seems likely to adopt, depends for its success on total secrecy."

"Why did you not tell the guards at the gate to stop me, then?" asked I. There was time enough for what lay before me on the hilltop, and I was curious to know more about this foreigner, who was clearly familiar with distant countries and events of which I would have liked to learn more. It also amused me to learn his views upon the affairs of the Island of Prydein and its proud kings.

Rufinus shook his head. "You must know that I have no authority within the camp," he explained. "I am accustomed to dealing with barb . . . federates. That was in Africa. They can make excellent soldiers, it is true; but of discipline they know nothing. It is all a question of tact, and God knows that is something of which long experience has given me a bellyful."

The unhappy man groaned, gesturing with his hand at the windy expanse of yellowed grass and dead bracken upon the slope about us.

"You turn out to inspect a unit on the parade ground. Ten to one it's a shambles: ragged marching, tarnished armor, ungreased boots. I'm talking about your Huns and Heruls, by the way; not these people here, whom I haven't got to know yet. They lumber past you, grinning all over their unwashed faces, while all you long for is the power to reduce the officers to the ranks, or turn them over to the navy; and discharge every tenth man—or at least confine them to the *praetorium* and deduct their pay for a month. I expect you're wondering about drill? Well may you wonder! I've often asked what we could have made of them if they'd been licked into shape by old Albinus, my *campidoctor* when I commanded *real* soldiers under John the Armenian. Well, you can guess, I suppose: They'd have lynched him the moment he set foot on the parade ground."

Rufinus was looking away from me now, across toward the dim outline of the mountains in the west. His thoughts were absent, and it sprang into my mind that, for all his harsh words, at this moment he wished himself back wherever he had been in Africa. His speech was directed more to the air than to me, though I guessed I was the first person to whom he had felt able to unburden himself for some considerable time.

"But what can you do?" he was grumbling, turning his face back to mine in the obscurity. "They serve only their kings and nobles, whom they regard as gods. In any case how do you fine an insubordinate soldier in a province which has abandoned the use of money? As for corporal punishment: Just let me raise my vine-staff to one of them, and his brothers and cousins and foster-brothers and foster-cousins and whatnot will cut the ropes of my tent at night and stick one of their long knives through me. No, I can tell you I have learned things the hard way. Still, I'm here to tell the tale, which is more than one can say for most of us who landed in Africa with the count Belisarius."

I leaned back against my rock, for I was still weakened by the sufferings I had encountered on my journey from the North, and the ascent of the steep hill had left me breathless and a little giddy. Though I had clambered up here to be alone, I was glad to talk for a little with this stranger. His tale intrigued me. There was a directness and matter-of-factness about him which set him apart from the men of Prydein, closely linked as they are by ties of blood and fosterage, and by common descent from Prydein, son of Aed the Great, and Don, the mother of Gwydion.

"What brought you to the Island of Prydein?" I inquired. "King Gereint mab Erbin told the council you passed the winter at his court, but he revealed nothing of the reasons that led you to cast in your lot with strangers in a land so far from your own."

The other glanced at me, as if surprised at my interest. "You are a strange fellow!" he remarked bluntly. "I noticed you at the king's council, and thought to myself: 'He knows more than he's telling, or there's something on his mind.' They are odd folk here in Britannia, scarcely Roman at all, for all their priests and the king's speaking Latin. Well, since you ask me, I will tell you. I never asked to come to this country, and to tell the truth I wish at this moment I never had done. I'm a soldier, and there's fighting to be done. But I can't see that it's going to be my kind of soldiering, which is unlikely to be of great use in some rough-and-tumble scrimmage between two yelping bands of barbarians. You must excuse my frankness, but I have had a troublesome past few days in the council chamber."

"Don't mind me," I replied in the same candid vein. "I am a stranger here too. I am Merlin, son of Morfryn, and I also am *alltud*, belonging to no tribe. Besides, I am possessed of an inveterate curiosity, and like to know all that is happening. Tell me, please, of your journey here. Were you taken by pirates of the Gwyddeliod or the Fichti, or were you wrecked upon the shores of Dyfneint?"

"I will tell you," replied Rufinus. "I was not wrecked, but sailed here on a ship bringing wine from Carthago to a port on the southern coast of Britannia. It was the last ship of the season, the merchant informed me, so I suppose I can count myself lucky."

"You came all the way from Africa, freely on a merchant's vessel? That is no short voyage. You came of your own accord, it seems, and yet you are discontented! Pray explain yourself, my friend."

"I did not say that *I* came from Africa," rejoined my companion brusquely. "The ship did, and I joined it when it put in at Malaca. I only needed to be taken across the Straits to my old base in Septem, but as we drew near, the captain took fright at two or three sail he spotted coming behind us. He swore they were pirates or Visigoths, and when I told him he'd be safe enough in the harbor at Septem, he just said he had no time to lose if he was to deliver his cargo, which as it appeared was the last of the season. I offered him all the money I had to set me down at Gades once we were safely through the Straits of Hercules, but he wouldn't allow that either. (Actually I don't blame him; all I had with me were the solidi we use to pay barbarian federates, and of no value in his line of business.) Besides, he said, he was late with his cargo, and had no intention of being caught by autumn gales in the Cantabrian Sea. So we sailed right past Gades, where I saw the light of its *pharos* shining out as near as that town down there. If I ever get back to Septem, and that pigheaded captain puts in to my harbor again, I'll see to it the customs keep him there for six months at least—or maybe as long as I'm to be stuck on this Godforsaken island."

I smiled at his vehemence. "Well, it seems to me that you will not have so long to wait now. The spring has come, and many ships ply the sea between here and Gaul. Perhaps you can accompany the merchant, Samo, who addressed us all in the council chamber. I presume he, too, will wish to attend to business at home now the winter storms are over."

The officer grimaced and shook his head. "It might be that his king in Paris would take it into his head (if they have anything under their long hair) to sell me to his cousins in Hispania, and that would provide a distinctly unhealthy prospect for me—in all likelihood, not to put too fine a point upon it, an abrupt end to the promising career of Rufinus Festius, lately tribune of Septem. Have you in Britannia heard anything of the present war the emperor is waging in Hispania?"

I shook my head, upon which he continued his story, glad at last (I flatter myself) to find someone prepared to listen and understand.

"As you heard me say in the council," he explained, "my name is Rufinus Festius. I have no wealth beyond my pay, though I come, if I may say so, of a family nobler by far than any of those proud barbarians drinking themselves silly down there. The villa where I was born had belonged to the Rufii Festi since the time of Septimius Severus. So my father used to say, and *he* was urban prefect of Rome. It was a great villa then, though for all I know a ruin now—or housing some beer-swilling Goth with his bandit followers.

"We had Gothic troops quartered on our estate then, of course; but that was in the days of King Theodoric, who maintained Roman order and treated my father in his prefecture as though the Empire still stood in the West. Our villa was only twenty miles from Rome: in the Ager Veientanus, between the Via Clodia and Lake Sabatinus. There was a tower window from which on a clear day you could see the red roofs of the city. I used to climb up there and spend hours looking southward beyond the blue-gray belt of olives that marked the boundary of our estate, to where the silent stream of traffic wound along the Via Clodia.

"It was from there, too, that I would watch each morning as the cavalry escort came to accompany my father to the Palace of the Prefecture. I believe he had a thousand officials working under him there. My mother said it was two thousand, but then, she was given to exaggerating these things.

"Then, when I was six and too big to continue under a tutor, I went to school in Rome—one of those by the porticoes of the Forum. Homer and Menander, Virgil and Statius—you know what it's like. Sallust was the only one who stuck in my mind, though, for it was the story of Rome's wars that gripped me from the beginning. My pedagogue and I were allowed to travel with my father in his carriage each morning to the city. Once or twice we were held up by the traffic, and he set us down right by the class in the street. That wasn't bad for my prestige, I can tell you! I liked my school, but I preferred it at home, especially in the summer holidays. Nearly four months at home! I formed the children of our slaves into a legion, and at the end of one holiday, I remember, we made war against the Gothic children who lived on our estate. My father put a swift stop to that when he found out; I can see why now.

"He always wanted me to be a soldier, though, from the beginning. In those days the Roman army had ceased to exist; the only soldiers you saw were Goths and federates. But my father used to smile and say that, as Rome was immortal, so must there always be a Roman army. I was not to believe that things would always be as they appeared.

"He used to play with me in the evenings, teaching me to lay ambushes in the olive groves, fighting with wooden swords and spears. He would tease me, I remember, calling me his 'little Goth.' There was one long summer, when his first term as prefect ended, when he and I made rival fleets of wooden boats which we floated in a huge cistern about half a mile from our villa. The water was low enough for us to wade about, and it was wonderfully cool in there, I remember—it was such a long, hot summer, and the cistern was high and vaulted, dark and damp.

"It was my father's practice to lose in all our combats, crying for mercy and holding the point of my wooden sword to his throat. With the boats, though, he played quite seriously, discussing tactics with me at length. He sank my little fleet at the end of a great battle, and landed his troops of clay soldiers on the rocky island we had heaped by my wall. I laughed and was happy, for though I knew my father was indulging me in allowing me the victory, I knew in my heart it was impossible that so great a man should be the loser.

"But then I noticed he was quite grim and serious. He sat down beside me upon the stones, and told me how one day a great fleet would indeed come from the East; that I would hear the tramp of the legions on the Via Clodia, and that the emperor would rule once more in Rome, with the Senate restored to its former powers. Though at first he was whispering this tale to me, I remember he became so excited that by the end his voice was echoing about the vaulted roof. The time had come, he swore, to end the domination of Italia and the Sacred City by a heretical Goth in royal insignia, who forsooth had acquired all the ornaments of the palace! I fancy he spoke more than he should of the hopes (or were they plans?) of the great Symmachus; whether he did or not, that of course was what it was all about.

"Afterwards, though, as we walked back through the garden, he told me to say nothing to my mother of what we had discussed. And as we passed into the *vestibulum,* he suddenly turned to me, earnestly urging me never to forget my favorite heroes, Horatius Cocles and Mutius Scaevola, who sacrificed themselves that Rome might be great and free.

"That evening, after our bath, we had supper in the oil-press room. That was always a treat. My father enjoyed listening to the farmhands cracking jokes at one another's expense. You would think, to see his cheerful face as he sat sharing their beans and onions and herrings, that he had never a serious thought in the world. But once, turning to him unexpectedly, I caught him gazing at me with a look both fond and sad. Was he thinking of my future, or his? I don't know. We neither of us said anything, but I knew he had been reflecting on our conversation in the cistern. Then he clapped me on the back and asked me in broad Etruscan (he was a wonderful mimic) how my pigs were fattening, and we all roared with laughter again."

"Then you enjoyed a happy childhood?" I murmured in response, after Rufinus had fallen silent for a space of time. I felt some envy, for I knew it would be long before I entered such a fair garden as that which this foreigner had known. But there was little enough elation in his expression, which, as I had remarked at the council meeting, was of a markedly pessimistic cast. Looking at him now, though, in the wan moonlight that lay upon our side of the hill of Dinleu, I decided that "pessimistic" was the wrong word. It was more that he appeared resigned to whatever fate might fling at him; resigned, but resolute and dourly determined to do his duty—whatever that might be.

Rufinus ignored my question, his gaze passing meditatively over the Vale of Hafren. The gray undulating landscape, remote and unformed, isolated us on the spot where we had paused, and I in my thoughts joined my companion within the cistern of his childhood. Water lapped faintly at its edges, and high above in the chill air hung the shadowed vault. Only through tiny chinks in the masonry could one be aware of the heat and golden light of the wider world without, its gorgeous burnished colorings and song of a thousand birds.

The soldier laughed shortly. "Yes. I don't know how many times my thoughts have flown back to that cistern. It was just a great concrete-and-brick water tank, but there were my father and me, and no outside world at all. You see, it was not long before I found out that the game we had played was no game at all, and it was to be my father who was the loser. Whether there really was a conspiracy or not I don't know. It was the time when Theodoric executed Symmachus and attacked the Senate. My father was too great a man to escape the fate of those around him. Theodoric was a virtuous king as barbarians go, but they say that my father's death was a very cruel one. My mother had the gossiping slave flogged, but not before I, too, had heard the tale. They bound a cord about his head . . . I don't know . . . My mother took us to our estate in Sicilia, and we lived there."

"What a terrible history. To lose such a father; and how must your mother have suffered!" I muttered awkwardly.

"Oh, as for that, I don't know that she did. She was very angry, as I recall, saying that he had no business to become involved in conspiracies against the government, and that he had ruined us all. Don't misunderstand me: My mother is a very fine woman, pious and virtuous. Perhaps she could not understand men; I don't know, as I never spent much time with her. She turned over much of the Sicilian villa to some monks, with whom as far as I could see she spent most of her day discussing the nature of the Trinity and other mysteries I've never been able to fathom.

"Like my father, I am a good Catholic. But Rome's greatness lay in a former age, and it seems to me that we have a duty to honor those powers which brought the whole world beneath the sway of the eagles. Neither my father nor any self-respecting senator would have dreamed of missing the July games in honor of Apollo, and what if disorderly women continue to be disciplined by the Wolf's Masks at the Lupercalia? I myself made my offering at the Twins' temple in Ostia before crossing the sea, and I cannot say that they brought me ill fortune. Still, these are not matters to bother a soldier's head; all he needs are his orders and his luck, and it seems to me that to invoke Christ and Minerva before a battle is but doubling one's chances of emerging safe at the end of the day.

"My mother saw how ignorant I was in these matters—as well as others, I fear—and sent me to school in Alexandria. I was to be a lawyer, so it was rhetoric and law for me. Naturally I was hopeless at both. 'Imagine you are Thetis lamenting over the body of her son Achilles, and deliver her funeral oration!' I couldn't do it, and that's a fact. Our master said I was too literal-minded, and I've no doubt he was right. I don't have the imagination with which you poets are so well stocked. I can tell you what use a king of the Mauri will make of a certain hilltop escarpment and lay my plans accordingly, but I can't think as he thinks. Someone told me he heard Count Belisarius say before the Battle of Ad Decimum that it was his habit to put himself in the enemy general's shoes, and then think his thoughts. I couldn't do that, which I suppose is why I reached the rank of tribune but will never be *magister militum*."

"It seems to me that you have a much more lively imagination than you think," I ventured gently. "I see your life unfolding before me as though I lived it myself: your villa, your father, the cistern . . . If you cannot, as you say, enter *my* mind, you have drawn me to enter *yours!* But if you studied law, how did you come to be a soldier? I cannot imagine the law possessing any great appeal for you."

"I hated it," replied the tribune shortly. "I did my best, because I knew my mother wanted it, and I suppose I wanted her to be proud of me. You should have heard my father talk away about literature at dinner! He could compose poetry to order, and sometimes even amused the guests afterwards by taking over the hydraulic organ and playing just as well as the slave whose task it was! Well, my mother sent money for my keep and tuition (she owned ships in the grain trade), but she never wrote to me. Mind you, the ships never arrived in Alexandria before May; and in any case I feel certain she must have been very busy with her monastery, for she is pious and much given to good works. Anyway, when I heard nothing for two years, I decided it could not matter that much to her what career I adopted; though doubtless she would be proud enough if I could only distinguish myself somehow. I knew that would never happen if I became a lawyer, so I joined the army.

"One of my fellow students, Apollos (he was an Alexandrian Greek of good family), bore a character the very opposite of mine. He was forever laughing, chattering, and up to as many tricks as a squirrel. He became bored with legal studies from the start, and in no time at all was caught up in the disorders of the colors. He was a fanatical supporter of the Blue faction in the Hippodrome, cutting his hair in the Hunnic fashion like all the rest, sporting their loose blue tunic, and so forth. The emperor himself is a Blue, of course, and we had the great Uranius driving for us then, so the Greens had something to grumble about! There was no charioteer like Uranius, not at least until old Porphyrius came out of retirement—but that's another story.

"You will laugh at an old man reminiscing over his youthful follies, and you are right. But we had fun in the Hippodrome in those days—and outside as well on occasion. As often as not, Apollos would return late at night boasting a black eye or cracked rib, after he and his drinking companions had run into a band of Greens in some unpoliced back street. Then he'd lie back on a couch with pretty Helladia sponging his wounds, sipping wine and telling us of scrapes which had us laughing till the tears ran down our cheeks.

"I was very taken by him from the first. He had a way of drawing you on one side, telling you a long tale with great gravity which entirely absorbed your attention—until all at once you saw that twinkle in his eye which betrayed the fact that all you had just heard was a string of complicated nonsense. He was a very different person from me in every way, but that side of him reminded me of my father. *He* was grave and awe-inspiring as Caesar himself, but with him, too, you never knew when he would not glance around with a half-smile and a joke that turned everything on its head.

"My father teased me and I think loved me because he was my father. But I could never quite understand what Apollos saw in me. As you will have noticed, I have no sense of humor at all. All my pleasure lies in making complex matters simple, and producing order where there was disorder. What is a joke but the misunderstood message which sets the parade ground in confusion? I suppose that is why my friend Apollos enjoyed my company; my solemnity was the perfect platform upon which he could set up his onager, discharging missiles at everyone who passed."

"It appears to me," I returned, "that you possess humor as well as imagination, and are not aware of either! You knew your role, which was as essential to your companion's pranks as is the platform to the onager—which I take to be some form of catapult?"

Rufinus paused, deep in exhumed memories. I found myself wondering at the littleness of our talk, floating alone in the emptiness of eternity. It was growing cold, the coldness of the empty cosmos at whose center we stood like two pips in an apple. Yet when my new friend talked, we were among the crowded streets of Alexandria, where the warmth, the shouting, the tavern music, the braying of donkeys, and the burning sun above the shop awnings shielded us from the indifference of eternity. Between our speech and our silence we moved from the lit-up king's hall, where a laughing retinue receives its mead-portion about the hearth of blazing logs, out onto the chill moor where winds howl bleakly, and only those formless beings that dwell by fen and mere shift about in peat and ooze.

Our poor bodies are perched upon the heathery slope of Dinleu, but where are our minds? Reflecting upon their wanderings, I murmured aloud:

"I was seated by my Monarch, when bold Lucifer he fell
From the airy halls of Heaven to the stagnant pit of Hell;
I who bore the oriflamme of Alexander forth,
Knowing every star's name, southwards to the north:
I was in the Fort of Gwydion,
And in the Tetragrammaton;
It is *my* name in the canon
That tells the death of Absalon;
I strolled the starry Court of Don
Before the birth of Gwydion,
Dropping seeds in dewy Hebron—"

"Ah, I was in Hebron once," interrupted the tribune, whose thoughts had, I saw, remained in Alexandria. "We halted our march to let the men see the grave of Adam, and the sepulchers of Abraham, Isaac, and Jacob. There's nothing to mark Adam's grave, though, just a grassy mound. The monks told us that the ruined town by our camp had been a great stronghold in the days of the patriarchs. I couldn't see it myself; there's a hill covering it to the east, well within the range even of our medium-strength *ballistae*. Curiously enough, that was soon after my recruitment, of which I was telling you. Am I boring you? I expect so."

"Not at all," I replied sincerely. "It is just that my thoughts do wander. Your story intrigues me; besides, it is you and not I who have work to do tomorrow morning."

"Work? After this night's feasting there'll be no early reveille. I hope we'll get the troops in better trim as we march south. Things usually improve once you break camp.

"Yes, my lively friend had made himself at home in the mess of the *protectores* whose quarters are in the palace of the Augustal prefect. The young sparks accepted me, too, as one of them. Everyone knew who my father had been, you see, and they were all young noblemen preparing to join the army. Oh, they teased me for my solemnity, but not ill-naturedly. Though my father could not save himself, I have always known myself to be under his protection. Do you remember that piece in 'The Dream of Scipio,' when Cicero sees his dead father, and Scipio Africanus tells him that 'those are in fact alive who have escaped from the bondage of the body as from a prison, and what you call life is in reality death'? I have often felt my father beside me, and I think it was he who preserved me until now, when as far as I know all my companions who were with me at the taking of Carthago are dead. Do you believe that all our departed comrades are quartered up there?"

He gestured upward, in the direction of the dim luminosity of Caer Gwydion, continuing, "That is what our good priest used to tell us on Sundays, in the garrison church of the Blessed Virgin, and I think a soldier has to believe it, for otherwise all his campaigns and decorations and promotions end up as an inscription on a tombstone in the garrison cemetery—a dogs' urinal when the *numerus* finally gets its marching orders. But of course you might say that proves the Afterlife as false as the rest. How proud you feel when the master of soldiers calls you forward to receive the *corona aurea,* and yet what is it after all? A shiny piece of metal whose special value lies in the minds of the troops and nowhere else. Would we risk death and wounding if we were not persuaded there was a land beyond, with my father and Scipio Africanus awaiting us there? Mightn't the whole thing be a *corona aurea,* put out in order to keep us steady in the ranks when the going gets hard?"

My first inclination was not to reply to what I took to be a rhetorical question, which busy men such as this tribune put up in passing as they pursue their ordered path. But I caught an appeal in his eye which told me that the question was for him by no means a frivolous one. His was a lonely life, and I could see he dearly loved his father. Rufinus was a practical man and doubtless hoped for a practical answer. That was, in the nature of things, an impossible expectation, but I tried my best:

"In the beginning were the gods, and at the end are the gods; there is nothing in between. It is through our lives the gods enact parts, like mummers in a play. It is a mistake to conceive of all things as proceeding in succession like an army on the march, and of your father's part as having been played out before yours. Nor may you expect to understand immortality, which is not of this world, where all things are mortal—even this hill upon which we rest."

"That is all very well, and much what I have heard before from others," responded the tribune gruffly, "but the fact remains that my father once lived among us and does so no more. How am I to know where he has gone?"

"I think you must dream of him when you are sleeping," I ventured. "Which is the reality, your dreaming or your waking?"

"My waking, of course."

"My friend, you must avoid that 'of course,' for which there is no occasion," was my reply. "How can you be so sure of the answer? You are awake now, so you believe waking the reality. When you are asleep, then it is your dream which is real. It may be that dreaming *is* reality, for in dreaming there is no time, and there is no time in reality."

"How can you say there is no time?" rejoined the soldier brusquely. "I know my age, and the number of years I have served with the eagles. I know I was with my father, and that I may be so no longer, much though I wish it."

"There is no time because there is neither past nor future. Consider: The past you can see, it is true, because it lies stored in your memory. The present is a moment so fleeting it does not exist; no sooner do you attempt to seize it than it is swallowed up by the past. As for the future, it exists as certainly as the past, though as yet you may not see it. Now, if time be anything, it is motion: our movement from one scene to another. Yet, since past and future exist equally at any one moment—this one, if you like . . . there, it is gone!—then there is no movement, only contemplation of the whole."

"That is all very well in its way," replied Rufinus skeptically. "We had a teacher in Alexandria who used to argue something along those lines. But the fact remains that *we* cannot see the future, so that it unfolds before us in reality just like a book in a library, when you cannot tell what the next chapter will relate."

"To us it does appear to unfold in the way you describe, though there may be those to whom it is given to see a little further ahead in the darkness," was my reply. "The immortal gods, however, being all-powerful and all-seeing, view everything that was and will be, from the first spark in Gofannon's forge to Doomsday and the death of Leu. If they see it all, they see it all at once, and thus there is no movement—which is No-time."

"But we are not immortal gods, and must judge of matters by what we experience," urged the tribune, seating himself beside me upon a rocky outcrop.

"No, we are not. But inasmuch as they perceive that which is concealed from us, it is they who know reality and not us. Our existence is an illusion in that respect, and it may be in all others too."

Rufinus tugged thoughtfully at his grizzled beard. I could see that in his lonely existence he had pondered on these matters more than he gave himself credit for.

"Well, my friend," he conceded with a short laugh, "you may be right. I receive (or received) orders at Septem from the *dux* of Mauretania, he from the *magister militum* in Africa, and he in turn from the emperor in Byzantium. The emperor knows all that passes throughout the whole Empire, and I only that small part over which he has delegated to me my authority as tribune; so God clearly sees His creation in its entirety, and we only that small plot upon which our role is cast. Though in my case I think I may say it is no very small plot, for I have received postings across the Empire from end to end: from Daras in the east to Septem in the west!"

Nodding in concurrence, I unfastened the brooch from my cloak. With the pin I scratched a design in the lichen upon the rock-face beside me. "Have you seen that before?" I asked, pointing.

Arising, he came near and peered closely. In the clear moonlight he saw the square:

$$R \quad O \quad T \quad A \quad S$$
$$O \quad P \quad E \quad R \quad A$$
$$T \quad E \quad N \quad E \quad T$$
$$A \quad R \quad E \quad P \quad O$$
$$S \quad A \quad T \quad O \quad R$$

"I think I have," he murmured. "Soldiers sometimes inscribe it on their barracks walls. It is some sort of charm, I imagine. Do you know its meaning?"

"It has many meanings; possibly as many as you search for. 'The sower guides the wheels of the plow.' There will be a rich harvest when the seed is ripened, but which way does the sower move, and at what point is the seed's ripening? Read it backwards or forwards, it is the same, is it not? Gaze long enough, and within the pattern you will see other patterns: the sun, for example, or the cross. If by computation you convert the letters into numbers (so have I heard) you may find the age of the world, or that of the rotation of the celestial millstone. A whole mountain may be reflected within a dewdrop, and the solitary pluck of a harp string arouse an ocean of submerged feeling. You and I here, with the whole bright world about us, are, as they say, but compounds of the nine forms of elements glowing at the beginning within the molten blazing heat of Gofannon's furnace, which Math then quickened with his wand, multiplying forms beyond computation. However, it is not for me to vouch for these things, who am as yet but a child in wisdom."

Rufinus sat intent and brooding, his mind set less, I suspected, on the conundrum of the ROTAS-SATOR square than on times past, and upon one time perhaps in particular. To lure him from what might be painful memories, I gently inquired again concerning his recruitment to the army. After a pause he started abruptly from his thoughts, and plunged back into his narrative.

"Ah, yes. It was in the second year of our present emperor's reign. The patrician Pompeius was raising forces to relieve Belisarius, after the defeat at Daras. Most of the troops were Illyrians, Thracians, Isaurians, and Scythians. But our young men were chafing to earn their laurels in the coming campaign, and off they went, myself with them. It was the magic of Belisarius' name that carried us all away. He was only twenty-five, but we were all convinced that any army under his command would defeat the great king of Persia and all his legions, marching onward to the east to achieve all that Alexander gained. Belisarius! We all slung our cloaks in his fashion, picked up his Illyrian accent, and had our mess lyre-player strumming out the marching song of the general's *bucellarii* a dozen times a night.

"One or two of our young bloods even swore they would marry their actresses (*focariae* we had to call them now, of course), each like Belisarius with his Antonina! Apollos' mistress was the famous dancer Helladia. In their case they were so close, you might almost say she was his wife. I liked her; she had very fetching ways, and I don't think grudged me my friendship with Apollos. As everyone knows, all the best dancers come from Alexandria; but I never saw one as pretty or graceful or kind as our Helladia.

"Well, I was carried away like the rest, pawning everything I had with a rich barber to purchase my equipment (there was no time to ask my mother for funds, and she wouldn't have agreed to my abandoning my studies anyway). The day I passed my *probatio* before the prefect was the only time in my life when I was the worse for drink—drunk as Silenus, to be precise. We started the evening with thirty-three *amphorae* of the best Knidian wine (expense no consideration), and when I woke up next afternoon all that was left of them as far as I was concerned was a head throbbing like the kettledrums of the Hunnic cavalry, and a tongue parched as the dusty end of the Thebaid. It took me three days in the bathhouse to recover, I remember. I have a weak head, and it was the first and last time I tried that game.

"So that was it. We were soldiers now, thinking no end of ourselves. We picked up the army slang: Tents were 'butterflies,' and all the rest of it. It happened that no units were required from Aegyptus for the Persian campaign, but we managed to tag ourselves on to the escort taking money to Belisarius at Daras, the emperor having ordered much of that year's revenue from the prefecture to be delivered up for payment of the troops.

"When we reached the citadel we found everything beyond even our extravagant fancying. *Miles gloriosus!* The strongest fortress in the world, twenty-five thousand crack troops, and the most brilliant general in the Empire at our head! The Persians were said to have mustered twice as many men at Nisibis, just across the frontier, but who cared for that? Their general, Perozes, had sent a message to Belisarius, telling him to have a bath ready for him in Daras, as he was coming soon to bathe in our city. Oh, we had a bath prepared for him all right!

"The Augustal prefect had provided me with a letter of commendation, pointing out who my father was and all the rest of it, so I was lucky enough to be appointed *ducenarius* in a crack cavalry *vexillatio*, the Equites Mauri Scutarii, and to start my military career by taking part in the first of our general's great victories. Our *vexillatio* was under Marcellus' command, on the right flank.

"The battle began on our left, and I remember now (though I have passed through so many battles and years since then) the excitement and glory of it all. Naturally I knew nothing of the careful plans laid by Belisarius and Hermogenes beforehand, and imagined that everything just went as it should. Even the wind was with us, deflecting many of their arrows during the exchange of volleys that started the action. The enemy pressed our left flank hard, until Sunicas and his Huns hit them from one side and Pharas and his Heruli from the other. Apollos and I (he had joined the Mauri too) watched all this, boiling over with impatience. The Persian right was in full retreat, throwing their weapons away on the sand, and the battle would soon be over without the participation of its two most promising young officers! Why didn't Marcellus order us into the attack?

"Well, everyone knows now what happened. We could see Belisarius all this time, as he had ridden up onto the horn of the trench protecting our front. His helmet flashed from time to time, and I remember wondering why he and his staff were continually looking toward us, ignoring Pharas' great fight on the left. We soon found out when we heard the enemy left, facing us about two spear's-throw off, give three great shouts. They were coming straight for us, and I felt my stomach jump in the manner that every soldier experiences in his first action. It had reason to jump, though the full extent of the danger I only understood afterward, when Marcellus made us ride over the field to receive our first practical instruction in the art of war.

"For their general, Perozes, was no novice, as Belisarius well knew. As we were drawing our swords, confident of giving their left wing the same treatment as that just received by the right, Perozes was quietly moving up the cream of his army, the famous Immortals, to take *us* in flank at the moment of impact. Marcellus realized what was happening just too late; but what could he have done anyway? We were stuck into the attack beyond recall, and in any case . . . the Immortals! There are no soldiers like them in the world, except maybe the *bucellarii* of Belisarius.

"I don't recall what happened next very clearly. You never do when you're in the thick of it; no idea of time passing, or danger, or what the orders are—except the last one you received. You don't hear anything either, not the trumpets, the yelling and the neighing—not, at least, until it's all over, when you hear it ringing in your ears all right for days afterward. It's like a dream in a way. But I wasn't in so much of a dream that I didn't see them coming all at once: rank upon rank of armored veterans moving in perfect order, more like a *testudo* approaching a city wall than soldiers in open battle. I can't remember if I knew then it was the Immortals, but I sensed all at once they were men who knew what they were about, and that it might well be *we* who were to be cut to ribbons. We all turned around and began pushing to the rear. Marcellus' trumpeters sounded for the Laconian countermarch, and that is what we liked to call it afterward; but the truth is that it was each man for himself. 'Turn to the spear!' I could hear an officer shouting again and again; but, sword or spear, it was in truth 'Turn to the rear!' I wasn't frightened, so far as I recall. At such times you just do what everyone else is doing. I sensed we were beaten, though, which is always a nasty feeling.

"How long we were in this state I don't know; probably only a few minutes, though now I see it all like a picture set down for all eternity. Everyone was milling about, officers shouting orders no one could distinguish, horsemen pushing forward to get into the fight, horsemen shoving back to get out of it: total chaos, if you like! Then suddenly I glimpsed out of the corner of my eye Marcellus shouting and pointing with his sword. I couldn't hear a word, but I glanced to our left, where I saw the prettiest sight of my life.

"Belisarius, of course, had been waiting for this moment, which he knew would decide the battle one way or the other. It was the move of the Immortals which would betray Perozes' thought to our general, and it was now that Belisarius divined that thought. We had been driven back from our trench, which on our left was angled to the rear. Now it was their flank which lay exposed to our center. Over the ditch, full-tilt on the Immortals' right, came Sunicas with the pick of his Huns and the general's *bucellarii*. That was a fight and a half! The Immortals squared up and turned on Sunicas, and what was left of our lot rode back to join the Huns. The Immortals certainly earned their name that day, for they fought like the Myrmidons before Troy. But the day was with us, and when their general finally fell, even his Immortals fled the field, casting away their shields.

"We pursued the enemy just far enough to make sure he wouldn't rally. Belisarius wanted to guard his victory, which was the first the Romans had gained over the Persians for many years. Mind you, the troops were in such a state of exaltation I think they would have stormed Nisibis, if Belisarius had given the word. However, I don't doubt that he knew best.

"We swaggered back into Daras—those that were left of us—bawling out the old song that Caesar's legions bore across Gallia and Britannia:

> 'Gallias Caesar subegit
> Nicomedes Caesarem.
> Ecce Caesar nunc triumphat
> qui subegit Gallias!' "

I laughed. "When you were speaking then, you might have been young Run mab Maelgun or Prince Elffin, dreaming of their first battle! And I took you for a wise counselor who foresees his own and his opponent's moves like an experienced player at *gwyddbwyll!*"

Rufinus paused in thought, and I feared lest I had broken the thread of his narrative. It is my business to know many things, and this foreigner possessed a deed-hoard I was, I confess, eager to plunder. Fortunately he proved not to be offended by my interruption, and continued:

"You are right, of course. But I recall my friend Apollos (he was killed, by the way, in our next great battle, at Callinicum) claiming that a soldier's first battle is like his first woman. I cannot vouch for the latter, for to be frank, women have played but a small part in my life. But that day before the walls of Daras was as intoxicating for me in its way as was our revelry on the evening we joined the army in Alexandria.

"We were all more than a little drunken with victory. *Pie zeses!* The whole army regarded old Hermogenes as a Ulysses in council, and would have ridden to India or Arabia next day if Belisarius had but given the word. For us youngsters, though, the real hero was neither Hermogenes nor Belisarius, but Sunicas. Sunicas! He was an ugly-looking little fellow, like all his people; but like all his people he rode like a centaur. He had a squadron of thirty picked chieftains of his tribe, who came trotting behind him with a horse's mane flying from a spearhead above them. It used to be said in the army that there was no need to ask which way the attack was directed: 'Just ride for Sunicas' horse-mane standard!' was the cry.

"After we had ridden back that evening from pursuing the enemy into the desert, there was a great feasting in the camp, each *numerus* in its own lines, and a division of the spoils taken from the enemy. But by the time the sun went down everyone was coming and going from the encampment of the Huns, trying to catch a glimpse of Sunicas, with his flat nose, scarred cheeks, and hair thatched round as on the huts of his people's homeland in Pannonia. I caught a glimpse of him through the crowd.

"There he sat on his couch, ugly and expressionless, just glancing about from time to time at his officers as they drank to his health. A couple of singers were droning out an endless chant; I imagine it was a song of victory, though in their barbarous Scythian speech it might have been a couple of bullfrogs croaking in a Dacian marsh for all I knew. The Huns appeared moved by whatever it was, but Sunicas went on sitting motionless and expressionless as a figure on a tombstone. Then a hunchbacked Gepid buffoon came on to perform tricks which set them all weeping with laughter. But old Sunicas, he just sat silent and brooding as before.

"Well might they celebrate! By now everyone had heard the tales: how Sunicas headed the first charge, singling out the Immortals' standard-bearer for himself, and driving his long lance through the fellow so that it stood out an arm's length and more between his shoulder blades. That drew the Persians onto him like bees around a bear, and *that* was what Sunicas wanted! They say that before the Huns were received into the true faith they worshipped a sword, and well they might, if it were but the sword of Sunicas! How many Persians he killed that day none could tell, but the climax of it all everyone knew, so that by the end of the summer I doubt if there was anyone in the Empire who had not heard how Sunicas fought with the one-eyed Persian commander, Baresmanas, splitting his helmet with a blow that sent him spinning from his saddle into the dust. That was when the Immortals fled the field. After that, Sunicas tied a noosed rope around the feet of Baresmanas, dragging his corpse through the sand at full gallop right up to where Belisarius was waiting at the head of his staff, crying out that the Persian chief was come to take that bath in Daras his envoys had requested the previous day."

The tribune chuckled at the memory. "For the rest of that year's campaigning, it was thought the height of wit to inquire politely of Persian envoys when their great king was coming to bathe at Daras: 'We have an expert *balneator* in attendance—just ask for Sunicas!' The joke lasted less than a year, though, the fortune of war being what it is. Next spring at Callinicum we met the Persian army again; whether it was they or we who won I cannot say, but I do know we got as good as we gave. We were near to disaster, and it was there my friend Apollos died, when our federates fled the field, leaving our right flank exposed. It was a real dog's breakfast. The center was on the point of giving way, had Belisarius and Sunicas not dismounted and fought alongside the foot soldiers. It was unwise to laugh at the Persians: They are dangerous foes. Next year our emperor and theirs signed what they called the Perpetual Peace. Well, if the truth be told, the war broke out again eight years later, but that was after my time."

My companion paused awhile, lost in thought. I guessed that his spirit was troubled, and in his mind he heard still the wheel and crash of the armored cavalry, imagining himself in the glare and heat of barren lands far from the misty green Island of Prydein.

"What brought you then to Africa?" I asked eventually, seeking to ween him from thoughts which I guessed were not all happy.

"To Africa?" he replied, starting from his reverie. "Ah, that is a long story, with which I will not trouble you. Apart from Apollos, who died as I have told you at Callinicum, I had no companion I could call a friend. I don't know how it was; I drank little wine and did not keep a mistress, so it may be my brother officers thought me a dull dog. I did not in any case object to keeping my own company, and found my military duties so fascinating as to exclude all other interests. At first I served with the cavalry, remaining for a while like everyone else infatuated with the glory of Sunicas. I studied while others drank, and soon mastered the Gothic tongue, which enabled me to command a cohort of Hunnic horse.

"The master of soldiers, Belisarius, remarking upon their smart appearance on parade one day, seconded me onto his staff. So it was I became a *bandifer*, bearing the standard of the general's *bucellarii* during the invasion of Africa. After we had beaten the Vandals, I imagined myself a cavalryman for life, but chance willed it otherwise. Having regained Africa for the Empire, the emperor ordered Belisarius to reconquer Italia from the Goths. It was at the taking of Panormus that I was wounded by a Gothic arrow, which severed the tendons of my right wrist. I lay sick with a fever for several months; there may have been poison in the wound. In consequence I stayed behind in Sicilia, and by the time I came to rejoin the army, Belisarius had taken Rome, which was then besieged in turn by the Goths.

"This chance proved a turn of good fortune for me in my military career, for though Belisarius made as good use as ever of his cavalry at this time, he had still greater need of skilled engineers and artillerymen. My experience had lain with neither of these branches of the army, but I had spoken often with those of my colleagues who were expert in these matters, and had studied until I knew almost by heart the manuals of Vitruvius, Heron, Biton, Philon, and the rest of them. Now I was able to apply myself to the practical aspects of artillery and fortification."

I had increasingly been struck by the solitary nature of this much-traveled man, and his mention of the Island of Sicilia brought to mind something of which he had spoken earlier.

"Did not your mother retire to Sicilia, following your father's untimely death?" I inquired.

Rufinus grimaced a little, or so it appeared to me.

"My mother was living on our Sicilian estate, and it is true that at my suggestion I was taken there by my staff to recuperate. However, shortly after the invasion of Italia, when Belisarius had crossed the straits to Rhegium, she explained to me that my quarters were needed for the care of the sick whom the monks of her household tended. She is, as I told you, very devout. Indeed, I think her piety was greater in some degree than that of the monks themselves, for I overheard the abbot remonstrating with her when she requested me to evacuate my quarters. It is true that the villa contained more than thirty rooms, a luxurious suite of baths, and all sorts of other facilities not needed by the monks; but I expect my mother had good reason for acting as she did.

"By now I was able to ride again, so I bade farewell to my mother and set off to rejoin the army. I was disappointed with my stay, I remember. It seems ridiculous, but from the day I enlisted at Alexandria, I had nurtured a childish dream that one day I would appear at my mother's gateway at the head of a glittering cavalcade of soldiers, and prove to her . . . I don't know what! In the end I did come with my escort, but nothing turned out as I had pictured it in my fancies."

"Did you see her again?" I asked casually, not liking to probe what might be a matter of some delicacy.

"No," replied Rufinus shortly. "I was told that she married again about six or seven years ago, when Totila conquered Sicilia. The man who informed me had spoken with those who had reason to know the truth, but I still find it hard to credit that she, who had been married to such a man as my father, could have consented to wed a Goth, however noble his blood according to the estimation of his people.

"At times I wonder if I had not been at fault, for I believe (though she never spoke of it to me) that she disapproved of my marriage, and it may have been that which made her a little cold toward me, and so the less mindful of the duty she owed her true husband."

Here I started involuntarily. "You did not say you were married?"

"Yes, like many of our officers I married my blue-eyed Vandal bride in Carthago. And like many of those marriages it did not last very long. She lost her property not long afterward, when the government ordered the confiscation of Vandal allotments, and then wisely sought a husband better able to support her than myself. It was all a mistake, I fear; there are men who are not made for marriage—or even friendship, it may be. I was married for nearly two years, and yet I can hardly remember what my wife looked like. Almost the only thing I remember from our time together is how to order a meal in her barbarian tongue: *scapia matzia ia drincan!*

"Yet Helladia—she was Apollos' mistress—springs to my mind as if not a day had flown of the thirty years since last we spoke. Poor thing—it was when I returned to Alexandria after Callinicum to tell her the news of Apollos' death. She had received word some time before I could get leave, but she stood before me white and weeping as though mine were the first news. She looked so beautiful that I saw in a trice that it was Apollos who was the lucky one, not I, though it was I who had escaped unscathed from the butchery at Callinicum. Well, I envied him in that moment, I confess.

"Poor, dear Helladia. She clung to me, weeping, I recall. Why, she even asked me to take her with me, bestowing such a melting look upon me, urging that she and I were Apollos' dearest friends and that together at least we could share his memory! I felt temptation then such as I have never known before or since; but I am happy to say that my loyalty to my friend triumphed over that other feeling. I told her—rather gruffly, as I fear—that I had to rejoin the eagles at once, and left her alone in that room where we'd spent so many hours of irresponsible happiness. She clung to me and tried to kiss me as I left. Her cheek was wet against mine, and I had to leave in a hurry. How could I tell her that I feared I might find it impossible to be faithful to the memory of our dear friend if I stayed for any time with her? I am relieved I did the right thing, though sometimes I wonder if it would really have been so bad if what I feared had taken place?"

The tribune paused, embarrassed as I thought. But I did not reply to his question, for which I could provide no happy answer even if I knew it. He cleared his throat awkwardly and returned briskly to his story.

"Poor, pretty Helladia," he murmured, "I wonder where you are now? I am sorry, my friend. Sometimes my tale seems to run away with me, like an untrained cavalry mount with a recruit at his first parade on the *campus*. Where was I? Ah yes, back in the days of my youth. Well, after the siege of Rome was lifted I was greatly tempted to visit my childhood home. During my years in Aegyptus and the prefecture of the East, I dreamed time and again of that glimpse of Rome from the tower window which as a child had so excited my imagination. I pictured in my mind the pall of dust which hangs above the busy traffic on the Via Clodia beyond the olive groves; I recalled expeditions my father and I made on occasion to Lake Sabatinus, where we would sit for hours, angling or skimming potsherds. I heard the creak of wagons and cheerful shouting of slaves returning at evening from the grape harvest, the gong in the villa summoning us to our midday meal, the morning clatter of the escort in the courtyard coming to accompany my father to the Senate; and many other things. Well . . . I suppose the image that came most to mind was that day when my father and I played with our toy fleets in the cistern building. I can remember every word he said, every expression on his face. Don't ask me why I remember that day more than the others, because I don't know."

"And did you visit your home? Was it changed at all?"

"I don't know. I put off going several times when there was an opportunity, and then in the end I never did. I don't know why; perhaps I feared the Goths had destroyed the house, and that would be upsetting to discover. The strange thing is, though, that during the months of siege when we couldn't get out, I used every day to ascend a tower by the Salarian Gate, and strain my eyes in an effort to pick out our villa among the hills to the north. I never did, even though you could certainly see Rome from our tower.

"Of course I saw many other familiar sights, now sadly altered. Most of the citizens had fled or starved during the Gothic occupation. By the time of my arrival (I accompanied the reinforcements commanded by Martin and Valerian), matters had been going very hard with us. Many public buildings had been demolished in order to employ the materials on the new walls constructed by Belisarius. The statues on the Mausoleum of Hadrian were lying broken on the ground, our garrison having been obliged to lever them onto the enemy below at a critical moment.

"But Aeneas' ship was still perfectly preserved, looking just as it had done years before when my father first took me to its boathouse by the Tiber, telling me of Rome's foreordained glory. Don't ask me how it survived, where so much else was lost. For me at least it was a symbol of the Empire's enduring strength. Was it not in that very ship that her founder, a friendless wanderer tossed upon a waste of seas, survived those terrible storms with which Juno assailed him during his escape from Troy? It had survived the destructive rage of the barbarians, to witness Rome's regeneration in our own time; and I believe its ribs and keel are so stoutly and skillfully joined that it will ride out a second Flood, or whatever further storms God sees fit to unloose upon the world from the Cave of Aeolus."

Darkness lay upon all the land below the precarious pinnacle by which the tribune and I crouched talking together, and as the wet wind from off the flooded plain whirled through bushes and branches about us it seemed for a moment as if we too might be cast adrift upon a hostile ocean. My companion's words briefly bore the ring of poetic inspiration; it may be his thoughts had conjured up old verses instilled in him as a child.

"Once or twice during the siege I went to visit the site of my old school by the Capitol," continued Rufinus at my ear. "It seemed strange to stand, as an officer with so many responsibilities, where long before as a lad my only care had been to jostle with my companions for those stools which provided the best view of the busy street. Where was our old *magister* now, whose ferule had aroused such terrors in my childish mind? I stood on that spot where my father came once to conduct me to my class, and recalled—no, not recalled: I saw it all again just as before—the look he gave me, full of affection and pride. And I remembered bitterly how I did not linger as I might have done, but ran eagerly to join my fellow pupils.

"It was not that I did not value my father's love, but in my foolishness I longed to earn what I later came to see was freely given and required no earning. When we turned our heads to see King Theodoric's cavalry riding through the street past our little school, I burned one day to ride in majesty like that, glittering in burnished armor, up to our villa gateway.

"Once again I had achieved my ambition, but to what purpose? I was valued, I knew it, in the council of Belisarius, and had played my part in restoring Rome to the Empire. It might be that I was all my father could have wished, and more; but what did it amount to now that he was dead? You will laugh at an old soldier, whose right arm can no longer wield a sword, playing the philosopher. True, I am no philosopher, but a soldier sees something of life which may profit him to know. The emperor Marcus Aurelius was a soldier and a philosopher, and there is a saying of his so true (as it seems to me) that I have committed it to memory: 'The man in a flutter for fame fails to realize that each of those who remember him will himself also very shortly die, then again the man who succeeded him, until the whole remembrance is extinguished as it runs along a line of men who are kindled and then put out.' What then may a man do? He cannot stay the present moment, nor return to it when it is past. He must persist and do his duty, but for what purpose I confess I sometimes find it hard to see."

"I think that you are wrong, my friend," I urged gently. "Through the inspiration of poetry, men and deeds may live forever. It may be, for example, that King Brochfael of Powys is fated to die in this summer's campaigning against the Iwys. Let it be this summer or another, or let him die peacefully in old age; he will live on from this to the world's ending on account of the fame which Taliesin has bestowed upon him in his praise-poem."

"You may be right," returned the tribune without conviction. "Nor will I shirk my duty, whatever its worth. Still, it was hard then, after all Belisarius' campaigning, to be a witness to the destruction of Eternal Rome. My father's town house and those of his friends were occupied by Hunnic, Herul, and Isaurian troops of our garrison, whom I regularly witnessed squatting around their campfires blazing on the tessellated floor of some senator's atrium—the owner himself probably lying strangled in a Gothic dungeon. The Senate, where my father's eloquence had been so often acclaimed, was now an arsenal, while the remaining senators had been carried off to be murdered by Witigis in Ravenna."

"It seems to me you had much for which you and your general might congratulate yourselves," I pointed out. "Between you, you had restored nearly the whole of the Empire in the West, previously lost to the barbarians. And for that the emperor must have regarded you highly."

The tribune shook his head gloomily. "The emperor is far off in Constantinople, and there is a little matter called *suffragium* which even his laws cannot stamp out. A friend at court is what you need if it's promotion and recognition you're after. I never had any money beyond my pay, and no means of placing my name before the praetorian prefect of the East. As for the emperor himself, the promotion prospects of general staff officers in distant provinces are no more his concern than is it mine whether this or that centurion of my garrison is responsible for the morning's patrol. Besides, matters went badly for us in the end. After Witigis was captured and sent a prisoner to Constantinople, the Goths chose Totila for their king. Now we found we had exchanged King Log for King Stork with a vengeance, and Totila gave us more than a run for our money.

"I was with the garrison when he recaptured Rome. By the end there were four hundred of us left, cooped up in the Mausoleum of Hadrian. We had our horses still and decided to break out and cut our way through the besiegers. But Totila knew our desperation, and decided to offer terms. We could swear an oath never to take up arms against the Goths again and go free, or join his forces, each retaining his old rank and pay. Most of the men went over to the enemy. I am not sure that I blame them, and their commanding officer and I were the only ones who rode away.

"Eventually we reached the camp of the general, Diogenes, who made much of us. But of what use was I to him? I could no longer serve in Italia, on account of the oath I had taken to Totila in Rome. I returned to Sicilia, thinking to recuperate at my mother's home (my arm was giving me renewed trouble). But nowhere was safe at that time. No sooner had I crossed the Straits than Totila marched south and invaded the island. I was cooped up in Panormus, where the Imperial garrison had managed to hold out.

"I think that was the worst time of all for me. There had been much to distress me in Rome, but despite all the destruction and change it was within sight of the old villa and there was much to remind me of my father. Now, after all our hard fighting, it seemed the Goths were victorious again and all had been for nothing. Belisarius had returned to Byzantium to sort out some political business; and here was I, a crippled, useless fellow, prevented (even if my wound allowed it) by my oath from advancing my career in Italia.

"They gave me a room in a tower overlooking the sea, that the salt breezes might do me good. I sat there, day after day, looking across toward the Italian coast, kicking myself for not having visited the old villa after all. For I lived in my childhood memories, foolishly nurturing the idea that they would have been revived by days spent wandering around the house and garden. I could have made a fire of vine twigs on the spot where my father and I used to grill sardines in a rocky corner by the edge of the olive grove. There were just the two of us, whom I imagined to be quite on an equality because he listened with such a smiling look of intentness to all my prattling!

"Now I found my memories artificial, like a young officer's formal report drawn up after the turmoil of the battlefield. Only that far-off day, when we paddled in the dark, cool cistern, and he, too, was like a child, pushing the wooden boats about and shouting so as to make the vault echo: only that came back in a rush in my sickroom at evening, or in the silence of the night. Perhaps the washing of the sea at the foot of my tower brought it back to mind, do you think?"

I thought it very likely, for the sea is awash with memories. I recited:

> "When the wind gusts in from the east,
> And the waves surge out of the swell
> My heart is drawn out to the west
> To the broad green meadows of foam,
> To the land where the sun sinks home."

"Strange you should say that," responded Rufinus, aware again of my presence, which had obtruded not too harshly upon his reflexions. "I was never one for poetry myself, but there was one I learned at school. Everyone knows it, of course, but it always carried me straight from the hot crowded street where we had our lessons back to a roadside inn I knew. It's just at the point where you leave the Via Clodia for the road home among the hills, at the fifth milestone beyond the *mansio* at Careiae.

"When I came home with my father we used to stop there after all the dust of the crowded highway, sitting and sipping under the vine trellis of a little *taberna*. For once I had no difficulty in learning the lines, and felt very proud of myself as I recited it to my father that afternoon in the carriage on our way home. Naturally he knew it, too, and often afterward we would recite it together as we approached our *taberna*—'To get up a healthy thirst, my boy,' as he used to say. How did it go? I know:

> "A dancing girl from Syria, Greek scarf about her hair,
> Flashing in the smoky bar soft glances that ensnare;
> Swaying 'neath her castanets, smiling from the wine,
> Clack-clacking out the rhythm as her feet keep time:
> 'O hot and thirsty traveler, just stop a moment here,
> Forget your dusty journeying: come try my wine and beer!
> We've strumming on the lyre-chords, we've flagons, fruit,
>   and flowers,
> And under our thatched arbor know but cool and shady
>   hours;
> A goatherd in the corner piping plaintively his reed
> That haunting little ditty which will never leave your head.
> Our wine is of the cheapest, yet while dozing in your nook
> Hear it pour into your goblet, tinkling echo of the brook!
> Flowers yellow as the sunlight and purple as the vine,
> Garlands 'round the trellis basking in the noon sunshine;

Pale lilies laid in manchets, fit to deck a siren's hair,
Gathered by a dryad where our lapping stream flows clear.
Then we've cheeses piled in baskets and fruit of every type;
The autumn plums have mellowed and are bursting richly
   ripe,
Chestnuts sweet, and apples weighing down the branch
   above.
Just take us as you find us: There's food, and sleep—and
   love;
Mulberries in clusters overhang the donkey stall
While the melon wallows basking by the garden wall—
Hey, donkey driver! Join us! Your beast's all in a sweat.
Tie him to the olive tree; you know he's Vesta's pet!
Cicadas are chirping in the thickets of the vine;
Lizards flicker on the rocks below the resined pine.
If you're wise you'll settle down, letting all the noontide
   pass,
Learn what thirsty work it is lounging lazy with your glass:
Lounging on our well-worn bench, slouching sleepy in the shade,
With a garland on your forehead and your arm around a maid.
Perish all those gloomy folk who sport a serious frown!
Can they smell that flowery wreath, when they're underneath
   the ground?
Bring the dice and pour out wine; some other time for sorrow!
Death tweaks your ear, and whispers, "Tis *I* might call
   tomorrow." ' "

Despite the expressionless monotone with which the tribune recited his favored poem, the words momentarily conjured into my
mind a vision of the hot and dusty road, with its crowded clatter of
vehicles rattling to and fro toward unknown destinations. Beside it,
free from the urgent shouts of hastening travelers and the wheel's
endless rotation, lie the shaded delights of the little inn, where time
stands still.

The verses spoke of purely sensual pleasures, yet despite their
grim conclusion I could not help wondering whether they might not
bear an allegorical interpretation. Certainly the images recalled to me
others with themes strikingly similar composed by the bards of the
Brython, extolling the pleasures of Caer Sidi. At the same time they, or
songs very like them, may be heard bawled out by boors in taverns as
praise-poems to wanton pleasure. The analogy was if anything strengthened, I felt, by the soldier's concluding reminiscence.

Intending to interrupt a train of thought that appeared to be becoming increasingly melancholy, I asked Rufinus how he had come to be (as he had explained at first) recently in Hispania.

"That is swiftly told," he replied, "though it was long and at times weary enough in the happening. I told you how my noble chief, Count Belisarius, was recalled to Constantinople. Had he stayed, I am certain my fortunes must have remained linked to his. With his departure, however, and the defeats we suffered everywhere at that time, I was without influence or prospects: an old, crippled veteran locked up in a besieged city.

"But Fortune is fickle even in awarding misfortunes, as I have noticed, and an unexpected chance came my way. The emperor chose as successor to Belisarius the old senator Liberius, who, before he settled in Byzantium, had been my father's dearest friend. He arrived the following spring with a fleet to relieve our garrisons in Sicilia, putting in at Panormus. When I learned who was the new master of soldiers, I sent in my name. The old man (he was eighty or more) received me like a son, and was concerned to do whatever might be done for me.

"I told him I was of no use to the army, with my injured wrist; but he would hear none of that. He had heard (perhaps from Belisarius) something of my work with the artillery during the sieges of Rome, and told me to return next day, when he would suggest a posting appropriate to my seniority and health. When I appeared before him next morning, he embraced me and handed me my appointment as tribune of Septem, in the province of Mauretania Tingitana. I was to succeed John, an old comrade of mine from Belisarius' guard.

" 'I should like to do more for you, my boy,' he told me. I could see there were tears in his eyes, for he had loved my father dearly and I believe saw something of him in me. His was the softening that accompanies great age, I believe, for though I was proud of my achievements I was not so foolish as to compare my narrow professional skills with my father's virtue, or his understanding of Rome's great purpose in history.

"Liberius told me that, even had I not been obliged to give my parole to Totila, my crippled arm debarred me from service in Italia, where the fortunes of our arms were so uncertain. Frequently the most senior officers were compelled to wield sword or spear in the breach of a besieged town or (as I had myself nearly experienced when serving with Diogenes at Rome) head a cavalry charge cutting the way out of a closing trap. In Septem, I would be my own commander, with minimum interference from higher command. I think he was alluding to the advantages of removing myself from the attention of the powers that be, so long as the fortunes of Belisarius remained clouded at the Imperial court."

"Well then, it seems that the gods favored you after all," I ventured. "Indeed, your father might be said to have interposed from the Otherworld on your behalf, for it was a strange chance, was it not, that brought you before his old friend at such a time and place? How did matters turn out at Septem?"

The tribune grunted noncommittally. "I cannot say that the governorship of a frontier town was the summit of my ambitions, and had the star of Belisarius remained in the ascendant I believe I had reason to hope for greater things. But matters might certainly have been a great deal worse. Shortly after our meeting Liberius was replaced as master of soldiers by Narses, whose victories have regained nearly all Italia for the Empire. But Narses had his own men to promote, and a worn-out companion of his old rival Belisarius would have sued in vain for promotion. In Septem no one interfered with me, and so long as I did my duty I was left alone.

"I had been in Africa before, of course, in the great days of Ad Decimum. But Septem was different. It is a thousand miles or more west of Carthago—'or anywhere,' as our soldiers used to say. Nothing but desert and a few naked Mauri with their stinking camels for four or five thousand *stades* between us and Caesarea! As far as I was concerned, though, there were much worse spots: beyond the mountains in the south on the frontiers of Numidia, for example. We at least had the sea, and ships calling regularly on their way to Hispania and Gallia, and even so far as Britannia. We were desperately concerned, of course, to follow the fortunes of Narses' army, and this we were able to do. The news improved with every year: Busta Gallorum, followed by Totila's death; Mons Lactarius, Capua, and finally Rome firmly in Roman hands once more! How we rejoiced, exulting to think that the Empire would after all be restored! Naturally I felt some sadness that it had not been accomplished by my valiant master, who might have achieved the same result ten years earlier had he received half the forces the emperor lavished on Narses. No doubt, too, I felt a secret selfish regret that I had played no part in all these triumphs.

"But I must not grumble; it is a sickness of old soldiers. There was, I confess, something about the tribunate of Septem that took my fancy. Long years before, as I told you, I served my apprenticeship in war at Daras, fighting the Persians on the easternmost frontier of the Empire. Now, I told myself, I commanded the westernmost outpost of the whole civilized world.

"For Septem, as you must know, stands at Gadira by the Straits of Hercules, at the point where the Mediterranean Sea flows out into the Ocean. Indeed, it is known as 'the threshold of the Empire,' for only the Ocean lies beyond. Just outside its walls there stands the pinnacle men call the Hunter's Rock, erected by Hercules (they say) after he slaughtered Geryon's cattle, which marks the boundary between Africa and Europa. Across the Straits—a mere eighty-four *stades* away—we could see Hercules' other pillar, the great Rock of Calpe. It kept our garrison on its toes when they knew that there, just over the water, the Visigoths were watching and waiting for another chance to take our fortress by surprise attack. This indeed they had actually accomplished four years before my arrival as tribune, when our forces were hard put to it to recapture the *castrum*.

"It made me content to see that before me lay a task for which my experiences made me well qualified. The defenses of the city and *castrum* were new and in good order, but my predecessor's placing of his artillery left much to be desired. The *ballistaria* were poorly sited with regard to covering fire from one tower to another, and the ditches on the landward side were angled in some places so as to give more protection to besiegers than besieged! Can you imagine it?

"Then the *ballista centenaria,* the reliable old hundred-pounder, while a useful enough weapon for maintaining heavy fire on concentrations of infantry or ships anchored in the roads, is virtually useless once the enemy approaches the walls. We had discovered this during the siege of Rome, so I applied the same remedy we employed with such good effect then, placing light field onagers at intervals along the walls mounted on rotating *ballistaria*. However, if I had my way, the enemy would never be permitted to approach so near. I set the men to work felling timber and weaving sinew-ropes for a battery of *ballistae fulminalis,* such as they use in the forts along the Danubius frontier. No one in Septem had ever seen one in operation before, and I'll never forget the day I demonstrated the first one to be completed. An artillery officer who had served at Singidunum boasted to me once that one of his machines flung its spear more than a mile. I don't know if that was true, but after six months my own artillerymen could put a missile through an old fishing boat towed by one of our *dromones* at anything up to a quarter of a mile's range. Beyond that it depended on the wind.

"The beauty of the machine is that, for all its incredible power, it takes but two men to wind it up, and only one to alter the range and angle of fire and discharge it! From fearing another Visigothic attack, the men turned to longing for an opportunity to try out their new weapons. This shoved morale right up, and as I kept them constantly up to the mark with drill, desert patrols, and mock attacks by day or night, we had at the end of six months a garrison as well disciplined and ready for action as any I've seen in more than twenty years' soldiering."

I smiled to myself, for there was a glint in my new friend's eye that told of real happiness. "Our bards sing of that place," I ventured:

> "Stark columns great and grouped by four,
> Red gold is glinting where they soar:
> Great Ercul's mighty pillared gate.
> No coward passes by that strait,
> No craven dares to raise his head,
> Where scorching sun would strike him dead.

"I should like to accompany you there some day," I said, "for it seems to me that you were on the boundaries of all things: set between Europa and Africa, Rufein and the barbarians, the Ocean and the Middle Sea. The Sun himself, after lighting in his daily course all the peoples and nations of the earth, wearies after passing your stronghold, dropping down to his resting place in the Ocean. As a soldier you must have experienced numberless occasions when your spirit was poised to fly from your body, and now your watching post was set at the very point where men take their final voyage from this world to the Glass House beneath the sea. For a man who wished to observe the course of nature, and understand the hidden workings of things, might do worse than construct an observatory at that point."

"You are right, my friend. From our little nest in Septem, I could keep my eye on much more than the Rock of Calpe across the Straits. Through our naval squadron I could check on every movement of enemy shipping from Gades to Carthagena. I prided myself on making the enemy coast the frontier, not ours. But, as my old master Belisarius used to say, it is a general's duty to have eyes so sharp they penetrate stone walls.

"My brief was to know everything that passed in Hispania, Gallia, and Francia, and this I flatter myself I did. I learned much from merchants whose trade took them to Visigothic ports both east and west of the Straits, and much more from agents with whom I kept in touch throughout their kingdom. As you may remember, Mauretania Tingitana came under the Diocese of Hispania before the barbarian conquest, and though that was so long ago, we still had many links with Europa.

"For while luck plays a great part in battles and campaigns, war on the frontier is (so I maintain) a matter largely of skill and foresight. True, you must anticipate all contingencies, but then you are provided with ample time for thought and preparation. The defense of a fortress or frontier calls for a thorough understanding of military science, whereas in a war of movement, flair and instinct may be even more important. I think I speak from some experience, for I believe my master Belisarius to possess all these qualities in greater degree than any commander since Julius Caesar or Alexander.

"Mind you, my responsibilities were not confined to ensuring the safety of the *castrum* and city of Septem. 'The end of the world' was what Septem was called by the troops. But, as Liberius hinted to me as we parted on the quayside at Panormus, 'the end of the world' is a place affording especial responsibilities—and opportunities. It was not long after taking up my new appointment that I began to appreciate the significance of his words.

"Mine was not simply the command of Septem and its garrison. I possessed authority over the coastal defenses of Tingitana, and maintained a squadron of *dromones* patrolling the Straits from the Promontory of Sestiaria in the Mediterranean to any point of my choosing in the Atlantic. From spies and agents established by my predecessors, and the interrogation of sea captains passing by, I learned much of the internal affairs of the barbarians in Hispania, Gallia, and Francia.

"Soon after my arrival the flow of orders began to increase, and I thought often of my patron Liberius' parting words, sensing that something big was in the offing. Orders came from headquarters at Caesarea that our intelligence reports were to be dispatched on a monthly basis, and any indication of unusual Visigothic activity to be reported without delay to the *dux* of Mauretania, who passed it on to the master of soldiers in Carthago. Copies of these reports and all records of dealings with our agents in Hispania were required to be kept under lock and key in my office, and no one—not even my staff—was to be permitted access to them.

"All this activity intensified as the months wore on, and at the end of eighteen months I was instructed to make especial provision for the reception of an emissary from across the Straits. No one, myself or anyone else, was to inquire concerning his name or the purpose of his visit, as he traveled under the direct authority of the master of soldiers. In due course this personage arrived, and I sent him on, under escort, to Caesarea. Six weeks later he was back again, with a sealed order from the *dux* of Mauretania requiring me to ensure his safe return to Hispania. This I did, placing one of my swift *dromones* at his disposal.

The ship was gone five days, and on its return I learned of an approach by night into the Bay of Tartessus, a beacon fire burning in a lonely cove, and a hasty transfer of our mysterious visitor to a waiting fishing boat.

"I respected my orders, making no attempt to pry into what was going on. Inevitably, though, as our visitor came and went with increasing regularity, I learned a little. He was a Jew of Merida, named Jacob, who trafficked in the wool trade. Though the Jews in Hispania are generally not maltreated by the Visigoths, as I understand it this Jacob bore a grudge against their king on account of a false charge brought against him of attempting to convert his Christian slaves, which had resulted in the confiscation of most of his property.

"It was at Jacob's fourth or fifth such visit that I discovered just how important was his role. He sailed into our harbor, flying the recognized signal as usual; this time in one of those swift low-slung vessels sailors term 'gazelles.' His manner was always respectful, but there was something about him on this occasion which almost amounted to an assumption of superior authority. He requested access to the *castrum* strongroom, and when I jibbed at that, he took me a little into his confidence. He would show me what goods he had brought, he assured me, and then I would appreciate the necessity of complying with his request.

"From the way he spoke I knew at once he had behind him the authority of the master of soldiers, but curiosity gripped me, and I seized the opportunity of learning a little more of what lay behind all these mysterious comings and goings. After two weighty chests had been deposited within the stone chamber, Jacob invited me to bar the door, and then showed me what he had brought.

"Well, I was certainly surprised by what I saw, I can tell you! The Jew unlocked his chests, and when he lifted the lids I saw they were filled with money. It was less the quantity that amazed me than the quality. For these were not the wretched lightweight solidi we receive for donatives to barbarians serving the Imperial interest, nor even the miserable dribble of substandard gold coins dispatched from time to time in partial commutation of *annonae* for my garrison.

"No. There, neatly packed between large sheets of paper, were layer upon layer of beautiful gold solidi. And by that I do mean beautiful! None of the wear or clipping, which has been the rule ever since Alexander (the one they called 'Snips') was sent out as *discussor* to 'reform' the currency. No, these were the perfect four scruples each, to a hair! The last time I had seen coins like these was at the prefect's palace in Alexandria. I asked no questions, but my guess was that

Jacob must have received them freshly minted from the palatine Offi-
cium of the Sacrae Largitiones in Ravenna itself. As the procurators
responsible for their issue are closefisted enough to make an Isaurian
seem generous, and as the emperor has of late years been exercising
severe economies in the intelligence field, it did not take a Ulysses to
sense something of what was in the offing.

"My suspicion became certainty when, a week later, Jacob removed the chests under guard to an old fishing vessel he had purchased
in the harbor. He refused my offer of escort, setting off alone westward through the Straits. One of my *dromones* reported sighting his boat
making for the Bay of Tartessus, and then I knew for certain that the
great game was afoot. If the gold was going to Hispania, then the
emperor himself must have authorized the operation. For, as you
know, it is strictly illegal to export gold to the barbarians.

"Swiftly we began to learn more and more, it being impossible in
my position not to do so, whatever my superiors' restrictions. Septem
is the watchtower from which the Empire overlooks Hispania, and all
news from that country passed through my office. We greeted with
delight, of course, news of the revolt of the citizens of Corduba against
King Agila, and when the king's repulse was followed by the rebellion
of one of his most powerful followers, Athanagild, we began to hope
for great things. The emperor has always been very skillful in profiting
from dissension among the barbarians, and here was our opportunity
at long last.

"My hopes were clearly shared in high places, for the master of
soldiers swiftly sent orders requiring our *numerus* to be established on a
permanent battle footing. This I prided myself they were in any case,
but to the customary drill I added, on my own account, regular
exercises designed to prepare the men for landings on a hostile coastline.

"Though nothing official had come down, all the men were
cock-a-hoop, fancying the long-awaited moment had come for Hispania to be restored to the Empire. King Agila and Athanagild were at
each other's throats, and with every ship putting in at Septem from the
east came news of a mighty armament being fitted out at Byzantium.

"At long last the spring arrived, and with it such a flurry of
orders, stockpiling of arms, and requisitioning of ships as I could
scarcely recall since Belisarius invaded Sicilia. Then came the news that
was a godsend for me. For who was to command the invasion fleet but
my father's old friend and my benefactor, the senator Liberius!

"In due course the Imperial fleet arrived and anchored in the
roads, its sails covering the whole bay. When I went on board the
flagship (I knew it of course by the purple sail), Liberius received me

like his own son; and I confess I wept as I reflected how close he had been to my father. For he was the only survivor I knew from that vanished world, and now how like a father he was to me!

"I could not believe it when first I learned the joyful news, since Liberius as you know was by now a very old man. For all his years, though, he displayed the enthusiasm of a man a quarter of his age. At our first council of war he brandished his sword over his head, declaring that he had arrived for the purpose of avenging in person injuries he had suffered at the hands of the Visigoths 'some little time ago.' This was a standard joke in the officers' mess. It was true that a party of Visigoths had once attacked Liberius and nearly stabbed him to death. The attempt had been made at the time when he was praetorian prefect of Gallia . . . a mere forty years earlier!

"No sooner had my squadron of *dromones* joined the Imperial fleet than we made sail for the coast of Baetica, where we landed the army. It was by no means so strong as rumor had led us to believe it would be, for the major part of the emperor's forces were earmarked for dealing the final blow to the Goths in Italia. But we could scarcely grumble, for we had a very potent ally (so we thought) in the person of the rebel Athanagild. He was at that time being besieged in Hispalis by King Agila, and Liberius wasted no time in advancing to his relief. The troops adored the old man, whose litter was always at the forefront of the column, and who knew how to talk to them in their own rough tongue.

"We achieved our disembarkation in good time, bringing our artillery and supplies on boats upriver, and trounced King Agila outside the city walls. He and what was left of his army managed to cross the mountains back to his capital, and we in our joy thought that a summer's campaigning would see the matter through. But Liberius—bless him!—was no Belisarius, and in any case he returned to Constantinople the following spring.

"For two years we enjoyed fighting, as hard as any we knew in Italia. If we ever thought that the Visigoths' hardiness might have been softened by the sunny skies of Hispania, we soon learned our lesson. A *thiufa* (that's roughly a *numerus* in our army) of Visigoths makes tough handling, as I found out all too often to my cost.

"Up to the spring of last year we were beginning to wonder if we would ever break out of Baetica, and there was even talk of establishing a fortified frontier along the River Baetis. Then word came from Ravenna in February that Narses, having defeated the Goths, Franks, and Alemanni and restored order throughout Italia, was sending an expedition to our assistance. After two years' frustration we could hardly credit the good news. But it was accurate for once, and in March a fleet arrived and landed a large force at Carthagena.

"I hastened to the city to confer with the Imperial general. With the combined forces at our disposal we felt confident we could crush King Agila once and for all, and resolved on a two-pronged advance on his capital. The Imperial army would reembark, sailing on through the Straits of Hercules to join my—our—forces, who were at that time encamped around Myrtilis. Together we would advance up the Anas, our siege-train and baggage accompanying us on a flotilla of boats I had assembled. Meanwhile, word had been sent to our ally Athanagild, urging him to proceed by forced marches through the passes of the Saltus Marianus to join us in a combined assault on Agila in his capital at Emerita. Victory appeared within our grasp at last, and in our excitement we felt ourselves on the point of crowning the conquests of Belisarius in Africa and Narses in Italy by restoring Hispania to the Empire. Agila, of course, was to be dispatched by us to Byzantium, just as Belisarius had done with Witigis fifteen years earlier.

"But what happened? The wheel of fortune is ever revolving, as I have had frequent enough occasion to observe, and once again the cup was to be dashed from our hand. The Visigoths, possessing more intelligence than we allowed them, and observing our policy in Italy and Africa, saw that the emperor had no interest in supporting one or other barbarian leader, and that the invariable result of our victories was the restoration of Imperial rule and the Catholic faith.

"Our Gothic ally, Athanagild, had always regarded us with suspicion, refusing to permit the entry of our troops into Hispalis or Corduba. We never deluded ourselves that he bore us overmuch love, but thought his rivalry with Agila had wedded him irrevocably to our cause. Well, that was true enough so far as it went. What we had *not* appreciated, however, was that the Gothic people would understand their own interests sufficiently shrewdly to adopt drastic measures designed to forestall our victory.

"We made good progress along the Anas, arriving at Emerita at about the time agreed with Athanagild. And Athanagild was there, too, just as arranged—not as our ally, however, but as commander of the combined Visigothic hosts, drawn up in hostile battle array. What had happened, as we soon discovered, was this: When the Visigothic chieftains in Emerita learned of the arrival of the Imperial fleet at Carthagena, they realized at once that the destruction of their whole race was imminent. For where now were their former neighbors, the Vandals and Ostrogoths, once-great nations destroyed by our arms? It was the civil war between Agila and Athanagild which had provided us with our opportunity, and this they at once resolved to end in order to oppose us with a united front.

"Athanagild, so Agila's followers decided in secret conference, would not give way, since he was supported by the Imperial army and could in any case never safely submit to being the subject of King Agila again. Accordingly, the leading Visigoths in Emerita decided that if one rival king would not go, then the other must. King Agila was murdered at a banquet by men of his own retinue, who sent emissaries to Athanagild, recognizing him as king of all the Visigoths. Athanagild lost no time in uniting the two Gothic armies, formerly hostile, and prepared to attack our expedition, now approaching his newly acquired capital.

"Knowing nothing of this treacherous development, and seeing Athanagild's camp and banners flying outside the walls, we pressed forward to join our 'ally,' falling into as neat an ambush as I have had the misfortune to encounter. Taken by surprise and heavily outnumbered, we were soundly defeated and forced to make a fighting retreat. As the news of our defeat spread, the whole of Lusitania was soon ablaze, and Gothic *thiufas* marched posthaste to harass us and if possible cut off our retreat.

"Fortunately I was able to bring out three *numeri* in good order, and my veterans from Septem were still able to give a good account of themselves. Our ships controlled the river, too, so with some pretty agile maneuvering I was able to keep our surviving units together. It took the whole summer, though, to fight our way to the coast. By August we were back in Myrtilis, where we were able to make ourselves impregnable, having virtually our whole siege-train still with us. I then set off by sea to summon reinforcements from Carthagena. Instead, as you already know, I was borne off by my pigheaded merchant captain to this remote island. Well, just let him beware of falling alongside one of my *dromones* in the Straits! A few years' diet of barley in the Septem jail might serve to recall him to his duty to the Empire."

When I had fled from the oppressive atmosphere in Caer Gurygon an hour or so earlier, my only thought had been to seek solitude on the hill of Dinleu. But I had found the tribune's confidences increasingly absorbing, despite initial irritation at his forcing himself upon me in the way he had. His was a tale of remarkable adventures and reversals of fortune. He had participated in great events, and as a personality greatly intrigued me. He was by his own account a man of limited imagination, whose sole concern lay in the profession of arms. Though there was something touching in his loyalty to the memory of his father, and tragic in the coldness I judged he had suffered at the hands of his mother, his was scarcely what you might term a warm personality. I took the unburdening to me of his life story to be a rare, if not unique, event, possibly prompted by his unexpected isolation in this remote land. His mind, I suspected, was normally bound up with the hostings of warriors, the conduct of battles and sieges, and the construction of ingenious devices for hurling rocks and spears across great distances.

But there was something alien and, I had to confess, invigorating about the world and ideas in which he had passed the span of his existence. The contrast was great indeed between his Empire and the timeless Island of the Mighty; with its Three Adjacent Islands, its Three Oppressions, and its Thirteen Treasures, fenced about by cliff walls, alone upon the tossing ocean; Precinct of Merlin, Island of Beli, conquered by Prydein son of Aed the Great; with its Four Quarters set about its Navel.

Poised, as we say, in the divine balance that sustains the whole earth, the Island of Prydein is but the reflection of the canopied tent of stars which rotates about the bright Nail of the Heavens. Provided the mysteries be observed and the games undertaken at Kalan Mai and Kalan Gaeaf, the Head of Bran be not disinterred, and the succession of her kings proceed in the manner preordained in the Prophecy of Prydein, then will the perfection of the Island of the Mighty and the people of the Brython be upheld by Leu with His Sure Arm, until the time comes when the earth is to be destroyed by fire or water.

It is in the Island of Prydein that men and gods and the Fair Folk live each in their own dwellings, and (save for twice a year, when the Hosts of Annufn are loosed, and Gwyn mab Nud rides out with his Wild Hunt) the ordering of things moves with the regularity and resistless strength of the tide's swell. But when the emperor of Rufein acquired the empire of the world, extending his sway over all neighboring regions and islands, it was his soldiers and masons and artificers who imposed their own order upon the face of the earth. The emperor in Caer Custennin is himself a god, and the law of Rufein the law that binds the earth. He has overthrown time and space and the harmony of all created things.

In the Empire of Rufein they know neither night nor day, summer nor winter. When the sun plunges to his rest in the Ocean, their palaces are lighted bright as noontide, while their ships are guided across the sea by lanterns of stone set before their harbors. Throughout the chill winter the men of Rufein feast in heated palaces and recline in steaming baths. Let the sun discharge its scorching rays upon them in summer, and they foregather in cool courtyards, splashing fountains playing about them, while they sip wines cooled by ice brought from northern lands. They are ever on the move, seeking new things, fighting new wars, subjecting the whole earth to laws of their own devising, binding its surface with new knots and chains, so that it may barely stir. The earth itself is refashioned according to their desires. Mountains are leveled with the plain, and swamps and seas made firm beneath their tread, as their roads cut straight lines across the earth's rough surface, and their fleets traverse the widest ocean. Deserts are made fertile, and water is carried by bridges and pipes from the springs of the foothills to the cities of the plain.

The men of Rufein reckon up years from the creation of their city or the beginning of their emperor's reign, count them in their passing, hastening to mark them by new exploits and achievements. All that they do or think they commit to writing, so that their wisdom is no longer the breath of the Cauldron of Poesy, but a dead thing of its own which may be mutilated or scavenged by all who find it on the wayside. Time for them is not the mighty stir of ocean, bearing a coracle upon its windless surface, but a racing chariot upon the highroad, rattling swiftly past the milestones.

Among us it is true that each king ruling in his country is set upon his chariot. But it is not a chariot that plunges forward on a heedless, headlong course: Its driver looks before him; he looks behind him; east and west, south and north he looks. He is a protector, whose task it is to see that the foundation below him is neither neglected nor violated. He may neither lie nor suffer physical blemish, lest there be cattle murrains and failing harvests. Set upon his chariot, upon the Stone of Destiny, the king is the guardian of his truth which preserves the kingdom, his *gwir deyrnas*. For it is through *gwir deyrnas* that the appropriate weather arrives each in its proper quarter: winter bright and frosty, spring dry and windy, summer hot and showery, autumn fruitful and heavy with dew. But let the king utter the lie of kingship, the *celwydd deyrnas,* and it will bring false weather over false people, so that the fruit of the earth dries up.

It appeared to me as I pondered the matter that the earth resembles that shapeless monster, the Adanc of the Lake, which men dragged with teams of oxen from the depths of Lin Sifadon. The strength of the Adanc is greater than that of the oxen, but men draw it and tease it and entice it, so that the monster moves as it wishes and as men wish. That is the way of the Brython in the Island of the Mighty.

But the emperor of Rufein bids his armies surround the monster with their spears and swords, and cast a net of ropes about it, drawing the strands so tight the monster may not move. Then he causes his masons and carpenters to build a great pen of dressed stone to hold the creature safe. The soldiers' spears are sharp, the net is strong, and the masons' work of consummate skill. Yet there must surely come a day when the guards are sleeping, the ropes rotted, or the cement moldered. Then will the monster recall his former days and shake himself with his former might, so that the net is burst open, the walls shaken down, and the guards crushed beneath the fallen ramparts.

For did not the Island of Prydein fall for a span of time beneath the Empire's sway? About us still we see the two great Walls in the North, and the network of roads, straight as stretched cords, which link the Twenty-eight Cities of the Island of Prydein. Now, however, the roads are blocked by fallen trees and broken bridges, and lie like a rotten piece of netting across the surface of the Island. The Adanc has shaken himself free of his bonds, and is returned to Lin Sifadon.

I looked up at Rufinus with my one eye, and he started when, for the first time, he glimpsed my scarred and ravaged face in the clear moonlight. Struck by a sudden thought, I inquired with a sly grin whether the emperor intended to restore the Island of Prydein to his Empire, now it seemed that Hispania might fall the way of Africa and Italia.

The tribune glanced at me with a quizzical expression. "It is not for me to interpret the emperor's will," he replied after a brief pause. "I am a soldier, and I obey my orders. There are those who say the whole world belongs to the Empire, and that those provinces which are now in the hands of the barbarians will in the fullness of time be restored to civilization. I myself stood beside Count Belisarius at Rome, when he offered to deliver Britannia over to the Goths. But that was just his humor, ridiculing the Goths' offer to recognize our rule in Sicilia, which we had already recovered by force of arms.

"It is generally held, as I believe, that Britannia fell under the sway of native tyrants when Rome first fell to the Goths. I do know that twenty years or so ago, Belisarius conducted a correspondence with the greatest of them, Artorius, whom he urged to cross into the kingdom of the Franks and fall upon the rear of the Goths, who were pressing us hard in Italia. But the truth is that few people speak of Britannia nowadays, and there are even those who believe it to be the island to which the souls of the dead are ferried!"

"That is no answer to my question," I countered a little sharply. "You are a commander of distinction, high in the councils of your army. Suppose that this summer your armies were victorious in Hispania, and you were ordered to embark with an expedition for this Island. Would that surprise you, and would you consider it a worthy enterprise?"

"Nothing surprises me, as it is my duty to be prepared for all things which may arise in the course of my service. As to whether it would be a worthy enterprise, who can doubt it? Perhaps you think me a frivolous person, since I recited to you 'The Syrian Castanet Dancer.' But that my father taught me; and, besides, it used to amuse the men at the end of a long day's marching in the heat to hear a humorless old veteran like myself extol the charms of

> "A dancing girl from Syria, Greek scarf about her hair,
> Flashing in the smoky bar soft glances that ensnare;
> Swaying 'neath her castanets, smiling from the wine,
> Clack-clacking out the rhythm as her feet keep time!

"As I told you, I've never been much one for the ladies, but I've still a soft spot for my Syrian castanet girl. In Alexandria my friend Apollos often took me to the theater. That was a year or so before the pantomimes were banished and the emperor ordered universal baptism, and I'm afraid in those days we young fellows weren't as pious as we might have been. I can't say the theater appealed to me much, but even now I remember the first time I saw our Helladia coming on as Venus, with a troupe of scruffy little Cupids trailing behind her. She seemed to leap with her eyes alone; and though she never noticed the lonely law student in the middle row, when her glance met mine (well, I thought it did!), my heart bounced within me as it did when I saw the Immortals coming for us at Daras.

"To be honest, the poem bears a great charm for me. No matter how often I recite it I can make the image return. I would close my eyes, letting my horse keep his own place at the head of the column—and there I was, back on the Via Clodia. Just ahead lay the *mansio* at Carreiae and the turning that leads to our villa, with the little inn on the corner, vines drooping over the trellis and fat melons basking in the sun. There would be time for a leisurely drink (the castanet dancer came only in the poem!), and then home to the dark, cool cistern, where I would sit with water up to my knees, listening to my father talking of Rome's departed glory.

"I have been fighting on the Empire's frontiers for nearly thirty years, from Daras to Septem as I have told you. During all that time it was a matter of no little pride to me that I was playing my part in restoring that glory. It was a silly fancy, but I confess that it was the thought that I was fulfilling my father's will that spurred me on, as much as my devotion to Rome and the emperor.

"I always bore in my mind my father's words concerning Rome's mission in the world. I was fifteen when he bestowed the *toga virilis* upon me; it was shortly after that he was taken away from me. It was a very solemn occasion: the festival of Liber Pater. The entire household was paraded in the atrium, with the busts of our ancestors watching from their niches. My father drew off my purple-edged toga, replacing it with the uniform of manhood. How proud I was, not to be degraded any longer by the hated purple! And what would I not give now to resume it!

"Then he took me by the hand and led me around past my forefathers' images, beginning with old Rufius Sextus, who rode by Emperor Septimius Severus' side at the conquest of Parthia. My father reminded me of the antiquity of our line, which in turn reflected the twelve centuries of Roman rule, emphasizing the comparative brevity of the recent cloud which had obscured the Roman name. He was no longer praetorian prefect at the time, but when we went to register my name in the *tabularium* he foresaw a day when I would earn a place by his side in that venerable Senate which was the custodian of Rome's virtue.

"Then my father turned to the assembled household and recited that wonderful eulogy of Rome, which every schoolboy knows but which (to my shame be it said, especially in view of the fact that I recall every line of 'The Syrian Castanet Dancer') I have almost entirely forgotten:

" 'Consul close to the gods, protector of the city . . .' But if I cannot recall the verses, I shall never forget the intent. Raising her golden head to the stars, her seven hills reflecting the seven regions of heaven; mother of arms and law, cradle of justice; it is Rome which has extended from one small place upon the earth to stretch from pole to pole. She has conquered Hispania and Sicilia, humbled Gallia and Carthago. Though defeated at Cannae and Trebia, she rose up with renewed strength to cross the Ocean herself and vanquish the Britanni. But those whom she conquers are received like children into a mother's bosom, drawn together by common citizenship and bonds of affection. The world has become one country, at peace with itself, whose citizens may explore the wilds of Thule and drink the waters of Rhodanus or Orontes without straying from their homeland. Nor can there be any limit to Rome's Empire, which alone has not succumbed to luxury and vice. For was not Athens humbled by Sparta, and Sparta by Thebes? The Assyrians conquered by the Medes, and the Medes by the Persians? Then Macedonia subdued Persia, yielding in her turn to Rome.

"I have been fortunate indeed in witnessing the truth of those words. At the very time my father uttered them, the Eternal City was in the hands of the barbarians and he, three-time praetorian prefect, about to be dragged off to a felon's death in Ravenna. Yet in the bare thirty years which have passed from that day to this, what have we seen? Our victories in East and West have recovered nearly all the lands bounded by the Empire's frontiers in the days of her former greatness. In the prefecture of the East the frontier is held against the Persians, and the barbarians are barred from Thracia by our defenses on the Danubius. In the West our armies have recovered Dalmatia, Italia, Sicilia, Sardinia, Corsica, and Africa, while Hispania even now succumbs to our arms. The emperor has restored fortresses and cities beyond number; from Byzantium and Rome his legions may march unhindered to the bounds of the civilized world, while his fleets hold undisputed sway upon the Mediterranean Sea. He has reformed the laws and improved the revenues. He has suppressed mutinous heresies in the Church, which is now fully under the command of the pope in Rome herself, fulfilling operational orders from the Council of Chalcedon.

"As some poet put it not long ago: 'Let the Roman traveler follow the steps of Hercules over the blue western sea and rest on the sands of Hispania, he will still be within the frontiers of the wise emperor's rule.'"

From somewhere far away below us floated up the mournful cry of a flower-faced owl, the old wide-eyed catcher of mice, screeching her summons to the hounds of night from the hollow of a rotten tree. The ugly scream echoed an oppressive sensation of fear and foreboding which assailed me increasingly as I listened to the tribune's reminiscences. It was not the wise Owl of Cwm Cawlwyd that was calling in the night, but the Owl of Gwyn mab Nud, conjuring up nightmare images of the Wild Hunt. "Hw-ddy-hw! Hw-ddy-hw!" wailed out her eerie screech through the dark trees beneath us. Into my mind it brought, too, a vision of the cruel betrayal of Leu, hanging pierced and rotting upon his Tree.

The air was raw and chilly, and cold had arisen upon a wind blowing the full length of the world from the hard unyielding planets set in the void above Dinleu Gurygon. The rough shoulder of the hill against which I leaned felt icy cold, and icy cold was I becoming myself. I knew that Rufinus' words disturbed me, yet scarcely understood why. I saw the ordered pattern of roads flung out upon the world, smacked down upon its surface like a fisherman's net when he flings it wide from his coracle upon a seething sea. Like a boulder under the stonemason's saw, the world was being refashioned from its former roughness into lines and squares. The lines led to the squares, and upon the stone-paved squares men and women congregated in numbers large enough to populate an upland kingdom. But though they shouted, gesticulated, and wrangled with one another, they did not savage one another like staghounds in an overcrowded kennel. For from the City at the center stretched laws written on parchment and transcribed to stone, and learning set in books, which marshaled and cajoled the people to live each in his allotted place beside the street.

Below the spot where we two stood lay buried in darkness the half-ruined city of Caer Gurygon, once the remotest township of that great Empire which Rufinus and his emperor were even now industriously repairing. Roads which had their beginnings in the city of Rufein and Caer Custennin by the Middle Sea crossed straight as spear-shafts over land and sea to take their ending here. Before their arrival they had tunneled through mountains, bridged great rivers, spanned marshes on timbered causeways. One obstacle only could they not surmount, and that was the holy hill upon which we stood: Dinleu. Here alone, at the end of its journeying, the broad street was compelled to skirt about to the north in a curve like a reaping-hook, almost doubling back on itself to enter the city by the shining Hafren.

Rufinus was speaking, but I could feel the draw and power of the hill exerted upon me, and his words became faint and distant. Other sounds were replacing those of his broken Ladin speech. A nightjar, twisting silently in the night sky above us, uttered a guttural "churr, churr" from his great gaping mouth; like the tribune, he was newly come from Africa, and like the tribune his voice was harsh and broken. From all about me in the heather and upon the rocks came a rustling and squeaking and grunting, as the myriad creatures inhabiting every footfall of its surface flew and crept and glided upon their secret paths.

I heard bats squeaking in the rimy dark and felt faint breeze upon my face from the wings of blundering moths. The cold had become yet more bitter: cold, cold, cold. I felt as if I were frozen into the hard ground, like the exposed outcrop against which I leaned for support. The owl's discordant shriek heralded the rising of a night mist, a vapor from each hollow, an encircling gray hood about the hilltop. I did not doubt that it was the mist of Gwyn mab Nud, smoky unguent of the Witches of Annufn, a shaggy mantle over the land.

Rufinus still stood before me, but his outline was dimmed by the gray mist of Dinleu and his features had become difficult to distinguish. He seemed to be speaking, but I could no longer comprehend the words despite the clarity and succinctness of his Ladin speech. It was jumbled and drowning amid the incoherent scraping, hissing, and coughing of those creatures whose lairs and trackways comprised as integral an element of the hill of Dinleu as the rocks beside me, the bracken and grasses bending in the wind about us, or the density of soil and rock below. Their bones, feathers, and shells, living and dead, carpeted its surface and were sealed deep below within the heart of the stone of the mountain.

Dimly I saw the tribune's face peering into mine, dissolving like a reflection in a mountain tarn when a flurry of wind turns upon it from the cliff-face. He had come close, clasping my shoulders and staring in bewilderment at my expressionless face. But I was cold and still—oh, so cold! Eventually he stepped back, took a final gaze at me and the rough crags beside me; then, shrugging, my friend turned to descend by the way he came.

CHAPTER TEN

THE DESCENT
OF MERLIN INTO
THE PIT OF ANNUFN

Rufinus descended the hill, and I was alone upon Dinleu Gurygon; the peak bright-crowned beyond all other peaks, with its summit round and green and rugged, wooded haunt of roe deer and badger and polecat. The breeze dropped, and a rank, warm scent uprose. By the shadow of the rocks a red fox was sitting upright upon its haunches, like a dog at his master's hearth. For a moment he sat, alert and easy, gazing out across the hillside. Then he rose silently and, turning about, slipped through the portals of Annufn, down into his earth. The harsh stench that assailed my nostrils and made my head swim flowed, as I guessed, from his bone-strewed litter, where his vixen lay suckling her cubs. It might be that they lay beneath my feet, drawing the warm milk from her teats.

There was a world beneath us, the departing tribune and I, upon which we had not bestowed a moment's thought as we spoke of the extension of the City's rule over the face of the earth. Yet it was we who had but paused upon Dinleu in our random wanderings, like the shadows of passing clouds obscuring the silvery sheen of the moon-lit hillside. *We* came and went as we chose, but the heather sprang up behind us as if we had never passed. It was to the red fox, slipping easy as an auger into the belly of the hillside, that the hill belonged, while our chatterings were snatched from our lips to be hurled to the winds, broken as the speech of a foreigner.

This sudden realization was accompanied by no reflexion on the earnest strivings of my friend the tribune, whose weft and warp of roads constrained the land over which they pass no more than does a salmon net the whale which, blundering among the cordage, lies momentarily supine before thrashing free. I knew that I too, Merlin mab Morfryn, was possessed of a deep desire to impose order and protection upon the Island that bears my name, through prophecy and enchantments and runes.

But vain and frivolous are our imaginings, our laws and hosts and treaties; vain and frivolous when they lack the oath that binds: of sun and moon, water and air, day and night, sea and land. Immobile and chill, I was stuck fast in earth. I was being drawn deep into the crust of the hill by a power strong as the water that filled the scabbard of Osla Cylelfawr. And though it was the mid hour of night, I heard about me the glorious singing of a flock of birds. They were the Birds of Riannon, which rouse the dead and make the living sleep. So it was that the false sense stole upon me.

I was wedged in the belly of the hill, my body stiff, cold, and inert. Before me, cross-legged upon a mound, sat a huge skin-clad herdsman, beside him a curly-haired mastiff bigger than a stallion of nine winters. Its breath was such that it would consume dead wood and yellowed tufts of grass upon the open Plain of Powys beneath. In his hand the great swart figure bore an iron club that would be a burden for two men to carry.

I asked him what was his power over the creatures assembling upon the hillside; for now I heard their scuffling and grunting and squealing all about me beneath the bracken, behind the boulders, and among swaying branches of birch, beech, and yew. "I will show thee, little man," he replied in a voice that rumbled like the roll of Taran's Wheel in storm clouds above the snowy peaks of Eryri. And, taking up his club, he struck a great stag that stood beside him such a blow that it roared as if at its rutting. As though in answer to the stag's bellowing, there gathered about us the boundless flocks of creatures that dwell upon the hill, in its depths, upon its surface, and in the windy air that sways the tops of bracken and trees. It appeared to me that they were numerous as the stars in the sky, so that it was difficult for them all to find space upon the hillside.

I saw spotted, high-antlered deer, roebuck of the mountain; great clumsy bears who shambled upright as the sons of men; bristle-coated boars of bright tusks; wild wolves of rapine with bloodshot eyes and slavering jaws; beavers, otters, and martens of sleek coats and lithe motion; badgers, which were men and women transformed; and other creatures innumerable. At that hosting it appeared to me that there were a hundred of every kind of four-footed animal. There, too, glided glistening serpents, each upon his belly in dire penance, venomous and twisting.

But great though that host of beasts appeared to me upon the hill of Dinleu Gurygon, it was as nothing to that which swarmed about the earth and rocks and bracken stalks beneath their hoofs and paws and bellies. Until the stars of heaven can be numbered, and the sands of sea be counted, and flakes of snow, and dewdrops in a dawn meadow, and hailstones in a storm, and blades of grass beneath the hoofs of racing horses about the hill of Leu at the Kalan Mai, and the white-maned daughters of Gwenhiduy in a sea tempest: until all these may be numbered, I say, there is no telling the number of the myriad host of insects that covered the brown slopes and summit of the knoll like a moving multicolored coat. There were armored stag beetles that gnaw the sides of sleeping men; golden-cloaked humming hordes of bees, each legion under the sway of its queen more numerous than the tribes of the goddess Don; and teeming cities of ants (they that brought the nine loads of linseed to Yspadaden Pencaur), whose streets and gateways and many-chambered palaces outrival those of the emperor of the world in Rufein and Caer Custennin.

When all the creatures were assembled, serpents and dragons and every sort of beast that glides or walks or flies, the Black Herdsman gazed around upon them and told them to return to their feeding. They all, serpents and dragons and creatures of all kinds, bowed their heads and acknowledged the Black Herdsman's sovereignty over them. They had entered his house and paid him tribute and delivered up hostages to him, so that he was the chief of their household and they were one and all of his kindred. I alone remained stiff and upright, for I was not of their blood, nor had the Black Herdsman's shears and comb passed over my head. That time was yet to come.

The Black Herdsman spoke to me with a voice which sounded through the bracken of the hill and among the host of creatures that paid him homage, so that it seemed to me it arose from all around like a summer breeze which stirs the leaves of a forest without revealing whence it comes.

"Do you see now, little man," he asked, "what power I hold over all these creatures?"

I acknowledged his power in trembling tones, and asked him faintly what I was to do and where I should go.

The Black Herdsman answered me in a rough and angry voice: "You must take the path that leads toward the head of this glade, and then ascend the wooded height until you gain the summit of the hill.

There you will find an open space like a large valley, in the midst of which is a tall tree whose branches are greener than the greenest pine trees. By the tree is a cleft in the rock which is ever filled with water, from which the Birds of Riannon drink. That is the Raven's Bowl. By the Bowl is a silver cup, attached to it by a silver chain. Take water in the cup and throw it upon the rock. You will hear a mighty peal of thunder, which will cause you to believe that heaven and earth are trembling with its fury. What follows the peal of thunder you will discover for yourself."

After these words the Black Herdsman departed and all his multitude of beasts with him, save one. I was alone once more upon the bare hillside, my sole companion one of the wild goats that grazed the hill Dinleu. As I drew myself free from the rock and soil and moved to resume my ascent, he stepped before me as if to guide me on my way. The path became rocky and steep, but fortunately the creature paused from time to time to crop grass at the wayside. I was exhausted, and my steps painfully slow.

Despite the difficult climb, my companion proved a sure guide. Swiftly we gained the edge of the summit, which was ringed by mighty earth dykes built in days long past by men or gods. Scrambling behind my sure-footed guide, I found myself gazing over the open space like an upland valley which had been described to me by the lord of the beasts. This I knew to be the enclosure of Leu, *clas Leu,* where the king and his druids had enacted the mysteries that day. In its center stood the tall Tree whose branches are greener than the greenest pine trees.

Above us the horned moon gleamed pale in the night sky, while the spangled array of lights in the dark vault beyond glittered brightly. The air was unusually clear, for a bitter wind blowing from the north had driven off the clouds, dispelling also with its drying breath a misty vapor that hung about the perimeter of the enclosure.

I approached the Tree, with the goat stepping ahead of me as before. Soon I came upon that recess in the rock which the Black Herdsman had termed the Raven's Bowl. It was filled with water, whose black and glassy surface perfectly reflected the rounded dome of heaven above, with its stars and its moon. There, too, lay the silver chain and cup. I took it up, scooped water from the crevice, and splashed it down upon the surface of the water.

At once the image of the night sky was shivered and broken. All about the hilltop crashed and rolled and echoed a mighty peal of thunder. As its reverberations died away, the skies seemed to open up over my bowed head and a shower of hailstones pelted down upon the enclosure, so severe as to make me wonder how I should survive its onslaught. From head to foot my weary body was struck as if by an unceasing volley of slingshot. I fell upon my face by the pool, bruised and aching in every limb, until the shower ceased as abruptly as it had started.

From the Tree I could hear birds singing strains more beautiful than I had ever heard before, but when I rose and looked, I saw that every leaf upon the Tree had been borne away by the shower. At its foot my goat was busily engaged in gnawing at its bark. I brought to mind the goat upon which Leu mounted to ascend the fatal Tree, when he was pierced by the fated spear that wounded his fair side. From the wound his blood poured out until he was naught but rotting skin and bone; but the blood at the foot of the Tree nurtured its roots, causing it to grow ever more green and fair and tall.

Far, far above me, set in that wonderful firmament which was crafted by the skill of Gofannon mab Don, glittered the aery palaces of Leu's divine parents, the wizard Gwydion and silver Arianrod. Their gates were opened in that moment, and for one brief blinking of my eye the whole world was irradiated by a wonderful light whose warmth and brightness were not of this world.

The night was about me again, but the warmth remained upon my body. I stripped off my clothes and lay naked, pouring with sweat, beside the pillar-stone that stood by the side of the Tree. Drawing a large stone upon my belly, so that I lay between the rock and the rock, embraced by the rock, I began to chew upon a morsel of pork from the kings' cauldron which I had borne away with me from their hall.

Pressed between the stone that lay upon me and the bare rock beneath, bedewed by the sweat that continued to seep from my emaciated frame, I felt my manhood seep away from me with it into the hill. Mine alone of all creatures whose dwelling place lay upon the hill of Dinleu Gurygon was the power to sweat, and it was my sweat that seeped through a crevice in the rock below me. It trickled past the badgers' set, where they frolicked with their cubs in fortresses of fifty gates, and down the walls of the foxes' earth hard by the portals of Annufn.

The red ravager, his vixen wife and robber brood were busy with bloody flesh and cracking bones, and so saw me not as I stole past their lodge down into the shadowed Halls of Annufn. I had passed from the land of the living to that of the dead, and as I stole along its endless descending galleries, I glimpsed through the murk beasts more strange and terrible than any conjured up in soothsayers' prophecies. Out of the darkness there glared forth dragons, Adancs, winged serpents, and other monstrous creatures too huge and horrible to describe, all ribbed, scaled, and armored in cold rock. Shadows shifted on their gigantic forms, claws curved like sickles and teeth edged sharp as dagger-blades seeming to menace me in my furtive descent. But all were cold, dead, and turned to rock by enchantments potent as those by which the Jet-black Witch, daughter of the Bright-white Witch from Penn Nant Gofud, binds the figures of stone that stand in her dripping cave by the borderlands of Uffern.

It is not for nothing that the pit into which I had tumbled is termed *Annufn:* "bottomless." Lit by no sun or moon or stars, its windy vaults contain a realm as spacious as that arching over the bright earth above. But here you find no joyous feasting around a blazing hearth, no lit-up doorway to welcome the purple-clad stranger, no talkative men waxing merry over ale, no trysting of lovers beneath the yellow broom. There the shades of the dead flit like bats through the endless maze of corridors and descending stairways, culminating at intervals in chasms so vast that their depths enclose worlds abandoned and lifeless as the crow-haunted ruins of royal forts, the genealogies of whose kings have long passed from the mouths of bards.

So I passed through passages and cells of time, which exist without number in the vasty Halls of Annufn. At times I journeyed in obscurity black as a raven's wing, traversing chambers roofed with a starless sky. At others I glimpsed distant holds, lit by the glare of furnaces where the hammers of elves rang upon tiny anvils; rooms fiery, melting, peopled by demons, screeching, cursing; shelves of rock with water dripping into pools of pitch-black water; pelting rain driving through darkness across an endless waste of upland peat bogs; veins of gold encased in stone, gleaming in the murk like kings' brooches; jewels of value and jewels of curing; huge bones of monsters; voices jabbering afar off in languages spoken on earth before the pure speech of the Brython emerged from the Head of Bran. I passed hard by the stinking lair of the Cath Palug, and the grove of stone-bolled trees where dwells the Witch of Caer Loyw with her Nine Daughters. Their poison eyes burned at me in the murk with hateful glare as I hurried past.

Much that I witnessed was noxious, vile, reptilian. But I saw also sights that were golden, glorious. I saw the stronghold where lie guarded the Thirteen Treasures of the Island of Prydein, which I might not enter. I opened the iron chest with its nine locks which contains the Writings of Prydein, within which are inscribed all the secret matters and holy of the Island of Prydein: the spell-books of Gwydion and Math, the Book of Laws of Dyfnwal Moelmud; works containing all the lore of earth and heaven—the movement of the stars, the size of the universe and the earth, the order of nature, and the strength and powers of the immortal gods. My heart beat fast when I glimpsed among the heap the volume which you who hold this book now read. Then it was termed by the learned the Book of Merlin, *Llyfr Myrddin,* but to a later age it has become the Yellow Book of Meifod. The black-cowled monks who transcribe its lines dread my name, yet they hope to make use of my words! It is a matter of sorrow to me that scholars of such littleness should have the Writings of Prydein in their keeping, after the druids and wise men who preserved them of old.

As you may shortly see, the Pit of Annufn is an unchancy place to visit. Yet it is there that Wisdom lies, and poets and prophets in search of their *awen* travel a hard road to the Fountain of Leudiniaun, where they may sip of the water of inspiration which flows out of the Pit. Not for nothing is the place beneath termed Puil Pen Annufn, which signifies, as well you know, "Wisdom of the Head of Annufn." Foolish men and dwarves, scratching their own heads in perplexity, scrape below earth and rocks for gold and silver; but it is not Wisdom which they discover within their mines. Far deeper far must you delve if you are to discover the true wealth of the Head of Annufn.

For when He whose seven words went forth to create all that is, has been, and will be beneath the firmament, began His mighty work, what was it that He summoned to Him for assistance? *Puil,* Wisdom, was there at the beginning, before the hills were heaved up above the land, the sea sunken below the circle of the deep, fountains flowed, or stars sparkled from the tent of the night. Wisdom was the workman by His side when He crafted lovingly His creation; Wisdom lay within the ten words of creation; Wisdom was as one with Him—yet likewise His separation when He spoke with His Wisdom, saying, "Let us make man!"

Wisdom is the labor and understanding of creation. The courses of the sun and moon were established firmly from the beginning, and men learned mysteries in the first age which are now but dimly remembered, so long is the cycle of centuries which has passed. The jeweled casket was no bungler's work, and understanding of its hoarded wealth may be attained by those who possess the key and do not fear to lift the lid.

Now the *Puil* which is the Head of Annufn was set in the midst of the starry void, and void indeed are the windy wastes that stretch beyond measuring to the outer spheres. When He wished for a companion, it was for a Son He wished. For the saying is, "A man lacking a son is as a lone tree opposed to the wind." And though the Tree be rooted fast with nine roots in rock of the Underworld, and its top soar even to the Nail of the Heavens, yet is the moan of the wind of the planets through the empty universe chill and friendless. Do I not know it in my lone refuge within the Forest of Celyddon; how it bends trees, heaps up snow, and hurls breakers roaring against the land? Wild is the wet wind and white the tree stumps; the stag trots over the bare hill; weak and worn is the exile, plodding painfully.

So it was that out of the Tree there grew a man. And when the craft of Gofannon mab Don had fashioned a bony armor of protection about His creation at the center of the void, He placed therein store of His Wisdom, that He might not be without a fellow being whom He might love.

Now within the Head of Annufn lie numberless chambers, containing each its portion of the divine Wisdom. To these chambers men have more or less access according to their nature, inclination, or skill. But to none is allotted knowledge of more than an infinitesimal section of the whole, for the life span of the oldest of men and women is but brief, and it is their deeds and thoughts that are continually accumulating in fresh chambers within the Pen Annufn.

Like the cells of a honeycomb are the galleried chambers of the Head, and like a bee I hovered before first one, then another, glancing with importunate curiosity from room to room. Delighted with my newfound pastime, I set myself to divining varied patterns from what I saw, much as a skilled harpist plucks here and there along the range of his instrument. And, just as the harpist moves from brief lilting interludes, tricks and practices of his art, to full flowing harmony of his creative mind, so I, too, found myself unconsciously adjusting the range of objects about me into patterns which were swift to assume their own course and identity.

I recalled a time lingering in my memory from long ago, when I with my lovely white-limbed companion spent all of a long summer tending goats by upland *hafodai* among the languid lawns of Leudiniaun. In the heat of the afternoon we would lie beneath the shade of a sweet-apple tree, the tinkling of goats' bells mingling with limpid plashing of a rill below our secret knoll. For long, long hours we lay, gazing upward at the dappled host of leaves, our half-waking minds absorbing from them fanciful shifting shapes of ships and serpents, castles and coastlines, lions and lonely landscapes.

So, between dreaming and waking, I created imaginary kingdoms of the mind, peopled by fantastic beings whose purpose became gradually half-apparent to my understanding. From the galleried cells of the Head of Annufn they passed into the chambers of my mind; and it was my mind, playing across them like the wind which, caressing the strings of the Harp of Teirtu, aroused harmonies of elegance and order. Within our heads there lies an Annufn in miniature, and upon the walls of their skulls men may contemplate the constellations, seeking their fortunes among the planetary spheres.

You see these twin serpents upon my staff, O Ceneu mab Pasgen; you who bear your adder about your throat? Look how they spiral, and how one writhing body is indistinguishable from the other! Follow either upward, and you will arrive at the same destination.

Let mad Merlin be your guide with his serpent-staff, and you are unlikely to lose your way! For the one serpent is male, the other female, like the sun and the moon, the sky and the earth. From their union derives the harmony you seek, and when your goal is attained you will find the sun but a step from the ocean, glorious Leu with His Sure Hand dying in the wilderness of dark Cernun, the body returned to the bourne from which it sprang. Follow the rainbow's arc, travel the Twelve Houses which are set about Caer Gwydion, return whence you came, into the harmony which was at the beginning:

Lord! Would that I were lying upon my love's smooth breast
When people here in Prydein have closed their eyes to rest;
Tired men and wearied women all slumbering till morn
While my darling love and I take pleasure's play past dawn!
O soft-skinned, yielding, gentlest of lovely maidens far,
My mistress, maid, and sister: my guiding Morning Star!
Nor priestly malediction, nor threat of vengeful kin
Shall ever make me misconceive our coupling as sin.

Such were my reflexions and discoveries as I passed through Puil Pen Annufn, the Head of Wisdom which lies within the Deep. In Annufn there is neither day nor night, so there was no measuring the length of my journey. For long I trudged by a black strand that bounds a sunless sea, that dark salt ocean from which all creation arises with the dawn and subsides with the coming of evening. Below a surface that glimmered dull and smooth in a pale predawning light filtering down from far above me lay the *Ty Gwydr,* the House of Glass, the elements within it endlessly dissolving and re-forming.

Pacing onward through corridors dusty, very smoky, I came to the entrance of Arthur's castle at Celliwig in Cerniu. There he sat in his hall among the warriors of his *gosgordd,* all still and cold as a ring of stones, awaiting the day when he shall be summoned to save the Island of Prydein from the Oppression of the Foreigners. As I moved on my way, I heard far off a dismal groaning in the darkness. When I inquired who it was that groaned and what was the cause of his sufferings, I heard a faint voice murmur:

"I am that Idawg Cord Prydein whose lying words brought about strife between Arthur and Medraud, from which proceeded the Slaughter of Camlann. And three nights before the battle I departed to the far North, to the stone which is called Lech Las in Prydyn. And here I must do penance and suffer torments, for it was through my deed that oppression came upon the Island of Prydein, and the false race of the Iwys set their claws upon the southern part of the Island."

The torment of Idawg is a terrible one, commensurate with his crime. For his role it is to play the part of the hinge of the door that leads below the stone into Annufn, and ever the hinge turns within his eye. When that door is turned the rust within the hinge screams and Idawg Cord Prydein screams likewise, and which of those two screamings is the more terrible no man can tell.

I left that dank spot, for my purpose brooked no further delay. It was among the twisting roots of that mighty Tree which grows at the Center of the Island, joining earth and heaven, that I arrived before a cavernous entrance set in coldest rock. By this gateway, seated upon a great knotted root, sat a huge churlish fellow, a club across his knees. When I inquired of him his name (though I knew it full well), he replied in a surly tone:

"I am Glewlwyd Gafaelfawr, the porter of this place, which it is forbidden to enter."

"Who forbids it?" I asked sharply.

"My master," grunted the porter, raising his huge club. "It is he who does not desire you to enter."

"And who is your master?"

"That I may not say, nor will I permit you to pass."

I became exceedingly angry at this base-born fellow's insolence, and told him what was in my mind:

"It comes into my mind that your master is none other than Hafgan, Lord of Annufn. And it is he you may tell that, unless you allow me to pass through his entrance, I will utter satires upon his name which will raise upon his face the three blisters of stain, blemish, and defect. And when the three painful blisters have come upon him, I will shout them with a cry which men will hear as readily at Penwaed in the south as at Penrin Blathaon in the north, and which will echo from the accursed Ridge of Esgeir Oerfel in Ywerdon. And from that cry all the women which dwell at the court of Hafgan will abort, and those that do not abort shall be sterile as an empty snail's shell until the end of time. Think upon this matter, Glewlwyd Gafaelfawr!"

"Is that the choice which you present to my master?" asked the porter.

"It is," I replied. "Remember: But one part of my life is nearly gone, while six parts of yours are departed."

Glewlwyd Gafaelfawr grumbled for a while into his beard. But he could not deny the potency of my reasoning, grudgingly moving aside to grant me entrance.

Immediately before me the tunnel plunged downward into a darkened abyss. As I groped my way down the narrow stairway I was seized by stark fear such as I had never known before—no, not even when I was menaced as a babe by the murderous Custennin Gorneu upon the strand below the Tower of Beli, nor when I hung upon the tide in the fishing-weir of Gwydno Garanhir. I was approaching the holy place, about which the very air was impregnated with danger.

After stumbling for some time blindly through what seemed to be a maze of galleries, feeling my way along the stone walls, I glimpsed ahead a faint iridescence. At first it was no more than that of a glowworm lying concealed below a thick hedge, but after turning two or three corners I came suddenly upon a long gloomy gallery. It was illumined with squat candles of animal fat, set in niches along its walls. They burned fitfully, emitting an acrid-smelling smoke which hung in a pall below the sooty arches of the roof.

On first entering this Hall of Wonders (as it proved), I gave an involuntary start of surprise and fear. For all around me were gathered herds of huge beasts, looming out at me from the shadows. There were bisons, wild horses, reindeer, and other creatures of the borderlands of the North. For a moment I thought myself upon the frozen plains that gird the North beyond Lychlyn, lost in a starless night among the creatures that lord it over that desolate region.

Recovering myself swiftly, I saw presently that what I took to be living creatures of forest and plain were but beautifully executed paintings upon the gallery walls, their features molded to the contours of the rock-face. Russet-brown, ocher, black: the coloring was reproduced to perfection. Even when I knew them to be but representations of the living beasts, I found it hard to believe that warm breath was not steaming from the horse's nostril, that the bristle-backed boar was not honing his tusks against a stone, or that a graceful antlered stag was not cropping lichen at my feet.

All were in truth alive, though not alive. It was here that the spirits of beasts roaming the windy world above were gathered, preserved to all eternity, while their mortal frames were struck down in succession by the arrows of disease, the spear of the huntsman, and the axe of old age. Beyond, in the upper earth, their flesh is devoured by their enemies, who gather up the bones within their stiffened, withered pelts. Then they perform the rites restoring to them the forms which lie in safety here, ever vigorous in their pristine splendor and power.

It was a place of purity and sanctity, and my fear passed. Moving onward, I encountered further herds of painted animals, each more lifelike than the last; some, fashioned in clay, seemed to pace beside me in shadowy relief. Turning into a fresh gallery, I glimpsed to my delight among the crowd of beasts jostling about me the Wolf of Menwaed and the Eagle of Brynach, who were conceived at my conception and born at my birth. There, too, bristling in giant relief, was the sow Henwen, who gave birth to them upon the cold slope of Riw Gyferthuch all of a long age ago. From a cleft above me peered down the old wide-eyed catcher of mice, the Owl of Cwm Cawlwyd, nighttime screecher, whose back is ever hunched against rain and snow, bird of death and companion of Gwyn mab Nud; while swimming upon the edge of the shadows at my side was the ancient one-eyed Salmon of Lyn Liw, who guided me safely from the lair of the Adanc of the Deep.

Now I rejoiced within me, for the herds of beasts and birds and fish provided me with strength greater even than that provided by my muse, my *awen*. For the expression of the *awen* is of the surface of earth, the yellow of primroses, and the wind that blows from the planets. It is strong, and may create worlds upon worlds. But they are worlds that live out their time and then, like summer at the Gwyl Aust, slip down into the Pit of Annufn. Among the animals, however, I shared the strength of the life-bearing and life-giving *enaid* that flows through them all like a breeze imperceptibly stirring the leaves of a thicket on a summer's day. With a man it is but one *enaid* he possesses, which at his passing leaves his body and passes over the waters to Caer Sidi. But among birds and beasts and fishes the *enaid* belongs to all, as it belongs to the earth and the universe in which they have their being. That is why, when men kill a beast in hunting, they perform those rites which placate the creature's *enaid* and that of its fellows who hold it in common.

So we arrived at the sanctuary at the heart of the labyrinth. I knew well the hatred its Guardian bore for me (with reason, be it said), and moreover that it is no easy matter, having descended the warren of tunnels, to return to the upper air. There was a thread that linked me to Rufinus, with his roads and aqueducts and host of officials compiling reports in Ravenna and Caer Custennin. Stronger still was the thread that joined my mind to that of Taliesin: his understanding of the earth with its Four Quarters about its Navel; the seven words spoken at the creation of the earth, the seven planets and seven notes of the Harp of Teirtu; and the nine elements of things.

But now I feared lest somewhere in the labyrinth's tracings behind me my lifeline's threads were snapped, for strongest of all bonds is the navel-string of earth from which I had been severed in my windy chamber above the Sea of Hafren, but which now drew me as I sensed down to the place of nocturnal repose.

Who would not linger in his downy bed of a morning in the black season of deep winter, when snow is piled high upon hills, fish frozen in ice, wolves finding neither repose nor sleep, no bell heard, the voice of the crane silent in the land, and the strands of the world washed by angry breakers? At eve the same snug couch awaits him, within it his wife warmly waiting, her breasts whiter than a swan's and her eye brighter than that of a thrice-mewed falcon. After fond play he sinks to rest pillowed on a white arm, bodies and dreams mingled in sleep. Yet, like Dinogad's father, he must be up and doing the livelong day; spear on shoulder, hounds in couples, tracking boar and roebuck amid a host of bare trees on the frozen shoulder of the mountain. For him is there a rising and a resting, regular as that of Beli the Great as he soars upon his golden arch, the reign of a king within his *gwlad;* a soaring of the falcon, his stooping, and his plunging to the kill; a loosing of the arrow and burying of its sharp head beneath the green turf. We may not look behind us, nor see whose Sure Arm and Unerring Eye it was that bent the bow.

Yet, once back at rest, how good it is to lie at peace! Broad is the full moon, pale are coverlet and pillow, and distant the rain wetting the deep and wind whistling through frozen reeds! Among the sleek-furred host of animals that padded about me in the grotto that lies almost at the heart of the kingdom of Annufn, I had returned to the warmth of my mother's belly, safe before the star fell from the sky through the window of the Tower of Beli. Through us all there floated the breeze that lifts the stars, which is seed in soil, sap in trees, blood in beasts. I was possessed of the floating grace of the Eagle of Brynach upon the wind, the fleet racing of the Wolf of Menwaed across the open plain, and the resistless strength of the sow Henwen as she burrows with tusks and snout deep into the recesses of the earth.

And now all those beasts, serpents, dragons, birds, myriad creatures having their origins within the abyss, followed as one a patterned course flowing like the *enaid* which linked them all in a chain of being;

dancing in an encircling stream of vibrant life throughout the vascular grottoes of the galleried labyrinth of Annufn.

Coursing convoluted as a heap of entwined serpents, we penetrated its inner passages. Our pulsating flow divided within the damp dark galleries. Encountered anew, it spiraled coiling about itself, palpitated for a space as if with a single heartbeat, unwound at length in sinuous languor. For thrice fifties of years the White Dragon ravaged the Red, after which for thrice fifties more the Red came to surmount the White; from that conjunction would the Island of the Mighty be reborn in pain and travail.

Like embers in the dark smoldered the eyes of jaguars and lions; like flickering flames of crimson and gold burned the dappled pelts of tigers and leopards. Kingly power soared in their effortless strength, and likewise sun and heat and light. From the regenerative writhing of snakes about the *pwynt perfedd* uprose the lion's majesty, high as a tree in the upper darkness upon crested antlers of antelope and stag.

A thousand birds sang upon the branches of the tree, and I with them in my bird cloak, floating upon the enchanted strains of their song. At times the melody was the rise and fall of the single heartbeat palpitating through all the animal host, but ever the notes soared higher over the pulsating rhythm as thrilling and compelling as a lark's solitary caroling in the empty aether over a windy upland. It is a song that summons golden glances from the sun's glad eye, unfurls green shoots from branches, and quickens wombs to procreative warmth. Tossing trees are jubilant, wavelets dancing, the earth alive with bees' murmuring.

The dancers' hearts leaped ever higher, mine I felt higher than all. Each ecstatic bound seemed to draw me forth from the abyss I had unwillingly penetrated, cadences of unseen music becoming steps ascending to the light. I was possessed of the serpent's sinuosity, the wolf's endurance, the eagle's soaring. I laughed aloud; soon would I pace the seven planets, step out the starry studs of the Chariot of the Bear, pluck the seven strings of the Harp of Teirtu!

"Question me: I am a harper!" were the words You uttered when You entered the Hall of Heaven, with its sooty roof and twinkling torches; and with Your Sure Hand You plucked the strings, set time in accord with eternity, harmonized the elements of the tune to which we danced throughout the coiled entrails of Annufn. It is a round that returns whence it began. It began upon the lofty peak of Dinleu, bright-knolled enclosure beneath the silver moon, and thither will it ascend once more when all is done.

About that fair peak the bright god maintains His protection, whirling the winds with His long arm, spinning the firewheel of fierce-rayed stars. His is the dance that causes the earth to sink, fires to flame, makes mountains leap. Bright is His brow, bright as the silver moon, flashing His radiant eye; forth from it winds the pure Hafren.

But only after death within the darkness of the cave beneath the Lech Echymeint does new life come with the call of the cuckoo at the Kalan Mai. Unless the adversary be vanquished and the great stone rolled aside, there may be no *kyntefin*, no Resurrection. Not until the beast be slain is the spirit free to fly aloft. Not before then may the dance reascend on wings of song; without that victory all lies covered in clay, beetles sucking at blood in the darkness.

Now I knew it before I attained it: I stood once more before the entrance to the sanctuary that lies at the very heart of the Halls of Annufn. Through the doorway shone a cold luminescence, like that of the reflected moon from a mountain tarn. I was weary from the dance among the innumerable twists and coils of the labyrinth, and faint with fear of what lay before.

Suddenly, amid the alluring languor of my dreaming, I was aware that our Master was in the midst of us, and that we were caught up within him. In form he was gigantic, and there was no part of the living earth that was not an attribute of his greatness. From his head spread the broad antlers and ears of the Stag of Redynfre. His eyes were deep and staring as those of the Owl of Cwm Cawlwyd. His tail was that of a horse; and there was no animal or bird or fish that runs or flies or swims upon earth that had not its part upon the Lord of the Beasts. But his body was that of a man.

He towered in our midst, for he was greater in size than the greatest of tusked, fanged, and winged creatures that paid him worship and fealty. The Stag-specter, as I will call him, was seated cross-legged upon a raised shelf of rock. About his neck was a torque of gold, and in his right hand he held up a greater torque, whose dominion encompassed the host of beasts assembled below him. From a shadowy crevice beside him emerged the shimmering, sinuous coils of Ifor's Daughter, who seemed to whisper with flickering tongue in her Master's ear. He grasped the cold reptile by its throat, yet seemed entranced by the mutterings of the perfidious, powerful being, who alone of all creatures succeeded in stealing the secret of immortality from the deathless gods. The faint hissing of the serpent was the only sound that broke the stillness of the cavern. Stags, wolves, lions and wild beasts innumerable, myself among them, crouched subservient and expectant about their Master and his counselor, like hounds at the feasting of kings.

All at once I found myself alone before the dread lord of that cold place. I felt as if the weight of the world were upon my shoulders and that death, the beginning and end of all things, awaited me in the chamber. Sodden with the cold sweat of despairing dread, I longed to depart. Yet my leaden feet bore me relentlessly forward.

It was death indeed that confronted me in the vault. The Stag-specter gazed coldly upon me with his predatory owl's eyes as I limped across the rock floor, which as I saw was worn smooth by the feet, hoofs, and paws of countless generations of men and beasts since the world began in the dance of time. A chilling luminosity irradiated the massive figure who squatted in the midst of the chamber. The glare of his owl's eyes was terrible to see, and I saw that his foreclaws were encrusted and dripping with gore. He had supped with death; the stench of death hung in the fetid air, death was among the lifeless forms of the beasts whose representations were traced along the roughness of the walls, death was old in the mildewed pelts and bared teeth and bones of a rotted heap of corpses scattered around, and death was fresh in the clotted blood upon the demon's fur-fringed lips and talons. It was the death of slaughter, the death of putrefaction, and the death of oblivion. It was Death who opened his jaws before me. Resistance was fruitless: I had danced the round, and the circle was complete. I shambled forward, wondering only (as men in their foolishness always wonder) in what manner it was that death would take me.

Broken in body and spirit, I stood with head bowed before the lord of this dreadful place. I, who had the power to know all things in earth and sky, had willingly entered the place of annihilation! What power could it be, greater than knowledge and prophetic foresight, that drew me on? Why had my *awen* failed me? When I played my solitary game of *gwyddbwyll* in the council chamber of King Brochfael, I had glimpsed the move of treachery, but not of death. What trickery had exerted its power over me, who knew all the spells of druids and smiths and women? All, all had been false: false the distillation within the Cauldron of Ceridwen; false the baptism of Abbot Mawgan and the sacred waters of the Sea of Hafren; false the images I had encountered with Taliesin upon the crag of Mellun above the forests of Argoed Lwyfein.

If these were false, then all in existence was false. The black hosts of the Coranieid, swarming on the confines of creation, would engulf all in chaos and dissolution; the White Dragon would overcome the Red, and the Monarchy of Prydein crumble to ruin with false kings and wasted crops. I could feel their decay within me. The blood was parching in my veins, the flesh shriveling upon my bones, and the bones drying and cracking within the frame of my body. I was dying, dying, dying, and the fairest isle that is in the world, the Island of the Mighty that bears my name (or I its), was sinking beneath the black tide. In the darkened skies the stars were plunging into the ocean, where the Adanc of the Deep was uncoiling his mighty length, setting the muscles of his ribs between the rocks that support the ocean depths, and splitting the earth asunder.

I saw all this in the cold gaze of the Stag-specter, and I heard ringing in my ears the last dreadful verses of the Prophecy of Prydein. Now the demon was holding me in his cold embrace, and it was the embrace a warrior knows as he suffocates in darkness beneath a heap of slain on an abandoned battlefield. I was sinking into the River of Death, and the floodwaters were closing above my head. A swarm of memories clambered upon each other within the chambers of my brain, like the hateful hosts of the Coranieid when their Oppression is unleashed from frontier wastelands.

Strongest of these memories, surfacing even as the grasp of the Stag-specter tightened about my throat, was that evil hour when at the orders of King Custennin Gorneu, I was launched as a babe out onto the turbulent waters of the Sea of Hafren. Death had intended me for his own even then, and but for the protection of Nud of the Silver Hand, I must surely have died almost before I lived. But Nud saw me from the precinct of his hillside temple in the pleasant land of Gwent, stretched forth his Silver Arm, and bore me safely upon nine great green-shouldered waves out onto the bosom of the Sea of Hafren, so that I might come under the tutelage of His servant, the wise Salmon of Lyn Liw, oldest of all created beings.

I gave one silent shriek from a throat dry as a tanned goatskin: the last utterance of Merlin mab Morfryn; the last war-shout of the kings of Prydein; the last breath of the *awen* from the Cauldron of Poesy. Though the words would not emerge from the portals of my lips, they were inscribed upon the tablets of my brain. They were the verses of "The Great Praise of Nud," and even as I dangled dying in the grip of the Stag-specter the alliteration and internal rhymings proclaimed the coming of the company of the gods who brought order, fruitfulness, and kingship to the Island of the Mighty:

> *Seith meib o Veli dyrchafyssyn*
> *Kaswallawn a Nud aches tudyn.*

My opponent knew my thought, and laughed aloud as his talons choked the last breath whistling faint within my gullet. But even as I sank beneath the River of Death, the Praise of Nud and the exultant laughter of the Stag-specter whirled together in a wind of consciousness gusting through my mind. I knew that laugh of old! Was it not that of the sorcerer with whom Nud fought in his deserted hall, the length of the longest nighttime that was in the world?

Even as the memory of his combat flashed through my mind, I resolved that my end was not yet come. I would fight as Nud fought, whatever the odds, and perhaps it might be I that worsted the Stag-specter even as Nud had worsted the sorcerer. I threw my arms about his huge furred body, striving with all my might to deprive him of his balance. He laughed his cold laugh again as he released his grip on my throat and grasped me in my turn about the chest and shoulders. As we strove each for the mastery, I sensed that he mocked at my futility, pitting as I was my weakened frame against the effortless might of stag and horse, bear and bison. I was feeble as the brothers Cacamuri and Hygwyd, when they suffered the hug of the Pitch-black Witch in the Cave of Penn Nant Gofud on the confines of Uffern.

But it was the valiant struggle of Nud with the sorcerer that I held to mind, so that it seemed to me as we wrestled up and down the chamber that I was Nud and my adversary the sorcerer. I felt an accession of strength and vigor, as if my sinews had been forged at the furnace of Gofannon. The rancid animal scent of my opponent had hitherto dominated my understanding of him. Now, however, the overpowering stench receded, and I was aware of attributes of sight and sound.

I perceived the beasts within him, and sought to use arts of skill and cunning to bring their strength beneath my sway. The bull I would harness to my plow, the reindeer to my riding and sledging, the bear to dance at my piping, and the owl to extend his protection over my granary. The creature grunted savagely as I soothed him with words of enchantment, and by wrestling-feats brought his might to assist me as much as it did him. Our feet gripped and slithered upon the smooth floor of the world-cave, as each struggled to overset the other's balance, securing that position of vantage empowering him to deliver the decisive blow or throw. No easy task was it to wrestle with the Stag-specter in his sanctuary at the Heart of Annufn.

There came a moment when we paused as if by mutual consent, neither giving ground, each harvesting what residue of strength he had managed to retain. Earlier, as I have said, I knew my adversary almost by scent alone in his murky lair. Now I saw him face to face, and I saw what brought cold fear to heart and belly. In his eyes was hatred putrid as a pestilence, and they were eyes and hatred that I had met before, when as a helpless babe I lay upon a shingled storm-lashed beach beneath the shadow of the dark Tower of Beli.

It was the hideous dying glare of my oldest enemy, King Custennin Gorneu, in the instant that he slipped upon the sea wrack and was spitted upon his own spearhead. Never had I forgotten that moment, when I believed the sharp war-beak upon its ashen neck was destined for my throat or heart. Even as I floated, at the good abbot Mawgan's skilled intercession, over the ninth wave out into the void, I knew more fear of the king's envenomed stare as he hung in death than I beheld upon the waste of waters spread about me.

I had myself been witness to the death of Custennin Gorneu, and I had not thought to encounter him again in this life. Now I saw him before me, glorious and terrible in the strength of the beasts whose lord he had become. The bony protuberances upon his forehead, sad deformity of a royal brow, had burgeoned into the glorious spread of antlers which crowned the creature in whose grasp I hung with a splendor like that of the Tree of the World. The once wasted body, suspended sacklike upon a spear-shaft, possessed the effortless might of the wild bull in the frenzy of his goring. And the pale poisoned stare reflected no more the clouded impotence of spite frustrated, but scorned me from depths unfathomable as those of the Pit of Annufn itself.

The Stag-specter read through my eyes' windows what passed within the chambers of my mind, and again he laughed aloud. I had thought to slay him, pitting my puny strength against that of the Lord of the Beasts by his own hall pillars! Derisive laughter rang dinning in my hearing, as the venom of the demon's spittle burned my back and shoulders. With nausea and loathing I sensed below a filthy asperging on my thigh, as he marked me for his own with a pungent baptism of misprision, derisive discharge of warm urine.

Greedily he grasped me with redoubled might, scouring my flesh with talons curved and cruel. The cold and damp of the cavern whispered chill upon my bared bones and severed sinews, laid open where the shredded skin hung in ribbons from my back and sides. I was sorely wounded and weakening fast. My feet slipped upon blood that streamed from gashes innumerable, and I could scarcely breathe from the suffocating heat and stench of the creature's exhalation as he bent his head, curled back his lips, and thrust his huge yellowed teeth ever closer to my lean throat. I tried in vain to scream; the bellows were broken, and the fire of the forge cooling to a dying spark.

I saw my moment was come: If I did not achieve it now, then I must indeed be swept away by the River of Death. And I believed, too, that a *tynged* was upon me that the Island of the Mighty which once bore my name was also fated to succumb in the same hour to the rushing rough flooding of high tide, the wave-breast of the blue-topped stormy floodtide, which at the end of all things will roll over the islands of Ywerdon and Prydein at one mile-high sweep. Reflecting for the first time, I saw with that inward eye which the Hawk of Gwales plucked from its socket that I must ply what enchantments were left to me without delay.

Somehow I began to sing, gently—oh, so gently! And as I sang, the Stag-specter swayed with the song, gripping me no less fiercely than before. I sang of the gray-bearded man of the forest, with his hat of fir sprigs and coat of lichens. My verses told of his passing through the woods, his clothing the aspens in shimmering gray, the pines in deepest green, and beeches in laughing gold. As he passes below them he scatters from his leathern satchel primroses pale as the moon in her fullness, dandelions yellow as the noonday sun, and bluebells cerulean as the summer sky. Warm winds stir trees and flowers as he moves by, spicy scents of pine branches in a hazy blue wilderness of honey. He plucks a switch from a thicket, tests it with his thumb, marshals the wild creatures from fen and copse and meadow, and escorts them in procession through the wilderness.

The demon's fell grasp remained fast upon me as I chanted, even as he raised his mighty head to toss his antlers and sniff the air. He was crouching lower now, his huge genitals pendant and his tail twitching. Then I told of the old man's leading the reindeer herd by the forest track; with his wand he displaces rotted tree trunks barring their way, traces bridges over brooks and fords through rivers; birds rise singing from every treetop, and fish slip silver through the wavelets. Now the antlered host steps delicately over foam-washed boulders below the roaring of the rapids, until under the old man's guidance they reach their favored grazing meadow, plucking at tender shoots of heather and nibbling lush lichen on charm-patterned rocks. On a black pond beside their placid grazing a troop of swans swoops down with sighing wings and long scuttering of the water's polished surface.

My opponent groaned and shuddered, clinging to me like a drowning sailor to a broken masthead. I sensed within him less a desire to overcome me in struggle than a desperate effort to imprison me forever within his still halls; imprisonment more certain even than that which Arthur knew in Caer Oeth and Anoeth, or beneath the Stone of Echymeint. The Stag-specter had fallen to his knees, oppressed by the weight of internal strife, but yet his bull's face and branching antlers towered above me. In his owl's eyes I glimpsed an unexpected expression of pain amidst the pride and power.

As a man he strove to stand erect, to flaunt his antlers high in the starless night of his vaulted roof; and as a beast he sought to set his hoofs firm upon the rocky floor of his sanctuary. I saw that the struggle between the upper air and lower earth, which drew my mind this way and that, warred within this mighty being on a scale of suffering beyond my imagining. He wrestled within himself, so it seemed to me, and the striving of his two natures represented a combat eternal as that of Gwyn and Gwithir in the upper air, or that of Arawn and Hafgan in the Underworld of Annufn.

Now was the moment of truth arrived, which I must grasp or lose forever. Whether it was You with Your Sure Arm who steeled my arm for the blow, or my own resolve and dread of dishonor, I can no longer recall. All I know is that there was a strength within my heart and my limbs and my muscles beyond that which existed at my own calling. The demon had me by the waist in a grip I might not loosen, but the state of our struggling was such that my arms were for a moment freed. With my left hand I seized my assailant by his bull's snout, grasping my fingers within his hot nostrils, and wrenching his head back between his shoulders. He was shaggy all over, save for one spot at the base of his neck, which I saw had but short hairs upon it. Then without pausing I drew the knife Carnwennan which once was Arthur's, and plunged it deep, deep into the monster's throat, hard above his shoulder at the spot which I had marked.

Grim fear seized me as the monster gave no groan of pain nor relaxed the bondage of his arms about me, which encompassed me fast as Caer Gwydion encloses the vault of heaven. I closed my eyes and knew fear which tormented me, not as the imps and demons that confront men in hours of sleep and darkness, but with a sickness hideous as the Yellow Death itself, which corrodes a man from within, hollowing out his strength with sweat and poisoning, and leaving him empty as the carcass of an ox from which a swarm of bees has had its conception.

The Stag-specter's head and mine rested each upon the other's shoulder, and I felt his lips' rancid breath whisper hot upon my ear:

"O stripling strong, be not afraid
To say what father's son thou art?
I feel my blood drip down that blade
Which your hand plunged into my heart."

Glancing aslant, I was aware of the creature's gaping jag-toothed grin hovering hungrily about my throat, and easy it was to guess his inward thought. Not safe is it to make a gift of your name to a dying man, lest he make use of it to curse you. My reply was guarded and cunning:

> "Sea-fortress is my only name;
> My father was to me unknown,
> Nor mother have I, to my shame;
> And so I walk this world alone."

But the demon made reply no less astute:

> "If fatherless you roam this earth,
> Pray tell what wonder gave thee birth?"

To which I answered sharply, growing ever more confident:

> "A wonder you had cause to rue,
> When on the wintry, sea-blown strand
> A lance the king of Cerniu slew:
> Horned tyrant slain by his own hand!"

Then the Stag-specter gnashed his teeth and, looking wild, asked angrily:

> "A Sure Arm must you have indeed
> To serve you thus in time of need;
> Was it your Father wrought this deed?"

I saw he knew me for who I am, and that the last anger was upon him. Now the fancy struck me that the monster's clutch lay upon me now more for his support than my destruction. His bristled black lips were flared wide, with a bloody froth foaming from between bared yellow fangs, as he strained to twist his head about and hold my eyes to his poisoned gaze. I felt his hairy muzzle and hot stinking breath upon my cheek, as gloating yet he muttered:

> "You seek my treasures here below;
> Instead, my venomed vomit know!"

Forthwith he opened his jaws wide as the Cave of Penn Nant Gofud in the North, and amid the red recesses of his gullet I saw the poison seething like fermenting honey in a greasy vat. By the gulping and wheezing and coughing within his throat I sensed my adversary was about to inflict upon me the doom for which he had been preparing from the moment I rashly set foot within his kingdom. Three venomous vomits were gathering in the thraws of his throat: a cold belch, an iron belch, and a liquid belch. Between them they would scorch the hair from my head, flay the flesh from my bones, and melt the entrails of my belly into a pottage for dogs to guzzle.

Not readily would I succumb to this worst of fates. I, too, summoned up the shards of my shattered strength, shouting back into the monster's reeking muzzle a rune of binding, blemish, and wounding. Within my heart I knew it to be but a cry of despair and call for aid, but for him I prayed that nevertheless it would provide shame and shearing, chains and chafing. These were the final words I was able to utter, which were a plaint and *rhaith* against the *ellyll* of the chill chamber in which we wrestled up and down:

> "Ah, spitting serpent, specter strong,
> I see your heart is filled with hate;
> Vile poison which will do *you* wrong!
> For ugly ogre, ugly fate!"

As I uttered these words, it seemed to me that there shone through the hall a ray of light, terrifyingly bright, and it shone directly into the Stag-specter's eyes. At sight of this he turned so faint that I felt much of his strength and vigor drain out of him, and he began retching in repulsive judders. Then all in a rush his vomit spilled out over his own jowl and breast; but it was I that was near to death from the loathsomeness and stench of it.

Horrible, too, was the piercing look of agony and hate which my enemy turned upon me, which of all the things I ever saw was that which brought me into greatest fear. I saw his poison gaze in the light that shone down the hall, and I heard him say with a choking rattle:

"You have made a hard journey, barefoot upon a sword-bridge, to seek me out, Merlin, but I think you will not be surprised to learn that you will gain no great fortune through me. I can tell you this: You have attained but one half of the strength which would have been yours had you not sought me out. I cannot now take away from you what strength you already possess, but I can so arrange matters that you will never become any stronger than you are at this moment. Despite this you possess a strength that many will encounter to their cost.

"Already you are famous for your deeds and your wisdom, but a time of battle-fog, manslaughter, and treachery is coming, and many of your deeds will turn out unchancily for you, and at the end will prove your undoing. You will be driven into outlawry, and will live a solitary, hunted, hateful existence.

"And now I lay this upon you, that these eyes of mine, as you see them in this moment, shall ever return before your sight. You will find it no pleasant experience to be alone with them, and it may be they will lead you to your death."

I cannot deny that the baleful glare of the dying eyes of the *ellyll*, even now glazing over with a film of death, filled me with fearful foreboding. The curse of a dying creature, whether man or wraith, possesses a malign potency few have encountered with impunity. And though death was undoubtedly spreading a cold mantle about his failing frame, the demon's strength and power were by no means departed.

I felt a grasp grim as that of Glewlwyd Gafaelfawr laid fast once more upon my throat. In my blindness and the dark I plucked in vain to free myself. The more I tore and wrenched, the tighter grew the hands that strangled me. Indeed, it seemed to me that the creature's strength was mine and that it was my convulsive struggling with which he sought to master me. I opened my eyes again, and for a moment wrestled on, before I was able to believe what they told me.

For I was standing alone, and the fell creature of the grotto clutched me no longer. He lay at my feet, a mountainous heap of rotten flesh-filled pelt, within which were already a writhing of worms and movement of maggots at their feasting. Of the long, broad-bladed knife Carnwennan, I could glimpse only the handle set fast in the thickness of his neck base, thick fur about its hilt matted with congealing gore welling up from his life-spring. Even as I gazed upon the huge hill of the expiring beast, I heard afar off shuddering screams in rocky chasms and distant groanings of the abyss, echoing through the Halls of Annufn to die far away among swamps and stagnant peat pools in the uttermost confines of windblown Uffern.

So it dawned upon me that (for how long I knew not) I had been fighting, not with the Stag-specter of Annufn, but with myself! It was my left hand that was clasped tight about my throat, and my right that sought to wrench it free. The more my left hand squeezed the air from my windpipe, the more my right strove to draw it back; then the left in turn resisted, and the right more angered still. Like a drowning man, I had struggled blindly with my own impotence as I sank ever more inextricably into the elements that sought to absorb me.

Idiot! I laughed aloud: "Well now, friend Merlin, what sort of person are you? People have called you a madman, and scoffed at your mutterings and talk of winged lions, fighting serpents, and fox-tailed boars. Was it not the young men of King Gwydno's court who sang of you:

> "Merlin the Mad, ugly and wild,
> Stuck up a tree like an idiot child;
> Singing as long as you care to hear
> An ode that's quite as crazy as queer,
> To birch tree white and piggy-wig pink:
> More than enough for *us,* we think!"

Oh, they thought I couldn't hear, but I have ears pricked sharp as those of Math mab Mathonwy! Well, but weren't my tormentors in the right of it? What if they were to see me now, in a blind panic, fouling myself in my terror, all through wrestling for dear life with my own self? Left hand versus right: oh, dear! And all the time the enemy was lying dead at my feet.

I looked down at him who had been my adversary—or whom I had taken for my adversary. I was in such a state of confusion, exhaustion, and self-mockery that I was no longer certain what had happened. But what with my naming myself, and my involuntary inappropriate laughter, I saw the cavern and its inmate for what they were: repulsive, dangerous, and destructive. Their earlier allure was departed utterly, the remembered spectacle of myself prancing about with the beasts seemed an absurdity I was only relieved no one could have witnessed, and the Stag-specter a menacing creature indeed, but one whom a ready wit and skilled dagger-play had proved sufficient to lay low.

I looked at his huge prone form with what might have been pity, had there been life left to pity. His eyes alone burned coldly upon mine in the fixed malignant stare he had foretold would never leave me. Fascinated, I watched as he gave up the strength that had been in him to the creatures who crept upon him from out of the shadows. It was a dog that licked the blood that gushed like a cataract from his shoulder, the great ram-headed snake he clasped when first I saw him that drank the life-seed spilling from his toppled pillar of regeneration, and a crab which squeezed his great genitals, that the warm moisture might flow forth.

From the blood and semen a new creation was forming itself. The great tumbled body lay heaped broad upon the sanctuary floor. By now it was encircled by a spreading lake of blood, upon which it seemed to float in a void of darkness. The sagging hide hung upon its bone frame like a worn cloak laid out to dry. The great skull, bare and bony, seemed lofty as the highlands of Prydyn. A ridge of vertebrae ran from north to south, a serpent of bone like the rugged Range of Cefn Prydein which divides the Island of the Mighty to east and to west. His ribs were valleys down which trickled streams of blood and sweat. The tufted hide was a fell of woods and bracken, among which crept a host of parasites, worms, and insects, engendered by the heat within his left armpit. Soon their race was spread upon the plains of his flesh, the hills of his bones, and the lakes of his eyes. To the north of the golden torque which was about the carcass's neck the insects, swarming and malevolent as the Coranieid, ravaged a wasteland of poisonous boils, rashes, and putrefaction of flesh upon the skull that was there.

From dead lips of sundered sovereignty floated up the last whisper of the conquered *ellyll*, as he paid fealty of his life for the taking of it:

"By perfidy you prised my life—
And treachery may take yours too.
For me is death come after strife;
Now let my strength to you accrue."

True it was that the life strength was returning fast upon me. But I saw, too, that about his limbs and trunk the Stag-corpse began once more to seethe and pulse with life. At the creature's side the great snake coiled about him, writhing up to breathe within the chasms of his mouth, nostrils, and ears. The bull is father of the snake, as is the snake of the bull. Where I stood and how I saw these things I can no longer tell. You may see it as a dream, O king, for so it seemed to me. All I can tell is that the isle of bone and skin floated before me upon an ocean of blood that encircled it in motion, and that about us in the darkness rose a wall of flickering fires: fires that are ever burning in the Heart of Annufn.

I felt a deadly fear such as I had not experienced even when the living Stag-specter sprang upon me with his bull's bellowing. I was alone in endless space and darkness. No friendly moon gazed down upon me, sending its swift silver bridge to my aid, as when I floated in a bag upon the still waters of the Sea of Hafren. I was hanging in the time that is No-time, the time between, the crossing of life and death, the black brief endless instant when those who understand the runes may learn the lore of the gallows corpse.

With the knife Carnwennan I had applied the searing fire that separates earth and heaven at the close of the old cycle and the beginning of the new. The spindle rotates, and not hard is it to mark the spot to which it shall return. My friend Rufinus the tribune, who seeks in vain to tame the world to his desires, has seen it written on a dirty barrack wall by the hand of an ignorant soldier who suspends his whole desire upon the fall of the dice in the dust of a parched courtyard. The soldier knows not what it is he draws, nor the tribune what he reads; and yet all is there.

I inscribed the rune upon the boulder on the windy hillside above, and see it now written in letters of light within the bony shelter of my skull. For the skull is like the kernel within the eagle-stone laid upon women in their pregnancy, a tiny egg within a greater. What is writ large upon the surface of the crystal sphere, my *Ty Gwydr* beneath the transparent ocean, is reflected by concentration of light upon its center:

R O T A S

O P E R A

T E N E T

A R E P O

S A T O R

Multiply the four consonants about the center, and what do you find? The sum of the degrees through which the golden Chariot of Beli travels in its yearly journey through the Houses of the Heavens. About them may be traced the circle, which is Beli's golden orb, and before all is held the cross TENET, which it may be is the Tree upon which divine Leu hung with the spear Rongomiant thrust deep into his side for thrice three windy nights: a sacrifice that shatters for all mankind an eternity of bondage to the wheel you see behind the cross.

Nor is this all, but a beginning. I may not commit to writing what must be learned by word of mouth during long years of tutelage, but it is my allotted task to protect the boundaries of things. A mystery is to be entered, not understood. If I draw you toward the mystery, I shall have performed no unworthy labor. The letters are numbers, and by harmony of numbers is the balance of the universe sustained. Multiply the corners of the square (RSSR) by the outstretched hands of the cross: that is six. Multiply that sum in turn by the TTTT (which is twelve) at the arms' ends of the cross, and you have seventy-two. Next, multiply *that* sum in turn by the value of PRRP upon the exposed face of the sun PRRP which glows from behind the cross, and this is the whole: 72 × 360 = 25,920. Or add the vowels excluded in the corners and multiply them by the corners; not hard is the answer: (400 + 32) × 60 = 25,920 again.

Now, 25,920 years make up the great year of being, at the close of which will come the fire and flood of which druids, wise ones, speak as bringing about the world's ending. And should druids and men of art and skill, *llyfyrion*, reproach me for writing that which should remain unwritten, I make reply that this alone is no arcane lore, dangerous to reveal. It is not I who would tell (if I knew it) where is Mabon mab Modron, and whether he be alive or dead.

But what is ROTAS-SATOR but the *gwyddbwyll* board upon which men play in palaces for idle amusement? In its center rests the king, the axle of the revolving wheel which is the sun in glory. About the king is the protection of the cross, whose arms attract the limits to that center whose focus is unity and order. Beyond, at the four quarters on the margin of things, unfocused and disordered, lie excluded and threatening the opposed forces of chaos, the hosts of the Coranieid.

The slaughter of the Stag-specter, Bull of Darkness, was the ending of a world-age. With the knife Carnwennan I had exposed the cliff-face, severing the old from the new; and even as I gazed upon the repellent sacrifice, with its stench of decay and involuntarily discharged ordure, its drying hide and seething host of lice and worms, I witnessed a transformation wonderful to behold.

CHAPTER ELEVEN

THE
MORNING
STAR

So I stood in a maze, not knowing where I was or what I did.
The ordering of the centuries and the corners of the earth had spiraled
out of existence, and my brain was whirling around within my skull. I
was confused and drunken, wandering the length of passages that had
neither beginning nor ending. There is no escaping from the Halls of
Annufn without the aid of the thread which fell from my grasp as I
wrestled with the Stag-specter.

The slain bull's hide appeared to my eyes as a wasteland, desolate
as if traversed by the Three Red Ravagers of the Island of Prydein,
beneath whose tread neither grass nor plants survived, neither for one
year nor for seven. Peopled it was, but by oppressions troublesome as
those of the Coranieid, the Gwyddyl Fichti, and the Saeson.

Now, however, I saw it grow green and lush as the meadowlands
of Powys and Gwent at the Kalan Mai, when mistle-thrush and yellow-
billed blackbird are loud in tree and bush, gulls cluster upon the
ox-furrows, and the sun casts a slender beam upon bright hills and
dales and islands of the sea. Mother of poets and lovers is that time,
kyntefin, and a poet and lover have I ever been. Seven times nine did
my heart beat wild with sickness and longing when I beheld this
transformation, with growth of green hazel shoots and loud cry of the
cuckoo upon the highest branches, whose melancholy cry arouses dear
and painful memories of youth and love.

I raised my eyes to see what it was that wrought this transformation, and saw you before me, a spindle in your hand, golden as a buttercup in the clear light of day: Gwendyd, my golden girl! Not less bright are your eyes than sunlight sparkling on merry wavelets, not more smiling than your red lips and white teeth the blue sky and chasing clouds, and most impudent and taking to my fancy is the curve of your fair cheek. Green was your robe, golden the torque about your slender neck, and lighter your tread than a butterfly's settling upon sweet-apple blossom.

Green and golden were you, my darling, and the withered landscape could not but arise refreshed at your passing, green shoots everywhere breaking the rough crust of winter's pall. But it was I to whom you looked, tormented as I was in spirit and broken in body. To me you came, until you stood so close I felt the warmth of your breast against my palpitating heart. Your beautiful face looked up into mine, and never have I seen or ever will such a look of love and fellowship and communion as that which flashed from the warmth of your brown eyes, seizing my heart and mind in bondage closer by far than the grasp of the Stag-specter.

Oh, my sister Gwendyd! Yes, though I knew you not until that moment, I came to you and you to me as though we had walked hand in hand through all the myriad meanderings I had known since my descent into the Otherworld. For you came up to me, standing expectant before me, your beautiful brown eyes turned up to my poor wasted face with such a look of trust and love as made me sick at heart and near to fainting.

I have seen beautiful women in the courts and castles of the kings of the Brython, and places loftier yet. I have seen Creiruy daughter of Ceridwen, Arianrod daughter of Don, and Gwen the daughter of Cywryd son of Crydon. They are fair, and fairest of all of the maidens of the Island of Prydein. Their beauty was a delight to me, who am a poet and lover of all that is loveliest in creation. I have slept in the bed of the young wife of Elffin mab Gwydno, and known languors and temptations—caresses, too—which consumed me with a wildness I shall not readily forget.

Despite the cruel power of that knowledge which is a scorching and consuming fire before which all things on earth are reduced to their elements, I have felt the power of love. But those loves were like that of the mountain for the lake, or the wave for the shore. There was a meeting, but not a melting.

But now, my Gwendyd (I draw you to me even by utterance of your name: Gwendyd, Gwendyd!), I was held by your brown eyes and gentle smile and dimpled cheek in that shadowy passage which had neither beginning nor end. There stole throughout my whole being a love mightier than Cynon mab Clydno knew for Morfyd daughter of Urien, Caswallon felt for Flur daughter of Ugnach, or even that which Dristan bore for Esylt amid the waves' moan upon the rocky shore of Cerniu; and I saw in your brown eyes that love likewise filled you from the arch of your foot to the crown of your head. I felt not an aching nor a longing such as men feel when they approach the mistress of their choice, but a warmth that stole upon us both, enveloping us as if within one radiant garment. We were of a single flesh and mind, my sister Gwendyd and I.

And so it was—do you remember, my Gwendyd, and will you ever remember?—that I caught you to me and kissed your lips; while you clung to me and kissed me with a sweetness sweeter than the juice of apples from the orchards of Powys, and a warmth warmer than that with which the sun caresses their rounded rosy flanks when he is at his summer zenith. Then I whispered boldly in the Labyrinth of Annufn, through the fluted spirals of your white ear: "Shall we sleep together this night, my golden darling?"

I was not so bold as the question might suggest, for I felt the answer within us both as we clung together there; the pair of us alone within the abyss. From chambers afar off came the murmured talk of those who dwell in the Halls of Annufn, but we two were alone and could not be disturbed. You neither blushed nor looked downward, my Gwendyd, but smiled up at me wisely and kindly, reaching up upon your toes to kiss me once again.

"Why me?" at first you asked. And then: "I will," you answered in a happy murmur. Then, with a glance of reproach or teasing that took my breath away, you added, "That is, so long as you promise not to hasten from me at dawn?"

I hugged her to me, and kissed her once again. That was a promise not difficult to make!

"I will stay with you until the dawn and afterwards, my dear. I will hold you in my arms this night long, and I think it will be you that is the first to cease from kissing. For I love you, Gwendyd, *araf eurfun.*"

"You must not say that!" she whispered reproachfully. "You do not know me yet. But you shall sleep with me. Prepare yourself, and come to my bed."

I felt no shadow of shame or fear of what the morrow might bring, such as men will often feel even when the giddiness of their nighttime passion is at its highest intoxication. *Post coitum omnia animalia tristia sunt.* Who knows that better than I? Knowledge is the quarry I pursue, and yet how often at the highest moment of truth have not wanton images and hot desire entered my heart, blotting out with contemptuous ease all my cherished wisdom. To my shame (I say to you) and longing (I confess to myself) it is that I find the study of stars and springs and winds melted away all of a sudden, just when I least expect or desire it. Then is every thought bent toward bed and boudoir, all the skills of my mind toward that genial flattering speech for which my name has since become a wicked byword; and I hasten with pumping heart and footsteps swift as the arrow of Gwiaun Lygad Cath to our snug trysting place beneath the yellow broom.

Then (I shall forget my tale if I continue) does my trouserful of wantonness make play with his eager jerking: a long night's roaming across smooth soft plains, twin rounded hills, white slopes for wandering; and at last the choice warm, wet cavern whose ferny entrance awaits the stiff ram-headed serpent's gentle entrance. Do you recall what followed, my Angarad of the golden hair, that evening when our fingers met by chance about the goblet's stem at King Ryderch's feasting? Long ages of the earth have passed between us since the night that followed, but it is not I who can forget each move and moan and murmur of our brief meeting.

Smooth white serpents coiling in nighttime solitude! At times it is but one remembered slender stroke or lithe arching or whispered joy that catches all my breath away, and with it those thoughts that but the flickering of a serpent's tongue before had sought to span the universe with all its mysteries. Thick and glossy-haired Afan, Brochfael's niece—oh, that glance as the mantle slipped from your white shoulders; standing straight you were as a spear-shaft by the dying hearth in the hospice of Meigen. What would the good monks have thought as we moved together, you and I? And Peruir, daughter of my friend Run mab Maelgun—ah! It was from your lusty father, I think, that your shameless tricks and gambols came, and a good inheritance he bestowed upon you and me; upon our mattress of down, and the scents of your secret places in my breathing. Shameless as Gwenhuifar the wife of Arthur were you, and never a night that I wished it but you were awash with desire and longing, clinging and fondling.

Now, in my exile of despair, snow up to my hips and icicles in my hair, what would I not give for but one of those deeds of enchantment, more ravishing to my senses even in contemplation than any raised by the arts of Menu mab Teirguaed? And yet—when I might myself have perpetuated the magic by marriage or mistress-taking—what did I do? When I wakened beside your sleeping warmth, heard the half-murmured longing from those lips whose kisses I had snatched but three hours ago without ceasing, and glimpsed the white breast which had slipped from out our tossed coverlet, what was my thought? It was all for books and learning, disputations of druids and counseling of kings, seeking of the outpourings of the Cauldron of Poesy. A cold cruel clarity of vision led me to flee your couch with the pale breaking of day, wan lingerings of guilt or pity a cowardly substitute for the blaze which had but a fleeting hour before illumined our pleasurings in the protecting darkness.

It may be that this unwelcomed dawning is but one of the many torments which assail those who tread that painful path which leads through thought and study to the release of the spirit from bondage of the body's prison, to attainment of the prophet's mountaintop vision, and the *awen* of the poet's darkened vigil. No moment is its own, but it must have its gloss of self-knowing: hateful, destructive, and ravening as the Cath Palug.

But why do I speak of all this now? Not for one night is my love for my sister Gwendyd, and not fleeting the rapture of our encounter in our hidden chamber in the Halls of Annufn. Not Taliesin himself, nor Talhaiarn father of the muse, could bring alive for me in words what love and worship and union of breast and heart and mind were ours that night. But I must utter the words as best I may, that you who hear me may know that I, Merlin mab Morfryn, have known happiness here upon and under earth: happiness of which mortals glimpse but the still lake's reflection, the shadow of the hawk under the sun's blaze, before they come at last to the glassy portals of Caer Sidi.

As you see me now, O king, you mock at my withered, aged frame, my thin gaunt beard, my puckered empty eye socket. Beneath the bare branches of the Forest of Celyddon I am condemned to wander amid wastes of snow and time; the wind is keen and the sky darkly low upon the surface of the moor, reeds are withered and their stalks broken by the frozen lake, and cold is the bed of the fish in the shelter of the ice. I am persecuted by the rancor of Ryderch Hael, hunted like a wolf upon the mountainside by the horsemen of Gwasawg, oppressed with guilt for the death of the son of Gwendyd. A heart full of longing leads to sickness.

But once—laugh if you will; the foolish are prone to laughter—I bore a torque of gold and mantle of purple, and was honored above all poets in the court of Gwendolau the son of Ceidiaw. And more, much more than all, when I was in my right mind I lay at the foot of my sweet-apple tree, a red-blossomed tree, which grows by a riverbank in the verdant vale of Arclud. By my side was the fairest of maidens, slender, queenly, and wanton. More beautiful to me was she than lovely Branwen daughter of Lir, whom Matholuch came a-wooing in Aberfraw with all the hosts of Ywerdon, or fair Esylt for whom Dristan pined and died beyond the stormy Sea of Udd. Now Gwendyd loves me not and greets me not—as once she did, turning her face up to mine to be kissed beneath the shade of our sweet-apple tree. And not more bright were the primroses that pillowed her curling auburn hair than were her shining eyes as they gazed into mine.

It was within the Halls of Annufn that we met and kissed. I knew in the moment of our first kiss that the love I bore for Gwendyd was as deep-flowing as the liquor that flows from the Horn of Bran Galed, plentiful as the riches of the Hamper of Gwydno Garanhir, and inexhaustible as fare from the Dish of Rigennyd the Clerik. Throughout my being in all times, past, present, and to come, I knew the first gushing of a spring sweeter than white wine, more fruitful than the Fountain of Caer Sidi. From the depths of my existence was flooding that dark, deep, green swelling ocean of feeling, of which our first unwitting kiss was the imprint. More to me than the Thirteen Treasures of the Island of Prydein was that kiss in the shadows, my Gwendyd!

My Gwendyd had gone to her couch, and as I undressed and came to her, I saw she was lying in her shift beneath the coverlet. At once her cool arms were about me, and I saw the tears start to her eyes as she felt the cruel lacerations disfiguring my torn body, the bones bare as the ribs of a lobster creel. Like a mother she rose upon her elbow to cradle my broken frame, kissing each gaping wound and muttering endearments of tenderest enchantment. I felt the skin heal beneath her soft touch, and, salved from kisses that moved from the crown of my head to the tip of my toe, I found myself grow young and hale as when I shone forth in purple and gold at the court of King Gwenddau.

Life coursed afresh through my veins, like spring watercourses at the snow's melting. Now it was my turn to rise at her side and, taking my Gwendyd's curly head between my hands, lay her softly back upon the pillow. Of the murmuring and laughter, kissing and caressing we knew that agelong night and again at the languorous coming of gray dawn, it is hard for me to tell. And yet I have a poet's privilege, which is to grasp such a moment in an eternity of verse blown upon the wind of the stars, binding us through all the ages like two swans linked by a silver chain.

And when the time of consummation was come upon us, our bodies were one body, conjoined in warmth and moisture, one seed within us, just as we ourselves are sprung from a single seed and suckled by a single breast. With our bodies, naked and warm, inter-mingled in confusion of delights, were our twin minds likewise united. It was as if sky and earth were one once more, as they were in the former time before man's overweening pride led to their separation. We had dissolved into that time which has neither beginning nor end, father nor mother, brother nor sister, neither gender nor species nor nine forms of elements. No more a man was Merlin, no longer a girl my Gwendyd: man-woman, element of the nine forms of elements, were we.

Long serpents coiling and writhing together, indistinguishable as those upon my staff of guidance. Long was the struggle, the Red Dragon at times upon the White, and the White upon the Red; until the Red achieved his mastery upon the White, so fulfilling the Proph-ecy of Prydein which is born out of that union. The red sun had risen, and the pale moon in her gentle beauty had softly succumbed to the hot vigor of his dawning, dropping a pale beam about the pillowed red-gold hair of my beloved.

My descent into the world-cave and my union with Gwendyd had returned me to the abyss of chaos before this world was made, the chaos of my mother's womb; and so for a space all things reverted to their beginnings. Naked, we were free, and in our erotic whisperings all social codes were ruptured. Not far were we from the dissolution of death, and yet was it also the moment of regeneration and creation. So will it be when, at the end of our earthly strivings, we arrive in the eternal refuge of Caer Sidi. For there, as they say, is a large house in which are waiting women of rare beauty: a bed for every couple, even thrice nine beds.

After the long dreaming moment had passed, we lay upon our sides gazing with deep fondness each into the other's eyes. Now earth and sky were parted, though linked inseparably by the Tree which rises from earth to Heaven. It was by the passage of that Tree that I attained enlightenment. Departed was my union of scent and feeling with the beasts, among whom I danced and growled in our rhythmic tracing of the labyrinth. I had risen upright and firm, my head in the bright daylight. In you, my dearest Gwendyd, I sought and found invention and understanding. I was possessed with a clarity of vision, cool as a cataract, soaring as a sparrowhawk, broad as the noontide arch of heaven. *You* gave me all that, my lovely sister, and it was *you* who brought me safe out of the Pit of Annufn into which I had stumbled and well-nigh perished. Not all the waters of cruel Ocean can wash one word or motion from my mind. Ah, but it is painful now!

Now it was my sister Gwendyd who led me unscathed from the

lair of the Stag-specter. It is I alone of all men who have penetrated into the Halls of Annufn and emerged once more into the upper air. But without the aid of Gwendyd, my pure white star, I should have wandered for all eternity among its twisted tunneling; lost within the web, the slain spider at its center. First she stooped to kiss the pillow which still bore the impress of our two heads, lip to lip, as they had been the livelong night. Then she took my hand and, with finger upon her lips and ever glancing smiling into my eyes, led me to the doorway of our chamber.

I have said that when my sister came first to me across the hide of the slaughtered Stag-specter she bore in her white hand a spindle, about which was wound a round clew of flax. The thread of the clew lay upon the rocky floor, stretching forward into the darkness. It was this that we followed through spiraled tunnel and steep stair. It seemed to me that for all our walking we did but mark time, for often and again I glimpsed some grim stone skeleton set within the wall, or painted image upon its surface, which I was certain we had passed before.

But I trusted in my Gwendyd, and with her was never lost. The pressure of her hand seemed to say she divined my thought and bade me take comfort. And ever as we went the clew of flax spun about its spindle, gathering up the twine into knotted convolutions as intricate as the maze in which we wandered. It passed through my mind that by memory of the knots one might recall the coilings that were past and predicate those to come. I glanced at my merry auburn-haired maiden to see if this could be so, and the radiant gaze she returned to mine bestowed the knowledge I sought.

Gwendyd's spindle glowed in the cruel darkness like Gwydion's silver path, and the length of that path we trod together. How many ages of years we traveled that path it is not easy to say. Hard was the way and wearied were we, my sister and I. But, oh, the ache at my heart's foundations as I gaze back upon it! There is a rift between us now, Gwendyd and I, since the slaying of Gwasawg, and I alone in the snowbound forest with wolves for companions. What would I now not give to be back there, dancing at your side, your yielding grasp in mine, your rounded flank ever pressing, your bright eye glancing! But an ocean of time flows between us which I cannot pass, though I can never forget.

We were aware as the end at last approached, for as we ascended through the twelve households of Annufn the flax wound in its length. By calculation of the knots and intricacies it might be seen that the span of the thread was the span of the number contained within the

ROTAS-SATOR square, and when that number was told, the clew would have attained its plenitude. Then, as I imagined, it would begin again an unraveling of equal time, and so on for as long as the clew be fated to rotate about the spindle.

It was cold, cold in the tunneled Halls of Annufn; but I had clad myself in the reeking hide of the slaughtered monster, and more—much more—was warm in the love of my sister Gwendyd. Ah, though I told it a hundred thousand times I could not tell the extent of my love for you! Not all the spells of druids and enchanters could extinguish it, nor yet the potency of the cloak of Manawydan mab Lir itself.

About us in the windy tunnel was the sound of laughter and song, sweet as any that arose from the enchanted strings of the Harp of Teirtu. Glancing back, I glimpsed behind in the shadows a following train of happy celebrants springing lithe as apes, lissom as the silvered serpents who glided among them. There were the badgers, foxes, and silky-haired martens who dwell within the sacred hill of Dinleu Gurygon. There too, gamboling among the winding throng, cavorted marvelous beasts of the abyss: sharp-beaked toads, whale-bellied dragons, golden-crested boars, and others too strangely multiformed for description.

Over these creatures there reigned the harmony of the dance. Drunken, wanton, and rejoicing were we, whether serpents, beasts, or humankind. It seemed to me that many of the creatures that sported in wild abandon were but men bearing masks before their faces, even as I, Merlin mab Morfryn, bore the stag's head and hide. It was Gwendyd alone, smiling and beautiful at the head of our giddy train, who belonged to the race of men, goddess-born descendants of Don. I laughed in abandon, and her dear eye reflected my wild laughter with the depth and calm of a brown tarn which gazes upward from the protection of walled crags to racing sky and ragged clouds.

We had escaped the place of death: the enclosed labyrinth of the Stag-specter, from whose coiling there is no escape, and whose path returns ever to its point of departure. *Hic inclusus vitam perdit.* We were drawn upward to the clear air by the skilled guidance of Gwendyd's thread. Our path was the path of an ascending spiral, the way to the lighted chamber. Love it was, the pure-bright star, which led me winging up the spiral stair. Unerringly did Gwendyd's thread trace the enchanted spiral whose fluted whorls lead on through all that is in existence, sustained by Your Sure Arm and Unerring Hand, bright Master of all arts and skills.

Throughout the serpentine sinuousness of snail-shells, twisted tree-fibers, and veins of insects, the road winds on. It traces with circumambular directness the tracks of minutest cells of living dust, lively specks darting within the primeval waters; and it rises about the swathed muscles of a man, binding protection strong as the encircling walls of a king's fortress about each organ of his frame. Unceasing are the writhing waves of its woven course, river round a royal fortress, stream of ocean encircling the corners of Caer Sidi. The ever-flowing current holds the *enaid* in its seed, through which are transmitted the minds of men through successive generations of birth and rebirth.

It is time that changes all things, and what is Gwendyd's winding thread but time's silken tracing? Not time itself can straighten out existence's eternal encircling, but being itself the essential element within the nine it diverts the curvilinear course of creation. Thus it devours not its own tail, like the destructive Adanc girdling the globe, but lies in spiraled curls, such as those inscribed upon the mighty monoliths of our forefathers' tombs by the Western Sea—or that which curves behind the white ear of Gwendyd.

But to those within whom is the blessed gift of the *awen,* who chew upon the pork and are inspired, it is given to see that the tunnel, though endless, lies coiled about itself. Those coils which have been lie not behind us, but beside; not past, but parallel. Ascension to the Center is hard but not long to those who discover the way. Transparent to them, seers sleeping upon their yellow calfskins, are the walls of the successive whorls. Transported by their *awen* to the Center, all that passes about the endless unwinding is perceptible as pictures arising within the prophet's glass retort.

Men marvel that I, Merlin mab Morfryn, who confronted Gurtheyrn the Thin beside the Dragons' Pool, should in Gurtheyrn's grandsons' day have performed enchantments for Arthur the emperor; and that three long reigns after the slaughter of Camlann, I was yet singing before King Gwendolau in the courts of the North. More, far more, than this have I seen: I, who was in Caer Nefenhir when grass and trees waged cruel war, who was enclosed in the rampart with Dylan Eil Ton, and who was so cruelly wounded by Goronwy from Doleu Edruwy.

But had they seen what I have seen, they would cease to marvel. There is the long road, which is the weary track they traverse. That is the straight and dusty road upon which my friend Rufinus marches with all his legions: from the founding of the City, and the birth of the Crist-Mabon child, and the crownings of consuls and emperors. It is the road, too, of the black monks of Meifod who hate me, with their chronicles of passing time, stretching cycles of forty years and forty and four.

In King Ryderch's court by his blazing hearth they scoff at me, homeless wanderer in the Forest of Celyddon, companion only of wild stags and wolves in the Wasteland of Godeu. Yet what is their road but a line without beginning or end, save in horizons beyond attainment? Our spiraled stair, that of my Gwendyd and me, is the rotating spindle that passes through the whorl. It joins the bright Nail of the Heavens to the Head of Bran which is the Navel of the Island of the Mighty. It is the Tree whose roots spread over the earth and whose branches cover the heavens.

Upon bark at its base feed goats whose horns form ring by ring, year by year. Like entries in the cowled ones' calendars, you cry? Aha! Year by year they grow indeed, and the rings indeed may mark their passing. But here is a spiral within the horn, and a generating curve which is the greater spiral, and the greater reflects the lesser in perfection.

Gaze, too, upon the broad antlers of the stag who bells in his pride from the peak of Newais Mountain, straining his sharp-peaked spreading to the sky. What do you see? The ragged branching of a wind-tossed leafless elm? Yet come with me, where in the cold Forest of Celyddon I crop beside my herd upon lichen from boulders in the snow. Look close: The twisting tines spread forth in no corrupt confusion; within their arched embrace lies the perfection of a sphere.

So the spiral stairway embraces all creation within its nine forms of elements. About the Tree that links us in empty time and space, honeysuckle and hop ascend by the warm sun's right-hand highway, field-convolvulus by the enchanter's tenebrous left-hand track, while woody nightshade twines now by one path and now the other. It may be there is but one understanding of all that is: understanding which is of differing natures, that of the left-hand spiral, and that of the right.

No matter! Though we never glimpse each other upon the way, the spiraled courses run from Gwendyd's whorl in parallel threads, whose color it is not for the Porter at the Door to examine. About her blazing spindle we pass until the clew is unwound and the winding starts anew. For now you know enough and more than enough of what I have seen during my ecstasy upon the bare mountain. Not hard is it to divine that Gwendyd's spindle is one with Gwydion's mighty Path, starry girdle of the heavens. About that jewel-studded cincture rolls Beli's golden chariot, glorious fiery-maned lion of the skies, while the lamps of heaven dance their glittering spiraled round in the chamber of the void. And when Beli's Chariot has completed its circuit of Gwydion's Path, then is an age of creation complete.

So our winding and unwinding dance drew to its climax. We who had merged in the deep-flowing subterranean stream of death were now emerging into the light that shines upon the mountaintop. Glancing fearfully over my shoulder, I saw that now it was I alone who followed in Gwendyd's footsteps. The motley company that had wound behind us in leaping harmony had fallen back, one by one, upon the tortuous ascent. Their masks abandoned on the stairway, they had resumed the bestial shapes of hair or scales they sought to shed. Others, less fortunate still, had flown back into the abyss, flitting like bats who squeak about the rooftrees of the halls of the dead.

I alone survived. That I did so was owing to no skill or courage of my own, but to the saving hand of the maiden who dwelt by the darkest recess of the Pit of Annufn. It was she who had given me strength to overcome in my wrestling with the horrible Stag-specter, and she who had led me up the spiraled staircase to the upper world. Her maiden purity and truth, the *gwir deyrnas* which is the king's when he weds the maiden sovranty of the land, was my sure guide and protection. Those who wish to emerge unscathed from the Labyrinth of Annufn must shed all impediment of base desire and worldly wealth, for its tortuous track is too roughly rocky to be traversed by him who bears a useless load—be it books or worldly wants—upon his shoulders. In order to scale the serpent-spiral unscathed it is necessary to become the serpent, sloughing off old skins which are cycles of ages of the world swallowed up in pitch-black whirlpools on the skirts of a sunless sea.

I tell you more than is fitting for me to do. Long ago it is that I passed into the Glass House with the Thirteen Treasures of the Island of Prydein, Treasures long concealed in the Wasteland of the North. Not by giving thought or pondering the books of *llyfyrion* is wisdom gained. Round about the coasts of Prydein, where the nine waves roll unceasingly, have I set up pillar-stones with runes of protection inscribed upon their corners. For the beguilement of the learned also have I written this, the Book of Merlin.

But I do not boast or mock, I who have known such torments as I hope may never be your lot. As Gwendyd turned to smile upon me for the last time, a longing gripped me with a grasp more dreadful than that of the Stag-specter—a longing to linger forever within this dark abode. Why seek the cold daylight vision which leads but to the biting winds of the Forest of Celyddon, when I might remain sheltered here, lost in my Gwendyd's warm embrace? Once already I had slid from out my dear mother's womb, to find that the *dihenydd* which was upon me brought but the hatred of an evil king, the savage spearpoints of his followers, and my setting adrift upon a boundless sea. Merlin Wyllt—"the Mad"—men call me, and mad must I have been to seek rebirth when I might have remained warm within my mother's womb, fast in the embrace of Gwendyd, safe in the cistern of my friend Rufinus the tribune.

But there was a *dihenydd* upon me strong as that which Abbot Mawgan revealed in the wave-lashed chamber of the Tower of Beli over the stormy Sea of Hafren. Once again the spiraled courses of my ear were filled with an onrushing roaring of waters. It was a bursting up of lakes, a plunging of cataracts, and a gushing of springs from the Ocean of the Underworld through the membrane of the earth's surface. The understanding I had briefly balked at achieving was upon me now, and from that there can be no returning.

> Flows the river deep below,
> Not too deep for me to know.
> Why it drops I understand,
> Why it floods the meadowland,
> Why it surges on its way,
> Why it ebbs in dying spray.
> Just as well is known to me
> Every imp beneath the sea,
> No matter what variety,
> Each in its own company.

The gush and surge and roar came upon me in a torrential rush, engulphing and permeating me with the ponderous might of its headlong course. I was deafened and bemused as when I seek the *awen* in my refuge by the Cataract of Derwent. Spume and spray enclosed me as if within a druids' hedge, a crushing weight of waters beat down all flight of thought, and an unceasing booming thunder drove out every waking image. All the myriad forms I had glimpsed within the Halls of Annufn were jostled into confusion within the chambers of my brain, as the Cauldron of Annufn was split as it had not been split since Efnisien mab Eurosui sundered it within the courthouse of Matholuch, king of Ywerdon.

After the clangor and quaking died away, there was stillness for a space. I opened my eyes, to find myself lying alone upon the peak of the sacred hill Dinleu Gurygon. My heart palpitated convulsively, echoing the drumming of the waters which still thundered in my ears. Gradually my mind cleared itself of its frenzied confusion, disparate birds and beasts, emblems and symbols, assigning them into an ordered polarity such as one sees about the edge of richly illuminated books wrought by scribes in the courts of the kings of the Fichti.

I lay upon my back on the bare face of the hill, protected from the chill night air by the stag's hide wrapped around me. His flesh I had eaten and his blood had I drunk; his power and strength were within me, and I lay somnolent and heavy from the fullness of my belly and the drowsiness of my eyes. There lingered a faint drumming in my ears: the drum that is made from the stretched stag's hide.

I closed my eyes again, and directed the onslaught of my mind toward an understanding of all that had befallen me during the long age of night. Determined was the surge of the nine billows of my thinking, and furiously did they foam upon the surface of the ocean of understanding below.

But though I knew the *awen* had come upon me since my slaughter of the Stag-specter, the images it conjured up remained turbulent as the racing steeds of Manawydan mab Lir, opaque as the green depths of ocean where the blind sea-specters sail. I saw brave warriors assembled about a rampart, white-faced shields and four-edged spears borne before them, swift long-maned steeds beneath them. Bravely did they earn their mead-portion in the place of slaughter. Savagely did they attack; like thunder was the clash of their shields; like the tearing of eagles' talons was the piercing of their spears. There were cries in the wind about the place of battle, upon the hillside, upon the bright brow of the king. Food for ravens and wolves was there aplenty, blood flowing from flashing sword blades, biers in abundance for the slain who lay with the light in their eyes.

Bitter was the laughter of the warriors, and glorious their mead-portion. Blood on the ground and flesh to the wolves were dearer to them than a wedding feast. There was rejoicing among bards, for the fame of the warriors of the Brython would live forever upon the lips of men at their mead-drinking. Better the long line of biers, better the deaths of princes, better the guerdon of yellow ensnaring mead, than coughing and old age, disease and sorrow. For before they were slain, they slew.

The old live on, but not on the lips of poets, whose songs endure till the world's ending. Not for the lame outcast is a welcome in the taverns of Powys, paradise of Prydein. Old age is a mocker from the hair to the teeth; in winter, trees are bare, the wind chill, and the lake frozen. Lusty maids laugh by the byre, the war horse stamps his foot in the stable. It is not they who are for the old man filled with longing; for him there is long labor without release.

Amid the turmoil upon the dyke and within the gateway I could distinguish feats of foeman, widowing of warriors, and the victory of a great host. But when I put the question "How do you see our

army?" I received only the reply "I see red on them; I see crimson."
"To which king will be the victory?" "I see red on them; I see
crimson." "Who will prove the masters of the Island of the Mighty,
the noble *llu* of the Brython or the mongrel hosts of Loiger?" "I see red
on them; I see crimson."

It was the voice of Gwendyd which answered me, teasing my
eager seeking after foreknowledge. "Not easy will it be for soothsayers
to predict the outcome," she replied at last. "Not within the Island of
the Mighty alone is red war being waged this summer. In the Otherworld also is strife and discord. In the Halls of Annufn the hosts of
Arawn and Hafgan are preparing to contest the mastery, and it may be
that in the sky above, you will see the clash of arms when the *gosgordd* of
Gwyn mab Nud encounters that of Gwithir mab Greidawl. Not with
kites and ravens alone will the place of slaughter be darkened, nor will
it be badgers and foxes who dispute within the Portals of Annufn
beneath the stamping of the war horses. The place of the Bear will be
soaked in gore, which the Island Dragon will lick with his fiery
tongue."

"But which Dragon is it to be, my sister Gwendyd?" I implored.
"The Red or the White?"

"Not easy is that to say," replied the voice on the dark hilltop. "I
see treachery such as has not been within the Island of the Mighty since
Idawg Cord Prydein bore his lying message from Arthur to Medraud
before the slaughter of Camlann. There will be deceit and illusions
impenetrable as a druid's hedge of mist, perplexing and bedeviling as
the enchantments of Math mab Mathonwy, Menu mab Teirguaed or
Coll mab Collfrewi. It will require all your skills, my brother, to
preserve the Monarchy of Prydein in the hour of its peril. And this
time there will not be your sister Gwendyd to unravel the clew and
guide you forth from the Labyrinth of Annufn."

"But what must I do?" I pleaded. "Help me, my sister!"

"It is for you to protect the kingdom, not I," replied Gwendyd,
her calm voice a gentle breath upon the empty ocean of my despair.
"You have played at the *gwyddbwyll* with Taliesin upon Mellun Mountain; the Hawk of Gwales has dropped your eye into the Fountain of
Leudiniaun; and you have supped upon the flesh and blood of the
king of Annufn. There can be little you do not know, though you
know it not yet. I shall be distant from you at this time, though our
love shall not be sundered by oceans of ages, and in life as in death are
we linked like swans with a silver chain."

Then the false sense stole from me, and I awoke within my
bloodied stag's hide. A faint gray light was stealing from the east

across the fertile plain of Powys, across whose broad morning expanse
lay, like a sleeping silver serpent, the strong-flowing Hafren, a faint
mist hanging upon her flanks. Dawn was approaching, though the
lamps of heaven still shone bright in their tented roof. Failing in the
east was the mighty Hunter with his dogs, whose vow it is to consume
all beasts and cattle that dwell upon earth. Already the scorpion had set
its grip fast upon his genitals, and the Hunter with his jeweled belt was
sinking among the faint hills smudging the eastern horizon, where the
highway runs on to Caer Luitgoed.

It was that unchancy moment which is neither dawn nor day,
dark nor light, when a man's wraith, *ellyll,* seems to stand beside his
body as a stranger. But even as I gazed, the malevolent Hunter and his
baying couple departed below the blue haze of the distant hills, and in
their place the pure white star of the morning shone forth, fresh from
her bath in limpid crystalline waters, wafting across waking woods
and meadows the warm breath and moist scents of the deep-blue
Middle Sea, home of splashing dolphins and laughing mermaids. High
in the House of the Bull she hung, radiant beacon of the firmament,
diamond of purest water, my *Ty Gwydr* in the skies.

So you arose from your nocturnal sea, my Gwendyd—Bright
Star—and with your ascent uprose my own flagged spirit. Your
iridescent glow outshone the mighty mansion of the Bull upon whose
rampart you had ascended, and I likewise upon my bed of stag's hide
felt the vigor of your vision suffuse my being. The beam that shone
upon me from the scented warmth of your white breasts, pillows of
my night's dreaming, quickened the blood within my veins and the
seed within my loins. Green was the *enaid* that breathed with the first
faint golden glow in the east, coursing through trees and flowers and
blades of grass, quickening them with the consummation that was
ours, my Gwendyd, when our limbs and lips were conjoined in
ecstasy. Purest white is the diamond, but each shimmering facet reflects the seven rich colors of creation.

> Fairest Mai Day, springtime's morning,
> At your flower-spangled dawning
> Blackbirds sing out their joyous lay,
> Awakened by the beam of day.
>
> Loudly the plaintive cuckoo's cry
> Rings dark against the summer sky;
> Fled is the icy winter night,
> Ranked green the trees in order bright.

Stilled is the rage of roaring seas,
Lulled by the balmy western breeze;
Like sleeping ocean, blue and still,
Blossom-white flecked are dale and hill.

Throughout the burning noontide hours
Droning bees toil midst the flowers;
Slow by sludgy tracks are treading
Cattle to each summer steading.

Strums Teirtu's Harp within the brake;
White sails are skimming on the lake;
Blue, green, and gold clothe every hill;
White rolls the haze on pond and rill.

Men at labor, up and doing,
Maidens under heather wooing,
Fair the forest treetops swaying;
Now the time has come for Maying.

Leaps the urge to gallop courses;
Warriors mounting mettled horses.
A bright shaft loosed throughout the land
Reflecting each blue-bladed brand.

For now the sun had risen in his shining glory, spreading his
radiant light over the fairest Island that is in the world. My bright
Gwendyd fled away, as a golden radiance, ruddy and aureate as her
soft-curling hair, filled all the land of Powys, Paradise of Prydein. I
was content with the thought that in time beneath the shadowed
coverlet of night I would return to her yielding embrace and soft
caresses. For now was the time to be up and doing! The sign of the
Bull, under which was gathered the hosting of King Maelgun the Tall at
Caer Gurygon in Powys, is red and orange: colors of blood and flame;
of hostings, cattle raids, and destruction of strongholds.

There was a stirring from all the land below me: a clangor of
smiths, a clatter of weapons, and a trampling of steeds. I rose to my
feet upon the flayed skin of the dead king of Annufn, and as I did so I
saw a shadow pass across the bright-bushed summit of Dinleu Gurygon.
Gazing above me, I saw the soaring form of the Eagle of Brynach, his
plumage golden as the sun's scorching sphere, and the spread of his
mighty pinions broad as the sky itself. The Eagle screamed, and I

turned obediently to descend the sacred hill. I was a warrior before I was a prophet, and I knew that the work of sword and spear lay before me and the men of the Island of the Mighty.

Through my mind passed the words I had uttered before Taliesin, when we played at the *gwyddbwyll* upon Mellun Mountain:

> For the strife of Arderid provides the cause
> From their lives' preparing to the last of wars.

CHAPTER TWELVE

THE WASHER AT THE FORD

The pale pure morning drew near, and Dawn caressed with her soft fingers the dewy summit of Dinleu Gurygon, bright-knolled peak beyond all hills of the land of Prydein. Stealing light-footed in her fair mantle across the heaving Sea of Udd, she began to brighten all the eastern sky above the somber hills and forests of Loiger. The candles of the firmament were extinguished one by one, as divine Leu flew upon His pale yellow steed in pursuit of His faithless Blodeued along the fading radiance of Gwydion's Path.

Fair, bright, and clothed in white arose smiling, rosy-fingered Dawn from the darkness, conscious of the beauty of her young body as a girl bathing emerges bare-breasted and cool-skinned onto a meadow bank. Chaste, fair, and endlessly reborn upon the margin of time past and time recurring is she, daughter of the sky and begetter of the day. Mother and sister is she of my Gwendyd, the Morning Star, and mistress of the Hunter whose starry cluster lies sunk in the eastern night from which her beauty arises. Sweet and soft and warm was the touch of her lips upon fecund plain and heathery hillside, dewy dell, and cold crag: kisses that quickened to life and vigor grasses and trees, cattle and roebuck, armored beetle and soaring sparrow hawk; and not least of all the ravaged heart of her lover of the night, Merlin mab Morfryn.

Now was the time come upon me to become the Hunter, for I shared with my mistress the Dawn a long and weary path whose end was death and darkness of night, and plunging dissolution in the Glass House of Ocean. Light filtered through my eyelids into the outer chambers of my mind, obscuring at the same time in swift-moving shadow those subterranean caverns I had explored during my nocturnal voyaging. Closed was the Head of Annufn, and I must be up and doing! With care and caution I passed from sleep to sight, for sleep is so near to death that the spirit of the unwary may unwittingly glide from one to the other with the sinuous ease of a serpent departing into his crevice.

As I arose from my grassy couch I felt the cruel shadows of the night pass from me. I was bathed in dew that cleansed and purified all the fair land of Powys below me, arising reborn among dispelling vapors upon that memorable Kalan Mai. It was *kyntefin,* the season of summer, the breeze fresh, grass verdant and dewy, birds joyous and loud-trilling. I mounted upon the eastern rampart encircling the crest of Dinleu Gurygon, and raised my arms to the lightening sky in solitary greeting:

> "Joyous tidings through every land!
> Lapping ocean, fishes brimming,
> Washing waves on golden strand;
> Smiling woodlands, swallows skimming.
> Rout of spectres, imps and witches;
> Orchards blossom, apples coming!
> Green corn-shoots for harvest riches,
> Bee-hosts in the warm air humming.
> Our cheerful world of warmth and light
> In peace and justice ordered right:
> Ah, happy, happy summertime!"

With that, the rim of Beli's golden Chariot appeared above the eastern horizon, and its glorious light shone out upon every long ridge and in every hollow. I gazed upon the fair plain beneath me. Just as Beli's golden gleam drew forth the young green spearheads of the corn and scattered primroses over meadows, so the hearts of men uprose and set them up and doing. From each steading wafted smoke of burning rowan twigs, dislodging hideous bone-shanked witches straddling every rooftree. Not long did the malign beings linger, but fled off shrieking to darkened chasms and pitchy pools high among the snowy crags of Eryri. Freed of the noxious brood, the upper sky was left alone to the crooked-taloned Eagle of Brynach, who soared above in majesty, his brazen plumes reflecting the radiance of Beli the Great, after whom this Island—the fairest that is in the world—is named.

Jubilant were the clarion calls of red-combed cocks, each exulting on his hill-fort of dung. Deep-throated was the lowing of kine, shrill the shouts of herdsmen, and sonorous the sounding of their horns as cattle were driven forth in preparation for the long day's ascent to upland grazings. For six drear months of winter they had been assailed by driving rain and heavy snows; since the melancholy festival of Kalan Gaeaf it was boar and stag alone that cropped the hillside pastures, and the gaunt wolf of the wilderness who sought shelter within the herdsman's deserted *hafod*.

Merry, too, were the choruses of the lovely maidens of King Brochfael's realm as they greeted the coming of summer. "Joyous are maidens when the Kalan Mai comes to them," is it said, and joyous was I as I watched them pass below me, barefooted and beautiful, upright and eager, no burden on back or in heart, free from sin and sorrow, chanting their clear chorus of greeting. My heart flew out toward cheeks flushed and rosy as Dawn herself, to golden tresses wafted by the willow breezes, and lithe forms lissome as fawns picking their way down hillside trackways. As readily might evil enter their bright young minds as a witch pass through the labyrinth traced in mud before each cottage threshold. Ah, that I might reattain that purity and innocence which was mine before the shattering of the Cauldron of Ceridwen!

Only for a dark moment did the shadow pass over me. For now, from the hazel branch above me rang out the clear liquid warbling of the mistle thrush. I laughed, and sprang from the rampart to descend the winding track of the steep hillside. For if one paradise lay far behind me in the deep combe on the bounds of Cerniu where I had my conception, did not another lie at the end of it all, beyond the hazy horizon? And was I not even now descending to join the joyous hosting of King Maelgun upon the green plain of Powys, Paradise of Prydein?

So my friend caroled on high while I plunged humming down the bright-bushed hill to the level green plain beneath. It was there that the greatest host that was in the Island of Prydein since the emperor Arthur went up to Din Badon was assembling. On the lower skirt of the holy hill I came upon King Maelgun mab Cadwallon Lawhir, who stood with his druids and priests to watch the rising up of that mighty battle array. The great king stood upon a large rock, his chief druid upon his left side and his chief priest upon his right, and he himself faced ever to the east. Close by awaited Taliesin, prince of poets, who smilingly signed to me to join him by his side.

I stood and watched, wondering, as the battle hosts of Prydein arose together at the summons of the great king Maelgun the Tall and the behest of his under-kings, and the cries of the heralds who passed sunwise around the encampment. Then the men of the Brython arose as one man stark naked, save for the weapons which they bore in their hands. And each man whose tent door faced the rising sun cut his way westward through the leather of his tent, deeming it a delay and shame to go around.

"How do the men of Prydein rise for battle?" cried Maelgun Gwynedd to Maeldaf the elder.

"They rise bravely," responded Maeldaf. "All are stark naked. Each man whose tent door faces to the eastward has plunged westward through his tent, deeming it too long to go around."

"That is good, and worthy a great host," uttered Maelgun the Tall with satisfaction.

Next the king turned to his messengers, namely Mawgan and Arianbad, and instructed them as to the words they were to bear to the kings of the hosts of the Brython:

"Go now, my heralds," he cried in his deep voice, "and restrain the men of Prydein. Do not permit them to come to the hosting until the omens and auguries are propitious, and until the sun rises into the vault of heaven, filling the glens and slopes, hills and mountains, elf-mounds and hero graves of the land of Prydein."

So Mawgan and Arianbad bore the king's message throughout the host, and every man remained in his place until druids and soothsayers had consulted the omens. It was long that they gazed upward at the sailing shapes of clouds, and longer still that they pondered the meaning of the cries of birds from green wood and brown hillside. To them from out of a certain grove called a capercaillie, with resonant rattle as of dishes set out in the well-lit hall, a plopping as of a cork drawn from a wine-crock, a bubbling as of rich liquor from narrow-necked vessels set before the glorious drunken war-band—followed by grim grating as of edged blade upon a whetstone.

Between the sucking, gurgling sound of the rushing liquor and the scraping of the sword blade there is a pause, and it is the length of this pause that druids and wise men interpret in their divination. Unchancy, it seemed to me, was the bird's pause, and unchancy the thoughtful looks of the great king's druids.

However, the talk of the birds was at length pronounced propitious, and the sun broke through the gliding clouds with a light that filled the glens and slopes and hills and mounds of the fair land of Powys from east to west and north to south. And King Maelgun demanded of his chief druid foreknowledge of what would occur during that summer's hosting in the Southland:

"There are many here who will part this day from wives and brothers, sweethearts and friends," he said, "from kingdoms and lordships, from father and mother, and if not all return safe and sound, it will be upon me that their curses and repining will light. Yet none goes forth and none stays here who is any dearer to us than we ourselves. I ask you therefore whether we shall come back or not?"

The chief druid remained plunged in thought for a space of time, while the capercaillie called again from a yew grove beyond us. Then he replied thoughtfully: "Whoever it is that comes or comes not back, you yourself will return."

Then the king and his companions rejoiced, flourishing their spears above their heads in jubilation. For, just as it is said that "It is not usual to continue the fighting after the prince has fallen," so it must be that if the king's life be preserved, the victory is his.

For my part, though, I drew my hood down over my brow and remained pensive and brooding. That the druids had interpreted the bird's cry aright, and that the king would indeed come back, I did not doubt. But it was what they had left unsaid that one would surely wish to know. Would Maelgun return exulting at the head of his war-band, or would it be a bleeding corpse upon a hurdle that was borne through the gates of Degannwy in Ros at the close of the summer's hosting? I shuddered as I seemed to hear once more the sneering laugh of Gwyn mab Nud in the chamber of shadows at Caer Gurygon, and thought of the misplaced piece upon the *gwyddbwyll* board.

"There will be flowing of blood from the bodies of men, and tears from the eyes of women," I murmured. "Long will the conflict be remembered and its deeds recounted in kings' halls. Limbs and trunks will be hacked about, great will be the feasting of kites and crows, and long and bitter the weeping of warriors' wives. The hounds of battle will sup their fill."

"Is that your vision, O Merlin mab Morfryn?" murmured Taliesin, whom I suddenly found by my side. "Is it chancy or unchancy? The omens are good, as you have heard. The kings of the Brython are very leeks of battle and bears in the trackway, and the hosts of Prydein are assembled to the number of a hundred thousand to do battle with the skulking whelps of the Iwys. This is scarcely a time for downcast looks and muttered forebodings, my friend. You had best take care, for the king's heart is up, and mighty is the shield upon a brave shoulder. He will look askance upon such ominous talk as yours, should it come to his ears."

Glancing aside at my companion, I saw him smiling quizzically at me, his radiant brow gleaming in the morning sunlight. My lips had barely stirred, and it came into my mind that he must possess the hearing of Math mab Mathonwy. I nodded in assent, and clasped his hand. But my thoughts remained momentarily clouded in melancholy premonition. The poet's fame would be as resplendent and his guerdon as great whether it were an elegy he came to compose at the Kalan Gaeaf or a praise-poem for victory. I bear a heavier responsibility, that *tynged* visited upon me at my birth which there is no evading. "Merlin's Precinct" men call this Island, and it is for me to ensure that the foeman does not violate its borders.

Now horns were sounded throughout the encampment, and like bees from a hive the kings and hosts and tribes of the Island of Prydein with its Three Adjacent Islands gathered together about King Maelgun the Tall, son of Cadwallon of the Long Hand, and gave him the cry of a king. And there was no numbering the hosts that were assembled that day in shining array, with their bright mail-coats and ash-hafted spears and blue-bladed swords and lime-white shields. For a king is a bulwark and stronghold to his people, a surety for the peace of the land, and a tree beneath whose shade the tribes may flourish. Fostered on his sweet yellow mead, no boasting was so expansive as theirs, and their fame shall be honored so long as there live poets in Prydein.

Then Maeldaf the elder spoke to the men of Prydein, recalling the hospitality dispensed at the court of Degannwy over the winter and the oaths and boastings proffered in return. Now was come the time for a mead-earning and a reckoning with the heathen hordes of the Iwys:

"Of old it was said of the king of the Brython that 'He judged Prydein with its Three Islands,' and that in wedding the kingdom he was as one with the land. But now is our ancestress Branwen slighted and the Island of the Mighty violated by the stranger, even as Gwenhuifar wife of Arthur was plucked from her throne in Celliwig and ravished by the traitor Medraud. The land has been faithless to its consort, and there must be a Restitution of Prydein!"

The kings and princes and warriors clashed their spears and shields and cried aloud in assent, whereupon the king's counselor continued as follows:

"Well you know, O people and tribes of the Brython, that the Truth of the kingdom was assured so long as the king's bride remained true and inviolate. You know, too, the Law of Dyfnwal Moelmud, which is the Law of the Land:

"Whoever shall commit rape upon a woman is to pay honor-price to her lord. But if the thief deny his crime—even as Cynurig, king of the Iwys, has impudently denied his fealty—then is the woman to take hold of his member in her left hand and swear to his having committed rape upon her, and in that way she loses nothing of her right."

Maelgun nodded in approval at these words of Maeldaf, for had he not himself ravished and taken in marriage his nephew's young wife? She had held his member, too, Tree of the Island of Prydein, though not, it may be said, in token of ravishment.

"Such is the law of Dyfnwal Moelmud," concluded Maeldaf, "which must be sustained if the Truth of the Land is to continue."

Here the king held up his hand for all to listen, and pronounced this exhortation: "You have heard the words of Maeldaf the elder, O princes. Now, at the time of the Kalan Geaef, I swore an oath upon the altar of the blessed Cubi which lies in his church beneath the holy mountain by the Western Sea. In the presence of the man of God and of Crist and His saints I took pledges by sun and moon and dew and light and by all elements visible and invisible and by every element in heaven and in earth that the Island of the Mighty shall be restored this summer to her lawful consort. I vow moreover that the ravisher of the Island, Cynurig the pirate, shall be compelled to pay honor-price for the rape he has committed. And this he shall perform, laying his hand the while upon that stone which stands at the Center of the Island of the Mighty, being called the Penis of Prydein."

The redemption was fitting, and throughout the encampment there followed an oath-taking, at which truth was pledged for the vow of the king: that is to say, truth of breast and cheek, of heaven and earth, of sun and moon, of dew and drop, of sea and land.

And when that was done, Maeldaf the elder declared before all the company that, should Cynurig fail to do as Maelgun commanded, then would the penalty exacted by the Law of Dyfnwal be exacted without pity: "If the culprit cannot pay, then let him be gelded."

At this a shout of laughter swept through the host, rolling from wing to wing like foaming breakers rolling out of a hazy summer sea across golden strands of the Western Sea. The consultation of the omens had caused a brief chill to pass like a shudder through the host, a chill dispelled and fleeing before gales of merry laughter.

The great king Maelgun the Tall, who towered in the midst of his host like a bull among his heifers, caused his heralds to cry for silence that he might utter the words of departure:

"Wisely is it ordained that no king is a true king unless he have each year a hosting from his country to a border country. And what better cause have we than that of expelling from our borders the heathen Iwys, whelps of false Hengys and his brother Horsa? Before the summer be out, they will suffer death and tribulations without number, burning of homes and taking of hostages. For never has such a host gone forth from the Island of the Mighty since the emperor Arthur went up to Badon Hill: a host of a hundred thousand, tribes of Edeyrn and Coel and Cadell, kings of Dyfneint and Dyfed, Gwynedd and Gwent, and the noble war-band of Elffin mab Gwydno from the North. No more shall the kings of the Brython strive one with the other, but all will combine to combat the enemy of all!"

Maelgun Gwynedd paused, gazing about him upon the hosting of the Brython. The rays of the morning sun glittered from one to another of the spearheads of the war-bands as they dance over the wavelets of an upland tarn. Or they might be likened to a host of bees moving upon a meadow of marigolds. And so King Maelgun concluded with these words:

"There shall be a Restitution of the Monarchy of Prydein, and we who speak the pure tongue of the Brython shall be as brothers, dwelling within one border. For this cause I declare this day, standing before the sacred hill of Dinleu Gurygon, that the people of this land shall henceforward be called Cymry, 'fellow countrymen,' and it will be to the Cymry of the Island of the Mighty that victory will be brought as the outcome of this summer's hosting."

Then the cry of a host was uttered again within the encampment, so loud that it caused great flocks of birds to rise from the groves and woods and forests of the land of Powys, darkening the sun as if it were nighttime. And so the birds passed away crying toward the Southland, whither the armies of the Cymry were about to direct their march. And this was pronounced by the king's soothsayers to be a good omen.

It happened, too, at this time, while all stood momentarily silent upon the Plain of Powys, that a certain jester perched in a tree hard by the camp called out in a loud voice, "Fu, fa, fum! I smell the smell of a lying, thieving son of the Iwys. Cynurig, you are too big for one bite and too small for two. I do not know whether I will boil you in a cauldron or take you as a pinch of spice between my five fingers!"

Merrily laughed the kings and princes and warriors of the Cymry as they set about striking their tents and preparing for their great march to the south. But of the jester it is said that he fell from the branch and broke his neck.

This was the manner in which the Cymry began their march toward the South. The blessed Gwydfarch exhorted the assembled hosts of the baptized, kneeling as one man upon the greensward before him. The occasion was fitting, for it was upon the Kalan Mai that Crist began his noble preaching to the people of the Jews. Fourteen nights had passed since the celebration of Easter, and it was the significance of the festival that the saint interpreted before the people. He spoke with such golden-tongued, honeyed words that the kings and people gathered about him seemed to see the triumph of Our Lord as if it were happening before them in Powys, the Paradise of Prydein.

They saw how upon the third day the Lord Iessu Crist ascended into Heaven, where He assembled about Him the greatest of hosts that was in the world. There was within His camp the war-band of Michael, archangels fierce and unyielding; the war-band of Noah from beneath the sea, who saw the earth reborn; the retinue of Esaias, prophet undaunted in battle; the battle host of Stephen, martyrs whose faces are ever toward the foe; the troop of Garmawn the bishop, whose "Alleluiah!" laid low the hordes of the heathen: These were the van of the army. Of the remainder of that host there is neither counting nor reckoning, with their noble over-kings, the numberless host of saints, bright and pure—a mighty assemblage!

At the head of the host rode the Holy Crist Himself, with the twelve apostles—each a leek in battle, a bear in the trackway—beside Him. Like the Thirteen Princes of the North were they, with Urien Reged, Bull-protector of the Island of the Mighty, riding at their head. May You be helping us in Heaven and upon earth, O tender Son of Mary, meek and mild!

All have heard tell how the Devil was at this time holding captive within his hostage pits many of the noblest of humankind, guileless and sinless men of faith. Strong were the palisades and earthen dykes of his dark fortress in the hot Southland, and grim and fierce the legions of fiends who assembled at the sound of his horn. But it was not they who would defeat the armies of Crist's saints, with their strength of psalm-singing and book-learning.

When Crist and His saints pitched their camp before the dark gates of Caer Uffern, it was the Devil whose heart became loose and liquid within him. And when Crist knocked thrice with His spear-haft upon the doors, the Enemy barred himself trembling within his stronghold. Vain hope! What need to say more? There was a trampling of steeds about the fortress, a raising up of spearpoints, and a burning and breaking of ramparts. Crist Himself, bull of battle, wolf of the army, herb garden of the war-band, thundered these words before the gatehouse of Hell's fortress:

"Thine enemies shall cast a trench about thee, and compass thee round, and keep thee in on every side.

"And shall lay thee even with the ground, and thy children within thee; and they shall not leave in thee one stone upon another; because thou knewest not the time of thy visitation."

Then Iessu Crist Himself it was, the man-slaying champion, black slayer of the band of brigands, who first broke through the breach. Bloodstained blades covered the ground and kites wheeled above, awaiting the flesh-feasting as the torque-bearing Savior made of the demon-host food for beaks of eagles and teeth of wolves. Then did the dark Lord of Uffern, enemy of mankind, sue for peace. To the King of Heaven did he raise the knee and suck His nipple, granting hostages, rendering tribute and releasing prisoners. Thus was the might of the Devil weakened, together with that of his dark despicable host, and the Lord Iessu Crist rode back triumphant in majesty to sit upon the right hand of God.

"It is recounted of that expedition that when He returned to Paradise from the realm of Uffern, not a cow lowed to her calf, so great were the herds of kine which the Lord Iessu Crist brought back from His cattle raiding. The fortress of Hell had He plundered of its wealth, and subjected its people to tonsure and collar of slavery. Joyous was the drinking in the Hall of Heaven that night! Would that it were I who provided that mead-feast for the King of Kings, so that He and the people of Heaven might be drinking it eternally!"

Raising his crucifix on high, Saint Gwydfarch called down the blessing of Crist, abbot, and king upon the hosting of Maelgun the Tall, son of Cadwallon of the Long Hand. Should victory that summer lie with the Cymry, then would they deliver a third part of their plunder to Crist, who is overlord of the tribes of Prydein:

> "The king asked me a question bold,
> What it was the Lord foretold?
> The prey of Hell He hath set free,
> Its host held down in slavery."

King Maelgun frowned to himself, for he had thought to pay but a tenth of all he should seize from the halls of the Iwys in tribute to Holy Church. But he said nothing at that period, for it came into his mind that there would come a more fitting time for dispute in the matter of tribute, once Crist had delivered the foe into his power.

Apart from these secret thoughts of King Maelgun, however, the words of the blessed Gwydfarch were received with high acclaim by the men of the Cymry, and from one as from all came a cry of *Alleluiah!* Then the saint and the monks of his household proceeded to the rushy banks of the winding Hafren, singing tuneful psalms and ringing delightful bells. So lovely was that music that it is said the beaver-folk who dwell upon the riverbanks ceased from their labors to kneel upright in prayer to Our Lord, Savior of Mankind. They were joined by many of the army, who assembled in the water meadows to receive the cleansing waters of baptism in the flowing wave of the holy river.

"The stream's flow makes glad the City of God," pronounced the man of God, blessed Gwydfarch, when the triple immersion was completed. Thereupon he led the pious host back to where in the midst of their camp he and his monks had built a church of leafy branches. Fervid in faith, though wet from baptism, the soldiers paraded to perform penance.

After this, while the kings and hosts made ready to march, Maelgun Gwynedd ascended the hill Dinleu Gurygon with his druids in order to wash his hands and his royal face in the well called the Bowl of Bran. For the kingdom of Gwynedd, with its snowy mountains and dark lakes, was in former days known as the Land of Bran, and it was there that Bran with his Ravens held lordship before he departed across the Western Sea to Ywerdon.

From the eve of the Kalan Mai the king's druids had kept watch and ward upon him lest inadvertently he violate one *kynneddyf,* or obligation, of the seven which lie upon a king of Gwynedd. They it was who ensured that the sun did not rise upon him in his bed upon the Plain of Powys; that the steed he rode that morning was not a dapple gray; and that he made his circuit of the camp sunwise with his head leaning to the left. Fortunately no other *kynneddyf* was of pressing danger at this time: that he should not eat by candlelight at Lanarmon-yn-Ial, spend a wet autumn night on Ynys Seiriol, hear the groans of the women of Arfon in their birth travail, nor undertake a cattle raiding in Cardigan when the cuckoo calls to his mate. None of these things did he do, and so all appeared propitious for a summer's hosting in the land of Loiger.

All was ordered as it should be, and the Red Dragon was unfurled before the baptized host of the Cymry as they set forth upon their march, with every tribe about its idol and every war-band about its king. And in the van of the army rode two great kings—that is, Maelgun the Tall of Gwynedd and Brochfael of the Tusks of Powys.

So it was upon the Kalan Mai, with the sun shining gloriously on every long ridge and in every hollow, that the host of the kings of Prydein set forth upon the great paved causeway that leads from Caer Gurygon to the southwest. Neither floods nor tempests of forests hindered the hundred thousand men of the Cymry as they marched upon their way, for King Brochfael had earlier dispatched messengers to the *pencenedl* of each kindred throughout all the broad lands of

Powys, requiring them to provide craftsmen and slaves to repair bridges and clear the roadway of fallen trees.

On rough-maned horses like swans rode the host around the bright-bushed hill of Dinleu, and with the day we passed through the splendid, spacious city. At the tombstone of Cynyr Gwydel we halted for a space while the blessed Gwydfarch bestowed upon us all his benison, before returning to his vigil in the rocky bed on the slope of Galtyr Ancyr above his church of Meifod.

Joyous were the warriors of Prydein as they rode, for they scented victory in the clear spring air. Now would they earn the wine and mead they had drunk through the long winter's feasting in the halls of Maelgun Gwynedd and Brochfael of the Tusks! Wine and mead from golden vessels had been their drink for a year, according to custom; three men and three score and three hundred gold-torqued princes of the most valiant of the Cymry.

From the hills around us, cattle lowed and sheep bleated, driven to their summer pasturage along upland trackways through heather and gorse. What slashing of swords and splintering of shields would there have been by the time of their return to winter steadings! Woe, woe to the heathen Iwys, who must even now be crouching in fen and ditch as the thunder of the approaching host reached their ears! For who was there in all the Island of the Mighty who had not seen the passing of the fiery star at the time of the changing of the year, and lights hovering in the frozen northwest which bore unmistakably the appearance of flaming lances? And even now from the northwest was moving a forest of spearmen whose weapons would make prostrate the rabble-rout of Loiger, and cause the crying of widows to be heard throughout the land. Happy, happy summertime!

I rode behind the two kings, with Taliesin at my side. By the traces of foam upon his lips I could see that he had sought out his *awen*, and that in each night's encampment there would be songs of battles past and victories to come. For what are the gains of conquest and plunder unless they be sung by the bards of the world, so that the warriors' fame be told in kings' halls until the world's ending?

Now I have spoken enough of the hosting of the Cymry, and must tell something of myself. Mine was no mean role, for I was to perform the task Cynddilig Cyfarwydd enacted for Arthur. That the host might proceed in due order, without mishap, and without causing offense to the people of the Mother's Blessing who dwell in elf-mounds upon the hills and pleasant plains of Prydein, it was necessary for me to expound as we went the lore of the land. And who indeed could better perform that task than I, Merlin mab Morfryn, who it was (if all that is told be true) first named the hills, rivers, and plains at the time of the first peopling of the Island of the Mighty by Prydein son of Aed the Great?

From Penrin Blathaon in the north to Penwaed in the south I have seen the sixty cantrefs and hundred and fifty-four districts of the Island of the Mighty, its Three Adjacent Islands, its Three Great Rivers, and its Twenty-eight Cities. And of each I know its naming and its story: the kings who judged the islands of old, the queens for whom the rivers flow, the craftsmen who dressed the stones, and the heroes who established their lordships within each shining city.

Every mountain and forest, lake and river, glen and down, hill-fort and homestead throughout the Island bears its name and its tale. The preservation of each name and tale is no ignoble task for men of learning. For should the lore of the land become lost to the recollection of men, whether by forgetfulness of tradition or invasions of men of alien race and tongue, then will the land revert to what it was before its naming and settling: to the nine forms of elements, a formless mass, unfeeling, unmeaning, inchoate; with its kings unwed to the Sovranty of the Land, their courts unfrequented by poets, and poets unvisited by their *awen*, and its tribes a lost horde wandering upon the face of the country, lawless barbarians lacking hearth and home, land and kinship. Order and significance will depart from the land, strangers will possess our twenty-eight cities and revel in our deserted royal halls, the truth of the land will be dissolved, and with the end of all things the dark hosts of the Coranieid will violate the borders.

> *Dysgogan Myrdin, dysgogan derwydon, dysgogan awen:*
> *dechymyd tristit byt a ryher.*

As we advanced day by day toward the southern marches of Powys, I told of the bursting forth of rivers and lakes from the Waters of Annufn below the ground; of each monstrous Adanc skulking in its slimy depths or beauteous lady dreaming within her subaqueous palace of clearest crystal; of the giants of the *Cewri* who inhabit the mountaintops, and the rocks great as houses which they tumbled from the summits; of those green swelling mounds which are the breasts of the goddess Don, within which dwell the Fair Folk men term the Mother's Blessing.

Not for me was there need of that potion which confers the quality of knowing every stream, every river, every estuary, every battlefield, and every place of combat of champions. I recounted the names of heroes whose graves lay to east and west of the track we trod: graves which the rain wets, the thicket covers, the shower sprinkles. Speechless beneath mounds and heaps of stones they lie, in lonely places upon airy mountainsides, by rivers roaring swollen from the molten snows of springtime, and in leafy glens where only the wolf's whelp howls. They are mute beneath the greensward, yet so long as the History of Places is told, they live upon the lips of men.

During the day's march, and at night about the campfires, the name of Arthur was ever upon the lips of the warriors of the Cymry. For all men know the prophecy that one day he will come again to aid us in our hour of need, and lead our armies once more to Badon Hill. I felt his presence brooding as I slept, and wondered: Would he receive us among the slain in his hall beneath the dark mountain, or would he head the battle-host when it should come to encounter the pale-faced Iwys on some foreordained ford or predestined down? At this thought the sweat would break out upon me once more, as it did during my night of trial upon the summit of Dinleu Gurygon.

Nothing hindered our march southward. The hills were clothing themselves afresh after the winter with greening of birch and beech-woods, and the meadows by the roadside were spangled with spring flowers. Each night when I ascended a hillside to watch over the host I would gaze upon the sparkling array of campfires in number not less than the spangled canopy of the roof of heaven overhead. And with each succeeding night I observed how the light that blazed through the rents that mark the Hunter's sword flared ever more fiercely—sure sign of impending war.

It was at the point where our road crossed that which spans the ridges westward toward Caer Luitgoed that we received curious tidings of an old acquaintance. In a clearing hard by the crossroads, Prince Run mab Maelgun, who was riding with the men of Arfon in the van of the army, came upon the encampment of a certain chieftain named Iorwerth mab Edeyrn from the uplands of Elfael. This Iorwerth had heard that King Brochfael of Powys was accompanying the host, and was waiting to claim a due from him.

Brought before the king, he explained that it had been his practice for many years to provide salt to the courts of Gurtheyrnion and Buelt, for which privilege their kings in turn dispatched tribute to King Brochfael at Caer Gurygon. Each spring Iowerth mab Edeyrn and the men of his tribe journeyed to the town of Caer Halwyn, on the eastern bounds of Powys beyond Hafren. It is there that is found one of the Marvels of the Island of Prydein: that is to say, wells of salt, springing out of the earth far from the sea. The lord of the tribe dwelling about that town has many slaves who toil within those wells, cutting salt out of the ground with picks, hammers, and wedges, refining it in ovens, and sawing it into bricks. It is salt of rare quality, much to be preferred for its flavor to that collected on the seacoast by the men of Cardigan.

However, it happened this year that the merchant brought with him but two wagonloads of salt-bricks. Hitherto he had been accustomed to bring away twenty or thirty loads, which he exchanged for hides and furs from the mountains. Great was his anger when the lord of the salt wells told him that a foreigner from across the sea had passed through some nights before and bought the bulk of the winter's salt-mining with rods of silver. At this, Iorwerth had considered following the stranger and slaying him with all his people. However, his host warned him that his rival had arrived claiming the protection and authority of King Brochfael of the Tusks, from whose court the foreigner had lately come, and so he desisted from the enterprise.

Brochfael was angered at this, for he had no desire at such a time to be obliged to avenge his missing tribute upon the kings of Gurtheyrnion and Buelt, and had in any case no recollection of providing the assurances claimed. But his anger turned to surprise, shared by myself and others present, when we learned that the foreigner was none other than Samo, that merchant of the Freinc who had provided the kings at their council in Caer Gurygon with invaluable intelligence concerning the disposition of the Iwys and the plans of King Cynurig. But why should Samo have bought such large quantities of salt, and where had he taken it? How could he dare to risk the anger of the king of Powys, when the latter should come to return from the summer's hosting?

There were many suggestions, but none that gained acceptance other than with him who advanced it. That the salt was of great value was incontestable—King Brochfael's father, Cyngen the Renowned, had wrested it after fierce war from a neighboring king in the East— but its value could only be realized at the court of a powerful king. The merchant had not traveled westward, of that Iorwerth was certain. Yet the South was closed to trade on account of the oppression of the Iwys; it had not been permitted to anyone to bear goods across the borderland since the emperor Arthur erected the dykes and forts enclosing their kingdom.

There ensued long and sometimes acrimonious discussion of the matter as we rode upon our way. At each town and fortress we passed, inquiry was made concerning the movements of Samo and his baggage train, but of news there was none. The tribune Rufinus, who appeared to regard me as the one person in whom he could confide, sought me out where I rode in the bright, busy cavalcade. The incident I discovered provided him with fresh opportunity to reflect upon the standard of discipline and organization in our army.

"As salt is an essential commodity in the army," he grumbled, "it is vital for the master of soldiers to send out his *delegatoriae,* well before the opening of a campaign, whose task it is to requisition essential supplies, issuing receipts to those who furnish the revenues. In special cases the *optio* of a given unit may draw rations in kind, again issuing his *recauta.* Neither of these regulation practices seems to have occurred, which is a dereliction calling for severe punishment upon the officers concerned. The supply of salt is no laughing matter for military men, my friend! Are you not aware that there was a time when it comprised the basis of the soldier's pay, *salarium?*"

Thus after several days' march we came to the old fort at the confluence of the rivers Tefaid and Colunwy, in which it is said Bran dwelt before his departure to green Ywerdon. That night the kings feasted with the chieftain of that place, a descendant of Cadell and so cousin to Brochfael of the Tusks, while the hundred thousand men of the Cymry camped in the fields without the walls.

Next morning the princes slept long and deep after partaking of their host's profusion of yellow ensnaring mead. King Maelgun and I arose early, however, and stealing past the bodies of our companions where they lay sleeping prone as sacks among the rushes, made our way out of the mead-hall through the gates of the fortress to the dew-sodden meadows beyond. I bore with me an image of sprawled limbs and gaping mouths, rich robes stained with blood-red wine, groanings and stifled cries from within the shadowed flesh-heap. I liked what I saw little enough, and least of all a glimpse of King Brochfael, his tusks gleaming pale in the half-light, lying sprawled among his mastiffs like a slain boar at the close of a hunt. It was for me an unchancy sight, and once again I felt a surge of apprehension pass over my heart like a cold wave rolling the length of a winter beach.

It was the moment when it is neither night nor day, and the still landscape gray as a wolf's back and empty of the cries of birds, save where solitary from a grove upon the hillside behind us came the hoot of an owl. Whether it was the wise Owl of Cwm Cawlwyd, or the ill-omened bird of Gwyn mab Nud, I could not tell at that time. In any case it was my task to follow the king, who pressed on with great strides that I matched only with difficulty. The great back before me was bowed, as if beneath a great weight which even the mighty shoulders of Maelgun the Tall might hardly bear.

I guessed at the oppression of sins that lay upon him: the usurpation of his uncle's throne, the rupture of monastic vows, the violation of his nephew's young wife. Beyond the bounds of Gwynedd there were few who had not heard the excoriations of Gildas the Wise, and it came into my mind that the king feared lest the saint might fast against him during the hour of battle.

Without uttering a word, we made our way down to the point hard by the fortress where three rivers meet, mingling their essence in triune sanctity. While I stood watch with a rowan twig in each hand, the king knelt down on the bank and bowed his head toward the pure running waters. There he paused in prayer until a ray from the rising sun suddenly darted forth like a javelin from the hand of a chariot-borne hero, dispelling the misty phantoms that ride upon the rivers' coursing, and gilding in glory the ramparted peak of Caer Caradog among the mountains to the westward.

This was the moment for King Maelgun to stoop his cupped hands swiftly into the chill stream, upon which the young sun was dancing, and bathe his royal face in the ocean of his gathering. As the pure element coursed in glistening drops down his broad cheeks and dark beard, he uttered aloud this prayer:

> "O God, you see me bathe my face,
> Washed by the sun's nine golden rays,
> As gave fair Mary—no disgrace—
> Milk to her Son in bygone days.
>
> Let sweetness now my face display
> And wealth be in me every day,
> Sweet honey on each word I say,
> My breath smell sweet as flowers gay.
>
> Black the land where the Iwys dwell,
> Black their hearts as the pit of Hell;
> White as the swan on ocean's swell
> Is he who rides his foes to quell.
>
> To thy great name I ever cling
> With strength of stag and serpent's sting,
> With speed of horse—and I am king
> On my foes' faces galloping!"

The king knelt silent upon the riverbank as the sun came up, bringing around us the joyous caroling of birds and the stir of insects leaving their tiny homesteads within the thicket which was the turf beneath our feet. Then he rose, embraced me in silence, and led the way back to the fort of him who was born of Bran. King Maelgun's step was lighter and his back straighter since his encounter with the purity of the running waters.

The host was stirring like bees at their swarming time when we returned. The smoke of campfires arose on every side, and there was a clatter of cauldrons and clashing of arms. Within the hall of the fortress, Maelgun joined the kings at their drinking, for it was the custom of that host to arise early in the morning and drink off mead at one draught on their journeying.

I parted from the king at the doorway with an excuse, for my mind was troubled and I wished to be alone. As solitude is not to be found in the midst of a host, I ascended the stone ramparts and made my way to a tower above the gateway, whence I could observe without interruption all that passed. It was not long, however, before my reverie was abruptly disturbed. Immediately below me I heard angry shouts, orders and remonstrances.

I leaned over to observe, being curious as ever concerning the buzz and fuss of mortal men in the surrounding emptiness of eternity. Bitter wrangling had arisen within a small group of men clustered below. Four were the spearmen of Gwynedd who comprised the gate-guard; they were endeavoring to restrain two men whose voices were raised in angry dispute. Of these one was at once familiar to me: It was that of my old friend the tribune, with whom I had spoken on the slope of Dinleu during the Nos Kalan Mai. He spoke scarcely a word of the tongue of the Brython, but this he appeared to have forgotten, for he shouted and swore at his uncomprehending audience in the language of his own people. It was time for me to come to his assistance, for it is not the least of my accomplishments that I have as great a command of the languages of the race of men (to say nothing of those of birds and animals) as ever did Gurhir Gwastad Ieithoed.

Hastily descending the steps, I turned the corner of the gateway to come upon a curious scene. Rufinus was attempting with his good arm to hold a lithe, active-looking youth, while he urged the puzzled sentinels to assist him in restraining the fellow. The tribune's commands bore an air of authority which carried some weight with men accustomed to obedience. On the other hand, they seemed to know his prisoner, whose vigorous protests they could at least understand.

"You appear to be having some difficulty here," I murmured at the tribune's elbow. "May I be of assistance?"

He glanced around, a little startled, for my approach had been, according to my custom, silent and sudden.

"Ah, it's you!" he cried, with evident relief. "Perhaps you can prevail upon these oafs that it is their duty to take this fellow into custody."

"Why, what has he done?" I inquired, flashing a glance at the others which bade them be silent.

Rufinus released his hold, upon which the young man shook himself like a dog emerging from water and stood sullenly by, regarding the tribune with no friendly eye.

"What has he done?" repeated the tribune impatiently. "It is not what he has done, but what these thick-headed sentinels—men lacking the wits even of a Cappadocian—have *not* done which concerns me, and should concern everyone who wishes to see this army maintain something approximating to Roman discipline. I have been posted to some out-of-the-way spots, and have seen a *campidoctor* trying to drill recruits who seemed to think they were rehearsing as a troop of buffoons for the circus. Well, I should have experienced enough in Libya not to expect too much of federates, but on this point I think I have reason to complain to the commander! I think it may be necessary to post a double, or even triple, watch."

I saw that it was necessary to placate my impatient friend before serious trouble ensued. A crowd was collecting about us, among whom a growing mutter of "Gray wolf" showed that anger was increasing that one of their following should be abused in this way by one who was *alltud,* a stranger in blood and kindred. I too was *alltud,* but by now the men of Gwynedd were aware of the favor in which I stood with the king. Moreover, I possess powers, and a gaze that not everyone might care to encounter.

"Surely it is not for an officer of your standing to exact punishment for each and every dereliction of duty?" I inquired tactfully. "Cannot this matter—whatever it is—be left to the man's captain or chief of his kindred? This army is not like those of your emperor, moving to order like pieces on a *gwyddbwyll* board. Surely you must make do with what you have to hand?"

"You are right, of course," replied Rufinus, who appeared calmed by my intervention, and more perhaps by the signal I gave to the guards to hold the object of his wrath—at least until a full explanation should be forthcoming. "An army of federates must needs conduct matters in its own way, of that I have reason to be aware. But there is one matter which I have urged upon the king, with which he is in full agreement, and which he has given me full authority to enforce.

"We have still several weeks' march before us before we enter the enemy's country. It is true that we have received intelligence concerning the disposition of the enemy's forces, but the truth remains that we do not know what to expect once we leave friendly territory. If we are to preserve the initiative, the enemy must know as little as possible of our movements until we appear among him. Security is everything in these matters, as I impressed upon the council in Viroconium. Yet what do I find? Security is so lax that I find these dunderheaded guards on the point of permitting an unauthorized person to slip out of headquarters, under circumstances which I can only describe as suspicious. Who is this man? Where is he going?

"Doubtless you think me overmeticulous, but I have seen a greater army than this go down to disaster for no greater a cause. It was betrayal of our march route that led the army of Areobindus to disaster at Thacia. Areobindus was no Belisarius (the whole of Africa knew his appointment was owing to his marriage with the emperor's niece), but there was no shortage of excellent officers serving under him. My old companion John, son of Sisinniolus, was among those who died at Thacia, and you don't find officers like him growing on every bush. Forewarned is better than forearmed, if you want my opinion. I can tell you, my friend, that security is the name of the game, and with security you don't make exceptions. This man should be held in custody pending questioning, or I wash my hands of the business."

I saw the force of the soldier's reasoning, though how anyone could hope to maintain secrecy over the movements of our great unwieldy host as it dragged itself across the country, proclaiming its mission with pride to the skies, was, it seemed to me, more easily ordained than enforced. Still, I thought I saw the way out of our present difficulty. Resentful of the prolonged talk in an alien tongue, the warriors crowded around had begun jostling and hemming us about with an increasing air of menace. Further cries of "Gray wolf!" arose, and the hubbub was only stilled when I explained that we—that is, Rufinus, myself, and the prisoner—would proceed at once to explain the matter before King Maelgun the Tall. Impressed by my coming and going at dawn with the king, the guards forced a way for us through the busy throng to the king's quarters.

He was not at home, and eventually we found him seated with Brochfael on the lawn outside the eastern gateway. The two kings were watching their sons Run and Cynan, together with my friend Elffin mab Gwydno, casting javelins at a mark before them. The young men were skilled in their exercise, shouting joyfully to one another with each successful cast, and pausing on occasion as they passed one another between the throwing place and the mark to wrestle in good-humored superabundance of strength and vigor. The kings laughed merrily at the sight, and it was with good humor that they addressed themselves to the troublesome matter we brought before them.

The tribune began by saluting stiffly, setting out succinctly the transgression he had detected, and concluded with a vigorous complaint such as no native-born Brython would have dared to utter before a king:

"It was agreed, O king, was it not, that priority should be assigned to the strictest security in our march? Yet here I find the sentries in your very *praetorium* in the act of permitting this suspicious-looking rascal to depart the camp without authority. We may still be many weeks' march from the enemy, but if discipline is not enforced now it will be too late when we come to maneuver before hostile lines. Permit me to quote to you the words of my great master, Belisarius: 'Talk borne about a camp will keep no secrets, for it spreads little by little until it reaches even to the ears of the enemy.'

"Permit me likewise to point out how these things are arranged, O king. You should dispatch your *exploratores,* men cunning by nature and skilled in languages, to haunt inns, markets, and other places of public assembly in hostile territory. It is not needful to think such a measure unworthy a great king, for does not Frontinus tell us that Hannibal himself captured many cities in Italia by sending ahead of his army spies dressed as Romans and speaking Latin?

"Your army should be accompanied likewise by men who exert vigilance in its van; these we call *speculatores.* Their returns must be dispatched as swiftly as may be, so that the *protectores domestici* on your staff have time to prepare intelligence reports for the generals' consideration. Do all these things, and I think little will go wrong."

Maelgun listened affably enough. His mood was benign, and I could see moreover that he respected the soldier's professional skills.

"Doubtless you are right, O tribune, and the matter will be looked into. But so long as we are on this side of Hafren, I think we need have no fear of spies from Loiger, nor that news of our movements may reach the halls of the Iwys. Is that not true, my cousin Brochfael?"

King Brochfael grinned, his protruding tusks providing an air of ferocity that he appeared not to feel. "You are right, Dragon of Mon. There is not a bird that flies beyond the bounds of my kingdom of Powys, nor a beaver that crosses the Hafren, but it is known to the men of the tribes of Powys and whispered in the ears of the king. Within the four corners of my kingdom my hearing is that of Math mab Mathonwy or the Coranieid. There is as yet no reason for excessive caution, my friend."

King Brochfael spoke carelessly, but I guessed that there lay more than idle reassurance behind his confident words. I had seen the smoke of signal fires on distant hills during our southward march, and noted also the continual coming and going of messengers from outlying regions of the kingdom.

The kings were content, but the tribune was not, as his countenance made plain. Maelgun, it seemed to me, felt the necessity to smooth the ruffled plumes of a falcon on whose skills he placed reliance.

"I will instruct each *pencenedl* and *uchelwr* to see to it that matters are arranged in accordance with your orders. Meanwhile, let us learn who is this fellow whose departure you have intercepted. What is his name, and what his tribe? On what errand was he traveling?"

His name, he explained respectfully enough but with a sullen reservation barely detectable, was Lofan Law Difro. From his epithet and tonsure it was plain he was *aillt,* and he revealed frankly that he was indeed a kin-broken tribesman from the North, who had taken service with Maelgun's cousin of Meirionyd. Though of middle stature, he was a bold, muscular, resolute-looking fellow. This, as I suggested when called upon for my view, was a factor in his favor. Had he wished, he could without difficulty have slipped away from the grasp of the maimed tribune. His motive for leaving the walled stronghold was reasonable enough too. He merely wished to relieve himself beneath a briar bush, and as a kinless exile had no desire for his lean buttocks to be exposed to gibes and mockery.

The kings and princes laughed loud and long at this, as they saw Lofan shift with increasing discomfort from one foot to the other. A sheltered corner behind a hut was allotted as the spot where he might relieve himself of his unwanted burden, and guards assigned to protect him from annoyance.

At that moment, however, there occurred an unexpected interruption. It came from Maelgun's counselor, Maeldaf the elder, who appeared silently, as was his wont, as if from nowhere, and announced to everyone's surprise: "This man speaks falsely, and it is not for the purpose he relates that he desires to leave the fortress!"

"What is this?" exclaimed Maelgun, turning to his adviser. "Do you know the fellow?"

"I do, lord," replied Maeldaf, "for surely he is my servant, and travels upon my mission and thine."

Maelgun frowned. "There is a mystery here. If he travels for such a purpose, why did he attempt to depart without permission, and why did he lie when apprehended by the tribune? You are our trusted counselor, Maeldaf, but it seems to me that you have much to explain."

"There is little mystery, lord, and all is readily explained. Now that our host is approaching the bounds of the kingdom of Powys and will before many weeks are out cross Hafren and enter the hostile land of Loiger, I thought it necessary to adopt certain precautions. Prince Einion in Caer Vydei is protected by strong walls but by few soldiers. If our plans are to succeed, he must continue to defend himself valiantly against the Iwys until our host crosses the emperor Arthur's dykes to the westward."

"All this is true," broke in Rufinus angrily, "but what has it to do with the clear violation of standing instructions? How often have I explained at the council of war that *no one* is to be permitted entry or exit from the *praetorium* unless he provide the watchword? We are at war, man, and yet we act as if we were engaged in escorting a column of recruits to a general's headquarters at the outset of a campaign. I'll wager sixty solidi to a denarius that those dozy fellows at the gate had not even inscribed last night's watchword on their *tesserae*. It is service such as the circus factions provide upon the walls of Byzantium, a rabble of armed civilians. Were we in Africa I would have had them paraded by the centurion and condemned to the *fustuarium*. A sound cudgeling is the least they deserve after dereliction of duty of this seriousness. There has to be discipline, even among federates. What is Rome without discipline? Would we have conquered Africa, Italia, and Hispania had each soldier acted just as he chose?"

Maeldaf bowed his head in silence, and the two kings gazed in bewilderment from the tribune to the elder. The brow of Maelgun Gwynedd was clouded as the lofty peak of Eryri as he demanded an explanation, swift and full, from Maeldaf. Leaning upon his wand of office, the latter raised his head and looked about him.

"Perhaps I was mistaken in my intent," he acknowledged after a pause. "However, my purposes were fair, as I see them. This man Lofan has performed many tasks for me, tasks requiring exceptional skill and discretion. I erred, it is true, in not informing you, O king, of my plan. But I told no one of the mission, lest news be borne to the pale-faced foreigners—the winds will bear it, if the times be bad, as once they bore every utterance of the Brython to the ears of the Coranieid. I wished this Lofan to bear news to Prince Einion of our approach, and to re-join us at a later stage of the march, when he might confirm that Caer Vydei continues to block the path of the Iwys. For if that gate be opened, then will it be not the *gosgordd* of Einion mab Run but the host of the heathen which awaits our coming."

After some discussion it was adjudged by King Maelgun the Tall that Maeldaf had acted wisely. Indeed, he bestowed upon the messenger a curious ring, as token that he came from the camp of the Dragon of Mon.

The tribune alone remained discontented, muttering darkly to me: "There is a saying among the Huns, Merlin—do you know it? It runs like this: 'A wolf may change the color of his fur, but he cannot alter his character, which is determined by nature.' And if ever I saw a wolf, it was yonder swarthy rascal."

So it was that Lofan—who had returned from his refuge and stood waiting, impassively heeding a discussion which might for him have had no very pleasant outcome—was permitted to depart. With a salute to the kings and a flash of his dark eyes at Rufinus, he bounded through the gateway, sprang upon the back of a horse saddled and bridled for his purpose and held there by a slave, and was off like the wind, clattering along the causeway to the southward.

As this Lofan Law Difro will enter my tale again, O king, I will tell you briefly what I learned of his history at that time. Dark of hair and black of eye, supple as a serpent and lithe as a lynx, he came of a people of the Fichti dwelling far in the North beyond the River Gweryt. Having slain a kinsman in some quarrel, he was driven forth from his tribe. After many adventures, he came to be cast up in a coracle upon the Strand of Menai, though how he escaped being sucked down into the Whirlpool of Pull Ceris is more than man may say. Thence he made his way unspied by Maelgun's watchmen through the passes of Arfon and Ardudwy to the court of King Cadwalader mab Meriawn at Cynfael, where he found refuge.

It was on account of his skills as a tumbler and a juggler that he found favor with the king, and many tales were told of his feats of knife-casting. It was said of this Lofan that he would permit the most skilled warriors to cast their javelins at him, evading their thrusts with such turns and twists as if he were an eel. It was believed there was an enchantment upon him, for he would come and go before men's sight in the well-lit courthouse as unexpectedly as does the dark-dappled trout flitting from beneath a fisherman's trident.

According to the custom of his people, he bore upon his cheek a tattoo incised deep within the skin. Though it was but the mark of his tribe, it was an image not false to his nature: a wolf, prowling, watching. I was to see that wolf again, cut upon the face of a stone in the desolate land of Fidach. That was during my perilous journey to the Cave of Uffern in the far North—but that is not a tale for today, nor one that I care to dwell upon at any time. Here I will say no more of this Lofan, save that it was hard to think of any man more meet for the mission laid upon him by Maeldaf the elder.

Rufinus followed me as I went to join Prince Elffin at his break-fasting, grumbling at evidences of indiscipline he saw about him and confiding darkly (as was his wont when alone with me) as to what regular troops might accomplish in a country like this. I was reminded of what his emperor's soldiers were achieving in Hispania at this time, and of what I suspected of his designs upon the Island which once comprised part of his ancestors' Empire.

Next day we broke camp and marched on our way, with the rising sun on our left. To the right lay the land of Cynlibiug, where Prince Elffin and some others departed for a while from the host in order to visit the celebrated Fountain of Helyg. No stream flows into or out of it. It is twenty feet square and steep-banked, holding water no deeper than a man's knees. And yet there are four types of fish to be found there, each of a different tribe frequenting only its own side. This is one of the Wonders of the Island of Prydein.

In the absence of Elffin mab Gwydno, I rode by the side of my friend the tribune Rufinus. Since his altercation with Maeldaf's messenger Lofan Law Difro, he had become unusually pensive and withdrawn, refraining from comment upon our failure to post adequate scouts upon the army's flanks, to employ our cavalry to best effect in checking rivers' flow at fords, or to dig in effectively when encamping. I seized the opportunity to question him about a matter that had exercised me ever since our conversation upon the mountain.

"How do you think your emperor regards this hosting of King Maelgun?" I inquired abruptly.

Rufinus flashed a quizzical glance at me.

"How should I know?" he replied after a moment's pause. "As you have seen, we are taking every precaution to ensure that the Iwys in the South of Britannia learn nothing of the matter. How then should the emperor in Byzantium know anything of it?"

I edged my steed nearer to his, and pressed my question in a lower voice. "We have been marching for over a month, and the expedition has been discussed in the mead-halls of the kings ever since the Kalan Gaeaf. But let me put the question in another manner: What would your imperial master's attitude be were he to have learned of our planned campaign?"

The tribune snorted. "Naturally he would wish you well. Are not your people Christians, and are you not citizens? Who constructed this road upon which we are riding? Is it not our mission to restore the bounds of Empire, driving the barbarians back to their swamps and forests?"

"Do you have authority for what you say?" I asked suddenly and looking him full in the face.

Rufinus gave me look for look, smiling as gleefully as his melancholy expression would allow. "You know full well, friend Merlin, that it was the chance of an unexpected and unwanted voyage that brought me to these coasts. You may inquire of the prince Gerontius, at whose port I made landing. It happened at the time of the rising of Arcturus, as I have good reason to recall, and even in the Mediterranean, ships do not make sail after the third day before the Ides of November. But for the lateness of the season I should have returned at once to my command in Hispania, so that my presence here is entirely fortuitous. Who could provide me with authority for what I had no reason to expect? However, it requires no knowledge of what passes in the Imperial Consistory to vouch for what is known to every soldier in the army."

"True, you have told us how it was you came to Prydein," I replied affably, "and it was indeed fortunate for you that you found haven on the coast of Dyfneint before the winter's gales broke up the Sea of Udd. I do not doubt your good intentions, but it has occurred to me that the interests of the emperor in Caer Custennin and those of King Maelgun might not be in every respect the same. A passing thought, but one perhaps worthy of consideration?"

I was watching Rufinus closely, but he made no response beyond a short laugh and laconic comment:

"You are right to ponder every exigency, however improbable; that is a soldier's duty. All I can tell you are two things which you know already. I came to this island by an ill chance not of my making, and the Imperial Government must naturally wish good fortune to all Christian kings who make war upon the barbarians."

Our route had led us from the hills toward the fertile vales where the rivers Gwy and Lugwy meet. The air was sweet with the scent of apple blossom, laughing with the lay of the blackbird, and melancholy with the cry of the cuckoo. Faint across the orchards chimed the delightful clangor of the monastery bell at Mochros. The place of strife seemed far off, yet I felt a need to learn more if I might.

"The emperor views the whole world from his palace window," I observed reflectively, "and must needs set by small issues while he grasps the greater. Where the law of the land is enforced by a strong king, there will be those who receive retribution beyond their meed; theirs is a necessary sacrifice to the greater justice, without which the kingdom must perish. Could there never be a time when the emperor's policies were best served by an embroilment between the Cymry and the Iwys? And might not that embroilment be of greater significance to him than its outcome?"

Rufinus did not reply, but I was determined to pursue the matter, which I had been pondering for some time.

"Could it be, for example, that the emperor would see his interest lie in a war here which would draw many of the barbarians northward, away from the war your armies are fighting in the South? Forgive the suggestion, my friend, but something of what we discussed upon Dinleu Gurygon steals into my mind. Did not your lord Belisarius offer to deliver this Island to the Goths, in exchange for their recognition of his reconquest of Sicilia?"

Rufinus snorted indignantly once more. "That was but in jest, as well you know. Sicilia was ours, retaken by force of arms. Britannia belonged neither to the emperor nor the king of the Goths, and so was not either's to be offered or received. In any case, were what you suggest true, the emperor would wish for a British victory, would he not?"

"Doubtless he would. But what he would wish still more, if I am not mistaken, is for more of the barbarian peoples to be engaged this summer in warfare on *our* side of the Sea of Udd than on *his*."

The tribune urged his horse forward into a trot, as if he would be rid of me and my troublesome questioning, but I kept pace with him.

"Well, what is it you wish me to say?" he grunted impatiently. "We are in this war together, you and I, and it is useless to expect me to know what is in the emperor's mind. From what I have seen of you, Master Merlin, you may have readier means than I of discovering what passes within the heads of others. All I know is this: Your general Artorius by all accounts worked well with Count Belisarius, it is said, invading Armorica at the time of the first siege of Rome, and I see no reason why you should suspect double-dealing at this time. The Saxons, I believe, have no love for the Goths, so that whatever the disposition of their forces here and overseas it will have little enough effect on the war in Italia. Have you spoken of this matter to the kings?"

"No, no," I exclaimed hastily. "Mine are but the random thoughts of one who is, as you see, no soldier. I have heard tell that in past years the emperor paid gold to the Freinc to turn their arms upon the Goths, and it occurred to me that a less scrupulous ruler might in the present circumstances contemplate bribing the Goths, and perhaps the Freinc as well, to cross the sea and seek easy prey in far-off Prydein. But I agree that all this is most unlikely. You must forgive a poet his overbounding imagination.

"I fancy you are in error on one small point, however. If, as you say, the Goths and the Saeson bear no love one for the other, how comes it that King Ida of Bryneich, wolf of the Eingl upon our northern borders, has named his sons Tewdwrig and Tewdwr? Would it not appear odd that he should bestow Gothic names upon his promising whelps, were such hostility as you ascribe to exist between Saeson and Goth?"

Rufinus turned in his saddle and looked me firmly in the face. "It seems that you know more of these matters than I. You may draw what conclusions you like—you will get nothing further from me. I am not here on authority or engaged in any secret mission, as you seem to be hinting, and would, to tell the truth, be glad to get back to my men in Hispania as swiftly as possible. But since I am here I shall do my duty, and I do not think you will find me backward when it comes to hard blows."

I felt some shame at this, for the man's honesty was patent. Moreover, it was not in my mind that he was engaged in any conscious deceit: Were his emperor employing him as a pawn upon his *gwyddbwyll* board, he would have neither desire nor necessity to confide his purpose to the instrument of his larger policy. Leaning across, I clasped my comrade's arm in a gesture of apology. He glanced sideways at me with a sour smile, which I valued as the nearest I knew him capable of expressing in friendship.

Troubled thoughts still clouded my mind, however, and when shortly afterward we turned the direction of our march eastward to ford the Lugwy, the waters washing our horses' tails, I still suffered misgivings. *A dwfn rhyd; berwyd bryd brad,* as we say in the tongue of the Brython: "Deep is the ford, and the mind plots treachery."

Ahead of me the princes Run mab Maelgun and Elffin mab Gwydno were laughing as they tried to force their steeds into a sluggish race through rushing waters that rose above their knees. The tribune Rufinus had left me, to engage in his customary frustrated efforts to persuade a detachment of horsemen to station themselves upstream in order to check the force of the current's flow at our fording. All about me were men of valor and skill, golden-torqued warriors like wolves at the ford, their eyes like spears, shining in their loricated armor like snakes coiling in their nest. And yet, and yet . . . What lies beneath in the darkness of the waters? Is it a shoal of speckled trout to be speared one by one by the sure javelins of my young princes? Or is it the evil war-goddess in ill mood, looming below in the shadows in the form of a slippery black eel—the eel that coils itself about the legs of men and horses, dragging them down into the dank void?

Venom breeds in treason's brew;
Wounds and weeping are its due:
Hollow gain and much to rue.

For much of our ensuing march it was with such premonitory
misgivings passing through my mind that I rode with my hood pulled
forward over my brow, sunk in a deep reverie. The young princes
avoided me as an unfit companion for their triumphal progress as we
rode through rich pastureland, patrimony of the brothers Peibio and
Nynio, sons to King Erb of Ergyng. They afforded increase of men
and fat cattle for the sustenance of the host.

The kings, princes, and great men of our host (myself included)
passed a night in the rich monastery that is named Henlan, by the
River Gwy. Right well did the good monks regale us at our feasting,
with fine beef and pork and strong wines from their vineyards. Much
compassion was felt for our host, King Peibio, from whose mouth
flowed a continuous stream of frothing saliva, which two slaves standing might scarcely wipe away from his sodden beard, let them apply
their cloths as assiduously as they would.

This affliction had come unexpectedly upon the king shortly before our arrival, as I recall. It was a misfortune for him, though no
very bad chance for me. For Peibio mab Erb was son-in-law to my old
enemy and would-be slayer, King Custennin Gorneu of Cerniu.
Now, however, he found his face so covered in frothing spittle, filthy
phlegm, and slavering saliva that he might not recognize among the
company the man who as a babe had brought about his father-in-law's
untimely end upon the strand of the Western Sea.

It was on account of this affliction that Maelgun Gwynedd assented
gladly to King Peibio's request to be permitted to remain at home in
his kingdom throughout our campaign, for it was thought his appearance would bring ill repute and misfortune and ridicule upon the
hosting of the Cymry. Throughout the time of the Affliction of
Peibio, the land of Erging suffered continual rains, foaming up of
watercourses, and inundation of river meadows. At the estuary of the
Aber Lyn Lywan the customary encounter between the incoming sea-
flood and the swollen course of the River Hafren created a whirlpool
which at the tide's recession belched forth a spumy fog covering the
coasts around like a druid's mist. Such was the state of the kingdoms
of Ergyng and Gwent during the Vomiting of King Peibio, as his
affliction was named.

Though I have bestowed many blessings upon the Island of Prydein,
O my king Ceneu of the Red Neck, it may be no bad thing even for

kings to remember that Merlin mab Morfryn—mad as they term him—can be an ill person to cross. However this may be, it happened that not long after our departure, the unfortunate king was healed of his disease by the touch of the blessed Dyfrig (or so they say in the region of Ergyng), until he and his brother Nynio came in time to be altered into the shape of oxen for their sins, and were banished in that form to the far north of Prydein, to the windy slopes of the Mountain Bannog.

The regrettable spectacle of King Peibio's infirmity aroused unease among some of the company, and it was to allay this that I explained at our feasting that we were passing through a land of wonders. I recounted the famous tale of the plunging of Gwyn mab Nud and his Wild Hunt on a night of gale and storm into the River Gwy nearby, and told also of the enchanted island in the river, Ynys Eferdyl, where Peibio's daughter Eferdyl and her newborn child had emerged unscathed from a blazing bonfire.

Moreover, as I explained, we were within but two days' march of the shining city of Caer Loyw, about whose walls lamentation and groaning may be heard continually. And that lamentation and groaning is the grief of Mabon mab Modron, one of the Three Exalted Prisoners of the Island of Prydein. Yet more terrible is the sound of the warring of the Two Kings of Hafren, when the Sea rushes upon the River and the River upon the Sea in two billows like those which will engulph the world at its ending. Then is the sun hid by the spray and the screaming of gulls drowned by roaring of waters as the Two Kings collide in turn, withdrawing and advancing upon each other like raging bulls. And this they have done from the beginning of the world until this day.

My words aroused the spirit and curiosity of the kings and tribes of the Cymry, who arose early in the morning and pressed on with their march. We passed through a land of low hills and pleasant woods until we descended into the broad fertile Vale of Hafren. But though the sun beamed down upon our brave company, lighting lance-heads like lanterns, there was for a long space fear and foreboding in every heart. Upon our right for many a mile hung a huge dark forest, impenetrable and savage, at which men glanced ever and awhile in trembling and dread. Limitless and unknown it stretched beyond somber hills heaped upon the horizon, its sunless glades and dense thickets untouched by light or air or song of birds.

Like a moving grove were we upon the forest's gloomy flanks, for there was not a warrior but held a rowan branch above him to ward off the evil of that place. Of this great forest, Coed Mawr, I had told nothing at my tale-telling, nor did I need to do so. For who in the Island of Prydein has not heard fearful stories of its evil denizens, noxious creatures dwelling among its broken rocks, foul fens, and thorny brakes?

Through its maze of moonlit avenues flies a stag which bears but a single horn upon its brow, and that long as the haft of the longest spear and sharp as the sharpest blade. Every creature he meets is brought to its death, and the woodland pools he sucks dry after his midnight gallop so that every fish is left exposed on the mud, gasping and dying. Within a cave set in the side of a broken hill dwells an Adanc; leading to its entrance is a waste of burned grass and broken bushes, marking the trail where his great carcass is dragged forth to spoil and ravage. At the mouth of the cave lies a blighted area where no blade of grass may grow, such is the destructive venom of the Adanc's puddled breath.

Of noxious beasts, reptiles, and vermin within that forest there is no numbering. There are beings, too, who have the semblance of men or women, but whom no man or woman would wish to encounter. There is the Black Man of Ysbidinongyl, whose enchantments it is said turned a wealthy kingdom of former days into the wooded wasteland which even now the hosts of the Cymry were skirting. Worst of all are the Nine Witches of Caer Loyw, daughters of the Witch of Ystyfacheu. Robed blood-red and bearing bloody tridents, they are a torment to the whole Island of Prydein, and the evil of their fell enchantments is known from Penwaed to Penrin Blathaon. Until the coming of Peredur of Steel Arms will they remain a blight from the Cave of Uffern upon the fair face of earth.

There is one marvel of that forest, however, that is known to me alone, and that is the Castle of Wonders which lies at its center, like a spider's nest at the heart of its web. No man dwells within its vasty halls, where the chill winds of the earth pass through each dark gallery, rustling the hangings upon the walls. In a chamber that lies deepest within the hold is an enchanted *gwyddbwyll* board, whose pieces play ever against themselves, age after age, deciding the destinies of kingdoms. And the pieces that obtain the victory give a shout which reaches my ears faint and clear as a bat's cry, were I as far off as the accursed Ridge of Esgeir Oerfel in Ywerdon.

After many hours of hard riding, the shadow that lay upon our host was lifted, the songs of minstrels were heard once again, and the princes Elffin and Run returned to their delightful boasting. The hills and hideous wood were behind us, and the mightiest host that ever was in Prydein since the levy of Yrp Luidog in the time of Cadial mab Eryn descended into the lush Vale of Hafren. Great was the laughter and happiness of the kings and tribes of the Cymry at that sight. No need for herding of kine to upland pastures was there in that rich land, for every meadow provided tribute of green grass and purple clover sufficient for the cattle of the Island of Prydein, each beechwood provided mast in plenty for the broad-backed beetle-black swine who frequented their pleasant shades, and within golden kingcups in profusion the bees of the region sipped their fill, buzzing about their banquet of spring in the sunlit royal halls of Dyffryn Hafren.

Above the hymn of the bees' hum and the lovely lowing of cattle arose the caroling of blackbirds in the brake: joyous sounds soaring aloft to where larks were singing in the upper air. And as the land and its creatures rejoiced at that time of rebirth which is *kyntefin,* so devout monks in monasteries throughout the land sang pure psalms and pealed clear bells, whose melodic clangor floated likewise upon the buoyant breeze. Thus a harmony of all that lives upon the land, a fusion of the nine elements, is plucked from the chords of the Harp of Teirtu, which is the lyre of the world.

Louder yet grew the warriors' laughter and more glorious their glee as they glimpsed beyond sun-dappled meadows and willow-fringed rills the silvery back of mighty Hafren, as she wound through the verdant vale in sinuous coils, glimmering in her silent strength like the Adanc of the Deep. The Holy River! From the spring on the broad breast of soaring snow-capped Pumlumon she drew her being, the well at the world's pivot which gazes out over the Western Sea. Thence by gorges and cataracts she plunges headstrong as any Prince Run or Elffin, until she emerges from the hills into the broad plain of Powys, Paradise of Prydein. Beneath the bright-bushed knoll of Dinleu she curves, where the god presides and where I descended to my ordeal of terror in the Pit of Annufn; and so she meanders southward in strength and majesty, mighty as Maelgun Gwynedd and beneficent as Brochfael of Powys. And just as the great kings with their war-bands are descending into the plain in order to restore the Monarchy of Prydein, so fair Hafren sweeps on to swell out into the broad sea itself: the silver Sea of Hafren, watched over from his temple by Nud of the Silver Hand, who delights in the play of gulls above wind-scattered spray.

Proudly upon the broad causeway curvetted the steeds of the warriors of Prydein, with stamp of hoof and jingling of harness. Cheerily chanted their riders, their golden torques and brooches glinting in the noontide radiance of lovely Dyffryn Hafren. Brave was the trumpets' blare, and dreadful the clatter and clash of sword and spear and white-limed shield! Not for the hosts of the Cymry was the broad-backed bridge which spans the stream before the citadel. Breasting the broad flood, they would set their horses swimming through the pure water, so purifying themselves of maleficent spells arising from the fetid exhalations of the grim forest of the Nine Witches of Caer Loyw.

My mount reared up and all but threw me, as two horsemen passed by at full gallop. Then I laughed as I recognized the backs of Run and Elffin, who were driving their horses forward swift as stags in a race to be first to enter the river. A belt of woodland ahead abruptly concealed the headstrong youths from view, and I continued at a sedate trot alongside my friend Rufinus, whose looks conveyed little satisfaction at the impetuous conduct of the princes.

I was about to rally him on his overly high expectations of discipline among soldiers whom he himself opprobriously termed "federates," when we in turn emerged through the copse ahead. The princes we found to our surprise waiting on the other side, having drawn aside their steeds onto the greensward at the roadside. At the sound of our horses' hoofs upon the causeway, they signaled urgently to us to join them. Though boys in years they were men in vigor, and their sharp eyes had clearly glimpsed something of moment in the line of our advance.

At once Rufinus urged his horse over to our left, shouting to a chieftain behind us to halt the advance and summon the kings. Joined by myself and the young princes at the wood's fringe, the tribune gazed down the white road ahead, sheltering his eyes from the glare of the risen sun. Taking his elbow, Prince Elffin directed his attention ahead to where the shining city of Caer Loyw lay in languid might a bare two miles off by a loop of the Hafren. With its mighty whitewashed walls of dressed stone, its lofty towers and huge halls of glorious colors and dimensions, its gigantic gateways and brazen-fronted portals, its red-tiled roofs and glazed windows glinting, it was a stronghold fit to compare with that which the emperor Macsen Guledig saw in his dream from his palace in Rufein.

But it was not at these that young Elffin pointed, and I heard the tribune draw in his breath as he caught sight of the spectacle that had halted the princes' wild gallop. Others of our company pressed about us, who hurriedly gave ground as the towering form of Maelgun Gwynedd broke forward through the throng like a bull through a herd of heifers.

"What do you see?" he asked shortly.

"See there, O king," responded his son Run. "There, below the walls of the city, beside the river!"

We all gazed ahead, and wondered at what we saw. On the open plain were drawn up three great hosts, dark before the glare of the morning sun in their rear, the shadow of their spears and banners thrown long before them upon the ground. Each host was a mighty war-band, three men and three score and three hundred, wearing gold torques and bearing great red blades with dark-blue sockets, such as even the hosts of the Cymry might reflect upon before engaging in battle. And even as we watched, the three hosts gave a great shout, loud almost as the scream that echoes every Nos Kalan Mai about every hearth in Prydein. Numerous were the points of their spears as the stars of Caer Gwydion, deep the murmur of the three hosts as that of Taran's Wheel when it crashes above the echoing cliffs and gullies of Eryri, and harsh the croaking of flocks of crows thirsty for their gory mead-feast who were roused by the clamor.

"Whose are these hosts?" inquired King Maelgun, frowning.

No one replied, for there was no knowledge of the matter.

"What say you, tribune? Do we await their onslaught here, or do we descend into the plain and fall upon them where they await us?"

I was delighted to see in my friend's eye a zest and sparkle I had glimpsed but once before: that night on the slope of Dinleu Gurygon, when he told me of the first battle in which he was engaged in the deserts of the East. He glanced swiftly about him with the rapt expression of a skilled player at *gwyddbwyll*, taking measure as I guessed all in a moment of the disposition of the rival hosts, the lie of the land, and the choice of moves at his disposal. He turned back to the king.

"Two things are clear to me, O king: firstly, that our arrival was expected, and that it is accordingly likely that the enemy is apprised of our strength. Secondly, he is so little afraid of us as to neglect the defenses of that strong city and face us in the open field. He has even placed the river to his rear, which is the act either of a very rash general, or one with strong reason for confidence in his superiority. As I see it, therefore, we must proceed with due caution though we be strong."

"What do you recommend, then?" inquired the king. "Is the bull to be diverted from his course by the ram? Have we not the hosts of the Cymry with us, and the tribes of Cunedda and Cadell and Brychan Brycheiniog? What of Gereint of Dyfneint, whose shout is ever in the forefront of a battle array?"

The great king's words were true, yet all present looked for direction to a maimed veteran, possessing links neither of blood nor fosterage, tribe nor kindred, with the hosts of red-speared warriors, Prydein's lofty sons. The tribune possessed the privilege of a poet who travels from one king's court to another; he was a craftsman and artist, fashioning victory out of defeat, and order from confusion, just as a scribe pens the subtle scrolling that borders a book's margin, or a poet attunes words by means of skillful alliteration and measured conjunction of syllables into verses of enchantment.

"If we are to fight, it will do no harm to let the enemy encounter us on our terms, and not we on his," Rufinus pronounced decisively. "Let a detachment of cavalry be dispatched through that valley on our left and seize the first ford encountered upstream. See there, where that farm and ruined villa face each other on opposite banks—most likely they are linked by a ford."

All present turned expectantly to the king, who nodded his head. "Let that be the task of the war-band of Meirionyd!" he commanded, and at once a messenger turned his horse's head and departed through the trees.

Rufinus, who had not ceased surveying the countryside ahead, continued speaking, as much, it appeared, to himself as to us.

"The land is open, and they have much room for maneuver on their front—they appear well-disciplined too. We must try to open up their ranks and see what may be done. Prince Run"—turning to the king's son, who like a hawk sighting his prey gazed eagerly upon the host confronting us—"you are an enterprising officer, I have reason to believe. Do you take a cohort down to the right there, crossing the river where you may, opposite that wooded hill beside the city. Once you gain the other bank I leave it to your wits to find some means of diverting or annoying the enemy without taking excessive risk."

Run mab Maelgun laughed and glanced with flashing eye at his friend Prince Elffin.

"Fear not, O stranger. We shall annoy them! I am as greedy for corpses as for drinking mead or wine in the hall of Degannwy. The ravens of Dyffryn Hafren shall glut their fill this day!"

"That is the right spirit, prince," rejoined the soldier. "However, there is more to be gained here by the fox's stealth than the bull's charge. A skilled cavalry officer may achieve much once behind the enemy lines. The walls of Neapolis proved too strong even for Belisarius, as I recall, and yet the city fell when an enterprising Isaurian found his way in with six hundred men through a broken aqueduct. Do you see what may be done."

Run mab Maelgun laughed again, clapped Elffin on the shoulder, and rode off at speed to find his men. The tribune turned to the king.

"First we must see if we may entice them forward, for they will be hard to come at where they are—you see how the loop of the river protects their flanks. It is a pity we have few archers, or we might have tried the game Narses played at Busta Gallorum. Still, we shall see what may be done. This is what I suggest, O king. Bring forward the inferior sort of foot soldiers whom you employ to guard your baggage train, and station them with maximum display of banners, noise of horns, and raising of dust before us where we stand here. That should hold the enemy's attention, and perhaps even draw him forward to probe our strength."

The king nodded; he had been knowledgeable in the ways of war since the campaign in which he overthrew the king his uncle and gained the throne of Gwynedd.

"Meanwhile," continued the tribune, "you must divide the remainder of your army into two equal bodies, and move them on either side of our rear as far down each side of this hill as may be done without drawing the enemy's attention to the move. Then, when the signal is given, let our left flank advance under cover of those trees lining the stream you see down there, while the right makes with all speed to where the river thrusts out an elbow toward us, so that they may hinge their right upon its bank. But let neither flank take up its forward position until I give the word. And when they move, it should be seen that the cavalry reverse their lances and cover their helmets and armor with their cloaks."

Maelgun the Tall and the kings accompanying him at once rode back to enforce the tribune's plan, which appeared good in their eyes. For the moment, but four of us remained upon the road before the wood, gazing down upon the serried ranks of the three mighty hosts which lay ominously passive athwart our path. Between the enemy and the river and the city it seemed to me that we faced three obstacles of no little difficulty to overcome. Prince Elffin had watched the departure of his foster-brother Run with some envy, as I guessed, and was impatient for the tribune to allot him some similarly daring task. Rufinus, however, had turned to Maeldaf the elder, wise counselor to Maelgun Gwynedd, and myself. The three of us had dismounted, bestowing our steeds to the care of slaves, while Prince Elffin remained in the saddle, leaning upon his spear-shaft, whose butt rested upon the ground.

"You see my intention, I imagine," the tribune confided. "I am glad the king sees matters as I do. I do not anticipate that anything can go very far wrong, though much depends upon the skill of the enemy general. I hope he may advance all or part of his army upon our center here, so that we may take him in the flanks with our main forces.

Frontinus recommends this move in his manual, though as he points out, one must guard against the attendant risk of the enemy's pressing home too effectively through one's weakened center."

Maeldaf, who had observed all these proceedings with close attention, inquired what the tribune proposed to do should the enemy host remain where it was.

"It seems to me that they would be wise to do so. Numerous as they are, they are the weaker party—at least in numbers."

Rufinus explained that in that case he would enclose them with the flanking forces already deployed, each pincer closing in with the river as a protection upon one flank.

"Meanwhile our forward scouting parties may be trusted to bring about some diversion in their rear, beyond the river. Two things may then happen. Either the enemy will stand and fight, in which case I think we need not fear for ultimate victory. Or, as I hope, they may try to recross the bridge, in which case they will suffer certain destruction. All I ask is that the assault take place when I order it, and not a moment sooner."

Maeldaf nodded, adding reflectively, "It comes into my mind that it is a bold man who plays such a game as this with you as his opponent."

"Oh, as to that, I have seen battles enough lost in my time," replied the tribune impassively. "But I think we probably have this one in hand."

"So you are confident there will be an assault shortly?" asked Elffin in high excitement, his war horse pawing the ground beneath him with impatience equal to that of its master.

Rufinus smiled grimly. "If the enemy will stand and fight, you shall have your fill of fighting, young prince."

Elffin's gaze was attracted at this moment by a movement in the forefront of the opposing host, and it was Maeldaf who took up the discussion once more.

"You arrive at your decisions very swiftly, O tribune," he remarked in a tone of admiration. "What if despite all your precautions matters should go wrong? The goddess of war is fickle, and it will be upon your head that the ire of the kings descends should aught go amiss. Were there to be a council of war, then blame would fall upon all who favored the plan adopted. It seems to me that yours is a vulnerable situation: You stand like a lone tree upon a windy plain."

The tribune grunted impassively. "I am accustomed to making my own decisions," he grunted, "and know just how much may emerge from a council of war. Much talk, little work. I am glad to see that your king is of my mind. When things go wrong in battle, then blame will be apportioned where the defeated see fit, let the true responsibility lie where it will.

"In any case, I foresee little danger here. The situation, from what I learned in Hispania from officers present at the battle, is not a little like that facing Narses three years ago when he routed the Franks and Alemanni on the Via Appia at Capua. In fact the lie of the river here is much to our advantage, while there, as I understand, the Vulturnus flowed on one side alone of Buccelin's camp. . . ."

The tribune's reflections were cut unexpectedly short by an excited cry from Prince Elffin. Glancing in the direction of his pointing lance, we saw that a lone horseman had emerged from the center of the enemy host. He rode at a steady trot toward us along the broad paved causeway, his spear raised before him, the metalwork of his armor gleaming in the sunlight.

"The valor of a hound on a dunghill!" cried Elffin joyously, glancing gleefully down at us. "Now shall I ride to encounter this pale-faced mongrel of the Iwys!" With which he couched his lance and clattered off down the causeway with a loud cry. The rider approaching responded with a similar shout, brandishing his broad-bladed spear above his head.

"A hotheaded boy," grunted Rufinus. "And yet it is no bad thing to begin battle with a single combat between champions. It heartened our men when on the eve of Busta Gallorum the Imperial champion Anzalas slew the traitor Coccas in front of the Gothic forces. Coccas was a very Hercules for strength, yet Anzalas' Armenian cunning got the better of him. He had a trick of swerving his horse and driving in his lance all in the same moment which was very effective. I was not present, yet I have seen it performed on the parade ground."

"You rate skill very far above force, O tribune," remarked Maeldaf reflectively. "Perhaps, too, you consider that a conflict of champions upon the highway before us may entice our foes' gaze this way rather than another?"

Rufinus acquiesced silently with a grim smile and approving nod. For my part I watched the approaching collision with some apprehension. A vision of Elffin's princess floated into my mind as she looked when she gazed down upon the departing cavalcade from the wall of Porth Gwydno, at the time of our departure from the North. Her dewy eye and pale cheek bore messages of sorrow and longing that I would not care to encounter again as the bearer of unhappy news.

The two horsemen met at about two hundred spear-shafts' distance from us, and we heard faintly borne on the western breeze Prince

Elffin's defiant challenge and his rival's ringing response. From soldiers stationed among the trees about us came a murmur of approbation as they saw a champion of the Cymry not slow to uphold the honor of his king and tribe. In a moment, however, this turned to muttered exclamations of surprise, and then dismay.

When within a few yards of the other, Elffin reined in his charger and engaged in a parley, of which only broken sounds reached us beneath the trees. Then he rode a little nearer, so that we thought the fight about to begin. But then, to the accompaniment of a sigh of shame and despair from all about us, we saw him tug at his bridle with a shouted exclamation, and swing his horse about. Next moment he was galloping back toward us, his adversary riding hard in pursuit.

That this should be the outcome had never occurred to me. My dashing young Elffin a coward! Now, how much harder an errand would it be even than that I feared at first, to tell the princess of the outcome of this day's work. For is it not a byword among the Brython that "Cowardice in a man is an evil possession." Moreover—and this is very true—"The brave escape from many a strait."

All in a moment the prince was among us, swinging out of his saddle and shouting in a state of high excitement for Maelgun Gwynedd.

"Call the king! Call the king!" he shouted repeatedly, while his pursuer sat his horse impassively about a spear's cast off before us. The rising sun behind him left his features in shadow, but it was not hard to see that he was a warrior of noble degree and high prowess.

By the time Maelgun the Tall had returned, an angry scowl upon his face, Prince Elffin had regained his breath and announced his unexpected tidings. There followed a brief moment of disbelief and discussion, and then a cry of rejoicing went up shrill and joyful as that of gulls following the ox-team at spring plowing. The rider encountered by Elffin before the armies was no enemy, but a prince of the Brython: and the triple host gathered before us was that of allies unexpectedly confederated to ride with us to the summer's hosting against the pale-faced Iwys in the land of Loiger!

Loud was the laughter and joyous the carousing in the mead-hall of Caer Loyw that night, as the kings exchanged gifts and drank deep of the yellow ensnaring mead. The bountiful host who led us up to the bright fire and to couches cushioned with white fleeces was the high-born king of Dyffryn Hafren. Cynfael Hael was he, who ruled his rich dominions from the Shining City, built in days of yore by Gloyw of the Long Hair and his three noble sons.

Though he was in consequence of the kin of Gurtheyrn the Thin, who first brought the oppression of the Iwys upon the Island of the

Mighty when he bestowed upon Hengys and Horsa the Island of Ruohim in Cent, King Cynfael was a doughty Bull-protector and Pillar of the Island of Prydein. When he learned of the hosting of Maelgun Gwynedd at Caer Gurygon, he caused horns to be sounded throughout his kingdom and named a trysting-place for his war-bands in a green meadow by the banks of the Hafren before the walls of Caer Loyw.

Then, too, he sent messengers riding hard by day and night along paved roads to great kings with whom he was linked by ties of fosterage. It was not long before there appeared before his gates the mighty war-band of King Ffernfael of Caer Vadon, the walls of whose city enclose one of the Chief Marvels of the Island of Prydein. Within a structure of brick and stone lies a hot pool into which men go to bathe. And for those who wish the water to be hot, it is hot; and for those who wish it cool, it is cool. Men come from afar off to cure themselves of sickness at that place, and rich are the gifts which they bestow upon the goddess who dwells within the waters.

At King Cynfael's summons, too, came Cyndidan of Caer Ceri, his warriors' cheeks glowing like live coals from the galloping of their long-maned steeds. Like pastures freshly plowed was every green field by reason of the passing of their horses; like waves of the sea against a sheer cliff, like the wind beating upon a copse of oak trees was the noise of the fluttering of their banners.

Now were the Iwys doomed indeed! As the kings and princes of the Cymry dipped their flesh-hooks into the cauldron of seething pork, each according to due order of precedence, there was laughter and talk of smoke above homesteads, raiding of cattle, seizing of slaves. As the mead-horn passed from hand to hand, though the laughter was stilled, there was joy in each heart as Taliesin sang of ravens screaming above blood, corpses of the Iwys staring open-eyed at the sky, long weeping of widows and shrieking of orphans.

By campfires sparkling the breadth of the plain without the walls were gathered the hosts of the kings of the Island of the Mighty, the butts of their spears thrust into the yielding turf. There were gathered at that time of the hosts of the Cymry men from every one of the sixty cantrefs of Prydein, with their ash-hafted spears and lime-white shields, their spirited high-neighing horses, and their snarling white-fanged war hounds. From the sixty cantrefs of the Island of the Mighty, from Cantre'r Gwaelod in the North to Dyfneint in the South, flocked brave men bound for battle-tumult, stalwart spearmen swift in assault and stubborn in defense; men who will scatter the foreigners fleeing like foxes to sea-swamps and estuaries, shifting to their ships and wandering far beyond the ninth wave.

Eager were the princes for the fray, and none more eager than the foster-brothers Prince Run mab Maelgun and Prince Elffin mab Gwydno. It was at their earnest desire that Maelgun Gwynedd at the council of the kings held in the hall of Caer Loyw resolved that the feasting at this time should last but a week before the march of the augmented host was resumed southward.

And so it was that upon a fresh spring morning, King Maelgun raised his gauntleted hand against the heathen, horns sounded at the eastern gateway of Caer Loyw, and the hundred thousand men of the Cymry rode southward across a region of stony hills to Caer Ceri. Beside the great causeway we paused by many a cairn to add stones in memory of warriors of old who had died defending the Island of the Mighty from invasions and oppressions. I named them every one, together with the hills and forests and streams which we passed, lore of earth and wood and water.

At Caer Ceri we halted but a day and a night before continuing our journey, every heart now eager to reach the place of strife without delay. It was in that city that an unchancy event occurred. After Maelgun the Tall had retired to rest, Maeldaf the elder revealed to King Brochfael and the princes of the Island of the Mighty that a certain jester had through ignorance or malice placed the seethed flesh of a dog in the king's dish that night. By great misfortune had the king eaten of this flesh, which as is known is a thing prohibited. For it is *cynneddyf* for a man to eat of his namesake, and since "Maelgun" signifies "great hound," so the king violated his *cynneddyf*.

When Maeldaf learned of this matter he slew the jester with the iron-shod butt of his staff, and caused his body to be cast into the pit where the butchers of Caer Ceri place their offal. But the deed was done, and it was necessary to consider how its ill consequences might be avoided. There was apprehension among the princes of the Cymry when they learned these tidings, and Maeldaf conferred long with Idno Hen, chief druid of Gwynedd, and others accompanying the host, that they might find some way of voiding the violation.

As we resumed our journey we encountered signs that we were nearing the place of strife. On the bare hillside the wind whistled shrill in the cairns of the dead, whispering it may be of death by spear-thrusts and sword-slashing. In sheltered valleys serpents lay sunning themselves upon boulders, slithering away into the Underworld of Annufn at our approach, bearing the secrets of the dead to the land of the dead.

At the edge of the hills, where we made our last encampment before the road drops down to the Vale of Temys, an unchancy sight appeared at the mid-hour of night before King Dinogad of Dunoding, cousin to Maelgun Gwynedd. He was greeted at his tent door by a repulsive hag whose buttocks were round and evil-smelling as cheeses rotten from bog-storage, and whose breasts, were she to drape them over the branch of a tall tree, would yet trail their hirsute warty nipples upon the ground before her.

Dinogad started up in fear upon his couch and strove to address the witch, but his tongue was dry and clave to the roof of his mouth. Then he saw that the slab-faced crone bore blubber lips upon her breasts, which emitted these words:

"Dogs of Gwern, beware Morddwyd Tyllion!"

With which she departed from that place, and Dinogad dared not pursue her to demand the meaning of the words, for he saw how she watched him ever from four eyes set in her back. Then he knew her for the Aderyn of Cirf, the Bird of Corpses who alters the form of children.

Next morning the prince of Dunoding appeared pale and drawn at the kings' council, and told his tale. None knew the import of the witch's words, which were related to the druids accompanying the host, that they might interpret them. Long and fruitless were their deliberations. The hag's saying was without doubt an augury of that which was to come, yet her words were misty and difficult of conjuration:

"Guern gwngwch uiwch Uordwyt Tyllyon!"

There were those who held "Guern" to be an alder-grove, *gwern,* the place of battle where would take place a piercing of thighs, *mordwyt tyllon.* Others recalled Gwern, sister's son to Bran, who departed with Princess Branwen to Ywerdon in the former age. For had not King Maelgun the Tall, descendant of Branwen, likewise departed from Gwynedd, the Land of Bran? But who then, or where, was Morddwyd Tyllion?

I listened to the druids' debate, returning with much misgiving in my heart to the council of the kings before the tent of Maelgun Gwynedd. I found them listening attentively to the tribune Rufinus, who was expounding the necessity for daily parades now that we were within a day or so's march of the enemy frontier.

"I have explained the importance of right wheelings in quick succession for your frontline cavalry," he was urging. "Meanwhile, masked behind the *equites alares,* the second line of *equites cohortales* should be preparing themselves for the major shock, which as you know is the Cantabrian gallop in good order. This has not always proceeded in the orderly fashion necessary, I regret to say."

At this, one or two of the kings hung their heads a little, for the tribune was held in good esteem by the host, and his reproofs regarded with dread almost as great as the blistering verses of offended satirists.

"No names, no pack drill," continued Rufinus tactfully. "At our last parade the cohort of King Gerontius distinguished itself, and is in consequence awarded the *congiarium* for good effort. Let each commander strive today to gain it for his unit. We shall start with ranked javelin-throwing at the point of impact, and then return to the Cantabrian gallop."

The kings departed, each to summon his own war-band, while Taliesin and I stood aside to discuss the implications of Dinogad's dream.

"Where is the alder-grove, and who think you is Morddwyd Tyllion, O prince of poets?" I inquired.

Taliesin shook his head doubtfully, pondered a while, and then from his word-hoard drew the distich:

> "I was with Bran in blue-green Iwerthon;
> I saw the slaying of Morddwyd Tyllion.

"It is a prophecy of old known to soothsayers, and for its meaning we must consult the *awen* when the time is propitious. For the present I find the future as veiled as are those fields and woods before us by the Mai mists of the Temys arising yonder upon our course. I fear we are approaching the place of darkness, and must find our way as best we can."

For much of that day our march was conducted in obscurity, and only the paved causeway beneath our horses' hoofs, lying straight as a spear-shaft athwart the plain, enabled us to continue the advance without confusion. A wet mist came in gray ranks upon us from out of the west across the miry waste of the water meadows. An enormous bruise upon the hillside it was, a cold vapor hanging in every hollow, a shaggy shroud upon the land. The horsemen rode on in silence beneath the covering of its hooded cowl; a silence broken only by the sullen tramp of hoofs and muffled clink of mail-coats mantled within sodden cloaks.

With the mist came trailing skirts of rain, and at noontide we were hedged about by darkness, thick and ugly almost as that of night.

The horsemen were as drenched with dew as was the yellow calfskin upon which Maelgun Gwynedd dreamed his dream the night before the hosting at Dinleu Gurygon. Once or twice we heard a far-off sound in the obscurity, as of dogs barking.

"The Hounds of Annufn," I heard Taliesin mutter beside me. "This is the hold of Gwyn mab Nud, the mist with which he seeks to bind the world. See how it hangs heavy upon those spiders' webs, and mark how the spider watches from the center. Follow which strand you will, and you come to where he waits. He is not busy now, nor pursuing his prey with horn and hound, for he knows we must come to him at the end, betide what may."

"Let's have no talk of that sort here!" sang out the voice of the tribune behind us. "Now is the time for cheering the men—not binding on about mists and spiders' webs. It is not a spider that waits where all roads meet, but Immortal Rome! This mist is precisely what we need to cover our approach from observation by enemy outposts. I take it as a sign of our luck."

Taliesin and I fell silent, though once or twice I caught his eye glancing gloomily across at me. However by midafternoon the mist was dispelled by bright sunshine, which swiftly restored the spirits of the army of the Cymry. Golden kingcups reflected the glory of the Chariot of Beli, and his burning eye was mirrored in every puddle upon the road. Birds sang upon every branch, and once again it was the season of summer. Prince Elffin and the men of Cantre'r Gwaelod sang in lusty chorus the ditty of "Dinogad's Cloak," which had become the marching song of his *gosgordd*. Laughter and talk of cattle raids and sieges passed back and forth among the long gleaming column of the host, like dipping swallows across the surface of a dew-pond.

A messenger rode up, requiring Taliesin to attend upon King Maelgun and sing "The Monarchy of Prydein." Every heart was uplifted by the magic of that song, and each warrior's heart longed for the place of slaughter, where men are cut down like rushes, bodies are mangled, and ravens glutted upon the blood of corpses. Maelgun the Tall laughed at the head of his mighty host, pointing ahead to where three horsemen had appeared, riding abreast in the track of the army.

"Son Run," he commanded, "do you go forward and ask who are those three red ravagers that ride with the hosts of the Cymry!"

Run galloped off, but spur as he would he might not come up with the horsemen, though they maintained a pace no greater than at the outset. Then Run knew them to be specters from Annufn, for red were their mantles, red their shields, red their spears, and scarlet the steeds they bestrode. Red was the hair upon their heads, but when they turned about, their faces were the faces of skulls, and their bodies but bones lacking flesh.

No nearer than a spear's length might Prince Run come to those three dread horsemen, let him lash his horse as he might. At his third vain attempt, the first of the riders turned his skull's face around upon his shoulders, calling out in a voice of icy cold to Run:

"Weary are the horses which we ride. We ride Hafgan's horses from the Stables of Annufn. Though we are alive we are dead. Great are the signs we show you: glutting of ravens; feeding of crows; whetting of sword-edges; shattered shields with broken bosses after the sun's setting."

And the second horseman cried out likewise in a fell tone: "I smell scarlet! I see crimson!"

And the third, with a shriek like the wind at its howling from the mouth of the Cave of Chwith Gwynt: "Dogs of Gwern, beware Morddwyd Tyllion!"

Then Run rode back in fear to tell what he had heard, and all knew from the portent that the place of battle could not be far off. They rode rejoicing upon their way, which was now become a trestled causeway extending over half-flooded water meadows lying on either side the Thames, which gushes forth from the Realm of Annufn not many miles to the west of the spot where we found ourselves.

Before us, reflected in the river heavy with recent rain, lay upon the bank a deserted settlement. The vale about had been devastated during the time of Arthur's wars with Ceredig and the Iwys, and few of the Brython had cared to return after the peace to towns and homesteads haunted by the spirits of the slain. Before the coming of Arthur, men of the Iwys had settled in the valley, where their descendants still lived, providing hostages and surety to King Cyndidan at Caer Ceri. They had been baptized into the faith of Crist, farming lowland meadows scorned by the Brython, who preferred the free air of the hills above. But for all this, few trusted the settlers should the pale-faced Iwys ever break forth again in conquests and invasions. For they clave to the barbaric language and customs of their forefathers, and as it is said, "A coward plans many schemes."

Sad it was, how sad, to see the noble Temys, one of the Three Great Rivers of the Island of Prydein, reduced to little more than a muddy, swirling stream with frothed scum along its banks. Truly, the men of the Brython were giants in former times, when their kings judged Prydein with its Three Islands and its Thirteen Treasures lay in safekeeping. Gloomy thoughts stole upon me as I sat alone upon a fallen stone lintel in the ruined town. The serpent and the fox now dwelt where once the pure tongue of the Brython had been spoken in every hall and hut.

But even as I brooded, a long shadow fell athwart me, and I looked up to see standing before me the king who was indeed a very giant, who had moreover sworn to effect the Restitution of the Island of the Mighty. Maelgun the Tall it was who addressed me with his deep laugh:

"Ah, Merlin mab Morfryn, has it come to this, that you have taken up quarters in a roofless house? Come with me, and it may be that you will yet wear a purple mantle and dip your hand in the gold-hoard of the heathen!"

I smiled and rose to join the king, who explained as we traversed the briar-grown street that it was in his mind to be the first to set his foot in Temys, just as he was the first Pendragon of the Island since Arthur to go up against the heathen in the Southland. Together we walked to the water's edge, where we found the wharf and quay of a small harbor, silted up and partially delapidated through rotting of supporting timbers. Protruding from the mud beneath us was the rib cage of a sunken craft, slime and river-wrack streaming from it like the tattered banners of a beaten host.

"It was from here in earlier times that the men of Caer Ceri used to transport goods from their cantref downriver to Caer Lunnein and the sea," reflected the king. "Now this harbor is abandoned and Caer Lunnein itself lies in ruins. It is a shame and disgrace upon the kings and tribes of the Cymry that these things should be, son of Morfryn."

"A shame indeed, O Maelgun the Tall, mighty son of Cadwallon of the Long Hand!" came a voice unexpectedly from beneath where we stood. Looking down from the edge of the quay, we saw a woman crouching at the water's edge. She was washing clothes at the point where the road ran down to the ford beside us. Her head was bent over her task, and there were nine dark loosened tresses upon her head.

"Who are you that know me?" asked Maelgun Gwynedd.

The woman made no answer, neither did she raise her face, but continued at her task.

"It is in my mind to lie with this woman," said Maelgun to me.

"Return from the land of Loiger by harvesttime, O king," rejoined the woman harshly, slowly raising her face to meet that of the king. "Then will be the time to speak of lying with me—should it come to pass that you do return."

Hers was not a gaze that was pleasant to meet, and her voice had a rasp like that of a crow.

"Will my hosting go well, O Washer at the Ford?" inquired Maelgun.

"I cannot say," replied the woman. "The Temys is defiled from its source to its mouth, but a time is surely near when there will run a river of blood in the Southland of Prydein beside which the Temys will appear but a stream."

"I have heard indeed that bondsmen of the Iwys have established a settlement at her springhead, polluting the pure source of the Temys; and it is true that blood will surely flow at a royal hosting," concurred Maelgun Gwynedd. "But tell me now, woman, is it to be that of the Red Dragon or the White?"

The woman at the water's edge laughed a while, as she scrubbed upon stones at a cloak with a broad purple stripe upon its edge. It was a cloak caked in blood, which reddened all the river beneath us.

"It is not long," said the woman, "since I sat upon the pillar-stone by Degannwy and spoke there with Brech, the cow of Maelgun Gwynedd. And it was to her I uttered these words, which now I relate to you, O king: 'Look you now, unhappy one, Brech of Gwynedd, be on your guard lest the men of Loiger come upon you unawares and drive you off to their encampment. For it is this may happen unless you look to yourself, taking care continually.' We live in a time of destruction, and nothing is what it seems, O Dragon of Mon."

"Whose is that cloak you are washing?" I asked. "And whose is the blood that flows from it?"

"They are the cloak and the blood of one who must die where the hosts meet at the place of battle, son of Morfryn. Great will be the slaughter and glutting of crows, and it is I who can tell the mustering of the dead."

"I know as well as you, O Washer at the Ford, that where there is a battle there will be blood," cried the king in anger. "Will you not tell us the outcome, that we may avoid ill *tynged*?"

The woman laughed a second time.

"Of what avail is it to be forewarned of what is foreordained?" she inquired bitterly. "If you knew all that you are about to undergo, it is in my mind that the knowledge would take from you the blood of your heart and the kidneys of your valor; your weapons would lie lifeless beneath you, every ground upon which you trod would be slippery as the raw flesh of an eel, the pangs of a woman in childbirth would be yours, and the life of the mists you see gathering about the riverbanks here would be as the stronghold of Degannwy in Ros to yours."

Indeed, the vapor of evening was upon the river and water meadows and woods about us, and the walls of the ruined town beside us floated upon the fog like rocky islands of the sea. A chill breeze uprose, causing Maelgun and me to shiver and draw our cloaks about us. It was time for us to return to the campfire. Next day at dawning the army of the Cymry would cross the ford.

The woman in the water laughed a third and last time, raising her cupped hands toward us. Through the swirling vapors we glimpsed blood, thick and red as wine lees, dripping from between her fingers onto the cloak floating at her feet.

"Here is the cloak for you to wear, Maelgun Hir and Merlin Wyllt! It will cover you both with its protection, as you shall see, and the man whose covering it is shall sleep snug in a close bed beneath a coverlet of turf. And now I must depart to my own, as must you to yours. I have watched you, and now I warn you: Dogs of Gwern, beware Morddwyd Tyllion!"

As the mist drew thicker between us, it seemed to me that beneath the surface of the water, there lay heaped a cairn of mutilated heads and trunks and limbs, from whose open veins and pipes streamed gouts of blood which reddened all the river. It was but a glimpse I gained, and yet I fancy it was these the woman washed beneath the cloak she showed us.

With this the Washer at the Ford departed from us, bat-winged, lynx-taloned, and black as a scald crow; and we knew her to have come from the elf-mounds in the guise of a fair woman.

Amid the gathering dusk we departed likewise from the wharf, returning to find the campfire of the kings. I had no mind at that time to partake of the feasting, standing apart muffled in my cloak and leaning against the cold wall of the empty town, outside which was clustered the encampment of the Cymry. Around the ruddy glare I saw come and go as they dipped their flesh-hooks in the cauldron, Maelgun Gwynedd, his son Run, his cousins of the house of Cunedda, Elffin mab Gwydno, and the tribune Rufinus. Emerging from the shadowy gloom that enveloped them, their faces appeared detached and pallid, estranged from daytime kindness and warmth; not a little like the row of impaled heads which I was one day to see surround the sanctuary of death.

I thought of the words of the Washer at the Ford, and knew that now was come the moment for me to depart the company of my fellow countrymen. I made my way through the darkness back to the ford. I was all but there, with the water glimmering dully in the pallid light of an obscured moon, when I caught sound of a footfall behind me. Turning abruptly, I recognized the form of the tribune and laughed.

"You keep a close eye upon me, Rufinus! I recall another such moment on the slope of Dinleu Gurygon. What is your errand this time?"

"That might I inquire of you, Merlin, who come and go like a guardroom cat. It was not wise of the king to absent himself from the army, and I thought it best to keep watch upon him—and you. It was but four years ago near Illyricum that Goar and Ildigisal slew four Roman generals who were rash enough to leave their camp, venturing down to a river at night in the way you have done. But in your case something tells me you are proposing to absent yourself from duty and leave the army. Am I right?"

Pondering a moment how much I might confide in this man, I decided to acknowledge a little of what was in my mind.

"I am not deserting you, tribune, though you are right in supposing that I am about to depart for a while. My mind is disturbed by many things, which it is necessary for me to consider in solitude."

"Do you fear for the outcome of this campaign?" inquired the tribune, looking me close in the face. "If so, you are in duty bound to inform the king. Or will you confide in me, upon whom lies the burden of advising on matters of strategy? Should you be in possession of military intelligence of which I am unaware, I must warn you that you would be acting irresponsibly were you to withhold it at this critical moment of our advance."

Brooding briefly, I glanced first at the intelligent gaze of the soldier and then at the somber swell of the river emerging from the dark to plunge onward into the dark.

"I know nothing of that sort," I replied at length. "There have been signs and portents upon our way, and I wish to place myself apart from the host to consider their import."

The tribune laughed shortly. "Signs and portents indeed!" he retorted gruffly. "Signs of the grossest violations of discipline, and portents of a total failure to grasp the basic principles of warfare as laid down by Vegetius and Frontinus! But seriously, my friend, you should not take on so at the grumblings of an old soldier. I grant you there has been overmuch straggling by certain units, and that the outposts were improperly placed at some of the river crossings. But the king is backing my recommendations admirably, and there is nothing like a long route march for licking raw levies into shape. You'll see, all will be well. After more years than I care to recall of frontier campaigning in Libya, I am the last person to hold exaggerated expectation of tight discipline among federates. Try talking to them of prostaxis, entaxis, epitaxis, hypotaxis, parembole—why, they do not even know the terms, let alone the duties, of professional soldiering!

"But our morale is high, and I would imagine we must have overwhelming superiority in numbers over anything the enemy can put into the field—particularly since we were joined by the armies of the three kings at the crossing of the Sabrina. Remember: Eternal Victory is the destiny of Rome, whose Empire is bounded not by land, but by the heavens. It was Cicero who wrote that, I believe; I am not entirely illiterate, you see!"

I clasped the old man by his shoulder and smiled.

"I have little doubt you are right, and in any case you know very much more of these matters than I. But still, there are certain matters troubling me, and it is necessary for me to withdraw myself for a while to contemplate how best to resolve them. Like you I am a 'gray wolf' from across the sea and have a viewpoint of my own. To each is his own skill, and if you and I apply ours effectively I see no reason why the outcome should be unsuccessful."

"Well, be it as you choose," rejoined the soldier. "I have no power to stay your departure. I hope we may meet again, for I think we could make a strategist of you yet. I never was a man of letters, and I left Alexandria knowing little more of rhetoric and law than does a newly enrolled recruit of *limitanei*. As for the *Organon* of Aristotle and Porphyry's *Isagoge*—well, I made about as much sense of them as I do of your ROTAS-SATOR square! But it is not hard for me to see that you possess much hidden wisdom and, I think, not a little goodness of heart."

Rufinus paused a while; and then he uttered words which I confess puzzled me, and which I was long to turn about within my mind:

"It may be that we are not destined to meet again in this world, my friend. It may be, too, that not all will happen as you and your king would wish in this campaign. But I hope you will believe me, however things may appear or whatever men say, when I declare to you that I shall perform my duty as a soldier of the emperor of the Romans. This, they tell me, is the River Tamesis. Well, perhaps we shall follow it together to Londinium, and there see a Roman and a British ensign wave friendly together!"

As Rufinus spoke, the moon emerged briefly from the rack of murky clouds moving slowly overhead, and I glimpsed a glistening in the old officer's eye as he turned on his heel to depart. I said nothing, but felt an unexpected pang something like that I had experienced when Elffin's princess turned to me for aid in her bower at Porth Gwydno in the North. There is a wretchedness about things which is at times hard to bear, and I felt momentary impotent indignation at the solitary lot which had been cast upon me at my conception.

"My complaint is not hard to conceive,
By this dark river, taking our leave,
To whose bank the rotten hogweeds cleave.

By bull of battle, seeking the fray;
Pillar of hosts and candle of day;
Lord of the stars, guide Rufinus' way!"

However, it is useless to repine. It is no more possible to stay a fleeting moment of warmth by a chieftain's hearth than it is to dam that hurrying flood which even then surged past my feet. Like a juggler performing his skilled balancing, I must turn every thought to the business in hand or all might tumble into ruin overnight, as did King Gurtheyrn's fortress in the mountains of Eryri. Below me in the gloom I heard the hurrying swirl of the river which Maelgun's host must pass tomorrow: a borderline of danger.

Behind us lay the ordered kingdoms of the Cymry, each tribe arranged in structured kinship about its prophesied king, wed to the land which supports the sky with its holy Tree. There is kingship in the sky above, where the Tree meets the Nail of the Heavens. Up there, across that spangled dome half-hid by angry clouds, the gods are playing that great game of *gwyddbwyll* upon which rests the fate of all creation. And here below, it is the Monarchy of Prydein which is beset by foes and whose pieces are advanced about their king. Upon earth as in heaven all will end in battle-storm and fire and flood, and for us it was a time fast approaching:

For the strife of Arderid provides the cause
From their lives' preparing till the last of wars.

Beyond the Temys lay a land under shadow, wasted, peopled by wild beasts and ravaged by men whose nature was fanged and pelted as wolves or wildcats. There is chaos there, deposition of lawful kings, dissolution of kinship, destruction of towns, man-slaying between fathers and sons, incest between brothers and sisters. Like the water-logged meadows behind me upon which the moon glimmered faintly, it was the louring Wasteland which is neither land nor water.

Before me flowed the river, once a holy stream that sained a land of flower-spangled meadows, fecund as the Caer Gwydion across the night sky. No fell being from an elf-mound might cross its healing waters, and even now it formed a barrier confining the foul hosts of the Coranieid and their confederates, the ocean-sailing men of Loiger, the Iwys.

I much misliked the unchancy aspect of the grim Washer at the Ford, and her words laid a chill upon my heart which might not be dispelled. They were a warning and a mockery, as I guessed: "Dogs of Gwern, beware of Morddwyd Tyllion!"

What were the dogs of Gwern, and who was Morddwyd Tyllion? It was for me to master their meaning, that the radiantly caparisoned hosts of Prydein might not be swallowed up in the abyss approaching. There is a dread spot all sailors know upon the Strait of Menai, which lies between Arfon and Maelgun's Island of Mon. It is a rushing spiraled descent within the turbulent waters, that warped abyss in ocean which is called Pull Ceris. Beneath its roaring depths the Sucker of the Sea awaits each passing keel, eager to draw it down into the jagged entrance of her jaws. And it is I, Merlin mab Morfryn, who am the pilot of our ship in her time of peril, and whose task it is to work her warily around the raging brink.

Forty years had I passed in the dissolution of the deep under the guidance of the Salmon of Lyn Liw. My emergence at the culmination of that ordeal onto the surface of the sunlit Sea of Reged had been for me a rebirth and regeneration. Yet even at that moment, when I hung in agony upon the stake in Gwydno's weir, I knew that it heralded also a time of trial and torment. Now I must return for a space to formlessness, that through the power of the goddess I might become purified and regenerated, initiated into wholeness and understanding.

Here I stood at the brink of all things. On my left the sky was paling faintly, and I found myself upon land and within water, at a time which was neither night nor day, on the borders of kingship and chaos. The river was become the limit of all things, a rampart to be paced lest the hosts of the Coranieid find a breach. Over my face and about my body I drew the black mantle of Caswallon mab Beli which is the *llen hut*. Thus enveloped in darkness and changed in form, I slid down the muddy bank into the rush of cold waters.

CHAPTER THIRTEEN

AT THE FORGE
OF
GOFANNON

Once again, as at the time of my birth, the waters closed above my head, but this time there was no wise Salmon of Lyn Liw to guide and protect me. There was danger above and about and below, and I with but my loricated *llen hut* about me as a protection.

There was scant time to spare on thought as I sped downstream with frantic haste of darting and turning. Had speed been my only consideration I should have maintained a headlong course midstream, where the current flowed strongest. But I had reason to prefer the river marge, skirting forests of bulrushes, lush groves of watercress and brooklime, stretches of solid mudbank from which willows trailed their silvery-leaved fronds upon the limpid surface. Best of all was when the bright gaze of the sun was hidden from view by an interposing roof of lily pads, for then no watcher from the bank might espy my furtive progress.

After the turmoil of the camp of the Cymry, I found myself plunged into a silent, slow-moving bowl of filtered light, opaquely illuminated from above. Water-boatmen skated the surface in zigzag sallies of placid purposelessness, while rowing beetles of varying size shot past trailing spangled clouds of silvery bubbles. Mine was a tiny kingdom, teeming with close-packed life. Occasionally its sky was darkened by the passage of a great white full-bellied swan sailing his smooth course overhead.

At times I passed by a muddied ford, where cattle came to thrust their broad pink muzzles into the refreshing waters. Once only did I come upon humankind, where at a place of stones I stayed a brief while to contemplate the fair pink feet of girls washing clothes. Drawing near, I heard their muffled speech and laughter floating in the clear air above me. The water dulled the syllables, bringing to my ears only the murmured resonance of speech, so that I could understand nothing of their talk. It may be they spoke the barbarous broken tongue of the Iwys, for throughout this time I knew myself to be gliding through territory which had long been their sword-land.

As I pursued my course I uttered inwardly an invocation to the clear-welled, pure-streamed, strong-flooding Temys, heart-artery of the Southland of Prydein, salmon-bearing sister of Hafren and Hymyr. Her lore I recited, her birth, her rearing and her naming; the wells and streams and lakes from which she draws her being; her passage from the depths of Annufn to the Sea of Udd and the blessed haven of Caer Sidi.

However, my time in the river was not the idyll lovers know as they stroll its banks, each with his arm about a rose-cheeked, white-limbed maiden. Nor was it that delightful place of contemplation chosen by the poet, where he seeks the *awen* from his mossy vantage point at a turbulent confluence. For I knew well that the Washer at the Ford, burning-eyed Morgan from the elf-mounds of the North, had marked my departure from the camp of the Cymry. Somewhere in the shadowy wasteland of the waters she would be lying in wait for me, eager for my destruction, coming to take me when I was least aware.

And come she did, as I turned the end of an aspen-grown island. She was there in the current before me, her webbed five-toed forepaws held close to her silky-furred belly, so that she curved and lunged through the water like a serpent. Her eyes, black and brilliant as ebony, were fixed fast upon me as I floundered fruitlessly to beat a path to right or left. Short and squat were her pug ears, stiff-streaming her bristled whiskers, and mocking the fierce glare of her broad flat head.

Even as I plunged in a frantic effort at escape, she swooped beneath me and sank sharp her thirty-six needled teeth into my belly. I uttered a long silent scream of impotent agony as my enemy paddled me with quick strokes of her short strong-finned legs toward the riverbank. Next instant she emerged into the daylight with me between her jaws, casting me floundering and gasping upon the boll of a fallen tree emerging from the water to the land, where its leafless branches thrust black and broken into the chill air above.

I was at the mercy of my inveterate foe, and could but heave convulsively upon the rotten bark as I awaited the tearing and ravaging of my soft-skinned underbelly and throat. She arched her head above me, her bright little eyes exulting in the kill, and I knew myself to be at death's entrance. Her tiny red opened jaws, with their serrated spiky pinnacles above and below, were for me without evasion the yawning gates of Uffern.

There had been a time of trial on Ynys Gweir when I had longed for the comfort of the deep, extinction in endless sleep and safe return to my mother's womb. But now, with the warm-scented air of summer breathing upon me, the hum of bees about buttercups, and the slow slap of cows' tails in the meadow beyond, I longed for life under the sun in the busy world of men. And what of the Monarchy of Prydein, the hosting of King Maelgun the Tall, and the fate of my friends Elffin and Run and Rufinus the tribune, now that I was come to perish alone and unknown upon this ancient tree?

A soft tread upon the turf drew near. I gazed imploringly up at my assassin as she crouched poised to lunge at my exposed throat or belly. Her little, wicked, black-beaded eyes turned momentarily from mine, she paused in a frozen instant of time too long for me to tell, and then she was gone, with a dull plop slipping back into the hurrying water. With a convulsive jerk of spine and muscle I flung myself after her, slipping sideways as I floundered down into the cool depths. From a crevice within a thicket of close-packed bulrushes I saw what it was that had driven my ruthless adversary from the scene.

The surface of the stream above was broken as a red tongue lapped greedily of the water. Wriggling back as far as I might in my place of concealment, I caught a glimpse of gray muzzle, keen fangs, and a brown-eyed gaze that seemed to seek me out of my fancied obscurity. Then I knew it for a great gray wolf, who had come to slake his thirst at this fortunate juncture. Next moment he was gone, and I knew that I must depart as swiftly, ere my tormentor return to complete her task.

It was with terror in my heart, I freely confess, that I swam on my course. My belly was sorely scored by the marks of Morgan's teeth, and all about me in the shadows I seemed to see her mocking mask watching and waiting. My flight was flurried and frantic, lacking the long easy strokes that would have borne me with surer speed toward my destination. There came a point after many miles when I felt I must pause to regain my strength, be the danger what it might.

It was a space of clear shingle, a haven hemmed about by clean sandbanks. It was not safe, but if pause I must, then at least it was a spot where my foe lacked grove or thicket in which to lie. I swam into the clear enclave, whose water was warmed by the noonday sun now darting his long ray upon me.

There I hovered awhile, midway between earth and air, recovering from my exhaustion and fear. All the time my eye glanced this way and that, but of the squat whiskered mask of the Washer at the Ford I caught not a glimpse. My apprehension lessened a little, though I knew full well that so long as I was within the water's obscurity, the peril was omnipresent. It was time once more to be up and doing!

Poising myself for departure, I found myself unexpectedly fetched up against what I took to be two tall bulrush stalks rising from the riverbed to the water's surface. Twisting to avoid them, I glanced momentarily downward—where I saw to my surprise and terror two triple-toed and spur-heeled feet, shaped like broad-barbed arrows! Not beside or below me was my remorseless pursuer, but standing high above: gray, gaunt, and motionless as a specter. I saw how, high in the sunlight, she was even now arching her narrow twin-plumed head upon its long serpentine neck. Long greenish stilt-legs astride, poised to drive a great long-bladed yellow spear deep into my feebly palpitating heart.

Now I knew dread greater by far even than that I had experienced at the Washer's first attack. For I knew that spear which was sharper and surer and fiercer than Rongomiant the spear of Arthur, deadly as the flashing bolt of Mabon mab Mellt, and its thrust more cruel than that which the giant Ysbaddaden received through his eyeball and out through the nape of his neck. Let that lance-blow be loosed and I would be lacerated through heart and liver, spitted to the stream bed, and the ford gore-red with my blood. There was hate and venom in the eye behind the spear, and supple strength of sinew and muscle about her who poised it.

I glanced wildly this way and that, desperate with one flick and a jerk to be away, but aware that my persecutor awaited the pleasure of that moment to inflict her lightning death-stroke. My mind was disordered and confused as the watery waste in which I was suspended; what seemed an age of ages was perhaps the passing of a moment. A diving beetle passed busily at an angle before me, while a handsome orange-bellied newt suddenly floated aloft from the stony stream bed, its legs dangling and delicate fingers outstretched. Our eyes met without recognition. How I envied him his careless ease; not for him was the lance-thrust lingering.

But for me the moment had arrived. The legs that bestrode me in exultant power stiffened and shifted, the shadow above me darkened, and the water stirred with a cold current. She was preparing for the kill. It was between my narrow shoulders that I fancied the stab would be directed, and I hunched myself together in mesmerized anticipation. Next moment came a swift flurry of movement, a swirl of mud from below and beating of water above—a turmoil of power and motion, a lifting and splashing, a beating and whirling, a lightening of the dark and lifting of oppression from my soul—and the long thin bony shanks of the river murderess disappeared as the shadow upon me was replaced all of a sudden with a shifting spectrum of spangled light.

As the wavelets settled and muddy spume subsided, I found myself alone once more in the bright clear stream. I felt a cool rush of relief such as the land knows when the sun emerges after a fierce spring storm. Paddling up to the light, I gazed upward from the smooth surface of my backwater to the pellucid sky. No trace of my persecutor or of any other living being could I espy; none, save where far above me soared in an ascending spiral a great wide-winged bird.

At first I took it for Morgan, the Washer at the Ford, departing in some form of enchantment. But then I saw it was a mighty eagle, golden, glorious. I followed him with my watery eye until his ascent brought him below the burning ball of the sun at its zenith, when my eye was dazzled and it was no longer possible to distinguish the gold within the gold.

That the sovereign of the skies had frightened away her whose steady pursuit I had hitherto been unable to evade I did not doubt. But there was no time to be lost: My journey was a long one, and who knew when the chase might not be resumed? She knew my every move, of that I was certain. In my mind's eye I saw the river laid out small as on a map, over which the poisoned eye of Morgan pored ceaselessly, tracing my every move with sardonic ease.

Still, twice had I avoided her, and I would persist so long as I was able. I must reach my destination before dusk; only then could I drag myself forth from the shapeless element in which every advantage of skill and strength and surprise lay with my opponent.

Mile after weary mile I alternately swam and floated, nearing exhaustion, but driven by abject fear to a resilience more than my own. Eventually I found myself in a place where the river meandered through meadows level and low enough for it to overspread its banks in a broad flood, making it hard at times to distinguish my course. The sun was descending in the west, waterlogged alders and poplars marking ever longer shadows pointing me upon my way. I was nearly there, and a moment's pause would give me strength for the final spurt.

Recalling my recent narrow escape, I found a pleasant pool formed where two great trees had fallen across each other and lay rotting athwart the current. Beavers had brought logs, branches, and leaves to build a fortress, and were even now busy about their task. As I have often heard huntsmen relate, it is their custom to post spies in willow-woven turrets along the ramparts of their *caer*. I reflected therefore that in whatever form Morgan approached me, she would disturb these industrious folk, whose agitation or sudden silence would in turn be a warning to me.

My pool was light and spacious, with but a few sparse rushes insufficient for a foe's concealment. I was wary from my experience, and was learning something of the arts of evasion. A living branch still thrived upon the dead trunk of its parent, through whose leaves the sun dappled the deep in which I lay suspended. Dappled was my flank, too, with variegated spotting, and I turned myself to the sunlight so as to be indistinguishable from the setting of my refuge. As the waters lapped, so I attuned myself to their motion. In color as in movement I was as one with every element around me, and I fancied that, provided I did not allow her time, it would be long ere the fell ravager detected my temporary refuge.

Above the firmament of my aquatic sphere darted and hovered a host of dragon and damsel flies, brilliant in blue, green, and red fluorescence, their bright armor a dart of vivid sheen within the blurred oscillation of their vibrating wings. Marvelous was it to me to contemplate the contrast between the motionless gleam of their suspended bodies and the imperceptible multitudinous fluttering of diaphanous wings.

It is in the tiny beings of the earth that the wonderful work of Your creation is seen to perfection, O You with Your Sure Hand! Not more radiant than the moonlit dance of the Fair Folk is the flitting of these gorgeous beings: dance of a moon's duration. And yet where is it that these gay creatures of light and air and color have their birth and conception? Where if not in the slime and filth and rotting sediment of the river bottom, foul rectum of the stinking Pit of Annufn? Who but You, O Divine One, could work such a miracle of craftsmanship, greater than that of the skilled goldsmith who fashions to enchantment a king's brooch from that which once lay prisoned within an earthbound rock?

Even now I saw one of their heavy-bodied larval nymphs dragging its ungainly length painfully up the pillared stalk of a yellow flag, its blind blundering gait standing in stark contrast to the golden flower at the summit, whose smiling face was raised in adoration to its father the setting sun. Heavy and repulsive was the creature of the flood's excrement, stagnant slime adhering still to its unwieldy, long-bellied carcass. Could *this* abomination of the primeval filth emerge from its evil husk to become *that* aery being of grace and beauty? But yes, for it was from the chaos of the nine forms of elements, the essence of soils, that You uttered the enchanted verse, spring of the *awen,* whose inspiration wafted over the waste of waters; until upon the foaming of the ninth wave the perfect forms enshrined in Your Cauldron of Poesy became primroses and flowers of the hill, dappled fawn of the brake, eagle whose pinioned sweep soars over sixty silvered estuaries.

Such were my tranquil thoughts, when all at once they were dispersed by a sudden silence of the beaver-folk from chattering over their unending task, and swift slithering of their bodies into the water. A bare moment later there came a heavy grunting at the riverbank and squelch of strong feet in the mud, and the placid surface of my refuge was shattered by the intrusion of the bristled snout and sabered tusks of a great wild sow who had come to this spot to slake her thirst.

Though I had no reason to fear her savage strength, my apprehension of danger from every quarter was so great that I jerked sideways in a spontaneous convulsion. In doing so I inadvertently avoided a danger more dire than the two attacks I had sustained earlier on my voyage. Seared into my consciousness was a horrible vision: staring me in the face with horrid glare was the dragonfly nymph whose ungainly ascent had attracted my attention a moment earlier. No more the lumbering mud-encrusted crawler of my contemptuous contemplation, it had detached itself with unexpected suddenness from its perch and darted for my exposed underbelly.

The face of the creature had altered horribly. Where before had been but blind stupidity and shapeless deformity, there was now revealed a monstrous mask, hideous with hatred. From beneath its head had shot forward a grotesque visor, in whose jaws were set two ravening claws which nipped together viciously at the spot where, but an instant before, the unprotected underparts of my body had lain exposed. Behind the deformity of prognathous jaw and protruding claw I glimpsed the face of the Washer at the Ford. Were it not for the abject nature of my blind panic I might almost have pitied the look of tormented frustration I saw set in the horny features of that repellent creature. But for the chance appearance of the boar and my unpremeditated movement, her claws would even now be ripping the entrails from my torn stomach.

With a mighty thrust of mind and bone and muscle I flung myself clear of the witch's swift darting, floundering for the opposite bank.

Though I knew that the evil being within whose husk she had made a home could make but one swift lunge, I sensed her presence looming near in the darkness of the void. Until I was safely upon land, stretched exhausted beside the rushing river, there was no ease within me. Thrice had I been near a cruel end: first, upon the fallen tree with the evil creature's teeth in my throat; second, by her lance-thrust at the water's edge; and third, by drowning, disemboweled and dragged down into primeval slime by the most loathsome of dwellers in the Pit of Annufn.

Yet even now, as the sun beamed down upon the meadow, suffusing my chilled and battered body with loving warmth, it stole into my mind that, if death had indeed thrice held me in his taloned grasp, so also had I escaped his clutches by as many times. I had achieved my purpose, traversing the most dangerous of courses, and was come through hale to achieve the task upon which hung the fate of the Monarchy of Prydein.

For a brief while I lay upon the bank, huddled still within the protective membrane of the *llen hut,* my knees drawn up to my chest, my heels against my buttocks. The constriction of my joints was such that it was hard for me to move after my long immersion in shadow and shape-shifting beneath the nine waves of the floodtide of Temys. But now came the warmth of the risen sun upon my back and side, and soon I felt my strength as it were triply renewed, for had not this been my third immersion within the watery deep, the third drop of baptism upon my radiant forehead? The first time was at the bursting of the lake of the breaking of my mother's waters; the second when the Salmon of Lyn Liw drew me from the ocean to the surface of the Sea of Reged; and now was come the third emergence upon the farther bank of the River Temys.

I rose unsteadily to my feet, shedding into the lapping wave the loricated cloak of which I had no further need. I was naked now as the day I was born, and alone as when King Custennin Gorneu had me cast upon the empty waste of ocean. Despite this it was with exultation that I pursued my path southward from the riverbank. My initial purpose was achieved, for all the malign attempts of the Washer at the Ford to frustrate it. I had traced the length of Temys where it lay like a serpent across the path of Maelgun's host, naming its places and rehearsing its lore. A cleansing of the host would the passage of its waters prove as they crossed the ford this day, a lifting of the Defilement placed upon it by the barbarous men of Loiger.

Beyond the flooded meadow before me lay a long dark ridge, toward which I traced my steps. This was the lesser rampart I must ascend before attaining the realm of darkness lying beyond in the Wasteland of Loiger. Over the crest I trudged, and so on across a bare upland heath coursed by a cruel wind and bearing but a few stunted trees, their boughs bare and bent to the westward. After the confinement of the riverbed, the blowing of the breeze and limitless expanse of the aery vault above my head were an exhilaration and a quickening of my pace. With each step I took there flew up before me the iridescent forms of green tiger beetles, running and dancing in my path like bright emeralds, and seeming to invite me to pursue a southward path.

And now I saw before me, not many miles off in the south, a great shadowy wall of downland upreared against the sky. Not pleasing was its aspect as it frowned upon me, blocking the horizon from left to right. Gray rain clouds trailed upon its slopes, and a heavy mist lay sluggish upon its summit. Even now I was within the bounds of Loiger, where every man's hand would be against me. But it was up there, upon the Plain of Bran, that danger skulked beside which all that I had hitherto passed through was but preparation and foreshadowing and initiation. And but one night was I allotted to ready myself for the ordeal!

Ah, King Ceneu mab Pasgen, what do you reck as you feast in your brightly lit hall in Caer Luelid of the travails and torments of him who placed your kingdom where now it stands? You summon me from my green mound to tell you of things to come. Would you have done so had you thought them to be unchancy things present and future, unleashed each year at the Kalan Gaeaf, riding on the storm clouds with Gwyn mab Nud, tearing at your frontiers with the swart hosts of the Coranieid?

Before me, on the lower slope of the ridge I was descending, stood a mighty yew, dark, full-skirted with spreading green branches, a pillar upon the plain, a bow bent against the rampart. High as the racing clouds it raised its barbed summit, across which they scraped their fleecy bellies. A pelting rain came on, driving northward until it flung down its heavy drops upon me as I ran, lashing my naked skin and washing my hair into wild elflocks.

It was to the shelter of the great yew that I made, where it stood upright and alone in the wet waste. Between the waste and the wet it stood ward, for its mighty roots were set deep in earth and rock at the edge of the descending slope. Beyond extended a sodden level which was neither land nor water, a broad expanse of dully shimmering wetland, sparsely studded with broken willow clumps. From all about me came the racing sound of hidden watercourses, hurrying like me down from the sharp-backed ridge which lay between us and the deep-flowing Temys.

Leaping the brooks and stumbling over stony banks, I swiftly gained the shelter of the yew and leaned panting and dripping against its trunk. The outstretched arms of three men might barely have encompassed its great trunk, and its branches formed a canopy above me broad as the roof of a king's tent. Protection and sanctuary were mine, for had I not traveled the length of the River of Death to find *naut* at the Tree of Life?

Even as I paused and pondered upon these things I heard from behind the Tree a piteous moan. Stealing around, I came upon a great gleaming white sow who lay against the roots in the throes of death. Upon her bristled flanks were gashed many wounds, from which the blood flowed fast as the stream bubbling beside us. It was in my mind that wounds of that nature could but be the handiwork of Drudwyn, hound of Mabon mab Modron, from which cause there lay now upon the eye of the stricken sow the glaze of death. Be that as it may, the unhappy creature gave forth a grievous groaning, and expired at my feet with a shudder that shook the ground beneath my feet.

At this the Tree above us groaned and shrieked likewise, shaking gusty winds from within its branches. From its side, too, there seeped a rush of blood, which never ceased to ooze and trickle the while I spent under its protection.

Crouching over the dead beast, I drew my knife and slit open its belly from throat to hindquarters. Working swiftly—so swiftly that when I came upon the creature's heart it was yet palpitating—I set about flaying the thick hide from flesh dripping with gore. Before my task was complete, my naked limbs were no less bloody, but once all was done I gathered the warm pelt about me as a cloak, knotting the dangling forepaws before my throat and setting the tusked muzzle upon my head as a hood.

Thus warmly clad, I beset myself to a yet more arduous task. Not far from the Tree beneath which I stood lay a great gray stone, its square-edged surface heaving up from the mud by the track I had traversed on my way. Now, with the power of the creature whose mantle I wore within my heart and bones and sinews, I heaved the rock from its resting place and dragged it to an open space beyond the yew. No easy task was it for me to cut out a recess within the dark earth, levering into it the end of the mighty slab, so that at the last it stood erect upon the plain.

Beneath the boar-hide my body was running with gore and sweat. Blood from wounds inflicted upon me by the hag Morgan mingled with that of the noble sow whose death was my deliverance. I lay for a space of time, exhausted and gazing from my stone to the grim bulwark of the downs to the southward.

Solitary in the field stood my great stone, growing out of the earth from which was its conception. Indissoluble was its strength, and imprisoned within its hardness was the essence of that place, the vigor of the soil, and the spirit of Him who presided over it. Who can tell when it was wrought within the remotest recesses of earth's time of labor? Those curves and crevices upon its rugged surface:. What runes of dwarves or arts of elves are they? Longer than the span of mortal man is my life, and longer still that of the yew soaring above me into the eternal sky. But that stone will endure until time itself has an ending, and only then will the stiff gray substance of its structuring deliver up the secret lore of the age of ages before the touch of Gwydion's wand set sap in tree, blood in beast, and mind in man.

I had set my mark upon the earth, a banner before the ramparts of Loiger, a mighty menhir, penis of the land. Crouching cross-legged before its majesty and ease of strength, thrust of power, upsurge of creation, I saw that upon the world it was a pillar, above which rested the gray, coursing sky, as did it also upon the crest of the great yew. It was the center of all things, the point from which my mission moved. From the Stone, I drew eternal strength, poised at the pivot beneath the revolving sky, while the Tree was the bow upon whose arrow I would fly soaring over yonder deep-dyked rampart.

Rising to my feet, I returned to the foot of the Tree, where I found a great hound tearing at the bloody carcass of the sow. Though I bore the bristled hide of the creature, the dog looked up and wagged its tail at my approach. His black muzzle dripped gore, but his eye betrayed no hostile glance. Then I knew the great hound to be an *ellyll* of the great king, *maglocunos*. For where the Center is, with its Tree and Pillar, there must the king be also.

Together we returned to the Pillar-stone. Upon one side of it I let spill the warm lifeblood of the slain sow from my cupped hands, while the huge hound lifted his leg and urinated upon the other. Long would the stains of the blood and the urine remain soaked upon the Stone's flanks, marking our unity with its potency.

Next I took a morsel of raw pig's flesh, placed it before the Pillar, and prayed to him who lords it over boar and bear, fox and foumart, owl and eagle, that there might be a Restitution of the Island of the Mighty, *Atbret Pritein,* the dark stronghold falling to the noble war-riors of the Cymry, skilled in secrets of spear-craft:

"Lay low their dwelling in the dust,
O Lord of the Circling Stars!
Be mine the name upon the rock
Throughout the cycle of the years."

Thus did that Stone come to bear my name, *Maen Merlin*. And there it stands to this day, O king, as a sign upon the wetland which lies between the full-flowing Temys and her tributary the island-studded Ehauc, home of gliding queenly swans. And it may happen that it will in years to come be cast down by wind or rain or wiles of the false brood of Loiger, so returning to dwell once more for a space of time in the cold earth from which I plucked it. But after that it will come about that the heir of my blood and my spirit will appear to raise it up, that men may know that the mantle of Merlin is yet a protection upon the Island which bears my name: *Clas Merlin*.

It will be a grim time, when once again there will come an Oppression upon the Island, when men small of stature compared with those who guarded it of old will have it in their keeping, and when the scattered remnant of the Brython, seeking refuge in hills and forests, will long in their hearts for the return of Arthur as a deliverance from their torments.

I must return to my tale, though it is hard for me, who have ridden the years upon a pale-yellow horse swift as a seagull, sleeping in a hundred islands and dwelling in a hundred forts, to rest my recollection overlong upon any one resting place upon the way. The time was upon me when I must cross that grim margin which lies between the formed and the unformed, the tilled land and the waste, the precinct for the unhallowed turbulence without. Like a chieftain who leaves the joyous mead-hall to pass water in the windy darkness of the courtyard without, I would pass from the known to the unknown, from that which is familiar and protected, enclosed and ordered, to that which is ruined, blighted, desolate.

Mine was the despairing cry over the Abyss of Annufn of the *car*-shattered, kin-wrecked man who, lacking inheritance or portion within his kindred, is driven with sounding of horns and barking of dogs to the sea marge, to put out upon the watery waste until he shall have passed three score hours beyond sight of man.

Now I returned to the flayed carcass of the sow, a shapeless mass of bleeding flesh at the foot of the Tree. Cutting off a portion, I chewed it for a while. Then, returning to my Pillar-stone, I took the morsel and placed it at its base. Kneeling down upon the wet grass, I spread the palms of my hands upward, breathing a prayer across the right to You with Your Sure Hand, my bright shining suffering one, who watched over me during my long years submerged in the ocean. Skilled master of the *gwyddbwyll* board, guardian of kingship and maintainer of the tribes, aid me now as I seek to execute Your will among the world of men, as Your Sure Hand sustains it throughout the unnumbered host of stars!

And across my left hand I breathed a supplication to the Horned One, who sits cross-legged upon the mountain with his stag and his ram-headed serpent. "O Little Pig," I groaned, "there is a troubled world before me; I hear the shrill cries of the gulls tossed in the wind! A specter from afar has told of kings with strange connections, Gwyddel and Brython and Rufeinwyr, who plan conflict and chaos throughout the Island of the Mighty. O Little Pig with your sharp claws, by your dark pool in the wilderness: Unless I receive from you a portion of mercy, then it will be ill that befalls me and wretched indeed my ending!"

Then I prayed for sleep to come upon me, lying down upon the damp turf. I placed the palms of my hands upon my two cheeks and closed my eyes, while the great war hound who was Maelgun's *ellyll* watched over me as a protection. And through the tips of my fingers, which touched the bulwark of my brow, stole images of time as yet untold. In nine, eighteen, and twenty-seven nights were revealed shuttered glimpses of what lay beyond the threshold, of which my flagstone was the gatepost.

At first I was with Arthur and Gwyn and Gwithir at the entrance to the cave of the Pitch-black Witch, daughter of the Bright-white Witch, in Penn Nant Gofud, which is the cold mouth of Uffern in the North. Already Hygwyd and Cacamuri had entered to do battle with the witch and failed to return. Now was come the hour for me to follow, tracing the labyrinth in a dizzying dance.

Then the Pillar-stone above me groaned through the starry night, and spoke. For the thoughts that the specter implanted in my brain that night were drawn into the elements of the Stone, where they remain. It is for this cause men come to consult the Stone, not daring to pass it without dismounting. Let any man remove my Stone, or set his dwelling place beside it, and I will place a curse upon him that he suffer from a worm which gnaws without ceasing at his entrails, that he be consumed with desires insatiable as the thirst of a parched wanderer in a desert, and that his place in the generations of his kindred be void as though he had never existed. His wife shall be faithless, foolish, and chattering, and their children without mind or shape or purpose, gibbering at their own reflections in a muddy puddle. And the worst of this curse shall be that he who suffers it knows not that it is a curse.

With the dawn I awoke, chilled to the marrow but prepared come what might to pursue my allotted course. A pallid light gleamed above the line of the downs in the south, and upon a branch above me in the yew there alighted three black ravens. Three harsh cries they uttered, blood-curdling and ill-omened enough to raise a corpse from the clay, or lift the hair from the head of their hearer.

But even as my resolution dwindled I saw that which calmed my perturbation of spirit and set warmth and strength within me. There in the southwest of the dawning sky hung my Morning Star, more bright and dazzling even than before! Flashing across intervening oceans and estuaries of the void shone her bright beam upon me, conferring the *awen* of understanding and consolation of courage I so sorely lacked. O my Gwendyd, was it in my dream that I saw you steal, white, warm, and lissome, from that cleft in the trunk of the bleeding Tree, with splendor of love glowing in your dear brown eyes and laughter upon your dimpled cheek? Was it you who wrapped us both about with the enveloping mantle of your soft limbs and velvet cloak? And those endearing words of comfort which whisper still within my ears, they were yours, and will wing me upon my dreadful journey!

Even as I stood proudly upright, gathering the bristled boarskin about me, I saw what it was to which Gwendyd was leading me with her fair hand. For I glimpsed afar off, upon the right shoulder of the distant down blocking my path, a fainter gleam which appeared an earthly incandescence of my Morning Star. Like the reflection of a hilltop fire at the Kalan Mai twinkling ruddy upon the surface of a still lake beneath, it burned faint but unfailing as a glowworm in a brake, or the last ember upon a royal hearth at dawning.

Now the sun rose in glory, and my smiling Gwendyd slipped from view. The glow upon the hill faded, and in its place I saw against the sky a plume of smoke, whose ascending column linked low clouds above with the land. There lay my destiny, and it was time for me to speed thither like a lance from the hand of a horseman in the battle-throng. My eye might traverse the journey swifter than the impulse it conveyed to my mind, but between me and my goal lay many a weary mile of miry meadowland and wandering waters.

From Rufinus I had acquired a certain skill in judging distances, and it seemed to me that my destination lay some ten miles or so to the southwest. That was no great measure to traverse before nightfall, had there been a paved causeway or upland ridgeway for me to pursue. Unfortunately there lay between me and my goal the course of the

River Ehauc. Though little more than a vigorous brook, it wandered within the level vale upon a haphazard course which flooded neighboring fields with great sheets of standing water, swampy and treacherous to traverse on account of hidden dykes and potholes. Trees felled by winter storms or the industry of beavers diverted the river now to this course, now to that. It was easy, gazing from some small eminence, to select what appeared the surer of different tracks—only to be obliged to retrace every difficult step and start anew.

Still, it was a place of peace and beauty, as I found when pausing to regain breath after struggling out of a slime-filled boghole or renegotiating an impassable thicket of scrub and bramble. Bumblebees and hover flies hummed about yellow flags gilding the water's edge; bronze-backed leaf beetles raced about on floating lily pads; dragonflies and swallows darted and dipped in the clear air on the rim of the running water. Tadpoles clamored in silent greed beneath the bank where I crouched, clustering about trailing willow fronds affording me brief shelter, while all about the waterlogged vale echoed the melancholy call of the curlew.

Motionless beneath the tree shade, I observed the breeze lifting leaves of poplars, their undersides glinting against the gray curtain of a drifting cloud. Now that the sun was moving into his zenith, tribes of honeybees flew forth in forays, searching for sweet pollen inside each golden goblet proffering itself upon lush green stem.

There was a whispered scurrying beside my little grove as a mother shrew emerged from a grass tunnel, her tiny progeny clinging blindly to her tail. As she peered anxiously about, her babies squeaking faintly as if in fear lest they be abandoned by the wayside, I bethought me of the host of Maelgun the Tall, which must even now be marching down the causeway yonder in the west. Like the shrew-babes they were clustered around their king, who was for them a pillar and protection.

Beneath the hum of insects and exultant chorusing of birds murmured a continuous gurgle and rush of running watercourses, tumbling undercurrent of movement which reminded me sharply that this was no time for reflexion or delay. There was a sudden flurry in the air above the river, a flutter of falling feathers: The broken body of a swooping swallow was trapped in the taloned grasp of a hobby, falling upon it from the sky with silent suddenness, swift and terrible as a lightning bolt from the hand of Mabon mab Mellt.

Agitated by the unexpected affray and relieved by my brief respite, I betook myself once more to my headlong course. Much, too much, rested upon the outcome of my solitary mission. There was danger everywhere in the air, as the mangled swallow had discovered too late. Running beside a deep dyke, across which I sought to find a passage, I heard not far off an ugly noise which as I guessed boded no good to me. A horn brayed harshly but two fields away, followed by a fierce baying of hounds. Men's voices, indistinct but drawing near, were raised in excited outcry. Then I knew it: They were after game, and what could the game be but myself?

Harried and hunted I was indeed. Next moment I saw a great mastiff's head glare through a hedge gap, and I was off. Without calculation of distance or danger I sprang sideways for the farther bank. Losing balance as I landed, I rolled heavily upon my side. Now it seemed to me as if I moved in water or within a dream, so sluggish were my reactions. As I staggered to my feet I saw the hound, followed by another and another, clear the hedge and come floating toward me across the grassy space in great long low bounds.

Across a place of tussocked reeds I blundered, crashed through a thorny brake unheeding of brambles ripping my bleeding sides, sped the length of a long green trackway that unexpectedly opened up before me, and so flew on without any thought save that of escaping the jagged fangs that every moment seemed to bring nearer upon me. Turning a sudden corner, I all but slid over as the thin covering of turf was sliced from the slippery mud beneath. Recovering my balance, I sprang forward—to sprawl headlong into the cold embrace of the river, which at this point skirted a small island.

As I turned over and over in the water, struggling at first vainly to right myself and regain the bank, I was no longer able to tell whether it was death by drowning or at the hands of my pursuers that I feared more. Fear gripped me and possessed me, and to my shame I say that all else—Maelgun the Tall, the fate of the Island of the Mighty, even you my Gwendyd, my Morning and Evening Star—sped from my mind as I was borne rising and sinking upon the racing river.

Some seven spear's-casts or more did I drift before I found a place of refuge. The current's force was dissipated where a reedy fen stretched stagnant across its path. Invisible, save where it lay exposed in black peat-bound pools, the water seeped beneath the swamp, seeking an outlet in the unknown beyond. A heron arose angry and ungainly from my path as I blundered across a tract of bog toward the only sanctuary in sight. Birches growing upon a low green knoll rose from behind a dense screen of bulrushes, into which I forced my way until I could penetrate no farther.

There I lay among the tall reeds, my breath coming in great gulping gasps like those of a smith's bellows, and my heart beating

loud as his hammer upon the anvil. But at least I was safe for the
present—however long that might be. As I collected my thoughts, it
occurred to me that I had no idea in what direction my flight had taken
me. It might be that I had turned back upon my tracks, that I was lost
or might lack time to attain the hills before dusk. A night in the fen did
not appeal to me, and time was short if I were to attain my purpose.
Still, it was not for me to repine could I but escape my savage
pursuers, and that it seemed I had succeeded in doing.

But O my Gwendyd, how often and gently have you comforted
me when that dreadful moment returned to my mind! For as I lay
wedged among the reeds, the pumping of my heart and the soughing
of the wind loud in my listening, what should I hear but a crashing and
shouting and baying of hounds all about me! Harsh cries resounded
everywhere: cries as it seemed to me in my dwindling place of concealment which were those of the broken-tongued speech of the barbarians, or it may be the tongue of a race older than that of the Brython,
yet dwelling in remote regions like that I sought to traverse.

What could I do? Save for the small birch copse, there was only the
open mere to which I could fly. There my foes would surely run me
down; all I could do was lie still and trust to my Morning Star to ward
over me. The cries and crashing drew near: Men were beating the
rushes as I guessed with their spear-butts. But then the noise grew
fainter somewhat, receding toward the birches. I closed my eyes, and
hope stole, small and apprehensive, upon me.

Next instant there was a violent sweeping and crackling, so it
seemed, immediately above me. I looked up, to see that the reeds had
parted and that three men were standing grinning down upon me. The
edged blades of their spears they held thrust forward, and close behind
was a crashing and plunging of hounds, summoned by the yell of one
of the huntsmen. Horns and a horrid yelping sounded from all about
as the whole troop of men and beasts converged on their victim. After
all my perils and escapes, I was brought to bay at last. Not in a green
mound upon an aery hillside would my body rest, to mark a tale
which a minstrel would relate before kings in their smoky halls. My
flesh would be torn to bloody rags, meat for the curs of barbarians,
and my bones whiten within a water hole.

At this, anger, red and burning, dispelled fear within me, and I
rose and made a fierce rush at my adversaries. I felt the spear-blades
gash my flesh, but the stout bristled boar's hide warded off the worst.
Not slow were my movements either, as I knocked one of my assailants over with a thrust of my shoulder and trampled a second into the
slime beneath me. The third drew a short sword and stabbed vigor-

ously at my throat. I think the thrust caught me somewhere, but I did not pause as with sudden convulsive jerk I ripped open his belly from loins to breastbone. A bare glimpse did I gain of him slowly vomiting black blood and clutching vainly to retain the disordered mess of entrails emerging from a yawning rent dividing his stomach.

I blundered onward through the reed thicket, mud sucking vainly at each flying step. As I emerged onto the tree-crested knoll, two or three hounds, great ragged scarred beasts with slavering red jowls, sprang furiously for my neck. Turning upon them directly, I stabbed viciously to right and left as they fell upon me. There came upon me might of muscle and strength of shoulder such that I sensed little could stay me now. There was a sobbing and yelping of gored hounds upon the ground beside me, and as the third sprang with ravening open jaws for my face, I hurled him circling high above me, so that he fell heavily upon his back some way off. His legs flailed the air as he endeavored to right himself, but from his tortured whimpering I guessed his spine was broken.

This was no time for thought, however, as a horn sounded loud and clear behind, and from all about me arose excited shouts and ferocious baying. Two or three spears flew close, and I fled swift as thought across the sward before me. Sufficient presence of mind had I preserved to mark where lay the shadowed line of downs ahead, and I set my general course toward the haven of the hills. Fear and anger lent me wings, and neither bramble thickets nor watercourses stayed my headlong course. It was long before I dared relax the frantic pace of my retreat, but finally the horrid yelping of savage men and savage dogs died away, and only the occasional faint far-off sounding of a horn told me that my enemies had not abandoned their vain pursuit.

I paused and looked about me. So swift and unrelenting had been my flight, I found that unawares I had drawn close to my destination. The distant gray rampart upon the horizon had become a towering green cliff stretching sheer above my head. A long broad tongue of raised scrubland extended from its base toward me, and across this I trotted at an easy pace. Soon I found myself in dark shadow at the cliff's base, for the sun was hidden beyond its crest. Despite my frenzied flight and warm covering of stout boar's hide, I felt a sudden chill steal upon me, and with it a fresh upsurge of fear. This was not the terror that gripped my vitals when the huntsmen came upon me, however, but a chilled perturbation of spirit, dank and menacing as the clasp of an invisible demon who takes you in his cold clasp at the mid-hour of night.

I had not survived so many perils to succumb to intangible fear, however menacing. Above me arched the cliff, curving over at its crest like a green breaker of the sea. At its foot lay a small shape, dark and square, which I discovered on approaching to be a great brownish-red stone set in the turf. Reaching to the level of my chest, it was penetrated through the middle by a narrow orifice. The grass for a space around was cropped close in a circle, like those which the people of the Mother's Blessing leave at the place of their dancing.

As I stood marveling at the meaning of this lone rock, I marked how beside it there was set firm in the ground a peeled yew stave, and that upon that yew stave were inscribed runes. Fortunate it was that there is none more skilled at rune-reading in the Island of Prydein with its Three Adjacent Islands than I, Merlin mab Morfryn. Not for naught did my mother Ceridwen gather herbs of the earth on certain days and hours within her Cauldron, boiling them day and night for a year and a day, and from three drops of their distillation did I receive understanding at my birth.

Thus I read the rune-writing upon the yew:

"Into the net the hunter drives his prey, and in its entanglement lies the path of death. Straight is the spear-shaft and bent the bow, and which is the way? By Caer Gwydion lies the ascent to the Bear, and all about the Head of Bran. By fire and by water is the blade tempered; take care lest you pass the House of Gofannon, and take care lest you linger long, O Black Frenzied One!"

I smiled as I read the words. Not readily would I permit myself to be outwitted in matters of magic and lore of enchantments! Hopping upon one foot, closing one eye, and using but one hand, I entered the precinct and inscribed upon the reverse of the yew stave these runes:

"What does my rune say, ascending by seven and by seven up the glen? The witch-wife culled cresses by the brook secretly; the head of the herring was in the slender tail of the speckled salmon, and the salmon's tooth in the tusk of the boar."

Then I placed my lips to the socket of the hole in the stone, and sounded a deep-roaring note that moaned away over the valley, dying within the woods and hanging faint about the hollow places of the hills. At once there came an answering clap of thunder, on the heels of which I seemed to hear in the gray sky above me a yelping of hounds, rattle of hoofbeats, and braying of horns, as though a hunt were passing overhead. For a moment alarm gripped me, as my recent narrow escape in the vale surged back into my mind, but the careering confusion of sounds swiftly died away. Nothing was left now, save the bare steep incline and the gusting of errant winds which plucked angrily at my flapping boar's hide jerkin.

Without more ado (perhaps I feared lest my resolution might dwindle unless I acted swiftly), I began my ascent of that great grass rampart which encircles the forbidden land of Loiger, the Plain of Bran mab Iweryd. So steep was it that its summit appeared looming over me, and barely could I maintain my hold as I scrambled slowly upward. The grassy face of the escarpment was cropped close by wild goats, one of whom stared curiously at me as I ascended upon my painful way. As if angered by my impudent violation of the great sanctuary, a gale uprose from the north and flung itself frenziedly upon me, howling in my ears and plucking fiercely at my cloak.

After scrambling upward for some time in this fashion, I made my way around to the lee of one of the sloping green buttresses that projected some way up the declivity. There I crouched, regaining my breath and wrapping my protective hide more securely about me. Below me stretched far into the cloudy distance the level vale, its expanse so remote from my precarious perch that it was impossible to distinguish the scenes of my recent adventures. A great belt of wood and water separating the hills from the kingdoms of the Brython far to the north, it was void of human habitation, save where once or twice a thin plume of smoke betrayed the spot where an isolated settlement of the barbarian Iwys lay hid amid the marshes. Far, far was I from the hospitable mead-halls of the kings of the Cymry, and now I was bound for a land more remotely cold by far than any I had yet encountered!

Squally rain clouds were ranging in a ragged curtain southward across the watery plain; while above me a belt of fog hung heavy upon the ridge like a druids' hedge, blotting out the sky and, I doubt not, warning me to desist from further rash ascent. Squatting for one brief moment of gathering resolution, I glanced to my right to where the cavorting wind gusted in confusion within a steep valley cut in the slope. As I looked, the mist broke and I glimpsed the wonder of which druids, wise ones, speak to initiates.

Galloping upon the hillside, legs spread in easy stride and head stretched ardently forward, was a majestic pale-white mare. Riderless and free she ran, ascending the hill above us in effortless grace. And yet, though her stride was greater than hills and valleys, and her long loose limbs bounded swifter than eagles, it seemed to me that her pace brought her neither nearer to me nor farther. Drawn by her lissome beauty and effortless power, I resumed my upward scramble. Yet, drew I nearer or drew I farther, she appeared ever the same distance from me.

Then I saw how the rampart to which I clung like a fly upon the flank of a cauldron, together with all the lost land of Loiger within it, revolved slow and steady as a mill wheel. Giddily I clung to the rim of that great wheel, fearful lest any moment I might be spun from its surface out into the dizzying abyss. At times I might do no more than rest my weary head against the wet grass, slippery as a slug's belly, and pray for strength to climb but a little more before I perished. The mist closed thick about me, drenching me with a soft rain, so that I knew not where my precarious perch held me.

Then it broke again briefly, to reveal the giant white mare racing close beside me. I felt the warm breath of her nostrils upon my dripping side, and it was a warmth that comforted my crushed spirit. Now I knew her for Riannon, the Great Queen, mother of the Fair Folk. From the great elf-mound she came, daughter of Hyfeidd Hen, and faster than any horse did she run beneath the sun in the racing at the festival of Kalan Mai.

But then at the time of the Kalan Gaeaf, when summer had passed, under concealment of rain and cold and darkness came ravaging the Hosts of Annufn, who stole her darling babe and bore him deep down into the endless night of the Underworld. Pryderi was he named from the anxiety, *pryder,* which his mother felt for him without ceasing. Weeping wildly she sought him throughout the land, upon which there descended for a space a thick heavy mist. And when the mist lifted, men saw that where previously there had been flocks and cattle and lofty halls, there was now neither bird nor beast, smoke nor fire, house nor hall. In their place was only desert and wasteland, fit for neither men nor cattle, and only ruined habitations to be seen, desolate, deserted, destitute of comfort or protection.

For seven years the cold Oppression lay upon the land, until the enchantments of the Wicked One were thwarted by Manawydan mab Lir, by seven and seven, by three and by three. Then was Riannon's golden child liberated from the dark chasm, the sun shone gloriously again upon every hill and hollow, and fields and forests became once more clothed in richest green. And it is at every Kalan Mai that men and maidens relive that joyous restitution.

So it is that Riannon rides in unceasing gallop about the rim of the seven cantrefs of the Wasteland of Loiger, and men gaze up in wonder from the vale upon the lithe-limbed apparition coursing between earth and sky upon the southern horizon. By the warmth of her breath and the song of her birds I knew her to be a protection about me. The gale abated for a space, enabling me to gain the rim of the cliff and fling myself down upon the summit beyond.

It was exhaustion that felled me a few paces from the precipice, and well it was for me that it happened so. For over the empty plateau came howling the winds of the world, shrieking and raging as if fresh from their unleashing within the Cave of Chwith Gwynt. Down upon me they tore, in anger and envenomed weeping, purposing as I guessed to hurl me back over the cliff. The sow's mask was whipped from my head and my hair streamed out in sodden elflocks.

With no time to lose, I arose and darted for the safety of a deep trench I saw before me. It proved to be the great ditch of a mighty fortress, long abandoned by a forgotten race of kings when all the land around was blighted by the filthy enchantments of Lwyd mab Cilcoed.

> Where lies today a ruin cold
> Once feasted mighty kings of old.

Crouching low, I encircled the earthwork's protective serpentine coiling and sprang out onto a great highway that passed hard by. Beyond I caught a glimpse through the driving rain of a bare, tempest-torn, blighted wilderness, stretching as it appeared deep into the hinterland.

The road upon which I stood, or rather crouched, passed east and west, skirting the ridge I had but now ascended. Not far off upon my right I saw that it was sheltered by low leaning trees, where the way dipped through a hollow. Gathering my thick hide about me (without it I should certainly have perished of cold), I ran as best I could down the road, until beneath the anguished rattle of battered branches I found the brief respite I sought.

Safe at last from the worst of the wind, I beat my arms about me and tried to recall the nature of my mission, which the squalling turmoil of the rainstorm had all but driven from my mind. Then I recalled that out there, somewhere to the westward beyond that darkening sky, the host of the Cymry must likewise be entering the lost land of Loiger. Only now did I appreciate in full the danger to which the fortunes of the Island of the Mighty were now exposed. We were entering the gates of Uffern, and I brought to mind that yawning black hole which once I glimpsed (or will one day glimpse) at the foot of the rugged coast of Prydyn, northernmost bound of the earth.

Tracing a circle in the mud around me, I closed my eyes and invoked with this *englyn* the protection of generous Riannon, that she might inspire the hearts of King Maelgun's bodyguard with courage and their steeds with strength and speed:

> "If your lord has ascended the rampart of Iweryd,
> Ah! war-band, seek not safety in flight;
> Earning mead, avoid a coward's plight!"

For a while I remained with eyes tightly shut, listening to the swish of the wind in the thornbush over my head, and the heavy drumming of rain upon great puddles spanning the road. It seemed to me that I heard the hosts of Prydein riding southward from Caer Ceri upon the long straight road which leads to the desolate uplands of Iweryd. And all in a moment I recalled the ominous words of Gwyn mab Nud, at the time when he visited the hall of Gwydno Garanhir on Kalan Gaeaf:

> "I saw Iweryd, where fell
> His son Bran, whose fame men tell;
> Ravens croak on him as well!"

As I murmured the verse reflectively to myself, pondering over its meaning, I heard a low, cold voice within a thornbush utter the words:

> "Dogs of Gwern, beware Morddwyd Tyllion!"

Startled, I sprang up and saw to my surprise that, though the chill wind still shrieked overhead and gusted about the sunken trackway, the fog formerly hemming me in had been dispelled. The stars glittered hard and bright in a velvet-black sky, those set in the sword of the Hunter burning more fiercely even than during the southward march of the hosts of Prydein. A waxing moon shed its unearthly light wan upon the upland expanse and glimmered in the puddled path, whose dappled luster stretched before me.

At once my eye was drawn to another ruddier light glowing within a copse of tall trees to the right of the road. Fierce as a beacon fire it burned, though it lacked the leaping flames. And as I wondered at this solitary blaze amid the water and the wind of the empty waste, I saw an eructation of sparks fly out, followed by a pealing clangor like that of a monastery bell in a woodland glade. Remote and desolate as it was, this was just the spot for some devout hermit to have sought out as his refuge. I recalled the ascending plume of smoke I had espied from my Pillar-stone that morning, and it came into my mind that Gwendyd had guided my steps in this direction.

Elated at the thought, I advanced lightly along the miry lane, until I came to where a lateral track led to a grove of tall trees hard by. Now I saw the fire clearly; it blazed beside the linteled doorway of a house that stood beyond. The ruddy glow played upon the broad trunks of the nearest trees, putting me in mind of the comfort of a royal hearth illumining its master's hall pillars. The clangor which I took to be the clapper of a great bell rang ever more clamorous in my ears as I approached. But then, as I drew close enough to feel the welcome warmth of the blaze upon my bruised and chilled body, it fell abruptly silent, its echoes merging with the murmur of leaves high above and dwindling to the furthest chambers of my brain.

As the tolling ceased, I sensed a human presence. Someone was observing my approach, of that I was certain. The bright fire dazzled my eyes, so that all behind appeared black as a peat bog, while I knew myself to be clearly illumined against the night behind me. There was more of hope than fear in my expectancy, however, as I drew nearer still. After my long immersion in the river, my frenzied flight across the ground that followed, and my aery ascent of the cliff-face, I longed for a hospitable hearth. Any confrontation with a fellow-being would be preferable to further abandonment among the elements, where the distant light of my beloved Gwendyd provided the sole guiding beacon for the friendless, battered wanderer.

When visiting a stranger's abode it is wise to allow him the first greeting. Accordingly I came and stood silent by the hearth, extending my open hands toward it for warmth—and also to convey to my unseen watcher that I bore no weapon. The fire was of glowing charcoal held in a furnace of clay, and hard by stood an anvil of iron. This did not surprise me, for a man in holy orders may be a smith, and in such an outlandish spot as this might be expected to ply many a trade.

As I reflected thus in the ruddy glare of the forge, I heard a laugh from the darkness above me, and a deep voice which startled me greatly:

"Welcome to my hearthside, son of Morfryn!"

I peered into the darkness, and my eyes, becoming gradually accustomed to the firelight, made out the form of a huge man who stood by the anvil. He wore but a leathern apron, fastened over his right shoulder, and bore in the one hand a great hammer and in the other a lengthy pair of tongs. His arms were bare, and not puny was the might of muscle and sinew they displayed. There was a thick curling beard upon his chin, and shaggy eyebrows overhung his piercing eyes like the turf eaves of the smithy behind him. I saw I had reason to fear his power and strength, yet the glance he gave me was not an ill one.

"Who are you, O smith, who knows the name of the unexpected and uninvited guest?" I inquired boldly.

"Uninvited maybe, but not unexpected," replied the smith with a mocking smile. "I have been awaiting thee, my Merlin, for this many and many a year, and now is come the time for me to provide a welcome for the wanderer of the Island of the Mighty."

"Since you know my name, O smith, then may I ask yours?" I ventured, my courage returning as the blood coursed once more warm within my body's veins. "What do men call this place, and what is it that you are fashioning there?"

I saw there was somewhat which gleamed upon his anvil, and which even now he took between his tongs and tapped with delicate rhythm for a brief moment.

"Ah, so there is knowledge which evades even the vaunted wisdom of Merlin, I see!" answered the giant with a chuckle. Pointing to where a great grass-grown mound heaved up behind him from the hillside, its stone-portaled entrance framing a rectangle of night, he intoned derisively: "It may be that report has reached you, O wise one, of the Graves of Gwanas? If so, you may gaze upon one of their number:

> "Long graves on Gwanas, earthly wonder;
> Despoiled in vain by robbers' blunder;
> Not safe such sanctuary for plunder!"

The sarcasm irritated me, and relying on my doubly privileged position as poet and guest, I continued abruptly:

> "Oeth's war-band and Anoeth's in vain
> Sought man and servant to obtain;
> You seek them now? Dig Gwanas' plain!"

The smith chuckled and resumed his task. For a while there was heard only the metallic tapping of his hammer and a sighing in the branches high above us. In the silence that followed I heard a lone wolf's howl in the darkness at my back. Eventually the smith paused and turned again to me.

"Well, little man," he said, "I see you are glib with your verse-capping! It may be that I will invite you one day to sing before the banquet when I hold my feasting; it is no liquor for maids which I provide. Meanwhile, you may feel inclined to explain the purpose of your visit, which confers such honor upon my poor smithy?"

With which he laughed loud and deep, striking the unformed iron upon his anvil such a blow that white-hot sparks sprayed forth from each side of the hammer's head.

"If your mead be strong," I rejoined with spirit, "not feeble either is my verse, nor unworthy of a winter's guerdon at the courts of kings as great as you, O smith of the sky!" For the shadowy form of the wright was silhouetted against the night, blotting out a shape of stars above him.

"Tell me more then, little man. It may be you will find me also not unskilled in arts and enchantments, and that I may match riddle for riddle!"

"Very well," I replied, my courage comforted by the furnace's fires, though for all the giant's geniality I was not altogether easy in his company, solitary as we stood upon the dark and windswept hillside. There was no turning back now, and boldness must be my friend.

"I have heard of the fame of your distilling, and that none is known to leave your board without his breath stinking of good ale or mead. I have heard much, O smith of the sky, for I am old and I am young. I am Gwion Bach, and I have drunk three drops from the Cauldron of Ceridwen. The chips of metal from which you fashion that weapon, were they not gathered from the faeces of your chickens? And was not I once a grain of corn within a hen's belly? I have been in Caer Oeth and Anoeth; I have seen the mouth of measureless freezing Uffern, and I know who wrought the starry firmament. Is not this dwelling before which we stand Caer Gofannon?"

The giant bestowed a quizzical look upon me from beneath his arched eyebrows.

"Before, or below, manikin? Not within this bare barrow can you contain the spangled ceiling of Gofannon's fortress, with its soaring rooftree, its lofty columns at its four corners, and its mighty moat of encircling waters. Try again, my little elfkin!"

"Very well. What say you to this? Was I not there with Math and Gwydion when you raised the roof upon your courthouse? More than most men have I seen. I plucked my harp before Lleon Llychllyn, and was in Gwynfryn at the court of Cynfelyn. Three beasts were born at my birth, and know you of what quality is my flesh: fish is it, or meat, or aery inspiration of the *awen*?"

"Not bad, not bad," grunted the giant, ceasing from his toil and leaning upon the haft of his hammer. "Not bad are you at the boasting, my poor mouse. Now, though night and day are all eternity, not eternal is *this* night. Is it permitted for me to learn at last the purpose of your visit?"

I replied with two testing *englynion*, for I knew full well that my merits were being proved as surely as is the iron, when the smith heats his bloom white-hot within the forge until the slag starts to drip forth.

"Elffin took me home to test my bardic lore,
First above a leader lying on the shore:
The bed of radiant Rufawn, now no more.

Elffin took me home to test my bardic lore,
First above a leader lying on the shore:
The bed of little Rufawn, cradled sure."

"Not hard to answer!" scoffed the smith. "Such riddling speech might bemuse buffoons at my banquet, O Merlin mab Morfryn, wise one, druid!—but it is child's play to such as me. Was not Prince Rufawn the infant son of Gwydno Garanhir, a child of promise whose sepulture is set upon the seashore in Cantre'r Gwaelod as a defense, lest one day the hosts of Manawydan mab Lir engulph King Gwydno's realm? Do you think I know naught of what passes in the North, little fellow? Not for nothing do they call you Merlin *Wyllt,* 'the Mad'; it seems to me you lack the brains even of Gwaedan the Half-witted, daughter of Cynfelyn Ceudod!"

"I see you are too shrewd for my humble talents to master," I confessed. "Still, a mouse may warm itself beside a king's hearth. How foolish a creature I am. Why, will you believe that my next question concerned the watch which Gurthefir the Blessed keeps upon the coast of Cent, lest the oppression of Hengys return to the Island of the Mighty? It was in my mind to inquire which port it is in which he stands ward? How foolish was my thought, for surely you know the answer already!"

The smith guffawed good-naturedly, though behind it all I detected a growing menace.

"Foolish indeed, my child—and as a child's cries when sporting beside the heavy roaring of the ocean is your lore to that of the wright of the world. Not in one port does dead Gurthefir repose, for his bones were concealed in every haven that stands upon the coasts of Prydein. It is in my mind that you had best depart before you come to mischief, manikin! I have a task before me which is not to be hindered by such as you. Away with you!"

I turned as if to go, and then said, "There is truth in what you say, O smith. A child upon the sea strand places a shell to his ear, and fancies he holds in his weak grasp the immensity of Ocean. For true understanding, we who profess the arts must raise our gaze from laborious study of books compiled by *llyfyrion* of old, who it may be knew no more than we."

I paused, watching the giant take up his tongs, shaking his head as if to drive my meddling intrusion from his mind. Then I added calmly (though trembling within, despite the heat of the glowing charcoal), "For within the waves do we not hear the weeping of Dylan Eil Ton, their serried ranks breaking battle twice each day upon the coasts of Prydein, seeking to avenge his murder? Is that not a sigh of the deep, where wisdom's hoard lies garnered?"

There followed a pause so long, it seemed to me that in it I lived for a year and a day in Caer Gofannon. The trees moaned as their branches slid one upon another, the sky wept cold drops, and the moonlit glade about the forge became troubled by a rising mist. All the land lay still, so still that I fancied I had the hearing of Clust mab Clustfeinad, who could hear an ant stirring in its hill fifty miles off even though he were buried seven fathoms deep in earth. For an age of ages the giant stood poised tongs in hand and head bowed, immobile as an enchanted statue. The fire splattered and hissed with the rain-drops, but he heeded neither that nor me. Were it not for my peril, and still more that of the hosts of the Cymry, I could have pitied him his pain and wished to have spared him.

At length he gave an anguished groan, so deep and terrible that it was heard blown about rocks upon the accursed Ridge of Esgeir Oerfel in Ywerdon, and turned his head to cast upon me a look of deepest reproach.

"I see you are not so foolish as I held you, Merlin; though it may be you are wiser than is good for your safety. So you know me, and all my story?"

"Not all, for who knows that? But I know you for Gofannon mab Don, and I know also who slew your nephew Dylan Eil Ton. Was not that one of the Three Wretched Blows of the Island of Prydein?"

Gofannon swayed like the great beeches arching above him, and sighed like the night wind in their branches.

"If you know that, then you should know also that it was not willingly that I encompassed his death. After he was baptized with the three drops of water, he partook of the sea's nature, swimming as readily as the most agile fish that plunges within its depths. No wave ever broke under him, but it was I who broke his back with a cast of my spear. It was an evil deed, yet until I violated the darkness and freed myself from the formlessness of the void, in no wise might I accomplish the task assigned me. And it is that which you see about you, the glory of my mother Don and the company of the gods, which I think you will confess is no small feat.

"It was not a deed I wished to perform, but there was a *tynged* upon me which I might not disobey. When men construct a fortress, do they not lay the body of a slaughtered child beneath its wall as a security? And what earthly fortress may compare with the handiwork of Gofannon mab Don?"

I shivered at the allusion, which I had more than one reason for misliking. But the skilled wright, master of magical crafts, was too deeply troubled to attend to my small concerns. His look was dark and angry as he conceded gruffly, "It may be you have mastered me for a moment, O Frenzied Black One. Dwarfish folk have ever possessed keen eyes and sharp wits. Tell me swiftly, what is it you wish of me?"

I felt a surge of joy, great as the ninth wave breaking upon a strand, and turned back to the forge.

"I seek the knowledge which will enable me to place protection upon the hosting of Maelgun Gwynedd, ensuring that he prevail over the oppression that lies upon the land. I know well enough the pain and danger that await me; but my heart goes with the princes, and I fear lest they ride unwitting toward the gates of Uffern, falling into the taloned clutch of the Pitch-black Witch, daughter of the Bright-white Witch."

For answer the smith took a strip of glowing metal from the furnace, placed it upon his anvil, and began striking sharply with his great hammer. I knew I must be patient to achieve my end, and waited until his angry rush of energy was spent.

"Do you see what it is that I am forging here?" he asked. "These are the fragments of Arthur's sword, Caledvulch, which was shattered upon the helm of the traitor Medraud at the field of Camlann. They must be forged and reforged, folded and beaten, time and again, until I have wrought a restitution of the sword of Arthur. Twice the length of a man's forearm from ridge to edge will it be, bringing blood from the breeze, swifter in its slashing than the flash of dewdrops when the dews of Mehevin are at their wettest."

Three great blows and seven lesser taps in succession did the smith rain down upon the white-hot metal, until it began to cool and he paused again. The blade glimmered like summer lightning, and the furnace hard by growled as though distant thunder were rolling in the hills.

"Never was there, or is there, or will there be such a sword in the Island of the Mighty, from its peopling by Prydein son of Aed the Great until the destruction of all things by fire and by water. Its first forging was at the hands of dwarves, dwelling beyond the vast black whirlpools of the strong-maned sea raging about Penrin Blathaon in the north. For seven years they toiled beneath the great stone which bears their name, even upon the Island of Orc, until they had forged the sword Caledvulch, brighter and cleaner and fiercer than any lightning bolt launched by the hand of Mabon mab Mellt.

"They say the sword spoke after its final forging, and the words it spoke are those incised in runes upon its blade. It has many qualities, not the least of which is that it will when unsheathed set forth the deeds of its possessor. None may escape its blow if once it be drawn from its deadly sheath, none may resist it, and when it goes forth it will slay a circle before it be sheathed once more. And the tribute it desired was that it be burnished by the best sword-burnisher in the world."

With seven taps drummed the hammer of the smith, and triple heavy blows that followed. I saw the blade's temper grow, with ninescore fiercenesses, and marveled at its beauty, which was that of a maid at her first flowering; and its strength, which was that of an ox at its plowing; and its vigor, which was that of a fleet steed at the racing of Kalan Mai. Not another sword like that enchanted weapon would I ever see, and I felt drawn to it as I was to my sister Gwendyd that first night of our encountering.

The smith laughed harshly. "Not for you, O Merlin, not at this time, is the sword Caledvulch—great though your arts and enchantments may be! The sword knows to whom it belongs, and like myself it will serve only a true king, upon whom is the *gwir deyrnas*, the Truth of the Land."

"I know that, son of Don," I conceded. "Until the slaughter of Camlann it was Arthur's. For whom will be its next unsheathing?"

"Do you not know, Merlin the Wise?" grunted the giant as he plied his hammer afresh. "Is there then some small thing that is beyond the boundaries even of your omniscience? Strange it is to me to hear that!"

"You are pleased to mock me!" I retorted angrily. "Much I know, and much I do not know, and whether you know aught is what I know not at all. You who forge the sword would do well to know for whom it is intended."

For answer, Gofannon took the burning blade between his tongs and limped across to place it within a cauldron of cold water beside the forge, where it hissed and frothed furious as a scotched serpent. Darting a suspicious look in my direction, he remarked sardonically, "It is children who put questions whose answers they know well, my wise friend. Who was it stood by when night fell upon the bloodstained field of Camlann, hearkening to the words of Arthur in his death agony? Was it not thus the king spoke:

'With my piercing spear and the good sword Caledvulch have I fought a hardy fight. Prydein! I have received my death blow; but this I say now as my lifeblood flows forth back into your soil: Lay by and preserve this sword, until there shall come a Dragon out of the wave-washed West who shall be a fitting lord for you. And his name shall be my name, even that of the Bear of Prydein.'

"So spoke the king, before he departed to a bourne, which it may be another here knows as well as I."

My heart misgave me at these words, for there was but one Arthur among the princes of Prydein in that age, and that was the child of Pedr, grandson of gray-haired Gurthefir of sea-girt Dyfed. He was but a babe at home in Arberth. Were it for him that the sword was destined, then what would be the fate of Maelgun the Tall and the men of Prydein at their summer's hosting? The blade of Caledvulch was a protection, *naut,* upon the Island of the Mighty. Were we fated to suffer the Oppression of the Iwys until Arthur mab Pedr was of age to wield it?

While the submerged blade of Caledvulch whispered sibilant its secrets within the water, lame Gofannon prised another length of white-hot metal from his furnace and set it upon the anvil. It was smaller than its brother, and yet it, too, bore marks of enchantment.

"What is that weapon, O Gofannon, and what *tynged* does it bear with it?" I inquired.

"Not difficult to say, Merlin," replied the other. "What should it be but the spear Rongomiant, which likewise was Arthur's? No battle was ever sustained against it, and no victory over the man who grasped it in his hand. Many are its qualities, and not the least is that it preserves a man from the enchantment of sleep, were the Birds of Riannon to be singing about him. Is it you that desires possession of this weapon, son of Morfryn—my fatherless friend?"

I shivered, for a reason that I knew and knew not, and said nothing as the giant continued:

"Not the dwarves of Orc was it who forged Rongomiant, but I myself, the son of Don, toiling for a year and a day, and without making any of it save upon the fortunate days of the fortunate months. I fitted the shaft to the blade with three chippings, and made the three rivets with three strokes, driving them home with three throws. Yet the wonder is that the head of the spear comes off its shaft, drawing blood from the wind, and returns again to its shaft.

"Whether its quality is a blessing or a malediction I cannot say. People are made, remade, and made anew. Brilliant is His name, strong His hand, and with lightning He governs the hosts. Though

tamed and bound on high, men scatter before Him like the sparks I
strike here upon this molten metal. A dreadful day is dawning, my
Merlin, when this spear will speed upon its destined path once more.

"Seven years and seven and three is the duration of my task. Each
year will I take the iron from the earth, blowing with my bellows
upon the fires beneath, separating the elements, bloom from slag. In fire
and water will the steel be tempered, and with clanging blows here
upon this windy hill will I forge the spear."

"And what is to be my role in this?" I cried in an anguished voice,
words snatched forth by a gust of the night breeze; for the smith's
words were couched in mystery, and I saw that he wished to end our
converse and return to his arduous task. "How shall I know when the
times be come?"

"Time runs out, little man," grunted Gofannon, shifting the blade
upon the anvil's head and reaching for a greater hammer that lay near to
hand. "I must be about my task. You will know well enough when
time has come again. The sword will be a sign which not only you,
but all men, will recognize when it is displayed. As for the spear, once
it leaves the unerring hand that casts it, then neither you nor any man
may stay its flight. For that is a *tynged* beyond the gods' controlling. Do
you not recall the rhyme Taliesin related upon Mellun Mountain:

" 'For the strife of Arderid provides the cause
From their lives' preparing to the last of wars'?

"However, for you alone will I provide a sign. Upon the spear-
shaft I shall place silver bands and rings of gold, and when the day of
strife be come it may be you will see the silver bands rotate about the
golden rings. And much good may it do you to know when ill times
are to hand, lacking the power to stay them!"

"I am not so foolish as to believe it possible for any man to evade
his *tynged*," I cried, "but this much surely you may tell me: I it was that
played at the *gwyddbwyll* with Gwyn mab Nud in the king's chamber
at Caer Gurygon, and I saw that the fiend played me false. There was a
misplaced piece upon the board, and a move made contrary to the right
ordering of the game. That is an infringement of the *gwir deyrnas*, a
violation of the truth of the land. Am I not entitled to guidance?"

The smith frowned in evident anger.

"Gwyn mab Nud was ever a meddler and mocker! Not for
nothing was my toil in constructing the board of Ysbidinongyl, checkered in silver and in gold, with its pieces of silver and gold. Not
crooked is the work of the craftsman, and the game must be ordered

aright. What will happen at the end, when the glittering hosts ride to the slaughter of Arderid and the Cad Godeu, is not now to be known. But until that dread day the pattern must be preserved and the laws obeyed. Impatient is the Lord of the Wild Hunt to claim his own, but he must bide his time. Come with me, my Frenzied Black One!"

Beyond the turf-roofed smithy lay the doorway I had glimpsed at my arrival. It was set at the mouth of a huge earthen mound, and on either side of the entrance were set upright four towering stones, whose puckered surfaces glimmered pale in the moonlight. That by the right-hand gatepost of the doorway thrust itself upward from the ground sharp and angular, as if in mimicry of the spear of Gofannon; while that upon its left squatted rounded, globular, ovoid. It was upon the left-hand boulder that the moonlight played with especial gleam, throwing into relief its swelling protuberances and darkening its hidden recesses.

As my eye lighted upon the boulder, I saw how all things were merged beneath the moon into a silvered harmony. By daylight we see a riot of color and movement, minds in turmoil, dogs barking, birds singing, seasons changing. Now here beneath the moon all was still and blended together into a bluish haze, a single silvery hue which pervaded the whole landscape, laying it as it were under an enchantment of pacific unity. The colors remain, but we see them not: only the still luminosity. So it is with men of learning, *llyfyrion*. Let them scan where they will, if they lack the inspiration of the *awen,* they see but the pallid outward form of matter; its beauty and essence remain forever hidden from them.

Beneath the golden glory of the sun there is a warmth and vigor that intoxicates, leading men to thoughts of hostings, cattle raids and sieges; feastings, voyages and adventures; wooings, abductions and elopements. There is a time for such things, but who does not feel at the evening's end the need for a sinking back into voluptuous softness, repose upon cushions of down? It is as golden figures glittering upon the *gwyddbwyll* board that the king and his protective pieces must make their moves; but the board which was there before the game began, and which remains at its ending, is of a single shimmering silver sheen.

Now the moon stood naked in the heavens, and below us upon the broad vale hung a wide ocean of mist, a sea of stillness upon which my spirit floated in placid content. All lay spread bare and open about me: silvered trees and grass, sleeping creatures furred snug within warm burrows, shapes soft and scarcely stirring in their sleep.

Gofannon stood, his mighty arms folded upon his leathern apron, beside the entrance to the Underworld. His parting words were of a keeping with the sardonic disdain he had vouchsafed throughout our conversation:

"May a fruitful journey be yours, manikin! Bear my greetings to the barrow-ghosts, ranked seven and seven; you will discover whether they be sleeping or waking!"

Then I stooped and entered that narrow, black, dark little house. I found myself within a low passage lined with cold flagstones. By the wan light of the moon which followed my path, I could see that twin doorways lay upon my right hand and my left. It was the right-hand door I entered, creeping into a little stone chamber, scarcely larger than the burrow of a badger. Very weary after my day's exertions, I lay upon the floor of beaten earth and composed my mind to contemplation.

It was a little while before my exhaustion and perturbation departed, as the events of that momentous day faded beneath the soothing serenity of the moon's majesty. I was lying upon my side, my gaze fixed upon the rock-face for strength of concentration. An aperture above my head admitted a clear shaft of moonlight, whose light glistered silver along the strands of a spider's web hanging on the wall beside me.

I have always been fascinated by the work of the eight-legged wright, spinning from within his own belly his perfect piece of spangled network. At its center he hovers, roads dry and straight as those of Rufein radiating from him, intersected by encircling viscid reticulations which are dykes dug for unwary invaders. Secure is his stronghold as the triple-fossed hilltop fortress of a king in Prydein. And yet, upon a warm morning breeze, how often have I seen him and his fellows, their delicate palaces shimmering like shards of gossamer, floating free in aery grace above the waving grasses of a summer meadow?

I watched, momentarily entranced by contemplation of the spider's microcosmic realm, as a gleaming bead of moisture slid slowly down one of the spokes of the wheel. Then, while I wondered how the king at the center would react to this intrusion upon his board, I noticed that the web upon the rock-face formed a light palimpsest reflecting a darker, hidden spiral within the shadows beyond. Traced upon the stone face was a carved coiled labyrinth, entwining the contour of a natural protuberance upon the rock.

Adjusting the focus of my gaze from the spider's silvered filigree, I turned my mind to contemplation of the spiral set within the rock behind. It soothed my mind strangely to pursue the course of its serpentine coiling, tending ever inward until my eye lighted upon the heart of the vortex. There was a strange, sinister restfulness about the process, as if all power and agony of will were seeped from me, and I sucked willy-nilly into the apex, like a coracle spinning down into the Whirlpool of Pull Ceris which lies between Arfon and Mon.

There was, I saw, a spread of lichen upon the left-hand side, the north, from which oozed a trickle of reddish-colored water. I watched fascinated as the insidious stream passed along the barely perceptible ridges of the spiral, seeping through the greenish growth, until it reached some small irregularity in the stone's surface, from which it dripped red in measured pauses upon the ground at my side.

I glimpsed before me a mystery. Above lay stretched the angled regularity of the spider's skilled craftsmanship; below, a half-hidden encircled writhing, chiseled out it may be by dwarves in some forgotten age. The drop of water upon the web entranced me too. For what is that tiny globule but the wide world itself, which to an attentive eye reveals itself imprisoned within the convexity of the silvered surface? There it hung, poised as though in indecision, while behind it in the murk welled up a darker drop from within the stony sinuosity: oozed blood from a freshly incised wound.

Now I was troubled, and where previously I had found comfort and repose in entering this womb of the earth, I was now exercised by an agitated seeking after knowledge. Far from me still was that return to rest for which my suffering spirit longed with much of its being. Twelve tasks had been assigned me at my birth, twelve treasures and a greater had I to seek, and twelve houses in the heavens must I tread before it would be my lot to sink once more into that blessed boundless ocean, where once the wise Salmon of Lyn Liw had been my guide.

> There are monsters who creep upon land,
> And sea-beasts that lurk in the deep;
> And the child that once lay on the strand
> Shall slay him who slaughters in sleep.

There was a wrong to be righted, and an ugly pit dug within whose hollowed jaws were sharpened stakes set to impale the unwary. But who was the predator, whose the prey, and where the place of concealment? My thoughts ran riotous and confused, until all of a sudden within me I heard a quiet voice utter as if from the depths:

"Dogs of Gwern, beware Morddwyd Tyllion!"

I knew those sweet and gentle tones, as who should not? I was no longer alone: there was one with me whose love was an enchantment strong as the serried spears of an envious war-band, linked to me close as a king to the land of his rule. High in the heavens above, shining down through the ragged entrance of my world-cave, sailed serene the Evening Star. Pure and pale was the shaft of light through which her essence poured, conjoined with mine, and purer yet and paler still were the white limbs and slender flanks of my Gwendyd as she came together with me in the cavern of the night.

Brown as the waters of a warm woodland pool were her smiling eyes, and laughing the dimple in her rounded cheek. She was not drowned in Ocean's depths, but born anew for me. And then as she slipped beside me upon the boar-skin rug, I felt warm as if by a fireside; rosy she grew, round-bosomed, placing her protective arms about me, kissing and murmuring within the spiral of my ear.

"Ah, Merlin, did you think that I would fail you, when now you have most need of me?" she whispered, taking my head between her hands and gazing smiling at my startled face. "I know—you need not tell me—you fear the one who slithers in treacherous insolence, the flesh-worm who saps your strength and seeks to destroy the kingdom. Am I not right?"

"Ah, Gwendyd," I replied, half choked with love, and finding every fractured thought focused upon the one alone who guides and comforts me upon my lonely course, a lantern burning before a mead-hall gateway. "Gwendyd, my love, who brought you here, and what am I to do? My burden is too heavy for me. May we not leave this place together and find a home far from strife and struggle? I know what is my allotted task—you have no need to remind me. But why is it my doom to tread this barren track alone? Is this weak world worth the sacrifice?"

For answer Gwendyd clasped and kissed me long and lovingly, until I forgot my feebleness and took her gently to me. How long we lay and loved together I cannot tell, for time was not within our cave. Surge after surge of passion passed over us, rolling through the aeons, until at the ninth breaker there swept over us the flow of the tide in his dragon's strength, golden and glorious; to be followed by the shattered wave's effortlessly extended sweep across the level sand, down into which it sank at last. Love's languor, stillness, peace, and calm of eternity stole upon us where we lay.

How long we clung enmeshed within each other, whispering together in the darkness, I cannot tell. Along the stone passageway stole sounds of the smith at his work: the sonorous heaving of his bellows, the sobbing moan of its wind's breathing, the rise and heavy fall of his mighty hammer, the shrill responsive clamor of the anvil, the deep regenerating roar of his raging furnace, in its heart the molten slag heaving, writhing, and spilling.

From the earth it is the smith's task to take lumps of unformed rust-red ore, where in fear of fire it secretes itself. Into the fiery recess he plunges and withdraws it, vigorously plying his bolt-headed weapon where it lies receptive upon the yielding anvil. In this manner he fashions from inspiration of his *awen* those blades which, forged in fire and tempered in water, form flashing spears which poets justly term "the wings of dawn."

On wings of dawn were I and my Gwendyd met, and to my broken body and misprised mind came healing and a fierce clarity of vision. Mind to mind were we conjoined, and there was no need of speech when it was as one we thought. Ever faster beat my heart, its palpitating rhythm echoing the drumming throb of the smith's hammer. Once more into my mind there floated in cadence the chill words of the Washer at the Ford:

"Dogs of Gwern, beware of Morddwyd Tyllion!"

At that did Gwendyd's brown eyes look deep in mine as, laughing lightly, she took my hands in hers and laid my fingertips upon her smiling lips. No word did she utter, but my heart leaped high within me. Outside in the rain I was but a lone broken fugitive clinging to the rampart of Iweryd, the mock and prey of beasts and men, neither man nor beast myself. But here, within the barrow's womb, under protection of lovely Gwendyd of the red-gold hair, what secret might I not master? Our cave was become a hollow of the night, its dripping roof the rainy dome of heaven, about it the obscurity of darkness, and we within it merged in unity with the sky and stars:

"Swift is the wind, and wild is the sky;
The books of the *awen* are not nigh;
Seek them, loving brother mine, on high!"

Then I knew Gwendyd to be my *awen,* twin daughter of song, and forth from my body floated my mind. Pace for pace with her, pulse for pulse, I felt my tread aery as that of Gwendyd, as we spun dancing on our spiraled way. I became lightheaded, fancying that we passed by way of the vent in the dome above into the night sky, and so floated freely toward the shining stars.

My resolution was fierce, and my heart beat high: high as the leaping hammer-strokes of the smith at his gateway. Triple blows of angry power rang hard upon the sturdy steel, echoed faintly by a gentler ringing rhythm whose triple cadences swelled and sank in shimmering undertones. Of a sudden the levin-bolt lashed fierce once more, and I leaped with it like a salmon ascending the first fall of the Cataract of Derwent. There was an access of vigor, followed by a lyrical lull where the water turned idly in the first pool of the ascent. Like triple waves radiating from the salmon's spring was the spreading strength that suffused my being, heart-easing in the pool's pause as the song's ascent arched upward through the screening spray, through which shone diffused the changing colors of creation. An enchanted melody played above me in trees that clung to crags about the cataract; though all was as yet but an unfulfilled imagining.

My heart and head beating in unison, I leaped higher still with redoubled eagerness, until I felt steal over me the strength a galloping horse gains when first he finds his stride, racing upon the yellow sands of Morfa Rianed. A threefold drumbeat repetition of the rising and falling of Gofannon's hammer, a last oscillation between promise and pathos, and I found myself caught up unresisting upon the golden brow of ecstatic contemplation. The force cascaded below me, and I emergent in the upland air!

It was the moment the poet knows when his verse flows free from the Cauldron of Poesy; when measure, harmony, and imagery pour forth conjoined into a single irresistible flood. The tasks and travails which had oppressed me then with their cruel complexity fell from me like the larval husk from an ascending dragonfly. My mind floated free and transcendent on wings of song: harmony of the Harp of Teirtu, whose chords are strung across the boundless deep upon the seven planets, meridians of eternal mind and axes of the sphere's infinity.

No sense of corporeal being clung to me; rather I felt myself to be a white glare about the myriad stars, irradiated in the silvery brilliance of the Evening Star. Through purple courts I danced in the great emptiness, treading out the measure of the seven stars, mounting the fiery sky, coursing upon comets, and leaping with the lightning.

All around me and within were ranged the jeweled glories of the galaxies, a lavish hoard dispensed to those who crowd the kingly mead-hall by the Sure Hand of a Monarch, generous in gift-dispensing beyond all the kings of the Island of the Mighty. I saw great hearths glowing, within whose embers lay expiring a multitude of worlds. Devouring dragons plunging through empty oceans; woven webs of red and blue filaments; fiery suns setting in unknown seas; flaring

flowers erupting into bloom upon a filigreed tapestry of myriad diamonds; circling spirals, whirlpools of the night; spinning discs, white-
hot in flame: I saw them all.

I saw, too, black shadows that engulphed the serried hosts; dark
shapes that assumed the guise of horse's heads, scorpions, swart blud-
geons of destruction, abyssal pits black and freezing as the mouth of
Uffern. Into their gaping, spiraled hollows they swallow the unwary
bright ones who pass singing too close to their unfathomed chasms,
voiding them into other alien worlds. Sugyn mab Sugnedyd is the
name they give to that vortex of the night, which might suck up an
estuary in which there lay three hundred ships, until there was nothing left but a dry beach. A red breast-pain is his, which is the worm
that gnaws at the entrails of the universe.

Now was the time for me to tread the void, dancing with care my
destined measure, that I might interpret the silvered lettering within
that dark-velvet book lying spread before me which comprises the
infinitude of all things. For all that numberless host of the heavens
moves in due order, a kingdom upon which lies the Truth of the
Land, with its king wedded fast to its Sovranty. Like a chariot wheel
the glorious array passes in majesty about the golden hub at its Center.

The chariot trundles the length of the heavenly highway, that
glorious trail we call Caer Gwydion, the trail which each man treads
from his going forth to his lying down. It is the jewel-studded belt
which binds the heavens, the road which runs from north to south the
length of the Island of the Mighty. May the day of its loosing be far
off, O Bright Shining One!

As I gazed upon Your glorious creation, an exaltation stole upon
me, which was, as I knew, but a feeble reflection of what is known to
You. For the sphere is without beginning or end, encompassing all
things, knowing all things, perfect in proportions of beauty and
order. And what am I but the imprisoned image within the alembic,
which when released reveals some measure of that essence? And when
once I have displayed the mercurial essence, transmuting base metal of
ignorance into golden gifts of futurity, then am I confined once more
by a touch of his wand of enchantment within Gwydion's glass vessel.

But I do not repine. Let the conjuration be conducted according
to rites known to smiths and druids, preserved in the books of
llyfyrion. Was it not I who uttered the Prophecy of Prydein, and is it
not my awen which enables the princes of Prydein to learn a little of
what else lies hid in its bottle beneath the roots of the Tree, deep
within the Realm of Annufn?

So I hung poised above the gale that blows from the planets, like a hawk hanging upon the wind. I saw worlds made and unmade, stars contract to the size of skulls, stars explode at the instant of their death into the brilliance of a thousand suns, trailing spirals of flame igniting gases in the surrounding aether; eerie lights that flare and fade upon the marges of reality.

There, borne like bubbles on a stream, float bright-rimmed globes of fire, enchanted spheres sustained by angry-eyed luminaries poised at their centers; meet vessels for contemplation by divine Gwydion and Math, whose wands of enchantment trace across them what has been, is, and will be. Though there, in the vastness of the void, space does not permit delusions of history, chronology, futurity. What is prophecy but contemplation of totality, whose fitting image is the unbounded circularity of the sage's sphere?

There are clouds that collide, clouds compressed by the shattering of stars marking the deaths of kings, from whose conjunction are conceived new stars, reigning in their stead. From the new star to the old passes that effulgent halo whose encircling sparkling river purifies, rejoices, and enriches the nimbus of sovranty. The Silver Wheel rotates, king succeeds king, the fiery fluid flows through the royal race in perfect order. After Arthur will be Maelgun the Tall, and after Maelgun the kingship is Urien's. And who is it reigns after Urien of Reged, my sister Gwendyd asks me? Gaze upon the book of the stars, and you will see. Gwendolau, patron of bards, will exercise gentle rule. Next, Ryderch the Generous it is who reigns upon the Rock of the Brython, about which flows the river of poesy; and after him Morgan mab Sadurnin.

Today resounds unceasing throughout the firmament the labor of Gofannon mab Don, skilled wright of the universe. Hard by the Hub of the Heavens, around which revolves the celestial Wheel, shine out in splendor the palace of his mother Don and the silver fortress of your pure mother, Gwendyd: radiant Arianrod; strongholds whose jeweled walls and gilded roofs the mighty smith erected at that first dread dawning, whose lambent glow and swirling mists were fire and smoke of the craftsman's crucible. Ah, Arianrod,

> Sunbeam's brightness, and beauty's boast!
> Shameful your death by Prydein's coast;
> Around your court rough torrents coast.

Most majestic in the eyes of mortal men, as they scan the night-time heavens after Beli's chariot of fire has dipped boiling beneath the Western Ocean, is that other wondrous chariot of the night, which men term the Great Bear. Upon four wheels of whitest bronze is it mounted, with hubs of ruddy gold shining like glowworms in the dusk. Smoothly did the adze of Gofannon carve out that fine wooden framework, and skillfully did he set the wickerwork about its sides, framed in copper, rounded, firm, very high. Its pole is of white silver, set with three golden harness mounts of intricate enameled inlay.

Just as the Chariot of the Guledig of Prydein is the sign of his sovranty over her Three Adjacent Islands, her Sixty Cantrefs and her Twenty-eight Cities, so stands the Chariot of the Bear as emblem of kingship in the heavens. Eternally vigilant must the driver of that chariot be, and not calmly may he sleep. Before and behind he looks, west and east, and south and north. A protection he stands, four-square, taking care lest the wheels beneath him be shattered through neglect or violence. He must pity and protect those who are given into his charge, destroying not the foundations that support him. For a false king, unwed to the Sovranty of the Land, shall surely be tilted and thrown when once he mounts upon its frame.

Gazing upon these marvels, I wondered at the power of Your Unerring Hand which sustains this eternal wheel in motion, so that every spangled cluster—a numberless host—maintains its due order in accordance with laws undeviating in their measure as the Chariot of the Bear upon its royal trackway. I wondered, too, at the love which filled Your kingly heart, leading You to pluck forth from trees the race of men, bestowing upon them a little kingdom which reflects Your own as does a clear pool the broad sky.

For is not the Island of the Mighty but a mirror of that mightier monarchy whose canopy is the tented hall of heaven? The land of Prydein is likewise ruled by a just king, free from blemish, staunchly set upon his chariot of power; drawn by descent and empowered by prophecy from the beginning, when Beli Mawr first raised his creation from out the formless azure main. The tribes of her hundred and fifty-four districts are governed by immutable laws, inscribed within the Book of Dyfnwal Moelmud, bringing harmony among the or-dered degrees of kindred.

Then, too, is the land itself, from Penrin Blathaon in the North to Penwaed in the South, from Crigyl in the West to Ruohim in the East, bounded by pellucid walls preserving it from the waste without, cruel chaos of the Coranieid. It is studded with twenty-eight shining cities, whose lamps in the night match the rents in Your canopied pavilion.

So pondering, poised in the void like all else by the protection of Your Sure Hand, I saw the belt bounding the heavens, which men call Caer Gwydion, passing likewise across the land of Prydein. It is a road old as the Island itself, winding from north to south. From sea to sea it stretches, and you may see to this day beside its track arrowheads of stone flung down by the Fair Folk, who trod its length long before Prydein son of Aedd the Great colonized the Island. Each enchanted blade retains a spark within, weak remnant of the blazing light it bore when set within the Path of Gwydion on high. Gofannon mab Don it was who set his forge upon its wayside and brought the fear of iron upon those people, who fled in anger to the elf-mounds where now they dwell.

Even as I thought upon these matters, there stole into my mind a notion cold and insidious as a serpent from a rock. High above me curved Caer Gwydion, spanning the heavens in luminous grandeur. Within the apex of its arch lay the Chariot of the Bear, brightest of the hosts of heaven. But even as I contemplated its splendor, it darkened before my gaze, the stars tracing its outline dimming and twinkling as if reflected in the oily waters of some filthy fen in the upland wilderness of Prydyn. One of the vast dust-clouds which float upon the whispering wind of the stars had interposed itself above the Seat of Sovranty. Enshrouded in fog, the jeweled Chariot glinted dully; blood-red and morbid now were the spots that marked the outline of its frame.

There was a shadow upon the Chariot of the Bear, and over gulfs of unmarked time and boundless space crept an uncanny chill. It was cold, cold as the Pit of Uffern. I gazed in fear upon the firmament, within which I heard no longer the faint singing of the spheres or gentle breeze from the planets. Silence falls upon the sacred precinct of the abyss, the silence of a deserted temple: Within the house, at the doorway, and in the fields beyond, all is motionless beneath a mantle of silence.

Not upon a rock is the firmament founded; it is sustained only by the skilled exercise of Your Sure Hand. Should You make one faulty move upon the board, then may the pieces tumble into chaos: that chaos of the Coranieid which was before You established the checkered Precinct, and commenced the moves which preserve it from the Oppression which ever encroaches upon its borders. And am *I* the piece whose moves may cause the kingdom to be preserved—or to perish? If so, it is a heavy burden You have placed upon me, and a weary path I must pursue.

The length of Caer Gwydion rides the furious hunt of Gwyn mab Nud, the hounds of Hell howling before him and the ghastly cavalcade of the dead sweeping behind. Even now I fancied I heard in the stillness the faint winding of his horn, as he approached the dimmed outline of the Bear's Wain.

Then I recalled his words in the darkened chamber of King Brochfael at Caer Gurygon, and the false move he made upon the *gwyddbwyll* board. Treachery! I was cold in the sunless void, cold as when I came to lie with snow to my hips and icicles in my hair in my frozen refuge below Newais Mountain. Melancholy was the howling of the wolves, and keen the wind in every wound. King Ryderch's men rest snug among quilts and featherbeds; not for them is the biting frost and flooded ford!

But swift and fierce as the gale upon the mountainside was my thought in that moment, edged sharp as hoarfrost and piercing as red sunlight glancing low across the snowy plain. When men of science and enchantment, *llyfyrion,* gaze upward from their books to contemplate that greater book whose secrets they seek to unfold, they divide the night sky among meridians reticulated neatly as a spider's web, striving thus to impose lore of order and understanding upon the matter of their study.

But what are those meridians of the mind save gossamer threads floating upon a wall of reality, screening from sight the spiraled labyrinth that lies behind? *There* winds the true road of the heavens: Caer Gwydion, bridge of the soul's ascent.

And here, in Prydein, what are the straight roads of Rufein but meridians of the mind imposed upon the Truth of the Land? No mortal mind saw clearer than that of Iul Kassar, emperor of Rufein, who conquered the Island of the Mighty in requital for Meinlas. He it was who set the roads upon the Brython, as a net to hold the ensnared bull. Yet the bull has burst its net, as ever it will, and today it is briers and beavers that unravel the handiwork of the emperor of the world.

As the spider's handiwork is brushed from the rock, so more clearly reappear the raised coils of the ancient road springing from the center. While fen and swamp and winter's flood make mockery of the roads of Rufein, high upon ridged hills and ramparts rides against the clouds that mighty track which men yet call Caer Gwydion. From the Mines of Flint to the Forest of Nwythoniog it stretches, skirting the Head of Bran (which is the Center of the Island), until it plunges down to the stormy Sea of Udd.

Like the heavenly Path of Caer Gwydion, then, it skirts the Center. And what is more, as I saw all of a sudden, it skirts likewise the Chariot of the Bear! Now I understood too clearly what lay behind the mocking laughter of Gwyn mab Nud as he cast his final piece at our last playing of *gwyddbwyll*: Not orderly from square to angled square are his hostile pieces closing in upon our king, but winding deviously by the older road I had forgot!

There is a warp and woof men impose upon the wild, and it is the seer's task to mediate betwixt the two, stealing back and forth across the border. Swift into my mind stole the reflexion—as if I should not have thought it long ago in Caer Gurygon: Must I not in truth be Merlin the Mad? King Maelgun the Tall of Gwynedd and the hosts of the

Cymry were marching by the direct road from Caer Ceri, and where was it they purposed to establish their strength? Was it not upon the ramparts of the deserted fortress of Dineirth, upon the outer rim of the Plain of Iweryd?

Straightway I saw it all, or nearly all. I experienced enlightenment, sudden and full as that of the brief magical flood of light which bathes the whole earth when a falling star rends the roof of the tent of heaven. Just as we in Prydein possess an earthly Caer Gwydion, traversing the Island of the Mighty as its lustrous counterpart does the heavens, so too we have beside it an earthen Chariot of the Bear. For Din-eirth signifies "the Fortress of the Bear": that is, the Bear which was Arthur, who took the ancient stronghold and refortified it, making it boss of the shield which wards the pastured land of Prydein from the Wasteland of Loiger, over which reigns the oppression of the Iwys.

It was from the night sky that Gwydion and Math acquired their enchanted lore, which they set down in the Books of the Brython, and writ clear upon the night sky was that which I sought. *From behind by the ancient way, the winding track of Caer Gwydion, was the enemy approaching;* while the reckless princes of the Cymry rode unwittingly along the causeway, there was a trap being prepared for them even now at the Bear's den!

Hunched with my knees to my chest upon the earthen floor of the cold chamber of Gofannon's smithy, sweating within my boar's hide and chewing upon the beast's rancid flesh, I saw it all through that eye which the Hawk of Gwales plucked from me in a dark hour upon Ynys Gweir of the white gulls. Hid from my waking eye by interposing mists was the landscape of Loiger, the Plain of Iweryd, the Plain of Bran. But upon the sooted roof above, sustained by its seven shining pillars, starlight gleaming through rifts in the rafters reflected all as clearly as though upon a mirror of polished bronze.

It was a map I saw, more skillfully designed than that exhibited by Maeldaf the elder in the palace of Brochfael of the Tusks. *There* smoldered savagely the Hunter's Dog, star of the barbarians; *there* meandered the wandering way of Gwydion's Path; *there* hung the Chariot of the Bear, besmirched by *migedorth*, druids' mist or fog of war; *there* beside beamed bright the Star of Arthur, Driver of the Bear, whither men say he repaired after suffering grievous wounds upon the dreadful field of Camlann. But is he the Arthur who led the Brython upon their twelve tides of victory? Or is he that translated Arthur, whose corpse-filled wagon trundles at the head of the host of the departed, guiding them to their final resting place beneath the hollow mountain? There was much that now I knew, but much yet to learn and more to achieve.

For long I lay midway between sleeping and waking, my *ellyll* floating downward like a feather to rejoin my drained body. It was the dear time of dawning, and I fancied my Gwendyd stirred in sleep beside me, turning to entwine her white arms about me, murmuring endearments in her guileless slumber. But when I woke and was no longer *wyllt,* there was no Gwendyd near. Only the dying gem of the Morning Star smiled down upon me through the crevice in my chamber roof: a bright speck upon the sky's cerulean face, like the dimple upon my darling's rounded cheek.

No longer did my *ellyll* float free above the galaxy. The starpatterns I studied were graven within the bony sphere of my skull; shrunk back into that fragile shell was that spirit which, as I fancied, had briefly been dissolved afresh into the nine forms of elements collected by my mother Ceridwen within her Cauldron of enchantment at the time of my conception: a bridge spanning sixty estuaries, a coracle swimming upon an endless ocean. What was without was now within; I was a drop in a shower, a bubble in beer; like the enchanter's alembic, reflecting distillation of all eternity.

> My little hut upon the hill,
> No palace quite as fine;
> Its every star bent to my will,
> Its sun and moon incline.
>
> None made it but skilled Gofannon
> (This tale I tell to you);
> My dear one, son of radiant Don,
> No thatcher quite as true.
>
> No rain falls through its hallowed guard,
> Nor stabs the sharpened spear;
> And it wide open in its yard,
> With no wall standing near!

Exhausted with my vision, I slept long within my chill rock chamber, dreaming dreams deep and strange. And after a while it appeared to me that I was translated, that I spoke with unknown men who jabbered in broken tongues alien to the pure speech of the Brython, and that I journeyed far to a wild cold land remote from the seagirdled Island of the Mighty.

CHAPTER FOURTEEN

WESTWARD
OVER THE
WHALE'S PATH

I t was in the time of Arthur the emperor, when he was leader of armies and ruler of battles, that the hosts of Prydein inflicted slaughter beyond reckoning upon the rascally crew of gallows birds who, at the invitation of Gurtheyrn the Thin, first set their talons upon the Island of the Mighty. At the siege of Din Badon, Arthur charged before the armies in the front rank, a leader who would sooner be flesh for wolves than go to a wedding, sooner be prey of ravens than kneel before an altar, sooner his blood soaked the ground than be borne upon a peaceful bier. With his spear Rongomiant he pierced the carrion race of the Iwys until blood flowed down his cheeks; upon his shield Winebgurthucher he bore the image of the Virgin; and there fell before the blade of his sword Caledvulch three three-hundreds and three twenties of the pale-faced men of Loiger.

It is said by some that after Badon, Arthur purposed to put to the sword all the host of the Iwys and the tribes of all the Saeson and of Loiger, vowing to cut them down so that the trunks of men would be piled high on the trunks of men, and arms of men piled high on arms of men, and the crowns of men's heads piled on the crowns of men's heads, and men's heads piled on the edges of shields; so that all the limbs of the Iwys scattered by him would be as numerous as hailstones upon a causeway along which a king drives his royal chariot.

But Ceredig the king of the Iwys having provided submission

at the spear's point, he was permitted to raise the knee before
Arthur and suck his nipple in token of fealty, delivering up his nephew
Creoda and others of his nobles to languish in Arthur's hostage pit at
Celliwig in Cerniu. And as the coastlands south and east by the Sea of
Udd were laid waste and uninhabited by the Brython after the long wars
which had devastated the region, Arthur the emperor permitted Ceredig
and his people the Iwys to dwell there as a subject people, dogs
without his hall.

Nevertheless (so it is related by druids, wise ones), Arthur had
sworn an oath by truth of breast and cheek, of heaven and earth, of
sun and moon, of dew and drop, of sea and land, that he would strike
three mighty, warlike blows upon the men of Loiger. Now Caledvulch,
the sword of Arthur, was wrought in the elf-mounds by Gofannon
mab Don, and there was that power within it that when it came to be
wielded it was as big as a rainbow in the air. Since he might not violate
his oath, Arthur did not stay his hand, but swung the sword above the
heads of the kneeling hosts, so that he struck three mighty sword-
strokes upon the hills and downs about them, shearing great dykes out
of the land which may be seen to this day. And those, if the tale is to
be believed, are the dykes which compass about the land of the Iwys.
And at the points where the sharpened tip of Caledvulch broke the
ground are situated the three great fortresses of Caer Caradog, Dineirth,
and Caer Vydei.

Then were the Iwys as bondsmen to the kings of the Brython,
paying annual tribute of pigs and oxen and brooches when Arthur
made his circuit of the kingdom. At that time there was not a smoke
from a house in Loiger which did not lie under his tribute. There was
tribulation throughout their region, and many were the children of
Loiger who were sold into slavery throughout all Prydein and Ywerdon.
And for the slaying of a king of the Iwys or of Loiger the blood-fine
was but ten cows; for the slaying of a noble, six; and the value of a
bondsman was no more than two goats. For they were not as the
people of the Brython, being *lletieith,* speaking with broken tongue;
alltud, possessing neither kindred nor oath-value; and pagans, knowing
not the faith of Crist. Thus were they speechless, kinless, faithless:
exiles from across the sea, strangers in the land.

Oath-breakers, too, the men of Loiger proved themselves to be,
for they rose up in after years in the disgrace of rebellion, slaying the
prince Nuithon mab Cathen, whom Arthur had placed in authority
over them, raising up Ceredig together with his son Cynurig as kings in
Prydein, each with his own status and *sarhad.* This was a violation of
the Law of Dyfnwal Moelmud, for it is forbidden to a prince of the

alltud to maintain *sarhad* within the bounds of the Island of Prydein with its Three Adjacent Islands. Then was Arthur angered, and ordered the slaughter of Wigmaer and other hostages whom he held in fetters at Celliwig. And when summer came he assembled the hosts of Cerniu and Dyfneint and made a great hosting into the land of Loiger.

At Longborth he met in battle with Ceredig and slew him and untold numbers of his following, a bare remnant only escaping together with the prince Cynurig:

> At Longborth saw I where Arthur drank,
> After slashing sword and bleeding flank;
> Emperor, and bull of battle-rank.

As for the remnants of the ungrateful race of the heathen, they and their prince Cynurig were subjected to greater oppression and bondage than heretofore, so that when Arthur was slain by his false nephew Medraud upon the field of Camlann, the Iwys remained quietly in subjection beyond the dykes with which Arthur had hemmed them about.

It was only after his death (or translation, for as men say, he is but resting in another place until the time be come for him to return and deliver the nation from its oppression) that men understood fully the greatness of this work of Arthur's. For there was war between the kindred throughout the Island of the Mighty, as five great princes strove to take unto themselves the inheritance of Arthur. Yet not once did the Iwys seek opportunity to violate the frontiers, but continued to pay their annual tribute and live peacefully in their own land. In the courts of the Brython it was said scoffingly that Cynurig was not the son of that warlike Ceredig who fought with Arthur, but a base-born changeling unfit for war.

So matters rested until the return of Maelgun Gwynedd from the monastery of the blessed Iltud, when he swiftly proved himself as much greater in power to the other princes of the Brython as he was superior in stature. Far and wide ranged the hosts of Gwynedd, until all Prydein south of Dygen acknowledged Maelgun the Tall, son of Cadwallon of the Long Arm, as pendragon of the Island.

It was this destructive war among the kindred which led the men of Loiger at last to believe they might with impunity withhold the tribute imposed upon them by Arthur, and it was the rash defiance of Cynurig that led Maelgun Gwynedd to assemble a hundred thousand of the men of the Brython at Dinleu Gurygon in the land of Powys. Now was he marching with his invincible host, gathering fresh armies upon his march, in order to root out and utterly destroy the pestilential brood of Loiger. Soon would the work of Arthur be completed and Sovranty restored to the Island of the Mighty!

Never since the year of Mount Badon had the coming of summer brought such joy to the hearts of the young men of the Brython, and it was as Cymry, fellow countrymen, that warriors of kingdoms once at war rode knee to knee rejoicing down to the place of slaughter. And of all the princes of the Cymry, none rejoiced more than Einion mab Run, lord of Caer Vydei upon the confines of Loiger.

Among the ring of dykes and fortresses established by Arthur to gird about the Iwys within their place of refuge, none was stronger than Caer Vydei. Built long ages ago by the men of Rufein, its seven-sided walls of dressed stone were a bulwark to the Brython, a strong stake in a weir, a promontory before an ocean wave. When Ceredig in the folly of his rebellion slew Nuithon mab Cathen, his son Prince Run withdrew to this strong place together with those who survived of his father's retinue. Run mab Nuithon was high in the councils of Arthur the emperor, dying by his side upon the field of Camlann, leaving the great city Caer Vydei as a surety for his son Prince Einion.

Thus it was that Prince Einion mab Run was known as one of the Three Noble Exiles of the Island of Prydein. (The others were Heled and Lemenig—he whose grave is at Lanelwy.) For once there had been a time when his dynasty ruled over all the fertile land of the southern Gwent, having their principal stronghold at Caer Went. Noblest of all princely families in the Island of the Mighty were they, for Prince Einion was sprung of the tree of that renowned King Cynfelyn who maintained sway over the Island of the Mighty before the coming of the men of Rufein. Together with Iul Kassar, emperor of Rufein, King Cynfelyn ruled over the whole world, and it was in his time there was born Iessu Crist, the Son of God.

Wretched is the life of an exile; was not the Lord Iessu Crist Himself, a sister's Son of man, the Son of an exile from Heaven? Oftentimes did Prince Einion ascend the southern rampart of Caer Vydei to gaze out over the fair green land that was once his forebears' domain, but which now suffered the oppression of the foreigner. In Caer Went now was heard only the mongrel tongue of the Iwys, and the hounds of Loiger disported themselves over his grandfather's grave. All that was left to him of that rich kingdom was a solitary stronghold standing sentinel upon the marge of the Wasteland as a bulwark against the barbarians:

When after its ebb there returns the broad tide,
It is well for an island in the great sea.
But exiled affliction for me will abide;
Around my lone refuge comes no flood for me.

So it had been; but now at last there had come a spring to which
the voice of the cuckoo brought not melancholy reminders of departed
kingdoms and dead companions, but hope of restitution and lifting
of oppression. Since the Kalan Gaeaf there had ridden messengers
from the court of Degannwy in Ros to Prince Einion in Caer Vydei,
telling of the mighty mustering that would take place at Dinleu
Gurygon at the Kalan Mai, and of the great hosting which King
Maelgun the Tall planned to hold in the land of Loiger. As the days
grew longer and the wan sun warmer, there came with every envoy
fresh tidings of great kings who had heard King Maelgun's horns
sounded at their gates, and who had sworn to attend upon the king's
hosting.

Though he stood as it were as a sentinel upon the bounds of the
kingdom, few knew more than young Prince Einion mab Run of the
unfolding preparations for combat which were toward, and none rejoiced more in his heart at the prospect. The mustering was appointed
for the Kalan Mai, when a hundred thousand of the most valiant
of the Brython would assemble in Powys and begin their march southward. Three Silver Hosts went forth in past times from Prydein, and
they were the hosts of Yrp Luidog and Elen Luidog and Caswallon
mab Beli; but greater than those (it is told) was the host of Arthur at
Din Badon. Now was it said that the host of Maelgun Gwynedd was
great as that of Yrp or Arthur, and it was not the false brood of Loiger
that would be able to resist the flood at its tide.

Then in the month of Maurth came Samo the merchant to Caer
Vydei, passing with his baggage train northward to Powys. He told of
the departure overseas of Cynurig with many of the chief warriors of his
people, and the heart of the noble Einion was filled with joy. Assuredly the day of retribution was drawing near, when he and his
fellow exiles would play at football with the skulls of the Iwys!

Though young in years, Prince Einion was a man in vigor and
skilled in the ways of war. It was with pleasure, therefore, that he
learned of the ruse by which King Maelgun's skilled counselor, Maeldaf
the elder, planned to deceive their cunning adversary. For it had
happened in the past that the men of the Iwys, foxes for cunning,
had concealed themselves in the forests of Loiger when invaded, emerging afterward unscathed to renew their oppression upon the Island
of Prydein.

As Maeldaf's messenger explained, it was Prince Einion's task to hold the city of Caer Vydei until the great host of Maelgun the Tall should appear before his western gate; after which they would sally forth together, marching resistless upon Caer Went in the South. Meanwhile the great king's son Run would with his *gosgordd* throw himself into the empty fortress of Dineirth upon the high downs westward along the dykes, where he would hold the main body of the Iwys at bay until the hosts of the Cymry should return from the burning of Cynurig's hall beside Caer Went.

Eventually, as expected, there came a day when a great host of the Iwys came and encamped south of the dykes barring the way before Caer Vydei. The sentinels of Prince Einion espied the gleam of their spears amid the birch groves, and when they summoned their young lord it was the banner of the White Dragon that he saw fluttering among the treetops. Then he smiled to himself, for he saw that the first part of Maeldaf's stratagem was come to pass.

As the sharp ears of Samo the Freinc had learned when he stayed in their great hall by Caer Went, the lords of the Iwys planned to dispatch a war-band to make play of strength before Caer Vydei, as if with the intention of seizing the city. In the meantime, however, the greater part of their host was marching with all dispatch upon Dineirth, intending to seize and fortify it. But thanks to the quick ears of Samo and the sharp wits of Maeldaf, the crafty foe was soon to be plunged into the very pit he had dug for his adversary! Prince Einion had but to stand fast within his impregnable walls until the great host of Maelgun Gwynedd appeared from the north, and then he would join them for the final march upon his slaughtered grandfather's stronghold at Caer Went, too long defiled by the presence of interlopers from over the sea. Confirmation of these tidings was brought by Samo himself, when after some months he passed southward through Caer Vydei on his return from the court of Brochfael of the Tusks at Caer Gurygon.

On the morning following the appearance of the White Dragon before his walls, Prince Einion dispatched scouts from the city, who entered the shades of the forest with caution. In the evening they returned, to report that the war-bands seen moving all day about the glades were but two in number, who by continually exchanging their dress and arms provided semblance of a great host.

"The fox has learned the ways of the forest!" Prince Einion said, and laughed.

At night he sent forth other men to espy the disposition of the foemen. The messengers returned, telling how woods and plain south of Caer Vydei, even as far as the Brook Leidiog, were covered with campfires numerous as stars in Caer Gwydion. But upon closer inspection it was easy to see that, though guards came and went, most of the hearths were unmanned.

"Blaze without burning, and fires without feasting!" laughed Prince Einion again. "Now we may see that King Cynurig is indeed departed abroad, and the wits of his people must have passed over with him. A king so old and wise would not have resorted to so simple a ruse."

Though he knew the mind and disposition of the men of Loiger, Prince Einion did not relax his vigilance one whit. For if the purpose of this display by the barbarians before his city were to draw King Maelgun and his host hither, then who knew that they might not be planning some fierce assault the better to assist in provoking that end? Guards on the walls and at the gates of Caer Vydei were doubled, and the three hundred chosen warriors of his household exercised themselves daily at spear-throwing and swordplay.

Upon the third day after the arrival of the Iwys before Caer Vydei, there came a lord of Loiger before the walls to parley with Prince Einion. With him was a man who spoke the tongues of the Brython and the Iwyss with equal facility, and he it was who interpreted between them.

It was thus that the lord of the Iwys spoke in his pride:

"The noble King Cynurig, Woden-born son of conquering Cerdic, has sent me to thee, that thou mayest hand over rings of gold in tribute and deliver up hostages, rather than that we, so hardy and invincible in war, should unleash the arrow-storm upon you. We need not destroy each other, if you will but consent to these things and place this fortress in the hands of the king. If you will consent to these things, who have no choice in the matter, we will permit you to depart in peace to your own people."

At this Prince Einion, proud upon his battlements, laughed loudly. "We will give neither rings nor hostages!" he cried, smiling, though with anger in his heart. "We are not ready for this; no, nor never will be, though our fighting last like that of Gwithir mab Greidawl and Gwyn mab Nud from this till Doomsday. My grandfather Nuithon mab Cathen would have suffered torture stoutly rather than cede anyone as hostage, or deliver up a stronghold in his care."

The barbarian laughed grimly as he heard these words. Then he spoke in words guttural as the song of a nightjar to the interpreter who stood by his horse's head:

"It seems, lord, you forget, or do not know, that your grandfather did indeed suffer tortures innumerable in the snake pit of King Cerdic, who took his lands and cities into his hands long ago. And now is come his son Cynric, Woden-born, together with his heir Ceawlin the *aetheling*, to require you to comply with his demands. I advise you to do so, lest you suffer your grandfather's cruel fate."

Prince Einion turned aside for a moment and wept, for it grieved him sorely to think of his noble grandfather's treatment at the hands of the barbarians. That the heir of Cynfelyn the Conqueror should have suffered thus at the hands of the landless scavengers of Gurtheyrn Gurtheneu! Then he turned and gazed proudly down once more from the rampart, marking the features of the boasting foreigner. It was in his mind to seek him out upon the place of battle, and avenge with his stout ash spear the poisoned words that galled him like barbed arrows.

"Those are ill words that you speak, O fox of the estuaries! It may be that you will come to rue them, you and your people. For it is known throughout all Prydein that old Cynurig, lord of slaves and hucksters, whom you term king, is departed across the seas with his hosts to plunder in other lands. He is greedy for treasure, and has left you here as sheep unprotected from the wolf pack. Stay but a little while, and I and my company will ride out and destroy you and yours."

The envoy from the Iwys spoke in a low tone with the interpreter, then cried up to the prince upon the parapet: "It is not as you think, *wealh;* King Cynric is not departed overseas, but is here with a host innumerable. I ask you for the last time: Will you deliver up hostages and give the city over to us? For I tell you this: If you do not heed these words of mine, Cynric has sworn upon the white holy stone to dedicate all within the city to Woden, and not one of you will be left alive! Remember how the crows feasted when Aella the Bretwalda took Anderida! Now is Cynric the Bretwalda; he has sworn to be revenged upon your wretched war-band. He will come in a day or so, and those whose blood he does not spill with the sword's sharp-filed edge will he hang upon the gallows tree as sport for the birds! Mine is no idle threat. I have spoken, and you have heard."

Once more did Einion mab Run feel bitterness pierce his heart like a serpent's bite, for there can be no greater insult for a prince of the Brython in his own land than to be termed *wealh*—that is, "foreigner"—by a homeless barbarian.

"*If* the dog Cynurig be still within doors, and *if* he can make his way through these strong walls, then let you and he do your worst to me and mine. We are strong in the faith of our Risen Lord, Iessu Crist, who will frustrate your purposes and those of the Devil you worship. Begone, before I cast this spear into your false heart!"

The messenger spoke no more, but returned to his people within the obscurity of the forest. Prince Einion descended the stone steps and spoke with the chief men of his retinue. One that had been with him upon the wall understood the tongue of the Iwys, and had overheard somewhat of the talk which passed between the emissary and his interpreter when they spoke aside. The interpreter, it seemed, had briefly questioned whether he was to say that it was Cynurig himself, or but his son the *edlyng,* who led the besieging host. Here, were it needed, was confirmation that the words uttered by the foeman were but lies, designed to make the men of Caer Vydei believe that Cynurig himself with his whole army lay before their walls.

Einion was joyful, explaining the master plan devised by Maeldaf the elder, lord of Penardd, in the councils of Maelgun the Tall and the princes of the Cymry. Soon would the king of Gwynedd and his host draw near from Caer Ceri, entering the western gate of Caer Vydei before passing on to scatter the weak war-band that made pretense of strength before them. After that would the warriors of the Cymry march southward together, irresistible as the Wave of Ywerdon, the Wave of Manau, the Wave of the North, and the Wave of Prydein, as far as Cynurig's royal hall beside Caer Went.

Meanwhile the *edlyng* of the Iwys, with such forces as his father had left behind in Prydein, would be laying siege to Dineirth, westward along the dykes. Unknown to him, the old fortress would by now be restored and garrisoned by Run mab Maelgun; and even as he attempted its capture the hosts of Prydein, returning from the capture of Caer Went, would fall resistless upon his rear. Death would come to the black host, preventing them from escaping as heretofore into their forest refuges, biding their time until the Brython were departed each into his own kingdom for the winter. The cities of the coast would be fortified and defended and the fleet of Gereint of Dyfneint would sail the Sea of Udd. In this way would Cynurig be prevented from returning, and the oppression of the Iwys would be lifted forever from the Island of the Mighty.

Rejoicing in their hearts, Prince Einion and the chief men of his *gosgordd* rode to the church which stood hard by the center of the great city. The sun beamed down upon their glittering array, warming the red-tiled roofs of Caer Vydei and gladdening the hearts of its inhabitants. Within the portals of the dwelling place of God they received from the bishop of Caer Vydei the sacrament of the Body and Blood of Crist; for now must they live in daily expectation of war with the crafty men of Loiger. Einion mab Run placed gold ornaments of value upon the altar and did penance for his sins. Afterward, he and his lords rode about the streets, where the people were gathered to sing the *"Sancti Venite."* And thrice from every throat went up the joyous war-shout "Alleluiah!," which Bishop Garmawn had bestowed upon the Brython in token of coming victory.

Matters stood thus when next day arrived further tidings of great comfort. There came a horseman galloping up to the western gateway who brought news at last from the camp of Maelgun Gwynedd himself. When last he left the great king, the messenger explained on being ushered into the council chamber, he was marching through southern Powys toward the shining city of Caer Loyw. Indeed, by now he might well have reached the Hafren, after which he would divide his forces, the main body advancing upon Caer Vydei while Prince Run his son with the war-band of Arfon made all haste to occupy Dineirth before the arrival of the enemy.

The messenger was none other than that Lofan Law Difro whom Rufinus had encountered at the moment of his departure from the camp of the Cymry. He was of the people of the Fichti who dwell in the distant mountains of the north. Lithe, dark, and cunning was he, and neither robbers by the wayside nor men of the Iwys settled beyond the frontiers had been able to stay his passage. He bore the ring of Maelgun Gwynedd as a sign, and told how within a few days Prince Einion might expect the war-band of Prince Elffin mab Gwydno, which was riding in all haste ahead of the army to strengthen the defenders of Caer Vydei.

Prince Einion ordered the fellow to be rewarded richly for his pains, and retired rejoicing into his palace. That night there was great feasting in the hall, and by blazing pine-logs the heroes quaffed sparkling wine from glass vessels, laughing and recounting deeds of valor so soon to be renewed upon the ranks of the heathen. The hour at last was nigh which was foretold by Merlin at the disclosure of the Red and White Dragons before King Gurtheyrn. For a long space of time had it been fated that the White Dragon should ravage the Island of the Mighty, even as far as the Western Sea, which it would lap with its venomous tongue. Thus ran the prophecy: Though the Red Dragon at first appeared the weaker, and was almost driven from the tent which was above the cistern, yet in time it proved the stronger, even driving the White beyond the tent's edge.

Three days later the skillful Lofan, who was permitted to pass in and out of the gates, appeared before Prince Einion to report that he had encountered Elffin mab Gwydno upon the highroad, and that he might expect the arrival of the war-band of Cantre'r Gwaelod within his walls that very night!

It was with a joyous heart that Prince Einion laid him down to rest at eve. Deep was his sleep, until of a sudden he was awoken by a light touch on his arm. It was the mid-hour of night, and the prince could see nothing in the darkness. Springing up, he reached for the sword that he kept ever hard by him. But then his hand was stayed by a whisper at his ear; he recognized the soft voice of Lofan Law Difro, the messenger of Maelgun.

"Keep silent, lord!" hissed the night visitor. "It is time to be up and doing."

"Are the enemy attacking?" inquired Prince Einion, hurriedly lacing on his shoes and buckling his sword belt about him. "How came you past the sentinel? I gave orders for every man to keep watch with eyes as sure as those of Gwiaun Lygad Cath."

"Blame not your guards, lord," whispered Lofan, leading the prince down the stairway. "I pass like a cat in the darkness, and it will be a sharp eye that detects Lofan Law Difro when he chooses not to be seen. We must take great care, for Prince Elffin mab Gwydno has arrived at the gates."

As they hastened through the empty streets, lit only by a glimmering moon and the occasional flare of beacons upon the battlements, Lofan explained to his lord that Prince Elffin had come to the western gate with but three of his following, the remainder of his *gosgordd* lying in wait within a grove not far off.

"He fears lest the foemen discover his arrival, and attempt an assault during the time of his entry," explained the prince's companion.

Einion nodded in approval, and a moment later they stood below the twin flanking towers of the western gate.

Recognizing the prince by the light of the guardhouse lantern, the officer of the watch silently drew the bolts of a small door set within the great gates. Accompanied by the captain of the guard and two or three of his spearmen, Einion stepped out onto the paved way which stretched away toward Caer Vadon and Caer Ceri. Before him in the half light he found standing a tall young man, cloaked and hooded. Behind him stood three other figures, while a little beyond, Einion glimpsed the shadowy outline of a wagon, its wheels and the hoofs of the oxen that stood in the traces swathed in sackcloth.

"Are you the prince Einion mab Run, lord of Caer Vydei?" inquired the newcomer in a low voice.

"I am," replied Einion, "and you must be the prince Elffin mab Gwydno, from Cantre'r Gwaelod in the North?"

For reply the stranger raised his hand, and at once Prince Einion felt himself gripped from behind as if by bands of steel. He saw the hangings of the wagon thrown back, and armed men spring silently out onto the road.

"Animith seax!" hissed a harsh voice in the darkness, and a score of bright blades flashed forth, piercing the gloom like angry flames. Then a thick cloak was cast over Einion's head, so that he might neither see not hear what further passed about him. He knew then that he and all the princes of Prydein had become victims of a mist of deception, such as assailed Pryderi and Manawydan when they sat upon the mound of Arberth in the former time.

Great indeed had been the deception and great was the exultation of King Cynric, when upon the following evening he sat upon Prince Einion's throne in the great hall of the city. Loud were the acclamations of his people, the Gewissae (or Iwys, as the foreigners, *wealh,* termed them), and fierce the rejoicing of the chiefs of the Angle-cynn and their allies from beyond the seas. The streets of the city had run with blood that day, and its treasures were theirs for the plundering.

It is related by Heorrenda, gifted scop of the Gewissae, that high upon his throne—*gif-stol,* source of gifts—sat the Woden-born Cynric, son of Cerdic the Conqueror, lording it over the captured city. Long ago, in the days of his youth, he came with Cerdic his father in five ships to the coast of Bryttene, landing at the place men call Cerdicesora, where they fought with the Bryttas and put them to flight. Afterward they slew in battle their lord Natan, together with five thousand men of his following. After that they captured the Island Wiht, which Cerdic bestowed upon his nephews Stuf and Wihtgar.

Then there came upon them ill-luck, when Arthur king of the Bryttas fought against the assembled kings of the Angel-cynn at Mount Badon, slaying many and exacting tribute from the remainder. And when Cerdic fought again against Arthur, the king of the Bryttas had slain him by wizardry, and Cerdic the king was buried at Cerdices Beorg. Then Cynric became king in his turn, after the death of Arthur making war once more upon the Bryttas. By skill and cunning he took the fortress which men have since called Searo-byrg, "Trick-stronghold." And now, four years later (it being the twenty-second of his reign), Cynric had captured the second of Arthur's great strongholds by a ruse as deceitful and cunning as the last! Truly could it be seen that the luck which deserted the father Cerdic had returned to the son Cynric.

This was not surprising, for was not Cynric the true heir of Woden, frenzied leader of battles, master of guile and guardian of the slain? Here follows the descent of Cynric: Cynric Cerdicing, Cerdic Elesing, Elesa Esling, Esla Gewising, Gewis Wiging (from

whom are the people of the West Saexe known as Gewissae), Wig
Freawining, Freawine Frithugaring, Frithugar Bronding, Brond
Baeldaeging, Baeldaeg Wodening. To Cynric, even as an aged man
fierce in the fray, his ancestor Woden granted success in war and glory
in battle so that his band of young warriors swelled to a mighty array.
At his feasting he distributed rings and wealth beyond measure, his
luck was great, and his word law far and wide.

After the slaughter at Natansleaga, Cynric's father, Cerdic, had
seized the great city of the Bryttas called Wintanceaster. Great was the
killing in the streets of that city, and bountiful the burning of battle-
corpses. I believe that the crows feasted for weeks within its walls,
while wolves lapped the lifeblood streaming through its streets. So
sang Heorrenda, the scop skilled in song, a man dear to his prince.

But Cerdic dwelt not within the city, mighty work of giants a
hundred generations past, who wondrously worked its encircling walls
with wires. Bright were its bulwarks, lofty its pinnacles, numerous its
bathhouses, mansions, and mead-halls, and pleasant the stone-paved
courts where kings of old feasted in their pride, flushed with wine,
glorious in their battle harness, gazing upon jewels and costly weapons
without number in this their bright castle set like a gem in its broad
kingdom.

Now were the tiles fallen from its roofs; grim frost worked
wrathfully within its mortar; lichen stained and ivy spread about the
huge walls and gateways. The place was sunk into ruin, the multitudes
who thronged its streets long laid beneath the earth. The wind alone
moaned about its courtyards, and the fox and badger dwelt within its
palaces. The *wyrd* which rules the destinies of men had ordained the
destruction of the kingdom and the breaking of its wall-stones. For
though there is nothing nobler in life than to fight on against overwhelming odds, yet as even Thunor found in the hall of the Frost-
giants, there is one thing against which men may strive in vain, and
that is time. One by one the greatest kings, Earmanric and Theodoric
and Aetla, have departed from their hall floors. So does this world,
each and every day, droop and fall.

Not Cerdic the king nor Cynric his son dwelt within the city
after its fall; they abandoned it to elves and trolls and spirits of the slain
who watch from its empty windows, lingering lustfully in doorway
shadows. An unchancy place it was at the stillness of noontide, when
the sun clothes the heavens with his brilliance; and worse by far in the
louring nighttime, when shapes shrouded in shadow come stalking
through the streets, black beneath the clouds.

So it was that Cerdic summoned skilled men from near and far to build him a mighty mead-hall, *heal-reced,* without the walls of Wintanceaster. Not long was it before there uprose a lofty towering hall with broad horns, where was heard the clear song of the scop, the melodious sound of his harp. And there Cerdic, according to his promise, distributed rings and riches at his feasting to gesiths and thegns who flocked with their warlike companies to his renowned court from lands far and wide throughout the world. Of all buildings beneath the skies, this palace of the mighty ruler was the most renowned among all men. Light blazed from it over many lands.

With the passing of Cerdic, that hall was Cynric's, who for fifteen years ruled the people of the Gewissae alongside his mighty father. Not long after that was their mighty foe Arthur slain also, he who was Bretwalda of the Bryttas, whose fame and power were as great in the west part of the world as was that of Hrothulf, mighty king of the Gar-Dene, in the east. Not many years after that, Cynric captured by cunning the fortress Searo-byrg, and his fame began to grow great in northern lands as that of his father. It was seen that he was *sigoreadig,* blessed with victory-bringing luck, bestowed upon him by his ancestor Woden, one-eyed bringer of victories.

At his birth a serpent had been seen to glide from his cradle, and a serpent's guile had remained in him from that moment. There were those who said that a fire-breathing serpent had been his father, and that his childhood was spent in the Forest of Ytene, in the company of serpents and firedrakes. When the heroic frenzy came upon him, men said that he bore within the pupil of his eye the likeness of a coiled snake.

When the scop sang of Cynric's valor and generosity in his famed mead-hall, it was of Hengest, too, he told. For was not Cynric a second Hengest, who crossed the cold sea to take a kingdom to himself within the wealthy land of Bryttene? Like Hengest, who ruled the kingdom of the Cantware in prosperity with his brother Horsa, Cynric and his father together brought victory-luck to their tribe. Like Hengest, Cynric locked his thoughts fast within the bony coffer of his mind. For it is known how Hengest dwelt for a slaughter-stained winter in the hall of Finn, brooding upon that vengeful killing of his host which he contrived in the spring. He preferred the avenging of his companions to the joys of his hearth at home.

And when Cynric took Searo-byrg by skillful wiles, men remembered how skillfully Hengest had deceived Wyrtgeorne, king of Bryttene, when he invited him to meet him in council that bonds of peace might be forged between their peoples. At a shout from their lord, Hengest's men drew knives concealed in their boots and slew every one of

Wyrtgeorne's royal retinue, so making the king their prisoner. After that, Hengest deceived Wyrtgeorne into wedding his beautiful daughter Hrothwyn, upon whom he was obliged to bestow many broad kingdoms as a dowry.

When it was seen that Cynric had taken Hengest's place among the Angel-cynn, and received Hengest's luck, the grandson of Hengest fared to the hall of the king of the Gewissae to place in the lap of Cynric the flashing battle-blade, brightest of broadswords, which had been Hengest's when yet he dwelt upon earth. It was an ancient sword, blessed with *sigoreadig,* wrought by Weland, a weapon worthy of Woden, sharp of edge, an object of glory to fighting men.

The giant smith wrought that sword, toiling within his barrow, and upon its hilt he engraved runes telling of the ancient strife between gods and Frost-giants. Also set down in foil of shining gold was the name of him for whom that blade was wrought, with its wave-curved hilt and gleaming serpent-coils: the name of the most terrible of kings who lived upon earth, even Aetla, king of the Hunas, the World-ravager. Hunlafing was that sword, light of battle, whose sharp-filed edges were renowned among the Eotenas.

There is an ancient song of that sword, known to Deor and to Heorrenda, gifted scops, which is called the "Lay of Hunlafing." There it is told how a certain shepherd of the Hunas noted among his herd a heifer limping. He pursued its trail of blood until he came upon the glorious sword lying in the grass of the broad Plain of Huna-land. At once he bore it to the hall of Aetla, who grasped it by its gleaming hilt, rejoicing in his heart. For he knew it to be the gift of Woden, and that it had been bestowed by the god upon him as a mark of victory in war.

So the sword became known to all the tribes of the earth over whom Aetla bore sway as Hunlafing, the Hun-sword; and they worshipped the sword, making *blot* of many prisoners and slaves before it, that their blood might be pleasing to Woden and gain the Hunas the kingship of the world. Afterward, when Aetla had conquered and laid waste the cities of the Rumwalas, he placed Hunlafing in the lap of Hengest. The World-conqueror desired to extend his rule to the islands of the ocean, and upon Hengest and his people the Eotenas he bestowed the kingship of Bryttene. Moreover Aetla had learned from a certain sibyl that his end was approaching, and he wished to bequeath his luck to the prince of the Eotenas, that it might be preserved safely beyond the seas from his enemies.

Thus it came about that, after avenging the death of Hnaef, when Hunlafing drank greedily of the blood of Finn, Hengest fared forth over the West-sea to Bryttene, which he conquered in the name of his lord Aetla. And he named his son after Aetla's uncle Octha, conqueror of Gifica, king of the Burgendas; for the name of Aetla himself none dared take. So the bright brand brought the doom of slaughter among the Bryttas, continuing the work of the world-ravager even after his death; though Casere regained his kingdom which Aetla had destroyed.

There was a doom laid upon that sword that it should be dreadful in battle as were ever the blades Hrunting and Miming, and that it would strike three blows of dolor and shame. The first of these was the slaying of Finn, king of the Fresan, by Hengest, who was his hall-guest; the second was the slaughter of the war-band of King Wyrtgeorne of Bryttene, with whom Hengest and his followers were conferring under pledge of peace; and the third Cynric now vowed would be the death blow of Maelgun, presently ruling over the tribes of the Bryttas, whose host he had enticed into a snare from which they might not escape. So the Hun-sword wrought mischief in the world, even after its master the world-conqueror was laid in his barrow for worms to gnaw.

Thus was the protection of the runes of the sword Hunlafing placed upon Cynric, so that he was among other kings as a noble ash over thorns; or as a young hart upon the dewy grass, towering above the other deer of the herd, its antlers glittering against the very roof of heaven itself. He struck terror into his foemen and their kindred, so that they were like goats that flee fearfully before the wolf. Mightiest of kings was he under the sun, and the spinning of the threads of his *wyrd* lay over all lands.

Many young men, *wreccan*, flocked to his court, as has been told, upon whom he bestowed fine rings and brooches, promising much more when war should come again between the Angel-cynn and the Bryttas. They were eager in their hearts for the joyful day when blood should drip from sword-points, and bees of battle sting the hearts of their adversaries. The fury of Woden was upon them, and when the king drew Hunlafing from its sheath, the runes inscribed upon its blade sang to them of looting and slaughter, burning of homes and violation of virgins.

Next there came to Cynric, being old and full of the wisdom of years, tidings of the mustering of the Bryttas beside their holy hill to the north. Much he learned by skillful means of the doings of their king Maelgun: how he had subdued all the kings of the Bryttas, and planned war such as there had not been since the time of Arthur against the people of the Gewissae.

These tidings bore no fear to the heart of Cynric, where lurked the cold guile of a serpent, the slow-dripping venom of a dragon; upon him lay Hengest's luck. He knew all the strength and disposition of the Bryttas, and he had especial reason to respect among them the skilled leadership of Gerent, chief of the West-wealas. So it was that with a spider's skill he wove a web about his foes.

With the coming of winter he sent to the court of the king of Bryttene a merchant of the Francan, Samo by name, who told the kings and thegns of the Bryttas assembled there that Cynric and all the bravest champions of his people were departed overseas to fight in wars being waged afar off by the shores of the Wendel-sae. The merchant Samo told, too, how the feeble remnant of the Gewissae left behind in Bryttene intended next summer to attack that fort in the high country which is called the Bear's Fort, Beran-burh, after Arthur the Bear of Bryttene. At the same time there was a trap baited, whereby the great host of the Bryttas would be drawn to approach a great city which they believed to be held by a prince of their own people. However, if all passed as was purposed, they would find of their city a hostile rampart. Moreover it was there that their guileless king would be ensnared, were Cynric's cunning to earn its fair reward.

Meanwhile it happened that, long before winter locked the waves in fetters of ice, there came to stay at the hall of Cynric by Wintanceaster a man skilled in song beyond all others. Heorrenda was his name, he who had been scop to the Heodeningas, who rule over the people of the Glommas dwelling where the sun rises far beyond the wild waves of the West-sae. Heorrenda was greatest of singers of men in those days, wandering through many lands, seeking lords skilled in songs and bounteous in gifts who desired the poet to exalt their fame, so that their honor might not pass away in the mead-halls of mortal men, until all light and life that is under the heavens shall come to pass away.

Through many lands had Heorrenda wandered far from his kindred, among most tribes and peoples throughout the broad earth. The wide realms of the Gotas and the Francan, where once Theodric, most mighty of all the race of men held sway, knew he well. The winter before had he passed in the great mead-hall of Aelfwine and Eadwine, kings of the Longbeardas; it was there he uttered the lay of victory of their people over the fierce Gefthas. Of all men, so the scop recounted to Cynric, Aelfwine possessed readiest hand for deed of praise, heart most generous in the giving of rings. Upon Heorrenda he bestowed a precious jewel, reward of his song.

Then Cynric gave Heorrenda an armlet of refined gold, and broad hidage of arable land in the country of the Meonware, with many *wealas* working plows in its fertile valley, and woodland rich in mast upon the hills above. For Cynric knew that when the scop unlocks his word-hoard within the halls of kings, then is their fame great in the mouths of men. Not among the warrior peoples of the North alone, Myrgingas and Hundingas, Engle and Swaefa, Brondingas and Wulfingas, had the poet wandered. Beyond the wilderness of Wistlawudu had he fared, even to the glorious court of Casere, king of the Creacas: he who has rule over the bright-blue waters of Wendel-sae, with its towns innumerable filled with revelry, riches, and rejoicing throughout the realms of the Rumwalas, whose *wyrd* it was once to rule the world—until Aetla arose to wreak his work of destruction upon them.

Many a marvelous tale could Heorrenda tell: He sang of Alexandreas, mightiest of men, who conquered all the earth. Of the wars of the Hraedas and the Hunas did he speak; how Offa with his single sword held the dyke against the Myrgingas at Fifeldor; of Hagena and Heoden he spoke, of Hrothulf also and Hrothgar; and of Wade—he who ruled beneath the waves.

While Heorrenda sat at his lord's feet, receiving wealth, plucking swiftly and skillfully with his plectrum at the strings of his harp, delighting the noble thegns of the Gewissae, Cynric stroked his gray beard and pondered long. Then, on a day, he took the scop aside and told him something of that which lay hid within his mind.

"For two and twenty seasons have I ruled the mail-clad Gewissae beneath these skies, and before that for many a long year I sat upon the gift-throne beside my mighty father Cerdic. In war have I protected my people with spear and with sword-edge against so many foes that I thought no more might remain beneath the broad sweep of the sky. My deeds are known to all peoples dwelling upon the coasts of West-sae, and far beyond. Of all the Angel-cynn dwelling in Bryttene, mine is the mightiest of kingdoms."

The poet nodded, plucking a soothing string, as the king continued.

"I have rewarded you with gold and with land, Heorrenda—not beyond your merits. I am wealthy, and much do I bestow upon the thegns who frequent my court. But for a great king to set a bound upon himself is a bond not to be sustained. It is in my mind to take into my hands wealth greater than the gold of the Herelingas, which they say lies below the River Rin; mightier than that for which hamstrung Weland toiled in the cold exile of King Nithad; more dazzling even than that jeweled Brosingamene which Hama stole from Earmanric. More than these things: It possesses the power of the Ring of the king of Sweon, in that its wealth begets wealth, as a swine is delivered of her litter. Think you that this treasure should be mine, O Heorrenda?"

The scop made reply: "For a great king there must be great wealth, that he may distribute it among the thegns of his following and the scops who sing of his glory. Nor is it right that goodly gold and hardy warriors should exist without the one falling into the hands of the other. Eager are fighting men to receive gold, when he who sits upon the high seat possesses abundance. But what is this treasure, O Cynric the king, and where is it to be found? Does it lie within some dragon-guarded barrow, whose guardian drips venom upon the rash man who enters the portals of his dark domain?"

Cynric laughed harshly and, veiling his serpent-gaze, looked sharply at the scop where he leaned over his harp by the dying hearth.

"Your arrow is near the mark, scop! I will tell you all. The treasure of which I speak is this great Island of Bryttene, within whose walled cities lies store of wealth untold. Her kings are weak, and war one with the other. The greatest, Maeglcon, who calls himself Dragon of the Island, is a faithless tyrant who dwelt long in unmanly wise among monks, afterward slaying his own nephew that he might wed with his wife. For this is he hated by his kindred and held unworthy of a great throne."

The scop plucked awhile at the strings of his harp, deep in thought. He saw the flames flare up fiercely upon the hearth of that royal hall, lighting its great pillars which stood like ranked warriors among the shadows. In his mind he glimpsed the arrow-storm, when sped by bowstrings the darts come flitting in over the shield-wall, and the eager feather-clad shaft does its duty, guiding the barbed arrowhead deep into the foeman's heart. Of such matter is the scop's song, and so he glories in war.

"It seems to me," replied Heorrenda at length, "that all this fair Island should be yours, O chieftain of the Gewissae and bulwark of the Angel-cynn! Was not your *wyrd* that of the supreme kingship, when your mighty father bestowed upon you the name of the kingdom, *cyne-rice*? Now you are old, and it may not be long before you receive the summons to join the immortal host of Woden. You should gather your tried warriors, who long for spear-work and slaughter, and take into your own hand the strong places of the kingdoms of the Britons. Thereafter you may distribute rings of gold to those who sit upon your mead-benches, securing yourself in strength until the time comes for your son Ceawlin to sit upon your gift-chair. After such a deed, never will your name be forgotten beneath the broad sky, when I bear the tale of your courage and generosity to all tribes and peoples throughout the earth."

"Mine shall be the fame and the greatness, and thine the guerdon of praise," agreed Cynric. "But what if I wish the kings of the earth to partake of the glory as well as the gold? Is it not an affront to all of Woden's stock, dwelling about the West-sae and this side of dark Wistlawudu, that here alone in the North does the fierce foe of the gods, Crist, erect his banner and summon his hosts to the place of slaughter? I believe that dread day may be near when, the World-serpent being loosed and the Wolf's jaws yawning wide, the gods must wage fierce war against their foes, so that either the battle throng of Crist or that of Woden will be driven down into the windy halls of Hell. Which is to prevail, the Cross or the Spear? Each is a weapon of strength and enchantments, and it is not within the same Island that they may rest peacefully upon the mead-hall wall. There are signs; I have made sacrifices. The dark waves roll angrily against the tall cliffs."

Heorrenda glanced up at the king, whose brow was darkened and his eye turned inward, and made cautious reply: "I, too, have heard such things, Cynric. There are preparations for war throughout the folk, and northward in Beormaland beyond the snows, men have seen bright hosts shaking their lances to the heavens. There is talk, too, among the wizards of the Scride-Finnas, who understand these matters, of a bearded star which will tear apart the tent of heaven some time next year. That is a portent of much blood to be spilt upon the earth. But tell me, O king: Why do you wish the kings of the earth to join your battle array? You are strong, and the enemy is weak. Would it not be wise to garner the plunder for yourself alone, rather than share it among so many? The Woden-born kings will be like wolves about the carcass of a stricken auroch, each tearing at his own portion. May it not be thought that your strength is the less, that you require assistance upon your battle road?"

Cynric shot a glance at Heorrenda from beneath the thatched eaves of his white eyebrows, a glance so sharp that the scop feared he might reveal the serpents coiled within each pupil.

"I am old and, it may be my foes think, crippled with age," growled the king, stirring upon his high seat, "but for all that, men would be wise to bear my words in mind. I have slain forty tens of men in single combat, feeding them as fodder to the swart-feathered raven. I have gained a name for manslaughter. Let the fiends gather me to their pit when I am no longer able to wield this sword! The sooner I am borne to my barrow then, the better. Then will I be in the shameful dwelling place, where worms, black creatures, voracious and greedy, may feed upon my body, tearing away the sinews. That day will come. But meantime I have some little killing to accomplish!"

He gnawed his beard awhile in anger, and the scop divined that battle frenzy had warmed the manly heart of the Woden-born king. Heorrenda touched his harp strings, singing of the serenity of the sea when the wind does not arouse it, and the peacefulness of peoples whose disputes are reconciled by a masterful monarch. Cynric's ire was softened by the song, and he resumed his tale with the calmness of a king upon whom is the gathered wisdom of years.

"You misunderstand me, Heorrenda!" he exclaimed. "I have no need of aid from kings beyond the West-sae when I wage war upon the false folk of the Bryttas. All the kings of the Angel-cynn who rule upon the coastlands of Bryttene own me as their warlord, even from the East Engle south to Cent and Wiht. The Beornice, too, have received the rune-summons graven upon the war arrow. And I have made a bond of alliance with the great king of the Peohtas, dark people who dwell beyond the River Gewaed in eternal shadow beneath mountains in the north whose summits touch the sky. He has sworn by the oath which is customary among his people that he and his hosts will fall upon the Bryttas of the North Country, putting them to the sword without mercy. Like grain between the flail and the floor will they be beaten, and their bodies blown as chaff to the four winds of the world.

"The kings of the Bryttas will I dedicate to Woden the All-father, and to him will they be a blood sacrifice. But I have received doom-laden news from a merchant of the Francan, who has come here to my mead-hall with rich goods. He has heard strange tidings from men dwelling by the Wendel-sae; tidings which it is fitting that all who fear the wrath of Woden should hear and ponder. It seems that the god of the Rumwalas, who also is the god of the Bryttas—I mean him they call Crist—has lately sent a sign to all men upon earth who own him as their lord: a sign which is a summons to war!"

"What sign is that, lord?" inquired the scop curiously. It was his task to learn all things that passed among the kingdoms of the earth, that he might bring them forth from his word-hoard wherever kings hold their feastings.

"It is a message, cunningly written in runes," continued Cynric. "The champion of Crist's war-band, Michahel, bore it as they say upon his spear to his chief sanctuaries about the Wendel-sae: to Ierusalem, Bethlem, Romaburh. Men skilled in rune-reading have interpreted it, sending it here and there wherever men worship Woden's fell foe. They are to observe rites upon the day they hold holy, and with enchantments counter spells which the one-eyed lord of learning mastered for mankind when he hung his nine dread nights upon the windy tree. They are to pay tribute to the priests who conduct sacrifice in their temples."

The scop nodded his head, saying to the king: "All these things are in my belief true, O Cynric, and I saw something of the false ways of the Crist-folk when I was at the court of Teodbald, king of the Francan, who alone of the heirs of Aetla worships the devil Crist. But surely this is nothing new, for such have long been the ways of their wizardry. And how else can Crist communicate with his war-bands save by means of rune-staves?"

"You interrupt me, scop," replied Cynric sternly. "The worst of the tale lies, like that of a dragon, in its end. The rune-message of Crist concludes by forbidding his followers upon the holy day we call Sunnandaeg to wash their clothes, or cut their hair and beards. What can this mean but that Crist himself is preparing for war against the holy gods who dwell in Wael-heall? Is it not my intention neither to wash nor comb my hair until I have devastated the whole of Bryttene with fire and sword? Must it not be likewise the intention of Crist and his warriors to take such an oath until, as they believe, the time has come for them to destroy the Woden-host? Believe me, Heorrenda: The end of the world is approaching, and there is an assembling for the slaughter!"

In the hall of Cynric all was dark, so neither king nor scop might see the other's face. Only the king's eyes, with their serpent pupils, glowed dull as dying coals. His war-band lay sleeping still and snoring soft beneath the benches of that royal hall. Outside, the wind moaned in pain about the timbered walls, where the ugly prowler of the moorlands roves beneath the moon in search of his prey. The wicked ravager purposed to devour one of the human race within that lofty hall, could he but lay his taloned grasp within the ribbed rampart of his breast.

The harp of Heorrenda struck forth a plaintive chord, for Cynric's words had plucked a verse forth from the scop's memory-hoard:

> "In the Halls of the West shall Hrind Wali bear,
> Who after one night shall avenge Woden's heir;
> His hands he'll not wash, nor take comb to his hair,
> Till Balder's bold butcher be brought to the pyre."

Cynric shivered upon his high seat, for the night was chill. A log on the dying hearth, or it may be the serpent within his eyeball, hissed angrily.

"That deed is one that will happen upon the eve of the world's ending," he muttered. "There are those who hold that Balder and Crist are one, for of both is it said that all nature wept at their passing. I think that dreadful winter may be nigh, when the sun will turn black, the sky fall, and the waves batter the mountaintops. The *wyrd* is unfolding, and who may stay the three sisters' weaving?"

Long in the darkness sat king and scop, silent and pensive. Then came the first pale light of dawn, and with it three cockcrows were heard in the distance. The thought sped into Cynric's mind that they were the three cries that presage the world's ending: the cry of the blood-red cock who will settle on the gallows tree, the cry of the cockerel that struts the earth, and the cry of the sooty-red cock echoing through the hateful halls of Hell. Cynric the gray-haired king, ancient warrior, rose in his pride leaning upon the sword Hunlafing, and addressed the scop sitting at his feet with these grim words:

"Dawn is breaking in the east, over the waves. But the light which will blaze forth over this Island will not be that of the sun alone, clad in his heavenly brilliance, nor that of a flying dragon's fire, nor that of the hearth of a great hall! Rather will it be the glint of moonlight on bright sword blades, for which few will be prepared. Then will the gray-coated wolf be howling, the spear sing forth, the shield echo to the shaft's splintering.

"We have spoken much upon these matters, you and I, Heorrenda. Now hear my words. I wish you to fare far and wide to the kings of the earth who follow the All-father, urging them to gather their war-bands and serpent-fleets for the conflict. The last age is upon us, an age of anger and slaughter. Brother will slay brother, and father his son. There will be a bitter time for humankind: ties of kindred and wedlock unloosed, adultery and whoredom no crime; an axe-age, a sword-age, when shields are splintered; an age when an icy wind from the east howls loose across the land; a wolf-age at the world's falling—none shall be spared! Spread the word among the kings: The World-serpent is unleashed and lashes the waves of ocean; the eagle is screaming, pale-beaked marauder ripping at mounds of corpses. Tell them that Woden is summoning all to the place of killing and rapine, where blood shall splatter upon the earth like red rain!"

Thus it was that Heorrenda fared forth from the great hall of Cynric beside Wintanceaster, riding to the place of ships at Cerdices-ora. Thence he set sail in a swift high-beaked vessel bestowed upon him by Cynric the king, passing over that arm of the Ocean Garsecg which embraces the land of Bryttene, until he came to the fair coast of Froncland. But there he sought no anchorage, for already the king of the Francan had sent word secretly to Cynric that he would send a mighty host of his people to Bryttene when the trysting time were come. King Teodbald did not wish this matter to become generally known, for he was himself a Crist-worshipper. Moreover, he feared the vengeance of Casere the great king, who had dispatched armies forth from Constantinople conquering all lands which were formerly his about the Wendel-sae. For Casere was the friend of Crist, speaking often with him in the great temple which towers in the midst of his stone-built city.

So Heorrenda's ship flew eastward along the coast, until he came to the long land of lakes and islands where dwell the Fresan. There he found the gaping mouth of Rin, mightiest of rivers flowing forth into the gray West-sae, along whose flowing flood he made his way. From its broad bank a chieftain of the Fresan, hardy beneath his helm, questioned Heorrenda concerning the purpose of his journey, and whence he wended. But when he learned that it was Heorrenda, greatest of scops that was then in the North, come to sing before his king, he welcomed the stranger, riding swiftly to inform the mighty heir of Finn where he sat in his hall among his retinue of thegns.

The king of the Fresan is the wealthiest of kings ruling by the West-sae. His people dwell in long halls upon mounds raised out of the sea, pasturing their cattle on rich marshlands stretching boundless about the lakes and estuaries of that level land. But it is not from fat cattle, nor yet from netting of countless shoals of herring that the king of the Fresan derives the chief part of the gold that crams his coffers. His is the town of Dorebyrg, to which fare merchants from all lands. Down the Rin float full-bellied ships from great peoples of the South, Thyringas, Behemas, Begwara, Swaefe, bringing rich wares over the mountains called Alpis in the country of Carendre, even from the mighty cities and teeming markets of the Rumwalas by Wendel-sae. And at Dorebyrg they trade in wine and grain, rich clothing and bright jewelry, with merchants plying about the West-sae and the Ost-sae, whose ships in turn are laden with the wealth of the North: sable and salted herring, beaver pelts and walrus teeth, amber and slaves. And all these ships and merchants must needs pass through Dorebyrg, paying tribute to the king of the Fresna-cynn.

Many of his people dwelt also in Bryttene, dealing in slaves and other goods. From them had the king learned something of King Cynric's purpose, and as it was not his way nor that of his people to be absent where wealth was being garnered, he had made preparations in anticipation of Heorrenda's visit. When the scop arrived he found assembled in the king's hall not only the thegns of the Fresan but also kings and thegns of neighboring tribes: Hocingas, Eotenas, Secgan. Before them Heorrenda sang the "Lay of Finnsbyrg," which all men know but none may sing so stirringly as the scop of the Heodeningas.

It is a tale of true and bitter grief, in which the forefathers of all present in the king's hall had played their part. Their hearts swelled within them as they recalled the champions of old, each now lying cold within his barrow, or blown by the cold wind in ashes over the sea.

But even as they grieved, Heorrenda struck up a joyful lay of battle: how Hengest and his brother Horsa fiercely fought, Angel-cynn and Fresan together, with four war-bands against the Bryttas at Crecganford. There they put to the sword four war-bands of the Bryttas, so that they fled in fear to Lunden-byrg, leaving Centlond to the conquerors.

Thus was the scop's lay sung to its ending, and merriment arose from the ale-benches as cupbearers bore about the brimming liquid. And the king of the Fresan spoke to his people and to the thegns of the neighboring tribes, pointing out that fratricidal strife had brought his mighty forefather, Finn Folcwalding, to a cruel death by the sword. But when their four peoples, Fresan and Eotenas, Hocingas and Secgan, joined in war against the foreigner, then was the glory and the booty a subject for merry song and rich revelry.

"I will send word to Cynric the king of the Gewissae," declared the king, "that there will be such a hosting of our people as has not been seen riding the waves of the West-sae since the time of my great-grandfather, Finn Folcwalding. For are we not of one kin and one language, we of the Fresan and they of the Angel-cynn?"

So the king purposed; but though he spoke of war and woundings, burning and butchery, before the thegns, in his heart I believe there lay another thought. Fiercely would his warriors fight, true, for there are none braver than the champions of the Fresan. But after victory, would there not be a numberless train of captives in the hands of the victors? By the ruined walls of Lunden-byrg the king purposed to establish traders, men skilled in slave-dealing. Thence from the Estuary of Temes to that of Rin would shiploads sail without ceasing, until the whole Island of Bryttene was emptied of its people, making it habitable for the Angel-cynn and the Fresan by the extermination of the *wealas* and their enslavement in foreign lands.

And the best of it was that every shipment must pass by Dorebyrg, which was, as it were, the funnel through which liquid passes from one vessel into another. Not difficult would it be to empty Bryttene of its inhabitants, for bottomless was the vessel into which the Fresan would pass their imprisoned people. The kingdom of the Rumwalas, with its mighty stone-walled cities, paved roads, docks, and lighthouses, marvelous machinery for lifting what a tribe of men unaided might not shift, required slaves innumerable as stars set in Iring's Path for its manning. In farms and factories, mines and merchantmen, they toiled; cheap on the frontiers, dear by the Wendel-sae.

Like a ship manned by oarsmen who row in unity did that greatest of kingdoms move, and it was by the unceasing toil of a myriad slaves that it was enabled to do so. Casere, king of the Rumwalas, scorned the kings beyond his frontiers, terming them "barbarians." But did not his officers and those of his thegns come every year to Dorebyrg to purchase the oxen without which their plow might not move? And in return he sent what gladdened the hearts of those who worshipped the one-eyed leader of hosts, making glad war upon all the world: the rich red wine of the South; wine that warms the hearts of men when winter's icy grasp closes upon sea and land, gladdening them and bringing their minds to battle frenzy. So Casere wreaks his own wreck, but cares not so long as his farms and factories afford him luxuries despised by the stouthearted sailors of the North. Such were the thoughts of the king, which he held locked within the coffer of his mind.

After the departure of the scop of the Heodeningas from Dorebyrg (for it was not to the Fresan alone that Cynric had bid him travel), the four kings, accompanied by their principal thegns, sailed in their eager warships to that holy island which lies in a deep recess of ocean; that is, in the midst of the watery waste of the storm-tossed West-sae. On that craggy rock, girt about by rocky walls and surrounded by the screams of sea birds, dwells Foseti, the god of the Fresan. He is son to Balder, and his is the power to resolve all disputes at law between merchants who sail from port to port across the West-sae, which is also called the Fresna-sae. And before Foseti the four kings performed blood sacrifice, vowing to repay him with rich trophies and many corpses should they gain victory and slave-tribute from the Bryttas in the following year. They swore also to divide the booty fairly, abiding by those laws established of old among the Fresan.

But Heorrenda the scop parted company from the kings' fleet at the mouth of the Rin, sailing eastward toward the land where formerly dwelt the Angel-cynn before they came to Bryttene at the invitation of King Wyrtgeorne. A warrior of Cynric's war-band, a man skilled in sea lore, guided the ship along the coast. When they came to Aelfe-mutha they turned and sailed northward along the coast of Scedenig past Fifeldor, where Offa with his sharp spear marked out forever the boundary of his kingdom against that of the Myrgingas. Leaving the land upon their starboard and the open sea on their backboard, they flew on before the wind until they came to the point where the sea inclines southward. It is there that the West-sae flows into the Ost-sae.

From the headland Heorrenda was hailed by a proud chieftain of the Wendlas; Godwulf son of Wulfgar was he named. "From where do you come, and for which king's hall are you bound? I believe that within that bag of beaver-skin you bear a harp, whose six strings may chant charmed songs, and that you are a scop of renown whose songs may entrance the ears of a great king."

To which Heorrenda made reply: "A scop am I indeed, and that of no little renown. For long was I dear to the prince of the Heodeningas, at whose feet I plucked the strings of this harp, singing lays of Earmanric and Aetla and Theodric, mightiest of kings who have ruled beneath the broad sky. And now am I come from the court of Cynric, conqueror of the Bryttas, seeking out the courts of kings to whom I bring news of no small advantage."

Then the mighty lord of the Wendlas laughed from the cliff-top, and bade the scop sail on: "Your songs recall the fame of great kings of whom all men speak, friend. But now, if I mistake not, you are bound for the court of a king whose fame has spread wide as that of Aetla or Earmanric. Southward beyond this sound lies glorious Heorot, where the lord of the Scyldingas dispenses hospitality to all the kings of the earth. If that is indeed your destination I will send my young thegns ahead to bear word to the king of your arrival."

Heorrenda thanked the noble chieftain, and made sail southward across the gray-green whale-ridden sea, where gannets bathe, until he came to the shore of that wondrous island which is the home of the greatest of halls which is in the world: even to glorious Heorot, hall of Hrothgar, king of the Dene. Leaving their broad-bottomed vessel held fast by its hawser to the shore, Heorrenda and his companions made their way along the bright-stoned street which leads to the royal hall.

Soon before them they saw the towering building, wide-gabled and gleaming with gold. That was a mightier mead-hall than any of which the children of men had heard tell. Of all buildings that stand beneath the skies, this palace of a mighty prince was brightest in fame among all the men of the world. Light blazed forth from it over many lands. To it flocked kings and thegns of nations beyond numbering, eager to earn the bright mead which the generous king dispensed at his feasting. To them he gave rings and riches, in return for which they plied their spears upon his foes.

Hrothgar, the old king who built the hall, had long been dead when Heorrenda came to Heorot. In his stead sat in the gift-seat his nephew Hrothulf son of Halga, who for many years had ruled over the Scyldingas alongside his uncle. But when Hrothgar died, Hrothulf slew his uncle's sons, Hrethric and Hrothmund, making himself sole king over the Scyldingas in their stead. And this he did at the instance of Unferth, the dark counselor, who sat at his lord's feet. Thus by means of cunning and treachery did Hrothulf take unto himself a great throne, fulfilling the baneful forebodings of Hrothgar's queen, the gracious Wealhtheow.

Never, so I have heard tell, was there a greater company assembled in that hall than when Heorrenda the scop came among them to dispense Woden's theft: that poetry which was the eye's price of the skilled All-father. On learning of his approach, King Hrothulf had ordered that Heorot be beautifully bedecked, so that men and women made ready the banquet chamber in haste. Upon the walls shone the fierce weapons of the Gar-Dene, and there too hung wonderful woven hangings depicting the deeds of the deathless gods.

Here in his great hall, Hrothulf, helm of the Scyldingas, made Heorrenda the scop welcome. One bench of the banqueting hall was cleared for him and his company, stouthearted men of the Gewissae, stern in their strength. A thegn of the Dene fulfilled his duty, bearing about the bench a richly adorned flagon of ale, pouring out the flashing liquor. In that hall men lacked nothing; men moved about from seat to seat, mingling their talk and dallying over their delight. Richly dressed were the warriors, with brooches and rings of finely wrought gold. They lacked nothing that wealth might supply: The attendant thegns were active; the hearth blazed; spears and shields sparkled brightly upon the iron-clamped walls.

To Heorrenda where he sat came Hrothulf's gracious queen, mindful of the dues of hospitality. To him she brought a goblet of chased gold, bidding the famed scop welcome to the hall of Hrothulf, bestowing upon him beer which he quaffed with a happy heart. Thus she moved about the hall, the noble ring-bedecked queen, bearing intoxicating beer to the mighty kings assembled within the hall Heorot, each with his own war-band upon the benches beside him.

To Godwulf, lord of the Wendlas, she bore the beer: even to the bold chieftain who watches ward upon the sea-cliffs of the sound, that no foe may pass undetected to harry the land of the Dene with a ship-borne host. From her noble hand also did Helm, king of the Wulfingas, receive the bright ale; he was of close kin by marriage to King Hrothulf and his faithful follower, a shield before him in the spear's pathway. To Heoden, lord of the Glommas, at whose hearth Heorrenda formerly sang, stepped the queen; and likewise she bore the brimming beer to Hagena, lord of the Holm-Rygas, who dwell upon the distant misty islands of the Ost-sae, hard by the coastland of the Gefthas, waging war continually upon the Winedas.

With winning words of courtesy, too, did the lady of proud

descent give the goblet to Eadgils, king of the Sweonas. For when Eadgils seized the throne of the Sweonas from his uncle Onela, Hrothulf it was who aided him with mighty men of war, dispatching Beowulf, lord of the Geatas, with a host of armed men to assist Eadgils in that bold venture. Upon the frozen waters of the lake they battled in bitter cold, all in a swirling mist of snow; and there Eadgils plunged his thirsty sword deep into his uncle's heart, depriving him of the life that was dear to him.

Beside the Sweonas stood the mead-bench of the Geatas, where sat the glorious son of Ecgtheow: even Beowulf, mightiest of all men in that day and age, noble by birth and huger far than all of humankind. Though he was old, his strength remained unabated since the day he carried the boar-standard before the warriors of Hygelac against the hosts of the Hetware and the Francan. And before Hygelac was slain amid shattering of shields and clash of battle-blades, he bestowed upon Beowulf seven thousand hides of land, a princely hall, and—noblest gift of all—laid in Beowulf's lap the gilded sword of Hrethel which is named Hrunting: No finer blade was there among the Geatas.

Not few were the mighty deeds of Beowulf, since he rid Hrothgar's hall at Heorot of that monstrous troll whose realm was the moors, and the swamps his sure retreat. Him he slew, hacking the clawed arm from the creature, severing its sinews and tearing apart its tendons. Then did Hell's thrall howl horribly his song of pain! Not content with this mightiest of feats, the hero sought the creature's dread mother in her underwater lair, stabbing her with a wondrous sword he found hanging upon its stony wall, and hacking off her head, which he bore by the hair all bloody back to Hrothgar's hall at Heorot.

Away in his homeland among the Geatas, Beowulf had heard of Heorrenda's purposed visit to Heorot. He heard, too, that the scop's song would be of warfare such as had not been in the North since Hygelac fared forth against the Hetware, and that the inspiration of his harping might send forth fleets westward over the waves, seeking plunder and carnage beyond reckoning. From such a banquet the lord of the Geatas might not be absent, and so it was that the prince of war-leaders was once more honored in Hrothulf's hall.

Now in the presence of the warrior who once led Hygelac's hosts to battle was there singing and music. Hrothulf's thegns plied the kings and chiefs with strong beer, until all were merry and began to boast one to another of slaughters committed upon many a blood-stained field, where gray wolves gorged themselves and black ravens quenched their thirst. Then, when the revelry was at its height, there fell a sudden silence, as Heorrenda passed between the mead-benches to sit at Hrothulf's feet. He plucked deftly at the six singing strings of his harp; the notes pealed clear throughout the smoky hall, the music made melody, swelling ever louder until the great horned hall trembled, shivering beneath the frosty stars in the dark nighttime of the North.

Unlocking his word-hoard, Heorrenda sang first a familiar lay: that of Sigemund son of Waels. Few chiefs could rival far-traveled Sigemund for fierce and bloody deeds, wrought upon many a distant shore. Many ogres and trolls had he slain in his time; and, greatest deed of all, he slew a fiery dragon in its gray den, bearing away the treasure-hoard upon which it squatted. With this deed did Sigemund become most famed of men; whereas before was Heremod most renowned for prowess, might, and valor.

After this the scop paused awhile from his playing, as men brooded upon the mighty deeds which had been wrought upon earth in times gone by. Then he struck a vibrant chord, which drew their minds back into the mead-hall. Now he sang a song of his own making: It was a lay of Cerdic, great chieftain of the Gewissae. In his youth he had known exile, suffering hardships, sorrow, and longing for old companions, the cold winter of exile. His mind filled with the bitter chill of adversity, of cruel wounds endured, of kinsmen slain, he fared with but three ships across the watery ways of the icy sea. So it can be for the greatest of kings in troubled times, when by the treachery of a close relative he is driven from the warmth of his own hearth.

But Cerdic was a man of infinite cunning, biding his time, neither overcautious nor overrash, calm in speech and sparing his boasts until his foe was nailed to the ground by the bright spearhead. To the Island of Bryttene he came, and there he fought fiercely with the Bryttas, killing their kings and slaughtering their thegns, until he and his followers had laid low many thousands with their swords. Thus Cerdic gained a kingdom, who had but been a thegn in another man's hall.

At last came a day when the great king, mighty in fame, rich in gold, and gray with years, came to be hid with a sad face in the earth-cave. But after him came Cynric his son, who long had shared the gift-seat with his father, taking the throne unto himself alone. Valiant son of a doughty father, he was a scourge to the Bryttas. Now, in the spring, he purposed to make war upon that proud people, grown rich and sluggardly after former victories gained by their renowned king whom men called the Bear of Bryttene.

Valiant are Cynric's thegns, deadly their spears, and keen their swords. But not by valor alone did Cynric purpose to destroy that

treacherous tribe by whose swords his father fell. Lest it be thought he
had taken a boar by the snout or a wolf by the tail, he had set a snare in
the forest for the Bear's cubs. By skill of lies and cunning had he laid a
trap for them, so that their king and all his host would be drawn into it
as a wild beast plunges into a net skillfully masked by leafy branches.

"Then will all their walled cities stand waste," sang Heorrenda,
"blown upon by winds, hung with frost, falling into ruin. Their
mead-halls will crumble, their rulers lying low with the dust, deprived
of joy. Their flesh will be carved and torn into morsels: one piece
borne off by a raven over the stormy sea, another dragged away by a
gray wolf to his forest lair. Who then will fall heir to the gold-plated
flagons, precious drinking horns, burnished coats of ring-mail, and
bright brands without number lying within the empty halls of the dead
kings? Cynric, lord of the Gewissae and chieftain of the West Seaxe,
is no niggardly ring-dispenser. To me has he entrusted this message:
Let all kings of the earth know that this spring will he dedicate the host
of the Bryttas to Woden the All-father; and to all who join him in this
venture will there be equal pickings of the plunder!"

As the kings pondered, each with his own thoughts locked within
the citadel of his mind, Unferth the cunning counselor arose. To him
had Heorrenda revealed Cynric's plan, which pleased King Hrothulf's
counselor well. For long had King Hrothulf, and Hrothgar his uncle
before him, been angered that the fame of Arthur the Bear had been as
great on the far side of the West-sae as was theirs on the hither. It
seemed to Unferth that it might indeed come about that the king of the
Bryttas, heir unto Arthur, would be ensnared as is a fierce boar in a
net, into whose flanks any man may thrust deep his broad-bladed
spear.

"For it stands thus," explained Unferth to the kings and thegns
who drank deeply of the clear ale dispensed by King Hrothulf in his
hall: "Not only will the heir of the Bear of Bryttene, who vaunts
himself as Dragon of the Island, be netted and slain, but his whelpish
brood, too, will be destroyed. And that is no small thing, for a small
serpent with vengeance locked within its heart may in time grow to a
great worm breathing deadly venom upon the land far and wide.
Alone among the peoples of the North, dwelling about the shores of
the gray-green sea, the tribe of the Bryttas worship the false god whom
they call Crist.

"I believe that the company of the immortal gods is angered that
this Crist, friend of Frost-giants and trolls, should have established
his temples within the inhabited enclosure of the world. For three
years now have we not performed the sacrifices at *Blotmonath,* fol-

lowing the four-oxed plow around the Island, and bestowing gifts upon Gefion? And has she not bestowed upon us in return three years of blighted harvests and withered crops, with plagues ravaging the halls of men?

"It is not hard to see that the Terrible Winter foretold by the sibyl has come upon us:

" 'Snow will drive from all quarters; there will be hard frosts and biting winds; the sun's heat will dwindle. Three such winters will pass with no summer intervening. And before that will there be three other winters accompanied by great wars throughout the whole world.' "

Unferth the wise counselor paused, that men might recall the truth of what he told them. Then he continued with skillful words, which entwine a man's thoughts as surely as the lime-strewn snare entraps a bright-plumed bird.

"I say to you, kings and thegns from many parts, that these things have come to pass. We have undergone snows and cold such as no man ever knew before, so that halls are buried, roads lost, and the ground hard as Weland's anvil. Even as I speak to you within King Hrothulf's welcoming mead-hall, I hear the wind howling about its eaves like a ravening wolf within the dark skirts of a wood beside a sheepfold.

"Have there not, too, been wars throughout the world such as no man can recall from former times? The mailed hosts of Casere have conquered all the lands about the Wendel-sae; deadly war is waged between Longbeardas and Gefthas; the king of the Francan has cruelly ravaged the broad lands of the Thyringas, avenging the rebellion of the Seaxe; even here in Heorot, as all men know, Hrothulf and Hrothgar humbled the host of Ingeld, hewing down the host of the Heathobardnas.

"More than all these, are not the portents clear within the Island of Bryttene itself? Did they not enjoy the Peace of Frea for the space of a generation, while the Bear-king ruled the Bryttas? Under his rule they of all nations prospered beneath the skies, so that all neighboring races across the whale-ridden seas came to obey him and offer him tribute. Upon his shield he bore the image of Crist's mother, whom we call Frea, and Crist raised his sharp-filed cross in rebellion against the rampart of the All-father. But then the Bear was slain in battle by his nephew, and there followed (so I have heard tell) three years of war with the West Seaxe and three winters wicked as the World-serpent. Now some say that Bryttene is itself the world, raised up by Wade from the whale-ridden ocean. If all these things be true, which I doubt not they are, then is the last age of conflict come. The world is breaking up, and its cities lie open to plunder. I believe that the time has come for all the kings of the earth, congregated here within this mighty hall of Heorot, to assemble their keel-borne hosts and harry that rich island."

So spake Unferth son of Ecglaf, sitting at the feet of the lord of the Scyldingas, unloosing secret words to stir up strife. For he was the king's *thyle,* whose task it is to advise the king and speak on his behalf to all the company.

Then was there delight in Unferth's words among that noble company, where they sat upon the benches at their beer. They approved the lovely song of Heorrenda, and the wily words of Unferth, revealing their thoughts each to the other. Many boasted of their swords and skills and triumphs in battles past, while others spoke of deeds yet to be done when springtime came, and their ships should sail over the briny ocean to the Island of Bryttene.

Delightful was the merriment, and mightier than men proved the mead they drank. For it became a binder and a scourger, and at the last a thrower. Sometimes it cast a champion upon the ground, where he grappled in vain against its mighty assault, hitting the bright-tiled floor with his back and beating it with his heels. Robbed of his will, boisterous in speech, deprived of his strength, he might no longer control his mind, his feet, or his hands.

Each drank to each, a horn drained at every health. Helpless were the heroes, happy and given to song. Some spewed upon the floor while others made their way out through the door to empty the enemy of wit upon the frosty ground. Others fell by the fire, whom maids helping at the hearth saved from roasting by drawing stoppers from casks, so letting the good beer which had been their downfall become instead their savior.

Nor were frothing beer and sparkling mead the only liquors that the good earth beneath the hall of Heorot drank with eager greed. It happened that Hagena, hardy king of the Holm-Rygas, crossed over to the bench where sat sturdy Heoden, king of the Glommas. No good-will lay between their peoples, but upon the hall of Heorot at that time was the Peace of Frea. It was in Hagena's mind to proffer friendship to Heoden, such help as hand gives to hand, or foot to foot. However, it happened by misfortune that as he stood hard by Heoden, there gushed up from within his stomach a great spew, which flowed upon Heoden's face, entering his nostrils and his eyes and his mouth, and running down his chest until he was all but smothered by the extent of that great spew.

For a short space Heoden might hardly breathe; but when he did he likewise puked forth against his will a mighty spurt of spew, enveloping King Hagena as it were in a veil of vomit from head to heel. Some men made mirth at this, especially when both kings were also seen to have fouled their breeches, fore and aft, so that they were entirely besmeared in filth, wallowing like hogs in their own mire; but warriors of the Holm-Rygas and the Glommas who possessed power still to stand grew enraged with one another. Seizing spears from the iron-clamped wall, they thrust blindly at one another in their anger, though in truth it was not they who fought, but the good ale which gripped them fast. Nor does the slaying spear like to lie idle upon a king's wall!

In this manner were the sworn oaths of thegns violated on both sides, and many were stabbed and slain, so that they fell among those whom beer and mead had already laid low between the benches. Blood spurting from slit gullets mingled with the foaming ale that gushed from casks beside the slain, the flesh of some of whom sizzled upon the cinders of the royal hearth of Heorot. Then was the hall filled with the flash of darting weapons, the screams of the wounded, and the smell of roasting flesh. Hawks within the hall swooped screaming over the heads of the warriors, while outside in the darkness steeds stamped in the courtyard.

It was wrong that the Peace of Frea should be broken in this fashion, and King Hrothulf was angered. He signed to his counselor, Unferth son of Ecglaf, who passed between the benches until he came to the place where sat the old champion of the Dene, he who saved Heorot from the murderous assault of Grendel long years ago. There the cunning counselor whispered into the ear of the lord of the Geatas, who uprose and cried out that all men should be still, permitting their swords to sleep once more within their sheaths.

Then did the slaughter cease, for upon the hero's head was set a helm surmounted by a boar-crest, emblem of Frea. Never did the son of Ecgtheow slay his hearth-companions, even when roused by drink. His heart was not savage, even though he had received from the gods the greatest strength that man may have. But none present in the hall of Heorot dared put to the test the might of the prince of the Geatas, though his hair was whitened by fifty winters. For great and grim was Beowulf, wolf of the bee, furred shambling thief of the hive. Far-famed for fighting was he, and in his embrace was the strength of thirty mighty men. Swords thirsty for their drink of blood were sheathed at his glance, and the worst of foes sat side by side in peace upon the mead-bench to hear his words.

Thus spake Beowulf, upon whose broad shaggy breast there glistened a ringing shirt of mail, web cunningly woven by Weland's skillful craft, growling fiercely:

"Hail to you, Hrothulf! And hail to you, kings and thegns from many countries of the earth! I think many of you have heard of my fame, for from my youth I have accomplished many glorious deeds. My father Ecgtheow was famed among many peoples and came of a noble race, the Wederas. Faithfully in my youth did I serve Hygelac, king of the Geatas, until he died in battle fighting the Fresan. After that I guarded the gift-seat of the Geatas for his son Heardred, until he in turn was slain by Onela, king of the Sweon. After the thirsty sword drank Heardred's blood, Onela bestowed upon me the princely throne of the Geatas, and now it is I who rule in my royal hall at Hreosnabeorh.

"You who feast here in Hrothulf's hall have heard the song of Heorrenda. He unlocked his word-hoard before us, he who of all men has wandered among most tribes and peoples of the earth. You have heard also the wise words of Unferth, the king's skilled counselor. They urge us to fare west over sea, once chill winter be past, when freezing fetters of Frost-giants become loosened upon ponds and estuaries. Then should we scan the omens and take to our curling-prowed ships, sailing away over the swan-ridden seas, driving onward like swift birds with foam-ringed necks, until we gain the gleaming cliffs, broad headlands, and deep estuaries of the land of the Bryttas.

"That, as I have heard, is a land of wealth long unplundered. In its cities lies hoard of treasure and gold uncounted: goblets and bowls, golden arm-rings and jeweled brooches, gilt-hilted swords once clasped by ancient heroes. I am old, and have fought battles unnumbered for my people, Wederas and Geatas. Now it comes into my mind that my *wyrd* is well-nigh woven and I must pass from this bright world of men to that other place beyond the boundless encircling ocean. For fifty years have I protected my people; no neighboring king dared attack me with his trusty sword. I have sworn no unjust oaths and pursued no spiteful feuds. When I ascend the rainbow bridge to join the war-band of the All-father, he will have no cause to reproach me for the treacherous slaughter of any kinsman. I shall die content, my *wyrd* fulfilled as it was ordained. But before that happens, it is my desire to rest my eyes upon a heaped treasure-hoard of lovely gems and glorious gold. Then shall I depart from among you content with my lot, though there be for me no longer bestowal of riches and weapons to those who follow me, nor delight in my own land and my beloved home.

"King Cynric, who dwells among the Bryttas, promises us gold beyond counting and slaughter beyond reckoning, if we join him at his summer hosting against that bold people which follows the false dragon-standard of Crist. Their proud king calls himself the Dragon of Bryttene. All here have heard tell of Sigemund, lord of the Waelsingas, who slew a deadly dragon, guardian of a treasure-hoard. I believe that what Sigemund, hardiest of fighting men, was able to perform, may be achieved by me."

So spoke Beowulf, shield of the Wederas, gazing about him upon the company. It had grown dark within the hall of Heorot as the hearth burned low, and to many it appeared that it was no chieftain in singing coat of ringed mail who addressed them, but a great gray bear, such as suddenly towers aloft, fierce and terrible, before a lone traveler in the forest.

"So this is my advice to all assembled here," concluded the hero, hardy under his helm. "Dene and Wendlas, Sweon and Geatas, Wulfingas and Wederas, Holm-Rygians and Glommas: that you sound the battle horn and send 'round the war-arrow throughout your lands, summoning your hosts, from the boy of twelve years and the foal of two winters, to fare over the swelling deep to the place where white shields will be cloven, cruel spears fly whistling and shrieking, and the arrow-storm sting home above the shield-wall. Then will we see all Bryttene drenched in men's gore, and the dark raven, eager for doomed men, will have much to speak of as he tells the eagle how he fared at his feeding, when with the wolf he devours the slain. Sae-Wicingas shall we be upon our sea-steeds; through deeds of valor alone, glorious and rash, does the highborn hero make his mark upon this earth, defying the darkness, before death steals away the spirit once clothed with flesh."

Then was a great cry raised within the hall, as thegns of high renown swore to become Sae-Wicingas and put the whole Island of Bryttene to fire and sword. Hearts were high and spirits ardent in Heorot, when the thegns heard the words of Beowulf, hardy son of Ecgtheow. Hrothulf's queen, a noble lady bedecked with gold, of illustrious lineage, brought a goblet to the king her husband, guardian of the homeland of the Dene, whom she bade drink beer with a light heart. King Hrothulf, whose victories were famed throughout the world, drank gladly. Then the lady of the Woingas moved about the hall, proffering the bright vessel to noble kings and great thegns who crowded the court of Heorot. To Beowulf, lord of the Wederas and Geatas, she came first, for it was to him that Hrothulf looked first for protection of his kingdom.

The fighter fierce in forays received the goblet from the hand of the highborn queen and drank deep of the strong ale. Then, towering above the tallest like a mighty yew upon the plain, the stalwart son of Ecgtheow once more poured forth his word-wealth. Thus spoke Beowulf, shield of the Geatas:

"Hear now my vow, O shepherd of the Scyldingas, and you his noble queen! Upon the holy ring I swear next spring to take to my ships with my war-band of trusty warriors, Wederas and Geatas. Westward over the whale-path shall we fare, and in that rich land across the waters where gannets bathe shall I bear a fearsome storm of blades upon the Bryttas. With their proud king, who calls himself the Dragon of the Island, shall I myself do combat; or it may be that I shall exchange fierce blows with the demon Crist he worships, should he venture from the halls of Heaven to wage battle for his people.

"Upon the holy ring I vow to perform these deeds for you, O king, or else fall slain, held fast within the foeman's deadly grip. For I scorn to bear sword or spear or broad buckler to this fray: With these bare hands and nails will I grapple with the proud king and the false fiend that sustains him, fighting them to the death, foe to foe. All men know how I ripped the arm from the monstrous Grendel's shoulder, so that he perished miserably in his gore. Now limb from limb will I tear the enemies of my lord, who has bestowed upon me twelve treasures, and much else besides. If once the Bryttas' king or his demon-helper come within this embrace of mine, then will they know no gentle hug, but one which will squeeze the lifeblood forth from the veins beneath their hair. This deed of heroic valor will I achieve, for else must this be my last meeting day within your bright mead-hall, prince of the Scyldingas!"

This proud boasting of the noble son of Ecgtheow pleased well the gracious lady of the Dene, who resumed her seat beside her lord. Once more brave words rang out within the hall of Heorot: the joyous vaunting of a victorious host. The whole company rose, as Hrothulf the wise king kissed and clasped about the neck Beowulf his bold champion.

"Mighty in actions and shrewd in mind are you, Beowulf, who utter such wise words. Not until the dreadful day of Muspilli will your deeds pass from the minds of men, chief of champions!" cried Hrothulf from his high seat to all the company. "Remember your glory; display your resistless valor; watch carefully the crafty foe! You shall lack nothing you desire, should you return alive from this great venture. I can think of no finer man to choose as king and guardian of the warriors' hoard. Of all men that live, it is you that I love dearest.

"But it grieves me that you should set forth in your sea-steed without a trusty weapon by your side. Once you gave my uncle

Hrothgar the ancient weapon which you took from the cavern of that fell being, mother of the moor-prowler, slaughtering her with it and bringing her blood-drenched head to Heorot. For long after Hrothgar's death have I cherished that noble weapon, Naegling, and now it is my desire that you take it with you to the land of Bryttene. Take that well-loved steel to be your friend in the fray and guardian of victory!"

Hrothulf laid Naegling, the serpent-striker, in Beowulf's lap. The wise son of Ecgtheow gazed upon its gold hilt, which he well remembered. Upon it was engraved the wondrous work of Weland: images of that ancient strife when the immortal gods banished the giant-race beyond the rim of the world, and the sun and moon were stablished in the sky as radiant lanterns above the hall of earth-dwellers. Upon the blade, too, was inscribed in runes the name of the god

for whom lame Weland forged it in the former time. With its hilt of writhing patterns and its steely serpent-blade, that was the choicest of weapons.

Sheathed within its scabbard stayed the blade, for while the Peace of Frea was upon Heorot, no sword might rightly breathe the air. Beowulf pondered awhile, gazing upon the images he saw upon its hilt, then spoke again:

"Once was this brand wielded at the establishment of the earth's enclosure, when the glorious company of the gods smote the Frost-giants, and the one-handed one braved the fen-wolf. A second time I myself bore it against that destructive prowler of the borderlands, whose realm is the moor and swamp; the fiend from Hell who ever stalks the Wasteland without the homestead's palisade, seeking to drain Heorot of men and mirth and music, so that the best of houses shall become empty and useless, as when all things come to fall beneath the shadow of darkness. And now, as I think, is come the third time for its steel to be brandished against the foeman's skull. For men say that fierce final fray is now to come upon us, when the sun shall go down for the last time into dreary darkness beneath the surge of encircling ocean. But before that happens, there will be a goodly time of slaughter, when steel will sing out upon ringed mail-coats, the woven mesh be torn apart, and sharp-honed spearheads cluster within men's bellies! I think this sturdy sword, king's gift, will strike true, even against the keen-edged cross of Crist!

"Never did the gray glinting blade, the ancient sword Naegling, fail me in combat. From Grendel's fell mother I took it, striking her death-doomed flesh, so that I severed the sinews and rent the ring-bones of her neck. The grim prowler of the mere I slew, and nine sea monsters likewise. What Sigemund did, I may do; and it will go hard with me if Naegling does not bite deep through the brain-rampart of this Dragon of Bryttene.

"Once was the West-sae called the Fresna-sae, when the ships of the Fresan plied its waters in peaceful trading. Tyr is the warrior-god to whom they sacrifice, and a sturdy fighter is he indeed, though he has but one hand. But his is not the glorious battle-frenzy of Woden, reveling in battle-slaughters and blood sacrifice, like the tempest-lashing ocean which destroys all within his raging path!

"To all assembled here within Hrothulf's hall I have this to say: Next year shall the wild ocean which lashes the coasts of the Dene and the Bryttas be named neither the Fresna-sae nor the West-sae, but the Wicinga-sae, when we Sae-Wicinga will turn its gray-green waters red with the blood of the Bryttas! Welcome is war to Woden's kin! Though generation after generation pass away from this fair earth, yet is the hero's struggle maintained against overwhelming odds, cruel conflict alone rekindling each warrior's strength. Though the odds be hopeless, still shall the sons of men rear their boar-crested helms against whatever *wyrd* has been woven about them!"

As the hero, hardy under his helm, resumed his place upon the mead-bench, a roar of acclamation rang up to the rafters of that glorious hall, and Hrothulf the wise king felt a deep love for the lord of the Wederas, whom he knew to be a stalwart champion of his own people and of the Dene likewise. He who slew Grendel and his hideous dam would bear his blade well against the Bryttas!

As the heroes' shouting died away, they heard from without the iron-clamped walls of Heorot a sobbing moan, as if Hell's slave were howling yet over his grievous wound. It was but the wind sobbing around the hall, whimpering beneath its eaves, and shifting the tapes-tries like sailcloths when first blows the sae breeze within their bellies. A storm was stirring out to sea; that men knew, for with the gale's groaning sounded the moan of Wade's waves lashing high upon the nearby strand. Swirling breakers were whipping high against a louring sky. Out over the Ost-sae a bitter squall was arising; the air grew dim and the skies wept upon the waters. Now beyond the warmth of the hall and its protective palisade were creatures of the night ranging: wolves and warlocks, waves and wind, murk and mists, enveloping moor and sea in darkness and disarray. Afar off was heard the gather-ing growl of Thunor's hammer; the smoke-hole in Heorot's roof

became momentarily a dazzling doorway as the heavens suddenly split
asunder.

Now began black-bellied clouds to roll together, one against the
other, clashing their bucklers together with dire din. Racing over the
ruined earth they came, dusky demons sweating fire in the void,
letting fall black pattering rain from their breasts, water from their
wombs upon the roof-shingles. Black gliding specters shoot their
sharp shafts hard upon the lonely halls of frightened men, and foolish
is he who does not fear their deadly onslaught. Death is the lot of him
at whom the god directs his shrieking spear, and wise is he who knows
it. The moist clouds clash in the scattered sky, the flint-gray flood is
turbulent beneath their blows, the forest sways, and the earth shifts.
Vast plains beneath the sea are shifting, the ocean floor is shaking, the
World-serpent is uncoiling; all that is under the roof of heaven is in a
ferment: wild, rushing, a chaos of intoxication.

So men drank hard of Hrothulf's good beer within their little
haven by Heorot's hearth, until their hearts too were wild as the wind
that screamed across the wilderness without. Once more merriment
soared high as the leaping gale; shouts from the mead-benches rang
louder still; cupbearers bore about wine in wondrous vessels from the
generous hoard of the lord of the Scyldingas. Heorrenda, scop of the
Heodeningas, plucked a wild strain from the chords of his sounding
harp; the yeasty draught of Woden began to bubble, frothing upon the
poet's lips, as he sang loud the lay of Aetla: whirlwind of nations, he
who of all men under the wide sky rode upon the storm, a tempest to
the tribes, crusher of kingdoms and breaker of nations.

Out of the wastes of the North he came, out of the frozen forests
and across the windy steppe, until he settled with his war-band about
the banks of the deep-flowing Danais. Wandering there about the
wilderness they encountered those unclean witches, *helrunan,* upon
whose shrivelled shanks and bloated bellies they begat the demon race
of the Hunas: barely human, stunted, slant-eyed; lacking speech, barking like dogs and howling like wolves. There upon the desolate plains
they multiplied until their host rivaled that of elves and ogres and the
walking dead.

Then out of Asia rode Aetla with his army, a demon-host with
flaming eyes and upswept hair engulphing the horn-decked halls of
mortal men, until he came to the Wilderness of Wistlawudu. Long
within that broad forest did battle rage between Hunas and Gotan, until
the swift-flowing Donua ran red with blood and the mountain passes
of the Maroara were choked with corpses. Eagles screamed over the
slain, and vast was the host that Woden welcomed within his hall.

With the Hunas lay the victory, and all the wide kingdom of wolfish Earmanric fell now beneath Aetla's sway, even from the Ocean Garsecg in the west to the Riffen Range in the east, from Cwenland in the north to the mountains of Alpis in the south. His, too, were the islands that lie in the Ocean, even Burgenda-lande and Bryttene.

After this, Aetla gathered together the warlike tribes of the earth and rode through the wilderness and over the mountains even to the realm of Casere, he who sat upon the throne of all the earth, ruling all the kingdoms that lie about the Wendel-sae. With the rage of Aetla the world itself writhed in turmoil, so that before his approach the walls of Casere's castle collapsed into chasms of the earth. Casere was driven by Aetla from his throne, who put him to an ill death; and all the kings and thegns of the Rumwalas he slaughtered likewise. Cities he burned, giving over this kingdom to slaughter and that to enslavement. No town remained unburned, no hall unstripped of its treasure: The world smoked as in a single pyre!

Men learned that the world was waning, and the last age come upon all that lies spread beneath the skies. Kingship would fail and the gift-seat no longer be a source of wealth; debts accrue, old age corrupt courage, evildoers brawl openly beneath the sun, the war-arrow be sharpened, the spear seek the hero's heart, and death pursue all as every hour of hate and shame tottered toward the worse.

But not yet was that hour come, when the heat of summer shall be no more as three endless winters vent their rage upon a freezing land, and men become wanderers upon the world's face like Wudga and Hama. By a woman's arts, they say, died Aetla the bold champion, flail of mankind, conqueror of cruel Earmanric, killer of Casere, mightiest of kings. Bewailed by his people the wolfish warlord died; the storm has subsided, the rain clouds lifted.

Wild was the wail of Heorrenda by the hearth of Heorot, shrill above the dreadful drumming of Thunor's hammer overhead and the pelting onslaught of the rain. Each warrior sat with his thoughts locked within him, staring before him, unmoving by the dying hearth-glow. Each hero's heart had soared like an unfettered falcon as he hearkened to Heorrenda's lay. Each bethought him of the axe-age Attila had brought upon the earth, when blades were broken, spear-shafts splintered, shields shattered—to be forged anew within the fierce furnace. It had been a mighty wind indeed which blew about the world when the king of the Huns rode wild through Wistlawudu! When the trees are shaken, then the fruit falls: Within the realms of Casere had the tribes taken treasure rich as the jeweled necklace of the Brosingas. Like a ravening wolf within a sheepfold, a bloody froth dripping from his maw, was Aetla amid the halls of Earmanric's realm and the fair cities of the Rumwalas.

Heorrenda, seated at the feet of Hrothulf, read the minds of the heroes. Fame is found on the field of corpses; but fame may not be destroyed, though the body lie cold within its barrow, prey of devouring worms. Whatever be woven within the woof of his *wyrd,* there is not more that a man may do than defend his lord, practice no unwarranted deceit upon his companions, and at the last die defending his own eternal fame.

Throughout the bright hall of the ring-giving sang out the harp of Heorrenda, as he concluded his song with these words:

"There are signs in the heavens, omens in the entrails, that the age of Aetla is to come again upon this falling world! The dread day of Muspilli approaches, when the immortal gods will wage deadly war against the giant-kin, foes of humankind. The World-serpent will arise from the deep, its open jaws reaching from the sea to the sky. In the East the Wolf's fetters will be shattered, and his howling will be heard among the poisonous fens.

"Who is that Wolf but Aetla, returned to ravage the war-wasted world? Within his yawning red gullet he seeks to swallow Woden himself. The earth is shaken with the tramp of armies; forth from his rabid jaws drips down envenomed blood. As the blood drips, so the mountains run aflame, every tree that stands against the sky is consumed, rivers run dry within their courses, the dark moors are sucked down within themselves, the heavens smolder with scorching heat, the moon tumbles from the livid sky, all Middle Earth is burned, no stone remains erect, and the sea seethes with smoking gore.

"Then must Woden's warriors fight fierce as wolves and bears, and every hero who bears his shield before the battle-host do his utmost in the conflict. Each thirsty blade will drink its fill of foeman's blood. Where the danger is direst, there is the glory greatest! Hearken to the song of Heorrenda, O shield-bearing thegns who quaff the strong ale of the Scyldingas! Sharpen your sword blades and burnish your boar-helms! Make ready your sea serpents and summon your hosts! The war-arrow of Cynric has passed among the Woden-kin, and the age of Aetla is come once more upon you!"

The strains of the scop's song surged over the host like a draught of strong ale when it captures a warrior's heart, filling it with wild longing for fine weapons, journeyings over the swan's bath, and ringing of keen-edged swords on war-helms. It was the power of Woden which held them fast; for what is verse but Woden's mead, and the waging of war Woden's frenzy?

So it was that boasts were uttered and oaths sworn within the hall of Heorot. Over the ale-drinking hovered he who is the heron of confusion, stealing the wits of men and entangling them in a fury which boded but little good for the land of Bryttene, once the passing of winter should come to unlock the ice-fetters which hold the waves in check. Westward over the waves would the sea serpents glide upon the whale's path, bearing upon the breast of the briny sea the storm-tossed battle-frenzy of the father of feuds and harvester of corpses.

The dark cowl of night was black and the blizzard still buffeted the iron-clamped beams of Heorot, when the benches were stripped bare and bedding bestowed about the hall for the repose of the warriors. By their heads they bestowed their stout bucklers, bright shields of linden wood; upon the bench above each sleeping hero was set his lofty battle-helm, his webbed shirt of shining ring-iron, and his sturdy spear. At all times was that numberless company of heroes ready to do battle for their liege lord; battle-hardened and bold was that hardy host!

Thus the winter passed among the numberless tribes of the Wicinga-cynn who dwell about the West-sae and the Ost-sae. The kings dispensed good ale and golden rings in their halls, while those who were bound to them by bonds of fealty harbored fell thoughts of hammer-forged swords stained with gore, cruel of edge, shearing the boar-crests from their foemen's helms.

Meanwhile Heorrenda the famed scop took to his ship and returned northward through the Sound of Scedenig, past the Promontory of the Wendlas, until once more he was riding the wild waves of the West-sae. It was not, however, his purpose to return to the court of Cynric in the land of the Gewissae, nor did he seek the coasts of Bryttene. Northward he pursued his path through the lashing gray-green sea, passing beside Northmanna-land until he came to Halgoland. No man dwells farther north than Halgoland, but it was in Heorrenda's mind to fare farther yet.

For three days he sailed northward along the land, leaving the wasteland to his starboard and the open sea upon his backboard. He passed the deserted havens where the whale hunters go at their farthest, and fishers of cod seek the last fishing grounds in the open ocean. Thither witches passing over the sea draw the catch by lures of enchantment, changing the surface of the waters to a lightish green above their watery lair. Among the islands on that chill coast there is much magic, where footless scaly ones watch each from his barrow-haunt upon a headland. For Halgoland in the North is a region given over to hiding places, things cunning and slippery, secret, slant-eyed.

Not rashly had Heorrenda made his way hither over the seal's path to this waste of ocean and craggy islands, however. In Heorot were heroes enough to put an edge to the sword and a point to the spear for a splitting of helms and shearing of limbs; sufficient, too, were the ships of the Fresan to bear those of the Bryttas who survived the slaughter-field into thralldom of chains and wretchedness. But if the time of Muspilli be approaching, then are swords and slave-collars not all that need be garnered for the red harvest. Words of wisdom, spells, visions, blood sacrifices: All these must be assured were King Cynric's royal luck to hold for his enterprise.

Far in the frozen wastelands of the North, on the borderland of Middle Earth, dwells the troll-race of the Scride-Finnas, over whom rules Caelic their king. Masters of magic and wizardry are they, practicing their arts each year in a drear cold night which endures for three whole months. An unchancy land is that to visit for those who voyage unprepared. Concealed within his cloak the scop bore rune-staves inscribed by the *blotere* of King Hrothulf's court. A skilled seer was that man, whose arts enabled him to loose and bind with rune-charms, once won by Woden as he hung upon the windy tree. And the rune he wrote was this:

"Heorrenda am I called, wise among travelers, bringing good luck."

Heorrenda's ship coursed ever northward. South of Halgoland the coastland was fertile, supporting many kings; but now the mountains pressed ever closer to the whale-ridden sea, until a bare three miles lay between coast and crags. Dark was the shadow they threw, and darker still the skies ahead. The sun, that bright candle of the sky, but showed his rim above the sea in the south as he passed on his daily journey into the depths of the Ocean Garsecg.

Heorrenda stood watch at the prow, his feet nipped with cold, frost-bound in chill fetters, hunger tormenting his soul. Winter wandered over the ice-cold sea, whose mighty breakers beat roaring against the rocky cliffs. Icicles hung from spars and rigging of stout walrus-hide, the sail flapped stiffly, and hail, coldest of grain, lashed the length of the strong-ribbed craft as it plunged painfully onward through the shifting swell. There was nothing in the scop's mind but the endless roar of white-crested breakers and the lap of the ice-cold sea. Not the laughter of men in the merry mead-hall did Heorrenda hear, but the plaintive cry of the gannet or the song of the wild swan. Above him screamed the sea mew, ice upon its pinions; the tern replied from its perilous cliff-perch.

Onward plunged the ship, through the fierce surging sea, until the scop became long wearied with the wave-path. Thick fog, witch-summoned, hung low about him, so that he might hardly breathe. At times the monsters of the deep drew near, spouting forth pillars of water that seemed to support the sky. Gaunt guardians of the deep, they open wide their grim jaws to entice unwary hordes of fish. Drawn by a sweet smell, their myriad victims are drawn unwittingly to their doom. Just so, thought Heorrenda, might be the outcome of his rash voyage. For he was entering the realm of eternal night, and a snow blizzard blew out of the bleak north. Dark waves dashed themselves fiercely over the prow; the unquiet ocean sought to draw the vessel down into the deep, beneath the dead waves. Within the whale's maw, beneath the dark waves' surge, might the ship with all its company be swallowed up into that swart void which existed in olden days, when there was neither sand nor sea nor cool waves: Earth did not exist nor heaven above; there was no grass, but a great emptiness.

Out beyond the skirts of the earth, deep below the surface waters where sea dragons and water monsters plunge in search of unhappy prey, down upon the ocean floor, Eagor's nine maidens were grinding the host-destroying skerry-quern. Ever faster whirled the Ocean-mill, its twin stones large as islands in the abyss. Ever wilder rang the laughter of the flowing-haired daughters of greedy Eagor, wild as the wet west wind, as they ground out their spiraled stream of salt into the thirsty main. A grating whir spread through the silence of the sandy ocean depths, as the rough round stone rotated ever faster.

Then, as the quern-wheel swirled more fiercely still, the maidens began to grind with giant-fury. The pole-frame shook, the earth shuddered; the quern-bin collapsed, the massive millstone was split asunder! Nine years the mill-maidens toiled beneath the earth, and now in frenzied rage they flung the mighty stone against the earth's face. Within them was the pitiless plight of bondmaids, grit-gnawed, frost-nipped, hate-drawing. The sea floor trembled, the earth shook, rocks clattered down from cliff-faces, and cliffs collapsed amid fog of spume and splash of spray into the turbulence of land and sea. It was to their own minds' liking they ground, not to that of mortal men, among whom they spread discord and cruel strife. Brands they reddened, as ring-mailed warriors flew to the battle-throng, and thrust their spear-shafts into the open wounds of bleeding foes.

Heorrenda's beak-prowed vessel was flung by Eagor's nine foam-haired daughters tossing toward jagged-jawed reefs and sharp-prowed cliffs. Then, as it seemed the frail bark must be shattered upon the sea-swept stones, the terrible whirling eddy, the mouth of the great World-mill, gaped gushing open out in the West-sae, seeking to suck down through its throat the scop's ship, into the maw where the skerry-grinder ceaselessly grinds all things to grainy sand.

Heorrenda glimpsed through the gathering gloom cold cliff walls, at whose feet were thrust forth ragged-edged rocks. Bright stars now banished to obscurity yet drew the tide racing toward narrow inlets, upon whose ramparts squatted Frost-giants exulting over their prey. He who guided the ship upon its way was skilled in sea lore, a man of the Haerethas accustomed to the ways of the West-sae. Yet even he felt terror as he sought to set a safe course beside the cruel cliffs of stone. For lumbering ice-islands, splitting and cracking in the cold, came rolling in upon them from the sea, seeking to splinter their frail wooden walls between the blue cliffs and the gray.

One night, between sleeping and waking, Heorrenda believed he saw upon a floe a huge white bear, who raised himself upright and shook his paws toward them. Fearful what this might mean, he asked the ship's master, who told him it was a sign that the weather would worsen, waxing to a gale: There would come a snowstorm from the east. And so it was, for the ocean floor was convulsed by the juddering of the Ocean-mill, and writhed within the clutch of the encircling World-serpent, until it seemed certain all within the ship must be swallowed up within the whale's lake.

"I foresee our deaths!" lamented the scop, fingering his rune-stave. "Our souls are fluttering between this world and the next. Doomed are we to die in the dismal Northland; frost and cold and horrors lie all about us!"

His heart near failing from fear and freezing cold, Heorrenda flung open wide his word-hoard to the winds, uttering this *gealdor:*

> "Fly forth, fleet keel, before the gales,
> Forth from fair land of songs and tales;
> My comrades seek a southern breeze
> Such as we knew in time of ease.
> Should courage fail the war-word's lost,
> And Woden's vessel overtossed.
> The cordage creaks, the strake-bands slip;
> Scarce floats at all our song-borne ship.
> On Woden's errand are we bound
> And fail it must if we be drowned;
> Cracking ice-floes, blizzard and snow,
> Hem 'round our boat; which way to go?"

A fierce, cutting northern wind snatched the words from Heorrenda's

lips, and the foulest of bitter weather and a louring night came rushing
suddenly upon them. But just when death seemed nearest, there arose
out of the deep before them a white whale who sported upon the sea,
guiding them onward in safety through many a dangerous sound and
around many a razor-backed reef. In that whale's wake the sea lay calm
about the foam-ringed vessel, so that its ironbound prow with serpent's head coursed swiftly and smoothly over the currents. And so it
came about that the sea with its rolling tides swept them onward over
a flood of coursing waters until they came to a lonely inlet, where the
wave washed the shore in the land of the Scride-Finnas. There is no
more northerly place than that in the world, nor none colder; for
afterward the coast inclines eastward, or the sea into the land—men
know not which.

There the wanderer, skilled in songs, made his landing. Masking
the dragon prow of his swift vessel, lest the land-spirits who teemed
on every hill and headland be affronted by its gaping jaws, he threw
down the anchor upon its hawser. Upon the frozen strand he found
men of the Scride-Finnas cutting up a great whale of fifty ells' length
beside a blazing fire. At first it was hard for the scop to tell whether
they were indeed men and not beasts, for they were garbed in the skins
of wild beasts, fastened together with sinews. Moreover they seemed
to bark and growl one to the other rather than speak with the tongues
of men. Nevertheless the men of the Scride-Finnas made Heorrenda
and his comrades welcome, for in his ship's hold lay cargo of amber
and honey from Estland, and other gifts dear to the Beormas and
Scride-Finnas who dwell most northerly of all men.

The scop and his company stayed with these people for a time,
dwelling within the tents of the Scride-Finnas while they awaited a
sign. For eternal night lay upon that land, and it was by the movements of the stars alone that men might reckon the passing of time. In
this way Heorrenda spent thirty-five nights, dwelling in the tents of
the Scride-Finnas. Finally there came a day when a man came riding on
a reindeer from a certain high mountain, who bore news that the
sun would return within five days.

Then the Scride-Finnas rejoiced, making preparation to perform
rites in honor of the returning daylight. It was at the ninth hour of that
day that Heorrenda saw where an old gray wolf approached him
where he stood at his tent's entrance. At this he went inside and put on
a hooded coat of sealskin and a pair of snowshoes. Bidding farewell to
his dear companions, he set off after the wolf across the snow plain.

For five days Heorrenda traveled thus, alone save for his wolf
guide, over the cold wilderness which the Scride-Finnas term Pohjanmoa.

And on the fifth day the rim of the sun was seen ascending over forests to the south. Pohjanmoa is a world formless, frozen and empty, realm of icy-fingered Pakkanen, whose breath is a wind sharp as a whetted knife. Along the boundless coast of Pohjanmoa he roams, freezing coves and ponds, icing up the shores of the sea. For long he did not freeze the sea fully over, but with the arrival of the poet he grew violent, spreading himself about at first in mischievous mood, then growing dark and dreadful.

Then all things became utterly frozen; Pakkanen's power froze hard. It froze ice a forearm thick, flung down snow a ski pole deep. It froze Heorrenda's ship to the frozen beach and froze the tents of the whale hunters until the leather was hard as pine planks. Next Pakkanen thought to freeze Heorrenda, too, pursuing him through the mountain passes, demanding his nose and fingers and toes. His laughter was heard in the tinkling of icicles, in the splitting of stones, the cracking of pine branches, as he pressed upon the track of the poet's snowshoes.

And as he raced after his victim, Pakkanen paused to freeze fens, freeze stones into the landscape, and the landscape into one icy element. Willows shivered and were still, gall was stripped from aspens, bark from birches. Crags became as iron, mountains as steel; cataracts congealed. Upon the settlements of the Scride-Finnas, the Beormas, and the Ter-Finnas, he laid snow in thick layers, while under the snow he extended his thin fingers until he froze the cauldron to the hearth, the coals within the hearth, the wife's hands within the dough. Further he felt within, freezing milk in ewe's udders, the foal in the mare's belly; nipping the child in the maiden's womb.

Harsh was Pakkanen's laughter in the silver moonlight upon the ice-glare. He mocked at Heorrenda, treading upon his heels, howling about his ears. He blew about the pine groves, roaring in the pines, frolicking in the birch copses, frisking among the alders. He swooped across the surface of the marshes, turning quagmires to hard plains. Then he whisked about and tore across the mountain slope, withering grasses where he passed and flattening fields. The trees he bit leafless, pinched off the bloom from the heather, scraped scales of bark from tall larches, broke branches from the pine.

Heorrenda felt Pakkanen's ice-cold fingers pluck at his heels, tweak about his ears, pinch his nose. He hunched his head within his hood of warm sealskin; he slid onward in the wolf's path. His guide's breath hung like woodsmoke upon the cold air; his gray fur glinted with frost. In the wind about his pinched ears, the poet heard Pakkanen's mocking vaunts:

"Do you know who I am? Have you heard of my fame? All men

know my lineage, know Pakkanen's upbringing! Among the willows was Pakkanen born, born in a birch grove, behind a tent of the Lappalainen—a rascally father, a shameless mother! Who suckled Pakkanen, nursed him to vigor, he whose mother lacked milk, was born without breasts? It was a serpent suckled Pakkanen, suckled and nurtured him, with tipless teats and empty udders. The north wind bore him up; the icy air rocked him among clogged willow-lined streams, by heaving quagmires. Cold over Pohjanmoa is the breath of Pakkanen, cold serpent's fosterling, and cold is the message he breathes at your ears, about your fingers, into your snow-dampened boots of reindeer skin, and down into the chill caverns of your lungs, O traveler upon the wastes!''

Heorrenda sped on, clasping his rune-stave, closing his ears to the demon's taunting, invoking the protection of his gods against the long-fingered Wizard of Pohjanmoa. He felt himself near to death: death, not leading through lofty gates into Woden's glorious hall, but death here upon the shrieking snow-fields; death where the River of Tuonela winds, where Tuoni's son with gnarled fingers and iron nails draws men down into the sucking quagmire where frogs spawn in the slime and seething reptiles crawl. He grew weak and faint; his lungs were choked with frost. Upon the snow-plain approaching he glimpsed a snow-cloud coming on before, as fast as Pakkanen pursued behind. He looked east and west, south and north. There was no escape, for the sky was white with snow, white was all the earth, and there was neither up nor down, east nor west upon the shapeless, lifeless wilderness of Pohjanmoa. There was little Heorrenda might do, but he feared Pakkanen most of all, and continued to follow the wolf. It was not long before the snow-billow loomed before him and he was engulphed within the white whirlwind.

Heorrenda's sight was blinded for a while by the gusting snow-flakes, but soon he found his sight again. Then he saw that which made him marvel. The rolling cloud of powdered snow was raised by the running of a great herd of reindeer, thirty score in number. In their midst coursed a gilded sledge, reindeer-driven, upon which sat a squat figure, slant of eye and broad of brow. Though he spoke no word, pointing merely to the poet to mount the seat beside him, the poet knew him for the king of the Scride-Finnas, he who rules all Beormaland from the West-sae to the Cwen-sae.

Even as Heorrenda sprang up beside the king, the reindeer herd wheeled about the sledge's turning, and the cavalcade spun onward in the midst of the snow-cloud. Silently they sped across the glaring desolation of Pohjanmoa; a land uncultivated, without brushwood even; a land given over to the bear and the elk, the wolf and the otter, where was neither sun, nor moon, nor dawn in the east. Endless night lay upon that accursed land, *talvidja*, such as was in the darkness of the void before the earth's conception, when earth and sky and sea still lay within the womb of Ilmatar.

Recklessly the little king's sledge skimmed onward, over fens, over the countryside, over open clearings in the boundless forest. Fire spurted from its runners; smoke started from the hoofs of the reindeer team. They glided swiftly over hills, over swamps, over regions beyond the sea; skied through all Hiisi's backwoods, through Kalma's graveyard heath; skied past death's domain, past Kalma's hateful homestead. Now Hiisi's jaws were opened, opened wide to devour the wayfarers; and barely did they skim out beyond his closing trap. For ever as they coursed on across the silvered snow, a small bird flew before them, sure guide upon their journey, sure helper on the way.

Along the sledge track of the cold north wind they flew, on the road of the blizzard, the path of the storm. From the farther side of the heavens yelled the gale, from the cradle of tempests, from the boundless back parts of Pohjanmoa. But not heaving quagmires might halt the little king's sledge with its reindeer escort, nor black ooze of a thousand fathoms, nor rustling spear-grass, nor reeking gore. By broad black lakes, across the crests of windswept ridges, past the mouth of Hiisi's dank cave, ever onward flashed the king's sledge, until they came to Syojatar's filthy snake enclosure, where reptiles writhe behind an iron wall which stretches from earth to heaven.

As the sledge flashed by, the ogress Syojatar looked out at her gateway. She had drawn her clothes over her head and was walking backward, her head bent down between her legs, and it was no kindly look she gave as she darted troll-glances at the travelers. She began to raise about them a thick mist upon the forest and the valley, and it was easy to see that she planned their destruction. It was a fog such as Terhen-neiti pours out upon the unwary traveler who finds himself yet from home at evening: a mist ascending to the heavens, a fog ascending to the sky. But the little king threw something that looked like ashes from a sack above their heads and over their tracks, which concealed the progress of their sledge from the witch-wife.

Then she grew angry, and her eyes flashed in the mist like marsh-lanterns. They heard her muttering in baleful wise; at once the land began to quake and heave and make as if to turn over, so that the landscape would be altered and grass never grow there again. This time the king threw three pebbles over his shoulder, which made appearance before the ogress of a range of hills, a snowdrift, and a rushing river. So her pursuit was stayed, and the reindeer host galloped on around the sledge, coursing upon its smooth runners of alder wood.

Thus it was that the little king's sledge came to the Falls of Kaatrakoski, ascending three glassy rapids, crossing three steely lakes, passing over three iron mountains. Fear lay upon the heart of Heorrenda, and he inquired of the little king what was their destination?

"We travel but a short distance now," responded the king. "A day's journey will bring us to a fiery river, within whose flood is a fiery current, within whose current lies a fiery island, upon which stands a fiery knoll, and on the knoll a fiery eagle. By night it whets its beak upon a stone; by day it quietly sharpens its talons."

"For whom does it make these preparations?" asked the scop in fear.

"For you, if your purpose be a false one," replied the king shortly.

Heorrenda clutched his rune-stave, uttering to himself runes of protection, which none knew better than he. So they passed the river and the island and the eagle in safety, but barely.

And now at last the scop found himself approaching that holy place which he had sought so far from the warm hearth of Heorot in the realm of the Scyldingas. The little king's sledge came over the snowfields to a hill; it traveled along the foot of it, along the left side of it. It came upon a river; it traveled upon the side of it, the left bank of it. It flew by three rapids, came to a long headland, came to a great shimmering lake upon whose expanse blazed the reflected lamps of the stars. Most brilliantly of all glittered the figure which is known to the people of Pohjanmoa as Vainamoinen's Scythe.

Beside the lake uprose a great fell, a hill of rock, a copper mountain. Once that fell had floated on an empty ocean, stood alone above the billows, lonely island on the broad expanse of the sea, on the unbounded open ocean. At the foot of the fell the little king halted his sledge and turning to his companion, told him his thought:

"Here you must ascend alone," he said, speaking further: "This is cold Pohjola, the gloomy fell. I advise you to keep your wits about you if in truth you are rash enough to enter the enclosure upon its summit. You may not see it now, for that weeping cloud obscures it. The ascent is clear enough, but beware! Behind every boulder lies a wizard, *turjalainen*, who will seek to destroy you with spells more potent than any in the land from which you hail. Naked they are, those snakes in the grass; coiled without clothing, not boasting even a belt. If they may, they will thrust you into the ashes, burning ashes, between red-hot boulders.

"However, if you sing this spell, they will be unable to touch you, though they lie there under their high-peaked hats until the grass grows through their shoulders."

And the little king recited a charm to Heorrenda, which may not be repeated in this place.

"If you succeed in gaining the summit," continued the little king, "you will come to the home of my mother, Louhi, and a fierce woman is she. About her yard is a ring of stakes; upon each stake stands a head, save upon one. Unless you are wiser and warier than other men, it may be they will cut off your head to adorn that stake. Should you evade your fate, however, I believe you will find that which you seek. For my mother, Louhi, is wise beyond all other witches of Pohjanmoa.

"Moreover, beneath Pohjola's hill of rock, inside the copper mountain, beneath its roots, behind five locks, lies the lovely Sampo; with its many-colored lid, sprouting all the seeds, grinding all the grain, milling all the salt that is in the world. Three roots it has reaching down to wretched Tuonela; it is the mainstay of the earth, and prop of the skies. That which you wish to know, and much more, you may learn from the whirring of the Sampo.

"Now, go upon your way! Should you return, I shall be here to guide you once more upon your way."

So Heorrenda thanked the little king, and proceeded on his journey. A long and rocky path it was that he found before him; behind every boulder watched a wizard, a singer of spells, a mutterer over salt, a binder of blue threads. As Heorrenda wound upward on his way he played upon his harp, singing the charmed song taught him by the king. The wizards succumbed to the spell, falling asleep each behind his own rock; their evil charms were frustrated, their spells spilt upon the wind: all save one.

Into the traveler that one shot darts of forgetfulness, tossed bundles of oblivion about him, plucked forth the roots of his memory. Heorrenda forgot the purpose of his voyage upon the ocean, no longer recalled the meaning of his journey on the mountain. He trudged upward on the stony path, slipping his foothold in the frozen snow. His memory-hoard was emptied; purposeless was his journey.

Once safely upon the summit, Heorrenda found the air about him resonant with rhythmic throbbing, like the beating of his wearied heart within, like rolling thunder in the valleys. At length he was come to the crest of the holy fell, a place of dread, and saw before him the knoll surrounded by stakes, as foretold him by the little king. Upon each was a severed head, dripping blood; upon one alone was the sharpened point bare, awaiting its prey. But since he was come so far upon his longest journey, the scop was determined to persevere, whatever danger loomed. Not upon that empty spearpoint should his head be impaled—on that was he resolved.

The cloud that rested upon the fell was now a dripping fog about him, and it was a little time before the scop of the Heodeningas might see what lay before him, what stood within the enclosure. Then he saw before him a high platform, and upon it a giant image of wood who bore both a shovel and a club. About the platform was assembled a host of kneeling wizards, a gathering of *noidi,* wearing hoods high and pointed, hoods bedecked with garlands of dried leaves, and belts of enchantment girt about their bodies. Their clothes were turned inside out and back to front; and the sound which Heorrenda heard, echoing about the place of dread, he found to be their drumming—a drumming of forked sticks upon drums painted with rune-signs: animals of the mountain and forest, stars, sun, and moon.

Even as the scop himself knelt amid the company of wizards, he saw that the sacrifice was about to begin. A number of men gripped fast a reindeer ox by its horns and muzzle, seized the stag and bore him down. A little old man with iron-gray hair, a *noidi* from out of the gray sea, from out of the gentle swell, from out of the wide ocean, approached the glaring-eyed steer. He bore a knife of gold, with copper-ornamented handle. As the beast struggled and screamed, screams that echoed in the ice-cloud, the chief *noidi* sliced off pieces of its ears and rump, placing them upon the platform as an offering to the god, invitation to a feast. Then was the beast's throat cut, and its blood caught in a large bowl. This the *noidi* bore up onto the platform, smearing the wooden image all over, so that it dripped from head to foot with life-bestowing gore.

All this while the fog clung close about the holy place, and the throbbing of the wizards' drums grew ever louder. It seemed to Heorrenda that amidst the strident din he could distinguish the cries of beasts and birds from forest and mountain, and human voices jabbering in tongues unknown even to him who had fared more widely than any other man. Every moment the frenzied drumming increased in vibrant volume, until the congealed air enclosing the assemblage, the deep-rooted mountain itself, began to reverberate in concert with the crouching *noidi,* with the palpitating heart of the flayed reindeer lying before them.

The poet felt the pulsation steal over his body, the humming fill his hearing, the strange speech of the drums engulph his mind. There were voices which it seemed he half understood amid the baying, snarling, droning, and squeaking that surrounded him. His companions were loosening their belts and shoelaces, and he did the same. They were nodding, swaying, writhing beneath the spell of the incessant drumbeat; their eyes were glazed, and froth stained their lips. Their jaws champed upon alder bark, and the juice dripped down their frozen beards like a seeping stream of blood.

Heorrenda swayed like a birch bending before a sea gale, and as his head lolled helplessly about, he saw that the mother of the little king stood among the company. Louhi was she called, and it was in the form of a huge she-cat that her face loomed out of the fog before him. The fur on her forehead was erect, her eyes wild, and her ears pricked sharp. A drop of blood stood upon the tip of every hair and whisker. The fierce mask came and went before the poet's gaze in the gray gloom that swirled about the sacred knoll, and it was now that he felt the greatest fear. Louhi's stare was mocking and cruel, and the far-faring scop felt himself to be but a mouse within the clasp of her curved claws.

Heorrenda closed his eyes, when in a moment a savage screaming raised his fearful lids once more. His companions' drumming was now so wild and swift, it seemed one endless shriek of ecstasy and pain. Their faces haggard, drained of blood, devoid of manhood, were lit by a strange light. No longer bent over their baying drums, they were raised in sightless adoration toward the bloodstained column, which stretched ever higher into the dense cloud hanging overhead.

At last it seemed to Heorrenda that he understood something of the barking, screaming ululation about him. The *noidi* were calling, crying out to the god of the pillar: Bieg-Olmai, ruler of the wild winds that race all winter long about the desolate snow-plains of Pohjanmoa. He it is who sends the blizzard whirling down from the mountains, dropping snowdrifts large as hillsides down the scree. He dwells among high rocks and upon inaccessible precipices. With his shovel he holds the winds within their cave until their time be come; and then he takes his club and lashes them upon their way.

Bieg-Olmai's laughter cackles harshly over fell and lake as he whips up storms along the seacoast, overturning in an instant the frail craft of the walrus hunters. Driving blizzards of snow he flings in the faces of the reindeer herdsmen as they skim the snow-face, returning to their settlements at dusk. With volleys of hail sharp as elf-shot he lashes lake and forest, fen and moor. And as he howls through the forest he tears up the tallest trees, so that their agonized tearing and rending, snapping and splitting, echo sharply over the snowfields, leaping across cold crags and spinning along blue rivers of ice. All Pohjanmoa groans and shivers beneath the wind of Bieg-Olmai's club, so that the wilderness itself howls continually in pain.

It is within the rocky halls of Huodno that the winds of the earth
dwell, a place of misery and wretchedness. But if the blood sacrifice be
to Bieg-Olmai's liking, then may he relent the keenness of his temper.
If the drumming draw his heart down toward pitiful mankind, shivering within their leathern tents, then may he in his mildness drive the
winds back into their cave with his shovel, sending soft breezes that
draw reindeer back to the valleys.

Despite the clustering fog, the wind was icy cold upon the holy
fell that night, and the *noidi* drummed and screamed with a noise of
wolves and eagles, dispatching into the upper air spirit-birds, spirit-
reindeer, spirit-fish, that they might summon *noida-gadze* to inhabit the
bodies of the *noidi,* revealing the words which Bieg-Olmai might wish
to hear upon his mountain-peak:

"Put away thy club; take up thy shovel, Bieg-Olmai! Lock up
your mighty winds, Bieg-Olmai! Leave behind only balmy breezes
such as reindeer relish, Bieg-Olmai! Bieg-Olmai: we have bestowed
blood upon your pillar, and life-giving blood will we give you in
abundance!" throbbed out the drums, wailing across the wilderness.
With one voice the *noidi* pleaded with Bieg-Olmai, chanting together:

> "Bieg-Olmai, take back your winds!
> Bind the weather with bonds of copper, bonds of brass!
> Seize your shovel! Slam the door!
> Fling down black slime upon the clear waters!"

But Bieg-Olmai's laughter shrieked mockingly about them; not
this winter would he be placated! Howled the wind from around the
mountain, yelled the gale that lashed the chilly land. The boulders
whistled wildly; the rocks clattered harshly. The frozen rivers stirred;
the lakes shivered; the copper mountains trembled. Shaken was soil
above rocks, rocks above gravel; stirred was the world upon its black
underwater ocean. All creation juddered dizzily. Blurred was the vision of the voyager from overseas; darkened before his gaze was the
snowy summit of the fell, dark as the time before Varalden-Olmai set
the sun upon its golden birch tree, placed the moon above its silver
pine; a time when men crouched in a dank ditch, without sun, without
moon, searching the hard ground with their hands, the marshes with
their fingers.

The moment passed, the cloud was lifted, and the scop saw the
noidi drew out their sharp knives, slashing and stabbing at their faces,
so that the blood coursed down their cheeks, mingling with the froth
that foamed from their gaping mouths. Heorrenda gazed about him

mistily within the throbbing murk, upon the gnashing teeth and bloody brows of the frenzied *noidi*. Why he was there he knew not; the purpose of his journey was unknown to him. Barbed were the arrows of oblivion which the wizard of the mountain slope, *turjalainen*, had lodged within his flesh; not easily may they be loosened. But the shaking of the earth by Bieg-Olmai loosened them, shook them to the frozen ground, stuck them to the ice. Jarred was Heorrenda's thought-coffer, and memory spilled from beneath its opened lid.

The pillar of the earth upon the platform, pillar which linked the ice-gripped ground to the cloud-bellied sky, staggered and lurched. The giant who lies imprisoned within the iron-clamped smithy beneath the roots of the holy fell was straining at the chains that bind him, striving to break the bars that hold him in. Stayed he must be, strapped down within the rock, for once freed he would fasten a ring to heaven, fasten a chain to the ring, drag down the sky, overturn the earth, confound earth and sky in unmarked turmoil. Goaded by hot venom dripping unceasingly upon him, he strives with all his might to loosen the bonds, untie the knots, unspell the runes of binding which preserve Middle Earth from being overwhelmed by the energy of his convulsions.

From the bloody pillar's axis spread the turmoil of earth's shaking, shuddered and jarring. All about it were bloody blades that carve dead faces, gaping mouths that shriek the charms. As he gazed about him upon slashing knives and into open-lipped wounds, slowly into Heorrenda's mind from afar off there stole a long-forgotten lay of the Hunas, which he had learned from a scop of their race when dwelling among the Swaefe. Was not this the screaming and stabbing and the icy wind off the steppe of which the lay the Hunas call *strava* told? The world-pillar was rocking for the time of Muspilli, as it did when Aetla the World-conqueror raised his fierce whirlwind which laid low all the world.

When Aetla came to die, his people mourned his corpse about its silken tent, hacking their cheeks with weapons in token of mourning according to the custom of the Hunas. Amid the shrieking of the *noidi,* the howling of the storm, and the groaning of the world-tree, Heorrenda raised his voice aloud in utterance of the *strava* of Aetla:

"Here lies Aetla, great king of the Hunas,
Mighty son of Mundzuk,
Lord of the bravest tribes upon earth;
His was power unheard of before,
And his were the realms of the earth east and west of Wistlawudu.

He wrought destruction upon the twin empires of the Rumwalas
After seizing their strongholds; then,
Heeding their plaintive pleas
That what remained might be free from plunder,
He took from them yearly tribute.
After gaining this glory with unstinted success,
He died; not by foeman's wound, not perfidy of faithless friend,
In the midst of the people he protected,
Merry and mirthful,
Unpunished by pain.
How may that be deemed as death,
Which none need swear to avenge?"

As Heorrenda's chant rose high, so the *noidi* stabbed and screamed
in harmony, echoing the potent song, delivering it up as a plea to
Bieg-Olmai, that the earth-tree might not be shaken, that the giant's
bonds be not broken, that the lake of blood which is in the house at the
end of the earth be not overspilled. Then from behind them in the
darkness Louhi laughed horribly, scraping her cat's claws upon a tree
where *seidi* dwelt, drawing a hair from her pelt which emitted a
poisonous stench.

"Now let what is ready come!" she shrieked with a cat's yowling,
and the *noidi* flung themselves face downward upon the bare face of the
copper mountain.

Alone stood Heorrenda before the platform, upon which he seemed
to see the corpse of Aetla lying on its bloodstained bier, stark amid the
swirling mist. About the body of the ravager of the earth flickered
unearthly lights, burning ever higher about the bier. Upward they
flared, until they hung draped in a spiraled curtain from earth to sky.
Gazing upward, Heorrenda saw myriad warriors fighting amidst the
encircling flare, spirits of the slain whose spears and swords do not
remain idle even in death.

Encircled above, as if reflected within a fiery well-shaft, glittered
the eternal stars: Vainamoinen's Scythe now burned so fiercely, it
seemed it might sear the roof of heaven itself. Into the vortex was the
scop's gaze drawn, his thoughts impelled, his vision drawn. Pulsing
streamers of blazing light shot upward, converging upon the tunnel's
starlit mouth. Rays played about the head of Heorrenda, whistling
about it, and singing gently in his ears.

The bird which had flown above the little king's sledge across the
snows was singing sweetly, and upon its pinions was the scop wafted
curling upward within the hollowed pivot of the whirlwind. On every

side flared fluted curtains of many-colored light, leaping and sinking, brilliant-colored, yet never burning him with their giant blaze. The gales of Bieg-Olmai gusted about him, buffeted him, swept him aloft through their throat, sucked him toward their source, drew him beyond the shimmering tunnel of light.

Heorrenda knew the danger, feared he might fail upon his journey. How might he ascend the flowing force of fire, climb the raging cataract, fly to the ridge of the lustrous cascade? To his helping bird he cried pleadingly, his *saiva-leddie*, his guide upon the way.

Then the bird beat its wings strongly, fluttering through the glowing gallery, bearing Heorrenda on the drumbeat safely past gaping jaws and grasping talons, through the river of fire, and over into the beyond. So fast they sped that he saw nothing, and heard only the wind whistling loud. Over the boundless forest they soared, even over Mearc-wudu, which stretches over the face of the earth, dividing this from the next. In the midst of Mearc-wudu lies a mountain wall, which Heorrenda's guide might barely ascend; about the passes were scattered the bones of those who had failed upon this dread journey; the rock-face was piebald with the bones of horses.

Southward over the yellow steppe they flew, where no raven ever flew before, over the yellow sands beneath a burning sun which scorched to dust whatever paused beneath its glare. Seas stiff with salt they crossed by bridges narrow as a hair, sharp as a sword blade. Under heavens that blazed like a blacksmith's furnace, over deserts which burned like a heated coal, the *saiva-leddie* bore the far-journeyed one; until at last they approached the mouth of the North Wind's Cave, the entrance to the earth's windpipe. Beyond it towered those mountains whose tops touch the stars. The sky was still through which they skimmed; but he who approached heard from afar off the hurtling roar of tempests howling about the precipices, saw boulders torn from crags tumbling slowly down from cliff to cliff, saw snow flung spinning in frantic flurries that hung in frozen fog across the arc of heaven.

In the deserts of the sun, below the high-fanged mountains of the sky, lies a steaming salty lake whose waters no dog would ever drink. In the midst of that lake stands an island, and in the island gapes a black vent, at the bottom of which lies a forty-lugged copper cauldron in which the North Wind has his birth. When he sleeps, the lake is still; but when he wakes, his lower jaw plows the earth, his upper jaw plows the sky. He shakes the bottom of the tide, rocks the bottom of the ocean, does the son of Erlik Qan! His mouth is a giant ripped fish, and about him glide his *dutpalar*, their flanks green, their breasts pale, and their jaws yawning like large boats.

Here lies the source of fury and frenzy, feuding and fighting: vagina of peoples, womb of nations, from which fare forth the tribes of the earth across the trackless desert, whipped onward by the hot breath of the hurricane into the sunless glades and swamps of Mearcwudu; driven forward through the pillared gloom of that unlit hall, until they emerge onto the windy moors and hazy-blue wilderness that lie about the marges of Middle Earth. There the tribes gather, confused and chattering, outside the palisade of stone which surrounds the citadels of kings. From within the enclosure they hear the clatter of golden goblets, melodious singing and merry laughter, where the lords of the earth feast amid jeweled luxury.

For a time the teeming tribes shiver together, crowded outside the cold wall, listening in envy to sounds of joyous revelry within golden-domed palaces, majestic chanting from churches lit bright as the sun by a thousand candles. Beyond in the chill darkness crouch the teeming wanderers, excluded from the princes' banquet, marveling at the distant laughter. But then upon their heels tread other tribes out of the East, in numbers untold; and so, driven by rage of despair and delight of destruction, they swarm over the wall and into the streets of the cities. There they pause a brief moment in wonder, awed by wealth beyond reckoning, work of skilled wrights, treasure fit for the company of Heaven.

But not long is that pause. What men cannot make, they may break. Soon does the North Wind blow icy-keen through brazen gates swinging loose upon shattered hinges, tear down woven hangings from marbled passages and halls, and burst like a raging bear into the banqueting chamber. Then is music stilled, laughter hushed, and a stillness stolen over the place of wealth, as the wintry wind makes sport of all: golden goblets rolling idly on the tessellated floor, blood spilling over images and mingling with the wine! An autumn of torn leaves flutters from the windows of burning libraries, wisdom piled on dead wisdom, until weary man can bear learning no longer: He must be up and doing!

A tempest is blowing through men's minds, and they will be marching, fighting, shouting; plucking down what is high, uprooting what is old, defacing what is beautiful. Away with the dead hand of ancient lore, the ordered road, the softened curve! A cruel winter is coming, one in which youth and vigor and consuming energy alone may match themselves against the cold and dark. It may be that spring will flower once again; but of what avail is that, when now nights are long and frosts sharp and glittering?

Heorrenda's feathered helper had laid him on a rocky outcrop by a reed-bed. The rushes shifted uneasily; beyond, on the heat-shifting horizon where lay the lake of his seeking, the island-cavern was opening its mouth. Beneath him crouched a group of gray wolves, whose fur was stirred by the coming breeze. They moved about restlessly, growling from time to time and displaying their fangs. Fear and rage gripped them, and the scop of the Heodeningas grew fearful when they glanced up at him with their blood-red eyes. In the distance the lake steamed sultry beneath the sun's suspended furnace, eight rivers flowing into it from every side, fast-flowing torrents over which the scop with the aid of his *saiva-leddie* had struggled during their frantic flight.

Even as the scop shielded his eyes to gaze upon the island-tower arising from the midst of the waters, he saw white-crested waves rise lashing about its base and racing toward the banks. The cavern mouth was opening, the wind beginning to gust forth. Now the heat-haze was sundered by sudden puffs of breeze, and a dark shadow arose upon the arid plain. The surface of the lake was whipping high, breakers frothing fiercely. Then the base of the pinnacle at its center became obscured, as did the foothills of the mountain wall rising to the sky in the distance beyond.

Dark storm clouds were gathering upon the waters, swiftly concealing the lake from view. They were boiling angrily over, rolling about violently, emitting streams of white vapor. As they gathered their strength, a brief calm descended upon the shallow gully where Heorrenda lay hid. But then there came a low murmuring sound, like that of the tide turning upon a distant strand, increasing to a roar of uncontrollable rage. Lightning flickered within the somber rampart as it rolled resistless across the plain; trees were torn up and flung about like grass at its base.

There was a great rushing in the sky as the whirlwind flew forward across the desert; a shock that shook the heavy air as if with a fierce blow, then cut it with an ice-keen knife. A swaying column at the angry, swarming center coiled serpentlike from its island source, then glided out like a giddy dancing seer when the fit is come upon him. As it crossed the surface of the lake, it sucked the waters spouting mountain-high and flung them furiously down upon the desert in blinding sheets of rain and sleet.

Darkness swept over the land as if at the onset of night, and Heorrenda looked about him for a refuge. The wolves below were clustered together, diving their heads beneath one another's bellies in search of comfort. Then all at once their courage blew away and they broke and fled, howling wildly onward before the path of the storm. It was too late for the scop to think of flight; the reeds were blasted level with the ground, trees ripped up by their roots and flung from sight. The darkness increased, great clouds of sand high as mountain pillars engulphed the sky, and the wind shrieked like a warrior when he flings himself upon the foe.

Heorrenda lay upon the ground, gripping vainly at bulrush stalks, setting his fingers into shifting sand. He closed his eyes, though the darkness that flew over the land was no less than that of his closed vision. Next it seemed to him that the land turned over, revolving with the sky, and he taken up with it until he must be clinging to the roof of the abyss. In his ears there was a rushing, as if all the cataracts of earth had joined the broad river of the heavens in a foaming torrent of destruction; a booming as of winter breakers bursting cliff-high upon northern capes, a frantic shrieking as of every icy wind that screams across the frozen steppe during the sunless winters of the empty backlands of the North.

The stars shuddered in their courses, plunging in fiery streamers from the roof of the tent of heaven into its abyss; the wind of the planets was a raging tornado, tossing about the elements as dust within a murky void. Like the lashing of the World-serpent at the world's ending was the pelting rain and streaming arrow-storm of hail upon the helpless back of the abandoned scop. Not like the warm hearth of Heorot was this tearing, whirling, freezing, blackened maelstrom! Like the cracking of northern ice-floes in spring was the harsh laughter of shattered creation, as it writhed and danced and drummed in orgiastic abandon.

As the laughter rang in his ears and echoed about the vault of his skull, Heorrenda, too, felt the elements of his mind dashed about, and the frenzy gripped him within its taloned grasp. He laughed aloud, a shriek of ecstasy, as he felt the bonds that bound his thoughts snap and part. Let loose were the wild thoughts that had lain there fettered fast as the Wolf of the Fens, from whose slavering maw flows the river of expectation which will burst its banks upon the dread day of Muspilli.

Wide-open gaped the scop's staring eyes, and he saw before him the one-eyed All-father astride his eight-legged steed, galloping before the blast out of the gates of the Hall of the Dead. From the draught of the deepest of wells had he drunk, bestowing an eye upon the Giant of the Abyss in recompense. He seduced the old Frost-giant's daughter, stole away the secret of foaming mead which drives men from their senses, bore himself off upon eagle's pinions, laughing at the lie he told! Stretched was the stride of his eight-legged steed, stretched back its lips from its yellow teeth, and stretched forth streaming its long mane, as it galloped with distended nostrils and shrill screaming neigh before the yelling gale. And the drumming of its hoofbeats upon the way of the storm clouds was the drumming of distant *noidi* echoing across the eternal darkness of the North, vibrating over iron-gripping ice beneath leaping lances of light ascending ever higher into the starry midnight sky.

Two swart ravens sped above the helmed head of the Lord of the Gallows, and wolves and wolf-men, bears and bear-men, savage outcasts of the tribes, raced beside him lusting for battle. Aloft he brandished the broad-hafted spear with which he marks down the slain, pointing with exultant screaming toward the West, where the departed sun still left a ghastly glow. Like fire raging over a burning city was the red-streaked sky, and like the screams of its slaughtered citizens the yelling of the hosts of the departed, as they raced forward on the storm clouds, plunging headlong on their wolfish journey.

It was the Spear they followed, the Spear of Woden; the Spear that Weland welded, consuming a forest at its forging, draining a river at its tempering. He who wields it bears a name which is raging fury, intoxication of wine, and battle and destruction! For what is wine without excess, combat if the sword be denied a slaking of his greedy thirst, a woman if she be not stormed against her will, like a stronghold defended until its gates are splintered apart, rich red blood seeping from within the palisade? Sweeter than the kiss of the softest lips is that of the keen axe's edge! There is a wolf-age and a wind-age sweeping out of the East; there is ice on the gale and lightning in the blast; shields will be shattered and no man spare his brother, none keep faith with wife or kin, now the lying rune-reader treads his Hell-path!

Over desert and mountain and landlocked salty sea swept the angry throng; in the whirlwind's track lay the untilled waste of empty steppe, the torn and broken forest. A chill draft blew about the courts of kings afar off before the storm's path. Not yet did they know what was moving in the East, but the curtained casements of their palaces shivered as the first breeze eddied in. The carrion-gulper was drawing near, stirring the sea yet never seen, fell wind from under the eagle's wings!

Now was the whirlwind passing over the untracked thickets of Mearc-wudu, which marks the bound between the wilderness and Middle Earth. The dark forest's branches billowed and tossed like wintry waves on a sunless ocean. In mossy lairs huge bears stirred beneath the passing shadow after their long winter's sleep, their frozen blood began to flow, and across their shaggy limbs stole afresh that strength which is mightier than that of oak or elm. Sharpening curved claws high on pine and birch trunk, they lumbered forth from bank and brake to pursue the battle-host. Not wise is the warrior who stands in their path, seeking to stay with his frail blade the resistless strength of the bold bee-wolf!

Behind the white steed of the worker of all ills, battle-inciter, bestower of victory, rode three dead kings erect in their saddles. Their eyes glowed dully in their pallid faces beneath boar-crested helms, and from gaping wounds upon their breasts and flanks dripped black gore upon the earth below. All Huna-land shuddered at the shadow of their passing, as well it might, for they were the three world-destroyers who in life broke down the walls of Middle Earth. Beneath their horse-mane banners bowed all the purple-clad princes of the earth; through waving fields of wheat passed the torch-blaze of their conquests. Upon ranked and ordered vineyards their hundred thousand horsemen tramped; from the vintage of their bruising bled a ferment rich and wild.

The first horseman was Aetla the great king, riding upon a blood-red steed with a ringing mane, encircled by battle-blades, bearing a great sword: symbol of unceasing war. As he rode behind the All-father he swore an oath upon the southward-curving sun, upon Woden's lofty crag, upon Wuldor's holy ring, that no more should peace prevail on earth. The sword was a token that strife grim and great among the kindred would continue until universal slaughter reigned throughout the land.

The second horseman was Earmanric, king of the Gotas, fell and faithless, whose cruel kingdom Aetla ruled when the allotted time had come, when the dice tumbled rightly beside the *taefl* board.

> When his twigs leave the field,
> Then must the king's tree yield.

Earmanric bestrode a pitch-black horse, and in his hand he bore a balance with which he measured out barley and wheat, oil and wine; for he was the first to seize the kingdoms of the world into his hand, when their wealth became his for the taking. So Earmanric thundered onward on the storm cloud, flung his head back, laughing as he stroked his whiskers, spurring fiercely in his wildness, wildness rising from the wine. Backward he shook out his brown locks; firmly he gripped his white shield.

By Woden and his two fierce kings rode a fourth horseman, set stiffly upon a pale steed. That king bore no name, but was called the Yellow Death, and in his train were all the torments of Hell. More terrible was he even than his dreadful companions, and more feared by men. The ravages of Aetla and Earmanric caused all the plains of the world to be sown with the bones of the slain, and its hills to be heaped high with their skulls. Yet is there great breeding of children in time of war, and the race of men is not utterly destroyed by the sword.

The fourth horseman follows hard on the heels of war, and it is his pallid glance which brings pain more terrible by far than that inflicted by greedy sword or stinging arrow. For he is the corpse-tearer, bringing death that creeps upon a man unawares, poisoning his blood with venom like liquid fire, rotting his organs, wrenching his vitals, splitting asunder the skin of his flesh, inflicting suffering in this life unendurable as that doomed upon the wicked when they pass away, down into the fogbound Hell which lies in the ninth world. Seeping sores and poisonous pustules will strike down the greatest king, penetrate the strongest fortress.

Behind Woden and the kings rode the cavalcade of the dead, their wounds still fresh and gaping upon their bodies as though they were newly slain. On over Mearc-wudu flew the Wild Hunt, and onward ever across the featureless swamps and windswept plains where dwell the Winedas and the Gefthas, the Aeste and the Holm-Rygas, until they came to the coast of the cold Ost-sae. Woden pointed downward from the sky with his spear, and the ice that bound the sea began to loosen its cruel grip. Sea serpents, curving-prowed vessels of war, for long months locked within its strong fetters, at last floated free upon their hawsers of stout seal's hide, ready with the coming of spring to bear their warlike lords westward over the whale's path.

The dark cowl of night had thrown darkness over the earth, save where the smoldering ember which was the great hall of Heorot glowed red among the murk below. The All-father reared up his gleaming-gray eight-legged steed and, laughing harshly in the abyss, pointed with his Spear down at the glorious horned hall, where Hrothulf and the kings were gathered. The warriors stirred from their sleep, where they lay beside the mead-benches, gazing upward to where a first faint light from the east shone pallid on boar-crested helm, on webbed shirts of mail, and on renowned swords, filed and tempered. Then the strong ale and mead that filled their bodies began to course again within them, exciting their thoughts to deeds of valor in foreign lands. They rose, the stern companions of generous Hrothulf, and began to gird their weapons about them.

But Woden and his Wild Hunt stayed not their flight to see that mighty armament, but galloped madly onward along the broad bridge in the sky which is Iring's Path. Over the wild waves of the West-sae they flew, until they saw far below them set in the sea a fair island, bounded by high cliffs, lying secure upon the western ocean like an emerald brooch pinned in an emperor's purple cloak.

Twenty-eight fine cities studded its jeweled surface; three mighty rivers watered its fertile meadows; three gracious adjacent islands ornamented its coasts. Through its rich meadows meandered softly flowing streams, by whose banks kingcups and cuckoo flowers clustered in profusion. Snowdrops and primroses adorned every rounded hillside, and its woodland glades were carpeted with bluebells. From royal fortresses and humble homesteads, hearth smoke hung upon the sweet-scented air. From byre and pen lowing herds of cattle and bleating sheep wound forth upon their way, seeking summer pastures on warm uplands; while over all rang out the delightful call of the cuckoo, recalling dear companions and pleasures of yesteryear.

It seemed as if a great tree were sprouting from the center of the island, its branches rich with fruit hanging even over to the sea that was about the island. The birds of the air flew about it, finding sustenance from the fruit, whose abundance was beyond reckoning. Under the protecting shade of that tree the land abode in peace and prosperity, untouched by demons, plagues, or perils of the night. For it was an island enshrined within an ordered kingship, ordered by unchanging laws, hallowed by the Truth of the Land. The rule of a great king was imposed upon its districts from sea to sea, and the peace of Crist preserved it in wealth and virtue.

Poised in middle air, Woden laughed as he gazed down upon the island, against whose shores the surge was beating angrily, and his laugh was the wild whinnying of a war horse amid the place of carnage. The three kings who rode behind him grinned wolfishly in deadly pallor, their tusked teeth glinting beneath the stars; the time of breaking of nations was come again upon the earth. In their train the legions of the dead gibbered in intoxicated anticipation of the impending onslaught. Blood would flow in rivers and gather in lakes upon the plain: blood which is life for the walking dead. Trolls and witch-wives, elves and Frost-giants, wolf-men and bear-men howled in exultant frenzy upon the east wind which bore them over Iring's Path.

Above the breadth of the island hovered Woden's Host, swarming in stinking fogs and miasmal mists, until a dark cloud hung dank upon the whole realm. It seemed as if the abyssal Ocean Garsecg had swept up in a mighty convulsion, swamping the lone sanctuary beneath its black flood. The bright star Earendel, herald of dawn, whose beam had warded every threshold in the land during the hour of darkness, twinkled for a while through the obscurity, flickered thrice, and then was extinguished from view.

Now Woden plunged exulting, as long ago he tumbled from his high seat in the heavens, down on his eight-legged steed until he approached a certain green valley. Above it he hovered, screaming in the blast, until he saw where upon a steep headland there rose up a green barrow from the ground. Straightway he galloped thither, leaping from his saddle onto the firm earth, landing upon the earthen house, secure upon the soaring spur, whose treasure was protected from intrusion by rune-magic. Upon Wodnesbeorg stood the leader of the slain, looking out far and wide over his lordships in the hazy plain beneath.

Harsh was his laughter as his single eye stared down upon a hollow way, carved out of the cliff-face as if by his immortal spear. The Way of Slaughter was that called, Walweg, a runnel for blood flowing from the uplands. Upon the barrow and upon the hillside and upon the Slaughter Way, Woden laid runes of mischief and deceit, so that a day would come when cousin would fight cousin there, the blood of kinsmen mingling in a common stream. Well does the Wise One love trickery and deception and mutual destruction, for that is the worst slaughter of all, bringing new hosts to swell his train as it crosses the night sky!

Over all lands he looked. His eye ascended the hill, peering through the mist until it came to where the road over the downs passed by a great earthen-dyked fortress. Within it stood the tall king of the island, surrounded by a scanty remnant of his war-band. Woden laughed mockingly again, within the hollow of the dyke, as he saw the handful of warriors seek in vain to strengthen a rotten palisade that stood upon the rampart. The tide was rolling in, and not by such sticks and stones might its waves be stayed! Alone in the midst of the *taefl* board stood the king, and his protecting pieces were departed from him.

Woden's all-seeing eye roved onward still, following the rutted track until, upon a northern cliff top, the track wound across another road: a road that sped straight as an arrow from north to south. A third time the Lord of Dykes and Tamer of Roads laughed loud and long, hurling harsh echoes about the embanked Slaughter Way. For there, marching away into the Southland, moved a mighty host, with brave pennons fluttering aloft, kings riding with their war-bands, and a young prince trotting gaily at its head. There were the king's missing protectors, who were leaving him helpless upon his undefended square!

The inspired seer oversaw all with his eye of wisdom. He whispered with the ravens who crouched upon each of his mailed shoulders. They beat a moment angrily with their wings, then sailed off with his thoughts into the eastern sky. It was not long before they were perched upon the gift-seat of Cynric, king of the Gewissae, where he sat in his great mead-hall. There they muttered into his mind Woden's wily words.

Meanwhile Woden stood beside his eight-legged steed upon Wodnesbeorg, horned helm on head and spearpoint soaring to the sky. Huge as the hillside he appeared, and around him now clustered like crows above an elm copse his cruel host of *waelcyrge*. Over the barrow they flew, those sharp-toothed maidens, squeaking shrill about their lord. To them Woden spoke words of doom, and then over the downs they sped upon the wild wind, until they came, some to the old fort beside the ancient trackway where the great king had been seen to rest, others to where his departed host wound away down the long straight road to the south. Like flies about a slaughtered steer they hovered, all unseen, shooting whistling spears at those whose names the Lord of the Gallows had marked down for death upon his rune-staff.

Borne upon the keen wind from the northeast, Woden heard the shrill rasp of file on bill-blade, as Weland in his barrow-smithy made weapons ready to sing their greedy war-song in the coming fray.

"Now am I in Wealland, fraught for the fray," screamed the Thief of Runes, "goading great kings to the field of swordplay! To Thunor the thralls: Thegns are mine that day!"

Now Woden took his horn and drained the dwarf-brew. He became drunken and wolfish, and knew a hammering and drumming within his head loud as Weland's hammer when he welds the war-blades, so that each hair stood out stiff and straight from his skull. And upon each hair-tip was a scarlet drop of new-shed blood. The empty socket of his one eye dwindled until it was no wider than that of a needle, while the other opened wide as the mouth of a mead-goblet. His mouth yawned open from his jaws to his ears, so that the fluttering of his liver and lungs was plainly seen, even down to the tormented labyrinthine writhing of his entrails. From the top of his skull played a fountain of black blood high as the mast of a ship, spreading in a cloud over the heavens like the dark smoke of a king's hearth upon a winter's night. From his forehead extruded the hero's light: a bony twin-horned crescent, thick as a whetstone, whose points were anger and fear.

The battle frenzy was come upon the Friend of the Raven. He was no more the gray-bearded husband of Frig, but Grim, the Masked One. The All-father, host of the Hall of Happiness, had donned a different aspect. Now was he Fire-eyed, the Evildoer, Blind, Double-blind. Out of decay arises growth; from destruction, rebirth; from fire, fertilization. The god bears more than one face, though he be one behind the masks. Is not the warrior all in an instant fraught with battle fear and battle fury? Does he not at once long both to fight and to flee? The mask of rage lies upon the face of fear, and the face of fear grins angrily from behind its wolf-mask.

Distorted was the guise of Grim upon the windy pinnacle of Wodnes-beorg: *grimes wrasen,* masked and twisted. His skin shuddered loose upon his bones like a bush in a storm or a bulrush in a torrent. Within his skin his bones rotated, so that his feet and knees faced backward and his calves and buttocks forward. The sinews of his calves came before his shins, and each contorted round knot of them was big as a warrior's fist. The sinews of his forehead were stretched over to the nape of his neck, and his face became a red raw hollow. His heart beat loud against his ribs like the baying of a bloodhound when he scents his prey.

Round spun the Masked One, revolving ever faster in his frenzy, the gale gusting over tossing furze and waving grass, the rain pelting upon his barrow-seat. His skin split; his blood burst. As he turned about, he passed water in stinking squirts upon each quarter of the rounded hillside. Whirling in his war dance, he grew giddy, and it seemed that the encircling landscape turned with him. The great round plain upon whose rim he perched slowly began to spin; like a great wagon wheel it revolved below the sky, until the mighty host that marched upon the straight-spoked road knew no longer whether it traveled east or west, north or south.

And so the Wily One brought it about that the king of the island, pivot of the wheel and guider of the Chariot of the Bear, was whirled away from his protection, which is a host about its king. Upon the outer rim was he abandoned, within the terret which is the Bear's Fort. The pole and axle tree of the Island of Bryttene had been drawn, and its chariot was foundering. Darkness out of the east lay upon the land, and the Chariot of Ing began to sink beneath the surrounding sea.

CHAPTER FIFTEEN

THE WIND-
COLD
WOLF-TREE

Thus it came about at the season when woods blossom forth youthful and green, cities are humming and bright, fields carpeted with flowers, and the world breaking into life, that the greatest of storm clouds began to gather over the Island of Bryttene. So sang Heorrenda, scop of the Heodeningas. Only the melancholy cry of the cuckoo, harbinger of summer, warned of bitter foreboding sorrow. Cynric the old king had sent forth the war-arrow to the tribes and peoples of the North, the wizards of the Scride-Finnas had wrought dark spells among the snow forests, and Woden was gathering his hosts riding upon the wolf-path. Against the northern sky were seen spear-shafts and sword blades leaping high before the stars in token of fratricidal strife, of war among gods and men. Those who read the runes foretold that year the passing of a terrible bearded star.

Before every royal mead-hall which stands about the West-sae sounded the horn of the king of the Gewissae. To kings dwelling afar off, on the skirts of the forest of Mearc-wudu in the border regions of Middle Earth, came many a witch riding on wolfback in the gloaming, bringing tidings of red war in the West. From all the bounds of the earth, spearmen were gathering: even from Mearc-wudu to the Holy Grave which lies in the realm of the Gotas, and from the Holy Grave to the famous Stone which stands by Danpar.

Not of the harp, or love toward women, or delight in the bright world did the heroes think, nor on anything but the surge of the waves, the shrieking of spears, and the call of the field where ravens gather. When the scop plucked at his melodious harp, sitting at his lord's feet, he sang of the cleaving of white-shining shields, the striking of cold spear on spear, and of men sinking lifeless to the grass. Then did the warriors' hearts become restless within their breasts, their thoughts ranging out over the ocean flood, over the home of the whale, ranging over the wide world. They heard the scream of the lone sea bird, and so their hearts were drawn resistless toward the whale's path leading westward over the ocean plains.

Over the broad sweep of the floods flew the message, and from each timbered hall poured forth a thousand thegns, bright in their singing ring-mail, a forest of spears moving upon the highways. To havens around the West-sae they rode, where freshly tarred curving-necked ships waited at anchor, eager to bear their dear masters over the sea's currents, across the swan-ridden seas. By each high-beaked prow the heroes stepped aboard, placing their splendidly wrought weapons and mail-shirts safe within the hold. Currents eddied; sea lapped the tarry timbers; desire pressed upon each heart to explore the rolling deeps, to set forth upon the dancing salt waves.

As dawn's brow arose warm upon their backs, the highborn heroes furled the bow awnings and hoisted the woven canvas to the yards. Then there arose a plashing of oars and clashing of iron, shield clattering against shield, as the Sae-Wicingas rowed forth beyond the broad headlands. A foaming path frothed in their wake as the dragon-prowed ships, sped by the wind, flew onward like birds with foam-ringed necks. Westward over the sea were they bound, and when the long keels clashed together, it was to the ear as if surf and cliffs were breaking each upon the other.

"Hoist higher the topsails!" came the joyous cry, and the oaken keels breasted the tossing waves like fleet steeds racing over a spring meadow. The wild gale blew strongly, and the serpents of the sea flew onward under broad wind-filled canvas until their gunwales all but passed beneath the racing billows. The dragon prows of renowned princes clave the waters, horns brayed from ship to ship, the hollow-straked hulls plunged rejoicing over the rolling breakers. Though the nine dreadful daughters of Eagor buffeted their bows, the brine-steeds leaped laughing over the ocean furrows.

Onward across the whale's path! Westward over the waves! Let the dragon-prows rattle, the masts quiver, the ice-sprinkled bulwarks shrink! The ocean boils about us, the billows toss; the whole sea is plowed by our sharp keels! The grim foam dashes in over the forecastle, the stiff gale sets the ship dipping within the gannets' trough; never sped more famous ships under more glorious kings. The gilded war-dragons gleam like beacons, like the breasts of swans are their billowing sails; a golden light hangs over the fleet of the Sae-Wicingas.

Stoutly the thegns strive at the oar-pulling; strained is the tholepin when with a single stroke forty oars smite the sea. Into the strong surf slashes the oar-blade; with a salmon's leaping it flashes forth from the wave's pull. Over Eagor's wide plain fly onward nailed dragons, serpents who glide on the stricken stream, over the waters where gannets bathe.

Huge was the number of that sea-borne host, greater than any that rode the seas since Woden's wooden-bladed vessel bore the company of the gods over Eagor's realm. Of the Sae-Wicingas who fared forth over the West-sae that summer there were sixteen hosts of warriors; in every host, five thousand; in every thousand, thirteen hundred; in every hundred, four times forty men.

Not a few of that mighty host were *wreccan,* young men exiled from ties of tribe and kindred, seeking service in another lord's hall. Not in times of peace and order could they find advancement, nor did their battle ardor incline them to idleness beside a royal hearth. To them Woden's raven-message bore especial allure, for in time of war alone might they attain great wealth, as did Sigemund when he gained the dragon's hoard. Or it might be that fierce blows struck by a keen-filed sword in the place of slaughter would earn a young *wrecca* a wide lordship, a kingdom even. Was that not the path which led Eadgils and Heremod each to his glorious throne? Had not Sigeferth, a prince of the Secgan, likewise been *wrecca,* serving in the war-band of the lord of the Scyldingas?

The heart of each bold *wrecca* longed for the gathering place of ravens as a maiden longs for her lover. Their spears were thirsty for blood; they would raise piles of corpses so high among the Bryttas that forest-prowling, wide-ranging packs of wolves could not climb them! But *they* in the hardihood and vigor of their youth would scale that hill, gaining each a kingdom in the ascent!

Of Eadgils and Heremod they thought, of Wudga and Hama; but most of all they thought of Hengest and Horsa, princes of the Eotenas who left their own people to range forth as *wreccan.* Now it was known that the luck of Hengest had fallen upon Cynric, a king old in years, wise and cunning. And had not Cynric also girded on Hengest's famed sword, even Hunlafing, upon which were engraved runes foretelling a glorious *wyrd* for him who bore that wondrous blade?

The sixteen sea-kings whose keels now cut the ocean's smooth side had performed rich *blot* in propitiation of the immortal gods.

Delightful to Woden, Friend of the Raven and Lord of the Slain, was the blood-sacrifice of Hagena, king of the Holm-Rygas. For with his own hands he bound his queen to the rollers upon which his warship slipped down to the welcoming waves. Her screaming and the snapping of her bones echoed about the haven of the Holm-Rygas. Thence was it wafted to the heavens, where it was heard by the gods who feast within weapon-hung Wael-heall.

Dark war-clouds rolled out over the skies, and rain poured down from all quarters upon the wind-vessel's wide bottom, lashing the turbulence of the West-sae and menacing the coasts of Bryttene as they approached. Troll women from the Isles of the North, their hair hanging wild and loose on the wind, gathered over the sea and over the ocean. Gand-riders were they, and it is said that certain whale hunters from Halgoland witnessed their muster. That was an unchancy sight, for they saw a black rider upon a black horse bearing a blazing firebrand, traveling in a circle of fire. She hurled the firebrand southward toward Bryttene, and where it landed beyond the mountains a great blaze was kindled.

Also in the North were seen the seven sons of the Dark Moon, riding. From brimming horns they drank the clear mead which flows from the Ring-rearer's rill. There was a lulling of the gale, even the waters that rage in the Firth of the Peohtas south of Orcaneg were stilled awhile. But then there came a dreadful distant roar as the heavens opened and the sea swelled cliff-high once more. Faithless women were grinding dust into meal for their adulterous lovers; stones squeezing out blood were their whirling querns; their gory hearts hung out from within their rib cages; heavy with grief were they. Scorched souls flew heavenward, thick as flies; many maimed men were seen treading that hateful path, their faces besmeared with witches' blood.

For sixty nights the swarming sea serpents coursed the waves of the West-sae, even during the months of Eosturmonath and Thrimilchi, when the glorious sun of battle rises ever higher in the heavens. And as they flew before Woden's wind blowing out of the east, many heard the chanting of his *waelcyrge* squatting over the frozen Cwen-sae in the North, where lances of light leaped ever higher into the cold starry sky. It was the *wyrd* of the hosts they wove, those three weird sisters, and as they wove, this was the song they sang, the song that Woden loves.

"Wide-stretched is our warp which foretells the slaughter, a cloud stretching from sea to sky, a rain of blood splattering down the woof. The gray web of the warriors is borne aloft on the spearpoints, web which we, Woden's women, work with red weft. It is a web warped with the guts of men, weighted with human heads; bloodstained spears are the shafts, cold iron are the stays, sharp arrows the shuttles! With swords we weave the victory web: swords shall sing, shields ring, the axe-blade kiss heads through helms!

"Wind, my sisters, wind away! Wind web of spears where banners are streaming, where warriors bear boar-standards to battle! Woven into our web is the *wyrd* of summer warfare; and it is we, Woden's *waelcyrge*, who shear the threads of each hero's *wyrd*. Death is fated to a mighty king, for whom the gates of Wael-heall will fly open wide.

"Now is our web woven, and green fields start to run red. Look about you in horror; gaze about in fear, you who dwell in Middle Earth, for gory clouds are gathering over all lands west of Wistla-wudu, and the air itself will be moist with blood-froth spurting from hewn heads and severed limbs! Such is our song; now must we three *waelcyrge,* weird sisters of the North, ride with bared blades upon unsaddled steeds back to the welcoming hearth of Wael-heall!"

So it came about that, by the end of the month of Thrimilchi, the shadow of that ancient yew which is the Gallows of Woden was spread over the whole Island of Bryttene, even from the West-sae to the Sea of Iraland. The war fleets of the Woden-born warriors fenced the Island about with a forest of masts; the levies of all northern lands locked in every bay, encircled every skerry; walled about was the whole land of the Wealas, so that the heroes who had feasted all winter long within King Hrothulf's royal hall might step dry-shod from deck to deck the Island round.

The serpent-prows scraped the shingled beach; the steeds of the ocean were made fast to the land with strong hawsers of walrus hide; their grinning heads and carved beaks frightened the land-spirits of the Bryttas. Hardy under their masked helms, the Sae-Wicingas sprang ashore; they possessed the land, they were possessed. Not among their own tribes or peoples were they; they owned neither kindred nor family; they knew not the weakness of womankind; the woods and hills of their birthplaces were forgotten. Theirs was no place beside a royal hearth; from no prince did they receive rich land to till: They were *wreccan,* exiles from humankind, roaming strange lands like wolves and bears about the forest.

Like wolves and bears were they, the youthful *wreccan,* and wolves and bears they became. Casting aside their clothing, they rubbed their naked bodies with potent herbs, with henbane and mandrake juice, mandragora and deadly nightshade. They donned shagged coats of bear- and wolf-skin; they became bears; they became wolves. They were *beorn, freca,* with tearing claws and grinding fangs.

The bear-frenzy overcame them; the wolf-fury possessed them.

Flinging off their furred pelts, they danced naked over the bared blades of their swords, bounded over upturned spears whose hafts were set stiff in the soil. Wildly they leaped in the wind, like those who follow in Woden's wake upon his nightly death-ride along Iring's Path, twisting their limbs and heads about, eyes staring and mouths yelling. Then in the evening they grew drowsy and sullen, seeking the shadow of the forest, the shelter of the reed-bed. There their shapes changed as, warm beneath the wolf-fur, their spirits altered within them. Now were they sons, not of the distant mothers from whose wombs once they sprang, but of wild Woden alone, lord of the midnight ride, exulter over the slain! No chain of love or loyalty bound their boldness or sapped their youthful vigor; let loose upon the world were their passions and strength. The runes Weland inscribed upon the blade of Hunlafing sang to them across the sedges and swamps of eastern estuaries: the song of the sword, which bites with two edges!

Inspired by the rune-magic, they vowed to give over the bodies of the Bryttas to the pyre of destruction, so that a mound huge as a hill might be made of their lopped limbs, and the carcass heap be big as a burial barrow. Next they made *blot* as a propitiation to the Friend of the Raven, and also to strike fear into the land-spirits of Bryttene, who clustered chattering about them on empty riverbanks and in mist-hung fens.

The young men seized a certain princess of the Bryttas, whom they hung bound upon a post upon the beach at Ypwinesfleot. That was the place where Hengest landed and first took possession of the Island of Bryttene under the authority of Aetla, despoiler of Middle Earth, and in the name of Woden, host of the Hall of the Slain. Then there went up to the girl a young thegn of the Gefthas, a *wrecca* in the service of the king of the Cantware. He it was who crooked his finger into her eye, so that it spilled out over her cheek. This was a sacrifice to Woden, One-eyed Lord of the Gallows. At this the girl screamed like a vixen, for she suffered the nine torments which come from the black stone beneath the sea. Then the *wrecca*, laughing, placed a bag of wrinkled skin over her head and pulled it down to her neck. He drew the draw-laces fast and, after torturing her in ways that were pleasing to him, battered her in the face so that in a while she was dead. There the thegns left that princess until the tide should turn, when Eagor would send his nine daughters washing over her and claim her body for his own.

So the fleets and hosts of the Woden-born set fast their grip upon the coasts of Bryttene beside the West-sae, even from the Island of Wiht in the south to the Isles of Orceneg in the north. To them flocked the kings and tribes of the Angel-cynn long established in Bryttene: In the south, about the dragon-banner of Cynric of the Gewissae, king of the West Seaxe; in the north, to the island fortress of Bebbanburh, where ruled Ida the son of Eobba, king of the Beornice. Thus the numbering of the hosts was beyond reckoning, and from Hunlafing came a humming of rune-staves, where the bright-hilted blade gleamed upon the weapon-hung wall of Cynric's mead-hall by Wintanceaster.

Beset were the Bryttas by fell foes; both by those who voyaged across the whale's path and by ancient enemies within the land. Beneath the snow-clad mountains of the North, in deep valleys unvisited by the winter sun, dwells the oldest of nations, the Peohtas. Not even the armies of the Rumwalas, when Casere's rule was extended over Bryttene, could conquer that vast land of windy crags and troll-haunted glens.

Bruide mac Maelchon succeeded to the throne of the Pecti in the year that Cynric sent his war-arrow about the West-sae. He was a prince of great power, ruler of the kingdoms of Cait, Ce, and Cirig; Fib, Fidach, Fotla, and Fortrenn. To him the kings of the islands of the Catts and the Orcs in the northern ocean paid tribute. He was son to the king of the Brython, for it is the custom of the Pecti that the inheritance of their kingship passes by right of the female. And this has been their custom since first their race came to Prydein out of the north, when they bound themselves by sun and by moon to fulfill this custom until the end of the world.

To the court of Bruide's grandfather, Drust son of Girom, came Maelgun the Tall, when his father Cadwallon Lawhir still lorded it over Gwynedd. All one winter Maelgun lay with the Princess Nesta, Drust's daughter, until the druids of the court pronounced her womb quick with child. Maelgun then departed southward over Gweryt to dwell once more in his father's realm. This was the custom of the Pecti, but after he had seized his cousin's throne, King Bruide pondered whether he might not likewise lay claim by virtue of his father's blood to that of his father Maelgun Gwynedd.

From the prince of the Orcs, whose galleys fared far and wide over the ocean, Bruide learned of the passing of Cynric's war-arrow about the courts of the North. The bard of Bruide's court sang of his forefather, Drust son of Erp, who fought a hundred battles and gained a hundred victories in the South. Bruide mac Maelchon became pensive at this, and later sent a fiery cross throughout the seven provinces of his kingdom. Beyond this he made no move against the men of the

Brython, dwelling to the south of the River Gweryt, but waited the
length of the winter to see what might come to pass.

With the melting of snows in the springtime came news that
pleased King Bruide but little, for his spies on the frontiers brought
news of a great hosting of the Brython of the North. King Urien of Reged
had ordered a mighty mustering of the three hundred swords of the
tribe of Cynfarch, and the three hundred shields of the tribe of Cinuit,
and the three hundred spears of the tribe of Coel. Urien likewise sent
word to him who ruled over the Western Isles, Gabhran mac Domhangart
of Dal Riata, who was no friend to the Pecti. When King Gabhran
received this news, he gathered together the fleets of the tribes of
Gabhran, of Oengus and of Loarnd; and from every twenty houses of
them came sailing two seven-benched ships.

When King Bruide learned of these musterings upon the southern and western skirts of his kingdom he was much vexed in his mind,
and consulted with his wise druid and foster-father, Broichan son of
Temnan. Bruide feared lest the fleet of Gabhran harry his coasts while
he was engaged in war with Urien south beyond Gweryt. Yet he
misliked much the thought that the Saxain from over the sea should
plunder the Island of Prydein without his being present at the division
of the spoil.

Broichan pondered long upon these matters, consulting a glass
vessel within which he saw floating images. At length he gave sound
advice to the king. He pointed out that Urien himself would be
threatened by the Eingl settled upon his eastern coastline, together
with the numberless host of their kinsmen from beyond the sea. As for
Gabhran mac Domhangart, Broichan advised Bruide to send word to
his overlord, Diarmait mac Cerbaill, king of the green Island of
Ywerdon lying in the Western Ocean beyond Prydein, from whence
came the men of Dal Riata before they settled in the islands lying west
of Bruide's kingdom.

Bruide mac Maelchon was well pleased with the wizard's advice,
giving orders for the hooded horsemen of his seven kingdoms to come
riding out of the gates of the North and assemble their hosting in the
mouths of the glens when winter floods were abated, freeing fords
across the Gweryt which lead to roads crossing Manau Gododdin deep
into the heart of Urien's realm. Meanwhile he dispatched his foster-
father Broichan across the sea of the Orcs and the cold sea of the
Brython, even to the court of Diarmait mac Cerbaill in Ywerdon.

Broichan's heart leaped within him, joyous as the dancing waves
that rocked his coracle, when he came to the coast of that dear green
island of the ocean. *Ywerdon* is it termed by the Brython, but to the

happy race of men dwelling within its surge-encircled bounds it is
known as Eriu. Merrily bounded Broichan's bark as upon the dancing
wavelets of Mannanan mac Lir it approached that island of green
lawns, round elf-mounds, beautiful women, brave warriors, and strong
ales; and cheerful were the thoughts that welled up within the wizard's
heart. And it is I, too, Merlin son of Morfryn, who love that land as
though it were my own:

> Delightful it is for the bard of King Bruide
> To hear on the sea a faint shout from Sliabh Slanga;
> The wave of Rudhraighe is striking the strand,
> And yonder the gulls are screaming 'round Rechra.
>
> How lovely to sleep by the banks of the Boinne,
> After coursing of deer in the broad plain of Midhe.
> Clear trilling of blackbirds on Druim Fuar,
> Loud roar of the stag beside leafy Rath Crinna.
>
> Shouting of huntsmen before Tech Laisrenn,
> Belling of stags about Ath da Loarg;
> Bleating of fawns at Ferta in Lerga—
> Croaking of ravens over the hosts.
>
> The toss of the hull of my ship on the wave,
> Howling of wolf-packs 'round Breslech Mor,
> Baying of Bran by the stone of Crich Roiss,
> And laughter of streams which converge at Ath Tamuin.
>
> The call of King Diarmait as he rides to the hunt,
> The bay of his hounds ranging wide on the hill;
> Seated among the bards of green Eriu,
> Broichan the bard is filled with delight.

So it was that Broichan the druid of Bruide mac Maelchon came to
the court of Diarmait mac Cerbaill, even to Temair of the kings in the
Plain of Midhe. And there he found Diarmait upon his couch within
his banqueting hall, with his host seated about him. And the Center of
Eriu was about Diarmait in that house, with the king of Laighin seated
on the couch opposite in the east, the king of Mumha on his right hand,
the king of Connacht at his back, the king of Uladh on his left hand.

There in the great hall of Temair, Broichan sang to his harp
before the kings and hosts of Eriu, telling them of the hostings and

expeditions and sieges which would take place that summer over the sea. He told, too, of the truculence of Gabhran mac Domhangart, who was assembling fleets and armies for war against Bruide without the leave of his overlord, the king of Eriu. Diarmait mac Cerbaill gnawed his lip and was angered at this news. Were not the men of Dal Riata of the race of Cairbre Righfada, and so tributary to the heir of Niall of the Nine Hostages and Conn of the Hundred Fights? What business had they to be making a mustering of hosts and levying of fleets beyond the sea at all?

This was a defiance and reviling of Diarmait mac Cerbaill, who had ever ruled his kingdom according to the Testament of Morann son of Moen, that Testament bestowed upon his forefather Feradach Finn Fechtnach. All men knew of his fitness to rule, for had he not driven his chariot by the Stone Penis of Eriu, so that it screeched against the axle a screech which was heard throughout all the five kingdoms of Eriu?

And this was how Diarmait spent the days of his kingship: In the morning he watched the noble youths of Eriu playing at hurley upon the green beside Temair, and loud was his royal cry about the ramparts when the youths drove the ball between the goalposts. In the afternoons he played at *fidchell* upon a silver board with golden men; and not often did he fling his king-piece at the *fidchell* player's head. And every evening he was drinking strong ale until sleep overpowered him where he sat in his drinking-seat. Rarely did he permit the stain of vomit to foul his royal robe; not frequently did he void foul air in the place of revelry. He preserved immunity as a privilege of the place of mead-drinking, so that foolish and wise, friend and stranger, might become intoxicated without penalty. In this kingly wise he cared for the tribes of Eriu, in this way he helped them, soothed them; so should they care for him, help him, soothe him.

Beneath the sway of such a king, maintaining justice, truth, and order throughout his realm, there should have been rich harvests of corn, great yielding of milk from cattle, goodly fattening of pigs; freedom from plagues and lightning-shafts; and obedience of kings and tribes throughout the land. Yet matters had not passed well with Diarmait of late. His noble son, Colman Mar, had been slain that year when his chariot collided on the highroad with the swift-driving car of Dubsloit of the Cruthin. Not niggardly had been the draughts of ale the princely youths imbibed upon their drinking-seats in their hostels before their racing, and dire was the consequence of the wager laid between them. Upon the broad highroad of Assail they had coursed, axle to axle, until the iron wheels of their chariots plowed furrows deep as fortress-dykes upon the way. It was there perished Colman Mar, driving heedless and hasty, when his axle-bolt was lost and the car-tire broken. His belt of protection had he left with his charioteer, and so he perished.

Before that there was the groin-pestilence, *Crom Connaill*, which caused grievous discomfort to the kings of Eriu where they sat at their drinking, bringing death to many. Men said openly that the Truth of the Land was not upon Diarmait mac Cerbaill, and there were those who recalled his father's blemish, even his twisted mouth. And when Broichan the druid revealed before all the hosts of the five kingdoms assembled within the banqueting hall of Temair the defiance of Gabhran of Dal Riata, the king grew fearful and angry, resolving that throughout all Eriu men should see that his power was unabated.

To that end he sent forth his servant Aedh Baclamh, who bore in his crooked arm a great spear. To every fortress throughout Eriu traveled Aedh, where with much reviling he compelled the kings to widen their thresholds so that the spear of King Diarmait might be borne breadthways between their gates. So he came, upon a lovely summer's day, to the stronghold of Aedh Guaire in Connacht.

"Hew down your palisade, that the spear of King Diarmait may be borne in breadthways!" commanded Aedh Baclamh.

"You may order these matters as they please you!" replied Aedh Guaire, greeting his guest kindly.

With these words Aedh Guaire dealt the head of Diarmait's spear-holder a side-stroke with his sword, so that he struck off the head from the trunk. Then he raised his hand swiftly again, dealing Aedh Baclamh another blow upon the trunk so that he split his body down the middle to the soil. After that the severed parts of the spear-holder tumbled upon the ground.

Then it came into Aedh Guaire's mind that King Diarmait might not be best pleased when he learned of this deed, and so with the godly assistance of Saint Ruadhan he fled away out of Eriu, over the sea to the court of Maelchu the Tall, king of Brettain. For it happened that the grandmother of Maelchu was a princess of the Goidil dwelling in that country, and so the king spoke the pure tongue of the people of Eriu. To Maelchu, Diarmait at once sent messengers, demanding the return of Aedh Guaire, that he might be avenged of the death of Aedh Baclamh. To this the king of Brettain made no reply, for at that time he was busy with other matters.

So it came about for many reasons that when Diarmait mac Cerbaill learned from the druid Broichan of the great hosting that was to be throughout all the world against King Maelchu and the Bretnaig, he resolved to summon the hosts of the five kingdoms of Eriu and cross over into Brettain in order to compel the king of Brettain to deliver over Aedh Guaire for punishment.

Diarmait summoned the hosts of Eriu to assemble on the appointed day about Temair, upon the Plain of Murthemne in Midhe. Likewise he gathered together a great fleet below Benn Edair, bright peak above the sea of gulls, loveliest of promontories in the land of Eriu, haven of ships beyond numbering. Then the hosts of all Eriu from wave to wave, even the hosts of Midhe and Mumha and Uladh and Connacht and Laighin, entered into their ships, preparing to sail over the sea's mane to do battle with the king of Brettain. It was their task to bring back Aedh Guaire to the hostage pit of Temair, that he might be blinded for his ill deed. And whilst they were about that errand, it was their thought to ravage the Island of Brettain as far as the Sea of Icht in retribution for the asylum which its king had granted to Aedh Guaire.

Now that was the greatest fleet and mightiest host that set sail from Eriu since Niall of the Nine Hostages and Loegaire mac Niall conquered Brettain after the departure of the Romanaig. It was sustained upon the sea by the might of Mannanan mac Lir, rolling with his three legs about his watery realm, from whose son-in-law Benn Edair receives its name. To the sea god dwelling in his Island of Mann, the men of Eriu made sacrifice of pigs and other animals upon the strand below Benn Edair.

Diarmait mac Cerbaill watched the assembling of the hosts and fleets of Eriu from the cliff of Benn Edair, and by him stood Broichan the druid of King Bruide.

"I have power to raise up a favorable wind, O king," said Broichan, "and I may put all who dwell within your enemy's land under edge of spear and sword, if you choose."

Diarmait was pleased with these words of Broichan's, so the druid turned his face thrice toward the south, upon the fleet, and a westerly wind arose. All men could see it was a wizard's wind, for it rose no higher than the sails of the ships.

"I may also bring a mist of darkness upon the fleet," declared Broichan, "so that its approach may not be observed by the men of Brettain. Shall I do that thing?

"Do that thing," replied Diarmait mac Cerbaill.

Then Broichan wrapped a goatskin about his head and cried out, "Let there be mists; let there be fogs and phantoms confusing all who gaze upon these ships!"

At once a thick sea mist uprose about all the vessels of the warriors of the five kingdoms of Eriu, so that no man might espy them as they neared the coast of Brettain. After that, Diarmait mac Cerbaill returned to his ale-drinking in the banqueting hall of Temair, much pleased with all that had passed. He sought to stay the druid's departure, vowing that no hour of his stay should pass without his lips bearing the froth and his mouth the reek of the strong ales of Eriu. But Broichan returned to the fortress of Bruide mac Maelchon among the mountains of the kingdom of the Pecti.

With the passing of winter the waves were locked no longer in fetters of ice, and summer came to the courts of men, bringing with it days of glorious sunny weather, as is the due of the seasons. Groves blossomed; fields grew fair; the earth stirred. The cuckoo, herald of summer, sang out his mournful note from the treetops. To Cynric in his mead-hall came from all sides tidings of the encircling of the whole of Bryttene by the war fleets of the kings. The Angel-cynn dwelling upon the coasts had answered his summons; the war-arrow had passed about the courts of the North beyond the West-sae; the kings of the Peohtas and the Scottas were dispatching great hosts from out of the mountains and over the sea.

The noble king of the Gewissae smiled within his gray beard, as he foresaw the doom of the king of the Bryttas with all his people. Their hosts would be slaughtered, and their people sold into slavery by the Fresan. With gold and jewels and the daughters of slain princes would Cynric reward his allies, taking to himself the kingship which Arthur in turn had torn from the grasp of Aelle. He would be Bretwalda of the Island, in succession to Aelle. The White Dragon would tear with its talons the heart from the breast of the Red!

Upon the gift-throne in his mead-hall sat Cynric the old king, with his war-band about him on the mead-benches. Upon his head was set the boar-crested helm of kingship; in his right hand he bore the spear of sovranty, in his left the royal whetstone. With the holy lance, weapon of Woden, would he dedicate his foes to the one-eyed Lord of the Gallows. Upon the whetstone were set these rules:

$$\text{ᚹᚠᛏᛗᚻᚠᚳᛁᚾᛁᛏ᛬ᚩᚻ᛬ᚩᚱᛏᚠ}$$

$$\text{ᚻᚠᚾᚠᛋᚣᚠᚦᛁᚾᚠᚠᚦᚩᚳᛁᚷᛁ}$$

Runes of mischief and destruction are they, uttered once by Woden, when with his whetstone merrily he sowed confusion among the nine thralls, so that each cut the other's throat with his scythe!

Across the knees of the bulwark of the Gewissae lay the deadly sword Hunlafing, humming softly. To the warrior king would it bring dominion of the overlordship of the Bretwalda, conferred by Aetla upon Hengest before his departure to Fresland; likewise it brought to Cynric the luck, *speth*, of the crafty king of the Cantware.

Thrust into the soil beside the Woden-born warlord stood the iron-shafted standard, *tuuf*, which would lead the West Seaxe and their allies to victory. It likewise bore the king's luck, and one day it would lie beside him within his royal barrow. Upon its crest was set a branching-antlered stag, while from a frame below hung down on every side banners bearing the emblem of the White Dragon. Beside it upon the field of battle would the banner-king, Segncyning, stand as he directed the hosts to the onslaught.

To Cynric, as he sat receiving the war-gathering of the Angel-cynn and the Sae-Wicingas from over the seals' bath, came one day Heorrenda the scop, returned from faring far among many lands and peoples. Cynric's heart grew glad within him, for he saw that now the time was come indeed.

"Fan the fire with constant blowing, my thegns!" he cried. "Here at last is Heorrenda, come from over the sea with news to gladden our hearts. Sweep clear the hearth and scatter the ashes! Strike up sparks from the fire; rouse up the sleeping embers; draw forth the smothered blaze! Bring light from the failing hearth; kindle the coals to a ruddy glow with a burning log! Too long have they lain coldly slumbering upon the floor of our mead-hall. The time is come for leaping flames, and ardent action!"

So Heorrenda returned to the hall of Cynric, sitting at the feet of the mighty king, gray with years. He plucked with his plectrum at the cords of his harp, uttering words of praise to his ring-giving lord.

"The bright sun shall turn black, the earth shall sink back into the dark sea, heaven shall be rent apart, the ocean shall sweep over the hills, before there shall be in Bryttene a better king than Cynric! I bring good news from beyond the West-sae, from the courts of the Fresan and the Gar-Dene. Great kings are mustering their fierce shield-warriors in bands, setting forth in their dragon-prowed ships, crossing the swan's path to obey your summons to battle. The wizards of the Scride-Finnas have made *blot* and foretold victory, and Woden himself is riding on the wings of the storm to bring victory to the White Dragon and destruction upon the Red. An axe-age is coming, a bitter wolf-age is blowing in upon the cold east wind!"

Then was there joyous laughter among the warriors; merry words rang out, and their words were cheerful. Full of happiness, too, was the ring-bestower, white-haired with age and famous in the fray. The prince of the Gewissae, shepherd of his people, felt strong in the faith of the aid brought him by these mighty princes.

About him in his hall were gathered the rulers of the Angel-cynn who dwell in Bryttene. There sat his valiant son Ceawlin, to whom the West Seaxe looked for the kingship when Cynric should come to lie within his barrow. Beside Ceawlin on the mead-bench sat likewise Cynric's nephew Stuf, pillar of the Eotenas, who held the Island of Wiht as his inheritance. Other highborn heroes, hardy under their helms, drank bright ale within the smoky hall: Earmanric, king of the Cantware; Erchenwin, prince of the East Seaxe, of the line of the sword-wielding god Seaxneat; Wiglaf son of Weohstan, a prince of the Scyldingas exiled from his kingdom, who with his hardy band of Sae-Wicingas established a lordship in the fertile levels of East Angeln. From the land of the Suth Seaxe beyond the boundless forest of Andredsleag came riding bands of youthful warriors, *wreccan;* for there had been no kingship among their tribe since Arthur slew Aelle the Bretwalda.

From over the sea, too, came shield-bearing warriors, kin to Cynric and others of the Angel-cynn, for whom was there no need of summons by the war-arrow. Between the Cantware and the Francan have there long been ties of kinship and companionship in war. King Teodbald had died during the winter, and his brother Chlothar feared to act openly in alliance with Cynric against the Bryttas, lest the emperor of Romabyrg be offended with him. Secretly, however, he dispatched his son Charibert to Bryttene with a great host of axe-bearing warriors of the Francan. Many pigs and people were sacrificed at their departure, ensuring victory for their arms. These were men of highest mettle who had met and defeated in war even the mail-clad battle-hosts of the Romane. With them, too, was a war-band of Wendelas, spear-bearing heroes from Hispania, whose fathers had been driven from Africa by the Romane, seeking refuge with the king of the Gotas who rules over Hispania. Thus were they, too, *wreccan,* seeking the place of blood where ravens gather.

Lastly there came to Cynric's court the champion of all tribes dwelling about the West-sae, even the dread son of Ecgtheow. Beowulf, lord of the Wederas, he who slew Grendel and Grendel's dam, came on a day with his shield-bearing band to the mead-hall. The entrance was darkened as the savior of Heorot bowed his head to make entrance under the lintel, for his was the size of a giant, and in his grip was the strength of thirty men. A shout of acclamation arose throughout the hall as Beowulf entered, for now all men knew that victory must lie with the hosts that rode beneath the banner of the White Dragon.

Beowulf came and stood by his kinsman Wiglaf, lord of East Angeln. To Cynric he gave greeting, saying: "Hail to you, Cynric! With my war-band have I come at your summons, westward over the whale's path. With me I bear the sword Naegling, given me by noble Hrothulf in his hall at Heorot, with which have I sworn upon the white, holy stone to drink the life-blood of Maeglcon, whom men call the Dragon of the Bryttas. It is my custom to return three blows for each one I receive, and alone in battle have I delivered over the bodies of so many men to the pyre of destruction that a lofty hill could be raised up from their lopped limbs and severed heads, and their heaped-up carcasses make a mound large as a burial-barrow.

"Who is this king of the Bryttas, who puffs himself up with the empty praise of his household scops, vaunting himself with his own praise, slighting others with his haughty words, and scattering vain taunts, as though his one body enclosed twelve lives?"

So saying, Beowulf seated himself at the mead-bench and drained a horn of bright liquor deep as that which Thunor quaffed when he visited the giants' hall. Then did the heart of Cynric, the old king wise with years, know great joy and battle-longing as he gazed about him at the heroes. Of royal lineage were their princes: from the spine of Charibert of the Francan, sea-beast's offspring, sprouted the bristled boar's crest which was the mark of the royal house of the Merewioing; the head of Earmanric, king of the Cantware, was shagged with the wild horse's mane which grew from the heads of all his house; while within Beowulf, prince of the Geatas, wolf of the bee, was the strength and rage of the furred shambling one who prowls the forest in search of wild honey. Among the champions were many whose hair flowed uncut to their shoulders, dyed red in readiness for war. Like a mid-night gathering of fierce forest beasts was the warrior-host assembled beneath the shadows of Cynric's lofty hall pillars. Wolf-coats and bear-sarks were they all, roaring and howling in the swirling mist of the hearth smoke, as they hammered with their sword blades upon their iron-bossed shields.

At last silence fell upon the angry host, as Cynric rose to speak the words that gathered within his mind. His royal words they knew to have sprung from the inspiration of him who is the beginning of every speech:

"Os hyth ordfruma aelcre spraece!" cried the king. Men shivered, knowing that Grima, the Masked One delighting in strife, might even now be moving unseen about the hall. They cast down their gaze to the rush-strewn floor, for within the pupil of the king's eye the serpent was beginning to uncoil.

"A forest of spears have we here, borne across the broad sweep of ocean-flood from all surrounding tribes!" declared Cynric, leaning upon his spear and gazing about him with the look that none save Beowulf, hardy son of Ecgtheow, dared meet. "To the feast of which wolves and ravens partake are you invited, for this summer's hosting will place all the wealth and lands of the Bryttas within our power. After hewing with swords and casting of spears will come acceptance of riches, bestowing of blades, and delight in conquered lands and new homes. That this is no idle boast or empty promise I will now show you.

"As all here well know, the kings of the Bryttas have been led on by trolls and by Crist, lord of the giant-race, to conspire against us. They have gathered to the northward, in their city beneath their holy hill, to plot the downfall of the Angel-cynn and that of all who follow the path of the Spear. All winter long over their ale-horns have they been putting their noses together and wagging their heads into each other's beards.

"Snares and pitfalls have they laid for us, and even now their hosts are marching to outwit us. However, it may be that it is they who will tumble into the trap which they have prepared. The fox's cunning may be met with serpent's guile. I remember the words of the High One:

" 'When a man enters the hall, he should look about him, checking and noting all the doorways, for it is hard to know whether enemies may not be lying in wait for him. And when the guest has seated himself upon the mead-bench, he should be ever wary, silently glancing about him, listening sharply with his ears and looking here and there with his eyes; in this way a wise man watches out for himself.'

"You have seen for yourselves how we took the strong stone city beside this hall through skill of lies and deception. I speak no false-hood, too, when I tell you that we had looked to take the Dragon of Bryttene himself within our snare. That day is yet to come, though not far off. However, it is no small deed we have achieved that the proud prince whose stronghold it was now stands bound to yonder hall pillar. The once-mighty warrior is become the butt of bondsmen, whom the thralls of our household treat as a target for the bones they have gnawed!"

The warriors gazed to where Prince Einion, a lord of the Bryttas who had been guardian of the city which now lay in their power, hung bleeding within his bonds, a heap of knucklebones about his feet. His head hung forward, so that it seemed he might be dead. Now a hero flung a heavy thighbone hard against his ear, and the prisoner groaned and stirred; so it could be seen that yet he lived, though hardly.

"Now will you learn, my son Ceawlin and my kinsmen of the Angel-cynn, and you kings ruling beyond the West-sae, and you, mighty son of Ecgtheow, how the whole host of the Bryttas, together with their king Maeglcon the Tall, will shortly be delivered into our hands, when they will one and all suffer the fate of that wretched prisoner. Once he bestowed rings of gold to his followers in his merry mead-hall; soon will he be food for carrion!"

Cynric paused a moment, then turned toward a man who sat near him beneath the shadow of a hall pillar.

"Stand forth, Samo!" commanded the king. "Stand forth, O merchant of the Francan, and reveal to the heroes your thoughts and your skilled deceits, speaking as your own heart moves you!"

So he whose business it was to trade in wines and oils, salt and grain, cloaks and brooches, stood up before the shield-bearing warriors and told them of the words of guile he had dispensed to the princes of the Bryttas at their council. He told also of what he had learned of their plans, which with the coming of summer they must even now be putting into effect.

"My noble masters," explained Samo, "ring-bestowing princes, hearken to my words! The king of the Bryttas knows nothing of the mighty hosting which has gathered about all the coasts of his kingdom, nor of your capture of his great stronghold here upon the frontier. He believes moreover that Cynric the great king is departed overseas with the chief thegns of his kingdom, and that the *aetheling* Ceawlin remains alone here among the West Seaxe with but a scanty following.

"He has laid his plans accordingly, which with my own ears I heard him recount to his chief thegns. He believes this citadel to be still held by men of his own people against a weak war-band of the West Seaxe, who feign strength to draw him hither. Meanwhile the prince Ceawlin (so I led the Bryttas to believe) marches with his chief host to seize the empty frontier fortress which the Bryttas call Dineirth, and your people Beranburh.

"King Maeglcon accordingly plans to forestall these measures, dispatching the young whelp his son to Beranburh, while marching himself with the host of the Bryttas upon this stone-walled stronghold. Thence he purposes to advance onward into the heart of the region of the West Seaxe. There will he lay waste all the land, and (so he boasts) give over to the flames your royal hall beside Wintanceaster. And after these deeds are done, then will he march back to the old fort you call Beranburh, which he believes to be assailed but by the war-band of the noble Ceawlin."

Samo fell silent for a moment, while each warrior took his words into his heart and pondered them. Then was there glad laughter among them; merry voices rang out, and their words were cheerful. Each king believed his host alone to be a match for that of the Bryttas, and now they knew King Maeglcon's every thought, they could compass him about, as skilled huntsmen do the wolf whose tracks they espy entering a certain brake.

King Cynric looked about him with his serpent's eyes, smiling within his gray beard.

"Such is the plan of the great king of the Bryttas!" he exclaimed with a bitter laugh. "He thinks to outwit us, but you will see now how he is to be entrapped. His host will march as it lists, all the way to the sea at Cerdices-ora if it chooses. But Maeglcon himself will not march with them: He will be our prisoner before ever the Bryttas reach Wintanceaster! A message has reached my ears, whether brought by a bird or borne on the breeze I do not say. It is this: The king of the Bryttas will not accompany his host, but by means of enchantments will be persuaded to remain upon the way within the crumbling walls of Beranburh. With him will be but one poor war-band, for he will believe his own host to be pressing upon the heels of ours until they reach the place of fighting at Wintanceaster.

"And while Maeglcon waits within the broken fortress, all unknowing of our movements, we with our great host here will march fast by secret ways and take him—as easily as a man takes a bird upon a limed twig."

These vaunting words pleased well the host of the Sae-Wicingas and *wreccan* within that hall. They knew that once the king of the Bryttas was taken or slain, the men of his host must cease their struggle. For whither may they turn once they have abandoned their lord? Heavy of heart, bereft of joy, separated from their lord, they must depart to face the hatred and contempt of people everywhere. If the king were taken, the game was won! The gracious princess bedecked with gold, wife to Ceawlin, now bore about the mead-horn to the champions. Then were brave words spoken, the sound of a victorious host, for all rejoiced at Samo's news and the words of the wily king.

After a time Samo made sign that he wished to speak further, to which Cynric made agreement—though there were those who glimpsed a sharp glint from the serpent's eyes set beneath the thatch of his gray brows.

"Noble princes and thegns!" declared the merchant. "I believe this great king's words are wise and his plan good. Nevertheless, I fear that there may be reason for caution in your actions. I am no warrior, but a man of trade who has many rich wares within his booth beyond these walls worthy of your inspection. Still, I have lived in the great town of the Bryttas and heard the talk of their kings. It seems to me that, though their kings are brave and their host numerous, yours are braver and still more numerous. But there is a man there, a warrior of the Romane, old in years but well skilled in matters of war. It may be—perhaps you should consider this—that if they heed his advice their moves will be more artful than you think."

At this there arose loud scoffing laughter, for who among that host feared the wiles of a foreigner, and he an exile from his home? Long had the Francan and Wendelas fought with the men of Romabyrg by the shores of the Wendel-sae, and none there but had a tale of triumph to his name.

"It may be that you are right not to fear this man's guile," conceded Samo, "but it is not him alone whose words I fear. The Bryttas have also among their host a wizard with but one eye, who I believe can read runes and practice enchantments of power. He is a companion of the king's son, accompanying him out of the North at the ending of winter. I saw that he spoke much with the old chieftain of the Romane. He said little to the council when I was among them, but I misliked his looks and feared lest he guessed my purpose, reading my heart through skills of magic."

Now was the laughter louder still; for were there not witches and warlocks enough among the West Seaxe to raise up spells against this wizard of the Bryttas? Had not Heorrenda the scop sailed northward to Beormaland, consulting Caelic the king and making sacrifice with the witch of the Scride-Finnas upon her holy mountain? None knew more of magic and of the unfolding *wyrd* of men than the Scride-Finnas, for they dwell at the very edge of Middle Earth, upon the cold margin where it meets the yawning void beyond.

Samo sat down, silent and dismayed. He saw that the king was angered, and wished now that he had withheld his counsel. Cynric darted at him his serpent's glance, and that was an ugly troll-look which he bestowed upon the merchant.

"What do you know of wizards and warriors, merchant? It is your lot to exchange salt-blocks in the spring for wool and hides, or to bargain for slaves in the markets of the Fresan. We seek information, not counsel, from such as you. That was an ill moment when your tongue wagged then: Never before has a wretched huckster and exile, *wraeclast,* sought to raise his voice in the company of thegns, as though he were our *thyle,* counseling the Woden-born king of the Gewissae! Receive now your reward, and betake yourself out of this hall as you may!"

Then Cynric took up a silver goblet from the table and cast it upon the ground, where it rolled before the feet of Samo. The merchant, who had a yearning for wealth, and also a yearning to depart swiftly from the royal mead-hall, stooped down in haste to lift the ancient king's lordly gift from where it lay upon the ground. Cynric laughed harshly, and cried out, "See how he stoops by the hall pillar, like a pig rooting for mast among beech-roots!"

And while Samo groped about him in the shadows, Cynric drew his sword Hunlafing, best of all blades borne in the North, and sliced off both the merchant's buttocks down to the bone. Samo fell to the ground, screaming like a horse, and loud was the laughter of the heroes at the sight. Then Cynric bade his young thegns shear off the man's feet, which was done with a sharp axe; after that they shaved his head and befouled it with tar and feathers. Then was he taken to the great door and turned out shrieking into the night.

"Must the swine squeal?" cried Cynric, seating himself once more upon his gift-stool. "He travels the road his sire and grandsire traveled, and still he squeals! The home of exile is the reward of treachery. I think that he whose trade it is to buy and sell does not retain his goods for longer than he need. The news he brought me from the hall of the Bryttas was worth a silver cup, and maybe more; but it could be that news brought back to them from the hall of the Gewissae would be worth another. The merchant has a heart as filled with falsehoods as that of the traitor Becca, lord of the Baningas, of whom scops sing. Now, however, I believe his walking will be but slow!"

Then all men made merry at their feasting, and the scop who sat at Cynric's feet sang to them the lay which told of Sigemund son of Waels, of his faithful nephew Fitela, and of the slaying of the dragon who slept curled about his serpent-hoard. Men's hearts uprose at the great tale, each vowing within himself to wreak havoc among the swart Wealas when the time of conflict was come.

The scop who sang that song was not the far-faring Heorrenda, but another. While Samo spoke of the coming moves of the Bryttas and the Angel-cynn, Heorrenda arose from the mead-bench and crossed to where lay the colored board upon which two warriors had been playing at *taefl* before the royal feast began. Heorrenda invited none to play with him, but sat gazing at the pieces where they stood set about their king. At times he threw the dice, then sat back once more plunged deep in thought.

It happened as he sat thus that another came and sat opposite him before the board. He was not a man known to Heorrenda; moreover he wore a cowled cloak with the hood pulled forward over his brow. Heorrenda asked the man who he was, and why his face was hidden.

"Men call me Blind Stranger," replied the other, "and the reason that I remain hooded is that my face is not one pleasant to look upon."

Then Heorrenda thought he must be a man suffering from the scurvy, for it is the practice of such men to wear cowled cloaks and never push back the cowl.

"What do you wish with me?" inquired Heorrenda again.

"I wish to ask you a riddle, my friend. May I do so?"

"Ask what you will, and I will tell you whether I can answer you," returned the scop, whose word-hoard was filled with many deceits with which he was wont to entertain kings at their feasting.

Then said the Blind Stranger:

> "What thegns are they
> Riding in bands,
> Hosting as one
> Over the lands;
> Spearmen sending,
> Settling fresh vales?
> Answer me this,
> Teller of tales!"

Heorrenda laughed as he shook the dice within his cupped hands. "The riddle is a good one, O Blind Stranger! However, I have guessed it, have I not? Woden is playing at *taefl* with the Frost-giant, each skillfully moving his pieces upon the checkerboard."

"Who are these, then, of whom I heard tell?" returned the Blind Stranger:

> "What men are they
> Watching about
> Their helpless king;
> With each new bout
> The dark withstand
> Oncoming fair?
> Answer me this,
> O poet rare!"

The scop laughed again, as once more he made reply: "Not difficult is that either, Blind Stranger! You speak once more of cunning play at the colored board, where the darker pieces defend the king, and the fair ones attack. Two men may sit long playing at that game, until sorrow slips from them and they forget what harsh *wyrd* the sisters may be weaving for them. Will you not play with me now?"

The stranger nodded, studying the checkerboard intently from within the shadow of his cowl. For some time he remained silent, gazing from one piece to another. Finally he spoke:

"There are misplaced pieces upon this board, Heorrenda. The game has been played false. You who have fared so widely among the courts of kings, do you not know how to play at *taefl*?"

"I know well enough, friend," replied the scop in cordial fashion. "I have this to say: It was not I who set up the game; the pieces stand as I found them. Another than I must have played amiss."

"Then it is not for us to alter matters now," muttered the Blind Stranger. "The world is as we find it. Shall I take the king?"

"I know not what you mean," replied Heorrenda in perplexity. "Do you intend to take the king's part, or is it that you see a move whereby he may be taken by his foes?"

"It may be I mean both those things, or it may mean either. However, let us arrange matters thus: I, who am dark, will take the dark side, while you who are fair, the fair."

"So be it!" rejoined Heorrenda, well content to find an opponent who, as he guessed, possessed great skill at the dice-throwing.

So they played together at *taefl*, the scop of the Heodeningas and the Blind Stranger. Skillful was the scop's play—he who was accustomed to utter good counsel, master runes, compose verses, expound dooms. But he found it hard to gain the victory over this stranger, who moved the dark pieces back and forth about the king's side. The luck of the dice-throwing lay for the most part with Heorrenda, but it was the Blind Stranger's way to turn those lucky casts to the advantage of his dark pieces.

Nevertheless the king was compassed hard about, in the main through openings arising from that faulty placing of the pieces on the board by him who played before. Heorrenda could by no means see which way the game would go.

"How say you, O Blind Stranger," he asked, "is it good fortune in the dice-casting, or cunning thought given to moving the pieces which plays the greater part in the contest?"

For answer the Blind Stranger took up his king, holding it out upon his open, withered palm.

"Do you see what is written there, scop?"

The poet gazed narrowly at the piece, reading the runes which he saw inscribed upon its flat surface:

ᚱᛖᛁᚺᚨ

"I see them, but know not which way to read them," he replied.

"Throw the dice; then read from right to left!" commanded the Blind Stranger.

"The runes are faint, and waver before my eyes," complained the scop. "Still will I do what I can. *Naeh,* 'near,' is how I read the first three runes. Then must I move a piece beside the king, it seems!"

"Read the next three before you do so!" again ordered the stranger.

Heorrenda held the king over toward the hearth flame, which licked its ruddy light across the level surface, throwing the runes into momentary relief.

"I read the other three thus: *hwaer,* 'where.' Ah, where indeed, my friend? I think here, to the north, where it seems you have left me an opening."

The Blind Stranger withdrew a forward dark piece, setting it beside Heorrenda's. Another move, and the fair would be trapped between two dark foemen.

"Beware, Heorrenda!" murmured his adversary warningly. "This time see if you can read the runes from left to right."

Again the scop's gaze traversed the twice-triple lettering, until he achieved understanding and raised his eyes to the hooded face before him. Was it the sparkle of the firelight, or did he see for a moment the gleam of an eye like a distant star? It was but his poet's fancy, but it seemed to him that in the darkness beneath the stranger's hood he saw the night sky beyond the royal roof.

"Rahwhan!" he exclaimed. "So that is it! It is a game of enchantments and rune-spelling you play with me, is it, O traveling cowled one out of the night?"

"Are you surprised?" inquired the other coolly. "Is not all strife beneath and about Middle Earth concerned with *rahwhan:* strife of gods, or strife of elements, or strife of men? Without *rahwhan* would all binding be loosed, the World-serpent set free, and the ancient chaos come again upon the world. Must not then our game, which is the image of that struggle, be governed likewise by power of *rahwhan?* Of what worth is rune-spelling if you lack the knowledge to make use of the spells? That is *rahwhan,* and if you take my advice, friend, you will pay heed to it or abandon our game!"

"I am master of rune-lore, as all men know," exclaimed the scop angrily, "but I fear your skill is greater than mine. Or are yours moves of deceit? I saw that the pieces were not established in due order from the outset. Perhaps it was you who altered the board, before I came upon it? If so, perhaps you will now lend me a little aid upon my way?"

"It was not I who tampered with the setting of the pieces, but another," muttered the Blind Stranger in a sullen tone. "Very well, I will help you, though not to win a game in which it may be I have a stake. The game itself shall be played out in another place than this, and I doubt not you will see its ending, good or bad.

"I will expound the matter a little to you, so far as my understanding permits. After that it is for you to learn how to make use of the *rahwhan* by which the conflict is influenced and, it may be, directed. I see you have much to learn, though you have journeyed to the holy fell of the Scride-Finnas. But even the gods do not possess its full mastery, or else would there be an end to a struggle which outlasts that of Hagena and Heoden."

Heorrenda wished to reply, but the words would not pass his lips. He feared the old man whose face was hidden within the dark shadow of his hood.

"Take these letters one by one. Together they spell a word of power, and each in turn bears its own spelling. What is the first letter? You know it, I see: *rad*—that is, the Driver of the Wagon. But who is the Driver and what his Wagon? Step outside this small enclosed space onto the face of Middle Earth, and direct your gaze upward. There, hard by Iring's Path, drives the Chariot of the Bear; the Lord's Wain, *Carles waen*—that is, *Wodnes waen*. It is the Chariot of the King of Men, whose trundling and creaking precedes the passage of the host of the slain toward Wael-heall.

"There, already I have told you more than I should! Let Cynric seek the kingship in the Chariot of the Bear, if such be his purpose. But let him remember also that the Wagon 'wends eastward over the waves,' as they say among the Heardingas. By that I believe they mean the place of death, for that is whither Woden's Wagon rolls. Know you this, or not?"

Heorrenda nodded, still unable to speak the words that surged within him, and his adversary proceeded.

"Not hard to know is the next letter, for in *Os* lie the beginnings of every language; and Os is the name borne by the Lord of Runes, who for nine fell nights hung in torment upon the World-tree, when screeching he grasped the runes.

"*Os* is the second letter, and likewise the fifth. For He hangs about the third letter, which is *Eoh*—that is, the windswept Yew upon which He hung, given to Woden, Himself to Himself. That yew is the best and greatest of trees, whose branches reach up to heaven and encompass the whole world; no man knows from what roots it rises. Within the well lying at its foot He hid His eye as a pledge for the wisdom which is His.

"By *Eoh* you see *haegl*, 'hail': elven-shot, and also arrow-storm. For the Lord of the Slain is the battle-inciter and foe of peace. Where arrows come whistling in over the shield-wall, there is he laughing at the mischief which he delights in stirring up among the princes, scattering runes of strife among the kinsfolk.

"And so we reach the last letter, which is *ned*. For 'need' is of necessity the end. It is that which binds each man's *wyrd,* and which of all things there is no avoiding. I mean Death, my friend, which is the end even of *rahwhan*."

The Blind Stranger replaced the bone king-piece upon the colored board with a mocking laugh.

"Now there is no need for further play, Heorrenda, far-faring scop! I have opened my knowledge-hoard, permitting you a glance within. If you understand what I have told you, then it may be you will win this game yet—upon the *taefl* board, and elsewhere too. Meanwhile I bid you farewell!"

With this the scop's opponent rose, gathering his dark cloak about him. Heorrenda looked up, and for a moment glimpsed the face beneath the cowl. He saw one who was very aged; gray, worn, and one-eyed.

Then the scop believed for the first time he knew with whom he had been playing at *taefl*. He sprang up, seeking to stay him, but words froze upon his lips and he might not move from the mead-bench. He saw the Blind Stranger pass swiftly beyond the hearth, slipping silently behind one of the great tree-pillars which sustained the roof of that greatest of mead-halls.

Then Heorrenda went up to Cynric the king where he sat upon his high seat, and told him all he had seen and heard. Cynric commanded men to search about by the hall pillar, but no trace was there of him who called himself the Blind Stranger. However, it was whispered by many that he was no other than the Masked One, *Grima,* Lord of the Gallows. By means of runecraft and magic had he entered the hollow post, and so escaped unmarked from the midst of that great company.

A chill now fell upon the feasting, and Cynric gave orders for his thralls to make ready foot baths and kindle fires for each warrior, to bait the horses and give the hogs their swill, before all men laid down to rest within his mead-hall. It was not long before the company lay sleeping on the ground, save only Cynric's prisoner, the prince of the Bryttas. Palely glimmering in the dying light of the hearth embers, he dangled from a pillar soaring upward to the unseen darkness, his life-blood seeping down tight-knotted thongs, dripping onto bones about his feet cast by the thegns during their feasting.

Then did the noble son of Ecgtheow, Beowulf lord of the Geatas, dream he was in Heorot upon that night long ago, when through the dark came stalking Hell's evil slave: he who prowled in the shadows, sharp-clawed offspring of a monstrous dam. The hero stirred in his sleep, gripping the gilded hilt of his sword Naegling. Others, too, suffered ill visions of the night-troll; gnawer of the moon, giant of the gale-blasts, curse of the rain-hall, friend of the night-roaming hag, swallower of the bright loaf of heaven. The owl called shrill from within the dark forest; the wolf howled long from the cold hill. No man wished himself without the iron-clamped walls, whilst black bat-frequented night hid all beneath the shadow of its hood!

But after the chill night comes at length the dawn, when warm light shines forth over mankind, and the sun, clad in golden glory, mounts the eastern sky. A gray light stole through the doors and smoke-hole of Cynric's hall, warriors rose weary from their uneasy sleep beside the mead-benches. They rubbed their eyes, gazing about them, puzzled by dawning memory of their visitor of the night before, and disturbed by their ill dreaming.

Then, as the heroes gathered about their lord, there entered running with frightened looks a thrall, who summoned the kings and thegns to the stables. That was an evil sight, for one had entered their stalls during the night who had chopped off their tails close to the rump, cut off their forelocks so close that the skins of their foreheads were shaved off also, and snipped off their ears down to the bone. Thus shamefully had the horses been treated, and that was a bitter insult to the kings of the Angel-cynn and their comrades from over the waves. Likewise they found that the tail-feathers of their fettered falcons had been plucked out and scattered about the mews.

Beowulf, lord of the Geatas, grunted angrily like a bear, gripping his sharp-filed sword and peering about him fiercely. Others were dismayed, though, for they feared the malice of the Father of Mischief. Seeing this, Cynric bade Heorrenda strike up a cheerful song:

"Bright day is dawning,
Cocks loudly crowing,
Summoning heroes
To wolf-feast going!
Wake now, my bold friends,
Saluting the morn!
Raise up your bright shields
Round the Woden-born!

"Proud prince of Geatas,
Wiglaf the Scylding,
Foes never fearing,
Corpse-barrows building!
Not for wine waking
Nor women at play;
Spears to the slaughter:
Rejoice in the fray!"

At this, the heroes' hearts became high within them. They made ready their weapons, donned their ringed mail-coats, and set off with the king to the place of sacrifice. There they purposed to make *blot,* so that the Lord of the Slain might mark down the foe with his Spear, giving victory to his followers. In this way they came to the sacred field by the forest which is called Aet Weonfelda. There had the chief *blothere* of Cynric's court prepared a great *sige-blot* for the Giver of Victories.

Cynric ascended the royal barrow which is there. Upon its holy summit stood his kingly platform, *stapol,* from which the king utters those dooms which make the year. Upon a throne set upon the *stapol* was Cynric seated, with the palms of his hands turned upward on his knees in sign of suppliance to Him who dwells beyond the Rainbow Bridge. About the sacred field were assembled the warriors of the West Seaxe, the priests who perform *blot* and *husl,* and the husbandmen whose thralls till the land. For nine nights was there to be peace about the sanctuary; no man might bear his weapons thither, for the king's peace was upon Aet Weonfelda throughout the time of *sige-blot.*

When the king had taken his place upon the *stapol,* with all his people seated about him upon the barrow, then Cynric's son Ceawlin appeared naked before them all. He was clothed by the air, stripped that his oath might have effect, unmasked from the elements, open to the eye of the god. He made obeisance to the elements before he approached the foot of the royal barrow. It was there that men had borne that prince of the Bryttas whose fortress Cynric took by skill of deception. The royal prisoner lay spread upon a great slab of stone, gaping gashes in his sides, his skin bedewed with blood. There appeared, too, a radiance about his white body, which was marked by many.

His hands and feet were tightly bound by cords of sinew, for men feared lest he bear rune-staves about him, with power of unloosing. Had not Crist himself, god of the Bryttas, freed his spirit from his body, cold prison of the soul, by utterance of magic runes when he hung upon the gallows-tree? That was a mighty rune-master indeed, and among his followers were known to be many sorcerers, *leodrunan,* to whom their Troll-lord had accorded powers of enchantment.

Now Ceawlin took a sharp-bladed knife from the chief *blothere* who stood by, and approached the captive. Holding the flashing blade high above his head, the prince of the Gewissae turned to all the people, crying, "Now I give this man to Woden, that we may have victory in war and plenty in peace!"

So saying, he turned the prisoner over upon his face, and tore his shreds of clothing from him. Then, setting his brawny knee in the small of his hapless victim's back, he raised high his knife and plunged it between the bound man's shoulders. With care then he cut the ribs from the backbone, and drew the lungs and heart out through the hole he had carved. From the dead man's severed windpipe wound forth a long whistling shriek, like that of a slaughtered pig whose throat a butcher slits at Blotmonath.

Thus Ceawlin made the blood-eagle upon the back of the prince of the Bryttas, who died there beside the barrow-mound, his gore soaking the stone and splashing the grass around. And so perished the noblest young prince of the Bryttas, dedicated to the Lord of the Gallows in the holy field Aet Weonfelda.

His long throbbing scream sobbed among the surrounding thickets, while from the worshippers there went up a great sigh of joy and awe. For all men saw that Woden was pleased with the *blot*, when a great raven perched in a yew nearby uttered a harsh chuckle before it flapped off, black against the bright roof of heaven. The crowd of warriors swayed together in ecstasy, their eyes half-closed. King Cynric ever sat upon his *stapol,* palms upward on his knees, his aged face closed fast in prayer. Together he and his people prayed that to him might be granted the luck of Hengest, a kingdom broad and cruel as that of Earmanric, and slaughter grim as that which Aetla brought upon the peoples of the earth. To Aetla, Cynric dedicated his son Ceawlin, could he but obtain victory over the foeman.

Next the chief *blothere* filled a bowl with the blood which still welled forth from the life-spring of the young man, and placed it upon a slab of stone. With twigs he sprinkled the blood, examining the patterns, and foretelling those things which were to come. Then the kings came forward and drank toasts in the blood of the prince of the Bryttas: first to Woden, bringer of victory; then to Cynric the king, that his rule might be prosperous; and lastly to the company of the gods, each in due succession.

After that, men took the body and carved it in pieces, hanging them from the branches of a tree in the grove hard by. From other branches they hung wolves dragged forward in nets by thralls. Then Cynric descended from his royal mound, and going up to where the limbless trunk of the young prince hung all bloody from its branch, he made the mark of Woden upon the flesh with the point of his spear: the rune of glory, and sign of the Chariot which keeps well its faith toward princes. Such a sacrifice was pleasing to the Lord of the Hanged.

Before him Ceawlin the young *aetheling* danced naked over the sword blades, beside the shade of the gallows-tree. Like dawn arising in the east was the leaping light of his lithe body, like a dragon flying flaming across distant downs, like the moon shining forth, wandering behind clouds. And as the noble young *aetheling* bounded beneath the clear sky, kings and champions sang together, howling and stamping upon the green ground.

"Away! Come away!" cried the carles of King Cynric. "Come away where the *waelcyrge* seek out the slain! Follow our march to the mouth of the cave whence but few will return! From the forest comes stealing the strong time of darkness, darkness of death and delight in the slaughter! We ride on the *herepath* leading to Wael-heall, winding the hillside to Woden's bright hall! Wisest All-father, grant us all our desire! It is you who give gold to the shield-bearing heroes, you who gave helmet and ring-mail to Heremod, who set before Sigemund the sharpest of swords: helped him to Hrunting, bane of the barrow-fiend! To some you grant glory, treasure to others; loquacity lavishing, *Os,* upon many, willing your eye-price, wisdom, on kings. To serpent-ships sailing, over seas faring, fair winds you blow; skill at the rune-rhymes on scops you bestow; give heart to the warrior wielding his blow!"

Upon the side of the *blot*-stone a rune-master carved these runes:

> Not by an iron blade is it to be cut,
> Nor by the sun will be sought,
> Nor any man read these rune-spells here
> While wanders westward the waning moon.

No witless wight shall steal it forth.
It is splashed with the red heart-lake,
Scraped on the stout thole-pin,
Pillar of Bryttene, bent by our oars.
What mask was that the Warrior-God wore,
Wending west from out of the war-land?
Scale-coated shoals swimming the slaughter-stream,
Bird of slaughter screech over the foes' throng:
Warning to Wealas, workers of woe!

The *blot* was performed, the runes traced by the *blothere's* blood-twigs he read as tracing a path of *speth*, and the omens observed by the heroes as they proceeded to the holy field were good. The dark raven had pursued their path, two proud warriors had been seen standing upon the wayside, and a gray wolf howled twice beneath an ash tree. Thralls cut from the sacred sod the turf necklace, which was set arched upon the point of Cynric's spear. Every ring-mailed hero in that glittering host passed in turn beneath the Earth-necklace, swearing not to wash his hands nor comb his hair until the cold lips of the axe brought victory to Cynric. Wealth greater even than that of the necklace of the Brosingas lay within that turfed entrance, for it was a taking of the Island of Bryttene itself, richest land that is beyond the kingdom of the Romans around the Wendel-sae.

Garbed now in his singing coat of mail and high-crested boar's helm, Ceawlin the *aetheling* brought forth the *tuuf*, White Dragon banner of the West Seaxe, from its resting place in a sacred grove. Grim barrow-dweller, he sallies forth breathing fire and dripping venom when fell foes seek to take from him the treasure-hoard which is his alone. From the royal barrow it fluttered free, from the bloody rune-stone at its foot, out onto the broad *herepath* which leads to the field over which ravens are screaming, pools dripping with heroes' blood, teeth struck from the mouths of the slain flowing in torrents of gore, rubbed smooth by stones upon their course, glittering in the slime among splinters of bone and lopped limbs. The place of conflict is soaked in gore, the red flood stagnates far around, and rich blood gushing from steaming veins engulphs the tumbled battle-corpses!

The moment was arrived when Cynric must part from his son Ceawlin, and he spoke to him his mind before all the warrior host: "Now has come the time, my son, for you with your hundred hardy spearmen to preserve for us the stone-built stronghold of the Bryttas. It will not be long ere their host appears before its walls, all unwitting that now it is held by the hosts of the One-eyed Lord of Victories!

Your task it is to hold them there in play, while we make our way by secret paths to where their king, left unprotected within the broken walls of an old fortress, all unknowing awaits the arrival of our unconquerable army. And when their host comes to learn their king is slain, then will they make but feeble fight as I and all these noble kings return like a raging wolf pack upon the highway in their rear.

"But take care, my dear son, that you do not engage the Bryttas in combat beyond the walls, for your band is but small and theirs great. Remember that I your father am old, and that our kinsmen among the Gewissae and the tribes of the West Seaxe look to you for succession to the kingship!"

Ceawlin swore to fulfill all his father's wish, vowing that the shield should be ready, the notched shaft set upon the string, the edged sword filed sharp. Courage for the brave, helms for the bold—and the least of treasures for all cowards at heart! Then the lord of the Gewissae, son of Cerdic of noblest birth, kissed his son and clasped him around the neck. Tears fell from the eyes of the gray-haired warrior. He was old and full of the wisdom which years bring, and he knew that there were but two things which he might expect. Less likely was the second, though who can know what *wyrd* has been prepared for him upon this earth? Never again might he see his noble son amid such a warlike gathering. His son was so dear to him that he might not contain the wellsprings of his heart; a longing for his dearly loved son burned in his blood and was held fast by his heartstrings. He wept, and his heart was sore.

So Ceawlin remained with his company, few but fearless, to accomplish his father's bidding within the strong walls of the ancient city built by skilled men from Romabyrg in days long gone by.

With the banners of the *tuuf* fluttering before them, horns braying, men shouting, hoofs clattering, the great host of Cynric set forth upon its march. From the city which had once been the Rumwalas' and then the Bryttas', but which was now a hold of the Angel-cynn, the heroes issued by the western gate. Before them, set straight as a spear-shaft through the forest, lay the great road, a wondrous work which the men of Romabyrg built of old. The broad paving of the highway gleamed pale beneath the morning sun; its course guided the warriors as they marched together. Each ring-shirt of mail glinted from its hand-forged links; each glittering ring in their harness sang out as they strode out upon their foray. Woe betide the foeman who placed himself in the path of that mighty war-band!

Over hill and dale flew the causeway, like an arrow through the yielding air, rather than a road which must trace brake and fen, river and upland moor. At last, after many days, came Cynric with his host to Cerdices Beorg. There he made blood-sacrifice, *blot,* by the howe of plenty; even to his father Cerdic, prince of the Gewissae, who was slain in battle by Arthur, king of the Bryttas. Within that great hill, raised by the warriors of the Gewissae about the ashes of their dead lord, lay hid abundance of arm-rings and jewels, plunder of the Bryttas, wealth of thegns. Now the earth guards it, gold in the ground, where yet it lies, set apart from the use of men.

High on the barrow-crest Cynric set up the *tuuf* of the White Dragon, and beside it he stood awhile. His thoughts were bitter as he recalled the day when burning coals consumed the mighty chief of fighting men, who so often endured the steely shower, when storms of arrows sped by bowstrings came darting in over the shield-wall, when the eager feather-cold shaft did its duty, aiding the arrowhead upon its way.

Then Cynric swore by the southward-swooping sun, by Woden's lofty Crag, and by Wuldor's holy Ring, to avenge his father's death, and that of Wigmaer the thegn who died within the prison-house of Arthur. With these three oaths he vowed to ravage the land of the Bryttas, watering its soil with the blood of its warriors, taking it for his own, and putting their king Maeglcon, heir of Arthur, to a cruel end. After that his *blothere* uttered spells about the barrow, so that the howe might not open, the bale-fires not be seen blazing, and the barrow-ghost lie still within his grave. But before he placed the rune-staves about the king's mound, the *blothere* saw how dead men bearing sword scars dripping gore flitted from its banks, and he knew that they departed to tread the red road of war.

After this the battle host rode onward until at last they came to where another great causeway crossed their road from north to south. Southward it led to Cynric's great hall by Wintanceaster, whither the host of the kings of the Bryttas purposed to ride ravaging, all unaware that their plans were known to the wise king of the Gewissae. It was their purpose to stain that finest of houses with blood, wetting it with drops that drip from sword points. But quite otherwise had the *wyrd* been ordered!

The princes rode some miles upon this road, until they came to another crossing. Here Cynric and the numberless hosts of the Woden-born kings turned westward upon the track which crossed the broad highway. Theirs was now no paved causeway, built by skilled wrights of the Rumwalas, but the holy way, *hearh-weg,* marked out by the Lord of Dykes before the Angel-cynn came to people the Island of Bryttene. The road crosses the Island from sea to sea; even from the kingdom of the

Cantware, which Hengest seized from Wyrtgeorne, to the promontory of Cornwealas, where once the Bear of Bryttene held his court. And at its midpoint lies the Giants' Circle, which is the Navel of Bryttene.

Upon the *hearh-weg*, where it winds across hills and ridges, over distant downs and around upland bogs, the forest of spearmen now made their march. Far below them now lay the straight roads of the Rumwalas, among level pasturelands green and misty in the warm sunlight; roads frequented by the hosts of the Bryttas. It was fortunate for their crafty foes that the mailed horsemen who serve the Red Dragon did not think to direct their gaze upward to the hills, to the thorny rock-strewn wilderness, where now upon a furze-clad downland wound the dark war-band of the White Dragon, lithe and secret as a serpent about its barrow. Beneath torn clouds beaten about a thudding sky, borne by black pinions on the racing wind, soared screaming a dark raven, that bird which is ever greedy for slaughter. From this the princes of the Gewissae and the hosts of the Angel-cynn knew that the Bestower of Victories, he who loves the waste places of the earth, watched over them and guided their march.

Thus the army wandered across a great wilderness, their steps guided upon the *hearh-weg* by the Lord of the Spear, their march accompanied by the dark bird whom the Friend of the Raven had sent to guide them to the place of slaughter. By day they followed the feathered plunderer, holding to the course of the *hearh-weg* upon the line of the ridges. At night, when they rested beneath the stars, they saw afar off a pale light gleaming like a distant lantern before a hall gate.

Then at last they came to a spot where the road plunged deep down to a lush green vale, through which a swollen river wound its tranquil way between sedge-swamps and summer meadows. Ranks of waving willows marked its course, where yet it flowed beneath spring floodwaters. At first it seemed as if the sad cry of the curlew piping faint upon a lifting breeze were the only sign of life within that lone green sanctuary sunk in the midst of the barren downlands. Gazing down upon the hither side, however, the kings saw far beneath them smoke curling up from homesteads huddled along the spring-line. The setting sun lit up long shadowed lynchets, where hardworking husbandmen had tilled the light chalk soil. Whether they were the dark foes of the Angel-cynn, speaking the chattering Wealas tongue, or whether they were far-flung settlers of their own people, bold worshippers of Woden, might not be known. Whoever their inhabitants might be, that sparse line of hutments huddled amid the gorse below appeared to the watchers upon the hillcrest as if it were the outermost bound of Middle Earth.

For upon the far side of the broad valley reared up a grim rank of steep dark hills, their face hidden from the ruddy light of the sinking sun, walling off all the land to the north. Upon the soaring slope of that harsh escarpment could the kings but barely descry where their way, after passing below by a broad causeway across the water meadows, crawled upward by a deep cleft within the cliff-face.

Sitting his horse upon the brow of the southern hills, hard by a lone ash tree bent beneath the wind, Cynric surveyed the desolate scene. Now he saw that the Raven had indeed guided them aright, for there upon the crest of the ridge before them, somber against a louring sky, reared up a mighty barrow. High over the vale it towered, sullen and swart as a crouching wolf, its broad head thrust forward to receive the keen-edged wind gusting in from the east. As if echoing his thought, the dark bird croaked harshly overhead where it hovered upon the wild wave of the beating wind.

Cynric knew he must meet his *wyrd* before that barrow, and gave orders for the army to cross the water meadows and ascend the opposing height. Hardy in their helms, they clattered across the causeway, splashed by way of the ford, until they came to the foot of the rocky cliff. There they were obliged to dismount, leading their steeds up the cold steep slope, clambering bravely by the narrow way. The dark cowl of night was coming on; it was the time of half-light, when the fiery guardian of the barrow-hoard ranges about his howe, burning and coiling in ruthless rage. Those brave men pressed upward on their path until they came all at once upon the summit, where they saw the dark shape of the howe looming up against the night sky.

All about the barrow burned the bale-fires which had been as a beacon to the host in the nighttime of its march. Around its base they flickered pale and leaping, a ring of shields red and white, rim to rim, which no warrior might break; a river of flame coiled about the mound as the World-serpent encircles the earth. No man might pass through that fiery fence and live; but Cynric the gray-bearded king old in wisdom, and Beowulf the son of Ecgtheow, greatest of warriors that dwelt upon earth, left the hosts upon the roadway and approached its rim.

Beyond the shifting shadows within the flame-fence, it seemed to the kings that they glimpsed a great tree, springing from the summit of the high place. So high it soared, it seemed to tower aloft into the starry sky, where Carles-waen glittered bright upon the sooty-raftered roof of heaven's hall.

Upon the trunk of the tall tree hung a naked figure, his wasted frame shifting in shadows cast by the cold light of the fire. Upon his shoulder perched a raven, who plucked the eye from his head, picked the flesh from his bones. From the hung-up naked man fell rotten flesh and maggots, upon which a great boar at the foot of the tree was feeding.

Broken and twisted was the hanging man's body, and his face shielded by shadow: *grimes wrasen*. But now the old warriors understood that they were come to the wind-cold wolf-tree west of Wael-heall, and that it was the Lord of the Gallows who swung there, riding that dread steed which gallops to the mouth of Hell. For a space they thought him dead, but then they heard him laughing harshly in the cold night upon the windy cliff-top.

"What have you come for, raven?" he croaked to his dark companion. "Whence come you at eventide, with your bloodstained bill? Flesh clings to your claws; the reek of rotting flesh breathes from your beak. I think you have been by the place where ranks of corpses are lying!"

The dark-hackled brother of the eagle dried his beak and, cocking his head, made reply:

"I have been following the path of Cynric son of Cerdic since I came out of my egg."

The figure hanging from the tree was silent for a space, then made reply in a voice which seemed racked with weariness and pain: "Then that is a red road upon which you come, friend; a wet way, a slaughter-way. If that be the road you follow, then will you feast well at your journey's end, well as the heroes in Wael-heall! You will come to a field where corpses are ranked so close that the heels of those who fight will slip upon the split faces of the dead. Many will there be who become the prey of ravens, whose flesh will be gobbets in the curved beaks of hungry eagles; the corpse-goose will gorge his fill upon a banquet of bodies! But that is the way for fearless princes to fall in war, clasped about their king in a common death.

"But why should you fear such talk, you, gray-bearded son of Cerdic, and you, mighty lord of the Wederas, slayer of monsters in hall and mere? What warrior king seeks the shameful Anathyrm, Worm of On, dying in old age without agony? Only the hero who is slain by the spear-thrust or hewn down by the sharp-filed sword may enter the great gates of Wael-heall, there to partake of my feasting!"

Then the two princes knew with whom they spoke; whose was the body hanging from the barrow-yew.

"I believe that to be the Lord of the Hanged," said Cynric to

Beowulf, "mighty in combat, ever content with his single eye. If you would look upon him face to face, then lower your head and gaze under my arm here, where I hold it akimbo. You must hallow your eye with the victory sign if you would safely know the war-god's gaze."

But the mighty son of Ecgtheow, troll-slaying lord of the Wederas and Geatas, laughed angrily at this, growling grimly: "Not even for the Lord of the Slain does the killer of Grendel and Grendel's fell dam feel fear. Within this grasp of mine I bear the strength of thirty men; with this bright sword Naegling will I face the Inciter to Battle. I believe it is lawful to lay low in war the war-waging god, if he come against me with his Spear!"

The hung-up naked man laughed through the night at these bold words, though ever the raven pecked at his falling flesh.

"You are a bold man, Beowulf son of Ecgtheow! Such words are pleasing to me, and much will I make of you when you come to sup in my mead-hall. I think you do not fear me; and yet why do you seek me, here on my windswept tree? I will read you a rune: Do not go out at night unless you are posted as a lookout, or you seek a place to relieve yourself. It is my belief you have come hither for neither of those purposes. Though you scorn my Spear, my words may be of some avail to you.

"Never laugh at an old withered man, troll-slayer! Often will wise words come from out of a shriveled skin, arise from hanging hides, dangle within dried skins, swing among worn entrails! Not always was I, not always am I, as you see me now. Many a time have I clasped a thegn's daughter in bed; white when we woke was her fair skin under shafts of morning sunlight. Among the reeds I waited, under the eaves of the byre, under the wagon in the muddy yard; let fathers and husbands watch as they might, always I achieved my end!"

"Men say that you were ever a deceiver," replied Cynric from beyond the bale-fires. "Though you swore faith upon the holy ring, still you stole from the giants the mead of verse and runes of magic. Is that true, or is it not, O Bringer of Victories?"

The gaunt frame of the hanged one gave forth a bitter groan at these words of Cynric's. The moon shone forth for a moment from between racing clouds upon his shattered body, and the sight of his scarred and torn flesh aroused the pity of the battle-hardened heroes.

"Your words are true, son of Cerdic. I stole the mead indeed, and took the runes. But I believe it is not for men to complain of my deceit, for bitter was the price I paid. For nine nights I know I hung upon the windy gallows-tree, nine whole nights together, wounded with a Spear; dedicated to myself, myself to myself, upon the gallows-tree. Who knows whence its roots spring? Then none came to bring me bread, no horn was handed up to me; I peered down about me, I seized the runes, screeching I seized them, and fell back fainting."

The breeze about the hill fell back among the woods below, upon the Barrow Wodnesbeorg descended a stillness of the night. The broken body hung motionless against the tree, until it seemed the sufferer might be dead.

At last the lord of the Geatas broke the silence, calling manfully across the flame-barrier: "Will you not help us, Bestower of Victories? Westward across the whale's path have I fared with my noble follow-ers, to aid Cynric gain a kingdom such as Earmanric achieved, or Aetla broke. See, here is the sword Naegling, with which I slew the dreadful troll-woman within her cave. Now I swear not to sheathe it until it has passed between the head and shoulders of Maeglcon, calling himself Dragon of the Bryttas. He is a worshipper of Crist, dread lord of Frost-giants, who I believe to be no friend to you and yours."

With which Beowulf drew forth the mighty blade, skilled work of dwarves, which flashed with a brilliance reflected above in the night sky, where the Sword of Tyr glowed radiant upon the cowl of night.

Cynric, too, that king wise and gray with years, spoke also: "It is the wisdom which comes from rune-reading that we seek, O High One. Brave are our warriors as this doughty foe of the bee, and numberless are their war-bands from over the whale's bath as stars in Iring's Path. All we fear is that the foe will escape our vengeance. Through our own wiles have we separated their king from his host, and now we seek to find his fortress in this wasteland, that we may slay him swiftly before his thegns discover the deceit. Will you not guide our steps, O Road-practiced Father of Victory?"

Once more the naked figure upon the tree trunk hung in silence for a space. The flames about his holy howe flared ever lower, fitfully flickering until it seemed they must sink back beneath the frost-whitened grass of the sheer hillside. The hosts of the Angel-cynn upon the highway hard by witnessed the death of the doom-light with dismay. They feared lest their kings be taken from them by trolls of the mountainside, or by those elves whom men glimpse flitting over barrows. At length Cynric heard the sufferer's words faint in the murk.

"Guidance will I give you; riddles will I unravel; runes will I read," muttered the hung-up naked man. "I know a charm whereby, if I see a gallows' corpse swinging from a tree, I carve and paint runes, enticing the man to descend and speak with me. Such a man I saw but recently within your sacred grove, son of Cerdic, and it was with him I spoke. Upon you and your hosts will I work powerful enchantments, strong staves of power, which the wisest of men painted and the foremost of gods carved.

"My strength is waning, like that of yonder moon, and you must wend your way to meet your *wyrd*. I shall not refuse your request; you have no long road to travel. Cross the dyke; go past the dell. An hour to the stock, an hour to the stone; keep by the left hand, keep by the right, until you see the Seven Barrows. If you read the rune-staves aright, then within Wuldor's Ring will you find yourselves, the Ring upon whose faith I vow to preserve you and yours—who are also mine. There will the golden-bristled one, Frea's friend, he who leads the armies, guide you by the passage which leads to Woden's Hall."

The sky was now fully overcast, and a weeping rain had extinguished the sinking flame-circle. The mighty tree sank back into thick darkness, and of the hung-up naked man Cynric and Beowulf might now see but a faint glimmer within the gloom.

"Tell us these last things!" pleaded Cynric, with a last loud cry. "Shall we be there tonight, and what shall we find when we arrive?"

About the king's ears stole a feeble, failing voice: "With toil and trouble will you reach it, about the time of sunrise or thereabouts. As for what you will find, I believe you know that already. For my part, I see *waelcyrge* and ravens about the Victory-tree, and blood in pailfuls spilled upon the grass. Skillful has been your deception, which will earn you honored places among the ranks of heroes, and rich will be your reward. Nor am I without gain, for now I see I have gained a little of that which even Thunor failed to raise within the giants' hall: little enough, but it may be enough!"

So the Hanged Man vanished, falling back into the darkness; and of the raven which tore his flesh, and the boar which ravened below his feet, nothing might now be seen. Cynric and Beowulf returned to the host, telling them of all they had seen and heard by Wodnesbeorg. Though some of his words were puzzling, the advice of the hung-up naked man was thought good and worthy of adoption. It was ever the way of the Masked One to speak in riddles: that all men knew.

So the host resumed its march northward over the down. They were in a wild place, wet and dark, uncheered by the warm sun. There dwelt no men by warm hearths where the weary traveler might find good cheer and friendly talk. It was a secret land of wolf-haunted slopes, windswept craggy outcrops, perilous fen-tracks. Dark dells lay concealed about it, steep rock-filled clefts cutting the ways, ugly brier-bound brakes impenetrable as fortresses. Within its thickets prowled the bear and lurked the lynx; the grunting black boar rooted about the beech woods; the gray prowler on the moor smelt out his prey. Upon the pitch-black surface of moorland meres fared a deadly wonder: fires flickering upon the water's face. Within their dank depths dwelt fell beings, Hell's hateful offspring, with whom none save the valiant son of Ecgtheow had ever dared exchange blows.

Like plague-boils on the earth's hide heaved up earthen tombs of long-forgotten lords. From some, still gleamed the light of a bright brand lying beside a dead hero's bony hand. Others, rash men must have raided for treasure in times of yore, for all the land about was blasted and blackened by the burning breath of scale-skinned barrow-guardians, angered by the impudent theft of their beloved hoards. Man's rich estate was become the inheritance of the venomous foe of mankind. Silent over the face of the wasteland rolled vapor white and thick as Eagor's daughters, when they break high upon a winter's strand. The huge one was passing over the earth, swallowing woods and water with his whiteness, gulping in men, waging war on the sun. It is wind alone which is feared by the fog, and runes of the Road-practiced alone which may guide a man through that thick hedge.

The heroes' hearts were not daunted in the darkness of that deserted wasteland. Following the runes received by Cynric at Wodnesbeorg, their hearts beat high with hopes of bloody war. The she-cat, mother of dragons, was abroad sowing confusion across the waste. The mouths of howes were opened: over some, elves flitted; at the doors of others squatted witches, blood dripping from their nostrils, awakening hatred among men.

Ever as the army marched upon the muddy trackway, their tread was echoed by a distant muffled thud. The wind, too, blowing in hoarsely from the northeast, came in heavy whistling gusts as if breathed in and out by a hugely distended belly upon a distant ridge above the plain. Then those who rode in the van glimpsed a livid far-off glare, like a star reflected in the troubled waters of a muddy mere. Not long was it then before all men knew that the lame son of Wudga, Weland, had burst Nithad's cruel bonds of sinew, and must even now be toiling hard within his forge, wielding his hammer above the flames, beating upon the fierce brother of the earth, who in his turn works wounds far and wide upon earth. From every man is that mysterious might concealed, and the course of its secret skill; but all knew for whom the weapons were being newly welded. The wind shrieked shrill about the winding forest of spears, and shrill rasped Weland's file upon the greedy sword's edge.

In the forefront of the army rode the two mightiest of men that were in those days: Cynric the old king, and the grim lord of the Geatas, Beowulf the son of Ecgtheow. Upon their way they crossed the great dyke built by the Masked One in another age, passed by the dell; saw the stock, saw the stone; came to a flooded valley. The moon emerged from its refuge to guide their way with a silver lantern; beneath the far-flung level they glimpsed the stony track. Across the vale the great host made its way, and it seemed to the princes as they turned to gaze behind them that they were an army riding out across an empty ocean. Darkness lay behind and before; spearpoints glinted like stars as the horsemen moved slowly across the silver-rippled expanse.

Upon the other side rose up a hill, and it was not long before Cynric counted the Seven Barrows named by the Lord of the Gallows. Faintly gleamed the frosty grass upon their rounded flanks, their number reflecting the seven stars which shine in Carles-waen. Behind the Wain careers blindly the Wild Hunt of the Slain, and likewise beside the barrows galloped forward the Woden-born king at the head of his host.

Now Cynric saw the Lord of the Gallows had read the runes aright, for of a sudden he found himself all unawares encircled by Wuldor's Ring. Within a double circle of high stones had he halted his gray steed: four times four gray rocks standing stiff about him, and six times seven encircling them in their turn. Who first raised up those gray markers, setting them upright in the soil, might no man now know. Before the arrival of the Angel-cynn, before even the Bryttas sailed hither to set their name upon the land, there reigned kings for whom the Island was an especial sanctuary floating upon the Ocean Garsecg.

"This must be the Ring of which the hanged wretch spoke," growled Beowulf at the king's ear. "Now which way do you think we must ride?"

But no sooner had the words fled from the mouth of Grendel's bane than an unexpected answer came. A great bright-bristled boar stepped from the shadow of a column and careered suddenly across the princes' path. Gazing after the creature, the two highborn lords of men saw where a broad stone-lined highway wound westward down the hillside into the shadowy vale beneath. High beat the hearts of that valiant host as they rode in file down that lordly road! Before them ran their four-legged guide, tusks and bristles glinting brightly. Upon either side, as posts upon their way, were set stone after stone, each one more than a fathom high. Pillars and diamonds were they, ranged in pairs. No man might lose himself upon that fair highway!

Like the coils of the World-serpent around the whole world wound the pillar-lined road; proudly pranced the steeds of that numberless host of spearmen, as if they trod upon the curved bridge which leads to Wael-heall. Long and broad enough it was to accommodate all the hosts of the earth, from the famous forest of Mearc-wudu to the holy grave in Gota-land, to the wondrous stone which stands by Danpar. It curved to the right; it curved to the left, where hard by swelled up a marvelous holy hill, rounded, smooth, perfect as the breast of a woman or the boss of a shield. Long must dwarves or giants have toiled to raise that great work, for certain it was that it had been a task beyond the achievement of the mightiest of men.

After riding for a dark space of time up what seemed an endless ascent, Cynric and all his company came to where a great gaunt earthen rampart stood foursquare before them against the sky, a broad-shouldered giant blocking the way. It stole into their thoughts that the Mischief-worker had led them astray, until it was seen how the boar who led them turned sharply to the right and then, as they followed, sharply again to the left. Not without their guide would the warriors have traced that crooked entrance, but there was a road for the Road-practiced; within the gloom stone markers loured yet to left and right.

Where at first there seemed no entrance was now a great gateway driven through the towering ramparts. The gateposts were two mon-strous boulders, each high as the rooftree of glorious Heorot. And as the army advanced between them, they saw a marvel such as those of which scops sing, but is not to be seen by men upon this earth, unless it be beyond Wistlawudu, where lies the shining city of the king of the Creacas, which men say is walled thrice about as if by golden rings linking the Wendel-sae to the Sweart-sae.

For there, girdled about by the soaring rampart which enclosed the circle of the starry sky, lay a great bare city of stone. Each stone was huge as a house, and halls and passages innumerable led about its winding ways. None that might be seen dwelt within those windy chambers, nor passed along its twisting tunnels. No men, glad of heart and flushed with wine, caroused there; none laughed upon his mead-bench, nor gazed at glittering weapons hanging from tapestried walls. Silent upon the springy turf moved the hoofs of the heroes' horses; stilled were the warriors' voices as they stared about them upon those ancient works of might.

For that was a holy place to which the High One had directed their steps. Six hundred doors it had, from each of which might eight hundred men emerge when the time came to do battle with the fell being who ever skulks about the bright enclosure. Twin circled cham-bers lay within, a sun and a moon within the earth's girdle. All about their corridors and chambers coursed the boar, and ever after him the cavalcade. A low mist rolled in over the ramparts, like a sweep of the tide little more than fetlock-high; while heavy clouds settled upon the ranged heads of the columns. It appeared as though the company might be riding among the clouds over the four corners of the earth, where stand the pillars which support the sky.

Blood-red glared the fog as the wild ride careered onward, and darker with each stride grew gray shadows around the stone shafts. Barely now might those in the forefront glimpse the boar's golden crest in the obscurity before them; it seemed as though a drop of bloody dew glistened on each bristle-point upon its back. The darkness grew deeper and the air denser, so that soon Cynric and his company might scarcely breathe.

"Will our journey never end?" cried Beowulf in anger. "I believe we are betrayed. The pig is a deceiver!"

No sooner had the words escaped him than their guide vanished amid the mists that swirled about them. The horsemen pulled up their steeds and peered about them in the nighttime.

"We have fallen into an ill path!" exclaimed Cynric. "I cannot believe it was for good we were brought to this strange place. What think you, valiant son of Ecgtheow?"

"I think the Mischief-worker has ensnared us, that he lied to us from his Gallows," replied Beowulf. "Like a wolf he hung there, and like a wolf he lured us to the place of danger. I would I had him now within the sweep of my sword Naegling. Then would he hear the wind whistle between his shoulders and his head!"

But Cynric, fearing further deceits by the High One, invoked his name, calling upon him to help those who waged war on his behalf: "Not for gain or greed did men leave their hearths beyond the swan's path to fare hither, but to strive against the friend of Frost-giants, foe of the gods: he who brandishes his sharp-edged cross high over the land of Bryttene. Will you betray those whose blades are borne hither to help you, O Bringer of Victories? Men term you Worker of Mischief, but are you not fearful lest the victory-luck pass from you and those who worship you, to Crist and his champion Michahel?"

At this the host gave a great cry of anger, which arose harsh as a crowd of disturbed rooks up to the heavens. Woden, dwelling in his hall in the North, heard it and gazed forth from his window. He saw what had happened and became wrathful, flinging away the mists that hung about the center of the ancient city of stone. The dawn arose, pale and reluctant, above the eastern hills, casting a gray pallor upon the hill of the Seven Barrows. High in the wakening sky above hung faintly yet the Seven Stars of Carles-waen, rolling remorselessly as the lost host of Cynric about its inaccessible axis. And the rim of that revolving wheel is the fiery belt of Iring's Path, highway of hosts hurtling headlong toward the windy halls of Hell.

From the Seven Stars, from the Seven Barrows, light stole softly westward from the encircled sanctuary upon its hill, down across the mist-hung vale below, stealing sinuously up the farther slope, until it shone between the giant portals of the great gateway set in the revolving ramparts, shooting a bright shaft into the heart of the holy city.

Standing silent amid the stones, the kings and thegns of Cynric's host remained for a moment still and pallid as the gaunt gray boulders soaring to the sky above them. Then they looked about in bewilderment. Before them towered three gigantic slabs set upright edge to edge, roofed over by a fourth. No image stood within that huge ark now, staring westward to the hills, but none doubted that once a wizened bent one crouched there, with his mists and gloom and blood about him. Many bones and skulls lay about the empty place: men and women long since dead, bruised and bled to satisfy the old one's hunger and his thirst.

The sky-ceilinged chamber in which his stone coffer stood was ringed about by twelve lesser giant-stones, sloped and sinking little by little below the turf of that grim garth, who for age of ages had stood ward about the bent one of the hill. Twelve gateways were there: four times three, while beyond them lay further openings three times nine. Mist-swathed was every passageway; which they should take to retrace their steps none knew, for no runes were written there, and their guide was gone.

"This is a trick of the Deceiver!" cried Beowulf, lord of the Wederas. "Never again, at any rate, will he skulk within this shelter, sowing mischief among men!" With which he dismounted from his steed and, setting forth his strength, plucked the topmost slab from off its supports. For a moment he held it high above his helm, then hurled it several fathoms from him. There it sank half into the ground, and there men may see it lie even until this day.

At this, light shone into the coffer, from which bounded forth the boar who had led them to that wondrous work of giants. He flew toward a gateway, careering beneath the stamping horses, anxious to escape the warlike throng. At once Beowulf seized his skillfully strung bow and, setting a barbed arrow upon the string, sent a sharp-piercing dart speeding toward the creature as it ran. The arrow struck it behind its shoulder; the boar stumbled as if to fall but, recovering, made its way off, swerving amid the serried lines of stones.

"See him bleed!" The noble son of Ecgtheow laughed. "If it is indeed the High One who has deceived us, he has that lodged within his hide which may help him to recall his childish trickery!"

There was laughter among the thegns when they heard the words of Beowulf, but the face of Cynric the king was clouded and grave.

"It may be we would do wisely not to laugh until we have retraced our steps out of this place of passages," he exclaimed. "I believe we have been misled through this maze of mists and stony whorls into the heart of that web which men call Weland's House. If so, it is a place difficult to enter and harder to leave. We must find our way out without delay!"

As he uttered these words the heart of Cynric became for a moment cold within him. If there lay mist in every gallery around, there was no smoke before his eyes, and he began to think he had not acted as wisely as he should. For there stole suddenly into his mind the parting words of Him with whom they had spoken as He hung upon the Tree:

"I have gained a little of that which even Thunor failed to raise within the giants' hall: little enough, but it may be enough!"

CHAPTER SIXTEEN

THE DEBILITY
OF MAELGUN
GWYNEDD

How long I lay within the cold chamber of Gofannon mab Don I do not know. Bruised and exhausted as I was by my journeying and travails, mine was a restless sojourn upon its damp earthen floor. I experienced many visions and dreams between resting and waking, and which were waking and which dreaming it was not easy for me to know. Beyond the entrance of my involuntary refuge the smith toiled on unceasingly.

At times the rhythmic tapping of his hammer and dull murmur of forge-fires lulled me into a quiescent restfulness. Then I felt myself curled once more within the womb of all things, suspended in the innermost enclosure. Above and around me slowly spun the millstone of the skies, the Chariot of the Bear drawing it surely about the eye of the quern. Other stars pass in endless succession beneath the sea, but the Chariot is set just and true upon its wheeling course; its cycle is not broken. My sleep was restful; upon the gently swelling waves of ocean was my vessel borne. I passed in my dreaming back to a time before the Cauldron was shattered, the waters broken, the herbs gathered together.

But then of a sudden I would hear the bellows begin to breathe heavily, gasps of heaving wind growing ever hotter, the giant grunting with exertion, striking fierce blows upon a molten mass of white-hot metal boiling out of the bursting blaze. With his tongs he took the shapeless slag, and upon his anvil beat it with skilled harmony of hammerblows into emergent form. Then came the convulsive drawn-out hissing sigh, as if a gasp of pain or pleasure, as the fresh-formed blade was thrust deep into the cauldron's cooling waters.

I felt the heat of the hearth even within my stone-slabbed coffer beneath the earth; I saw the ruddy glow flicker upon its sides, as if bale-fires leaped up all about me. Feverishly I turned about, my spirits troubled as the tossing tongues of flame. The hiss of the tempered steel was transformed in my troubled mind into the hiss of the uncoiling Serpent of the Deep, the roaring of the fire into that of the pyre which will engulph heaven and earth at their ending.

I glimpsed horrid images of war; gazed deep into red chasms of oblivion, into yelling mouths and gaping wounds, into roofless infernos. I heard the cracking of a child's skull crushed in by an iron heel, the helpless screaming of a girl passed about by loveless hands, seemed to see her unbelieving stare of shattered innocence. And upon all thundered in crescendo, echoing in every ear, the measured tramping of a thousand metaled hoofs; masked helms, faceless hosts, a blind hundred-headed monster.

About the barrow flames were leaping, growling around the ring. I rose, stooping within that strait place, resolved upon flight from all that mocked and menaced me about. But not easy was it to leave the house of Gofannon mab Don. Many false entrances present themselves within its subterranean halls, passages doubling back upon themselves, fluted spirals within spirals, encircled circles, a vortex sucking ever to its center. Renowned among all the company of gods is the feast over which Gofannon presides, and his hall does not accommodate the departing guest!

For long, how long I know not, I wandered with my mind in a maze, hearing the harsh cries of the angry host behind me. But I, too, have mastered enchantments. I, too, can read runes. Am I not Merlin the son of Morfryn, who slew the *ellyll* in the Cave of Annufn and emerged to tell the tale? I saw once more the serpent coils carved upon the rock, felt your loving strength, Gwendyd, within my heart. I traced the serpent's twining, gained the stone-slabbed entrance, saw once more beneath the moonlight the giant guardian pillars that stand before the forge of Gofannon.

The smith was absent; his coals burned low. Gone, too, was the vengeful blade I had heard him forging, and I knew that but little time lay before me. But time had I bought, and that is not the least of achievements. It is a gift of the *awen,* and that indeed is timeless.

A dawn wind was rushing cold out of the east over the downs, swirling about the holy place upon the hill, rippling bright-bladed puddles upon the rutted road as it tore down the slope to shake tall trees growing about the forge of Gofannon mab Don. Their branches swayed wildly, creaking and bowing before the pitiless gale. I shivered, drawing the tattered boar's hide which was my only covering close about me, and stumbled upon my way.

Dawn was breaking cold and gray over the dreary expanse of the raised empty plain, about whose outer rim I made my way. The only living being visible on that desolate landscape, I felt myself the cynosure of the unfeeling elements about me. But when, after trudging some way along the road, I let my mind gaze coldly back upon myself, I perceived that I was but a fly perched upon the iron tire of a chariot wheel. And the fly must be careful lest he be crushed by the wheel's turning, by the relentless revolution he barely discerns and may never stop.

Nor was I entirely alone in the solitude, though my companions were not such as I would have chosen. Twice I heard a wolf howling some way off on my right, and from a yew grove in a hollow a round-eyed owl, night bird of Gwyn mab Nud, hooted mocking and melancholy its unchancy cry across the abyss. A moment later, and my blood froze as there wound up from the dark patch between the hills which was the huddled skulking copse a piercing wail of tortured pain. I started fearfully, then mocked myself as I realized it was but the cry of some poor mouse being torn apart by the curved talons of the dweller in the hollow.

It was a cruel, empty, wind-tossed road I trod. In the dawn of another age great kings had ruled upon these once-fertile heights. I saw about me their gorse-grown burial mounds, graves which the rain wets and the thicket covers. Once the proud princes dispensed hospitality within their brightly lit halls, but now none made libations upon the earth heaped above their bones; no poet sang their praises before a gracious company; their names and deeds were dispersed by the gusting wind. I had thought the *awen* deathless, that *awen* which I have felt course about my whole being like a cataract over a crag; but now I saw how all that is born of the elements is dispersed at the last into the inchoate waste which was there before Gwydion raised his enchanted wand, before my mother Ceridwen gathered herbs for her Cauldron.

You see, O king, how I set down my thoughts as they occurred to me at the time. There is a place where every cairn is counted, every mound named, the dynasties of kings recorded. But I had long been alone, a hunted and tormented creature. I felt closer in that hour to the mouse within the owl's clawed grip than to the kings and bards of Prydein whom I have known. I was but a passing speck upon the brown waste. The Forest of Celyddon is a wilderness indeed, and no very welcome place to me. But there every crag and plunging stream had its shape and memorial in my mind, pleasing or fearful. Here all was of the same sad, dun-colored uniformity: long level uplands, with here and there scattered boulders, a solitary barrow, or a stunted tree. My feet were clogged with great lumps of clinging clay, so that I might hardly place one before the other. Before me the winding upland road reached forward to a broad empty horizon, which when finally attained gave way to another of grim sameness.

However, every journey has its ending, even if that be but a renewed beginning. At first my road had taken me northward, grad-ually ascending until I was moving upon the spine of a broad ridge. After a while the height afforded me glimpses of a great plain over in the west, stretching far as the eye could carry. The open view allevi-ated a little the shapelessness, the lack of direction and purpose, which so oppressed me. The sky was overcast, despite the time of year, and hitherto only the ancient road stretched silent across the plain told me that I moved at all. And it was the road itself that seemed to wish to hold me, sucking at my feet, encumbering them with ever greater loads of cloying marl. Reappearing as it did at intervals beyond the hillside, the recurring view provided at least a semblance of ground gained.

Few sounds disturbed the dreary waste, which undulated about me like a shipless ocean. At times a lark sung his unheeded lay in the high air above, but for the rest there was no sound save the wind sweeping the thin grasses. No fellow being could have sought out such a wilderness for home or occupation. Upon the distant plain I thought once or twice to have caught a glimpse of a thin spume of hearth-smoke rising, but here the muddied highroad bore but the occasional slotted imprint where boar or stag had passed across. Though I saw neither boar nor wolf nor lynx, I guessed that they abounded in a realm long abandoned by man to their rough sway.

Scarcely more empty than the low sky above was that desolate spot. Eddied crowds of crows smudged the gray cloud-wall above a hanging wood in a grim descending hollow to my right, while high above me floated a crook-winged hobby. All unconsciously he seemed to follow my clumsy ascent, hovering overhead, adjusting himself to my snail's crawling with an easy tilt of his wing upon the wind. I welcomed his presence, studying with pleasure the careless skill with which he stooped and flung himself in hurtling flight down upon some hapless small bird flitting between the gorse clumps. Within the black pool of his frowning eye the broad expanse resolved itself into a tiny focus—like that strange glass through which you and I, my Gwendyd, have so often gazed out upon the wider world. Nothing moved upon its surface but he marked it.

Perhaps it was this reflexion which brought me to direct my gaze more sharply around me from my vantage point upon the ridgeway. At once it seemed to me as well that I had done so, for the first object upon which my eye lighted was an ancient grass-grown earthwork. It lay perhaps but a bow-shot's distance from me, no different from a dozen other such I had seen upon my way. But as I swept its hunched summit with the solitary eye the Hawk of Gwales had left to me, I saw that which made my heart stop a moment.

Something glinted sharp against the brown heath beyond: It was a spearpoint raised a little above the rampart! Instinctively I crouched low within the sunken way—for too long had I been a helpless quarry harried about the land—and listened hard. Veering sharply, as was its wont upon the hills, the breeze bore across to me a snatch of voices raised as if in dispute. Such was my plight that, where hitherto I had suffered nothing but pity for my wretched solitude, now fear flung loneliness to the winds.

The eddying of the limbless creature, lacking bones or blood yet irresistible in his rushing strength, now wet and now dry, old as the earth and broad as its face, shook the squat thornbushes beneath which I skulked, preventing my distinguishing the words or even the tongue of those who lay so near me. But it was not an encounter I dared chance. I was being hunted by an enemy cold, cunning. and cruel.

It might be these unseen men were but wandering shepherds or huntsmen: men, it might be, of that ancient race who settled the Island of the Mighty before ever Prydein son of Aed the Great sailed hither with his company, and who, fearing iron, dwell among these wild upland wastes, speaking yet the ancient tongue of their people. But also upon the skirts of the downs (as I had discovered already) settlements of the Saeson had long been mingled with those of the Brython. True it is that all are tributary to the lord of Caer Ceri, whose task it is to ward over this section of Arthur's frontier. But now, with the hounds of war running loose across the land, who would be so rash as chance his life upon their surety? Still more likely—and, if anything, worse—a prospect was that they might comprise one of those bands of brigands calling themselves "sons of death," who bear a mark upon their foreheads and undertake a vow of evil to cut the throats of a given number of men. For it is upon the frontier regions of kingdoms that such lawless gangs abound.

At once I resolved to make a circuit across the open heath upon my right, which might afford me shelter where it fell away from the crest. The ridge in any case was curving to the east, and I could cut across and rejoin it at some point where it met the sky to the northeast. The wind being momentarily in my direction, I was the less frightened by the loud squelching my feet made as they were sucked up with each step from the wet clay upon the trackway.

But for the fact that it was my only guide, I wondered that I had not thought to leave the trackway earlier. Kicking great lumps of heavy mud from my feet, I found myself bounding almost gaily across the open turf. No longer buffeted by the northern wind that scoured the ridge above, I found the warm damp air of the valley-head invigorating. The wound upon my back, where the huntsman's spear-blade had gashed me, was sore indeed, but not insufferable, and I felt my strength returning. A track trod by deer (as I guessed) made my way easier yet, and like a deer upon the heath I bounded forward!

The hill grew steeper, the horizon renewed itself each time I thought its summit near, but tirelessly I flew upward. After the cramped confines of Gofannon's dark halls, I was intoxicated by the unbounded expanse of light and air. Suddenly I came upon a broad path crossing my green winding way. Looking leftward, I followed it up the hill-side, where what should I see but the ramparts of a mighty fortress upreared against the sky! Huge earthen dykes, sullen upon the hillside, stood surmounted by a palisade, while the path ran on below massive timbered gates which blocked its passage.

Smoke curled upward from within; I heard the cries of many men, sounding of horns, baying of hounds. Now was my heart filled with gladness to which it had long been a stranger, for high above the walls fluttered bravely in the breeze a banner: It was the Red Dragon of the Cymry! When last I saw it I had been with King Maelgun and the hosts of the Brython in their camp beside the Temys. Why it should be here in this deserted spot, when the host's march had been directed southward upon the straight road leading southwestward away to Caer Vydei, I could not for a moment tell, nor did I wait to consider such matters.

Up the hill I ran, laughing and crying, so that it was not long before figures appeared running dark against the sky upon the rampart to gaze down in my direction. As I neared the gates I cried out a greeting, wondering which of my comrades I might find within. You may judge of the surprise I experienced, if only for a moment, when a flurry of arrows smacked in swift succession into the turf about me, and I felt a sharp stab of pain in my side! By now no stranger to this sort of thing, however unexpected, I flung myself sideways behind a boulder and lay there panting beneath my boar-skin.

My respite lasted but a brief moment. I heard a creaking of gate hinges, and the shouts of men approaching. "It is there, behind the stone!" cried one, now very near. At once I laughed out loud. Once again have you made a fool of yourself, Merlin the Mad! What could the poor fellows have thought, when they saw me approaching in my cloak of hide, but that a great boar was charging across the hill? For I recalled how I had coursed over forest and field, my bristled covering glittering like wings of silver. Doubtless they looked forward to a savory filling of their cauldron as the meed of their skilled shooting. Well, I had better disappoint them before matters became more dangerous!

I was clumsily attempting to strip myself of my animal guise, when a dozen soldiers shot up around me, their broad spear-blades converging on my breast. "Hold!" cried their captain, with a look of amazement. "It is no boar, but a man. What sort of unchancy fellow can he be who roams the wild in such a guise? Perhaps we should kill him after all!"

"Just a moment, my friend," I exclaimed, struggling to my feet and striving at the same time to untie the knotted forelegs of the dead beast which held his pelt about my throat. "I implore you to stay your hand, at least until I have been brought before the king!"

The chieftain came closer, staring at me in some disbelief. "Why, I know who you are," he cried. "You are the bard of King Gwydno Garanhir, whom Prince Elffin brought with him out of the North! I have heard you singing in the hall; what are you doing here in so strange a robe? I think that you have not been kindly treated upon your journey, wherever it was, whatever it was?"

"That I have not!" I replied. "And to tell the truth, I am exceedingly hungry and tired. Will you not help me back to your fort up there?"

The man saw my plight at once, which was no very difficult thing, and signed to his followers to help me. At the sight of their friendly faces, and the thought of rest and food and the homely tongue of the Brython once again within my ears, I felt a happy weariness steal over me so heavy that I fell forward in a faint. Strong arms gripped me fast, before I suddenly slipped away into sleep.

How long I slept I do not recall. It may not have been more than a few hours, for, as perhaps you will have appreciated by now, O King Ceneu of the Red Neck, mine is a hardy constitution. When at last I woke, I thought at first I found myself still reposed within a delightful dream, after the wild and frightening nightmares I had experienced within the forge of Gofannon mab Don.

Not upon his hard earthen floor was I lying, but in a warm bed between freshly laundered sheets and my head resting upon a feathered pillow. Above me I saw, not the cold wet slab of Gofannon's chamber, but the thatched roof of a snug booth. Best of all, and scarce believable after all I had undergone in my troubled travels and visions, I saw stooped above me the faces of men I knew and loved. For there beside me looked smiling anxiously down Prince Elffin mab Gwydno of Cantre'r Gwaelod, and Taliesin, chief of bards!

My eyes were opened, and I seemed to float on air; but my surprise and delight were such that for a time I might not speak.

"He is awake!" cried Elffin in high delight, beaming across at his companion. Taliesin leaned forward, peering closely at my face; it was easy to see that he shared the youth's concern.

Chuckling loudly, he declared mockingly, "A hard task it is, Elffin, to wring the neck of such a tough old bird as this! Whoever they were who received him upon his way were no very hospitable folk, that is clear. It may be he tried singing his bad verses in the halls of kings less indulgent than your father Gwydno Garanhir, or Maelgun the Tall of Gwynedd!"

Elffin grasped my hand where it lay upon the coverlet; I saw there were tears in his eyes. "There are many at my father's court at Porth Gwydno in the North who would have grieved sorely had you been lost, my Merlin. There is one in particular very dear to me, whose weeping I believe would not have ended swiftly. Do you remember how Taliesin and I found you hanging from the weir-stake? No, for you were but a baby then. Where have you been all this time? The king told us how you left him by the banks of the Temys, but a month has passed since then with no sign from you. Many times in our councils we longed for your advice, and for my part I would like to speak to you of home: of galloping upon the Strand of Traeth Reged, of bull-netting, hawking, and playing at *gwyddbwyll* and kiss-in-the-ring with those who loved you as if you were their own wise child. Where have you been, and what have you learned?"

Taliesin signed to the young prince to cease from tiring me with questions, and indeed I was still so weary that confused memories of dreams jostled within my mind against my present waking vision. A broken snatch of verse surged up from somewhere within the chambers of my brain:

"Whence came Woden's whetstone which he threw among the thralls,
Leading them a merry dance throughout lame Weland's halls?
Checked them on the checkerboard, laid snares within the ring;
Winked wisely from the treetop, spread dark as raven's wing?"

"Now truly is our mad Merlin returned to life once more!"
grunted Taliesin in satisfaction. "When he rises I do not doubt we shall
hear much of winged serpents and talking eagles, inspired pigs and
sweet-apple trees, more jumbled and in faultier meter than ever before.
And to think I believed him seated beside some distant cataract, seeking the gift of the *awen* that he might rival my enchanted verses in the
courts of the kings of Prydein!"

I smiled at this and fainted away once more. It was not for long,
though, for when I opened my eyes my two friends were still beside
me. Now, however, they were seated on stools, watching the court
physician (whose duty it is to accompany the hostings) make his
examination of the wounds and bruises innumerable I had received
during my traveling. The physician's name was Melys mab Marthin,
and he came from the land of Arfon.

"How do you find him?" asked Elffin anxiously.

"He is in a sorry strait," replied the physician, whose fingers I felt
pressing my body gently about. "He has received knocks and blows in
abundance, but what he has not received is one of the three dangerous
wounds, which are a blow to the head reaching the brain, a blow to
the body reaching the bowels, or breaking of one of the body's four
posts. But see here, prince, where beside his shoulder blade the arrow
struck him. That is a sore cut, deep as the gash of a bear's claw.
Nevertheless it is no mortal wound, but one as I judge given unwillingly by one of his own blood."

"You are right, O Melys mab Marthin," cried Elffin, "for it was
indeed one of the archers of my *gosgordd* from Cantre'r Gwaelod who
all unwitting sent the shaft that struck my friend! But tell us swiftly:
He will live—that is not to be doubted—but how soon may he rise
from his bed?"

The physician pondered a moment, then rose and looked porten-
tously about him. "I will apply red ointment; I will let blood. The
wound should mend; the scar should heal. It will be a hidden scar,
whose *dirwy* will be of the value of one cow. As to when he rises, that
may be for you to say, O prince. There lies a choice before you: Either
the sick man may endure a long illness, and afterward certain help and
succor; or else he may after three days and three nights have a temporary healing, with longer sickness to follow. Men customarily adopt

the second choice when they wish to exert all their strength against their enemies."

I heard these words with satisfaction, for I knew that I was needed within the camp. Three days even might prove too long, for aught I knew.

"I choose the second cure!" I cried out, then groaned from a sharp spasm which seized about the shaft-hole in my back.

Prince Elffin laid his hand gently upon my arm, saying, "Are you wise, Merlin? The fighting is far off, where Run mab Maelgun leads the men of Arfon with reddened spears to victory over the Iwys before the walls of Caer Vydei. Nor is it right for a bard to lend his hand to combat. Take rest after your troubles, which I think have been many. We will have much to talk of later, you and I. Besides, there is someone at home in the North who will not forgive me should harm come to her Wise Child!"

I clasped Elffin's hand with my own in weak gratitude, but I noted also the look which Taliesin bent upon me. My thoughts were still wandering and confused, but his glance told me that, even were my arm too weak to wield a spear, my words might be required within the council chamber sooner rather than later. My choice was made, despite Elffin's protests, and Melys busied himself with preparations for the temporary cure, giving orders which all obeyed, for in matters of herbs and enchantments he had no rival in the courts of Prydein.

"Cause a marrow-mash to be brought to this booth!" he commanded; and straightway men busied themselves within the encampment slaughtering kine and sheep and pigs, whose flesh and bones and hides they ground up together into a pulp. Then was I lifted and laid back upon the marrow-mash spread within my bedding, so that the marrow entered my grievous wounds and gashes, my aching sores and stabs. As to the wound itself where it suppurated, Melis applied an unguent of which I afterward learned the secret. He took sheep's suet and oaten flour and leaves of foxgloves and maidenhair, boiling them together into a porridge which he applied hot upon the lips of my wound. Lastly he spat with healing saliva into the orifice, providing pledge for restoration after cure, and plugged it with dry wisps of tow.

Prince Elffin himself requested the post of guard about my person; upon which the physician stood with him by the door, directing him as to what he was to do.

"You are to see that the women who attend upon him supply the sick man with honey, fresh garlic, and an unlimited amount of celery; for it is celery which prevents thirst and does not infect wounds.

"Then you must take care that the following prohibited persons be not admitted to his bedside, that is to say fools, lunatics, half-wits, or persons with whom he may be at blood feud. No games are to be played within the house, no tidings announced, no children chastised. Neither are women or men to exchange blows with fists or rods across the bed; no beating of hides, no fighting, no sudden awakenings. No conversation may be held across his pillow. Neither dogs nor cocks are to be set fighting beside him within the chamber, nor even outside the door. Lastly, you must see to it strictly that no pigs grunt about the walls, that no shout of victory in sports be heard, nor mutual cursing by angry women.

"However, should he suffer from excess of lust, a woman may be brought to him. These are the Judgments on Blood-lyings, and if you wish your man to recover you must abide by them without fail."

So the physician departed from my chamber, as I learned later by no means pleased with the outcome of his labors. For a perquisite of his attendance upon a man stabbed in the middle of his body is that he should receive the bloodstained clothes he wore when stabbed. Now in my case I had worn nothing but an old torn boar's hide, which was of scant value to Melys mab Marthin.

Elffin returned from his conversation with the physician, laughing, to my bedside.

"Now, Merlin, I hope you recall all that I need to know, for I fear it is more than my poor brain will hold! And do not forget to tell me when the excess of lust is upon you, for that is one medicine whose nature I do recall."

"It is not a cure to which I would normally have objection," I made reply, taking care not to laugh myself, lest the spasms in my back start up again. "But whether the woman upon whom your choice falls will enjoy tumbling in this stinking stew in which I am swimming is more than I would care to say."

My young friend came and sat beside me, his face growing grave again.

"The truth is, my dear Merlin, that as I see it you are fortunate to be alive. You are a strange fellow, are you not? This is the second time I have retrieved you from imminent peril, and on each occasion I find you wrapped in nothing but an animal's hide! What are you: some sort of shape-shifter? Sometimes I wonder whether it was woman or beast that gave you suck. But you must not mind my babbling on like this; I am so delighted to see you again. You are old and I am young, and yet I feel you understand me better than any of the young men of my *gosgordd*. You are no fool, and that's a fact!"

"Perhaps I am a strange person," I replied. "But that does not make me any the less fond of you, my young friend. I hope I may pass this winter again at your father's court? We should have much to tell them by then, and many songs to sing."

No sooner had I voiced these words than memory of our present predicament washed back over me like a flood. Uttering an exclamation of alarm, I made an involuntary—and painful—effort to sit up. Elffin seized me firmly by the shoulders and forced me gently back onto my pillow.

"Remember, old fellow, you are not to excite yourself! Keep calm, and if what the physician says is correct, you will be walking about within three days."

Three days! I groaned aloud; as Elffin thought, from pain.

"Are you all right, my friend? Shall I send for Melys? Perhaps I had better leave you. You need more sleep."

He rose as if to leave, but I grasped his arm in a grip which made him wince.

"Don't leave, I implore you!" I cried. "You must tell me everything. Where are we? How many men have you here? Are the hosts of Prydein about their king? What news of the barbarians? Tell me everything, only quickly!"

Elffin sat down again and leaned close to me. "Now don't agitate yourself about these things; there is no need at all. Of course, I had forgotten that you know nothing of what has been happening these past few weeks. I was wanting to ask you where you have been, but in view of your condition perhaps I should start. You will see then that you have no cause to fret. You have missed no battles, and you assuredly will be present when we come to play at football with the heads of the Iwys!

"How shall I begin? Well, I am here with the three hundred men of my *gosgordd* from Cantre'r Gwaelod, and it is our task to guard King Maelgun the Tall within the walls of this old fortress of Dineirth. Arthur built it, they say, in the time of my grandfather Caurdaf; now it is somewhat ruinous, but we are repairing it fast. The earthworks are strong and high, as you may have noticed, so we are making something of it."

I interrupted him here, striving not to betray my mounting anguish. "But where is the army? And why is Maelgun not leading them, wherever they are?"

"The army is marching, as you may recall was agreed in the council held at Caer Gurygon, as fast as it may by the straight road over the land of Iweryd to join Prince Einion mab Run in Caer Vydei, which he holds against the Iwys. Have you forgotten? We know all the enemy's plans, which were revealed to us by the merchant Samo. Old Cynurig himself is abroad with the chief men of his tribe. The young whelp, his son, has mustered forces before the stone walls of Caer Vydei to the east, where Prince Einion will bid them defiance as long as he chooses. At the same time another warband of the Iwys is said to be marching hither, imagining the old fortress lies empty for their occupation.

"As we know what they are planning, our own actions are simple to conceive. After relieving Prince Einion, the hosts of the Cymry will continue southward into Loiger, where they will seize and burn Cynurig's royal hall. After that they return to join us here, assisting us in destroying whatever host has come against us in the meantime. All we have to do is sustain ourselves here against such attack as comes."

It was hard for me in that moment to recall how little we of the Brython knew of the enemy's wily plans, nor of the overwhelming strength of his hosts. Gathering my scattered thoughts, many of which appeared still but as troubled dreams, I could only blurt out, "But why has Maelgun remained behind in this unprotected place? Why is he not with his host?"

"He is not unprotected," replied Elffin a little stiffly, patting the hilt of his sword. "We have walls and men here sufficient to keep at bay whatever wandering war-band the Iwys send against us. And not long will we have to hold the fortress, in any case. King Brochfael of the Tusks commands the hosts of the Cymry, and Prince Run mab Maelgun rides in the van with the men of Arfon, as is their privilege. It will not be long before they return."

"But he plans to march all the way 'round by Caer Vydei and Caer Went, and only then back here. . . . Besides, nothing is as you think it!" I blurted out in lame conclusion. In truth I was too agitated for a moment (as well as weakened from my wound) to consider how to begin to unravel these tangled cords.

Elffin patted my hand consolingly. "I see it must seem strange to you that the Dragon of Mon is not at the head of his host, and it was indeed a strange chance that brought him here. I doubt if you will remember (I thought nothing of it at the time) what took place during our stay at Caer Ceri? Through grievous oversight a foolish slave gave King Maelgun a dish to eat which contained the flesh of a dog. It appears the king unwittingly ate of it, thus violating his royal prohibition. It is *cynneddyf* for a man to eat of his namesake, and since 'Maelgun' signifies 'great hound,' it is easy to see that the king indeed violated his *cynneddyf*."

"True enough," I replied, a little puzzled. "But what has that to do with his absence from the host? A man may purge himself of such a violation, if he follow the counsel of his druids and fulfill all things in order."

"True, O wise one. That is just what has happened! After your departure from the host, we marched southward upon the highway until we came to that point on the ridge of the downs where the paved highway crosses the ancient road along the ridgetop, which they say was made by Beli Mawr in the beginning. It is on the cliff-face there that you see the huge white mare, which is the goddess Riannon galloping about the revolving plain—you will know that, Merlin. Well, the time had come to ensure that all things were arranged as they should be, for we were entering upon the Wasteland.

"Maeldaf the elder, the king's chief counselor, summoned together Idno Hen and his other druids beside the crossroad, and there they made sacrifices and deliberated the matter, sitting within a circle which the witch who dwells beside the crossroads keeps clean with her besom. Afterward, Maeldaf told us that they saw but one way to remove the peril from the king.

"It had already been agreed at the council in Caer Gurygon that a small part of our army should occupy this stronghold before the Iwys reach it. As all men know, this ancient fortress of Dineirth takes its name from Arthur, the Bear, who made it his chief stronghold about these parts. So it was decided that the Dragon of Mon must dwell for a time within these walls. In this way would he become a Bear within a Bear's fort: no more a Hound who had violated his *cynneddyf* by devouring the flesh of a hound. Then again, as you will know, it is the starry Dragon in the skies which is known as the 'bear-ward'; so that it can only be fortuitous that the Dragon of Mon should come to ward over the Fortress of the Bear."

"That is certainly ingenious," I mused, "and of course the king's *cynneddyf* must be strictly observed, especially at the outset of a hosting. Tell me, Elffin, how long have you been here? Have you had news of Brochfael and the hosts of the Cymry since you parted from them?"

"We have been here, as I think, not more than twenty nights," replied the young prince. "As for the host, we have heard nothing, nor do we expect to do so until they begin their return march hither."

I groaned inwardly at this, and asked whether a messenger could be dispatched to Brochfael: "How long would such a man take to reach the host, and how long for Brochfael to return as swiftly as may be?"

Elffin looked appropriately startled. "But why should we wish the host to return? We have repaired the palisade upon the ramparts, and I have here the three hundred men of my *gosgordd*. Run mab Maelgun was to have been here with me, until our plans were required to be altered. But my men will be sufficient to drive off the small band Samo told us the Iwys plan to send here. After all, they expect to find the fortress empty! My dear Merlin, you must not fret yourself about these things until you are recovered from your sickness. It must seem perplexing to you, but I can assure you we have everything in hand!"

This time I groaned openly, striving despite the searing pain to raise myself and grasp his arm. I sank back exhausted, bitterly frustrated by my physical inability to convey the urgency of what was needed.

"Elffin, my young friend, I have to tell you that you have nothing in hand. Nothing is as we believed it at Caer Gurygon. Cynurig himself, with all the hosts of the Iwys and barbarian hordes beyond numbering from beyond the seas, is hastening hither as swiftly as he may. It is he who will hold our king within his hand if we do not act at once. Even now it may be too late, for he is a ruler of skill and cunning, with great power and luck accompanying him.

"Now, Elffin, please listen, and don't argue. I am still very weak, and cannot repeat myself or explain my meaning as fully as I should like. Just take my word for it: You must send the swiftest messenger you have, riding night and day, to summon Brochfael back. If you do not, Cynurig will take Maelgun, and there is an end of the whole game which started so promisingly."

Elffin placed his hand upon my brow, which was sweating profusely.

"Calm yourself, my dear old friend! Your mind is confused by your travails, as well it might be. One day you and I will sit by my father's royal hearth, where you will recount all your adventures, which I think have been considerable. Cynurig is not in Prydein—we know that from Samo. Even if he were, the whole mustering of the Iwys could not match that of the kings whose warbands were gathered about Dinleu Gurygon. Lastly (if you were not so sick, you would surely have thought of this yourself), you must reflect that were all you fear true, still would Cynurig encounter Brochfael upon the highway as he advanced. I assure you, all is going precisely as it should, as wiser heads than mine will confirm to you."

I had no strength to counter what he urged, nor did I see that it was possible to do so effectually.

"Will you not at least send a messenger to warn Brochfael of my words?" I pleaded.

"My dear fellow, as you know I would do anything to oblige you. But this I cannot. I am certain you are mistaken. Besides, such a message would require the authority of Maelgun Gwynedd, or at least Maeldaf the elder."

I grasped at this straw: "Then will you ask them to come and see me without delay? None of you has any idea how desperate this business is."

Elffin shrugged good-naturedly and left my chamber. To my relief but a short space of time passed before a shadow fell upon the entrance, and the grave figure of the lord of Penardd stood before me. Elffin hung a little awkwardly behind him, an expression of mingled apology and sympathy upon his handsome face.

"Maeldaf!" I cried, without wasting my feeble powers on preliminaries. "Do not ask me how I know these matters, but I assure you I have learned many things since my departure from the army. The barbarians have mustered hosts greater even than those led by Hengys or Cynurig's father Ceredig. By means of skill and treachery they have discovered Maelgun's presence here, and are marching with all their strength to seize him. Brochfael and the others are departed on a fool's errand; they must be called back without delay!"

Maeldaf stroked his beard, looking at me shrewdly from beneath his dark brows. Unlike Elffin, he spent no time in challenging my assertion, unsubstantiated though it must have seemed. Instead he seized upon the central issues.

"Prince Elffin has told me something of your fears, son of Morfryn. I see there may be more which you have not the strength to relate now, but I have to say that I cannot believe your fears justified. And even were you right, then it is a fact that any host the Iwys directs hither, whether led by Cynurig (as you fancy) or his son, may in all likelihood encounter our army on the way."

"But there is more than one way!" I exclaimed heatedly. "You must believe what I tell you! The Monarchy of Prydein, the Chariot of the Bear, depend upon the outcome of this day. It is for Brochfael to venture himself upon the place of slaughter, and for Maelgun to be preserved from danger and wound-blemishing. As you know, if the king be taken or slain, it is not the custom for a host to continue the conflict. Our enemies know this, and for that end they are hastening hither."

Maeldaf looked doubtful, though he listened patiently enough to my words. When I had finished, he looked up and addressed me thus:

"All men respect your words before the council, son of Morfryn. For myself I find it hard to credit what you say, for we have deep knowledge of our enemy's battle planning. Nevertheless I will bear your counsel to the king, and see what he says."

This was little enough, in truth, but at this stage was the best that might be done. Without Maelgun's authority in any case no messenger could be sent. I watched Maeldaf depart with some small feeling of relief, and when Elffin urged me now to find some sleep I was glad enough to do so.

"I am indeed very sore and weary," I confessed. "But promise me this, Elffin: You must wake me the moment Maeldaf returns with the word of the king, whether it be for good or ill."

Elffin adjusted my pillow, wiped my fevered brow with a cloth, and resumed his seat beside me.

At once I succumbed to sleep, though in truth it was a troubled one. The shadows seemed to be closing all around me; I was back in the deserted chamber of Brochfael's palace in Caer Gurygon. I was playing at *gwyddbwyll* with a shadowy hand which reached for the pieces out of the surrounding darkness. Pieces were missing from the board; they came where they should not be; they went from where they had rested; the king stood alone upon an empty board. I heard a chuckle in the nighttime; I heard an owl's hooting. I thought that it was Gwyn mab Nud who mocked me in the moonlight. O Merlin the Mad, fatherless child, one-eyed waif of the waters: Who are you to believe that the mighty Monarchy of Prydein, divinely descended dynasty of Beli Mawr, is a tree whose felling is to be stayed by your weak hand? Back to your orchard with you! Back to your nineteen apple trees, your piglet, and your wolf-mate!

The owl hooted harshly again: a long, long discordant shriek which seemed to wake me within my dream. For though I dreamed, I fancied I knew it was but a dream. But though my eyes were opened, I still saw darkness all about me. Glancing about in confusion, I saw a pale face glimmering faint beside my head. Fear snatched at my heartbeats, and with a sudden access of convulsive strength I reached out toward my enemy. I felt my grip close around his throat, and frantically I sought to squeeze the life out of my ancient foe.

But strong hands seized hold of my wrists, wrenching them away, and as if I were a child I was thrust back upon my blood-soaked bed. Without shame I confess I wept at my impotence. For what purpose was I rescued from the weir, if all was to be engulphed once more into the deep? What was I but the plaything of beings whose thoughts embraced all that has been, is, and will be: Gwyn, and Gofannon, and dark Cernun, whom I slew in the Pit of Annufn? Could my poor wits, sharp as I thought them when in the sunlight, save the king from his *tynged,* when pieces, board, and all belonged to others than myself?

A distant light approached out of the gloom. It came so near I felt its warmth upon my cheek. I could not move my head, but screwing my eyes to my right I found a face floating within a foot of mine. It was my young friend Elffin mab Gwydno.

"Steady, old friend, steady!" he whispered in a soothing tone. "I hope you do not really wish to strangle me?"

Feeling foolish, I muttered some weak apology. "I had thought I was dreaming—but why have you brought that candle? What brings this darkness about us?"

"Fear not, my friend," replied Elffin. "I have been with you all the time. I am thankful to say you have slept for many hours, and it is now nighttime. Go back to sleep now. You will feel better in the morning!"

"But where is Maeldaf?" I cried. "You surely did not let me sleep on when he returned?"

Elffin shook his head. "He did not return. He went to see the king, as I believe."

I grew still more sick at heart than before, were that possible. Hour by precious hour was slipping over into the abyss. I was struggling to emerge from the sea, with each step the sand giving way beneath my feet. All about me were kind, foolish people who could not help themselves.

"Elffin," I cried with sudden energy, "will you do this for me? Forgive my fears—they may be but a dream—but will you see that sentinels are properly posted by the gates? Something is amiss, and I shall not sleep until I know that all is secure."

Elffin nodded understandingly, and departed. No sooner was he gone than I summoned all my strength and scrambled from my bed. For a moment I stood swaying, grasping the bedpost, my mind giddy as if tossed upon an ocean swell. Before I knew what was happening my stomach was seized with cramps, and I was retching blood upon the ground. But then the fit passed from me, and wrapping myself in a bed-covering, I staggered from my hut.

The mantle of night had fallen upon Dineirth, whose dark ramparts lay like the world's rim beneath the starry night sky. Looking above me, I saw the studded frame of the Chariot of the Bear ride out in glittering glory, to all appearance secure as the day Gofannon mab Don first thatched the roof of heaven. But hard by it ran the great curved highway of Gwydion's Path, along which comes nightly galloping the furious host of the dead.

The dark Wasteland around was excluded from my sight by encircling ramparts, upon the glancing spearheads of whose sentinels the skirts of the night sky appeared supported. But as if within a wizard's glass alembic—or that *Ty Gwydr* which one day Gwendyd and I may come to know—I saw reflected overhead a perfect plan of all which lay without the walls upon the revolving Plain of Bran.

As I clutched at the doorpost for support, all became clear to my vision as before it was hidden when I fled like a hunted wolf across the cloud-coursed contour. High in the northern skies hung the enchanted necklace of Caer Arianrod, about whose labyrinthine whorls the barbarian host of Cynurig roved in search of her saving clew. Past the magic palace of the goddess wound the meandering road *Efnys Afon*, River of Rage, by which the enemy must in time approach the Chariot of the Bear; beyond in the night, upon the abyssal edge, glowed the fiery forge of Gofannon; there beside Gwydion's ancient Path galloped Riannon's Steed; while stark over all flared fierce the Hunter's Sword, red and bloody.

For a moment a bloody mist passed before my eyes. I wiped it away, finding myself revived a little by the clear night air, and focused my vision on that dazzling diamond which is set in the center of the nebular dome. From it there filtered down a beam of evanescent light, straight and narrow as the silver rod which is the lawful measure of a man. About that shaft spun all that Gwydion created with his wand of enchantment, all that his brother Gofannon wrought with ringing blows within his glowing forge. I saw how the beam stood as an axis to the earth, striking the Center of Prydein to the southward of Dineirth. There it passes through the convoluted Navel of the Island, mightiest of stone circles, which men call the Head of Bran.

It was there that the Head of Bran the Blessed was brought from Gwales: the Head of Him for whose Pierced Thigh all the land about lies blighted and barren. Scattered memories surfaced upon the sea of my memory, sinking back, barely glimpsed.

"Dogs of Gwern, beware of Morddwyd Tyllion!" a voice had warned me, when first I set foot upon the wasteland. Again I recalled the ugly words of Gwyn mab Nud when he paid his unwelcome call to the court of Gwydno Garanhir upon All Hallows' Eve:

"I saw Iweryd, where fell
His son Bran, whose fame men tell:
Ravens croak on him as well!"

The double-fossed fortress of Dineirth stood as it were a terret
upon the rim of an ever-revolving wheel: wheel of the Chariot of the
Bear, drawn upon its frantic course by tireless Riannon, whose form
men yet see traced upon the frowning cliff-side. I had heard the
warning, but not heeded it. Was there in truth not time to make it
known to Brochfael and the hosts of the Cymry, who even now
advanced upon a spoke of the Wheel toward that dread axle?

There are, as all know from the writings of the *llyfyrion* Three
Unfortunate Revelations of the Island of Prydein: the Revelation of the
Bones of Gurthefir the Blessed; the Revelation of the Dragons which
Nud mab Beli interred at the Center of the Island; and the Revelation
of the Head of Bran the Blessed. The first Revelation was accomplished by the treachery of Gurtheyrn the Thin; the second I accomplished in the former time, in fulfillment of the *tynged* of the Island of
Prydein; the third is yet to come, though there are those who say that
Arthur accomplished it, for he sought no protection for the Island but
that which might be gained by his own skill and strength. Whether that
was wise in him will perhaps be seen in the outcome of events.

Now must I see the heir of Arthur, he who in expiation of his
violated *cynneddyf* had assumed Arthur's role within Arthur's fortress.
Maelgun the Tall was the Pillar of the Island of Prydein with its Three
Adjacent Islands. Were that Pillar toppled, then all would crumble
down to ruin with it. Gwydion's heavenly Path cast a faint gleam along
the well-worn track which led from the eastern to the western gates of
Dineirth, and it was upon this I set my faltering footsteps. Many huts
of wickerwork and leathern tents had been erected within the enclosure. Which was that of Maelgun Gwynedd?

Not hard was that question in the resolving. Just as Caer Gwydion
winds about the Center of the heavens, so the road that crossed
Dineirth curved about a large tent set in the middle of the enclosure.
Thrust into the ground beside it was a tall spear muffled in drapery
which must be, as I guessed, the drooping Red Dragon of the Cymry.
Tottering to the entrance, I clung to the edges of the tent for a
moment, steadying myself, and then made my way into the darkness.

At first my vision was dazzled by the light of a small taper set
upon a table. It was not long before I was able to see about me,
however, and not a little startled was I by the sight. For I might have
been within that cave at Craig y Dinas, where, as they say, Arthur lies
surrounded by his warriors, waiting for the summons to restore the
Island of the Mighty to the Truth of the Land.

Stretched upon the ground, or slumped upon their seats, sprawled
sleeping the principal officers of Maelgun's court. Beside them lay their

burnished swords, spears, and shields, ready to hand should the moment of battle arrive unheralded. None stirred at my entrance, however, and it seemed strange that no sentinel challenged my entry.

In the center of the pavilion, supporting its ridgepole, lay the sacred stone from the Mountain of Presseleu, which had accompanied the host upon its march south. Upon that slab was set the royal throne of Maelgun the Tall, king of Gwynedd, heir of Cunedda Guledig and Dragon of Mon. There sat Maelgun enthroned, garbed in a white robe, a white wand clasped in his right hand. Upon him was the Truth of the Land, *gwir deyrnas,* the maintenance of the tribes and kingdoms of the Cymry, and the guardianship of the Three Tribal Thrones of the Island of the Mighty. His gaze was fixed and staring, and though he looked straight at me, it did not seem as though he saw me.

Before the king stood a small table, upon which lay a silver *gwyddbwyll* board, its pieces made of gold. On either side of the king were set two seats. Upon the one sat the blessed Cubi, who bore upon his breast a cross; and upon the other sat Idno Hen, chief druid of Gwynedd, who held in his hand a sprig of rowan. A little way off sat also Taliesin, chief of bards, whose eyes alone were turned in my direction.

"What do you seek here, in the tent of Maelgun Gwynedd, son of Morfryn?" he asked me. "Are you not sick, under the care of Melys mab Marthin?"

"I am sick, Taliesin," I made reply, "and much travail has it cost me to come here. But the Monarchy of Prydein is in dire danger, and I am come to warn the king of his peril. Will you ask him to heed my words?"

"In time of war all the land is imperiled," responded Taliesin, "and it is for that reason that we place ourselves under the protection of Mabon, who is also called Crist:

"*Kat ynracuydawl a Mabon
Nyt atrawd adurawt achubyon!*"

"You are a wise man, Taliesin, and well versed in the writings of *llyfyrion.* No one doubts that 'Mabon in the decider of victories,' nor can it be false to assert that 'No survivor will have cause to cavil.' But whose is to be the victory? And should it happen that there are no survivors, what need then for Mabon to suffer reproach?"

So I pleaded: to which Taliesin replied out of the darkness of the king's tent: "The omens have been consulted; the flight of birds is propitious; the princes' plans are skillfully conceived. What more do you seek?"

The taloned pains about my body ripped me with renewed rage, as if to draw me away from this deathly spot back to my bed; the stag bowed by wintry gales seeks a snug glen. The arrow hole in my back burned as if an envenomed blade yet rested within it. Mine was a struggle to overcome my own infirmities of mind and body, no less than the vigorous strength and subtle wiles of the enemy.

"I must speak with the king, Taliesin," I pleaded. "Have you not heard what has been said:

> " 'Treason undoes every knot;
> Grief the outcome of the plot:
> Little sold where much is got'?

"You have gained lore from the books of the *llyfyrion*, but I have spoken with Gofannon mab Don. I have visited strange places, seen strange things; I have read silver runes inscribed upon a book bound in black velvet. I have seen a great sadness upon the hosts of the Cymry, *gormes* upon the Island of the Mighty, a swarm of bees lacking its queen."

"Speak then, my friend!" urged Taliesin in a voice of sympathy. "But I question whether you are pursuing a profitable course."

I turned to the king, who looked down upon me with a look of great sadness.

"Maelgun!" I cried. "There is no time to be lost. A hundred thousand of the hosts of the Iwys, and others besides beyond numbering are marching upon this place. You have not here the strength to resist them! I urge you, return forthwith back to Caer Ceri until Brochfael and your son Run return with the hosts of the Cymry!"

Maelgun Gwynedd sighed softly, remaining silent for a space so long that I thought he intended no reply. But at length he spoke, wearily, and as if oppressed by a great burden.

"If what you say be right, Black Frenzied One, then of what use is it to flee? A man must meet his *dihenydd* when it is due; he may not escape from Mabon, though he fly with wings."

"But why should you believe your *dihenydd* awaits you here, rather than in another place, O king?"

Maelgun remained seated stiff and upright as the stone upon which he had taken his stance.

"You mean well, son of Morfryn," he muttered at last, with a groan, "and it may be that all you say is true. Indeed, I fear it is. But not yet may I leave this place, since I have violated my *cynneddyf* by eating the flesh of a dog in Caer Ceri. There is a *tynged* upon me, which I may not flout. The gods are angry with me, seeking to kill me if I evade what must be done. Unless I remain here for four times nine nights, in this lair of the growling honey-seeker, I may not live.

"The druids of my household have consulted the omens: Mabon is angered at the violation of *tynged*. What happened to me after I ate of that unchancy dish? Since I came to this barren land of Loiger, I believe that nothing but ill-luck has attended me. Against my own wishes have I done forbidden things: I have entered a dark country; I have overtaken a galloping gray; I have drunk of water between two darknesses."

The king's massive head sagged forward as he spoke, he was muttering into his beard, and I saw with sinking heart that there was a great debility upon him. Still, I must do what I could, though my own strength was ebbing fast.

"Take thought, O king!" I urged. "These things may or may not be as you fear. But here beside you sits the blessed Cubi, the pure sound of whose bell echoes like the call of the cuckoo across the wave-lashed Strand of Durgynt. May he not call upon the strength of Iessu Crist to overcome these ill omens?"

Cubi appeared deep in prayer, but Maelgun shook his head wearily.

"Mabon may have abandoned me to my enemies, but Crist Himself is my foe. He has cursed me through the mouth of His servant, Gildas the Wise, who has sent a book about the Island of Prydein listing my sins, which are indeed heavy. Did I not vow myself to become a monk within the monastery of the blessed Iltud, a vow broken when I departed to regain the kingship in Gwynedd? Consumed with lusts, to which even now I am not wholly rid, did I not wed my nephew's wife while my own yet lives? Worse by far, I slew my nephew that I might gain the fair object of my desire. What does Gildas say of me—that the dark flood of Hell shall roll around me with its deadly whirling and fierce waves; it will continually torture me without wholly consuming me. I shall long to repent, but it will be too late!

"Since you are here, Black Frenzied One skilled in interpretation of omens, I will tell you of a dream I dreamed last night as I sat here. I saw myself here upon this bare grassy plain; I saw a whole host slain; I saw before me a great growling honey-eater, evil flaring from his red eyes; I saw ravens gorging their fill upon heaps of naked corpses! Can you read me this dream?"

But I could not, for I was fainting with pain and weakness of my limbs. My thoughts swam sickeningly about my brain, and now I longed only to regain my couch. Stumbling from the royal tent, I made my way out once more into the open space beneath the stars. Glancing up, I saw them whirl wildly around as if in that infernal image Gildas conjured up for Maelgun. I tottered, and would have measured my length upon the dewy greensward had not strong arms seized me about and guided me back along the path.

Who had taken upon himself to help me I cared not. I cared no longer about anything, save to sleep again within my bed of pain. Let the hosts come; let them kick open my door, drive the steel through my flesh. What suffering could be greater than that I now endured? Death is but sleep, and sleep was all I longed for.

"Bear up, comrade!" murmured a voice at my ear, and as through a fog I recognized my companion's voice as that of my friend and rival Taliesin, chief of bards.

"I will guide you to your hut. Lean on me! You have done well, Merlin, but nothing you nor any other can say will move Maelgun now. The nine-days sickness is upon him, and that not priest nor druid may deflect. Here now is your bed. Lie back, and take the rest you need!"

I was asleep before I fell upon my pallet, and when I woke, daylight was streaming through the open doorway. I must have slept long, for though still enfeebled I was calm and my pains more sore than sharp. At the foot of my bed stood Melys mab Marthin the physician, a cup of blood in his hands.

"How are you now?" inquired a voice at my side, which was not that of Melys. Shifting my gaze sideways, I saw Taliesin smiling down at me.

"Better than I was," I croaked, surprised to hear my voice so clear.

"You have slept long, my friend," murmured the bard, "which is good. After all, you are lucky to be alive. Did you know that? You might have had a dozen arrows meeting in your heart. To be truthful, it could be said that you invited them! You appear mystified. Shall I tell you why?"

I nodded, whilst I collected my thoughts. How long had I been here? How long before that had the king and his *teulu* occupied the fortress? And above all, how long had we before the wave of Cynurig swept in a tide of blood over this forgotten spot?

"You see," continued Taliesin, "when we first arrived here, the king's druids adopted the customary practice when an oppression arrives and threatens the land. They took a wild pig, decorated its ears and throat with red and green wool, and by means of invocations placed upon it every sin, every evil thing, every pestilence, that was with the king's *teulu*. Then they drove it away southward, so that all our ills should be borne to the enemy and remain with him. You can imagine how the watchmen on the rampart by the gate felt, when they saw you in your boar's hide racing up the hill toward them! Naturally they believed that the Iwys had driven the sin-bearer back upon us, in the hope that the pestilence would enter our camp.

"Next time you take to wandering about the countryside on your own, I recommend more respectable garb than an old boar-skin—you might be safer too! By the way, you do tend to make your appearances a little dramatic—or eccentric—do you not?"

I saw what he meant. Last night (was it last night?) I must have appeared a weird spectacle in the shadows of the king's tent, naked as I had been, and smeared all over with mangled flesh and blood. Small wonder, I reflected, that they ignored my pleas. Merlin the Mad they would have thought me, my every appearance stranger than the last.

"Taliesin!" I implored him with all the energy at my command. "Do you not understand the danger? There is an oppression great as that of the Coranieid upon the Island, and it is directed hither. The king is unprotected, separated from the hosts of the Cymry which should be about him as a protection. Can you not persuade Maelgun to withdraw before it is too late?"

I tried to take his hand, but could only flutter my fingers feebly. Taliesin took them gently in his, and smiled down at me.

"I see that you are really troubled, my friend, and it may be with good cause. I will speak with the king, and also with Maeldaf the elder, whose advice at times he heeds. But you have seen the way things are: The king has the nine-days debility upon him, and I doubt much whether he can be persuaded now. There is another here, too, to whom the king has hearkened in the past; I will try him. Rest assured, I shall do what I can. A man cannot do more, and if in truth there be a *dihenydd* upon us, then no effort will avail to alter it. You know that—or should."

With which he departed from me, leaving me in a high state of agitation. Tossing feverishly between waking and sleeping, I saw a succession of bloody visions: lopped limbs arranged in butchered heaps, severed heads grinning in ghastly array. In my distress and confusion I tried at times to rise, tearing the bandages from my wounds. Melys mab Marthin came and went with his attendants, chanting spells and applying healing herbs to my contusions. A harpist was sent to play at my bedside, and the sleep-music, plaintively plangent as the trickling of a mountain rill, brought me to rest at last.

I traveled that time upon a rough journey, through the Forest of Celyddon, over the Mountain of Bannog, across the River Gweryt. I traversed the glens of Prydyn, until at last I came to the Sea of Orc, beyond which lies nothing save the wild waves. Beneath the desolate cliff upon which the waves hurl themselves twice in every day lies the Cave of Uffern. I stood on the narrow strand before its mouth, while mocking laughter screamed about me from cleft to cleft.

Upon a great rock at the cave's entrance sat three filthy unkempt hags, whose names are Lewei and Rorei and Mederei. Upon three crooked twisted sticks of holly had they hung enchanted hasps of yarn, which they began to reel off left-handwise before the cave. Upon them were three coarse heads of disheveled hair; their eyes were rheumy and red-bleared; within each of their three black wry-mouthed gullets was set a ragged rank of curved venomous tusks upon raw ramparts of bleeding gums; their hideous heads shuddered upon their scrawny bony-jointed necks; their six shriveled shanks were shagged with gray hairs coarse as broom-fronds; their six arms were hugely long and dangling, while upon each shriveled finger was set a dirt-encrusted nail sharp as the claw of a lynx.

As I watched the witches at their weaving, two men stepped up beside me. Without turning I knew them to be Maelgun Gwynedd and Taliesin the bard. Moving forward to gaze closer upon the hags' hasps, they swiftly found themselves meshed about by the web of enchantment which those sisters spun about them. Then I saw that their strength had passed from them, that the witches' hasps drew them forward unresisting to their doom. For there behind the rock gaped the pitch-black maw of ice-cold Uffern, and king and bard possessed now no more strength than does a newborn babe to resist the power drawing them onward to their destruction.

All strength had likewise departed from my thews and sinews, and the clinging hasps clutched fast about me too. I felt myself being sucked into the dank cave from which none returns. I gave myself up for lost—when all at once I felt a strong hand grip me by the shoulder. A thick mist rolled in from the sea, enveloping me in its protection, and I was whisked with an arrow's speed through the upper air.

I woke, to find Prince Elffin mab Gwydno grasping my shoulder and beaming down upon me.

"To judge by your angry expression, that was no pleasing dream you saw just then, no wanton maiden gamboling with you beneath the golden broom!" He laughed. "How are you now? Perhaps I am mistaken, but it seems to me that your strength is returning. How goes it with you? It is a shame my wife and her handmaidens are not here to tend you."

"Better still," I cried, "were this bed within her bower, and you and all within these walls feasting at your father's hall. Death lies all about us, yet you are as lighthearted as though upon a hunting expedition. Do you not understand: It is you that are the prey, and there are those approaching whom you have not the means of resisting!"

From weakness of body and frustration of spirit I spoke with anguish and distress. At the same time I was a little gratified to find that the prince was right, and that health was beginning to return to me.

"Not altogether helpless!" replied Elffin cheerily. "Those who built these double ramparts knew what they were about, and I will match the three hundred men of my *gosgordd* against any champions in the world. The battle cannot come too soon for us, Merlin, of that I can assure you! Well, I will confess to you I am a little afraid—afraid that Brochfael and his host may destroy the foxes of the Iwys in their lair, and we here never enjoy a fight at all!"

"That you need not fear," I assured him grimly. "Three hundred men—is that all you have within the camp?"

Elffin stroked my arm reassuringly. "Full three hundred of the most valiant young nobles in all Cantre'r Gwaelod, and that is no lie. Not one is less eager than I for the fray, that you will see for yourself! But if you are still fretting, here is someone who will reassure you. He is old, but I think he has seen a hundred battles."

I heard a cough at the entrance, turned my head, and saw . . . who but my old friend the tribune, with whom I had spoken so often on our march south! He came forward and stood at the foot of my bed, scratching his bald head. There was an awkward smile upon his weathered, lugubrious features which told me he was pleased to see me.

"You here!" I exclaimed. "I never thought it. I imagined you must be with King Brochfael."

"I should have been, but there comes a time when an old horse can no longer match his pace to the rest of the troop. I am not sick, as you have been, but the fogs and rains with which Britannia appears so beneficently endowed have cramped this game arm of mine." He gestured with his right arm, which moved awkwardly, like the damaged wing of a fowl.

"Still, that is little enough and to be expected, I fear, at my age. 'Off the bridge with the sixty-year-olds!' my father used to say. Well,

I am not sixty, I am thankful to say, but perhaps a little beaten about the bows after the wars. I did not come here to talk about the state of my health, however. Our friend the poet tells me you are agitated about the state of our garrison here. As I have been entrusted with the command of this fort, I should certainly be grateful for any intelligence you may have gained along the way. As I understood from what the merchant of the Franks told the council of war, we are to expect an attack eventually. But since the enemy's thrust will in large part be met by our army to the south, any major assault here (assuming they can find us, that is) appears unlikely, I take it, to be more than a rough-and-tumble skirmish. They believe the fortress unoccupied, and are dispatching a light-armed force to take it. Am I right?"

Elffin nodded wisely in agreement, smiling from me to the tribune. With a little pain, though not as much as I had expected, I managed to raise my head and shoulders from the bed.

"I am afraid you are very wrong, Rufinus!" I replied as emphatically as I could. "There is little enough time to explain how matters stand, but I implore you to believe me when I tell you that Samo deceived us! He has deceived us utterly, as surely as Idawg Cord Prydein deceived Arthur. The enemy host is great—great as any which has inflicted its oppression upon the Island; great as that which Yrp Luidog took with him to Lychlyn. It has been swelled by untold levies from across the Sea of Udd. The hooded horsemen of Prydyn are stirring in the mountains of the North, the fleet of Ywerdon is on the sea, and it is Cynurig himself who is marching hither by secret roads to take the king."

I sank back, exhausted by these few words, and still more by the impossibility of conveying adequately all I knew—or fancied I knew, for the tramp and movements of mighty hosts seemed to thunder within my mind until my head swam, and I saw all dimly, as in a mist.

"You see?" urged Elffin brightly. "I gave you the message correctly, did I not? The enemy is great; the pale-faced dogs of Loiger may swarm about our gates; but each man of my *gosgordd* is a leek in battle, a bear in the trackway. If Merlin be right, then will Taliesin have much to sing of when the day is done!"

I groaned at this, but could not at the same time dismiss a touch of admiration (envy, too, it may be) for the young man's bounding confidence. Eager and athletic, he possessed that rash optimism and effortless energy which may accomplish astonishing things. Incapable of contemplating the odds against him, fearless of death, longing only for glory, he might soar like the leaping steed which ascends higher even than its practiced rider believed possible.

But gallantry and youth were not enough now. I looked inquiringly at Rufinus, who frowned, momentarily lost in thought.

Then he spoke: "I am less surprised by what you say than perhaps I might be, Merlin. I never liked the look of that Samo, nor the fact that upon leaving us he would have once more to pass through the land of the Saxons. How many men do you think they have?"

"I cannot tell. I am sick, as you see, and my memory is confused. I have seen so many things, some it may be in dreaming as in waking. But you must believe me when I tell you of our mortal danger!"

"Well, the precise number is immaterial at this stage," murmured the tribune to himself, "and it may be we shall be able to gain an estimate in due course. By which route do they approach us? Do you think they know our disposition—how many men we have here in garrison?"

My heart leaped a little: The old soldier did not disbelieve me.

"They are avoiding the straight roads of Rufein, which they know to be preferred by the Cymry," I made reply. "They have made a great circuit to the south, and are even now approaching by the ridgeway which runs along the western crest of the downs from the southwest."

Elffin gripped the tribune's arm in his excitement; his eyes were shining, his limbs alert. The old soldier winced a little, and I could see his arm pained him still.

"Shall we ride down upon them now?" cried the prince. "I have but to sound the horn, and you see three hundred spears upon the highway!"

"That is the spirit, prince!" Rufinus nodded approvingly. "We do not march yet, but I advise you to see that your horses and equipment are ready at all times. Perhaps you should see about it without delay?"

Beaming upon both of us, Elffin left with joyful springing gait.

Rufinus looked at me quizzically. "We need young men like him," he grunted. "He reminds me of Photius, the stepson of Belisarius. He, too, was always eager to be first into the breach; I remember how I had to hold him back from leading the Isaurians when they discovered the hidden way through the aqueduct into Neapolis. But we need many more like him than we have, if all you say be true. Now to business: How many days have we before they are upon us? Do I take it they are mainly horse, and do not bring siege-engines in their train?"

"I believe that is right. They ride hard, and are doughty men of war. They have enough of Elffins of their own, and to spare, unless I am mistaken. How long you have precisely is not easy to say. I lost them upon their way, but old Cynurig has the cunning of a fox and will not be long off the scent. Do you think Maelgun will pay heed to your advice, and depart northward in time? If you and Maeldaf together—he respects the advice of his elder—"

"No, no," interrupted the tribune. "I believe the king's mind is made up. We have no time for discussions of that sort; besides, were we to break camp now, the risk would be great that the enemy might catch us on the move. We have no real choice, which is not always a bad thing when one is in a fix. We have but two things to do, neither of them easy of accomplishment: We must send word to our army to return as swiftly as possible (if necessary dispatching their cavalry ahead), and in the meantime we who are here will have to stand and fight. All we need is time, and that at present I take to be in short supply!"

"I believe I have bought you some, though scarce enough," I ventured as the soldier stood momentarily plunged in thought.

"You have achieved much, my old friend," returned the veteran, with a brief flash of gratitude. "Time is everything in war. Now, I wonder how far they have come? I have an outpost about a mile down the highway in that direction, and no signal yet has come in from them. We have a little time—a very little. I had better see to things without delay."

He rose and, coming to my bedside, gently grasped my shoulder for a moment.

"We have not known each other very long, you and I," he said, smiling faintly, "but I have told you matters concerning myself that no one else has heard—not since my misspent youth in Alexandria, at any rate. We must put a good face on things now, but should matters go ill with us all, then perhaps we will resume our conversation in that place which Scipio saw in his dream. Farewell for the moment!"

"Wait!" I cried, raising myself on my elbow. "How long have I lain here, do you know?"

"Your arrival was reported three days ago. I should have called sooner, but I am afraid I have many duties, and few to whom much may be delegated . . ."

"That is nothing!" I cried joyfully, thrusting my legs over the bed's edge, and easing myself into a sitting position. "The physician said that in three days I could rise, and the time is up! Help me to dress, my old friend, I implore you!"

Rufinus looked doubtfully at my battered and emaciated frame.

"Is that wise? You would do better to rest, I believe. That arm does not look ready yet to bear a javelin."

"I am well, I tell you!" I cried, half angrily. "I have seen the foe, and may be able to help you a little."

The tribune shrugged his shoulders. "Very well. A sensible head can be more useful than a strong arm at such a time, and if things happen to go wrong, then we will all be laid to rest. Up with you, then!"

Wrapped snugly in a thick cloak, and walking in boots of supple deer's hide, it was but a moment later that saw me emerge into a daylight by which I was momentarily dazzled. I heard Elffin's merry voice give a cry of joy nearby, and found myself limping along upon the support of his strong arm.

During the period of my sickness I had hovered long between waking and sleeping, and was troubled endlessly by turbulent memories and fears. As a result, the hum and clatter which now buzzed about my ears from all around the encampment struck suddenly upon me, almost as if it had arisen at my appearance. Everywhere men were coming and going, on horse and on foot. Huts and tents had been erected in rows, cauldrons were steaming over peat fires, and there was a ceaseless clangor from smithies set up at different spots. Only the royal tent of Maelgun Gwynedd remained closed and silent, as the king sat on (so I pictured him) in the lassitude of his nine-days debility. Above his tent reared the Red Dragon, banner of the Cymry, bounding in a warm breeze gusting over the downs.

What surprised me was to see how swiftly the defenses had been restored. On the ridge of the dyke about us had been erected a stout palisade of logs with a narrow passageway behind, where men might stand guard and pass in safety about the whole circuit of the walls. Each of the two gateways at the western and eastern entrances was dominated by a lofty gate-tower, beneath which all who entered must pass.

"This must be your doing, Rufinus!" I remarked as we ascended a timbered stairway by the western gate. He grunted noncommittally as a warrior opened a door leading into the tower before us. Inside, a ladder led up to a square of light in the roof. We clambered up it, Elffin bringing up the rear, ever solicitous that I might stumble. "I am not a child, you know!" I snorted as he gripped my waist.

"Not quite," he said, laughing, "but very near!"

We emerged onto a level platform, protected by wicker fencing sturdy enough to stop an arrow. Despite my defiant words to Elffin, I found the light and height and universal clatter a little dizzying, and clung to the parapet for support. Now could I see how well the men of old who built this stronghold of Dineirth had selected their site. To the north the ground fell away abruptly, down to a level plain stretching as far as the eye could see. The track emerging below us passed steeply down, too, linking the fort to the great road that wound below, coiled like a sleeping serpent about the crest of that ridge upon whose rim the mighty encampment crouched like a watchful mastiff.

It was a hot, sunny day, and the horizon was obscured by haze.

"Your road follows the ridge of those three hills," observed the tribune, touching my arm and pointing. "Is that the way the enemy approaches?"

"It is. Do you think we could espy them from here?"

"Possibly. Possibly not. But we have an outpost on the second hill who will give us warning."

As far as I could judge, that was the point at which I had taken fright and plunged across the rough ground falling away to the east. It crossed my mind that the men whose presence so alarmed me had in all likelihood been but the tribune's guards.

Contemplating the strong defenses, and the old officer's skill and efficiency, I felt an access of confidence and strength. Feeling a little foolish, I confessed I might have appeared unnecessarily fearful while on my sickbed.

Rufinus gave me a sharp look. "We have done the best we can, but if their numbers be anything like what you have led us to believe, then it behooves us to neglect nothing that tends toward our safety. Look at our numbers: what reserve have we if the enemy breach the rampart at one point—let alone several? There is however one satisfactory matter, for what it is worth. Now I know where the enemy is, I can pull in my other scouting parties closer to our base."

"What do we do then?" I asked. "Await Cynurig's arrival? Should you not be sending a messenger to Brochfael?"

"Two have been sent already, each by a different route. If we are to pull through this awkward affair, much depends on the fleetness of their horses. No, Merlin, the answer to your first question is that we do not sit meekly waiting for our throats to be cut, like a bull before the altar. Our weakness compels us to take the initiative. It is for us to act."

"Ah, you are right, old warhorse!" cried Elffin jovially. "What good can my horsemen do cooped up in here? What glory is gained by casting our lances from behind this fence? Let us to horse, set spear in rest, and be upon the carrion-eating Iwys before they know what we are about!"

Rufinus pursed his lips, and I looked doubtfully at him.

"How may we be the attacker, when we are so weak?" I inquired. "Surely we cannot afford to lose a single man before they reach us?"

"True enough, true enough," the tribune replied. "Nevertheless, we must make them think us stronger than we are, and do everything to delay their arrival. Once here, they will soon sound out our true strength, which is what I am anxious to avoid. Prince Elffin, you shall have your fill of fighting, since that is what you desire! Come, let us go below and talk this over. Summon thirty of your best riders, and assemble before my tent in half an hour. You will receive your orders then."

Elffin clattered excitedly down the ladder before us, eager to perform his duty. So far from resenting the tribune's brisk manner of conveying orders, I believe it pleased the young man, enabling him to imagine himself one of those loricated warriors of Rufein whose arms conquered the world. Descending more slowly, Rufinus and I made our way across the busy enclosure to his tent, which stood beside the king's. Inside, he motioned me to his couch and, drawing up a stool beside me, poured out two horns of wine.

"You need strength, Merlin, as do I. I may say nothing before our young wolfhound which might sap his courage, but between you and me, I fear matters do not look as promising as they might."

I nodded in cautious agreement, but could see that the tribune had more to say. Nor would he, as I judged him, voice any sentiment needlessly likely to depress our courage, whatever the reality as he estimated it inwardly. I was right, for he continued as follows:

"Our numbers are so small that they provide us with very little room for maneuver. The worst that can happen is that which, were the odds not so heavily loaded against us, would normally prove the downfall of an assailant: and that is, that he should press on regardless of his disposition and overwhelm our flimsy defenses before reinforcements can come up. A smart ambush upon the way might make him halt to gather his forces, advancing in more orderly—and leisurely—manner.

"Do you think my plan a risky one? Perhaps you are right, but when the overall situation is risky, then it is only a bold taking of risks which can see you through.

"I am not altogether inexperienced in this sort of warfare, as it happens. The emperor considered Septem of such importance to his long-term strategy that he stinted no expense to make it impregnable.

Even if they managed to ship across siege-machines, I had no fear of what the Visigoths might do to us there.

"My principal duty was to preserve Septem until the day came for the invasion of Hispania. However, I was also in theory responsible for the whole province of Mauretania Tingitana, and since my squadron of *dromones* kept the Visigoths safely on the northern side of the Straits of Hercules, I saw no reason to neglect my responsibilities inland. Besides, I needed something to keep my men on their toes.

"A couple of hundred miles to the south, beyond the mountains and desert and across the Subur, lies the land of the Baquates. They are Christian, and their king and nobles continue to speak Latin. It is said that their capital, Volubilis, was founded by Joshua the son of Nun, though of that I know nothing. The Baquates are Romans, and there is much trade in black slaves and other wares between Volubilis and the sea at Septem.

"Though there was in reality no need for me to have done so, I decided to accept the request of the king of the Baquates to send troops to police the road. My forces were scanty, especially after the great plague which devastated the world thirteen or fourteen years ago. Still, I established a series of small signal-stations, sited in secret places among the hills and manned by troops from a light-armed *numerus* of our garrison, serving fifteen days at a time, turn and turn about. They were Sclaveni from the Ister; the native Mauri are themselves renowned for their nimbleness and fleetness of foot, but for cunning and skill at concealment there is no tribe on earth to compare with the Sclaveni. By a system of smoke and other signals they were able to call up cavalry detachments disconcertingly swiftly when there was trouble with the mountain tribes dwelling on either side of the road.

"There are no people more treacherous and wily than the Mauri. Neither fearing God nor respecting man, they care neither for oaths nor hostages. Fear provides the only means of preserving peace among them, and I preserved the peace. Well, at least the caravans came through, and that is saying a lot. Some bands we beat into submission; others were bribed. Either way we kept them too busy to collect forces large enough to tackle caravans accompanied by military escorts. . . . Here, you, shift those stones out of the way, will you!"

Sipping our wine and continuing our conversation as we went, the tribune and I had emerged from his tent to stroll about the encampment. As he talked, the tribune kept a keen eye open for every detail of the work which was in progress all about us. The ramparts were faced with unmortared stone, and the palisades erected above appeared complete, but sections of logs and piles of stones lying about told how recent and hurried had been the work. Though bond and free who toiled away could understand nothing of the foreigner's broken tongue, they gathered his intent and obeyed him cheerfully. Incapacitated from labor himself, he would clap a hardworking fellow on the shoulder, smiling to indicate appreciation, or frown and shake his head at another, were all not as it should be.

"We must keep them at it, Merlin, keep them busy! There is much still to be achieved. Besides, occupation will keep the thought of danger from their minds. It applies to the enemy, too, you know—that was the lesson we learned in Tingitana. 'Keep them busy, and keep them guessing!' That's the motto for me!"

I felt my weakness coming on again, and seated myself upon a beam projecting along the ground from the inner revetment of the rampart.

"But truthfully," I inquired, "with but three hundred men to guard so large a space, can you afford to lose any fighting men beyond your walls?"

"Can I afford not to?" was his grim reply. "When once the enemy reaches the ramparts, he will know our weakness, and unless he is very foolish he will not wait to profit by it. The plain truth is, my friend, that three hundred men cannot defend so extended a line, however strongly fortified, against such odds as you have described. Only the return of the army can save us, and only time gained will permit that to happen. But do not despair, Merlin! At least there is an army whose return is, well, *possible*. In Mauretania, I had no troops beyond my poor garrison upon whom I could call in need. The nearest command, in Caesarea, is a good four days' sail away—with a favorable wind!"

We were interrupted by the arrival of Elffin and his chosen troop of horsemen, who made a brave show on their stamping steeds.

"We are ready!" cried the prince, brandishing his lance above his head and whooping joyfully.

"Good," replied the tribune. "I will explain what I wish you to do. Beside the ridgeway, over there on the left of the skyline below that clump of trees, lies an earthwork in which are stationed scouts whose duty it is to warn us of the enemy's approach. When that happens, and they have fired their signal-pyre, they are to ride back here as swiftly as they may. Now a skillful general, such as I take this Saxon king to be, will make every effort to capture the scouts in order to learn from them our strength and disposition. Whether or not he is aware of their position, he will, the moment he sees the smoke, order some of his best horsemen to gallop forward and seize them.

"Something of this sort is bound to happen, unless I am much mistaken. Now, what I wish you to do is this: Below our scouts' enclosure, on this side of the road, I noticed a birch copse in a fold of the downs. Each day, from dawn until dusk, I wish you to ride out and take up position there, making yourselves as concealed and comfortable as you may.

"At the same time, you will send forward one man on foot to the nearest vantage point where you may still see him, and where he in turn commands the longest possible stretch of road lying to the south. When this man first sights the enemy vanguard, he is to return unobserved at once to you. Then you are to wait (by the way, you must ensure that every horse in your *turma* is a gelding, for one neigh will give the game away), until the enemy outriders pass above you in pursuit of our returning scouts.

"Then will come the chance for which you have been waiting, young Elffin. Ride down upon the rear of the advance party, and do you make sure that not one escapes alive!"

Elffin nodded and grinned and his followers shouted loudly, so that all within the camp paused from their labors to look.

"Do this," urged Rufinus, "and then make display of strength upon the highway, sounding trumpets, waving banners, and riding about this way and that so that you appear at a distance greater in numbers than you are. But whatever happens, let no man of your *turma* fall into the enemy's hands, or all our purposes are defeated."

"I understand," responded Elffin with a gleeful laugh, throwing his thigh over his saddle. "It is a skillful plan, and not difficult of accomplishment. And so, farewell!"

A horn was blown, answered by others at the western gateway. The heavy beams which held the gates secure were withdrawn, the iron-clamped doors swung open, and Prince Elffin's thirty horsemen trotted out beneath the tower, curvetting proudly past the sentinels. Word having been sent to the watchman upon the tower, enjoining him strictly that the tribune was to be summoned the instant the outpost signal was seen, he and I made our way to the spot before his tent where our midday meal was being prepared.

"How in truth do you see our situation, Rufinus?" I asked, after we had sat eating in silence for a space.

The tribune chewed reflectively upon his chicken leg for a moment, then replied: "I do not see it at all, if the truth be told. At present the odds against us appear overwhelming, and it is unfortunate (to say the least) that the king is with us. But Fortuna is a fickle goddess, and we do not yet know how far off is our own army. It may be my messengers will find them soon. For the rest, we can but do our duty as conscientiously as may be. A man cannot do more, and much is to be achieved by that alone. Were Belisarius or Solomon in command here, I doubt not they would conceive of plans more skillful than mine. But win or lose, at least a commander cannot be reproached who takes every precaution he sees lying to hand.

"When I was laid up with this arm of mine in Sicilia, and studying the military manuals, I read a piece of advice which has stuck in my head, and which I believe is worth all the rest: 'A general should never have to say "I didn't think of that." ' I trust none will be able to say that of me."

The tribune's coolness I found reassuring—until I thought of what I knew to be approaching from the south.

"Well, I must be about my duties," he exclaimed abruptly, interrupting my reverie. Flinging away his chicken bone, he buckled on his sword belt and made to leave.

"If anyone inquires for me," he added, "I shall be at the western gate. As a matter of fact, I have something there which may amuse you, if you have time to call 'round. Farewell for the moment!"

Being of little enough use to anyone, I was content to lie for a while in the sunshine upon the turf. The sky was dazzlingly blue, and the sun at its zenith poured down its kindly heat upon me. My pains were lessening hourly, just as the physician had promised, and the four posts of my body were losing their discordant stiffness. "Joint to joint, and sinew to sinew," I chanted softly. The fragrance of healing herbs was all about me, red juice of the alder Rhun Rhuddwern, juice distilled within my mother Ceridwen's Cauldron, all sweeping warm and refreshing over the three hundred and sixty-five sinews of my body like cleansing water of the ninth wave.

Close at hand, bees buzzed from bloom to bloom; ants toiled imperceptibly upon their forest floor beneath the grass; faint and seemingly far away floated all about me the sound of men shouting, hammers tapping, saws rasping. That was the busy world which Gofannon constructed: confused, intricate, delightful under the sun. I felt myself gradually withdrawing from it; I was becoming drowsy. Over that disordered hum Rufinus had cast a frail network of harmony, from which my mind receded fast. Shouted orders and repeated instructions subsided into a distant babble; words and phrases merged until they had regressed within my absent hearing, first to the meaningless prattle of childhood, and then to the silence that preceded the earth's parturition.

Closing my sound eye against the glare, I began to explore inwardly with the other: that which the Hawk of Gwales stole from me

long ago upon the rock of Ynys Gweir. It is entering a world hard of
access, whose entrance traces an entangled skein. Coiled and wandering are the skillfully dug entrances of Dineirth, ensnaring the unwary
foe who seeks to intrude himself within its looped double-fossed
defenses. Just so does it require depth of knowledge and charms of
unloosening to penetrate the inner place which is the world's focus; to
negotiate the vortiginous entrances of the ears, trace the springheads of
the veins, unravel the convoluted ciphering of the entrails, pace the
myriad chambers of the brain.

Images, symbols, patterns began to swim up out of the darkness,
as I who am Merlin became no longer Merlin, but the nine forms of
elements upon which that name was foisted at my beginning. I was
what has existed; I was within the world's expanse; I was slipping with
Dylan Eil Ton into the earth's rampart. Stillness and clarity stole over
me and I into them. I was gliding like a serpent into the hill; I was
between sea and shore. In a moment, so I sensed, I would know what
has been—and what is to be before.

All in a moment my reflexion was shattered, like the image on a
lake's surface when a stone is flung upon it. A voice spoke suddenly
beside me: a voice I had thought to hear within, not without.

"I think you are mending at last, Merlin mab Morfryn?"

I opened my eye, to see Maelgun's trusted counselor, Maeldaf the
elder, lord of Penardd, standing over me. His head was between me
and the sun, so that I could not see his face. Dragged from my
dreaming, I found difficulty for a moment in recollecting my thoughts,
and listened perforce to his utterance.

"You are a fortunate man—and so are we, for we had not thought
to see you again. But I see you are hard to lose as the swine of Ol
mab Olwyd, who disappeared seven years before his birth, and were
yet recovered when he came to manhood. Indeed, the guards took you
for a pig, and would have shot their arrows through you, had I not
been by to stay their hands!"

"Scarcely so very fortunate, Maeldaf," I replied. "I received a shaft
in my back which, had it traveled a little deeper, might have left me
low as now you see me, without the power of thanking you for your
aid."

"I see you have suffered, Merlin. 'The cheek does not conceal the
hurt of the heart.' You have been away from us for a while now.
When first we talked within your hut you spoke of great dangers
threatening us; of the advance of the Iwys upon Dineirth. May
I ask how you came to know of these things, and what more you
learned of the movements of the hosts? I suppose you may have

discovered something of Cynurig's thinking—what his spies have told him?"

"Much and little," I replied, a bit gruffly, for I was not best pleased at having my thoughts interrupted, nor was I greatly taken with this Maeldaf. His sage saws and endless questioning irritated me not a little, and I saw he placed a high value upon his own wisdom, seeking to approach me upon an equality.

"Did you learn anything more precise than that which you have already told us of the foemen's movements, their plans—their knowledge of our deliberations?" he persisted.

"Little enough. As I said, I suppose there will be an attack here before long, for which the tribune appears to be making due preparation. It is most unfortunate that the king cannot be persuaded to leave."

"Very unfortunate," concurred the elder. "He violated his *cynneddyf*, you know, so there seemed to be no way of arranging matters otherwise. Naturally I urged another course, but in time of war little heed is paid to the advice of men such as you and I."

"Very likely not. Warriors are confident and rash."

There was a pause, which I did not permit my natural politeness to break. I remained lying on the comfort of the turf with my eye closed, though I could tell from the shadow upon the lid that Maeldaf had not moved.

"How could the Iwys have come to know of the king's presence here?" he asked, after a further pause.

"Do they know? Who said they do? From what Samo told the council of the kings in Caer Gurygon, I gathered it was their intent to seize this place regardless of who was here."

"True. I had forgotten. What is your opinion of that Samo? Did you think his information trustworthy?"

"Who am I to judge of these things, lord of Penardd?" I responded a little sharply. I opened my eye and contemplated his face. Though I could not see it clearly against the bright sky, it seemed to me that he was in a state of barely suppressed agitation. I knew more than I had chosen to tell him, but did not feel in the mood to elaborate. We were caught in a cleft, where the larger issues no longer counted for much.

"Remember what Gwydion said when his enchantments were placed about Caer Arianrod," I observed laconically: "There is no counsel now but to shut ourselves within this fort and defend it as best we may."

"You are right, Merlin, as always. But as the king's elder it is for me to consider how best to arrange matters. I cannot help but feel that things have gone astray, and that not entirely through ill chance:

"Paths are slippery, sharp is the shower;
The ford is flooded in the plotter's hour.

"Do you think it possible that someone has betrayed us? If you know anything I do not, I think you should tell me. It is essential for me to know all, though it be but conjecture, if I am to judge matters aright. I will tell you what is in my mind, Merlin, since you are wise and I value your counsel.

"The king is not to be advised while he suffers under his debility, and I am of little use here. What say you if I were to leave the camp and return to Degannwy in Gwynedd? I think you know something of the struggle for the kingship which took place before Maelgun came to accept his cousin's fealty upon his winged throne at the Traeth Maur? It was I who assisted him not a little at that time. Now I am fearful lest the king's predicament become known among the princes of the tribe of Cunedda, and there arise once again contention among the kindred, each royal heir striving to seize the kingship for himself. Whatever happens here, Prince Run mab Maelgun's inheritance must be made safe; and I might do much at home in Gwynedd to preserve it until he or his father returns home."

I did not trouble to answer, since the drift of his speech told me that he was already resolved on a course of action which no words of mine were likely to alter. I wished he would be off, if that were his desire; but still he lingered a little.

"When they find that I am gone, there may be those who call me coward, woman, or some other bad name," he muttered awkwardly. "I hope that you, who know what it is necessary for me to do, will defend me. The wind is keen about the oak, and the birds chatter upon its branches; the envious and contentious are ever noisy.

"I regard you as my friend and, like me, a faithful counselor to the king. Farewell, son of Morfryn, and may we meet before long in happier circumstances!"

The shadow lifted, and I knew that Maeldaf was departed. Cowardice in a man is an evil property, but I did not think that his weakness. Foul weather brings wet paths upon the hillside, and an experienced rider will keep careful watch where the brink breaks beneath his horse's hoof. Matters did not appear hopeful, that was certain. But the defense of the fortress was in as good hands as might be; what Rufinus could not achieve, I did not think any other man could do. Maeldaf had his own purposes, which for better or worse could no longer affect the critical issue about to be enacted on this desolate spot. It was for me to observe all things about us, playing the greater game against an adversary whose face remained veiled from sight.

I closed my eye once more, preparing to redirect my gaze inward, seeking to acquire by reflexion what was denied to the crowded waking image. Those who seek hidden knowledge or the *awen* of creative inspiration search out spots far from the inhabited places of the earth: mountaintops, cataracts, forgotten forest glades. Small wonder, for in my case no sooner was the ordered confusion of the encampment once more fading from me than again I received a less than welcome interruption.

Opening my eye with a start and a frown, I saw one of Elffin's men smiling politely down at me.

"I have been sent to request your attendance on the tryffin," he explained. "Tryffin" was the nearest the tongue of the Brython could get around Rufinus' rank, and so I rose wearily. I could not see that I could be of any assistance to a man who knew his profession so thoroughly, but if my presence cheered him, then that in itself could contribute its mite to sustaining us.

I rose creakily, and stumbled after the fellow, who irritated me by continually stopping solicitously and trying to cosset me along like an old woman. What pests these young men can be at times! There was a time when I, too, wore golden spurs and bore a gallant spear, when this wasted body was welcome in the taverns of Powys, Paradise of Prydein! But the leaf flutters away before the autumn wind; it is old, though born this year.

At the western gateway my companion paused, ushering me ahead of him up the planked stairway. Ascending to the parapet, we passed a little way along the walkway to the left, until we arrived at a spot where a space opened out onto a projecting spur of the earthen rampart. This was protected by a low stockade, broken by a broad embrasure at its outward end. There stood Rufinus, perspiring freely and looking as near to cheerfulness as I had seen him since my return.

"Ah, Merlin, there you are! Now, what do you think of my little toy here?" He slapped his hand on the flank of a massive beamed construction lying squat upon the rampart beside him, looking at me with an expression of considerable pride. I could see my approval was called for, but at first found some difficulty in appreciating what it was I should approve.

"Very fine!" I exclaimed, moving around a little delicately and touching it at different points in vague indication of judicial assessment. "Very fine!"

A crowd of carpenters stood around with similarly expectant expressions; clearly it was they who had constructed this object under the tribune's directions. If my description appear a little confusing, I can only plead in extenuation that the apparatus was quite unlike anything I had seen before, and from its immediate appearance seemed to serve no comprehensible purpose. What was it? Well, all I can say is that it looked to me like a huge flat wooden chest, with some odd adjuncts tacked on about it.

In height it came up to my hip. Its length was about two spearshafts; in breadth, one. On either side of the end facing into the fortress were two large wheels, which at first glance appeared designed for trundling the structure about. However, not only did it seem unlikely that any wheels could possibly have supported so bulky a structure, but even my inexpert eye told me they were of relatively flimsy framed construction, and also so situated that their rims rotated clear of the ground. Very useful! Knowledge is the summit of all human attainments, but when men attempt to apply their deficient understanding to any practical purpose, the results are all too often lamentable.

Enough of this sententious cant—particularly as not for the first or last time I was quite wrong in my assessment! Let each man stick to his chosen profession, that which fate has allotted him. "The carpenter's son to the adze, the smith's son to the coal," as it is said; "it is fitting for each to follow his family." Concluding my inspection, I remarked a high arch of iron spanning the center of the frame, its bases firmly riveted to the principal lateral beams of the engine's framework.

"Neat, do you not think?" reiterated my friend, whose eye shone bright as a falcon's, seeking my instant approval.

"Very," I concurred. "It has been well put together, that I can see. But I freely confess to you, Rufinus, that I have no idea what it is. I fear you will have to excuse my ignorance in these matters, which is far from matching my interest. As you know, I am intrigued by all conceptions new to me."

The tribune nodded benignly. "Naturally you would not know what it is—why should you? Unless I am much mistaken, it is long since one of these has been seen in Britannia. I will not keep you in suspense, my clever friend. What you see before you (a little crudely constructed at points, I grant you, but we will let that pass) is an approximation of the heavy *ballista* which the Roman army deploys for the defense of fortified towns. This little fellow, so I am told, can fling its missile across the Danubis downstream of Vindobana, hitting a target no smaller than a forage-wagon. I had a battery of them protecting our harbor at Septem, which must have had something like that range. On a calm day we could hit a towed target-boat well beyond the mole four times out of five."

"Ah, I remember your telling me about such things when we spoke months ago upon the slope of Dinleu Gurygon!" I exclaimed with genuine enthusiasm. "I imagine their effect must be deadly?"

"Pretty fair," rejoined Rufinus, chuckling to himself. "Would you like a demonstration?"

"I certainly should. Where would you like me to stand?"

"Go back there, by the stair-head. You have been in the wars enough of late, and I don't want any accidents. Mind you, you do not have the problems with a *ballista* you can have with the onager, where a stone faultily placed in the sling may rebound and strike the unlucky operator. It is not a pretty sight, from what I hear: Your man can end up smashed into so many pieces that a surgeon would be hard put to it to match them up again!"

I backed away hastily, as recommended, watching with great eagerness and a little trepidation to see what would transpire. At a brisk command from Rufinus (I should mention, by the way, that he was assisted by a young attendant of Maelgun who had accompanied his master during his stay in the monastery of Iltud, and who when necessary interpreted the tribune's orders), the men standing about jumped smartly to and set about their work. After each task Rufinus called a pause, in which he explained briefly what was being done.

"First we take the spear and lay it along the stock," he intoned, as a man brought up a thick-hafted javelin about the size of those used by our horsemen, with tapered flights of wood inserted at the butt end.

"Good. Now this man places the iron hook over the sinew-rope, which draws it back. Of course no man would be powerful enough to accomplish that of his own strength, but these two hefty fellows will demonstrate what can be done with an effective winch system."

I saw now that the two wheels I had noticed at the rear of the engine were in fact devices for drawing back an immensely thick knotted cord which linked the bases of the iron hoop spanning the timber frame. A man dived behind each wheel and, setting his shoulder to a spoke, began with considerable effort to turn them around.

"Now do you see how the missile is drawn back on the sliding stock? Steady . . . that's far enough for this time! This is our first firing, which I thought you might like to see; we shall have to try its strength by stages. The base and frame are sturdy enough, if a little clumsy—the king's carpenters know their business. But I am not entirely satisfied with the cord. All our manuals recommend the back and shoulder sinews of any animal save the pig, whose sinews are useless. Women's hair is excellent, by the way, but (fortunately in every other respect) there are none in the camp. Our material will do well enough (so long as one remembers to oil it well once an hour when in use) but the plaiting is a matter of great skill, which I confess lies outside my expertise. If I had my *praeceptor* Serenus from Septem here I should fear for nothing. Still, we will get there in time—a commodity in scarce supply at present, regrettably. Now, my lads, are you ready?"

The men operating the winches darted out and stood by the palisade while Rufinus himself approached the machine. Glancing to see whether I was observing the operation, he suddenly jerked at a cord dangling from the left-hand base of the hoop. At once there followed a sharp thud and clatter, as the hook spun from the cord, the cord sprang back taut beneath the hoop, bringing the stock below sliding violently forward on its base, so that the spear lying upon it shot forth with astonishing velocity over the embrasure. Dashing to the rampart's edge and leaning out over the palisade, I caught a faint glimpse of it hurtling across the valley toward a grassy slope opposite.

Beyond a brief glint in the sunshine it was not possible to detect precisely the course of the missile. However, a moment later we saw a man spring up from behind a boulder, brandishing a white cloth upon a pole. The distance was about two bow-shots, as I guessed. From all along the battlements rose up a mighty cheer: As many of Elffin's warriors as had heard what was impending had flown to the spot to witness the demonstration. Clearly it had impressed them deeply, as well it might.

The tribune now invited us to descend and inspect the effects of the launching. Running down the declivity and up to the point where the signaler was waiting, we found the javelin buried halfway up its shaft into the chalk of the hillside. This striking evidence of the engine's devastating power brought a brief silence upon the awestruck assembly. It was followed in a moment by a babble of excited comment.

"Why, if that had been discharged at a host, it would have impaled six warriors in a row—just like larks on a spit!" cried a merry-looking fellow at my side.

"True enough, it would," confirmed the tribune tersely, "if they were obliging enough to present themselves in the line of fire in file, that is."

This remark did nothing to dampen the enthusiasm of the crowd, all of whom had to come forward and tug at the shaft sticking stiffly from the hill, each commenting to the other on what all had seen for themselves. So it is with most men, as I have observed. A picture Taliesin could conjure for you within a single pithy phrase, they must bury beneath a mound of superfluous chatter. Rufinus and I left them to their pleasure. Spades had been brought, and the buried projectile was being dug from its lair, buried deep in the hide of Annufn.

You must not misunderstand me: I was at heart as impressed as any by this astonishing display of forceful energy. Also, I am greatly intrigued by the dissection of things into their elemental compounds, their mastery by ingenuity of hand and eye, and the valiant if fruitless attempt by man to master nature.

"Does this not place a different complexion upon things?" I asked the old soldier as we trudged back to the fortress. "There is no mail forged on earth which could withstand a blow from that sling. I think even Gofannon mab Don would be hard put to it to construct a shield to stay its course!"

"You are right, Merlin, as ever," grunted Rufinus. "Indeed, I myself saw a Gothic chieftain in a fine coat of mail to whom our people made a present of one of these little missiles. It was at the first siege of Rome; he was sheltering by a tree outside the Salarian Gate, loosing off arrows at our fellows on the battlements. Then some bright spark thought of lining up such a *fulminalis* as this against him. The first missile took master Goth in the chest, straight through his corselet and out the other side, so that it nailed him to the tree with half its length buried in the trunk beyond. There he stayed, but the Goths did not—of that I can assure you. The whole detachment cleared off, keeping well out of range from then on.

"It is an effective implement of warfare, I grant you. *Fulminalis,* 'lightning,' it is called, and that not for nothing. Still, its effect may not be quite as magical as our men appear to think. Stop here a moment, and look up there. What can you see?"

"The outer rampart of Dineirth; and very steep and inaccessible it looks, too, to my eyes at least."

"Steep enough, but scarcely inaccessible. But where is our *ballista?*"

"Beyond, upon the inner rampart, of course."

"Precisely. You see the weakness? Let the enemy collect his forces at the foot of our outer wall here, and he is as safe as may be from all our missiles. Yet is he also within a stone's throw of our true line of defense, which is as thinly held as can be conceived."

There was obvious reason in the tribune's words, and my elation was proportionately dampened.

"Then is the machine useless?" I asked. "Is our position hopeless?"

"Not hopeless," muttered Rufinus. "Not hopeless. Desperate, maybe, but not hopeless. Indeed, we must regard it as hopeful. Our sole chance of survival lies in the return of the army, to whom we have already sent word. How long they will take to return is anyone's guess. We must buy time, and time is bought with hope."

"But if your arrow-flinging engine can do nothing, how can the three hundred men of Elffin's *gosgordd* withstand the onslaught of such a host as Cynurig brings with him—even for a day?"

Rufinus halted and, leaning upon his staff, turned toward me. "Stay a moment, Merdinus," he commanded. "I would have a word with you here, where no one can overhear us."

Men were riding and running down the track beside us toward the crowd gathered around the magical spear, but they paid no heed to us who had halted a little to one side. At once I paused likewise, full of curiosity to learn the tribune's inner thought. There was more than a touch of unreality in all this reflective discourse, when the whirlwind of war might at any moment sweep us and all about us from existence.

"As I see it," began my friend in his usual matter-of-fact way, which quite prevented one from anticipating his coming thought, "we are in an awkward spot. These old forts were probably intended as a defense for an entire tribe together with its cattle in time of war; not to be held as an outpost by a single cohort. I had to be my own *mensurator* when we first arrived, and I estimate that the walls here enclose an area of between twenty and twenty-five *iugera*. We have barely enough men to patrol the wall of such a space. Where are my reserves, my replacements as units come off duty?

"Now, if we had effective artillery—"

"But you have!" I interrupted. "Have we not just witnessed what can be done?"

Rufinus grunted dismissively. "What we have witnessed can accomplish nothing, or nearly nothing. I will tell you all the truth, which no one else must know—not even the king. The king brought with him many carpenters and masons, for it was known that the fort's defenses were old and in disrepair. They are men of some skill in their trade, and I was able to repair stonework and re-erect the palisade more swiftly than I had thought to do. When that was done, I set a group of the more enterprising to constructing a *ballista*.

"There are three standard artillery-pieces used by the army for the defense of fortifications: the lighter arrow-shooting *ballistra*, the heavy *ballista* which you see before you, and the stone-throwing onager. Of the three, the *ballistra* is the lightest and most maneuverable, and hence most suitable for our purposes here. The onager is powerful, and has the advantage as a stone-throwing catapult of not requiring specially constructed missiles. In fact there are, as you may have noted, numbers of large flint stones lying about here on the open ground eminently suitable to its purpose."

"From what you have just told me, you appear to have selected the least effective alternative. May I ask why is that, or have I misunderstood the matter?"

"No. So far as it goes, your assumption is correct. The truth is that none of these machines is of much use for defending such a place as this. The double dyke is very effective, it is true, in providing a killing ground within the trench at the final moment of assault. However, it also prevents the use of artillery at any but a fairly long range. The plain fact in any case is that a circular defense is the very worst that can be devised. No artillery emplacement is positioned to cover more of the defenses than its own platform; only the troops at the point where an assault takes place are enabled to play any part in its repulse."

"Do you mind my inquiring, then, why you devoted so much labor and thought to constructing an engine which, by your own account, is of no value?" I asked, suspecting nonetheless that a man like the tribune must have had some reason for his action.

"What can be done for the defenses, I have done. Moreover, I did not say that my *ballista* was entirely without use. To have any appreciable effect upon an attack in force I would require a full battery, and for that there is no time, nor have I the men to man them. But now you have told me from which direction to expect the attack, I can at least prevent the enemy from concentrating his forces preparatory to an assault, and perhaps unnerve him a little—since I doubt he expects such a reception in such an out-of-the-way place as this!

"If we can damage the enemy's morale, at least for a time, so that he is compelled to pause and consider the best method of attack, that in our case is a great deal better than an immediate head-on assault, which would, I fear, have every chance of success. And, as far as morale goes, you have seen for yourself how my little demonstration cheered our people. It has kept them busy and curious at a time when waiting and wondering are the most insidious enemies there are, and a brief initial effect may do much to steel their hearts when the siege opens. We have made one or two other little toys, too, which if deployed at the appropriate moment may give the enemy a nasty turn and our own men a fillip. Come with me, and I will show you."

A little way within the gates lay a squat timbered building, to which the tribune led me. We had to stoop our heads to enter, and at first the darkness inside prevented my distinguishing anything. When my eye had become accustomed to the obscurity, I saw that this must be a workshop for the finished products of smiths and carpenters. Turned and partially turned sections of wood lay about, together with rivets, stanchions, and other products of the metalworker's art. My gaze was at once attracted by a great tube or funnel of copper gleaming warmly where it stood propped in a corner. Before I could inquire its purpose, however, Rufinus summoned me across to his side.

Stripping off its cloth covering, he revealed a small engine which I could see was another form of catapult. It was mounted on a tripod set in a wooden base, and comprised a squat oblong box not more than a spear-shaft in length, with a curious sort of broken-armed metal bow at one end and a small winch handle at the other.

"Now what do you think of that, eh?" asked Rufinus.

I was a little unsure how to answer. From the evident pride in his expression I guessed that this instrument particularly pleased him. Yet its size suggested there could be no comparison with the huge engine squatting on the bastion which we had so recently inspected. The span of the bow was little greater than that of the ordinary weapon borne by huntsmen. I noted, too, a considerable pile of arrows neatly stacked in a box against the wall. To my inexperienced eye they appeared decidedly inferior to those regularly employed by archers. They were not more than about six palm-breadths in length, and their flights, though long, emerged scarcely a couple of barleycorns from the shaft. Surely that would affect their steadiness in flight?

Rufinus actually grinned cheerfully when I put this tentatively to him.

"Ah, I see you are learning something of the military art, Merdinus. As a spy you have already proved invaluable, and I will make a soldier of you yet! Your objection is valid, so far as it goes, and yet this machine has some compensatory advantages. So much so, indeed, that we have actually constructed two of them." He gestured toward a structure of similar shape, hunched beneath drapery by the opposite wall.

"Will you not enlighten me, then?" I inquired. "It seems to me that, with such marvelous machines at your disposal, it is small wonder that the army of Rufein should once have conquered the world—indeed, appears to be on the point of reconquering it all over again? Could you not surround the frontiers of your Empire with such devices, and overawe the barbarians for all time? It seems to me that an engine like your spear-throwing machine which you demonstrated just now might take the place of a detachment of soldiers. With large numbers of them, then, you could greatly reduce the size of your armies, devoting yourselves to the acquisition of wealth and cultivation of the arts of peace?"

Rufinus stroked his machine with the affection another would bestow on a favorite hound, stooping to wind back the winch a little whilst aligning his eye along the stock. Then he rose erect and looked back at me.

"This is what we call the Little Scorpion, invented by Dionysius of Alexandria, which is not in fact in regular use with the service. When I was laid up in Panormus I read up the account in Philon's artillery manual, and later had the chance of inspecting an old model in the arsenal at Caesarea. It was preserved more as a curiosity than for use, I would think.

"It is true that advanced new military machines have proved of great benefit in defending our cities from the attacks of the barbarians. There will never be peace so long as they are pressing on the frontiers, howling 'round it everywhere. Within their inaccessible forests, protected by deserts or marshes, they remain more or less immune to destruction. Their numbers are limitless, and to combat them we need stone walls and powerful artillery of different capacities.

"Nevertheless I question whether we should place as much reliance as we do on complex engines of war. The barbarians are by no means foolish in this respect, and for the most part quite capable of imitating our skills in engineering. You may recall how Gainas invented the system of raft transportation by which he moved his Visigoths across the Hellespont—a system we copied and have employed on occasion since. And the most effective battering ram in our siege-trains is that devised by the Sabirian Huns, still named after them.

"No, my fear is that the more we rely on engines and the less on men, the more we are in danger of placing ourselves eventually on an equality with the barbarians. It was not artillery that gained us the dominion of the world, but Roman virtue and Roman discipline. If we lose sight of those qualities, then what will there be to choose between Rome and her adversaries? Just the fortune of war, which is to say the throw of the dice! Mark my words, Merlin: The day we place our reliance in machines and not men will be one which ends all order in the world."

I was about to suggest that in a tight spot like the present any effective contrivance might be of advantage, when a man came running up to the entrance of the storehouse, shouting for the tribune. The enemy was approaching! At this we both hurried out into the open, making our way up the slope until we gained a point from where there was a clear view of the hills to the southwest. Sure enough, a plume of smoke was streaming up from the left-hand end of the ridge! More than this we could not see, though I thought I detected the faint echo of horns being blown.

"Prince Elffin and his men will be back shortly," exclaimed Rufinus. "Dispatch a troop to meet them on the way! If they follow their orders they will not need assistance, but it is better to be sure."

The man vaulted into his saddle and was off without a word. The gates swung open before him, and by the time the tribune and I had gained the rampart, the messenger and half a dozen companions had ascended the hill opposite and were disappearing along the ridgeway stretched at full gallop.

Needless to say, there was great excitement in the camp, and men came and went, shifting piles of arms, clearing obstructions, and seeking orders from my friend. Once or twice I saw him glance toward the king's tent, but there was no sign of movement there. Clearly the nine-days debility was still upon Maelgun Gwynedd, defender of the Hosts of Baptism, and we must abandon any thought of last-minute withdrawal.

All at once a shout went up from those with us, and we gazed back over the parapet. The ridgeway ran for the most part along the skyline, and horsemen could be seen moving at a spot where the trees thinned out. Clearly the scouts who had fired the signal-pyre were withdrawing under escort of Elffin. I could only hope that the ruse Rufinus had ordered was effective. I will confess to a nervousness suddenly arising within me. In the ordered atmosphere of the camp, surrounded by familiar faces, I had almost forgotten the reality of the danger that drew ever nearer. We were surrounded by exultant faces, but of all that company, the tribune and I alone knew how slender was the thread upon which our lives now hung.

It seemed an age before we glimpsed our horsemen riding hell-for-leather down into the declivity lying between the ridgeway and the western gateway of Dineirth. Up the slope they spurred their steeds in headlong haste, until they passed beneath us into the fortress. I looked in vain for the familiar figure of Prince Elffin, and it was for news of him that Rufinus called when we clattered down the steps of the gate-tower to interrogate the riders streaming in by ones and twos.

"Prince Elffin has been taken by the Iwys!" cried one in an agitated voice.

"What!" shouted Rufinus, seizing the man's horse by its bridle.

"What has happened, man? Did you not follow my orders? This was no time for seeking after glory!"

Distress, mortification, shame were written on the face of the whole troop, as they stared wildly about them. Their horses' heaving flanks and frothed muzzles told of frantic flight. I was angry, and shouted harshly at the man who had spoken:

"How is it you have returned in safety, leaving your lord dead or a prisoner? Never will you be able to return to Cantre'r Gwaelod. You will become shameful exiles, ranked with the Three Faithless Warbands of the Island of Prydein!"

The rider appeared confused by my reproach, almost as much as he was afflicted by his dreadful predicament.

"Is it you, Merlin mab Morfryn? You are right: No warrior may survive with honor the death of the prince whom he accompanies into the place of battle. But what were we to do? Before ever the enemy was seen approaching on the highway, Elffin mab Gwydno called us all together, compelling us to swear the oath 'by sun and moon and sea and dew and light' that we were to return here to continue the combat should he fall in the fray or into the hands of the foeman. What choice had we? We have sucked his nipple, as well as that of his father Gwydno Garanhir. We are the foster-brothers of his *gosgordd*, fostered by his father's wine. It is not to be supposed that we will be honored in the mouths of poets, but we have drunk of our prince's mead and are bound to obey his command."

Though the warriors' words rang true, still in my distress would I have continued my abuse, had not Rufinus seized my arm and dragged me away up the slope of the enclosure.

"You loved Prince Elffin, I think," he exclaimed forcefully, as he hastened me along. "I, too, had a dear friend who was killed in battle. It is hard to bear, very hard. But we cannot alter Fortune's decrees, and there is some consolation in memory, as I have found. Now, however, there is no time for regrets or consolations. If we do not keep our heads and act decisively, it is unlikely that any of us will live long enough to fret about his lot."

He was right, that I knew, but my heart swelled up with grief. Before me, vivid as in life, floated a picture of the lively, artless son of Gwydno. With the gallop of a colt, bringing uproar to the battle-slope, a racing fire, he was an impetuous, flashing spear before all the hosts of the Cymry, the hope of all who dwell in the fair northern land of the Cantre'r Gwaelod beside the Sea of Reged, white-bosomed haunt of gulls and gannets. But now the eagle of the graceful swoop was left beside the ford with the falling of the dew, and the bards of the world would lament his manly heart. As grievous to my heart was the image, surging unsolicited continually before my inward eye, of Elffin's beautiful princess in that moment she stood pale and fearful at our departure from Porth Gwydno in the North.

At the same time I remember that a confusion of fear, excitement, and movement jostled my grief about, so that I scarcely knew what I thought or felt in that hour. It is hard to believe that any man is in truth departed when his death is recent, and now we were caught up in events so far beyond our controlling it seemed as though Elffin remained one of the pieces being moved this way and that upon the gaming board.

"We must assume the worst, I fear, whilst hoping we are in the wrong," urged Rufinus, gripping me by the shoulder and compelling my attention with his decisive energy. "If Prince Elffin be alive, they may have extracted from him some impression of our weakness. In that case they would know, too, that we are awaiting the return of the host, in which case they will press forward as swiftly as they may to take the fortress before we can be reinforced."

"It is not the fortress that matters, but the king," I groaned. "If Maelgun the Tall be captured or slain, then there is an end of the Island of the Mighty."

"Then neither he nor the fortress must be taken!" rejoined the tribune, with an air of resolution so persuasive I could hardly bring myself to believe it delusory. "Come, there are matters I did not confide to Prince Elffin; young men are little concerned with stratagems of war, desiring only to measure their sword blades with those of the enemy. Ask that fellow to lend me his horse, will you? And take one yourself if you wish to accompany me."

The sight of the tribune being assisted into his saddle served to bring me to my senses a little, for I was distressed to note the extent to which he had concealed from me the pain his right arm was giving him. He uttered no complaint, but I saw him bite his lip and turn pale as he was obliged to make use of it in righting himself in the saddle. I also suffered from affliction, in particular a recurrent pain like that of burning elf-darts in my back, but my thoughts had drifted for a time into a self-indulgence I doubted the tribune would have permitted himself.

Declining the use of a horse myself, I clung to my companion's saddle and trotted at his side as he made his way through parties of warriors, artificers, and slaves hurrying to their various posts, until we reached the western gate. Ascending to the parapet of the tower, we looked first in the direction from which we knew the enemy to be approaching. The tribune permitted himself a grunt of satisfaction when he saw no sign of movement upon the rolling line of hills. Next he directed my gaze toward the southwest.

I should explain here that the fortress of Dineirth is poised high upon a spur of the downland wilderness, looking out over an unbounded expanse of level green plain to north and west. The crest of the downs is bounded by a steep horseshoe-shaped escarpment, at the center of whose arc lies the ancient stronghold refortified by Arthur, and restored again by Maelgun Gwynedd. The ridgeway which stretches from the Center of the Island of the Mighty to the misty Sea of Udd straddles the western face, passing in its course below the western gate of Dineirth. It was upon that road that Elffin had taken his post, and along which we now awaited the march of the barbarian hosts.

A lateral track leading from the ridgeway passes through Dineirth itself, leading out of the gateway where now we stood and passing along the eastern curve of the horseshoe. It was by this approach I had first made my arrival, having struck across the valley from the ridgeway in my fear of being taken by the armed men I had seen—more likely than not, as now I saw, Rufinus' advanced scouts! Where this other road led we did not know; from its course one might suppose it directed toward the heart of the desolate Plain of Bran.

"You see that ridge, Merlin," indicated the tribune, pointing with his staff. "Now, picture things to yourself in this way: Suppose yourself the barbarian king approaching us. What if you had reason to believe our force no mere cohort holed up in a temporary strongpoint far from its own territory, but a powerful force of legionary strength, drawn up in battle order? Imagine our front extending the length of this ridge, and this fort but the strong point upon which we pivot our right flank. Were that in truth the case, would you not be compelled to withdraw as speedily as may be? Standing our ground upon the bluff, we should be well-nigh unassailable in defense. Between our left and his rear lie sunken stream beds and small ravines ideal for the concealed approach of an assailant, should we choose to outflank him as he is strung out upon his march. Not a pretty situation for a general who moves in any case through uncharted territory!"

"I suppose you are right, Rufinus," I made reply, "but why should he believe any of these things?"

"Perhaps he will not, but I think he may. Judge of the effect for yourself!"

The tribune signed to a guard, who at once set the head of a resined pine-torch into a glowing brazier until it flared alight, applying it then to a cresset set high at the corner of the gate-tower. The iron basket must have contained cloth steeped in pitchblende or the like, for at once a dark stream of smoke began pouring upward into the clear air.

Following the direction of the tribune's gaze, I could at first detect no response to his signal. But then upon the eastern ridge there curled up an answering gray smudge, a lick of flame, and then a steady stream of smoke poured upward to the low-hanging clouds. All along the ridge sprang up similar puffing columns, until it did indeed appear that a mighty host of men was encamped the length of the bluff.

"Very ingenious!" I conceded with a laugh. "Have you many more such tricks up your sleeve, Rufinus?"

He gave a grunt of satisfaction, glancing to his right. There was still no sign of the enemy. I felt hope returning, accompanied by a sudden recollection of the fate of young Elffin. For a while we stood looking out over the still landscape, until the tribune silently pointed to where a lone horseman came cantering along the track beside the bonfires. We followed his approach with our gaze, until finally his horse's hoofs thudded on the turf below us, and he reined in his mount with a shout for the gate to be opened.

"Ask him what is his message, will you?" requested Rufinus at my elbow. The man looked up, recognition springing at once to his eyes.

"Ah, Merlin!" he cried. "I think the news is bad. See what we found beside our tent when we returned from lighting our signal-fire!" He bore a sack slung across his saddle, to which he pointed in some distress.

"Tell him to say no more, but wait for us there!" ordered Rufinus urgently. I complied, and we tore down the stair as swiftly as we could. The gates were unbarred, and we joined the messenger at the entrance.

"Tell no bad news that others may overhear, man. What have you there?" muttered Rufinus in a tone of anxiety.

"See for yourself," replied the rider, as I translated. "I think it may not be we who are to play at football with the heads of the Iwys; the game is now 'Badger in the Bag,' in which they have been playing with no unskilled hand, as I fancy."

He handed me the sack, which I was about to open and empty on the ground. But Rufinus stayed my hand, and instead we opened the neck and peered inside. I gave an exclamation of disgust, for forth from the darkness stared out at us a pale and bloody face. With a cry of dismay Rufinus drew the bleeding head up a little by its hair: beneath it lay another, whose sightless sockets were dried wells of congealed gore. The tribune dropped back the head he held, swiftly drawing tight the thong once more about the neck of the sack.

"Return at once to your post and conceal this! We must try to keep the news from the garrison. Recall all the posts along the ridge as you return, and bring them back inside the fortress! No delay, do you hear?"

The man nodded and took back the sack. "There was this beside it, lord, which may tell you more."

About his neck I had noticed a branch of oak sapling bent and bound into a circle, with marks carved upon its length. The rider flung it to me, turned his horse's head, and was off to fulfill the order.

"What do you make of it?" I asked.

"Nothing good," grunted my companion, whose face for the first time I saw to be drawn and pale, as if suddenly assailed by a great weariness. "The faces upon which you looked were those of the messengers we dispatched three days ago to recall the army. This puts a different complexion upon matters, Merlin, as you see. Each hour I had hoped to gain for our deliverance has in reality been one in which our army has moved ever farther from us. I suppose there is some polite message cut upon that stick; can you read it?"

I turned the ring about in my hands, reading the runes incised within it:

"Here is a ring. What is its meaning? What is its secret import? How many placed it here: one man or many? The Bear who mangles flesh is come upon you, who will bring death and destruction upon you, spilling blood, sparing none. It is for that this ring was made."

Rufinus looked up at me.

"The barbarians must know just how we stand. The old fox has outwitted us. I fear much, Merlin, that we are compassed about in this place, from which it may be there is now no escape."

CHAPTER SEVENTEEN

THE SLAUGHTER OF DINEIRTH

Now it happened, when the ninth day of King Maelgun's debility was passed, which was also the day after the enemy's approach became known to the defenders of Dineirth, that Idno Hen, who was chief druid of Gwynedd, consulted with the druids of the court who were present within the fortress, and likewise with Melys mab Marthin and the physicians of the court. It was their purpose to consult concerning the king's malady, that a cure might be effected.

And as they spoke upon the green by the king's dragon standard, they heard a desperate moan coming from within the king's tent.

"That is a moan of sickness that the king emits!" pronounced Melis.

"It is a moan caused by the point of an enchanted weapon!" declared Idno Hen.

"It is necessary for him to be given treatment!" was the judgment they uttered together.

Then they entered the king's tent together, driving forth all those who were assembled about Maelgun, save the blessed Cubi, who bore with him a vessel of healing water from his holy well in Arfon. Idno Hen took wands of yew upon which he inscribed runes of knowledge and power, standing the while upon one foot and using one eye and one hand. It was the words he wrote which revealed to him the nature of the king's malady and the means of its expulsion. Orders were sent to the smith of the king's court, he who was master of spells and enchantments, that he keep the bellows of his forge blowing until the coals were blazing, and upon them place the coulter of a plow. When the coulter was become so hot that it was red, the smith bore it in his tongs into the tent of Maelgun, where he made a feint to plunge it into the king's belly.

Even as the smith made this feigned thrust, so Cubi and Idno chanted together a charm of healing:

"In nomine patri et filii et spiritus sancti. Telon! Terula! Tilolob! Ticon! Tilo! Leton! Patron! Tilud! Amen."

With that the king leaned forward and vomited forth all manner of beetles, reptiles, blood clots, and other harmful matter which was within him, so that the maleficent creatures lay heaped swarming upon the ground before him. Thrice did the smith approach Maelgun with his coulter, and three times the king voided the creeping things that infested his inside. In this manner the enchantment which was upon him was lifted; no longer was there left in him either moan or sickness, but his strength was returned and he was whole. Idno Hen pronounced the words which ensured that the debility would not return to the king, provided, that is, he did not again violate his *cynneddyf:*

"Maelgwn gwell gwyd vwyt noc arthes."

With that the druids and physicians and priests who were with Maelgun departed, and I hastened to him together with Rufinus the tribune. Entering the royal tent, we were delighted to see the king restored to his full health and majesty. He was seated in his royal robes upon his royal throne, bearing within his hand the wand of kingship. He greeted us kindly, pressing us at once for news of Brochfael and the hosts of the Cymry whom he had last seen passing onward into the land of the Iwys.

It was not long before we had told him all we knew: of the approach of the barbarian host, the death or capture of Elffin, and the fate of the messengers dispatched by the tribune to recall Brochfael. And even as the king pondered these ill tidings, there came running a soldier from the ramparts who told of sounds of turmoil, trumpet blasts, and cries filling all the land.

"It seems our situation is a sorry one," said the king.

"It is," replied the messenger. "We have heard trumpets and shouting all about us. What are we to do?"

"It seems to me," replied Maelgun, "that there can be no other counsel than to shut ourselves up within this fort and defend it as best we may. Meanwhile I will ascend the rampart and see who it is that approaches."

So Maelgun Gwynedd, accompanied by Rufinus and myself, went up onto the tower which was over the western gate and looked out across the valley and the ridge. The air was filled with shouting and horn-blowing, though there was nothing to be seen but the green hillside, trickling rivulets, and the wind that moved the trees. The pale light of dawn was over the land, and few things appeared as they do when daylight lies bright upon them.

"What is that noise?" asked the king. "Is it the earth quaking, or is it the sea flooding over the land, or is it the sky falling?"

I looked out over the parapet, and it did indeed seem to me as if the sky with its showers of stars were falling to the surface of the earth; or as if the fish-stocked, blue-rimmed sea were sweeping across the face of the land; or as if the earth's hide were being rent apart by tumors erupting from the Halls of Annufn. The shrieking which filled the air and assailed our ears was terrible as the cry annually resounding upon the eve of Kalan Mai above every hearth in Prydein, which goes through the hearts of men so that through terror they lose their color and their strength, women miscarry, sons and daughters lose their senses, and all animals, forests, earth, and waters are left barren.

The sky seemed to fall upon the earth, and the earth to be swollen by convulsions which set it rolling like waves across a winter's strand. The trees which clothed the landscape swayed and tossed as if enchanted by the wand of Gwydion mab Don into a host numerous as the creatures of the deep, or the sands of the seashore, or the radiant stars of the firmament. Elm and ash and oak marched in serried ranks upon the fort; holly brandished his spiky leaves; hazels raised their shafts against the sky. I thought the forests of the earth locked in battle about us.

I feared lest hills and fields and valleys should be leveled with the ground, all things confounded into their nine forms of elements, chaos of the Coranieid be come again upon us, heaven and earth commingling in one tempestuous turmoil, and the world rushing to universal ruin.

"What means this tumult and crying and turbulence of the world, Merlin?" asked Maelgun.

Now the sun rose above the hills behind us, and I saw that it was not the cracking of the sky nor the splitting of the earth nor the ebbing of the sea which was about us, but the angry advance of a mighty host. What I had thought to be tall trees was a forest of ash-hafted spears approaching in dense array. What I thought were tops of hills were helmets of champions riding in ranks to the fray. What I thought were stars falling in clusters from the sky was the flashing of the eyes of the angry foemen, and the sparkling of sunlight upon their gleaming armor. What I thought were bright streams dividing meadows were burnished blades borne by countless men of valor. What I thought was the rush of roaring cataracts was the galloping of the steeds under them, and the froth which flew from their bits and bridles. What I thought were clouds descending upon the earth was the dust raised by the hoofs of that unnumbered host. And the shouts which seemed to shatter the sky around were those of a host of barbarians, which in numbers and strength and ferocity was greater than that of any array of foemen that brought its oppression upon the Island of the Mighty. I told these things to Maelgun the Tall, the son of Cadwallon Lawhir, king of Gwynedd and Dragon of Mon.

"Then we shall hold this fortress upon whose walls we stand," replied the king, "and unless the ground indeed quake beneath us, or the heavens collapse upon our heads, we shall not flee from this spot."

The king had spoken, but now he turned to the tribune, asking what counsel he would give in the matter.

"It seems to me we have very little choice," replied Rufinus grimly. "We are holed up here whether we like it or not, and must make the best of our plight. But since you ask me, O king, I will tell you what I think. First, you should at once give orders to entrench the two entrances of the camp, sowing a thorny path of *triboli* in the ditches. This will not only hinder the enemy in his attack, but also prevent our own people from being lured out into a sally.

"Second, you should ensure that the men on the walls are subject to regular relief, each sector being the responsibility of a particular troop. In that way they will not become demoralized, nor will different units impede each other as they move to and from their posts.

"Third, if there be any means of doing so, we should attempt to dissuade the enemy from attacking until the evening. This is always to be recommended where the enemy enjoys the preponderant strength. You may then display what eagerness you will for battle, since night will shortly put a stay to fighting. It is the stratagem which Frontinus tells us Jugurtha employed against our armies in Africa, and I do not doubt that what was undertaken by the enemies of Rome may effectively be used by Romans against barbarians.

"Beyond these measures, I have only this to say: Rely on God's help, allow no hesitation in issuing or obeying orders, and by God's favor we will achieve victory."

Maelgun expressed satisfaction with these words of the tribune. "Then let Dineirth be the station of the whetter of armies!" he exclaimed, gripping us each by the arm before turning to descend the stairway.

As the king left the wall to resume his royal station before his tent beneath his banner, the warrior host of the Iwys uttered the loud, terrible cry of an army. So fierce was that cry about the walls of Dineirth that there was not a spear on a rack, nor a shield on a spike, nor a sword on a shelf that did not fall clattering to the ground.

Then the company of the Cymry who were within the fort gave forth likewise a joyous angry cry, and all their weapons were replaced just as they had been before. And the cries of those two opposing hosts were taken up by screaming of goblins, ghosts, and specters in every glen and hilltop around them, to which the demons of the air responded with a shriek of exultation in contemplation of the rain of blood which they foresaw would drench the soil about that stronghold.

"Who is that horseman who approaches us?" asked Rufinus at my side; for as the screaming echoes died away on each stony headland, a troop of riders detached itself from the host of the barbarians and advanced before our gates. At their head rode an aged warrior, gray-bearded and grim of aspect.

"I believe that to be Cynurig, king of the Iwys," I made reply.

"Tell him to beware of approaching too near," muttered Rufinus to me. "Even a herald must not be permitted to glimpse anything of a garrison's disposition."

"You may come no closer!" I shouted down. "Disclose your name, and declare your purpose!"

The old man upon the horse removed his masked helm, and I saw that he was indeed Cynurig, cruel lord of the Iwys.

"I am Cynric, son of Cerdic, Woden-born king of the Gewissae!" cried the gray-bearded rider, "and I have come to demand hostages of Maelgun, falsely calling himself Dragon of Bryttene. I think you will be wise to heed my words, for as you see I have at my back the greatest host that has been in the world. Every tribe that lives about the West-sae has sent its war-band; every people dwelling between the land of the Fresland and Mearc-wudu has levied a forest of spears.

"See, here I bear the enchanted sword Hunlafing, which Aetla the World-conqueror gave to Hengest in token of rule over the Island of Bryttene! Each time this blade is bared, it slays its man; it never misses its stroke, and no one recovers from the wound it gives. Open your gates and deliver up your king, before my wrath becomes aroused!"

I wished that young Elffin had been there to deliver the reply of the Cymry, for I knew how such words must have galled him. Still, I had heard the young princes boasting at their feasting, and it was for me (Rufinus could understand nothing of this exchange) to speak as I fancied Elffin might have done.

"The kings and princes of Prydein assembled with their hosts within this mighty fortress regard your threats as but the crowing of a cock upon a dunghill!" I shouted back, in that harsh voice which some have unkindly likened to a jay's cry.

"You incite us and revile us and speak evil of us, which does but raise our anger and ire the higher. For the dispossessed rabble from overseas which stands at your back, Cynurig, I say that shortly those few who are found still alive will be exhorting and praising and speaking well of us. And as for you, bold blusterer from the outlands, there is a king here will shear the head off you, who will trample on your cheek."

Cynurig turned his serpent's glare full upon me, but before he could speak, a giant warrior among his company cried out in a voice of thunder:

"Ah, is it you, one-eyed deceiver of mankind? Now I think you find yourself in a trap from which even your cunning cannot deliver you! Do you not know me? I believe you will have cause to do so before the day be out: I am Beowulf, the son of Ecgtheow, lord of the Geatas, and there are few who can boast that they have escaped from my grasp, once set about them."

The champion raised his masked helm, grinning up at me with his bear's fangs, and brandished a great sword above his head.

"With this good blade Naegling I sought out the fell prowler of the mere, slaying her in her lair. It is a weapon whose hilt you may yet feel grind against your breastbone. I am not Woden-born, as is Cynric, the shadow of whose sword Hunlafing lies over all this land; but I think it likely I shall become the Woden-slayer before the sun seeks his ocean resting place!

"Likewise will I seek out the prince who calls himself Dragon of the Island, and it will be no maiden's embrace which he feels about him in that hour. There is a good fight coming. We shall stand on slaughtered Bryttas, on heaps of sword-sated slain, like eagles on their crags. Our fame will be great whether we die today or tomorrow. No man may live beyond that evening in which the shears are destined to slice the thread of his *wyrd*!"

With this speech Beowulf concluded his battle-boast, swelling out his huge chest until it seemed it might burst his weighty coat of mail asunder, exulting with a deep growl of laughter which was taken up by the innumerable host of the barbarians, rolling from rank to rank like the deep-throated roar of ocean at the time of incoming tide.

"You rail at my one eye!" I called down mockingly, though glad enough of the steep rampart and high palisade which stood between me and the doughty subject of my jibe. "Yet I can see enough to tell me that a steadfast talker wins more by his words than his deeds. As has been said: 'Usual after arrogance is lasting death.' I am no warrior, but a bard of the Brython whose task it is to speak as a herald on behalf of the great king Maelgun the Tall, son of Cadwallon Lawhir, ruler of Gwynedd and lord of the tribes of Cunedda. My muse is my ash-spear.

"It is this that I am required to say to you, and afterward I think it will be with sharper tools than tongues that our armies speak each to the other:

"As long as rocks remain over shores, and streams continue to flow, and the sun ascends his bright arc, and the moon passes through her changes, and the earth stays steady upon its pillared base, we will not flee from this place."

The giant who called himself lord of the Geatas growled in his beard at this, and I confess that I hoped devoutly that I would have no occasion to feel his hug that day. He looked as if he would have made reply, but Cynurig the king flourished his spear above his head and spoke what was in his mind:

"The sea is angry, the ocean stormy. Dark waves will shortly dash themselves angrily against this cliff, when we shall see how firm it stands. Spearmen of the Angel-cynn and you, valiant warriors from beyond the West-sae, look above you: The Raven is circling, dark and dusky! Look about you: The gray wanderer of the moors does not hide the slaughter-rune! Raise high the White Dragon, the *tuuf* of the heirs of Aetla, ravager of the world! Follow the bold bee-eater, valiant son of Ecgtheow who slew Grendel and Grendel's dam, over the wall and into the hold!

"I go now to perform *blot*, that the gods may grant us the victory we have been promised. But first I invoke the Masked One, dedicating the foe as a blood sacrifice for him to trample down upon his eight-legged steed."

With which the old king drew back his spear and flung it with all his strength, so that it whistled over the heads of Rufinus and myself, falling somewhere within the fortress behind us.

"Woden owneth you all!" he cried in a terrible voice, which thundered echoing from the throats of every one of the hundred thousand warriors of the barbarian host assembled outside our ramparts. Theirs was the shout of a victorious host, as I recognized with mounting dread in my heart.

Almost in the same moment the gate-tower upon which we stood echoed to a sudden loud clatter reverberating below us to our left. This was followed in swift succession by a heavy jerk which made the gate-tower shudder upon its supporting timbers. The triumphant yell of the barbarians was stilled as suddenly as if muffled by a cloak, and their faces turned as one to gaze above them.

As if in reply to Cynurig's spear-cast, something glittered overhead like a lightning bolt, flashing over all the host, high as larks soar on a day of fair weather when there is no wind. Scarcely curving in its arc, it disappeared in a moment somewhere far off upon the dark hillside beyond. Then every awestruck face turned back as one to the bastion beside us.

Rufinus uttered an exclamation of anger. "Fools!" he yelled. "Who gave you the order to shoot?"

It was men manning the great engine he showed me earlier who, unable to resist the opportunity, had released a missile against the besiegers. Following the tribune as he hastened down to the rampart, I overheard his furious grumbles:

"Idiots! But what can you expect of men who have never seen a real war? Wet behind the ears, they think the *fulminalis* a sling to be shot off whenever an idle moment comes their way. Don't they understand the purpose of heavy artillery? Now, men, perhaps you can tell me who gave the order to shoot, and who drew the cord? If you must take matters into your own hands, perhaps you might consider recalling my instructions concerning the elevation and depression of the *cochleae machina*. Remember: when in doubt, wind the roller low. A missile aimed too high is a missile wasted, whereas one too low will at least throw up dust and provide your attacker with food for thought."

The men stood around looking sheepish, while Rufinus stooped lovingly over his engine, examining its workings, and glancing up from time to time to deliver a running commentary unintelligible to his hearers. I for my part stood at the parapet, watching with satisfaction the unexpected effect of the accidental demonstration upon the enemy. Cries of distress were emitted and looks of dismay displayed by many, and there was a confused attempt at a general movement to the rear.

Seizing the opportunity, I leaned over and called loudly to Cynurig: "Did you think to offer us up to the god whom you worship, O pale-faced Saeson? I think, however, it is you, skulking foxes from the estuaries, who have passed beneath the Spear of Leu!"

Cynurig scowled savagely at me with his serpent's eyes as he turned his horse's head to follow his host. I misliked much more, however, the ill glint his giant champion bestowed upon me.

"You need not think to frighten such men as we with your jesting tricks," he snarled, opening his jagged fangs toward me. "There are warriors here who many a time have encountered such wired engines, which spit forth deadly spears from their dark bellies. We have men who have fought with the Rumwalas beside the Wendel-sae, Francan and Wendlas, who understand such arts."

I translated this for the tribune's benefit. He rose and, looking searchingly at the enemy, nodded his head.

"He is right enough. See, those with the red heads and short-hafted axes are Franks and those with the plaited fair hair, Vandals. I see no siege-engines among them here, but they are not the men to be frightened by them without cause. I think the time has come, Merlin, for us all to make ready. They have been startled for a moment, but it will not be long before they are back. Then it will be for the purpose of exchanging deadlier objects than insults, if I am not mistaken. I intend to observe their movements here from the gate-tower for the present. What will you do?"

"I will go to the king. It is him they seek to slay, for should he fall, then all is lost."

"So you think the day may yet be saved?" asked the tribune, with a quizzical smile.

"I do not say so. Who can know the when and where of his *dihenydd*? Like leaves from the treetops will each man pass away when his *tynged* is fulfilled. We have a task before us, and this is no time to ponder what may or may not be, before night closes upon this scene."

So saying, I made my way to the king's tent. Maelgun was seated upon his throne unarmed save for a fork of white hazel in his hand, his cloak wrapped about him, and a gold brooch upon his cloak. Idno Hen, his chief druid, sat upon his left, and the blessed Cubi upon his right. Maelgun and the officers of his court were listening to the recitation of a *cyfarwydd,* skillful teller of tales, who recounted stories of cattle raids, battles, and sieges, of deeds of champions and heroes, and of victories of great kings of former times: Cunedda, Emrys, Arthur. When the *cyfarwydd* ceased from utterance, there was heard a sudden fluttering and whirring as the banner of the Red Dragon was borne about the enclosure, that banner whose habit it was to cause bones and skulls to be split asunder, and blood to flow to the ankles.

All was then silent within the fort as Taliesin placed himself in the midst of the royal *gosgordd* and sang before them the sacred song "The

Monarchy of Prydein." That was a fitting song for the glorious company of the Cymry: uproar, fire, and thunder and spring tide.

Next Idno Hen gathered his druids about him and flung three goblets of water upon the wind, uttering these words as he did so:

"Three showers of fire will be rained upon the faces of the false Iwys, with which will I draw forth from them two thirds of their courage and their skill at arms and their strength, and I will bind their urine within their bodies and in the bodies of their horses. Each breath exhaled by the men of the Cymry will increase their courage and skill at arms and strength. Should they remain at war for seven years, no weariness will they know!"

Strength came to the hearts of the men of the Cymry when that charm was uttered. And there was strength likewise in the water from his holy well at Fynnon Gybi which the blessed Cubi sprinkled upon the rampart and upon the host, uttering these words:

"It is a city of protection; it is not a weakness to sing it. It is a strong rampart without reluctance against men, against devils. Unto God is this the strongest of prayers; against the Devil it is a great strength; it is a sword-psalm, a shield-hymn. The war shout of this host will be a noble song, heard throughout the halls of Heaven; it is this host which will raise the knee to Crist, will grasp His cheek, will suck His nipple.

"The redoubtable host of the king is that along with whom I will fight; this cry of mine will be a match for the Devil. I will be a surety on their behalf!"

Now when the host hearkened to the spell of the druid and the spell of the saint, not easy was it for them to decide which of the two was more potent in enchantments, in wizardry, or in binding. Thus it was not possible to say that there were not druidical powers nor secret spells protecting the place of refuge.

But then came one running from the ramparts to say that the hosts of the foemen were assembling in waves like the daughters of Manawydan when at the worst season of winter they dash against the headland of Penrin Blathaon in the north, overwhelming rocks and cliffs and land. Moreover, the men of the Iwys had erected a great scaffold, and upon it a black tent, and within the tent squatted a sorceress who was raising a storm of sorcery against the men of the Cymry, so that few could withstand it. From each of her fingers she shot sharp arrows, and every arrow found its man.

I saw Maelgun turn pale on receiving this ill news, and I guessed he thought upon the ill deeds he had committed, the curse of Gildas the Wise, and the violation of his *cynneddyf*. He remembered, too, the ill dreaming he had undergone upon Dinleu Gurygon, though of that at that time I knew nothing. For a witch's arrows are wont to seek out the weak places about a man, where his unchancy actions have laid open the orifices of his body so that noxious things may enter.

"Merlin," said Maelgun, "will you play at *gwyddbwyll?*"

"I will, lord," I made reply.

Then a youth of the king's household brought before us the king's board of silver with its golden pieces, and we began to play. And that was the *clas* of Leu upon which we played, the board being within the rampart of the *caer,* the *caer* encircled by the rim of the world, all reflected in the firmament above, where the great game is likewise played. Each corner of the board was lit by a precious stone, even the four corners of the Island of Prydein: Penrin Blathaon in the north, Penrin Penwaed in the south, Crigyl in the west, and Ruohim in the east. I misliked what I saw before me, for that was an ugly checkerboard to me, and there was upon it a move of banishment.

"For what stake do we play?" asked Maelgun Gwynedd. "It is usual when playing at *gwyddbwyll* that there should be a stake."

"For the Thirteen Treasures of the Island of Prydein," I replied. "That is to say, for the Mantle of Tegau Eurvron, Dernwin the Sword of Ryderch Hael, the Hamper of Gwyndo Garanhir, the Horn of Bran Galed, the Chariot of Morgan Mwynfawr, the Halter of Clydno Eidyn, the Knife of Lawfroded Marchog, the Cauldron of Dyrnach Gawr, the Whetstone of Tudwal Tudglyd, the Coat of Padarn Peisrudd, the Crock of Rygenyd the Cleric, the *Gwyddbwyll* Board of Gwendolau mab Ceidio, and the Mantle of Arthur in Cerniu."

Maelgun Gwynedd laughed shortly at these words.

"You are a strange man and a bold, Merlin mab Morfryn. That I will say for you. The most part of those Treasures are held in the North, and that is no very chancy place to visit."

"That is true, O king," I answered. "Still, that is the stake for which I must play, for good or ill."

"What will you do with the Thirteen Treasures should you chance to win them?" asked the king.

"I will return with them to the Ty Gwydr, where Gofannon mab Don wrought them, toiling nine years below the deep."

"I do not think that will be the easiest task in the world, but if such be the stake which you have chosen, then it is for that we will play."

So we played, Maelgun the Tall and I, while the battle raged about the walls of Dineirth. In the air about us was darkness and tumult from the flapping of the wings of ravens innumerable, gathering from afar to croak over the place of slaughter; while without the rampart arose another tumult and nebulosity from the groaning of men tearing each other asunder in the conflict. We marveled at the extent of the carnage and destruction and confusion which shook the fortress and surged about the Chariot of the Bear, of which Maelgun was the rider and I the driver. We who directed the ancient wheel-rim might not sleep; it was for us to look ahead, to look behind and before, to right and left. We looked, we defended, we protected, so that the wheel-rim running under us might not be shattered through neglect or violence.

And while we were playing at *gwyddbwyll* in this manner, there came running to us where we sat at our table a youth with yellow curling hair and blue eyes, who bore in his hand a heavy blue-bladed sword.

"Lord," he exclaimed, "there is bad news from before the gateway, where men are withholding the assault with blood pouring down their cheeks!"

"Move your piece," said Maelgun to me. "What is that bad news?"

"It is that the witch of the Saeson is sending arrows against us from each of her fingers, and every arrow grievously wounds the man it strikes."

"That is bad news indeed," replied the king. "It seems the day is going ill for us."

So we played at *gwyddbwyll* until a second young man came running to where we sat before the king's tent. He was a ruddy-complexioned warrior with auburn hair and a freshly trimmed beard.

"Lord," he shouted, "there is ill news from without the walls, where leaders charging before the armies are being cut down like rushes!"

"Move your piece," said Maelgun to me. "What is that bad news?"

"The witch that is with the Saeson is employing her magic arts, reciting her incantations, sending spells upon the wind, so that those of the Iwys whom we slay are restored to life and returned to the fray."

"That is bad news indeed," replied the king. "It seems the day is going ill for us."

Again we continued to play at *gwyddbwyll,* when of a sudden there arose a great and terrible shout from the summit of the ramparts. The king looked at me, and I at him. It was in our minds that the host was destroyed by the enchantments of the evil creature who aided the barbarians with her enchantments. We feared lest it be the Witch of Ystyfachau, or the Hag from the Hall of Afarnach, or one of the Nine Witches from the Uplands of Ystafengun; we feared that the time of the Cath Palug was come upon the Island of the Mighty, as foretold in the lore of the land.

Then there came running to us where we sat below the banner of the Red Dragon a third young man, of noble bearing, with ruddy cheeks and large hawk's eyes. He bore a spear with a square-pointed head, and there was a deep wound-mark bleeding upon his brow.

"Lord," he cried, though he was spare of breath, "I bring you news from the rampart!"

"Move your piece," said Maelgun to me. "I believe, Merlin, that this is bad news he brings us."

There is good fortune and ill fortune when playing at *gwyddbwyll,* and so I threw the die.

"What is your news?" asked Maelgun Gwynedd of the youth.

"It is this, lord. The witch of the Saeson has sent a storm of sorcery about the men of the Cymry, so that we might scarcely see the field, fighting one with another in our confusion, one champion falling across the other, warriors wandering from the shield-wall in their weariness. And when we slew the warriors of the Iwys, she raised them from the dead, so that they fought with us once more with renewed strength. There was a cry of despair from the host; though we fought like bloodhounds in close ranks and stubbornly, yet might we not withstand the battle onslaught of the whelps of Hengys. Our shields were shattered, our spears no protection. It is a conflict of a hundred thousand with three hundred, bloodily splashing spears upon a field of slaughter."

"Then that is bad news indeed," said Maelgun, moving his piece upon the checkerboard.

"There is bad and good, lord," exclaimed the young man. "For the lord of the Rufeinwyr, the *tryffin* whom Gereint of Dyfneint brought to the hosting at Dinleu Gurygon, has constructed a monstrous creature of wood and wire which squats upon a bastion by the gateway of the stronghold. From its belly it shoots forth spears greater than any man might bear, flying faster and farther than a javelin flung by the hand of a mighty prince. He calls it 'Lightning,' and indeed its darts are like those which Mabon mab Mellt hurls from within black rolling clouds when thunderstorms gather about the uplands of Godeu."

"Has he discharged this weapon against the enemy host?" I asked curiously.

"He has indeed. The first shaft flew over the heads of the whole host of the Iwys, and I heard the *tryffin* cursing the men who aid him, in the broken-tongued language of his own people."

"Did he not shoot another spear at the enemy?" inquired Maelgun, shaking the die.

"He did," replied the messenger, who was short of breath from his exertions.

"And did that one also pass over the host?"

"It did not. It slew three chieftains of the Iwys who were standing at the foot of the witch's tower, nailing them together like quails on a spit."

"Then that is good news," said Maelgun to me, "though it may be that the slaying of three men among a hundred thousand will not turn the tide of battle. Play your game, Merlin."

"There is better news than that, lord," continued the youth, wiping the blood from his eyes.

"And what is that?"

"This: that the *tryffin* was angered once more, and his cries sounded fierce and harsh as yonder kite which circles above us. With his own hands he moved one of the monster's limbs, and then drew the leash by which he guides it. A third spear flew forth, so fast that all I saw was a glint such as the sunlight makes upon the ripple of a lake."

"Was its aim more sure this time?" I asked, removing a piece from the board as I turned toward the man.

"Sure enough, Merlin. The witch whom the Iwys brought with them was screaming shrill spells from her scaffold, when the great four-sided ash-hafted spear-blade entered her gap-toothed mouth. Passing through the length of her body, it emerged from her anus as swiftly as it had entered her mouth, and upon its barbs were clustered the entrails and intestines of her body, which were borne dripping away into the hillside beyond. And from the witch's empty body there wailed forth a scream as piercingly wild as though the Cave of Uffern were opened wide, and all the Hosts of Annufn riding upon the gale with Gwyn mab Nud at their head.

"The *tryffin* cried out, too, though I think from pleasure: for he clapped the men that serve him upon their shoulders and smiled upon them. It is not usual for him to smile."

So the messenger departed, returning to play his part in the battle.

"Play the game, Merlin," said the king once more. "What do you make of this news? Is it good, or is it bad?"

"It is both good and bad, lord," I replied: "good that the witch is slain; bad that we are but three hundred men fighting against a hundred thousand."

"Then let us hope that the good enjoys better fortune than the bad," rejoined the king, shaking the die long within the dark hollow cave of his hands.

All these things which had passed thus far had taken place beyond our vision, though we heard the terrible yelling of the hosts and of the demons who resided within their weapons and in the air above the place of battle. But now even where we sat, Maelgun and I at our checkerboard, could we see arising in the sky a storm of spears and arrows and sling shots, which descended upon the ramparts like a swarm of stinging bees from heaven on a summer meadow, and clustered about the gate-tower like a cloud of rooks over elm groves at autumn, striking the strong palisade like a winter hail-shower lashing the shingled roof of a kingly hall.

Now was the tempest truly arisen, and the king and I bent our heads over the board, playing the hardest of games of *gwyddbwyll* that ever was played. The king which stood at the center of the board trembled from the fury and shock and savagery of the fighting, and seemed like to be shifted from his place.

"Men of the Cymry, children of Prydein mab Aed Mawr!" cried Maelgun aloud. "Fight against the pale-faced sons of Hengys, crush your foes utterly; behead them and scatter them in revenge for your kinsmen and comrades who have died at their hands! And may the protection of Heaven, the longed-for land, the home of enlightenment, be yours in the place of strife! May you have a welcome there among the host, in perfect unison with the Trinity!"

But the king's hair had grown dark and his eye dull, and he was changed from his usual form and figure. No man heard his prayer save I, Merlin mab Morfryn; for the wrath and anger and blood-frenzy which was upon the hosts was such that none who were engaged in the battle had his mind on any matter in the world save fighting and slaughter. Pitiless and cruel was the combat: Champions, reapers like leeks of battle greedy for corpses, hewed at each other with bright blue-bladed swords, and thrust at each other with thick-shafted crimson-headed spears, so that arms and legs and heads were hacked from bodies, and pieces of flesh so cut about that they flew off like lightly driven leaves at autumn. Such was the strife between the men of the Cymry with the mongrel hosts of Loiger before the gates of Dineirth.

We who played at *gwyddbwyll* before the king's tent heard only the harsh shouts of the battle leaders, men laughing loudly, shields resounding like the thunder of heaven before the onslaught of the foemen's spears, snorting of horses, screaming of eagles eager for blood. Earth and sky shook, and the outcry and tumult echoed among rocks and crags and distant hills. Not long was it before we heard, too, the clatter of swords ringing against the stockade, and the clatter of shields in the gateway.

Black ravens were glutted upon the rampart; bloodstained checkered cloth was trampled into the thirsty earth; the trees of battle were trodden down in retribution for earning of mead. The pale mead which the heroes drank at their lord's feast was their poison; fighting in order as was their due, the inescapable tryst with death overtook the lords of the Cymry. Though they went to churches to do penance, both old and young, strong and feeble, the inescapable tryst with death overtook them. After the exultation of battle there fell a silence upon the field. Blood lay wet upon the green grave-mounds.

Though our men slew seven times their number of the crafty men of Loiger, yet were their lives short and the grief for them long among their kinsmen. Many wives were made widows; many a mother had tears upon her eyelids; the blows of the warriors rang in the heads of women. All the land about the rampart was taken and ravaged by the surge of the heathen rabble. Like the rushing rough flooding of high tide, the wave-breast of the blue-topped stormy floodtide, was the onrush of the enemy. Now was Dineirth abandoned like a rock washed by the incoming tide, a slab of rock in a cleared country, a lone hill on the borderlands of Prydein.

A messenger hastened to us from the gate-tower, a look of fear upon his face.

"What news?" inquired Maelgun without raising his face from the board.

"Bad news, lord," cried the messenger. "It is said that a huge bear has been seen advancing in the forefront of Cynurig's army, and always he is nearest to where the king is. He slays more men with his iron-clawed paws than any five of the king's champions, and there is none among your *gosgordd* who may stand against him. Blows and missiles glance from his hide, he tramples underfoot both men and horses of the Cymry, and he crunches everything near him between his teeth. His grip is greater than that of thirty men, and each one of the men of the Cymry that he takes within his grasp he crushes within his arms so that he makes of him a marrow-mash, flesh and bones, sinews and skin broken up together. His strength and ferocity are such that murmurs of dismay have arisen throughout the host. There is fear and distress among them, for he is approaching the gates, and I do not believe that bolts and bars may withstand his strength."

"The news is bad indeed," groaned Maelgun. "Will you play your game, Merlin?"

It was in this moment of despair, when the mail-clad hosts of the enemy were come like a gray swarm about us, that I learned the noble measure of Rufinus the tribune. He was truly an unyielding gate, an unshakable fortress of refuge. He was calm and civil to those who pressed about him; he was a pillar of the army, which trusted him. None called on Rufinus but he would be there. As Taliesin sang, he was,

> Like a wolf at his feeding, raising eyes in grim glare;
> With his spear-eyes keen-gazing, a snake's stare from its lair.

I saw him descending briskly from the rampart, just as there came a dreadful crashing at the gates. Catching my eye resting on him, he called out cheerfully: "Things are warming up, Merlin! I have not been in so tight a spot since Totila took Rome and cooped us up in the Mausoleum of Hadrian! We were surrounded and starving, nothing to eat but our horses—and we drew the line at that. But despite all, our commander refused to surrender—and here am I to tell the tale! We shall pull through yet, mark my words."

I could not share the tribune's confidence; nor, I felt sure, did he believe his own words. But his quick eye and calm manner cheered the young men of Elffin's *gosgordd,* who desired only that it might be said of them in after times:

> "Before they were slain, they slew."

Now Rufinus summoned to him the war-band whose duty it was to guard the king, who had until now remained beside his royal tent, chafing for the fray. Together they went to the hut I had entered with him earlier, dragging out the small war-engines the tribune had exhibited with such pride. Even as they did so, there came a splintering crash like that of a mighty oak uprooted at the height of a tempest's rage, and the gates of Dineirth were burst asunder. Bolts, bars, and broad oak planks were splintered and shattered, as through them broke a huge stone, greater than any two strong men could lift.

Every eye within the fortress was turned upon the dark opening of the entrance, while for a space all was quiet and it seemed time stood still within us. Rufinus alone remained busy supervising his men. His task swiftly completed, he swung on his heel and returned to the place where the king and I sat bowed over our board.

"How goes the game, Merlin? I was never one for such myself, though long ago in Alexandria, I used to watch my friend Apollos gamble the night away. I suppose I lacked the brains; besides, I never enjoy leaving anything to chance. *'Iacta alea est,'* Caesar said before crossing the Rubicon. That is true. However, as I recall, he had taken the precaution to have the Thirteenth Legion at his back when he said it!"

"Well said, old friend!" I replied, looking up at him while I shook the dice briskly. "I believe that what can be done, you will do. But it is necessary also to take chance into account. Look at our game here, which lies between Maelgun and myself. I make a skillful move, having pondered long; the king counters it with another. Our minds are pitted one against the other, and he whose thought is keenest, who looks now this way and now that, like an eagle upon his pinnacle, will outwit another whose thought is lax, or who possesses too much or too little confidence.

"Skill seems all—but then comes the dice-throw, when chance may overthrow the adroitest move. It is necessary, therefore, so far as one may, to make allowance for the intervention of chance, as well as the reasoned move your foeman makes. Nor is chance to be neglected or despised because it appears random or unreflecting. For it is by means of chance that the gods intervene in our affairs: This world and all that lies beneath the blue arch of heaven are ruled and directed by chance."

"Still the old philosopher, eh? Even when the barbarians are battering at the gates, you ponder these questions, wise Merlin! Well, each to his own task. Rest assured, I am leaving nothing to chance here!"

The tribune uttered a grim laugh, glancing keenly about him as he spoke. I believe that even now he was calculating the effect his apparent coolness would have upon the spirits of the soldiers who watched his every movement.

"You see how it is, Merlin: In a moment such as this every soldier's mind is bent upon decisive action, leaving scant room for the element of choice or chance which attends upon your more leisurely meditations."

"True," I replied, flinging down the die. "But the more decisive the differing actions of many men assembled in one place may be, the more fiercely they conflict with one another. The outcome of all those conflicting actions is the aggregate of all, which, as I have said, is chance. Not one of the chain of events which brings you here, so far from your home, but was the consequence of an infinite number of different decisions, made by you and others. But did you or they ever intend that you should voyage from Africa to Prydein? I think not, though at one time I confess I thought you came here on purpose, and that a purpose other than that which you avowed."

With these words I cast down the dice upon the board. It was an ugly number, an ill throw, that I saw before me.

"You see?" I said, removing the king's principal defender. "Chance achieved that mischance, though the pieces had been skillfully set out. Yet now we know that, from the moment the king and I sat down to play, it had been decided the game would go in this way and not another. And who, think you, was it that made the decision? Not I, nor Maelgun, but another greater than either of us."

"Point taken," rejoined Rufinus affably. "And now, if you will excuse me, I will return to the humdrum business of issuing orders and enforcing decisions. For, if I am not mistaken, the moment which we may call the pivot of the battle is arrived."

A cry arose about the western entrance of Dineirth. Looming out of the shadows beneath the gate-tower appeared that gigantic champion of the barbarians with whom I had rashly exchanged taunts at the enemy's first approach. His mail-coat now hung open, and was encrusted with broken flesh and running gore. He bore no blade in his huge hands, no lime-white shield or holly-hafted spear; but the nails of his fingers dripped blood, and blood oozed out of his great rough-toothed jaws. A grizzled beard covered his cheeks up to his blood-red eyes, and like a furry pelt was the hair upon his hands and massive column of his chest, so that he did indeed appear a very bear upon the trackway.

"What seek you here, in the king's fortress?" at length cried out a lord of the Cymry.

For a space of time the barbarian said nothing, but glared about him, reared up upon his hind legs, so that his helm all but scraped the beam of the lintel. His red eyes were glazed, he snarled and growled by angry starts, seeming to search for a victim upon whom he could unleash the storm-rage of his strength. It could be seen that the battle frenzy, *angerd,* was upon him; he ground his teeth upon the broken jamb of the gate, leaving upon it fang-gashes and blood-froth.

"I am Beowulf son of Ecgtheow, lord of the Wederas and a prince of the Geatas!" he roared. "I am a warrior hardy under his helm, whose fame is known in many lands. Kites and crows follow my path, and the gray wanderer upon the moors is gorged wherever I pass. I am here to seek tribute from the dark Bryttas for the Woden-born king, Cynric son of Cerdic, lord of the Gewissae! I am here to bear off your people into thralldom, to bind them with sinews, and sell them overseas in the marketplaces of the Fresna-cynn! When you have consented to these things, we will depart from this place and leave you in peace.

For we do not intend to allow one among you to remain behind alive within this stronghold!"

At first none answered the barbarian's demand, for he was dreadful to look upon, appearing rather a monstrous creature out of Annufn than a warrior of human form. It was the tribune who replied at last in a level voice:

"None of these things will happen as you have devised them, barbarian! None here will give tribute to such as you or your king; none will be sold into slavery. I am the captain of this fort, which I hold for the great king whom you see here. It belongs to him whose ancestors received it of old from the hands of the emperor of the Romans. You have no right to it, and I have these words to say to you, which I heard my great master Belisarius utter to the heralds of Witigis in the Senate of Rome itself: The time will come when you shall be glad to hide your heads under the thornbushes, and shall be unable to do so. It is impossible for me to surrender this stronghold while I am alive."

The giant in the gateway turned his bloodshot gaze upon the officer, and it was not a look that anyone would care to receive. But Rufinus appeared unruffled, calling out a command to the men beside him.

"Your words are brave, old man," growled out the enemy champion scornfully, "and it may be we shall see shortly how your deeds will match them! That is not for me to try, however. Before long I shall set these arms about yonder king, who vaunts himself the Dragon of the Island, and it will be no maiden's embrace he feels in that hour, I assure you! I have slain sea monsters and fen-dwellers, as well as men unnumbered, and it will go hard with me if I cannot measure my strength against that of this Dragon.

"Now is the last hour come: Ravens are screeching; the gray-coated wolf is howling; the spear rings out; the shield will echo to the spear-shaft. Soon will arise such deeds of woe as will satisfy even the deadly spite of Cynric of the serpent's eye.

"As for you, bold-spoken chieftain of the Rumwalas, I believe that you are looking for the last time upon this earth, though, as I see you are a cripple, it is not for strength such as mine to measure itself against your weakness.

"So I leave you, though it may be not for long. Soon will these walls echo to the cracking of that great king's ribs; soon will the blood start from his veins; soon will the Dragon's eyes be squeezed from their sockets and glazed in dreaded death."

The champion departed, and I felt great pity for Maelgun that his son Run was not by, nor any other champion of the Cymry, to answer the stranger's taunts. For the king himself might not fight, since it was his part to perform the rites and play at *gwyddbwyll* in the Center.

"Well, if words were arrows, we should all be dead by now!" called out Rufinus cheerfully. "To your posts, men. It is ever the way of barbarians to puff themselves up with vain boasts before a battle. I have seen the backs of better men than that lubberly fellow in my time, and will do so again. Ah, I thought as much!"

The tribune's exclamation sprang from the appearance of shadowy figures looming within the gateway. If the grim champion had aroused involuntary fear in many a breast, those who replaced him appeared no less daunting. Crowding for protection against the timbered walls of the entrance, sheltered by the remnants of the gate, a score or so of savage-looking ruffians I saw skulking in the shadows at the threshold of Dineirth. At once I recognized them as warriors of the Freinc, those whom Rufinus had pointed out to me from the parapet.

Just as the champion of the Iwys appeared a shambling beast from the Otherworld, so these men resembled demons from the Pit of Annufn. With their long hair died crimson, swept up stiff and spiky, they were naked to the waist, clad only in leather trousers. Their eyes were set and sharp and cold as those of snakes, and the frames of their bodies, bare above leathern trousers, were hard and sinewy. Each bore in his hand a heavy double-edged axe, mounted on a short wooden handle. My heart missed more than one beat as I recalled what Rufinus had told me: that it is the practice of these people to run in fearlessly upon their foes, hurling their axes (which they call *francisca*) with such deadly force and accuracy that they shatter shields and pierce breastplates.

What affrighted me worst of all was the way in which their killers' eyes were fixed unwaveringly upon the figure of Rufinus, where he stood among his men not a bow-shot from them. Their shadowy forms came and went within the gloom, but always I saw each gaze directed toward one target. It was not hard to guess that the person of the tribune was being pointed out to each in turn.

It is the custom of kings to maintain on their borderlands bands of young men whom men call Sons of Death and the like. They obey the laws of neither gods nor men, and possess no fief but that which is bestowed in a wood or a mountain. Between the ages of fourteen and twenty they live severed from all ties of kindred, outside their tribe, filled only with desire and willfulness. It is their way to go a-wolfing, committing lawless depredations upon men of property, maltreating women, and fighting with rival bands of their own sort. Each youth bears upon his brow a demon-mark, that the friends of his band may know him and his foes fear him.

At times kings find employment for these Sons of Death, dispatching them against those foes within or without the tribe at whom they may not strike openly. Then the Sons of Death make a vow of evil to slay or mutilate that man against whom the king points his finger. There is no kingdom but sustains its Sons of Death dwelling upon the margins of territory of the tribe, but of all nations upon earth it is the Freinc who supply the greatest number of these landless wolfmen, undertaking contracts for foreign kings as readily as their own.

I sat with a *gwyddbwyll* piece poised in my fingers, gripped with fear. Rufinus paced about, calmly instructing the warriors and workmen with him. I longed to give a warning cry, but the word froze on my lips. It was impossible to believe that the tribune was not aware also of the danger that menaced him from the black-mouthed gateway, and a shout might precipitate that which was held back but for a suspended moment.

Others besides myself had grasped the danger, but paused likewise transfixed where they stood about the enclosure and upon the ramparts. Rufinus alone moved and spoke quietly in the stillness, as if he were a sole living man among the dead. Indeed, I saw him for a moment as the last man alive on earth, in the awful moment when the busy life of man comes to be extinguished by lawless encroachments of the Coranieid, leaving a world forever silent in the empty frozen wastes of Uffern. That he was not of the people or tongue of the Cymry, but a foreigner, *alltud,* but made the image the more poignant and terrible to me. For it was as a man unsustained by links of law or kindred, custom or tribe, that he met his fate; and that is what we all must do at the end, when the sudden moment comes to tread alone the windy Halls of Annufn.

Then of a sudden, after what seemed a cycle of stillness, there came a harsh cry out of the shadows: a cry out of Annufn, a cry taken up by ravens strutting on the battlements and perched on every rooftree. It was the cry of the captain of the Sons of Death, and like wolves the wolfmen sprang forth from the entrance, each with his keen-bladed axe swung back for flinging. At once several spears were raised among the men of the Brython, but the gleaming gray wolves' eyes were fixed without wavering upon that man alone at whose head they had launched their vow of evil.

Like the stoop of a peregrine was the lithe pounce of the wolfmen of the Freinc, as each whipped back his axe for its hurling; like the rasping scream of the airborne predator was their howl of hunger for blood; and like a helpless heron straddling a stream in the path of the death-stroke was the tribune in my eyes at that instant.

"Now: before they are clear of the portal!" shouted Rufinus sharply. Still the scene was frozen before my numbed mind, frozen as it remains now in my memory, even as I recall it to you, O king. There stood Rufinus, hands on hips with his back to me; beyond, sprung like bent bows, bounded forward his murderers.

And then everything changed with marvelous rapidity, so that for a moment it seemed in truth that one picture had been substituted for another. Immediately following Rufinus' shout came a sharp, rhythmic clatter, like that which is heard within a winnowing shed when a team of slaves is engaged in flailing wheat in orderly succession, the first man in the rank beginning his task anew exactly as the last leaves off.

From the chest of the foremost Freinc there suddenly sprouted a short shaft, no more than a man's forearm in length. His gray snake's eyes were dilated in disbelief (so, too, were mine, I confess) as he stood staring in mid-poise. And then, slowly it seemed, but in reality as swiftly as I may strike my staff here upon the grass, there sprang out another shaft next to the first, and another. I heard the dull thud as each smacked home among the man's ribs, and saw the dark blood well about the place where each arrow planted itself. The fellow staggered; and then, as shaft after shaft struck him, he was flung heavily over upon his back.

Next it seemed as if the scene was being repeated, for the bare-chested barbarians behind the fallen man were in turn spinning and falling, as bolt after bolt whirred and struck deep into their soft flesh. They were tumbled in a heap, neither groaning nor moving, but the darts still flew with unceasing rapidity over their bodies and into the milling throng of their comrades clustering behind in the gateway. Their rage and frenzy spent all in a moment, they were jostling frantically in an effort to flee. But even as they turned, the arrows came streaming in among them. Smack! Smack! Smack! I heard the missiles go driving home, one after the other in perfect regularity. Spinning down to the ground, dead before they reached it, the attackers' flanks and backs were pinned by an orderly progression of the deadly darts, which struck again and again at the same spots, nailing themselves into whatever presented itself before their pitiless stream.

The frozen moment melted away before my eyes. One instant the would-be murderers were bounding out of the gateway, axes poised for hurling; the next they were heaped before it, shafts still pouring past them into the shadows, striking unseen screaming victims crowded behind, unrelenting until a sharper thudding told that no man stood longer in their trackway, and the death-strokes were being vented upon the logged walls of the camp entrance. All fell suddenly still; only a limb continued to shift convulsively upon the heap of white bodies.

The mass of smitten flesh, jumbled together without life or distinctive shape, brought to mind a netted heap of game I had examined at the end of a day's hunting with Prince Elffin in the uplands of Cantre'r Gwaelod. The resemblance was the greater, for along the spine of each man of the fallen Freinc grew a stiff gray-brown crest of boar's bristle.

"Halt!" cried the tribune to his men. "Cease firing! Now, you men, make a shield-wall in the gateway, while these others throw up a barricade!"

Evidently well-rehearsed, those about him dashed forward, leaving the tribune standing alone. As if conscious of our fascinated gaze, he turned about to face Maelgun and myself. I saw that his face was a little set and drawn, though not so much so that any but I might notice. He clapped his hand upon one of the two engines standing beside him, calling out to me in a cheerful voice:

"What do you say, Merlin? Do you think those fellows enjoyed the Scorpion's sting? Old Dionysius of Alexandria should be pleased with himself, wherever he is now, for there are few nowadays in the artillery who set much store by this little one-cubit engine!"

A sound of hammering from within the gateway told that the blockading was proceeding unimpeded, and I could not resist leaving our game for a moment to talk to my friend.

"I should think so!" I replied with enthusiasm. "Why, if we had but a dozen of these we would need no spearmen at all to defend a stronghold such as Dineirth, surely?"

"Don't you believe it, old fellow," rejoined Rufinus. "It is an ingenious toy, I will give you that, but distinctly limited in its uses. We were lucky just then, but now they have seen what the little fellows can do, I doubt they'll be of further use." He patted the engine where it stood stolidly upon its tripod, much as a huntsman bestows affection on an ill-trained hound who has surprised his master with some unexpected feat.

"See, this long block is the case which contains the missiles. They are inserted into that slot, ten at a time. The bottom one falls down onto the slider, which is drawn back by the windlass. Here, try it: Rotate the handle. You see how the stock is withdrawing and the bow being bent all in the same action? There is a double claw raised automatically upon a bronze wedge inside there, which draws back the cord. Right? Well, when the bow is bent this far—keep turning, just a little more—an arrow drops out of the case into its path. You can hear the movement. The missiles are not nocked, so the angle of fall does not affect the firing. Turn the handle a little more, and there you are: Away goes your dart!"

Sure enough, an arrow thudded into the side of the gate-tower, the tribune having raised the machine's alignment by rotating a little screw-headed bar in the base.

"Keep turning!" urged my friend at my ear. I did so, and the cord was drawn back as before until I felt once again the sudden spasm as another arrow was released, striking within two inches of its companion. Greatly delighted with my prowess, and still more fascinated by the beautiful precision with which the machine performed each one of its several tasks of drawing, loading, and loosing, all to the simple rotation of the windlass, I continued winding away until a dull thud told me I had emptied the arrow-case of its contents, which were now set fast in a close-packed clump in the wall of the tower before us.

"Brilliant!" I cried with enthusiasm. "But there are several things I do not understand. Why, for example, do not all the arrows tumble down together before the cord, shooting simultaneously or jamming together inside the machine? And how do the claws manage to release the cord at precisely the right moment, instead of continuing to draw it back? To tell truth, seeing that it can in fact do all these things, I find it hard to understand your lack of enthusiasm for what has proved so effective a weapon."

Rufinus laughed. "I fear we have little enough time for me to act the *praeceptor*. You are right: The machinery for selecting each arrow in turn from the case is extremely ingenious. The slot in the case tapers at the bottom, so that only one arrow may drop out at a time. At that point it is selected by a long roller (operated, like everything else, by the action of the windlass), which has in its side a shallow channel like a groove, in turn bearing the arrow 'round until it drops onto the slider.

"It certainly served its purpose beyond expectation just now, but it is not in general a very serviceable weapon, and I doubt if repeating catapults will ever find much favor in the army."

"But why not, when it seems you can loose off six or seven arrows within the space of time an ordinary machine—like that monster you placed on the bastion, say—can launch one? I found the effect terrifying, I confess. As for the Freinc, they had no time to think at all!"

"True enough," replied the tribune. "But there is much in warfare which appears effective in theory, or even on the training ground, which does not apply in the field. At one time, for example, there was talk of introducing catapults powered by compressed air, but it never came to anything; apparently it is impossible to synchronize the power of the cylinders. Personally I have never seen one of these Scorpions used in action before, but from those who have, I hear the snags are several.

"For instance, what is the point of hitting a man with six darts where one suffices? As you saw for yourself, the missiles have no spread; since the aperture has been laid on a single target, the trajectory is more or less along one segment of a circle. You may hit one man, but the others, if they have any sense, will shift before they can be hit.

"Then again, you must recall that you are not merely wasting good missiles, but actually supplying the enemy with them. Against that, though, it could be said that they are not of immediate practical use, since they are not notched. Notching, as you know, is a major operation which requires a deal of work. No, the art of warfare depends on maneuverability, swiftness of movement, instant adaptation to fresh circumstances. None of those are the characteristics of our friend the Scorpion, I am afraid."

"Well, I think you at least have reason to be grateful to your 'toy,' as you term it!" I rejoined, with what I recognized to be a nervous laugh. Rufinus' words dashed the elation I had momentarily experienced while operating the Scorpion. I am possessed, I think most men will allow, of some versatility and range of knowledge. Warfare, however, was not something to which I had applied my mind greatly. I had experienced an exhilaration when loosing the engine's bolts into the gate-tower which made me temporarily forget the terrible predicament in which we were circumstanced. You feel your mind fly forward with each arrow: a wonderful sensation of vigor and achievement. But that and everything else about us was illusory. Time seemed momentarily suspended; a sinister passivity lay upon our enclosure and all within it.

Rufinus excused himself and departed toward the gateway, while I resumed my place at the *gwyddbwyll* board before Maelgun. The heavy hammering that resounded around the ramparts died away, telling that the broken gates had been replaced with an improvised barricade. Amid much shouting and some laughter I saw men under the tribune's direction trundling a wagon into the entrance, smashing its wheels with axes, and heaping stones and other lumber around it.

The brief hubbub subsided, to be replaced by a renewed oppressive stillness. Our men patrolled the parapet, frequently collecting in groups to discuss some object of interest beyond the walls, but from where I sat it was impossible to distinguish any sign of movement on the part of the enemy host. Yet from what I had seen of them, I could not but believe that the cunning Cynurig was planning some new and devastating assault against our severely depleted band of defenders.

"It is very quiet," Maelgun remarked, gazing reflectively upon the board. "I remember such a day at another time. It was when I was returning from the monastery of the blessed Iltud in Gliwising to regain my patrimony in Gwynedd." He paused, shaking the dice pensively.

"I was traveling alone through the region of Arfon along the causeway of Sarn Helen toward the city of Caer Seint, which lies beside the straits which divide Mon from the mainland. It was there that Macsen Guledig found this silver *gwyddbwyll* board and golden pieces at which we now make our play, which in after time, so it is said, brought about the downfall of that prince of the Rufeinwyr to whom the Brython looked for aid at the first coming of Hengys and the hosts of the heathen to the Island of the Mighty.

"My way led me over many weary heights, steep precipices, and dark valleys. I wandered among the mountains of Eryri, stronghold of Gwynedd, haunt of eagles. I came to a narrow pass, whose mountain walls supported the sky on either side. Sullen slate were those craggy ramparts, somber were the clouds which roofed the pass, and pitch-black was the water of the lake beside which I rode.

"There was no sound in all that huge empty place save that of a wild foaming stream tumbling among rocks, which was silenced when it entered the long cold lake. It is an ill place in which to be at any time. I have heard that the Fair Folk preserve their treasure beneath one of the mountains, and at Fynnon Beris, I spoke with the sacred fish. The water of his well was murky, and the answers I received cloudy, doubtful: boding ill for my enterprise.

"Among the mountains of Eryri it is customary for there to be noise of cataracts tumbling, eagles screaming, stags belling. But in that hour there was a heavy silence, still and threatening. I did not know whether to pursue my course, or return whence I came."

The king paused, frowning to himself, deep in thought.

"You would have been wise to return to the protection of your holy teacher, the blessed Iltud, O king!" ventured Saint Cubi. "You imperiled your immortal soul when you violated those vows you took at the monastery of Laniltud Fawr to remain within the embrace of Mother Church."

"You had no choice," interposed Taliesin sharply, "but to ride on to undying fame and imperishable glory. It was your *tynged* to win back the kingship, and who but Maelgun the Tall, heir of Cunedda Guledig, might sustain the Truth of the Land?"

I said nothing, and the king continued.

"At length I heard the faintest whisper among the rough grasses by my stony track. I thought it at first, so gentle and caressing it sounded, the conversation of the Fair Folk, who I sensed watched me from all around. But then it grew louder; it stirred in the still air; it rippled the surface of the lake. Ahead in the north, at the mouth of the pass, I saw the tops of trees tossing and spray gusting in sheets from a distant waterfall. A storm was brewing—I felt it approaching.

"When it came, it rode at me thundering like the rush of the ninth wave, like the gale which howls from the mouth of the Cave of Chwith Gwynt. Nor did its rage come tearing up the pass alone; it flung itself down between the crags above, wind beating against wind, flinging down rain in torrents from each black drizzling crag, lashing the length of the angry tossing waters of the lake. A bolt of lightning lit that place of rocks for one brief blinding moment, leaving a broken yew blazing like a pine torch in an empty hall. So air and fire and water fought with each other in confusion around me.

"A voice within me urged the advice you pressed but now, Cubi: Go back, Maelgun. Return to the safety of the sanctuary whence you came! Be at peace; be still! And another voiced your words, Taliesin: Go forward. Take up arms; bear down the tumultuous rage of envious foes!

"Which word should I heed? For long I sat motionless upon my sodden steed, hidden in my cloak, unable to turn back or ride forward. You know what choice I made at last, but how or why I made it, or whether I was right in what I did, I do not know. What do you say, son of Morfryn, who have said nothing yet?"

I pondered a moment, then made reply: "I believe you were right to remain as you did, in the eye of the storm, sustained by the sky above you, the earth beneath you, and the water around you. For a king must stand as a stone pillar, a tall tree, a safe chariot, at the Center of his kingdom. Throughout his lands he maintains peace and justice and fertility of crops, and it is through the truth of his rule that the rooftree of every tribal lordship is upheld in lawful inheritance. Yours, Maelgun, is what your head and tongue may claim, so long as the wind dries, the rain wets, the sun moves, as far as land and sea reach."

The day and year were drooping, drawing to a close. Even as I spoke these words, the stillness which surrounded us broke. A breeze began to blow in out of the west, rustling stunted thornbushes clinging about the ramparts of Dineirth, and causing ravens perched upon the palisade to strut uneasily, croaking harshly to one another. Maelgun shivered, drawing his cloak about him.

"It is in my mind that this is no good wind for me," he murmured. "That is a wind off the Western Sea, where the men of Ywerdon and Prydyn are sailing their fleets over the rough ocean toward the Island of the Mighty."

The wind increased its force, chasing clouds in ragged shreds whose torn shadows flew over the walls and across the enclosure. It whined through the crevices of timbered walls, flapped tents, and caused the Red Dragon to beat angrily overhead. It was a wind keen as a sword's edge, cruel as a wolf's fang, high and cold. It was the raging wind of war, breath of the poet's inspiration. Taliesin swayed back and forth upon his bench, his eyes half closed, his lips murmuring. I knew that if we survived this day, his would be a lay recited beside royal hearths so long as kingship stands in the Island of the Mighty, and the pure tongue of the Brython remains upon the lips of its people:

Beird byt barnant wyr o gallon.

Sweeping out of the endless emptiness of the firmament across the pit of the world, the wind moaned as if in pain upon the hillside, groaned as if wounded by the keenness of its whetted edge, howled furiously a shrill battle-yell. From the mouth of the Cave of Chwith Gwynt it flew, bearing upon its unseen wings the cold chill of Uffern, the turbulence and shrieking of the hosts of Gwyn mab Nud riding out of the Pit of Annufn.

"But three men escaped, they say, from the Battle of Camlann after Arthur died," muttered Maelgun. "Do you think as many will survive this day, Merlin?"

"That I cannot say," I replied. "A wave is thundering; breakers are covering the coast; warriors are engaging in battle. I think there will be many a sad tale upon the green dyke before this evening has passed."

"Is it clouds, or smoke, or warriors engaging in battle that I see now about the stronghold?"

"It is the *migedorth*, the battle-fog," I rejoined. "Now I fear the enemy host may be upon us."

The wind was stilled as suddenly as it had arisen, and a thick gray bank of fog came rolling in over the battlements. With it came an eldritch screaming, as the men of Loiger swarmed howling over the ramparts in three mighty hosts. One host broke through the barrier of the western gateway; they penetrated the protection of the labyrinth, broke down the bars that bind. Another scaled the northern rampart. A third passed over that to the south. The men of the king's *gosgordd* rose up to meet them: Three hundred clashed with a hundred thousand.

The heathen hosts of Loiger broke into the enclosure like a hawk passing through a flock of small birds, like a wolf through a sheep flock, like the heavy rush of a mad swollen stream in spate. Chalk flew from riven shields; they were shattered in fragments. Spears passed through bodies. So dense was the press of the battle throng that a chariot might have been driven above it. There was no withstanding the onslaught of the Iwys and the men of Loiger and the barbarians from across the Sea of Udd, and it seemed the day was lost.

There was a fog of blood and mist upon the battlefield, a cloud of white lime rising from shattered shields, a rain of blood from severed limbs, a haze of dampness from the hillside. Blade rang against blade, spear against spear. A blood-red sun hung low overhead, burning dimly in the murk like a lantern behind a thin curtain. I saw the masked helms of the Iwys and their allies, rank upon rank, driving back the valiant men of Prydein, so that the conflict approached the spot where we sat playing at *gwyddbwyll* beneath the Red Dragon. The stamping of the warriors' feet upon the soil of Dineirth rattled the golden pieces upon the silver board. Blood was splashed upon the white robe of Maelgun.

"This is no good, Merlin. We must break out of the fortress!"

I found Rufinus standing beside me, and his expression was grimmer than I had ever seen it.

"You must tell the king to bear the standard, and I will form up the men in a phalanx. We have to try to fight our way out of the eastern entrance!"

Maelgun understood, and rising to his full stature, he drew the pole of the banner of the Cymry from the soil of Dineirth. He bore the Red Dragon high above him, as Rufinus drew up the residue of our *gosgordd* into a stronghold in the face of battle, a bristling wood of spears. Slowly, like a mortally wounded boar at whose flanks the hounds are tearing, we cut our way back toward the entrance.

The enemy raised an exultant battle cry, clustering about us, wave upon wave. I glimpsed the shining *gwyddbwyll* board as it slid to the ground, saw the golden pieces trampled down, glimpsed the king, splattered with blood, tumbled from his high place. But there was no time to think of these things. The press of the throng bore us backward; it was all a man could do to keep himself upright. Those who fell were trampled and gored all in an instant. I clung by the king, who strode head and shoulders above all around him, Bull-protector of the Island of Prydein, bearing aloft the Red Dragon of Prydein, beneath which Arthur twelve times rode to victory.

What we would do once beyond the walls I could not see. But there was no time to think; the battle-fog enclosed us all about. Gaping mouths and grinning wounds filled my sight; cruel cries sounded in the spiraled thresholds of my ears. Now we halted—why, I could not tell—and I closed my eye to shut out the hateful vision. I seemed to see trunks of bodies, headless and bleeding, tumbling about me; heads bouncing upon the ground, severed limbs flailing one against the other.

"You are mad, Merlin, mad; your wits are scattering!" a voice seemed to scream in my ears. "The wilderness is all about you—where will you hide yourself?"

Then it seemed that the bottomless ocean had come flooding in over the land, engulphing the plain, rising until it spilled over the crumbling ramparts, moaning and murmuring in disjointed confusion. All was awash in a dark sea of blood, from whose depths floated up and receded before my terrified vision a confused congeries of dismembered elements of men and women, no head answering to its trunk, no limb to its fellow.

I recalled the dreadful verse which Taliesin recited to me upon the summit of Mellun Mountain:

> For the strife of Arderid provides the cause
> From their lives' preparing till the last of wars.

But that time was not yet.

I made to stop my ears from the cry of tortured pain which came winding up out of the abyss, but before I could do so I heard a louder roar which caused me to open my eye and gaze ahead in surprise. Beyond the protecting hedge of spears and white-limed shields which warded us about I saw looming the eastern gateway of Dineirth, through which Rufinus had said we must make our retreat. It was as if through a film of water or beyond a haze of mist that I saw the front rank of our warrior band break apart, dividing like a white-crested wave when it encounters a ragged-fronted rock at a cliff's foot.

There in the gap stood that terrible figure—whether man or bear it was hard to tell—who had uttered grim threats against us at the first assemblage of the enemy without our gates. Within his mighty grasp he lifted and crushed breath and blood out of the bodies of the bravest warriors of the Cymry, so that none might stand against him and all hung back in fear. In the gap he loomed, each of his great arms bloodied up to the shoulder, mangled flesh embedded in his nails and teeth, snarling and growling at those who ventured to raise sword or spear against him. Then he turned the glare of his blood-red eyes, glinting within the mask of his helm, full against Maelgun Gwynedd where the king stood in the midst of the shield-circle. Like the brooding blood-red sun itself in the thick swirling fog above was the malign scowl which flared forth from beneath the boar-crested helm of Beowulf.

"Now hear what I have to say, you men of the Bryttas, and you who call yourself Dragon of the Island!" thundered the heathen champion. "I have seen here many limbs sheared off and shields split apart, helms and mail-shirts hewn in pieces, chieftains hacked apart. I have fought as champion of the three greatest kings who bore rule on earth: Hygelac and Hrothgar and Hrothulf. I have fought twelve pitched battles; I have slain water-monsters; I put Grendel and Grendel's foul dam to shameful deaths.

"Now will I end this slaughter, where blood enough has been spilt to satisfy even the gray prowler of the moors, and the dark devourer of carrion has glutted his sharp beak. I am come to measure my strength with thine, O Dragon, and it will go ill with me if I do not slay you with this my good sword Naegling. No host may fight when once its king is slain, and you have not long to live. I have heard of dead men fighting on after their lives have ended, and so that all men here may know you are truly dead I will hack off your hand and foot, and slice your head from your body, and your body into four pieces!"

At this the giant laughed a dread laugh, and the numberless hosts of Loiger encompassing us about uttered likewise a laugh of scorn and derision and enmity. Holding high his great sword, Beowulf strode forward across the open space toward the great king. Maelgun Gwynedd stood rigid at the center of all. The banner of the Cymry hung limply from the pole above him; the Dragon drooped in the fetid fog of war. No man was there to stand as champion between the Dragon of Mon and his cruel adversary.

Now the champion of Cynurig, the heathen lord, halted a bare three spear's-lengths from where awaited his onrush the king of the Cymry. Exulting in his resistless strength, he cried out once more:

"Hear my last words, men of the Angel-cynn, and you, men of my own people, Wederas and Geatas! As all men know, it was I who slew Daeghrefn, who bore away the standard of the Hugas, placing it in the hand of my lord Hygelac. Nor did I slay him with the sword's edge, but with violent grip I crushed his heart's beating and the framework of his bones.

"I would not now bear this good sword Naegling against my foe, but that in fighting a Dragon, I believe my adversary will fight with scorching fire and envenomed breath! It is for that reason I wear a shirt of mail and bear a shield. Now is my heart eager for the fray, so I cease my taunts against a failing foe. Wait by the dyke, my comrades. This is no exploit in which you may share, nor is it for any man to pit his strength against the fire-breathing barrow-guardian save myself. I alone will achieve this heroic deed, winning gold through my valor; or if I fail, then will warfare, life's dread destroyer, bear away your lord!"

So spoke Beowulf, mocking the mighty king his adversary, and the Red Dragon beside which Maelgun took his stance. Then he swung aloft his broad blade, an ancient sword prepared by ogres long ago, high above his boar-crested helm, and stepped forward. For what to me seemed an endless space of time, there fell a ghastly spell of silence upon the place girdled about by the ring of warriors, by the ramparts of the fortress, by the encircling rim of the earth: a silence broken only by the advancing tread of the mail-clad giant.

I stood immobile as the king, images of the approaching end clouding my vision. The scene before me began to whirl about giddily, so that I thought myself fainting. And in that moment, of a sudden, there burst forth beside me a blazing oily stream of flame, a roaring torrent of scorching fire, long evil flames running forward through the air like winged serpents darting from their rocky crevice, hot venom spitting from red gaping jaws. The scorching heat struck my side with sweltering force; it was accompanied by a black stinking smoke which choked me with its hateful acrid stench.

Before I could take thought for my preservation, or wonder at the sight, or turn to gaze whence came this hideous cataract of devouring racing flame, I saw it strike Maelgun's mighty foe full upon the breast, so that the blazing liquid poured and spread itself about his whole body. He towered before us all, blazing from helm to foot like a beacon fire upon a high hill at the Kalan Gaeaf. Angry fires melted his steel-ringed mail-shirt, consumed the hairy-pelted flesh revealed for one briefly illumined moment within the blaze beneath, flared briefly as they burned away his grizzled beard. Black smoke floated upward, as flames spiraled and sported serpentine about his wasting body. A stench of roasting flesh hung upon the air, such as rises from pork-gobbets drawn by princely flesh-hooks from a cauldron seething upon a king's hearth. The roaring of the body-pyre sounded like a winter's wind about the smoke-hole of a king's hall. The champion's blood fizzled and ran dry all in an instant, like water splashed upon a furnace; his bones crackled amid the blaze like those which a king's mastiffs chew upon his rush-strewn floor.

Like a falling star on a summer's night descended the sword of Beowulf, until its point stooped to the ground, slicing a great gash in the blood-soaked turf. From out of the empty mask of his great helm whistled a thin wailing scream, as the bellows providing breath of life to the bony framework of his chest were withered, tautened, punctured in the crackling pillar of flaring, dripping flame which had but a moment earlier been Beowulf, champion of all heathen peoples dwelling about the stormy Sea of Udd.

The river of flame sank back as swiftly as it had started forth, and upon the ground before us we beheld only the proud boar's helm, the bright sword, a smoking heap of half-molten metal rings, and a scattered pile of scorched skin and burned bones. A terrible cry like that of a wounded beast went up from all the angry hosts of Loiger. A valiant kinsman of the fallen hero, Wiglaf son of Weohstan, started forward, gathering up the remains of his dear lord to bear them away upon his shield. While this happened, the serried ranks of Loiger stood mute, momentarily stunned by what they had seen.

I was not a little startled myself, and then surprised to hear a gruff chuckle beside me.

> "*Tam magis illa fremens et tristibus effera flammis*
> *quam magis effuso crudescunt sanguine pugnae,*"

murmured Rufinus at my ear. "A telling demonstration, undeniably; though if truth be told it is one normally employed in destroying siege-engines, wooden *ballista*-emplacements, and the like at the storming of fortified cities. However, one may always find a new use for an old weapon. As you know, Merlin, I have taken more than a passing interest in such devices of war."

I turned in astonishment, to find the tribune standing with an air of great satisfaction beside a long copper tube, about a spear-shaft in length, which rested upon a light wheeled framework. A fume of black smoke hung in the air about its hollowed end, and an acrid stench envenomed the air.

"Why, is this more of your work, Rufinus?" I inquired, still a little dazed by a demonstration which had left us as stunned as were the enemy.

"Guilty again, I'm afraid," he replied cheerfully. "You see, with nothing else to do and no serious attack expected here, I could not resist keeping the men occupied in constructing toys at which I fear my professional colleagues might smile."

"But how did you manage to throw that fearful tongue of flame so far in that devastating manner? What is the material that burns so fiercely? Is it blown with a bellows?" I asked with eager interest.

"That, my friend, is what the troops call 'Medea's oil,' for like that oil which Medea of old persuaded old King Pelias would provide him with renewed life, it translates those who encounter its invigorating warmth from one existence to another.

"It was the invention of a certain Proclus, an Athenian scientist, who supplied it to the emperor of the Romans at the time of Vitalian's rebellion. In my case I learned the formula and techniques of construction and operation of the tube from a skilled engineer named Theodorus, whom I came to know when I was serving under Hermogenes in the East. No, there is no need of a bellows. This man here is my *siphonarius,* and the combustible matter is essentially a compound of sulphur, bitumen, and naphtha, which is ignited . . . But I fear this is neither the time nor the place for a discussion of chemical principles, nor for me to betray state secrets. I have gained us a brief breathing space, of which we must make effective use without delay."

"What do you propose we should do?" I asked. "It seems to me we are in poor straits whatever we attempt." For I saw around us a forest of spears, and our own people, though heartened by the destruction of the heathen champion, wounded sorely and few in numbers.

"It is true that the balance of forces is not what I would choose voluntarily," the tribune conceded, "but still, we must do what we can. This place is become a deathtrap for us, for if the enemy have but the sense to place archers upon the ramparts, they may shoot us down like dogs over the heads of their fellows."

The old soldier turned to the king and, saluting, addressed him in these words:

"It seems to me, O king, that we would do well to force the gateway which lies ahead, before the enemy recovers his wits and strength. For the present our men have had a little time to regain their courage and their breath. If you will accept my advice, O king, you will exhort them with words something like these: 'Citizens, Romans! Let us advance in a manly and steadfast fashion. Show the enemy our strength; let them see they are facing men who will strike rather than be struck. Our foes are barbarians; they are not made of stone or bronze which cannot be wounded; their bodies are not iron which does not wear down or feel nothing. Let the gate but be taken, and we will yet gain the day!' "

I saw that nothing could be worse than to stand like sheep awaiting the butcher's cleaver, and, together with Taliesin, I urged Maelgun
to comply with the tribune's request. At this Maelgun looked about
him, grim and angry, his head high above all, and flourished aloft the
Red Dragon above the hosts.

"Come, warriors of the Cymry, men of the Brython! Have you not
drunk bright mead in my hall? Let us now rise up, and charge forward
upon the pale-faces, each man like a hundred. Make streams of blood
flow fiercely before you, like the mead you drank while laughing at
the banquet. Strike down corpses with swift sword-strokes. Advance
like serpents with terrible stings; lead uphill like wild boars!"

At this there arose the mighty cry of a host about its lord, and the
gosgordd of Maelgun Gwynedd advanced fiercely through the battle-fog,
passing through the eastern gateway and so out onto the green on the
ridge beyond. Then were the hundred thousand men of Loiger angered, when they saw their champion slaughtered by means of fire and
their enemies passing from out of their grasp. So Cynurig led his men
out of the fort and around its ramparts, until they formed a warlike
battle-pen about the men of the Brython and fell upon them in an
innumerable host, making wounds of spears and causing many to fall
dead in gory pools within the borders of their shields.

It seemed that we must shortly be overborne by weight of numbers, and all that might be done by our people was to preserve for a
little space our bristling wood of spears, our battle-pen of lime-white
shields, about the person of the king and the war standard of the
Cymry. Above the hateful whistling and shrieking of spears and arrows, the clash of blades on splintered shields, and the cries of wounded
men, rang out the deep battle-shout of Maelgun Gwynedd. Amid white
clouds of chalk arising from smitten shields could be heard a brave
warlike psalm chanted by the blessed Cubi, and from within a crimson
mist of spurting blood Taliesin sang the ancient song "The Monarchy
of Prydein." Blood was streaming down his face, yet he sang on for
the sake of his brilliant *awen.*

All was foreseen by soothsayers from the beginning, yet would
not the Cymry give way before the pale-faced heathen. Though they
were slain, they slew. One by one they fell, those who would never
return to their dear homes. How sad I felt, I, Merlin mab Morfryn, as
I witnessed the dreadful battle-slaughter of Dineirth! I had seen the men
of Cantre'r Gwaelod hasten forth, had been with them when they
feasted together for a year over the mead which was their portion, had
heard their valiant boasting. How sad the tale; with what grief I longed
for another outcome!

Cruel was the resting place of the fallen; no mother's son succored them. How long would be the mourning for them, the yearning, after the fall of the fiery Men of the North from the fair lands of wine-feasting! It was a famous feast which Gwyndo Garanhir contrived at his courthouse by the Sea of Reged, and a costly one when it came to be paid for at Dineirth. The recompense of the heroes was bitter.

With lime-white shields hacked small, their bright mail-coats stained red, showering spears from diminished numbers, the men of the Brython defended the blessed *awen* of Merlin. The mighty king, a tall pine above the forest, even Maelgun Gwynedd who sustained us, bull of battle, wearing a golden torque: He confronted the foemen with his brave battle cry. So sang Taliesin, chief of bards, as the Men of the North fell one by one beneath the blade-shower, the dauntless chieftains' heads laid upon the gory turf.

At last the crafty hosts of Loiger desisted for a brief space from the battle, while our small warrior-band stood leaning on their spear-shafts, bleeding and weary so that they might scarcely stand. From Maelgun's side, where I had taken my stand, I could see where the gray-bearded king of the Iwys, Cynurig, was consulting with the lords of the Angel-cynn and the confederate princes from across the ocean. I could see that he was preparing them for the final onslaught, which it was not hard to see we lacked further strength to withstand.

At length he came forward and spoke mockingly to Maelgun: "You fight as if you believed this the conflict of Hagena and Heoden, O king, which continues from this day to that of Muspilli! But now your shields are shattered, your numbers small, and I think you should prepare to enter the windy hall of Hell. If you do not wish this dreadful thing, then I call upon you to deliver yourselves up to our judgment!"

Maelgun replied with anger: "I should like to see a gush of blood and gore from the mouth from which that talk comes! My father, Cadwallon of the Long Hand, would have suffered torture stoutly before he acceded to such a demand. We are weary and we are few, but still shall we fight on until you return to us with arms crossed upon your breasts in token of submission. This fair Island was gained for us by our forefather Prydein son of Aed the Great, and never shall we see it become the patrimony of crafty heathen kings, scavengers of Gurtheyrn!"

Then Cynurig laughed mockingly as he returned to his host, saying: "Now will you discover your own ruin, meeting destruction huddled together upon the ground, your king beheaded and cut to pieces with this my good sword Hunlafing!"

With this Cynurig was gone, and Maelgun exhorted us to fight for
kith and kin, raising our spears on high and our shields before us, that
we might make ravens red with the blood of the false brood of Loiger.

His words were brave, as befitted so great a king, but did not
seem to me to bear much hope. With deepest anxiety I watched the
king of the Iwys as he made his preparations for the final assault. I saw
how he drew up his host before the eastern wall of Dineirth in the
form of a wedge, its point directed toward our shield-ring. It was
easily seen, too, that the tallest and most valiant warriors were stationed at the point of the wedge, which was clearly intended to be
driven into the heart of our dwindled and failing host.

Then came a loud braying of horns and trumpets, and the great
wedge began driving heavily across the greensward toward us. My
mind was assailed once more with a confused medley of ghastly
visions and jumbled thoughts. I wondered for a moment how Rufinus
would regard the enemy's battle order, but glancing about could not
detect him amid the close-packed throng. The evening was drawing on,
the drooping sun but a dying ember glowing from the darkening
battle-fog above the rampart. Blood and mist and gloom were closing
in upon us with the approach of the earthshaking tramp of the heathen
foe. I heard Saint Cubi praying beside me; I believe it was his confession, but the whirlwind was upon us and all time for thought blown
away.

There was a shrieking and a clashing and a howling as the van of
the heathen host struck and divided our shield-fence, as the coulter of a
plow divides a light sandy furrow. There was a din of horns and
clangor of ring-mail and a shout which seemed to shake heaven and
earth. I heard a voice cry out in triumph, a voice laughing, a trumpet-
voice which yelled a familiar cry I had never thought to hear again upon
this earth.

In astonishment and disbelief I looked about, and saw a great host
riding in array along the ridge behind us. At first I thought that Cynurig
had sent a second war-band to encompass us behind, but then I saw
riding before the army three battle-horsemen in bright mail-coats,
three princes wearing gold torques, three bold horsemen, three battle-
peers bounding forward together. And as they drew nearer still I saw
that they were Brochfael of the Tusks, king of fertile Powys; Run
mab Maelgun, stalwart heir of Gwynedd; and Elffin mab Gwydno, who
once rescued me from the weir of Erechwyd!

Elffin must have glimpsed my straining face, for he shouted joyously, brandishing his spear at me. Now all our men saw who was
come and raised a mighty battle shout, though they were so few.

Cynurig heard it, too, where he sat on his horse directing the march of his host, and I saw him chew his beard in surprise and rage and mortification.

A moment later came a shock like that of the Four Great Waves of the World striking against the cliff of Penrin Blathaon in the north, as the dauntless hosts of the Cymry rode headlong into the midst of the heathen array. In the forefront, behind the three princes, rode the spearmen of Gwynedd, in whose vanguard were the men of Arfon of red spears, whose privilege it is to ride in the forefront of the host. Behind them came galloping in glittering array like wolves in fury the six war-hosts of the tribe of Cunedda: even Cadwalader mab Meriawn, lord of Meirionyd; Dinogad, fierce prince of Dunoding; Serwyl mab Usa from sea-bound Cardigan; Cynlas mab Owain from Ros, his flaming hair streaming from beneath his bright helm; gray-haired Elud of Dogfaeling, his slashing spear held high; and brave Breichiol of Rufoniog, whose lofty stronghold at Dinbych is famed for hospitality throughout the world.

I saw kings and heroes without number gathered in that great company: a host of horsemen with dark-blue armor and shields, spears brandished aloft, and sharp swords and bright mail-coats glinting. Foremost in the fight on that day of wrath flew fierce chieftains of Dyfed, Brycheiniog, Gliwising, and Gwent; proud princes of three mighty stone-walled cities, Caer Vadon, Caer Loyw, and Caer Ceri. Though the hosts of the Fichti and of Ywerdon were to come against their land, they would ensure their shields were broken. Last of all, though not least in might, came riding the glorious hosts of deep-delled Dyfneint. Gereint from the South raised loud his battle cry before his men; flashing and bright was the whiteness of his shield. Lord of the spear, lavish dispenser of mead and brooches, liberal as the boundless ocean are you, courteous son of Erbin!

With a mighty shout that echoed over the land the hosts came together in the clash of battle, warriors striking one another with deadly blows. How many noble heroes fell in the stalls of death that day I do not know. Great was the slaughter and grim the grave-filling which took place; pride and shame lay side by side. I saw anger and indignation, blood pouring in rivulets from the white skins of young warriors mangled by the sharp-cutting blades of foemen. Harsh was the din of multitudes of champions as they hurtled together, spear striking shield, blade against blade, flesh mangled and torn—a prey for the wolf and the raven. Harsh was the hideous tumult: shouting of warriors, clashing of lime-white shields, slashing of swords, clattering of quivers, humming of javelins, and whirring of arrows, grinding and smashing of death-strokes delivered, groaning of men lying gored and trampled underfoot.

For as the champions hacked at one another, the press of men was so great that their fingertips and feet almost touched. So slippery with blood was the earth beneath that men were slithering and falling, their heads hacked from their bodies where they stumbled. No spear-shaft was there but it was running with blood to the haft; no sword blade but its blood-groove was dripping with gore.

Now when Cynurig, lord of the Iwys saw that the battle was by no means going as he had hoped, and found the whole host of the Cymry arrayed against him, he became as one beside himself. The serpents which lay within his eyeballs dilated until they seemed almost to dart forth hissing at whomever he glanced, his beard grew stiff and bristled as a gorse-bush, and he gnawed at his lower lip until it was running with fresh blood.

The White Dragon of the heathen peoples of the coasts and the sea flapped angrily in the heavy air above the spear-forest of the men of Loiger. Evening was drawing on. The battle-fog swirled ever thicker about the struggling warriors; eagles and ravens darkened the air, exulting over the blood banquet that would shortly be theirs. For a brief space there was a lull in the fighting, men pausing with blades poised, considering how matters might come to pass.

A sullen drowsiness seemed to descend upon Cynurig and his people. Their pale faces became white as their shields, their eyes and tongues dry as those of snakes; the spittle that flowed in their throats was stopped, and they knew a consuming thirst which set the blood throbbing and drumming within their veins. Many stripped themselves of their shirts of mail, rubbing themselves with foul-smelling ointment which made the thick hair upon their bodies shine with a dull glistening in the failing light that lay upon the place of slaughter.

No longer did they chant the war cries of their tribes, but growled and snarled and ground their sharp teeth, spitting and hissing in the face of their foes. They were become, as they say in their tongue, *beorn, freca,* and all saw them for what they were: wild beasts consumed with a raging hatred for the Red Dragon floating above the bright spearpoints of the princes of the Cymry, blades that reflected the ruddy hue of the vanishing sun and the gore-sodden battlefield.

Like bears the men of the Iwys, of Loiger, and of the heathen tribes from beyond the sea roared and growled; like wolves they howled against the baptized host of Maelgun Gwynedd; like boars they whetted curved blades upon the wet grass, stamping the heavy clay beneath their feet. For Cynurig had made a profane sacrifice in the form of a blood offering to a boar, and the boar-crest upon his masked helm and upon those of his champions appeared in that hour to pant and heave as if alive.

Then Cynurig cried loudly to all his men: "Now is come the hour which all men dread: that of Muspilli, when gods and men gather to wage the final war against the Frost-giants. Yonder you see the World-serpent flying over the hosts of Crist, the Dragon which seeks to consume all that lies in Middle Earth! All about us is the fiery vapor of his venomous breath. The sun is failing in the west; unless we gain the day, there will arise no new dawn for the children of Woden, One-eyed Leader of Warriors!

"Bear forward your blades. Hearken to the raven's croaking, the gray wolf's howling, the ringing spear, the echoing shield. Soon will the moon, wandering among the clouds, shine down upon your exploits. Now shall arise such grim deeds as will satisfy the deadliest spite of the Woden-born.

"So awake now, my champions! Take up your shields; recall valor to your hearts; fight your way forward in the van. Make high your courage!"

And when Maelgun the Tall, son of Cadwallon of the Long Hand, Dragon of Mon, lord of the Land of Bran, and chieftain of the tribes of Cunedda the Guledig, heard those words of Cynurig, he cried out likewise to the host of the baptized, defenders of the faith of Crist:

"Soldiers of Crist! Valiant defenders of the Island of the Mighty! Men of the North and Deheubarth, Gwynedd and Gliwising, Dyfneint and Powys, hasten forth to battle like noble hounds; form the battle-pen in the presence of the spears! Be dragons in bloodshed, generous wyverns in the javelin fight! Be reapers like leeks in battle. Recall the bragget and mead you drank to the warm light of tapers within your kings' halls!

"Children of Cunedda, good hound of Gododdin, remember the deeds of the guardian of the Wall; protect the court and girdle of the Guledig! Tribes of the Coeling, whelps of Ceneu, be valiant in defense of the inheritance of the protector of the land of Mabon! Torque-wearing princes of the Brython, companions of the Cymry, scatterers of the mongrel hosts of Loiger: Be swift as staghounds upon the track of the deer, fierce as wolfhounds sighting their prey, stubborn as bloodhounds in the battle slaughter!"

Thereupon arose a mighty battle shout among the hosts and warriors of Prydein. But I for my part recalled the words I had heard uttered from the thornbush by the forge of Gofannon, and wondered yet what might be the outcome:

"Dogs of Gwern, beware Morddwyd Tyllion!"

Then the lords of the Brython unleashed the three hundred ban-dogs that were with them, huge mastiffs reared in the courts of kings. Hitherto they had lain with their heads couched upon their paws, raising their great heads from time to time to sniff the air, which reeked of blood. Furrowed were their brows and melancholy their expressions as they awaited patiently their masters' bidding. But when their triple chains were slipped, they rose up large as young colts, their swart masks scowling, white fangs gaping; and wild, untamable, furious, savage, ferocious, and eager for battle were those hounds when their chains were loosed.

So the hounds of the Brython bounded forward upon the foes of the Brython, and with them rode all the hosts of the Brython. Not slow to meet the attack were the men of the Iwys and of Loiger and of the tribes from the coastlands of the Sea of Udd. Dreadful was the conflict between the White Dragon and the Red. The champions of the heathen seized upon warriors of the Brython, crushing their bodies until bones were splintered; hacking their throats with jagged, broken knives; ripping up stomachs and flanks with sharp, curved blades. For their part, the defenders of the faith of baptism leaped and bounded this way and that, evading the flailing weapons of their foes, slipping within their guard, flinging themselves with bared weapons upon those who opposed their Lord.

Again I recalled the verse which Taliesin told me:

For the strife of Arderid provides the cause
From their lives' preparing till the last of wars.

But that time was not yet come.

At the fore of the host of the Cymry rode Maelgun the Tall, great hound of Gwynedd, baying the battle shout of his host. To him came riding in anger Cynurig, crafty king of the Iwys. Beneath his boar-helm he appeared no smaller than a three-year-old ox, wolf-gray in hue, and from each of his bristles it seemed that there flew an arrow which laid low a man of the Cymry with every stroke.

It was not long before he came up with Maelgun, and Maelgun with him, and the two kings became locked in deadly combat. So they fought, with all their hosts tearing and slashing about them. So terrible was the clamor and uproar, tumult and thunder, which arose from the clash of shields, the rattle of spears, the clangor of swords, the hoofbeats of horses, and the hoarse shouts of heroes, that elves and goblins and spirits of down and barrow and demons of wind and fog screamed from the rims of shields and from the edges of swords and from the points of spears. And the warriors' war cries were echoed every one by yells of hate and terror uttered by sprites and specters and dogheads haunting every crag and swamp and wooded hollow of that desolate place. The air above was black with demons, seeking to drag all who fell in battle down to the Pit of Annufn.

And it was in the darkened Realms of Annufn far beneath the tramp and tread and groaning and gashing of the fight about the rampart of Dineirth, that the twin lords of Annufn, Arawn and Hafgan, waged deadly war one against the other. And in the unseen aether high over the battle-fog of Dineirth, men heard faint and muffled howling and horn-blowing, as Gwyn mab Nud passed by exulting at the head of his Wild Hunt.

Then I met Taliesin's gaze fixed upon mine, and a third time I recalled his unchancy verse:

> For the strife of Arderid provides the cause
> From their lives' preparing till the last of wars.

But not even now was that fell moment come.

Meantime the warring hosts fought on with such unwearied rage and vigor it seemed the conflict might last as long as that of Gwyn mab Nud and Gwithir mab Greidawl, which as all men know endures from this till Doomsday. They pierced and wounded, slaughtered and slew, until if birds might fly through men's bodies they might that day have done so, bearing lumps of flesh and blood through their gaping wounds into the crimson battle-fog which enveloped them around. The swords and spears of many were splintered and broken, so that men rent and devoured each other with the weapons of their bodies. In this way many lay clasped in a death embrace, with the lips and nose and ear of his foeman in the teeth and tusks of the other after they had set aside their arms.

So fierce was the fighting and so dire the fate of the noble race of the Cymry that I did not disdain to take up a spear and join in the conflict, though my weapon is the divine one of the *awen*. It happened that I stood near the place where the wedge-point of the heathen host had penetrated our battle fence, until it approached the space about the banner of the Red Dragon. It surprised me to see that the tip of the enemy van was not led by any mail-clad chieftain, but by a man in a black hooded cloak, with the hood pulled low over his face. His only weapon was a spear, with which he directed the heathens in their advance.

I watched this man approach, and saw that whenever a warrior of the Cymry hewed at him with his sword, the blade snapped in two upon the haft of the stranger's spear. I saw, too, that when men of his own host fell with deadly wounds in their breasts, the hooded man touched them with his spearpoint, upon which they sprang up with their strength renewed and resumed the fight. It seemed that none might withstand his advance, for King Maelgun was striving a little way off with Cynurig. Thus I took it upon myself to interpose myself in his pathway.

"Go back!" I commanded, standing upon one leg and leaning on my spear. "This is the Red Dragon banner of the Island of the Mighty, upon which no gray wolf from overseas may lay impious hands!"

"Who are you, little man, who opposes himself to the Masked One?" inquired the other in an ugly voice, raising his hood a little as he spoke. I saw he bore but one eye, and that it was with no friendly gaze that it glared forth upon me.

I was angry at this, making reply: "I am no little person, as you think, but a man possessed of the *awen*. Once was I Gwion Bach. 'Black Frenzied One' some call me now, and I am no stranger to the Cauldron of Poesy. I was in many forms before I was conceived; I was lanterns of light for a year and a half; I am a bridge stretching over sixty estuaries; I was created from water of the ninth wave. I have dwelt in the courts of kings, and am foster-brother to Prince Elffin mab Gwydno, to whom the kingdom of Cantre'r Gwaelod looks forward."

The hooded stranger, exulting in the midst of the place of killing, a black raven gripping upon each of his shoulders, smiled sarcastically at this vaunting.

"You are a very great person in your own estimation, I see. But it may be that I shall make my mark upon you with this spear—and what think you then will be your fate?"

It seemed to me for a moment that he spoke with the voice of Gwyn mab Nud, when last he conversed with me from out of the shadows within the palace of Brochfael at Caer Gurygon in Powys. But then it came into my mind that he was not Gwyn, but another. I had seen him elsewhere. I knew him as well as if he were my brother. Who was he?

"It may be that the day will come when this proud banner will fall and the tides wash in over the Island of the Mighty," I made firm reply. "But I do not think that day has yet come, or why was I preserved when I lay in the watery rampart, and for what did I slay the Stag-specter of Annufn in the heart of his labyrinth?"

My adversary peered at me from the unsounded depth of his single piercing eye, and gave a cracked laugh.

"We are in the place where ravens glut themselves upon blood, and the bravest warriors fall before the arrow-storm or lie toppled by the spear, whistling and shrieking. This is the place I love, where men are frenzied and destructive, breaking all they have built, exulting in their foolishness. Why should I spare you?"

I knew he might slay me if he wished, marking me down for slaughter with his spear. However, I was not afraid. I felt flooding over my being the wisdom of the Salmon of Lyn Liw and the pure love of my sister Gwendyd, the consolation of the sow Henwen, the soaring protection of the Eagle of Brynach, and the grim companionship of the Wolf of Menwaed. Of a sudden I knew why I had been permitted to survive as a babe within the watery rampart of Dylan; how I had succeeded in returning safe out of Annufn; and what was my protection about the Monarchy of Prydein. I stood at the point of contention, and that must continue until the time be done.

I was told afterward that it was at this time that Gwydfarch and Cubi and others in the hosts of the Cymry saw Iessu Crist Himself striding in the sky above our army, wielding His cross against the foe.

"You may not touch me now," I cried, "great though I know your power to be!"

"Why not, little man, why not?" asked the Hooded One, raising his spear-blade to my side. "What is there I may not do, here on the field of blood?"

"There is one thing you may not do, and one only!" I shouted above the clangor and outcry, fear at last mounting within my breast. "You may not violate my *tynged,* which as yet is unfulfilled."

"And how are you to know when it is fulfilled? What if this were the moment of your death, painful and unwelcome? After all, it steals unexpectedly upon every man, like a wolf entering a sheepfold. Tell me *that,* little man, and it may be I will spare you this once!"

Then I approached the Hooded One and whispered words within his ear. And though they are words which it is not fitting should be spoken by those who are not initiates, I set them down here that men who have passed through the cleansing waters may know the truth of this my tale:

"Gwareis yn llychwr, kyskeis i ym porffor;
Neu bum yn yscor gan Dylan Eil Mor,
Yg kylchet ym perued rwg deulin teyrned,
Yn deu wayw anchwant o nef pan doethant;
Yn Annwfyn llifereint wrth urwydrin dybydant."

Then he whose face was shadowed by a cowl of night laughed and lowered his spearpoint.

"That indeed I cannot answer—at any rate, not at this time," he conceded, still regarding me with much scorn and (as I fancied) a little amusement.

"Did you think I did not know you, Merlin son of Morfryn? You are he whose *wyrd* it was to be named Sea-fortress, are you not? And all this"—here he traced a circle about us with his spear—"is the Enclosure of Merlin, as you fancy. Well, we shall see! For the moment the day is yours and you are saved, though whether you will thank me for that when you come to that which awaits you remains to be seen. Fear not, we shall meet again. For you, perhaps, it will be no very fortunate encounter. Farewell, Merlin, one-eyed scop of the Bryttas!"

With which, darting a blighting look at me from beneath his hood, the stranger turned upon his heel and departed from that place. It seemed to me I saw him spring upon a great gray steed, eight-legged, with streaming mane, and gallop at speed away into the north. But such was the fog and din and confusion that I have no certainty as to what passed that day. Indeed, I will relate to you a strange matter, O king. It happened by chance that I was looking upon the shield of Maelgun, where it lay at the foot of the Red Dragon. There, in the reflection of the polished metal, I saw my own image—which is something I am not accustomed to do. And it seemed to me that the face of my adversary was not so different from my own, so that in after times I began to wonder whether in my confusion I had been but speaking with my own shadow!

With the departure of he (whoever he was) who had formed their battle-wedge, the hosts of Loiger were of a sudden turned to disarray. A dreadful torpor descended upon them out of the fog, so that they might lift neither limb nor blade against their foes. A net which no man might see was flung about them, binding them about with battle-fetters, *hualogyon,* which grip tight a man's heart and nerves, drawing away his strength and courage. Runes of enchantment were wound around each hero's valor, entwining his sinews and nerves in knots, so that in a moment he who would have fought unflinchingly with giants was become weak and timid as a maiden gripped with panic. As the

World-serpent encircles the earth, so the war-band of Cynurig was ensnared by rune-fetters of the Frenzied One.

Maelgun and Cynurig were locked in ferocious combat. Casting away their weapons, they rushed each against the other bare-breasted and barehanded. The king of the Iwys gored the Dragon of the Island with his tusked eyeteeth; whereupon Maelgun bit off Cynurig's ears and the flesh of his cheeks as well, swallowing them down as though they were gobbets of seethed pork.

And that was one of the Three Honorific Portions of the Island of Prydein.

Then was Cynurig likewise netted in a shroud of impotence by the *hualogyon* decreed by his *dihenydd*, falling back immobile and helpless before Maelgun, with a mist of confusion reflected in his unseeing eyes, from which serpents white and red were departed. Then it was that Maelgun the Tall, king of Gwynedd, raised up with both hands a mighty sword flashing blood-red in the glow of the setting sun and, brandishing it thrice above his head, brought it down upon the helm of the king of the Iwys.

It was that blow which split Cynurig's body, slicing his spine in twain even down to the navel. Then very swiftly Maelgun dealt him a second blow crosswise, so that the three sections into which the barbarian's body was cut fell at one and the same time onto the ground. And Cynurig coughed up his heart as it were in a great lump of blood through his mouth. And in this manner he died.

Those who were at that moment standing upon Maelgun's right hand heard Saint Cubi, his chief priest, cry out in a loud voice:

"Occidisti insuper et possedisti!"

But those who stood upon the king's left heard Idno Hen, his chief druid, call out in a wolf's voice:

"Rincne marincne!"

Now it was told to me afterward that the sword with which Maelgun struck down Cynurig was no other sword than Caledvulch, the sword of Arthur. That is a sword which contains this property: that if a man let it sweep out in a circle it will bring slaughter upon a whole war-band. When I heard this I recalled the words of Gofannon mab Don, which he uttered to me while toiling at his forge. For though no man might make use of that sword unless he were Arthur, had not Maelgun become Arthur when in expiation of his violated *cynneddyf* he became a Bear within the Bear's Fort?

Then were those of the Iwys and the men of Loiger, and their confederates from across the seas who had survived the battle, compelled to come forward with arms crossed before their breasts, seeking submission at the sword's point and the spear's point. For now their king was slain, and their courage and strength bound as it were with a net of sinews, they might in no wise continue the conflict. The manner of their submission was that they lay upon the ground, swearing oaths of slavery and subjection and leave-taking, the while a sword point or spearpoint was placed into their mouths between their teeth.

Just as the Island of the Mighty was raised up by Beli the Great from the watery chaos, and the *gormes* of the Coranieid dispelled beyond the ninth wave, so the ordered battle-pen of Maelgun the Tall trampled down the howling hosts of the barbarians, and the ramparts of Dineirth resumed their lofty protection about its green enclosure.

Thus it was that after the victory at Dineirth, the kings of the Cymry sold many of the heathen into servitude; others they permitted to remain within the bounds of the Island of the Mighty upon provision of surety; and yet others they drove down to the sea's edge, even beyond the ninth wave, never to return. And it happened that the heir of Cynurig, the prince Ceawlin, following hard upon the heels of Brochfael's host when they withdrew from the walls of Caer Vydei, had come up with his war-band as the battle was drawing to a close. He, too, was in consequence compelled to submit to the mercy of Maelgun, being allotted a wretched portion of his father's patrimony, on condition of sucking King Maelgun's nipple and swearing upon the cross of Crist to undertake fealty to him and his heirs forever.

There was no numbering the extent of the men of Loiger who were slain that day. Until the stars of heaven may be counted, and the sands of the sea, and flakes of snow, and dew on a lawn, and showers of hailstones, and grass beneath the hoofs of horses, and the horses of the sons of Lir in a storm at sea, there will be no counting of them at all. The men of the Cymry made a high hill of their heads and a mound of their weapons and armor.

Thus was victory taken by Maelgun. The head of Cynurig was brought before him, which he ordered to be washed and combed and placed in a satin cloth. That he might not be overlooked by Cynurig's death-glance, Maelgun ordered seven oxen and seven wethers and seven pigs to be cooked and placed before Cynurig's head. It is said that the face of Cynurig reddened before this sacrifice, and that he opened his eyes for a moment. Afterward the meat was consumed by the host.

Maelgun also permitted the kinsman of that champion of the Iwys who had fought in the form of a bear to take away what remained of his lord's body and burn it upon a pyre, according to the rites of his people. It is said a woman of his tribe, with her hair bound up, passed wailing about the smoking pyre, chanting a dirge in the barbarous language of their people. But its words I could never discover. It is said that to this day no grass will grow upon that hill. Some great lords of the Iwys who had perished in the conflict were likewise permitted to be buried hard by the same hill; and that is the hill upon whose slope gallops forever the fair goddess Riannon.

Some of these things happened afterward, and so here I return to the field of battle. The peace which Nisien brings, the peace which he lays upon two opposing hosts when they are at their most wrathful, now mantled what was lately a place of bitter strife. With the destruction of the heathen host, the battle-fog of Dineirth was lifted, and for a space the glorious light of the dying sun illumined the triumph of the Cymry. Fiery red glowed the Red Dragon against the sunset, and red was all the land beneath the ramparts. High above me in the ruddy-tinged sky I saw an eagle soaring, the sun's rays gilding the breadth of its wings. That I believe was the Eagle of Brynach, for in "The Battle of Dineirth" Taliesin sings of "The Eagle of Brynach, victory grasped in his talons."

I stood by Maelgun, where he sat upon his throne gazing about him upon the place of slaughter. As thin evening mists arose like wraiths along the ridge, the plain of blood seemed like a distant sea, out of which arose islands which were cairns of heads. The groans of the dying were like the moaning of Dylan Eil Ton among the waves of the Aber Conwy after he received his death blow at the hands of Gofannon mab Don; and the screams of the wounded were like those of white gulls about the Promontory of Dinbych.

Now it was that I heard approaching us a galloping of hoofs. Looking around, whom should I see but my dear young friend Prince Elffin mab Gwydno, whom we had all thought slain, and who had yet appeared at the eleventh hour with the hosts of Brochfael to deliver us! A boy in years, he was a man in vigor; he would sooner attend a battlefield than a wedding, would sooner be food for ravens than receive peaceful burial. I gazed up at him in pride and delight.

Rearing back upon his swift thick-maned steed, which bounded free as famed Torllydan, the horse of Collawn mab Teichi, he brandished his spear exultantly above his head.

"Hail to thee, Maelgun!" he cried. "And greetings to thee, my brother Merlin! I had not thought to see either of you again in this life; nor, I fancy, did you look to meet me!"

He sprang from his saddle and came forward to raise his knee to the king. Then he turned to me, and we threw our arms around each other's necks.

"What happened to you?" I asked in wonderment. "The men who

were with you told us you were slain by the Iwys. I believed I was
dreaming when I saw you come riding with the kings of the Cymry—
indeed, it still appears a dream. How did you come to escape the
enemy, and how did you happen upon Brochfael and the kings?"

Elffin laughed delightedly, setting his foot on the head of one of
the slaughtered Iwys and leaning easily upon his lance. He appeared
so flushed and handsome that I wished his wife could see him in that
moment.

"My dear friend Merlin," he cried, "I have so much to tell you I
hardly know where to begin. And I think you must know much that I
should wish to learn. My loving friend, you shall return to spend the
winter in my father's hall at Porth Gwydno in the North. We shall be
comrades together, ranging through the woods and upon the hills of
Cantre'r Gwaelod. We shall share one bed, use one flesh-hook. We
shall sleep a deep sleep after our weary fighting in this strange land, and
we will tell all our tale. Do you remember how we used to sing
together that childish song:

> "Dada's gone a-hunting grand,
> Spear on shoulder, club in hand;
> Calling to his clever hounds:
> 'Giff and Gaff, now make your rounds!'?

"Now I tell you only this. Fearing that the messengers we had
dispatched to Brochfael had been taken by the enemy, and knowing
that in any case the fortress was clearly compassed about, I resolved to
make my own way as best I could to bring back the host. Since I
feared lest the enemy in some way learn my plan, I resolved to deceive
even the men of my own *gosgordd* as to my purpose. The moment we
detected the approach of the heathen, I concealed myself in a brake,
and then rode day and night, sparing neither my horse nor myself
until I came up with Brochfael and his host before the walls of Caer
Vydei.

"And this perhaps you will find hard to believe, though you will
find in time that it is true: We had been betrayed from the outset of our
march! Prince Einion mab Run had fallen into the hands of the Iwys,
by whom he was cruelly slain, and Caer Vydei lay in the hands of the
heathen! Cynurig had left the young whelp his son with a single
war-band to guard its walls against us. When King Brochfael learned
of the peril of the Dragon of the Island, he at once broke camp and
rode hither as fast as he might."

"You did very well, Elffin," declared Maelgun, "and it seems to me that your praises will be sung throughout all Prydein after this day's work."

"Will they not!" Elffin laughed, clasping me by the hands and looking me in the face. "What do you think, Merlin? Did I not save the Monarchy of Prydein, I alone, and does not Taliesin possess meet subject matter for a mighty praise-poem? 'Though he was not Arthur'— this is what the bards sing of heroes; will they not now exalt a chief by recounting that 'his courage was that of Elffin'? Am I right, Merlin? What will my father Gwydno think when he hears the news? What will be the thought of Urien Reged? What will warriors say of me in the courts of the Thirteen Princes of the North? I believe that Urien Reged may appoint me his champion when he goes forth to fight the men of Deifr and Bryneich! Aha, Cynurig, pale-faced fox: where are you now?" With which he kicked the skull beneath his foot some way off, and skipped jauntily.

"You have done well indeed, Elffin," I responded warmly, "but I wonder you do not think of someone who will honor your exploits more even, it may be, than the Thirteen Princes of the North? Have you forgotten?"

"No, Merlin, I have not forgotten. I am glad that it will be no small thing for her to find that it was her husband who saved King Maelgun the Tall from death at the hands of the heathen Iwys of the Southland, and men will honor her the more for that! Ah, I cannot wait to tell her, my dear one."

Dusk was falling fast, and soon we would have only the dim light of the stars for our lantern. Men were moving about with torches, accompanying those who bore away the bodies of the slain upon long biers. The physicians of the kings' courts busied themselves in applying unguents and sewing up wounds. Warriors who were whole searched for plunder among huddled heaps of corpses. Elffin had earned his boasting—I did not resent it. After all, it is from the fry the salmon emerges; it is from the young man comes forth the king. But suddenly I felt very weary. Making my excuses, I departed to find a resting place for the night, leaving Maelgun to question Elffin further.

Making my way between the tumbled heaps of corpses, I came to where many men were gathered in a solemn company. A strain of singing came from among them, and making my way forward, I knew them for Cynan Garwyn and the men of Powys, who were assembled to lament their fallen lord. I saw the place where Brochfael fell, where eagles screamed above the slain. Saint Gwydfarch was praying for the king's soul, a cross held above his head. Torchlight lay upon the face of Brochfael, glinting upon his bared tusks, so that he appeared for a moment fiercely alive beneath the shifting shadows. His body was wedged among a tumbled heap of slain, Brython and Iwys intermingled, mangled limbs writhing and twitching like coiled adders at their spring awakening.

"*Altisona carminalia et valde suavia audivi angelicorum coetuum cantica,*" intoned Gwydfarch in a high melodious voice. "*Eodem momento egresionis inter angelicos sanctae ipsius animae ascendentes choros.*"

I looked up toward the canopy of bright stars, to which the bird-soul of the king of Powys must but now have ascended. Then I gazed once more upon the face I would never see again in life; soon his flesh would be the prey of worms, and his blood seep down to the realms of Annufn. I believe he knew beforehand that his last hour had been named. Kings reign in glory and they die, time careering past them the while as fast as the white chariot of Brochfael's son Cynan. The ghostly faces of the mourners took on for a brief moment in my mind the semblance of a procession of kings, the history of this world emerging from darkness into brief light, to depart once more into the shades.

Chilled by the raw night air of the downs and, despite our victory, somewhat melancholy at heart, I made my way through the eastern gateway of the fortress. The tower was unguarded and the gates swinging loose, and I was inside the walls when I heard a painful groan not far off. There appeared to be no one but myself about, and so I peered to see who it was who needed aid.

There was a figure slumped against the base of the rampart, that I could see.

"Who are you, and of what name and race are you?" I inquired cautiously. Another groan was all the reply I received. Since the poor fellow was clearly past harming me, I approached him more nearly. "Are you of the Brython or the heathen?" I asked gently.

The faint reply in the darkness made my heart leap in surprise and horror.

"Merlin, is that you? You know me, surely. I am Rufinus the tribune."

"Rufinus!" I cried, darting down beside him. "You are injured! Is it painful? I wondered where you were, but had no idea that anything like this could have happened."

If truth be told, I had forgotten his existence for the moment, so great had been the strain and confusion of that dreadful day.

"It is bad, my friend, I believe," whispered the soldier, so softly that I had to bring my face close up to his. Faintly I distinguished his familiar features, so reserved and lugubrious in health that only the trickle of blood which seeped from the corner of his mouth down his beard told of grievous pain and injury.

"Where is the wound? Let me bring you a physician at once!" I urged.

"No, do not leave me. The truth is, I valued your company more perhaps than you knew, Merlin. I have spoken to few people as I have to you. I think if you leave me now, you will not see me again. It is in my back—my shoulder."

Despite himself Rufinus groaned in agony, clenching his teeth in vain attempt at restraint. Very gently I eased my hand behind his shoulder. At once my fingers encountered an arrow shaft embedded firmly up to its feathered flights.

"You see? It is hopeless, is it not? It is not to be drawn out," he whispered yet more faintly. His face stared up into mine, appealing—though not for medicine or physician.

"I know what the surgeons say," he murmured to himself. " 'If the extraction would occasion much laceration, the attempt must be declined, lest while we do good we expose ourselves to the reprobation of ignorant people.' And that would never do, would it?"

Rufinus closed his eyes for a minute or so, then opened them and looked once more into mine.

" 'Bring the dice and pour out wine; some other time for sorrow!
Death tweaks your ear, and whispers: " 'Tis *I* might call tomorrow." '

"That is the way it goes, is it not? Do you remember? I wonder if I am to meet my father. I did my best to maintain the peace of the realm and Roman rule. But what a place to die: the last of the Rufii Festi, left to the wolves in a barbarian hill-fort!"

"You will not be left to wolves, or any other carrion—that I assure you," I promised earnestly. "You have done your duty, it seems to me, and much more. I never knew your father, but I am certain you will see him, and that he will be more proud of you than any father. How could he be otherwise? It was you who saved the day. Did you hear about the victory?"

Rufinus shook his head feebly. Weakened with the effort, he closed his eyes once more. So long did they stay closed I feared he must be dead already, and gently took his hand. It was cold, but I felt a feeble responsive clasp.

Without opening his eyes he spoke again, his lips scarcely moving.

"I was thinking earlier: Is this place not called the Chariot of the Bear? It is strange; a little as if, like great Porphyrius whom we cheered in the circus at Alexandria, I had been brought out of retirement to win one final race. But what is it all for, eh? The emperor has reconquered much of the Empire, but how long will it last? How long? My father feared that there were so few men of culture left in the world, that the Latin tongue might one day die completely."

Night had drawn on; it was growing colder, and the cries of men about the fortress were few. A wolf howled outside the rampart, to be answered by another farther off, and then another near at hand. Rufinus paid no heed; he seemed lost in his thoughts, which I feared were beginning to wander.

"Strange. Porphyrius was our hero, you know. Apollos always said he would come back, when everyone believed him retired for good. But who will drive the chariot now? I took up the reins from my father, but now I am the last of my line, which must shortly be no more.

" 'The wicked god of war runs wild as unknown fate,
Like chariots fast charging through the starting gate;
Curb them when they gather speed racing up the straight—
Horse and car beyond control; both are checked too late.'

"Was that Virgil, or Petronius? You see my ignorance—who am I to talk of culture, who know only about the defense of frontiers and stringing of catapults? I am fifty. I am old, Apollos. The drinking and racing were all finished, long ago."

I said nothing, for I could see his vision was turned away from me. There followed a long pause in the darkness; all that could be heard was a group of wolves snarling together by the gate and an owl calling shrill from a distant thicket. At length—when I was persuaded that Rufinus was asleep, so that he might not be woken—he called out more loudly and clearly than hitherto:

"Apollos, I am dying. I need a priest—I must be baptized before I go! I have led a sinful life, but if I be not baptized, how shall I join my father in the cistern?"

"Wait!" I urged, with my lips to his ear. "I will be back in a moment! Only a moment. Keep up your strength, my friend."

Hastening back through the gateway, I made toward the spot where I had seen Gwydfarch conferring the last rites upon Brochfael. But all was darkness; there was no one there. Looking desperately all around me, I saw only flickering campfires, heard only the groaning of suffering men and the cracking of bones as wolves feasted undisturbed. Where could I go? To whom could I appeal? In the whole camp I knew of but two priests of Crist, Cubi and Gwydfarch, and by now they must be asleep in their darkened tents.

All at once I saw a gray form that moved like a specter across the battlefield. Who it was I did not know, but were he of the men of Powys or Gwynedd he might be able to direct me to one of the two saints. Drawing close, I discovered the visitant to be Idno Hen, the king of Gwynedd's chief druid. He knew nothing of the sleeping quarters of the saints, and I sensed from the brusqueness of his reply that he concerned himself with rites of which no Crist-worshipper should be aware.

"What may be done then, Idno?" I exclaimed in despair. "The lord of the Rufeinwyr, who this day saved and protected the Monarchy of Prydein from the oppression of the Iwys, lies mortally wounded within the gateway. He seeks baptism into the faith of Crist, and I fear he will die troubled in spirit if his wish be not granted."

"I do not know how to help you, Merlin. The priests of the god Iessu Crist are few in the camp of the kings. They mislike these wild upland places."

I groaned out loud. "We must do something, Idno, and that swiftly. He is a dear friend of mine, and he must not leave this life unsained."

Idno pondered a moment, tugging at his white beard, then said, "In that case, were it not best that I perform the rites? Many is the man's spirit I have eased from his body, and I may do the same for this valiant man who, though a foreigner, has accomplished so much in the service of Maelgun the Tall."

"But he and all his people are worshippers of Crist!" I exclaimed in dismay. "Your power and knowledge of the rites are great, Idno, but they will not serve one of a different faith. It is a good thought, but we must seek some other way."

"The only way is that which all men must take: through the Gates of Annufn," rejoined Idno Hen grimly. "It seems to me that what serves one man may serve another. What choice have you, or he? Take me to him!"

What else was there to do? The druid was right: A few more moments and the tribune would be lost to us, whatever happened. To search for a priest in the scattered darkness of the camp would be a hopeless task, and I longed to return to my friend's side without delay. We would have to comfort him in what manner we could.

I led Idno back through the gateway, and we found Rufinus lying just as I had left him. Seating myself on the bank beside him, I leaned my head close to his. In the murk I could detect the faint outline of his face, but might not distinguish his features. I feared him dead already, but my warm breath on his cheek seemed to arouse him, for I heard a faint murmur emerge from his set lips.

"Did you find a priest, Merlin?" I barely caught the words, which the darkness seemed anxious to extinguish as they emerged.

"Here is one come to see you," I replied evasively, drawing Idno down by his sleeve to the grass beside the sufferer.

Mistaking (I suppose) the white robe in the gloom, the tribune inquired hoarsely, "Are you a priest? I wish to be baptized at once, for I am dying."

He paused, choking a little. I had my arm about his shoulders, and felt warm blood trickle upon my hand. Rufinus spoke in his own tongue, for he knew but little of the tongue of the Brython, and I translated his speech to Idno. Before he could make reply, Rufinus continued in brief, broken tones:

"Doubtless you think it strange that I, who am a Christian, have not been baptized before? But a soldier leads a sinful life, killing and causing others to kill. It is better to wait until all the killing is done. This was how even Constantine, emperor of the Romans, acted—so I have heard. Proceed at once, I beg you, before it is too late!"

Idno asked me what the man said, and I explained.

"He is right, Merlin, and I shall perform the rite at once," returned the druid. "Fetch me water from the well!"

Startled, I was about to protest, but seeing the futility of any objection I desisted, and rose to fulfill the task. Meanwhile the druid bowed his tonsured head and began to murmur close in the tribune's ear.

When I returned, bearing the little water requisite within a ram's horn, I found the druid deep in speech. Rufinus lay with eyes closed, but on my feeling his wrist I found the blood yet flowed (though but feebly) within his veins. As he appeared without pain and rested, I crouched beside him, hearkening to the words of Idno Hen. He was a man of great learning and wisdom, and I myself found his words comforting, though I knew poor Rufinus could understand nothing of them.

Idno Hen was speaking of the wonders created by Gwydion mab Don, whose glittering Path flowed, a river of silver, across the expanse of heaven above Dineirth. Before the creation of the world, Gwydion it was who with great magic from his wand of enchantment flung fire among the nine forms of elements, so that they combined into a wondrous growth: essence of rich soils, water of the ninth wave, primroses of the hillside, bloom of woods and trees. In the night sky he set his jeweled Path as a sign to men, a bridge spanning sixty estuaries; he traced a bound between the sea and the land where the ninth wave rolls.

Then Gwydion touched the earth with his wand once more, raising up a man, not from father or mother, but from the nine forms of elements, from fruit of fruits, from fruit of the creator at the beginning. Next he took flowers of oak trees, and flowers of broom, and flowers of meadowsweet, and through his enchantments created from them a maiden who was the fairest above all, and the most beautiful creature that man has ever seen.

So men and women dwelt within Gwydion's fair garden, for a time well content with their lot, reading his name in wax tablets. But though chaos had been dispelled without the enclosure, still and ever the dark hosts of the Coranieid strove to break down the rampart. The great scaly, hundred-headed animal, a fierce host beneath his tongue, souls suffering by hundreds in his skin, heaved up his dripping bulk from out the ocean. Him Gwydion wounded, bruising him beneath his heel, but tumult remained in the world, forest trees tossing and splintering beneath the gale, warriors locked in grievous conflict, maidens uttering bitter sighs, grief breaking forth throughout.

Then glorious Gwydion was filled with pity for men and women. To virgin Arianrod, chaste, white-armed wise one, was born a son, even Leu of the Skillful Hand, the most beautiful youth that man had ever seen. Master of all skills was he, of cadences of music, of craftsmanship, of playing at *gwyddbwyll*. He it was also who established kingship on earth, which is a reflection of that in heaven: without His blessing no king may ensure the Truth of the Land, nor may the ordered community of earth stand secure about its Center. This is what is meant when men speak of the Enclosure of Leu.

Many and wonderful were the blessings which gracious Leu bestowed upon men, and the brightness of His countenance was like that of the sun at his zenith. But envious men plotted His death, which he suffered willingly for all upon the Tree. A triple death of the elements was that, for He was hanged on the tree, pierced by the spear of false Gronwy Pefr, and drowned with a poisoned draught. For nine nights He hung there in torment, while His precious blood watered the Tree, from which derives its strength, sustaining the heavens above the earth.

But though bright Leu was slain and left hanging from the Tree, so that His body decayed and was devoured by swine, He Himself was not dead. For His spirit flew Heavenward in the guise of an eagle, and He left behind Him the richest of gifts: even wax tablets, inscribed with the runic lore by which wise men guide their lives. And for this reason each year men mourn the death and hail the birth of divine Leu at the hill of Dinleu Gurygon in Powys and other holy spots.

Now Leu Himself dwells ever in Ynys Afallach, the Island of Apples, where is neither hail nor snow, lightning nor thunder, nor venomous serpents, nor any form of deprivation, but only feasting and music and good fellowship. And there He receives those who have voyaged in the right manner from this world to the next, appearing before them once more in the guise of a beautiful youth, guiding them through a land of emerald meads, limpid streams, fragrant flowers, and honey-distilling dew, there to dwell with Him forevermore.

Moved as ever by the familiar story, my mind strayed for a space from the cold corner of the rampart where we crouched. Then, with a guilty start, I recalled the pitiable plight of the old soldier. Unable to understand the soft tongue of the Brython, he remained still, as if sleeping. Once again I thought the final moment had passed by us unmarked, but after a time he opened heavy lids and looked at me.

"Why does he speak in Greek?" he complained feebly. "I am no Greek, but a Roman. Why, it is the privilege of a soldier to speak Latin even with the emperor in Byzantium!"

I muttered some evasive reply, content that he had unwittingly adopted this self-deception.

Then Idno Hen took from me the vial of water, pronouncing the names of the Three Waves of the Sea, even the Wave of Ywerdon, the Wave of Manau, and the Wave of the North. Those are the waves which mourn the death of Dylan Eil Ton; and the Fourth Wave is that of Prydein of Splendid Hosts.

> "Ton iwerdon, a thon vanaw, a thon ogled;
> A thon prydein toruoed virein yn petwared,"

chanted Idno, for that is the verse which is uttered on such occasions. With which he scattered three drops upon the brow of Rufinus, where they were absorbed into the moist sweat and blood-dew faintly glistening there. Thus the enchanted *dwr swyn,* which is a crushing of the black hosts of the Coranieid who gather like insects of the night about a dying man, was mingled with the fluids of his body. It is two streams which emerge from their confluence in a single river flowing down to the boundless ocean where lies the sunlit isle of Ynys Afallach.

After this, Idno Hen busied himself in carving the rune-stave which is interred with the body. The tides were ebbing about the coasts of the Island of the Mighty, for Rufinus' strength was slipping fast. As I sat supporting him with my arm, I saw his lips move a little, and brought my ear close to hear what his words might be.

At first I could distinguish only an unintelligible mumbling, in which the name of his long-dead friend featured once or twice. I thought he still confused me with Apollos, but then he turned his face a little toward mine, and whispered:

"Thank you, Merlin. Though I could wish the priest to have performed his duty in good Latin, like a Roman. But at least I know I die an honest Catholic, and with the assistance of fortune may join my father and the dear friends of my youth in the company of Our Blessed Lord, who died upon the Tree that we might be redeemed by His precious blood.

"I am old; the time has come to strip the belt. Will you do something for me? They will bury me here, I know, but I would like something of me one day to lie in the garden of the villa of the Rufii Festi."

He paused awhile, his breath rasping in his throat as a spasm gripped his body, bringing a momentary expression of intense pain to his set features. Then he attempted unavailingly to raise his left hand to his throat, pointing feebly with a gesture of frustration.

"What is it, my old friend?" I whispered in his ear. "What can I do for you?"

"There"—he gestured—"around my neck, you will find my lead identification disc. Will you take it now? And if in the course of your travels you ever come to Rome, then perhaps you might journey out to my father's villa. You remember the directions? Turn right at the inn on the Via Clodia, at the fifth milestone beyond Careiae. Ah, that dear little inn, where we would sit for a whole hour together, he with all his wisdom listening to my prattle! Listen:

"O hot and thirsty traveler, just stop a moment here;
Forget your dusty journeying. Come try my wine and beer!
We've strumming on the lyre-chords, we've flagons, fruit, and
    flowers,
And under our thatched arbor know but cool and shady hours.

"*Still* I remember that jingle, while everything else seems to be slipping away.

"If you would do me a kindness, you will take that road some day and bury my identification beneath the floor of the cistern in the garden, of which I once told you. Will you do that?"

I clasped his limp right hand reassuringly.

"Of course, Rufinus. You may rest easy on that score. You must fret yourself no longer. This world is a profitless and uncertain place, a passing possession of every one of us in his turn. Everyone that has been, everyone that will be, has died, will die; all have departed and will depart, until the board is left as cold and empty as it was before its peopling by the race of men."

I do not think he was listening, for after a yet longer interval than hitherto he fixed me with an agitated look, saying, "Do you remember my telling you how long ago in Alexandria I came to break the news of my friend Apollos' death to his mistress? Dear, pretty, funny Helladia! So lithe and lovely on the stage, her eyes could draw the heart out of your body, though you sat in the farthest seat of the auditorium. And yet she was as good a friend as any man could have, comforting a lonely, awkward youth at a time when his mother . . . Where can she be now? She must be old, too, like the rest of us—but never old in my memory."

"Wherever she may be, I fancy she remembers you too," I ventured, filling the ensuing pause.

"No," resumed Rufinus at length. "But I remember her. I remember that last moment, when she came down to the street to say farewell on the threshold. She was very pale and weeping pitifully, but beautiful as ever—I could see her face quite clearly by the light of the streetlamp. Our house stood, you know, in a street just behind the church *Arcadia*—the one which used to be the temple of Dionysus. Do you know that she asked me to take her away? Of course she was not thinking what she was saying. She would never have betrayed Apollos, and what was I to his bright spirit? Fortunately I was self-possessed, and the dangerous moment passed. But I fear I may have betrayed my friend a little in my heart in that moment on the doorstep. I had to return to the eagles, and she to the theater; both of us to mourn our dearest friend. She called out after me as I left, but I could not hear what she cried for the rattling of cartwheels in the cobbled street.

"But lately—these last few days, when I knew that death was drawing close—I have wondered whether I was right. Would she have been faithless to Apollos had she left with me, Merlin? Would I have been disloyal to my dearest friend? Do you think Helladia could have loved me too?"

Rufinus closed his eyes and seemed to be sleeping.

"I believe she would have done, for you are an honest man, Rufinus," I muttered lamely. "You have done your duty upon this failing earth, shoring up walls which will crumble in time whatever efforts you, or I, or any man may make."

It was a feeble enough reply, for what can be said appropriate to such a moment? In any case I do not think he heard the words, for he never opened his eyes again. Nor did he speak again, except once, when slaves summoned by Idno Hen approached us with spades upon their shoulders.

"*Auguste, tu vincas!*" I heard him cry faintly, and then he was dead.

They buried him within the rampart, in his armor with his sword by his side, facing toward the barbarians in the east. Next day, as I heard, the saints Cubi and Gwydfarch uttered prayers upon the spot, so that he received the rites of his own people as he had desired.

Not caring to see earth flung upon my friend's face and his descent into the dark Realm of Annufn, I turned away and wandered back through the fortress. The enclosure was heaped high with bodies, their sightless eyes torn out by black ravens. Walking was not easy in that place, for the ways were slippery with wet clay and blood. Picking my way with care among the scattered slain, I made my way by circuitous meanderings until I gained the center of the ringed enclosure. Maelgun's tent had been knocked over and trampled during the desperate struggle, but the pole stood yet from which the Red Dragon flapped proudly in the hilltop breeze. Someone had thought to return it to its place after the conflict, though I could see nobody near.

Steadying myself against that sturdy column, I looked about me upon the ghastly scene. Dawn was breaking faintly, and men moved like wandering wraiths about the field. For long it seemed the fortress had been darkened by an oppression, a *gormes* come upon the high-rimmed redoubt, so that it was hard to tell whether it was cloud, or smoke, or warriors who defended themselves. Now the fog had receded from the field, lingering only in departing wisps about the encircling palisade. Outside, however, the valley around was awash with swirling forms of morning mist, so that the Chariot of the Bear appeared to be floating upon an insubstantial sea.

Beyond in the east the rim of the dawning sun was glowing through the gateway like a blacksmith's forge, preparatory to accomplishing his diurnal ascent from the depths of Ocean. Across the intervening sea of clouds ran straight his blood-red road, passing athwart that transverse trackway within Dineirth which reflected his daily passage across the heavens. Above me the Red Dragon was suffused by his touch with yet more sanguine hue.

The morning stillness bore within it a calming property which seemed to still in my hearing the excited cries of the warriors of

Prydein who encircled the rampart. Still fainter sounded the angry snarling of ravening wolves out in the wilderness gloom beyond the dyke, tearing at the bodies of the slain, feuding over gobbets of flesh dragged off between bloody jaws. Calmness and quietude stole over my weary body, like a cloak which a fond wife places upon the shoulders of a weary loved one. I thought of the tribune's Helladia and, like him, wondered where she might be in that moment.

The king was established firm upon his throne; he judged Prydein with its Three Islands. The Island of the Mighty was safe about its Center, the Truth of the Land was established throughout its one hundred and fifty-four districts and its Twenty-eight Cities. There was peace within the enclosed space which was my enclosure: *clas Merlin.* Now surely might even the son of Morfryn find rest after labor: a lifting of the *gormes* which oppressed my aching spirit, a restitution of the four posts which sustained my worn body!

"It is through the royal justice, *gwir deyrnas,* that there is a state of quiet, peace, tranquillity, happiness, well-being, health, ease, throughout the Island of the Mighty, even from Penrin Blathaon in the north to Penrin Penwaed in the south." So it is written in the Testament of Riannon, which she delivered to Macsen Guledig. After sore travail it is customary to seek rest. High summer was come; the morning was warm, the crickets chattering, the dewy grass sweet-smelling. The chairs upon which Maelgun and I had sat when playing at *gwyddbwyll* yet stood among the tumbled slain fallen about the foot of the Red Dragon standard. I felt as it were a lifting of the load as I resumed my seat, closing my eye in blessed relaxation. My head nodded forward. I slept.

It must have been long that I slumbered, for when I awakened, the rim of the sun was once more passing below the western hills. Among the debris of men and weapons festooned about my feet, my glance was caught by an aureate glint, which in turn reflected the last departing glance of Beli's Eye. Stooping, I retrieved the golden king-piece of Maelgun's silver *gwyddbwyll* board. Dashed from the board during the conflict, it had lain among shattered shields and broken blades, severed limbs and puddled gore. The board itself had been replaced upon the table by my side; I raised the king and restored him to his central peg-hole within its double-ringed enclosure.

But where were his twelve companion pieces, without which the game cannot be played? The jewels set in each corner of the board sparkled bright as glowworms in the gathering dusk, bright as the stars of the Chariot of the Bear, wheeling foursquare about the center of the night sky above. But absent were the attendant pieces, who should each be encircling the other around the central enclosure, without and within, and the courts locked. Toiling nine years beneath the sea was Gofannon mab Don when he wrought those twelve golden pieces, together with their king. Through Twelve Houses must one pass to find them, performing Twelve Dire Labors of Retrieval.

In the heart of the night within the ramparts of Dineirth I sat, alone and sorrowful. While all men slept I alone must perforce remain awake. I have seen slender steaming yellow-maned chestnuts racing at the festival of the Kalan Mai, their tireless vigor sustaining the delightful fern-fringed peak of Dinleu. The Center alone is still; unresting, the Charioteer guides the Chariot upon its endless circuit.

I raised my gaze to the dark domed roof of Gofannon's hut. Amid the obscurity of its sooty rafters a waxen torch flared, a glowing jewel of the night. Even as I watched, the pure white star dilated, dazzling as the silent explosion of a thousand suns, into a refulgent flood whose nimbus was the unperceived bound of all that exists within the *Clas* of Leu. For one twinkling, the five hundred and sixty-fourth part of a moment, a blinding radiance flooded earth and sea and sky, suffusing all my waking being with a vivid moment of illumination.

The cloak of darkness was flung once more about the fortress; the vision receded from the bony coffer of my mind. But I knew that for the second time I had been permitted a fleeting glimpse of that ethereal light which lies beyond the awnings of the tent of heaven. And who but you, Gwendyd, my Star of the Evening, had thought to throw open to my *awen* that aperture into eternity? My destiny was clear: though the trackless way across the wasteland be uncharted, beset about with impenetrable thorny brakes, gaping quagmires, and beasts that raven in the night, there was a lantern in the distance glinting over the gateway. Let me fix my gaze on that, hitch my chariot to the star, and the way would be made clear.

Above all, I knew now that I was not alone. Side by side and hand in hand we two would strive to tread the Twelve Chambers, attempt the Twelve Dire Tasks, and garner the Thirteen Treasures of the Island of the Mighty within the House of Glass lying beyond the portals of Caer Sidi!

Now this tale is called the Coming of the King, *which is the first* cainc *of the* Tale of Merlin, Hanes Myrddin, *and thus it ends.*

A portrait of the author by Clifton Pugh, 1958

To JEANNE

WITH ALL MY LOVE & BEST WISHES
FOR CHRISTMAS 1992
& THE NEW YEAR

John

x + x
x x
x

By the same author

BOOKS

TID (*a case history*)
Chinese Drama in the Goldfields (*a treatise*)
The Blue Lamington (*a novel*)
Bizarre (*a compilation*)
(with N. Garland) The Wonderful World of Barry McKenzie
(*a comic strip*)
Barry Humphries' Book of Innocent Austral Verse (*an anthology*)
Dame Edna's Coffee Table Book (*a compendium*)
A Treasury of Australian Kitsch (*an excavation*)
Les Patterson's Australia (*a panegyric*)
A Nice Night's Entertainment (*a retrospective*)
The Dame Edna Bedside Companion (*a soporific*)
The Traveller's Tool (*a manual*)
My Gorgeous Life (*an adventure*)
The Life and Death of Sandy Stone (*an obituary*)
Neglected Poems and Other Creatures (*a nosegay*)

ONE-MAN PLAYS

A Nice Night's Entertainment
Excuse I
Just a Show
A Load of Olde Stuffe
At Least You Can Say You've Seen It
Housewife-Superstar!
Isn't It Pathetic at His Age
A Night with Dame Edna
An Evening's Intercourse with Barry Humphries
Last Night of the Poms
Song of Australia
Tears Before Bedtime
Back with a Vengeance
The Life and Death of Sandy Stone

in preparation
Look at Me When I'm Talking to You

BARRY HUMPHRIES

MORE PLEASE

He was always a seeker
after something in the world
that is there in no satisfying measure,
or not at all.

Walter Pater
From *Imaginary Portraits*

1992

VIKING

Author's Note

The people portrayed in this book are real
and the events described took place, but
fictional names and descriptive detail have
sometimes been used.

VIKING

Published by the Penguin Group
Penguin Books Ltd, 27 Wrights Lane, London w8 5tz, England
Penguin Books USA Inc., 375 Hudson Street, New York, New York 10014, USA
Penguin Books Australia Ltd, Ringwood, Victoria, Australia
Penguin Books Canada Ltd, 10 Alcorn Avenue, Toronto, Ontario, Canada m4v 3b2
Penguin Books (NZ) Ltd, 182–190 Wairau Road, Auckland 10, New Zealand

Penguin Books Ltd, Registered Offices: Harmondsworth, Middlesex, England

First published 1992
1 3 5 7 9 10 8 6 4 2
First edition

Typeset by DatIX International Limited, Bungay, Suffolk
Printed in England by Clays Ltd, St Ives plc

A CIP catalogue record for this book is available from the British Library
ISBN 0–670–84008–4

Dedicated with much love
to my sister, Barbara,
and my brothers, Christopher and Michael,
who would probably tell you
a very different story

Contents

Acknowledgements

I wish to thank the following for their encouragement and assistance in this daunting task: my wife, Lizzie Spender; my sister, Barbara, and my brothers, Christopher and Michael; Katherine Brisbane, Peter Coleman, Geoffrey Dutton, Ramona Koval, David Marr, Lewis Morley, Colin and Neil Munro, C. K. Stead, Paul Taylor and others who helped me in Australia; in America: Earl McGrath, Jean and Brian Moore, Evgenia Sands and Stephanie du Tan; in England I'm indebted to Helen Crisp, Nicholas Garland, Candida Lycett-Green, Charles Osborne, Stephen Spender, Ken Thomson, Ed Victor, my secretaries Annabel, Beverley and Nicole, and, at Penguin, the book's designer, Caz Hildebrand, my copy-editor, Judith Flanders, and especially my editor Fanny Blake, who had faith that this book might be written even when I did not.

'More please'
– the author's first coherent utterance

Alzheimer Remembers

I ALWAYS WANTED MORE. I never had enough milk or
money or socks or sex or holidays or first editions or solitude
or gramophone records or free meals or real friends or guiltless
pleasure or neckties or applause or unquestioning love or
persimmons. Of course, I have had more than my share of most
of these commodities but it always left me with a vague feeling
of unfulfilment: *where was the rest*? Is it possible that while
still at the breast my infant gaze was fixed on the adjacent
mound of nourishment fearing that it might be snatched away
before I could clamp it with avid gums?

Now I have passed middle age and achieved enough fame to
be sought after by hostesses, AIDS charities and a few well-
meaning Australian thesis-writers. I am already the subject of
two generous biographies and it is only the fear that my
adventures might for a third time be profitably chronicled by
another man that prompts me to relate my own story.

Vanity plays lurid tricks with our memory, as Conrad has observed, but the well-intentioned biography or earnest thesis can
also play lurid tricks with the truth, as its author squeezes and
pummels his subject to fit a convenient or fashionable theory.

I cannot say that this has yet happened to me, but if I do
not immediately sink into obscurity or cease to be funny
tomorrow, it might. I had intended to call this volume of reminiscences by the above title to illustrate the selective pathology

of all such memoirs. Yet as I begin this task aspiring to total candour, it is inevitable that I will rearrange the facts of my life in an attractive tableau, in much the same way as we arrange our features when we are about to be photographed. In that fraction of a second before the shutter clicks, our faces undergo a subtle but dramatic transformation. I am sure that all authors, however bent on frankness, also perform some last-minute act of moral titivation before embarking on self-portraiture.

From time to time I have stepped into a lift or washroom, or some other chamber lined with mirror, and for a second been perplexed by the sight of a round-shouldered, middle-aged man, dewlapped and disconsolate, a few feet away from me and looking in the other direction. It is when I see he is wearing my suit and my necktie and carrying my briefcase that I know him to be my *doppelgänger*, lurking in the far corner of my field of vision; the man who will never catch my eye. Unlike the friendly fellow who confronts me from the shaving mirror with his rehearsed and jaunty grin, this, though I am pained to confess it, is the *real* me. You may meet him on these pages, but only, so to speak, when I am not looking.

The Reader will be relieved, I hope, to see that this book is not prefaced by a page of pompous epigraphs, obscure apophthegms from Kierkegaard, Borges, F. Scott Fitzgerald, Kafka, Turgenev and the letters of Arnold Schoenberg. It is an indulgence of the provincial opsimath; a highfalutin' mannerism beloved of Australian and American authors keen to parade their multi-lingual skills and sophistication in the face of strong suspicions to the contrary. I will also try to avoid a lot of unnecessary name-dropping. Thus, in the illustrated section, the *here's me with . . .* pictures will be mercifully few.

But the retrospective posture is uncomfortable. Long periods spent looking over one's shoulder can lead only to a painful case of Orpheus' Neck. So I must proceed with my story.
Alzheimer! Erinnern Sie!

Beverly Hills, November 1991

MORE PLEASE

Ghostly Golfers

I WAS BORN at Number 38 Christowel Street, in the Melbourne suburb of Camberwell, or I would have been born there had my mother not been rushed to a nearby hospital; but it was to this address that my infant self was conveyed, with throbbing fontanelle and abridged foreskin, in February 1934. A lazy breather, I had been given a good whiff of oxygen soon after my advent, and to this balsamic inhalation my mother liked to attribute my precocity – in matters of no importance.

My white wicker bassinet, shrouded with net, and later my play-pen were usually placed in the garden under some protective bush. White cabbage moths flitted just out of reach beyond my translucent canopy, and the earliest scent I can remember is honeysuckle. A long way off, the thin nasal voice of the wireless transmitted a popular 'coon song' of 1934 called 'Oh Mona'. The melody was at once jaunty and melancholy, and the words as mysterious now as they were then.

> Down by the hen-house on my knees
> *Oh Mona!*
> I thought I heard a chicken sneeze
> *Oh Mona!*

My parents both came from the distant suburb of Thornbury, and had been at Sunday school together. Thornbury was one of

BABY'S RECORD

Barry put his toe in his mouth on July 23. 1934. for the first time. He loves to play with his toes.

Barry's hair was quite fair, but I think it is going darker now. (5 months)

Barry is still fair. 12 months. He is such a happy little man. He never cries. He plays all day-long.

the city's older districts, created by speculative builders in the 1880s and linked to central Melbourne by the extended cable tramline. After their marriage my mother and father made their gigantic move to the new 'garden suburb' of Camberwell. The Great Depression was receding and my father began building houses on a recently subdivided Golf Course, called somewhat anomalously – it was ten miles from the sea – the Golf Links Estate.

I can still remember those remnants of fairway, tee block, bunker and rough between the pristine brick homes, and the puckered grey golf balls we sometimes dug up as we planted our new garden. Hydrangeas, rhododendrons, geraniums, zinnias, pansies, stocks, snapdragons and phlox, all from Chandlers Nursery. There were no roses, which my mother dismissed as 'a bit old-fashioned'. Down the hill by the railway line there remained a sizeable wedge of vestigial fairway, a derelict weatherboard clubhouse and even a couple of ragged and reprieved gum trees. If that hillside were ever haunted, it would not be by the Aborigines, but by some ghostly golfer of 1910, plus-foured and Fair-Isled, prowling through those suburban gardens at dusk in search of a long-lost shanked drive.

Number 38 Christowel Street (or Christowell Street, depending on which end of the street you read), in the 'Tudor style', was my father's first speculative villa and we lived there until he had built a mock Elizabethan dwelling four doors up the street. Soon after I was born the Tudor house was sold to two maiden ladies called the Misses Train and we moved into the Elizabethan bungalow, while my increasingly prosperous father drew up the plans for a two-storeyed cream-brick neo-Georgian monolith on the very crest of the hill. Dwarfing all its neighbours, this was to be our final family home. Or it *would* be if he got a good enough price for the Elizabethan at Number 30.

They were 'homes' in Christowel Street, Camberwell, and there was a magazine called the *Australian Home Beautiful*

SUBDIVISIONAL AUCTION SALE

CAMBERWELL GOLF LINKS

SATURDAY 30TH APRIL

at 3 O'CLOCK

The Spirit of the Camberwell Golf Links

AUCTIONEERS

SYDNEY T. HAYNES & CO.
COMMERCIAL BANK CHAMBERS
339 COLLINS STREET · MELBOURNE

NORMAN D. MACKAY
258 RIVERSDALE ROAD, MIDDLE CAMBERWELL
PHONE CANTERBURY 1860

especially addressed to enterprising young couples who no longer wished to live in houses. 'Houses' were rather common weatherboard affairs, they were old-fashioned, dark, close to the street and sometimes joined together, or semi-detached. If you had survived the Depression and had liberated yourself from a working-class suburb like Thornbury, you deserved a nice brick home with a thirty-three-foot setback, picture windows, a terrazzo porch, a bird bath, a 'nature strip' and a driveway with 'provision for motor-car accommodation'.

In old Thornbury there were few trees, and they were mostly 'natives' – shaggy old eucalypts and pittosporums. Often in the back yards of the narrow artisans' houses there survived a few battered peppercorns, dropping their sticky aromatic drupelets or brushing the tin roofs of fowl house and outdoor dunny with their feathered leaves. Sometimes there was a perished Goodyear tyre roped up to one of the old tree's stouter boughs to make a swing for the scabby-kneed ragamuffins of that distant age, long before Thornbury became, amazingly, an Equadorian and Laotian enclave.

On the Golf Links Estate, however, the eucalypt was banished. A few, as I have said, lingered along the railway line, or survived in small parks – ghettos for gums – but in the new gardens on the hill the vernacular, even the arboreal vernacular, was considered bad manners. The New Gentility demanded silver birches, liquid ambers, pin oaks, prunus plums and magnolias, and every back garden had its lemon tree, which thrived on the sandy soil. And everyone had a Japanese maple, although after Pearl Harbor most of these were patriotically poisoned, ringbarked and extirpated.

Because the Golf Links Estate was to be a model suburb, builders had to observe special covenants ensuring that they would not erect timber dwellings and corrugated-iron roofs or paling fences within thirty-six feet of the frontage. These measures were to keep our estate respectable, free of ramshackle outhouses and, above all, chicken coops. These were emblems of a working-class background from which the young couples in Finsbury Way, Maple Crescent, Marlborough Avenue and Christowel Street had at last emancipated themselves.

Our new house had a tradesman's entrance, the only one in the street, with a discreet sign which said no hawkers or canvassers. Sometimes I kept watch on the other less protected houses in the hope of glimpsing one of these strange mendicants. The hawker I imagined festooned with black birds like a sinister Papageno. On our gatepost at the entrance to the driveway was a large brass plaque and the legend:

J. A. E. HUMPHRIES
MASTER BUILDER

which my mother regularly burnished with Brasso. In the opposite gatepost there was a cavity in the brickwork containing our letterbox. Cold and slightly damp, it was the popular abode of snails which left their silver signatures on our post.

In the thirties, when our street was created, it was experimentally paved with cement, not bitumen like all the other streets in Melbourne. It felt different even to a child, living on a white road, and I can remember the many horse-drawn vehicles that clopped up and down it through my childhood. There was the ragged 'Bottle-o', with his strange yodelled call which could be heard streets away, and a Chinese greengrocer. Then the baker, with his elaborately painted van, and the milkman, whom I never saw; though if I woke early I could always hear the sound of his draught-horse snorting outside the house, the chink of the bottles and the snap of the tradesman's hatch. There was a brightly decorated ice-cream cart too, drawn by a pony with a tinkling bell, which on a hot summer afternoon made the slowest progress of all up our street. In spite of the warning on the Tradesman's Entrance, we had a procession of tradesmen to the front door from whom my mother might buy something, depending on whether they wore an ex-serviceman's badge, or how few fingers they had. We had a Honey man, a Needle-and-Thread man, a Scissor man and a Rawleigh man, who carried a small Globite suitcase of Rawleigh's medicaments, like Ready Relief and Goanna Salve, which my mother always purchased, and never used.

Over our new back fence of wooden palings coyly camouflaged with a brushwood screen, was a dark alleyway paved with bluestone and smelling of a dank ferment. If you scrambled up the fence and looked beyond this lane, you could see the broken back fences and the old unpainted weatherboard houses in Bellett Street. Once on the fringe of Melbourne, these were now the houses my parents and their neighbours literally turned their backs on. They had flaking red-tin corrugated roofs, collapsing back verandas, grimy windows and their rusted fly-wire kitchen doors were constantly being slammed open and shut by ragged kids and mongrel dogs. The lazy rhythm of the lawn-mower which chattered through every summer afternoon of my childhood was never heard in those derelict back yards with their coarse and piebald grass, and their clutter of improvised fowl houses, ramshackle sheds and lopsided dunnies overgrown with Morning Glory. There, at our back door, was another world; the world of the poor!

We stared at each other sometimes, the poor and I. Me, on the top rung of my cherry-red ladder propped against the brushwood, and they, across that sour narrow lane through the gaps in their disintegrating fence and a tangle of briars and rusted hoop-iron. We never spoke, just stared. They always seemed to have very healthy brown faces and bloody kneecaps. The boys wore knotted handkerchiefs giving them an insolent piratical appearance and, with their heads on one side, they gawked at me for a while before running off to scrabble once more in the dirt amongst the dogs and chooks. Once an unkempt urchin-girl gave me a sheepish smirk before grinding her nose with the back of a frayed knitted wrist and releasing a trapeze of lettuce-green mucus.

Family snapshots show me romping around in the back garden at Christowel Street in various exotic disguises. From an early age I had a 'dress-up box' and my parents' little black

Kodak captured me coyly posturing in the costume of red Indian, sailor, cowboy and Chinaman. My first memories are of the garden in these small black-and-white photographs. The poplar and tulip trees newly planted, the big hydrangeas merely cuttings, the beds of phlox, pansies and petunias only seedlings, and the new English lawn, a timid gramineous haze.

My father had installed an elaborate underground sprinkler system to maintain both front and back gardens in a state of perpetual verdure, even through the most scorching summer. It must have been one of the first of its kind in Melbourne and it did away with the need for an unruly – and slightly common – garden hose. On hot afternoons we simply adjusted a series of taps, and miraculously, from nowhere, there sprang bouquets of sparkling water ticketed with rainbows. Amongst these I loved to play, bare soles squeaking on the wet grass. There were no water restrictions then; no neighbours eager to report a frivolous waste to the authorities.

We had only one set of neighbours anyway, the Train sisters who had bought our old house. To the left of Number 36 was a vacant allotment full of blackberries and coarse grass. For years afterwards my father bitterly regretted his failure to purchase this land and build a tennis court. Instead it was snapped up in 1939 by a Mr and Mrs Tootell who, to our horror, built *another* two-storey house, irritatingly like our own, and covered with a disagreeable buff stucco, like dried sick. Although we remained on polite terms with these childless architectural plagiarists until their ultimate relocation to a nearby twilight home, we exchanged no more than the most perfunctory courtesies; nor once crossed each other's threshold. Moreover, if half-cups of sugar, cream of tartar, bicarbonate of soda or any urgently needed ingredient was to be borrowed, my mother preferred to ask the furthest neighbour than importune the stand-offish couple next door.

From my earliest recollection, my father's habitual nickname for me was 'Sunny Sam' because of my blithe disposition. I was blithe, of course, for I was the centre of attention, the focus of my parents' affections and those of my many aunts and uncles. There was no brother or sister to deflect the flow of adoration which streamed towards me. Yet.

At bedtime my mother would come into my room to hear my prayers, a litany of gibbered 'Godblesses' in which I tried to mention everyone I knew. I most enjoyed prayers when my parents were going out to the pictures or to a 'card night'. Then my mother would be wearing her silver fox, its sprung tortoise-shell jaw snapped shut on its own tail, and its sly glass eyes staring into mine. With my nose buried in that musky pelt, I gabbled my vespers in my mother's perfumed embrace. The longer I protracted my prayers the longer I could bask in Evening in Paris, Charmosan face powder and the faint vulpine odour of her wrap.

I cannot remember precisely when my sister, Barbara, was born. I can only recall a day when there was suddenly and unexpectedly another focus of attention in our house. It lay on my mother's bed, shawled and swaddled, a black hairy caterpil-lar. My sister's arrival, when I was nearly three years of age, caused me no great concern at the time. I must have adjusted quite quickly and comfortably to this new presence, which failed seriously to challenge my position. But what was terribly worrying, inexplicable and grossly unjust was that, seven long months later, she was *still there*.

Licking the Beaters

MRS FLINT WAS my very first teacher. I have thought of changing her name in case some litigious descendant recognizes his venerated great-grandmother. But I can find no better name for her than her real name; grey quartzy sharp-edged hard. She ran a small kindergarten in her own grey pebble-dashed Californian bungalow down the hill from our place, and her two best rooms, the lounge and dining-room, to the right of her dark hallway, had been turned into a classroom for local tots. Edna, my first and favourite nanny, would escort me every morning down the steep pavement of Marlborough Avenue until after several twists and turns and carefully crossed, sparsely motored roads we arrived at Mrs Flint's front gate, already jammed with tricycles and mothers. Mrs Flint, wearing a large apron to keep the chalk off her faded if flocculous print dress, stood on the front step screwing her face into what she imagined to be a friendly and motherly grimace as she welcomed her little pupils and reassured departing parents. She was a good actress, this old battle-axe, for the mothers all went home fondly believing that their littlies were in wonderful hands in spite of the panic-stricken screams that most of Mrs Flint's pupils emitted as soon as they realized that they had been abandoned to her care. No sooner had the last mother gone and the drone of the last parental sedan faded up Orrong

Crescent than Mrs Flint's true mineral nature asserted itself. Once she was alone with her infant charges the ingratiating smile of the kindly old widow who adored children quickly faded and she would swing around from her blackboard and exhibit to the class a very different and frightening countenance on which rage, spite and ignorance jostled for supremacy.

It always took a long time for the crying to stop at Mrs Flint's kindergarten. One little girl called Jocelyn cried all the time and no amount of cajolery could stop her. In the end Mrs Flint put her out to graze in the back yard where, still bawling, she executed endless circuits on her trike. Inside we sat at miniature tables on stools enamelled cherry-red, one of the most popular hues of the late thirties. Because the classroom occupied Mrs Flint's lounge and dining room there were a few of her more substantial pieces of furniture – a Genoa-velvet couch, a bookcase and a Jacobean-style dining table with matching sideboard – shoved against the wall to make room for our small chairs and tables. Mrs Flint made it very clear that if anyone so much as laid a curious finger on one of her trumpery treacle-coloured sticks they would be put out in the yard with the eternally blubbering Jocelyn.

Mrs Flint was no great reader; except for the *Pears Cyclopaedia*, a couple of Ethel M. Dells and a Netta Muskett, her bookshelves accommodated faded family snaps and gewgaws which she called her 'ordiments'. However, every morning, seated in one of her deeper fawn-and-russet Genoa-velvet lounge chairs, with her dress hitched up so we could see her surgical stockings, she read us a story. Her favourite was Hansel and Gretel and even the least imaginative child found a painful empathy with this tale and its themes of parental abandonment and persecution by a cannibalistic crone.

There was a mid-morning break and we all filed out the back to our trikes and lugubriously circled Mrs Flint's prickly lawn. When I first saw Doré's engraving of convicts dismally revolving in their bleak exercise yard, I had only to imagine them with gaily painted Cyclops tricycles and scooters between their shanks to be grimly reminded of playtime at Mrs Flint's.

One day two bikes rammed into each other just in front of me, and my friend Graham Coles fell off his seat and crashed to the ground, breaking his arm. There was a big fuss and Mrs Flint's face nearly ruptured itself, feigning expressions of compassion and concern. Poor Graham's arm wasn't set properly and it had to be operated on again. The operation was not successful however and Graham's arm never grew. Years later when we were no longer the friends we had been in childhood I would see him as he passed our house on his way to Scotch College, one sleeve especially shortened to accommodate his bonsai appendage.

Apart from her fawning attentions to our parents and nannies there was one other human being to whom Mrs Flint displayed an amiable demeanour. Her daughter Nursie. Over half a century later I can only assume that Nursie was a nurse and that she had a real name like everyone else. But Mrs Flint always called her Nursie and something resembling warmth crept into her cold dry voice when she announced Nursie's presence in the house. For Nursie came and went, and we glimpsed her but occasionally sitting at the linoleum-covered kitchen table having a cup of tea, as we filed out to the back veranda for our play lunch. She had plucked eyebrows and a blonde perm which stuck out in a wedge at the back like Garbo's in the last scene in *Queen Christina*, or like the 'art deco' windswept hair-do of the woman whose white glass profile appeared on top of Atlantic petrol pumps; a crude commercial descendant of Lalique's opaline car mascots.

Between sips of Robur tea and puffs on her Du Maurier, Nursie flashed us a flirtatious smile while Mrs Flint fussed about refilling her cup and fetching her ginger nuts and Marie biscuits as though she were a nice person pleased to see her daughter.

Mrs Flint was keen to show parents that their children didn't just listen to stories or ride their bikes in endless circles in her back yard, so she decided we must all learn to count. I must have been the slowest to acquire this doubtful skill, for I remember being kept back while the other children played. Alone amongst the chipped cherry-red stools while Mrs Flint, terribly close so that I could smell her damp surgical stockings and her odour of stale talcum, forced me to count and count and recount until, weeping, I finally stumbled to one hundred. When would Edna come to rescue me? I wondered, peering up towards the lozenged leadlight windows through which grown-ups could be seen on their way to the front porch. But on that dreadful day each shrill chirrup of the doorbell announced someone else's mother, so that I was alone with my tormentor and all those numbers for what seemed like an eternity before deliverance finally came. Since those early struggles with innumeracy – as I believe it is now called – I have shunned every form of mathematics, leaving the counting to accountants and trusted managers, a task they have often performed with a surprising display of imagination.

I am not certain at this distance in time whether, having counted to a century, I graduated from Mrs Flint's Dame School, or whether my mother, detecting my misery, rescued me. I may well have complained, for I remember my mother saying, in her defence, what a 'refined' woman she thought Mrs Flint to be. Already at four years of age I had begun to apprehend that refinement was very often an extenuating virtue; one that excused and eclipsed almost every other unappetizing trait. But it was hard for me to share this adult view of Mrs Flint's refinement. No doubt the hag had once patronized my mother with a long word or an unfamiliar locution – a verbal crooking of the pinky – and had thereafter acquired her dubious epithet.

I preferred to be at home anyway; pampered by Edna and spoilt by Pat Bagott, our gardener and handyman. Pat was my father's favourite employee, and in Australian society of this period he was that great rarity, a childless Roman Catholic. This may have been the main reason why my mother spoke more generously of him and his little wife than she customarily did of their more fecund co-religionists.

As Mrs Flint's saving grace had been refinement, the Bagotts' was their cleanliness, not an attribute my mother's family associated with the adherents of Rome. She had made a point of seeing where the Bagotts lived; in a flat working-class suburb far from our undulant and lawned oasis. And she had pronounced the dwelling 'spotless', '*small, but spotless*'. One of her favourite sayings was: 'You don't have to be well-off to be *particular*,' and she frequently attributed this apophthegm to her late mother, lending it a kind of genealogical veracity. Much as Field-Marshal Goering sought to confer Aryan status on the Jewish tenor Richard Tauber, so my mother spared Pat Bagott her usual strictures against Catholicism. Without knowing it, the spotless and particular Bagotts were granted a unique amnesty; in my mother's eyes at least they were honorary Protestants.

My father was a builder of sturdy suburban villas whose business reached its first peak of success in the years before the Second World War. He built houses in all the popular styles; mock Tudor, Spanish mission, neo-Georgian, Californian bungalow and moderne. In the very late thirties, if the client was especially rich and daring and my father able to procure enough glass building blocks and aubergine-coloured 'manganese' bricks, he would build them a 'jazz moderne' house with curved corner windows, a flat roof, a nautical-looking sun deck and *no front fence!* It is still odd to see in the suburban streets of Melbourne these once startling architectural hybrids; chubby colonial relations of their austere German cousins in Dessau and Stuttgart.

As a toddler, long before Mrs Flint's kindergarten, I would often be taken off by my father on his daily rounds visiting building sites. In that epoch before seat-belts I would roll around on the back seat of his streamlined putty-white Oldsmobile, or stand precariously on the hot grey leather clinging to a sturdy tassel. We would arrive at a 'job' and while my father strode fearlessly across the raw yellow joists remonstrating with brickies, or pored over flapping blueprints with the foreman, I would amuse myself with a drill and an offcut of Oregon pine. Sometimes we would arrive during the lunch break and I would see the men rolling their 'smokes' and making their billy tea over a mound of blazing wood chips on an improvised hearth. Just as the water in the blackened tin came to the boil Alec Gibson would open a sachet of wax paper his wife had packed with his doorstep sandwiches, and fling the contents of sugar and tea-leaves into the seething water.

I used to love watching the cement being mixed, as I enjoyed a similar process at home when my mother ran up a sponge. Alec warned me against getting too near the concrete mixer with a story about a nipper who had only the other day got too close to the grey-lipped maw of that relentlessly sloshing drum, and got sucked in. With a calloused finger he pointed to a small cement-encrusted boot lying amongst the builders' debris. 'That's all that's left of him, Bun,' said Alec lugubriously, 'so don't get too near that bloody doover, or *you'll* be a goner yesself!'

Alec and Pat Bagott and the other men called me 'Bun', which was probably short for currant bun; a reference to my innumerable moles. One day, at smoko, while we were sitting around on piles of bricks, eating our sandwiches and waiting for the billy to boil, Alec stood up, 'See you in a jiff, Bun, just going to strain the potatoes.' And he ambled off in the direction of the narrow galvanized iron dunny, screened with a hessian curtain. That night at dinner I rather pointedly left the table and on the way to the lavatory I called back to my mother, 'Just off to strain the potatoes.' When I returned there was an 'atmosphere' and I overheard my mother saying in the low voice children are not supposed to hear, '. . . and just make sure the more common element amongst your men watch what they say in front of little Barry, or who knows what he'll be coming out with next'.

The South Camberwell State School was a raw red-brick two-storey building in a small street off Toorak Road. It stood in an extensive asphalt wasteland, bounded by the palings of adjacent houses. This was the playground. Far away, against the back fence and partly shaded by a mutilated peppercorn, stood the only other structure in that desolate schoolground, the shelter shed. This was a sort of wooden box with one wall missing in which children presumably sheltered from the extremes of the Melbourne climate. At lunchtime on a wet day it would be packed with damp urchins delving into their sandwich tins and screaming at the tops of their voices. The noise in that confined space under a reboant tin roof was appalling, but worse was the overpowering and nauseating stench of gooey brown banana sandwiches and other nameless fillings. It did not surprise me in the least, when years later I learnt that the artless expression, 'Who opened their lunch?' was 1930s Australian slang for 'Who farted?' Only then did I realize that others before me had reeled back from the effluvia of cut lunches.

My parents sent me there for about a year until I was old enough to attend a nice Junior School. I had seen the brochure for Camberwell Grammar in my father's den. It had a sky-blue crinkly cover, embossed with the school's mitred crest, and glossy pages with pictures of some brand-new manganese brick buildings photographed from oblique angles to make them look more monumental than they actually were. It was supposed to be a 'very good school' and it charged *fees*. It catered for boys only, and mostly boys from 'comfortable homes'.

But Camberwell State, which I was forced to attend in the meantime, was free and co-ed. The hardships of life in Mrs Flint's back-yard jungle were nothing compared with the shrieking, thumping, yelling, wrestling maelstrom of human maggots into which I had been hurled.

Quickly I became aware of the gulf that divided me from them; the gulf that separated the Australian working class from the newly arisen 'affluent' middle class. It was wider, bleaker and more inimical than the grey tundra of the playground. In my effeminate little blue Aertex shirt which laced at the neck, pleated linen shorts, fawn cotton socks and leather sandals with side buckles, I felt uncomfortably alien to the other boys. Many of them wore scuffed and splitting sandshoes and a few even arrived at school barefoot. Our classroom was full of densely darned and threadbare maroon sweaters, patched britches, grubby lacunose stockings, scabby knees, bloody noses, verminous hair and ears erupting with bright pumpkin wax. The slatternly girls were no less alarming to a mollycoddled little Lord Fauntleroy from the Golf Links Estate.

The first form was presided over by a gorgon called Miss Jensen. She was the first woman I ever met with her hair in a bun, and she had a knack of making the chalk squeal on the blackboard. She favoured bottle-green 'twin sets' and fawn tweed skirts and she looked uncannily like Mrs Bun the Baker's wife in Happy Families. Miss Jensen and I took an instant dislike to one another.

We lived only about half a mile from the school, so I was mostly spared the ordeal of sandwiches in the shelter shed. Instead, punctually at 12.30, my father would collect me in the big putty-white Oldsmobile and drive me home for a peaceful lunch at my own little table on the lawn, or with my mother in the sun-room amongst her new cane furniture and shining brass knick-knacks. Everything in our house was new, or 'up-to-date' as they said in the thirties. We had a new Frigidaire with a light inside which went on when you opened the door. Every now and then it shuddered rather violently, as if from the cold. Most other people we knew still had ice-chests, and I rather envied them the iceman's visit as he shouldered those great glassy blocks up their sideways. On top of the fridge stood our new Sunbeam Mixmaster. This was a streamlined bullet-shaped appliance rather like a Buck Rogers spaceship, in the popular colour combination of cream and black. We had all the attachments and the brochure, but we only used it for juicing oranges and making cakes. When the twin whisks plunged into the bowl of glutinous sponge mixture my mother tweaked a mammiform control knob to the appropriate speed and the engine whirred into action, the whisks churning so that their blades seemed to vanish until they were just two chrome rods suspended in a fragrant yellow vortex. The kitchen filled with a miraculous aroma of heating machinery, compounded with vanilla essence. Once the Mixmaster was silenced and the whisks detached, I was allowed to lick off the ambrosial emulsion. Licking the beaters was one of the great privileges of an Australian childhood.

Our other modern appliance was a Radiola 'mantel model' wireless set. Chubbily ziggurattish in moulded brown Bakelite, it had a vertically fluted front panel rather like the fascia of a modernistic building. Behind the organ-pipe grille could be glimpsed a curtain of sheeny brown cretonne through which the music and the voices shrilly filtered. 'The Girl on the Pink Police Gazette' and 'My Merry Oldsmobile' were popular airs of the period, and it seemed strange and inexplicable that the radio could be singing so intimately about our family car.

> Come away with me Lucile
> In my merry Oldsmobile,
> Down the road of life we'll fly
> Automobubbling you and I.
> To the church we'll swiftly steal,
> Then our wedding bells will peal,
> You can go as far as you like with me,
> In my merry automobile.

I had been given a toy submarine made in Japan, containing a clockwork mechanism which, when wound up, propelled it realistically along the bottom of the bath. One day I took it to school, a big mistake. It was one of those rare days when

I didn't go home for lunch, so, avoiding the hellish shelter shed, I took my sub and my sandwiches to a peaceful corner of the playground. Soon I found myself encircled by a group of rough kids who demanded my submarine. A tussle ensued in which my lunch got trodden into the asphalt and as the jeering circle of larrikins drew closer and more threatening I picked up a handful of gravel ready to defend myself. The bullies fled, but they did not disperse. They must have formed a delegation to Miss Jensen because immediately after recess she hauled me out in front of the class for 'throwing stones', a heinous violation of the school rules. I denied doing any such thing, but the testimony of the smirking yahoos carried more weight than my tearful protestations, and I was pushed in the corner for the rest of the afternoon with a sign on my back: I AM A BULLY. Much later, when the class had been dismissed for the afternoon, Miss Jensen told me that if I persisted in denying my guilt she would take me to see Mr Fraser, the headmaster, a ginger-haired functionary whom I had privately nicknamed 'Duckface'. I stuck to my guns, however, and only at the entrance to his study, and threatened with imminent expulsion, did I finally break down and recant, confessing to a crime I had never committed. Grudgingly, clemency supervened, and I was allowed to go home, my heart pounding with shame and rage. For some reason which remains obscure, I never told my parents of this incident – perhaps I feared that they might share Miss Jensen's view of the matter.

Since then I have entertained fantasies of vengeance. Supposing Miss Jensen had been, say, twenty-five at the time, she might now, in 1992, be a sprightly seventy-seven-year-old living with her daughter, sitting peacefully knitting in some honeysuckled garden bower, or quietly watching television in a Melbourne suburb. For my purposes it would be more convenient if she were installed in a sunset facility or oldsters' terminary. There I could visit her, explaining to the nursing staff that I was a concerned relation who required a few moments' privacy with the titubating inmate. I would need very little time to attach the small placard, concealed under my raincoat, to the back of old Miss Jensen's bobbing matinée jacket.

The Master Builder

M Y NEW SISTER did little to spoil my excursions with my father. On the contrary, so that my mother could devote herself to this squealing, coconut-faced intruder, we spent more time together than before. Occasionally his business took him 'into town' and sometimes I would be left for what seemed like an eternity in the locked Oldsmobile while he rushed into banks and insurance companies. Once, I am told, he returned to find the car surrounded by a large crowd of amused pedestrians watching while I performed some sort of comic mime on the back seat. My father was sufficiently entertained by this incident to relate it proudly to my mother on our return home, but far from pleasing her it had, to his dismay, the reverse effect, and he was severely told off for 'neglecting' me.

When my father took me into town and he was not on business, we would often visit two places: the Museum and the Aquarium. At the Museum he would hurry me past the paintings and the stuffed bandicoots and the mineral samples, and stop only before one exhibit – Phar Lap, the famous racehorse, who stood, impeccably stuffed, in a large glass case. There was always a small group of awe-struck spectators around this mysterious effigy.

People would pop into the Museum in their lunch hour to pay their respects to the most celebrated dead horse in Australia;

some were eating sandwiches and sausage rolls as they stared up at those unblinking glass eyes. I had noticed on my visits to the city how often people seemed to eat in the street, many of them hurrying to catch a tram, but with their noses buried in paper bags, rather like the horses they so much admired. These ravenous pedestrians were not just office boys and shopgirls, but men in business suits wolfing hot pies as they stood at traffic lights, and with a spare handkerchief – this was before the age of Kleenex – unselfconsciously mopping up the sauce and scalding gravy as it trickled down their wrists. Even today, the lifts in office buildings throughout Australia reek with the smell of sandwiches, pies and pasties – and with the more exotic smells of Vietnamese and Laotian takeaway. Eating on the run may well be an atavistic custom inherited from convict days.

Our other pilgrimage was to the Aquarium, then a run-down and gloomy establishment. Few went there, however, to see the fish, just as the Museum and Art Gallery was rarely attended by the admirers of Tiepolo, Manet and Van Eyck. On a damp wall of the Aquarium hung an object which looked like an old rusty bucket, and beneath it, a larger crudely shaped carapace of dented iron; it was the bullet-grazed armour of Ned Kelly, the legendary bushranger, which he wore in his last confrontation with the police.

My father told me that Sarah Meadows, my grandmother, as a small child near Benalla, used to hide under the bed when the Kelly brothers rode by. I had the feeling that my father, and all the other people who shuffled in a silent semi-circle gazing up at this assembly of scrap iron, had rather a soft spot for Ned Kelly, though I no more understood why his armour hung amongst the fish than I comprehended why the mummy of a horse stood in an art gallery.

Apart from regular visits to building sites, he would also take me to the Camberwell market to buy oysters from a Greek 'reffo' (or refugee) whose shop window was perpetually veiled by a sheet of running water. This custom, now long obsolete, gave an illusion of freshness; as though the shoals of schnapper, whiting and flathead and the serried jars of oysters and mussels that lined the parsley-upholstered marble slab were submerged in their natural element.

Unlike the decorous little shops my mother frequented, the market was raucous and pungent, filled with the stench of fish, the scents of fruit and the acrid odour of chrysanthemums.

Sometimes we would have a haircut together and, because I was too small for the chair, Mr McGrath, the barber, would sit me on a box high up on one of his adjustable cast-iron thrones. A towelette would be tucked into my collar over which he draped a large sheet, so that, seen in the mirror, my head appeared to project from the summit of a white wigwam. From a glass-fronted cabinet bearing a crudely painted Red Cross, he then removed a greasy comb and a pair of scissors and proceeded to slice away at my hair, which fell in pale mousey stooks upon the folds of my voluminous tent. During this operation Mr McGrath conducted a loud and esoteric colloquy, mainly on sporting subjects, with the other customers, who lounged on a long pew against the wall, smoking and leafing through *Smith's Weekly* and copies of the Melbourne *Truth*.

As he snipped, Mr McGrath's white-coated tummy pressed so firmly against me that the labyrinthine progress of his lunch, and the peristaltic rills and tricklings which accompanied it, could be plainly heard.

Next came the clippers, which were kept, like all his other tools of trade, in the same magically sterile cabinet with the chipped Red Cross. I felt the steel mandible coldly gnashing at my nape and travelling ominously upwards. Finally the time came for a squirt of water and a swift anointment of cherry-coloured brilliantine. His last savage gesture with the comb never failed to decapitate a small mole on the crown of my head, which, undeterred, always managed to heal – and enlarge – by the next haircut. To this day, deep in my scalp, I can still feel that hidden wen; legacy of the McGrath method.

After the comb and the cowlick, the barber, with the flourish of a matador, would sweep the sheet off my shoulders and lift me down from my box on to the pilose linoleum.

Haircuts were frequently interrupted as Mr McGrath hurried to the counter at the front of his shop to serve customers with smoking materials. Behind the small lino-topped counter was a positive reredos of cigarette packets and smoking slogans: We too smoke Turf! Three Threes Always Please, Country Life, City Club, Temple Bar, Ardath, Craven A, Capstan and the less popular filtered lines designed to appeal to women and pansies, like Garrick and Du Maurier; names that aroused a distant resonance of sophistication even if you didn't know they were named after dead actors. Mr McGrath also did a roaring trade in Havelock Ready-rubbed Tobacco, Boomerang Cigarette Papers and, on very rare occasions, a packet of Spud, Australia's first mentholated cigarette. Spuds, as I later discovered, tasted of strong mothballs and had a habit of emitting small but startling detonations as the chunks of saltpetre embedded in the tobacco exploded.

Mr McGrath lived above and behind his shop. I was often in the chair or waiting when his two burly sons came home from school. With caps askew, grumous-kneed and with concertina socks, they stormed through the dark shop and disappeared into the mysterious sanctum beyond. Mr McGrath usually glanced up from his victim and eyed them reproachfully in the big mirror on which was painted a First World War infantry officer lighting a comrade's cigarette. Beneath the puzzling rubric: 'The Greys is great!' On a dusty shelf below the mirror was a display of Spruco, a popular lolly-pink hair lotion of the period which came in chunky Cubist bottles distantly related to the sculptures of Henri Laurens and Archipenko.

I envied all shopkeepers. How exciting it must be to own a shop and live above it in a 'dwelling'. I had learned from my father that accommodation above shops was always called a dwelling whereas people who were slightly better off, i.e., didn't have to sell things, lived in houses and we, who were already, to employ my mother's favourite epithet, 'comfortable', lived in a home. Indeed, a *lovely home.*

My mother's unmarried sister, Elsie, was lucky enough to have a dwelling. She sold wool, cotton and knitting accoutrements in a dark but thriving little shop in Burke Road, Camberwell. While Aunty Elsie gossiped with her customers and doled out the bright skeins of wool to her zealous clientele of knitters, I, as her nephew, enjoyed the exciting privilege of going 'backstage'; parting the cretonne curtains behind the shop and entering the arcana of her premises where my grandfather sat in a small parlour smoking his pipe and listening to the wireless. Because Aunty Elsie was single, she had inherited the spinster's task of looking after her widowed father. His wife – my mother's mother – had died before I was born, but there was a large sepia photograph of her in my aunt's dwelling; a handsome, unsmiling and curiously implacable woman. It was impossible to tell, as with many women, whether she wore an expression of goodwill or disdain. As I write this, it occurs to me that nobody ever smiled in formal portraits of that period, since one could never sustain a smile for the length of the exposure. There must have been a moment in history when it became fashionable to grin unconvincingly at the camera. The age of the snap.

Papa Brown, as my mother's father was called, had a large repertoire of music-hall songs, my favourite being 'The Mystery of the Hansom Cab'.

Stop the cab, stop the cab, whoa, whoa, WHOA!
Somebody hold the horse's head and don't leave go,
But nevertheless they had to confess although they made a
grab,
They never discovered the mystery of the hansom cab!

Many years later, I discovered Fergus Hume's mystery yarn of the same title. It was set in Melbourne in the 1880s and had a worldwide success, though I can find no record of the catchy but frustrating song it inspired.

At this time in my life, with little thought to the irreparable damage it might have upon my future character, my father willingly translated my every whim into reality. It may have been to compensate me for the unwelcome persistence of a sibling, but I was horribly spoiled. Soon his carpenters were busy in our back garden constructing my own shop, my name in flourishing cherry-red calligraphy, painted on the shingle by a professional sign-writer. I would spend every afternoon behind my counter selling miniature groceries to the neighbours' children for hard currency.

My father had always wanted to be a dentist and, whenever any of us had a loose tooth, would eagerly volunteer to separate us from it. He had only followed the building trade in obedience to the wishes of my grandfather who had set himself up in that business in the country town of Benalla soon after emigrating to Australia from Manchester in 1888. When my father was five my grandparents and their young family moved to Melbourne, but Great-Uncle Jack Meadows, my grandmother's brother, stayed in Benalla, and, with dubious credentials, opened a dental practice. In those far-off days when my mother still joked, my father's amateur extractions usually inspired a satirical comment: 'I don't know why your father never became a dentist like his Uncle Jack,' she would say, adding with a whimsical smile: 'not that *I* would ever have married a man who liked putting his fingers in other people's mouths!'

Respectability began to grow up around us like the garden, putting down its roots and stretching forth its tendrils and branches. We had special words for things which 'common people' didn't use. Indeed, my mother never employed the word 'common'; she preferred the epithet 'ordinary'. The children at South Camberwell State School, for example, were 'ordinary', but the boys at Camberwell Grammar School were, on the whole 'nice', from 'nice homes' (not houses) and their families were 'comfortable', that is to say, they had enough of the wherewithal. 'They' only had a back yard but we had a back garden. They had a wash house, we had a laundry. They pulled the chain, we flushed the toilet. They had 'blood' noses, we had nosebleeds. They had buck teeth, but my teeth were slightly prominent.

As soon as my father recognized that we had a dental problem in the family, I was whisked into town to see a specialist. This dentist occupied rooms in the T&G Building, one of Melbourne's first skyscrapers, and to reach him we had to ascend by lift to the giddy height of twelve floors. However this dentist did not merely occupy an architectural eminence, he had attained such distinction that he was no longer Dr Morris but *Mr* Morris, an elevation in rank which mystifies me as much now as it did then. Mr Morris looked at my rabbit-like incisors and recommended a long and costly treatment. But my father already had other ideas. Whatever these fancy Collins Street specialists might suggest, a second opinion must be sought. And the man to pronounce that opinion? No one more qualified – though his surgery was 120 miles away – than Uncle Jack.

At Spencer Street Railway Station, armed with tickets and, if not books, Reading Matter, we set off on the long train journey to my father's birthplace, the township of Benalla. The war had begun and the train was full of our men in uniform, smoking, shouting and endlessly filing up and down the swaying corridors. My father in his civvies looked slightly out of place and nervous amongst all that khaki. He had bought me a copy of a cheaply produced magazine called *Humour*, containing cartoons and a great number of short jokes like the ones found in Christmas crackers. Though I did not get the point of a single joke, I ploughed doggedly through its dully printed pages. I noticed when my father glanced at the same periodical that he smirked a couple of times and even laughed, so I realized that what was incomprehensible to me could be funny to adults. And I marvelled that an entire magazine could be devoted to making people laugh.

We were travelling at night and sometimes the train stopped

inexplicably for long intervals before rumbling off again on its endless journey. There were uncomfortable visits to the lavatory when we lurched down dim corridors through a gauntlet of somnambulistic soldiers until at last we reached the mephitic cubicle. Locked therein and struggling to keep my balance without crashing against a contagious surface, I watched my father fastidiously drape the wooden horseshoe with swathes of toilet paper.

Uncle Jack, dapper and rubicund, was waiting for us in the early hours as we alighted, ashen-faced, at Benalla Station. During the short drive in his old Ford through the wide dusty streets of the township, my father excitedly pointed out surviving landmarks of his boyhood: the iron-lace-verandaed Coffee Palace his grandmother had established and where my grandmother had worked as a girl, his old school and Great-Uncle Frank's tinsmith's shop. From the bridge I saw some ragamuffins diving into the Broken River. At last we arrived at Uncle Jack's abode, a rambling Victorian bungalow, shaded by big gnarled peppercorns, where an attractive woman with a long sallow face called Mrs Black ran us a deep Rexona-scented tub and prepared a large country breakfast of bacon and eggs. There was no sign of Aunty Gertie, who I gathered lived more or less permanently in Melbourne, and Mrs Black seemed somehow, even to childish eyes, a little more than a housekeeper.

Uncle Jack, donning a starched white double-breasted overall, ominously flecked with rust-coloured stains, vanished into his surgery only to reappear half-way through the toast and marmalade. 'Got the beggar out just before it burst!' he announced proudly, waving a pair of forceps under my nose. In the pincer-grip we saw an enormous nicotine-streaked molar and on its snaggled root the plump yellow sac of pus. 'Keep it as a souvenir, lad!' said Uncle Jack, dropping it with a clink on to the plate beside my toast. Soon after I was in the dentist's chair gagging horribly while my great-uncle's Solvoled fingers plunged around inside my mouth. As my father listened devoutly, he explained his revolutionary new corrective method. Three days later I was orally fitted with this contraption. It was a plate, similar to my father's denture, which supported a metal band extending in a semi-circle under the top lip. Between this band and the front of my teeth were wedged several thin layers of rubber which pressed painfully against the rebellious incisors. The advantage of this method, apparently, was that it forced the teeth back twice as fast as traditional braces and the effeminate methods of the city. I had only to travel up to Benalla once a month for a whole year so that Uncle Jack could remove the plate and add another layer or two of rubber.

Apart from the dull ache which I constantly experienced, the taste of blood, and the difficulty I had in talking with this false red palate in my mouth, there was another inconvenience which I perceived only after drinking an ice-cream soda. Between my monthly visits I had to live with the nauseating taste and smell of rancid food trapped under Uncle Jack's inextricable device.

The damage from this amateur dentistry has caused problems that persist to this day and a very large chunk of my life has been spent, drugged and terrified, staring at the ceilings of dental surgeries throughout the world, or hunched over a spit-bowl drooling the blood-freaked detritus of yet another reamed root canal or shattered crown.

On winter nights we would always burn Mallee roots, which the woodman regularly heaped on the 'nature strip' outside our front gate. Some of them were huge, knotted and noduled, and rather than leave them burning all night in the grate, my father would, at bedtime, lift the incandescent root on a shovel and, trailing sparks, run outside and deposit it with a loud hiss in the gulley trap. In late summer if there was a hot north wind we might get 'red rain', big terracotta teardrops on all the picture windows and the car windscreens, which took hours to remove the next day with a chamois. The rain, we were told, was from the Mallee, a horrible far-away place where the firewood came from. It never occurred to me, or to many others then, that the more these roots were ripped from the soil to make our homes cosy, the more red rain would freckle our nice clean windows. It was a tasteless reminder of a place where Aborigines had once lived, where explorers had died, and where none of us need ever set foot.

Very few people we knew had gas fires, which my mother regarded as dangerous, and even slightly common. However, both my Aunty Elsie's 'dwelling', my grandparents' house and Uncle Jack's surgery smelt faintly of coal gas, an olfactory novelty to one accustomed as I to an odourless electrical home. When I stayed with my grandparents, Sarah, my father's mother, could always be found in her gas-scented kitchen cooking and making tea on her old 'Early Kooka', which, with its avian pun – an enamelled kookaburra on the oven door – was so much more interesting than mother's scentless Moffat electrical stove. At Nanna's there would always be the scratch of a match, a tweaked tap, a little *phut*, and then, miraculously, a blue lotus of fire. She was a tireless baker of cakes and pavlovas, and after a visit to my grandparents no one left without at least one passionfruit sponge and a tray of kisses, butterfly cakes and yo-yos. Whenever I stayed with them my sweet, kind grandmother spoiled me terribly, and fed me almost exclusively on those delicious confections she had learned to bake in her country girlhood, when she and her mother ran the Benalla Coffee Palace.

I had been told that my father's father was as stern as his wife was saintly, and when I bathed or cleaned my teeth in their small, Rexona-green bathroom, I saw, suspended beside the towel rail, his leather razor strop. My father had told me how he and his brothers had lived in fear of this shaving accoutrement, yet I found it hard to see my grandfather as a punitive figure. To me he was always affectionate; too affection-ate in my mother's view.

'Eric,' she would say to my father, 'does Papa have to give

the children such wet kisses? I'm glad to say he doesn't do it to me any more.' And it was true, the tall Mancunian builder preserved a polite distance from his daughter-in-law.

My father's sister, Aunty Irene, lived with my grandparents before her marriage, and it was she who took me to my first motion picture. It was *The Wizard of Oz* and, apart from the Columbine caramels and the enchanting music of Harold Arlen, I recall few images from this film except that of Margaret Hamilton as the witch bicycling across a stormy sky. 'Could all women turn into witches?' I wondered on the many sleepless nights that followed my first movie matinée. *Snow White* was my next cinematic experience and for a long time thereafter, as my mother stooped tenderly over my bed to kiss me good-night, she may have been puzzled to see me looking up in terrified anticipation of a witch-like transmogrification.

The poisoned apple that Snow White nibbled greatly intrigued me and I was determined to make one myself and offer it to my sister's friend, Valerie, in the hope that it might immobilize her for many years to come. Carefully shaping some scraps of pastry left over from one of my mother's apple pies, I impregnated it with fly-spray, coloured it as realistically as possible with cochineal, and graciously presented it to my sister's pretty little playmate. Alas, I could only force her to take one bite before the odour of insecticide persuaded her that this was no ordinary Red Delicious, one of which a day would keep the doctor away. She must have shown my gift to her parents, for I was sternly rebuked and forbidden thereafter to offer artificial fruit to the neighbours' children. In vain I tried to explain that my poisoned apple was merely a gallant attempt on my part to hasten Valerie's encounter with Prince Charming.

Weatherboard Swastikas

S OME YEARS AGO I found myself in Paris in August. As
might be expected at that time of the year, the city had an
air of abandonment and the narrow streets on the Left Bank
were almost deserted. Today, irrespective of season, one would
find Japanese tourists milling about obediently photographing
each other, but on this afternoon I noticed only one elderly
couple peering into the window of an antiquarian shop that
was clearly *fermé*. I instantly recognized, even at a distance of
one hundred yards, two fellow Australians. Perhaps it was the
predominant fawn and bistre of the man's attire, or the manner
in which the woman's short-sleeved Orlon print frock exposed
the peculiar flaccidity of her pale freckled triceps – known in
our homeland as 'bye-byes', since it is in the valedictory gesture
that they most noticeably wobble.

To confirm my surmise, I sidled up behind them to eavesdrop,
only to discover that I knew them. Quite well. They were in the
Old Wares business in Melbourne, in a modest way. I had
sometimes visited their dim little shop full of over-priced
gewgaws invariably labelled 'art deco' or 'art nouvé'. However,
pleased with this chance encounter, we retired to a café for a
celebratory drink, and after an inevitable discussion about the
mind-numbing rudeness of the Parisians, Herb and Doris
Prentiss confided that they had yet to arrange accommodation

for the night. With a locution that only a Melbourne-born person of his generation would utter, Herb leant across the table and inquired plaintively: 'D'you happen to know a nice *guest house* in this particular suburb?'

Throughout my childhood the world consisted of homes, houses and Guest Houses. Hotels were taboo. They were 'licensed premises'; insalubrious buildings on street corners, sometimes with a gimcrack 'art deco' fascia, which I noticed from the car window when we lingered at the lights. Shabbily dressed men shuffled in and out of their doors through which I would glimpse dejected figures quaffing glasses of yellow beer. Often, drunks swayed on the kerbside outside them, a bottle of Foster's Lager in one hand and in the other a scarlet lobster swaddled in a few pages of the *Sporting Globe*.

Unlike these hotels, guest houses were nice, respectable affairs, mostly built of weatherboard, and nestled in some of Australia's more picturesque nooks and crannies.

The Warburton Chalet was one of the most famous guest houses in the environs of Melbourne. Probably built in the twenties, it was a rambling white weatherboard building in the pretty riverside hamlet of Warburton. Nearby, on the edge of the large moss-scented, bellbird-haunted forest, stood a famous sanatorium and surprisingly, in that sylvan retreat, a large modernistic factory in cream brick where Seventh Day Adventists manufactured 'Sanitarium Health Foods' (*sic*). There was little else in Warburton besides the gently purling waters of the Upper Yarra, the whispering tree ferns, and the giant eucalypts casting their shadows over the factory, the hospital and the guest house. With its peaceful atmosphere and babbling river sounds, it was the closest thing you could get in Australia to a European spa, and in 1937 the Warburton Chalet had already become a kind of half-way house for refugees from Hitler.

My mother and I stayed there just before my sister was born, and my most vivid memory is of one particular afternoon in the large chintzy sitting-room of the Chalet, where my mother sat ominously knitting something white and pink and monkey-sized. In the big 'crazy'-stone fireplace, flames fluttered around the hairy logs which drooled their amber sap. Outside the picture window the autumn sunshine slanted through a blue haze of wood-smoke. It was the afternoon tea hour, and at our end of the lounge cups clinked, and cakes and scones were silently devoured. But something strange and exotic was happening at the far end of the room. Who were those people? They seemed to huddle together in their odd clothes and spoke a little too loudly in a foreign language. There was much curious murmuring down our end amongst my mother's friends, until at last someone leant across the couch and, with her cake-crumbed lips close to my mother's ear, said in a whisper audible from one end of the room to the other, 'Jews!'

The sibilance almost riffled the chintz curtains. We all sat and stared; beyond the steaming crockery and the Devonshire teas, across the expanse of shining parquet, the rugs, the fringed standard lamps, subsiding armchairs and the toffee-coloured tables loaded with *Women's Weeklys, Home Beauti-fuls, Walkabouts* and *Table Talks*. Uneasily, awkwardly settling into chairs or sofas, at their own considerably draughtier end of the lounge, the Jews stared back. My mother's informant, this time with a small stalactite of strawberry jam depending from her forelip, once more lurched lobeward. 'See their rings!' she hissed. *'They carry all their money on their fingers.'*

It was thirty-three years later when I returned to Warburton which, unlike so many idyllic spots outside Melbourne, had been spared the desecrations of progress. The old Chalet was a little modified by fire and fashion, and much much smaller than I had remembered it, but still there. I climbed the nearby hill and looked down on the rusting corrugated-tin rooftops of the sprawling Guest House. Its extended accommodations projected from the central structure in four crooked wings. The old building, seen in aerial perspective, had exactly the same configuration as . . . a weatherboard swastika.

Many Guest Houses still bore the name of the old homesteads, before their conversion and extension for paying holiday-

Old house at Mornington, oils, 1952 (note Norfolk Island pine)

makers. Darva Lodge at Mount Martha, and Ranelagh at
Mount Eliza were two favourite seaside resorts on the
Mornington Peninsula, where we often stayed in the old days
before Melbourne's middle classes erected their own beach
houses. Like the Chalet, they were rambling, asymmetrical
structures spreading amoebically, like the private hospitals of
the seventies, until their wooden tentacles annexed the old
gardens, the apple orchards, the croquet lawns, the tennis
courts and neighbouring allotments. After each successful
season of maximum occupancy by the families from Malvern,
Camberwell and Kew, another century-old Norfolk pine would
be felled, another Victorian wistaria arbour deracinated, to
make way for yet another wing of chilly, linoleum-floored
bedrooms.

Before each meal, and all in black, with white starched
apron, cap and cuffs, a maid hurried down the labyrinthine
corridors sounding the dinner gong or strumming an inane
tunelet on a miniature marimba, and in her wake streamed the
famished families. Piebald with sunburn, sand chafing in each
secret crevice, they hurtled towards the dining-room. This was

located in the original part of the house, and invariably smelled of old gravy mingled with the more inviting effluvium of vanilla puddings. The walls were cheaply panelled in brown varnished wood in a debased Arts and Crafts style popular just before and after the Great War. Where the panelling stopped about eight feet up the wall, a 'curio ledge' supported a frieze of dusty knick-knacks, chipped Toby jugs and crockery with an Olde English theme. The tables, at which the elderly waitresses sullenly loitered, were all draped with white starched damask minutely foxed with old cigarette burns, and in the centre of each table on a small nickel-plated stand, beside a cut-glass vase of poppies and a fly-specked cruet, stood the day's menu card, crookedly typed on an ancient Underwood. Breakfast was always stewed fruit and rolled oats, and although we had porridge at home in the winter months – John Bull Oats, Sargeant Dan, Uncle Toby's and more refined derivatives like Creamota and Eazy-Meal, the generic 'rolled oats' was exclusively a guest-house offering, though it tasted exactly the same as ordinary porridge. With our eggs and bacon, toast would arrive; discreetly singed white triangles wedged in a tarnished chromium toast rack. As holidays progressed, there was a good deal of friendly nodding and smiling from one table to the next, and genteel 'G'mornings' as we walked the gauntlet of penguin-coloured waitresses to our table by the window.

Dinner was served from six o'clock until the late hour of eight, and in the corridors of Darva Lodge percussion instruments announced this repast twice; the first gong being a plangent reminder to bathe and dress. However, no sooner had the second xylophonic reverberation sounded at six sharp than the ravenous families, in their evening finery of skirts, cardigans and sports coats, once more stormed towards the dining-room. Soaped and scented with Cashmere Bouquet, Potter & Moore, Rexona, Cuticura, Pears, Palmolive and Faulding's Old English Lavender, the women's bouquet of aromas was modified by a medicated whiff of Lifebuoy from the menfolk.

Dinner consisted of soup, a joint, veg and pudding. The soup was usually as white as its main constituent (flour), meagrely flavoured with celery or tinned asparagus, although sometimes in the winter there might be a watery pea soup with 'sippets'. The joint was either mutton or pork, dished up with pumpkin, parsnips and an ice-cream scoop of mashed potato, submerged in coagulating umber gravy. All this was an irksome preliminary to the pudding, which was invariably steamed, and served in little glutinous igloos on a yellow lake of custard. There was Cabinet, Queen, Albert and Victoria pudding, and if these confections ever had a distinct character in the recipe books of the late nineteenth century, their identities had become blurred or lost on the way to Darva Lodge. Our desserts appeared to have been baptized quite arbitrarily; so that, for example, a 'Victoria' sponge might be seamed with delicious whorls of scalding apricot jam, and at other times studded with currants and sultanas. An 'Albert' pudding could resemble a lemon meringue pie or a treacle dumpling – or a synthesis of both – depending on a whim of the kitchen. They were all delectably viscous, adhering tenaciously to the roof of the mouth, and second helpings were generously proffered. Having spied on neighbouring tables where some impatient diners were already tucking into their sweets, I habitually ordered my second helping of dessert when I was half-way through the soup.

The point of being at Darva Lodge and Ranelagh was, of course, the beach, though in both cases it was a steep scramble through tea-tree and down a cliff path before we finally reached the sand. My father carried large tartan rugs and a beach umbrella and then there were the buckets, spades, baskets of sandwiches, thermos flasks, and presumably my infant sister. As I write this I suddenly see the portable wicker bassinet sitting in a shady corner of our beach rug, shrouded with white net on which the fat grey March flies settled like brooches. Deep beneath the milky drapery, my sister's small nut-coloured face seemed permanently puckered on the verge of tears.

We rarely holidayed without a few relations in tow, often one or two of my mother's sisters, who always doted upon me and thoughtfully paid little overt attention to the gnome-like interloper under the net. There was much uncomfortable wriggling and writhing under towels as we modestly changed into our swimming costumes on the beach. My own swimming 'togs' were made of some abrasive maroon jersey with a short 'skirt' to disguise impolite sexual contours.

We all wore sun hats with green fly veils and my mother insisted on lavishly anointing my freckle-prone beak with zinc cream. Then there were cooling applications of almond-scented sunburn emulsions before I was finally ready to paddle in the waves of Port Phillip Bay, which lapped apologetically a few feet from the fringe of our rug. At the water's edge, the waves stirred the bright lettuce-coloured weed, whilst further up the beach before the row of weatherboard bathing cabins the line of weed was dry, brown and fibrous and the sand sometimes so hot it was an agonizing dance to the water's edge.

The little crescent of beach, with its bright umbrellas and rugs like tartan islands, would be unrecognizable to a modern sunbather. There were no transistor radios, no thin crackle of pop or thumping rock 'n' roll to disturb those Kwik-Tan-scented afternoons. Strangest of all, amongst the stirring shells, cuttle fish and bleached driftwood at the tide's edge, there were no hideously writhing tatters of plastic or imperishable chunks of leprous styrofoam.

At night in the lamplit lounge, the adults sat in cracked leather chairs playing Solo or Five Hundred, reading their Ethel M. Dells, Dorothy Sayers and Angela Thirkells. We used to gather there to listen to the News, which in the early 1940s was synonymous with the War. There was much talk over the wireless of strange European countries being overrun by the Germans. It was odd to think that in the pencil case with the sliding lid which my Uncle Dick had given me, there were those beautiful hexagonally-bevelled blue and black Wolf-Staedtler HB pencils with a tiny gilded legend: *Made in Germany.* My father had boxes of them, bought before the war, which he used for drawing up his plans. He also had a drawer in his desk filled with rainbow-coloured aquarelles made in that other strange country they kept talking about on the wireless – Czechoslovakia.

In the Darva lounge there was one man who had been to some of these places before the war. Quiet and balding, he wore glasses so thick his eyes seemed to be looking at you through the bottom of a milk bottle. He smoked a pipe and was always reading a book called *Berlin Hotel* by Vicki Baum. Mr Hickman listened more intently to the news broadcasts than anyone else and every now and then explained something intricately geographical to the other less travelled guests. But politely and not like a know-all. Nevertheless, my mother, behind his back, often so described him. 'Know-all, know-nothing,' she would sagely mutter.

'Hicky', as the children called him, was in his quiet way the most popular person at the guest house. Perhaps a lonely schoolmaster, or a man of private means, nobody was quite sure. One night, he showed us some of his travel snaps including some pictures taken in Canada of a river choked with bits of wood. 'What do you make of that?' he asked me through his tobacco haze. Nobody else seemed to know. 'A beaver dam?' I said. By coincidence, I had been reading a book about beavers the day before. Hicky took another suck on his pipe and looked up at my father. 'You've got a very clever boy there, Eric,' he said, 'a very clever boy indeed.'

We were a bit upset when Hicky left suddenly without saying goodbye to anyone. None of the other adults at Darva Lodge had time to read us stories as Hicky did, or give us a push on the swings at dusk, even if his avuncular hand did sometimes accidentally slide a few inches too far up our shorts. They were all far too busy playing cards and ping-pong, though when Hicky left so inexplicably, I heard one of the men say: 'Good riddance!'

Years later, I thought I recognized Hicky, stooped and myopic, serving in a Melbourne bookshop. How many guest houses had he been expelled from since Darva? I wondered. How many boys' schools had he mysteriously quitted mid-term? Somehow I could not, under the circumstances and after such a lapse of time, bowl up out of the blue and introduce myself: the very clever boy from Darva Lodge who had beavered up on beavers.

Wilf

Uncle Wilf was my favourite uncle. He was married to Aunty Violet, my mother's oldest sister, who had once been a nurse and had tended victims of the Spanish influenza just after the First World War. Wilf had served in the Australian infantry in France and their house contained a number of souvenirs of those terrible battles. On their Arts and Crafts mantelpiece stood two gleaming brass shell-cases and, high up in a cupboard, Uncle Wilf kept a German helmet with a spike on it. Sometimes he showed us a sepia photograph taken from the pocket of a dead German soldier, perhaps the same soldier who no longer required the helmet. The picture showed a husband and wife, she seated with a certain wistful beauty, he in uniform standing stiffly at her side. In the background was the blurred hint of a bourgeois parlour – no doubt a tricked-up corner of the photographer's studio. They both gazed apprehensively at the lens as though it were about to go off like a rifle, but that would come a month or two later.

Uncle Wilf was the only person I knew who had served in the First World War, though casualties of that legendary catastrophe were often pointed out to me; legless lift drivers, blind newspaper sellers, and the door-to-door salesman from whom my mother bought our honey who always wore one stiff black glove.

Wilf always marched on 25 April, that most important day in the Australian calendar, Anzac Day, when a great cavalcade of Diggers walked in solemn procession to the Shrine of Remembrance. Every year we, and thousands of others, would line the roadside and cheer the old soldiers, many in uniform and others in their Sunday best blazing with medals, as the military bands played 'Tipperary', 'Pack Up Your Troubles' and 'Roses of Picardy'. At the end of that long procession came the wheelchairs and the stretchers and nurses leading the gassed and the blind.

Wilf and Vi had one son, who was a spastic, and my aunt and uncle were devoted to his welfare. John loved music and had a large collection of records which he would play loudly at family tea parties. No one listened to his carefully planned recitals, they only talked louder, though occasionally someone would glance over at him as he sat by the gramophone nodding his head to the music, his poor legs in chromium callipers.

'There's no doubt about John,' they would cluck. '*He loves his music.*'

Uncle Wilf worked for Imperial Chemical Industries and my father often took me to his office in the city where I would be given small sample jars of dye manufactured by the company. At home I experimented with these wonderful pigments: purple, fuchsia and gamboge, dropping a pinch or two into a full beaker, and watching the bright streamers of colour fall through the water and spread like tendrils, or making exotically hued potions in the new laboratory which my father had built for me at the back of the garage.

Wilf and my father adored each other, and the three of us would regularly lunch at the Wool Exchange Hotel near Uncle Wilf's office. It was my first experience of a restaurant, and there was a pretty receptionist who always greeted the brothers-in-law flirtatiously and made a fuss over me as she led us between the rowdy lunchers to our special table. There were stiff, starched napkins, a cruet holding the indispensable bottle of Holbrook's Worcestershire sauce and, in the centre of the table, an oxidized nickel trumpet from which a few crumpled poppies bloomed on their hairy stems. The vegetable fritter with hot tomato sauce was one of the Wool Exchange's gastronomic specialities, as well as the more conservative T-bone steak and crumbed whiting.

It must have been during one of these lunches that the two men planned to build a weekend shack together at Healesville, a beauty spot about forty miles from town. Accordingly they bought thirty acres of virgin bush about a mile from the township, up a dusty track. There, in a small clearing with a blue view of Mount Riddell and the lavender-coloured foothills of the Great Divide, my father, assisted by Pat and Alec, built a house, known thereafter as 'the shack'. It was a rudimentary structure of weatherboard, asbestos sheeting and corrugated iron and there were none of the cosy amenities of Camberwell. No water, electricity or sewerage, so we had a galvanized-iron tank at the side of the house, spirit lamps and an outdoor dunny, built of split logs over a very deep hole. This was furnished with little more than a huge desiccated tarantula on the ceiling and, for the hygienic convenience of visitors, a mutilated Melbourne telephone book suspended by a string from a bent nail. This popular cubicle buzzed perpetually with the sound of voracious flies and reeked of some am-moniac pink powder which Papa Brown regularly ladled into the abyss.

Soon our shack in the bush became a regular weekend haven for all the relations. There were beds everywhere, and at night on my lumpy mattress in my little 'sleep-out', I could hear the adults in the living-room playing Whist and Mah-jong late into the night, smell Uncle Wilf's sweet Wayside Mixture and hear my father pumping up the kerosene lamps until the guttering mantles glowed white again. In the forties we acquired a battery-powered wireless set, and on Sunday evenings everyone listened to the Lux Radio Theatre. There was great excitement if the hour-long melodrama happened to star Thelma Scott, my mother's sole theatrical acquaintance, or Thelma's talented young friend, Coral Browne.

When war came I would lie awake in bed watching the lamplight ebb and flow through the crack under my door and hear those urgent, ominous news reports of far-away catastrophes. The voice of Winston Churchill crackled over the BBC World Service as my family sat gravely listening to the war in the silent Australian bush 13,000 miles from Westminster. There was so much distortion and explosive static on those shortwave broadcasts that I pictured Churchill himself standing at the very heart of the battlefield, perpetually under fire and growling his famous rhetoric through a lethal fusillade.

One night in about 1943 I heard them playing 'Sweet Spirit', a psychic parlour game in which I was never allowed to participate. An alphabetical circle was arranged on the table top and everyone put their finger on an upturned glass in the middle. They all took it in turns to ask the spirit questions, and there were always crescendos of laughter followed by, 'Shhh, you'll wake the children.' My father was regularly reproached for cheating. One night I heard a voice, I think it was Aunty Dorothy's, ask the spirit when Cliff Jones, Phyllis's brother, was coming home on leave, and there was a strange silence in the room as the glass, carrying everyone's fingers with it, darted from N to E to V to E to R. They never played that game again.

In the long summer vacation my father built a log fort for me and a red bark tree-house high up in a shaggy old eucalypt. My tree-house even had an old-fashioned battery-operated telephone connected to the main house, so that I could order cakes and sandwiches without ever having to leave my eyrie. Here I played for hours in my new Gene Autry cowboy suit with its fringed white kid chaps and my Gene Autry ivory-handled cap gun. Watching out for snakes, my young sister and

I would explore the bush together, while back at the house cousin John played his portable gramophone, so that wherever we were we could hear from afar those wisps of tinny music like the horns of elfland faintly blowing. It was strange sitting on a mossy log in the Australian bush and listening to Fraser Simpson's incomparable Vocal Gems from *Toad of Toad Hall* or Richard Tauber's 'Dein ist mein ganzes Herz'. Especially strange, really, to hear the illicit language of the Enemy thrillingly wafted through the saplings and the sword grass and the yellow flowering acacias and the mauve bush orchids.

The hour drive to Healesville seemed, of course, interminable to a child. Camberwell was then on the outskirts of the metropolitan area and once past Box Hill we were in open country. Near Lilydale, my father always pointed out the long and impeccably shaved hedge of green privet that concealed from the road the vast estate of Dame Nellie Melba, and Coombe Cottage, the Australian diva's legendary home. Melba and Donald Bradman were the only famous Australians I had ever heard of, and it seemed an amazing coincidence that Melba's name should so closely resemble the city of her birth.

Half-way to the shack we crossed a billabong of the Yarra River on a low pontoon bridge, and there on a kind of island almost camouflaged amongst the tangled blackberries and the sloughed bark of the huge river gums was a small swagman's encampment; a few wretched humpies built from rusty kerosene tins and hessian bags. As our Oldsmobile rolled past, a starved yellow mongrel always started up and barked until we were out of sight. My father had only once pointed to this little camp, but thereafter our noses were pressed to the car windows whenever we approached the river bank in the hope that we might glimpse one of these legendary vagabonds boiling his billy, or stuffing a jumbuck in his tucker bag like the hero of that incomprehensible song 'Waltzing Matilda'.

Half a mile from the shack on the other side of the Don Road lived a real swagman called Smithy. Smithy dwelt in an improvised hovel of galvanized iron and sacking where chooks and dogs scrabbled in the dust. He had a wife somewhere in that kennel too, who was supposed to be, according to Uncle Wilf, 'as black as your hat'. Smithy was a lanky taciturn figure with a pointed Adam's apple and a grey beard and an old digger's hat. He still wore the threadbare remnant of a khaki uniform and after Uncle Wilf befriended him he used to chop wood for us, and do odd jobs. Sometimes I would sit with the men at smoko and hear Smithy tell some of his old soldier's yarns. He had a great and touching nobility, like a peasant in a story by Turgenev. In September, before the morning mist cleared and the magpies were gargling in the tall saplings, Smithy would show us the paddocks where we could find the best and biggest mushrooms. They were the ones with the blue-pink gills underneath: the colour of milky cocoa.

If we were at Healesville at Christmas time, and the heat became unbearable, we would set off with rugs and picnic baskets to Badgers Creek. There, where no badger had ever set foot, amongst the pungent mosses, and sheltered by tall tree ferns, we splashed about in a dark green pool. Then we would perch on the bank watching the icy water purl and gurgle over rocks like emus' eggs, and sip raspberry vinegar from Bakelite cups, while Peter Dawson sang 'The Floral Dance' on John's wind-up phonograph.

There was a terrible week in 1939 when the great bushfires which raged throughout Victoria nearly got the shack. Wilf and my father drove back and forth from Healesville all day, through the smoke and under a dark copper sky, bringing linen and portable furniture to safety. The house and its surroundings, however, were spared, though it was a close one, and on the crest of Mount Riddell there was always, thereafter, a bald white patch of bleached burnt-out timber.

Those bush holidays provide the happiest memories of my childhood, and during the war the house was extended to

The author's birthplace

The author aet. two weeks

John and Sarah Humphries, the author's paternal grandparents

The only child

Dressing

up

Siblings

At Healesville

Schooldays

Barbara, Christopher and Barry Humphries

furnish more bedrooms in case we decided to evacuate there when the bombs fell. For some reason it was felt that thirty-five miles from the General Post Office was a safe radius if the Japanese invaded Melbourne.

In the late 1930s the voice of Joseph Schmidt was always on the wireless, singing that evocative song of the period, 'A Star Fell from Heaven'. It was the voice of Europe before the Terror and, had I but known it, a Jewish voice. But the song which I most associate with the outbreak of war was 'South of the Border (Down Mexico Way)' crooned in the light tenor of Gene Autry. Whenever I am in Los Angeles, supping with my friend Roddy McDowall in Studio City; I gaze across his fence at the house next door where Gene Autry still lives, in the hope that I may get a glimpse of my childhood idol.

Papa Brown, my maternal grandfather, had an ominous ditty in his music-hall repertoire.

> Tramp, tramp, the boys are marching
> Knock, knock, the bobby's at the door.
> If you don't let him in
> He will knock the door right in,
> And you won't seen your daddy any more!

This cautionary refrain gave me terrible nightmares and Papa was forbidden by my mother to sing it ever again. Early in the war I must have overheard many discussions between my parents about whether or not my father should enlist. His younger brother, Dick, had joined the air force and my mother's brother was in the Australian Infantry Force, and I am sure my father, although he was just too old to be called up, had pangs of conscience about not doing 'his bit'. I can remember an argument between my parents once, when we drove past the Hawthorn recruiting station, but Wilf ultimately arranged for my father to do war work for ICI, building munition factories and nitroglycerine storage tanks at Deer Park, an outer Melbourne suburb. However, I am convinced the spectre of conscription must have hung over him during the early war years and I always feared that his father-in-law's minatory recruiting jingle would come true, and that my father might be snatched away by the army and I would never see him again.

When the war broke out he employed several very jolly Italians called the Angelo Brothers who created the terrazzo porches and bathroom floors in all his houses. They seemed to sing all the time as they worked and they wore paper hats made from Geelong cement bags to keep off the sun. But one day they disappeared and were never spoken of again. Although they had probably lived in Australia for years and had barely heard of Mussolini they were interned for the duration of the war in some dismal concentration camp outside the city. There was also a German carpenter called Fritz whom my father liked, and an attempt was made to save him from the same fate as the Dagos. One day my father asked Fritz to come into his den, put his hand on the family Bible and swear allegiance to King George. Agog, I witnessed this touching if somewhat naïve ceremony but, alas, it failed to save poor old Fritz from his inevitable sequestration.

Unlike my mother, my father sometimes spoke to foreigners, and often told a story of one of his uncles back in Benalla who had befriended a German tradesman during the Great War when the rest of the town refused to talk to him. When he finally died he left Great-Uncle Frank a house and several thousand pounds.

I had embarked on philately and I already had a large collection of British stamps, including a Penny Black. When my grandparents went back to England for the coronation of King George VI, I steamed the stamps off their many letters and postcards. I also had an exciting German section in my album thanks to a funny old lady called Mrs Vannemark who lived a few doors down Marlborough Avenue in a tapestry-brick, neo-

Tudor bungalow built for her by my father in 1938. Old Mrs Vannemark – though she was probably only about forty-five – spoke with a strange accent, which gave her an air of acerbity. Her house had quite a few 'teething problems' too, and I often heard her harsh voice on the telephone asking for my father. 'It's that Jewish woman making trouble again,' my mother would say. 'Why your father does business with them I'll never understand.' Mr Friedmann was another thorn in her side. He ran a local firm called the Suburban Timber Supply and although my father liked him, my mother was convinced that he was a cheat and a swindler. However, in spite of my mother's open hostility towards her, old Mrs Vannemark was very kind to me, giving me the stamps off all the letters she received from her family who were still in Germany. They were rather spectacular: most had swastikas on them and images of a bad-tempered-looking man with folded arms and a square moustache. I secretly hoped Mrs Vannemark's family would not come to Melbourne too soon or an important philatelic source might dry up. But as it happened she remained alone, and some time around 1940 the letters stopped.

My parents enjoyed a busy social life. Once a week they had a card night. Baize-topped bridge tables were erected in the 'best' room and my mother spent the whole day making sandwiches and cakes. Her specialities were matches – a delicious colonial millefeuille filled with jam and cream and covered with walnuts – and sponge fingers with passionfruit icing. The next morning we had what was left of the sandwiches toasted for breakfast and took the cakes to school in greaseproof paper.

When my mother took me into town on her shopping expeditions, we usually visited Mitzi of Vienna, her favourite dress shop.

The proprietrix, whose creations my mother found irresistible, was another of those exotic arrivals of the late thirties whose companions had given Melbourne chocolates, coffee lounges and chamber music. We would also visit the Myer Emporium, where my mother had once worked as a milliner, before she married my father. I noticed her voice changed when she spoke to the shop assistants, as though she had to make it very clear that she and they were now separated by a great distance, and the gap was getting wider. I always felt uncomfortable when she spoke in that unreal drawl, but I was coming to believe that my mother was perhaps several women; or different things to different people, and there was a life within her which excluded me.

Sometimes we lunched at Myer's in the Mural Hall, which for suburban shoppers of this, or any, period was the height of grandeur. Frequently used for fashion parades and receptions, it was decorated with large pale neo-classical frescoes by Napier Waller, a Melbourne artist who had lost his right arm in the First World War and immediately began painting with his left. More often, however, we had our lunch at the Wattle Tea Rooms in Little Collins Street. The Wattle was a long room in the Arts and Crafts style, with leadlight windows on the street, and dark wainscot within. Plates, Toby jugs and knick-knacks stood on the sempiternal curio ledge, and there were chintzy banquettes to the left and right, and white linen tables down the middle. These dark varnished surroundings emphasized the bright floral dresses and hats of the women who, talced and toilet-watered, thronged the Wattle every day, so that the whole café resembled a conservatory. Women like stocks, in mauve and heliotrope, or puffed up in brighter speckled hues like calceolarias. Blue delphinium women nodded to each other across the room and there were old ladies too, like bunches of violets and boronia huddled behind their Denby Ware tea sets, or sitting alone pecking at asparagus rolls. There was, of course, no shortage of snapdragons.

In the centre of each table at the Wattle there were real

flowers: gum-tips and luminous orange and yellow Iceland poppies in cut-glass vases, dropping their calyxes on the doilies as each new flower shook out its crumpled petals, the long hairy stems turning double-jointed in the water.

The speciality at the Wattle was Adelaide whiting, which all the ladies ordered if they didn't eat egg sandwiches or asparagus rolls. Afterwards there were scrumptious things on silver three-tiered cake stands: kisses, éclairs, butterfly cakes, neenish tarts, matches and lamingtons.

Sometimes, at the sound of too loud and imperious a voice at an adjacent table, or the appearance of a pink-cheeked man in a hound's-tooth jacket and corduroy trousers with perhaps, also, a spoilt child, behaving like a *little madam*, my mother, or one of the other seed-packets, would smile secretly at her neighbour and, with a roll of her eyes, mouth the mysterious initials, like a code: 'E.N.T.' The whisper ran around the Wattle; nudges and little moues were exchanged, serviettes would discreetly mask smiles as eyes swivelled in the direction of this rather stiff *loud* family. 'E.N.T. and no doubt about it I'm afraid, Coral!' I heard a tight-lipped Carnation exclaim to a Gladiolus. English Next Table.

Lou and Eric – my parents – belonged to the local tennis club and on Saturday afternoons I would sit in the small clubhouse with a book listening to the distant laughter from the mixed doubles and the soporific sounds of tennis floating in from the courts. After the tennis there was always an enormous tea dominated by something called a 'tennis cake'. They were carefree afternoons of perpetual sunshine which the war changed forever.

We lived quite close to the Camberwell Sports Ground and on Saturday afternoons, if I happened to be at home in bed sick, I would hear, borne with terrible clarity across the housetops, the spasmodic applause of the cricket fans and, worse, in winter, the frighteningly mindless roar of the football rabble.

Long before I was ever forced by school authorities to watch these horrible and pointless games, I had formed a lifelong aversion to them based solely on those first auditory impressions. Crowds have always frightened and appalled me unless they happen to be in a theatre during one of my engagements. Then the noise they make is benign; a great ecstatic whoosh like a fire going up a chimney or the word 'yes' chanted by a heavenly host.

My mother was always concerned about my health and the great bogy of my childhood was Infantile Paralysis. I was never quite sure how old one had to be to avoid this scourge, nor had I ever met a victim, but I willingly swallowed whatever my mother poured into a spoon and pressed to my lips. Usually it was just the sticky and delicious Saunder's Malt Extract. I had seen it advertised on a hoarding which depicted a muscular baby, decorously diapered, shouldering an enormous steel girder. A favourite tonic of my mother's was Hypol, which was a less palatable white emulsion of cod-liver oil. There was, however, one prophylactic against Infantile Paralysis and other ailments that always made me sick. It was the egg flip, a glass of milk into which a raw egg had been whisked. Threads and clots of albumen always wrapped themselves around my uvula like a tourniquet, and although I gagged horribly, favours were withheld until I drank the last drop.

The illnesses of my childhood, although brief, gave me time to lie in bed, reading and listening to the wireless. My mother put the Radiola set in my room on a table beside the bed, and between sips of barley water I would tweak the knurled Bakelite knob from station to station. Throughout the day there was a succession of what are now called soap operas. Many of them employed the same actors, so that it was disquieting to hear a familiar character in *Aunt Jenny's Real Life Stories* crop up again with a different name in *Dr Mack, Fred and Maggie Everybody, When a Girl Marries* and *Martin's Corner*. Somehow it gave all those radio melodramas a spooky homogeneity.

In the mornings, soon after *Daybreak Dan*, there was a popular programme of community singing; a type of entertainment that has almost died out. With Uncle Wilf, Aunty Vi and John, I once went to a recording of this entertainment in a small radio auditorium in town. It was thronged with women, a few accompanied by their children. Some of the ladies had brought knitting, very often khaki socks on five needles, and others had colanders in their laps into which they absently shelled peas. Led by a radio 'personality' called Charlie Vaud, with Mabel Nelson at the piano, they all enthusiastically sang such war-time hits as 'Run Rabbit', 'We're Going to Hang Out Our Washing on the Siegfried Line', 'Hey, Little Hen', 'Berlin or Bust' and 'The White Cliffs of Dover'. There was a vaudeville interlude when two comedians called Edgley and Dawe capered before the microphone and a strange woman called Nellie Colley, dressed in top hat and tails and smoking a pipe, sang a comic song called 'Burlington Bertie'. It was my first enticing glimpse of the Music Hall.

There were humorous interludes on the radio: mostly records of pre-war British vaudeville comics like George Tilly, Sid Field, Cyril Fletcher, Jack Hulbert and Cecily Courtneidge and my favourite, Horace Kenny. I would lie there in the darkened room through measles, mumps, whooping cough and scarlet fever, with my calamine lotion and Vicks Vaporub, laughing at those wonderful old-fashioned jesters. In the voices of some of these radio comics I recognized with a start the northern intonations of my father's father, whose Lancastrian accent had hitherto seemed so unique and outlandish. Here on the wireless were men with similar voices, interrupted by explosions of laughter. I later wondered why so many of the funniest comedians came from the North of England and why the idea of a 'Kent comic' seemed so anomalous. In the forties, yodelling was popular and there were many excruciating hillbilly programmes on the wireless, but in the afternoon the children's sessions began, and I would listen to rather arch transmissions of *Chums at Chatterbox Corner* and later, around teatime, *The*

Search for the Golden Boomerang, which used as its signature tune the voluptuous hothouse melody of Tchaikovsky's 'Waltz of the Flowers'. By the end of the day the bedroom smelt strongly of my medicaments mingled with the aroma of hot Bakelite.

One morning, when I was about ten, I woke very early, and as I went to the lavatory I glanced down at the skirting board outside my bedroom door. I then got down on my hands and knees and looked at it more closely. There was a small wire staple fixed to the wood an inch or two above the carpet, through which was threaded a thin cord. There was another staple on the opposite side of the architrave, and more, as I discovered, at regular intervals between my bedroom and the door to my parents' room, into which, like Ariadne's thread, the string disappeared. It occurred to me that I could easily have tripped on this filament on my way to the bathroom, and it was a mere fluke that I had not.

That morning, I was alone with my father for a few minutes after he had made my mother's breakfast, and when I told him of my strange discovery he became agitated and evasive. Finally, swearing me to secrecy, he explained that for some weeks he and my mother had been disturbed in the middle of the night by Barbara's sleepwalking, so he had installed this ingenious system of trip cords which connected to a bell beside his bed. Thus, whatever the hour, he would be instantly alerted to my sister's noctambulations and steer her safely back to bed. I must say, he looked particularly haggard that morning so I assumed the mechanism had been working all too successfully over the past few weeks.

I could not help but admire my father's ingenuity, though only one detail puzzled me; the cord did not pass across my sister's bedroom door, but mine. A few weeks later I noticed the whole system had been dismantled without a trace, and

my father looked considerably more rested in the mornings. I
assumed that my unconscious wanderings had come to an
end.

My father had secured a valuable contract to build a sausage
factory for Mr Prince of Prince's Sausages. I went along with
him to the old meat works for his first discussions. The noise in
the factory was deafening and there was an appalling and
nidorous smell. Very fat men in overalls and gumboots sloshed
around in pink water as machines masticated huge quivering
swags and chandeliers of offal; mauve, crimson and magenta.
At the other end dirty pipes extruded serpents and stools of
bright pink mince which the brutish men aimed into endless
frankfurter skins. I remember my father had to rush away to be
sick and thereafter never ate another sausage in his life. At our
children's parties we always had cocktail frankfurters – from
another firm – which we dunked in sauce and washed down
with raspberry vinegar. These lavish teas, usually a celebration
of a birthday, were held on Saturday afternoons and were
preceded by a matinée at the Rivoli Picture Theatre near the
Camberwell Junction. After the candles had been blown out
and the last frankfurter ground into a slice of bread and butter
and hundreds and thousands, there were party games in the
garden until the parents arrived to escort their invariably weeping children home to be sick. Uncle Wilf always turned up at
my parties and would organize the activities, which sometimes
got rather rough, and he would find himself playing 'Stacks on
the Mill, More on Still' flat on his back on the lawn beneath a
writhing pyramid of about fifteen small boys.

'Stacks on the mill,
More on still . . .'

chanted the children. My parents would exchange a glance and my mother once said, 'Poor Wilf. He loves children and he's only got John.'

Uncle Wilf always bought the latest parlour games which helped to fill in the long evenings after tea when we were up at Healesville. We loved Mah-jong until Wilf produced a pack of Belisha, a new card game inspired by British traffic signs. Each card had a picturesque view of England, Scotland or Wales painted in bright colours in a slightly primitive, Lowry-ish style. Although the cars in the pictures looked quaintly out of date, the landscapes, as green as salads, and the castles and thatched cottages, filled me with a yearning to go there.

After the family weekend at the shack, we used to drive back from Healesville in rather a long convoy, stopping occasionally for the children to go behind bushes or for Aunt Ella to be sick, or sometimes stopping too for Uncle Wilf to get out of their grey Chev and lean for a while with his elbows on the roof and his head in his hands. We would stop our car a few yards ahead and my father would watch his brother-in-law in the rear-vision mirror. 'Wilf's getting more of those headaches,' he said. 'Time he had a check-up.' A few months later he did, and had to go to hospital for a 'minor operation', as my parents, with their usual prudery about illness, described the removal of a brain tumour. I spoke to him on the telephone soon after he came home from the Alfred Hospital but he didn't seem to know who I was. When he died, leaving no will, the house and the land at Healesville had to be sold to provide money for his widow and son. And we left the bush forever.

Not long after Wilf's funeral, which I was not allowed to attend, my father and I were driving to one of his more important jobs to deliver a precious cargo of plate glass which was roped to the open boot. My father was driving a little too fast and as we went over an unexpected hump in the road there was an ominous thump and a dull crash behind the car. My father pulled over to the side of the road and got out to examine the disaster. I had never heard him swear, but this time he stood looking at the shivered panes and released a litany of curses. Then he sat on the kerb and sobbed quietly for a while. I didn't know what to do, but I felt he wasn't just grieving over the glass.

Hats and Glads

CAMBERWELL GRAMMAR SCHOOL had been built in the grounds of a large Victorian house in an older neighbouring suburb. The original gardens were still there, including two elephantine Moreton Bay fig trees and a tottering arbour, from which, in its season, wistaria mauvely dripped. There was also the inevitable Norfolk Island pine tree which every Victorian residence of any distinction seemed to possess. They rose like tall viridian fishbones over the suburban landscape and always denoted the presence of an interesting old house. Today, however, though many of the trees survive, their gardens are often subdivided and the houses demolished; replaced by nice 'units' and practical townhouses. Mr Tonkin, the magenta-nosed headmaster, lived in the original Victorian house in the school grounds that also accommodated a few wretched and dispossessed boarders on whom we well-fed, warmly housed day boys gazed with pity.

My teachers in the junior school were mostly women. But there was a bald and nervous little choirmaster called Mr Dennis who visited the school and led us all in rousing renditions of 'Nymphs and Shepherds', 'Bird of the Wilderness' (... blithesome and cumberless) and a muscular ditty called 'Clang, Clang, Clang on the Anvil' – a song that sounded particularly odd when rendered by boy sopranos. At home

65

Purcell's 'Nymphs and Shepherds' became my earliest party turn, after my mother had overheard me singing it in the bath, and much to my embarrassment she insisted that I sing it to all the uncles and aunts at the next family Sunday tea party. I only agreed to this on condition I was allowed to perform behind the curtain, so that my voice was disembodied like those on the radio. Thereafter, if ever my parents wanted to cajole me into a song or recitation, they would have to say – and I wince to recall the words – *pretend to be the wireless*. Needless to say I have pretended to be the wireless on many occasions since.

After the persecutions by Miss Jensen at my former school, Camberwell Grammar was a blissful respite, though a boy called John Bromley, who seemed tall for his age and had soft white skin like a slug, used to push me over whenever he saw me, for no reason that I could ever understand. I learnt to avoid him, and many years later in adult life, and when he was least expecting it, I visited an exquisite revenge upon him which I will describe in a later chapter.

Sometimes when Bromley's capricious bullying got too much for me I would, I am afraid, seek a victim of my own. There was a perfectly nice, but rather small lad called Gifford, whom I pushed over a couple of times, on one occasion causing his mother's beautifully cut sandwiches to scatter on the dusty playground. For years afterwards I experienced a sharp pang of guilt whenever I thought of this incident until, on a recent visit to Melbourne, I could bear it no longer and decided, half a century later, to make amends. By consulting the telephone directory I discovered that there was, in fact, a Bruce Gifford who was practising architecture in the city and to my delight he answered the telephone. I came quickly to the point, explaining that I was sorry about the sandwiches and hoped he was doing well and that there were no hard feelings. A wave of relief and absolution passed over me, though as I gently replaced the receiver, I could still hear his voice exclaiming, 'Who is this? Who *is* this?'

I loved history, art and English, but I was already having

difficulty with arithmetic, which seemed to be the one subject in which my father hoped I might excel. Even then I may have been vaguely aware that he wanted me to become an architect; something better and grander than himself. If only he had known, he could have adopted little Gifford!

One morning, through the classroom window, we noticed a strange figure prowling around outside in the school playground. He wore floppy green trousers, a red shirt and a bow tie, and his hair was very long and wavy. We laughed delightedly at the sight of him; he was the oddest fellow any of us had ever seen. Miss Ewers left the classroom and went outside and we saw her talking to the peculiar stranger for a few minutes and shaking her head. They could both see our grinning faces pressed to the window and the weird man glanced at us nervously, but Miss Ewers did not seem to mind. She was blushing, and trying not to smile herself. Soon the stranger walked off towards the school gate and our teacher came back into the classroom. She sat at her desk and exploded with laughter. She was convulsed. 'Who was that, Miss?' we all asked, but Miss Ewers took some time to compose herself. 'He . . . wanted to know if we'd like him to give us theatre lessons at the school!' She could hardly get the words out before a further paroxysm. We were all laughing now and the weird man must have heard us through one of the open windows. We could see him at the gate, gazing back at the school with a pale puzzled face. 'Who is he, Miss Ewers?' we piped in chorus. Miss Ewers had gone bright red. She looked very pretty with her eyes sparkling with tears. 'An actor,' she said at last, drying her eyes with a handkerchief, 'he said he was an actor!' Our peals of merriment must surely have reached him now as he closed the gate and trudged off towards the bus stop.

Sport was my greatest problem at school. I was always perfectly healthy and yet I could never see the point of games. Paradoxically, I attribute my excellent constitution and energy today to the fact that since school I have never engaged in more than a minute of athletic activity. We all had to traipse down to

CAMBERWELL GRAMMAR SCHOOL

REPORT FOR FIRST TERM, 19 46

Name _J. B. Humphries_   Form _VB_

Conduct _Excellent_   No. of Boys in Form _37_

Days Absent _1_   Position in Form _8_

SUBJECTS	Percentage	Form Average	SUBJECTS	Percentage	Form Average
Scripture	82	63	Arithmetic	65	77
Writing	A	—	Algebra	60	75
Drawing	95	63	Geometry and Trigonometry	78	71
Reading	A	—	General Science		
Spelling	88	83	Physics		
English Grammar and Composition	74	59	Chemistry		
English Literature	100	64	Mathematics I		
French	76	70	Mathematics II		
German			Mathematics III		
Latin	85	68	Mathematics IV		
History	74	63	Com. Principles		
Geography	90	66	Commercial Practice		
Economics			Physical Education	D	tries hard

GENERAL REMARKS: _Barry is a most satisfactory pupil. He is showing a distinct leaning to the literary subjects. His Literature paper is one of the best I have corrected for a boy of this age._ _H Brown_

Average 80.5%

H L Tonkin .... Headmaster

Signature of Parent or Guardian _H H Humphries_

a horrible building called The Gym. Here were coarse unscalable ropes, parallel bars and porridge-coloured mattresses, stained and pinguid from generations of brilliantined scalps and sweaty somersaults. This torture chamber was presided over by a man called Scotty, one of those repulsive and nuggety Caledonians with pale sandy hair and white eyelashes that gave him the look of a near-albino. Scotty was perpetually dressed in a short-sleeved Aertex, briefs and tennis shoes, which we called 'sandshoes' and 'ordinary' people called 'runners'. Scotty's piggy little eye fell on me immediately when he saw the difficulty I had in executing a pointless somersault. Much given to jocular nicknames, he decided that mine should be 'Granny Humphries', a soubriquet which met with the ribald approval of my schoolfellows. Needless to say, on subsequent sports days at which I was a reluctant participant and in the tedious brutalities of egg, spoon and sack races, the air rang with shrill cries of 'Come on Granny! Come on Granny!' As the reader may imagine, I had little affection for Mr Scott, but I am happy to say that very many years later a terrible sadness befell him in which I played a decisive, if anonymous, role.

An unpleasant concomitant of Physical Training was the cold shower we were forced to endure in a dank concrete basement near the gym. There were no lights and no proper drainage system, so we had to splash around in the dark with black water up to our knees, for no good reason that I could comprehend, except that cold showers were supposed to be 'good for you'.

There was a tuck shop at the school where two women sold pasties and pies to boys whose mothers, unlike mine, could not be bothered to cut their sandwiches or lovingly pack their leather satchels with fruit and cakes. The savoury effluvium which wafted from the tuck shop daily at twelve o'clock percolated to every corner of the school, and as I chewed my bland sandwiches I sometimes wished I was just slightly neglected, as I hankered for a succulent pasty, haemorrhaging sauce.

It would not be long before we would all be officially urged to devour something called the 'Oslo lunch'. At the time I assumed this to be identical with the lunches eaten by schoolchildren in occupied Norway. It consisted of a carrot, a slice of brown bread (in Melbourne, in those days, this was white bread coloured brown), a piece of Kraft processed cheese still half-wrapped in foil and bearing a parent's thumb print, and half a pint of milk. For a short while in the early years of the war my mother followed this edict and daily packed this austere and unappetizing collation in my satchel. However, on the journey to school the milk bottle often leaked and by the end of the term most of our school bags reeked with the smell of raw leather, ink and rancid milk. Soon, and in spite of the war effort, I persuaded my mother to supply me with a normal lunch of spaghetti sandwiches and cakes.

At the beginning of the war with Japan, trenches were dug in the gardens of the old school house and we were issued with gas masks and strange black rubber gags which, if bitten on when the bombs fell, would prevent our teeth from shattering. We all had to bring money to school to pay for these prophylactics, but I horrified the Head and was made to feel shamefully unpatriotic when, before the whole school, I innocently asked whether we would get our money back if the Japs didn't bomb us. It was a solecism I was never allowed to forget.

Meanwhile the school grounds became a muddy maze of trenches, and strips of cellophane were pasted in lattice patterns all over the windows. On the wireless Vera Lynn optimistically sang:

When the lights go on again
All over the world . . .

Many of our neighbours in Christowell Street were happily building air-raid shelters in their back gardens. These were exciting subterranean dwellings upholstered with sandbags, but my father refused to disfigure our back lawn and constructed an elaborate, but barely bomb-proof, bunker under the stairs. Carpenters made large hardboard panels that could be fitted to the inside of our windows in the event of aerial bombardment, though how this could be done at high speed in an air raid, and in a house that must have had at least forty windows, is difficult to imagine. Fortunately it was never put to the test. The back garden was converted from flowers to vegetables and fruits, and in a short time we were producing our own carrots, parsnips, beans, potatoes, peas, lemons, peaches and apricots.

There was some confusion, certainly amongst children, as to which war we should be worrying about: the Hitler one or the Tojo one. However, most streets had a Fat for Britain depot.

It was popularly believed that fat, or its absence, would be a decisive factor in the outcome of the European war, and that the more fat we could send to England the better her chances of victory. The dripping from every Sunday roast in Melbourne was therefore carefully decanted into suitable containers – old Farex tins, glucose canisters and jam jars – and these, hygienically sealed, were left on the front porch of Mrs Long's Spanish Mission Home on the corner of Fairmont Avenue, whence they were presumably collected, consolidated and shipped to London. To this day I have never met a recipient or beneficiary of this lardy largesse, but the Japanese sank many Fat for Britain ships and it is strange to think of this greasy residue of a million Sunday joints lying in some coral dell at the bottom of the Pacific, waiting to produce the biggest dripping slick in history.

Our vicar, Canon P. W. Robinson, was a Londoner, and his sermons rambled on at some length about the threat to what was then called The Old Country and the safety of the King, Queen and the little Princesses. To my father's disappointment, my mother always thought of some excuse for not going to church, though I knew that our sanctimonious vicar was the principal reason for her absence from Morning Prayer. My father, however, was a regular churchgoer, later a vestryman, and during the Offertory he would always slip a crunched-up pound note into the plate amongst everyone else's shillings, and insisted on saying Grace before meals: 'Forwhatweareabout-toreceivemaytheLordmakeustrulythankfulAmen.' This always embarrassed me when we had friends to stay, as my father's recitation usually caught them unawares mid-way through the first forkful. And sometimes, at night, I would see him through their half-open bedroom door – it was rarely closed – kneeling in prayer beside the bed. Canon Robinson took a great fancy to me and always patted my head vigorously after Sunday service. I had the uncomfortable feeling, later confirmed, that he envisaged some future for me in the Ministry, and at Sunday school he was always singling me out to read the lesson.

Sunday was the worst day of the week, because my father, with his north of England Methodist upbringing, forbade us to play with any other children on the Sabbath. Instead there were endless drives back and forth to St Mark's rather ugly buff-stuccoed nave, and the cold red-brick Sunday school beside it. In church, I liked the music, though I successfully resisted Canon Robinson's efforts to conscript me into the choir. However, the smell of everybody's 'Sunday Best'; the camphor, the talcum, hair oil and the toilet water, mingled with whatever disinfectant it was that the cleaners used, always made me feel like passing out as if I had inhaled carbon monoxide. Withal I struggled for some great faith; some transcendental religious experience. Great-Uncle Albert, always extolled to me as the most successful member of the Humphries family, had, back in Manchester, once written a seminal work, *The Holy Spirit in Faith and Experience* (Primitive Methodist Publishing Company, 1911), and though I attempted to read this book many times, it failed to yield up its mystery to me. Moreover, there was some evidence from its musty unopened appearance that previous readers had also abandoned their search for Truth amongst the closely printed pages.

Sunday lunch – or dinner as it was called – always consisted of a Roast; lamb, pork or beef. This was always cooked, as I still prefer it, until it was an attractive shade of grey. The roast was accompanied by potatoes, parsnips and pumpkin baked to a crisp, the pumpkin caramelized. This would be followed by tinned peaches or a steamed pudding in which apricot jam, golden syrup or sultanas were alternating constituents. Much as I looked forward to this meal throughout the tedious tracts of Canon Robinson's sermon, I dreaded the return home as well. For Sunday was the day that my parents usually had 'words'. It would be more truthful to say that they had no words at all, but there was a palpable atmosphere of tension which had no explicable origin. It may have been that my parents, to all appearances a happily married couple, found the prospect of one day in the week spent in each other's company unendurable. This oppressive atmosphere, which froze the heart of a child, may have had a purely gastric origin, as we consumed those large quantities of fat that would never find their way to Britain. Happily, the family's spirits lifted at last when we piled into the Oldsmobile and later the Buick and went for the traditional Sunday-afternoon spin.

There was nothing my parents enjoyed more than motoring around the new suburbs on the outskirts of the town looking at houses. For my father, the builder, it was an excursion of professional interest, and every now and then, as we drove down a brand-new street of villas, with their freshly planted lawns, bird baths and sickly silver birches, he might suddenly jam on the brakes and point an enraged finger at some crude, jerry-built imitation of one of his own designs. On the new roads, crescents and boulevards flanked by pristine triple-fronted cream-brick bungalows, other vehicles filled with gawking families also cruised. It was the thing everyone did on a Sunday afternoon, and it was called *Looking at the Lovely Homes*. On the hills of Ivanhoe and Eaglemont above the Yarra River, where the artists of the 1880s had painted their idyllic 'impressions', stood some of the grander new houses with tennis courts which especially interested my mother.

Mostly of brick, the colour of milky tea, they had curved nautical-looking terraces, balconies and picture windows, with satin festoon or 'veil of tears' blinds; and if these were raised, as they often were by the proud owners, there might be a glimpse within of blond veneer and peach mirror, and prowling along the window sill just inside the glass, a lithe white marble puma.

The lovely homes bored me. As we glided along in our big chubby car past the raw new houses, still smelling of wet cement, admiring the azaleas and the 'crazy' stone work, the 'feature' chimneys and the names of the houses or their street numbers scribbled across the façades in duck-egg blue wrought-iron, I hankered for hovels. There was a place I had heard of called Dudley Flats, a low-lying wasteland to the west of Melbourne, where 'slums' and *really* poor people could be found.

I begged my parents to drive me there so that I could see them for myself. But we never visited the older suburbs of Melbourne, except when we went to see my mother's sister, Ella, who still lived in a dark Victorian house in Thornbury where her parents had once lived and my mother had grown up. It had ruby and Bristol-blue glass in the panels beside the front door and a long central corridor with a curtain half-way down, so that when the front door was opened, visitors were not afforded a vulgar view of the back yard. There was even an aspidistra in the front parlour which Ella washed with milk, and I once asked my father, in the presence of my aunt and uncle, if their house was a *real* hovel.

Sometimes on Sunday afternoons we would visit the Melbourne General Cemetery with my relations on my mother's side. After much wandering through the maze of granite obelisks and tottering tombstones, overrun with skeleton weed and lantana, we came to a grave that was better kept than the rest. It looked rather like a narrow bed of grey stone, covered with marble chips, and on the headstone was my grandmother's name. My mother removed the old stalks and put some fresh flowers in a little vase buried in the gravel. Aunty Elsie pulled out the weeds and we all just stood and shuffled, looking at the grave and trying to feel something. Around us were sadly neglected plots and even a few that had caved in, so that kneeling down and peering through the cracks you might just see the skeletons of other people's grandmothers.

To earn extra pocket money I often went shopping for my mother. There was a small parade of shops not far away in Camberwell Road, and although their proprietors, Mr Hall, the grocer, Mr Ryal, the chemist, and Mr Ernie Young, the butcher, all seemed to me to be of normal height, my mother always referred to them as diminutive. 'Barry, would you please go down the street and get me a half a pound of nice lean lamb chops from my little butcher. Oh, and while you're there, pop in and ask the little man in the chemist shop for a bottle of Hypol and some Buckley's Canadiol Mixture.' I always took a basket with an orange ten-shilling note and a ration book.

There seemed to be no great shortage of anything, though butterless recipes were popular, but I would stand on the sawdust floor of little Mr Young's butcher's shop while he put his bloodied thumbs in a pair of scissors and deftly snipped a few squares off our meat-ration book. Sometimes, if there was a big card night looming, I would pick up a sponge, a lemon meringue pie or a few fairy cakes from the Misses Longmire who had the 'homemade' cake shop at the end of the Parade. There was always a delicious smell in their shop, though it puzzled me, since everything was baked on the premises, that the Misses Longmire could, with a clear conscience, describe their confections as being homemade when they were so obviously baked in a shop.

If I were not running simple errands after school, I might be in my laboratory mixing quite dangerous combinations of sulphur and potassium permanganate over a Bunsen burner or practising a few magic tricks. I had always had a hankering to be a magician like the top-hatted, opera-cloaked gigolo called

Mandrake who appeared regularly in a comic strip in my mother's *Women's Weekly*. Mandrake had only to 'gesture hypnotically' and people disappeared. That seemed to me to be the greatest gift imaginable; to make people and things vanish.

Sometimes, too, I might even play with my sister and her little friends, Maureen and Valerie. My mother had long ago whispered to me that Valerie was adopted, but never to say anything to her face because her adoptive parents had not yet told her. At the time this information intrigued and frightened me, since it occurred to me that I, like Val, might also be adopted and that my parents too could be keeping this a secret. It even occurred to me that my mother's confidences about Val's origins might be her way of preparing the ground for a confession of her own. It was true to say that her expressions of love for me were sometimes evasive or ambiguous. Once when I was quite young I asked her point-blank if she loved me and she seemed nonplussed and embarrassed. 'Well,' she replied evasively, 'naturally I love your father most of all, and then *my* mother and father, and after that, you and your sister, just the same.' It was clear from what she said that love had a strictly hierarchical structure, and was certainly not something that could be spontaneously experienced or bestowed. My unspoken adoption fears were not put to rest when my mother said, as she frequently did to others in my presence: 'Eric and I don't know *where Barry comes from*.' I have recorded this story as accurately as I can recollect it in order to show the warmer side of my mother's complex personality.

Every now and then there were special occasions; usually a wedding, or a dance at the tennis club. Weeks before these events my mother and I would drive to a distant suburb to the home of Miss Wilmot, my mother's dressmaker, and I would wait in the hall while she had another 'fitting'. These seemed to take forever, and from time to time, Miss Wilmot would put her head around the door and smile at me reassuringly, as if that were possible with a mouthful of pins. Taffeta was my mother's favourite fabric in that epoch; it was before the age of Thai silk. Taffeta was cool and it rustled and chafed upon itself, and before my mother's big night out it was, with a few drops of Bond Street perfume, the nicest textile to say your prayers against.

Once they went to a grand luncheon at the Town Hall, and my mother wore her best suit from Mitzi of Vienna, and a hat with a veil covered with fat black polka dots. Later I asked her what it was like. 'Lovely,' she replied. 'I'm pleased I went to a bit of trouble. It was all hats and glads.'

Gladioli, especially flesh-pink ones, were the floral symbols of respectability, success and thrusting, unquestioning

Mandrake the Magician – a fragment

optimism. They also seemed somehow to be the appropriate emblems of Mr Menzies, the reigning prime minister, who had such a nice 'speaking voice'. Never before had I heard a voice so described, and when my parents tuned in to the wireless to hear one of his public addresses I listened attentively to those sanctimonious, lah-di-dah tones, trying to detect why my parents had singled out this 'speaking voice' in particular. Did he have other more recondite voices, I wondered wickedly. A farting voice perhaps? Above all, Mr Menzies was extolled by my parents and their friends for his repartee and the swiftness with which he rebuked interjections from the Opposition supporters, whom he wittily described as 'that riff-raff at the back of the hall' to roars of laughter and applause.

His opponent, who was later victorious, was Mr Chifley, 'a pipe-smoking Labourite', who had once, Mrs Kendall whispered, 'been a *train driver*'. Certainly Mr Chifley had nothing which could be described as a 'speaking voice', and my father summed him up in three words, 'rough as bags'. 'Irish, too,' my mother added tartly. Since her only brother had married a Roman Catholic and been ostracized, my mother had little affection for the Irish. 'But didn't Nanna's mother come from Ireland?' I asked ingenuously. '*Northern* Ireland, Barry,' she averred warmly, 'that's the nice part of Ireland, and don't you forget it.'

I sometimes think I might still bear the ugly scars of my early indoctrination, when I read absurdly Anglophobic accounts of the Gallipoli Campaign and sensationalist works of Australian history like Robert Hughes's *The Fatal Shore*, where the British are uniformly depicted as shits, and the Irish convicts as misunderstood scallywags. 'He would write that, wouldn't he,' I reflect, 'typical revisionist Mick that he is!' A modern manifestation of this persistent sectarian split in Australian life is the Republican Movement with its cant about patriotism. It is, of course, no such thing, but just another form of pommy-bashing. One has only to glance at the names of its most vociferous champions: Keating, Keneally, Doogue, Conolly and

O'Horne. It is no surprise that the Australian Republican flag is green.

Today I keep my sweaters in a toffee-coloured chest lined with camphor wood. It is densely and rather crudely carved with dragons and ovate oriental bas-reliefs which I remember in the greatest detail from my earliest childhood. It was bought by my grandparents in Colombo as they returned from the Coronation on the Orient Line, as, indeed, were thousands more identical chests purchased by other voyagers. It used to stand in our upstairs hallway and contained my mother's best things: her furs, rugs, table linen, wedding dress, and a gold meshed evening belt encrusted with imitation rubies, sapphires and emeralds.

When I was eleven I noticed in the window of a small secondhand shop near Camberwell Junction a pair of earrings that seemed to match my mother's belt perfectly. I covertly inquired the price which, though I no longer recall it, may have been quite expensive for such cheap paste, but over a long period, and by secretly slipping into the shop and leaving small amounts, I finally paid off the earrings, brought them home and carefully hid them. As her birthday approached I wrapped the earrings, speculating excitedly on the surprise and delight they would bring. I had not even breathed a word to my sister or father.

The great morning came and my father brought my mother breakfast in bed. It was then that I proudly presented my small package. I watched my mother's face carefully as she unwrapped it, but when the tissue paper parted and she saw the earrings, she did not smile. Instead her face darkened and she turned angrily to my father. 'Where did he get these, Eric?' my mother said sharply. 'I hope he didn't pay for these out of his own money?' My father looked confused, and speechless. 'Where did you get them?' my mother asked me. 'Not from that little rogue down at the Junction, I hope. How much did they cost?' I muttered a price. 'Daylight robbery,' exploded my mother. She thrust the earrings at my father. 'Eric?' she commanded. 'I want you to go straight down to that little Jew and tell him to give Barry his money back. And you can also tell him if he goes on overcharging children for rubbish like this I'll have him reported.' Needless to say, that was one of my mother's more memorable birthdays.

My father often used to bring home carnations as a peace offering for some nameless transgression, and I always found them unsympathetic flowers: prim, sharply budded, pinked and serrated blooms in ice-cream colours, with a scent that smelled sprayed-on. They still fill me with a remote dread. Always wrapped in a cone of pink or purple tissue paper, they often lay on the hall table for a long while, depending on the time my mother had set for my father's sentence. But in the end she would always drop them in a vase and say with a smile, 'Look at the lovely carnations your father has given me.' They had worked again.

My father insisted that my mother have domestic help. I had never quite recovered from the sudden departure of my first beloved nanny, Edna, who left without farewells or adequate explanations; although later there was a succession of domestics and housekeepers, they never meant the same to me. After my sister was born my mother engaged a girl from the nearby Salvation Army home, euphoniously called Valmai Grubb. Although my mother admitted that the rest of Valmai's family were almost certainly 'ordinary', Valmai, she insisted, had a very kind heart and a sweet soft nature. Why otherwise would she cry so uncontrollably when rebuked? Valmai stayed a long time and was replaced by Mrs Lane, a woman of about sixty, who came from Welshpool and whom my mother described as 'very countrified'. They took an instant dislike to each other and my mother told me that as soon as she saw the down-trodden heels of Mrs Lane's shoes she knew that she should never have engaged her. On Mrs Lane's days off my mother would inspect the floor of the shower recess and with some satisfaction she always found it to be dry and the room filled with a cloying scent of Three Flowers talcum powder, Mrs Lane's preferred alternative to soap and water. In the mornings, as the housekeeper trudged up the stairs with my mother's breakfast tray, my sister and I often overheard her muttering under her frequently juniper-scented breath the malediction: 'I hate her, I hate her, *I hate her.*'

Having engaged a 'home help' who had quickly proved herself unsuitable, my mother found herself unable to dismiss her, so that thereafter Mrs Lane, having failed as a housekeeper, was retained – even became indispensable – as an example of incompetence and slovenliness. 'Look at the dust,' my mother would say with some satisfaction. 'It's that grub Mrs Lane. She thinks I don't notice.' My mother confided all her complaints about Mrs Lane to Mrs Shores, the woman who came to do the washing and ironing. Mrs Shores was a garrulous lady with a shrill laugh and a husband who enjoyed a drink. She laughed immoderately, though quite genuinely, at all my mother's sardonic jokes. Whenever Mrs Shores arrived my mother would hurry to impart to her Mrs Lane's latest outrage, at which Mrs Shores would burst into peals of incredulous hilarity. It began to look as though Mrs Lane would never be sacked, but be retained forever as a grim cabaret turn and an essential topic of conversation. Mrs Shores was another comic act on the same bill who frequently interrupted her tasks in the laundry to follow my amused parent from room to room gossiping; or she would stand in the kitchen recounting some long anecdote at the top of her voice, assuming my mother was listening in the adjacent sun-room. However my mother often went upstairs, or wandered into the garden to pick a few camellias, and after a wink at me would return to the house to find Mrs Shores still cheerfully soliloquizing.

Mr Dunt, the gardener, was another incompetent hired in order to provide my mother with anecdotes of incompetence. He was an old man, though perhaps little older than the author of this memoir, who arrived on a bicycle with a large pannier attached to the handlebars and who thereafter pottered about pruning the wrong things and digging up carefully planted bulbs. Mr Dunt had a special cup and saucer for his afternoon tea, from which we were forbidden to drink since it was rather uncertain as to where Mr Dunt might have been. It was only after a few years that my father noticed that small things were missing from his workshop behind the garage. The absence of an expensive electric exhaust fan finally aroused his suspicions and a telephone call was made to Mr Dunt's family who, sure enough, discovered a large haul of unused appliances, as well as hinges, nails, trowels and hammers, under the old man's bed. We never saw him again.

One day when I was about six my mother disappeared. My young sister and I were given no explanation of this terrible event and a kind family friend called Janet Ballantyne came to look after us. My father was rarely home, and seemed so stricken with anxiety that we were unable to demand an explanation. I would lie in bed feeling as though some calamity had taken place. Somehow it was even uncertain whether my mother would ever return. But she did. Perhaps she had only been absent for a few weeks, and quite recently I learnt that she had suffered a miscarriage and spent a period convalescing in hospital. My family were madly circumspect in matters to do with illness, sex and even reality, so that a misfortune combining all three taboos was veiled in absolute silence. To this day I can remember those feelings of childish desolation, so that if people close to me leave me now, even on shopping expeditions, I always need to know exactly where they are going, or that oppressive emotion of loss, with all its old force, comes back to me.

Dirty Hair

CANON ROBINSON PERSUADED my father to withdraw me from Camberwell Grammar and enrol me at The Melbourne Grammar School, an old and traditional establishment that was over six miles away. I hated the idea of changing schools and leaving my friends, but Canon Robinson had 'pulled a few strings' and had even talked to the Bishop. It was emphasized to me that I was jumping a long queue and should be grateful for the opportunity of going to what was described as a 'good' school.

My father seemed very nervous at the interview with the headmaster. He received us in his study, in a romantically decaying wing of the nineteenth-century bluestone school buildings. The room was tenebrous, and pale wistaria flickered outside the lancet windows, which were screened with wire mesh to protect them from cricket balls. Mr Sutcliffe wore a tattered subfusc gown and spoke in chilly, unfriendly 'English' tones, which seemed to intimidate my father, who became tongue-tied and deferential. (Many years later and long after his retirement, I met Mr Sutcliffe again at the Melbourne Club and was then struck by his rather broad New Zealand accent.) Canon Robinson had advised my father against describing himself in the enrolment application as a builder and had recommended that he call himself an 'architectural designer' instead. I think my father was embarrassed by this fraudulent snobbism but, since it had been recommended by a Canon of the Church, he reluctantly went along with it.

Our interview, it seemed, had been a success, and I was admitted to this famous institution. No longer could I ride my bicycle through leafy streets to school as I had done in my last few years at Camberwell Grammar. Instead there was a train to be caught and then a tram before I reached the iron gates in Domain Road, South Yarra, just in time for morning chapel.

The school uniform was a quaint version of the 1930s business suit: navy-blue double-breasted serge, remotely inspired by Ronald Coleman. Just as the dinner-jacketed waiters in today's restaurants ape the formal dress of smart diners a generation ago, so the attire of schoolboys (and bank clerks) in the 1940s was a sartorial throwback, echoing the angular-lapelled and tiepinned matinée idols of a former decade. The compulsory hair-style too, a skull-cap varnished with brilliantine, crudely suggested a sleeker pre-war mode. In the school chapel one morning, soon after I had arrived, the headmaster delivered an impassioned address from the pulpit in which he fulminated against long hair. Prefects were urged to catch and punish any boy whose hair touched his collar, and I can still remember Mr Sutcliffe's peroration, delivered in tremulous pseudo-English Kiwi tones: LONG HAIR IS DIRTY HAIR. Permissible only was the abridged Etonian forelock or quiff, which schoolboys of this epoch used to toss back with an automatic flick of the head, almost like a tic. To this day I have observed old Melbourne Grammar boys of this generation, now completely bald, still twitching their heads as though flicking back a phantom forelock.

The boarders of Melbourne Grammar were of a type I had never encountered. With their own stercoraceous jargon, these oafish hobbledehoys resided in a crumbling and evil-smelling wing of the old school. They wore grey trousers and khaki shirts since, unlike the day boys, they were not required to resemble little Christian gentlemen on public transport. Yet whereas many of the day boys were the children of the *nouveau-riche* middle classes, the boarders, often as not, sprang from the loins of Old Boys and their parents either lived in some remotely rural part of Australia, where they farmed, or within a mile of the school in the suburbs of Toorak or South Yarra, where they pursued a vapid social existence, released from the irksome necessity of feeding and housing a dim heir. Little wonder that these waifs, ill-favoured with intelligence and smarting from parental abandonment, should seek comfort in the muddy embrace of their football comrades, and for the rest of their lives pursue a bleak hedonism on ski slopes, golf links or behind the wheels of Porsches.

Our schoolmasters were equally unimpressive. Many of them had been hauled out of retirement during World War Two to replace teachers who had been 'called up', and most of these remained on the staff for the duration of my schooldays. Looked upon as wonderful 'characters' by sentimental Old Boys and younger staff members, and like my mother's home-helpers kept on for their eccentricities rather than their abilities, these ignorant dotards made no effort to communicate knowledge since they had no store of this article on which to draw. Basking in the titillating propinquity of small boys, they filled whole periods, terms and years with boring reminiscence, bluff and sadism. Thus, I was 'taught' mathematics and divinity by a senile football coach, art and algebra by a desiccated athletics instructor, and English literature by a Major of cadets.

Mr 'Tickle' Turner was famous for his intimate methods of corporal punishment. He would put the offending boy over his knee, hold him firmly by the nape of the neck and pat his buttocks rhythmically with a ping-pong bat for twenty minutes whilst delivering a history lecture. 'Bully' Taylor, a turnip-faced ignoramus, was retained by the school merely because he had once, long ago, been an effective football coach. He always took great delight in telling anti-Semitic jokes and then asking Nathan and Goldsmith if they'd got the point. The only schoolmaster I liked at all was Mr Albert Greed, the chapel organist, who took us for musical-appreciation classes one afternoon a week. Albert was usually in a convivial mood after lunch, having had a few beers up the road at the Botanical Hotel, and could sometimes be persuaded to break off a lesson on Schubert and, whilst still seated at the piano, launch in to a sprightly rendition of 'Nola' or 'Kitten on the Keys', during which he would blush and giggle immoderately. Albert also organized lunchtime concerts in the War Memorial Hall and to one of these he invited the Aboriginal tenor, Harold Blair. He was the first Aborigine I ever set eyes on, for if there were any of Australia's original inhabitants living in Melbourne, they were kept well out of the way of nice people; unless, of course, they could sing.

Meanwhile, beneath a cunning smokescreen of philanthropy, the school offered scholarships and endowments to talented state school boys, thus saving itself from gross academic disgrace in the public exams. My first form was something called Remove, which I took to be a class for dunces. I was still overwhelmed by the size of my new school. It was a disconcerting jump from being one of the tallest and best-known boys at Camberwell Grammar to being one of the smallest and least-known at Melbourne. I was to experience a similar emotion in adult life when I arrived in London as an obscure actor after a taste of hometown fame. I looked around the classroom and thought how unlikely it would be to ever make friends with a single one of these unprepossessing classmates, but I did. Slowly people got to know my name and the daunting scale of the beetling school buildings quietly subsided.

I missed the masters at my former school, especially Stanley Brown, who had encouraged my interest in books. I also missed the art classes. A 'real' artist called Ian Bow had come to teach us and though very few boys were interested in his subject he had become a kind of hero, arriving every day in a loudly backfiring Hillman Minx. It was rumoured that Mr Bow had *two wives*, one of whom my friend Richard Tolley had actually met. Mr Bow smelt of art, that is to say, turpentine. Sometimes he would bring his still-wet paintings to school and talk about the fun he had in painting them. He also told us stories about artists, one of whom, a Dutchman, had once cut off his ear. Mr Bow showed us some prints of this artist's work, including a picture of sunflowers which created a titter. He emphasized the need to use plenty of paint. I asked my father if I could have some oil-paints for my birthday – in advance, if possible, since my birthday was in eleven months' time!

So I came to possess my first set of Winsor & Newton student oil-paints, and a small easel which I set up in the middle of a paddock near Uncle Dick's house at Balwyn. The rolling green gorse-covered hills of this district have long since been built over and suburbanized, but then they were windswept and glorious and the nearest thing I could find to a Van Gogh corn field. Inspired by Mr Bow's exuberant example, I went on many painting expeditions; beside the Yarra River, where the Melbourne 'impressionists' used to set up their painting camps in the eighties and nineties, and on the red bluffs of Mornington, the bayside resort where my father had built us a new holiday 'shack', this time with a septic tank and a tennis court.

The beach at Mornington was unfrequented, almost private, and sometimes on hot summer days, when the bay seemed tideless, my sister and I would swim in the green glassy water, explore the cliff paths and search for shells. I liked to burst the small bladders of the antlered seaweed, or dabble languidly in the secret crannies of the rock pool, surprising the petals of the sea-anemones and feeling them sucking and nibbling at my fingertips. On such becalmed days, the tartan rugs would be drawn nearer the verge and the umbrellas planted close to the barely lapping water.

One hot afternoon I noticed on the shore a few feet from where I floated a dentist's wife my parents knew cooling her ankles in the water, squinting into the spangled brightness and brushing the sand from her knees. But then, suddenly, as she stretched across the picnic debris to have her Bakelite teacup

refilled from the orange-flecked Thermos, I noticed how her
woollen bathing costume gaped at the place on her legs where
her suntan stopped; and then I saw a kind of pleat, sutured
with hair like a dark V-shaped darn. Soon she drew her knees
together again and, sipping her tea, squinted out to sea where I
hid in the white dazzle.

Although I still painted during these summer holidays, trudging around with my portable easel searching for the Mornington
correspondences with Cézanne's 'Mont St Victoire' and Van
Gogh's 'Asylum at St Remy', there was no one at Melbourne
Grammar to offer much encouragement. In fact, no one seemed
to draw or paint at all. Some form of instruction in art must
have been compulsory, or why else would poor lugubrious Mr
Grant, known as 'Whizzer' because of his legendary sprinting
prowess, be forced to teach, against his better inclination, this
Cinderella subject? Not much happened in art class. There was
general disorder which Mr Grant, sunk in a post-prandial
torpor with his mind clearly on other things, did little to
subdue. At least our music classes were livelier, especially if
Albert had had a few.

Slowly, in spite of myself, I began to enjoy the new school with
its old buildings and the nearby Royal Botanic Gardens to
which we sometimes escaped during lunch hour. After school I
would take the tram along St Kilda Road, lined with English
plane trees, to the city and often, instead of catching the train
home from Flinders Street Station, I would spend an hour
browsing around some of the secondhand bookshops. At the
top of Bourke Street near Parliament House, where an
anachronistic hansom cab still loitered, there was the bookshop
of Ellis Bird. Mrs Bird, a good-looking woman with a grey bun,
and her assistant, Shirley, always seemed to be entertaining a
priest whenever I entered the dusty old shop. But Mrs Bird had
quickly learnt my name and always addressed me rather
formally, and to my intense pleasure, as *Mr Humphries*. 'Excuse
me, Father,' she would say to her sherry-sipping guest, 'but I

just want to show Mr Humphries a book which I think might amuse him,' and she would produce *South Wind* or *The Green Hat* or Richard Garnett's *The Twilight of the Gods* or *The Monk* by M. G. Lewis.

On the campus of the Melbourne University beside the Conservatorium of Music was a curious brick building that seemed to be permanently closed. It was also apparently windowless. A small plaque, however, proclaimed it to be the Percy Grainger Museum, and those wishing to inspect its contents might obtain permission and a key from the secretary at the Conservatorium. Percy Grainger was Australia's most famous composer, *outside* Australia. In the United States, he was largely celebrated as a conductor and concert pianist who had, in 1928, been married to his 'Nordic Princess' in the presence of an audience of 23,000 people at the Hollywood Bowl (the couple were later photographed with Ramon Novarro). The event must have come as no small surprise to his bride, who was expecting a 'cameo' wedding, and supposed the Hollywood Bowl to be a picturesque grotto in a quiet park.

If Percy Grainger had any renown in his homeland, it was only as the composer of 'Country Gardens', a jaunty ditty which the Australian Broadcasting Commission used as a theme tune for their rural broadcasts. Grainger, undeterred by the indifference of his countrymen, had built this museum in Melbourne to house his own memorabilia, and he had designed it himself, so that its ground plan was identical, from the air, to an Icelandic burial ground. Unfortunately there were few, if any, Australians inclined to recognize this similitude, even had they been vouchsafed an aerial view of the building. Consequently, although it had been conceived as a modernist structure, it most resembled a large and inaccessible public lavatory.

About once a decade Percy would revisit Australia and spend a few days in Melbourne dusting his unfrequented museum and adding to its contents: a Greig manuscript here, a bust of Sibelius there.

There had been a small paragraph accompanied by a photograph in the *Melbourne Sun News-pictorial* announcing Grainger's latest visit, and on one of our Sunday afternoon drives I spotted him strolling along a quiet, leafy street at Kew, on a nostalgic jaunt. I asked my father to stop the car, and rather boldly accosted the maestro. I told him that I had what I thought to be a rare recording of one of his compositions for solo cello, and asked if he would accept it as a gift to the museum. He seemed very pleased and invited me to call on him the following day.

Thus was I taken on a personal guided tour of the museum's many treasures and curiosities, including a pair of breeches worn on a walking tour of Norway by the forgotten composer Balfour Gardiner. But I, a mere Melbourne schoolboy, had now shaken hands with the creator of *The Magic Flute*; for had not Percy shaken hands with Greig who had shaken hands with Liszt who had shaken hands with Beethoven who had shaken hands with Haydn, *who had clasped the hand of Mozart?*

Quite recently I revisited the Grainger Museum. Percy, being long and safely dead, was now acknowledged as an important Australian, and the museum doors stood proudly ajar. At a desk within I saw a young female archivist earnestly cataloguing the avalanche of letters to and from the composer, which Grainger had bequeathed to his own museum. It was a task for the stout-hearted, however, since Grainger's sexual vocation was, to say the least, exotic. Even as I entered the room, I observed the young woman holding an envelope at arm's length, and, with a pair of tweezers, disdainfully extracting from it a fibrous tangle of pubic hair.

Every Anzac Day there was a special assembly in the Memorial Hall, usually addressed by some purple-faced old general with a knighthood and a rainbow of ribbons on his khaki chest. Then, while the whole school stood silently to attention, a group of impetiginous prefects would recite the Roll of Honour; the Old Boys who had died in the Boer War and the Great War. There was one family called Snowball, which produced a titter every year, though the laughter died on our lips as we counted seven Snowballs. The list of the fallen was a long one, and many students fell in sympathy and had to be carted out, grey-faced, into the quad.

Over the next few years I gained friends and confidence. Some of my poems about theological doubt and pacifism were published, if in expurgated form, in the school magazine and I appeared every year in the school play, usually in a minor role, except for my most spectacular cameo as Mrs Pengard in Walter Hackett's *Ambrose Applejohn's Adventure,* a precursor perhaps of a later theatrical invention.

I became involved with the debating society also, and in my third year we sometimes debated against other schools on Friday evenings. Girls' schools. These exciting expeditions were organized by our history master, Mr Olsen, a dapper Englishman who wore the first double-vented sports jacket seen in Melbourne. He had a knitted tie and an effeminate habit of tucking his handkerchief in his sleeve. He was also known to possess a pair of suede shoes, a sure sign in the Melbourne of this period of sexual ambivalence. Mr Olsen, however, had a rather vivid wife, who, it seemed, was interested in Art and completely understood, according to her husband, Paul Klee. The girls at our debates impressed me then as being much more clever and quick-witted than us; and to someone like me, whose female acquaintance was limited to my sister's friends (who hardly counted), my beautiful, fierce and witty debating opponents from Merton Hall, Lauriston, Shelford and the Methodist Ladies' College, seemed at once ravishing and unattainable.

My sister Barbara and I began to attend ballroom-dancing classes given by an Austrian couple called Myer. No doubt they were Jewish refugees from Vienna and they seemed to move

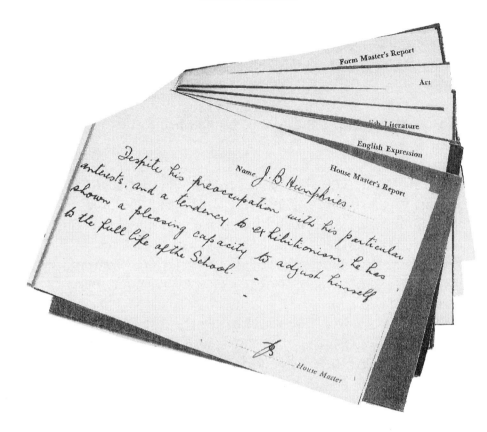

Form Master's Report

Art

...ish Literature

English Expression

Name *J. B. Humphries.*

House Master's Report

Despite his preoccupation with his particular interests, and a tendency to exhibitionism, he has shown a pleasing capacity to adjust himself to the full life of the School. –

House Master

Melbourne Grammar report, c. 1948

perpetually to the tempo of the waltz. I dreaded their classes, and I was convinced that I had no dancing ability whatsoever. During these excruciating *soirées* in a rented church hall I was forced into the apprehensive embrace of all my sister's girlfriends: Valerie, Maureen, Gillian, Margot and Wendy; the latter always, it seemed, clutching in one hand a slightly damp handkerchief. At the end of what felt like an interminable evening of hopping and shuffling to a thumping piano accompaniment, Mr Myer commiserated with my bruised and disgruntled partners, and in a last desperate attempt to inculcate in me the basic steps of the waltz or the foxtrot, would take me in his powerful arms and sweep me imperiously around the room, his chin held high, his eyes blazing and his knees locked

into mine. 'VUN two sree, VUN two sree, VUN two sree . . .'
Out of the corner of my eye I could see Mrs Myer and the
other pupils watching this demonstration with patronizing
smirks as, growing giddier by the second, I was propelled past
them.

Most boys joined the school regiment and became known as
'cadets'. Every Tuesday afternoon after school they paraded for
hours in uniform, and the time approached when I would have
to enrol. I had been reading some of Sassoon's pacifist First
World War verse and I also knew something of Bertrand
Russell and the other conscientious objectors whom Lady
Ottoline Morrell had sheltered at Garsington, so I decided to
be a conscientious objector myself. Mr Sutcliffe, to whom I
made this rather priggish declaration, took it, to my surprise,
extremely well. He even seemed impressed and I was immediately excused from the pointless hours of drill into which
the other boys were grimly conscripted. I have a picture of
myself – not an altogether attractive one – strolling jauntily out
the school gates past a rigid platoon of my classmates, their
faces sullen with envy. Mr Sutcliffe always called me by my
first name after this and it was difficult to imagine that he was
the aloof and snobbish figure who had intimidated my poor
father years before in his office. Perhaps, I reflected, the
headmaster was a secret pacifist himself.

With a few carefully chosen friends I formed a small
subversive gang. From the back row of the classroom we would
submit some of our teachers, who were not fully the masters of
their subject, to relentless raillery. I became Secretary of the Art
Club and arranged exhibitions of work in the cricket pavilion,
in which my own paintings predominated. Some of these were
bright-hued post-impressionist oil-paintings of Mornington
views, and others, in stark contrast, were in the cubist and
Dadaist manner, designed to shock. I also invited some 'real'
artists to speak at the school; an unprecedented event. One was
an academic old duffer, Max Meldrum, and another was Noel
Counihan, a notorious communist whose scurrilous caricatures

of the prime minister, Mr Robert Menzies, appeared regularly in the *Guardian*, Melbourne's only communist newspaper.

Senator McCarthy's witchhunts in the United States had distant reverberations in Australia, and the Melbourne *Herald* was gleefully publishing the shameful confessions of an ex-party member under the unimaginative banner 'I Chose Freedom'. For years the *Guardian*, full of old-fashioned anti-capitalist cant and naïve pro-Soviet propaganda, had been sold on newsstands and by 'workers' on the steps of Flinders Street Railway Station without anyone taking much notice. Now there was talk of banning this anodyne little rag. The very idea of communism, rarely thought of before, sent a shudder down every respectable back.

I decided to become a communist. Furtively I bought a copy of *The Communist Manifesto* in a back-street bookshop in the industrial suburb of Brunswick, but I found it practically unreadable. The next best thing, so I thought, was to *appear* to be a communist, and this was a path down which I was sure Mr Sutcliffe would not follow me. My political period – the only one in my life – was short-lived, since the *Manifesto* left ostentatiously on my desk so that it could be seen by the most fanatically right-wing schoolmaster in Australia was swiftly confiscated and I never saw it again. However I had discovered that there was a very special pleasure and excitement to be derived from shocking people. I suppose it gave a schoolboy, who was in fact completely powerless, the illusion of power.

In spite of some of the freedoms that I was claiming for myself at school, there was one principle that was ruthlessly enforced: it was something called *School Spirit*, or the compulsory attendance at games. Precious hours of after-school leisure were wasted in those dangerous and futile exercises upon the playing field. Only the sickliest boys escaped, on medical grounds, the ineluctable twice-weekly 'turnout'. First, one entered the dungeon-like tog-room beneath the Memorial Hall, and in an atmosphere reeking of jockstraps and carbolic acid and thunderous with cold showers, one hastily donned the foolish motley of cricket field or footy pitch. Thereafter one would ascend to the oval's miry brink to have one's name ticked off by a yahoo prefect. Like sheep to the slaughter the boys would then subject themselves to hours of health-impairing sport, often returning to their homes after dark, too ill and exhausted to study. Not I.

Twice a week for several years I dutifully 'turned out'. No sooner was my name ticked off on the roll than I would furtively skirt the playing fields and vanish into a cubicle of the school lavatories. Minutes later, in response to a tapped signal on the door, I would open it, and my accomplice, now an advertising tycoon, for whom I performed a similar service on *his* turnout nights, thrust into my grasp a Gladstone bag containing my school uniform. A quick change, an all-clear whistle, and I was outside the school gates, off on a tram – to freedom!

Amazing, really, that this ruse should have succeeded as long as it did; and inevitable, as I now apprehend, that the day should come when, emboldened by habit, I should hear the familiar knock, open the door, and behold a glowering Neanderthal figure. 'The game's up, Humphries,' said Peter Beer, the Captain of the School, for it was he. I was led away to his study, if a room without books may be so called, where I received six strokes of the cane.

Shithouse Spaghetti

I NOW HAD TWO younger brothers, Christopher and Michael, who were enrolled at the junior school, but I saw very little of them during their childhood, except on school holidays which we spent in the new house in Mornington. With an army of workmen, my father had built it in two weeks and I remember our first Christmas there, when the paint was still wet. It was in the bay at Mornington that we all had our swimming lessons from a deeply suntanned, wiry German called Willi Fritsch.

Willi had been a champion at the Berlin Olympic Games in 1936 but had somehow been stranded in Australia, where he spent the war in custody. If swimming could be called a sport, it was the only one that ever gave me any enjoyment, as it still does. Willi lived quite close to us in Camberwell and I once had to call at his house for some reason, perhaps to pay swimming fees. I was admitted by his attractive blonde wife, and whilst waiting for Willi, I noticed an interesting framed photograph of my swimming teacher taken some years before, being presented with a silver cup by Hitler. It was not the sort of snapshot one was used to seeing on a surburban mantelpiece.

My parents expressed concern when I began to form closer friendships with Jewish boys at school. 'Robert seems a very nice type of boy,' my mother would say, unconvincingly, 'but can't you spend more time with people of your own kind?' My mother had dark hair and olive skin, and it was by no means certain that if her ancestry were ever traced it would necessarily reveal a purely Anglo-Saxon heritage.

Jews were admitted to Melbourne Grammar on a very discouraging quota system and even then were only grudgingly excused from attending chapel. They had about them an aura of separateness which I identified with. I felt somehow 'different' and they *were* different.

Robert Nathan, my new friend, was obviously a gifted boy and I felt drawn to his circle. It may have been my parents' suburban anti-Semitism that made these classmates seem somehow brighter, funnier and more attractive than the rest, but, I reflected, weren't the Marx Brothers Jewish? Nathan, though not a brilliant scholar, had the aura of talent about him, and on Sundays he often held musical evenings at his parents' house. These consisted of record-playing sessions and Robert, whose musical tastes were very advanced for a schoolboy's, liked to play works such as the Brahm's *Requiem* and Walton's *Belshazzar's Feast*. I brought along my 78 recordings of *Façade*, the most thrillingly modern and witty music I had ever heard, with the voice of Constant Lambert, and Edith Sitwell herself declaiming the insouciant verses.

By then my mother and father had been forced to relax their fundamentalist attitude to the Christian Sabbath, and I was sometimes allowed to spend a Sunday evening with my friends. On the one hand they were no doubt relieved to know that these evenings were supervised; indeed occasionally there was even a rabbi present in the same house, as well as my friend John Levi, a rabbi of the future. On the other hand, however, they felt as though the traditional Church of England 'values' which they and Canon Robinson had tried for so long to inculcate were being insidiously eroded. In fact, they were.

Some time before, I had become a Sunday-school teacher at St Mark's Church, Camberwell. Autocratic, sanctimonious old Canon Robinson had conscripted me, and every Sunday I had to teach the New Testament to a small class of bored and restless children in the hideous red-brick hall beside the church. I felt I was a terrible hypocrite, mouthing the teachings of the Church of England to these indifferent brats, and at the same time writing agnostic and frankly anti-clerical verses for the school magazine. The rapture of an authentic spiritual experience had always eluded me. I remember at my Confirmation I had hoped and prayed for such a transcendental moment, when Bishop McKay, the Bishop of Geelong, had placed his hands on my head in blessing. But as I knelt expectantly at the altar rail and the Moment came, I felt nothing. All I could smell was the odour of Brylcreem on the bishop's benedictory palms, and I pictured him in the vestry, just before the service, quickly caressing his dark greasy hair before stepping into the Chancel.

My fellow Sunday-school teachers were either devout and elderly parishioners whom I could see in other corners of the hall droning on to a circle of stupefied children, or young conscripts like me. There was a pretty girl called Rosemary Gair teaching the juniors, whom I sometimes met on the tram. Whenever I spoke to her I always moved my head vigorously, making it impossible for her to focus too intently on my acne. Eyeing her sideways at Sunday school, I secretly wondered if she had as little faith as I, or if, indeed, she ever entertained impious fantasies similar to my own. Probably not.

I befriended a fellow teacher called George Howe, who also played the piano and organ at Sunday school. We shared an interest in music and sometimes we listened to records at his home, where he lived with elderly parents. It was a dark Edwardian house in an old section of the suburb, and the streets were shaded with large elms and plane trees. The oldest streets and parks of Melbourne still have mature plantations of trees which have not yet succumbed to the 'Dutch' disease, so that the city has become, almost, a Museum for Elms. George had a large old-fashioned wind-up gramophone, and a complete collection of pre-war recordings of Delius, conducted by Beecham. It was strange sitting in that dim house on a still night in a city of South-east Asia, as this most English of music floated out the window into the heavy English foliage of Canterbury Road.

At last the day came when, not to be outdone by the Infidel, my parents cautiously agreed to let me hold a reciprocal musical *soirée* at our house. My father bought a large walnut-veneered piece of furniture called a radiogram, with a noisy and sometimes violent automatic record changer. Then the night arrived: a small group of my friends and a few serious-minded and very pretty girls from Merton Hall came to Christowel Street and sat in the sun-room in various attitudes of highbrow concentration, while I played them an opera by Ravel. The music wove its spell of chaste eroticism, a spell which was somewhat broken by my mother's periodic interruptions, 'Do you *have* to have it up this loud, Barry?' or, more archly, 'I hope you've asked your friends if they really want to listen to this,' and finally, at about 9.30: 'Would you all like a little nibble of something *before you go home*?' At which my mother, speaking in that distressingly genteel voice she always employed in the presence of strangers, would invite us all into the dining-room for tea and sandwiches and cakes.

I winced with shame and snobbishness when I thought of Mr and Mrs Spira, my friend Leonard's parents, who had escaped from Poland via Shanghai, arrived in Melbourne, started a small restaurant and helped to found a chamber orchestra. When I had gone to their place a few Sundays before to listen to the gramophone, Mrs Spira had offered the boys a glass of Chartreuse; and although their house was much much smaller than ours there were garlicky cheesy smells coming from the kitchen which my mother could not, and certainly *would not*, ever produce.

In the Spiras' small sitting-room it was somehow warmer too, and the lights were dimmer, and some of the boys rested their arms idly around the girls' shoulders almost as if Prokofiev and Bartók and Stravinsky were not entirely the point of the evening.

*

It is strange to think that I, who now leap around the stage performing nimble corybantics to a musical accompaniment in front of thousands of people, once had an aversion to dancing, and such a conviction of my own inadequacy that I would avoid all social gatherings where dancing took place. To arrive at somebody's house in my new dinner jacket and black tie and hear, even in the street, the ominous thump of Dennis Farrington's orchestra playing such popular hits of the period as 'The Roving Kind' and 'A Kiss to Build a Dream On' always brought me out in a cold, apprehensive sweat.

My mother was particularly anxious for me to attend one such event in the company of a friend's daughter, yet even as I collected this unfortunate girl and pressed upon her the obligatory corsage of gardenias and maidenhair fern in a celluloid box, I pitied her. Later that night as we stood by the bar I prayed that someone else would tap her on one of her bare, blue-mottled shoulders and whisk her on to the dance floor forever. Then, looking slightly past me with eyes that already seemed to well with tears of disappointment, she asked for a glass of punch. Eager for something to do – and say – I proceeded to tilt the large jug of fruit-choked liquid gently into her glass which she held close to her deeply *décolletée* ballerina-length dress. The punch merely trickled into her glass, so I tilted the jug at a sharper angle. The dam of pineapple, orange, strawberry and passionfruit ruptured, sending two pints of chilled cordial directly down her cleavage whence it pursued an invisible path to the carpet beneath.

She gave a sort of whimper, and fled to the bathroom where she remained for the rest of the evening until finally I drove her home in total silence. Strange to say, my pity for her completely disappeared and was replaced by a kind of rage against adolescence itself, and the cruel and pointless rituals of my class.

Another of my new interests, which disappointed my parents, was my enthusiasm for secondhand bookshops; indeed, for anything that had the patina of age. 'Do you have to buy those old bits and pieces?' my mother would say if I came home with some dusty old volume after a visit to Mrs Bird. 'You never know where things like that have been.' Some of my books, like the *Tales of D. H. Lawrence*, disappeared mysteriously from my shelves and when I mentioned this my mother said, passing the buck, 'Your father thought it was quite unsuitable, unnecessary and completely *Uncalled-for!*' I never saw the books again, though I suspect they were consigned to some secret bibliocaust in the incinerator at the back of the garden.

My father was beginning to see that the educational opportunities that he had struggled to give us – and barely a week passed when we were not reminded of his sacrifices – could have their disadvantages; could even introduce us to the seamy and seductive world of the Uncalled-for. On the whole, though, he was proud of the As I got for English, and, to gently discourage me from buying old and dirty books, he opened an account for me at Robertson & Mullens, which only sold new and germ-free editions.

My friend Robert Maclellan and I sometimes dined in town on Friday evenings before a meeting of the school Debating Society. To fill in time we would visit bookshops or art exhibitions, and then have a plate of pasta at a small, cheap Italian restaurant next to His Majesty's Theatre. The Spaghetti à la Bolognese was a total novelty for me, as were the strange twig-like fragments in the sauce that suggested that someone had shaken a dead bush over the plate. It was my first experience of herbs.

One evening at about 6.00, we were twirling our forks when a disturbance broke out at another table. There was the crash of a chair falling backwards and we looked across the small café to see a woman with dishevelled hair and a crimson face swaying slightly before she lurched against the wall. Her husband and a small child sat there looking at her with expressions of horror, and also with a kind of grief, that I can still see to this day. The woman pointed to her plate, and at the top of her voice she screamed, 'THIS SPAGHETTI IS SHITHOUSE!' I had never heard a woman swear. The owner hurried to her table. 'Get to the shithouse!' the woman yelled, while her husband made mute gestures of despair and apology to us all. The family was bundled out into the street. The other diners all looked at each other and grinned sheepishly as we heard cockatoo-like cries of 'shithouse' dwindling down the street. It was my first encounter with alcoholism.

My last year of school was almost amusing. Unfortunately, Mr Sutcliffe, of whom I had become rather fond, resigned under suspicious circumstances. It was said that he had tried to expel a group of hooligans who had disrupted a school dance with fireworks, forgetting that they were the sons of rich and influential parents. Some of the parents were on the school board, so Sutcliffe got the shove. He was replaced by a craggy-faced and hearty new headmaster from Sydney, who quickly instituted reforms. The incompetent 'characters' who had hither-to shuffled across the quad or, rather than teach, loitered before the blackboard, were expelled. Younger schoolmasters replaced them, a few of whom even wore casual clothes; crew-necked sweaters and knitted ties. Some of these, we noticed, even failed to bow to the altar in Chapel.

I no longer tried to be good at mathematics, though for years my father had sent me to a succession of coaches in this incomprehensible subject. It was not as though I got bad marks for maths; I got zero, term after term.

Instead I devoted most of my energy to the Art Club and to my new passion for the Dadaists and surrealists of the early 1920s. Everything I read about their antics and outrages excited me, and the work of Duchamp and Picabia and Schwitters seemed so much more amusing than the landscapes I had been painting in plodding imitation of Cézanne.

John Levi had a crony called Perry whom I persecuted by bombarding his desk with vicious caricatures. I am sure envy lay behind this behaviour since Perry was clearly an authentic artist, although what kind it was difficult to tell. Slowly I relaxed my mean-spirited vendetta and we became friends. Already he was writing brilliant and anarchic monologues and wild irrational tirades that anticipated Lucky's speech from *Waiting for Godot* by several years.

Sometimes our Dada Group went down to the seaside suburb of St Kilda to Luna Park, a large and tawdry fairground which was entered through a huge neon mouth. Between rides on the Big Dipper and mysterious River Caves, amongst the shrieks of plummeting roller coasters and the smell of sparks and fairy floss, we recorded our subversive improvisations in a tiny recording booth next to the Giggle Palace. The wafer-thin black discs we made there were crude and fragile, though a couple, miraculously, still survive.

After Luna Park we sometimes visited the Galleon Coffee Lounge, a raffish café filled with smoke, where I saw my first 'blue' comic, a man called Frank Rich who wore a suit and a moustache and looked like a successful commercial traveller. Next to the Marx Brothers, he was the funniest thing I'd ever seen, although I could never have guessed then that one day part of me would also be a 'blue' comedian.

A new club had opened in Melbourne called the Society for New Music. It met on Sunday nights in a theatre in the old bayside suburb of Middle Park and there, once a month, flocked the highbrows and *poseurs*, the precious, the pretty and the pretentious. The foyer of the theatre was painted black and was hung with photographs of Melbourne actors and actresses looking intense, all smoking and wearing black polo-neck jumpers. The photographs were by a young German called Helmut Newton. When the New Music Society met, the small theatre was thronged with long-haired youths in suede shoes and corduroy trousers smoking Turkish cigarettes with the wrong fingers. 'Window-dressers!' someone whispered, grinning. There were beards too, and women who, in the age of the perm, wore very long straight hair, sandals and not much makeup. And there was a loud babble of foreign tongues. It all felt, well, continental.

The society was founded by Kevin McBeath to foster an interest in modern music and we would sit solemnly in the stalls listening to recordings of Menotti's new operas and occasionally live performances of advanced chamber music. I had recently, after a long struggle, got my drivers licence, and one sultry Sunday evening I was allowed to drive my mother's car to a special Sunday-night recital devoted to the music of Erik Satie.

The three *Gymnopédies* were not then the slightly hackneyed works they have sadly since become, and as their breathless and limpid beauty unfolded at that arty little gathering, I glanced across the aisle and noticed one of the girls I had met at Leonard's house. She was transfixed by the music. There was coffee after the concert and for the first time in my life I found it possible to say the words, 'May I give you a lift home?' That night in a cream Austin A40 parked beneath an enormous lilac tree in full bloom, I fell in love.

Russian Salad Days

'I HOPE YOU'RE not turning pansy.'
Mr Hone, the craggy-faced headmaster, looked up at me interrogatively. What could he mean? It was impossible to know how to reply to such an unexpected and heartfelt expression of concern.'I hope not too, sir,' was all I could manage.

I had been called to the Head's study to explain why my final term's results had been so unsatisfactory; even in subjects like English and history I had gained disappointing marks, though I had won the poetry prize again – with very little competition, it must be confessed.

Mr Hone – soon to be Sir Brian Hone – was obviously sincere, but it was hard to know the basis for his concern. Throughout my last years at school I was always being told my hair was too long, and since the time when my elaborate ruse for avoiding games was discovered and punished by the School Captain, I had been called 'Queenie' Humphries by a few scurrilous boarders.

'You've got a lot of serious decisions to make over the next few years, my boy,' said the bluff old Head, rising from his chair and extending the five sausages of his right hand, 'and I hope you feel you can call on me for help at any time.' I didn't feel I could in the least, as a matter of fact, nor was I quite sure what the decisions I had to make were all about, but I allowed my hand to be lightly sprained by Mr Hone's rugger-toughened grasp, and sheepishly retreated.

It had been suggested that, like some of my dimmer classmates, I might stay back at school another year and repeat my matriculation. However the public examinations had yet to come when we all traipsed into town to that majestic Victorian folly, the Exhibition Building, and sat for our Finals, adjudicated by impartial examiners.

When, after Christmas, the results were published, it seemed that I had done spectacularly well, and to my father's amazement I even won a valuable scholarship to the University. I had hoped to read Arts, but due to an oversight at Melbourne Grammar, I lacked the prerequisite language. I decided to please my parents and enrol at the Law School. I would spend a year catching up on German at a famous crammer, and commence my Arts course the following year. I later heard that due to this blunder, my old school had been given an enormous rocket by the University, and Mr Hone had been hauled over the coals for failing to spot a star pupil. I was immoderately pleased. Most of my contemporaries at school entered the World of Business, the logical destiny of bores. No more than eight members of the entire sixth form went on to University. I remember that one of our masters proudly collected the names of Old Boys who had 'done well', and these he recorded in a small book. It was a very small book.

There was another interruption to the launch of my academic career; military service. I had vaguely known about this, but like many things in my life, had supposed it couldn't happen to me, or, if it did, I would gesture hypnotically like Mandrake the Magician and make it go away. At the medical examination I tried the Conscientious Objection tactic that had worked so well in the past, but it provoked only a derisory laugh. Then I found a doctor who wrote that I was psychologically unfit for military service, but his letter was ignored. And so soon after, I found myself at four o'clock in the morning doing kitchen duty at Puckapunyal Military Camp, seventy miles from Melbourne. Puckapunyal is an Aboriginal word meaning The Land of the Outer Barbarians.

I had sometimes, though rarely, gone to bed at four a.m. but I had never risen at that hour. Minutes after waking and dressing, I was in the camp kitchen scrubbing 'Dixies' – large aluminium vats to which the greasy and gristly remnants of stew tenaciously clung. I was sure that my attempts to dodge National Service had earmarked me for this brutal assignment. I stood all day at the sink, my hands raw with detergent, while the oafish and grinning kitchen hands from the Regular Army sadistically added to the huge pile of clattering aluminium to which the burnt residue of cabbage, cod and mashed potato seemed inseparably bonded.

The stench was the worst. In the kitchen it was pre-dominantly the fart-like odour of cabbage with a dash of onion and offal, but the whole camp was pervaded by the smell of dust and garbage. The surrounding countryside may have been attractive once, but now it had been wrecked and eroded by military exercises over many years so that it resembled an overheated, antipodian Somme or Passchendaele. The camp was huge and the prospect of having to spend three months' penal servitude there filled me with horror. Some of my school friends were in the same regiment and I would glimpse them through the greasy louvres of my kitchen as they marched past at 8.30 a.m. A few even seemed to be enjoying themselves. Should I too be relishing this healthy military life, or was Mr Hone right, and was I turning pansy after all?

At the end of a long day, around seven p.m., I was sometimes too tired to take off my fat-spattered boots. I lay on my horsehair palliase, in one of the long tents of the Melbourne University Rifles, sobbing with rage and fatigue, while some of the more enthusiastic recruits nearby whistled inanely as they scrubbed their webbing, polished their boots and oiled their rifles.

My parents were very pleased that I was in the army. The

fact that I hated it somehow pleased them even more. I was beginning to realize that this was an aspect of the Puritanism which governed most of my friends' lives as well as mine, so that later, at the University, I saw many men I knew doing courses only to gratify their parents or, as the phrase went, 'to get something solid behind them.' There was a moral virtue in suppressing all real talent; in flying in the face of impulse and vocation and doing something, instead, which was completely repugnant. That made parents happy.

At last released from kitchen duty, I did square bashing with the rest of them, though I quickly found that the more laughs I could win through incompetence, the more chance I would have of getting off punishing drills and manoeuvres.

In the evenings, as it cooled down a bit and the foul-smelling dust settled, it was almost pleasant to sit beside the tent on an upturned box reading, or teaching myself to smoke a pipe. Occasionally a surly officer from the Regular Army would strut past, eye one of us severely and bark, 'On your feet, soldier! What's the matter with your right hand?' At which we would spring to attention and deliver the appropriate salute, even though sometimes it was too dark to see the face of our superior. This gave me an idea which briefly restored my failing self-confidence.

With a false moustache of burnt cork and my hair plastered back, I would visit remote sections of the camp at twilight and catch slovenly privates unawares as I surprised them from the shadows. 'What's the matter with your right hand?' was a phrase which, if enunciated at close range and with sufficient savagery, would bring even the most vigilant corporal to a position of tremulous attention, and I was gone before they could, by squinting through the dusk, observe my lack of stripes or my anomalous uniform. I felt a little reassuring gush of illicit power.

By fraternizing with the Entertainments Officer, I managed to involve myself in the camp concert, which was to be a whimsical view of army life on Mars, with musical items pinched from Gilbert and Sullivan. I contrived to get the job of Scenic Designer, an official task which required more and more leave of absence from arduous military training. Luckily Lieutenant-Colonel Duffy, the commander of the camp, was enthusiastic about the whole project and I was given a disused aircraft hangar on the periphery of the camp in which to supervise the painting and construction of the large sets, which I had also designed. These were mostly backdrops painted on enormous sheets of canvas and hessian, and I arranged for a few of my less martially inclined friends to be seconded to my scene-painting unit.

At reveille, as the others clambered into their gear before shuffling on to the parade ground, my little team and I enjoyed an hour's more sleep before ambling over to our hangar for a leisurely few hours painting, or snoozing on the bales of hessian. It was important military work, though it did not earn us the affection of our foot-slogging counterparts. There was a particularly strong pink colour I needed for a sunset which proved to be unobtainable in the hardware stores of Seymour, our nearest country town. I insisted that it was absolutely necessary and, to my surprise, was given a staff car and a driver to take me seventy miles to Melbourne. It was a tremendous jolt to be in the city after two months' rustication at Puckapunyal and the very dull streets of Melbourne were suddenly glamorous and exciting. Even though I wore the drab, ill-fitting uniform of a private, office girls seemed to give me a little squeeze with their eyes. In an artists'-supply shop I found the pigment I was looking for, and to the surprise of the salesman ordered it in huge quantities, instructing him to invoice the army.

At the dress rehearsal of the concert I was a little disappointed to see how lacklustre this special paint finally looked under the lights, but the general effect of our décor was impressive, the show a hit, and my military training came to an agreeable end with a large programme credit and personal congratulations from Colonel Duffy himself.

Later that year, I read in the Melbourne *Age* that there had
been a military inquiry into certain excessive expenditures at
Puckapunyal Camp, and particularly the funding of a theatrical
event authorized by Colonel Duffy. One item was particularly
singled out: a quantity of red pigment made from the pulverized
wings of a rare Korean insect, costing over £700.

At the army camp I had taken up smoking, an addiction which
I only relinquished, with the greatest difficulty, ten years ago. I
did not indulge my nicotine habit at home for my mother
deplored it and, when quizzed, I always denied that I had been
smoking. At this she would regard me with an omniscient smile
and utter her favourite admonition: 'Don't bother to tell fibs to
your mother, Barry. *I can read you like a book.*' From a
woman who read very few books indeed, this was, paradoxically, reassuring. But it had not always been so.

As a child, I believed my mother absolutely when she warned
us that 'the wind might change' if we pulled faces, leaving our
countenances permanently fixed in hideous grimaces.

Once at the university I began attending lectures at the law
school. Here and there, amongst my fellow students, I noticed

with a premonitory shudder those who would later specialize in 'matrimonial law'; stirring up the acrimony and greed of their clients so that they might up-grade their cars or finance their wineries or their vacations at the Villa D'Este. There were girls too, lips now pursed in concentration which would remain forever pursed; for the wind changed early in the lives of these young professionals.

I recognized, also, a few fellows from Puckapunyal earnestly scribbling their notes. They were the ones who had always been keenest in their pursuit of rank and military prowess; the ones who had most loudly sneered whenever I dropped my rifle on the parade ground. Already at that early age they were priggishly, proudly unimaginative; preparing themselves for that day in the future when they would become Silks, with Mercedes Benzes and Saabs for their wives, and original daubs by Fred Williams, and macadamia farms and wineries and distinguished cellars of Australian reds, and big collections of that safest and dullest of all artistic commodities: Georgian silver. There was something about those conscientious young bores with Irish names furiously taking notes to my left and right that told me they would one day be running Australia.

In the evenings I had to present myself at Taylor's Coaching School in a narrow street of the city in order to catch up on my neglected German, but it was difficult to concentrate and I felt surrounded by dunces and dyslexics. My friends were launched on their University careers but I was lagging behind, forced to show up every day at incomprehensible legal lectures and later dreaming and dozing off in Frau Steinki's classes.

Now that it looked as though I had been successfully diverted from artistic pursuits, my mother thought it was safe to rekindle my interest in painting – on a purely recreational level. Both my parents were fond of saying, 'You've got a wonderful hobby there, Barry, and as long as you keep it like that you'll save yourself and your parents a lot of heartache.' They were pleased with my pictures too, or at least the nice ones that weren't unnecessarily 'futuristic'. There was a well-known private art school in a nearby suburb, run by George Bell, a failed Melbourne Post-Impressionist. Bell had taught a handful of quite famous artists and I began to attend his classes every Saturday morning.

Rather to my surprise, my mother insisted on paying the fees for my art classes, as she had paid for my driving lessons, with the caution, 'Not a word to your father about this.' I sometimes suspected she might even be my secret ally against the strictures of my father; someone with a great love of beauty who might have possessed artistic gifts herself which she had rigorously suppressed in order to be a respectable housewife and mother.

At the back of George Bell's suburban house was a studio, and there I would sit with my sketchbook in a semi-circle of chairs on which several real artists – judging by their beards and berets – drew and painted from a live model.

The studio smelt wonderfully of turpentine, and old George Bell, irascible and owl-like, strolled up and down behind us peering over our shoulders and occasionally making pencilled corrections to our work. The surprise to me, however, was the model; a naked girl. She sat there, right in front of me, next to the black studio stove, so that in winter one half of her blushed red whilst the other was pale blue and goose-pimpled. I found it very difficult to concentrate and manipulate my charcoal as I stared at this creature, and Bell's correcting pencil seemed to disagree with every voluptous contour I put on paper. Looking at some of the others' drawings, I noticed that I was the only one who seemed to have devoted much care and attention to the rendition of pubic hair, and it was fairly clear that my work was still well out of line with George Bell's austere anatomical precepts.

Sometimes we were set painting assignments, but when I propped my picture up with the others, Mr Bell never commented. Often I had the uncomfortable feeling that I wasn't there at all, though at other times I imagined that I detected a sympathetic glint in the model's eye as she rearranged herself, the soles of her feet black from the charcoal dust on the studio floor.

'What have you been doing today, Barry?' my mother would ask when I got home from art class. 'Nothing much. A bit of still life, as a matter of fact,' I would reply evasively. 'I'd like to see it,' said my mother. 'It's awful,' I said, 'anyway, I left it in the studio. If I do anything good, I'll let you see it.' Although I wasn't particularly enjoying Bell's grumpy tutelage, I knew that my parents would stop paying the fees if they knew what we were drawing every Saturday morning.

My attendances at the art school were, in any case, becoming more infrequent as I started experimenting again in creating 'Dada' objects and events.

Some of my old Dadaist cronies from school were now at the University and after lectures we mounted a series of impractical jokes, that is to say, jokes that had no rationale, or even satiric point, so they defied explanation.

These 'happenings' and examples of street theatre predate *Candid Camera* by many years. Sometimes, I'm afraid, they were deeply misanthropic. For example, we selected a small shopkeeper near the campus called Malouf. He was chosen entirely for the euphony and novelty of his name. He was a typical, modest, corner-of-the-street tradesman who sold a variety of merchandise, and once a day, at a specific time, one of us would enter his shop and buy a cake of Lux toilet soap. For this we would offer money that required change. When Mr Malouf put the change on the counter, we would take it and start to go, leaving the soap behind. The shopkeeper would say, 'Hey, you've forgotten your soap.' To which we would make the standard reply, 'I don't want the soap, *I just want to buy it!*' We would then leave and join our accomplices, convulsed with childish laughter. This simple but radical variation on a fundamental commercial principle was repeated countless times until Mr Malouf ceased, at last, to mention our failure to take the goods we had paid for.

Though by now he knew our faces very well, we occasionally conscripted a total stranger to go and buy the soap. Malouf's face would light up to see a new customer who was bound to accept the purchased item, but when he heard the same phrase, 'I don't want it, I just want to buy it,' Mr Malouf became crestfallen and confused. He had entered the world of nightmare.

By now the shopkeeper, with a sigh of resignation, had begun to put the same grubby package on the counter, and one day having paid for it, we actually took it. A minute later I ran back into the shop with a packet of soap. 'I'm sorry,' I said, 'I forgot to leave the soap.' Placing the shop-soiled item on the counter, I left and never returned.

As an epilogue, I should add that we had cut, to the correct proportions, a slice of cooking lard which we carefully wrapped so that it precisely counterfeited a cake of Lux toilet soap. It was this that we had substituted for the product which I had finally returned to Malouf, and, so we conjectured, it would be this that in the normal course of his business Mr Malouf would ultimately sell. The customer would have discovered under unpleasant circumstances, in bathtub or shower, the inadequacy of his purchase, and would have irately complained to Mr Malouf. He, in turn, relieved to have, at last, an explanation of the strange events in his shop, and assuming *a rational explanation*, would then have unwrapped every cake of soap on his shelves.

We were not surprised to learn soon after that Mr Malouf, severely depressed, had closed his business and moved to another district.

Another 'stunt' calculated to disturb and disorient a deeply conventional social group took place on a suburban train. My friend John Perry entered a non-smoking compartment one morning at a time, between commuters, when the compartment was customarily occupied by middle-aged, female shoppers. Perry's disguise was striking, and if the compartment was full

Homage to

Gene Autry

and Cézanne

Barry, Michael and
Christopher Humphries

Mrs Pengard in
Ambrose Applejohn's Adventure,
1949

Schoolboy surrealist

Rabbi   Ratbag   MP
John Levi, the author, Robert Maclellan, c. 1951

Marriage, 1956

Phillip's Street Revue,
l. to r. Max Oldaker,
the author, Gordon Chater

Sydney by night, 1956

Dr Humphries, 1958

*Forkscapes and
surgical gloves, 1958*

Student actor

The Bunyip

Mrs Everage at Home, 1959

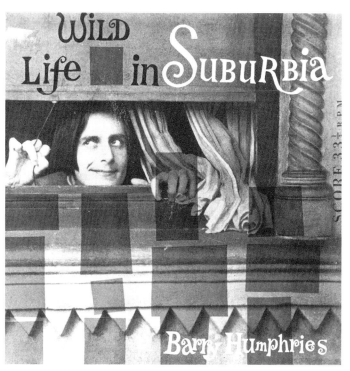

First albums

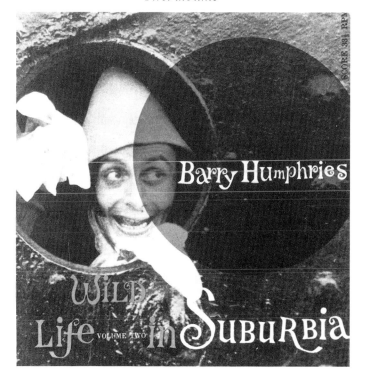

Venice, 1959

someone always sprang to their feet and offered him a seat. His leg was encased in a plaster cast and a neck brace supported his chin. He was, furthermore, apparently blind, wearing very dark glasses, and after travelling some distance in silence he fumblingly withdrew from his pocket a large rolled up sheet of Braille (which was actually part of an old pianola roll), and proceeded to run his fingers across its surface and quietly mutter to himself. The sympathy and awe that this spectacle engendered in his fellow travellers cannot be overstated and it was into this atmosphere that I stepped at the next station on the line.

My apparel was very different. My longish hair had been combed to make it appear even longer, and my fingers were heavily ringed. I wore garish clothes and although it was a non-smoking compartment I kindled a strong-smelling Turkish cigarette, at the same time producing a German newspaper which I read ostentatiously. Already I could sense the aversion of the whole compartment. From time to time I glared across at Perry, until the train pulled up at its next stop. I rose suddenly to my feet, snatched the Braille from his fingers, ripping it in half. I then delivered a kick to his leg, shattering the plaster, and, seizing the glasses from the sightless eyes, I smashed them to the floor of the train, at the same time shouting imprecations in German interspersed with words like 'blind pig'. The other travellers were always transfixed, immobilized with horror by this demonstration, and I always escaped easily. After my exit Perry travelled the rest of the journey and repeated the words 'forgive him, forgive him' until he could hobble off the train at an appointed station and be whisked away in a car.

Our theory was that events of sufficient strangeness and violence, such as this, would change the lives of those who witnessed them, and provide them, perhaps, with their most indelible, if mysterious, memories.

Disguising myself as a tramp and rummaging in garbage close to a bus queue was another enjoyable example of 'street theatre'. Previously, of course, we had planted a cooked chicken and a bottle of champagne in the bottom of the receptacle so that the large queue of staid travellers were at first repelled and alienated by a filthy scavenger and then astonished by the delicious trophies he fished out of the refuse. Wandering away swigging champagne and gnawing on a drumstick I always noticed that a few people detached themselves from the queue and peeked curiously into the bin searching for treasures for themselves. Wise men amongst them may have thought the chicken and champagne were indeed 'plants' but then they would be lead to the question 'why?' It was a question without an answer.

The firm of H. J. Heinz had an excellent product called Russian Salad. It consisted largely of diced potato in mayonnaise with a few peas and carrot chips. Surreptitiously spilt and splashed in large quantities on the pavement of a city block, it closely resembled human vomit. It was a simple and delightful recreation of mine to approach a recent deposit of salad in the guise, once again, of a tramp. Disgusted pedestrians were already giving it a very wide berth, holding their breaths and looking away with watering eyes. Not I, as I knelt beside one of the larger puddles, curdled and carrot-flecked. Drawing a spoon from my top pocket I devoured several mouthfuls, noticing out of the corner of my eye, and with some satisfaction, several people actually being sick at the spectacle. I have done this in many parts of the world and only in Fleet Street in the 1960s did I come close to being apprehended by a policeman. He, however, was too profoundly nauseated to take my name, and as he stood gagging on the salad-splattered pavement I made my escape.

Even more entertaining by far were the two Dada exhibitions held in the Women Graduates' Lounge in the old Union building, and our lunchtime revue, *Call Me Madman!* These are the highlights of my short University career.

The 'art' exhibitions occurred on consecutive years, but have merged in my memory. One of the most notorious exhibits consisted of a large tub filled with old books, one about Cézanne and another called *The Book of Beauty*. Over these volumes a large industrial-sized can of Heinz Russian Salad had been poured. By consulting their catalogues, curious art lovers could discover that this exhibit bore the title, 'I was reading these books when I felt sick'.

Perhaps it was as a revolt against the worthy, timidly modern academicism of George Bell that I developed the idea of making pictures and sculptures out of highly perishable materials, like cake and meat. There were a series of exhibits simply called 'cakescapes': framed, double sheets of glass, between which were compressed cream cakes, lamingtons, swiss roll and rainbow terrace. For a short time these looked rather pretty, even mysterious objects, until mould slowly and decoratively transformed them. An exhibit entitled 'Creche-bang' was merely a broken pram draped with raw meat, and on a pedestal hung with velvet lay a spoon containing the opaque eye of a sheep. This was called 'Eye and Spoon Race'. Most of the exhibits were deliberately infantile and calculated to test the shock threshold of undergraduates, which was surprisingly low.

My 'shoescapes', for some reason, irritated many people. They were framed panels of wood on which large numbers of old shoes, found on a rubbish dump, had been nailed. One of these leather 'reliefs' was called 'My Foetus Killing Me', but it was 'Pus in Boots' which caused the greatest stir: two old shoes brimming with custard. Throughout the exhibition a recording of 'I'm in Love With a Wonderful Guy' from the current musical comedy *South Pacific* was played on a small but strident gramophone. String had been attached to the pickup arm so that the needle repeatedly jumped, and the voice of Mary Martin could be heard singing the same phrase *ad nauseam*: 'I'm in love click I'm in love click I'm in love click . . .'

The apotheosis of the Melbourne Dada Group was a

1952 **FIRST PAN-AUSTRALASIAN**

DADA

EXHIBITION

ORIGINAL PAINTINGS by:—

picasso

cezanne

humphries

matisse

levi

laver-tree

perry

gawkgin

luigi-bop

van-goof

lunchtime revue inspired by a current Irving Berlin musical, *Call Me Madman!* The object of this 'entertainment' was to provoke the undergraduate audience into some kind of irrational demonstration, and it succeeded all too well. A small orchestra in the wings (the musicians were too frightened to expose themselves and their instruments in the orchestra pit) played an inane and repetitive tune throughout the performance. One of the most effective 'sketches' was 'The Piano Tuner'. The curtain rose revealing the back of an upright piano, which effectively concealed the player. The invisible pianist sounded the same chords and notes over and over again until the audience could stand it no longer and began stamping, jeering and throwing the vegetables with which I had liberally supplied it. At length the dissonance on stage ceased, and, after a long pause, the Piano Tuner came into view. He was blind, and as he fumbled his way towards the wings he smiled wanly and bowed crookedly to the audience over which, by then, had fallen the deathly silence of shame. Needless to say, once the actor had reached the safety of the proscenium arch he discarded his white stick and dark glasses but then revealed himself once more to the audience with a low bow. Having been duped into an expression of unjustified compassion, the audience went wild, and it took little more to goad it into storming the stage.

I hid in a cupboard in my dressing-room as angry students, many from the faculties of law and commerce, thundered past howling, 'Where's Humphries? *Get Humphries!*'

I began to absent myself from lectures, attaching myself more and more to extracurricular groups like the Film Society. I arranged special screenings of surrealist movies like *Un Chien Andalou* and *La Coquille et le Clergyman*. I also strayed into English literature lectures and special lunchtime events when, for example, the British poet Stephen Spender visited the University and addressed a lively student gathering where he was repeatedly heckled by a group of campus communists.

The Rape, c. *1951*

I had been chosen to take part in a play by Emlyn Williams called *The Wind of Heaven*. It was a mystical allegory about the second coming of Christ to a Welsh mining village, and I had the role of Evan Williams, an awe-struck peasant, who at the end of the play intones the Lord's Prayer in Gaelic. I had gone to a great deal of trouble to make this recitation as authentic as possible.

The production was chosen as Melbourne's entry in the Australian Universities Drama Festival that year in Adelaide, and I went off there in the train during the mid-year vacation with the rest of our troupe of student players. Amongst them was Graeme Hughes, a brilliant German student and gifted actor whom I had only recently met. Hughes was a troll-like figure whose most prized possession was a set of recordings of *Ariadne auf Naxos*. Older and more worldly than I, he highly recommended to me the merits of West End lager, the beer of South Australia. My parents were very abstemious and I had barely ever seen them drink alcohol; indeed, my mother used to condemn my father's parents for their open consumption of tawny port in front of children.

In Adelaide I was billeted with a nice suburban family, but to be away from home and beyond parental control for the first time in my life was a heady experience, and I was out every night at riotous student parties with Hughes, my mentor in the novelties of intoxication.

One evening, after the Adelaide Dramatic Society had given us Shelley's *The Cenci*, a production which did much to explain why this work is so rarely performed, we went to a party with a large bottle of the liqueur Parfait d'Amour, a viscid purple beverage scented with violets. The effects of this drink, quaffed by the tumbler, were disastrous, and I was volcanically sick in the middle of the Union lawn. The violet stain was still there several days later and inspired the song 'Mauve Chunder',[1] which Hughes and I sang with great success at parties. Thereafter we drank more conventional beverages, but I had discovered Mandrake's secret; a simple and accessible substance that made everything disappear.

---

1. **chunder** *n. or vb.* Australian (nautical) interj. Vomit. Like the golfers' warning 'fore!' the word derives from a popular expression on the early convict ships. It is an abbreviation of 'Watch under!' an ominous courtesy shouted from the upper decks for the protection of those below.

Shellac Smashing

ONE EVENING AT dinner my mother said to me rather abruptly, 'Look at your father, Barry.' I glanced up the table to where he sat tackling the large T-bone steak he had cooked himself. 'You're killing that man, Barry,' my mother said in a matter-of-fact voice, as though she were merely commenting on the weather or some other immutable circumstance. The family went on eating, though my sister looked as if she was going to cry. There was nothing more to be said. Who was I to disagree with my mother when I had the uncomfortable, guilty feeling that she might be right?

My undergraduate interlude did seem to be at an end and the future looked bleak. I had had fun during my two years at University but there were dark moments. Half-way through my year as a law student, Robert Nathan had died from a tumour. We used to go to see him in his private room at the Alfred Hospital and he was thinner and weaker on each visit. The last time I saw him he suddenly began to shout abusively at me, bitterly reproaching me for being well and alive.

Even my parents were moved by his death, though my father was horrified when, on the evening of Robert's funeral, a group of his friends and I went to see the Marx Brothers' *A Night at the Opera*. To us, however, it seemed the most appropriate way to mourn him.

When I finally scraped through German at the crammers and was able to abandon my irksome law course, I seemed also to have abandoned the last vestige of my ability to concentrate. I started to read Fine Arts, which I enjoyed, but I found myself drifting more and more into the amateur theatrical life of the campus. The Union Theatre was small but well equipped and I spent most of my time there. We were rehearsing, I think, a production of Hecht's *The Front Page* when a strange and cathartic event occurred. Standing at the stage door and looking across an expanse of lawn towards the medical school, I saw a vaguely familiar figure sitting studiously beneath a gum tree reading. I experienced a painful flashback to Grade One at Camberwell Grammar. It was John Bromley, the boy with the soft slug-like skin who delighted in giving me 'Chinese Burns' and 'Rabbit Choppers', the archetypal bully of my childhood.

How quiet and peaceful he seemed now, poring over his book in the feathery shadow of the foliage! Immediately I descended to that room beneath the stage used for storing scene-painting equipment. Looking quickly around, I saw a large sack of white paint powder and, seizing this, I lugged it upstairs and out the stage door. Bromley still sat there in deep shadow. He hadn't moved. Very quietly, with my heart pounding, I crept stealthily towards him until I was directly behind him, and then raised and tilted the heavy sack. A twig cracked sharply under my foot and Bromley looked around and up. By then the bag was evacuating a dense cascade of pigment over the seated student. Just when I thought the white torrent was petering out, it seemed to renew itself. When the bag was finally empty, I turned and cravenly bolted, only once glancing over my shoulder. Standing now, though seemingly rooted to the spot, stood a totally white figure under a tree. Back in my dressing-room, slightly puffed, I experienced the voluptuous satisfaction of vengeance. I remembered, with intense pleasure also, the victim's face as it turned towards me in that instant before the clown-white avalanche struck. It was *not* Bromley. Not, in fact, much like Bromley at all. But thereafter Bromley was forgiven. That blanched and bewildered figure on the Union lawn had unwittingly performed a noble act of expiation.

At the end of my University days I scarcely went to lectures and it became clear that my scholarship would cease. I was aware of a good deal of headshaking amongst my professors and mutterings about me being, what they suspected all along, a 'flash in the pan'. John Sumner, a young Englishman, had, amidst great scepticism, founded a professional fortnightly repertory company on the campus. Sumner had directed me in *The Front Page* and he now asked me if I would like to play a small part in *The Young Elizabeth* starring Alex Scott and Zoë Caldwell. I was not too busy to accept. The part was indeed small, a scheming courtier called Lord Thyrwhitt. Also in the cast was an Irish-Australian actor called Peter O'Shaughnessy who had just come back to Melbourne after working at the famous English repertory company at Leatherhead. He and his fiancée, Shirley, befriended me at a time when I really needed guidance and encouragement. At coffee breaks he would entertain the company with Kenneth Tynan stories and of all the cast he was the most experienced and urbane. I felt that money must have been rather short, because whenever he felt like a cigarette he would casually stroll some distance away from us, quietly withdraw a Turf cork-tipped from a packet of ten, light it and return to the group. O'Shaughnessy was deeply amused by stories of some of my Dada escapades which were still talked about around the theatre. He seemed to get the point of them and he was the first professional man of the theatre, apart from John Sumner, to suggest that there might just possibly be a future for me on the stage.

I rejected, however, all such warm words of encouragement, since I firmly believed, like my parents, that there was no livelihood to be made, or respectable career to be derived, from anything I was faintly good at. I also knew that my vocational *impasse* was causing my father perpetual anxiety, and I wanted to please him. But it was clear that he was disappointed. 'There's no doubt about you, Barry,' he often prognosticated, shaking his head, 'you're always going to learn the *hard* way.' It was a self-fulfilling prophecy.

When I came down to breakfast in the mornings he was always there in the kitchen, in a nimbus of toast smoke, scraping the black fur off carbonized crumpets, squeezing orange juice and juggling bacon and eggs. Still in his fawn plaid dressing-gown with shaving lather on his lobes, he would trudge up the stairs with my mother's breakfast. Moments later he would be fully dressed and down the stairs, two at a time, and off in his Buick to the office.

My father had taken his younger brother into partnership soon after the war and my mother was constantly expressing her doubts about my Uncle Dick's diligence and suitability. 'Never employ members of your own family,' she would say to us in my father's presence; 'it never works. They use you and want more and more, until in the end you're working for them.' At this my father usually sighed and held his tongue. After some years' experience in business, however, I now see that my mother's counsel, though intended as an oblique rebuke to my father, had some sound basis of sense, although it applies less to members of one's own family than to theatrical managers, lawyers and accountants.

My sister and young brothers were at school and I was at home and out of work. I had never thought of the future and never entertained the idea of a job. I always believed, absurdly and romantically, that 'something would happen'. John Levi, one of my best friends, was already in Cincinnati studying to become a rabbi. My other friends were working seriously at the University. All I did was sit at home like a droopy dilettante, leafing through the Sitwells and playing records of Bartók and Hindemith to myself. I had sent off to a special gramophone shop in London called Collector's Corner for some obscure recordings of Kurt Weill's *Threepenny Opera*, a then-forgotten work of the twenties, and when they arrived I would play them carefully with fibre needles. At that time, serious gramophone enthusiasts always followed a needle-sharpening ritual before playing their fragile 78s.

In desperation I decided to go to the Vocational Guidance Centre in the City, and there I spent a whole day answering elaborate questionnaires and being interrogated by a man who seemed like a defrocked Salvation Army Major. The whole family eagerly awaited the results of these tests, which finally arrived in our letterbox, mucilaginous from the vagrant attentions of the snails. The Vocational Guidance Centre had decided, after much deliberation – in those days before computers – that the job I was best suited to was that of a Vocational Guidance Counsellor. Even my father, eager as he was for me to find conventional employment, looked askance.

Then he had a brainwave. A friend of a friend of his at golf worked for EMI and they had a vacancy for a trainee executive in the wholesale record department. They were prepared to employ me for a small wage to 'teach me the ropes', he said. The idea was that I would ultimately become an 'executive', a word with which I was until then totally unfamiliar. This scheme was recommended to me as the perfect solution. It was business – *and it was music!* It was that noisy and inexplicable obsession of mine with the gramophone made respectable, bringing in a wage, and possessed of 'a future'. My father seemed to glow with pleasure and relief at the sudden simplicity of it all; as though this job had been staring us in the face for years and we had failed to recognize it for what it was: The Answer To The Problem of Barry.

Thus it was that I found myself on Willison Railway Station every morning at 7.45 with a folded copy of the *Melbourne Age* under my arm ready to step into a first-class smoking compartment and be borne to the terminus at Flinders Street Station. It was the same route that I had travelled three years before to school, but in a different uniform. Now I wore a new grey bird's-eye double-breasted suit specially made for me by Mr Warner, my father's tailor. My father had also ordered a single-breasted navy-blue worsted, an overcoat and a dark grey fedora to enhance my impersonation of a young businessman. The EMI warehouse was in Flinders Lane behind St Paul's Cathedral and a short walk from the station. Just inside its entrance there was a large time-clock, and at 8.25 I would remove the card bearing my name from its slot, punch the clock and report to the manager, Stan Deverell, for my day's assignment.

This is an idealized version of my morning routine. In fact, always late for breakfast, I would rush out of the house and down the steep hill of Lansell Crescent, lined with the houses my father had built, to the small station, only to see the train, *my train*, pulling out. Then, the interminable wait for the next train as the station began to fill up with a different kind of commuter, better dressed people who didn't need to get to work as early as me. With a knot in my stomach I would arrive in town at 8.30 and run, dodging along crowded pavements, all the way to EMI, with my heart thumping and the faint taste of blood in my mouth. After 8.30 the clock always printed my arrival time in red, and at the end of every week the black numerals on my card were few. No one ticked me off, strange to say, and the others just looked at me and exchanged winks and grins amongst themselves. It occurred to me that my father might well have been paying this company to employ me, and I later learnt that he had performed a number of 'favours' for the Managing Director.

In my first few weeks at EMI I had to wear a grey overall and push boxes of records around the warehouse at the back of the building. There didn't seem much point wearing a good suit into town in order to do such a dirty, sweaty job, and I reflected rather ruefully on the long and boring journey that lay ahead of me from the warehouse to the executive office suite.

I had, of course, met the Managing Director, Mr Dennis Hern, at my first interview. He was short, bald and bespectacled and I wondered at the time if this were the type of person my parents hoped I might come to resemble at the end of my long training period. Mr Hern's office was at the 'presentable' end of the building, just near the entrance and off the main carpeted showroom. Every time I arrived late, which was most mornings, I had to pass the open door of his outer office and Pat, his beautiful blonde secretary, always looked up from her typewriter and smiled.

In due course, having gained valuable experience pushing boxes, I was promoted to the wholesale record department, wandering amongst the aisles of steel shelving with a clipboard of orders, and pulling out the records. It was an historic time in the music industry, since the Long-Playing Record was being introduced, and old-fashioned shellac 78s were being phased out. Most of the small record stores in the City and suburbs of Melbourne were distrustful of the new 'microgrooves' and bought them in token quantities, one or two at a time. They saw them as a 'flash in the pan', a phrase with which I readily identified. Tom Goodridge, my immediate boss in the fledgling LP department, warned me that a lot of the Australian pressings were defective, and to be prepared for a few irate retailers returning warped or flawed copies of *Die Schöne Müllerin*, *The Student Prince*, and *Satchmo at Pasadena*. He explained that the official policy was to accept defective recordings and replace them with another copy. However, the returned disc was put straight back into stock and, to use a word that was unknown in those days, 'recycled'. Thus faulty recordings were constantly passing back and forth between the public, warehouse and distributor until the anonymous music-lovers grew tired of complaining. It was little wonder that the modest suburban retailers were so deeply suspicious of the new recording revolution.

When not searching the shelves for orders or taking a quick puff from a cigarette behind the storage racks, I would stand with Tom waiting for customers. Directly across the showroom from my counter was the door of Mr Hern's office, and there was Pat with jonquils glowing on her desk. I would try to catch her eye as she looked up from her typewriter.

One morning Mr Hern muttered something to Stan Deverell who spoke to Tom Goodridge who, like Hermes, led me to the lower regions; a small windowless room in the basement of the warehouse. There was an important job to be done, said Tom, and I was just the man to do it. 'Better get back into your overall, though, Baz,' he added with a wink. I stood in the room as a couple of storemen trundled in an enormous number of cartons filled with 78 records. They then dragged in a couple of tea-chests.

Mr Deverell entered with a hammer. 'Boy, oh boy, son,' said Stan, 'have you copped it sweet! I wouldn't mind a nice cushy job like this myself.' I didn't quite follow his drift. He plucked a shiny new record off the top of the pile and slipped it out of its paper sleeve. 'You see this, Baz? What is it?'

'It's a yellow label Decca.' I squinted more closely at the label. 'It's the Arnold Bax Nonet,' I added, rather wishing I could hear it.

'Wrong!' said Stan. 'It's *discontinued*!' Holding the record at arm's length over the tea-chest he struck it deftly with his hammer. The sharp black shards fell into the box. Stan warmed to his task and shattered a few sets of Sibelius symphonies as he explained: 'In the next few weeks you'll be seeing thousands more of these bloody deletions and this is all you have to do to them.' He brandished the hammer in front of my nose. 'We're moving into the future now, Old Son. It's the age of micro-grooves and the Powers That Be reckon we can't have too many of these old-fashioned buggers collecting dust and taking up valuable space. Are you with me?'

'But,' I protested, 'do they all have to be destroyed, can't you give them away to hospitals, to old people's homes . . .?' I refrained from recommending universities, suspecting that even Stan knew that recordings of classical music would be a most unwelcome donation there. 'Not on your life, Baz,' said Stan gravely, 'it's a question of copyright. They're deleted so we can't sell 'em and we can't give 'em away. All you have to do is break 'em up nicely so we can send the bits up to Sydney to be melted down.'

'But if they're not making 78s anymore, why melt them down?'

Stan Deverell looked at me with his head on one side and an expression of long-suffering patience. 'Listen, young fella, you can ask clever questions like that when you're an Executive, but until that far-off day you can do as you're flamin' told!' He looked around the small room which was now filled with teetering skyscrapers of deleted records. 'Sorry there's no windows in here, Baz, but someone will stick their head around the door later and let you know when it's knock-off time. And by the way, Baz,' he handed me back the hammer, 'don't go crazy; you only need to hit 'em once – about two inches *to the right of the hole.*'

After he had gone I sat down on a pile of deleted Diabelli Variations and picked a small record from the top of another box. It was a black label ten-inch Parlophone, and the title was *When the Lighthouse Shines Across the Bay*, featuring Conrad Veidt. There were five boxes of the same recording. I took it out of its sleeve, held it gingerly over the tea-chest and raised the hammer. Only then did I begin to wonder how exactly you located a spot two inches to the right of the hole on a round record.

My former life of freedom at the University already seemed remote and dreamlike as I sat in that small airless basement room all day for weeks on end pulverizing the combined repertoires of Columbia, Decca, Brunswick and His Master's Voice. The irony did not escape me; if there were a Dadaist's hell, this was it.

Sometimes my new life seemed so dismal that my only escape, however brief, lay in books. Perched in a patch of sunshine on the doorstep in Flinders Lane outside EMI, or on a bench in the Fitzroy Gardens, I ate my lunch and read the 'smart' fiction of the 1920s for which I had developed a voracious appetite. *The Madonna of the Sleeping Cars* by Maurice Dekobra, Harold Acton's *Humdrum*, *Peter Whiffle* by Carl

Van Vechten, and the novels of Michael Arlen and William Gerhardie. Immersed in their pages, I could almost forget that I lived in Melbourne in the feeble fifties.

In one of my lunch breaks Tom took pity on me and invited me down to the Cathedral Hotel on the corner of Flinders Lane for a counter lunch. I ordered a beer.

'Is that all you're having?' said Tom, handing me a State Express. 'I thought you'd be a Top-Shelf Man.' I must have looked puzzled.

'You know,' said Tom, indicating the bottles on a shelf of the mahogany back-fitting behind the bar, 'whisky, gin, drop o' rum.' I noticed with a shudder a dusty bottle of Parfait d'Amour, between the advocaat and the crème de menthe. I said I thought a rum might go down rather well after a record-breaking morning. After that I acquired a taste for over-proof Queensland Rum with beer chasers at lunchtime. They got me nicely numb and lightheaded to face the long, iconoclastic afternoon.

I was close to despair when relief came. Friends at the University had invited me back to appear in the annual Student Representatives' Council Revue, so after I clocked out of EMI at night my spirits would rise as I took the tram to Carlton to rehearse songs and sketches with the cast. My mother lent me her Austin A40 on rehearsal nights and these were often very late nights indeed, if there was a party somewhere, or if a few of us went on later to Val's Coffee Lounge. This was a wicked establishment at the top of a narrow staircase in Swanston Street. Here the walls were hung with black fishnet, the lights were dim and the toasted raisin bread more lubriciously buttered than at Gibby's or Raffles or Rumpelmeyers. Val, the proprietrix, was a pretty blonde of about thirty who dressed like a boy; an Australian *garçonne*. The waiters, as far as one could tell, were men, though they had a tendency to walk in time to the music which was quietly be-boppy.

My father had extended the back of our house to create a large flat for me. I supervised the decorations which, if preserved today and transported to a museum of decorative arts, would perfectly exemplify the avant-garde Melbourne taste of the period. Three sides of the room were pale blue and a fourth was a deep tan 'feature wall'. The curtains were yellow with a dark blue stripe. There were smoked-glass coffee-tables supported by spindly black suction legs, an Italian spun-aluminium anglepoise lamp, and a big yellow 'hammock' chair with a leopard-skin cushion. On the walls hung prints in natural-wood frames by Klee, Miro and Léger, and on the blondwood tablegram revolved microgrooves of music by George Shearing and Khachaturian. More than any other tune, Khachaturian's *Sabre Dance* seemed to dominate the early part of this decade. Whether played by Arthur Fiedler and the Boston Pops Orchestra or sung with silly words by the Norman Luboff Choir, its stabbing, sewing-machine rhythms could constantly be heard on the radio, and, with Auric's sweetly melancholy waltz from the *Moulin Rouge* played by Mantovani, will always evoke the fifties for me.

With such accommodation, it was impossible to explain to my parents, who had done more than their best to make my life exquisitely comfortable, that I would prefer to live in one ill-furnished room. I had made one unsuccessful dash for freedom. An artist's studio above a stable in the older quarter of East Melbourne had become vacant, and without discussion with my parents I rented it and moved in a few possessions. It was only a short walk through the Fitzroy Gardens to the record warehouse and I thought that propinquity might beget punctuality. Having secretly furnished my new 'bohemian' abode, the time came for me to announce my relocation to my parents. Naturally they found the idea wounding and incomprehensible, and I spent no more than two or three delicious nights alone in my studio before my father arrived in his new Mercedes, silently packed my case and drove me home. No subsequent reference was ever made to this truancy, but I learned later that other friends of mine had had similar problems escaping from the thraldom of their families. One man, who only felt able to leave home at the age of forty-five, after the death of his mother, is now convinced, with some justification, that she drugged his food, obliging him to return constantly to her steaming, heavily doped, addictive roasts.

I was still trudging off every morning to the record-smashing chamber, on my Executive Training Course, so my parents grimly indulged occasional forays into student theatre. As I had met my mother and father half-way in pursuit of a respectable career and abandoned my loft, they were now more lenient when I sometimes returned home very late indeed, smelling strongly of black Sobranie gold-tipped cigarettes, a ferocious fortified wine called Brandivino and, occasionally, the perfume of one of my more attractive female satellites from the show.

Unfortunately my flat did not have a private entrance and as I tiptoed past my parents' bedroom door, which was always ajar, a light would snap on, I would hear hoarse whispering from their room and my father's voice would croak, 'Is that you, Barry?' Then my mother's voice, more urgent and wakeful, would chime in, 'Do you know what time it is? Do you realize your father has been *worried sick*? I hope you know you have to be at work in three and half hours' time?' Most of these questions were rhetorical since there was nothing to be said, and my parents left no pauses in which to reply. I kept my lips tightly closed so as not to release further incriminating fumes of the night's excesses.

One morning, haggard and hung over from a particularly late rehearsal, I was running out the door already tardy for work when my father stopped me, and gravely led me to the Austin A40, crookedly parked in the driveway as I had left it in the early hours of the morning. He was ashen-faced and trembling slightly as he reached under the driver's seat and produced a small package of contraceptive accoutrements. My heart sank.

'What is this doing in your mother's car?' he said.

I heard a voice, which I recognized as my own, reply: 'I don't know. Perhaps you'd better ask her?' And I turned on my heel and ran for the train. It was one of the most courageous statements of my life yet paradoxically one of which I am least proud. My father made no further reference to this incident, out of embarrassment no doubt, and also perhaps out of a wish to make it un-happen.

Someone had recommended to me a product called Parafeminol, a gelatinous pessary which unfortunately left black and indelible stains on the upholstery of Austin cars. Until I became aware of this drawback I used to buy it from chemist shops in remote suburbs where I was sure nobody could possibly know me. None the less, in ordering this product over the counter, I was consumed with embarrassment, and invariably muttered its name so apologetically that the pharmacist almost always thought I had said 'paraffin'. I never had the courage to correct him, so that consequently, at this painful stage of my life, I acquired large holdings of paraffin oil in all known brands and bottles. They were very hard to hide, dispose of or, when discovered, explain.

The Birth of Edna

'TO BE A GOOD actor, Barry dear, you must have it here, and you must have it here ...' With an expression of Central European sapience, George Pravda pointed first to his head and then to his heart. Then, with a delicate gesture in the direction of his fly buttons, he added '... but most of all, you must have it here!' For a while he regarded me with a whimsical smile. 'You, I'm afraid dear fellow, have only got it ... *here.*' After this gnomic utterance, George tapped his high Slavic forehead quite loudly. It was my first experience of the backhanded compliment; my brains had been praised at the expense of my balls and any hopes I might have had of a theatrical career had been expertly dashed.

George Pravda, who resembled a shifty little concierge in a two-star Prague hotel, had come to Australia after the War and had, in a short time, carved an impressive niche for himself in the semi-professional theatrical life of Melbourne. Most actors I knew revered him as an emissary from the far-off World of Culture. Certainly in the early 1950s culture and foreigners were inseparable. At the Savoy Theatre in Russell Street, Melbourne's intelligentsia flocked to every screening of French, Italian and Scandinavian movies. Anything with a subtitle, however execrable, was received with awe-struck reverence and its merits earnestly debated afterwards over toasted raisin bread and Temple Bar cigarettes in the louche coffee lounges of the city.

One of the most successful continental films of this period was called *One Summer of Happiness*, a tedious Swedish idyll that reached the Melbourne screen only after severe excisions by the Censor, though it still retained a few titillating glimpses of nude silhouettes against a sparkling lake. Undoubtedly this film converted more citizens to a love of culture than the manager of the Savoy Theatre could have dreamt possible. *One Summer of Happiness* was to the Australian cinema of the early fifties what *Peter and the Wolf* was to music, and 'Sunflowers' to art.

The epithet which carried with it the very highest promise of artistic excellence was 'continental'. No more improving evening could be spent than in a continental restaurant eating a continental meal before a continental film followed by a continental supper in a continental coffee lounge preferably inhaling a continental cigarette. Black Balkan Sobranies were very popular with affected youths like myself, and black coffee was still a slightly exotic novelty in a society that either sipped tea or swilled beer. At symphony concerts in the Melbourne Town Hall, it was the visiting continental artistes who attracted the biggest crowds, although Australia's own Bernard Heinz (later Sir Bernard) was a popular conductor, probably because his name sounded foreign *and yet* reassuringly the same as the tomato sauce (Australia's alternative beverage).

In spite of the fact that a tiny percentage of Australians held all Foreigners in superstitious veneration as repositories of Old World Culture, the majority took huge delight in humiliating the new arrivals to our shores. 'Populate or perish' was the catch-phrase of the time, and Australians reluctantly accepted large numbers of 'Balts', not necessarily from the Baltic States. Then the word became a generic term for almost anyone from Overseas who did not speak English, and replaced the pejorative 'reffo'. I once even heard a Chinese restaurateur described as a 'bloody slant-eyed Balt'. For the privilege of dwelling in

Australia, the 'Balts' were obliged to spend their first years in the Land of Sunshine living in concentration camps and doing forced labour. Whatever their European qualifications may have been mattered little to the Australian authorities, and there were gleeful tales of brain surgeons obliged to work as night-soil contractors, and concert pianists conscripted as tram conductors. Thus, while a small minority hankered for the Old World, most of us sought to revenge ourselves against it. Soon, however, the coy euphemism 'New Australian' came into general use, as in: 'make Mine a Steak, that New Australian food gives me the shits!'

Almost a year before Mr Pravda had, with continental charm, given my budding career the thumbs down, I had toured the country towns of Victoria, absurdly miscast as Duke Orsino in a production of *Twelfth Night*. The offer of this role finally emancipated me from my enslavement at the record company. Looking back, I cannot imagine how I managed to tell my parents that I had decided not to be an EMI executive, but an actor instead. I think they still entertained some glimmer of hope that I would fail in the theatre and creep back into my old job, because they persuaded Mr Milligan to give me leave of absence. I never entered that building in Flinders Lane again, and for many years, until they recorded some of my early stage shows, I was unable to read the letters EMI with equanimity.

On the *Twelfth Night* tour we performed for the most part in one-night stands on an assortment of stages; town halls, cinemas and Mechanics Institutes, although in these last mysteriously named auditoriums we never stumbled upon a single mechanic.

I was still secretly unconvinced that I really wanted to be an actor, but touring with this jolly troupe of players was certainly better than smashing records. I envied Stanley Page, who took the part of Andrew Aguecheek, since that was certainly the role I could have played more convincingly than my hobbledehoy impersonation of the lovesick duke. I must be the only actor who ever got a laugh on the line, 'If music be the food of love, play on'. Well, it was not exactly a laugh, but a perceptible titter which rippled through the audience whenever I was on stage, and which was, somehow, worse than open hilarity. For some reason the costumes were vaguely Carolingian and I wore rather loose woollen tights beneath velvet breeches with a dropped crotch. I was convinced that my legs were to blame for the furtive merriment that greeted my every scene, so I kept dodging behind furniture and giving my sagging tights a surreptitious hoist. The barely suppressed laughter was more probably a response to my aura of absurdity in a serious role. What I did not realize at the time was that I was naturally, instinctively ridiculous, and would later be very grateful that this was so.

Then there were problems with the wig; an ill-fitting tangle of hennaed ringlets. The actress who played Viola was Zoë Caldwell who later became a star of Broadway and Stratford Ontario, and in all our scenes I could not help but notice how intensely she had to act in order not to burst out laughing. Her eyes blazed, her fingers clawed into my ruffled wrists and she enunciated her lines with such passion that I was almost blinded by saliva. If ever I saw her after the performance, I would invariably mutter the word 'sorry' as she flounced disdainfully past; as though she had been one of my sister's friends at dancing class whom I had almost trodden to death. If only I could have had a shot at Sir Andrew. I knew exactly how I should deliver that wonderful and pathetic line: 'I was adored once too.'

We travelled from town to town in a bus, amusing each other through the long hours of boredom with songs, jokes and little improvised performances by members of the company. Our play was directed by Ray Lawler, who also played Feste. Back at the hotel after the show, he would retire to his room and we would hear his typewriter tapping into the night. We later learnt that he had written a play with an unusual and highly unfashionable Australian setting called *Summer of the Seventeenth Doll*. Within two years this unlikely product of the *Twelfth Night* tour was playing to packed houses in the West End of London. My own creation took another twenty years to get there. I usually sat at the back of the bus improvising, in a flutey falsetto, a speech of gratitude by some fictitious female factotum. Wherever we went there was always a 'bun fight' after the performance provided by the Ladies Auxiliary or a more cultured member of the Country Women's Association. A forlorn affair usually, of trestle tables groaning with asparagus rolls, party pies and lamingtons on which the actors descended ravenously. Our hosts, who had all too recently learnt that great art is *meant* to be boring, stood sheepishly at the other end of the room in their bucolic finery and Sunday best, and there was an inevitable speech by one of the ladies thanking us for bringing culture to their township. Often one felt they were even more thankful when we left in our bus the next morning that we would be taking our art with us – and as far away as possible!

As the tour progressed, my improvised burlesque of these poignant votes-of-thanks grew more elaborate and absurd. Sometimes the *actual* remarks of a headmistress or mayoress at the after-show reception bore an uncanny resemblance to my most fanciful parody and I prattled away on the back seat of the bus, grateful that I could, at least, amuse and entertain by day the actors whom I dismayed by night. My nice, well-meaning lady who was so thrilled that culture had finally come to her town, and who was convinced that Shakespeare's Anne Hathaway was fundamentally just like any ordinary Australian housewife with a growing family of kiddies had, as yet, no name. It was only months later when we were preparing our end-of-season revue and Ray Lawler suggested that I revive the character that I decided to call her after my nanny, Edna.

Except for those jocose interludes in the bus, I cannot say I enjoyed the depressing cavalcade of country towns we visited. This was before the Age of the Motel which revolutionized rural accommodation in Australia. With its *en suite* bathroom, sanitized toilet seat, raw-brick feature wall and foam pillows artfully secreted behind a mustard vinyl lift-out headboard, the motel was still a thing of the near future. Our accommodations belonged to the pioneering past. Bedrooms were gloomy and sparsely furnished with a teetering wardrobe and often an old-fashioned washstand and chamber pot since the bathroom and lavatory were invariably a long walk down the coir-matted corridor. High on the nicotine-lacquered walls there was usually a sepia print in a cheap frame, representing some forlorn and coniferous glen in Scotland or Canada. The iron bedstead supported a sagging horsehair mattress, and the pillows, filled with a porridge of congealed kapok, were deeply impregnated with the beery exhalations of a thousand commercial travellers. In the morning, as your feet hit the cold sticky linoleum, you were greeted by the mingled effluvia of cigarette smoke and curried sausages – an Australian breakfast staple.

The dining-rooms of these establishments were always dominated by huge marble-topped mahogany credenzas loaded with cut-glass cruets, nickel-plated toast racks and domed Britannia-ware cloches. From the high anaglyptic ceiling, amongst the sparsely beaded electroliers, flypapers dangled in sticky convolutions. To the present generation of Australians, flypaper is as unknown and anachronistic as blotting paper or the gramophone needle, but in my youth no restaurant ceiling was without its viscid coil of brown paper palpitating a few feet above one's lunch with an iridescent harvest of trapped and vomiting blowflies.

No meal was ever placed on the table without an encouraging 'There you go' from waiter or waitress, who customarily left a gravy-brown thumb print in the mashed potatoes. I am sorry to say that 'There you go' – the Australian equivalent of *Bon appétit* or *Mahlzeit* – is now uncommon except in the remote provinces of Tasmania and New Zealand, although 'sumthin' t'drink, jellman?' is still current amongst *sommeliers* in those very few restaurants which remain in Australian hands.

Yet it was not the accommodation which made my *Twelfth Night* tour uncomfortable, but the conviction that I had been miscast, not merely as the romantic lead, but as an actor. One of the last towns we visited was Benalla where, as a child, I had been subjected to Great-Uncle Jack's orthodontic experiments. Sure enough, though greatly aged, he attended the performance in a black alpaca blazer, and sat in the middle of the front row watching the whole show through a large pair of racing binoculars, which he occasionally rested on the edge of the stage. The entire cast complained about him and I did not have the courage to admit that he was my relation until, to my embarrassment, he ostentatiously embraced me at the reception after the show. It was my only accolade.

Back in Melbourne, my first and last season in the repertory theatre began auspiciously, and my vocational doubts briefly evaporated when I had a small success as an eccentric cowboy in William Saroyan's *The Time of Your Life*. In Shaw's *You Never Can Tell*, my impersonation of William the waiter actually received critical acclaim, but after that the roles I was offered grew smaller and smaller. Learning my lines was a persistent difficulty and even as I was acting on stage before an audience I mentally turned the leaves of the script dreading that moment, a couple of pages on, where the text became suddenly illegible. Sometimes I could clear this terrible mnemonic thrombosis by letting my arms and legs turn to jelly and erupting in a copious sweat, but more often than not I had to stroll downstage left within earshot of the Prompter, whose voice was frequently more audible in the stalls than it was on the stage.

The nightmare became a reality during our production of Noël Coward's extremely dated three-hander, *Design for Living*. I had been studying my role at home, but in perfunctory fashion due to a distracting romantic entanglement, and even at the final dress rehearsal I was very far from word-perfect. Sure enough, on the first night, in my big scene in the second act, and like some chill, heart-stopping, self-fulfilling prophecy, the worst happened. As I mouthed Coward's brittle lines I mentally flicked through the pages of dialogue that lay ahead. The laughter from the audience grew more distant, the voices of the other two actors fainter as I hit that terrible blank in the script. I went on talking, acting, winning a few laughs, but the blank was getting closer, it was a page and a half away now, then a page, then two speeches. I tried going limp but could only feel my false moustache, undermined by perspiration, beginning to peel off. The blank moment was almost upon me, and once more I tried to visualize the text which lay in my bedside drawer in Camberwell. I was meant to be standing and doing something but instead I sank into a chair. I could see the other two actors staring at me now. Perhaps it was a moment they had dreaded even more than I. A silence fell, and I knew that was when I should have been saying something – *but what*? I could see the Prompter in his shadowy corner wildly gesticulating and uttering hoarse and quite inaudible noises, but I remained frozen in my chair like a man in a nightmare. At length my lips began to form words and I listened to them with a curious detachment.

'You'll find it in the drawer,' I croaked. *'It's in the drawer.'*

June Browne, my leading lady, looked at me goggle-eyed. How was she to know I meant the script, and that the drawer was locked and the key forever lost. But June was a resourceful young trouper and knew that given time I might accidentally stumble back into the real play. She crossed the stage, opened a drawer in the desk, looked into it and said in a brittle Coward manner, 'It's not in *this* drawer, Ernest. Are you sure you didn't leave it in some *other* drawer?' Noël's comedy began to assume a surrealistic character, and it was many unendurably long minutes before I finally regained an approximation of the text and careered towards the final curtain. The audience, aware that something rather unusual had happened but unable to identify precisely what, applauded politely, but as we bowed June quietly hissed, *'I'm never going to speak to you again.'* And she almost didn't, though I, strange to say, remained a sort of actor thereafter, and she married Helmut Newton, became a famous photographer and changed her name from June Browne to Alice Springs. True to her word, June never spoke to me again, but thirty-six years later Alice has.

After that, I became *persona nongratissima* in the company. The next offering was Steinbeck's *Of Mice and Men*, in which I played a walk-on, and in the penultimate production, which required the offstage noise of a barking dog, I did the barking. Then in the final show – the world première of *Summer of the Seventeenth Doll* – I had no role at all, human or canine. It was at this point, the nadir of my career, that Mr Pravda, the company's artistic advisor, whose estimation of himself as the incarnation of Stanislavsky was widely shared, proffered me his unsolicited advice, the three requirements of a good actor – cerebral, cardiac and genital.

I had not exactly been fired from the company yet but I received strong intimations that the Christmas show – a revue – would be my last production, perhaps even my last appearance as a professional actor. I knew my parents would be pleased to be proved right. I also knew that some of my friends who had been alarmed that I might be taking 'a nice hobby' seriously would be tickled pink to see me hounded from the theatre and back into the real world of careers and salaries and superannuation. The difficulty was that whenever I thought about a career, or what I might do with my life, my mind went completely blank. At home I had been brainwashed into believing that my few accomplishments were liabilities. The record company wouldn't have me back and I had stopped painting, even Dada was vieux jeu. Since I seemed to lack all the qualifications of my more ambitious acquaintances, I wondered if I would ever be given a passport to the adult world or would I end up as a perpetual undergraduate; the type who never really leaves the campus. I knew several grisly examples: former wits and wags and dilettantes now gone to seed. I had seen them, balding and corduroyed caricatures of their younger, more promising selves, rubbing along as part-time tutors or running the University bookshop or still dabbling in student revues. I could see myself being drawn into this grim fellowship of flops.

This may have been why I decided to get married, although it would be wrong to describe this impetuous and dramatic event as a decision since, at the time, I did not feel as though I had had much of a say in it. It was all rather sudden and unfair on both parties, but it did enable me to leave home.

This eventful year had started very badly with my twenty-first birthday. Most of the people I knew had elaborate coming-of-age parties with caterers, marquees in the garden and Dennis Farrington's ubiquitous orchestra, but I wanted none of that. I was still in my last weeks at EMI, sorry for myself and spending much of my time after work at the Swanston Family Hotel, a rendezvous for Melbourne's bohemia. My new mentors, Peter and Shirley O'Shaughnessy, had introduced me to this picturesque public house, which reeked of cigarette smoke, yeast, urine and some unidentifiable disinfectant, and it contained, it seemed to me, between the hours of five and six o'clock, the most interesting people in Australia. In those days pubs closed at six, and when the publican started yelling 'Time, Gentlemen, please! Drink up now, please, Gents!' there was a rush to the bar for last libations and bottles of beer to be consumed at home or in cars, on doorsteps and at improvised parties in nearby studios. This brief period after 5.45 was known as the 'six o'clock swill'.

Amongst the drinkers there were some older faces I knew; I spotted the historian, Brian Fitzpatrick, looking very much like W. C. Fields, sozzled and slobbering over a double Jubilee whisky. Often I bumped into John Eddy, the Financial Editor of the *Herald*, with whose daughter I had had a long and hopeless infatuation, or the painter Arthur Boyd, and his brother-in-law John Perceval. On Friday evenings a whole group of painters and potters would appear from the artists' colony at Eltham with their girlfriends, to join the 'Drift', as those relentless evenings of gatecrashing and party-hopping came to be called. The noise was deafening, but the atmosphere was heady and as I stood in that packed throng of artists' models, academics, alkies, radio actors, poofs and ratbags, drinking large quantities of agonizingly cold beer, I felt as though my True Personality was coming into focus.

On the afternoon of my birthday, my parents had arranged a small gathering of aunts, uncles, grandparents and a few respectable old family friends. They had had a special cake made, iced with birthday wishes, and they had prepared an elaborate supper. It was to be a surprise party for me when I came home from work that evening. Unfortunately, it was I who proved to be the surprise.

My mother had not driven her car for several years and although she never actually gave it to me, I could sometimes borrow it freely though at other times it was locked inaccessibly in the garage. On my birthday I had been allowed to take it to work, and it was in this vehicle that I wove homeward later that evening, having drunk some rum and champagne in an artist's studio after the Swanston Family had closed its doors. Half-way to Camberwell I had missed the brake at a set of traffic lights and collided with the back of a truck. The driver had jumped out but, observing no damage to his vehicle, had driven on. The entire radiator of my mother's car, however, was smashed in, and though it still drove, there was a strong smell of oil and burning rubber and a terrible groaning noise so that I had to drive the rest of the way home at a snail's pace. I can only just remember my arrival at the front door and the blank dismay on the faces of all my relations. My father ran out to inspect the smoking wreckage of the car as I was ignominiously bundled off to bed.

I woke much later the next day with a terrible feeling of guilt, shame and impending doom. Thereafter whenever I got drunk I always felt exactly the same, although strange to say it never discouraged me. I always believed it would be different next time; that I would somehow conquer the problem, and eliminate the side-effects. At any rate, nobody ever mentioned my twenty-first birthday again.

The announcement later that year of my intention to get married was a further blow to my already punch-drunk parents. The picture they were forming of their son was bad enough; but worse, what kind of a picture were *other people* beginning to form of *them*! Not only was I a university drop-out – though the word 'failure' was employed in those less equivocal days – but I was already, at the age of twenty-one, an unqualified, promiscuous, chain-smoking tosspot on intimate terms with Jews and Roman Catholics.

I had met my wife, Brenda, during a production by O'Shaughnessy of *Love's Labour's Lost*. She was an exquisite little dancer who captivated all the men in the company, and in spite of my parents' profound disquiet we were married within about six months.

My mother refused to come to the service but my father and brother Michael were present, looking rather as though they were attending a funeral. I rented a small flat in the old suburb of Hawthorn, moved in some of my books, pictures and records, and tasted freedom for the first time. Freedom, that is to say, if I ignored the presence of my wife.

Return Fare was the final production of the 1955 season: an intimate revue with an overture that was a crude plagiarism of *That's Entertainment*, and an amiable series of sketches and monologues, delivered by members of the company. Although I was no good at acting, it was generally felt that I had a contribution to make to the more frivolous theatre, so I was invited to write something for the show. Melbourne had been chosen as the site for the 1956 Olympic Games, but unfortunately there were not nearly enough hotels to accommodate the anticipated crowds. Half of Victorian Melbourne – including its grand hotels – had been torn down in the stampede to be modern.

At the time I was racking my brains in search of comic ideas, large advertisements were appearing in the newspapers inviting ordinary folk to billet visiting athletes. Ray Lawler suggested this might be a fruitful subject. 'Why,' he said, 'can't you write a sketch for that woman you used to do in the back of the bus? Edna, wasn't it? Wouldn't she be just the kind of person who would offer her spare bedroom to a Latvian pole-vaulter, provided, of course, that he was spotlessly clean and didn't hang his jockstrap on her rotary clothes-hoist in full view of the neighbours?'

Fired by this idea and encouraged by two of my fellow actors, Peter Batey and Noël Ferrier, I devised a two-handed sketch in which Edna (my average housewife) offered her home as an Olympic billet. I had hoped the role of Edna could have been played by Zoë or one of the other girls, but Lawler thought I should play the part myself like a pantomime dame, and so I did. The dialogue was full of glutinous descriptions of the amenities and appointments of Edna's Moonee Ponds villa, and there were very few conventional jokes. Occasionally Edna broke off to apostrophize her aged mother and her infant son Kenneth on the telephone.

The sketch had a galvanic effect on Melbourne audiences because it described their own homes and their own taste in something closely resembling their own dialect. When the Olympic Games official offered Mrs Edna Everage a cup of tea she beamed at him, and after a long pause exclaimed with a shrill note of ecstasy, 'Look, I'd love one!' The phatic and redundant 'look'[1] preceding a bald statement of fact or opinion had perhaps not previously been brought to the attention of an

---

1. New Zealanders prefer to say 'listen' before almost everything, though it is a completely unconscious locution or verbal tic, like that threadbare word 'basically' in current usage.

Australian audience, and they laughed with a mixture of surprise and empathy, as they did throughout the dialogue, at references to burgundy wall-to-wall carpets, lamington cakes and reindeers frosted on glass dining-room doors. It would be true to say that the audiences who filled that little theatre on the campus of Melbourne University every night positively swooned with pleasure at material which, however childish, required neither subtitles nor that elaborate process of translation and transposition that British and American dialogue always demanded.

I should explain to English readers that in this epoch, the cultural aspirations and vernacular of the Australian middle class rarely, if ever, found their way into 'art', so that Edna's simpering genteelisms and her post-war, house-proud rhapsodies had a kind of thrilling novelty that is hard to believe today.

For my first, and what I supposed to be my last, appearance as Mrs Everage I wore my own shirt under a rather large blue cardigan and a gaudy floral skirt. A clown-like effect was suggested by a pointed yellow felt hat which my mother had bought in a moment of folly, but never worn. Edna wore no glasses, and no makeup except for a line of carmine around the lips, and her legs were bare, hairy, and shod with flat black brogues.

My days in repertory theatre came to an end, but I was lucky. A telegram arrived from Sydney, that big wicked city to the north, which I had only glimpsed years before on a holiday with my parents, inviting me and my young wife to join the Phillip Street Theatre in a new revue. Air tickets would follow and we were to start rehearsals the next week.

My leave of absence from EMI was never mentioned again, and I had heard that the mild, bespectacled Managing Director, Mr Hern, that paragon of Executives, had left under a cloud. My father's brother, Dick, gave us a family post-wedding party and even my parents thawed a little. My mother, surprisingly, even apologized for not being well enough to attend.

But there was, none the less, an atmosphere of goodwill towards me, and relief, too, that I had a new well-paid job – a long way away.

Sinny

'I WOULDN'T TAKE Edna up to Sydney if I were you,' someone
said before I caught the plane, 'she's too Melbourne.
They've got a funny sense of humour up there.' I had not
thought of taking Edna anywhere. In fact, I had no intention of
ever getting into that silly frock again.

Brenda and I were met at the Kingsford Smith aerodrome by
Eric Duckworth, the business manager of the Phillip Street
Theatre and the partner of William Orr, the founder and
director. He drove us to our accommodation in the Rembrandt
Private Hotel, Kings Cross. We were in the heart of Sydney's
most notorious district: the Soho, the Pigalle of the city, and
certainly the liveliest, seediest, wickedest, most amusing and
most overrated place in all Australia.

Our room, which was a large bedsitter with a kitchenette,
was floored with khaki linoleum and we had barely put down
our suitcases and inspected the sagging fawn candlewick
bedspread when I saw something large, black and glossy dart
under the stove. It was my first glimpse of a cockroach, the first
of many. Having lived such a protected life all those years in
vermin-free Melbourne, I knew so little about cockroaches
that I experienced no revulsion whatsoever when I saw them,
and thereafter I saw them in their hundreds, scurrying industriously around our small apartment.

Just around the corner and only a few doors from the Rembrandt was the Hasty Tasty, a popular restaurant brilliantly lit with pink, blue and yellow neon tubes, and with miniature jukeboxes on every table. To attract visiting sailors and late revellers, it was open all night and the smell of fried onions from its kitchens seemed to be ducted directly into our bedroom window. On our first night in Sydney we had a hamburger there before catching the tram to the theatre in order to see the latest Phillip Street offering. The show had a few weeks to run, then ours would take over.

Phillip Street was a narrow thoroughfare which ran from St James's church, built in the 1830s by the convict architect, Francis Greenway, down the hill to Circular Quay. It still exists, that is to say there is a street bearing its name, but it is now a draughty chasm between blank, shark-grey office towers and it is impossible to believe that it was once, in the recent past, a street full of such history, charm and character or that the revues performed at its famous theatre were amongst the most fashionable and insouciant events in the Australian theatrical life of the period.

The little theatre which was to be my home for the next eighteen months was really the St James' Church Hall and it had a small stage and a tiny dress circle. For the past two years it had been packed every night with audiences enjoying that sophisticated novelty – intimate revue.

The management showed us to our seats and I saw, with surprise, that the star of the show was Max Oldaker, a musical-comedy figure of the thirties and forties who had been my mother's idol. She had taken me as a child to performances of The Gondoliers, The White Horse Inn, and The Desert Song, that famous production in which Max, disguised as the 'Red Shadow' and mounted on a white charger, had for six evenings and two matinées a week, enraptured the matrons of Melbourne and their wide-eyed offspring. When he sang, even the boxes of Ernest Hillier Chocolates in the stalls were momentarily stilled and the

Black Magic Assortments in the dress circle ceased their susurration.

That evening he appeared in a number of disguises but mostly in top hat, white tie and tails, singing sophisticated and ingenious ditties about champagne and caviare in which he was, from time to time, required to twirl a female partner. His most successful moments were a piquant song about his birthplace, 'I have got a mania to return to Tas-a-mania . . .' and the wildly applauded number 'I'm an Old Red Shadow of My Former Self', in which Max rather courageously mocked his most celebrated role. I noticed from my seat so close to the stage that he rouged his ears – a rejuvenating trick, I later learned, employed by many artistes of his generation.

In the interval, Bill Orr, the director, and Paul Riomfalvy, a charming stage-struck Hungarian and a director of the company, gave us some Australian champagne in their office and told us how the Phillip Street Theatre had helped revive Max's flagging career. 'The audience loves it when he sends himself up rotten,' Bill said. It was my first encounter with this curiously distasteful phrase, but I was to hear it many times over the next months, for it was for this especially that the small, hermetic theatrical world of Phillip Street was famous.

Ten years later, in the mid-sixties, the theatrical slang of the previous decade percolated into the middle-class vernacular, and even housewives were saying, 'Are you sending me up?' Just as America had, in Bernard Shaw's perception, moved from barbarism to decadence without an intervening period of civilization, Australian humour had somehow skipped the ironic and gone from folksy to camp.

The rest of the cast were very young and ebullient and we both felt excited at the thought that in a few weeks we would be on that same stage, 'sending up' similar things and possibly even ourselves. There had been a number of sketches and monologues which I recognized as revamped London revue sketches, and these had been given local colour by the introduction of product names, Sydney radio personalities and social 'identities'. In Sydney, as I later learned, there was a small group of persons who described themselves as 'socialites' and who were accepted by the press, and indeed the public, at their own estimation of themselves. They were always good for a laugh, though it turned out that most of them were on the board of the Phillip Street Theatre and luxuriated in the laughter and applause that the mere mention of their names nightly evoked.

The new revue was called *Mr and Mrs* and had a cast of four married couples, we being the youngest. Somehow the unequivocally heterosexual title of our show was at variance with those naughtier, more epicene tastes which Phillip Street had, in a short while, engendered in its suburban audiences. However the show did give me an opportunity to fly in the face of my Melbourne adviser and introduce Edna to a Sydney public.

The Olympic Games sketch was still very topical and it went down astonishingly well. The character of Edna was not, it seemed, a uniquely Melbourne phenomenon and in this strange, new, raffish city, I began to feel a little more at home. At the party on stage after the first night, suitably primed with Great Western champagne, I even performed one of the most expressionist of all our Dada sketches, 'Tid and the Psychiatrist', in which a cretin and his therapist slowly exchange personalities. In the absence of my old partner, John Perry, I played both roles myself and it was a party turn guaranteed to bring most social gatherings to a premature close. However in Sydney people seemed to sit through my tirades with an amused indulgence. I needed to draw attention to myself, for I was in a strange city, missing my Melbourne friends, scared of my marriage and worried that I might disappear forever.

Finally driven out of the Rembrandt by the roaches, particularly when it was discovered that their favourite refuge was the pop-up toaster, Brenda and I moved to a lodging house in a suburb called Centennial Park on the Bondi tramline. This was a street skirting the swampy, forlorn and, by Melbourne standards, sparsely arborated parkland, named in commemoration of Sydney's 1888 centenary. Its houses all faced across the road towards the elephantine Moreton Bay figs and coral trees of the park, and were formerly the unlovely mansions of book-makers, abortionists and speculative builders. Their style was indeterminate; an inflated yet debased variant of Arts and Crafts, where rusticated stone, stucco, 'tapestry brick', shingle and bottle-green half-timbering gauchely united.

The neighbourhood had been sadly declining since the Depression, so that when we arrived in Lang Road with our suitcases, these rambling villas were mostly subdivided into bed-sitting rooms. (In recent years they have been restored to private residences by people from Advertising and the Gown and Mantle business.)

In spite of the fact that we were working hard as revue artistes the journey 'home' on the tram, past the fumid and raucous taverns of Oxford Street towards the Centennial Park's gloomy portal, was dispiriting. Awaiting us was the small room with its treacly wainscot and curio ledge, a sagging pink chenille bed, and, in the morning, breakfast in the large shared kitchen where I caught glimpses of my fellow tenants; mostly aged and itinerant, and all lonely.

Sometimes I would go for long walks in the desolate park opposite. In those days it was not thronged with jogging bankers and their sun-wizened wives. On one of these walks I came across a cluster of young trees with a plaque stating that they had been planted in memory of somebody's son. The sight of this shivering little plantation in a bleak corner of the reserve increased my feelings of homesickness and alienation. Every day I walked past them I felt my rage and frustration grow, until early one morning I borrowed a small tomahawk from my landlord's toolshed and, skirting the empty park until I arrived at the memorial grove of trees, surreptitiously, angrily and to my eternal shame, I chopped one down.

My parents wrote to say they were off on a trip around the

world. There was a cheque for £500 enclosed. A great deal of money then, and, no doubt, a belated wedding present. Our boarding house had become intolerable and the last straw was the arrival of a couple called Cartwright, who looked very well-mannered and mild in the daytime but at night kept us all awake with bloodcurdling, drunken rows. We decided we could now afford to move to quieter premises and with a sense of relief we rented half of a large bungalow on the cliffs near Bondi Beach.

Mr and Mrs proved to be a short-lived attraction, but my contract was renewed for the subsequent revue called *Around the Loop*. Once more it starred Max Oldaker, a gifted young English comedian, Gordon Chater, and a large cast of pretty girls. Chater had come out to Australia in the touring company of *Seagulls over Sorrento*, liked it and stayed. Rather outrageous and given to scatological jokes, he achieved a great personal success in this revue, giving performances which, as I later realized, were an inspired combination of Max Adrian and Hermione Gingold. The best material had been carved up between Max and Gordon at rehearsal and I, who shared their small subterranean dressing-room, had to content myself with the leftovers.

From our first meeting Max Oldaker was friendly and generous. He put up with a great deal of macabre teasing from Chater and me. 'Isn't it funny, Max,' panted Gordon one night as he dashed down the rickety wooden stairs in a black suspender-belt to execute another lightning costume change, 'in a few years time, Barry will be thirty, I'll be forty and you'll be dead.' Max took such brutal sallies with an amused stoicism, seated at his cramped dressing-table rouging his lobes and patting his bald spot affectionately with a brown cosmetic.

I had written an old-fashioned recitation for Mrs Everage called 'Maroan', about a congenital Australian pronunciation difficulty, which I delivered in the same dowdy and rudimentary costume that I had worn as the Olympic hostess. I vowed it would be positively the last time I would ever impersonate this character.

MAROAN

You've read in all the magazines
About the Colour Question:
Should we be black, off-white, or beige?
May I make a suggestion:
Maroan's my favourite colour,
It's a lovely shade I think –
It's a real hard colour to describe,
Not purple – and not pink.

All our family loves it and
You ought to see our home,
From the bedroom to the laundry –
Every room's maroan!
When we bought our home in Moonee Ponds
It didn't have a phone,
But it had one thing to offer:
The toilet was maroan.

Look, I fell in love with it at once,
I felt the place was mine.
You see the day I married Norm
My bridesmaids were in wine.
Our wedding cake was iced to match
And glowed in splendour lonely,
And they drank our toast in burgundy
Which sparkled so maroanly.

The day my mother had her turn
We heard an awful groan,
I dropped young Ken, dashed to her room
And there she was – maroan.
And now she's in the twilight home,

We're going to England soon,
But one English custom gets my goat:
They call maroan, 'maroon'.

This, my only real moment in *Around the Loop*, was always politely received, but there was a feeling in the audience, none the less, that snobbish jokes about Australians getting it wrong were in poor taste. Years later the only person who ever seemed to remember this squib was the author Patrick White, who had just returned from Europe and was living in an outer suburb of Sydney.

In the evenings in our dressing-room, as we applied our makeup, I would sometimes improvise new characters for the amusement of Max and Gordon. There was someone called Basil Clissold, a youth who was so paralysed with inhibition that he could barely complete a sentence. Then there was Sandy Stone, an elderly and childless Australian who talked affectionately about his wife, Beryl, who was obviously a battle-axe. On one of my disconsolate walks, this time on Bondi Beach, I had met an old man whose voice was at odds with his rather sturdy appearance. It was high and scratchy with a sibilance caused by ill-fitting teeth. I had asked him the time and he had replied, 'Approximately in the vicinity of 5.30.' Sandy Stone's scratchy and pedantic utterances became quite successful in the dressing-room where my most memorable performances took place. My nostalgia for vermin-free Melbourne inspired a musical parody which Max Oldaker enjoyed singing before he went on stage. It began:

Deep in the Wheaties something stirred
Lo, twas a cockroach the size of a bird. . .

'How do you manage, Max,' I once asked him, 'to smile with such sincerity at the curtain call on a thin Wednesday matinée?'

'Dear Barry, it's an old trick Noël taught me and it never fails.'

He demonstrated, standing in the middle of the dressing-room in his Turkish towelling gown, eyes sparkling, teeth bared in a dazzling smile. 'Sillycunts,' beamed Max through clenched teeth, bowing to the imaginary stalls. 'Sillycunts,' again, to the circle, the gods and the Royal Box.

'It looks far more genuine than "cheese", dear boy,' said Max, 'and you've just got to hope that no one in the stalls can lip-read.' I couldn't help thinking of all my mother's friends at those Melbourne soirées, their palms moist and their hearts palpitating, as Max Oldaker, the Last of the Australian Matinée Idols, flashed them all his valedictory smile.

Yet, despite the convivial atmosphere at Phillip Street, I still felt like an exile in Sydney. I was stranded amongst people who could not even muster the glottal energy to pronounce the 'd' in the name of their own city. They looked so different from their Melbourne counterparts. They wore beach clothes in town, they were shorter and taller and flasher and poorer, and their faces told a story in which beer, cigarettes and strong sunlight played a dominant role. At the time, they seemed to me like parodies of people; like the Toby jugs on the curio ledge at the Wattle Tea Rooms. William Dobell, perhaps the greatest Australian artist, has painted the Sydney face a thousand times, and at the time he was vilified for being a mere caricaturist. At the Granville Returned Servicemen's Club, at 11.30 on Sunday morning, the faces looking up at me as I stood on the small stage were all Dobell creations.

One afternoon a week before, I had been in the back bar of the Criterion Hotel in Park Street where Jim Gussy and the ABC Dance Band used to drink. Someone introduced me to an agent called Ted James, a pushy little man in a shabby fawn suit worn over a maroon cardigan. He had that authentic aura of seedy vainglory which typifies all agents great and small. Ted was a small-time agent, but since I had never met an agent before I was impressed. A measure of his lowly standing amongst agents was that he, in turn, was impressed by me.

Several freezing 'schooners' later, and this little fox-terrier of a man was singing the praises of the Phillip Street Theatre, and all who performed therein. He had never, it emerged, seen a production there, but if I was one of the stars – here I feebly demurred – then he, Ted, would get me a club booking for a top fee, like *that!* He snapped a pair of Craven A-lacquered fingers.

I vaguely knew that the suburbs of Sydney were full of licensed establishments run by Football Clubs and Returned Servicemen's Leagues, and it was to one of the latter that Ted James directed me the following Sunday morning.

'But what exactly will I do, Ted?' I plaintively inquired after we had been drinking in that echoing lavatorial bar for about three hours. Ted ruptured the cellophane on another packet of Cravens, tapped one into his mouth and extended towards me the cork-tipped pan-pipes with his freckled marsupial paw.

'Yiz Act, Brian, jus do yiz Act!'

I wondered why so many people preferred to call me Brian. I later learned that getting people's names *almost* right was an Australian – and particularly a Sydney – courtesy. It was enough to call people something.

When Laurence Olivier, not then knighted, and his wife Vivien Leigh were touring Australia in 1948 the Lord Mayor of Sydney, at an official reception, introduced them as 'Sir Oliver and Lady Leigh'. When told the actors had been slightly miffed by this imaginative transposition of their names, the Mayor had merely shrugged affably and said, 'Shit, you can't win 'em all.'

'But I don't think I've got an act, Ted,' I ventured lamely.

''Course you've got an act, Bri,' said Ted, calling for more schooners. 'They wouldn't book you for the Phyllis Theatre if you didn't have a flamin' act! You'll kill 'em out at Granville next Sunny, and look out for Les Foxcroft, he's the other comic on the bill. He knows his stuff, and he'll show you the ropes if you get the wind up.'

*

164

The train trip to Granville took an eternity, the area was treeless and dismal and the Club, an insalubrious weatherboard structure, was thronged with men at eleven a.m., all drinking and noisily operating one-armed bandits at the rear of the hall. Backstage, Les Foxcroft introduced himself. He was a courteous man, and he offered to go on first and 'warm them up'.

'You'll find they're a hard nut to crack here in Granville,' he warned me. 'Do you work blue?' I had no idea what he meant. 'You'll find that they go for a bit of blue material out here.'

I looked down at my best navy-blue double-breasted suit made by my father's tailor, and I felt reassured. At least I had the blue material.

'How long is your act?'

'Oh,' I replied evasively, 'depends on the laughs!'

Les gave me an odd look, and went on stage. I could hear bursts of laughter during Les's act, but I couldn't concentrate. *What was my act?* Had I been drunk when I agreed to do this? Of course I had. Extremely drunk. As full as a Catholic School. In a minute it would be my turn to step on to that bleak platform, and at 11.55, when most people were still in church, I would be 'doing my act' in broad daylight in front of about one hundred and fifty rough, tough, well-oiled veterans. I thought of the 'top fee' – £5. I needed it. The back bar of the Criterion was an expensive habit. I decided I would go on and give them my old Dada party turn, 'Tid and the Psychiatrist'. It would be the first time that the expressionist theatre had ever come to Granville.

When Les left the stage to warm applause and a few stentorian 'Good on yiz!' he winked at me. On I went.

'We take you to a psychiatric clinic somewhere near the top of Collins Street. Dr Scott, brilliant graduate in Cretinology, is examining a new patient, called, for the moment, Tid. A rather big youth. The doctor is speaking . . .'

The Dobell faces looked up in silence. I had jammed a homburg hat over my lank hair, whitened my face and blackened

my eyes so that I resembled a personage in a Fritz Lang movie –
a resemblance that was probably lost on this audience.

'Well, Tid, my boy, what's the trouble old chap? By the way,
how old are you?'

Changing character to that of the imbecile, I took off the hat
and crossed the stage. Then, in a keening voice, 'Nearly sixty.'

A restlessness seemed to be spreading through the audience.
Quickly I became the doctor again. 'Well, Tid, I'm afraid I'm
going to have to take the dimensions of you.'

There was no doubt about it, my audience were beginning to
mutter amongst themselves.

'Your waist . . . one mile fat. Your height . . . six inches! Tid,
I'm afraid we're going to have to give you some special therapy
exercises for fear you'll grow up different from other boys.'

The members of the Granville Returned Servicemen's Club
were not merely talking amongst themselves now; they were
leaving their seats. They were actually turning their backs on
my performance – on my Act! I decided to talk louder, and
slower, in an attempt to regain their attention, but it was too
late. Soon all those backs, those cardigans and singlets and
little-boy shirts, were turned as they ambled to the rear of the
hall and resumed their assault on machines. One by one the
handles slammed down, the coins jangled, the talk and laughter
grew louder and the bar was back in business. It was as though
I wasn't there, and Dr Scott's final, eldritch scream as he
capitulates to cretindom was drowned in a cacophony of indifference.

Silently the club manager thrust a beer-soaked fiver into my
hand and, with a sour sideways nod, indicated the door.
Groaning inwardly, I wondered what he would tell Ted James
about my cabaret debut. Probably give him a real earful,
I imagined. Les Foxcroft travelled back with me in the train
and I sat in shame and silence as we rattled towards Wynyard
Station.

'Don't let them get you down, Brian,' Les condoled. 'There
are plenty of jobs better than this, son.' He offered me a

a nove calud Aid

bewildering—
exasperating—
insidious—
exciting—

*Tid, by Barry Humphries, from the title page of the exceedingly
rare first edition*

compensatory City Club, and a light. 'Being a comedian is a mug's game anyway.'

He was right. But what else could I do?

I was still uncertain of my artistic vocation; drawn to music and painting as well as to the theatre. Uncertain, too, of my choice between connubial life and creative solitude and between Australia and beckoning England. I vaguely knew I had to forge something original out of these contradictions and irresolutions.

The Assembly Hotel was Sydney's 'bohemian' pub. It was conveniently located one block from the theatre, and I took to calling in there every evening before the show. Very different from the Swanston Family Hotel in Melbourne, where amongst the boozers and hangers-on real artists could sometimes be found, the Assembly was patronized by actors from the radio studios next door. Here, propped up at the bar, and already the worse for too many gins and tonics, were the heroines of all the soap operas I had listened to as a child. Many of the old serials were still on air, and these permed and sozzled harridans who practically lived at the Assembly would, from time to time, fall off their stools and totter to the adjacent Macquarie Studios to impersonate yet another sexy ingenue, pert minx or warm-hearted wife and mother. Their male counterparts were equally unappetizing, with faces the colour of condemned veal. They possessed, none the less, voices that were famous throughout Australia, and on the wireless these burned-out old hacks became handsome doctors, benevolent family solicitors and likeable cads – whatever the script required. They took great pains to suppress their natural accents, since in the limbo of soap opera they were never asked to impersonate Australians. Hence they all adopted a fruity and adenoidal singsong which they supposed to be 'international', and can still sometimes be heard from older radio announcers. Today, Australian actors have gone to the opposite extreme. Convinced that they don't sound faintly Australian when speaking naturally, they assume a grotesque parodic accent unknown outside the Australian film industry. Consequently, the dialogue in most Australian movies is incomprehensible.

There were even a couple of child actors who drank copiously at the Assembly. That is to say, actors who *sounded* like children of both sexes on the air. One was a middle-aged catamite with a puffy, puckered face, like a balloon two weeks after the party, and the other, a stunted eunuch with a nicotine-stained forelip. Over this small troupe of men and women whose miraculously unravaged voices still thrilled the nation's housewives, hung a terrible Sword of Damocles – television. Few of them survived the new invention.

In the ladies' lounge, that is to say, in a cheerless tiled room off the saloon bar where rudimentary seating was provided, met another hermetic Order. It called itself 'The Push', a fraternity of middle-class desperates, journalists, drop-out academics, gamblers and poets *manqués*, and their doxies. These latter were mostly surburban girls; primary-school teachers and art students, who each night after working hours exchanged their irksome respectability for a little liberating profanity, drunkenness and sex. I belonged to neither group at the Assembly. The radio actors ignored me; I was too young and green for them. The Push shunned me as well because I was actually doing something vaguely and peripherally artistic. If they had any unifying credo which was endemically Australian, it was a snobbish philistinism and a distrust of success. In the Assembly, for the first time I heard a commercial artist bad-mouthing the painter Sidney Nolan, who was in the early flush of his European fame. ''Course he's pulling the wool over the Poms' eyes,' he was saying to a rapt and convinced circle. 'The only reason he's doing well is he's hired a big public-relations firm. Trust old Sid, the cunning bastard!' Few of those talentless tosspots who snarled their endorsement of this theory in 1957 had the faintest idea what public-relations firms were, though by the sixties they were probably working for one.

The radio actors also excoriated those of their number who

had 'got away'. Peter Finch, Coral Browne and Leo McKern had gone to London and quickly got 'too big for their boots'. They were called expatriates, a word I heard for the first time in the Assembly Hotel. Success was less threatening when it happened to a 'fuckin' ex-pat'.

'Finchie's back in town for a few days,' someone said. 'Jeez, that's nice of him,' said another. 'He won't be coming in here for a beer, that's for sure. Talking to his old mates would be a real come-down after all that hobnobbing with Larry and Viv.' But 'Finchie' did rashly look up his old mates. There was a party in his honour at our theatre after the show, and he arrived very drunk indeed, his face cancelled by a diagonal smear of vermilion lipstick. Someone, clearly, had been very pleased to see him.

The difficulty about a theatre job is that it interferes with party-going. By the time the curtain falls and you fly out the stage door and into a taxi, armed with a remote address, scrawled hours before on a sodden beer coaster, the party is either over or has moved elsewhere. Usually, however, the revellers have attained an alcoholic frequency you can never quite tune into. A concupiscent smile and a scribbled address from some girl in a bar at five p.m. can lead to many a wild-goose chase at 11.30 as you arrive, comparatively sober, at some reverberating bungalow in a distant suburb. Sometimes my poor wife would be woken in the early hours of the morning by a taxi-driver requesting her aid in waking me up or lugging me from the back seat of his cab to a convenient sofa, or the floor. Meanwhile Joe, the stage manager, was adopting the tiresome habit of confiscating flasks of St Agnes 'Hospital' Brandy discovered behind the mirror of my dressing-table.

I had taken to 'nibbling' between appearances on the stage. I was getting awful hangovers as well, until a barmaid recommended the Grappling Hook. 'Ever tried a Grappling Hook, luv?' It is equal parts Australian brandy and port wine and should be drunk very fast and as early in the morning as possible. If it stayed down, the hangover evaporated, and normal drinking could be resumed. To me, then, this seemed as pragmatic as it was civilized. Certainly it had to be imbibed in a hurry, because it was the most nauseating cocktail imaginable, and one to which the floor of the stomach rose in protest like a trampoline. The guilt of early-morning drinking was simply assuaged: I was not drinking alcohol at all – I was taking medicine. It was inevitable, of course, that with these health priorities, I saw less and less of my wife Brenda, and spent more and more time trawling for some obscure consolation in the bars and clubs of Sydney. Late one night at the Journalists' Club, a Scottish poet and drinking companion called Alan Ridell pointed out Kenneth Slessor. Slessor was Australia's greatest poet, whose work would fit quite snugly into any respectable anthology of later Georgian verse, between W.J. Turner and Wilfred Childe. He had written little in later years, when he toiled as a tame literary hack for Sir Frank Packer on the *Telegraph*. At the time I saw him, the great man was stooped over a snooker table, concentrating on a plant with a lot of right-hand screw. I introduced myself and mumbled something about my long-time admiration for his work. Slessor looked me up and down, took a long pull on his drink and said, 'Why don't you get your fucking hair cut?' I was always a reluctant lion-hunter after that.

Inevitably, at some noisy party, very late, I found myself locked in a bathroom with an exciting older woman. Not much older, however. After that there were the deceptions, assignations and all the dangerous stratagems of grown-up turpitude. The solvent and the catalyst was alcohol, my seductive new friend, which always kept its promise. I felt that I had successfully smuggled myself into the adult world on a forged pass.

Bunyip

O N MY RAMBLES around the secondhand bookshops of
Sydney, I had come across a copy of *More Pricks Than
Kicks* by Samuel Beckett, published in the year of my birth. It
contained a memorable phrase, 'No gardener has died, comma,
within rosaceous memory.' Poetry or hokum, one could never
be sure with this author. The volume, which I recently saw
listed in the catalogue of an American rare-book dealer at
$2,000, cost me 4s. 9d., a tidy sum, none the less, in those far-off
days. Searching for more works by the same author, I had also
read the novel *Watt*, so I was already a Beckett enthusiast,
when my early mentor, Peter O'Shaughnessy, wrote from
Melbourne to say he was planning to produce the first Australian performance of *Waiting for Godot*, and would I play
Estragon?

The long run of *Around the Loop* was drawing to a close, so
I accepted Peter's offer and hastened back to my hometown at
the first opportunity for rehearsals. Brenda and I were now
living apart, although I knew, with a heavy heart, that I would
have to return to Sydney and discuss our affairs, and mine in
particular. It was a desolate prospect. Fortunately my parents
were still abroad, quietly reconciling themselves to the idea of a
married son, who was meanwhile conspiring to unmarry himself. Their postcards kept arriving from Italy, France, Japan,

Canada and Switzerland, where my father had won a small prize in some tourist competition for his coloured slide of Lake Geneva.

This was a time when Australians were leaving for Europe by the boatload. Nice young physiotherapists, primary-school teachers and mothercraft nurses, all off on the Big Trip in order to make up their minds about some local beau to whom, after brief and catastrophic experiments with Italian ship's stewards and Austrian ski instructors, they would inevitably return and marry. The older couples, like my parents, usually had some Royal objective; a glimpse of the Queen perhaps, or several hundred Kodachromes of an English phenomenon known as 'pageantry'. They never returned to Australia without first purchasing several copies of the *My Fair Lady* album for culture-starved friends and relations. They also preferred to visit only what they commonly described as 'the clean countries', i.e., Holland, Switzerland, the Lake District and Scandinavia. And in handbags and hip pockets they carried, neatly folded, yards of toilet paper with which to upholster the lavatory seats of Europe.

While rehearsing for *Godot*, my friend Margaret and I shared a small flat in St Kilda with an obese British actor called Philip Stainton, who played Pozzo in the play. On his mantelpiece was an enormous glass jar containing a prescribed appetite-suppressant called Dexedrine. On the way to the theatre every night he helped himself to these by the handful and crunched them like Floral Cachous. Our eyes fell eagerly upon these innocent-looking tablets which, combined with beer, gin or fine wines, dispelled hangovers far more effectively than the traditional Grappling Hook, and Philip was only too happy to share his abundant supply of 'little yellow friends'. It may be that this generous self-medication has blurred some of my recollections of this period but, perhaps in spite of it, *Waiting for Godot* was a modest success. It was, however, almost too much for Melbourne audiences, who had only just acquired a taste for the last fashionable dramatist, Christopher Fry, and, had they but known it, were soon to be assailed by the turgid didactics of Brecht and his disciples. Yet after my fragmentary appearances in the Phillip Street Revues, it was wonderful to be on stage all night without a break. Gratifying, too, to hold those pauses, carefully indicated in the script, for as long as one dared. As I sat there in my filthy tramp's attire looking into my boot during one of these meaningful caesuras, I often wondered what I would say to Brenda when I saw her next.

Soon after the play closed, my wife and I formally separated. A Court of Law had ordered that I pay her what seemed to me then the extortionate sum of £4 a week in maintenance. I was therefore relieved to hear of more work on the horizon. O'Shaughnessy was planning a Christmas attraction; *Pygmalion*, starring him and his wife, and a new children's play called *The Bunyip and the Satellite*. It was proposed that I play Colonel Pickering and the 'Bunyip', for which Arthur Boyd had painted a ravishing backdrop. Since bunyips existed only in Aboriginal mythology, I felt free to create a prancing, bird-like clown, with a falsetto that inevitably got huskier after twelve performances a week in the stifling Christmas heat. With so much capering and singing before packed audiences of cachinnating kiddies, I was so exhausted when my time came to be Pickering that, during some of Professor Higgins' longer speeches, I literally fell asleep on stage. But I developed, with practice, a cunning method of leaning on the mantelpiece, chin in hand and half-turned upstage, so that my narcolepsy went largely unnoticed. I modelled my characterization of Pickering on the dean of Ormond College, Professor Newton-John, who had kindly lent us his house for rehearsals. His beautiful daughter Rona played Clara Eynsford-Hill and sometimes his wide-eyed youngest daughter, Olivia, would watch rehearsals.

The children's play, for which I had written several songs, was a hit and I must say I enjoyed the local celebrity the *Bunyip* brought me as I immersed myself enthusiastically in the wild bohemian life of Melbourne. Not far from the city was Eltham, a picturesque riverside hamlet, where, in adobe houses amongst the eucalypts, dwelt painters, potters and artistically minded and free-thinking academics and civil servants. On Friday and Saturday evenings, after the pubs had closed, the road to Eltham was thronged with a cavalcade of dusty vehicles, party bound.

Until the small hours the blaring gramophones filled the bush with the voices of Dylan Thomas, Lotte Lenya, Harry Belafonte and Bill Haley and his Comets; frightening the wallabies and traumatizing the kookaburras. Within the houses, the flagon claret flowed, as beard, sandals and sheepskin vest discussed Arthur Koestler, Jackson Pollock, Stan Frieberg, Saul Bellow and himself, with a long-haired, chain-smoking, breast-feeding, unmarried ceramicist. Improbably, a favourite author of the 1958 Melbourne intelligentsia was C. P. Snow, whose stupendously boring *oeuvre* was, I am now convinced, introduced to this circle as a joke. Beneath Brueghel prints depicting the bucolic revels of yesteryear, dancing to 'Island in the Sun' and 'The Alabama Song' from *Mahagony*, pissed architects made whispered arrangements with the barefooted wives of rustic abstractionists. Needless to say, I danced there in the midst of them all, feeling alive for the first time.

On the crest of a wave, O'Shaughnessy and I set about devising an intimate revue in Melbourne. He had strenuously opposed my efforts to drop Mrs Everage from my repertoire. Even in Sydney, Peter had urged me to develop this character with a monologue about the new Opera House and its lack of child-minding facilities and nice non-cultural amenities for those who disliked opera. The piece we wrote together was too overtly satirical for Phillip Street and was dropped after one trial performance. It was also thought to be too wildly improbable. In the following decade, however, all of Edna's prophecies came true. Sydney had something it could put on a stamp or a travel brochure and what happened inside it mattered little. The original plans for the Opera House were so drastically modified by the bureaucrats that the building can now only accommodate the most limited repertoire. When Benjamin

Britten visited Sydney soon after the building was completed, he unwisely remarked on the smallness of the pit. 'Pig's arse, it's small!' replied an indignant official. 'You could fit an entire orchestra of musicians in there.' 'Only,' said Britten drily, 'if they were all Japanese and playing piccolos.' More recently a senior member of the Opera Board was asked where their audiences came from. He might have been speaking for every opera house in the Western World when he replied, 'We'd be up Shit Creek if it wasn't for the Jews and the poofters.'

In the new revue Edna was encouraged to do what she had never done before; chat intimately to the audience. There in her twin set and pearls, frumpy blue floral skirt, hairy legs and flat shoes and with a rudimentary maquillage beneath her yellow felt hat, she expatiated on her favourite obsessions: her family, Royalty, culinary matters and interior decoration. For the first time, perhaps, audiences laughed at the mention of duck-egg-blue venetian blinds. An umber and more-ish yeast derivative called Vegemite that had anointed the toast and sandwiches of a generation of Australians here made its theatrical debut. Mrs Everage also reflected the fear and resentment that most Australians felt towards the new and, unfortunately, necessary arrivals to their shores; Italians, Greeks, Yugoslavians and 'Balts'.

Able to talk fluently on any subject whatsoever without drawing a breath, Edna became the living, glittering incarnation of Tristan Tzara's famous Dadaist dictum, 'Thought is born in the mouth.'

Shortly before our revue opened at the New Theatre in Flinders Street, I had made a 45 recording called *Wildlife in Suburbia* for a small Melbourne company. On one side was Mrs Everage's Olympic Hostess sketch, now updated as the Migrant Hostess, and on the other, Sandy Stone made his first appearance, enthusiastically describing a whole week in his vapid life. When Sandy 'had a bit of strife parking the vehicle' he was articulating a very new Australian problem, and one that has not gone away. My producer felt that this character would work on stage, and so, in a frayed checked dressing-gown and clutching a clammy hot-water bottle, I delivered my first Sandy monologue, with plenty of long, Beckett-like pauses during which the piano tinkled nostalgic and evocative airs such as 'When You Grow Too Old to Dream' and 'Little Man You've Had a Busy Day' and 'It's a Lovely Day Tomorrow'.

In the small cast of the revue was a former member of a New Zealand ballet company, Rosalind Tong, who looked exactly like Botticelli's 'Primavera'. I had met her at a New Year's party of nostalgic Kiwis, and soon after we began living together in a flat which I decorated with some of the pictures I had started to collect. A portrait by Tom Roberts, a Fragonard print and a small chalk drawing by Whistler of a French model who, in her old age, had come to live in Melbourne. My parents had returned from their trip, and, sadly, refused to acknowledge my new arrangements, believing that I had succumbed to the bad influence of older friends, which was roughly true. My father dolefully reiterated his favourite augury, 'There's no doubt about you, Barry, you'll learn *the hard way.*'

One of the most successful of the Eltham group was the painter Clifton Pugh. Dour and pipe-smoking, Pugh was a kind of outback academician who lived in a rambling mud-brick house on a large estate of native bush evocatively called Dunmoochin'. Rosalind and I often went up there to stay amongst the wallabies, bellbirds and the flies, and Cliff painted my portrait looking haunted, angular and aesthetic. My interest in art revived and I decided to have another 'exhibition'. Pugh offered to help and used his influence to secure the staid premises of the Victorian Artists Society. It was a large gallery to fill and I recruited a small team of helpers to realize some of the exhibits. One of my assistants was a beautiful undergraduate in a cobalt-blue shift and provocatively laddered black stockings; her name was Germaine Greer. A young sculptor called Clement Meadmore helped create a display of Platytox boxes, a new 'product' designed to eradicate the platypus, and most other beloved marsupials. There was small print on the box hinting that a liberal sprinkling of this toxin might also conveniently reduce the Aboriginal population. Needless to say, these boxes were filled with sawdust, but the effect of this display on the public was gratifyingly subversive, particularly on those who were embarrassed by the anthropological wildlife of Australia.

Pugh and I collaborated on some parodies of Aboriginal art, which was then just beginning to be taken seriously. On to the earth-coloured and patterned surfaces of these pictures we glued trashy modern objects like soup tins and photographs of the Royal Family. Back at our bed-sitting room, Rosalind helped me create some dangerous 'sharp reliefs', or pictures entirely constructed of broken glass or mirror. From some, the glass tusks and shards projected as far as three feet from the wall, like the Helictites which grow on the walls of caverns, and visitors to the gallery had to approach these works with extreme caution, and could be seen sidling warily past them. Unfortunately, in slicing up large sheets of glass there were inevitable depredations to a mushroom wall-to-wall.

Besides overtly satirical exhibits, I continued making pictures and sculptures out of rubbish, especially bent forks, which I discovered in large quantities in wasteland used for the dumping of hospital refuse. From this contorted cutlery 'forkscapes' were constructed, and although some of these possessed a certain lyricism, they deeply disturbed high-minded Melbourne art-lovers who had only just come to terms with the duller manifestations of Modern Art. Large numbers of people visited this show which, in the guise of 'Dr Humphries', I opened at twenty-minute intervals throughout the day.

Surprisingly, I also sold several exhibits, including a large 'shoescape' consisting of about thirty rotting and disintegrating boots, salvaged from the local tip and crudely nailed to a wooden panel. These had been sprayed white and upon this intricate 'texture' I had painted a conventional landscape. The whole picture was rather sportingly framed by my father who, it seemed, was slowly becoming resigned to the presence of

KEEP YOUR COUNTRY CLEAN!

A surviving Platytox box

insanity in the family. He regarded me at this time, I believe, more with pity than anger. To his surprise and mine, the 'shoescape' was sold to John Reed, a Melbourne lawyer and collector who was an early patron of Sidney Nolan, but unfortunately the work is now lost – or has shuffled back to the midden whence it came.

This exhibition, which was more like a theatrical event than an art show, attracted a great deal of publicity and I received many interesting offers. Channel Seven, one of Melbourne's first television stations, approached me to make a weekly appearance on a children's programme as the Bunyip. For the rather large sum of £9 a week I was to sit on a log on the studio floor and tell my juvenile audience a little story lasting for about fifteen minutes. Most television in those days was live, which lent a certain precarious intensity to these monologues. Every Monday morning I would have to dream up a new Bunyip story, often with Rosalind's help, and then arrive at the studio in plenty of time to apply the elaborate makeup, which included a long beak-like nose, modelled from nose-putty. My hair, always rather lank, had to be interwoven with leaves, another time-consuming procedure, and then, of course, I had to don the costume.

As the weeks passed, however, I began to devote less and less time to conscientious preparation. Sometimes it was even: 'Christ, I have to be in the studio in half an hour. What the hell will I tell the kids this week?'

One week I was especially late, and ill-prepared. My mind was a complete blank. *En route* to the studio I scanned the roadside for a suitable bush or peppercorn tree from which to pluck enough leaves to pin in my hair and, double-parking the old and slightly smoking Austin A40, which had been relinquished by my mother, I rushed into the dressing-room and furiously tweaked a lump of nose-putty into a vaguely recognizable beak, while someone pinned a few fronds and twigs to my scalp. By then, an anxious floor manager had appeared at the door, pointing imperatively at his watch, so that I had barely pulled up my tights and sat on my studio log when the red light on the camera announced that I was on the air. 'Hello, boys and girls!' I squeaked breathlessly. 'Have I got a funny story for you today . . .!' My brain whirred as a large clump of gum leaves detached itself from my hair and fell into my lap. The floor manager seemed to be gesturing at me, and pointing insistently at his nose. Improvising wildly, I allowed my fingers to stray casually to the place in the middle of my face where my beak ought to be. It was not there. I glanced down. It was on the studio floor. Applied far too hastily, it had refused to bond with my nose.

My Bunyip story that week got me into real hot water. Fables about leprosy in the Australian bush were not thought to be suitable or tasteful entertainment for children, even though, as an ex-Sunday-school pupil and teacher, I recalled that references to this malady cropped up rather often in the Bible. There were complaints, too, from parents about the Bunyip's free use of Australian slang, which large numbers of small, uncritical children were beginning to emulate. The following week a contrite Bunyip, with a restored proboscis, ritually washed out his mouth with soap and water, live on camera. But by then the damage was done. The producer had words to say; and, disgraced, I retired from children's television for ever.

I decided that the time had come at last to go to England, although I had not the faintest idea where I would find the boat fare. Peter, who was also contemplating a trip abroad, suggested we jointly give two farewell performances in Melbourne at the Assembly Hall.

My divorce had come through and, since Rosalind and I were seriously considering marriage, we flew to Auckland so that I could meet her parents and also perhaps write some new material for my valedictory concert. Alas, I had no sooner been introduced to my future parents-in-law than I was struck down with agonizing toothache, and I spent every day for the rest of my time in New Zealand in a dentist's chair having critical root-canal surgery on the very teeth which, many years before, had withstood Great-Uncle Jack's innovative experiments.

This orthodontal catastrophe cost me most of my savings and I realized that if the two farewell shows were not a complete sell-out we would have to remain in Melbourne for another year. The Australian Broadcasting Commission came to my rescue and invited me to do two half-hour television 'specials' of my own material. These were, again, live, so that no record of them survives, but they provided Mrs Everage with her television debut.

In one sketch, she exchanged beauty and fashion secrets with the famous Melbourne model, 'Bambi' Shmith, who is now, perhaps thanks to Edna's homespun advice, the Countess of Harewood.

I had had some experience of the world of fashion before this. A girlfriend of mine worked at the Greta Meirs School of Charm, which ran a special course for housewives. Twice a week, wearing my slightly threadbare EMI navy-blue suit, I conducted elocution classes for a group of eager young matrons and aspiring models bent on self-improvement. I cannot imagine what I could possibly have communicated to these comely and trusting souls. My own diction has always been slurred and scratchy, but I bought a book on voice production and spent most of the classes drawing diagrams of the throat and larynx on a blackboard and encouraging my young married pupils, some of whom I imagined to be of a libidinous inclination, to open their mouths as wide as possible and glossaly explore their soft and hard palates, whilst I peered between their lips and made knowledgeable noises. From time to time Greta Meirs herself would look in on one of my 'lessons' and listen sceptically for a few minutes as her ladies, dressed to the nines, with tight chignons and faces tangerine from their previous makeup class, performed their guttural and sibilant exercises. The money had been good, but the engagement, alas, was short-lived.

The Testimonial Performance, as our two-man show was

pretentiously called, attracted large crowds. Peter and I did several 'duets', including a very funny scene from Ionesco's *The Chairs*, but my Sandy Stone and Edna pieces appealed more strongly, it seemed, to the mood of the audience.

I also impersonated a park derelict in the uniform of army greatcoat and sandshoes which these 'deros' seemed always to wear. The performance was a lugubrious parody of Marty Robbins' popular air, 'In My White Sports Coat and a Pink Carnation', which I sang unaccompanied and *adagio misterioso*: 'In my white sandshoes and my army greatcoat I'm all dressed up for the park.'

At the end of the show, I'm afraid I may have rejoiced a little too overtly in the applause of the audience, for my colleague Peter rebuked me quite sharply for 'hogging the limelight', and his dressing-room door closed rather loudly. Although I have always had a reluctance to appear on stage which amounts almost to a phobia, I have found that once this has been conquered, the virtues of self-effacement and modesty quickly elude me.

Rosalind and I bought two third-class tickets on the Lloyd Triestino vessel *Toscana*, and in the beautiful garden of an artist friend we were married in the Melbourne suburb of Brighton. The ceremony was performed by the Reverend Douglas Tasker whom I had met in the saloon bar of the Swanston Family Hotel, and in gratitude for his services I presented him with a large and important Forkscape.

Our meagre savings were unexpectedly supplemented by the sum of £40; the proceeds from the sale of my Whistler drawing. About a year before, when I was very broke, a business-man friend told me that if I ever wanted to sell my picture he knew of a rich buyer. Morrie Bardas was an interesting character, who had established a thriving sportswear company since his arrival in Australia from Poland before the war. He had a great love for music and for books, especially the work of D. H. Lawrence, and an almost prurient fascination with

Melbourne's artists and writers. In his dapper suit and tie he was one of the many unlikely people who frequented the saloon bar of the Swanston Family Hotel. He told me that his wealthy acquaintance wished to borrow my pastel and would almost certainly give a good price for it after having lived with it for a couple of weeks. As a schoolboy I had paid the huge sum of £14 for this drawing over a period of many weeks so I plucked up the courage to ask £40 for it now. Morrie raised his eyebrows a little sadly, but took the picture. For the next year I kept asking him when his friend was going to cough up, at which he looked most uncomfortable and apologetic and explained that the buyer had gone 'overseas', but would *definitely* pay up when she returned to Melbourne.

When I got the cheque for my farewell show, I suddenly realized I wanted my Whistler back. What was forty quid? I asked myself. Morrie looked very ill-at-ease when I announced my decision. The lady, he said, had taken the drawing to London, had it verified at Christie's, and agreed to pay the money. He pressed the miserable sum into my hand, which, after twelve months, had not accumulated interest. Where is my picture now, I wonder. No doubt over-framed, under sticky non-reflective glass, with a gilded picture-light glaring above it, on the rag-rubbed wall of some hideous Melbourne mansion. I told this sad tale, with suitable embellishments, at a Sydney dinner party some years ago, and one young woman took a keener interest than the rest in my story. 'I know the picture well,' she said, 'but I never knew how my mother came by it.'

All our friends came to see us off at Port Melbourne, including my father, who, as a belated wedding present, had bought Rosalind and me two new suitcases. A photographer friend persuaded me to put on Edna's hat and look through the porthole waving a hanky. It was my next record sleeve.

Raspberry Ripple

I ALWAYS LONGED to live in a city where you couldn't drink the water. Here at last it was; a far cry from Melbourne, so prim and proper and *potable*. I had been woken soon after midnight by the sounds of running footsteps and excited cries outside my porthole, and I had rushed up on deck in time to see the amethyst lights of Venice, and the Doges' Palace, pink and nacreous, sliding past, as the *Toscana* nudged its way into the Canal San Marco. It was my first glimpse of Europe and of a city that actually smelt of something. In Venice, and in Vicenza, I hunted out everything I could find by the Tiepolos, father and son. In an old church on the Giudecca, late one afternoon, I peered up at a fresco on the ceiling which seemed to be in an appalling state. One could almost see the particles of paint detaching themselves from the surface of the picture and joining the other bright motes in the gold slanting sunshine. I felt that if I stood there long enough, arm outstretched, I might, a year hence, discover a cherub's rosy kneecap in my open palm. We spent the next few weeks there, then travelled through northern Italy, living cheaply, visiting museums and climbing every campanile in sight. In Rome we dossed down in the studio of my artist friend, Lawrence Daws, and met the old and ailing Martin Boyd, Australia's greatest novelist, whose nephew, Arthur, I knew. By then we were almost out of money, so that by the time we reached London, after an endless journey in third-class railway carriages, I had only 4d. left in the world.

The 1st of June 1959 was a hot day in Mayfair when I presented myself at the ormolu reception desk of the English Speaking Union in Charles Street. I had joined this highly respectable club in Melbourne years before, since they regularly held dances and 'socials' attended by very pretty girls, and I hoped that reciprocity with the London Branch might help me secure comfortable accommodation in the West End. However the lady behind the desk regarded me with not a little distaste. My hair was lank, and after nearly two months' rough travel through Europe in the same clothes, I must have presented a striking contrast to the neatly groomed middle-aged Americans and decorous English ladies who frequented the club. I was told firstly that they had *no accommodation*, not even for students, and a commissionaire escorted me, rather roughly, back into Berkeley Square. I looked at my 4d. It was enough for a phone call to my sister, Barbara, who was already living in Paddington. She lent me £20 and my European career began.

In Elgin Crescent, Ladbroke Grove, a Polish couple let us a tiny bed-sitting room in their attic for £4 10s. a week. Although the street was quite respectable, we were not far from the scene of the recent race riots, and only a few streets away from Rillington Place, where Christie had murdered and im-mured his pathetic victims. Notting Hill still had about it an agreeably seedy pre-war atmosphere, so well described in the novels of Patrick Hamilton. In winter the yellow smog, smelling slightly of brimstone, curled around the houses, and the air in the pubs was thick with Old Holborn tobacco smoke. The Portobello Market was only two blocks away and, in those days, surprising treasures could be had there. I remember one stall groaning with the unfashionable and unsaleable cameo glass vases of Émile Gallé, one of which I purchased for a pound.

I had been given the names and addresses of a few people who might help me; one was Charles Osborne, a fellow Australian who was the co-editor of the *London Magazine*. Another was Peter Myers who, with his partner Ronnie Cass, had written a celebrated revue called *For Amusement Only*. Myers and Cass had visited me backstage in Melbourne and urged me to look them up if I ever came to England. At his house in Bishop's Bridge Road, Myers gave us a very good lunch. Another person I had an introduction to was Eric Maschwitz, who was head of light entertainment at the BBC. He was a famous song-writer who had written the lyrics of 'These Foolish Things' and 'A Nightingale Sang in Berkeley Square'. He was very kind and helpful and told me to let him know when I was doing something.

My sister's £20 was running out fast and I decided to take a night job, so that I could attend some of the auditions advertised in *The Stage*. Lawrence Daws and his girlfriend, Heather, had come to live in a basement flat nearby. Lawrence needed a night job as well, and together we found one at Wall's Ice-cream Factory, Acton, a very depressing neighbourhood which could be reached by bus from Holland Park Avenue. Every night at about 6.30, Laurie and I would meet in the pub at the corner of Addison Road, have a pint of bitter and a Weights cigarette, and then catch the Acton bus for the night shift in the Raspberry Ripple section of the ice-cream factory. The clamorous interior, with its steel gantries, galleries and cat's-cradle of intersecting conveyer belts, was like something from the imagination of Piranesi.

There were no nitpicking hygiene regulations then; no inspections of fingernails or latex gloves. My task was to stand at a conveyer belt all night long, watching the swiftly flowing procession of Raspberry Ripple packets and ensuring their smooth passage. If there was a blockage, chaos very quickly ensued and before I could fumblingly wrench a squashed packet off the belt, or staunch the sticky leakage, a siren would sound, lights flash, and the entire plant grind to a throbbing halt. A foreman would then rush to my side and, after cursing me, he would restore order and set the machinery in motion once again.

Something seemed to go wrong in my part of the factory every night. At about 3.30 in the morning I had only to doze for a second on my feet or think about something else and the works would become instantly constipated. There would be a horrible pile-up and a massive loss of Raspberry Ripple from the ruptured cartons.

Finally I was relieved of this exacting work and placed in a bare room, not unlike the room in which, only three years before, I had broken gramophone records. It was, I soon apprehended, a sort of kindergarten for the terminally incompetent. This chamber contained a large galvanized-iron drum, surrounded by a circle of chairs on which sat a group of overalled and impassive West Indians. Every few seconds tins full of deformed ice-cream packets were thumped down beside us and these we had to unwrap, flicking the glutinous contents into the central receptacle. In Dante's description of the Torments of Hell, there is, to my knowledge, no scene depicting an ice-cream factory, though there should be. Glancing at my co-workers, I saw no real evidence of boredom, though by about five a.m. the fistfuls of Raspberry Ripple sometimes fell short of their destination or occasionally overshot it, leading to a playful exchange of creamy missiles (amongst my dark-skinned colleagues). The smell was all-pervasive and even after the hottest, deepest bath and the most lavish application of cologne I was convinced, as I performed my audition pieces by day, that my tenacious nocturnal aroma could be detected in the stalls. Bleary-eyed and somnambulistic after the sleepless torments of the night, I recited my monologues and sang my songs, imagining those anonymous producers in the darkened auditorium finding themselves inexplicably hankering for a Wall's Raspberry Ripple. I had become a subliminal human advertisement for ice-cream.

But I did get a job in the end. It was a brief appearance on a Rediffusion television talk-show hosted by Godfrey Winn, The

Novelist *Manqué*. One of my letters of introduction was from an Englishman who had worked in Melbourne for the Australian Broadcasting Commission. He was a fan of my new character, Sandy Stone, the boring old man with the hot-water bottle, and he had warmly recommended me to Winn who put me on the show, which was live, without ever having seen the act. My spot was preceded by a long and obsequious interview with the former Governor of Cyprus, and then I was perfunctorily introduced as a hilarious Australian comedian.

The camera found me seated in a chair with my dressing-gown and clutching my hottie, and I launched into an abridged version of one of Sandy's grindingly banal monologues about Melbourne suburban life. There was no studio audience but over on the interview set I could see Winn twitching and blinking in my direction, shrugging apologetically towards the Governor of Cyprus and running a fastidious finger around his cutaway collar. I had barely got into my stride before a floor manager started giving me a vigorous wind-up signal, and my first appearance in Britain petered out apologetically.

No one approached me at the end of the show, least of all Godfrey Winn, and I skulked out of the studio just in time to catch the tube and the bus to my night shift in Acton. In the *Evening News* that day there was a small paragraph about me on the entertainments page; the headline read,

A STAR HERE?

The piece had been written by Julian Holland, an English journalist who had been in Australia to cover the Test Match, and who had stumbled upon one of my performances. With not a little courage, he had given my debut on the telly a generous plug. I could not help feeling that I had let my champion down badly, and as the interminable night wore on I angrily shied dollops of ice-cream at an imaginary effigy of Godfrey Winn.

In Oxford Street in those days there were, for some reason, a number of near-tramps who sold plastic raincoats to tourists.

For such a character I had written a macabre little song with a sexually perverse undertone. Somehow I had contrived to rhyme 'plastic rainwear' with 'Mr Norris changes train-wear' – a reference to the fetishist personage in Isherwood's Berlin novella. It was a song that sounded sophisticated if you did not listen too carefully – which is probably true of most sophist-icated songs.

I was called back to one of my auditions twice to sing this decadent ditty and it got me a job. Colin Graham and his friend Disley Jones were planning a musical version of Sweeney Todd, the Demon Barber of Fleet Street, at the Lyric Theatre, Hammersmith with music by Anthony Bowles. They offered me the part of Jonas Fogg, a madhouse-keeper, with two very good songs to sing. With Jones' brilliant Pollock's Toy Theatre sets and Graham's witty direction as well as Tony's ingenious tunes we looked all set for a big hit. But the critics were lukewarm and to our dismay this elaborate little operetta which had taken so long to rehearse closed a few days before Christmas 1959.

The stage door was right beside a small market, and after the last matinée the street traders were so sorry for us they sold us our Christmas geese and turkeys at outrageous discounts. I did, however, have a few memorable weeks in a beautiful theatre which has since, inexplicably, been torn down, reconstituted and embedded in a concrete office tower. The old Lyric had a curious and convenient feature. Opposite the prompt corner in the proscenium arch was a small door and a spiral staircase. This led to a tiny cubicle or 'snug' attached to the dress-circle bar but hidden from the theatre patrons by a screen of frosted and engraved glass. Here the artistes, and especially I, could enjoy a quick drink between appearances on stage. It was a quaint amenity which may have depended too trustingly on the temperance of actors, and I have never encountered it elsewhere.

So, when the sixties dawned, I was out of work again. We had moved from our attic to a basement; this time a few doors from Notting Hill Gate's underground station and the rumble of the Central line was periodically audible in the cheerless flat, which we heated to a stifling temperature with an Aladdin paraffin stove. I resumed auditions and Rosalind, between ballet classes, got a part-time job in the local fruit shop. We also took in a lodger, a boy from the Royal Ballet, who lived in the dark back bedroom with a view of the light well. This fuliginous cavity resounded with clattering noises from the kitchens of an adjacent Lyons Corner House. It seems to me now outrageous that we should have charged rent for this dismal accommodation, but we did.

Occasionally we held dinner parties at which I provided Algerian red wine from Del Monico's in Soho costing 4s. 9d. a bottle. Special guests like the painter Sidney Nolan, the dancer Lynn Seymour and John Dexter, a young theatre director, were all offered this noxious beverage which could not be sipped without a violent shudder. In the end I took to mulling it with lemon, cloves and brown sugar, spiked with cheap brandy, and people rather liked it, especially those who did not mind having black teeth for several days afterwards.

Black was the colour of the early sixties, and everybody under thirty seemed to wear a black duffle-coat. The Campaign for Nuclear Disarmament was a popular cause and with friends from Oxford, I joined that long, black and rather inspiring procession which shuffled to Trafalgar Square from Aldermaston. I had found a theatrical agent in Regent Street called Myrette Morven, who had once understudied Cecily Courtneidge, and I had my photograph taken for the Spotlight Casting Directory by a famous theatrical photographer called Angus McBean, who looked as though *he* were understudying the role of Augustus John, with his Burlington House beard and carpet slippers. The photographs made me look rather soppy and unemployable.

The first stage show I ever saw in London was at the Metropolitan Music Hall where the Westway now hideously passes over the Edgware Road. To stand with a pint of

Guinness at the back of the circle and watch the show was exactly like being in a painting by Sickert. There was a wonderful bill of old-time players that night including Hetty King, the male impersonator, G. H. Elliot, 'The Chocolate-Coloured Coon', who sang his famous song 'Lily of Laguna', and Randolph Sutton who brought the house down when he sang, with tremendous poetic feeling, 'On Mother Kelly's Doorstep'. I felt that this night in the theatre alone had made that 13,000-mile journey to London worthwhile. Soon after this performance shamrocks were painted on the fire curtain and after a brief Hibernian interlude, the theatre was given over to bingo and within a year it had been demolished. Thereafter, except for the Palace of Varieties in Leeds and some small theatres in seaside resorts, the Music Hall died.

One day Miss Morvan put me up for a new musical comedy which no one thought stood a chance, though it had been written by Lionel Bart, who already had two big successes in the West End. I must say the thought of *Oliver Twist* set to music sounded unpromising to me as well, but I went to the audition and sang my Demon Barber's arias bravely into the darkened stalls. It was depressing to pour so much energy into what seemed like an empty theatre, and I was relieved to see the occasional flare of a match and the glow of a managerial cigar. They called me back three times and then Miss Morvan telephoned to say they wanted me to play the part of Mr Sowerberry, the undertaker, one of the smallest parts in the show, and to understudy Mr Ron Moody, who was to play Fagin. For this and some chorus work, I was offered £15 per week.

We started rehearsing at a hall in Bloomsbury and I met the director, Peter Coe, and the composer and librettist, Lionel Bart. It was then that Lionel Bart announced that he had enjoyed my audition so much that he had actually written a new song for the undertaker, called 'That's Your Funeral'. Thus I was to rehearse a number which, had I but known it, I would sing on at least seven hundred future occasions. *Oliver!*

soon became the musical success of the decade and I had suddenly become a West End actor without ever having set foot in the provinces or served my apprenticeship in 'weekly repertory', a discipline in which I knew, from grim Melbourne experience, that I would certainly fail. I had found my way on to the West End stage by a most agreeable shortcut.

It was exhilarating to be up there on stage every night in my assortment of Dickensian guises with an orchestra in the pit and a rapturous audience crying for more, even if it wasn't for more of me. Ron Moody looked discouragingly robust and I wondered if I would ever get a chance to take the leading role, even for a night. I didn't. The catch to being an understudy is that you have to rehearse with any new additions to the cast and in *Oliver!* the small army of pickpockets was constantly changing. Thus, I found myself in the theatre for several days a week, rehearsing with Oliver Twist's understudy and a succession of Artful Dodgers and precocious brats. During these endless rehearsals the wings were thronged with ambitious stage-struck mothers. I soon got to know the role of Fagin so well that I could leap on to the stage and perform it now; but then it was to no avail.

Working in the West End at night and often during the day gave me an ideal opportunity to explore London. Now that I was earning money I could venture into secondhand bookshops, and sometimes, for very little, I could pick up a treasure like William Beckford's first book, *Extraordinary Painters*, written at the age of sixteen, and in orange wrappers a rare copy of *Zang Tuum Tuum*, Marinetti's Futurist Manifesto on 1913, belligerently inscribed by the author. Then there were the pubs. In Australia they were no more than licensed urinals, but in London they were often more comfortable and congenial than the basement flat in Notting Hill Gate. Right next to the theatre was the Salisbury, which had an Edwardian gin-palace glitter and a camp theatrical clientele, but I preferred the Lamb and Flag in Rose Court and I persuaded the more convivial members of the company to drink there between the matinée and evening performance on Wednesdays and Saturdays. The jovial publican began to greet me like a long-lost friend. On one occasion I found myself without enough money for an expensive round of drinks and he, at once, offered me something which to a dedicated drinker is more precious than love: namely, credit. I had only been in the West End for a few months, and I had a slate. At last I was beginning to feel like an adult human being.

Alan, our ballet-dancer boarder, sometimes drove us into the countryside in his small car, when it had not been borrowed by an opportunistic artist *manqué* from Sydney called Robert who had come to London in the hope of becoming a critic. Why were people from Sydney always so pushy? Probably the convict background, I reflected.

Around north Soho there were the beatnik pubs where my long hair was less noticeable in the throng of black-duffle-coated men and the barefoot hoydens with their lewd mascaraed glances. In a bar near the Portobello Road I met John Gawsworth, a sub-Drinkwater poet and self-styled King of Rodonda, a title he had inherited from M. P. Shiel, the 1890s writer of fantasy whose books I avidly collected. Shiel's ashes were in a biscuit tin on the mantelpiece in Gawsworth's olid Westbourne Grove bed-sitting room. There he once made me, from cabbage leaves literally picked up off the vegetable end of Portobello Road and some cartilaginous scraps, a dubious stew, seasoned with a generous pinch of Shiel's incinerated residue. Gawsworth, charming and erudite in his rare moments of sobriety, was always on the cadge. Sliding deeper into alcoholism, he was rarely, as they say, 'in showroom condition'. But he had known so many of the authors I liked that we spent hours together in one pub or another talking about Havelock Ellis, Anna Wickham and Arthur Machen until he lapsed into total incoherence.

After about eighteen months, rumours circulated that Ron

Moody planned to retire from the role of Fagin and I immediately wrote to Donald Albery offering my services should the leading role be vacated. I knew the part backwards and I felt sure that my case would be sympathetically considered. However, I did not realize that I had become indispensable at the boys' rehearsals. As an understudy, I was *too good* to be wasted in the lead! The director began auditioning for the new Fagin, and I, with shattered hopes, had to go through the ignominy of priming and rehearsing the orphans, so that the new star could take over. It need hardly be said that I looked on the other contenders for my role with a jaundiced eye. The final insult came when the part was given to a recently arrived Australian actor *whom I knew*! As a matter of fact he was very good, but that was completely beside the point and I decided that I had had enough of this theatre and its managerial treachery and ingratitude. Mr Albery, soon to become Sir Donald Albery, had assured me that after eighteen months' service at my original salary, a release from my contract might be considered, *if I were offered something extraordinarily promising elsewhere.*

But nothing seemed promising or extraordinary enough. *Beyond the Fringe* at the Fortune Theatre had been a sensational success and I knew Peter Cook slightly and had met Dudley Moore at the Lamb and Flag. As the show was going to Broadway, auditions were being held for a replacement cast. I auditioned and they immediately offered me a job replacing Peter Cook when the cast changed, but *Oliver!* would not release me. The same thing happened with an offer to join the Aldwych Theatre Company, and a new revue by Steven Vinaver called *Twists* with music by Carl Davis for which I auditioned in the basement of the Cambridge Theatre. Apparently I almost scared Oscar Lewenstein to death with an expressionist monologue.

I was feeling trapped in my undertaker's shop, as night after night, and with growing resentment, I capered about on Sean Kenny's creaking and relentlessly revolving set.

An impresario from Melbourne proposed that I put together a one-man show of monologues for an Australian tour, and going back home to do something creative for a while suddenly seemed an attractive idea after the hack work which my West End job had become.

I was due for my first brief holiday from *Oliver!* and, at the suggestion of my Oxford friend, Ian Donaldson, we decided to take this vacation in Cornwall, at a cottage he knew near Zennor. There I hoped I could write my one-man show, even though I knew I would never be released from my contract to perform it. Loosemoore's Farm was only just across the fields from the house in which D. H. Lawrence had lived with his German wife, Frieda, during the First World War. Their persecutions there are peevishly described in Lawrence's curious novel *Kangaroo*, although reading it I tended to side with the locals. I took with me a suitcase full of Australian newspapers and magazines which I had got from a friend in Fleet Street. There were copies of the *Women's Weekly*, filled with tips for the fashion-conscious Australian housewife and illustrated recipes, mostly in colours of brown and orange with splashes of yellow, since every Australian dish of this period was garnished with pineapple chunks. The *Women's Weekly* also contained an interesting illustrated fashion section called 'What people are wearing Overseas', candid snaps of movie stars in their first-night finery with a sprinkling of bedizened Sydney 'socialites' photographed on the way to a Royal Garden Party in London. There was a strong bias towards Thai silk, which was *the* textile of the period.

Leafing through those pages, as we huddled beside a wood stove in a Cornish farm cottage in February, I felt instantly transported back home to a world of cosy certainties; a land of sponge cakes and pavlovas and curried Hawaiian spag hoops and gingham, seersucker and Thai silk. It was hard to believe that I was actually living in that mysterious unattainable place, which Australians call 'Overseas'. The *Australian Home Beautiful* was also a valuable inspiration with its decorating hints and strong emphasis on the 'latest trends from Overseas'. There was that word again, that mythological, paradisiacal place where every self-respecting middle-class person in Australia would rather be. It was Utopia, it was Serendip, it was the Land of Oz and the Isle of Cythera.

At night, dead on eight, as I tapped away at my typewriter, I was interrupted by a curious humming noise. It was me singing, under my breath, the overture to *Oliver!*, a tune which has never been completely flushed from the uttermost ventricle of my memory. Today, every time I do a new show it returns to me just before the curtain rises, like a virus. It is in my system like herpes. It is the first few bars of Lionel Bart's 'Food, Glorious Food', and I thank him for it.

In the evenings we would put on our coats and mufflers and walk the windswept mile to the Tinners Arms for a drink before dinner. I was getting on quite well with my script until one morning in late February, my wife and I decided to go for a walk along the cliffs. Patches of snow still lay on some of the fields like scattered laundry and as I crossed a small fast-flowing stream of melted snow, I put the heel of my Wellington boot very carefully on a central stone before swinging my right leg across to the opposite bank. But the stone was icy, my boot slipped and I sat rather absurdly, but with a freezing shock, in the shallow rushing water. Rosalind was close behind me and in reaching out to help, tripped and also fell. It was ridiculous, but there for an instant we sat. It was only when I tried to get up and slipped again that I realized how close to the precipice we were and how steeply inclined the stream. Unable to clutch at any vegetation on the bank, we had started to move, first slowly and comically, and then very fast, as the stream became a stone chute that abruptly turned a corner and jettisoned us over the cliff's edge.

I came to, sitting on a narrow rock ledge, my legs dangling over an abyss of some two hundred feet. Below were jagged black rocks around which the sea frothed and crashed. Over my left knee splashed the icy cataract which had deposited me on this precarious shelf. But where was my wife? I looked over my shoulder and saw her higher up the cliff, clinging to some gorse. I tried waving until I realized that my right arm was lifeless and there was a tingling sensation in my right shoulder. I only managed to call out and tell her to scramble to the top somehow and get help.

I was alone on the face of the cliff for many hours. I watched the light on the rocks below change, the sea grow calmer; I saw the shadow of my own cliff fall across the water and still no help came. It was a very unfrequented coastline and I began to entertain the idea of jumping. If I missed the rocks and landed on my feet perhaps I could walk to safety. The pebbles, two hundred feet below, began to look soft and inviting. I desperately tried to make my past life flash before my eyes, but nothing happened. Was this an omen? It had become bitterly cold on the cliff face and I was trembling; moreover my water-logged jeans began to slip, centimetre by centimetre, and with a minute squeaking noise, on the glassy rock. I must have dozed off, for I awoke suddenly to the sound of calling voices and there was a great wind ruffling my hair. Straight ahead on a bright patch of sea I saw another shadow hovering. Then there were cries of 'Hang on there, man!' 'Hang on, for God's sake!' As I became aware of the roaring helicopter above and the profile of the cliff's shadow on the sea bristling with other shadows, I heard cries growing louder and remember very little more, except for a tilted view of Cornwall in the late afternoon, as I shivered in a cocoon of blankets.

I heard later that Rosalind, badly concussed, had wandered aimlessly for several miles, finally appearing at the door of a cottage and saying blankly, 'There is a man on the cliff.' Armed with this slender information, the rescuers mounted my deliverance. Friends drove us back to London but the pain of my dislocated shoulder and fractured arm was so bad I was put in the Royal Free Hospital. The climax to our Cornish holiday had made the front page of every newspaper in Britain, and

Joan Littlewood sent me a telegram, 'GET WELL SOON, BIRDMAN'. Painfully, I had fallen off England, but I had also, it seemed, dropped out of the cast of *Oliver!*

A Nice Night's
Entertainment

S OME MONTHS BEFORE this successful struggle with the
forces of gravity, Rosalind and I had been the beneficiaries
of another rescue. We had been rescued from our subterranean
flat in Notting Hill Gate by a saintly couple. Bill and Deborah
Kellaway were two Australian friends who lived with their
young family in Grove Terrace, Highgate Road, one of the
architectural treasures of North London. In exchange for little
more than a modicum of household help, they offered us a
small flat at the top of their house with views of tousled treetops and Parliament Hill.

Here we lived until we returned to Australia to present my
first one-man show, which I had decided to call, rather flatly, *A
Nice Night's Entertainment*. This was always Sandy Stone's
assessment of an evening out, however dull, although in recent
times this has been displaced by the encomium 'thoroughly
enjoyable', usually with a strong emphasis on the adjective.

'How did you like *The Silence of the Lambs*?'

'Look, it was *thoroughly* enjoyable. In fact we all *thoroughly*
enjoyed it!'

Then London was a Mecca for Antipodean painters, and
Australian art was 'hot', largely due to the perfervid advocacy

of Bryan Robertson, the director of the Whitechapel Gallery. Arthur Boyd, perhaps one of the greatest and certainly the most 'European' Australian painter, had set up his studio in Highgate and other artists had followed.

One weekend Arthur, the painter Charles Blackman and I decided we would go to Paris to see major exhibitions of works by Goya and Braque. Leaving our wives in London we set off on that wonderful train which used to leave Victoria Station at dinnertime, enter the bowels of a boat at bedtime, and whisk its passengers through the landscape between Calais and Paris the next morning. As we enjoyed our breakfast I recognized at the next table Sir Herbert Read, the art historian, but I could not pluck up the courage to separate him from his newspaper in order to boast that I knew most of his pre-war surrealist poetry off by heart and that I thought his novel, *The Green Child*, was a masterpiece. I suppose I still remembered the brutal rebuff I had received from Kenneth Slessor in the Sydney Journalists' Club years before. Still, it felt odd watching that grey-haired stranger whose innermost reflections I felt I knew so well reading his paper across the aisle.

In Paris after a day of pictures, museums and a few cocktails here and there, Arthur Boyd seemed to become apprehensive. Charles and I certainly had delinquent tendencies, and Arthur keenly felt his responsibility for getting me back to London in one piece, so to speak. That evening, after a convivial dinner, Charles and I 'escaped' and went on an extended tour of the bars and clubs of Montmartre. Yet finally, even Charlie announced that it was time to go back to our Left Bank hotel or poor old Arthur would be calling the police. On hearing this I managed to give him the slip, and disappeared into the Paris night for several hours which are, alas, forever lost to my memory. I do, however, remember as dawn broke, creeping back into the room in which we all slept like the three bears. Just as I fell asleep I was aware of Arthur Boyd fumbling in the pockets of my jacket. Feigning slumber, I saw him in the dawn light carefully counting what little money remained in my pockets, and then retiring to his own bed with an audible sigh of relief. Like the dear man and conscientious chaperone that he was, he knew exactly how much cash I had had, and he had been checking to see if I had lavished any of it on nocturnal pleasures more expensive and dangerous than Calvados.

Meanwhile my Australian impresario, Clifford Hocking, wrote with renewed confidence that I could manage a whole evening alone on stage, although I was far from convinced. However, the tour was postponed when we fell off the cliff and it was two months later and much physiotherapy on my fractured arm before we could set sail.

John Betjeman and Elizabeth Cavendish came to see us off. John had recently visited Australia for the British Council and someone had given him my Sandy Stone gramophone records, which had reminded him of *The Diary of a Nobody*. We became instant friends and I would visit him at his small house in Cloth Fair near the Smithfield meat markets and in the shadow of St Bartholomew the Great. He described himself, not as a poet but as a 'senior journalist', and in his book-cluttered sitting-room lined with green Morris wallpaper and hung with pictures by Conder, Laura Knight and Max Beerbohm, he dispensed generous late-morning drinks to friends like Osbert Lancaster, Philip Larkin, Kingsley Amis and, very often, an Anglican priest or two. Then, in an exalted mood, we would all repair to Coleman's Chophouse in Aldersgate Street, where the atmosphere and appointments were immutably pre-war, and remained so until the enlightened sixties, when the entire eastern side of that old thoroughfare was razed to the ground and replaced by council houses in the Brutalist style.

At Coleman's we would tuck into roast beef and Brussels sprouts, and drink champagne from pewter tankards. John always insisted on paying, which was just as well. His *Collected Poems* was a bestseller and he was fond of exclaiming, with huge merriment, 'I'm as rich as Croesus!' The poacher's pockets in his jacket bulged with books and round canisters of Players cigarettes which he liked to smoke because the art-work on the tins hadn't changed in thirty years.

We shared several interests, especially in the Music Hall and the writers and artists of the 1890s, and he gave me many slim volumes of the period with wide margins and precious verses by dim and half-forgotten poets. 'Dimness' was his favourite term of approbation, and he knew I admired the rather dim, but once brightly hued, paintings on silk of Charles Conder, the English-Australian friend of Wilde and Lautrec, who had died of syphilis in 1909.

'There must be a few chaps who knew Conder who are still with us,' said John one morning, picking up the phone. 'I say, let's give Maresco Pearce and Augustus John a tinkle and ask them over for some bubbly!' Alas, neither of these octogenarian painters were in the reminiscent mood that day, and died soon after. Like me, John Betjeman relished such mysterious links with the past.

My pursuit of Conder, whose turn-of-the-century vogue had been brief, and who was now almost totally forgotten, led to a couple of curious incidents. Once, in the Crown, a pub near Leicester Square, which, in the early sixties remained unchanged since the 1890s when it was a poets' pub, I was accosted by a very old man with rheumy eyes, a greasy woollen muffler and mittened fingers around the handle of his pint of mild. He said he had been a doorman at the Leicester Galleries in the early years of the century, and that I reminded him of one of the artists who used to exhibit there. 'Who was that?' I asked. 'Well, Guv'ner, you wouldn't know him, and he's been gone these many years, but he was called Conder.' The hairs on the back of my neck twitched. 'Not *Charles* Conder?' I said, in astonishment. 'Can you remember what he was like?' 'Well, I've told you, sir, and it was over fifty years ago, but he was an *e-ffeminine* type of a chappie, very like your-self!' Later I was to befriend John Rothenstein, the author of a brilliant and evocative life of the artist, who remembered meeting Conder, then mortally ill, on his parents' doorstep in 1906.

I had noticed in a contemporary book on this artist that many of the illustrations were reproduced by courtesy of their owner, a Miss Amy Halford. I looked in the telephone book and discovered to my amazement that there was one Amy Halford listed with a Kensington telephone number. Impulsively I dialled it and a very old lady answered the telephone. Slowly and quite loudly I explained the purpose of my call, but she had got hold of the wrong end of the stick. 'Darling Charles!' came the Edwardian voice through my cream plastic receiver. 'I haven't heard from you for weeks. How are you? The fan you painted for me looks glorious and Edmund Gosse was here with Ricketts for tea yesterday and thinks it is one of your best. When are you coming to see me?' Our conversation was rudely interrupted by a brisk modern voice, 'This is Miss Halford's nurse. Miss Halford is not strong enough to speak on the telephone, I'm afraid. She should be having her rest. Good day.'

Although I had made some progress on my script in Cornwall before the accident, I had still a long way to go; so it was probably just as well that our voyage to Melbourne, via Rotterdam, Lisbon, Genoa and Auckland, lasted six weeks, and I could finish writing the show. We travelled on a Norwegian cargo ship with only twelve other passengers, and it was rather like being in a play by Agatha Christie. There were two nuns, an Australian honeymoon couple, and the Gillespies, a middle-aged pair migrating to Australia; a destination that we all knew they would detest. They actually began to complain about their anticipated social hardships when we were three hours out of Lisbon, and since everyone sat at the same table, the troll-like Norwegian captain had to exert great self-control in listening to this lady's ceaseless whinging. We were rather pleased therefore, when somewhere in the Indian Ocean during rough weather, poor Mrs Gillespie's chair capsized, throwing her legs over her shoulders, and she was seen by all, on that tropical evening at least, to have abandoned the humid confinements of her panties. From that undignified moment until we berthed at Auckland, Enid Gillespie never emerged from her cabin.

Also on board was an elderly German widow and her blond nephew; the son, we gathered, of a German industrialist in New Zealand. His urbane and smiling scepticism about the Holocaust was not the least of his charming attributes, though we were only privy to his political and racial views on those few occasions when he graced us with his presence. Most of his time was spent below decks providing amusement for rougher members of the Norwegian crew, who, given certain inducements, were prepared to overlook the German invasion of their country and had their own quaint methods of burying the hatchet.

In Auckland my wife was reunited with her parents, and with some success I tested my new material at a lunch-hour performance at the University. We got to know a few Kiwi poets and writers, especially Karl Stead and his beautiful wife, Kay, who to this day, remember more about my visit to New Zealand than I do. (See Asides.)

When we finally reached Melbourne, my parents were there to greet us and there was even a family dinner party to which we were *both* invited! My sister, now living in Melbourne, had married Robert, an engineer, and already had a daughter, Penelope; my brother Michael was in his final year at school and Christopher was studying architecture at the University. They were much changed since I had seen them last and seemed to regard me with a shy diffidence. I sadly regretted that my early marriage and expatriation and the inevitable age difference had created a gulf in my relationship with them.

Although I was nervous about my opening night at the Assembly Hall, my father, it seemed, was even more apprehensive. On the day of the final dress rehearsal, the box-office lady called me over. 'Had your dad in here this morning, Barry,' she said. 'What a nice man, and thinks the world of you too.'

'What did he want?' I asked.

'Look, it was funny really, and I reckon I shouldn't be telling you this, but he wanted to buy all the seats in the house to give to his friends in the Rotary Club.'

'*All* the seats?' I asked stupefied.

'Every blessed seat,' said Joan. 'He has to be your number one fan.'

'What . . . what did you tell him?'

'Well, I more or less told him I would if I could but I can't. You're *sold out*, aren't you?'

I told her I hadn't known that and I asked her what he had said.

'He didn't say anything really, just looked amazed. But I found him a single for himself right up at the back on the side, and he wouldn't take a comp either.'

A Nice Night's Entertainment was successful. Thanks, really, to Cliff Hocking, who had thought of the idea in the first place and John Betjeman, who had written a laudatory blurb for the programme. (See Asides.)

We extended the season, and then we did the show in Sydney in the Macquarie Radio Theatre, right next door to the old Assembly Hotel where I used to drink with the radio actors in the Phillip Street days.

Apart from Edna Everage and Sandy Stone, one of the most popular characters in my show was an Australian beatnik; a black-clad, suburban rebel in that period garment, the duffle-coat. These feckless hobbledehoys were to be found in the coffee lounges of most Australian cities, where they strove to resemble minor characters in the romances of Jack Kerouac. My beatnik carried a cheap guitar, which I had bought in Lisbon, and with exiguous skill I accompanied myself in a self-pitying ballad, which I whined and bleated in the manner of Bob Dylan. Such being the fate of satirists, this item was particularly popular with beatniks.

We took the show to Newcastle and also to Adelaide, which I had not visited since the days of Mauve Chunder. Hospitality, as usual in that most *gemütlich* of Australian cities, was lavish and although I was not unaccustomed to performing on stage with a hangover I usually found a 'hair of the dog' a helpful form of self-medication.

Then an imperious summons arrived from Broadway. *Oliver!* was to be presented there, and Mr David Merrick, the impresario, wished to reinforce the New York cast with as many members of the original London production as possible. The show was already touring; it was, in fact, about to open in Toronto and I was offered a tempting financial inducement to resume my old part as the undertaker and once more understudy the leading role of Fagin. On the one hand it would be exciting to live and work in New York but on the other I had little appetite for another long captivity in a show that I could sing in my sleep and to experience once again the demeaning and frustrating life of the understudy who never goes on. But when Merrick agreed to pay me even more money and limit the engagement to three months, I accepted. Moreover, Rosalind was expecting our first child, so it all fitted in rather well, and we could be back in London from New York in comfortable time for the birth.

It was agreed that my wife would join me in New York and I flew alone to Toronto. But I was not, in fact, entirely alone. I had been asked to be the unlikely chaperone to 'the Artful Dodger', a small boy called Davey Jones, who was later to become a celebrated member of the sixties band, the Monkees. He had been a star of the West End production of *Oliver!* and, like me, was another of David Merrick's last-minute replacements. What Davey and I did *not* know was that the two American actors whose roles we were usurping had no idea that they were about to be sacked. They had happily toured America, and Toronto was their last stop before Broadway.

We were met at the aerodrome by one of Mr Merrick's henchmen who smuggled us off to an hotel and invited us to see the show that night, but with a caution not to go backstage in case the cast smelt a rat. We realized that the management had, with despicable ingenuity, made us somehow to blame for the dismissal of two fellow actors. Since then I have often pondered on the anomalies of 'show business', which is not really a business but a game played with all the petty deceits, subterfuges and bitcheries one would expect to find in a provincial amateur dramatic society.

But an hour after I stepped off the plane there was another shock in store for me. Clive Revill, the actor playing Fagin, had laryngitis. Since I was the new understudy, I had to go on – *that night*. Except for rehearsals, I had never appeared on stage as Fagin before and had not studied the role for more than twelve months. As far as I was concerned, *Oliver!* was a past interlude, over and done with. Now, after a long flight, I had less than two hours in which to prepare myself for the leading role in a major musical.

The theatre, named after a munificent Canadian brewer, was new and enormous and that evening, as in a dream, I somehow pulled it off. I also, in a frenzy of compensatory over-acting, pulled off my false beard, although it is unlikely that the audience noticed this, since they seemed miles away; so far away, in fact, that the performance must have resembled a puppet show. I could, however, see the front row, and to add to my distractions I could see one man in particular, in the middle of the front row, leaning forward and staring at me balefully. His face was pale and cadaverous, and his lips seemed to move in time with mine. He was, of course, my unhappy predecessor, and he was there every night until Mr Revill's larynx revived. How could I complain and have him removed, if only to a less conspicuous seat in that vast auditorium? He had been ignominiously removed once already, so that every night I had to watch him down there, miming and muttering his way through all my scenes and songs. He was there at the stage door after every performance too, being stroked and embraced by commiserating chorus girls, whilst I, like a pariah, skulked into my dressing-room.

New York in the early sixties was an attractive place to be, even in the dead of winter. Like jetlag, mugging had not been invented, though neither phenomenon was unknown. There were no aerosol spray cans, so there was no graffiti except the decorous old-fashioned kind, and the tallest skyscrapers were still the venerable Empire State and the Chrysler Buildings, both pre-war. Harlem was visitable on foot, even at night, and Greenwich Village, where we rented an apartment, felt village-like and residential. From the women's penitentiary which loomed over Seventh Avenue the inmates screamed down their friendly obscenities to passing pedestrians, and at the nearby Village Vanguard you could hear Louis Armstrong, Sarah Vaughan and Art Blakely and his Jazz Messengers or Count Basie at Birdland on Broadway.

We lived in what was called 'a walk-up, cold-water' apartment on West 10th Street. This meant it had no lift and no heating. The latter inconvenience I failed to grasp, but on our first night there, as the icy wind off the Hudson rattled the windows and soughed under the door, I soon became aware of its disadvantages. Subjacent were two colourful establishments, Alex's Borscht Bowl and Ruth's Poodle Parlour and the co-mingled aromas of stewed beetroot and canine shampoo filtered up through our bare floorboards.

Directly above us dwelt Mrs Lyles, the Haitian supervisor of the small brownstone building, and wafting from her premises came an unidentifiable stench; the effluvium, we surmised, of certain arcane and unneighbourly rituals. Why else would I have surprised her on the staircase late one evening conveying to her apartment a caged and apprehensive chicken? Mrs Lyles and I disliked each other intensely, for it was to her that I had always to address my complaints about the discomforts and inadequacies, not to say the gelid conditions, of our accommodation. She was exasperatingly unhelpful, so that I was obliged to carry my grievances to the owner, a Wall Street business man and amateur artist, who kept our flat as a bohemian pad for the summer months. When I told him that I was almost certain, judging by Mrs Lyles' dusky and credulous visitors, and by the midnight incantations and aromas which filtered through my

*Rosalind, Emily, Tessa and
the author at Little Venice*

Christmas, 1965

Tessa and Emily, 1969

By Cecil Beaton, 1967

The author in Little Venice with his Conder collection

The Surfie

The bride's father

The author with Small Bigscape, 1968

Drunk: with and by David Bailey, 1969

Sober

Edna Everage with Barry McKenzie

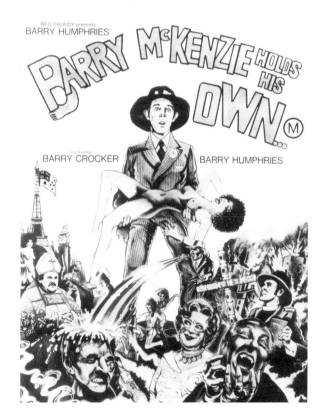

An historic encounter

The Republican (Sir Leslie Colin Patterson)

ceiling, that she was a fervid practitioner of Voodoo, he replied sententiously:

'It must be a difficult period of adjustment for you, Mr Humphries, being so fortunate as to have once lived in a homogenous society.'

Oliver! was a hit, but it was not the only successful British show on Broadway. Anthony Newley was appearing up the road in *Stop the World, I Want to Get Off* and Peter Cook, Dudley Moore, Alan Bennett and Jonathan Miller were starring elsewhere in their London success *Beyond the Fringe*. Rosalind and I began to see something of Peter Cook and his wife Wendy at their comparatively luxurious apartment which was not just full of Tiffany lamps but something far more precious – Central Heating. On Sunday nights Peter and I used to go to the Apollo Theatre in Harlem to see a new black singing group called the Supremes.

The cast of *Oliver!*, thanks to Mr Merrick's indefatigable battles with Actors Equity, swarmed with English actors, and since we were all being paid a great deal more than we were used to, and were in a constant mood of celebration, our dressers, like bewildered Ganymedes, were sent scuttling back and forth to nearby liquor stores during each evening's performance. A stranger glancing into one of our dressing-rooms might have supposed we were all throwing cocktail parties. One of the British actresses failed to appear on stage one evening and a duet became abruptly transformed into a solo, punctuated by anxious glances into the wings. The woman was found asleep on the dressing-room floor in her Dickensian finery with a gin bottle in her hand, like a figure in an engraving by Hogarth. The rest of us stumbled uproariously through our scenes, impatient to return to the Bacchanalia that reigned in our dressing-rooms. It was little wonder that the hard-working Americans in the cast, who earned a great deal less than we, looked on these boozy revels with the disdain of the Pilgrim Fathers.

After the show I did not always proceed directly home but

loitered in some of the more picturesque taverns of Greenwich Village. My favourite was the Ninth Circle, on West 10th Street, only a few doors from Ruth's Poodle Parlour and Alex's Borscht Bowl. The propinquity of my apartment enabled me to spend a few guiltless hours at the Circle every night, and I felt, as I stood at the dim bar of my 'local', ankle-deep in peanut shells, that I was as close to the threshold of my own home as any man need be. There was nobody I knew at the Ninth Circle and nobody who knew me, except for one drinker who always addressed me as 'the English Poet', probably because of my hair, which was unusually long for those days. I gathered he was some kind of minor academic because he told me he had been invited to Oxford University and earnestly besought my advice, as an 'English Poet', as to whether or not he should accept.

Although we drank together every night, I never quite caught his name, and one evening he insisted that I come with him to a party. With the aid of another drink, I suppressed a brief qualm about my wife sitting at home alone watching television, and accepted. But it was a difficult party to leave early. It was snowing heavily, and there, parked right outside the bar, was a large furniture van into which the other guests – and my friend had invited all our fellow drinkers – scrambled. Within the vehicle fitful candlelight revealed more people, sprawled and huddled, smoking and drinking, while a tape-recorder transmitted the music of John Coltrane and Miles Davis. The doors were slammed and slowly and silently the van glided off into the night. I have no idea how long this 'mobile' party continued, or at what hour it at last came to rest outside the Ninth Circle and we tumbled out into the snow, but I had, at least, overheard the name of my host. It was Jack Kerouac.

Rosalind and I attended many of the big uptown art shows in smart East Side galleries: Rothko, Rosenquist, Rivers and Rauschenberg. At one of these shindigs I was jostled against a picture which was still very wet, and I later found that I had one of the finest passages from Hans Hoffmann's best period imprinted on the sleeve of my beige corduroy jacket. At the Gotham Book Mart I met Salvador and Gala Dali, who invited me back for afternoon tea at the St Regis Hotel when they promised to visit Australia, and there were many big parties thrown by society hostesses for the *Oliver!* Company. At one of these, in the Waldorf Towers, where the champagne and caviare omelettes flowed and the walls dripped with Monets and near-Monets the colour of boiled sweets, I wandered off into a small study where a fat, ill-favoured woman in surgical hose sat alone watching *I'll Cry Tomorrow* on a small screen.

'Wouldn't you like to join us all at the party?' I urged her affably.

'There are more int-er-esting people on television,' barked Elsa Maxwell grumpily, as her eyes swivelled back to the screen, which at that moment showed a group of derelicts on Skid Row.

As the evening wore on the theatricals grew rowdier, until our hostess struck several loud blows with her Tiffany-topped cane on a Boule table. 'Would y'all hush your voices, ladies and gentlemen, *please!*' She pointed a Van Cleef'd finger at the ceiling. 'Mr Cole Porter is trying to get some sleep!'

Our time in New York was drawing to a close and I had not the faintest idea what I would do on my return to London. Very soon there would be three mouths to feed. Peter Cook told me he had started a nightclub in London called the Establishment. It followed the success of his fortnightly *Private Eye* and Peter felt I should present some extracts from my one-man show at this already highly fashionable venue. I was not at all certain that my vignettes of Melbourne suburban life were really attuned to the taste of a sophisticated late-night London audience. But Peter had listened to my Australian gramophone records and was sure I would be a hit. He even offered to pay me £100 a week. A fortune in that far-off epoch!

Rosalind and I sailed back across the Atlantic with our

baggage stuffed with gramophone records, books, glass, sheets and baby clothes. Since the *Sylvania* docked at Greenock in Scotland, we had to pack all our loot into a hire car and drive down to London. We had only parked the car outside Charlie Blackman's house in Highgate for about fifteen minutes, but it was long enough for thieves to break in and steal the entire proceeds of my New York engagement. Fortunately the police were able to retrieve from a vacant allotment in Muswell Hill the sleeve of one corduroy suit. It was my original Hans Hoffmann!

Between rehearsals at the Establishment I was attending Professor Norman Morris's special classes for fathers-to-be at the Charing Cross Hospital. Although I heard myself asking clever questions at the end of the Professor's talk, I felt more woefully ignorant of the awesome events that lay ahead than I ever dared let on.

The Establishment club was a long room in Greek Street which had been redecorated by Sean Kenny, the designer of *Oliver!*, in a kind of heavily timbered, Tudor–Constructivist style. There was a bar at the front at which young satire groupies loitered; pale-faced girls with fringes, pearlized lips and eyes like black darns. They said 'Yah' and 'Soopah' a great deal and they all seemed to know Dudley Moore quite well. Would these crack a smile at Edna Everage or Sandy Stone I wondered, as the cold hand of fear entered my breast and gave my heart a little squeeze. Late at night when the club was packed I watched a typical Establishment show. Eleanor Bron and John Fortune did a very funny sketch about middle-class pretentiousness, like a sort of Hampstead Nichols and May, and John Bird impersonated Harold Macmillan to a convulsed audience. There seemed to be a lot of jokes about upper-class politicians and once again my flesh crawled with misgivings about my own folksy act. I remembered the warning of those well-meaning Melbourne friends back in the fifties. 'I hope you won't be doing Edna in Sydney. *She's far too Melbourne.*

They'll never get the point.' I had got away with it in Sydney, but Soho in the sixties was another matter altogether. I sat at the bar morosely drinking until the Late, Late Show when they tried out new acts, usually wags from the Great Universities. One unprepossessing fellow seemed to get a lot of laughs with a none-too-hilarious monologue about the Royal Barge accidentally sinking in the Thames.

'He looks like a Methodist minister's son,' I thought uncharitably, as the birds around me hooted and soopahed. How was I to know then that David Frost *was* a Methodist minister's son?

As opening night grew nearer my portrait was specially taken by Lewis Morley, a Chinese photographer who later became one of the most celebrated photographers of the sixties with his famous image of a naked Christine Keeler straddling a chair. I was surprised therefore when an extremely truculent young man called Jeffrey Bernard attacked me in the French Pub in Soho for sitting for Morley and not him! Bernard apparently thought he was the Establishment's official photographer, though it was hard to understand how the fault could possibly have been mine.

On my first night on the pocket-handkerchief stage, I bravely launched into Mrs Everage's opening song. The pianist was an Australian girl who had failed to warn me that acute anxiety sometimes caused her to strike so many wrong notes that a tune could become unrecognizable. To this dissonant accompaniment I trilled Edna's hymn to 'The Old Country' as courageously as I could, but it was disquietening to look down and see, through the clouds of cigarette smoke, and at a round table only a few feet away, the critics busily scribbling in their notebooks. One in particular I recognized to be Bamber Gascoigne, the theatre critic of the *Spectator*, looking rather trapped, whilst others could be seen crawling out half-way through the performance. It felt horribly like the Granville Returned Servicemen's Club all over again, as the murmur of talk grew louder and the exodus to the bar more rowdily overt.

Backstage, after my performance had finished to the most perfunctory smattering of applause, I bitterly cursed myself for ever having agreed to trot out these whimsical provincial marionettes, who never made so much as a single reference to the Rt Hon. Harold Macmillan. The reviews confirmed my fears.

Bamber Gascoigne in the *Spectator* called my turn 'distinctly soporific' and Julian Holland, an erstwhile champion, said I lacked 'anger'. The worst part about it all was that I had to do the whole thing again the following night and the night after that and the night after that. Three weeks of public failure and rejection.

I was almost relieved when Nick Luard, the business manager, politely told me that they would have to cut my season short. I felt I had let my friend Peter Cook down badly, though I was pleased that he was still in New York and not in London to witness the disaster in person. However, there was another positive event in my life which alleviated all the pain and ignominy of failure. On the 14th of May 1963 my daughter Tessa was born at the Charing Cross Hospital.

By coincidence, on the same day Spike Milligan sent me a telegram asking me to play the lead in his new play, *The Bed-sitting Room*, if I were free to start rehearsals immediately. I was wonderfully free.

Ruth

THE ARRIVAL OF Tessa dispelled most of my feelings of gloom and self-reproach after the Establishment débâcle. Overnight I became a doting father and, as I held my daughter in my arms and felt her exquisite mauvely-mottled fingers patting my face and plucking at my tie, I little thought that, many years later, those same fingers might be playfully reaching for my credit card.

Tessa, Rosalind and I lived in a rented house in Highgate, not far from the Archway Road. We inherited it from Leonard French, an artist friend from Australia who had just gone back to Melbourne. I had never wished to live permanently in England, much as I loved it. Always, at the back of my mind, I had a picture of some idyllic abode in a garden by the sea. Portugal perhaps, or Tasmania? Sometimes, in my imagination, this prefiguration of my fantasy residence was more vivid than at others. There was a terrace, azaleas and a colonnade hung with wistaria. Once in the early seventies at the Paris flea-market I came across a painting of my dream house by a forgotten French artist. It matched my vision in every detail, my 'coign of true felicity'. The terraces, the gardens and the shining sea. The dealer asked far too much, of course, and I walked away with the intention of returning an hour later to haggle, but when I came back the picture was gone.

The Bedsitting Room, a post-nuclear farce by John Antrobus and Spike Milligan, had already opened at the Mermaid Theatre but just as the play was about to transfer to the West End there was some dispute involving firearms between Spike and his leading actor, Graham Stark. That, apparently, was when I was summoned, Spike having seen my show in Sydney. As if the job and the money were not enough, I even had an understudy, a young actor called Michael Gambon.

In the lunch break after the first day of rehearsal, I was taken quietly to one side by one of the actors. It was Valentine Dyall, a tall, haunted-looking man with a glass eye. Before the war he had been a classical actor of great gifts of whom much was expected, but he had, in later years, failed to live up to his early promise. Yet there was always a trace of hopefulness, of jaunty vanity – sometimes winning and sometimes merely ridiculous – attached to his decline. His voice was his most famous attribute; sepulchral, supercilious, aristocratic, it had become known throughout Britain on BBC Radio in Dyall's celebrated impersonation of *The Man in Black*. Spike Milligan often used him in *The Goon Shows*, usually in the role of an effete and crazed Englishman, but he was especially funny on stage in *The Bedsitting Room*, in a role which he hoped might re-establish his reputation in the West End.

It seemed that Valentine had drawn me to one side in the saloon bar of the Round Table to warn me about another member of the cast. Discreetly rolling his good eye in the direction of a balding and mild-looking man in a navy-blue blazer, quietly sipping a half of bitter, he hissed:

'Never lend money to that man over there, dear boy. He looks nice, and he is nice, but you'll never see your money again.'

Oddly enough, in the next few hours at least two other members of the cast drew me aside and confided the same warning, so that I began to feel slightly sorry for poor old Vernon, as he was called. He certainly didn't look like a sponger, but I tensed up a little at the end of the day when he sidled up to me in the bar, looked cautiously over his shoulder, and asked me casually how I was 'fixed' for cash. I was forewarned.

'I'm terribly sorry, Vernon,' I said, quite truthfully. 'I'm afraid I don't even have the price of a round of drinks tonight.' Vernon beamed. 'Just as I thought, dear fellow,' he said. Then, with another furtive glance over his shoulder, he pressed £10 into my hand and whispered, 'The ghost doesn't walk until Friday (this was theatre slang meaning that we did not get paid until the end of the week), and I had a feeling you might be a bit short. Pay me back any time you like.' He gave me a conspiratorial wink and patted my shoulder. 'I have a feeling we're going to become good friends on this show.'

I was too astonished to do any more than croak, 'Thanks, Vern,' and I pocketed the tenner very gratefully as a matter of fact, vowing to pay him back as soon as the ghost walked. 'What sneaky bastards actors are,' I thought. 'Why would they gang up and bad-mouth a sweet and generous chap like that? Envy, probably. Never underestimate the power of envy!' I paid Vernon back on the nail, though he was terribly reluctant to take my money, and there was lots of 'Are you sure, old chap? Are you really absolutely sure you can spare it?'

Once we had opened at the Comedy Theatre in Panton Street, with the cash flowing and the laughter from full houses rolling over the footlights, I realized with a sense of elation that I could still be funny. After the Establishment I had begun to fear that I might have lost the knack. Spike Milligan, though marvellously risible, was sometimes unpredictable; he once went home at intermission without any warning, so that the ill-prepared understudy was obliged to take over his role in the second half, to the confusion and bewilderment of the audience, and cast.

In the second act I had to spend a long time in bed on stage with a very pretty actress called Jacqui Ellis. We just lay there in the half-darkness for about forty minutes whilst Spike performed the most astonishing and hilarious improvisations. I was aware that Miss Ellis was married, but estranged from her husband who, she informed me, was an extremely jealous and violent man. Indeed, he had been seen lurking in the vicinity of the stage door on several occasions and had even made attempts to enter the theatre. I was especially alarmed when I learnt that her husband was none other than Jeffrey Bernard, that chippy photographer whom I had quite inadvertently miffed. I was fairly sure that his bark was worse than his bite, but I none the less dreaded the possibility that one night Bernard, after a few large ones, might overpower the stage door keeper, storm on to the stage and alter the course of the play in a manner transcending the surreal imagination of the author.

One Saturday morning in Highgate, Rosalind and I had had a leisurely breakfast and Tessa was rattling the bars of her play-pen when the doorbell rang. It was Vernon. I asked him in for a cup of coffee and he explained that, although he lived in south London, it just so happened he was in Highgate on business and so thought he would drop in. My wife suggested that he might like to stay for lunch and we could both journey into the West End for the matinée. Vernon, however, looked ill at ease.

'The silliest thing has happened, old boy,' he said. 'I've got a little deal going through up in this neck of the woods and I've come all this way and completely forgotten my bloody chequebook.' My hand had gone to my own chequebook almost before he had finished speaking.

'How much do you need?' I asked. Vernon was blushing, and was he perspiring slightly?

'Well, £75 would get me out of a terrible hole,' he said, 'but don't worry, I'll go back to Wimbledon and come up again next week, if the deal hasn't fallen through.'

I wrote him a cheque for £100 and stuffed it in the top pocket of his blazer. It felt rather good to help such an atrociously maligned fellow actor, and a man who had also been a Spitfire pilot in the War. 'Pay me back when the ghost walks,' I said magnanimously.

Later that week Vernon proudly gave me a cheque and I thought no more about it until the bank suggested that I re-present it. I did this a couple of times before confronting Vernon, who went very red and fulminated against his bank manager. At once he wrote me another cheque, which bounced as well. Terry, the publican at the Round Table, showed me a large pint glass filled with cheques. Vernon had written all of them. 'But how can he do it?' I protested. 'How does he *feel*? We're on stage with him every night.'

'There's not a pub in the West End where he dares show his face,' said Terry. 'Did he give you all that old moody about being a Spitfire pilot?' I nodded forlornly.

'He's a master!' said Terry, with something almost like admiration. 'But mark my words, he'll put the bite on you again one day.'

Weeks later, and incrementally, Vernon did cough up. But on the very last night of the show, and with exquisite timing, he touched me for a fiver. I never saw him or the money again, but only the other day I heard that he was still alive, well and working. No doubt living on borrowed time.

I drove a turquoise Mini Minor to the theatre every night, in those days before double yellow lines, and on some evenings, if a friend had come backstage, we might stop in Soho for a nightcap. Colin MacInnes told me about a wonderful club called the Colony Room which everyone went to after the pubs had closed. Colin had written books about Soho, although he had spent his childhood in Melbourne. His mother, Angela Thirkell, the granddaughter of Burne-Jones and the cousin of Rudyard Kipling, was a popular novelist of English upper-class manners who had improbably exiled herself in Melbourne between the wars. Colin told me that as a little boy she had sent him off to Scotch College in white lacy frocks, and when he had suffered the inevitable derision of his jeering classmates she had turned up and embarrassed him still further by castigating the schoolmaster in her loftiest Kensington accent.

When I knew him, Colin affected a manner of careless truculence. He wore his grey hair very short, dressed always in jeans, and seemed to prefer the society of 'spades', as London's West Indians were called. He was the most charming and generous of men until he had had a few drinks, and then he underwent a dramatic personality change, and he could turn very nasty if he didn't like the look of you.

Upstairs in Dean Street, amongst the membership of the Colony Room, there were about fifty personality changes every night. I had become quite adept at picking people with an allergy to alcohol, or those unfortunates without will-power who were obliged to construct their personal lives uncomfortably around their thirst. For example Terry, the publican at the Round Table, often allowed a select few of us to go on drinking after closing time as his personal guests. There was a childish, illicit pleasure in sipping away in a closed bar. And yet, around one a.m. I began to worry. *Should he be there?* I wondered. What about Terry's wife and kids upstairs? Was it entirely fair to keep this charming fellow up drinking large scotches, when his domestic responsibilities lay elsewhere? I completely forgot that my *own* wife and child were miles away in Highgate, and asleep, one hoped.

Sometimes I entertained fantasies of abstinence. What would it be like? I knew one or two people who did not drink, but *had*. Why on earth did they stop? 'Couldn't handle it,' was my invariable answer to myself. Perhaps, one day, I might cut down. I decided I would – one day – if it started to cost me more than money. Meanwhile I reflected how lucky I was to be able to take it or leave it. It just so happened that I preferred to take it. Such was freedom of choice.

The Colony Room was one narrow flight up, small and dimly lit, with a mirrored wall which duplicated the lucifugous drinkers. On a stool at the bar, just inside the door, sat the proprietrix, Muriel Belcher, a bawdy *jolie laide* with an air of successfully repressed refinement. A piano tinkled in a dark corner and Colin introduced me to the pianist, another Australian, called Malcolm Williamson, who later quitted the club and became the Master of the Queen's Musick.

There was no one in the club that I knew, but a few I recognized. Tom Driberg, the MP and old friend of John Betjeman, was talking about E. M. Forster to a very drunk and uncomprehending guardsman. Francis Bacon, the Vorticist artist, stood at the bar ordering champagne for everybody. He was the first man I ever saw wearing black leather from head to foot. There also seemed to be an assortment of ambiguous-looking businessmen around him; perhaps they were naval Commanders in mufti, doing a little cruising on dry land, or were they just some of Francis' placenta-coloured models, whom he depicted coupling smudgily on billiard tables?

A beautiful Canadian girl, whose lion-coloured hair hung down like a curtain over one eye and kept getting in her gin, took a fancy to me. She was called Elizabeth Smart, and she worked on a fashion magazine. A few words from her to Muriel, and I was a member! To what privileges I wondered, if any, would membership of this wicked little den entitle me? Perhaps only the dubious luxury of paying double, and sometimes treble saloon-bar prices for large and highly intoxicating drinks and, of course, the titillating propinquity of some high-class riff-raff.

Muriel took a liking to me too, or so I thought; in her fashion she was generally polite to all male members, unless they failed to settle their extortionate 'slates'. At the Colony one was always encouraged to buy large rounds of drinks without a demand for immediate payment, and this highly civilized procedure found extraordinary favour with the clientele until the time came, weeks later, for them to get out their chequebooks and pay the price of pleasure. Muriel lost her suaveté only when someone behaved very badly indeed; though the Colony's rules of bad behaviour were, to say the least, flexible. The girls who used the club, however, unless they were Liz Smart, or inebriates with titles, fared less favourably. 'Hello, cunty!' Miss Belcher would frequently say to wide-eyed debutantes on their first visit, as they stumbled in the door on the arm of some black-tied debauchee, and 'Fuck off, cunty!' as they left, generally alone.

I must say that I found this a most congenial and amusing haunt, and, perversely, the fact that it was so expensive lent it an added allure. As I mounted the stairs and heard the voices and the music floating down to greet me, with Muriel's psittacine laughter rising high above them all, I felt a curious anticipatory excitement. 'What was going to happen tonight?' I wondered. 'Where will it all end?'

It ended, of course, with a hangover, and a guilty apology to Rosalind. I always vowed 'never again' after an evening at the Colony, and, oddly enough, I always meant it.

I had arranged for some of my possessions, especially books and pictures, to be sent over from Australia to furnish the flat in Highgate. Tessa was growing fast and when *The Bedsitting Room* closed we went to Lisbon for a family holiday, for me the first of many visits to that beautiful Lusitanian land. At Highgate we entertained many of the Australian painters who had set up their studios nearby, and my closest neighbour was John Perceval, Arthur Boyd's brother-in-law, an old friend from Melbourne. John was a brilliant painter and ceramic sculptor, but he had started drinking heavily and developed an alcoholic *folie de grandeur*, disdaining all drinks except Johnny Walker Black Label, and I became very worried about him. He missed the Australian sunshine but contrived, in his flickering paintings, to make Highgate Wood resemble the bush.

A visitor of this period was Patrick White, whose early novels I hugely admired. Patrick and his companion, Manoly Lascaris, had loyally come to see *The Bedsitting Room* but were politely non-committal in the dressing-room afterwards. Patrick's aged mother still lived somewhere in Kensington, perhaps in a mansion flat next door to Miss Amy Halford. He was very censorious, indeed toffee-nosed, about Australians living abroad, however temporarily, even though he had lived in London and Greece for large chunks of the thirties and forties. After one of these chauvinistic outbursts, Manoly interjected: 'But Patrick, you know you hate Australia!' Patrick shot him his cold dowager's stare.

He had dedicated a short story to me and we invited him to lunch with Sidney Nolan. Sidney's wife Cynthia, a complex and saturnine woman, was excessively protective of her husband's privacy and their unlisted number was always being changed.

Later on the day of White's visit, after several bottles of Madeira, Nolan suggested that I telephone Cynthia and invite her to join us for dinner in the West End, but I had no sooner announced myself than she barked: 'How did you get this number? You can't speak to Siddy anyway, he's busy in his studio and doesn't want to be disturbed!' The phone slammed down. Poor Cynthia never knew her busy husband was standing right beside me, or that Patrick White, the great Australian novelist, was anxious to dine with her. She would have been mortified had she known, avid lion-hunter that she was.

In 1960 the wardrobe of Heather Firbank, sister of the novelist Ronald Firbank, was sold and dispersed. Gowns by Worth, Mme Vionnet and Patou, some never worn, others worn no more than once and all in storage, were snapped up by the Victoria and Albert Museum, and the remnant knocked down to the public. From this, on some absurd caprice, I bought a pair of fine cambric bloomers trimmed with lace and blue ribbon, and bearing Miss Firbank's embroidered monogram.

Once, as Patrick White and I talked about our mutual attraction to the author of *Valmouth* and *The Flower Beneath the Foot*, I showed him the Firbankian knickers. Never before or since have I seen him so excited, but as he tremulously fingered the fabric, his delight changed to an expression of regret. At the evanescence of this flimsy textile? Or perhaps also at the size of the garment – impossibly slighter than his own substantial loins.

Later I asked Patrick, who found the author's mantle an

intolerable burden, what he would prefer to do. 'Look after a few goats on a Greek hillside,' he said. 'I'd like to be a goatherd.' Years later, though in Sydney, surrounded by a small and bleating herd of caprine disciples who munched and swallowed everything he said, his dream came true.

Peter Cook, it seemed, was still a fan of mine, even after my ill-starred appearance at his club. He was back from New York, and he asked me if I felt like writing something for *Private Eye*.

A comic strip. When I lived in the Notting Hill basement I had made a gramophone record which included the plaintive monologue of an Earl's Court Australian; a youth called Buster Thompson who huddled together with his mates in an Anglophobic ghetto, drinking Foster's Lager, a Melbourne-brewed beer, which in those days could be obtained only at one pub in London. Cook thought that a character like this, an Australian innocent abroad, would make a diverting comic-strip hero, and he introduced me to a New Zealand artist called Nicholas Garland.

Humphries by Garland   Garland by Humphries

The origin of the name Barry McKenzie has been amiably disputed. I think Peter Cook came up with it, though my own name must have obviously inspired it. Nick certainly created the 'look' of the character: tall, gangling and lantern-jawed. I felt he should seem rather old-fashioned in a double-breasted suit and tie, like the former Australian Prime Minister Sir Robert Menzies, and we decided he would always wear a broad-brimmed hat, like the rural Australians sported when they came to town for the Royal Agricultural Show. It went without saying that Barry, like Buster Thompson, would have to be a *thirsty* person, with an idiosyncratic taste for the most obscure lager in the world: Foster's.

After a few script conferences Garland started drawing up the first strip, which showed Barry's arrival in England (by boat):

'' 'Streuth, this trip isn't the full two bob, I can't even see the flamin' White Cliffs!'

'This is Southampton, not Dover,' says a snooty British stereotype in a bowler hat, who is standing next to Barry at the rail.

Peter Cook wanted as much of the colourful Australian idiom as possible in the dialogue, although I realized that a great deal of it would be obscure to a British audience. It was necessary, therefore, in order to initiate readers into the mysteries of Australian colloquial speech, for Barry to repeat certain actions and forms of behaviour. For example, Australians had an enormous vocabulary celebrating incontinence in all its infinite variety. Thus Barry was always 'shaking hands with the wife's best friend', 'pointing Percy at the porcelain', 'going where the big nobs hang out', 'shaking hands with the unemployed', and 'draining the dragon'.

Since he mostly subsisted on a liquid diet, he was invariably 'chundering', a term I had first heard at Melbourne University, and which was not in general currency. If he wasn't 'chundering', Barry might be 'laughing at the ground', 'playing the whale', 'parking the tiger', enjoying a 'liquid laugh' or a

Barry Humphries in the sixties, as drawn by Gerald Scarfe

'technicolour yawn' or, simply, 'calling'. One could, depending
on the regurgitative pressure of the last few drinks, 'call' for
Bert, Herb, Charles or Ruth. Generally speaking, the most
painful form of projectile vomiting would be to call
'Rooooooth!' After a good party, healthy young Australians of
this generation would casually inquire of each other: 'What did
you call last night?'

Although the adventures of Barry McKenzie, when they first
appeared in *Private Eye*, met with the same stunned indifference
as my nightclub act, Peter Cook and his editor Richard Ingrams
nursed the strip along. Ingrams was an unkempt and acne-
flecked young man, rather like a neglected grammar-school
boarder, with dried shaving lather on his lobes and a demeanour
that suggested cricket and Best Bitter. As a National Serviceman
in the Korean War, he had made a brief excursion into adult
life and then wisely retreated to the more congenial milieu of
the sixth-form common-room, which the offices of *Private Eye*

resembled. In these raffish premises in Greek Street one could usually find the jovial actor and artist William Rushton, the poet Christopher Logue, who contributed a regular column, and often that guru of the *Eye*, the amiable Irish rogue Claude Cockburn. He was what used to be called a 'card', and had been married to Jean Ross, Isherwood's 'Sally Bowles'. Claude was that anachronism, a Communist with a sense of humour, who liked nothing better than to dish up propaganda as truth.

Also drifting through the office were sympathetic people like John Wells, the Eton Schoolmaster and wag, caricaturist Gerald Scarfe, the crusader Paul Foot, the pedagogue Christopher Booker and the gifted cartoonist Barry Fantoni. Unkindly nicknamed 'Sycophantoni' behind his back, he was the only member of Ingrams' circle from the wrong side of the tracks. However he made up for this solecism by laughing immoderately at all the Editor's jokes. Ingrams had a gruff and diffident charm, but also, as I later discovered, a strongly puritanical streak; so that whilst he and his cronies freely indulged, on the pages of the *Eye*, a scatological vein of schoolboy humour, he looked rather askance at jokes about sex. Luckily there was enough childish and excremental ribaldry in Barry McKenzie to satisfy the editorial policy.

After a few months Garland and I got into our stride, the drawings became surer and my balloons bigger. Our hero had started soliloquizing rather in the manner of one of my long-winded stage characters, yet whereas in the theatre I tried to get the dialect and vocabulary of a class or profession exactly right, 'Bazza' spoke in an invented idiom; a synthetic Australian compounded of schoolboy, Service, old-fashioned proletarian and even made-up slang. The comic strip ran, with a few interruptions, almost until the end of the decade and spanned that period of the sixties to which the Press attached the epithet 'swinging'.

Whenever I was on tour in Australia, I had to keep Nick Garland well supplied with material so that the strip could continue uninterrupted during my absence, but sometimes the

text dried up and I received urgent telegrams and entreaties from artist and editor. It was rather like the old Bunyip days, when I perilously left the writing of the script to the eleventh hour. On one occasion Garland had only enough dialogue left for half a strip so, rather wittily, he drew Barry McKenzie with empty balloons and a vignette of me lying unconcerned on a tropical beach with a can of something in my hand.

Richard Ingrams was extremely tolerant of these lapses and lacunae, although once or twice I was politely warned that the strip would have to be axed if I kept failing my deadlines. It may also be true to say that editorial good will and our very occasional raises in salary could have been due to Barry McKenzie's growing popularity; it might even have sold a few more *Private Eyes*! Although I had signally failed to make any impression on English audiences with my Australian stage act, it looked as though I might be reaching another audience through this comic-strip character who bore my name.

Only recently have I perceived the autobiographical elements in Barry McKenzie's adventures. Like Barry, as he wanders through the moral quicksands of the sixties, I felt I was always on the periphery of 'the action', waiting for something to happen. Like McKenzie also, I seemed to drink too much in those very situations when it would have been more prudent had I not drunk at all. It was a therapeutic release for me, at the time, to write scornfully about the affectations and excesses

Cartoon rough by Barry Humphries: 'Barry McKenzie,
dental practitioner'

of the 'poor old Poms', with whom I, Barry Humphries the artist, had failed to ingratiate myself.

Barry McKenzie's amorous ambitions were another matter. Always in a state of heightened sexual erethism, he invariably failed to make contact with the desired object or completely misread any signs of encouragement. In one episode Barry, confronted with an open invitation from a young woman, suddenly discovers that she is a fellow Australian. His desire turns to ashes and he showers upon her a vituperative diatribe, reminding her of her family back home, the fragility of her mother's varicose veins, her disabled brother Craig, her Sunday-school precepts and, even more obscurely, the threat of modern promiscuity to Australia's unblemished War Record. Here it is difficult to see exact resemblances between Barry's conduct and my own. There is no doubt, however, that I did from time to time, and after too many 'tubes' or 'cold ones' or when I may have been as full as a fairy's Filofax, put my hand on the wrong knee.

As the sixties progressed and my own life became more unmanageable, so did Barry McKenzie's. My first encounters with pyschotherapists are echoed in the comic as Barry, confined by a strait-jacket and interrogated by a slightly crazed, womanizing and Jewish doctor (Meyer de Lamphrey), rails against the injustice of the Brits. In a later episode the doctor himself is seen to have a drinking problem and there is an unpleasant accident, later transferred spectacularly to the cinema screen and much emulated thereafter, when Barry calls copiously for Ruth on the head of his therapist.

Spiked

J OAN LITTLEWOOD'S PRODUCTIONS, and Miss Littlewood
herself, had been for so many seasons a feature of the
London West End theatre, that any wonder at the extent of her
vogue would have seemed ignorant or provincial. I had known
her for some years and while I was still appearing in *The
Bedsitting Room* had even 'moonlighted' in a pantomime by
Peter Shaffer which she directed at Wyndhams Theatre. The
pantomime, which only played matinées, came down just in
time for me to sprint across Leicester Square to my evening job
at the Comedy.

Joan always wore the same clothes; a long pleated grey skirt
and a short grey jacket nipped in at the waist, like the already
very old-fashioned 'New Look'. White sockettes, flat shoes and
a knitted hat completed her habitual ensemble and spared her
from any accusations of being over-dressed for the rigours of
rehearsal. One of her early successes had been *Fings Ain't What
They Used to Be*, a musical by Frank Norman and Lionel Bart,
and Frank had just written another play with a Soho theme,
called *A Kayf Up West*, which Joan was to direct at a theatre
she had resurrected: the Theatre Royal at Stratford, in the East
End of London.

Frank Norman was an *habitué* of the Colony Room and the
French Pub and I had always been rather scared of him, since

his good-looking but fleshy face bore the scar of a razor slash, and he affected a surly manner, liking to 'put the mockers' on people he distrusted, or perhaps even feared. He had written several vivid and original books about his childhood and youth in boys' homes and Borstals, and had been taken up by the literary Establishment as a sort of home-grown, and anodyne, Genet. Frank usually wore a cashmere overcoat – a symbol of his success – and he was fond of flexing his shoulders like a pugilist under the fabric, but all of this belied a good-natured and sensitive man.

Joan invited me to join the company and play about four roles. She could coax remarkable performances out of very unlikely people and she was not over-fond of 'professional' actors. I suited her well; I was unlikely, and not too professional, but an even more unlikely member of the company was Jeffrey Bernard, who to everybody's surprise, including his own, gave one of the best performances in the show. I played, amongst other things, a Greek café proprietor, an old lag, a sinister toff called Lord Sexkilling and a nun. Bamber Gascoigne, who had found me 'soporific' at the Establishment, redeemed himself in his review of *A Kayf Up West* by calling my performance 'the main pleasure' of the evening.

On the tube journey home from Stratford East, Jeffrey and I enjoyed asking commuting Cockneys if they would kindly direct us to the buffet car. One needs to have had quite a few drinks to find this as hilarious as we did.

We did not, as we had fervently hoped, transfer to the West End, though Jeff and I spent a great deal of time there all the same, especially in dives like the Kismet; a dark basement in Cranbourne Street, which had once been an Indian restaurant and retained the old, curry-impregnated flock wallpaper. The Kismet was open during that inconvenient hiatus between three p.m., when the pubs closed, and 5.30, when they re-opened. Whenever I called in there for a quick drink on my own, I would notice several solitary drinkers whom life seemed to have passed by. It was distressing to see them still there several hours later.

A publisher called Paul Elek got in touch with me out of the blue to edit a volume of literary bad taste. It was to be called *Bizarre*, since much of the material was to be culled from a French periodical of that name, but ultimately I drew most of the book's elements from my own collection of oddities and curiosa. It was a vulgar and dissonant gallimaufry of *fin de siècle* decadence, kitsch, blasphemy, teratology and silliness, beautifully published. Most critics who reviewed it hated it. W. H. Smith refused to sell it and Philip Toynbee accused me of 'vile whimsicality'. It is not to my credit that as the sixties wore on many more books even viler and more whimsical were published in imitation of *Bizarre*.

I found myself, almost to my own surprise, in another Lionel Bart musical; a kind of industrial operetta with a fashionable Liverpool setting, called *Maggie May*. In the midst of this entertainment there was a scene in a club where a rock 'n' roll group performed a Beatles pastiche. But as well as a dash of the Beatles, there was also a dollop of Brecht in the person of myself as a sardonic tramp, with a drum on my back, cymbals between my knees and a harmonica wired to my lips. At intervals during the show, which was set in the docks, I would interrupt the action with an alienating chorus or two of the Weill-like 'Ballad of the Liverbird'. The money was wonderful, and the billing was not far below that of Miss Rachel Roberts, the star. I had, furthermore, taken special lessons to perfect my Scouse accent.

But when we opened in Manchester for the try-out, the play ran for over three hours. Ted Kotcheff, the director, had to make some drastic cuts and one of them was me. Thereafter, instead of materializing spookily in a spotlight throughout the evening, I now opened the show, and closed it. As Kenneth Haigh, the hero, lay on the stage fatally electrocuted, Miss Roberts sobbed and the dockers stood in a grieving semicircle around him, the ominous thump of my drum sounded in the wings, my cymbals whispered, and I shuffled to the centre of the stage to keen my valedictory lament. It was an affecting *coup de théâtre*, but the audience had to wait a long time for it. In fact, I had exactly two and a half hours in my dressing-room between appearances. If a member of the public was slightly late, they would miss my first entrance, and if they had a train to catch, they would miss my second.

Once we were installed at the Adelphi Theatre in the Strand, and the carefully pruned production was one of the hits of the season, I began to find my prolonged incarceration backstage irksome. I shared a dressing-room with three other actors who had lots of scenes and songs, and they darted in and out all night. Once I had sung my opening number I would slip the heavy drum off my shoulders, unbuckle my cymbals and slump at my dressing-table with a cigarette and a book. After a few weeks of this I decided it was probably healthier to go for a walk, but my walk was usually quite a short one, from the stage door to Yates's Wine Lodge next door to the theatre. Yates's was a darkly timbered Tudor-style corridor between Maiden Lane and the Strand. Its clientele was mostly old and Irish, and it served an inexpensive port in half-pint glasses which always seemed to contain a quarter of an inch of gritty brown sediment. Propping up the bar in this gloomy establishment soon palled, and I began to amuse myself by visiting the cinema opposite, where vaguely indecent Continental films were exhibited. I would always keep one eye on the luminous dial of my watch so as to be back in the theatre in plenty of time to re-apply my tramp's makeup, and to be harnessed with my heavy musical accoutrements.

After a few months, I began going to the theatre, and occasionally to parties. Often I would miss little more than the first fifteen minutes of the play, and, leaving immediately the curtain fell, I could make it comfortably back to the Adelphi. The parties were riskier. One was in Hampstead at Olivia Manning's, so I was obliged to keep a taxi waiting while I had a few drinks before retracing my journey. Another party was in Putney.

A close friend of mine at this period was Georgina Barker,

the daughter of George Barker the poet. Her mother was
Elizabeth Smart, my sponsor at the Colony Room. Georgina
was an acquaintance of Augustus John's family and, when she
told me they were throwing a big party at their Putney home, I
airily agreed to call in for a drink. I did not bargain for the fog.
That night I had not retained my taxi and when, after an hour
or so of dancing and drinking, I asked my hostess if we could
call a cab she laughed; 'Have you seen the weather out there?'
she said, pointing through the leadlights at the swirling
Thames-side mists. 'You must be joking!' I rushed out into the
night and by a sheer miracle discovered a taxi, which after
much haggling agreed to convey me, at a snail's pace, to the
West End. Thanking a God whom I had rarely addressed in
recent years for my deliverance, I reached the theatre with
barely enough time to transform myself into the Balladeer.
When the curtain fell, the company manager warned me that I
had caused some anxiety to himself and to Cuthbert, my
dresser, and that I was not to leave the theatre ever again under
any circumstances.

My old friend Spike Milligan was about to open at the Comedy
in *Son of Oblomov*, an eccentric version of a Russian classic.
'Come to the opening night,' he urged me. 'We don't go up
until 8.15, and when we come down you'll still have a quarter
of an hour to get to the Adelphi.' I shook my head, but Spike
was wearing his hurt look. 'Come and see me in my dressing-
room tomorrow night and I'll give you a ticket near the exit,
and don't be late, old cobbler.'

I knew I could probably sneak out of my show one more
time and Cuthbert, if suitably recompensed, would cover for
me. After all, I reasoned, I wasn't going to Putney, or drinking.
And if I left Spike's exit door dead on 10.30, I would be almost
over-prepared for my final dirge.

When Spike handed me my ticket, he gave me a glass of *vin
rosé* as well, and a vitamin tablet. 'I don't take pills,' I said
with the prudery of all drinkers. 'It's not a pill, mate,' said

Spike, 'it's a food. These are great for the liver.' My liver had been aching slightly, or the part of my body where I imagined my liver to be, so I swallowed the damn thing, washed it down with wine and wished my friend good luck.

Trust Spike to turn everything upside down, I reflected from my seat in the stalls. On stage the actors, with Milligan in the middle, were bowing to the audience and the curtain was rising and falling. The public, joining in the joke of a finale at the beginning, were applauding wildly. But something was wrong. People near me were getting up, looking for their coats and . . . *leaving*. The curtain remained down, and the house-lights came up. A chill seemed to grip my heart. 'Was this the end of the show?' I thought. 'Have I been asleep?' My mouth felt furry. That tablet . . . ? I had left my watch on my dressing-table back at the Adelphi to heighten the illusion of my presence thereabouts, but now I desperately needed to know the time. Clutching the wrist of a startled theatre-goer on my right, I stared at the face of his watch; *it was 10.55!* In five minutes I was due to appear, elaborately disguised as an old man wearing a drum on his back, cymbals on his knees and a harmonica, before an expectant audience and the full cast of a West End show, on the stage of a theatre on the other side of town!

I hurtled out of the exit into the street. Amazingly, at that moment a vacant cab rounded the corner. Pressing a salad of money into the driver's hand I leapt into the car and we careened in the direction of the Adelphi Theatre. I was drenched with sweat as we turned the corner into Maiden Lane on a couple of wheels and I saw the company manager standing in the street, beside him my poor little dresser holding a drum and a cymbal. I fell out of the taxi and bolted in the stage door to the concrete steps which led down two flights to the stage level, and, as I ran, Cuthbert hitched various instruments over my flailing limbs. The enormous drum, only tenuously attached to my back, crashed against the stairwell, as with a free hand I slapped some blackish greasepaint arbitrarily across my face until at last I stood, panting in the wings.

On stage all was silent. Uncannily silent. Kenneth Haigh lay prone, the dockers stood in a grieving tableau and Miss Roberts sobbed. How long they had kept their vigil I knew not; but the thump and crash of my descent to the stage must surely have transmitted itself to the audience. I took a deep breath and shuffled to the centre of the stage, trailing my abridged equipment. I glanced into the orchestra pit where Marcus, the musical director, gaped up at me. I realized, only then, that I was wearing modern dress; a figure who bore no resemblance whatever to the ragged old Liverbird who had opened the show two and a half long hours before. 'Perhaps they will read something allegorical into this,' I reflected, as I croaked my closing lines.

The company, who held me in a kind of amused contempt, let me off rather lightly, but I was hauled over the coals by Mr Bernard Delfont, and rightly so.

The next day Spike phoned and asked me how I had enjoyed the show. 'It was great,' I lied. 'Did you make the Adelphi in plenty of time?' he probed. 'With time to spare,' I said. Did I imagine it, or was there a little silence on the other end of the phone? And was it just a vitamin tablet, and an innocent glass of wine? Who will ever know?

Boudoir Fingers

THE MEMORY OF this incident had barely faded when I found myself travelling a very great distance indeed every night after the show. I was no longer living at home, but in a large hospital. Several doctors had conferred together over my 'case' and it had been decided that I should spend my days and nights in 'treatment' at Halliwick Hospital in remote Winchmore Hill, with special permission to commute every evening to the theatre to perform my job. There was a strict curfew governing the time of my nightly return to the institution. I had been given a course of capsules, and the doctors had told me to drink very little alcohol with them or, preferably, none at all. Since it was absurd and impractical to adopt the latter recommendation, I settled for a loose interpretation of the former.

This dramatic change in my circumstances had sprung from an unfortunate confrontation between Rosalind and my friend Georgina, whom I had hoped might never meet. A psychiatrist, who was called in to adjudicate in this delicate matter, decided that I had gone mad, and that I would benefit greatly from a sojourn in neutral territory; a lunatic asylum. I had had no previous experience of psychotherapy, or anti-depressive drugs, and had only once been in hospital, with a fractured arm, so the novelty of my new predicament kept me toeing the line – for the time being.

Although I was managing to give a good performance on stage every night – or thought I was – the rest of my life seemed to have slipped away into the realm of fiction, so that the things that were now happening to me seemed almost to be happening to someone else. The theatre was reality; reality was theatre. Above all, I felt it was prudent to do as I was told; and it was strangely comforting to slide back into a kind of acquiescent second childhood.

I have no memory whatsoever of what I told my therapists during many interviews. Monstrous self-justifications, probably, and grotesque alibis. If my increasingly abnormal drinking was ever mentioned, I was only too happy to chat about it, and it was almost with relief that I heard one doctor say he thought it might be interesting to investigate, over a long period of time, the causes of my growing obsession. It was the *long period of time* that appealed to me. I knew I was in good, sound medical hands when nobody told me to stop.

Although none of the doctors was explicit, I felt very strongly that they wanted me to give up one, or all, of my pleasures. God-given pleasures to which I was surely entitled, even if they did not give me very much pleasure.

I was not in Halliwick for long; in fact, after a month I was expelled as incorrigible, because, with my busy life and my many nocturnal preoccupations, I found it impossible to abide by the curfew. Some nights I would appear like a phantom on Georgina's doorstep, and at others I would implore Rosalind to let me come home. A kind and thoughtful friend of mine, seeking to cheer me up, would sometimes drive me back to the hospital in his car; and to sustain us for the long journey north we would stop for a nightcap or two at various bars, clubs and discothèques. I felt that the assortment of tablets that I had been given may have been mis-prescribed, since they seemed to interfere with the pleasant effects of alcohol. In the interests of my health, therefore, I stopped taking them.

By the time I was expelled from hospital we had moved house to Little Venice in Maida Vale, one of London's prettiest neighbourhoods. In my absence, the move had been arranged by Rosalind since we had slowly, and almost with relief, assumed the roles of efficient Organizer/Nurse and helpless Artist/Invalid. No sooner were we established in this charming maisonette than Clifford Hocking arrived from Australia and suggested another tour, this time in big theatres. I wondered if this was part of a conspiracy to get me as far away from Georgina's flat in Westbourne Terrace as possible.

It was over three years since I had last appeared in Australia; three years since I had last seen my parents, my brothers and sisters, and my old friends. I realized that I wanted nothing more in the world than to go home, at least for a while; and the prospect of writing a new show seemed to dispel all my daemons and provide me with a positive view of the future, not just for me, but for my growing family, for it was at this time that my second daughter, Emily, was born.

Often, I took Tessa for afternoon walks along the Regent's Canal, and on one of these, beside the Edgware Road, I spied a very interesting old house set back behind a neglected garden. An overgrown blue plaque informed the curious – and they were few – that the house had belonged to the Edwardian sculptor Sir Alfred Gilbert, whose masterpiece is the statue of Eros in Piccadilly Circus. The house and grounds were in a state of uttermost desuetude, and I wandered up the ruined driveway until I could see a building, slightly separate from the house, which had obviously been the artist's studio. There was not a soul about, so I made a pile of bricks and boxes and, clambering on top of them, I just managed to peep in at the high studio window. I saw an astonishing sight. There, ranged around this enormous room, were allegorical carvings and huge plaster casts, left as if the artist had just walked out of the room; and yet I knew that he had been dead since 1934. But there was one thing which was alarmingly wrong. The sculptures had been horribly vandalized: heads lay shattered on the floor, hands smashed off at the wrist, and there were fragments of stone, plaster and gypsum everywhere, as though some vindictive poltergeist had been let loose in the studio.

I was startled by a man's voice, gruffly reminding me that I was on private property, and asking me my business. It was a grizzled old caretaker who lived in some kind of shed behind a hedge, which I had failed to notice. I apologized for trespassing, but told him of the terrible sight I had just seen through the studio window. Had vandals broken in? I asked. He shook his head. It was the last Lady Gilbert, he explained. For years after her husband's death she would visit the studio every morning, and, with a stout iron hammer, fastidiously mutilate her husband's surviving works. 'She was at it for years, Governor; *at it for years!*'

I felt blenched and shaken as we walked back down Maida Avenue. Why should a woman, however wronged, bitter or envious, murder a man's work? Was it in the hope that by destroying this extension of the man she might somehow succeed in destroying him? But I was young and, happily, still had more illusions than I thought.

At one Christmas during the Little Venice years, I decided, rather magnanimously, to give my bank manager a seasonal gift. I carefully selected a bottle of Black Label Johnny Walker Whisky and had it gift-wrapped for presentation to the unsmiling, silver-haired curmudgeon who presisded over my 'active' account at the local bank. Alas, when I arrived on the morning of Christmas Eve with my tinselled offering, his secretary told me rather sourly that he was engaged with another client. I decided to wait and, instead of loitering in the banking hall, I found a comfortable bench round the corner beside the canal. The time seemed to drag, and I decided without too much deliberation that a very small swig from the bank manager's Christmas present would go unnoticed, especially if I was careful in replacing the elaborate wrapping. This proved easy, and after some fastidious peeling of sellotape and surreptitious uncorking I drank a yuletide toast to Mr Rogerson in his own liquor, with a epiglottal sensation that I imagined to be not unlike that regularly experienced by knife-swallowers.

By the time I got back to the bank the secretary told me Mr Rogerson had waited, but was now with another client and would be free in an hour. From beneath his mahogany door cigar smoke seeped, and I imagined the manager behind his gift-laden desk, sharing a Christmas Monte Cristo with some crass client with an account in obscene credit. Promising to return sixty minutes hence, I repaired to my bench round the corner and gazed on the sparkling canal. 'Why not?' I reflected, once more delicately tackling the gift-wrapped whisky. By the time I had finished the level in the bottle did look distinctly lower than it should, but I decided that was a detail which Mr Rogerson was unlikely to notice in the seasonal excitement. Back at the bank Miss Powell shook her head. I had missed him again. In fact, Mr Rogerson had gone around the corner for a drink with an old client but would be back directly. Would I . . . ? But I was gone.

By now the wrapping round the Johnny Walker bottle looked like last year's Christmas paper. The selloptape had lost its stickiness, and the silver ribbon and the red rosette had blown off into the canal as I sampled more deeply my placatory gift. I had, however, effortlessly crossed that invisible line beyond which such things ceased to matter. Besides, if someone gave me half a bottle of scotch for Christmas I would be exceedingly grateful. It was lunchtime when I returned, and Mr Rogerson, who had been in and who had waited, could wait no more, and had departed for lunch. Quickly I scribbled an effusive and insincere note on a pay-in form, and, thrusting my dishevelled and radically depleted gift into Miss Powell's hands, I dashed out of the bank for my own lunch and some leisurely shopping in the West End.

On subsequent and inevitably tense meetings Mr Rogerson, rather rudely, neither made reference to my gift nor expressed his gratitude for the inch and a half of festive cordial from which I had so generously abstained.

*

At last the time came to embark on the tour. We found an Australian journalist to house-sit our flat, and, with a French au-pair girl called Dominique, we all set off for Australia, this time by aeroplane. Since Qantas then flew on an interesting route via Mexico and Tahiti, I decided to stop off for a few weeks in both places to finish writing my show, which I had already started in Little Venice. It was to be called *Excuse I*, one of my favourite genteelisms, long remembered from talc-scented, Colombine-caramel-rustling matinées in Melbourne, as tardy floral ladies squeezed past our knees; ' *'Scuse I, 'scuse I, 'scuse I.'*

If not completely chastened by the recent events in my life, I may have been more than a little frightened; so I decided not to drink alcohol for a while. In retrospect, I am surprised that I found this so easy, but I see now that I was merely postponing the next inevitable drink. Besides, it was amusing to see the expression of incredulity on people's faces when I sanctimoniously said at dinner parties, 'Not for me, thanks, I don't use that stuff.' That was what teetotallers said all the time, I presumed, but they didn't feel as good as I did because they *meant* it, poor wretches.

None the less, my brain cleared and the ideas seemed to flow. My new stage characters included two outdoor hedonists, a 'surfie' extolling the cult of the waves in his almost incomprehensible jargon, and a loutish Public School skier, pursuing 'snow bunnies' on the slopes and in the chalets of Australia's newly developed Alpine resorts. Another invention was Neil Singleton, a character who gave a party on stage and did a lot of talking to invisible acquaintances. It was a good acting exercise and was bound to impress people, even if I did not perform it all that well. You don't really have to try very hard for critics to write: *'He peopled the stage.'*

Some insisted they knew Neil Singleton. He was a left-wing academic, not very high up in his department, an advertising executive perhaps, or a journalist with literary aspirations that never quite came off. Longish hair, and that fringe of beard around the chin, *sans* moustache, identified him very precisely according to my 1965 audience at the old Theatre Royal, Sydney. Someone else in Melbourne was positive that Neil was inspired by an annoyingly successful art critic, whilst the art critic in question asked me confidentially if a tall, bearded radio playwright had recognized himself yet, or was going to sue.

I had no idea how many Neil Singletons would emerge from the woodwork. Until the mid-sixties Neil's class of puritan, querulous, turtle-necked, elbow-patched, pipe-sucking, wife-cheating, wine-buffing, abstract-art-digging highbrow had been amongst my most enthusiastic fans, eager for a chuckle at the middle-class effusions of Edna, Sandy and the other Australians they never met at their own parties. Deep chagrin greeted this impersonation; and it was only after the birth of Neil Singleton that the arty periodicals began to launch upon me their rather snide attacks.

There was an uncanny moment after a matinée in Sydney when an importunate journalist, complete with fringy beard, muscled his way into my dressing-room dragging a reluctant and waif-like spouse. He *was* Neil Singleton, my fictitious character, dreamt up, or so I thought, whilst taking the waters at Puruandiro, in Michoacan. He seemed to be actually *imploding* with rage, which I gathered from his hostile and confused manner, had something to do with me living in England and having the cheek to write rude things about contemporary Australia.

'There's a cultural renaissance going on here, y'know,' he declared truculently. 'Things don't just stand still here because guys like you piss off to the bright lights and easy money in England. You're living in the past, mate, and so are your characters.'

'But surely the reaction of that audience out there today showed some recognition?' I interjected. 'I mean, would they laugh so much at people they didn't know?'

'They weren't all laughing, mate,' said the clone with a

complacent smirk. 'A lot of people I know are very worried about the direction your stuff is taking. We think it lacks . . .' He seemed to be searching for a word, and, when he finally found it, he spat it out so violently a little geodesic dome of spittle hit my nose '. . . *relevance!*'

I never saw this captious fellow again, but over the intervening years he has regularly flown into print with the same old carpings, to which have been added the fashionable accusations of racism, sexism, élitism, Fascism and misanthropy. I took to quietly observing this man's journalistic career, and when a novel failed and then a rock opera, I saw the full extent of his tragedy. He wanted so very much, I realized, to be an artist; a part of the Cultural Renaissance he was always on about. There is, perhaps, no more dangerous man in the world than the man with the sensibilities of an artist but without creative talent. With luck such men make wonderful theatrical impresarios and interior decorators, or else they become mass murderers or critics.

Excuse I seemed to hit the spot with Australian audiences and there were, indeed, long queues for tickets at the box offices in Sydney and in Melbourne. Edna, the character I had once thought of dropping altogether, had come up in the world. It was almost as though she were developing a life of her own, over which I had little, if any, control. She was also building up her part. On my first tour she had appeared on stage only once, but this time she opened and closed the show. In *A Nice Night's Entertainment* she had treated the audience to an old-fashioned slide evening, but this time she showed a short home-movie of her peregrinations around London, drawing attention as often as possible to Royal edifices.

Edna wore a different dress in the second half to the first; a long blue satin number, and a hat with one of those short projecting veils known as a 'fascinator'. She had also made a significant change in her appearance, by adopting a pair of upturned *diamanté* spectacles. These had no lenses and were as cosmetic as the moustache of Groucho Marx, but they suddenly invested her face with a sharper, beady-eyed and predatory look. They were also the kind of glasses which more fashionable ladies in the audience wore. From then on Edna's 'look' began slowly to converge with that of her better-dressed patrons. From having been, at her beginnings, a comical frump, she was now almost as attractively attired as the ladies at her matinées. Today – though this would have been beyond her wildest dreams – she is better dressed than the richest and most fashionable women in her audience.

It was during my extended season at the Theatre Royal in Sydney that Mrs Everage took pity on a woman in the front row who had been covetously eyeing the vase of 'gladdies' on the piano all night. At last, in exasperation, Edna hurled the dripping blooms with full force at their sedentary admirer, who unselfishly passed them to her neighbours down the row. It was the sight of an audience spontaneously wagging these evocative flesh-pink spears in time to the final number that inspired Edna to 'keep it in'. No show of hers is now complete without ritualistic gladdie-waving in the finale, and sometimes as many as two hundred gladioli, imported from plantations as far distant as Brazil, Queensland, Malta and Mexico, are showered nightly on the stalls, or catapulted by giant slings or cannons into the dress circle.

'Our Joan' Sutherland had just toured her homeland, and after singing through a comparatively highbrow repertoire, had endeared herself to those who might otherwise have pigeon-holed her in the expatriate 'traitor' category, by singing 'Home Sweet Home' as an encore. Edna did the same, and it was to this sentimental air that the sea of glads so suggestively oscil-lated. The standing, saluting, the trembling and the twitching and all the other virtuoso variations were to come in later years.

Although my recent compilation, *Bizarre*, was available in Australian bookshops, *Private Eye* was not. It was banned. The reason it was banned was because it contained my comic strip, Barry McKenzie, which was officially deemed obscene. Barry's occasional expletives, which were never worse than 'shit', were none the less thought to be demeaning to Australia's international image as a *nice* country. The word 'image' was just beginning to be bandied around, and in some prudish circles there was a fear, amounting to paranoia, that the closely guarded secret of Australian vulgarity might leak out.

But it had happened already. In 1946 a traumatic event had taken place. Debates and Question Time from the House of Representatives in the Australian capital, Canberra, were for the first time broadcast to the Nation. With shame and horror, Australians heard the voices and vocabulary of their governors.

Initially, this was thought to be a radio hoax perpetrated by students or some antipodean Orson Welles, in order to frighten listeners into thinking their country was run by yahoos and guttersnipes, but slowly the truth dawned. This was what our elected politicians and their opposition really sounded like! *This was us.* There were a few parliamentary pansies, it was true, who spoke in more expensive and grandiloquent tones, but they were a drop in the ocean. The enormous and prospering Middle Classes were appalled. What was the use of teaching the kiddies nice manners when our politicians carried on like that, squawking and braying like livestock? It was a crime against Niceness.

So was Barry McKenzie. Yet, despite the ban, the comic strip already had a large underground popularity; Bazza talked dirty with lyricism; he revived a dialect that had been vitiated by respectability, he was the Voice of Vulgarity.

After a triumphant tour, we returned to London slowly via Bangkok, Beirut and Prague. In Bangkok I committed a terrible gaffe by buying a durian fruit at the market and bringing it back to our room in the hotel. Supposedly an aphrodisiac, this fruit has a strong, gamey odour, or, as I preferred to imagine, the odour of the hircine bed-linen of an imaginative couple. I was not aware that durian was strictly banned in all good hotels, and, having been sniffed out by the management, we were, *en famille*, asked to leave.

Back in London at last, we settled into our lovely, if rented canal-side house, the walls of which were soon covered with pictures, many by our Australian friends. Throughout the mid-sixties I wrote a weekly column for Rupert Murdoch's national newspaper, the *Australian*. It was dispatched, often precariously close to its deadline, from London, but often too from wherever I happened to be, like Lisbon or Beirut, Vienna or Mexico City. But now I wondered what my next real job would be, and I did not have to wait long.

The Satire Movement, launched so brilliantly in the early sixties by Peter Cook, was by now showing signs of enervation, but late-night television 'satire' continued. I was invited by the BBC to join the cast of a new weekly programme to be called *The Late Show*. The other actors and writers were veterans of the Establishment like John Bird, Eleanor Bron and John Fortune, or *Private Eye aficionados* like John Wells and me, and our little troupe was supplemented by two Americans, Andrew Duncan and Tony Holland. A further and most unlikely addition to the cast was Malcolm Muggeridge, like a satyr in a dog-collar, who delivered a weekly sermon on some topical theme.

The programme was live and very uneven in quality and the producers had some difficulty in fitting me in to sketches, so that I mostly delivered songs and monologues, hastily written and often ill-rehearsed. The BBC Club was also a trap for people with my susceptibilities, though in retrospect it is extraordinary how many drunks, and convivial folk like myself, were officially tolerated, and managed to hold down respectable jobs.

The largesse of the BBC in this period was legendary, and for those of us without Jaguars, there was always a black radio cab at our disposal to take us to work, and to bring us home.

On leaving Television Centre at Shepherd's Bush for Maida Vale every evening, I was inclined to take advantage of the comfortable transport provided and break my journey at various places, not all of which were on my direct route home. Sometimes, for example, I might be so engrossed in some urgent discussion in a Soho bar that I would temporarily forget the black vehicle ticking away outside at the British taxpayer's expense. At other times I might call in at art exhibitions or late-closing secondhand bookshops, where time, so often, stands still. So long as the taxi was there, my conscience was salved; *I was on my way home.*

One evening, slumped in the back of the cab reading the *Evening Standard*, I half overheard the driver's radio broadcasting an emergency. Some child, apparently, had accidentally swallowed poison, and a driver in the vicinity of the accident was urgently needed to rush the victim to a hospital. The cabbie looked over his shoulder: 'Not far from your gaff, Governor,' he said. 'What's your number in Maida Avenue again?' I told him. 'Christ,' he said, stepping on it, 'looks like that kid's in one of your flats.' Then terror struck me. 'It's not a block of flats,' I said. 'It must be one of my daughters!' We screamed to a halt outside the house a couple of minutes later, and Dominique and Rosalind were outside the gate with little Emily, white-faced in a bundle. She had been prescribed some fancy anti-colic remedy with a strong sedative constituent, and had grabbed the bottle, carelessly left at child-level, while the nanny was out of the room. She must have guzzled most of it because she was unconscious as we rushed into the nearest hospital on the Harrow Road.

The poor little girl was there all night under observation, which gave me plenty of time to pace the floor and wonder what might have happened if my cab had not been a few short blocks from the emergency. I could easily have been on one of my selfish jaunts across town. *What if . . .?* I anguished. But Emily recovered and the au-pair lost her job. And yet the whole episode, which could have had such a tragic outcome, left me with an uneasy mind. '*I must remember I have a family, I must remember I have a family, I must remember I have a family,*' I said to myself, '*and not hear about it on a cab radio!*'

After a typical morning at the BBC, larking about the office, the cast of *The Late Show* would all wander down to Shepherd's Bush Green, where an old-fashioned Italian restaurant called Bertorelli's still stood. There we would have a long 'working lunch'. It was at one of these that I astonished my colleagues by drinking, at a single draught, a pint of crème de menthe, and being none the worse for it afterwards. I had secretly warned the waiter of my intention by phone, so that when I, amongst protests, demanded the drink, he brought me a pint glass brimming with water which had been thickened with sugar to give it a syrupy consistency, and to which a few drops of green vegetable dye had been added. After this feat it was generally thought that I had a remarkable head for strong drink, which was of course far from the truth, since I had begun to notice that my tolerance was waning.

I made two great friends on *The Late Show*, the composer Stanley Myers, and a young comedy writer called Ian Davidson with whom I work to this day. Stanley and I wrote what must have been the very first ecological song in history; it was dedicated to the Thames and it was called 'Filthy River'. Stanley arranged the song for a large string orchestra and choir – the BBC seemed to offer us unlimited funds – and I sang the refrain;

> River, Filthy River
> flowing,
> down to the filthy sea.
> Alone I stand
> gazing down at you,
> filthy river,
> you remind me of me!

The lyric rambled on in much the same manner as its subject

and there were lines like 'children paddle in you', rhyming with 'cattle straddle in you'.

But the sketch to which that cant word 'controversial' most aptly applied was a potted musical on the subject of the Pre-Raphaelite Brotherhood; an esoteric theme, even for a *very* late show. A young pianist and adroit lyricist called Richard Stilgoe collaborated with me on a scandalous segment in which the painter Millais, hearing a knock on the door, opens it to reveal a blow-up of Holman Hunt's famous painting, *The Light of the World*. Holding a lamp aloft, Jesus's lips suddenly animated, and he delivered a well-known commercial for pink household paraffin. Witless though this reads, it was visually very amusing to those unperturbed by blasphemy. However, the matter was raised in the House of Lords by the Archbishop of Canterbury, there were outraged letters to *The Times*. *The Late Show*, which was watched by so few, enjoyed a fleeting notoriety.

One evening after work, Stanley Myers and his girlfriend, and Rosalind and I, dined at a smart new restaurant in Holland Park called Chez Moi. The evening was going very well until Stanley suggested that it might be amusing if I did the trouser trick. This was a simple, and perhaps juvenile, stunt which worked only in a dignified or pretentious ambience. All that happened was that my pants fell down, apparently by accident, at a conspicuous moment. The 'trick' was that I should exhibit a high degree of embarrassment. That night, on my way back from the gents, I timed it to perfection. Barely a diner in that crowded restaurant could have missed it, and with a tremendous show of shame and apology and much bowing and shrugging I retreated to our table, where Stanley, at least, sat convulsed with laughter. Soon the maître d' was at our side, his lips to my ear. 'I am sorry, sir, but we must ask you please to leave the restaurant *immédiatement*. Lord Snowdon over zair is most offended by what just 'appen.' I had no time to protest, or even to get a view of Princess Margaret's outraged husband. Two burly waiters lifted me bodily from my chair and propelled me out the door into Addison Road, where I was obliged to loiter, undined and unwined. All I had to nibble were a few stale sponge fingers left over from my luncheon zabaglione at Bertorelli's, the kind which are sometimes known, rather suggestively, as Boudoir Fingers.

I attempted to get back into the restaurant, but the door was locked, and through a chink in a curtain I could see my wife and my friends enjoying a delicious meal as if nothing had happened; relieved, no doubt, that I was out of the way. On the corner of Addison Road was a telephone box and, after consulting a dog-eared directory, I dialled the number of the restaurant. The maître d's voice answered, ''Ullo, 'ullo?' I assumed the fluting tones of a middle-aged, upper-class Englishwoman. 'This is the Countess of Rosse speaking. My son Lord Snowdon is dining in your restaurant tonight. May I speak with him urgently please?' There was a long pause on the line and then a man's voice. 'Mother? How did you track me down here?' 'Tony, darling,' I trilled, 'there is a lovely and talented man in your restaurant tonight who has been far from well, his name is Barry Humphries and he has been accidentally locked out in the street. Please buy him and his party a large bottle of champagne and get the management to apologize.' On the other end of the line I could hear a voice cry: 'What, Mother? Who is this? *Who is this speaking?*' I rang off.

The door of Chez Moi, much to my chagrin, was not immediately thrown open, until Rosalind, Stanley and Yvonne at last emerged, but there was a sequel to this sorry incident, which will be told later.

Paint Over Rust

> Food glorious food
> Hot sausage and mustard
> While we're in the mood
> Cold jelly and custard . . .

The maddening chorus of small boys' voices leaked out of the tannoy in my dressing-room. Carefully I dabbed some spirit gum under my ginger moustache, which had come adrift after the last generous sip of South Australian claret. It was hard to believe I was back in the same old show, but this time I was Fagin – the lead! It seemed poetically just that I should accept the offer when it came along, and it was satisfying to have my name up there in lights in Piccadilly Circus.

The revival of Lionel Bart's classic musical at the Piccadilly Theatre suited me in every way, and now I even had two small daughters who were old enough to enjoy it. What a relief not to have to attend understudy rehearsals! The young actor who played Mr Sowerberry, the Undertaker – my old role – was no doubt dragged in to the theatre every day to rehearse with the boys, just as I had been, and no doubt also he watched me like a hawk – as I had watched Ron Moody – for signs of flagging health or laryngitis.

The so-called 'swinging sixties' were at their height. A few yards from the theatre, Piccadilly Circus in mid-summer was thronged with hippies from all over Europe, and on the steps surrounding Sir Alfred Gilbert's Eros, with nude, reasty feet the tie-dyed, patchouli-drenched girls from Holland and Germany and Denmark and North Finchley sprawled provocatively beside their unsuitable male companions. Gaudy, bell-bottomed tatterdemalions with guitars strummed plaintive songs about remote wars as tourists swarmed into Soho in search of Union Jack T-shirts, granny glasses, old ceremonial uniforms and Doors' albums.

During my season as Fagin I heard that auditions were being held down the road for the musical *Cabaret*, based on Christopher Isherwood's Berlin stories. I had listened to the Broadway recording, and rather fancied myself as the sinister Master of Ceremonies which Joel Gray had played in the original production. It would have been imprudent to inform my management that I was trying for a role in another show whilst I was still working successfully for them, so I enrolled for my audition under a false name.

I had not been to an audition for years, and I was as nervous as hell, but I launched into my big number 'Willkommen', with baleful energy, focusing my eyes on the small row of tiny red lights that winked in the blackness of the stalls; the terminal embers of the producers' cigarettes. At the end I just stood there as a disembodied voice reached me from the darkness. 'Thank you so much, Mr Harrison,' it drawled. 'Very nice interpretation indeed. I'm sorry we can't offer you anything in this particular show but please let us know when you have had some experience. NEXT!'

'*Experience!*' I muttered to myself, skulking angrily back up the Haymarket, to a position where I could see my own name up there in neon on the *Oliver!* sign. 'I'm only playing a West End lead, for Christ's sake! How much experience do these bastards want?'

My morale was greatly boosted when a letter arrived from Bernard Miles, who had launched the Mermaid Theatre.

This lead directly to my next engagement, the role of Long

MERMAID THEATRE

PUDDLE DOCK BLACKFRIARS LONDON EC4 CITY 6981
BOX OFFICE *Telephone* CITY 7656   RESTAURANT BOOKINGS *Telephone* CITY 2835

August 10th, 1967

Barry Humphries, Esq.,
25 Maida Avenue,
London W.2.

Dear Barry,

Brought grandchildren to see "Oliver" and must congratulate you. You are superb, incisive totally audible, finely characterised, larger than life and bursting with personality - and the voice!

Congratulations!

Yours,

Bernard Miles

John Silver in a stage adaptation of Stevenson's *Treasure Island*. Miles had created the role, and appeared in it every year, except for one winter season when the part was taken by Sir Donald Wolfit. In this new production Spike Milligan was to play Ben Gunn, and William Rushton, Squire Trelawney, so I would be amongst friends. As soon as my *Oliver!* contract ended, I started rehearsals at the Mermaid, but it was a long part, and I was a poor learner of lines. Spike suggested a brilliant hypnotherapist he knew in Harley Street, and in desperation I went to see this 'alternative' physician. I was wary, however, half expecting to find Spike in a white coat and a wig posing as a hypnotist.

I explained my learning block to the doctor, who told me to

lie comfortably on a table while he tried to put me under. Staring at the ceiling, and extremely sceptical, I felt not the least sleepy sensation. All I could hear were the rumblings of the doctor's stomach. Rather begrudging this old charlatan his exorbitant fee, I hurried back to the Mermaid for the afternoon rehearsal. I knew every line.

Knowing the lines, however, was only half the battle. Acting on one leg with a parrot on one's shoulder, and participating in a frenzied cutlass fight, was almost beyond human endurance. The parrot, a pet of Bernard Miles', hated me. It also had a keen appetite for human flesh, and when it was not flying into the auditorium and screaming indecencies at the children in the audience, it was pecking at my ear until the blood flowed.

We did two shows a day, and the weather was bitterly cold. After the first week I slipped on some ice outside the theatre and sprained my one good leg; the leg on which I so heavily relied every day for five hours of solid hopping, while the other leg was strapped up behind me. Switching legs was strangely disorientating, and far from being Stevenson's nimble old amputee, I developed a tendency to fall over rather too often. But since rum was Silver's preferred tipple, it became, in the interests of literary verisimilitude, my own. It was remarkable how little pain I felt, or how much manic energy I seemed to release, after a few breath-taking tots of this powerful Jamaican beverage.

As the season wore on, so did I. I seemed to need less and less character makeup, as my face began naturally to assume the lineaments of a ravaged old sea-dog, and a magenta hue that would formerly have taken me some time to achieve artificially.

As I became Long John Silver, I felt an increasing licence to take my own liberties with the text. Was it not possible that Silver was an escaped Australian convict? Why not introduce a few echoes of Barry McKenzie? Perhaps even a chunder scene from the poop? When Bernard Miles, returning from a holiday, looked in at a matinée he failed to recognize the show he had created. There were some acerbic notes, but a kind of anarchy had been set in motion, which could not easily be curbed. Long John Silver, being the ship's cook, occasionally produced his own specialities, and one of these proved to be a giant quivering pavlova which was sometimes accidentally planted on the face of Squire Trelawney or the dignified Dr Livesey. Spike was without reticence when it came to pantomimic anachronisms. When Ben Gunn appeared with a blunderbuss and fired, we were all showered with a great cloud of white flour. 'What was that?' said Squire Trelawney. 'Flour-power,' replied Milligan, topically.

In the midst of this highly professional jollity, the stage doorman told me he needed a word with me. In a quick break between scenes, and rums, I limped to his cubbyhole. He pointed to a large suitcase to which was affixed an envelope. It was a note from Rosalind. She was sending the rest of my clothes and personal effects to the theatre in the next few days. An anonymous member of the *Oliver!* cast had told her all she needed to know about my relationship with Delia, the assistant stage manager, and she hoped I would be very happy. It seemed to have gone very quiet on stage. 'My God!' I thought. *'I'm on!'*

'I hope you realize I'm just putting paint over the rust.' It was an offensive thing for anybody to say, let alone a doctor. And a doctor I was paying good money. I was in Sydney again, backstage at the old Tivoli Theatre, presenting yet another one-man offering, this time entitled, with mock modesty, *Just a Show*. The doctor was giving me a powerful shot of vitamin B_{12} and my cheeks were burning with the characteristic 'niacin rush'.

There is a type of medical practitioner I particularly loathe. The smug type. I had consulted just such a doctor a few months before in London, when Rosalind presented me with a legal ultimatum.

MERMAID THEATRE

PUDDLE DOCK BLACKFRIARS LONDON EC4 CITY 6981

BOX OFFICE *Telephone* CITY 7656   RESTAURANT BOOKINGS *Telephone* CITY 2835

8th February, 1968

Barry Humphries Esq.,
25 Maida Avenue,
LONDON W.2.

Dear Barry,

        Just a word of profound thanks for your
work in Treasure Island - you have enormous capacity
as an actor - most of all a life-enhancing vitality
and energy which is a gift from the Gods - besides
your intelligence and ready wit.

        You also have what I think is almost the
greatest gift of all, namely determination not to
give in. I know you were often feeling down and
hard-pressed and the three performances on Saturday
(I did them myself three years ago so I know what
I am talking about) are really like total war.

        A thousand congratulations and Bless
you Barry.

        Yours ever,

P.S. Do give me a ring as soon as you are in
circulation again and come and have lunch. Bring
your beautiful wife.

The late Dr László Zadór had rooms in Harley Street at the top of three flights of stairs, but I had to spend a long time in the waiting-room first, examining his other patients. They looked awful. 'Who the hell recommended that I see this quack?' I thought. 'Probably that smooth lawyer who is winding her up!' I felt angry, and completely sane. Hadn't I agreed to keep everybody happy by doing another Australian show?

One of the girls in the waiting-room was muttering to herself. Was she drugged? I had seen the junkies queuing up outside Boots the Chemist in Piccadilly Circus. It was a sickening sight to behold all those young people who had completely lost their will-power. Often, gazing at them pityingly from my comfortable seat in the back of a cab, I would need to take a quick swig of scotch from the half-bottle in a Harrods' bag.

I told the doctor a long and rambling yarn which I felt sure would amuse him, and he took copious notes. At the end of the interview, in his strong Hungarian accent, he asked me only one question: 'Have you ever thought of going to Alcoholics Anonymous?' I felt soiled and degraded. It seemed to me a disgrace that one should actually *pay* to be insulted.

This all came back to me in the dressing-room in Sydney. Paint over the rust? What moralizing shits some of these doctors were. I had agreed, at short notice, to do another Australian tour. Rosalind had magnanimously accepted me back into the fold on condition I got some sort of treatment. I'd seen this phoney shrink in Harley Street. Even done a stint in some private nursing home in North London, God help me. Then we had all gone to Mexico again where I had been a good boy and kept off the tequila, and I had even written an entire one-man show, which was now booked solid. What more did they want?

I was far from paranoid, but I knew that Cliff, the impresario, was having me tailed, if by any chance I managed to slip away from my 'jailers' after the show. Working under the pressure I did, didn't I deserve a few quiet drinks in a peaceful club to recharge my batteries? It was insulting to glance across a dimly lit room, in a louche part of town, and see Don Harris, my poor hard-worked stage manager, *who needed his sleep*, trying to look unobtrusive at a remote table. We never exchanged a word on those embarrassing occasions, but I guessed he was being paid a few dollars extra to snoop on me, though God knows what they thought I was getting up to. A nightcap or two, that was all.

When the doctor had gone, I looked in the mirror. My hair was short and blond for a new character called Brian Graham, a young fertilizer executive in the novel and ludicrous uniform such Australians were beginning to affect: shorts and long white socks worn with a collar and tie. Brian's chief aim was to hide his homosexuality from his tyrannical father and business associates. It was a nice dramatic piece.

Over the blond hair I wore a succession of wigs, including a pale blue one for Edna. She'd gone mauve in the last act, and she now wore Thai silk like every other Edna in Australia, and the audiences loved it. If only they knew the aggravation I was having to tolerate backstage. *Paint over the rust!*

I was rather proud of the richness of my new show, considering the troubles which had preceded it. Apart from Edna and Sandy Stone, there were five other characters, including Rex Lear, a coarse *nouveau-riche* father of the bride stumbling around at his daughter's wedding reception and, like his Shakespearean counterpart, railing against his daughter's ingratitude. It was an experiment to see if I could present single-handed on stage an entire (and invisible) wedding breakfast complete with bridesmaids, vicar, best man, caterers and Italian waiters.

I had made the show a little easier for myself by including a filmed segment. An 'underground' film. One of my new characters was called Martin Agrippa, a hispid Australian movie-maker with pretensions to being a kind of avant-garde Ingmar Bergman. The better half of the sketch was Martin Agrippa's film, which Bruce Beresford had made for me in London before I went out to Australia.

I had always wanted to include short films in my solo shows, both to give me a rest and a chance to transform myself into Edna or some other character who required an elaborate makeup or costume change. Patrick White had recommended a young Sydney film-maker whom he thought was destined for great things, on the strength of having seen one of Beresford's student efforts. When I met him, he was in charge of the production unit at the British Film Institute, and married with one son to a stylish and beautiful Irish girl called Rhoison. He was an enormously bright and attractive character, tousle-headed, opinionated, wittily intolerant and passionately fond of movies and music. Bruce sometimes wore an old-fashioned navy-blue chalk-striped suit which he proudly announced had been bought for £1 off a street vendor. His cars were equally picturesque bargains. It was Bruce, really, who put me on to the Underground Cinema joke, since he knew a lot of people both in England and Australia who had successfully applied for large grants in order to inflict their turgid and pretentious films upon an indifferent public.

Bruce and I created a hilarious and convincing parody of one of these movies; later shown at several International Festivals of Underground Cinema where it was acclaimed as a masterpiece of the genre. In *Just a Show*, following Martin Agrippa's monologue, the film brought the house down.

When Beresford and I were working together in London, I was unsure how much he knew of my domestic difficulties. On the one hand he was an indefatigable, indeed gleeful gossip; and on the other, curiously thoughtful and circumspect. After *Treasure Island*, when I agreed to incarcerate myself in a nursing home for a while, he made the long journey to visit me and never asked why I was there. This struck me as very odd. I managed to do some work in this foetid institution; some book reviews for the *Spectator*, commissioned by a nice-sounding girl called Hilary Spurling. She never inquired, either, why her correspond-ence was always addressed to me care of a private hospital. Very odd indeed. If Bruce or Hilary, or indeed anyone else, had asked me what a perfectly sane, talented and perhaps over-sensitive person like me was doing virtually locked up, I would have had to express myself very delicately – perhaps even pretend to be depressed – so that they would not think too unkindly of my wife.

I remember very little about this interlude in the nursing home, except that one day when I had been 'a good boy' for several weeks I was granted permission to go for a walk. I dressed excitedly, and set off into the nearby woods. Half an hour later I was still in sparse woodland and obviously lost. I increased my pace until I came at length to a large tract of common land, with a few houses in the far distance. I was running now, though not sure why. I reached the houses and at last came upon a small parade of shops. Breathless from my exertions I ran past them, around the corner and straight through the doorway of an off-licence. I had to lean on the counter for a few minutes to regain my breath. A friendly Irishman smiled at me interrogatively.

'Ahem, twenty, er, no, forty Dunhill please . . . and, er, a couple of boxes of matches, thank you.'

The Irishman smiled again, and put the cigarettes on the counter, and the matches, and then a package containing six miniature bottles of Smirnoff vodka.

'What are these for?' I asked, flabbergasted.

'You're up at Elm Hill, aren't you now?' he said.

I nodded.

'That's what they all order.'

I quickly paid my money and bolted out of the shop. A minute later I was back on the common beside a very large bush. I ripped the lid off one of the miniatures and held it to my lips. Nothing came out. There was an air lock in the neck. I gave the bottle a little shake and, with a glug, the entire contents poured down my throat with a sharp burning sensation. I took a deep breath before tackling the lid of the second miniature, at the same time tossing the empty bottle into the bush. There was a loud clink. I parted the foliage, and peered inside. There was a considerable pile of empty vodka bottles. Others had been this way before. I had the sudden, if fleeting, impression that I was not entirely alone.

There were flies everywhere. Australians are used to them of course; even in restaurants where they grow to the size of hummingbirds, but it was unusual to find them in an art gallery, and in such numbers. They crawled around the picture frames, they supped at the eyes and briefly formed loose scrums at the corners of people's mouths. High up, against the white ceiling, thousands of them moved ceaselessly in a decorous holding pattern.

The cause of this muscarious invasion seemed to be a large, circular, blue plastic paddling-pool in the centre of the gallery floor. It appeared to be filled with some clotted and pus-coloured substance which already bore in places the blue-green bloom of mould. Here the nimbus of flies was thickest, for the glutinous yellow liquid in the pool was custard, gallons of it; and here and there, projecting through its coagulating surface, were the corners, spines and covers of books. It was laced with dozens of books, which I had bought as a job-lot from a Salvation Army depot. This 'sculpture', for sale at $6,000 (with a discount to museums and learned institutions), was an inflated recreation of my notorious work from the early fifties: 'I was reading these books when I felt sick.' Unfortunately it was an exhibit that attracted more attention from the flies than from the public.

I had decided to hold this art exhibition to run concurrently with my Sydney theatre season. It was to be pretentiously called a 'Retrospective', in mockery of the retrospectives every young artist in Australia under the age of twenty-five seemed to be having. An old friend, Kym Bonython, had opened the smartest new gallery in town and he offered it to me for my show. In spite of performing solo for three hours every night, I had somehow managed to assemble enough 'works of art' to fill Kym's large gallery. There were a lot of my early landscapes of Mornington in an amiable fauvist style, some reconstructions of Dada objects of the early fifties, like 'Books', as well as a series of large and realistic portraits of Australian prime ministers, some of who were wearing real suits, glued on to the canvas. I had also executed a series of monumental 'Bigscapes', mainly to fill up empty spaces in the gallery. These consisted only of the word 'Big', fastidiously painted on canvas in huge letters.

The show attracted large numbers of people who did not normally frequent art galleries, but sales were few. One of the portraits was bought by a Sydney collector and someone else bought a drawing. The rest of the exhibits either got lost, rotted or were thrown out with the garbage. Kym told me years later that after my show the flies never forsook his gallery but loitered in their hundreds in the hope, no doubt, that in the fullness of time I would be mounting another delicious retrospective.

Just a Show played in all the Australian cities, ending in Perth. By then I was reluctantly beginning to agree with that impertinent theatre doctor in Sydney. The rust was starting to bleed through the paint.

By the light of a trembling match he stared at his watch. It was twenty to two. There was something very important that had to be done but he could not remember what. On the floor of the small unfamiliar room was a puddle of clothes; some were like his, except for the crumpled brown silk dress with an Indian pattern. Nearby in a tangle of linguini laces were a pair of Roman sandals that had fallen in first position. They were like the ones he had seen before, latticing a girl's brown legs. The girl asleep on the bed reminded him vaguely of the student whose eye he had caught in the front row at a talk he had given at the University of Western Australia. When was that? Yesterday? TODAY? The match had gone out, burning his fingers. He lit another and looked once more at his watch. Was it upside down? The time now seemed to be twelve minutes past eight.

By the time he got to the theatre, fortunately only a few blocks away from the shabby private hotel where he had found himself, the audience – in varying degrees of puzzlement, impatience and jocular irritation – had been seated for over thirty minutes listening to a jolly medley of recorded music. His hair was glued to his scalp with sweat from the mad dash across town, and the manager kept refilling a cup of black coffee which rattled on the saucer as he stabbed at his face with makeup and stumbled into the gaudy costume. Somewhere nearby, white-faced, stood his wife; but he looked no one in the eye that night, and felt at home and safe only when he had burst on to the stage, and for the next two hours struggled for the forgiveness of laughter. It was an evening which, for years afterwards, if he ever thought about it, made his flesh crawl.

During the Melbourne run I had a visit from a London producer, Peter Bridge. He was convinced that the show would be a huge hit in the West End and he told me he wanted to produce it himself. I patiently explained that no one in London really got the point of my Aussie act, except homesick Australians and English people who had been down there on a visit. I had even tentatively introduced Edna a few times on *The Late Show*, but the BBC switchboard had not exactly been jammed with calls from ecstatic viewers; nor had the mailbags overflowed with fan letters hailing a great new comic creation. Only Malcolm Muggeridge seemed to have found Mrs Everage risible. I also told Mr Bridge that my earlier attempts to win over a British audience to my essentially regional material had met with stony indifference. Better, I said, to stick to my comic strip, which I had heard had quite a few distinguished fans, like Kenneth Tynan, Bernard Levin, John Osborne and Alan Sillitoe. Bridge disagreed, and told me to let him know when I got back to London so he could present me at the Fortune Theatre, where *Beyond the Fringe* had been triumphantly launched six years earlier.

I heard a shrill cry of 'Daddy!' and, turning sharply in surprise, I saw little Emily running towards me along the pavement with her arms outstretched. I felt a tremendous surge of joy as I stooped ready to snatch the child up into my arms. But suddenly, only a couple of yards off, she stopped, and looked at me with horror. At the same moment I realized that it was not Emily at all; just a little girl who looked like Emily. The child was crying now and running towards a woman outside a fruit shop, who gathered her up and glowered at me resentfully. 'What have *I* done?' I thought, with a thumping heart and tears in my eyes. It was hardly my fault that the child mistook me for her father.

Of course it could not possibly have been Emily or, for that matter, Tessa, for I was now in London, and they were 13,000 miles away in Melbourne with their mother. When the tour of *Just a Show* had ended, or petered out in illness and disarray, Rosalind had moved into a flat and not disclosed the address.

For a while I had dossed down in a suburban motel, making a few desultory excursions to Sydney in search of consolation. But when they went to New Zealand to stay with Rosalind's parents, I followed, checking into a mean room, not normally rented, above an Auckland pub. By having my bed only a few yards from my chosen drinking haunt I had hoped to avoid the pitfalls and dangerous distractions which seemed always to entrap me when these two polarities of my life were widely separated. It was, I decided, the *getting home* that was the central problem, not the harmless conviviality which preceded it.

To the best of my ability at the time, I tried to make amends to my family, but to no avail. Rosalind had finally had enough. Briefly, I saw the girls again, and with a heavy heart set off for London, and work.

Peter Bridge was as good as his word, and as I began rehearsing for my first London one-man show, my spirits, and my health, seemed to revive. I had always directed myself in all my solo enterprises, but this time Eleanor Fazan, an old friend, was hired to direct the production, which was to contain most of the elements from the Australian show with a couple of extra ingredients. One of these was my old 'surfie' character, clutching a bucket of prawns and singing Barry McKenzie's legendary drinking song, 'The Old Pacific Sea'.

Oh, I was down by Bondi pier
Drinking tubes of ice-cold beer,
With a bucket full of prawns upon me knee;
But when I'd swallowed the last prawn
I had a technicolour yawn,
And I chundered in the old Pacific Sea.

CHORUS

Drink it up, drink it up,
Crack another dozen tubes and prawns with me.
If you want to throw your voice
Mate, you won't have any choice,
But to chunder in the old Pacific Sea.

I was sitting in the surf
When a mate of mine called Murph
Asked if he could crack a tube or two with me.
The bastard barely swallowed it
When he went for the big spit,
And he chundered in the old Pacific Sea.

CHORUS

There's a lot of ways that you can
Have a ball when you are pukin',
And the secret of it is variety
You can either park a Tiger
From the summit of the Eiger,
Or chunder in the old Pacific Sea.

CHORUS

I've had liquid laughs in bars
And I've hurled from moving cars,
And I've chuckled when and where it suited me.
But, if I could choose a spot
To regurgitate me lot,
Then I'd chunder in the old Pacific Sea.

CHORUS
Drink it up, drink it up,
Crack another dozen tubes and prawns with me.
Why kneel there all alone
By the big white telephone
When you can chunder in the old Pacific Sea.

On the opening night my producer Peter Bridge was very excited by the 'buzz' in the foyer, and even I, nervous and still sceptical, felt a frisson of hope as I hid in the manager's office next to the box office in my Edna disguise of cyclamen-and-peacock Thai silk. The show always opened with an overture on the Hammond organ played by my female accompanist in the orchestra pit. As she took her bow, Edna would enter shrilly from the back of the stalls, an ordinary member of the audience wishing to address publicly several popular misconceptions about the Australian way of life. That was the reason I was huddled in the manager's office and not waiting in the wings.

The audience was settling down. The house-lights dimmed, I took a discreet but fortifying nip of brandy from a small flask in Edna's purse and crept out of my hiding place to peer through a crack in the doors at the back of the stalls. Beside me, in black tie, and perspiring with nerves, was Peter Bridge. The organist he had hired seemed an apposite choice; Josephine Bradley. In Edwardian evening dress and wearing a feather boa, she looked like a musical Lady Bracknell. She got a large and encouraging round of applause too as she sat down at the electric organ, but she seemed a long time starting the overture, a medley of early fifties novelty numbers. Beside me Peter muttered profanely, but Miss Bradley's problems with her instrument, which had somehow become separated from its source of electrical power, seemed to amuse the audience, who tittered, as audiences do, at shows where things are *meant* to go wrong.

After an eternity, during which the sweat must have washed

The author with Sacheverell Sitwell

The author with Mischa Spoliansky, 1986

Sir Leslie Colin Patterson

Alexander Horace 'Sandy' Stone

Dame Edna, a recent Hollywood study by Roddy McDowall

Diane Millstead

Oscar and Rupert Humphries, 1992

Tessa, Oscar and Barry Humphries
at the Botanical Gardens, Sydney

Tessa and Emily, 1992

With David Hockney in California, 1992

Lizzie Spender

The author at dinner in Los Angeles

Lizzie, Barry and Stanley, 1992 by David Hockney

all traces of Edna's makeup off my countenance, the Hammond organ was reconnected, and the show began. I tensed for my entrance, but it was that moment that Mr Bridge chose to inform me of a minor adjustment he had made to the props in the finale. He hadn't worried me about it before because I had a lot on my plate, but the wholesale florists at Covent Garden were out of gladioli due to some bug that had attacked the crop, so he had taken the liberty of buying five dozen daffodils instead. I could throw those at the audience at the end of the show and they would be none the wiser.

'But, Peter,' I hissed, 'what about the song?'

'What song?'

'The song I sing at the end,' said Edna, frantically. 'To the tune of "Coconuts"!' With five seconds to go before her entrance, she sang a few bars:

'. . . I've got a lovely bunch of gladdies,
See them all awaving in the stalls
Big ones, small ones, some as big as your thumb
Give 'em a twist, a flick of the wrist
— There's lots of different ways of arranging them,
Just remember all you mums and daddies,
There's lots of flower power to be had
All you need's a lovely bunch of gladdies
And you'll never be sad, as long as you wave a glad!

Try getting "daff" to rhyme in *that* number,' I yelled over my shoulder as I bolted through the door and down the aisle to the point, just against the stage, where the spotlight hit the flurry of Thai silk and the sparkle of *diamanté*, and Edna trilled: 'Excuse I!'

I have a clear memory, however, of Peter's face as he got the message and his lips mimed the word 'Jesus!'

At the end of the show there were gladioli. Dozens and dozens of them. Poor old Peter must have dragged every florist in London away from his dinner to provide an Australian housewife with what remaining stocks they had of this endangered species.

Next day, we had some nice publicity. RARE PLANT INSECT THREATENS WEST END SHOW. Qantas Airlines must have read this because for the next few weeks they flew, from far Australia, large quantities of glads of a hue, size and succulence never before seen in London.

The papers also published the reviews. They were not all bad, but they were not all good. Harold Hobson dourly said, 'Most of Barry Humphries' *Just a Show* will give pleasure to most Australians living in London.' And Herbert Kretzmer wrote: 'The mood of those [last] ten minutes cannot be produced in words. It was one of those magic moments in the theatre where the audience becomes truly happy.' But, as I had feared, the show was ultimately a provincial curiosity; admired by a few, shrugged off by most, and attracting too few patrons for my valiant producer to be able to keep it going for more than six increasingly difficult weeks.

As we limped on, I viewed the attraction across the road at the Theatre Royal, Drury Lane with mounting envy and resentment. It was *Mame*, starring the already legendary Ginger Rogers. Even before I opened, Miss Rogers' renovations to her dressing-room had received more publicity than our modest production could ever hope to attract. Edna countered with a piece about *her* gorgeous improvements to her backstage accommodation, but as Miss Rogers' box-office queues lengthened, Mrs Everage's dwindled. Every night as I left the theatre I cast a jaundiced eye across the road at the stage door of the 'Lane', where Ginger's many fans were waiting for a fleeting glimpse of the star. When we finally knew we had only a few more performances to go, I decided to capture Ginger Rogers' audience, if just for a few minutes. Carefully timing the end of my show to coincide precisely with the end of hers, I dashed out the stage door the instant my curtain fell, so that Edna, in all her finale finery, was outside the Fortune Theatre before my audience had found their coats. Leaping on to the roof of a parked car, Edna executed a lively tap routine just as both theatres, Ginger's and mine, disgorged their patrons. My own meagre followers were, of course, dumbfounded to see the artiste they had just left behind performing an encore in the street, and the throngs evacuating the Theatre Royal stopped in their tracks as Edna shrilly exhorted them to come back tomorrow and patronize 'the Ginger Rogers of the sixties'.

Two weeks later, after we had closed and I was out of a job, I received a nice fan letter from a woman who had witnessed this event. She enclosed a large invoice from a North London firm of panel-beaters who had encountered extraordinary problems in removing the indentations of stiletto heels from the roof of her car.

Don't Wake Me For Cocktails

T HE ONLY REALLY hostile review *Just a Show* received was in Australia. I was now living in a small private hotel on Westbourne Terrace, and one night the telephone jangled at about four a.m. It was, of course, an Australian journalist under the impression that the time in London is identical to the time in Sydney, although such intrusions – and they still occur – always begin with the phrase: 'Sorry mate, what time is it there?'

The reason for this call was that a New Zealand impresario called Harry M. Miller, of whom I had vaguely heard, had come back to Sydney after a quick shopping expedition in London, and attacked my show on the grounds that it was unpatriotic. In Australia, a foolproof means of grabbing publicity and appearing to be a fine fellow is to impugn another man's patriotism; and no doubt Mr Miller hit upon this method to liven up his press conference. 'What did he say?' I sleepily challenged the transmitter. The journalist gleefully quoted:

'That man Humphries is an idiot ... We have enough trouble convincing the world Australia is sophisticated, yet we have this idiot ruining the country.'

I had a brief and comic vision of Mr Miller convincing the world of Australia's sophistication, where I had patently failed. Luckily, despite the hour, I managed to think up a few vaguely amusing ripostes to the charges levelled by this scurrilous Kiwi, who had, it emerged, not even been to see my show. In the intervening years, however, and as regular as clockwork, I have had to reply to – or ignore – similar charges; usually from disc jockeys and tenth-rate academics with chips on their shoulders. As a recipient of these attacks I have always been in excellent company. There is not one Australian singer, artist, writer, actor or film director whose success abroad has gone unpunished by an envious minority of his countrymen. A few of our film directors had quite recently been fulminating against their colleagues who had 'sold out to Hollywood'. They wanted to ban foreign actors and directors from working in Australia. One or two of these same film-makers are a little more circumspect now, I notice, as they recline beside their pools in Beverly Hills.

Someone at the BBC had seen *Just a Show* and I was offered my own TV series, *The Barry Humphries Scandals*. It was to be produced by a man called Dennis Main Wilson who, I was told, was one of those BBC comedy veterans who 'could do no wrong'. He had initiated many famous television shows, and he seemed very enthusiastic about my series.

Gradually I learned to live with that dull ache of loss over my little daughters back in Australia, and I felt a resurgence of energy as I started work again at Television Centre. It was as if my way of doing things, of living even, had been vindicated after all. Considering the way in which my life had been sliding out of control over the past couple of years, I seemed to have landed up on my feet again, so to speak. And my feet stood nonchalantly at the important end of the long bar at the BBC Club, where I could smile and nod to people like Frankie Howerd, Harry Secombe, Morecambe and Wise and Marty Feldman. I was back in the world of black taxis, too, which would whisk me 'as directed' around the West End of London, and wait obediently for hours outside smart Mayfair pubs as I purchased cigarettes, sampling a few Fernet Brancas and large Teachers while the bartender fetched them.

We now lived in Mayfair, that is to say, Roslyn Mackrell

and I, in a tiny flat in Park Street. Roslyn was a beautiful girl from Sydney who deserved a great deal better than the sporadic companionship of a dissolute, guilt-ridden, self-obsessed boozer, whose own definition of himself would have been *very* different. To cheer myself up, I had got a lot of books and pictures from the old house at Little Venice out of storage, and had stuffed them into our cramped accommodation; ballast from the past. On the mantelpiece and on the crowded tops of tables stood my collection of Gallé cameo glass, mostly assembled whilst browsing in junkshops during Australian tours, long before art nouveau had returned to fashion.

The *Scandals* were written by me and my old colleague from *The Late Show*, Ian Davidson, though the tapes of the series no longer exist, having been destroyed by the BBC to save space. This may not be a tragic loss to the world's archive of funny material, but the show had its felicities. There was an elegant film set in a 1930s nightclub in which I, disguised as Jack Buchanan, sang my own loosely autobiographical composition, 'Too Drunk to Dance', and a musical based on the career of the Australian bushranger, Ned Kelly. Various actor friends made guest appearances in the series, including Dick Bentley, June Whitfield and Michael Palin.

One of the most successful sketches concerned an unmarried man who, as he rushes out the front gate to work, is always intercepted by his mother with the question: 'I hope you're wearing clean underwear this morning, darling. No man knoweth the hour!' Of course the tardy commuter, summoned back to his bedroom to change his underpants, saves time by merely stuffing a clean pair into his briefcase, pecking his mother on the cheek and running to the bus stop.

In our film he could be seen crossing the road just as an enormous lorry bore down upon him at high speed. Seeing his peril too late, he becomes rooted to the spot as the camera goes into slow motion. Then, methodically, he puts the briefcase down on the road, removes his trousers and underpants, dons the clean pair, places the old ones in the briefcase, pulls up his trousers, straightens his bowler hat and stands to attention, only to be flattened by the lorry, as his mother's words echo through his brain: *No man knoweth the hour!*

This short film ended with a scene in which the old lady answers her front doorbell. A policeman stands in the porch looking grim. 'I'm afraid I have some very bad news for you, madam.' 'It's Basil, isn't it?' says the sweet old lady presciently. 'Tell me, officer, was he . . . was he . . .?' 'I'm happy to say he was, madam,' replied the policeman, handing her a small package. 'You'll be relieved to hear they were *absolutely spotless*.' The bereaved woman fell into the policeman's arms with the words, 'Heaven be praised, heaven be praised!'

A song I had written called 'True British Spunk' proved to be the swansong of the series. A swansong, moreover, that was never transmitted, though an audio-tape miraculously survives. 'Spunk' was a party turn of mine at the time, ostensibly about British courage and fortitude down the ages, but its humour resided, of course, in the equivocal meaning of the word, with its sticky schoolboy resonances, which nobody at the BBC dared to point out at that time.

Dennis Main Wilson, with his usual flair and extravagance, commissioned a large orchestra, and a chorus of soldiers, sailors, airmen, nurses, air-raid wardens and land-army girls to harmoniously ejaculate, in stirring Elgarian style, the rousing and spunky chorus. I might add that I sang the song myself, as Edna impersonating Vera Lynn. But it was only after the whole thing had been expensively recorded in the presence of a large and enthusiastic audience that a senior member of the BBC Board found the courage to draw me to one side, and attempted to explain to me that the title of my song had, in some circles, an alternative and unacceptable meaning, of which I, as a Colonial, was naturally ignorant. This was elucidated with much beating about the bush, which I suppose was appropriate under the circumstances.

*

No one ever saw the final episode of *The Scandals*, which remained, at the last, true to their title. Yet when the series ended and there seemed no immediate prospect of work, my morale quickly faded. I spent money as fast as I earned it, and my health seemed to be failing.

A doctor told me that my liver was inflamed and asked me how much I drank. It was a difficult question to answer. Did he mean, for example, before or after breakfast? Did he mean wines or spirits? How could a professional man expect me to know how much I drank, when much of my drinking was performed unconsciously and in those reaches of the night that were becoming increasingly blank.

In the small hours of the morning I would wake up in a cold sweat, with feelings of impending doom. I was convinced something terrible was about to happen, but could not possibly explain what it was that I feared. The sounds of cars outside in the street became ominous; would they stop at my house? Were they coming for me?

In the mornings, on waking, I would need to lie for several minutes with my eyes squeezed shut before daring to examine my surroundings. Was it my own bed? Was this my girlfriend? The relief at discovering that I was at least in my own flat would lend me the courage to examine my discarded clothes. Were they neatly hanging in the wardrobe or folded over a chair, or were they strewn, inside-out, on the carpet? If the latter were the case, as it all too often was, I would then begin an agonizing reconstruction of the night before. Where had I been? The stubs in my chequebook might hold an answer to this mystery. Feverishly I would riffle through them. Three were blank. My God! I must have cashed some cheques – but where? There was one cheque stub across which was scrawled, in unfamiliar writing, the cryptic word 'entertainment'. The pocket of my jacket yielded a clue: a book of matches which advertised the Blue Parrot Club. Where was that? There was a sordid-seeming address off the Harrow Road. A few smudgy memories filtered back, but not many. I vaguely recalled dinner in Soho. A room somewhere, ruddily lit, with a lot of people. Where had the evening gone wrong? I must have changed my drinks, I decided. If I had only stuck to whisky, and a little wine, everything would have been all right. Or I must have run into some boring crowd who insisted on pressing on somewhere else, and then somewhere else, ruining my plans of an early night. But I would not be so easily led astray next time. It would never happen again. *Never again.* They were the two words I repeated every morning of my life like a mantra.

This mental and physical anguish did not, fortunately, last for too long. A Radox bath, a sanguineous shave, a clean shirt, too much cologne and I was ready for the short stroll from the flat in Park Street to the Red Lion, which, miraculously, threw open its doors at the precise moment of my arrival, to permit my thirsty ingress. As I walked towards the bar the barmaid, without any command from me, placed a large glass of bitumen-coloured Fernet Branca on the bar. I had discovered this powerful Italian *digestif* and tonic several years before, but had only lately taken to imbibing it before breakfast. Politely, Veronica turned her back as I picked up the glass with an unsteady hand and contrived to steer it towards my lips without spilling too much on the way. Fernet Branca stains on ties and lapels defy the efforts of even the best dry-cleaners. Several deep gulps of air usually persuaded me that the balsamic cordial had been permanently ingurgitated, and I could safely order a little whisky and mineral water to banish, for the day at least, the phantoms of the night before.

Often across the bar I noticed a trembling copy of the *Daily Telegraph*, opened to its full extent. I never once saw the reader, only his right hand, which from time to time darted beneath the newspaper towards a large glass of clear and rapidly diminishing liquid, which it then withdrew behind the quivering screen of newsprint. Who was he, I often wondered. And how did he sneak into the saloon bar before me? Hadn't I arrived on the dot of opening time? Had he, perhaps, been there all night? Sadly, I made my own diagnosis: the poor man behind the paper must be an alcoholic.

One morning, with a worse attack of amnesia than was customary, and a conviction that some catastrophe had occurred that I would rather not know about, I wandered into our sitting-room. As usual, the telephone was off the hook and growling resentfully. I had come to dread this instrument, and the bad news it must invariably communicate.

Something in the room seemed to be missing. Where was my precious glass collection? The slender vase by Daum with its shouldered, swollen, cylindrical form and gently everted rim, on knopped stem and bun foot, acid-etched and enamelled with poppies in orange, black and green on a yellow acid-textured ground? The Gallé mould-blown triple-overlay vase, with acid-etched crocuses in pink and mauve, in frosted opalescent glass with the artist's intaglio signature? And where was the Gallé lamp with its hemispherical shade and double-overlay carved and acid-etched decoration of clematis, blue and amethyst, on a ground shading from yellow-amber to frosted coral, with Gallé's cameo signature on the base and shade? There were half a dozen more pieces which also seemed to be missing. I asked Roslyn if she had put them somewhere safe and out of range of the cleaning lady's duster. She gave me a look of incredulity. 'Don't tell me you don't remember what happened last night?' Of course I didn't. 'You just came home and threw them at the wall; every single one of them. I couldn't stop you. But surely you remember that?'

It appeared that my father had arranged my rescue, for I was back in my hometown of Melbourne. Back with Rosalind and the children. With my father's support, she had just turned up, minutes, it seemed, after sending me a telegram, and the next thing I knew was that there was a furniture van in Park Street, loading up the contents of the flat to be shipped back to Australia. The scene reminded me, dimly, of my expulsion from the artist's garret I had rented years before, when my father had unceremoniously packed my bags with the words 'Why the dickens do you want to live in a dump like this when you've got a perfectly good home to go to?' It had a kind of logic, too, if one wasn't an adult. Now, I felt I had forfeited all will of my own, and I was almost relieved to be a person to whom things just happened.

I remember little of the flight back to Melbourne, much of which I spent at the back of the plane obtaining furtive drinks from the obliging Qantas stewards, who always had a fund of amusing gossip. In the maroon leatherette wallet, containing my in-flight toiletries, sockettes and slumber-shades, was an adhesive disc intended to be stuck, if necessary, on the back of one's seat. It said: DON'T WAKE ME FOR COCKTAILS. I screwed it up and stuffed it into my air-sick bag.

My mother's arthritis, which she was convinced was an unavoidable and hereditary complaint, seemed much worse when I saw her again. She rarely went out, preferring the company of her domestic helpers, and communicating daily on the telephone with all her sisters. It was darkly hinted that her health was none the better for my antics. My father was working even more frenetically, and obsessed by golf, his only recreation. However, at this time he confided to a friend: 'I was so worried about Barry, I couldn't even play golf last Thursday.'

A quantity of my books, many purchased years before when I was a schoolboy in Melbourne, arrived from London in large crates. Because I had been the compiler of a lewd work, *Bizarre*, and since I was also the author of the banned comic strip, *Barry McKenzie*, the Australian Customs authorities took an interest in this much-travelled library, and when it finally arrived and was unpacked in Rosalind's sitting-room, there was a senior official from Customs in attendance over a period of several days, who gravely examined every volume for obscene illustrations and equivocal texts. Every now and then, having stolen a few drinks from a carefully hidden cache, I would put my head around the corner of the room in which this custodian of decency ponderously laboured, and make matters worse with smart quips and sarcasms. In the end the poor old dunce got his own back by confiscating a couple of books; one a

Victorian treatise on morality, misleadingly entitled *A Book of Strange Sins*, and the other a tame translation of a nineteenth-century adventure story with a North African setting called *Musk, Hasheesh and Blood*. It is amusing to think of these anodyne works sitting on his suburban bookshelf between *Arthur Mee's Encyclopaedia* and *Whitaker's Alamanack*.

On the Queen's birthday weekend, after a period of good behaviour, I was allowed to take the car to a nearby shopping centre to buy some groceries. On the way I stopped at a pub and drank several glasses of schnapps in quick succession. The local doctor had put me on a course of so-called anti-depressants, which doubled the effect of the alcohol. I returned to the car and was just about to turn the key in the ignition when two policemen appeared from nowhere. Some years before, in London, I had had brushes with the law, and I had once lost my licence for a year for driving in the wrong direction up the Tottenham Court Road in a state of chemical exaltation, but at least the London bobbies called one 'Sir'. Their Melbourne counterparts were less polite. I was hustled to the Camberwell police station, a stone's-throw from my parents' house, where I most unwisely muttered the word 'fascists' within earshot of my apprehenders. Seconds later I was in a cell.

My appearance in court the next day attracted a great deal of what is now called 'media attention', so that my poor family must have deeply regretted the part they played in my extradition from London. A lawyer friend, armed with medical reports that emphasized my 'depression' and its chemical antidotes, cleverly got me off most of the charges, so that I escaped with only a light fine. The police glared across the court-room, and I smiled back.

Two days later, my medication doubled, I was in town to discuss the possibility of writing a regular newspaper column for the Melbourne *Age*. I managed to slip out of a side door of the building and into a nearby bar frequented by journalists. Only very vaguely do I recall somebody saying, 'There are

some friends of yours in a car outside who want to talk to you.'
My next recollection is of distant lights and mud. It was night
and for some reason I was lying face down in some kind of
waste land surrounded by rubble and broken glass on which a
fine drizzle descended. I tried to crawl, but there was an
excruciating pain in my abdomen and I collapsed back into the
mud. Slowly, however, I dragged myself towards the edge of a
desolate road and, at length, attracted the attention of a passing
car which dumped me off, like a severely damaged parcel, at St
Vincent's Hospital. As I lay in Casualty, shivering in my ripped
and mud-soaked suit, my face swollen and bleeding, I heard
one of the doctors saying '. . . they must have given him a real
going-over. Could be some internal bruising . . .' Sick and sore
as I was, I remembered that scene in the court-room two days
earlier. Had I been entirely wise in beaming quite so broadly at
my captors?

I opened my eyes and saw my father beside my bed. He was
weeping.

I must have spent many months in the Dymphna Ward of St
Vincent's Hospital. John Betjeman wrote me a long and comforting letter containing much information about the life and good
works of St Dymphna herself. My father called regularly to see
me in my private room, bringing cigarettes and nougat, and
Rosalind came a few times without the children. I learned that I
was in the psychiatric section of the hospital and a very softly
spoken doctor saw me daily for a chat. I was constantly being
woken up and given tablets of various colours and quantities,
but they did little to alleviate my self-pity. I spent a lot of time
weeping into my pillow and thinking to myself, 'Why should a
thing like this happen to a nice person like me?' After a long
time I was allowed out to visit my children, but I had no sooner
left the hospital than I felt a craving to use the telephone. The
nearest telephone was in the nearest pub, so that I returned to
St Vincent's, in a sorry state, without having glimpsed my
daughters. 'Who's been a naughty boy?' said Sister Mann when

I had been put to bed and sedated even further. I liked that. I preferred to be thought of as a child. Children have only to close their eyes for problems to go away.

Somehow, I began my column for the *Age*, which I could spend the whole week polishing in the seclusion of my cell. I must have been one of the few patients in the psychiatric hospital who was earning a living. But my friends and most of my family had disappeared, or withdrawn from the danger zone. Still, I had other visitors.

Nuns popped their heads round the corner of my door and smiled compassionately. Salvation Army officers looked in and passed the time of day. I was a sitting duck for bores. Couldn't they see I was busy? *That I was an artist?* Hadn't they noticed that I had a portable typewriter on my lap? The fact that it contained a blank page was neither here nor there. Doctors of course were always barging in, and they were very interested in finding out what childhood events had led to my present predicament. I did not mind doctors so much, because it was their job to listen, and I was happy to talk to them endlessly on my favourite subject – myself.

One morning a man in a suit walked straight into my room without knocking, and sat on the end of my bed. I assumed he was a new psychiatrist, and I prepared to launch into another impressive monologue of self-justification, but he cut me short. He explained that he was a prosperous real-estate agent. It occurred to me that he was probably another psychiatric patient, and possibly dangerous. Then he began to talk about himself. His background was not unlike my own; respectable, Melbourne, middle class. His parents had given him everything on a plate, and he had been very successful in his work, but things had started to go wrong. His drinking had slowly and insidiously changed, so that alcohol, once a delightful adjunct to his life, had gradually destroyed him. He told me that only a few years before he too had been a patient in the Dymphna Ward.

I told Tony that I didn't believe a word of his story, hair-raising though it was. He looked far too well, he had made affectionate references to his family and he drove a Mercedes Benz. He then explained that he no longer drank, and that he was a member of something called Alcoholics Anonymous. I winced with embarrassment at the mention of those two words, and at my own plight, lying there helplessly in hospital, a prey to ratbags like this; salesmen and evangelists for some kind of temperance society, or middle-class Salvation Army.

Tony took all this with infuriating good humour. 'How can you be so sure you know how boring an AA meeting is if you have never been to one?' he asked with a reasonableness that I failed to perceive. 'I could, of course, get permission to pick you up from here next Thursday night, take you home for dinner and off to the Sandringham meeting; you could see for yourself then.'

It sounded deathly, and Sandringham was a bayside suburb of Melbourne I had always thought to be mind-numbingly boring. Still, I reflected, with the cunning of the crazy, what could be more boring than this hospital? Here was a simple-minded do-gooder, willing to sit me in his Merc, give me dinner and take me on a suburban drive. There were worse ways of spending an evening, and when his car stopped at the traffic lights, I would only have to turn the handle on the door to be off into the night to liberty . . . *to freedom!*

On the following Thursday evening, between St Vincent's Hospital, Fitzroy, and the Anglican church hall at Sandringham, six miles down the coast, there were green lights all the way.

My experience in that smoke-filled hall that evening, where I saw a number of people that I had known years before whom I had assumed must be long dead, had a profound effect on me. Although I had never thought seriously about Alcoholics Anonymous, I had pictured the gathering in my mind on the journey to Sandringham in Tony's car. A grim prayer meeting of derelicts, probably all wearing army-surplus overcoats and thumping tambourines. Doom, gloom, ginger-ale and Jesus. I was completely unprepared to find a large crowd of well-dressed people, many my own age, and younger, and women — some very pretty — and to hear laughter; gales of it. If you had seen that diverse group of people leaving the hall after their meeting you would not possibly have guessed what they could have had in common. As Lola said to me over coffee later, 'The only thing we've all got in common is that we don't need to drink anymore. If you can't smell us, you can't tell us!'

I wish I could say that my life changed immediately thereafter. In a sense it did, since, after a few meetings — and to Tony's alarm — I became a world authority on Alcoholics Anonymous. At the drop of a hat I would stand up at a meeting and give everyone the benefit of my insights — at length. I discharged myself from St Vincent's Hospital, and I decided that it was time to resume my trade as a comedian; time to do another show. But who would produce it this time? Why not Harry M. Miller, the New Zealand impresario who had attacked my London show in the Australian press? It was a piquant idea, and of course this fellow would jump at the chance of presenting someone like me, and of being photographed shaking hands. It was *delicious!*

Christmas was approaching, and I was still writing my weekly column for the *Age*, but the editor was being difficult over petty things: cutting out my best jokes, censoring my more outspoken material. I was in an irritable frame of mind when I caught the flight to Sydney for my historic *rapprochement* with Mr Miller. While I was in Sydney I thought I might even telephone Roslyn, whom I had rather caddishly abandoned in London, and tell her I was 'on the wagon'. She would be so pleased that she would undoubtedly fly out to Australia on the next plane. The stewardess asked me if I would like a drink. 'No thanks,' I smiled smugly, 'I don't use the stuff.'

'That's funny,' she said, pointing to the little plastic tray that unfolds from the seat in front, 'you've just had one.' I looked at the tray. There was an empty glass, and a miniature bottle of brandy. I must have drunk that automatically, unconsciously, I thought with more curiosity than alarm. An AA phrase came back to me: *It's the first drink that does the damage.* Well, it seemed that I had had the first, so a second would do no harm so long as I kept it at that. I thanked God that I had rediscovered my will-power.

He checked in to the Gazebo Hotel in Kings Cross, a brand-new cylindrical building, rather like a cocktail-shaker. The room was large, with a view of Sydney Harbour, but he telephoned the desk and asked to be moved to a suite. Then he telephoned a florist and ordered lilies, dozens of them. It was so exciting to be back in Sydney, with all those hospitals and doctors a thing of the past. A relief too, not to have to go to those AA meetings any more – he had helped those people enough.

The doorbell rang and a room-service waiter pushed a jingling trolley of champagne and glasses into the suite, followed by another waiter bearing oysters and lobster.

Harry Miller was not returning his calls. It was disgraceful under the circumstances, and he decided that it was demeaning to be always ringing those patronizing secretaries. Who did that shaygets and schlockmeister – he relished the Yiddish epithets – think he was? Instead, he would call around to Miller's apartment in person.

A housekeeper opened the door, Irish, and, he suspected, very slightly drunk. Mr Miller was not at home, she explained, and he couldn't come in. What nonsense. He pushed past and took a comfortable chair in the sitting-room. The pictures looked to him as though they might have been hired, and he mentioned this to the agitated woman who hovered in the background. He demanded a cocktail, but after several of these it was apparent that his unwitting host was not immediately returning.

Back in his suite at the Gazebo, heavy with the intoxicating efflux of too many lilies, he decided to have a party to celebrate the resuscitation of his career, and his new sobriety. He telephoned Patrick White and left an urgent message for him to come to dinner at his hotel. He telephoned his old girlfriend Margaret, who was now married to a charming property tycoon, and invited them both. He called all his old girlfriends. He telephoned everyone he could think of, he even telephoned the Sydney switchboard of AA. Someone there could surely do with a party, he thought.

But nobody came. He nibbled the oysters, drank some more champagne and obscurely wondered how he would ultimately pay for all this, for he had absolutely no money. No more, in fact, than his return ticket to Melbourne, and a chequebook on a bank account that no longer existed. He was sick a few times, unfortunately into the sunken bath, or as near to it as he could manage. It must have been nerves, he reflected. Nervousness from being in the world again after so many months 'inside'. The doorbell rang and a stranger called Guy stood there looking embarrassed. He said he was a member of AA, a pretty new one, too, but he had been told about a phone call, and did he need help? The man in the suite with the lilies, and the trolley laden with half-opened wine bottles, and the debris of several seafood suppers, laughed. 'Do I look as though I need help?' he said.

All night long, and well into the next day Guy sat there watching the man make phone calls, sleep, drink, weep and vomit. A secretary phoned to say that Mr Miller's housekeeper had been insulted yesterday and that Mr Miller never wished to hear from him again. The man then telephoned the florist and ordered twelve dozen gladioli to be delivered immediately to Mrs Nora O'Sullivan, care of Mr Miller's residence.

At some point he went off in a taxi to visit his friend Patrick (see Asides), and at another time Margaret arrived and fed the man with some potent vitamin B compound. Late the next afternoon a psychiatrist turned up and persuaded him to go to hospital, but at the very gates of the institution the man escaped and thumbed down a car-load of students whom he conned into buying him a bottle of vodka. With this in his pocket he somehow found the airport, and was reluctantly admitted on to a flight to Melbourne. There, it seems, some plans had been laid, by persons he did not know, for his admission to a small hospital called Delmont, run by a Dr John Moon. It was a hospital for 'thirsty people'.

After the doctor had been to see him, he was given, at his own importunate request, a large glass of brandy. It was his last drink.

As he sank deeper and deeper into sleep, he felt like a character in a remembered story by Kafka, who, as he dropped into the river Moldau, cried softly: 'Dear parents, I have always loved you, all the same.'

Rest for the Wicked

I WAS AT the very entrance to the departure lounge when I heard my name being called. A small bald man in a fawn suit was running across the terminal waving frantically. As he drew nearer I saw it was Jim Preston, from the Australian Film Development Corporation. He must have been in rather bad shape because he was panting heavily and gulping for air by the time he drew level with me.

'Just one thing, Barry, before you go, and can you pass this on to Bruce when you get to London.' A Qantas steward in his coral-pink blazer was standing only a few inches away looking interested. Jim stepped nearer and lowered his voice: 'I've been talking to the Board, and we all hope there won't be too many . . . er, *colloquialisms* in the fillum.'

I assured him, on my honour, that any 'colloquialisms' that might be in the script would be reduced to an absolute minimum. Jim, having done his duty by the Board and risking coronary occlusion on his dash through the airport, mopped his brow and looked relieved. 'It's not me, Barry,' he explained rather sheepishly. 'But Barry McKenzie does get a bit on the *permissive side* every now and then, and the blokes upstairs – who I have to keep sweet – are keen that we don't do anything to ruin Australia's overseas' image.'

On the long flight back to London I could still picture Jim

Preston's touching expression of simple gratitude. It seemed strange that the Film Development Corporation should have given Beresford and me $250,000 to make a film about Barry McKenzie, and then have last-minute scruples about the propriety of his language! If we cleaned up the dialogue there wouldn't be a movie; but with one foot on the aeroplane and the cash in my pocket I didn't dare tell old Jim that.

It was Bruce Beresford's first big feature, and my first film, not counting 'cameos' in a few movies during the sixties. Bruce had been talking about a Barry McKenzie film for several years, and in the end he had, with a little help from me, actually written a script in which Mrs Everage appeared, as Barry's aunty from Melbourne. I was not totally convinced that Edna would acknowledge such a common nephew, let alone fly with him to England as the script required, but we thought we could make it plausible enough, within the manifold implausibilities of our narrative. Apart from the role of Edna I was also going to play two other parts, a hippie and Dr Meyer de Lamphrey, the psychiatrist on whom Barry chunders.

The drawings of Nicholas Garland for the original comic strip largely governed our casting. My old manager, Clifford Hocking, had, years before, drawn my attention to an uncanny resemblance between Barry McKenzie and a talented Australian singer, coincidentally also called Barry – Barry Crocker – now renowned as the singer of the *Neighbours* theme. Crocker was engaged to play the eponymous Bazza. The cast also included Dennis Price, in his last performance, Dick Bentley, Julie Covington and my old friends Peter Cook and Spike Milligan.

Our producer Philip Adams had rented a small production office in Soho, not very far from the offices of *Private Eye* where Barry McKenzie had been born. It was a strange but exhilarating experience for me to be back in London after such a long absence – and not drinking. I would find myself walking past pubs in which I had formerly spent countless hours, and a great deal of money. Where on earth did I find the time? Or the money? Two years before, after a meeting at Delmont Hospital, I remembered asking Dr Moon a question over which I had long agonized: 'Now that I have stopped drinking, John, what am I going to do with my time?' He had smiled patiently. 'As you get well, a person like you will find more than enough to do. The danger is getting too busy.' But I had persisted: 'What takes the place of alcohol in a man's life?' Dr Moon said, 'How about gratitude, and concern for others?'

At the time, they were the most novel concepts I had ever encountered.

Two years before, I had resumed my acting career in Sydney on a modest scale. It was an anthology of early material, and my old adversary Harry M. Miller produced it. For reasons not totally unconnected with the desire for financial gain, we had succumbed to each other's charm. After the big theatres I had played in the sixties, I now adjusted myself to smaller venues, and rediscovered an intimate connection with the audience. Above all, my confidence, which had been badly shaken, returned.

In Melbourne I got to know my daughters Tessa and Emily again, and we spent weekends together in the countryside not far from Healesville, where I had had so many happy childhood years. Rosalind had divorced me, citing her near-namesake Roslyn, who had bravely returned. Then came the news about the Mckenzie film.

We were at first amazed that a new Government film-funding organization should have chosen, as its first project, a picture based on a comic strip which another Government organization had banned. However it was not for us to question the byzantine workings of the Australian bureaucracy. A few months later when we returned from London with the finished picture, yet another Government department – this time the Censor's Office – gave the film its most restrictive classification. Adams, Beresford and I appealed, and we got to meet the custodians of Australian morality themselves; an unprepossessing trio consisting of a one-armed functionary, a schoolteacher and a retired Olympic athlete. Root-faced, they watched the film again and delightedly reconfirmed their original classification.

Happily, far from sabotaging the success of the film, the Censors only gave it the allure of the forbidden. It enticed into the cinemas of Australia a totally new class of youthful hedonist, who ecstatically identified with McKenzie, imitated his habits and 're-cycled' his dialect.

The world première of *The Adventures of Barry McKenzie* took place in Melbourne and was an immediate success. This, however, was in spite of its reviews, which were almost universally disparaging. Like the Parliamentary broadcasts of the fifties, the film exposed an aspect of Australian speech and behaviour that many preferred to think did not exist. Australian journalists, never renowned for their refinement, sensitivity or temperate habits, went apoplectic with rage and denial at this jolly little picaresque saga. 'The worst Australian film ever made', shrieked Max Harris.

The manufacturers of Foster's Lager, that obscure beverage which the comic strip character had been cheerfully guzzling for nearly a decade, viewed the success of the film with mixed feelings. They had recently spent a large sum of money with an advertising agency to make commercials in which their product was depicted as a rather sophisticated tipple, to be consumed on yachts by men in blazers and girls in pearls. Now here was their beer being drunk directly from the cans, crudely described as 'chilled tubes', and 'ice-cold tinnies'. Worse, its incessant consumption on screen led directly to the film's two major climaxes: Barry's famous chunder attack, and the final scene where a fire at the BBC is extinguished by a group of Australians drinking Foster's Lager and urinating on the flames. For the London première at the Columbia Cinema in Shaftesbury Avenue, we had approached the distributors of Foster's for a couple of free cases of their product to serve VIPs at the party. They refused unequivocally. Our guests drank Carlsberg.

Years later, when Foster's had become available all over Britain, I noticed a television commercial for this frothy cordial. There was no yacht, or blazered gigolo, but a craggy-faced man wearing a wide-brimmed bush hat, exhorting the public, in unmistakably proletarian tones, to 'crack an ice-cold tube'. It had taken the brewery a long time to profit by experience. Alas, it was a profit in which Beresford and I were not invited to share.

When the producer and I had set off for London to make the film, both my parents and my brothers and sister had come to the airport to see me off. It was a touching expression of their new attitude to my work, and perhaps also to me. In the preceding two years we had become closer, and my father had even proudly arranged a special evening at my stage show for all his friends at the Rotary Club.

One evening not long before the film première, I called at our family home in Christowel Street, Camberwell for Sunday tea. As I arrived a dapper figure in a dark suit was climbing into his Mercedes in the driveway. I recognized Sir Clive Fitz, the famous Melbourne cardiologist. He explained that he had just made a professional call on my father, reassuringly adding that things were not serious. But my father looked very grey and older than his sixty-eight years. That night, as I left the house, we embraced. It was the last time.

Neither of my parents came to the film première. I could understand my mother's absence from a widely advertised evening of relentless vulgarity, though she diplomatically declined on the grounds of 'a headache'. My father would have had a wonderful time, but I suspect his last-minute apology was due to some gentle coercion from my mother, who would otherwise have spent the evening alone. He may also have been unduly nervous about critical reaction to the film. My family placed great store on what the papers said. I might have received rave reviews, but if one journalist even *qualified* his praise, my mother would say with a slow shaking of the head:

'I see you didn't get a very good write-up in the *Sun*, Barry.' No reference was ever made to a favourable notice.

A few years later, when I went to New Zealand with a show called *An Evening's Intercourse with Barry Humphries*, we had to cancel the Christchurch season because the local paper refused to publish the word 'Intercourse' on their entertainments page. The result was that the tour was less than financially successful. When I told my mother this news, she brightened perceptibly. 'You see, Barry,' she said triumphantly, 'you're not popular everywhere.' On hearing this, my pianist at the time, Tomi Kalinsky, said, 'Are you *sure* your mother isn't Jewish?'

The pompous, outraged reviews of Barry McKenzie were still appearing in the Melbourne press when John Levi telephoned to say that my father had died in the middle of a game of golf, just like Bing Crosby.

With the help of my new manager, Clyde Packer, I launched a new stage show in Sydney called *At Least You Can Say That You've Seen It*. Like many of the titles of my one-man plays, this was inspired by the sort of remark my mother or her friends made after attending the theatre. Again, this contained film segments which Bruce Beresford helped to create. Meanwhile Bruce and I were thinking about a McKenzie sequel, and since the first picture was such a money-spinner (the Film Development Corporation, to its surprise and irritation, recouped its investment five times over) we had no trouble in raising the money. A Brisbane entrepreneur called Reg Grundy backed the sequel and Bruce and I finished the script in a secluded hotel in Tasmania.

Before I left for England I went to see my mother, now alone in the big empty house. 'No rest for the wicked' was a favourite phrase of hers when she was a busy young housewife, invariably uttered with a short self-deprecating laugh. As a child I had found it startling, like a blasphemy against her goodness; worse, really, since spoken against herself. But now that she was widowed, reclusive and increasingly crippled with arthritis and a curious form of self-starvation, I still occasionally heard her use the same words, but this time they described poignantly, her loneliness and guilt.

Flying back to London once more, I took a detour to Prague to visit my old friend Jiri Mucha, the Czech writer, and son of Alphonse Mucha, the great exponent – if not the creator – of the art-nouveau style in Paris at the turn of the century. After his release in 1957 from six years' imprisonment in a Stalinist labour camp, he devoted much of his time to the rehabilitation of his father's artistic reputation, so that those floriated and tendrilled posters, many originally commissioned by Sarah Bernhardt, became a commonplace of the sixties, decorating psychedelic record sleeves and the boudoirs of teeny-boppers.

Until his death in 1991, Jiri lived in some style in a thirteenth-century house near the Castle, surrounded by his father's pictures, sculptures by Rodin and a harmonium that had once belonged to Gauguin. Always hospitable, this dear and loyal friend has been unfairly described elsewhere as an 'orgiast', but if a love of youth, a speculative intellect and a generous desire to accommodate the tastes of his guests, how-ever whimsical, is orgiastic, then so be it. It is true that sometimes in the darker moments of Prague's recent history before the liberation of his country – which happily he lived to see – he choreographed piquant gatherings of the city's Golden Youth for the amusement of visitors; and it was into one of these that I had, it seemed, stumbled late one evening, as I returned from a concert of Mozart and Martinů. As I mounted the stairs, the house seemed deserted, and on entering the large drawing-room I found it to be in pitch darkness, so that I had to feel my way cautiously across its length to get to my bedroom. Slowly, I became aware that the room was not empty. There was a palpable warmth, a faint susurration and a musky atmosphere suggesting invisible human presences; and here and there, as my eyes became accustomed to the intense and velvet darkness, I saw the pulsing glow of a cigarette. Just as I was reaching forward to touch what I estimated to be the panelled doors that would lead me to the chamber beyond I froze in my tracks, as a hand – warm, inviting and insistent – closed around my left ankle.

Barry McKenzie Holds His Own, starring Barry Crocker and Donald Pleasence, was, very loosely, a vampire story set in Transylvania, where the vampires, for the first time in the history of this genre, were Communists, determined to kidnap the Queen of England in order to attract tourist dollars. Edna Everage is mistaken for the Queen, and Barry McKenzie for Prince Philip. Soon after this the complex plot lapsed from plausibility; due, no doubt, to the insidious Tasmanian influences that surrounded its writing. There was a funny scene in the film when Edna, Barry and his twin brother, the Reverend Kevin McKenzie ('Kev the Rev'), visit Paris and meet Colonel 'the Frog' Lucas, an Australian intellectual long expatriate in France. This bereted, goateed and French loaf-toting personage – played by Dick Bentley – was based on Alister Kershaw, a Sydney writer whom I had met on my hectic visit to Paris years before with Arthur Boyd. Barry's rare filet mignon ('just knock off its horns, wipe its arse and bung it on the plate, *garçon*') is drugged by the Transylvanians, and 'calls Ruth' from the top of the Eiffel Tower. Although this film did not attract the audiences of its predecessor, it is memorable for this scene alone. The minor character of a drunken film critic was movingly played by Clive James, an author who has had the acumen to distribute his reminiscences over several volumes.

But at the end of this uneven film there was a moment which could truly be described as Epiphanic. It is the moment when Edna and Barry return triumphantly to Australia after their adventures. The script demanded that they be met at the airport by the Prime Minister of Australia, and we had difficulty finding an actor with sufficient grandeur to impersonate the

Right Honorable Gough Whitlam. I chanced a phone call to Canberra and Mr Whitlam himself, and his wife Margaret, agreed to appear as themselves in the climactic scene. As Edna emerges from Customs she is stupefied to behold the Whitlams awaiting her with open arms. As she fell into an embrace with the Prime Minister, Gough improvised: 'Arise, *Dame Edna!*' he intoned, as the camera rolled until Beresford cried 'cut'. Edna obviously took this accolade as a legitimate citation, and has ever since appropriated the title. The Prime Minister was later heard to mutter to an aide, 'She certainly picked up on that one.'

Not long afterwards, Whitlam's Labor Government ignominiously fell and, after the two Barry McKenzie pictures, Bruce Beresford, the future director of *Driving Miss Daisy*, dismissed as a director of broad comedy, found it impossible to get work in pictures for the next two years.

One afternoon I found myself a passenger in a London taxi travelling from Chelsea to Hampstead, and as we turned into Park Lane I had a sudden and curious impulse to see the house in Mayfair where I had lived five years before, at the nadir of my career. The driver, surprisingly, protested that Park Street was well off the direct route to Hampstead, but on my insistence he turned right at the Dorchester and into Mayfair. I cannot explain why it then seemed to me so important that I glimpse once more the uninteresting house in which I had so briefly lived, but as we neared it I remembered with a shudder the shattered Gallé, and my old pictures. Most of them were now back in Melbourne, at Rosalind's house; all except one, I recalled, a big oil I had bought in the early sixties from an art student in New Zealand, that had never turned up in the shipment. Lost forever.

Now we were in Park Street and travelling north. I leaned forward as we passed the Grosvenor House, and there ahead, on the right, I saw scaffolding outside my former flat. There was a pile of rubble on the pavement also, and I realized that this gloomy abode was at last being renovated. Just as the taxi drew level with number 62, two workmen strode out of the door, holding between them a large unframed canvas, the painted surface of which directly confronted my approaching cab. *It was my picture!* At that instant the two men tossed the painting on to the pile of rubble and went back inside. Several yards further on, at my urgent command, the taxi screamed to a halt and I leapt out, ran back to the building site and entered the derelict house. 'Where did you find that picture?' I said to the men. I must have been rather wild-eyed, because they looked at me oddly. 'That's our Gainsborough, isn't it, Terry?' laughed one of the men. 'We found her flat on her face on top of that wardrobe.' Terry chimed in, 'It's our table, too, Guv, we've been having our tea off it for the last few weeks, haven't we, Len? You can see the rings.' *'It's mine,'* I blurted. 'I used to live here once.' The men looked at each other sceptically, but I led them out into the street and pointed to my name on a torn label on the canvas stretcher. Then I showed them my passport. A decent tip, and the picture and I were back in the cab, and I vowed, then and there, that in future I would pursue as many impulses of that kind as I possibly could.

In Melbourne not long afterwards, in yet another taxi, I experienced again that mysterious prompting to diverge from the normal route, which on that day took me from the airport to my mother's home. Motoring down an unfamiliar street I saw, outside a terraced house, a shingle that bore the legend ART GALLERY in sign-writers' gothic. I stopped the cab, got out and, still yielding to impulse, knocked on the door. It was opened by a bearded young man who, when he saw me, stepped back with a gasp. 'Who told you to come here?' he asked rather rudely. 'Is this some kind of joke?' 'I just arrived from London this morning,' I replied calmly. 'I have never been in this street before, but I like pictures and I saw your shingle.' The young man looked confused. 'But I've just put it up. I mean to say, I've just opened the gallery this morning, you're my first customer.' 'Perhaps that's lucky,' I said. 'What can you show me?' But he was shaking his head and looking at me oddly. 'I believe I know who you are,' he said at length, 'and it's not quite true to say that you're my *very* first customer, because a man was here an hour ago who sold me a picture that might interest you.' He was leading the way up a narrow staircase, but said over his shoulder, 'You'll see what I mean when you see the picture, Mr Humphries, but I still don't believe nobody put you up to this!' Together we entered a bare, recently decorated room. One large painting stood against the wall. It was a picture which I knew had been missing since 1958, and had long been thought lost or destroyed. When I recovered my composure I asked him his price, which was not, under the circumstances, extortionate. I paid it and, still in a great agitation of spirit, took the picture home. It was a portrait in oils by Clifton Pugh, of myself. It is the frontispiece to this book.

In 1976, at the end of my Australian tour of *At Least You Can Say You've Seen It*, I took my daughters on a long holiday to California and Mexico. On my return I began living with a gifted young surrealist artist called Diane Millstead. Some months later she joined me in London where Michael White, the wunderkind of West End producers, had invited me, as Peter Bridge had done in the sixties, to present my Australian show.

This time it worked. At the unusual hour of eleven p.m., on Tuesday, 16 March 1976, at the Apollo Theatre, Shaftesbury Avenue, *Housewife-Superstar!* opened. It was an abridged version of *At Least You Can Say* . . ., with the addition of a new character called Les Patterson, the self-proclaimed Cultural Attaché to the Court of Saint James's.

Les had been invented in the previous year when I had ventured once more 'to do my act' at a Sydney football club. I still had grim memories of the Granville Returned Servicemen's Club on a far-off morning in 1956. But Clyde Packer urged me to invent a new character suited to the rougher milieu of a

Sydney Leagues Club. I decided that Les, with his nicotine-stained and snaggled teeth, padded stomach, powder-blue suit and stacked Engelbert Humperdinck shoes, could pose as the Club Secretary, and could in that way deflect possible audience hostility towards the next act – Edna.

Les Patterson was, perhaps, an oblique and long-delayed revenge on the Club Secretary at Granville who had, all those years before, thrown me a damp and grudging fiver, and shown me the door.

Leslie Colin Patterson inherited the Language of Barrington Bradman Bing McKenzie, although his discourse is today a great deal closer to that of real people; especially the more eloquent and verbally inventive Australian Politician, although, needless to say, Les Petterson's cheerful vulgarity is condemned on all sides in his homeland and is dismissed as a scurrilous anachronism. Les is by turns long-winded and laconic, and he has a knack of stating the obvious at length, which is particularly Australian.

Soon after the Berliner Helmut Newton, a fugitive from Nazism, arrived in Melbourne, he and his wife June were in bed one morning reading the newspaper. It was a warm day and the curtains were open on their ground-floor city flat, affording curious pedestrians a glimpse of the bedroom. Two men walked past, glanced in the window and stopped in their tracks. One said to the other:

'Jeez! Look at that fuckin' man and that fuckin' sheila lyin' in that fuckin' bed, reading the fuckin' newspaper!'

After this reflection they continued on their way with great merriment. Certainly the pedestrian's observation appears, at first sight, to be merely a brutal statement of fact, but it is more subtle than it seems, for it conceals an acrostic message; an oblique speculation on how Mr and Mrs Newton might, under the circumstances, more appropriately occupy themselves. Helmut remembers this as his first baptism into Australian culture. Without doubt it is a classic example of the art which conceals art in our vernacular.

In *Housewife-Superstar!* Les entered through the audience, as Edna had in the late sixties, and as he blundered on to the London stage on the first night, I realized, by the hush that had fallen over the audience, that they all believed Les to be a genuine Australian diplomat, the worse for liquor!

To the padding which constituted his false stomach I had added a large upholstered phallus, the contours of which were unmistakably discernible beneath the taut fabric of the diplomat's stained blue trouser. As Les rambled on discursively on cultural topics, I noticed women in the audience slowly becoming aware of the pendulous yet frisky protuberance which extended to a point only a few inches above the diplomat's knee. Deep within Les Patterson, I hoped at least one highbrow critic, whatever he thought of the show, might mention the persisting influence of Aristophanes' *Lysistrata* – or at least Brecht's Mr Punt.

Yet for all his gross ventripotence, some women love Les Patterson. His involuntary habits of projectile expectoration do not dismay them, for as he says: 'Don't worry, ladies, Les Patterson's saliva is *safe*!' One evening a very attractive, if chemically elated, young woman sat sprawling in the middle of the front row, legs akimbo. 'Spit on me, Les,' she cried imploringly, 'spit on me!'

It was strange, after all those years, to find London audiences laughing just as loudly, and in just the same places, as audiences in Melbourne. The penny, it seemed, had dropped at last. Soon there was a show album, and, thanks to my old publisher friend Ken Thomson, *Dame Edna's Coffee Table Book* was launched upon the world. 'Is it *meant* to be vulgar?' asked Harold Acton ingenuously.

After the show had been running in the West End for several weeks, *Vogue* magazine, I was told, wished to interview me, and they were sending a photographer to meet me at the theatre. When I turned up, as usual slightly late to the appointment, I was considerably taken aback to see that the photographer was already waiting at the stage door. It was Lord Snowdon.

Remembering a distant and acutely embarrassing incident, I effusively apologized for my lateness. But he was exquisitely polite. He didn't mind in the least, he said, because it gave him a chance to think about the pictures he was planning to take. 'I'd like to take up most of your day on this job, if you can spare the time,' he said. 'Perhaps we could break somewhere for lunch?' I told him I knew a good Italian restaurant near the theatre, and would be delighted if he would be my guest. 'Oh no, thank you,' replied Lord Snowdon. 'I want you to be *my* guest. There is an excellent French restaurant I know in Addison Road, Holland Park, called Chez Moi. I wonder if you know it?'

He gave me a broad Royal Doulton smile, and I think he might have even winked. Otherwise, no subsequent reference was ever made to that evening, so long ago, when for two minutes I had been his Mother.

Talking Back

FANNY, MY EDITOR, was briefly out of her office, and I noticed, upside-down on her strewn desk, a letter, still warm and gently undulant, freshly extruded from her groaning facsimile machine. I perceived that it was from her Australian counterpart, and concerned this book. Unhesitatingly, I read it. '. . . Thank you for sending me those sample chapters of Humphries' book. It is perhaps more serious than I imagined, but just as self-centred as I expected . . .'

I wish I knew how to give an account of my life that was less egocentric, but the art eludes me. Perhaps it is because, in the theatre, I am always a one-man band; my supporting cast is the audience.

Throughout the seventies and the eighties I continued to work in the same vein, commuting between England and my homeland, without ever being quite sure where I really belonged. In all my travels, but especially in Portugal or Tasmania, I went on searching for that familiar fronded gateway, the tunnel of trees, and beyond, in the folding hills by the still, argent sea, a house that seemed to say: 'Here, live your life out!'

In 1977 Michael White decided to present *Housewife-Superstar!* in New York, in association with Arthur Cantor, a fine producer, especially of solo performers, but a man, none the less, who could be said to give Melancholy a bad name. The theatre selected for my off-Broadway debut was Theatre Four, a long way from the beaten track. I asked Mr Cantor why he felt this was such an ideal venue, and he disarmingly replied: 'The Boys in the Band was a hit here for years. It's a good theatre for fag shows.'

But Mr Cantor poured a great deal of energy and optimism into the promotion of my show, and with Brian Thomson's sets, help from Ian Davidson in adapting the London production and moral support from Diane Millstead, I began to feel encouraged. The previews went wonderfully well. Stephen Sondheim forced all his friends to attend, and Charles Addams sat in the front row – and laughed. On the first night everyone was suitably embarrassed by Les Patterson, who had now become Australia's Cultural Attaché to the White House. Edna's beady eye fell on several choice victims, including the inimitable Earl McGrath, former president of the Rolling Stones' record company, art dealer, *flâneur*, wit, host *extraordinaire* and, in 1992, Dame Edna's godson.

After the show there was the traditional party at Sardi's, where the mood was cautiously ebullient. An hour or so later I went upstairs to read the notices. Arthur Cantor's offices were conveniently above the restaurant, but, when I opened the door and saw Michael White and Mr Cantor slumped silently over the early editions, I knew the worst. So did the guests at the party. By the time I had gone downstairs again, the restaurant was deserted.

A Jaffa is a popular Australian confectionery; a small sphere of solid chocolate, coated with a brittle orange-flavoured shell. At the time of my New York débâcle, an Adelaide newspaper carried the following banner headline:

BAZZA GOES DOWN IN NEW YORK LIKE A JAFFA DOWN THE LIFTWELL OF THE EMPIRE STATE

For its imaginative ingenuity, and as a classic illustration of Australian *Schadenfreude*, I was almost proud to have inspired it.

A sketch by the author

Diane Millstead and I were married in June 1979 and in the ensuing years she presented me with two wonderful sons, Oscar and Rupert. The marriage lasted nine years. Now I am very happily remarried to the writer and actress Lizzie Spender. My daughter Tessa is a successful young actress, and Emily is an artist now living in Melbourne. (See forthcoming volumes.) I still paint cheerful landscapes in oils, during rare holidays abroad, except that I am never quite sure what is abroad.

A few doors from my dentist's surgery in Mayfair I had for several years noticed a doorbell above which was the label: Spoliansky. Could it, I wondered, belong to Mischa Spoliansky, the Russian-Berliner who had written the first songs to bring fame to Marlene Dietrich – the composer whose insouciant music had, more than Kurt Weill's pervaded the whole Weimar period? It was. During our brief friendship we spoke of collaborating on a *Songspiel* for Dame Edna, but this gentle, cordial and humourous man died in 1985, at the age of ninety-one. Three years later Sacheverell Sitwell also died, a very different artist, but one whose rich creative life spanned the same period as Spoli's, and who like him, had remained artistically prodigal since his early fame in the far-off twenties.

A far cry from Mischa Spoliansky and the *Goldenen Zwanzige Jahre* is Mr Barry Manilow, the popular singer, who has expressed a desire to write a musical comedy based on the memoirs of Dame Edna. It seems strange that I am now making television programmes for the National Broadcasting Corporation of America, and planning new and energetic amusements in the land where, not long ago, I was convinced that my act was 'too British'. But I believe, as Gabriel Dalzant once wisely said to Vernon Lee, that 'one must be prepared to begin life many times afresh'. If I were granted one wish, I would ask to be a cocktail pianist.

Some of my friends are now retiring; a few, like me, remarrying, and others, sadly, have died. Since my father's death, my mother had increasingly withdrawn from life, though she still enjoyed family holidays in Mornington. She and I had long and affectionate international telephone conversations; her brain was active, and her sense of humour remained as sharp as ever. But the day we brought little Oscar to meet his grandmother for the first time stays in my memory. When we arrived on the back terrace of Christowel Street, my mother could be seen through the french doors in her usual chair, listening to a portable radio. As we entered, she pointed to the radio and with her finger to her lips made a gesture of silence. It was a 'Talk-back' programme, in which listeners are invited to contribute their views on a topic dictated by the announcer, and on this occasion, by a macabre coincidence, the topic was me. In the fruity tones adopted universally by all afternoon radio 'personalities', Patrick Tennyson was asking his female listeners whether or not they thought Barry Humphries was 'selling Australia short overseas'. Then came the phone calls, as one by one the ladies of Melbourne expressed their opinions.

'I've never seen any of Brian Humphrey's shows, Pat, and I don't want to. Australia is a beautiful country, and we don't need people like that Dame Edith and that horrible Len Peterson giving the world the wrong idea.' And so it went on.

My mother was listening intently, and only once looked up at us all. She was obviously quite distressed. 'You see, Barry,' she said, 'that's what they think of you.'

I felt helpless. I went into my father's old den, and after looking in the phone book I dialled the number of the radio station.

'This is Dame Edna here, I want to be put straight through to Mr Tennyson.' I was. I was on the air.

'Is that you, Pat, darling? It's Edna here. I *adore* your show, especially today. How I agree with all those wonderful women who are ringing you up. I know Barry Humphries better than anyone, and he is dragging Australia through the mud as often as he can, for base financial gain. The millions who laugh at his shows should be ashamed of themselves, and I HAPPEN TO KNOW THAT HIS MOTHER AGREES WITH ME!'

Trembling, I put down the phone and returned to the sun-room. As I entered, my mother switched off the radio and shot me a dry smile, as if to say '*touché*'. Then, as though nothing had happened, she held out her arms towards Oscar and said: 'Don't just stand there, I want to see my grandson.'

In 1985, in a private hospital in Melbourne, my mother died. I was in London, and unable to fly home in time. Shortly before the end I spoke to her on the telephone. Later, she said to her nurse: 'Look at the beautiful carnations Barry has given me.' But the nurse could see no flowers.

Twenty years ago, when I returned to London sober, I walked one sunny morning down Lower Regent Street to meet my old friend Paul Oppenheimer for lunch at his club. Half-way down the hill, I had to stop and sit on the doorstep of a shop. I had the most extraordinary sensation that something was seriously wrong, and I was convinced that I was having some kind of heart-attack. For a while I sat there, panic-stricken, breathing deeply and wondering when I was going to pass out. In front of me the legs of pedestrians endlessly scissored past. Which leg, I wondered, would I grab, and cry to its owner: 'Quick, for God's sake, get a doctor! On this sunny day in London, I am dying.' But I did not do that; I sat a while longer on my doorstep until I decided I was not dying at all. With a rush of joy I found at last the label to my strange and alarming condition. I realized I was happy.

Santa Fe, 9 May 1992

ASIDES

from
Colin Munro
Bruce Grant
C. K. Stead
Patrick White
John Betjeman
Julian Jebb

Dada days

W HEN BARRY WAS at Melbourne University doing a combined Law and Arts Degree he stood for SRC. His election speech in the Public Lecture Theatre was an extraordinary theatrical event. Immaculately attired, he appeared in what might be described as his persona of 'Dr Humphries'. Behind him on the dais sat a committee of friends wearing academic gowns and 'Tid' masks, large and vaguely circular disks of white card on which were drawn the childishly minimal features, dots for eyes and a single line each for nose and mouth, of a variety of cretinously vacant faces. Each performed throughout the speech some infantile repetitive task, such as the piling up and toppling of children's blocks. A toaster, despite audience protests, filled the theatre with the pungent fumes of burning toast. One of his election purposes seemed to be the deregulation of medical services. He described how a 'little tot' had written to his organization and had been supplied by post with surgical instruments which enabled her to perform a very delicate operation on her mother's eye. Humphries also advocated the rebuilding of the University 'along the present lines of Wilson Hall'. The speech, it must be explained, occurred shortly after the fire which had left Wilson Hall a smoking ruin. Referring to his well-known artistic talents, he admitted that he had received many requests to execute a painting before an audience. An ancient framed oil was then produced, and Humphries proceeded to chip it to pieces with an axe. At the end of the speech, perhaps fearing audience reprisals, Dr Humphries appeared to experience some kind of seizure, took pills and fled the hall to be whisked away in a waiting car. Despite the pure Dada of this performance, he attracted a large number of votes.

Another University event was the Dada Exhibition. This was held in the Women Graduates Lounge, rooms of the old Union which were transformed by the renovations of the sixties. I recall three of the exhibits. One was a glass retort whose bowl had been filled with cooked spaghetti coloured with blue dye. It was entitled 'Spaghetti Head'. Another was a drawing in which the letters of the word BOY had been arranged so that the inverted Y formed the body and legs of a stick figure, the O the head and the B, on its side with slightly projecting stem, the genitals. It was entitled 'What we are'. The third consisted of a large box containing old books with worthy titles, such as *The Book of Beauty*. Over them had been poured a tin of thick vegetable soup. The caption read: 'I was reading these books when I felt sick'.

Barry was at this time producing a variety of Dada works, notably the '-scapes' in various media. Cakescapes, Forkscapes, Shoescapes and Rubbishscapes. There was also a project, perhaps never actually realized, for abstract sculptures, even an entire exhibition of them, constructed from broken glass. Long, dangerous slivers of glass were to protrude from these works, and a trained nurse was to be in attendance to give first aid to viewers mutilated by too close an inspection.

An exhibition in which many of these varieties of artefact appeared was held at the Victorian Artists Society Gallery. The show was opened by the artist himself at twenty-minute intervals throughout the first afternoon. One exhibit, shown in this or more probably the University exhibition, caused considerable controversy. It consisted of a beer bottle around whose neck was an Old Melburnian tie. The title was 'Old Fool's

Tie'. As a result Barry was evicted from the Old Boys' Association. He claimed at the time that he had appeared, dressed in a pin-striped suit and homburg, and bearing a calf-bound edition of Burke's *Trials*, at the offices of the Association, where he threatened to subpoena the minutes of the decisive committee meeting.

No account of Barry's extra-curricular activities at the University would be complete without mention of the Dada Revue. This was a lunch-hour performance in the Union Theatre, and in many of its sketches the distinctive form of his later satire was already present. There was, I recall, a long, excruciatingly funny conversation about nothing between two solemn suburbanites, both named Jim. There was also the notorious final sketch, later to be included in the 'Wubbo Recording'. My memories of the stage performance are now inseparable from the recorded version.

The scene is a mission station somewhere in Bengal. The Reverend J. Big and his wife, Mrs Tum, are at breakfast. The minister reads from his newspaper descriptions of heart-rending incidents arising from the current famine. There is a picture of an old woman being eaten alive by a starving child. Suddenly Mrs Tum (played by Barry) interrupts him to shriek: 'I couldn't care less!' Before her on the table for some reason there is an incongruous pile of vegetables, cake and raw meat. In a kind of paroxysm of jubilation at her own sufficiency, she springs to her feet and begins to pelt not only her husband but also the audience with the contents of the table.

This was too much, even for the most devoted supporters of Dadaist subversion. The audience began to assail the stage.

Barry, fleeing to the dressing-rooms to hide from attack, euphorically quoted historical precedents for such events in the original Dada movement.

Colin Munro, 12.10.91

A Bunyip comes to Melbourne

The Bunyip and the Satellite, which can be enjoyed for only a few more days at the National Theatre, must be added to the growing list of original work which is contributing to Australia's theatrical renaissance.

The Bunyip, the strange likeable character which Mr Humphries presents with such sensitive artistry, is the Australian relation of the Harlequin, Pierrot, Joey, Touchstone and even Lear's Fool. I think we should rejoice at this. We might easily have had as our national Fool a swaggering bandicoot or a Koala footballer.

Here instead is a delicate hero. A courteous, gay, troubled creature who admires wit and intelligence and has no material ambition except the discovery of his identity. It is the touch of pathos – the sad, white face framed with a gumleaf wreath, the essential loneliness – which gives the Bunyip the power to inspire us with feelings that are too deep for laughter. This is not only good theatre, which can never afford to forget the heart of man. It also represents a fresh Australian line of heroes.

Barry Humphries has a voice with a range and melodic sharpness of a violin; he sings as he looks – angular, uncomfortable, determined on cheerfulness.

He also dances. Jean-Louis Barrault said that for grace, actors should walk 'with the pit of their stomachs'. Mr Humphries walks with the top of his head, as graceless as a pair of hedge-clippers.

Bruce Grant, *The Age*, January 1958

A Kiwi remembers

I FIRST SAW Barry Humphries on stage in the Phillip Street Theatre in Sydney in 1956 or 1957, and got to know him in Auckland in the early sixties after we had both come back from our first visits to London. Barry's second wife, Rosalind Tong, a dancer, was an Aucklander. Sometimes Barry would put on a lunch-hour show at the University, which was where I first encountered the then rather down-market but already very funny Edna Everage. There was an evening when Barry and Rosalind took my wife and me to a sort of teen-club under the street where there was a band and dancing. We were all aged about thirty and felt out of place; my inclination was to be inconspicuous, but with Barry Humphries for company it was impossible. The Beatles hadn't yet begun the fashion that allowed men to grow their hair long; and in Australia and New Zealand the short-back-and-sides was almost a moral obliga- tion, as was the jacket and tie. Barry's hair was long, partly as a protest (his headmaster in Melbourne was given to saying, 'Long hair is dirty hair'), and partly because at that time this was the hair that came out from under Edna's hat. He wore an overcoat and no tie, and looked rather like a tramp, and we hadn't been long at our table before he had made everyone aware of his presence. When the band began something with a strong beat he suddenly launched himself backwards into the crowd.

His dance was extraordinary, jerky, almost spastic, yet perfectly rhythmical, with something of that physicality with which Dame Edna still reminds her audience that she's really a big energetic male. Someone shouted angrily at Barry, calling him 'Jesus'; there was a precarious moment in which the mood might have turned hostile; and then by some magic of facial expression he swung it entirely in his favour. The crowd pressed around him clapping rhythmically and cheering him on, while Barry, still leaning backward in his dance and with the bewildered expression of someone not quite sane, but benign, danced with prodigious vigour. When he sat down I felt as if I'd watched someone go over Niagara Falls in a barrel and survive.

Not long after, I wrote a fantasy called 'A Fitting Tribute' about a character I called Julian Harp, who solves the problem of engineless flight. The figure of Julian Harp was modelled on Barry Humphries, and the scene I've described . . . occurs in the story, as does Humphries's remark to me that at night the timber houses of Auckland look like lanterns. The story first appeared in the *Kenyon Review* in the United States, and soon afterwards was translated into Spanish, where it appeared in *Reviste de Occidente*, and into Hungarian for an anthology of 'the world's best stories'. It seemed to me significant that literary persons in a Fascist and a Communist state of that time should both seize on it. New Zealand and Australia were political democracies: but the sense of moral repression, of the crushing weight of propriety, was extraordinarily strong. Barry Humphries's outrageousness – his dandyism, his Dadaism, his various stage personae – were all aspects of the one rebellion against that oppression. Whatever he has become since, that is where he begins.

C. K. Stead

A letter
from Patrick White

Patrick White to Geoffrey and Ninette Dutton, 27.7.70

. . . A few days ago Barry Humphries suddenly came up on the telephone (it turned out he had got my silent number from that strumpet at the British Council!). He was in Sydney, in a state, after blotting his copybook in several places. The *Age* had given him the sack after he had written a column sending up the rich Melbourne Jews who celebrate Christmas. He had then rushed (perhaps even escaped) from his hospital in Melbourne to come to Sydney to ask Harry Miller to take him on. Harry had given him an appointment at the office but before this was due, Barry had burst into Harry's flat in Harry's absence and insulted the housekeeper by saying rude things about the paintings and furniture. According to Barry he was confused by his first day of freedom after a year of hospital. According to the housekeeper, he was drunk. Next day he rang up the secretary and insulted her too, according to Harry; amongst other things he said, 'I'm trying to get in touch with a friend who's become an acquaintance: a Christian writer called Patrick White.' Barry's call to me was to see whether I would try to make the peace with Harry M. We had Barry out here to lunch. He arrived an hour late, after two more telephone calls announcing himself, and a taxi-driver at the door to ask whether I still expected to see Barry Humphries. Barry, in a grazier's hat and monocle, was looking rather strange. He says he has been 'weaned off one or two toxic breasts' but I felt he must have got on to at least one of them again on his way to Martin Road. I'd be most interested to see his medical report. He still has flashes of great brilliance, but moments of despair, one feels. Very difficult to assess. He is such an actor one can't decide when the acting has stopped. I spoke to Harry Miller on the phone, and he agreed to talk to Barry. Whether he did, I don't know, and I didn't feel strong enough to ring Barry and ask. He was staying at the Gazebo, in spite of being on the rocks financially, and was planning a party for the following night to which so far he had invited Sculthorpe, Peter Coleman, and Peter Scrivener. He said: 'I suppose you wouldn't care to come?' I didn't feel I wanted to. Nor do I like to think what must have happened to Barry when faced with the toxicity.

Patrick White to Ronald Waters, 8.1.71

[After an abbreviated account of the visit to the flat and the call to the office:]
How insulting the insults were, I don't know. Both the house-keeper and the secretary told Harry that Barry was drunk. Barry comes here and wants me to make the peace. I, in my Martita Hunt role, try to do so. At least I rang Harry and told him he ought to see Barry: although he's crazy, he's a genius and one can't dismiss him just like that. Harry said he would see him. Since then I haven't had a word from either of them. I expect both are angry with me: Harry because I tried to make him do something. Barry because Harry either made no attempt to get in touch, or did and gave him the brush-off.

A programme note by John Betjeman

IT WAS IN the British Council office at Sydney that I first heard of Barry Humphries. Someone there had his records and I played them over to myself dozens of times. I had already realized, as anyone who visits that marvellous and varied continent must realize, that Australia has an exciting and vigorous culture of its own which has more to give the Old World than it can take from it. Musicians, artists and writers from Australia have won international fame and when one considers the size of its population, the number is disproportionately large. It would be invidious to mention names, but you all know them. Barry Humphries is one who, I have no hesitation in saying, will become internationally famous, because he is an artist with words, imagination and mimicry who belongs to the great tradition of music hall and theatre.

I was surprised to find that in his own country he was regarded as a satirist by some people. To me he seems much more than that. He shares the tears of things, as well as the laughter. He has created in Sandy Stone a character for whom one can feel affection and sympathy, while laughing at him at the same time. He is a sort of verbal and Australian Charlie

Chaplin. He is also a figure whose prototype can be found in most parts of the Western World, the decent, honest, kind-hearted but deeply conventional man who takes life as it comes.

Sandy Stone is only one side of Barry Humphries' genius. He can see into the home thoughts and home life of the average housewife or teenage daughter, or tough young man who is little different in England from the Australian counterpart.

There is besides all this the brilliant subtlety with which Barry Humphries portrays his characters and situations. Not a word is wasted. Not a point is missed. He hits the nail on the head every time and his phrases linger in the mind for months after one has heard them.

As soon as I returned to England I made a point of searching him out where he was performing in a successful musical, *Oliver*. I was not surprised to find he was longing to return to his own country, for his inspiration is local and derives from Melbourne in particular. He knew, of course, all about the artists and writers I admired, and we had in common a liking for artists of the nineties and Edwardian times – Conder, Phil May, Streeton, Tom Roberts and the early McCubbin, as well as modern Australian artists and writers, and we shared an enthusiasm for English music hall with its local and broad jokes and moving songs with memorable choruses.

Here is no satirist. Here is a great artist who comes from a country which has grown up and can look back at itself with amusement and affection.

Over in England I thought, in my enthusiasm for all things Australian, that the genius of Barry Humphries might be a bit too local and specialized for my friends who had not been to Australia. Not at all. A course of Sandy Stone enchanted them and has made at least fifty people who have heard the records I have played to them want to go to Australia. That is because of the note of affection implicit in them.

John Betjeman

Julian Jebb on
Just a Show

'THIS IS the most expensive finale in London, Peter Bridge will go mad,' shrieks Edna Everage nightly from the stage of the Fortune Theatre as she hurls armfuls of gladioli into the auditorium. On a good night she reaches the gallery and, when all the absurd phallic blooms have found their place, Edna leads the audience in the Gladioli Song. This extraordinary woman, a vulture in bird-of-paradise clothing, exhorts the audience to wave, thrust and tremble their gladdies with an almost spiritual fanaticism. This finale is not only the most expensive in London: it is one of the strangest and funniest quarters of an hour you could spend inside a theatre.

Edna's creator is Barry Humphries, a young Australian who reverses the saw about the prophet not being honoured in his own land. He has recently returned from a six-month tour of Australia where he played to capacity houses in theatres nearing up to 2,000. Now he is playing the same theatre, and under the same director, Eleanor Fazan, as *Beyond the Fringe*. In spite of a note in the programme of *Just a Show*, which says he was born on 'the eve of Munich', he is 35 years old, the eldest son of a prosperous Melbourne builder. He recalls that the atmosphere of gross philistinism at his school encouraged him to champion

331

the cause of minor artists whom he might find precious today – Denton Welch was one. His image of England came, somewhat surprisingly, from the music of Vaughan Williams and Delius rather than from the poets and novelists. The cultural wallpaper of his own childhood was the Australian commercial radio stations.

After school he became a repertory actor and played one of the tramps in *Waiting for Godot*. Beckett is a very clear influence on the monologues which he started doing in revue and soon put on records. The most extraordinary of these is called *Sandy Agonistes*. A drunk old man (one suspects that he is drunk and old and a man, but the voice is sexless and ageless with disappointment) speaks a litany of names for nearly half an hour. Patent medicines, breakfast foods, old film stars, snatches of popular songs, Melbourne suburban stations, follow one upon another by every conceivable associative process. The final effect of this poem is anthropological: it is as if the listener had been present at the construction and decay of a mythical society.

There are two distinct sides to Barry Humphries's genius as a performer. The dionysiac reaches its apotheosis in the gladdie-hurling finale of *Just a Show*; and the introverted in *Sandy Stone's Wake*. Edna totters demently from side to side of the stage, released at last from the pent-up fears which haunt Sandy and the other pathetic creations. The doomed farce of parents' relationships with their children is the chief source of his inspiration. Rex Lear, lonely and drunk, boasts about how much his ungrateful daughter's wedding reception has cost him. Edna is hysterically refined in her vindictiveness against her son Brucie's mixed marriage (to an English girl). Even little Debbie Thwaite, the plucky Earl's Court girl speaking her amazing aria about the comparative prices of meat in London and Melbourne, is gripped by the fear that Mummy or Daddy will suddenly turn up. In Barry Humphries's world there seem to be only two absolutes, family life and death, and only the latter can free one from the former.

In England he is probably best known as the author of 'Barry McKenzie', the scatological comic strip in *Private Eye*. The fictional Barry is far less ambiguous than any of the characters he has created on stage or record. This mountainously jawed extrovert chunders (or vomits) his way through the kangaroo valley of Earl's Court in pursuit of Sheilas and notes (girls and money) buoyed up by innumerable tubes (bottles) of Foster's beer. He is the embodiment of grossness and anarchic good humour, the child which Edna and Sandy dread they may have borne. Unhappily, their fears are groundless: they could never have conceived a creature so free from repression.

In 1959 Barry Humphries came to Europe for the first time. In 1962 Peter Cook, the owner of the Establishment Club in Soho, heard one of his records and offered him a season in cabaret. He was booked to appear for a month, but closed after a fortnight. The audience, used to jazz singers, satire companies or stand-up comedians, could make nothing of his work. Were they meant to laugh? At that time he left the audience to distinguish between the poignant and the comic in his monologues.

To his admirers the critical reception of *Just a Show* has been dispiriting but predictable. His fans rallied, he made some conversions, while the rest of the critics registered shades of disapproval ranging from terse bemusement to open hostility.

Acknowledgements

The publisher thanks the following for permission to reprint from copyright works: *Mandrake the Magician* comic strip reprinted with the kind permission of King Features Syndicate Inc.; *The Age* for 'A Bunyip comes to Melbourne' by Bruce Grant, 1958; *London Review of Books* and C. K. Stead for 'Here to Take Karl Stead to Lunch'; Barbara Mobbs Agency on behalf of the Patrick White Estate for Patrick White's letters to Geoffrey and Ninette Dutton (27 July 1970) and Ronald Waters (8 January 1971); The BBC for 'Barry Humphries' by Julian Jebb, *The Listener*, 1969; Peermusic (UK) Ltd for 'Oh Mona!' by Weems and Washburn, copyright 1931 by Peer International Corporation, New York; Essex Music for 'Food Glorious Food' from *Oliver!*, 1967 by Lionel Bart; Music Sales Ltd (Campbell Connelly and Co. Ltd) and Carlin Music Corporation (Redwood Music Ltd) and MCA Music Publishing for 'When the Lights Go On Again' sung by Vera Lynn.

PHOTO CREDITS: 'Marriage' – Bruno Benini; 'Dr Humphries' – Australian Consolidated Press; 'Wild Life in Suburbia' – The Glenn A. Baker Archive, photo Gerrard Vandenberg; 'The author, 1967' – Cecil Beaton; 'The author in Little Venice with his Conder collection', 'The author', 'The author with hat', 'Moonee Ponds' – Lewis Morley; 'The Surfie', 'The bride's father' – Theatre Museum Crown Copyright, Houston Rogers Collection; 'Sober', 'The author with Mischa Spoliansky', – John Timbers; 'An historic encounter' 'Diane Millstead' – Press Association; 'The author' – Brian Savron; Melbourne *Herald*; 'Dame Edna, a recent Hollywood study' – Roddy McDowall; 'The author at dinner in Los Angeles', 'With David Hockney in California', 'Oscar and Rupert' – Lizzie Spender; 'Drunk' – David Bailey; 'Lizzie, Barry and Stanley' – David Hockney.

Endpapers: *A Nice Night's Entertainment* – John Tourrier; *Isn't it Pathetic at His Age* – Toby Purves; *Just a Show* – Geoffrey Goldie; *Back With a Vengeance* – Dewynters; *Tears Before Bedtime, An Evening's Intercourse With Barry Humphries* – Diane Millstead; *Excuse I* – Colin Munro.

Every attempt has been made to contact copyright holders. The publisher would be pleased to hear from any copyright holder whose work has not here been acknowledged.